ANNA LEE WALDO

PRAIRIE

THE LEGEND OF CHARLES BURTON IRWIN AND THE Y6 RANCH

JOVE BOOKS, NEW YORK

PRAIRIE

A Jove Book / published by arrangement with the author

PRINTING HISTORY
Berkley trade paperback edition / November 1986
Charter (revised) edition / August 1987
Jove edition / January 1991

For information address: The Berkley Publishing Group, 200 Madison Avenue, New York, New York 10016.

ISBN: 0-515-10696-8

Jove Books are published by The Berkley Publishing Group, 200 Madison Avenue, New York, New York 10016.
The name "JOVE" and the "J" logo are trademarks belonging to Jove Publications, Inc.

PRINTED IN THE UNITED STATES OF AMERICA

10 9 8 7 6 5

DEDICATION

Although Charles Burton Irwin, his family, and many friends actually lived, this novel about him necessitated a few additional fictitious characters to fill in blanks where people probably existed, but have been forgotten. Most of the conversation is made up; most of the stories took place. This work is dedicated to the real people, relatives, and friends of C. B. Irwin, because they left a precious legacy toward the growth of the American West, and should be remembered.

CONTENTS

BOOK II

PHOTOGRAPHS AND ILLUSTRATIONS

(This section follows page 496.)

The three girls have the same saddles, bits, and headstalls on their horses.

Charlie Irwin in the New York Stampede, 1916.

An advertisement for the Irwin Bros. Cheyenne Frontier Days Wild West Show. *The Wyoming Tribune*, Saturday, June 7, 1913, page 7.

Floyd Irwin on his horse, Fashion, in front of the Sioux camp outside Frontier Park in Cheyenne, Wyoming.

Buddy Sterling, in the driver's seat, and Roy Kivett. Sterling took care of Will Rogers' polo ponies. Kivett was raised as a member of the Irwin family.

C. B. Irwin and the Baron de Rothschild of France, standing beside the Buick touring car and Model T Ford.

Charlie was given his commission and star as an officer of the Wyoming Humane Society and State Board of Child and Animal Protection in 1918 and remained an officer for the rest of his life.

Frontier Days Parade on 17th and Capitol Avenue, Cheyenne, in the early 1920s.

Fire at the Tia Juana Racetrack in Mexico in 1924. All the barns on this side of the railroad tracks were destroyed.

Pablo Martinez, a famous jockey, Will Rogers, and C. B. Irwin.

General "Black Jack" Pershing and Charlie Irwin.

Douglas Fairbanks, Sr., and Charlie Irwin.

Chief Red Cloud and Charlie Irwin with three Sioux women.

A personal letter to C. B. Irwin from General John Pershing.

C. B. Irwin with jockey E. Taplin on Bonnie Kay at the Agua Caliente track in Tia Juana, Mexico, 1930.

Flood at the Y6 ranch, 1935.

Letter to Charlie's middle daughter, Pauline, from one of the Sioux, meant a great deal to the Irwin family.

Foreword

All America loves a Western story. Europe and Japan are enthralled by it. Western clubs are in all of the West European countries. Spaghetti Westerns (made in Italy) are in continuous demand in European and Japanese movie houses. Australia, Argentina, and South Africa, with their own prairie lore, adore the American Western saga. I submit its mystique is *independence*—personal, family, social, and local independence.

Although he heard the news by telegraph and newspaper, the independent westerner paid little heed to Victorian England, Russia's tzars, or Perry in Japan. The discoveries of Madame Curie's radium and the North and South poles were worlds apart from the independent cowboy.

The blacksmith in Chillicothe, Missouri, and Colorado Springs, Colorado, the corn and wheat farmer in Kansas, the rancher in Wyoming, the rodeo rider in Omaha, Nebraska, and Pendleton, Oregon, the railroad man on the Union Pacific, and the racehorse man of Tia Juana paid little heed to these world affairs, even World War I and the economies of the twenties. The West was his life; free and independent.

Such was Charles Burton Irwin. Big in voice and stature, big in deeds and heart, C.B. was also big in the West. As a cowboy, breeder, steer roper, showman, and trader, he loved the open sky, the crops and cattle, and the horse. His life from the 1880s in Missouri to the 1930s in Wyoming epitomizes every modern boy's dream of the Old West. His story crystallizes the dreams of today's man as he yearns for true independence.

Raised by the tough pioneer stock of a Missouri blacksmith and challenged by the horses and men of the Old West, C.B. and his family loved, ranched, rode, and lived the rugged individualistic life of the frontier. He could sit in the saddle for two days at a stretch during roundup time. He could bring in stray calves for branding and deliver feed to cattle during a blizzard, and he could always mend fences. As a rodeo contestant, he set records, but he also furnished livestock needed for first-rate rodeo productions. He sponsored the best cowboys and cowgirls, bringing topnotch contenders to the rodeos. This knight of the corral was always youthful in spirit. Graduates of his tutelage stuck their necks out and developed the Cowboy Turtles Association to increase prize money and to formulate fair rules for the events. The organization today is called the Professional Rodeo Cowboys Association.

He put together one of the top traveling troupes, displaying the popularity of the West. The Irwin Brothers Wild West Show played before tens of thousands each year from coast to coast.

As a livestock agent, general agent, and superintendent for the Union Pacific, he helped ranchers ship cattle to market on schedule. He moved racehorses from one track to another without injury. He contributed to the development of the racetrack at Tia Juana, Mexico, and Ak-Sar-Ben in Omaha, Nebraska. He was able to find consistent winners in bloodlines not previously considered worthwhile. C.B. was a transitional figure in the growth and development of the American West. He was, in fact, a bridge between the Old West and the New, tying them together, in his good-hearted, easygoing, but hard-driving personality of the open frontier. He treated all people the same, regardless of wealth or position, and could be flush with funds one day and broke the next. He loved risk and would as readily step out to stop a runaway team as someone else might jump for safety. No automobile went fast enough, and no horse was swift enough to satisfy him. He was the equal of any in a battle of wits. He never gave up. Persistence was his hallmark.

Warren Richardson, writing in the Cheyenne *Tribune* for March 28, 1934, commented: "If the right man ever writes the life of Charlie Irwin . . . every page will tell of an adventure. If Charlie had lived in Napoleon's day, he would have been a marshal of France in command of cavalry, and like Marshal Ney, would have been always in the front leading the charge." In these few words, Richardson, who knew C.B. for thirty years, summed up that wonderful spirit of the independent man of the West.

—A.L.W.

PRAIRIE

C.B. Irwin's Family

Charles (Old Charles) Irwin
b. July 17, 1805
Philadelphia
d. Nov. 9, 1870

Nathan
b. Aug. 12, 1850

Joseph Marvin
b. Oct. 16, 1846, Henry Co., Ind.
d. July 27, 1913, Colorado Springs, Colo.

Sarah
b. July 16, 1842

Rebecca
b. July 18, 1839

Riley Brassfield
d. Aug. 8, 1895

Rachel
d. Oct. 9, 1894

m. 1861 Mary Margaret Brassfield
b. Sept. 23, 1845, Livingston Co., Mo.
d. March 4, 1897, Colorado Springs, Colo.

Granville Marvin
b. Feb. 27, 1867
Chillicothe, Mo.
d. Jan. 10, 1868

William H.
b. Feb. 27, 1867
Chillicothe, Mo.
d. Nov. 27, 1942
Colorado Springs, Colo.

m. July 22, 1895
Margaret Rick
in Colorado Springs, Colo.
b. Nov. 21, 1880
d. Summer 1981

Letitia (Ell) Ellen
b. Sept. 30, 1871
Chillicothe, Mo.
d. June 26, 1950

m. Sept. 11, 1890
Frank Leslie Miner
b. Aug. 4, 1865
d. Sept. 23, 1953

Gladys Laye
b. Oct. 19, 1897
Timberline Camp, Colo.
m. Clay Foster
in Grover, Colo.

Charles (Sharkey) Marvin
b. Aug. 4, 1899
d. Feb. 17, 1984

Eugene (Gene) William
b. Apr. 9, 1907
d. July 22, 1943

Juanita Helen
b. May 29, 1911
d. Sept. 27, 1937

Floyd (Buddy, Boots) Leslie
b. Apr. 29, 1895 near
Goodland, Kan.
d. July 19, 1917
Cheyenne, Wyo.
m. Edith (Dee Dee) Stumph

Joella Mildred
b. Dec. 8, 1896
Colorado Springs, Colo.
d. Oct. 24, 1975

m. July 29, 1915
Frank (Deeke) Jones

Patricia (Patty) Enid
b. Nov. 24, 1916
Cheyenne, Wyo.
d. 1946
California

m. (2) Norman E. Waldron

Etta Elizabeth (Betts, Betty)
b. Aug. 24, 1915, Cheyenne, Wyo.
m. Kenneth L. Steele
b. 1913
d. 1983

m. Malinda
d. May 22, 1884

William
b. Mar. 10, 1837

Martha
b. Jan. 30, 1835

George
b. July 14, 1832
d. in Civil War

Elizabeth
b. Dec. 27, 1830

Charles Burton (C.B. Irwin)
b. Aug. 14, 1875
Chillicothe, Mo.
d. Mar. 23, 1934
Cheyenne, Wyo.
m. Jan. 1, 1894
Etta Mae McGuckin
near Goodland, Kan.
b. Nov. 23, 1874
d. Nov. 19, 1953

Frank R.
b. Aug. 18, 1877
Chillicothe, Mo.
d. Jan. 4, 1959
Colorado Springs, Colo.
m. Mar. 13, 1905
Clara Belle Patterson
in Colorado Springs, Colo.
d. May 1982
m. (2) Rose Mary

Maxine Eleanor
b. Nov. 13, 1907

Louise Adelaide
b. July 30, 1911
d. Aug. 19, 1975

Arlyne Lucille
b. Oct. 20, 1915
d. Dec. 9, 1976

Frank Leslie
b. Sept. 18, 1917
d. Nov. 20, 1948

Pauline Lorraine
b. Sept. 25, 1898
Colorado Springs, Colo.
d. May 13, 1966
m. Charlie Johnson
b. Jan. 23, 1893
California
d. Oct. 3, 1964
Oregon
m. (2) Claude Sawyer
d. March, 1985

Frances (Noonie) Gwendolyn
b. Oct. 6, 1901, Horse Creek, Wyo.
d. July 9, 1979
m. Joseph Edward Walters
b. Feb. 4, 1900
d. Mar. 1965
m. (2) Mannie Keller

Robert (Irwin) Charles
b. Feb. 22, 1924

BOOK I

ONE

Chillicothe, Missouri

"Charlie! Charlie Irwin, what in all get out are you doing?" Rachel Brassfield's voice was strident. She was disturbed. Her nostrils contracted as she moved from the fresh air outdoors into the tangy odor coming from the saucepan on her spotless kitchen range. The wood-burning range was a Majestic, cast iron with isinglass in the oven door. Rachel's eyes moved from the empty vinegar bottle lying on her white enameled kitchen table, back to the steaming, eye-stinging liquid in the pan. The room filled with the pungent aroma. Next her eyes settled on the disarray of her white kitchen chairs. One wooden chair was stacked on the wide seat of another in front of her cabinets. The high cupboard doors were wide open, revealing cans of pickling spices, several glasses of strawberry jam with thick paraffin covering the tops, and some of the latest, glass, quart milk bottles.

"Charlie, why do you annoy me? You come into my house and make a mess when I'm not here," complained Rachel. Her eyes watered from the irritating vapors.

"Ma sent me for those eggs you promised her," Charlie said, standing still, trying not to blink his eyes. "Grandma, I looked out the window and saw you out back feeding chickens. I waited for you to come in. I sat in the rocking chair. Then I looked out the sitting room window. You were stringing up pole beans on stakes. I thought you'd be right in. I drank some water and waited. Then I lassoed the kitchen chairs. I pulled them away from the table. Then all of a sudden I got this idea to try the trick Will told me about."

Rachel didn't say a word, but clicked her tongue and looked at Charlie.

Charlie was an average-sized, suntanned nine-year-old with sandy hair that hung over intelligent, deep brown eyes. He took great pride in the fact that he could throw a horsehair rope around his body and do a couple of fancy tricks that opened the eyes of younger boys in the neighborhood. Often he would let one of the younger boys try one of his tricks. It was his secret for drawing a crowd. He had learned that it felt good standing in the center of a bunch of wide-eyed kids.

"Don't worry, Grandma. I'll put your chairs back. Look, if I stand in the corner I can pull 'em back without moving a foot. Even the ones stacked together move. Wanna see how good I am using my rope?"

Rachel's lips were sealed as she pulled her four chairs back to the round, drop-leaf table. She motioned for Charlie to sit. She set the empty vinegar bottle upright on the table. She pulled the pan of boiling lachrymator to the back of her range, wiped her eyes on her apron's skirt, and paced across from Charlie.

Rachel Brassfield was in her late sixties, with graying hair braided and wound around her head and held at the back with two tortoiseshell combs. She was short, round-hipped, with large grayish eyes.

"It smells like pickles in here. Why are you boiling my vinegar?" sniffed Rachel.

"Grandma, it's a trick Will told me. It's with eggs and boiling vinegar."

"Mercy! Look at this mess by my range!"

"Can you put an egg in a glass milk bottle?"

"Of course not! No one can, unless it's a pullet's."

"I can. See, you cook this egg, shell and all, in vinegar. Then put it in the milk bottle—right through the skinny neck. Will swore it'd work."

Charlie's older brother, William, was born a twin. The other boy, Granville Marvin, was born first, but he grew listless, then died before he was a year old. After that, Will was pampered and treated as something special. Charlie knew he couldn't always believe what Will told him. But he wanted to show his grandma that he, too, was special and could do tricks.

"Will should have his mouth washed out with soap," said Rachel.

"The egg'd be like that ship in the bottle at Creelin's Jewelry Store. You know, Grandpa's friend."

"He don't count Creelin a friend since the elections." Rachel's breathing quickened and the sides of her neck throbbed.

Charlie's grandpa, Riley Brassfield, was a thick-chested, six-foot farmer and stock raiser. He had three hundred acres in Livingston County's Section 23. Twice he ran for mayor of Chillicothe. He lost both times to Bill Creelin, the jeweler.

Rachel picked up some broken shells, trying not to touch the slimy, raw eggs. "I mopped yesterday! Who's going to mop today?"

"I had to see if an ordinary egg'd go inside the bottle without busting. It didn't! The trick is to cook the egg in vinegar!" Charlie took an egg out of the saucepan with a wooden spoon and tried to push it through the top of the quart milk bottle. Finally he put the egg back in the pan. He looked up at his grandma. "Will told me about this here other trick. You put an egg in lime. Grandpa has lime in the shed. You leave the egg buried about a year and it shrinks so's it looks like a dark green jellybean."

Rachel's nose twitched and she rubbed it.

"Will says limed eggs don't stink and that the Chinese coolies eat 'em. Could I—?"

"Not on your life! That's disgusting! Those slant-eyes live in tarpaper shanties where they're laying railroad ties. What does Will know about that coolie camp and their strange ways?"

"He heard they keep coins in their ears. I'd like to see that!"

Rachel grimaced. "Don't ever put coins in your mouth! You hear?" She shook her finger under Charlie's nose. "Land sakes, you sound like Old Charles. He was always wanting to see, hear, smell, taste, and feel anything new. God rest his old soul."

Charlie looked at her from under his mop of hair and decided not to comment. Charlie never knew Old Charles, his pa's father. Old Charles died of heart failure in the fall of 1870, five years before Charlie was born. But ever since Charlie could remember, adults had looked at him and said he looked and acted like Old Charles.

"Wrench out that vinegar pan. The smell is nauseating."

"Yes, ma'am. But first I want to show you this amazing trick. You know, Frank is still sick?"

"Your poor mother. I suppose she's waiting on these here eggs in my lard bucket. I don't know how she puts up with your foolishness and a sick baby." Rachel pointed to the gallon tin full of eggs, sitting on her kitchen counter. "Charles Burton Irwin! You get going!"

"In a minute," he said. "This trick can't have me stymied. It's too simple. It's a present for you." He blinked to clear his watering eyes and forced a rubbery egg into the milk bottle. It plopped on the bottom.

"Well, I declare! There's an egg in a bottle. I thought you were full of beans, but you were right all along," Rachel said. "That's some trick! I'm going to show Riley. He won't believe it."

Rachel bent a little and put her arm around Charlie. "I'll have more eggs from my hens by tomorrow morning. Would you like some ginger cake?"

"Yes, ma'am!" Charlie smiled. He felt good. He'd found another secret. You get cake when the trick works.

Charlie was careful carrying the eggs home. He passed Orin Gale's Livery and his father's place, Irwin's Smithery, but he did not stop. He cut diagonally through the vacant lot. It was one of those hot summer days of 1884. The wind blew dust into Charlie's eyes and snapped the clothes on the Gregorys' line. Mrs. Gregory had a dishtowel fastened around her gray hair and a clothespin bag tied around her waist. She was taking in dry wash. She waved a handful of straight clothespins. "How's Frank today, Charlie?"

"He's really sick," Charlie said. He stopped a moment, shaded his eyes, and looked up to watch Mr. Gregory crawl stiff and slow on the house roof to replace weather-damaged shingles with new cedar shakes. "Is it hot up there?"

"Yup. Hotter'n hell with the blower on!"

"Hush, that's Joe Irwin's boy!" called Mrs. Gregory with a clothespin in her mouth. "You know, Old Charles's grandson!"

"Yep, I know!" shouted Mr. Gregory. He waved his arms. "Old Charles used to rive all the town's shingles! Look at the boy!" He pointed. "My, oh my! The boy's got a walk just like Joe's pa! You see the way he sort of cocks his head? He's the spittin' image of Old Charles!"

Charlie closed his eyes and felt the sun hot through his muslin shirt. He stood on the wood floor of the Irwin porch, where it was cooler on his bare feet than the dusty paths and sun-scorched boardwalks he'd come over. Through the screen door he could hear his mother talking to his sister, Ell.

"Oh, my dear, it's a scorcher today." Mary wiped the perspiration from her face with her apron. Charlie heard the rustle of the starched cotton material.

"Did Frank drink all the spicebush tea this morning? You know that runs a fever down."

Charlie thought his thirteen-year-old sister talked big, like she knew all about dosing with herbs. He yanked open the screen door.

"Grandma Malinda'd use yarrow brewed in the iron pot for fever," he blurted, coming into the house.

"Don't slam the door!" Ell hissed, holding her forefinger to her mouth. She was slim and light-complected. Her eyes were deep green like the moist spring sassafras leaf. Her long hair was shiny like strained clover honey. Charlie was too young to see that even in her walk was the promise of a vivacious, breathtaking beauty. Ell was hardly aware that she could stare into the eyes of a man and stir his primal urges. She was learning the use of incense, sweet herbal odors, and one day she would be completely adept at keeping a man in a state of desire and constant worship of herself. She took the bucket of fresh eggs from Charlie. "Oh, joy! Now Ma and I can make an egg pie. Charlie, you're an angel," Ell sang. She took the eggs to the kitchen. Charlie followed her so that he could talk to his mother.

"Ma, can I sleep outside tonight with the cheesecloth over me?"

"No! Of course not! The netting is for little Frank so's he can take a nap under the shade oak. Fresh air is good for him and it gives me a chance to redo his bed and sweep his room."

"But—he doesn't use it at night. And it's my room, too." Charlie saw his mother frown, draw in a deep breath, and let it out slowly. He said, "Can't I stay until the egg pie is done?"

"Your big brother is expecting you to help out at the smithery. I think he has a big job this afternoon."

"Oh! Jeems! Where's Pa at?"

"Charlie!" his mother rebuked. "Your pa left only moments ago for the smithery. He's taking the saddlehorse to look for Doc Reed."

Charlie's father, Joe, was the town's farrier, shoeing horses and treating their diseases.

Charlie was shocked. "Can't Grandma Malinda make Frank well?"

Malinda Irwin was distinguished not only for raising eight

children but also for knowing the healing quality of roots, barks, and herbs. She was not more than five feet tall, with nearly cotton-white hair that once had been the color of fine strands of amber. Inquisitive, clear, coffee-colored eyes seemed to see into the center of a person's soul. She competed with the medical physician, Dr. Art Reed, by convincing her clientele that she could foretell the future.

Mary's eyes watered and she swallowed. "No. It was Malinda's idea to get Doc Reed to look at Frank."

"I thought Frank only had summer complaint," said Charlie.

The humidity added to Mary's frustration. The summer sunlight seemed not only hot but oppressive and the air heavy. "We've tried everything to make Frank well." She rubbed her temples.

Charlie went into the bedroom he shared with his younger brother and looked down at the pale face with the mop of reddish-yellow hair lying in the white painted iron bed. Frank opened his eyes. They were luminous in the light from the open door, like the liquid bluing Mary used on wash day.

"Have you ever seen a real angel, Charlie?" Frank spoke barely above a whisper. Charlie thought the freckles on his nose looked like they could be picked off, like fly specks on the wall.

"Nope."

"Me, neither, but I was wondering what one looked like."

Charlie shrugged his shoulders.

Frank pointed to the inside of the doorframe. There were three forged nails hammered in a triangle. "Ell did that to keep witches and spells out. She closed my curtains," whimpered Frank.

"You want them opened? It's awful dark in here," agreed Charlie.

"It's all right. I feel like sleeping anyhow."

Charlie nodded and left the room, leaving the door open. He went to the kitchen and stood by his mother.

Mary said, "There's not only enough eggs for pie, but for rye bread, too." She had put several cups of mashed potatoes into a big bowl with rye and whole wheat flour, sugar, water, and her dough starter. She pushed, punched, and pounded the dough.

All the time Ell stood at the stove repeating charms and superstitions under her breath. They were ones she thought might heal Frank. Ell greatly admired Grandma Malinda and had dreams of also being a famous healer. All her life she'd heard Malinda's stories of the Union soldiers who looked for the "Lady Doc" to sew them together, holding their intestines in their hands. Lately

Ell carried a comb and scissors in her apron pocket because Malinda carried them in her black medical bag. Whenever Malinda performed her medical miracles, she cut the children's hair afterward.

Mary wiped her hands on her apron, divided the dough to fit into several pans, covered each pan, and set them on the oak stump to rise in the hot sunshine. Then she put some bread with thick, hard crust and some dried meat with grains of salt into the lard tin Charlie had brought the eggs in. "Charlie! Take this tin to the smithery quickly. Pa forgot his lunch and he may have to go as far as Brookfield to find Doc Reed. Straight to the smithery! Hurry! That's a good boy!"

Charlie stepped off the porch and saw the cloth-covered pans of rising rye bread dough. He nipped a hunk of dough from one and nibbled it. He enjoyed the mild sour taste. He headed back in the direction of the smithery, kicking rocks and dust. He was careful not to kick the barbed hawthorn hedge in front of the house. He watched a wide, black cricket hop through the dust. Charlie did not step on it, because to kill a cricket was to kill the luck in your house, according to his Grandma Malinda. The cricket sprang into the dry, yellowed grass and Charlie moved on, bucket in one hand, horsehair rope in the other. He twirled a loop in the air and whistled happily. He felt good because the rope didn't catch the side of the bucket as it usually did. He was getting better.

He wished it were he instead of his father riding the red-brown stallion, Flame. That horse had a lordly lift to its head and a dip to its aging back. Charlie liked horses.

The sun was a smidge past midway on the top of the blue sky. Charlie blinked as he walked through the open barnlike doors into the smithery's dusk. He'd finished eating all the sweetish-sour dough ball. He licked the palm of his hand and stood a few moments until his eyes were accustomed to the darkness. He could hear the men talking in the smithery's yard behind him. It was a meeting place where local farmers and itinerant cowboys waited to have a knife sharpened, a horse shod, or a bridle repaired, and they aired views on politics, religion, or stood around gossiping. These men had shown Charlie how to braid a horsehair rope, splice in an eye, and work the end so that it wouldn't unravel. To pass the time they'd shown Charlie tricks with the rope.

Charlie moved toward his father, who was showing Will how to operate the new sling. It had a canvas girth that went under a horse's belly. When it was tightened it raised the horse so that its feet were just touching the floor. Joe rigged this up so that it was easier to shoe the horses that were kickers.

Charlie admired his father, who was about three pounds heavier than an ox, six feet two inches tall, with straight black hair and brown eyes. Today Joe Irwin had his hair tied at the back of his neck with a piece of leather string cut from the bottom of his apron.

When Joe saw Charlie, he removed his apron and hung it on a nail on the wall. "Help your brother all you can," he said, taking the lard tin Charlie held out. "And when you are home, help your ma."

"Yes, sir," said Charlie. "How long you figure you'll be gone?"

"Until I come back with Doc Reed." Joe nodded to Will to continue the shoeing job.

Charlie's father had been gone before. He'd been gone a week burning hickory wood into charcoal. Charlie had practiced a lot of rope tricks then, ridden the saddle horse, and talked Will into letting him hammer out a couple of bucket bails.

"Pa, you suppose I could go down by the covered bridge to fish if Ma don't need me? Could I do some new rope tricks in the vacant lot, if I promise not to lasso Mrs. Gale's picayune?"

"Pekingese, son. Stay at the smithery. Will needs you here in case something big comes in. In the meantime sweep and tidy the place. Stay out of mischief."

Charlie expected that last. He asked, "What about Frank?"

"Pray," answered his father, going toward the back door with his soogan, a couple layers of blankets rolled with a bed tarp on the outside, and the tin pail of dried meat and bread.

Charlie settled himself on a pile of burlap. He could hear his father saddling the stallion, talking to it, then the clop of the stallion's hooves on the packed dirt, as his father rode off.

"Hey! Is the smithy here?" a voice called, startling Charlie. "This here gentle creature sorely needs a forward shoe repaired." The stranger was dressed in a tight-fitting gray wool suit. His face was red and shiny with perspiration. He pointed to the right front foot of his palomino. The horse seemed to sense the awe it inspired. Will stood open-mouthed by Charlie, looking at its flaxen-gold color and the ivory mane and tail.

"That fella looks like a newly minted gold piece, sir," stammered Will, aiming to translate a compliment.

"It is a using horse," said the man in the gray suit. His eyes squinted to get used to the darkness inside the smithery. "It can go over trails that would be highly dangerous to other horses." The man was rather tall and well built, except for the high belly up under his gray vest, out of which his voice thundered deep and slow. "You do shoe horses, Your Excellencies? If so, I have a gold piece for you."

"Oh, yes! I can, sir," said Will, finding his voice. He jerked his father's apron off the nail and tied it over his leather chaps. Will motioned for Charlie to start pumping the repaired bellows.

Charlie threw a handful of wood shavings next to a piece of charcoal that was holding the heat. Instantly they caught fire, and he tossed a couple splinters of dry pine on them, then laid a hunk of charcoal on to catch and glow red. He raked the old, unburned charcoal over the fierce little fire as if he'd been doing this for years. He caught the bellows' lever and pumped a rush of air into the hearth. When the fire was a mound of bright red, he nodded to his brother.

Will told the man to bring in the palomino. The stranger had an auburn mustache, which matched his hair and curled at the corners, like the ends of his long hair curled.

"This your establishment?" The man was inspecting the canvas sling around his horse.

"Why—yes, in a manner of speaking, it is," said Will, without batting an eyelid.

"Put considerable into it for a young man, I see."

"I believe in work and simple living."

"Well put, Your Honor. I say the same myself. No endeavor that is worthwhile is simple in prospect, but if it is right and good, it is simple in retrospect."

Charlie's ears perked up. This stranger sure knew how to use words. He'd try to remember them. He thought, nothing worthwhile is easy, until it's done.

Will's eyes squinted and he blurted, "You looking to sell this here horse? It's a mite flashy, besides its foot's bad with acute founder." Will spit out the side of his mouth. In his anxiousness he added, "I have a younger pony that I could make a trade with, if you'd be willing to judge good horseflesh. The pony has wide hips. They give a horse more power."

Waiting for an answer, Will took up a pair of pliers and pulled the broken shoe from the palomino's hoof. One nail had to be yanked out as the horse pawed the air. Will spoke to the nervous horse, "Whooaa, there now, this won't take long."

The stranger cleared his throat. "Chief, you ain't 'xactly hog-tied when it comes to making chin music." He hesitated long enough for Will to look up and let the words sink in.

Charlie thought he had a perfect way of saying Will sounded like an overblown rooster. He wished he could talk like the stranger.

"This horse of mine's got no more laminitis, nor founder, than I got a malarious poison. Front foot's not even hot. Shoe's broken and that's about the size of it. Nope—I got no intentions of making any trade nor sale."

The stranger winked at Charlie. "Never met such young smiths." He smoothed his mustache. "Unless I'm just getting old. I'm Colonel Johnson." He held his hand out to Charlie.

"I'm Charlie—Charles Burton Irwin. I'm glad to meet you, sir. This here is my brother, William Henry Harrison Faulkner Irwin. We just call him Will and on occasions some other things."

Colonel Johnson shook hands vigorously. "Say, either of you royal citizens ever see a real, honest-to-God medicine show?"

"Nope," said Charlie. "I ain't ever. But I heard they combine some singing and dancing with peddling conjure draughts."

"Nice job," complimented Colonel Johnson, looking at the new horseshoe. "I might have more work. Say, some harness hardware. You two young gentlemen are definitely invited to see Colonel Johnson's Medicine Show, completely free of charge, of course."

"You made the deal for a gold piece," said Charlie, looking Colonel Johnson in the eye.

The Colonel flashed a smile and handed a small gold coin to Charlie.

"Where's the show?" asked Will.

"Right here in this lovely town. At the end of this here main street, yonder on the prairie. Show begins promptly at sundown. Don't miss it!"

A gopher spoke in a thin, sharp squeal two, three times from the vacant lot. It reminded Charlie of the time he'd found a gopher's hole in the center of the tiny mound next to Old Charles's grave in the cemetery. Grandma Malinda filled it, smoothed it, and told Charlie not to say anything to his mother about the gopher digging into the baby's grave. Charlie had asked her who the baby was, but she had closed her eyes and not answered. Charlie looked up Washington Street and saw the emptiness of the land beyond town. The air hung heavy and warm. Suddenly something caught his eye in the last red rays of sunlight. A blue-green-bodied, four-winged dragonfly hung over the foxtails beside the smithery door.

The dragonfly's wings shimmered like liquid silver in the fading burnished light. A dust devil swirled along the road, stopped, started again, and whirled quietly out to the empty land. The breeze felt good on the back of Charlie's neck. He reached out in slow motion for the dragonfly as it hovered over the weeds. He caught a flash of light on its silver wings and closed a thumb and forefinger together. He tried to will the body to be still. Inside the smithery he found a clear Mason jar holding chain links. He dumped the links into an empty Hills Bros. can, then put the dragonfly inside the jar and screwed down the lid. He punched a tiny hole in the metal lid by pounding a rusty nail on the lid's center.

Charlie helped Will pack the forge fire down around a stub of hardwood for the night. A bucket of ashes was mounded over the fire to trap the heat. Will coughed when Charlie exhaled over the heap, blowing ash thick into the air. He made a face at Charlie and lunged as if to grab him by his mop of sandy hair.

Charlie dodged and hung up the tongs, scooped wood shavings back into the box by the wall, and picked up the spent iron shoe and threw it into the box of odds and ends. He looped his coiled rope over his shoulder, checking the end for frays.

Will closed the front doors and fastened the latch by slipping a wooden peg on a leather string through a notch on one of the doors.

"I caught an angel for Frank," said Charlie, holding the jar carefully and shuffling along home beside his brother.

TWO

The Medicine Show

Next morning Malinda showed up early with a basket of blackberries. "Came before it got too hot," she said, preparing to bathe Frank. "Found one of them white cedars in the woods. Rare as a thornless cactus in these parts."

Charlie looked at his grandmother through squeezed-down eye slits. "How could you tell it was white instead of red?"

She chuckled as if half expecting Charlie to check on her. "Its twigs is covered by overlapping scales fitting tight as any snake's skin. But you can tell red cedar in a wink by those small, sky-blue berries and them waxy cones with blue scales that look welded on."

"Where'd you learn all that?" Charlie now watched Will wolf down bacon and eggs in preparation for a day at the smithery.

"Some I got from dear Old Charles and most I learned by looking at the real thing. Not just seeing, but real deep looking and remembering what I see." Malinda's double-chinned face was framed with soft, curling white hair.

"Come on, Charlie, finish your breakfast so's we can open the smithery," said Will. He was looking for his straight razor. "Hey, Ell, you use my razor again to cut heads off clover or some stupid damn weed?"

"I hope Ma washes your mouth," said Ell. She was washing

breakfast dishes and the black iron griddle. "I haven't used your dumb razor. Maybe Pa took it."

"If I shaved I'd have a special place for my razor and things," said Charlie. He was looking out the front screen door. Rachel Brassfield was coming up the walk. She had come in her one-horse shay. Her horse was tied to the iron post beside the hawthorns. "Ma, here comes Grandma Rachel."

"Tell her how much you enjoyed the egg pie, Charlie," called Mary, who was helping her mother-in-law bathe Frank.

"Good morning!" called Rachel. "Think we'll have rain before the week's out? Is Joe back?" Her graying hair was twisted, not braided, back behind her ears and held in place with the tortoiseshell combs. She'd held her long, brown cotton skirt up several inches as she walked across the dusty path from the street to the house. Inside she went right to Frank's room to talk with Mary, not waiting for answers to her questions. "I don't think this sick baby should be taken outdoors. The thermometer Riley has on our porch says eighty-two degrees and it's only seven in the morning! I may have heat prostration by afternoon!"

"It's warm in this room already," said Mary. "I'm going to carry Frank to the cot under the oak; you can put the net over the hoops that Joe built. That'll keep out flies, but not the breeze. Frank always feels better after he's been out. By mid-morning, if it's too hot, I'll bring him in."

"What's this?" asked Rachel, holding up Charlie's Mason jar so close to her face that the dragonfly's blue-green iridescent body reflected in her eyes, making them shimmer.

Charlie paused at the bedroom door. "Grandma Rachel, it's something pretty for Frank to look at. Kind of lights up the room and makes Frank smile. He thinks it's an angel and in the middle of the night I heard him talk to it."

Rachel cleared her throat and looked at Charlie. "Do you want your baby brother to die?"

"Oh, no!" A lump came into Charlie's throat.

"No one talks to angels unless they are in Heaven where the angels live. This is one of those vile insects, darning needles, they're called. Many a time I've heard it said that one can sew a baby's nose and mouth shut tight." She shook the jar, causing the dragonfly to flit back and forth in the confined space.

Mary carried Frank outside. Malinda followed with the folding cot, hooks, and roll of cheesecloth.

"I never heard that," said Charlie. "But I did hear of cats jumping into a cradle and smothering a baby. Frank's too big to be smothered by a cat. He's probably too big to have his mouth sewn. Besides, the dragonfly can't get out."

"I'll make certain of that in a jiffy." Rachel took the jar to the kitchen, pulled the front lid off the range, opened the jar, and turned it upside down. She shook the insect onto the hot coals.

Charlie gasped. His bottom lip trembled and he clamped his top teeth over it. Suddenly he felt the oppressiveness of the new day. He opened the screen door and let it bang shut behind him.

Rachel called shrilly for Charlie to come back. He walked slowly to the front hedge. He heard Rachel, but he didn't turn his head to look at her. He respected his Grandma Rachel, but he was not overly fond of her. Nine-year-old Charlie felt she was picky about cleanliness and jumpy about tiny things, like mice, spiders, and garter snakes. On the other hand she made good ginger cake and was generous with the produce from her kitchen garden and her chickens. He tried to stay on her good side by giving her presents he thought she'd like. But he usually failed in guessing what she'd like. Charlie liked Grandpa Riley well enough. And he knew that Riley respected Rachel, because he gave her a wide berth whenever possible. He let her run the house in town. Riley must be fond of Rachel. He let her have most anything she asked for. Charlie heard a *pad-pad* of running feet and hoped it wasn't Grandma Rachel come to scold about him slamming the screen door. It was his mother. "She called for you to come back. Didn't you hear?"

"I heard. But Grandma Rachel burned Frank's angel—the dragonfly. I'm mad enough to kick Squirt."

"Charlie, the old dog is on its last legs. What good would it do to kick it? Don't let people get you down. You have a long time to live with them."

Mary and Charlie stood by the hawthorn hedge. It was cool in the shade.

"Ma, think. Grandma Malinda gave us Squirt a long time ago. He was a good pet and no one threw him away. That dragonfly made Frank feel good."

"Charlie, think. Grandma Rachel told you about the flying darning needle. She believes there's such a thing. When I was your age I heard the same story. But you and I know there isn't an insect in the world that can perform such a wondrous feat."

"She believed it and she burned it! It made Frank grin when it flew in the jar." Charlie's voice was choked. He felt his nose become stuffy and his eyes water.

"Maybe she is also dead-set against flies and pests and things she calls vermin. She's really trying to help. If it were you sick, she'd worry same as she worries over Frank. She loves us."

"Ma, she's pushy and won't listen!"

"Go back and see. Tell her you are sorry you slammed the door. She'll understand. She'll see that you worry about Frank, too."

"She doesn't have to worry about us. She has her own boys. Can't she worry about them?"

"They are grown and take care of themselves. Go back and say good-bye, then hurry on to the smithery with Will." Mary gave Charlie a hug.

He felt only a little better, and was not yet ready to admit he understood Grandma Rachel's feelings. He wiggled out of his mother's arms. "I'm going to find something else to make Frank feel better and she better not touch it!"

"Then keep it out of sight," Mary said.

They walked back to the house. Charlie lagged behind three, four steps. At the door Mary said, "Grandma Malinda believes Frank'll pass the crisis before your pa gets back with Doc Reed."

"Grandma Malinda told me the Irwins are nonbreakable. So don't worry, Ma. Frank'll get well," Charlie said. He thought his mother's eyes sparkled like a pair of will-o'-the-wisps. Then he blinked and the light was gone from her eyes. She looked tired and sad.

"Indestructible," corrected Mary.

"Yup, that's it. I'm going to take a lunch to the smithery today."

Mary did not go inside, but went to the little cot under the shade oak where Malinda was fussing over the netting. Frank had been ill more than a month. First he had a cough, then a runny nose.

Charlie went to the kitchen. He heard the sizzle as Ell spat on the flat iron to test the temperature. He smelled the freshly ironed clothes. He cut two slices of rye bread and spread on raspberry jam.

"Charlie, make a sandwich for Will, too. Wrap them in a clean dishtowel," said Ell.

Charlie licked off the knife and found the towel.

Ell fixed crystal green eyes on him, shook her head and sighed, then continued to iron.

Charlie called out so that his Grandma Rachel, changing Frank's bed, could hear, "Bye! I won't slam the door!" He rushed out, grabbed the screen, and eased it shut.

Grandma Malinda was coming in. "Slow down, the day is too hot to rush." Her brown eyes crinkled with her smile. "I thought you left a while back."

"I came in for bread and jam," said Charlie, looking for a way to escape. He licked his lips, tasting the sweet jam from the knife.

"Want to know a secret?" asked Malinda in a whisper.

Charlie held his head so that his grandmother could put her lips close to the hair over his ear. She tickled when she whispered, "I'm going to give you Grandpa's old rifle."

"For me?" Charlie's eyes grew wide. "The Henry rifle?"

"Yes. He wants you to have it."

"Did Old Charles say so?"

"Last night he told me." She kept her mouth straight. Her eyes sparkled.

"But, Grandma—he's dead."

"I know that. He's an angel now."

"Were you in Heaven?"

"No, he came to visit me in my dream. We all have dreams, Charlie."

Charlie felt as if the pull of gravity had suddenly been divided in half. He could breathe easier and he was lighter on his feet when he walked. "Next time you dream, tell Old Charles 'thanks a lot,'" Charlie said. He not only respected Grandma Malinda and her knowledge of local plants and animals, but he was not continuously on the defensive in her presence as he was with Rachel. He knew he liked Grandma Malinda. "I have to go to the smithery or else Will might wring my neck."

"Next time you come to my place, we'll get the rifle out and look at it. In my time every boy had a rifle by the time he was twelve. It was a symbol of growing up and kept the gopher population in check."

"Grandma, I'm not twelve. Did you forget?" Charlie edged toward the front walk. "You keep the rifle. When I'm twelve I'll look at it with you."

"I'm not senile! Some things I forget, but not your birthday. You are to have the rifle now. It's Old Charles's wish."

They both saw that Rachel was coming out the screen door. Charlie wanted nothing more than to bolt up the street. He took a deep breath.

Rachel came off the porch and swished open a fan she had tied to her waistband with a pink, silk cord. "Is Charlie telling you about the eggs he broke yesterday in my kitchen? Eggs are scarce in this heat. You pay twenty and a half cents a dozen if you buy them at Clem's Groceries."

Charlie looked from one grandmother to the other. "Did Grandpa Riley like the egg in the milk bottle?"

Rachel fanned her face so hard Charlie could feel the breeze. "Well—he was surprised. He couldn't believe it. He wanted to know how it was done."

Charlie smiled and pushed the hair from his eyes. "Did you tell him?"

"I told him about the mess in my kitchen." Rachel looked at Malinda for sympathy. "I remember when Riley gave Charlie thirty cents to help shock wheat. Charlie couldn't keep that money in his pocket. He rode my black mare to town and bought a star candle from Sherman's Merc. I told him not to light it. Why, he'd set fire to my place."

Malinda didn't move an inch. She looked straight at Charlie. "So that's where you got the money to buy me that star candle. I still have it in the bottom of the water glass, just the way you brought it over. It's a pretty sight when I light it. The flame flickers in the bottom of that clear glass like a firefly. Sometimes I have a cup of tea and watch it before I turn on the electric." She put her hand out and pushed the lariat straight on Charlie's shoulder. "Hurry on to help your brother."

"Good-bye—tell Ma we'll see her at supper!" Charlie ran down the dirt path to the street. Then he slowed to a walk. Halfway to the smithery he decided not to tell Will about the Henry rifle. It was a secret. He began to think of his grandmothers. He thought of Rachel as sour and Malinda as sweet. Life was sweet some days, sour other days. If a person let the sour take over, he could become blind to the sweet. He decided to avoid life's sourness any way possible. By the time Charlie got to the smithery he was in good spirits. Life was going to be ruled by the sweet for him.

At the smithery yard were two men sitting on the bench under the tree waiting for something to be repaired. Charlie nodded and smiled to them.

"Hello there, Charlie," said one, putting a wad of tobacco in front of his teeth next to his cheek so he could talk. The other, with gray suspenders, said, "You startled me, son. For a moment I thought it was Old Charles coming along the walk swinging his arms the way he used to do."

"I guess everybody in town knew him," said Charlie, trying to catch a scampering black ant between his toes.

"Yep, and liked him," said the man with the tobacco cud.

"I wish I'd known him."

"Some men are hard to forget. He's one," said the man with gray suspenders. "Everyone was a friend to him. He found something nice to say about the worst. Once a man shot his wife and Old Charles said, 'That man just lost his patience at the wrong time.'"

Charlie stood by the smithery's gaping entrance. Both of the double doors were pulled open to let in air and light. By his feet Charlie saw some gray stones, all about the same size. With a big toe he pushed them in a line. Then he put two of the stones side by side, silently calling them Ma and Pa. He put four smaller stones around the two, naming them Will, Ell, Charlie, and Frank. He stared at the stones. Then he took out the smallest and stared again. He thought, I can see there's a hole. Even the smallest is missed. He spread the stones apart and went inside the shop.

Charlie and Will worked on repairing farm equipment most of the morning. About noon Charlie shared the bread and jam sandwiches with Will. Afterward Will brought a tin can of water from the pump in back, near the horse shed.

"Listen," said Will. "Sounds like fiddle music coming from down Washington."

"Yep, I hear it. I'll go see what's going on."

"Sweep the floor first. Pa could come back while you're gone."

Charlie swept, hung up the broom, and took his lariat off a nail. "You'll tell Pa that you said it was all right for me to go?" he asked.

"You little runt! Don't you trust your big brother?" asked Will.

"Not much reason to," said Charlie, swinging his rope.

"Get that rope out of here. You could knock something over."

"If it's a medicine show, we can all go."

"I was thinking that," said Will back at the forge.

The music became louder and louder. Charlie walked faster and faster. The music made waves that enveloped Charlie. The waves put out invisible strings that made him swing his arms to the beat. He stopped and twirled the rope over his head, trying to hold the rhythm. He continued walking, letting the rope move over his head.

Charlie saw a crowd of kids standing around the back of a

large wagon, freshly painted red and yellow. On a small wooden platform a girl was fiddling "The Old Rugged Cross." She was in her late twenties. Her eyes were glossy gray, like a silver fox fur. Her hair was straw-colored, but dark close to the part down the middle of her head, and she had wound the braided ends to form two coils and fastened them over each ear. Her pink satin dress was none too clean. Charlie could see the dinginess around the high buttoned collar that was not buttoned as high as it could have been. There were dark patches in the material under her arms. Charlie felt the wetness under his own arms. The humidity was high and evaporation low.

She stopped playing as a well-dressed man stepped onto the platform. He took off his wide-brimmed white hat and waved it at the crowd of curious youngsters. "My friends, I am Colonel Johnson, and this medicine show begins at sundown. You saw the dress rehearsal. Now go home and bring your folks back after supper. Bring neighbors, aunts, uncles, grandparents, and a pocketful of change. There's something here for everyone." He pushed the girl through the curtain and he, too, disappeared.

"Are you coming back?" one of the girls asked Charlie.

"Sure, and so's my family." Then he added, "Of course, someone will have to stay home with Frank, who's sick. Boy! That little kid would like a medicine show. I'm coming so's I can tell him about it." The kids left in little groups, heading for different parts of town.

Charlie hurried back to the smithery to tell Will what he'd found. Near suppertime Will and Charlie closed the shop. When the boys were home, they found everyone knew about the medicine show because there were advertising posters nailed to the electric light poles down the main street of town. Ell was going to the show with Grandma Malinda, who had stayed for supper.

Since Old Charles's death, Malinda often stayed for supper. No one ever objected. She was a member of the family and well loved.

Mary asked Will to take Charlie to the show and said she'd stay home with Frank and keep a warm supper for Joe. "He surely will be back with the doctor tonight."

"Don't fret," said Malinda. "Joe'll do what he can to get the doctor. Frank is no worse. Sit by the screen door so you can hear that lady's fiddle music Charlie told about."

* * *

There were very few forms of entertainment in Chillicothe, except watching the railroad tracks being laid at the edge of town. A medicine man camped on the outskirts brought out most of the townsfolk.

Charlie twirled the end of his rope until Will told him to put it away. "Do you have to take that blasted rope? Geez, Charlie, I bet you'd take it to church, maybe rope the preacher." Will laughed.

Charlie was looking at the crowd of people in a large semi-circle around the wagon. He waved to Grandma Malinda and Ell standing together and turned to tell Will he was going to move closer so he could see better. Will was talking to a couple of friends, so Charlie squeezed through the crowd and leaned against the wooden platform which was hinged to the side of the wagon and supported by two blocks of wood in front.

Colonel Johnson stepped to the very edge of the platform and waved his hands. "Folks, move up. I am the one and only Colonel Johnson. You are lucky enough to hear this little lady sing. She also plays the fiddle." He pointed a finger at the girl. "The famous operatic star Ophelia."

Ophelia spread out her soiled satin skirt and curtsied. Her feet were as bare as Charlie's, except she had dirty pink ribbon pulled up around each big toe across the top of her feet and wound around her ankles and tied.

"Folks, now, listen. Tell you what I'm going to do! See this here packet of peppermints?" The Colonel took a small brown paper bag from a wooden crate. Ophelia had pulled it through the curtain to the stage. "Young, old, large, small, everybody loves peppermints!"

The sun was below the horizon and the western sky glowed deep crimson. Charlie thought it was the perfect background for the yellow and red medicine wagon.

The Colonel waved his big hat. "Breath sweeteners! Peppermints are the perfect breath sweeteners. They can settle a sour stomach. One packet is worth a nickel, one Indian head, five cents, or one buffalo. Dig in your pockets!

"Now, here's the deal! Tell you what I'm going to do!" His voice carried to the back of the crowd and on across the prairie. It vibrated on the floor of the stage and in Charlie's chest. Charlie had never heard a man talk so well, so loud, so clear. He thought if a man spoke loud he had to be shouting and then his words became garbled, almost incoherent. Colonel Johnson made no effort to get his voice out to the back of the crowd. It was formed somewhere deep at the bottom of his chest and rolled up his throat and out his mouth like fresh, crisp cracklings of thunder. Charlie was fascinated. Suddenly he wanted to do the same thing. He turned from the stage framed in the last pink light from the sinking sun, took a deep breath, held up his head so his voice would go out over the crowd. He waited two, three heartbeats until Colonel Johnson paused, then he called out.

"Colonel Johnson chose the Irwin Smithery to have his faithful, golden palomino's shoe repaired! Irwin's Smithery on Washington. It's the choice of the medicine man. It ought to be your choice. Irwin's Smithery!" Charlie's heart beat fast and hard, as if he'd been running uphill. He saw heads swivel around and eyes look at him. He closed his mouth. He thought the swell of his voice, high and loud, rippled over the crowd. He didn't dare look around again. He'd not realized the extent of the crowd. It seemed everyone from Chillicothe had come out. There were several snickers behind him and he heard someone whisper.

"Chip off the old Irwin block." The voice was Grandma Malinda's.

Will and two friends stood near Charlie. Will wanted to clamp a hand over Charlie's mouth, but he didn't want to start a commotion. Will moved a few feet from Charlie. He was embarrassed and did not want to be associated with a loudmouth for a brother. Yet, he admitted to himself, it was a clever way to draw attention to the smithery. Geez, the customers will razz us tomorrow, he thought.

Colonel Johnson glanced down and glared at Charlie. "Scram! Beat it! You're upstaging the act." He then looked up, ignoring the skinny kid with the sandy hair that nearly covered his eyes. "This is the deal! I'll sell one packet to each customer, for only one nickel. That gives you a real chance to win this here genuine Injun blanket you see behind me."

Ophelia held out a gray blanket with a red and black triangular border design.

"You pay one nickel for a packet of genuine peppermints and in addition you get free a chance to own this real Injun blanket. That's one chance to a customer! 'Course I can't keep track of names, so if you buy two or three of these here peppermint packets, you double or triple your chance to have this beautiful, genuine wool blanket." Colonel Johnson reached out and took the blanket from Ophelia. He shook it out so the people could see the bright-colored design in the center.

"This here is an authentic Navaho blanket. It's hand-woven by

Navaho hands and wove so tight that water can be carried in it for hours. Yes! Carry water in it for four or five hours before it leaks through.

"Folks, it took one Navaho squaw two, maybe three years to complete this one blanket. It will outlast a lifetime. Guaranteed! You can roll it in mud until every bit of color seems gone. Totally muddy! Then, when you wash it in water with kitchen soap, the beautiful colors come back out as bright and clean as new. Ain't no blanket anywhere as good as a genuine, hand-woven, Navaho Injun blanket.

"Tell you what I'm going to do! I have a hat full of numbers to match the ones on your peppermint sacks. Do not destroy nor lose the number on your sack. That is proof positive you bought peppermints and are eligible to match the number pulled from my hat.

"Stick around! Folks, this is one exciting show!"

The Colonel lit two torches that hung on the back sides of the wagon. The flickering light would be welcome in a few more minutes, as the twilight was nearly spent and the now gray sky was darkening fast. The Colonel had on a gray dress vest and pin-striped trousers topped off with a high, black silk hat. He seemed busier than a prairie dog after a rain as he passed out brown sacks of hard peppermints and pocketed one handful after another of nickels.

Ophelia came back in a tight red dress with three rows of ruffles. The bottom ruffle dusted the floor boards. Will whistled, "Wow! Is she stacked!"

Charlie called out, "Pipe down! She's talented, you know!"

Ophelia moved her ribboned feet in a little dance and began to clap her hands. She smiled and it was not long until most of the audience clapped in time with her. She began to sing, ever so soft at first, then it grew until "Skip to My Lou" filled the air between the flickering torches. People in the audience smiled and swayed in time to the music. Some sang with her. She picked up her fiddle. Charlie could not hold back, he sang, raising his voice to match hers. After a couple of songs she laid the fiddle on a beat-up chair near the curtain. She reached inside the curtain and pulled out a small dog, which she held in her arms.

The Colonel used a speaking trumpet to carry his voice into the darkness and to the far edge of the crowd. "Tell you what I'm going to do! Right here, before your own eyes, I'm going to let you see our Wonder Dog! He counts! He sings! He jumps through fire! That's what I said, he counts, sings, and jumps through fire!

He is undoubtedly the cleverest dog in this here county."

Someone shouted, "You mean Livingston County?"

"Yes. Now here's Wonder Dog, the most fantastic dog in Livingston County!"

Charlie felt the surge of the crowd at his back moving in for a better look. He leaned closer and saw that the Wonder Dog was a scrubby, yellow and black, wire-haired fox terrier. He turned to say something about the dog to Will. Somehow he'd lost Will as the crowd moved up. Charlie knew Will was close somewhere. He leaned on the stage for a good look.

"Hey, kid, come on up!" shouted Colonel Johnson, pointing a finger at Charlie. "Yes, you, the loudmouth. Hold this here hoop."

Charlie felt an electric tingle go clear through his chest as someone boosted him up on the stage. The hoop had rags wrapped around it. It smelled funny to Charlie.

"Soaked in alkyhall," whispered the Colonel. "Hang on to it. It's not hot enough to burn nor blister. Hold there. You'll be fine. Not as hot as a forge, you'll see. The tip'll love your show." He motioned out over the crowd with a wave of a hand. "I can't run you off for advertising your business to all these people, so you join my show."

Charlie swallowed and laid his rope on the battered chair beside the fiddle. He hoped his hands stayed steady. His mouth felt dry as dust. He held the hoop high. The Colonel brought one of the torches near and suddenly there was a bright flash and the rags on the hoop glowed an eerie blue, shimmering light. The Wonder Dog jumped clean through on Colonel Johnson's command. Just as Charlie thought the dog was going to run off the stage and into the crowd, it turned and ran back to jump through the hoop again.

Wild applause came through the air. Charlie felt the surge of cheers and heard the call for an encore. He inhaled deeply through his mouth as though sucking in all of it. He felt wonderful. He stepped forward a trifle and held out the smoking, blackened hoop for all to see. He hoped Will, Ell, and Grandma Malinda could see him. Charlie put his left hand to his waist and bowed as he had seen Colonel Johnson do.

Ophelia removed the hoop from his hand and replaced it with a black silk top hat with a false bottom. The motions of the pitchman, Colonel Johnson, were fast. The Colonel kept up a constant patter of words, making the audience remain relaxed and laughing.

Charlie laughed when the Colonel whispered for him to slide the latch on the bottom of the hat. He did this and a huge white rabbit popped up over the top. It was alive. Charlie's eyes were round as silver dollars. He took another bow and popped the hat on his head. The rabbit was bigger and fatter than any Charlie had ever seen. The long pink ears twitched. The rabbit hopped to the edge of the stage and wiggled its nose. Ophelia came behind the animal with a wire cage. She slid the door open and held a limp carrot so that it dangled from the top to the inside. At that moment the Wonder Dog yipped and ran between Ophelia and the rabbit, causing the cage to fall. Ophelia made a fast grab for the rabbit, but tripped over the cage and fell head first with her legs in the air. Her skirt went to her waist, revealing red satin bloomers.

Ophelia picked up herself and smoothed her skirt down over her hips so it covered her slim, white legs. From the corner of his eye Charlie saw the rabbit hopping around the front of the medicine wagon, then he was aware that the Wonder Dog was chasing it. The Colonel cried, "Oh, my Lord! There go the props!"

The crowd hooted back, thinking for sure it was all part of the act.

A voice called, "Bring on the dancing girls!" There were more whistles until someone else called out, "We want the liniment!"

"How am I going to get that fool rabbit and dog back?" moaned the Colonel.

Charlie had already figured that out. He picked up his horsehair rope and stepped down from the stage. He scooted around the wagon, where the crowd thinned out, and ran toward the high-pitched yipping. He prayed the rabbit would not lead the dog into a gully, where the sound would be so blocked that he couldn't follow it. As he ran he could hear the voice of the Colonel buffeting him from behind, "Tell you what I have. It's medicine all right! The show goes on! Step right up here!"

The dog stopped. The rabbit was cornered between two boulders. It was so big and unexercised that it could not quickly squeeze between the rocks, nor run past the panting dog. It was hunched and cowering, scared to death. The Wonder Dog barked in short yips, then longer yaps. The rabbit's breathing was fast. Charlie could see its sides moving in and out like bellows in the moonlight. Charlie was thankful his eyes became accustomed to the darkness, lit only by a pale yellow moon near the horizon, because rocks were everywhere. They were sharp as flint, hidden in the weeds, waiting to twist an ankle. He jumped back from sharp scratches in his knees. Blackberry bushes were in a patch of shadow. He skirted them now and saw the dog, a shapeless shadow that panted and yipped. The dog enjoyed the chase and wanted more. The rabbit, a talcum white in the moonlight, was not going to move.

Don't either of you move, thought Charlie as he steadied his hand. The rabbit's head came up and its ears flicked once in Charlie's direction. He was sure its nose twitched as the wind changed and brought his smell right over into the rocks. His arm reacted automatically. The loop settled over the rabbit and Charlie jerked. He ran to see what was at the rope's end. All had taken place in only a couple of seconds. He was beginning to think he might have jerked the rope too hard. An extra half-pound pull would mean disaster if the rope were directly around the rabbit's neck. Charlie exhaled and shook his head so that the hair was out of his eyes. He picked up the rabbit and hauled in his rope. The dog was by his side barking its head off. His hand felt the rabbit's heartbeat. He nuzzled his face in the warm fur. A hind leg pushed hard against his chest. "It's the cage for you," he said. "Come on, let's get you guys back in show business." The dog ran happily at his heels.

Charlie eased himself against the back of the stage under one of the torches. He patted the rabbit behind its ears and rubbed the dog behind its head. The dog licked Charlie's arm and ignored the rabbit. Ophelia came out with the cage. "Put the rabbit in here," she said, lifting the sliding door. She grabbed the rabbit and slammed the door closed.

Colonel Johnson hustled Charlie out to the back of the stage as Ophelia, in a pink satin dress, began another song. He gave Charlie a dozen bottles of tonic to sell among the crowd.

"I've never—I don't know—" started Charlie.

"You can sell! Damn-tootin'," he called after Charlie. The Colonel was not far behind, relieving Charlie of fistfuls of silver coins he collected. The Colonel had a rope holding a box of tonic bottles slung over his shoulder. He kept passing more bottles to Charlie.

A stranger asked Charlie if he were selling the famous Wizard Oil. Charlie's head came up and his eyes went to the left, where there was a shadowy figure. The figure was Charlie's father! Momentarily Charlie felt a spasm of faintness. It passed quickly and his eye caught Colonel Johnson. The Colonel put a steadying hand on his shoulder. "That rube someone you know, son?" whispered the Colonel.

Charlie swallowed. "Pa, I want you to meet my friend, Colonel Johnson."

"Pleased," said the Colonel, putting a fistful of coins into his pocket before extending his hand. "Fine lad—fine, mighty fine."

"You make a fine spiel yourself," said Joe. "Sounds like you use some tongue oil." Joe stared angrily at Charlie.

Charlie felt his mouth go dry. He rasped, "If you give my pa a bottle of this here medicine, I'll pay for it by selling more of the stuff."

"That's a fair, square deal, pal." Colonel Johnson shoved a bottle into Joe's hands.

"Take this to Frank," Charlie said to his father. "If the medical doctor does no good—this sounds like it cures everything."

Joe pulled Charlie around so they faced each other. "Doc Reed's not coming until morning. Frank's no worse. But your ma's worried about you. Will came in for supper. He said you were working the medicine show. I came in and couldn't believe it!"

Charlie forced a grin. "Tell Ma I'm all right."

Joe seethed. His face was red. "Ell and Malinda went on home, even Rachel and Riley left." His finger pointed in the direction of the Brassfield house. "I'm not keen about you staying! But you made a bargain with that—that colonel. I'll send Will back and when the show closes come home with him. Keep your nose clean!"

"Thanks, Pa. Don't forget, give Frank some tonic!"

Joe turned back and glared, then he was gone, concealed by the crowd.

Charlie held up a bottle of tonic and called in his clear voice, "This here Injun medicine is better'n blood from the amputated tail of a cat to cure a case of shingles!" The bottle sold right away. Charlie called again, "This medicine is more powerful than a calomel purge!" He sold several bottles and felt something rub against his legs. It was the Wonder Dog. He stroked the dog's back and it stuck close to Charlie's heels so as not to miss this rare demonstration of affection.

Colonel Johnson reached out to collect the coins and said, "That's right! Use the long con, slow and deliberate persuasion. Keep these lot lice buying."

Charlie spouted sayings he'd heard from his Grandma Malinda. "A little hair from this ol' Wonder Dog swallowed with your medicine is genuine proof against mad dogs. Or, if you prefer to use just one thin hair in a bread-and-butter sandwich, it will do the trick." Charlie enjoyed diving into his memory for medical hints. "Take one teaspoon of this tonic and put a pan of water under your bed. It will knock out any fever you got." Charlie's voice grew husky.

Colonel Johnson beamed from ear to ear. "We've activated this crowd! We've turned the tip this night." He closed the show down and Charlie helped him stack the empty bottle crates and push up the flimsy stage against the back of the wagon, after the torchlights were doused in water. Charlie stooped to pet the dog as he left, and when he looked up the Colonel was talking to Will. "Say, your brother there is a genuine, natural-born grinder, a medicine hawker par excellence!"

"Thank you and so long, Colonel Johnson!" called Charlie as he and Will turned together and started through the short dried grass for the street and home. Charlie felt as if he were as tall as Will.

Frank was asleep. Joe said the boy's face was cooler. Charlie couldn't tell. Will went to get some rye bread because he felt hungry. Charlie could see better with Will out of the way and thought his father sure used a wet rag because the pillow where Frank's cheek lay was soaked and his hair was plastered to his forehead.

In the living room Ell was telling Mary about the big white rabbit. "The dog chased the rabbit and Charlie chased both of them!" She stretched her arms upward and yawned, and Charlie remembered Ophelia in the pink satin dress. Ell went to bed and Charlie told his mother about the dog jumping through fire and the fiddling. "You would have enjoyed it," he said.

Then Joe asked Charlie to go into the kitchen. "How about a glass of milk?"

"Sure, and a piece of rye bread," said Charlie. "About half the size of the one Will just had."

Joe looked worn out. He slid into a chair at the kitchen table. "Son, there's something important that should be said before the evening is spent."

Charlie felt a soft explosion inside, like the breaking of a glass. The exaltation was gone. He could not get it back. He felt tired and empty even after the bread and milk. He looked at his father, who seemed to be formulating just the right words.

"Charlie, if you ever go into a business, whether it be blacksmithing, or even a medicine show, remember these words." Joe looked at his son, who was not quite ten years old. "If you use a hired man, always be honest with him. It's one thing to cheat your equals, as in a horse trade. But don't cheat helpers. That Colonel cheated you. You made him a lot of money. He paid you one bottle of tonic worth fifteen cents. You were worth a man's price, a dollar a day, or fifty cents a half, for all you did."

"Pa, I know he cheated people. But I felt good. I learned I could do something myself. He gave me two bottles—Will has one."

"No matter—be honest with your hired help. Your equals will look out for themselves."

Next morning before breakfast the doctor came riding his horse through a soft, drizzling rain into the yard. Mary wiped her hands on her apron and tucked her hair wisps into the braid circling her head. Her eyes were clear with blue lights in the gray. Charlie went with her out the door. "I'll take his horse to the shed and give it oats," he said.

Doc Reed was a small man, with blond hair and silver-rimmed glasses. He looked tired. Mary told him to go into the house and dry his coat and wide-brimmed felt hat, then have something to eat.

"I would like to eat before I see the patient." Doc Reed washed at the kitchen basin after removing his wet coat and hat. He had biscuits, scrambled eggs, and bacon. After a second cup of coffee he washed his hands again and went to see Frank. Mary followed. Charlie, Will, and Joe stood around to hear what the doctor would say. Ell cleared the table and washed the dishes. Will was ready to leave for the smithery.

"You see those silver-rimmed glasses?" Will said to his mother. "I guess a man can see razor sharp with four eyes." His head ached. He guessed that bottle of tonic hadn't agreed with him last night.

Mary shushed him and sent him out the door.

"Well," said Doc Reed, looking like he had his second wind, "your young man appears to have had an infection in his lungs. I'd say it was pneumonia. But he's outlived the crisis. His fever is broken." He smiled and patted Mary's arm.

"I knew it!" cried Joe. "Charlie and I thought he was cooler last night."

"Well—maybe so. But I gave him an antipyretic that works within minutes," said Doc Reed.

"I've given him willow-bark tea," said Ell. "Grandma Malinda says a fever can be broke by lying on a heap of willow leaves. The fever transfers itself to the leaves. They are warm where the person has lain."

"I've heard of your notorious grandmother," said Doc Reed. He cleared his throat and decided not to say more about Malinda's herbal treatments. "Keep your young man in bed another week. Feed him soft, bland foods."

"If he gets out of bed, his strength comes back sooner," said Ell.

Doc Reed looked at Ell over the top of his glasses. "Young lady, your pa rode clean to Laclede and took me away from a game of cribbage with the postmaster. I give you the best advice I have. You've had several weeks to make the lad well. I've had less than an hour and he's better."

Ell's face turned red. Mary and Joe looked at her with stern faces.

The doctor cleaned his glasses on a snow-white handkerchief. He started for the door. "The boy's blood is thin. He'd catch his death with a relapse. Keep him out of any breeze; one strong enough to blow out a candle is too much."

"I've been letting him rest outside in the cool morning air—when it's not raining. Maybe that was wrong," said Mary.

"Well—I can't be sure. But for now, rest and soft food. Don't do anything that could upset his delicate balance."

Ell could not be repressed for long. Her thirst for medical knowledge was stronger than her fear of reprimand. "Henry Clem broke his leg and I helped my grandma set it. Only the long bone was broken, so it pierced the skin. How should that've been doctored?"

"I don't give out advice on cases handled by another. But if the long bone were actually broken, the man has a limp today. I saw that man last week and he walks as well as you or I!"

Ell's face was red again, but she went on. "If we could exchange information, I could tell you that the fracture was reduced and cedar shingles were tied on each side of the break. To keep the leg straight, a traction apparatus was made with a rope and a flatiron and a couple of horseshoes for weights."

Doc Reed wiped the perspiration from his forehead. He took his coat and hat from the chair, where it dried in front of the open oven. "Is that a fact!" He stared at Ell. "Maybe you and your grandma do know something. My friend, John Pershing, that Laclede postmaster, told me that Joe Irwin knows more about horseshoeing and horse ailments than anyone in the state. Pershing warned me about Joe's mother, saying she'd delivered most of the children hereabouts. But he never said a thing about Joe's daughter." He chuckled.

"Warned you?" said Joe, standing up to help the doctor put on his damp coat.

"Well, yes. He said your boy must have one foot in the grave already or you wouldn't have sent for me. Your mom is the best healer around, according to local opinion. Pershing said if she couldn't make the boy well, I couldn't either. Looks like I owe you folks an apology." His head fell to his chest. He cleared his throat. "Maybe I didn't make the boy better. I think he probably passed the crisis yesterday. The fever broke then."

Charlie looked up, his mouth open. Joe was shaking hands with Doc Reed saying, "Thank you for being honest. I think I know what pulled my youngest through."

Doc Reed, with a wide grin, said, "If you don't mind my saying so—it was the love and concern of this family. Oh, oh, I almost forgot. There's a message from old Pershing. He said, 'Tell Joe to bring his farrier's tools,' because he has horses that need shoes! He'll have you playing a game or two of cribbage also, I'd bet."

The two men settled the medical fee. Joe would put a new rim on the wheel of the doctor's wagon.

Charlie saw that no more was going to be said. He went out to the shed and brought out the doctor's horse. The drizzle had stopped and the sky was clearing in the west.

"Did the Kickapoo tonic work on Frank?" Charlie asked his father when they were back in the house.

"Could have," said Joe with a wink, "but then, there were prayers. Say, Malinda ought to meet that young doctor. They sure have something in common. Honesty! I sure like that in a person."

The thought caused Charlie to think. That's the secret: People like Grandma Malinda because they trust her.

Frank was out of bed in a week, eating meat, potatoes, and string beans.

Joe and Charlie went to Laclede in the farrier's wagon, leaving Will to work in the smithery alone.

On the following Monday morning Joe was telling Mary about the trip. "We would have been back sooner, but old Pershing kept regaling me with stories about his boy's competition for the military academy. And listen to this, his boy taught school to earn enough so's he could go to that normal school in Kirksville."

"Why was that so entertaining?" asked Mary. "Will does not want to teach school and heaven only knows what Charlie wants. Frank is too young to decide anything."

"I was thinking of Ell, Letitia Ellen. If she went to school in Kirksville, she could be a teacher of anything."

"Ell wants to be a healer," added Charlie. "Ma, you should see all the books in the Pershing place. Ell'd go crazy. You know how she irons with a book on the board beside the shirts."

"Normal school takes money," said Mary.

"Charlie!" said Joe. "Your ma and I are talking. Follow Will to the smithery. I'll be along after a while."

Charlie took his rope and let the front screen slam shut behind him. The grass was still damp from the night's dew. The sky was a deep blue. Charlie thought he knew what his father wanted to talk about—sending Ell to school because she was the one who could read. He shrugged his shoulders and thought school could make a slave out of a person, so he craved nothing but books. He wasn't sure that was good. He wondered what old Pershing's boy was like. Probably the boy was pale as paper from reading and soft from staying inside all day. I'd rather juggle a rope or ride bucking broncs, thought Charlie, letting his rope settle on a fence post.

The next morning at the smithery Charlie pumped the bellows so that Will could fire up the forge. A shadow fell through the front door and caused both boys to look up. Auburn-haired Colonel Johnson came in. He let his eyes adjust to the dark interior. Neither boy had expected to see him again.

"Where'd you keep that braided horsehair rope, Senator? A man with a trick rope is a show stopper. What do you think?" The Colonel looked at Charlie but didn't wait for his reply. "If I could learn a few spins, maybe the big loop over my head and around my body—people go for that stuff."

"Sure, they like that," agreed Charlie.

"Here's the broken harness." The Colonel had on a pair of dark wool pants stuffed into black boots, a soiled gray shirt, and a huge, dirty white sombrero on his head. He looked wonderful to Charlie.

Will rubbed his temples and let the intricate network of leather straps, loops, and pads that were held together with iron fittings, such as rivets, rings, lengths of small chain, bolts, clips, and hooks, run through his fingers. "Fifty cents for repairing the fittings. Twenty cents for the leather, if I can fix it."

While Will worked, Charlie took the Colonel to the vacant lot and showed him how to whirl the lariat. Then he showed him how to keep the noose open by turning his wrist as his hand came around to the front, keeping the back of his hand parallel with his head.

Colonel Johnson learned quickly. "Now, where can I buy a rope and some eats?" he asked.

"Clem's Groceries on South Locust will sell you a hemp rope. Get one with a honda-loop; otherwise, you gotta make your own."

Colonel Johnson hurried down the street.

Charlie saw no sense in letting the forge fire go to waste as Will worked on the leather straps, so he tried his hand at mending a large discarded pot. He put an iron bolt in the worn hole. He put a washer over the end of the bolt and heated the bolt close to the surface on both sides. Gingerly he cut the long end off the red-hot bolt and dropped the end in the slake bucket. "I think I'll sell the pot to Colonel Johnson," said Charlie.

Will looked disgusted. "Charlie, he won't buy that. The pot's no good. Been around here a long time and never used."

"It's mended," Charlie said with a smile, "and he'll feel obligated to buy because I taught him how to twirl a rope."

In two, three hours the Colonel was back. The harness was mended. He inspected the work and said, "Uh-uh, I've seen better."

Charlie stepped up. "You've never seen better'n this." With some effort he said the next sentence slowly. "You can see it is worth a dollar." He held out the mended pot.

Colonel Johnson blinked his eyes, then stared at Charlie. He pushed the dirty white sombrero to the back of his head so that Charlie had the thought that his face was like a picture framed in a ring of white felt. The curled ends of his auburn mustache moved up and down as he talked. "Well, Your Honor, I found a nest of bird eggs that would fit nicely in that there pot you wish to sell as a blow-off. I thought to pick them eggs up, but with nothing to carry them in, except my hat, which I need to keep the breeze off my head, I'll take the pot for a half dollar. That will prove your high-pressure salesmanship and liquidate your stock."

"Bird's eggs!" Charlie's eyes were bright. "Really?"

"Have I ever lied to you, my good man?" asked Colonel Johnson.

* * *

Charlie bent a little to watch the Colonel dig at the base of a damp clump of wild honeysuckle. They were at the end of Washington Street, out in the prairie. "Lookee here! The eggs are just as pretty as I remembered. They'll make a fine supper for me and Ophelia," said the Colonel.

Charlie rolled over in his hand one tiny white egg, spotted brown and purple. He said, "You didn't pay for the pot."

"My Lord, I did not forget. I'll pay when I pick up the harness."

Charlie pointed to the mended pot. "It's a half dollar, remember?"

"It's not worth that!"

"All right," agreed Charlie. "Forty-five cents and let me have two eggs."

"Four bits and I'll keep all the eggs."

Charlie rolled the egg from one hand to the other in front of the Colonel. He held the words back until just the right moment. He looked up, squinted one eye against the sunlight. He opened the other eye wide to watch the Colonel. "You're the first person I ever knew that liked to eat snake eggs."

Colonel Johnson stood still. "Snake eggs? Live snake eggs!" He handed the pot to Charlie. He hurried back into the shop and came out with the harness twisted over his shoulder, several leather straps and chains dragging in the dirt.

"Good day, Colonel Johnson," said Charlie, deliberately making his face serious. He put the egg in the pot beside the others. "I hope to see you again. You pay for the smith's work?"

"You owe seventy cents!" called Will.

"Oh, snake spit!" The Colonel reached into his pocket. "Take this you—you Pharisee. He handed Will a single, large paper greenback. He did not look back at Charlie, who stood in the street holding the pot with the late-laid meadowlark eggs in one hand and his side with the other as he suppressed his laughter.

"I have a new present for Frank!" Charlie called out. "I'll make needle-sized holes in the ends and blow the insides out. Then I'll string the eggs on thread. Frank can hang them up wherever he wants for decoration. Aren't they pretty? Too pretty to keep out of sight."

"Better hang them higher than some grandma can reach," Will said and laughed.

"Some grandma don't like snake eggs."
"They don't look like snake eggs," said Will.
"But if I mentioned snake eggs—"
"You wouldn't!"
"Who sez?"

THREE

Catastrophe

In late April the sky was a hazy blue and sunlight shone on the tall, white spire of the Baptist Church, then filtered through trees and glowed on house windows. Early in the morning Malinda Irwin saw a lone pair of whooping cranes flying high overhead toward the Grand River on their northern migration. The cranes dropped low and dipped gracefully as they passed directly over her small frame house. Malinda had not seen cranes since she was a small girl. Her quick mind recalled the old superstition that cranes passing over a house announced a death within that place during the coming year.

She watched the birds' long necks pull straight out like taut clothesline rope as they moved upward to higher altitude. She imagined a sad summoning note in their shrill, prolonged cries. The wailing dirge of the cranes' call caused tears to well in her eyes. She breathed deeply, prepared herself for the final farewell, her last sensations of the glorious Missouri spring. She wiped her eyes roughly on her sweater sleeve and spoke out loud to herself, "I saw the sign and that's that!"

"Grandma! Why are you crying?" said Charlie.

He surprised her. His voice sounded so much like that of her dear, deceased Old Charles. She took a deep breath. "It's nothing. The sight of cranes brought back memories of old times."

"Tell me some," said Charlie, going into the kitchen behind her.

"I remember a day I really cried. Your grandfather and I left our home in Indiana, Henry County, and took off for some place called Chillicothe. It wasn't on no map, because most of the inhabitants were Shawnee Injuns."

"Why'd you choose this place?" Charlie sat at the kitchen table while Malinda poured hot water in two teacups that she'd filled a third of the way with milk.

"Old Charles did the choosing. Stir your cottage tea. Put sugar in it," she said, smacking her lips. "I'll tell you when you have to run to school."

"Did Grandpa rive cedar into shingles then?"

"Land sakes, no!" She blew on her tea. "Old Charles, he learned to make moccasins from them Shawnees. Then on his own he learned to make men's work boots and ladies' slippers. Made his own tools. Bought leather goods from the Injuns with a gunny bag of potatoes, a fat hen, even his home brew. He traded shoes with the settlers for food and livestock. He was Chillicothe's first cordwainer." She pressed her blue-gray lips together, thinking. "He told me this town was named by them Shawnees. In everyday language *Chillicothe* means 'the-big-village-where-we-live.'"

Charlie nodded. He wanted to hear more.

"When did Grandpa sell shingles?" Charlie asked again. He sipped tea from a spoon, copying the habit of his grandmother.

"Later. When the town's settlers wanted frame houses." She sniffed and looked at Charlie. "Did you forget your bath this week? What's that I smell?" She pinched her nostrils.

"I plumb forgot!" Charlie lifted the bottom of his bulky sweater and pulled out a package wrapped in newspaper. "Two catfish I caught yesterday where the Thompson and Grand rivers join. You know that sandbar? Will and I waded out there."

She tore off the paper and pulled away the green leaves that were supposed to keep the fish fresh. She ran her fingers over the broad heads and scaleless backs. "These are dandies. There's enough for two meals, maybe more. Didn't you all go to church yesterday?"

"Nope."

"Time to hie for school. Tell your ma and pa I'll stop by and we'll all go to church next Sunday. Thanks, Charlie." She dropped the fish into the galvanized metal sink.

Charlie hitched his coiled horsehair rope a little higher on his shoulder. "Pa ain't speaking to me."

"For how long?" asked his grandmother.

"Since yesterday when I roped Grandma Rachel's guinea hen on the way home with the catfish. I only wanted to see if I could. She told Pa and I got a whipping. I think she expected to get my catfish."

"Charlie, have you gone clean wacky? You have to realize it is all right to tie a horse to a stob and use the horse as a roping target. But roping things like chickens, cats, dogs, and toddlers upsets their owners." She pushed him gently out the door and off the porch.

"I know. Pa told me." There was a sad, frayed look in Charlie's eyes. "Pa can lay a kid across his knees and whip him harder and faster than any other pa in town."

Malinda did not smile; she gave Charlie a quick hug and waved as he trotted off for school. "Come back and we'll talk more about the olden times," she called.

Charlie figured the sooner he got through school the sooner he'd become a cowboy and own a horse ranch. He dreamed of showing other cowboys how to master roping and how to round up a bunch of wild horses to fill his corrals. Already he had the terse words thought out that would go with these exhibitions. He practiced by giving lessons to some of the young boys at the town's newly built Fair Street Public School. Charlie charged each boy a nickel. He called the group Charlie's Roping Academy. His father put an end to the academy when a neighborhood mother complained that her son's fresh-starched shirts were looking like dust rags after her boy was chosen the academy's roping target for that week.

During the pledge of allegiance Charlie decided to put on an exhibition of his roping prowess. He invited everyone in fifth grade to bring lunch outside in the open field where they played kickball. "Come watch amazing rope tricks for free!"

Every child waited, breathless, to see what Charlie would do with his coiled rope. He kept them wide-eyed with spinning the big loop around his legs, then up, up to his neck. He had good control of the wide open loop and this achievement gave him the confidence to ask the young fifth-grade teacher to come see his show. She came out when Charlie was winding up for the big climax—roping the flagpole.

"Watch me rope the pole! Oh, dear, bread and beer, if I was

home I shouldn't be here!" Charlie called in a loud voice to attract attention. He swung the rope a couple of times to get the loop well opened, then lifted it high over his head and let it sail upward against the clear sky. He felt wonderful. The loop was just shy of the pole when it slowly settled downward and astonishingly slipped around the teacher's head. There was a twist and quick pull and the rope tightened about her waist, pinning her flaying arms to her sides.

Charlie feigned surprise and a sudden muscular contraction of his arm, that was an innocent reflex action, brought screams from the teacher as she went down in the dust beside the flagpole's foot. The applause was tremendous, instantaneous, and short-lived. Charlie quickly apologized and untangled the rope from the teacher and said in a weak, squeaky voice that he needed more practice.

The teacher put Charlie's rope inside her desk and kept him inside the fifth-grade room during recess and lunch for the week. She also walked to the smithery and told Charlie's father. Joe pulled a leather strap from a nail on the wall and waited for Charlie. The moment he walked into the smithery his father grabbed him.

Charlie looked up and saw the dark, piercing eyes, the large nose with nostrils flaring faintly in and out, the slashed, large mouth half open, and the swatch of black hair over the sweaty, red forehead.

Charlie was sick about the whole episode. He thought, when Pa takes the strap to me—I won't sing. I won't open my mouth. He clamped his lips together and drew in a deep breath. He'd die standing up.

"For a week there will be no horseback riding. Understand?" The leather strap hung limp in Joe's right hand, then it was flung up and down, up and down.

Charlie gritted his teeth and held his breath on the down stroke. I'll be gritty as eggs rolled in sand, he thought. He gasped for breath on the up stroke and smelled the acridness of horseflesh and leather on his father's work apron.

By the week's end everything seemed swell. Charlie had his rope back.

On Sunday, Malinda stopped at Joe's house on her way to church. Mary was slicking back Frank's unruly hair. Charlie and Ell were in their best clothes. "Where's Joe and Will?" asked Malinda.

"Somewheres along the Grand, sawing cordwood," said Mary, letting Frank go put his shoes on.

"A whole family ought to attend church," Malinda said with a sigh. But she knew that Joe thought the outdoors was the best place for worshipful communication with the Lord.

Joe often said, "Alone, close to the earth, a person learns most about his Maker." Whenever he was unstrung he sought the recuperative power of the silent cottonwoods along a riverbank. He didn't want to hear gossip, nor back-biting, nor a preacher's high-flown language. He said that alone in the outdoors he could put his problems in their proper place and find they were always small compared to the Lord's great scheme of things. Nowadays his problems were the drought and hard times.

Will was easygoing and never cared much one way or the other. He could go to church, or work at the forge, or fish, or saw wood without complaint.

Ell ran her hands over her slim hips, making certain her silk skirt skimmed the toes of her gray kid, two-button shoes. "Grandma, I'm going to Teachers' College in Kirksville this fall."

Malinda's brown eyes flew wide with surprise. "How?"

"Quincy, Missouri, and Pacific Railroad."

"I mean, who's going to pay?"

"I can sell herbs. There's no herbalist in Kirksville." Ell smiled as if to add, don't worry about it.

"Maybe I have herbs you can have," offered Malinda, "and maybe a little extra money. I'll look. We'd better not be late for church."

"I've tried talking Ell out of this foolishness," said Mary. Her gray eyes reflected green flecks of light. "We'll leave as soon as I find my purse."

"Pa told us about the Laclede postmaster's son who earned his way. I know I can. I want to be a teacher. And it would be no trouble to heal and study teaching at the same time." Ell's voice turned soft and pleading.

Mary looked down at her homemade shoes, which were the shape of her feet and the color of dust. "Times are hard. Some of the farmers are doing their own smithing now, so Joe loses their work. Ell doesn't realize how much it costs to live away from home!" Mary tucked a strand of loose hair into the braid around her head. She held the screen door open so that the three children could go outside.

Charlie said, "Jeems, Ma doesn't want you to go anywhere, Ell. Can't you tell? Pa's not got enough money for teacher's school in case your stupid herbs don't sell."

"You stay out of it!" snapped Ell.

Charlie stuck his tongue out at his sister. "I'm never leaving. But if I had somewheres to go, I'd take everyone with me."

"You'll never amount to a hill o'beans."

Frank sat on the steps and stared off into space.

"That ain't true!" cried Charlie. "I'll amount to something. I have a secret."

"What's that?" asked Ell, putting her nose in the air.

Frank leaned backward so he could hear Charlie's secret.

"If you want to do something, don't stir everyone up—just do it."

"What if it's wrong and you don't find out until afterward?" asked Ell.

"Say you're sorry, and start over."

"Some secret," said Frank, sitting up and hitting his heels against the riser.

"Maybe when I grow up I'll be Livingston County's most expert rope spinner. That kind of expert don't cost a cent to learn."

"Charlie, that's not funny. You gotta have a real job," said Ell, holding the door for Grandma Malinda and their mother, who'd found her purse on the bureau where she'd left it.

They walked to the Baptist Church, Mary and Malinda leading, the children following one by one.

In the churchyard Ell grabbed Charlie's arm. "Who's that?" She pointed to a tall young man, maybe older than Will, with a firmer chin, but with the same stocky build. He was dressed in the uniform of the United States Military Academy. "He's a dream!"

"I thought you said men around here are stinko."

"Does he look like any men around here?"

"There's old John Pershing," whispered Charlie. "You know, Pa and I went to Laclede to look after his horses. That must be his boy in the army uniform."

"Why'd they come here?" said Ell, following Charlie right up to the newcomers and smiling at them.

"Howdy, Mr. Pershing." Charlie held his hand out. "I'm Charlie Irwin. Remember? Pa and I did some blacksmithing at your place. This is my brother Frank. My sister, Ell. You know my Ma and Grandma Malinda?"

Pershing looked at Ell. "How d'a' do, young lady. My, what pretty eyes. This is my son, Cadet Jack Pershing, home on spring holiday from the military academy at West Point."

Ell grinned and tipped her head coyly.

Charlie thought if she were a cat she'd purr.

"I've heard of your grandmother for years. Jack and I came looking for your father. We need him in Laclede again for a sick horse. I want someone I trust. We stopped in the churchyard to ask directions to your place." He turned. "So, you're Malinda Irwin, the famous lady doctor."

"Come to church with us," suggested Malinda. "Joe ought to be back early this afternoon."

"Well, I'll see what my cadet says." Pershing turned to his son, Jack, who was looking at Ell like she was the only person in the churchyard. "We'd be pleased to accompany you."

After the service, John and Jack Pershing rode horseback to the Irwin home. The Irwins walked home hurriedly. Mary and Malinda worried about dinner, Ell kept talking about the handsome cadet. Charlie thought she was bird-brained and said so. "Your senses have shrunk. Jack puts his pants on same as—"

Malinda put her hand over Charlie's face. "Hush, or I'll wash your mouth with yellow soap."

"Jeems, Grandma! Let me see where I'm walking!" Charlie cried.

At home Will and Joe were back from sawing cordwood and sat at the kitchen table drinking coffee. Joe saw the Pershings tie their horses to the shade oak. He was so surprised he knocked the coffeepot over. Ell cleaned up and told Will to change his sweaty clothes on account of the company they had coming in. "Cadet Pershing would never allow himself to be so grubby," she sniffed.

"I bet you a buck that dude wishes he had on baggy trousers and a flannel shirt," said Will, going to wash.

Joe and John Pershing talked as if they'd known each other for years. Finally they went to the smithery for the farrier's wagon and creosol ointment.

Malinda and Mary made corn pone, rice, beans, and slaw. Ell insisted on making a dried apricot pie. Her face shone and she became even more animated when Jack asked for seconds of pie. "I made—I mean—I like—you know—the pie," she gestured with her hands.

He smiled. "I like fancy apricot pie also," he said easily.

"That's what I meant," said Ell, then, with a playful singsong to her voice, "I heard you rode a mule, each time you went to school."

That made Jack laugh. "Believe me, you can't believe everything you hear."

Ell's eyes sparkled. "What do you know about the Teachers' College in Kirksville?" She bent her head so that her long blond hair spread over the yoke of her dress in front.

"It's small, founded in 1867, on weekends the students go to Columbia if they can find a horse or wagon—or mule."

Ell put out her hand as if to touch his arm, then drew it back slowly. "I'd like to be a teacher."

"That's the place to go, then. But if I were you, I'd start teaching in a rural school and get experience," said Jack. "The state will give you certification if you pass the exam. You can do it, I'm sure. Those one-room schools need school marms as bright as you."

"Really?" Ell was surprised. She took a deep breath and blinked. "You believe I could teach school right away?"

"Certainly. Haven't you been teaching your brothers? Self-confidence is all it takes." Jack looked around as if seeking someone, then he said, "Say, I want to see if your brother will show me how to use a rope." Jack went out the door to the backyard before Ell could take another deep breath or roll her eyes.

Charlie saw him and yelled, "Hey! You wanna see me lasso our dog, Squirt?"

The old brown spaniel got up and wandered out of sight.

"Some tree or post or stob in the ground is good enough. Your pa told my pa that you were real good with a rope."

Mention of being good made Charlie's fingers rush to uncoil his rope. He flung that fourteen feet of horsehair out and twirled the largest loop he could handle. He *kiyi*ed like an Indian and whinnied like a horse, then explained, "It takes both hands to do this, and a long time to get it right." Suddenly he felt wild and cocky, ready to show off all his fancy tricks. "That there eye through which my rope goes is called the honda."

"Doesn't it ever kink?" asked Jack.

"Naw! See, you let the end twist in your hand." Charlie looked at Jack and wondered if his brains were smooth. "Like riding a horse, you let the reins roll so's not to kink."

"Can you rope something high?" asked Jack.

Charlie looked around. He saw his pa's fresh-cut cord of wood; the pile of cow manure had been plowed into the garden.

His eyes moved higher, to the top of the utility shed, where there was an iron weather vane in the shape of a horse that Joe had made one winter at the smithery.

Joe was proud of that roof decoration and could foretell a storm by which direction the horse's nose was pointed.

Charlie lifted his wrist and with a tiny twist the rope settled over the fancy ironwork of the weather vane. With another upward thrust of his left hand and a slight bend forward from his waist, Charlie flipped the rope off the iron horse and to the ground in a graceful curve. "You try once," Charlie said.

The air was warm. Jack took off his dress jacket and rolled up his sleeves. He took the coiled rope from Charlie.

Nine-year-old Charlie began the instruction. He chose his words carefully and showed each move as though he were a ballet master. "Now stand with your feet apart, like this. Your arms should be down below your middle. Helps with the balance."

Twenty-four-year-old Jack listened carefully and followed Charlie's instructions exactly.

"The left hand holds both loop and end. Keep your fingers loose like you were holding the line of a fly rod," Charlie said. "Throw the right hand toward me." He pushed Jack's arm to the proper level. "Now, release the loop with both hands and hold the guilding end with your fingers of the right hand."

This last was as clear as the muddy Missouri River after a hard rain to Jack. He stepped back and laughed nervously. He didn't want the kid to think he was dense. Jack's wrist began to swing loosely and the rope began to whirl. The loop opened and Jack's fingers gripped tensely and the rope slid down over his neck like skin off a roasted snake. "I don't want to hang myself." Jack's face was red and his breath came in puffs.

"You didn't have the rhythm quite right," said Charlie.

Jack coiled the rope, and this time he let his left hand help with the turning, sliding rope. The rope whirled rhythmically by centrifugal force until it flew out of his hands and landed like a spent telegraph wire in the tall grass and bright hollyhocks beside the shed.

"If you could get something in between, you'd have it perfect," said Charlie. "I've taught kids younger than you and they caught on."

Jack set his jaw, flexed his knees, and tried again. The rope spun around as though it had a life of its own. Charlie was ready to whistle his approval. His lips were puckered and he drew in his breath, then Jack threw the loop out from his body and it sailed through the air in a graceful arc to the top of the shed. Jack's right hand jerked and the loop over the weather vane contracted faster than cooling iron in a slack tub. His left hand fell down at his side, putting more pressure on the wood molding at the base of the delicate, skillfully hammered iron horse. The horse bucked off the shingled roof, pulling a huge piece of ridgepole, several shingles, and the hollyhocks down with it as it bit the dust once, bounced up and back, bit the dust again, and then lay in a tangled mess at Charlie's feet.

"Boy! You managed that just dandy!" cried Charlie.

"I'm terribly sorry!" Jack was chagrined. "Can we go up and fix it?"

"Maybe you shouldn't overdo it." Charlie clamped his teeth shut a moment, then said, "Let's put the rope away. Say, do you manage men as well?"

"You mean can I persuade men to do what I want? Give orders?"

"Ya." Charlie looked over the weather vane. He felt better when he found there was no damage to it.

Jack began to pick up shingles and shingle splinters. He stopped all hunched over near the ground and said, "Charlie, I asked a similar question of a colonel, who was my instructor. He looked at me as if I'd come from some wide spot in the road west of the Mississippi that no one in the state of New York ever heard of and least of all cared about. He snapped, 'Cadet Pershing! You manage things! You lead men!' "

Charlie rolled his rope, propped the broken hollyhocks against the weathered boards of the shed, then put the weather vane and loose shingles inside. He crossed his fingers, hoping that his father would not come out before he had a chance to nail everything back on the roof. He was trying to think of something to say in case his father noticed there was nothing on the roof just as he and John Pershing came out the back door. Charlie wished he could sink into the dry ground as if it were quicksand.

"I want to show you my pride and joy," said Joe, strutting proud as a peacock toward the shed and pointing upward. "This weather vane moves with the slightest breeze and it's large enough to see from anywhere in the yard. I made it of cast iron and kept it rustproof with linseed oil. Just look at that stallion, you can almost imagine its muscles flexing as it—it—"

The words trailed off as if carried away by a fierce wind. Joe's face looked flat, as if it had been hit by an unseen force.

"Hey! What happened to my iron horse? Where's the weather

vane?" Joe's words were sharp as a guillotine to Charlie.

"A sudden storm—" Charlie's voice sounded like it was coming from a hollow log.

"I swear to God I saw it pointing southwest this morning!"

"That's the direction of the worst storms! Tornadoes come from the southwest!" Charlie felt as if he were going to throw up.

"We had no storm this morning, young man! What are you trying to say?" Joe's face was dark. His eyes bore into Charlie.

"I was practicing with my rope. A spinning loop—"

"You? You pulled my weather vane off with your rope? Charlie! How could you be so careless? So stupid?" Joe's face turned bright red and his big hands clenched and unclenched.

The Pershings stood at attention, side by side, stiff as boards.

Charlie felt hot tears form in his eyes.

Jack's face was the color of fresh-ground flour. "Sir, if I might—"

"Yes, you might wait until I have this out with Charlie!" said Joe. He pushed Charlie toward the shed.

Jack stepped forward. "Mr. Irwin, sir, wait a moment. It's not all Charlie's fault. I asked him to show me how to twirl the rope. I was all thumbs. The rope was all tangles. It flew out of my hand before I was ready!"

Joe ignored Jack's explanation. He pushed Charlie into the shed and across the wood chopping block and thrashed him with the palm of his hand.

It was a terrible experience for Charlie. He didn't crave witnesses. He felt like a jackass. He could not come out of the shed and face Jack. He hated his father. He wished he'd suffocate right there in the shed beside that damned iron horse.

Thirty minutes later Jack pounded on the door. Charlie didn't answer. Maybe he'll think I've died, Charlie thought. The door opened. Jack was smiling.

Charlie pulled himself off the floor and accidently kicked the iron horse. He jumped backward as if he'd kicked the devil himself.

"I told your pa that it was not fair for you to take responsibility for my transgressions. I told him you managed the rope, but I led you to the weather vane."

Charlie walked out of the shed, blinked in the sunlight, and dug his fists into his eyes to clear the tears.

Inside the house Joe's face was soft. He was telling John Pershing how he'd made the weather vane thin, but strong, on the forge.

* * *

The Pershings said good-bye a short while later. Joe sat in his wagon ready to go to Laclede with them and look after their prize horse. Joe suspected the horse had gavel and needed to be treated with mustard and hot packs. Jack shook hands with Charlie. "So long, friend. We'll get together again. Remember, manage things. Lead men." He winked.

Ell moped around the rest of the day thinking about her conversation with Jack. Suddenly she said, "I'm not going to Kirksville. I'm going to get a certificate and teach in a country school. I have the confidence I can do that right now!"

"That's what Jack said." Charlie made a face.

Ell glared at Charlie so that he felt mad as a rained-on rooster. "He had nothing to do with my decision. He paid more attention to you than he did to me. Charlie, you got all the attention. You took Pa's weather vane off the roof and got a whipping. But somehow, you are still a hero!" she cried.

Etta put down the newspaper she was reading to tell both youngsters to stop squabbling.

Charlie looked at Ell and said, "Crisis is the only thing people remember."

Ell's mouth fell open. Etta dropped the newspaper. Charlie grinned, feeling that he'd said something important. His anger faded.

By April's end school was out. Boys and girls were needed to plow and to seed. School wouldn't reopen until mid-October, after harvest. Charlie couldn't remember when he hadn't done the odd jobs around his father's smithery during the lazy summers, except when he wasn't school age and his family tried farming in Kansas for a couple of seasons.

This morning the *chunk chunk*ing of cardinals in the red cedar at the corner of the house woke Charlie. He got out of bed, pulled denim pants on. He and other youngsters his age called the straight-leg blue denims "shotguns." Charlie went to the back porch and saw that Will had gone. As he went to the kitchen and hunted for syrup to pour over biscuits, he thought of Will going to the dark smithery constantly, morning until night, getting no sun. No wonder Will was pale year-round.

Charlie understood that the smithery was dark so colors of cooling iron could be watched, the subtle greens and blue and the white hot cooling down to yellow, orange, then red. A good striker, and Will was that, knew just the right stage or color for striking. Will suffered from hay fever and the smithery was a kind of refuge from watery eyes, tickling throat, coughing, and sneezing.

Charlie heard Ell in the bathroom. Her bedroom was made from stringing a flowered curtain on heavy wire at the end of Mary and Joe's room. Ell was running the water, probably cleaning her teeth with salt and soda. The Irwins had had their inside plumbing for nearly a year. It was nice not to have an outhouse, not to carry buckets of water to the kitchen sink.

Charlie went to the kitchen where the thin, see-through curtains moved in and out with the breeze.

Mary came into the kitchen. Her hair was combed and her dress was fresh. It was the blue that Charlie liked, with little yellow daisies in the material of the long gathered skirt.

Mary sat down beside Charlie at the table. "Before you go to the smithery, I want you to take a loaf of bread and half a raisin pie to your grandma Malinda. She's not feeling well again."

At the door to Malinda's house, which was clapboard over the original logs, Charlie yelled through the screen, "Grandma! Hey, it's me!"

He was startled to see that her white hair was stringier than usual, and her skin looked paper-thin. She was still short and squat, but this morning, somehow, she seemed fragile. It was the first time Charlie had noticed she might be ill.

She had been drinking a mixture of parsley and willow bark tea to ease her sour stomach and dull her arthritic pains. She took the bread and pie and set them on the counter without taking off the dishtowel wrapped around them. "God bless you, Joe," she said, keeping her first fingers on both hands crossed for luck.

"I'm Charlie."

Her mind had wandered. She thought that this helpless feeling was nothing but age. Age was something everyone felt sooner or later. There was no escape. During her younger days work was done by hand and the old taught the young. Grass was cut with a sickle, dried and cured in piles made with hand rakes. Wheat was threshed on the barn floor. But today, there were mechanical tillers, reapers, and threshers if a person had money to buy. She looked at Charlie and said, "When you become a man, son, have a beard."

"Why'd you say that, Grandma?" Charlie felt she spoke a riddle.

"Look mature right away. Command proper respect. That's

how people know you are wise." This was not a riddle to her, it was good, common sense. "In my day a boy began growing his beard as soon as possible. But today—look, your brother, Will, is clean-shaven. My own son, Joe, shaved his beard when the town got the electric plant. These men resemble hairless boys. What is happening to American men? My dear Old Charles had both a beard and mustache."

"Grandpa Riley has a beard and mustache. They're salt and peppery," said Charlie.

"Riley's a damned fool. He looks old before his time," replied Malinda perversely. "Aren't you cold with no shoes on?"

"No, ma'am. I'd have come without a shirt, but Ma wouldn't let me."

"There'll be another drought. And the dry spell will be worse than in seventy-three or seventy-eight. Someone will find a way to use the Grand River water. Mark my words. Then this dryland farming will be about as popular as a pig's tail."

"Pa says the same thing." Now Charlie was beginning to feel unusually warm in the kitchen. "Grandma, why do you have the range loaded with wood? You fixing to do some canning? It's too hot for a big fire. That's why Ma sent you bread and half of our pie—so you wouldn't have to cook nothing."

"You're right. Women are the best thing that ever happened to men. Joe knows Mary is the sweetest thing in his life, same's Old Charles felt about me. Some men don't appreciate women. Hanging's too good for that kind." She got up from the table and seemed to forget what she was up for. She sat down. "Get yourself a cup and put some tea in the strainer, and pour in hot water. I'll read your tea leaves from those that slip through the strainer."

Charlie poured hot water into his grandmother's cup also. She took a spoonful of sugar and dipped it into her weakened herb tea. She sucked the liquid from the sugar and dipped the spoon into the cup again. It was something that many of the old-timers did. Charlie tried it.

"You sip tea just like my Old Charles," his grandmother said with a sigh.

When the tea was gone Malinda picked up Charlie's cup and looked at him. Then she bent her neck to study the bottom of the cup and the arrangement of the tea leaves. "Huumm—you want to be as big and good-looking as your brother Will?"

Charlie wondered if she could read his mind. He ran a bare foot down the calf of his leg. "Yes, ma'am."

"It will come to pass. You will be a big, handsome man. But

you won't be like Will. He had a twin, you know. The twin was in a bad fix with fever. He lived about a year. Cried day and night. Made your ma ragged. He's the baby buried in the cemetery near Old Charles."

Charlie pondered his grandmother's words. They sounded like a family secret. "I had a brother who died?" Charlie couldn't believe it. "You mean the baby buried in the cemetery was my brother?"

"Prexactly! A long time ago your pa bought Nash's barn for the blacksmith shop on Washington Street. Then he married the prettiest girl in Chillicothe. They had twin boys first."

"Tell me about that time," he said, holding his breath until she spoke again. Malinda laughed. She lowered her voice. "I laugh because if I didn't I'd cry. There were good olden times, and there were bad olden times."

Charlie could feel his grandmother wanted to go on. When she got going she was about as easy to stop as a raging prairie fire. Charlie sat still, his feet not moving off the chair rung. "What was his name?"

"Your ma called him Granville Marvin. Your ma's favorite brother is your Uncle Granville, and your pa's middle name is Marvin. About that time there was gossip about a no-good cousin of your ma's with the same given name. I told her the name could be changed. She was stubborn. I told her the name was cursed."

Charlie saw that the left corner of his grandmother's mouth had a droop even when she smiled. "What do you mean?"

"I mean the first Granville M. Brassfield was a traitor. He would do anything to get information to help the Confederates at Wilson's Creek during the War Between the States. Why, he got hold of a smart Chillicothe lad about your age, George Pepper, and tortured him with near hanging more than once. Pepper was stout-hearted, closed-mouthed, even though he got scars round his neck from rope cutting across his windpipe. Pepper was a Union Army hero the rest of his life. Your ma's cousin Granville was branded a bully and marked for treason for the rest of his life. The rascal was forced, by public opinion, to move west somewheres."

"Jeems! I never heard that! Why did the baby die?"

"I remember the day, like it was yesterday, that he drew his last torturous breath." She closed her eyes, but not her mouth. She talked on as though she were seeing what took place under her eyelids. "I dosed him with peppermint and put mustard and boiled onions in a little sack on that frail baby's chest to draw out congestion, and once I dared to blow mullein smoke into his tiny nostrils so he could breathe easier. Eventually I dosed him with red pepper in whiskey and it brought him out of his lethargy a while. Then he wouldn't eat a flummery of oatmeal gruel. Your brother Will ate everything his pudgy hands could push into his mouth, even the lucky charms on his flannel bellyband.

"The sick baby died gasping for air the morning we was having a terrible blizzard, with thunderblasts and winds that cut through a person like steel knives. Your poor, sad ma washed that tiny cold, blue-white body in the basin and dressed him in a long white dress. We burned all the other clothes he wore. Your grandma Rachel came, and before I or your ma knew what possessed her, she was kneeling on the floor in front of the chair where I rocked Will. Now, we know she was overcome with grief. That bad day she pressed her hands together, like this, and bowed her head and prayed like she was a Holy Roller, promising the Lord that Will would be raised in a manner not to shame Him. She said she knew Granville's soul floated toward Heaven as surely as dogs have little puppies."

"Grandma Rachel said that?"

"That's what she meant. Next day Old Charles transformed one of the babies' cradles into an aromatic cedar box with a lid. Your ma lined it with cattail down and covered that with a soft, sunbleached, muslin cradle blanket. Your pa used a pickax to dig out the frozen ground so that the cedar cradle coffin could be buried. Come spring he made a cross from cedar heartwood. Your ma planted them hollyhocks by the shed and started being overindulgent with Will. I'm going to tie a little bag of asafetida around my neck to calm my nerves. You want one?"

"Don't give me one of those little bitsy sacks of weeds. It'll make my nose run," said Charlie. He swirled the tea leaves in the remaining drops of liquid in the bottom of his cup and slouched down in the chair.

"Oh, give that here and I'll see about your fortune," remembered Malinda.

"Is there more to see besides me being handsome?" Charlie laughed, knowing she'd said that earlier only to please him. He felt a deep love for his grandmother.

She studied the inside of the cup, turning it this way and that way. "Don't get too set on staying in Missouri. Life will be what you make it, wherever you are. You'll see—I'm right." Her chin sunk to her bosom.

Charlie straightened up. "Is that in there? I ain't leaving! It's Ell that wanted to go. But, jeems! She's over that stupid stage."

"Wouldn't surprise me if all of you went somewheres."

"And leave you?" Charlie was shocked.

"Don't worry about me," she said. She got up, went to her bedroom, took her old maroon, handknit sweater off the hook, and put it on.

"Are you all right?" asked Charlie, wiping perspiration from his forehead.

"I'm just a little chilly. I can remember when the wind howled around the corner of this house and we kept the firewood inside to feed the stove."

"I'm going, but I'll be back tomorrow," said Charlie, baffled by his grandmother's unusually strange actions.

"We ought to have Grandma Malinda stay at our house until she feels better," said Charlie that night at supper. "She's acting addled. The heat from her cookstove has baked her think box."

Mary gasped. "Charlie! Where do you hear such awful things?"

"It's true. You should go there yourself and see. I hear stuff at the smithery, at school, you know, all over." Charlie reached for the butter. "Ma, she's cold when it's hot enough to go without a shirt. She called me *Joe*."

For the next few days Mary and Ell went to see Malinda each afternoon. Ell asked questions about lucky charms, scent-makers, or recipes for dyeing cloth. Malinda seemed fine when giving Ell this information, but when she tried to talk about present-day activities, her words sounded as if she'd stirred her thoughts in a butter churn and spread them in a heap on the table.

"Stay with us awhile," Mary begged her mother-in-law. "Let me cook for you."

Malinda smiled, trying to correlate a couple thoughts, but she didn't pick up the correct pieces. "Have you seen how big the woods violets are this year?" she said, making a circle with her thumb and forefinger to show the enormous size. Then she looked at Ell in a mysterious way and said in a whisper, "You'll teach school in a God-forsaken place, child. Don't be discouraged. In the end you'll be a healer of men."

"Oh, pooh, Grandma. I'll teach right here in Livingston County and prescribe herbs here. You can bet on that."

Malinda shook her head and whispered, "I wouldn't."

* * *

"Your mother is spooky," Mary said to Joe on Friday. "I do think we'd better have her stay with us. She's getting forgetful. Yesterday Ell and I found her cellar door left wide open."

Joe slapped his hand against his thigh. "After church, Sunday, you bring her here. Fix the bed on the screen porch. That's settled."

Saturday after lunch Charlie ran to visit his Grandma Malinda before going to the smithery. He liked to walk through her old shingle yard that still had piles of wedged cedar. He imagined the time his grandpa, Old Charles, had made those neat stacks. Charlie went to the back door of the little gray, one-story house. "I'm here! Grandma! It's Charlie!" He went inside. The kitchen was empty. The oak-planked floors were scrubbed white. Thin, lacy white curtains hung at the windows of the front room, and a flowered cotton material was strung across the two alcoves at the side to shut off the bedroom and bathroom. The material was drawn back so that Charlie could look right into the bedroom. He saw his grandma standing next to her massive, handmade oak bed. She was reading her Bible. Her lips moved and her finger traced the words. She cleared her throat and closed the book and snapped the silver clasp. She shuffled to the trunk at the foot of the bed, bent to pull the lid open. Charlie smelled camphor and saw the stenciled star lining. He watched her take out a yellow hair bracelet and hold it in the sunlight a moment, then she ran her hands over a pair of high boots with spool heels and laces on the inward sides.

Malinda closed the trunk, put her hand in the middle of her back as she straightened. She shuffled toward the flowered curtain and started to pull it closed. She saw Charlie and nodded fondly. Charlie moved slowly and eased his hand into the bony one of his grandma. They stood together several minutes. Charlie heard the soft stirring of the flames and hot air rushing up the chimney of the wood range. "Are you cold again?"

Malinda released her hand. Charlie looked up and saw the old, tanned, lined face washed over with tears. He heard a faint rush of air in his grandma's throat that was almost inaudible with the noisy blast of hot air going up the kitchen stovepipe.

"Cold for a day in May," she said. She added water to the teakettle and put it back on the top of the range. "The wind used to be so strong in these here parts that it blew the ducks' feathers onto the chickens, and the chickens' feathers onto the ducks."

Charlie laughed and sat on the leather couch. "Do you know more of those silly stories?"

Malinda sat in the rocking chair. "Not so silly. You know how the wind can blow. Well, once it scooped the cellar from under a house, but left the house alone." She chuckled. "And we had a dog called Shep. That dog dared to bark at a twister moving in on him and the wind came and left so fast it turned the dog plumb inside out." Her eyes began to sparkle.

Charlie had slid sideways on the couch and was laughing hard.

"In the hot dry summer I've seen grasshoppers so large they picked their teeth after eating the last ear of corn in a field. They picked their teeth on the barbs of the barbed-wire fence."

Charlie looked like he was having a spasm. He held his sides and laughed. "I have to get a drink," he said, catching his breath. "Even the guys at the smithery can't tell such good stories as you."

"Here, we'll both have some good, hot tea." She lit the kerosene lamp on the kitchen table. "I like it better than the electric."

Charlie looked up at the bare bulb above the table.

"It's more like home. The light is better, not so bright that it hurts your eyes."

"It's not dark, yet," said Charlie.

They drank steeped tea with milk and plenty of sugar.

Malinda hummed softly, enjoying Charlie's company.

"Pa said you could come and stay with us," said Charlie. He put his cup and spoon in the sink. "Oh, not so we could take care of you, but so we could see you more often. I could board up the screened porch so you wouldn't feel the breeze. It would be your room. Will could move in with Frank and me like he does every winter."

Malinda sipped her tea and did not answer for a moment, then said, "Thanks, Charlie. I hope you're as generous with food and board to all down-and-outers. I'm down for sure. I have to work this out my own way. I was looking for my leghorn bonnet with the pink roses framing the underside of the straw brim. I want to wear it. There's this thing going through my head. It's so loud, I'm surprised you don't say something about it."

Charlie was surprised. "I don't hear nothing, only the wood fire crackling in your stove. That thing is roaring!"

"In my heart lays a cold stone. I aim to thaw it. Listen now. I hear a whole choir singing, 'O, My Poor Nelly Gray.'"

"Will it ever stop?"

"In time, I suppose." She shuddered and hummed a while. "The days are flat, Charlie."

"Grandma Rachel says, 'In time everything heals.' You want to know what I say?" She nodded and Charlie went on, "Time makes some things worse."

She smiled. "Rachel can't think deep. You're right. You want the Henry rifle now?" She pointed to the rifle on the wall rack. "No one has used it for years. You ought to learn to hunt, even if it's for varmints, like gophers."

"Oh," breathed Charlie excitedly. "You really meant I could have it?"

"Of course. I told you Old Charles wants you to have it. Lookee here. The firing pin has a divided head. It strikes both sides of the cartridge rim at the same time. I learned a lot from Old Charles." Her laugh was cracky. "I'll find a couple boxes of cartridges for you in a moment. Old Charles always said, 'There's no chance of a misfire with this here baby 'cause there's no dead spot on the priming ring.' Holds fifteen rounds. But a sixteenth can be loaded in the chamber. Your pa, who's my boy, told me that the soldiers with Sherman carried these rifles clear to Georgia, and the opposition complained, 'That damned Yankee rifle is loaded on Sunday and fires all week.'"

Charlie looked at his grandma. He'd never heard her swear before, even telling what others said. He was brought up to believe that women never cussed and that men never cussed in front of women. Charlie turned the rifle over in his hands feeling the smooth, blue-black frame. He examined the metal plate on the butt, being careful the muzzle was pointed away from his grandma. A strange melancholy took hold of him. He thought of the grandpa he'd never known, Old Charles, stalking a buck deer in crisp autumn air. Charlie's fingers roamed back and forth over the side plate, and the sad gloom was suddenly replaced by an explosion of excitement.

"Here's two full boxes of forty-four cartridges and another half-full. That ought to last a while. You get more at Hoppe's Hardware," said Malinda.

"Thanks, Grandma—I've never felt so—so big," said Charlie, wanting to convey his deepest gratitude. He pushed the cartridge boxes into the front pockets of his shotguns. Then it dawned on him that Hoppe's Hardware had been out of business for five or six years. He looked at his grandma with his eyes closed partway so he could see clearly. She looked happy and her face had a rosy color. Her eyes shone.

"I know how you feel," said Malinda.

"Maybe Will felt this way when he got his pony, Scratch," said Charlie.

"It's not the same with Will. He's a taker, same as Frank. You're not. You're a giver. You can't see now. But your friends will know. Say! You want to spend your life in that there gloomy smithery?"

"Well, Grandma . . . I like horses and people—"

"Well, Hell's bells, excuse me, but times is changing. Ain't they? Know what I think will be next for a smithery?" Malinda pointed her teaspoon at Charlie. "Shoeing racehorses. Racing's in the East and it's moving West. You'll see. Might kind of keep that in your mind. I read the papers!"

"Will has cattle ranching in the back of his mind. He told me."

"The day will come when he'll ask you to stake him for a ranch. It had better be land you want also. And some more advice that won't harm none: Be beholden to no one. That goes for relatives, too."

"Grandma—you coming home with me, maybe just for a few days? You can watch me target practice." He held up the rifle.

"You go to the edge of town and shoot away from houses, shacks, cows, and stuff. A rifle is not like a rope."

"Yes, ma'am. I know. You coming?" Charlie asked again. "For supper?" He was marching around the room with the rifle held over his shoulder.

"Nope. I'm staying. This here is my home." Malinda laid the pewter spoon solidly on the table.

"Come by in time for church tomorrow. Ma's expecting you."

Malinda's voice was soft and sad. "Between the dish and my mouth all food turns to fodder; even my blackberry wine has lost its pleasure."

Charlie picked up his rope from the chair and shoved it high on his shoulder. Satisfied that it was comfortable, he held the rifle in the other hand. He gave his grandma a hug and kissed her thin, cold lips. She pulled out a paper bag from her large apron pocket.

"Take this to Ell. It's only a few rare herbs and things that are hard to find these days."

"Grandma, I only have two hands! My front pockets are filled with shells! I have the rifle and my rope!"

"I'll stuff it in your back pocket. It's not so heavy, nor bulky. Just don't lose it."

He picked up the rifle and went out the back door. Malinda followed him into the yard. She stopped at the pump and filled a bucket of water to take into the house. She hesitated as if forgetting what she wanted water for, then she offered Charlie a drink from the dipper. "Better than piped water, eh?"

"Yes, ma'am. Thanks." Charlie walked on through the shingle yard, passing rows of neatly stacked thin cedar shakes. Charlie had one hand on the rifle barrel and the other on the butt. He had to stop to hitch up his shotguns. The cartridges pulled them down over his small hips.

Malinda stood at the back fence. When Charlie turned, it was hard to see in the evening light, but he felt certain his grandmother waved. He waved and then grabbed hold of the rifle barrel. He'd spent the whole day with his grandma Malinda, not once thinking about going to the smithery.

Charlie did not go inside the house right away. He knew his father and Will were back from the smithery because he heard them talking. He sat in the old swing by the shed. The leather seat was cracked. Gingerly he tested the strength of the rusty chain links fastened to the wood beam nailed across two oaks. The swing creaked. He held the rifle on his knees. He thought of Grandma Malinda saying, "In a swing, waiting for the cat to die—watch one's life go by." He sat there a long time. He wanted to feel the rifle in his hands without anyone asking him questions or taking it from him. His father might say he was too young for a lever-action rifle and put it on two nails high on the front-room wall. Frank or Will would want to hold it and feel it.

The air was damp and cool. He had to hitch up his shotguns when he left the swing. He was hungry. The excitement in his belly had died down some. He went to the shed, fumbled with the wooden latch. The door squeaked. He was careful not to kick the weather vane. He stood the rifle against the wall and put the boxes of cartridges on the floor next to it. The dog brushed against his legs. He went outside, called the dog out, and latched the shed. He went inside the house.

Joe looked up from the paper. "It's late, son. Your mother worried about you. We missed you at the smithery."

"Ma knew I was visiting Grandma Malinda. She gave me some roots and things for Ell." He took the brown paper sack out of his back pocket. He hung up his rope. "Do you think she's really going to come here?"

"Really. We are going to tell her tomorrow. Did you eat supper with your grandma?" asked Mary.

"Nope, only tea with sugar," said Charlie.

"There's milk in the pitcher, greens and bacon on the back of the stove. When you finish, clean up the dishes and go to bed."

"Thanks, Ma." Then he added, "Pa, I'll work at the smithery all day Monday."

In the middle of the night Charlie thought about the rifle. Next to his rope it was the most important thing he'd ever owned. He heard the rumble of thunder and moved his legs stiffly and opened one eye. He listened and heard the thunder again, but this time it was a pounding on the front door. He climbed out of bed and heard voices. His father and mother were talking, but he couldn't understand what they were excited about. He put on his shotguns. Frank sniffed in his sleep. Then he heard a sharp, ear-piercing scream. He knew it was Ell. Charlie's breath came in short gasps. He ran to the living room.

Orin Gale was there with another man Charlie didn't recognize. They smelled like a bonfire. Orin was saying, ". . . so sorry, it was over when we got there. Nothing we could do. It must have gone up in blazes like a tinderbox."

Will came from the kitchen with a coal-oil lamp, which he set on the top of the cold potbellied heater. Frank got up and came into the living room, rubbing his eyes, and stood close to Mary. Ell was in a heap on the floor. Joe wiped her face with a wet cloth.

"What's the matter with her?" asked Charlie. He could feel his heart thumping.

"She burned to death," said Will. His voice seemed to come from a long way off.

"What?" Charlie thought his mind was befuddled with sleep.

Will's voice broke when he explained. "Grandma Malinda—her house. All the shingles—all burned. It was a catastrophe!"

Charlie felt like a hot wind hit him in the face and a hard-clenched fist hit his belly. His mouth was dry. All the air went out of his lungs and he sat on the floor, feeling like he was going to be sick.

Orin Gale said, "If there's anything we can do, tell us. I'll be at home or the livery all day. It's a pity. She was one of the best-liked old souls around here."

Joe shook hands with both men, hardly hearing what they said. When they were gone he sat next to Mary on the davenport. Will sat on the opposite end with his head in his hands. Ell was up sitting in the rocker. Her head was back and her eyes closed. She moaned softly. Frank stood with his back to the door, sucking on the corner of a small blanket.

Charlie was dizzy. He went to the back door. Outside everything was a gray haze. The morning light was beginning to lighten the eastern edge of the sky. He took a deep breath to clear his head and went to the shed to get the rifle.

Will heard the slam of the screen door when Charlie came back. "Where'd you get that?" he asked.

Charlie stammered, "She—she ga—gave it to me."

"Yesterday?" asked Will.

"Ya."

Slowly Joe leaned forward to examine the rifle. "This was my pa's—Old Charles's."

"Old Charles wanted me to have it," said Charlie.

"Did Grandma say that?" asked Joe.

"Ya."

"What else? What other things did she say?"

"She told me some funny stories and gave me some advice. She was cold. She had singing in her head. She said she was staying home, not coming to stay here."

"What do you mean—staying?" asked Joe. His voice was high-pitched.

Charlie swallowed to moisten his throat so he could talk. "I told her we'd like to see her more often. Like you and Ma said. I said she could sleep on the screened porch. She didn't want to come." Charlie licked his lips. "She wanted to wear a straw bonnet—one with roses. She said nothing tasted good." Charlie stopped. He felt a lump like dry, mashed potatoes in his throat, shutting off his wind.

"Did she say she *wouldn't* come?" Joe persisted.

Charlie's eyes burned. It was like using binding twine. Each question pulled and twisted and cut into his heart. "Ya."

Joe put his hands to his face.

Charlie said in a whisper, "Pa, I think she knew it was going to happen. She tried to tell me—in a way."

"Knew what, son?" Joe's voice was soft, matching Charlie's.

"That the kitchen stove was too hot. That she had a sickness."

Mary wiped her eyes. "I thought she was getting better. Her memory was more clear."

Charlie felt hot tears on his face. "Her old memory maybe, but for everyday things, no. She couldn't even remember who I was. She had something that time made worse!" Charlie choked.

Ell sat straight up. "She knew all the medicines!" she cried. "Why didn't she use them?"

Charlie went to the kitchen and brought back the sack Malinda had tucked firmly into his back pocket. "She sent this to you."

"Oh, joy!" sobbed Ell. "It's little packets of leaves and things all labeled. And lookit! A roll of bills!" She began to count. "One hundred and four dollars! This was for me to go to Kirksville! But I'm not going—and she knew that." Ell held the roll of bills to her breast and cried, "Oh, Grandma!"

Frank knelt before Ell. "She should have sent for Doc Reed. He would have fixed her."

Charlie moved his foot so that it touched Frank's. "Her sickness was different. It was a sadness. Like lonely."

"But she had all of us." Ell wiped her eyes with the back of one hand.

"She wanted her bonnet—and high-button shoes—and Old Charles!" cried Charlie. "Can't you see she wanted to live in her time, not ours?" His eyes went to Joe beseechingly. "Oh, Pa! She told me. I knew she was going to—to die, for a long time. I just didn't think about it enough to say anything. I knew, but I didn't believe." Charlie gasped and ran into the kitchen. He sat at the table with his head in his hands. He could not control his sobs.

The next morning Charlie put two nails in the front-room wall and hung the Henry rifle. He stepped back and let the look of it soak into his mind. He squinted to read the barrel mark: HENRY'S PATENT OCT. 16, 1860.

Joe came out of the bedroom, put his arms around Charlie, and held him like he was a little kid no older than Frank. "After the war in 1865 my pa put this rifle up on a shelf. It was his symbol that no one would use it for killing. It was a sign that killing of people was over."

Will came in from the porch. "I could get some good shots off with that."

Frank stood in his bedroom doorway. "Can I use it for shooting gophers?"

"It's up to Charlie," answered Joe.

Charlie could not answer. The mashed potato lump in his throat was back and much bigger. Hot, salty tears blinded him. He ran out into the yard, up the street to the stables behind the smithery. There Joe left horses that he would shoe that day or the next. Charlie sat on the stable floor with his head covered by his arms and cried. Finally he blew his nose in a clean rag he found poked on a nail on a feed stall. He got out the brushes and brushed down each horse, and when he was through his hand was steady and his eyes dry. It made the horses feel refreshed and took the edge off Charlie's grief.

Two days later Charlie was nauseated by the overpowering, sweet-spicy scent of yard flowers. There were white and lavender lilacs, late tulips, spirea with satin ribbons, and white cards with black names. The shades were pulled, making the house dark. No one spoke above a whisper and everyone walked on tiptoes.

Mary and Joe shook hands with neighborhood men and women. Rachel and Riley came all dressed up. Mary put her head on Rachel's shoulder. "Oh, Ma, you can't imagine how much I'll miss Malinda."

Rachel gave Mary a fresh handkerchief to dab at her eyes. "You know, the last time I saw Malinda she said to me, 'Do something foolish!' I thought she was insane. But she explained. 'Old age is creeping in and you ought to get around to doing what you want.' You know, she was right! You think she knew her time was short and she became sort of—careless?"

Mary's eyes were puffy and red-rimmed. "We all know Malinda had unusual perceptions."

Riley shook hands with Joe. Riley looked strikingly well dressed in his black suit, in place of his farmer's bib overalls. "Your ma was the beginning and the end of an era. She and me had disagreements. But I liked her." Riley shut his eyes and when he opened them the tears spilled into his beard.

"Thanks," said Joe, taking his father-in-law's hand.

Will sneezed and blew his nose loudly, causing people to stare. "The flowers make my nose and throat itch."

Someone said, "Malinda always had flowers in her yard."

Another said, "And she gave them away. She was always giving something. She gave love with all of it."

Charlie felt hollow inside and his head seemed to be filled with wool. He felt woozy and thought it was from the different smells coming from the covered dishes, cakes, and pies on the kitchen table that people brought. The disease burned her, not carelessness. Grandma Malinda would enjoy being with all these people who loved her. She was never naggy. Not like Grandma

Rachel. Right away Charlie was ashamed that he even thought to compare his two grandmothers.

There was no casket. There was a plain, square cedar box, which had been put together in the back of Spence Stone's furniture store. There was no body. In the box were ashes that Joe and Orin Gale, the plump, red-whiskered, livery owner, thought must have been Malinda—if she died in bed. That was where they found her platinum wedding band in a heap of black charcoal and gray ashes—where the heavy, hand-carved oak bed always stood.

Reverend Talbott came up the porch and into the house. He was out of breath. He shook hands with Mary and Joe. Then, standing by the purple lilacs, he spoke in a deep, somber voice that went from a crescendo to a diminuendo and back in full force. He praised Malinda Irwin as if he'd known her all his life, not just over a year. Then he left, saying he had another appointment.

Joe and Orin Gale went to the cemetery. They buried the square, cedar box beside Old Charles. "I'll have something written on a large shale stone," said Joe.

"I'll help you find a good-sized stone in the grass and weeds by them new railroad tracks, just outside the town," offered Orin Gale, brushing back the pompadour of red hair.

"I'll chisel out something on the stone. Make it nice and neat, with four straight lines around it, like a box," said Joe.

Later Will and Charlie took the flowers to the cemetery. Charlie thought loving someone was like going fishing. You caught the fish and were excited, beyond reason, brought the fish home, and were pleased above good sense to have them in your house. You talked about them and looked at them. You enjoyed them, then finally they were consumed, used up, and gone forever. You could talk about them, but you could never again enjoy their sight, nor feel nor smell. He wiped his mouth on his sleeve.

Will's eyes watered and he sneezed. When it was over he turned his back on the blanket of flowers, raised his face to the clean, fresh sky, and let loose a string of epitaphs and blue curses that would have embarrassed any farmer at the smithery.

Joe sat at the kitchen table. He took off his suit coat and rolled up his shirt sleeves. He put his head in his big burly hands. The windows were open and a breeze made the dimity curtains billow back and forth against the screen, like pressing air rhythmically into the hot forge. Joe got up and went to the cupboard. He reached to the highest shelf and pulled down a cigar box. On the outside were large letters printed in indelible pencil: IMPORTANT IRWIN PAPERS.

He put the box on the table and poured himself a cup of cold coffee. Inside the box the first paper was his clear title for a quarter section between the Middle Fork and the South Fork of the Sappa Creek in the state of Kansas.

I'd like to go back and try the irrigation, he thought.

The paper underneath was older, yellowed and brittle with the words: DEED OF TRUST—CHARLES B. IRWIN—CHILLICOTHE, LIVINGSTON COUNTY, MISSOURI. Underneath that title was a penned addition: GIVEN TO JOSEPH MARVIN IRWIN, AUGUST 24, 1865 by CHARLES BURTON IRWIN. Joe stared at the paper several minutes, thinking about the time Old Charles had written those words. Then he decided that tomorrow he and Will would go to the burned ruins and take all the scrap to the town dump. We'll hitch old Flame to the plow and turn the rest under. The lot won't look too bad. It's flat and already has an iron gate that can be built on to. I'll sell it to someone who wants to build a house in town. He folded the brittle paper carefully and brushed the small, dry, yellowed paper flakes onto the scrubbed wood kitchen floor.

FOUR

Splitlogs

Two years of too little moisture had piled the yellow dust of the Missouri hardpan against fences and farm buildings. Farmers feared another scourge of grasshoppers, which would strip the land bare of any green thing, as it did during the seventies. Some farmers pulled up stakes, rode away from their dried fields to seek work in towns. The grain-hauling flatboats from Chillicothe Landing on the Grand River forks to St. Louis were few by the autumn of 1887.

Transients, tramps, panhandlers, and bums, lean men with sunken cheeks, without work, walked Chillicothe streets singly or in pairs seeking handouts for menial labor. They swung down from empty box cars on the Hannibal–St. Joseph Railroad empty-handed. The woolen pants, shirts, and heavy work boots they wore were their only possessions.

Housewives believed these men marked the board or concrete walks next to their homes if they were especially generous with a free meal or a job of chopping wood for the jingle of pocket money.

The men congregated before Gale's saloon and Pool Hall and around the beer parlor of the Grand River Hotel, or on the U.S.

Post Office corner. They waited for the settlers and farmers coming into town for supplies and then pestered them with questions like "Need a hired hand?" or "Need an extra worker for harvesting?" or "Need a thrasher?" "I'm a dandy handyman—could you hire me for a month, or couple weeks, maybe a few days?" Less than half were lucky and found something for a dollar a day, working from sunup to sundown.

After fighting his way through eighth grade, always big for his age, Will could see no use for more school. For the last five years he had worked full-time with his father in the smithery. Ell at sixteen, with long, topaz-colored hair, taught in a one-room country school, getting there each morning on the back of Will's pony, Scratch. She dispensed herbs and roots to the children and their parents when they were feeling poorly.

Frank was physically small for his ten years and thought his schoolteacher was dead-set against him. He complained of her making him stand in the corner, staying inside during recess, and rapping his knuckles smartly with a ruler. "For what?" he complained. "Nothing. Well—once I threw a spitball and it stuck in her hair."

Charlie day-dreamed of being as tall and strong as a stretched-out grizzly bear. He still carried his lariat, but he used it for emergencies, such as getting a kitten out of a tree or catching the possum that got into the school's trash. Charlie was good in sums and take-aways and naming state capitals. Charlie completed fifth grade. It was his last formal education.

From that time on he had to learn by his own ingenuity and intelligence, because in mid-April 1888 his father announced that the Irwins were moving to Kansas. "We're going to be well-fed farmers. I'm sick and tired of being poor and skinny as a bed slat."

Joe said, "Crops here are so poor they bring only thirty-five cents a bushel, and that's ten cents less than it cost farmers to grow. Farmers are leaving this area like flies. The smithery customers have certainly slacked off, so I have almost nothing to do. The only income is from the cordwood I'll bring to town this fall."

"What makes you think it's better in Kansas?" Charlie was skeptical.

"I've been reading this here pamphlet. Lots of folks going West. I've been there and I know it's possible to use downhill irrigation and not have to wait for rain. Look, right here in black and white it says, 'A wheat field will ripen like golden waves in the sunshine,' and 'Fields of barley like crushed velvet, silvery, then green in the breeze.' Can't you just see it?" Joe was enthusiastic.

"Why can't farmers here use downhill irrigation?" asked Charlie. "Grandpa Riley never did."

Joe scratched his head. "That's just it. Riley's land is table flat and too far from the river. Your ma and me remember Kansas around the Sappa area; swales and swells. We'll make a go of it this time. So—we're going to sell this house and the smithery." Joe slapped his thigh to indicate the finality.

The next couple of days were spent sorting, throwing out, and packing.

"I hope there's country schools in Kansas," moped Ell.

Mary reassured her. "The most important thing is that we'll be together. Pa'll build a decent house, from lumber. We'll have chickens. There'll be a schoolhouse for you. Frank needs work on arithmetic and Charlie more reading. There's two pupils. We'll tell Pa to trade some blacksmithing tools for books."

"Ma! I want to teach real pupils, not brothers!" Ell moaned.

"It's funny," Mary said. "The things we want most are vague unknowns. The things we'll miss are commonplace, like the hollyhocks in the backyard. I'll miss the afternoon walks carrying fresh zinnias, cosmos, or marigolds to the cemetery for the graves of baby Granville, Malinda and Old Charles." She sighed and looked up at Ell's unhappy face. "My thoughts seem to be with those who have passed away."

"Ma, look forward to new things and stop thinking of the past. Kansas is a breadbasket," said Ell. She brightened, her eyes seemed to go from olive to clear emerald as she talked. "This move may be the best thing for all of us. I used to think I'd never find a school here, but I did. I'll find a place to teach in Kansas. There must be settlers' children who are eager to learn. Working with brothers will be practice until I can find a real schoolhouse." Suddenly her problem was resolved and she smiled.

Mary felt better seeing Ell smile. She brushed her hair and changed her dress. She took the old cocker spaniel, Squirt, to her mother, Rachel. For years Rachel and Riley Brassfield lived in nothing but log houses on their farmland. Now for the first time Rachel and Riley let their sons do the farming and they lived in town in a white two-story that had a porch on three sides.

Rachel was never happier. She called the house and everything in it hers.

"I'll be glad to have something of you and your family to take care of," said Rachel, taking hold of the leash and tying it to her clothesline. "See how the old dog runs. He likes it here."

Mary knew leaving the dog would break the children's hearts, but it was better than having it die on the way to Kansas. She was trying to be sensible.

While his mother was gone, Charlie took down his Henry rifle, cleaned it with a strip of cloth on the end of a rod. He oiled the barrel and admired the shine of its blue-black metal. He wrapped it in one of his shirts and laid it gently under his bed. He heaved himself on the bed and sobbed with his face buried in the soft, goose-down pillow. He'd grown up with the dog. He couldn't imagine the family without it. Utter sadness created a lump in his throat. Charlie had no ambition to do anything, only stay curled in a ball on his soft, comfortable bed. Silent tears wet his pillow. Taking the dog to Kansas could surely mean its death. Finally he reasoned that it was best to leave Squirt behind. His sorrow lessened and the lump in his throat subsided. He was ready to go West.

Two weeks later Joe was in Clem's Groceries to buy sugar, flour, dried beans, cornmeal, and salt pork. Then he took the wagon to his father-in-law's place in town. For a few minutes Joe and Riley talked about crop yield and soil conservation. Most of Riley's land had been timbered, and when it was cleared and grubbed it was as mellow as an ash heap. Riley planted corn easily with nothing but a hoe, then prayed for life-giving rain. Some years he was lucky and the rains came. Other years he was unlucky and the skies remained cloudless during the growth period, from June through August.

Joe bought a pair of workhorses and a milk cow, named Clover, from Riley. Riley scalped his son-in-law. Joe knew he'd paid too much, but would rather avoid the fuss of accusation. Riley was known to be tightfisted and cagey. Joe could bargain, but not with relatives.

Joe thought of the time Rachel wanted the electric lights put in her house in town. Joe was stringing the electrical wires, and Riley squinted his oval, faded blue eyes and said, "If the Lord wanted a light at night, he'd a'made the sun shine twenty-four hours a day. When it's dark I go to bed the way the Lord intended. Don't expect me to pay for this fool incandescent light.

It'll more'n likely make us all blind. If I charge around breaking furniture I can't see, you'll have to pay for it."

After pocketing Joe's wad of paper money for the horses and milk cow, Riley said to Joe, "You'll be planting late, I 'spect."

Joe said he'd probably not plant anything except winter wheat, and maybe he'd just begin some farrier rounds and plant nothing at first. "I saved some of my most useful farrier's tools, and I gotta get the lay of the land in Kansas, so's to make a go of it."

"Can't get no money from a farrier's business if Kansas runs into a blasted drought. That'd make it no different from here," said Riley.

Joe said that he'd heard there were fewer droughts. "And there are men traveling around the state of Kansas who make it rain."

That took Riley by surprise and he looked suspiciously at Joe. "Hell's bells, that's tampering with the Lord's business. A feller can't do that!"

Joe scratched his head and said, "I should think if he had the know-how and was paid, he could."

Joe went to Riley's back porch and said good-bye to the old dog, Squirt. He had to close the door fast before the dog came out to rub up against his leg for more scratching between the ears. It was enough to bring a pang to his chest.

Riley had more to say to Joe, so he caught his attention by jabbing him in the midsection with his thumb. "You're taking my girl, Mary Margaret, and all her young ones. Rachel and me'll miss 'em. Who knows when we'll see Mary and the kids again. You going to put her in a damn soddy like before?"

Joe's feelings were hurt. He couldn't take those words any longer, so he strung the workhorses and cow behind his wagon and pulled out.

Riley came running and yelling, "Cripes, I'd like to go! But I'm too old to start. Besides, Rachel wouldn't take the prairie heat, and the damn wind and cold. You take care!" He waved both hands above his head.

Joe leaned over and waved one hand, keeping the reins taut in the other. He couldn't remember when he'd heard Riley use so many *damns*. "I'm going to cut me a rusty!" he called, meaning he was going to make good come hell or high water.

The next day Will's pony, Scratch, and the cow, Clover, were tied to the back of the wagon. Joe and Mary sat on the wagon's seat looking toward the future. Frank, Ell, and Charlie sat at the end of the covered wagon looking back on the sights they passed.

Will rode the stallion, Flame.

Charlie could not remember when his father did not have old Flame. He could barely remember the drought of 1878, when Joe hitched Flame to a wagon and went from one farm to another as farrier.

Charlie tried to remember eight, nine years ago when he'd first ridden to Kansas in a covered wagon with his brothers and sister. He closed his eyes and could see his mother carrying baby Frank, Ell running through tall grass, his father and twelve-year-old Will stacking hunks of grass and dirt to build a one-room house that had no windows and a stiff cowhide door. Charlie had heard stories about his father paying ten dollars to file for a land patent in a town called Oberlin. Then six months later he spent his entire savings of two hundred dollars at the Oberlin Patent Office in exchange for a paper showing clear title for one hundred sixty acres. This paper had meant a lot to his father because it showed that his quarter of a section was exempt from attachment for debt.

At the end of two years of near backbreaking work, in the spring of 1880, Charlie's father reluctantly put his family and goods back into the covered wagon and returned East to Chillicothe. Joe's hopes were unfulfilled. He never had a chance to try his idea of irrigating from one of the creeks or diverting a stream into a series of ditches between his rows of grain.

Charlie's memory of going back to Chillicothe was more clear. He envied Will, who was tall and strong. He was solid with wide shoulders, thick arms, and thighs. His hair was golden and his large oval eyes were as brown as richly tanned leather.

Charlie's reminiscence was spoiled by a sharp voice near his right ear.

"By the time I was Charlie's age, I worked hard. Charlie ought to stop being an annoyance, stop playing with that rope, grow up, and learn a trade," said Will, riding by the back of the wagon and pointing to the rope Charlie was thoughtlessly tossing out to pop the heads off the tall, wild timothy.

"Who sez?" snapped Charlie, winding the rope over his elbow and shoulder. "The last time you suggested I do something I got so bee stung that I couldn't sit and it was torture standing."

"I told you to go at that hive careful to see if there was honey. I didn't tell you to poke a stick into the fool thing." Will laughed. He knew he'd told Charlie to put a stick into the center to see if honey clung to it.

"You're the one that gave me the stick!" cried Charlie. "I ought to tell Pa what you did!"

"Why, you wouldn't snitch! I ought—"

"Will! Charlie! Hush!" It made Joe mad as a wet cat to hear the boys raise their voices and bicker. "Or I'll see that you both get the razor strap. Now—neither of you open your mouth until suppertime!"

Joe followed the Quincy, Missouri, and Pacific tracks. By the afternoon of the second day they passed through St. Joseph, a border town.

Riding up alongside the wagon Will asked, "Pa, where do you suppose Jesse James lived? I heard he married and took the name Howard so's no one knew who he was, then he got hisself killed. Killed in his own house by his own brother for a ten-thousand-dollar reward."

"That's a lot of money for anybody's dim-witted brother," squealed Frank.

"We're not going by that place," their mother said.

"With that kind of money I'd go West and buy me a cattle ranch," said Will, dropping back to keep an eye on the cow and pony as they approached the ferry to cross over the Missouri River, which was an opaque, brown color. The river's banks were high cliffs on both sides that had been cut to make a sloping wagon road to the ferry docks. Charlie counted five floating logs going down river as they crossed the rushing water.

Joe leaned over and whispered to Mary, "The brother, Charles James, was pardoned for that murder."

Mary turned her head and faced her husband. "Joe, that's perfectly terrible!"

"Well, it's not a woman's place to worry about such. I just told you the facts," said Joe, looking out the corner of his eye at Mary.

The weather held fair and dry. Joe forded the wagon across the Delaware and Big Soldier rivers, ignoring the difficult and dangerous railroad bridges. The Kansas and Pacific train puffed across the prairie twice a day, one westbound, one eastbound.

Charlie waved at the trains. Engineers waved back. The powerful chugging sound was exciting to Charlie. He thought the tracks looked like there was no beginning and no end.

Going through Topeka, Joe told about Fort Folly, a roofless log structure that had been erected more than twenty years before as protection against Confederate raiders. Joe was only fifteen when he joined the Missouri Militia. Joe told how the Civil War brought Federal soldiers to Chillicothe, which was a base for supplies and operations for the militia commanders. Joe fought at Wilson's Creek and Pea Ridge. When he came back to Chillicothe, he said he was surprised to find the Confederates had burned Graham's covered bridge. There was no other way to cross the Grand River, so he went along with the Grahams and hauled oak timbers by oxen and hand-hewed a new bridge. "Then I got work with Earl and Foreman Sloan in their livery stable. That's where I learned blacksmithing and how to buy and sell horses. But it wasn't long before them Sloan brothers gave up the livery business and moved to Ohio, where they bottled and sold their famous liniment. It's good for sprains and bruises in horses as well as humans."

Charlie said, "You know how to make it, Pa?"

"Not the exact formula, son, but I know what's in it for the most part. Stuff farriers been using for years before the Sloans began making it for everybody and his horse."

The wagon road took the Irwins beside the Kansas River. When it was time to ford the Blue, Joe was thankful for the dry weather. They crossed the Republican on a ferry, not much more than a log raft. Near Junction City, Mary suggested she buy greens, such as string beans and cabbage. She found only potatoes and turnips for sale.

During the preparation of the evening meal Mary confessed to Ell, "We are about shut of meat. I should'a had your pa lay in another barrel of salt pork back there where I got these potatoes."

Joe overheard. "Don't fret. Salt pork gives me the trots anyways. Me and Will might find some fresh game."

During supper Charlie complained, "These potatoes taste like spoilt buffalo chips."

"That's turnip," said his mother. "It's good food. If you can't eat them, give them to your pa."

"They give me gas," said Joe, picking out the turnips that were mixed with the potatoes.

Mary looked exasperated with both Joe and Charlie. "Then leave them on your plates and say nothing."

Charlie broke into a broad grin, looked at his father, and shoved his plate to the center of the quilt that was their table on the flat ground. "Nothing."

Mary laughed until tears came to her eyes.

Joe couldn't see the humor. He felt his wife was far too tolerant, even on the borderline of indulgent, with the children. Joe tried to think of something to say and finally noticed some low, rocky bluffs in the distance. "It's hard to imagine what it was like on this plain when Injuns were riding over them flinty hills." He pointed and everyone looked and he could see they agreed. "Then came the traders and trappers, the army on horseback, and next the pioneer settlers, then miners, cattlemen, sheep herders, ranchers, and farmers. By jing! This country is so vast nothing can stop a man with big ideas. There's opportunity for everyone. The Irwins are getting their opportunity and high time, too!" Joe slapped his thigh.

Mary said mostly to herself, "The greater the risk, the greater the reward or—complete loss. I guess we know that." But still she felt the excitement of the wide rolling hills.

Now they passed fewer and fewer settlements and the sky was an immense blue dome overhead. Charlie anticipated the trains passing twice a day.

One morning Ell said, "I wish there was a little cloud of dust on the horizon, like a dust devil. I'd watch it until it grew larger and all of a sudden turned into another wagon."

"What if it was a band of Injuns?" said Frank, pulling his mouth down at the corners to frighten his sister. "You'd jump and hightail it over that bluestem grass like it was a boardwalk."

"Naw!" she said. "No Injuns can scare me. I'd give them the evil eye." She squinted and opened one eye halfway.

"Wanna know what I'd do?" Charlie eased himself between Ell and Frank so that he could still see the wide expanse of land and the bare rim of horizon where thunderheads formed.

"Naw!" repeated Ell.

"Aw, cripes! You're no fun!"

"Charlie! Watch your tongue!" Their mother turned on the front seat so that she could look inside the wagon.

Charlie decided his mother could hear cussing and secrets no matter how much noise the wagon wheels made nor how far away she was. He stuck his tongue out as far as possible and curved it upward and half closed his lids so he could easily look down.

"I did what you told me, Ma!" he called, smirking.

Mary shook her finger in Charlie's direction and tried not to smile.

Joe gripped the reins tighter and thought soon Charlie would go too far and get the thrashing he deserved.

"Tell me what you'd do if you saw Injuns," whispered Frank.

"Not now," said Charlie.

"Aw, why not?" Frank whined.

"All right," Charlie said, "but you have to stop whimpering like a lost pup. I'd use my Henry rifle. I'd watch and just before they nocked their arrows—Bam! Bam! I'd make some bite the dust before the rest left so scared they'd wet their pants."

"Injuns don't wear pants," whispered Ell, "just a skirt in front and back."

"And sides?" questioned Frank.

"Bare naked," said Ell sensuously.

Joe stopped to make camp early. This gave Mary and Ell a chance to wash clothes while Joe and Will went out with Joe's rifle to hunt for a deer coming to the river for the late afternoon drink. Will carried the fish trap made with willow switches so that it looked like a kind of basket. He'd used the trap often on the Grand River to catch catfish. To make the basket he'd wrapped young willow sticks around a small barrel, then wove more willow sticks up and down the sides. The barrel was removed, the open end closed, and a kind of door put in. This trap was weighted in water with rocks and left in a deep hole, but tied to the bank with grapevines. Usually Will threw a handful of corn in the trap—not ordinary shelled corn, but fermented about a week until it was sour. He had only some spoiled, old potato peelings tied in a bandanna he hoped would attract the fish. He could just see the basket full of fat, white-bellied cats eating on those peelings. He'd grab that vine and haul up the trap before the fish could get out. Then he wondered if he'd find any vine down by the riverbank. If his father and he didn't scout up a deer, he'd be sure to get a mess of fresh catfish.

"The sun bleaches good," said Mary, spreading dishtowels on the bluestem grass to dry.

"I hope Charlie's going to shoot away from the wagon," said Ell, looking at Charlie and Frank with their heads together. Charlie had talked his mother into letting him practice shooting the Henry at buffalo chips.

"Charlie's twelve," said Mary, as though age had everything to do with safety.

Frank was begging Charlie to let him try just one shot. "Only one?" A tear clung to Frank's long, dark eyelashes.

"I'm using three shells," snapped Charlie. "That leaves me only two." He looked at the colors of the spectrum on that teardrop and Frank's sorrowful face. "So, do what I tell you and don't waste your shot. Hold steady. Aim at the chip up there in the notch of that rock. Here, lay down on your belly and put the barrel on my leg. Is that high enough?"

"Huh, I see the chip in the sight! Charlie, I can see it! Can I squeeze the trigger?"

Charlie felt perspiration run down his back. "If you are aiming low the lead could bounce off the rock and hit Ma's Dutch oven. Then we'd both get a whipping. So, be sure what you see before you shoot."

Frank pulled the trigger. There was a sharp ping, like a hard object striking a rock at an angle. Then without meaning to Frank pulled the trigger again, only this time the gun was pointed halfway up the sky line.

Charlie pulled his leg up and grabbed the gun. "I told you not to! Jeems!" shouted Charlie.

Their mother had come halfway toward them. "Charlie! Charles Burton Irwin! Bring that gun here this minute!"

Charlie sighed and moved toward his mother, but not before he looked into Frank's brimming eyes.

"Were you trying to kill us? Look at the hole in the wagon cover!" She moved to look at it from the other side. "Two holes —Mercy! It went clean through!"

"Holy mackinaw!" said Charlie, feeling queasy.

Ell grabbed him by the shoulders. "You could have hit me—or Ma! You want us buzzard bait?"

Charlie understood their being upset, but he couldn't see why they thought he did anything on purpose. He glared at Frank, who was wailing in fright.

Their mother snatched the rifle from Charlie and hurriedly pushed it in the back of the wagon. Bam! She jumped back and looked around. The three children were staring. She was looking at Charlie. "Now see what you've done!" She was shaking.

Charlie pushed his sunbleached hair from his eyes. He could see his mother's face was pale underneath her suntan. "Ma, the safety wasn't on. You grabbed so fast! I'm sorry."

"Don't say sorry to me, young man!" She grabbed Charlie's arm and pushed him against the back of the wagon. "Don't move an inch!" She looked around and picked up the best thing she could find to whip Charlie with, the spatula. Charlie saw red spots in her cheeks and a mean look in her eyes that he thought would make an icicle feel feverish. He felt the blows, gritted his teeth, and dug his fingers into the wood of the wagon. Once he raised up on his toes so that the blows would not all fall on the same stinging spot.

When Mary calmed down, she said, "Get into the wagon and put the safety on that gun. Then don't shoot it again until you are sixteen."

He knew there was no use being logical and telling her that he hadn't shot it yet.

"Then you and Frank take the bucket to the creek for water. When your pa comes he'll see those holes in that canvas first thing."

"Yes, ma'am." Charlie moved fast with Frank sobbing at his heels. They went to the edge of the cutbank and saw the creek ten, twelve yards below.

"You let me shoot your gun! So it was all your fault!" cried Frank. "Get rid of it! It's nothing but trouble!"

Both boys grabbed at the slippery, dried grasses and eased themselves down the cutbank to a little gravelly beach. Charlie reached way out to fill the bucket. He watched the water edge up inside and listened as Frank scrambled around on the rocks looking for a flat one to skip in the water.

Suddenly Charlie felt Frank grab his arm and saw him point a jerky thumb over his shoulder. Charlie turned and nearly skidded off the tiny gravel bar. Behind Frank an unfamiliar brown face was smiling.

The stranger wore no shirt and looked as though he'd lost his pants. His underwear was short and split at the thighs, and made of a soft leather. Charlie's heart thumped. His mouth was bone dry. His legs were frozen, and he watched two other smiling brown strangers come alongside as silent as wildcats in the moonlight. All three were dressed alike and wore their hair in braids, except one who had his braids stuck to the top of his head with daubs of mud. Their eyes were deep brown, like the middle of a black-eyed Susan blossom. Charlie could see cheekbones beneath the skin because there was no excess fat anywhere on their bodies.

The first stranger looked from Frank to Charlie, then to the steep bank. He had a blue jay's wing feather in his hair. There were tiny laugh lines at the corners of his mouth.

"I'll help," he said as friendly and plain as morning light.

The words startled Charlie into action. He grabbed Frank and began to push him up the cutbank.

The man held the water bucket by the bail and wedged moccasined feet into chinks and crannies as if they were steps. Near the top the three strangers laughed out loud, and Charlie and Frank scratched and clawed at grass, rocks, and roots to pull themselves up. Charlie's bare feet stepped on loose rocks, causing tiny slides. Finally, at the top, Charlie paused to catch his breath.

Frank was breathing down his back and whispering real loud, "Injuns! Real Injuns! We'd better run!"

Charlie said, "Thanks for the help" and reached for the bucket in preparation to run right back to camp as fast as possible.

The man carrying a carved walking stick stepped in front of the bucket of water. "Have you food?" he asked. "Biscuits, corn bread?"

Charlie straightened and looked up. "Sure."

The man with the feather in his hair stepped forward. "We lost our gear. Cattle rustlers dipped into our small herd. We tried to scare 'em off, but we were caught in our own loop last night. They got away with our horses, clothing, grub, and cattle. We tracked 'em, but lost the tracks in the river over yonder. We were looking when we heard your three shots. That's a sign there's trouble."

Charlie was astonished. "You don't talk like Injuns. Injuns don't get stole from."

The man with the feather then spoke something that was gibberish to Charlie and Frank and the three men laughed. "That was Wyandot. If we spoke in our language, you wouldn't understand us. If Indians have something another person wants, they get stole from. It's the same anywhere. Those that don't have grab from those that do have."

Charlie nodded.

"We're from Kansas City and don't usually dress like this. How do you think our people are going to look at us when we walk into town?" He held out his arms from his sides.

Charlie could see it could be a funny situation. "You live in a house, not in a tepee?"

"A house in town."

Again Charlie was astonished. "What will Ma and my sister think when we walk into camp with you?" His eyes moved across the three near-naked men.

"We'll follow behind you," said the leader. "Tell your mama that we are friends."

Charlie and Frank ran excitedly. Once Charlie turned his neck backward to see how fast the three Indians were walking. The leader carried the water bucket real steady.

"Ma! Oh, Ma!" Charlie cried. "Give us biscuits! I need biscuits for my friends."

"Whoa," said his mother, catching Charlie and Frank in her arms. She had not seen the strangers. "You can't be hungry al—"

Ell screamed, "Lord 'a mercy!" She scrambled under the wagon and cowered behind one of the wheels. Her face was white as a bleached buffalo bone. Mary's mouth stayed open, but she could not speak.

Frank grabbed his mother's skirt. He tried to explain fast. "Wyandots. From Kansas City. Lost gear. Rustlers. Injuns. Friendly."

"Ma, these men are friendly. They brought the water without spilling a drop," said Charlie, breathing hard.

The lead man put the bucket beside the campfire that was mostly ashes and a few red coals. He hesitated only a moment to see if Mary was going to speak first, then said, "Ma'am, we mean no harm. We are sorry if we frightened you and your girl child."

Mary was amazed. To her knowledge Indians were not supposed to speak so well. She heard Ell sobbing and thought, these men look exactly the way we all imagined. But, God in Heaven, they act like real people! No wonder Ell is so frightened.

The man with the feather in his hair continued. "I am Matt Splitlog and these are my brothers, John and Mark." John had the wooden cane. Mark had dried mud holding his braids on top of his head.

"We're Irwins," said Charlie, feeling he was reminded that he was the man of the family as long as his pa and Will were out hunting and fishing and that he should be doing the introductions. "This is Ma and under the wagon is Ell and here's Frank and me, Charlie."

The Splitlogs nodded. Matt shook hands with Mary, then Charlie, and Frank, then nodded toward Ell. She was not crying, but hugging her knees and rocking back and forth.

Charlie wanted to show that he was courteous same as his pa would be to friendly strangers. "We're going to the Middle Fork of Sappa Creek. Pa has got a homestead and he's going to farm."

Matt hunkered down on his haunches and the other two men

sat in the grass, eyeing the lumps and bumps under the dishtowels near the cookfire.

Charlie rummaged around in the kitchen utensils and brought out three tin plates and three spoons and gave them to his ma. "Those men are awful hungry," he said.

Mary was caught off guard. She quickly took the plates and added lightly browned biscuits, which were still warm under the dishtowel. "I'll make some mush to go with these. Oh, you can have some boiled turnips, too."

"Never mind the turnips," said Matt.

Charlie was certain now that he liked these men. He sat beside Matt, who ate three biscuits before saying another word. Matt brushed the crumbs from his fingers and spoke loud enough for Mary to hear as she stirred the cornmeal in the hot water, over the fire's bed of coals. "I know the area you will travel going to Sappa's Middle Fork. When you get to Salina, past Abilene, take the wagon road north along the Saline River for a spell, then follow the road across country northwest. It's a shortcut and avoids a couple river crossings."

Mary tried to remember what he said. He went on. "You'll pass through some small towns and the only big ford is on the south fork of the Solomon near Nicodemus." His eyes lighted up and he smiled a moment. "Colorful place. Nice folks there. You can get fresh provisions. Then it's only a few days' travel before you'll be on your Sappa Creek—Middle Fork."

Mary spooned out the mush into each man's plate. She got the canister of sugar from the back of the wagon. "Tastes better with sugar." Then she passed Matt the dipper so that he and his brothers could drink from the bucket of fresh water. Mary repeated the directions for the shortcut to Sappa Creek's Middle Fork, and felt pleased with herself when she got them correct.

When the three men were finished eating, they used the dipper to rinse out the cooking kettle, plates, and spoons. They wiped everything dry with handfuls of grass. Matt put the kettle and eating utensils next to Mary's kitchenware in the back of the wagon. Then he walked around the wagon. He could hear Ell moving from one side to the other. Finally he asked, "Are you folks traveling alone?"

Mary hesitated. Charlie could tell that his mother didn't want to say that he and Frank were the only men in camp this afternoon. "Pa and my brother Will are hunting close by. They more than likely have a deer or some fish and are on their way back.

That's why Ma had fresh biscuits ready," said Charlie.

"I've not heard a shot for game. Did you?" he asked his brothers.

Mark kept a straight face. "I only heard those three—uh—misfires."

"Jeems! And you thought we were in trouble!" Charlie said, laughing.

"You were!" countered Mary. "Your target practice backfired into the wagon canvas. That's trouble." Her eyes sparkled and Charlie could tell that she was not so angry now. She was telling the story more as an incident that deserved a good chuckle.

"Pine tar ought to cover those holes," said Matt. He was sitting on his haunches again, chewing on a grass stem. Frank was sitting between the other two brothers, motioning for Ell to come out from under the wagon. "I suppose you'd never guess I went to Training School in Lawrence, Kansas?" said Matt.

Mary was again astonished. "Training School?"

"Yes, ma'am. I trained in United States history. In winter I teach our children. Some of our womenfolk also went to the Training School and teach the children. We have a good school." Matt's eyes had a way of sparkling so that the listener knew he had some kind of secret joke. "I'm like a schoolmarm."

Ell sucked in her breath, causing Matt to look out the corner of his eyes as she came out from under the wagon.

"Ell's a schoolmarm herself," explained Charlie. "She hopes to teach at our new place, if she can find pupils."

"Pshaw, you'll find kids anywhere that want to learn," said Matt, squinting at Ell. "Especially if you use those McGuffey's *Eclectic Readers*."

"That's just what I use," said Ell, sitting beside her mother.

"I saw them in the wagon close to the dishes. I guess you use them every day," said Matt.

"I work with Frank and sometimes Charlie after supper," said Ell.

Mary was rather enjoying the company. She had decided the three men were really friendly and harmless. She was glad that Ell had come out of her frights and was feeling easier around the strangers. Ell could not keep her eyes off the copper-colored men. She was fascinated by the smooth rippling of their muscles whenever they moved.

Charlie was wondering how the three men would get their next meal. "Do you ever make stone arrowheads?" he asked.

Matt laughed. "My pa can make a half dozen in just a couple of minutes if he finds a good flint bed. But none of us had to learn in order to keep meat on the table, so it's becoming a lost art."

"Isn't it cold at night, without—uh—shirts and—uh—trousers?" asked Ell.

"We can keep walking and it won't seem cold," said Matt. "But Lord help us, I'm hoping we can track down those buzzards and by nightfall have our gear back along with those six fat cows."

"What if you don't?" asked Frank.

"We'll just have to dog after them until we catch up," said Matt. "Don't you worry. We'll do what we can."

"If Pa were here he'd give you part of the deer he's bringing in or some of the catfish," said Charlie.

"If he gets a deer; I haven't heard the shot yet," said Matt, standing up. The other two brothers stood right away.

Mary wrapped the remaining biscuits in a dishtowel. "For your supper," she said, handing Matt the package. Then she gave them a lard bucket filled with fresh milk.

"Thank you kindly," said Matt.

Now Charlie's mind was racing. He was going over what had happened just before the Splitlogs had come to the water hole. Frank had yelled about the Henry rifle as if it were a red-hot piece of iron, "Get rid of it!" Next Charlie thought what Grandma Malinda had said about the rifle being used for peace. Today his mother told him he couldn't shoot it again for years. He climbed into the wagon and brought out the Henry rifle. It seemed the right thing to do. He handed it to Matt, saying, "It's mine. Take it. Maybe we'll meet somewheres and by then you'll have your own rifles. It needs cleaning."

Matt was so surprised his mouth fell open. His brothers' eyes grew big and they said together, "Kindness is its own reward."

Matt held the rifle out toward Charlie. "Nobody loans a valuable weapon, especially not to strangers."

Charlie shook his head and pushed the rifle back. "I'm not a nobody. I'm loaning it to friends. It's meant to be used to keep men alive." He reached into his pocket. "Here's a box half full of shells."

The three Splitlogs smiled. Matt said, "We'll see you in Abilene or Nicodemus. This will keep us in grub until we get our own gear. It may be a lifesaver."

Charlie felt good. He held out his hand and said, "Thanks for bringing the water up the cutbank."

Matt sighted with the rifle along the prairie's skyline, made the cutoff sign, walked past Mary, and put the rifle over his shoulder. He turned. "Your boy's certainly not an Injun-giver—is he? We honor him."

Mary's hand flew to her mouth and she nodded.

Matt waved John and Mark on. "The rifle will be preserved and returned. Don't stay out in the prairie sun long without your bonnets. If you get too dark you'll be taken for Exodusters. Not that there's a thing against Exodusters. But until you acquire some wisdom, you might find them a problem." Matt chuckled and moved behind his brothers through the dropseed and beard-grass.

Ell was quiet. She watched the muscles flex in Matt's jaw and neck as he talked.

Charlie did not move for a long time. He noticed the sun seemed brightest when a cloud just began to cover it and then again when it first came out from behind another cloud. A meadowlark flitted behind the wagon. Frank and Mary gathered dry clothing off the grass. Ell had her eyes closed as if she were sleeping against the back wagon wheel. She thought of the pleasing copper color of the Splitlogs' lean muscular arms and legs, chest and back. She found the graceful movements of their near-naked bodies strangely exciting. She wondered if that was what frightened her.

Charlie still felt good about letting the Splitlogs take his rifle. He felt his right thigh. It still stung where his mother had whipped him good.

Before dark Joe and Will came back with a small buck deer thrown behind the saddle of old Flame. Will rode his pony, Scratch, and behind its saddle was the willow trap, half full of fat, white-bellied catfish. "Nothing better than cats rolled in flour and fried in lard with a few onions. Fish are all gutted and clean for you to cook, Ma." He and Joe dragged the buck deer to the creek to skin. When they came back, supper was ready. No one said much during the meal. Charlie noticed that Will wolfed down his food. The Splitlogs must have been hungrier, yet they were more mannerly.

After supper Mary and Ell cut up the venison and put the strips over a wire Joe rigged on top of a long trough dug in the ground that held a grass-fed, smoky fire. The wire with the drying meat looked like a short clothesline to Charlie. He sat hunched over the back of the wagon reading one of Ell's McGuffey's books when he heard his mother telling his father about the stray bullets and the Splitlogs. Next he heard the tramp of his father's boots on the hard-packed ground as he walked to the back of the wagon.

"Charlie, you can kiss that rifle good-bye. For every privilege there is a responsibility. It was a privilege for you to have that old Henry and your responsibility to take care of it to the best of your ability. Do you understand?"

"Ya, I understand. I did that, Pa," said Charlie as steadily as he could muster.

FIVE

Abilene, Kansas

Approaching Abilene at the confluence of Turkey Creek and Smoky Hill River, Joe told his children about the numerous cattle trails that came in from the south.

One of the shortest but most traveled routes was the Chisholm Trail, which started south of San Antonio and went nearly due north to end in Abilene, Kansas. The Shawnee Trail also began in San Antonio and ran through Indian Territory, crossing the southeastern corner of Kansas. Before reaching Kansas this trail split into two; one branch went to Junction City.

The Western Trail began near San Antonio and crossed Kansas into Nebraska. A branch of this trail followed along the eastern boundary of Colorado and Wyoming. Cattle on this route were placed on the open range, not in stockyards. Longer than any of these was the Long Trail that began in Brownsville, Texas, went west along the Platte River into Wyoming and Montana after passing through Kansas and Nebraska, then ended in Canada.

"Will we see a cattle drive?" asked Charlie.

"The cattle leave Texas in May or June, and there may be as many as seven thousand head in a herd of young animals," said Joe. "But if the herd is of older and larger cattle, that are more nervous and the fighting type, there may be only one to three thousand in the herd. Yes, you'll see plenty cattle and soon."

"I think I can almost smell them," said Ell, holding her nose.

Abilene grew from a one saloon, one trading post, wide place in the road, to a rough town with a dozen soddies, to a booming town of three hundred people in a few years. The cattlemen were never known to hoard their money, so dancing, horse racing, and gambling became a thriving business. At one time Abilene had forty saloons with a dance hall or gambling room between every two saloons.

Joe said, "I've heard tell Abilene was one of the roughest towns in the West in the sixties. More than three million head of cattle were driven here in the sixties and seventies."

"What's the roughest?" said Will.

"The wildest place was Dodge City. It was headquarters for bandits and outlaws who come from the gold fields of Colorado and California thinking to make even more money robbing cattlemen and cowboys instead of miners and merchants. You can imagine the fights and shootings and robberies. The graveyard near Dodge City is called Boot Hill because so many men were shot in some quarrel while protecting themselves or others and they 'died with their boots on,' " explained Joe.

"I heard that more than five thousand cowboys were paid off at the same time once in Abilene," said Will.

Joe nodded. "If eight men are with every thousand head of cattle and each man has five to ten horses, in case one becomes weak and dies, or is stolen by Indians, you can see the number of people and animals that can come into Abilene."

"Pa, where did all those people stay?" asked Ell.

"Are there hotels for such an army of men?" asked Mary, suddenly interested.

"Cowboys sleep on the prairie and eat at their own outfit's chuck wagon," said Joe. But he didn't tell all he knew. For example, the only accommodations the cowboys really wanted were saloons, gambling houses, and brothels that were open all night. From the desire of these cowboys came the custom of rolling the chuck wagons of the various outfits downtown at night and parking them in front of the saloons to feed their carousing members.

It was near suppertime when the Irwins rode through "Texas Abilene" on the south side of the railroad tracks, where the longhorns were driven into stock pens to wait for sorting and shipping. Their Texas cowpunchers camped nearby. Both Will and Joe waved to the men meandering around their chuck wagons. The air was pungent with smells from the stock in the yards and the spicy foods simmering over cookfires. The air was dusty and flies buzzed everywhere. Some cowboys swaggered in and out of the Old Trail's End House facing the railroad tracks. This was a flat-roofed, two-story limestone building that had other saloons and gambling halls on the west side.

A cowboy standing on the boardwalk waved at the Irwin wagon.

"How do I get out of town, cowboy?" asked Joe, his lips pulled thin.

"Just keep going straight ahead past McCoy's Addition and you'll be out of town!"

"Good! Thanks a million!" Joe felt some better. He had read about Joseph McCoy. He was the man who originated the idea of driving cattle from Texas to the railroad in Kansas. The wagon lurched forward. Joe crossed his fingers and hoped that Mary and the children paid small attention to the ladies he saw who were talking and laughing farther along. He was so bent on moving quickly and finding a place to camp all night that he drove into the street along McCoy's Addition without seeing that it was completely blocked with household goods from the gray frame houses standing between saloons and dance halls. He had to pull to a halt fast. "What's this?" he yelled.

The answer came right away from a man who was obviously not a cattleman. The man had on a black suit and his thumbs were hooked inside his black suspenders, which lay against a starched, white shirt.

"This is McCoy's Addition, or better called the Devil's Half Acre! Pull up over there on the other side of the tracks and wait."

"I can't stay here!" Joe was offended and upset with this awkward delay. His wife and family were hanging out the wagon gawking at every passerby they could ogle.

The man in the black suit smiled and waved Joe on toward the tracks. "Stay overnight. It's safe here. Outside of town there are road agents, thieves, and robbers who scout for travelers the likes of you."

"See, Charlie! We could use that rifle you so gallantly gave away. You birdbrain!" Ell poked Charlie in the ribs.

"Yah, some thief will come after our stuff. We only have one gun to hold this gang of robbers off," added Frank, looking for a place to hide.

"Only a dumb jackass'd give their rifle to some Injuns," said Will, giving Charlie a dirty look.

Charlie hung his head, but he thought, they're a bunch of scaredy-cats. What could happen here to hurt us? There's cowboys everywhere for protection. It's a well-known fact that cattle drivers fight for fair play and justice.

Joe waved his arms and his face turned red. "Look, man, I have a wife and children—"

The man stepped off the boardwalk and came closer to the wagon. "Mayor Avery's my name. Carl Avery. Go on over the tracks. You can see the crossing from here. Keep your missus and little ones inside for the night."

"I'm not happy with this situation," said Joe, pounding his fist on the wagon's wooden seat to show his displeasure. "Someone should have told me to steer clear of this town—this, this Addition. Now I'm forced to camp in the middle of—wickedness." He sputtered with anger.

"I have explained why you are better off here tonight," said the man who called himself mayor. "By morning you can move on safely, as the bandits will be moving on to easier pickin's. We are fortunate to have plenty of cattlemen here during this year's purge. Oh, yes, there could be petty thieves taking furniture and clothing, or even the girls taking each other's clothing or satin sheets. You might hear gunshots, but it's safe over there, I guarantee. Have a good evening."

"Damn it!" Joe swore. He could not control his resentment even though he looked down on men who cussed in front of women and children. He could see no way out. He certainly didn't want to camp outside of town to be exposed to road agents and their ilk. Besides, it was getting late to look for a campsite.

"Water's fifty cents a gallon for as much as you want!" called the mayor. "Get it at the Abilene Oasis!"

"That's robbery!" yelled Joe.

Mary leaned out the wagon and said sweetly, "Thank you, Mr. Mayor. We'll camp right here and make the best of things. There'll be something to tell our grandchildren about the town of Abilene. And we can add that we met the mayor personally."

Mayor Avery waved. Joe drove to the crossing. When he finally stopped, he turned to Mary. "I swear I don't know what came over you. You spoke out and made yourself bold with little cause. Mayor Avery said for you and the children to stay inside."

"But we've already seen," she said, biting her lip.

The Irwin wagon was just north of Abilene proper. Here there were a couple dozen one-story frame houses, each with ten to twenty rooms. Between the houses were saloons, dance halls, and gambling rooms.

They ate a cold supper inside the wagon of salty smoked venison, milk that Will brought in from the cow, and some leftover biscuits. The children went to the end of the wagon to investigate a commotion across the road.

A couple men, not cowboys, carried furniture and bedding to a wagon beside the tracks. "Are they stealing?" asked Frank. No one answered, because without warning several shots rang out. Then pandemonium began. Frank ducked behind Mary's trunk. Cowboys and cattlemen ran down the road after the two men. One thief stumbled and fell, a clock rolled from his arms. Will hooted. Another shot, then two more. Frank was shaking.

"Aw, those shots are in the air," said Charlie, kneeling at the back of the wagon where he could see.

"That one man is still down," whispered Ell. "Is he dead?" She looked panicky, like she wanted to hide with Frank.

The crowd of cowboys converged and mingled and sent out shouts from the low buzz of voices. Then the cowboys moved away, leaving the street empty.

"Don't lean out. Keep your heads inside!" ordered Joe. He wondered what fate had led him here. He wished his wife and children would not stare so boldly at these women who seemed to be moving in and out of the saloons and dance halls, resigned to the ruination of their goods. The sprawling gray houses were dark beside the well-lighted saloons. The houses had never seen a whitewash. But Joe saw in the late afternoon light that they all had white lace curtains and the windows sparkled shiny clean.

Mary thought how much better were these houses than the soddy she was going to be calling home. Surely these places never had bedbugs nor fleas. She'd heard of the sheets with lace and the fine silks and fur pieces and brand-new high-button shoes. It took a roll of money to buy expensive furnishings and clothes. She pulled Ell back because she was leaning out of the tail of the wagon calling to girls as they passed.

"Where are you going?" Ell had called to a wiry, black-haired girl, who looked more Mexican than anything else.

"My friend," said the lean, dark girl, "in this place you go down like scummy water."

"Don't call those floozies over here," warned Joe. He saw that most of the girls stayed on the other side of the tracks, where the saloons and gambling houses were.

Frank crow-hopped his way from behind the trunk. "Some of the girls look about like Ell. Is this their home? Don't they have a ma or pa?"

Joe cleared his throat. He thought it was going to be hard to explain to a ten-year-old about the boardinghouse girls of Abilene, especially with Mary and Ell listening. "Son, these girls haven't the kind of home Ell has. These girls don't generally stay here permanent. They are looking for something better. But while waiting and looking they take a man's cash. Everyone has some hard-luck story and they expect trinkets of lace, or gold and silver, just for listening to their story."

"I know some stories," said Ell. Will glared at her for interrupting.

"These girls don't get attached to any one man, like Ell might one day," Joe said, hoping he was making some sense. "You see—they ain't looking to be married right off." The words were hard for Joe to put together. He wished the words would roll from his mouth like a full river in the spring. He saw Mary and the children with their faces toward him, their ears full of hearing.

"I'm not looking to be married either," said Ell, glaring at Will.

Joe scowled at his two oldest children and tried to go on explaining the best he could. "They don't use real names. They call themselves something fanciful, like 'Sweets' or 'Peaches.' They usually have some talent and can sing and dance and make their partner feel happy and waste a lot of a man's time."

Now Will, who sat cross-legged in the back of the wagon, put his chin in his hand, elbow on his leg, and listened attentively to see just how much his father would tell.

"It's said some take opium—they call it laudanum—to make the time go by, or spirits to make the time more pleasant, but I suspect most later on get married and settle down like everyone else. They probably try to keep their past a secret."

"Why would a girl do that?" asked Charlie. "If a girl can sing and dance, I'd think she'd be pleased to talk about it."

"Well, these—uh—dance hall girls are different," said Joe, taking a deep breath. He could feel the perspiration on his back and under his arms.

Mary thought he'd done very well and was about to tell him so, when he added a sentence. "The girls are what some call hussy, a jade, a dirty dove." Joe stood up and stretched. His explanation was over. He was not going to say more. He expected that if he went on, he'd say too much. Even so, he was prepared for Mary to ask him later how he knew this much. He wasn't going to discuss more of the seamy side of life with his family. He was a gentleman and showed them respect.

Joe had made the girls seem like performers to Charlie. He

listened to the fiddle music and singing and watched the lights that came across the tracks. It was like a circus and was as exciting as a medicine show. Charlie wanted to walk along the boardwalk and peek into each open door to see what caused the laughter and shouting he heard. "Ma, I could go across there and get water in the bucket."

"Oh, no, you can't! Neither can anyone else go across those tracks!" Mary was quick to say. "We have plenty of water in the barrel."

"If I go, you'll never know," smirked Will, teasing his mother.

"You do, I'll know," Mary said, slapping the comforters down so that Will and Joe and Charlie could sleep under the wagon. She moved boxes around so that she and Ell and Frank could sleep inside the wagon. "I'll unmend those two little holes in the wagon cover, so's to keep an eye on you," she said to Will. He laughed and winked.

For prudence's sake Joe divided the money he carried, giving Mary half. "God forbid either of us is robbed. But part of a loaf is better than none. You can divide yours with Frank and Ell. Sleep with it pinned on your undergarments. I'll divide some of mine between Will and Charlie."

Mary nodded and agreed. "Put your money in the inside watch pocket of your trousers. Then you and the boys sleep in your trousers."

Everything was quiet around the wagon, but Charlie could not sleep on account of the music coming from across the tracks. He sat up. The girls were in front of the saloons, or inside. The lights there were bright, mostly from coal-oil or kerosene lanterns. Joe snored. Will stirred.

Charlie whispered, "Let's go for a walk."

"If Ma found out, she'd kill me for letting you go over there," said Will, yawning.

"You said she'd never know," said Charlie.

The two boys sneaked across the track and stood around watching the cattle drivers go in and out of the saloon called Abilene Oasis. Charlie recognized Mayor Avery, the portly man in the black suit. "Good evening, sir," said Charlie. "Say, do you know the Splitlogs, three Injun brothers who brought a big herd of cattle here?"

The mayor looked quizzical. Then he brightened and his face shone as he moved under a lamp. "I never heard of that outfit." He brushed the flying moths away from his face. "But I heard something that'll put a couple of cartwheels in your pocket, right here at the Oasis in a couple of hours. So don't wander far."

"A couple of cartwheels!" repeated Will.

"A couple of hours? Much obliged," said Charlie, reaching out to shake the mayor's hand. The mayor turned and went inside the saloon. He was whistling.

Charlie stood on his toes trying to get a good look and at the same time listen to the piano music inside. He didn't recognize the tune but he found it catchy enough to hum.

Two girls, walking backward making eyes at the cowboys walking toward them, ran into Charlie and Will. "Pardon me," said the girl with long reddish hair and a brown wool cape around her shoulders.

"Excuse us," said Will, getting a sweet flowery smell of their perfume, which was more pleasant than the tangy odor of the stockyards.

"You cowboys need a drink?" She was blond with short curls and wore a man's black suit coat. Both girls had on rather short dresses of a flimsy flowered cotton. Like nightgowns, thought Charlie.

The blond opened her eyes wide and gave the two Irwin boys the once-over. "Red, you're as dizzy as a witch. Didn't you notice one of these cowboys is a baby. A kid, wet behind the ears!" She put her finger on Charlie's chest, making him blush.

"I'm not as young as you think," Charlie said. "I'm Charles Burton Irwin and this here is my big brother, William."

"Glad to meetcha. I'm Wild Honey and my friend is Red Stockings." She nodded but did not take the hand Charlie offered, so he pulled it back to his side. He thought the customs of Abilene were probably different from those he was used to.

Honey brought out a small, wooden box of thin cigars from her beaded reticule. She lighted one, striking the match on her fingernail.

"I'll buy some whiskey," said Will, feeling in his watch pocket for his father's money. He smiled and talked about shoeing horses and sawing hardwood as the four of them walked into the Oasis.

Charlie felt light-headed. Inside the saloon his bare feet seemed to barely skim the sawdust floor. The place was filled with noisy cowboys and cattlemen. Charlie wondered if anyone ever slept around here. Coal-oil lanterns were strung across the ceiling and over the bar. However, the corners of the huge room were in the dark. They edged their way through the crowd. Some bearded guy made a grab for Red, but she sidestepped.

Will looked confused. "Say, do I have to tip—pay anything under the table, so to speak?" he whispered, and wrinkled his forehead.

"Don't be a hick," sniffed Honey. "Get the bottle and let's get out of this stuffy place."

"I'm not a hick," said Will. "I feel like a nighttime hooty owl." He took the roll of greenbacks from his watch pocket and counted off two. The man at the bar took both. Honey's eyes were wide open the whole time Will had his father's money roll out.

"Come on, I'll show you where to put your tip, Cowboy," Honey murmured in his ear as she put her arm around his waist, her hand on his pocket. Will took a swig from the bottle and gave it to Honey. Charlie noticed that her teeth were yellow-brown. She cooed, "Sweet William, try a cigar. It's imported. A man looks sexy with one of these in his mouth. What do you think?"

Charlie was sure Will would roar laughing at that kind of simpy talk. But Will put one hand around Honey's waist and took the cigar with the other, giving it several puffs. His smile turned crooked and his face turned red and he coughed. Charlie thought it served him right. Will hunkered down like he was moving uphill. "You're a bear-cat!" he said. "My hands are sweaty and my heart's apounding."

"Oh yeah?" giggled Honey, her pink tongue traveling around her red lips.

"You have many cowboys as friends?" Red asked Charlie. She combed her long reddish hair. Playfully she ran the comb through Charlie's hair a couple of times. The stroke of the comb turned his brain to mush, his stomach to aching, his legs to noodles.

"Hey, stop that!" said Charlie, pulling himself together. "I can comb my own hair when it needs it."

"Yes, I'd say I've known a lot of cowboys. If you know what I mean." Red answered her own question.

"Like that one back there in the saloon? Is he someone special?" said Will, teasing.

"That's no cowboy. He was just funnin'. When times is slow he gets us business. He's an—an agent. Like when the hog drivers come in the fall. They don't have so much money, being paid less than a dollar a day, and they don't have much comfort, sleeping on the ground rain or dry. Hog drivers want to drink, shoot out windows, and race. They have to be told what we're here for."

Charlie asked, "What are you here for?" The minute he asked he wished he hadn't. All eyes turned on him. He felt like a clock whose time had run out.

Red's mouth turned down and her face looked flinty hard. "That guy in there is hired by Mattie Silks to see we serve the customers."

That information was meaningless. Charlie shut up. He wanted to know who this Mattie Silks was, but he didn't want Red to think of him as an ignoramus kid. He began to hum with the music coming from the dance hall two doors away, "Sweet Adeline," and fight off the black flies.

"You sing all right," said Red, her mouth lifting at the corners.

"I was born in 1875. My birthday is August fourteenth."

She gasped and grabbed for the whiskey bottle.

Charlie felt a delicious, undefinable longing somewhere in his midsection. He found that he didn't have to drink when he raised the bottle to his lips and no one knew the difference. Will and Honey whispered and giggled and nuzzled close to each other.

"Let's go to the train depot and lay on the benches," said Honey, nipping at Will's earlobe. Little gusts of wind blew the flies away.

"I wouldn't mind sitting on one," piped Charlie.

"Let's go round to the other side," purred Honey meaningfully.

"Charlie, you wait here," said Will. "Don't follow or I'll punch your teeth out. And don't get any ideas."

"How long you gonna be?" asked Charlie. A film of perspiration broke out on the palms of his hands. He felt dizzy. He wanted to go back to the wagon, but also he wanted to stay a little longer. Will didn't answer his question.

Honey patted Charlie's arm. "Don't do anything racy, Chuck." She winked at Red, who was pouting, then put her arm around Will's waist and pulled him into the shadows.

A prestorm stillness was in the air. Charlie looked around. "I wonder when Will's coming back?" There was a sudden splatter of raindrops on the boards. Red got up and moved with Charlie close to the side of the depot under the overhang. In one jagged flash of bright, white lightning he saw that her face was pale, thin, and pimply. He thought, she doesn't get enough to eat. She shivered and he moved close and put his arm around her shoulders.

"Hey!" called Will.

Charlie leaped away from Red as if he'd felt a spark from a bonfire. Red laughed.

Will's shirttail hung out and Honey's hair was wet and blowing. "We'd better get back," said Will. He cuffed Charlie under the chin. Will looked at Honey and said, "I'll stop by again when I get the cattle going on my ranch."

Charlie shook Red's hand and said, "So long."

The rain had stopped and Charlie heard the dance hall music, felt the dampness of the boards on his bare feet, and smelled the overpowering odor from the stockyards. Will tucked his shirt into his pants. They were halfway across the railroad tracks before Charlie broke the silence. "How was it?"

"What?" said Will.

"You know—with Honey?"

Will grinned and hit Charlie under the chin again.

Charlie felt a pulling spasm inside. He looked ahead at the wagon. Everything there was quiet. The moon came out from behind a cloud and made the wagon's canvas top glisten snow white.

"Wasn't so much. No better'n riding a horse full tilt across the prairie and coming back, out of breath and spent."

Charlie thought of that feeling, pure exhilaration, and it made him excited.

Will laughed softly and put his hand on Charlie's shoulder. Suddenly he stopped and put his hands in his pockets. He cried, "I've been robbed!"

"Sshh! You want to wake everyone?" said Charlie.

"I don't have the money Pa gave me. He'll tan my hide!"

Charlie grabbed Will and made him hunker down in the wet weeds. "I saw Honey eyeing your roll of money in the Oasis. I thought you noticed."

"Oh, geez, I feel terrible," moaned Will.

Charlie took out his roll of money. "Keep this in case I don't get back until daylight. Think of something to tell Pa."

"What are you going to do?" asked Will.

"I'm not sure. You crawl under the wagon and into your blankets. I'll get Pa's money." Charlie got up and walked through the weeds back to the tracks. He stopped halfway and looked back. Will was out of sight. He sighed and hitched up his damp shotguns. He had no idea what he was going to do. When he got to the saloons he looked for the mayor and found him in the Oasis.

"A girl called Wild Honey took my brother's roll of dollar bills. Ten of 'em. They belong to my pa."

Avery could see Charlie was just a barefoot kid. "Remember I said there was money to be made. Come with me, cowboy." They went into the Oasis. Avery said, "Your money's here!"

Charlie saw no money. He blinked so his eyes would water and he could see better in the smoky lantern light.

A ring was drawn in the sawdust about ten feet in diameter. There were four or five men standing at the circumference of the ring. "Get over there with those other cowboys and wait for my instructions," said Avery.

Charlie didn't know what this was all about. He stood on the edge of the circle and looked at some others who were doing the same. They looked like ordinary cowboys to Charlie. He rubbed his sweaty hands off on his shirt. Then he saw a man coming from the back of the saloon with a big, black, cast-iron frying pan filled with silver dollars. The man held the skillet with his two hands wrapped in dishcloths.

"Get down on one knee!" called Avery, "and when I give the word, reach for the cartwheels. Keep feet behind the ring!"

Charlie saw that the pan of cartwheels was going to be dumped into the circle. He dug his toes into the sawdust. He was sure he could grab ten. That was all he needed. He let his pent-up air go out just as the man spilled the dollars in the sawdust. The room was quiet. Charlie knew there was a wide band of men behind him waiting and watching to see who could grab the most coins.

"Make your bets!" Avery yelled. "Each contestant has a number."

Charlie felt someone pin a cardboard on his back and whisper in his ear, "Four."

Avery hollered, "One, two, three! On your mark! It's yours, cowboys! Go to it! Now!"

Charlie could feel his heart pounding and smell the sawdust in front of his nose. The sawdust smelled scorched, like it came fresh from a burn pile at a mill. He pushed for the pile of several coins lying together. His hand closed, then he let go with a startled cry. The others were hollering and yelling. One cowboy was holding his hands close against his chest and whimpering. Charlie looked at his own hands, one had the outline of a dollar in white and it stung as if he'd been hit with a dozen rattlers. The silver was hot, as though it had been in a forge.

"Go after it!" someone yelled. "Shovel up those there cartwheels!" "Grab in there, number three!" "I'm bettin' on ya', number one!"

Charlie tried again, using his left hand, thinking that the metal would be cooled some. He let out an awful yowl. The coins hadn't cooled much. He could never hold one coin long enough to claim it as his own. He tried scooting one, but that was not in the rules and Avery thumped him on the back with a fist. Avery's face was against his. "Be a sport!" Avery yelled. "The money's yours for the taking!" Charlie smelled whiskey on the mayor's breath and saw the bottle in his hand.

The tips of Charlie's fingers were sore. He spit on one hand and then the other. This helped some. Avery's face was against his again. Charlie saw the whiskey bottle. He heard laughter above him. Never in his life had he heard of this kind of entertainment. The excitement he'd first felt had gone sour. He felt bitter anger. He wanted to double his fists and punch in the face of Mayor Avery. Charlie got to his feet and lurched forward making certain his toes never went beyond the drawn ring in the sawdust. He grabbed for Avery's bottle, brought it over the ring with one hand and poured the contents on a dozen coins nearest him. They sizzled and steam formed down close around them, smelling like alcohol. A couple cowboys rolled into the ring over top of Charlie trying to scrabble their aching hands toward the cooler, wet coins. The wet sawdust was pressed against Charlie's shirt and face. His back felt as though it would break with the press of bodies. He could not turn his neck because someone had a leg clamped over it. He tried not to breath wood chips into his lungs. He prayed this game would end. Then he heard a shot from a pistol nearby.

"It's over, cowboys!" cried the Mayor. "We've had our fun! What's directly under you is yours if you can handle it! Get up!"

Charlie mustered all his strength, rolled over and with aching hands scooped eight coins into his pocket and grabbed for two more, but lost them to someone else. A man with a rake pulled the remaining coins to one side, shoveled them into a coal bucket.

"Here's your extra money! Don't ever say Mayor Avery ain't fair!" Avery gave each player two cartwheels from his own pocket. Charlie was declared the all-time winner. "Number four is top man! No one has ever had the guts to cool off his pile of cartwheels with my whiskey! This man is a thinker!" Then aside to Charlie he said, "Man, you look like a pup. They're taking cowboys young these days. You lose your boots playing cards?"

The men close by hooted and hollered and pointed to Charlie's bare feet.

Charlie didn't reply. He was sucking his fingers to take some of the heat out. He heard the comments and laughter before he found an opportunity to move out to the boardwalk for some air. He spread cool, damp, rain-laid dust on his burning hands. That eased the pain some. He drew in a lungful of clean, fresh air. He was going to have a hard time keeping his pants up where they belonged with ten silver dollars in his front pockets. The cook from a nearby chuck wagon had his head back chuckling to the sky as Charlie walked by. "Hey, you the kid what snookered Avery out of a handful of cartwheels?"

Charlie nodded.

"Hey, better let me give you some rope to tie up your pants. You got some weight in them there pockets." He cut two pieces of clothesline rope and attached them to the loops around Charlie's waist and made him a quick pair of suspenders.

"Much obliged," said Charlie, stepping down from the boardwalk and hurrying across the tracks, thinking how friendly some people were.

Back at the wagon he rolled under the blankets next to Will, who smelled like sour mash. Joe sleepily opened one eye and told Charlie to keep covered so he wouldn't catch cold in the damp, rainy air.

Charlie turned on his stomach and put his hands out in front into the cooling mud just outside the wagon wheel. Sleep came fast.

SIX

Nicodemus

The cookpot and dishes were washed and packed into the wagon. Charlie rummaged around in the pewter spoons trying to look busy until he found the can of venison grease. He rubbed some on the palms of his hands to keep the hardened, burnt flesh soft while new skin formed underneath.

Will milked the cow and put the fresh can of whole milk inside the wagon out of the sun. "We ought to cool it in the creek awhile," he mumbled. But no one was interested in waiting longer to be on the road.

Mary and Joe studied the black and white map printed in the back of one of Joe's pamphlets extolling the virtues of Kansas farmland. Joe said, "If we continue along this way, due west, we'll hit Fort Hays. That place is like Abilene, with cattlemen coming in daily with herds to be railroaded to the East."

"Well, then, do like I say," said Mary. "Follow the Solomon River northwest and when it splits stay with the southern fork."

Joe rubbed his eyes and folded the pamphlet. "We go as far as Salina today. So we cross the Solomon by bridge. Tomorrow we move northwest through farms and prairie and I pray there are wagon roads between the small settlements." He pulled his wife close to himself and looked at her contentedly, then gave her a quick kiss on the forehead. Joe did not believe in demonstrations of fondness in front of children. "This will be new land to me."

Charlie clenched his fists for courage and interrupted. "Pa, Ma, promise to hold your tempers until Will tells about the money he had for safekeeping?"

Joe made a growling sound in his throat.

Mary quickly spoke. "Don't say anything until you hear him out." She put a hand on Charlie's rope suspenders and nodded approval.

Joe closed his mouth.

Will looked at Charlie and scowled. He swallowed and said, "Did you feel the wind last night? It came just before the rain."

Joe's mouth was pulled taut into a fine line. He shook his head, indicating he didn't feel any wind last night. Mary kept a hand over her mouth.

"Well, it woke me and I began to worry about all that money Charlie and I were responsible for. I got up to make sure Charlie and I still had it. I felt in Charlie's pocket and sure enough there was his roll. I felt in mine and I had a roll the same size. I thought to be on the safe side I should count the money. And you wouldn't believe how strong the wind was. It blew all ten of my one-dollar bills all over the prairie before I could get them rolled up and into my pocket. Jeez, I knew you'd thrash me alive if I didn't figure out something before morning. So I figured I was in deep trouble." He looked at his feet and swallowed again.

Mary's mouth fell open. Charlie rolled his eyes skyward and he crossed his second finger over his index finger on his right hand.

"Well, when I was a little kid I had a trick for getting money out of the cracks between the boards in a walk. I put gum on the end of a stick. I scraped some wax off the top of one of Ma's jam jars, put it on the end of a stick, and here's what I brought back for you." Will looked out toward the wooden boardwalk across the tracks, then dumped ten cartwheels from his pockets at Joe's feet.

Charlie bit his lip and kept the backs of his hands toward his parents.

Joe was dumbfounded. "If you hadn't been so careless you'd still have those greenbacks. I never heard of anyone using wax to pick up money." Joe bent to look at the coins.

Charlie prayed his father would not pick up the coins. His prayer was answered when Ell scooped them into her apron and squealed with delight. "Will! Could I try? Could we look for more? Oh, Pa, please!"

Charlie put his aching hands inside his pockets. Joe shook his head. Mary shook her head and said, "Heavens, no! It's time to move on. There's no time to be greedy. Will retrieved his father's money and more. I for one am proud of him." Her face shone as she smiled at Will.

Charlie felt his aching fists relax. His breathing was easier. He heard Will sigh.

Mary rested her head on Joe's shoulder, feeling the roughness of his river-washed, unironed muslin shirt. "I feel like a true pioneer this day," she said. Charlie and Will climbed to the wagon's seat. Will held the reins, ready to move. Will called, "Pa, you want to ride Flame or hitch him to the wagon and give one of the workers a change of pace?"

Joe shook his head. "Will, you know better. You don't break up a good pair of workhorses. Suzie and Jed work best as a team. Split 'em and we'll have nothing but trouble. I'll ride Flame until noon anyways. Your ma and I talked of going to Salina, then heading off northwest. New country and it might be interesting. We'll see how other settlers do with cattle and crops."

"I'm ready," said Will.

"Giddap!" he called to the team.

The Irwins left Abilene. The wagon scattered half a dozen dogs that had come around to sniff and survey and Charlie was reminded of Old Squirt. Will began telling Charlie about the Kansas land and cattle raising.

Mary, sitting inside the wagon, watched her eldest talking serious, using his hands to make a point. She was struck with the notion that Will was no longer a child. He was nearly as large as Joe, although his coloring was sallow and pale. She stared at his face and was surprised to see a shifting in the eyes from her angle of view, not the same concern Joe possessed, not the deep interest in the big picture of a subject. Will would never be a thinker. She thought, he is destined to be a doer, and a great one for talking with no concern for consequences.

The wagon rattled on the rackety wooden bridge over the Solomon River, which was a shallow tannish stream flowing between banks fringed with willows ranging from small shrubs to moderately large trees. The willows were like green silhouettes, standing out against the sere prairie, making the curved pattern of the river visible for miles.

At noon Will stopped the wagon west of Salina against a wind-sheltered bluff. Ell found the cream-white rock rich in fossils of snails and tiny, prehistoric fishes.

Joe and Will were interested in staring at the rich wheat fields, still yellow-green and laid low by wind, then altogether moving upright, then pushed down, then straight up, then down.

Charlie felt a sense of awe and wonder, especially when they forded the Saline River. He thought, maybe no one has ever forded this water in this particular place since the world began.

Two days later near Sylvan Grove, Ell told Joe, who was driving, to stop the wagon. She pointed to a strange-looking bird she'd watched fly from cottonwood to cottonwood tree. It was big and black, about the size of a wild turkey. Charlie laughed because it looked like a carnival clown with wide stripes of red and white on its face. Its bill was yellow and its neck was longer than it seemed right for the size of its head. While Ell was pointing, the bird began tapping on a dead cottonwood trunk. Its head hammered the beak so that the sound was like an iron mallet on an anvil. When it flew off it appeared awkward and not sure of itself. The huge wings *whooshed* and beat the air. Charlie was amazed at the amount of sawdust and wood chips the bird left at the base of the rotten tree. His hands still hurt.

Joe said, "I imagine we'll see more unusual sights as we go West. Maybe that bird doesn't even have a name yet. There's probably some plants that haven't been named either."

They passed settlers' farms. Some were fenced with posts that were columns of split rock. They were the same off-white color as the limestone bluffs. Some posts had a brown streak running down through the stone, which was the color of rust. Barbed wire was fastened in tiny wedges in the stone. "If wood is scarce, man makes something else to take its place," said Joe. "I guess quarrying them rock posts ain't easy. Looks like a six-foot post'd weight near 400 pounds."

"How'd you suppose men come by them?" asked Charlie, holding his hands in his pockets.

"I suppose they use iron bits and wedges. Looks like the stone breaks clean. That first farmer to think of stone fence posts was mighty enterprising," said Joe.

"Look there! See the stone hill? Looks like someone has chopped it out pretty good," said Charlie.

"Well, I'll be!" exclaimed Will. "I'd'a gone right past and never seen that."

They forded the Saline River again and found some of the places they passed were more than wagon roads crossing; they were clusters of farms and a small general store next to the road. These infant towns had names like Lucas, Waldo, Paradise, Natoma, and Plainville. Often now Charlie pointed out skulls and bones of long-dead buffalo in the bluestem grass.

Joe explained to his children, "I should guess there were hundreds of men on these here plains after the Civil War. Some of the buffalo hunting was for sport, but there were others who took to trading for buffalo hides. Hides were better'n money. These men went in groups of a dozen or more with wagons and horses. They only camped where a big herd would pass. The ones that were good marksmen did the killing and the others took off the hides. Hides were made into bundles and cured back in camp, like we cured that deer hide. Once I heard that Bill Cody was hired by the Kansas and Pacific Railroad to hunt buffalo to feed the men who were laying them tracks."

Will let Charlie ride Flame and sat on the wagon seat beside his pa. "Remember that there buffalo skinner came to the smithery a couple'a years back?" asked Will. "He made out that skinning those beasts wasn't easy."

"I don't remember that," said Charlie, riding close to the wagon so he wouldn't miss anything. His hands were still pink on the palms, but they no longer were crusty and throbbing. He held the reins lightly.

"Punks like you were in school," said Will. "That buffalo skinner said sometimes he'd have to finish killing an animal with his knife 'cause it only had a broken leg from a stray bullet. Geez, that man's clothes were stiff with dried blood and guts!"

"Will, that's awful!" cried Ell, pretending she was offended by her brother's description.

"He ate only buffalo meat and hardtack and drank coffee laced with plenty of grounds. He slept in the same clothes and never shaved nor cut his hair. He looked like he'd been pushed out of jail 'cause he wasn't worth the keep," said Will.

"I gave him some of that leftover Sloan's Liniment on account of the bad bite, probably a blowfly, on his lip. Just getting close to him was a chore. He stunk something fierce," said Joe.

Mary put her hand to her nose.

"Don't worry, Ma," said Frank. "I'm not going to be a buffalo hunter."

They crossed the muddy Solomon River again, but it was

much more shallow here and there was no bridge. After the crossing Charlie lay on the floor of the wagon and stared at the swaying white canvas top. He listened to the wind and churning of the wagon wheels. His hands had healed. But when he was not doing anything, he kept in his fists a pad of raw wool he'd found in Ell's medicine box.

At night the family camped close to the rails. Charlie was lulled to sleep by the persistent song of the scalloping telegraph wires that followed the rails.

The wagon rolled along the slick mud ruts during thunderstorms and gentle rains and dried and dusty grooves when the days turned to scorchers in the treeless prairie.

Between Ell and her three brothers there existed a loose relationship. Will was for the most part condescending to Ell and his brothers. Frank looked up to the others, but never in a worshipful manner. Charlie had a fondness for all, which turned once in a while to unexpected sentiment. He was unalterably loyal to his sister and brothers and to his mother and father.

The day after the second crossing of the Solomon the Irwin wagon moved over low bluffs and dunes, keeping in sight of wagon tracks and telegraph lines. A mile ahead were a group of low buildings that looked like a small farming town. Joe drove the wagon through the town slowly so not to stir up dust. Mary waved to several women who sat in homemade-looking wooden chairs in front yards. A bandanna was tied around one woman's head. They all wore wide aprons that covered the entire front of their cotton dresses. Some were barefoot, others wore leather moccasins or sandals with the front cut open so toes were exposed.

Charlie watched from the back of the wagon. He pointed, "Ma, lookee there, darkies. See, Pa? What is this place?"

A youngster dressed in a pair of faded and patched overalls looked out from the doorway of a squat, stone hut. "This here is Nicodemus! Our church has a pumper organ!" The boy ran behind the wagon.

"I know what an organ is!" yelled Charlie, waving his hands.

The boy was about ten, Frank's age. "If you all want to picnic, the schoolyard is south a ways. Turn here; see the shade trees ahead?"

"Thanks!" called Charlie. "Ma! Should we stop? It's Nicodemus! The colorful town!"

"Why, this is an Exoduster place!" said Joe. He pulled the

wagon beside the creek close to the one-room, gray-white limestone schoolhouse. He let the horses and cow nibble the sweet grass laced with dandelions and drink creek water.

"That's the second time I've heard that word. What is an Exoduster?" asked Mary.

Joe said, "As I recall, a group of ex-slaves came into western Kansas. They built three towns. Hill City was one. Nicodemus the other. I can't recall the third—something biblical. These people from the South were so excited about a place of their own that they spent life savings on railroad fares and land patent fees. In the end they had nothing left to spend on home-building materials. They made dugouts or burrows, some used blocks of limestone from their fields. They burn sunflower stalks for heat. They're mainly farmers, but I heard there was some preachers and lawyers."

"Must be pretty smart to build three towns," said Charlie. "This is where the Splitlogs were to visit."

"I'd like to see those Injuns for myself," said Will.

Ell's hands were sweaty and she felt a tingling in the pit of her stomach. "Let's have our noon meal here," she said. "Maybe the Injuns are waiting for us. Something exciting might happen. I can feel it."

"Are there any Injuns in town?" Charlie asked the boy.

"Not that I know about this day," he said. "But I know Injuns, yes, sir."

Ell spread the quilt. In a few moments Mary found dry twigs and had water boiling over a stone fire pit. She put dried venison and sliced potatoes in the boiling water.

The boy stood at the back of the wagon sniffing the delicious cooking smell. "Hey!" he called softly, but clearly. "I could race you two." He looked at Frank and Charlie. "I'm Zach."

Charlie introduced himself and Frank, then drew a line in the dust with his bare toe. "This is the start. We'll go around the schoolhouse three times. The loser eats last."

Zach's face brightened; he wanted to ask if the winner ate first, but he'd already surprised himself with a flash of boldness. After the second time around Zach slowed and panted, "My side aches."

"Bend over and bite your knees," Ell suggested.

Zach bent double and the pain subsided. The three boys dropped to the warm grass. Mary and Ell brought them plates of meat and potatoes and each a spoon. Zach smiled and bowed his head quietly.

When no one spoke, he said, "We all give our thanks to You, Lord, for this here 'licious slumgullion." Then his head popped up and he said, "My ma says it's growin' pains." He pointed to his side.

"She's probably right," said Ell. "You go to school here?"

"Yes, ma'am, and to picnics." He turned to Charlie and Frank. "Man, you should see the watermelons and barbecues. Your ma and pa square dance?"

"Of course," said Frank.

"We all do if there's some fiddle music," added Charlie. "You, too?"

Zach laughed. "Fiddle music and square dancing makes us happy as a horse in spring pasture." He liked these white folks. "If you ever go up to Tindall Hill, you can get enough gooseberries for a pie."

"I like pie," said Frank.

"I can pick berries. We had wild blackberries back in Missouri," said Charlie. "You got a horse?"

"You see many horses on these streets, mister?" asked Zach.

"None, 'cept ours," said Charlie.

"Well, everyone has a horse, but it's out in the fields." Then he hung his head and rolled his eyes up to see if anyone was still looking for him. " 'Cept ours. It's standing in the shed waiting for my pa."

"Where's he?" asked Frank.

"Want to come to my place?" asked Zach, standing up. "You can see him and my ma."

"Huh-uh," said Frank. "I'll come if Charlie does."

"Not much else to do," said Charlie. Will and Joe were discussing where they were going to spend the night, and their mother was on the quilt, resting with closed eyes.

Charlie told Ell where they'd decided to go. She looked around and thought of reading for a while, then on impulse said, "Mind if I come, too?"

"Oh, no," said Zach. "Ma likes company. I'm Zach Fletcher."

"I'm Ell Irwin. I guess you know my little brothers."

"We're friends," Zach said, grinning broadly, so his teeth seemed like bright stars against a black night sky.

Inside the stone hut was one room containing a couple of wooden chairs, a table and stove, and a large iron bed. Charlie wrinkled his nose against the strong musty odor. Mrs. Fletcher was pressing prairie flowers in a wooden frame lined with blotting paper.

"I said to Zach this morning that this day, with white lamb clouds against the bright blue, was for adventure," she said. "You are friends of Zach's and welcome in our home." She saw Ell staring at the bed. "Yes, daughter, we all sleep in that there bed. That's Mr. Fletcher. Ever since he's worked on the town's church, he's been too tired to get out of the bed."

"How long does he need to get rested?" asked Charlie.

"Child, only the Lord knows. Mr. Fletcher had so much energy and enthusiasm, but since the town isn't growing and doesn't need a carpenter, or stone mason, Mr. Fletcher just laid down for a rest." Tears were in her eyes. "The Reverend Roundtree, he preaches at our church, has been here persuading Mr. Fletcher to get up out of that bed. But he hasn't budged."

"Do you feed him proper?" asked Charlie.

The man was curled in the middle of the bed. He was a bag of bones on the snow-white, flannel sheets. His brown eyes sunk deep into his head and his mouth looked shriveled like a plum hung on the tree too long in scorching sun.

It's become small from nothing to eat, thought Charlie.

Mrs. Fletcher looked at Charlie with large, sad eyes. She patted her glossy, kinky black hair and sighed. "Son, there has not been anything in the minds of the good people of this town that has not been tried. The Reverend comes once a week and reads my man passages from the Good Book. These same words my man once read by hisself."

"Maybe he read too much. Sometimes when I read, my head aches," said Frank with a sigh. Ell hit Frank in the side with her elbow to keep him quiet.

"Don't hit me!" cried Frank. "I'll tell Ma you hurt me."

Ell tiptoed closer to the bed.

Frank was breathing hard and making loud whimpering sounds.

Charlie tried to shush Frank.

"I'll tell on Ell if I want," sniffled Frank. "And I'll tell about you and Will going across them tracks at Abilene."

Charlie's mouth flew open.

"I saw you leaving but I couldn't stay awake to see you come back."

Charlie spoke between his teeth, barely moving his lips. "Don't be a tattletale. Mind your own business and someday you'll grow up in one piece."

Mrs. Fletcher got up and stood between the boys. "Do you

know how lucky you are to have a brother, each of you? The Lord sent you here and you're goin' make the most of it."

Ell looked away from Mr. Fletcher, who was staring at the whitewashed stone wall. "You sound just like our ma."

"God bless her, then," said Mrs. Fletcher. "She'll raise you right."

"The Reverend?" asked Zach. "Do you know him?"

"No," said Ell.

"He has a brand on one side of his face. When you look at him, it's the first thing you see. He got it because his master was mad. The master's son taught the Reverend to read and write. The master didn't want no *nigger* of his to know what he knew."

"Did he run away?" asked Charlie.

"Must have to get here," said Zach. "He teaches us at the school. Even the granmommies and granpoppies go to learn to read 'n' write."

"I taught first graders," said Ell. "During spelling bees I helped older folks with their writing."

Both Zach and Mrs. Fletcher looked up at Ell with respect.

"Land sakes, you're but a child yourself. Some of our folks would light up to see someone as pretty as yourself teaching 'em. Landsakes alive!"

Ell smiled, enjoyed the flattery, then went back to look at Mr. Fletcher curled in a tight fetal ball.

Mrs. Fletcher showed Charlie and Frank the kinds of flowers she put in the flower press. "I make pictures with flowers. Put them between waxed paper and iron over with a warm flatiron." She pointed to some of her pictures on the wall behind the kitchen table. There were wild daisy, goldenrod, columbine, prairie phlox, clover, primrose, morning glory, and verbena.

"He's not sick, just tired. His nerves are worn out," Mrs. Fletcher said again, nodding to Ell, who had her hand on Mr. Fletcher's forehead.

Ell came back beside Mrs. Fletcher. "Ma'am, my grandma knew about healing with herbs and all kinds of magic. She taught me some."

"She's a teacher?" asked Zach.

"Yes, in a way. She was known as the lady doctor."

"Daughter, if it's witchcraft and conjur medicine, it's been tried, besides both Baptist and Methodist praying and laying on o' hands."

"But," insisted Ell, "a growed man staying in bed when it's

daylight, that's not right. Something's wrong."

Zach started punching Frank in a friendly manner. "My pa used to show me how boxers punch."

Frank crossed his arms across his chest for protection and said, "He ain't doing that now."

Mr. Fletcher had not made a move since the three Irwin children came into the one room hut.

"Naw, you heard Ma. His brain stopped working when his nerves broke down, so all the rest of him quit." Zach's eyes fell to the floor and his bottom lip quivered. "He's a good pa. He jus' worked too hard on our church."

One look at Zach caused Charlie to feel sad. "Maybe I could sing for him," Charlie said. "My singing makes my pa laugh."

Charlie hesitated a second or two and when no one said "don't," he sang several songs and danced a little jig.

Mrs. Fletcher smiled, but Mr. Fletcher didn't move, not even to swat the fly crawling on his scrawny neck.

"I ate with these here folks," said Zach. "They had the best slumgullion." He began to describe what he had to eat and his ma's eyes grew round.

"You asked my boy to sit with you and eat?" She patted Ell's hand. "I'll show you how to make a flower press for yourself."

"I'd like—I'd want to try," said Ell, thinking hard what Grandma Malinda would do or say in this same situation. Then she decided she'd move straight forward. "Let's try to get Mr. Fletcher up on his feet. He has no fever and his heartbeat is strong. He needs nourishment and something to jolt his mind into action."

"Oh, daughter, if we only could. I'd do anything. You talk like a healing woman, but you look so young. Like you'd faint at the sight of blood and the smell of sickness."

"I don't, honest." Ell did not say that she'd gone on many house calls with Grandma Malinda and held torn flesh so that the stitches would hold the sides together without a pucker and leave little scarring. She did not say that she had seen birthing and broken bones pierce through the flesh and heard the screams of pain. She didn't say that she had made conjur tea and poultices and salves and had wrapped bandages tightly on sprained ankles. "I could make sassafras tea, but it needs strength, so if you have dried hollyhock roots and horseradish roots to add, I can say some words, and if the boys go outside to gather sticks and trash for the fire, you and me could concentrate."

Mrs. Fletcher looked skeptical, but she said, "Shoo, now boys, you heard this here daughter. We're goin' work something out. Shoo!"

The front door screen slammed three times as the boys went out one by one.

"I'll get my dried roots out here and you can pick what you want. I'll try anything, like I said, even from the medicine of sodbusters." Mrs. Fletcher rolled her eyes toward the ceiling and smiled to herself. "Your folks are sodbusters, ain't they?" she asked apologetically.

"Huh-uh," said Ell, now more interested in stirring the mixture in the black iron kettle on the top of the wood stove.

Mrs. Fletcher piled in kindling, getting a good blaze.

Ell mumbled words she'd learned from Grandma Malinda. She tried hard to think of each conjur line, wanting it just right.

"Oh, Lord, stay with us," murmured Mrs. Fletcher, "this daughter is so young in body, but old in mind. She knows life is not easy. Put Your hand on her arm. Guide her. Hear? You guide her. Keep Your Brother Satan out. This here is no Black Magic. Lord stay with us."

Ell heard and the corner of her mouth creased into a pleased smile. She sang her words softly, bending close to the supine form of Mr. Fletcher, looking for any movement. "Oh, body find the mind! Bring out the thoughts, share your voice! Come together! Closer! Closer!"

The boys came back inside the house with some flat limestone plates and smooth sticks. "Ma, you could use these thin rocks for a flower press, maybe frame them with these sticks if they was split just right," said Zach excitedly.

"Shhh!" said Mrs. Fletcher, then in a whisper she told the three boys to sit on the floor against the wall opposite the bed and be still as a hole in the ground. Charlie recognized the smell of sassafras and thyme and the head-clearing horseradish. Still whispering, Mrs. Fletcher said, "One whiff of that delicious aroma and Mr. Fletcher'll sit up by hisself. Watch, watch, watch."

Ell decanted clear hot brown liquid into a tin cup and brought it close so that Mr. Fletcher could smell. His eyes rolled under the opaque lids. Ell held her breath. His head moved. It moved slowly. Ell thought her eyes were seeing things not true. She looked at Mrs. Fletcher, who had stopped chanting with her arms held in midair over her head. Mr. Fletcher's head moved back and forth. Ell dipped her finger in the deep brown tea and dabbed it on his thin purple lips. A noise barely audible came from Mr. Fletcher's gaunt chest. Ell dabbed more strong tea on his lips so that some ran down the corner of his mouth and made a brown stain under his ear.

"Drink," Ell urged. "Try, please. Drink. You will feel refreshed as a bear coming out of hibernation."

"No, no," Mr. Fletcher's voice called from the center of his chest cavity.

"It could make you feel good."

"No, no."

Mrs. Fletcher let her aching arms down to her sides, tears streamed down her face. "Sassafras tea was once your favorite. Come back to us. Get out of the bed. We gather around you. Life is just so long. Don't throw it out. Find yourself and come back."

"No, no." Mr. Fletcher's voice sounded like a clock with a broken spring.

Mrs. Fletcher pulled back the quilt, then the soft flannel sheet, and held her man's head up. Something dropped with the quilt, which made Charlie look up. It sounded like a piece of stovewood. Charlie couldn't understand stovewood in the bed with an ailing man. He looked beside Mr. Fletcher on the white flannel. His eyes widened. He blinked, looked again. For certain, there on the bed, close beside Mr. Fletcher, was the Henry rifle he'd lent to Matt Splitlog. Charlie's Henry rifle!

Ell was on the other side holding the tin cup to Mr. Fletcher's lips. He seemed to be drinking, but his eyes were closed, not seeing what was happening in the hut.

"No one can expect miracles," said Mrs. Fletcher, wiping the tears with the back of her hand. Her black face had a sheen. The temperature in the stone hut was now ten degrees higher than outside. The fire in the stove flickered strongly.

Frank and Zach were sitting limply against the wall rolling an aggie marble back and forth to each other.

Charlie felt a shiver move up his spine. He was surprised that in this heat his hands seemed cold and stiff. He willed them to move. He forced his feet to walk close to the bed and reach ever so slowly for the rifle. It was his rifle!

All the while Mrs. Fletcher was singing revival songs and Ell was singsonging magic words, the healing medicine words she'd learned from Grandma Malinda. Ell's eyes were closed. Her hands were on Mr. Fletcher's arms, rubbing them back to life.

The blue-black barrel was in Charlie's hands; he felt the plate on the butt and his heart beat in his throat.

"This is mine," he said clearly.

Mr. Fletcher moved out of Ell's grasp and out of bed so fast that Charlie bumped and stumbled toward the door, then ran against the screen door. Outside Charlie tripped on the pile of sunflower stems the boys had gathered for the stove. The safety was pushed and Charlie blundered into the side of the stone hut. The gun went off.

Mr. Fletcher yelled louder than any Indian *kiyi*ing on the warpath. "You're shot dead!"

Charlie wondered how a man could sleep with a loaded gun in his bed! He grabbed the gun tighter and ran to the back of the hut. Mr. Fletcher was right behind him wobbling and stumbling.

Mrs. Fletcher was in the doorway. "Glory hallelujah! Glory hallelujah!" she hollered. "My man's on his feet! Mr. Fletcher's running! Praise the Lord!"

Frank and Zach squeezed out around Mrs. Fletcher and went out the screen door. They chased after Charlie, who was running headlong toward the back shed. Inside was an old workhorse. Charlie stood panting against the wall, trying to pull the door shut behind him. He heard the footsteps coming toward the shed. He held the gun so the barrel pointed toward the ceiling and pulled the trigger. The shot was loud and the kick knocked Charlie flat on the floor. The horse whinnied and shied away to the other side. Charlie was afraid the horse would be so frightened it would kick if he got near. Charlie hoped the shot would make Mr. Fletcher stop running after him.

It made someone yell and cry and holler for him to stop. He recognized Frank's voice yelling loudest. Charlie hid behind a large gray stone grinder. His heart pounded in his throat and he could not calm it, nor push it down in his chest where it belonged.

Mr. Fletcher's thin, charcoal face looked in the doorway. The door's hinges creaked in the breeze. His eyes were open because Charlie could see the clear whites around the deep brown centers. However, Mr. Fletcher evidently couldn't see so well. He left, leaving the door swinging and groaning.

Charlie could hear feet running hither, thither, and yon and he heard the calls for him. Then he heard great wrenching sobs. The running and calling stopped. Charlie put his rifle to his shoulder after making sure the safety was on and walked out of the shed.

Mrs. Fletcher was wiping tears from her face. Her shoulders jerked with her sobbing. Mr. Fletcher was beating some bushes saying, "He's shot dead. Shot dead. Dead."

Zach was standing close to his ma. Ell stood with her hand on Frank's shoulder scowling fiercely as Charlie came out of the shed.

Ell yelled, "Why'd you do that?" She shook her finger at Charlie. "Now look what you've done! You've spoiled the conjur words and the herb tea is spilled! And you stole his gun! I can't believe all the trouble you've caused, Charlie!"

Mr. Fletcher turned and said as clear as spots on a yearling deer, "Shame on you, son, causing so much commotion."

Charlie felt the shiver along his back as the breeze evaporated the wetness from his shirt. "But—but this is the Henry rifle Old Charles gave to me. It's mine! Can't you all see that!" Now Charlie was doing some shouting himself.

"It *is* his!" yelled Frank, running to examine the stock. "Geez! How'd it get here?"

Mrs. Fletcher seemed dazed, looking from her man to Charlie.

"Lord a'mighty!" Mr. Fletcher said, pointing a stick-thin finger. "You're only a puny paleface. You give that there rifle back to me straightaway. I promised by my life to keep it for *a man*."

"It's mine!" insisted Charlie, feeling his hands ball up.

"A man—you are not a man! You danged whites are all alike," said Mr. Fletcher, shaking his bony shoulders. "You see someone has something, you say it's yourn. This was given to me while I lay worn out inside that house, on the bed. I promised I'd keep it for the rightful owner, who is *a man*."

"I'm the owner." Charlie started to back away, thinking that a crazy, sick man, a woman, and a boy couldn't do much to him, and besides, he had the rifle. "Let's go to the wagon," he said, and motioned to Ell and Frank.

"Mr. Splitlog say I should keep the rifle!" called Mr. Fletcher in a thin watery-sounding voice. His hands shook like aspen leaves in the breeze. "He say the owner is *a big man*. This man, he will come here, and then I will let him have the Henry rifle. If you take something belonging to this big man, all the Wyandots in Kansas will be down on you. You hear of scalping? This will be not hair removal, but head removal!" The speech was long and tiring. Mr. Fletcher leaned against Mrs. Fletcher, who was still bewildered.

Charlie's mouth gaped open. Frank and Ell's mouth gaped open. Charlie grunted, then the words formed in his head and he licked his lips so that he could speak. "Matt Splitlog? The three Indian brothers? They came to our camp."

"You know Matt, John, and Mark?" Zach asked.

"Sure. Ma gave them biscuits and mush."

"Wait here!" Zach ran into the stone hut. When he came out he was waving a white cloth, like a surrender banner.

Ell's hands flew to her mouth. She took her hands away and cried out, "That's Ma's dishtowel, the one she wrapped around the biscuits! See—it has blue forget-me-nots embroidered in the corners."

Zach smiled. "She's right. It has blue flowers sewn in the corners. My ma thought it was so pretty she used it for a tablecloth."

Mrs. Fletcher stood with her hands to her mouth.

Mr. Fletcher stood on weak, bony legs, stock still, staring at the three Irwin children.

By this time several neighbors were standing around whispering among themselves.

Mr. Fletcher stretched out a long skeletal leg from under his white nightshirt. Charlie moved back a step. Mr. Fletcher moved one step forward and held out his trembling polelike arm. Charlie backed off, hugging the rifle. "This rifle is mine and I aim to keep it."

"No—I ain't goin' take that gol-durned gun. I believe it's yourn. I want to shake your hand and say thank you. I haven't felt so good in a long time."

"A miracle!" called Mrs. Fletcher. "Praise the Lord! We have witnessed the unbelievable. Thank You, Lord. Many thanks!"

"Hosanna!" shouted one of the neighbors. "Amen!" cried another. Soon the neighbors were down on their knees with their arms in the air shouting praises to the Lord.

Charlie moved closer to Mr. Fletcher. Ell put up her arm so he wouldn't move too close. "What made you see the truth?" asked Charlie, puzzled by all this emotional ruckus.

Mrs. Fletcher pulled out a rickety wooden box from a patch of wild currant brambles and pulled Mr. Fletcher over to sit there. He sighed and slumped over as if sitting were a chore. He explained that the Exodusters gave the three Splitlogs flour, ham, and dried grapes for the town's well they'd helped dig a while ago. The Splitlogs dug rock for posts around gardens to keep the deer out of the grain and vegetables. Matt left a rifle with Mr. Fletcher to shoot the fox that was raiding chicken coops. Mr. Fletcher shot the thieving fox and went back to bed to wait for the owner of the gun to come and claim it.

"What if we'd not come home with Zach?" asked Ell.

"But, daughter, you did, and you brought life back to Mr. Fletcher," said Mrs. Fletcher, full of faith.

"Who's that *big man?*" asked Frank.

Mr. Fletcher folded his hands in his lap and closed his eyes, as though resting so that he could say what he had on his mind. Everyone hushed to hear. "A child will be a big man, my son. Your brother fed the Splitlogs by loaning them his rifle. That sounds *big* to me."

"Amen," said the neighbors in unison.

"Mr. Fletcher, don't forget the power of this sister," reminded Mrs. Fletcher. "She has a power most has forgot to use. She has a soft heart when it comes to the ailing. She'll help many a destitute folk."

"Glory to the Lord!" cried the neighbors.

Ell smiled and wiped tears from her eyes. She could not speak. She put her arms around Mrs. Fletcher.

Charlie shook hands with Mr. Fletcher and was surprised at the strength in the grip. There were tears in his eyes.

Mrs. Fletcher invited the neighbors in for tea. They stood or sat where they could, some on the empty bed. They sang praise hymns and sipped the hot herb tea. "What is this?" the neighbors asked.

"Mostly sassyfras," Mrs. Fletcher whispered.

Mr. Fletcher drank as though he'd had a pile of rock salt for breakfast. His eyes were wide in his cavernous face. He did a couple skips and a hop to show how well he was.

Everyone smiled and clapped for his dance. Charlie thought his arms and legs looked like burnt willow sticks poking from the white nightshirt.

Ell gave Mrs. Fletcher another hug and whispered some conjur words of safekeeping in her ear. "We are going now," said Ell. "Keep the—tablecloth."

Charlie invited Mr. Fletcher to come to the Sappa country to go fishing if he ever got the urge.

"Maybe I'll bring the Splitlogs," said Mr. Fletcher with a grin. "Those boys get restless and have to get away from their own place once in a while. It's the Injun blood in them."

Frank fingered an aggie in his pocket, debating whether to leave it with Zach. Charlie noticed the debate Frank was having with himself.

"Give it to your friend," said Charlie. "It won't hurt."

Frank grinned and rolled the marble toward Zach. Zach said in a playful way, "Put up your dukes," and feigned a couple friendly little jabs toward Frank's jaw.

Mrs. Fletcher ran after them. "Here, take this." She gave Ell her flower press, explaining that her man could make another first thing tomorrow morning. "Praise the Lord for today's adventure," she said.

"Sassafras 'n' hollyhocks, thyme 'n' horseradish makes a powerful cure," said Ell with a smile. She ran ahead. She could hardly wait to tell her mother and father about the herb tea and Mr. Fletcher, all arms and legs, chasing after Charlie, who found his Henry rifle.

Mary had the stewpot, plates, and spoons packed inside the grub box and the quilt folded and put on the wagon seat. The three children talked at the same time, spilling over with the story of Charlie retrieving the Henry rifle.

"It's hard to believe," said Will. "How do we know Charlie didn't make all this up?"

"He couldn't," said his father. "The story is too fantastic."

"I kind of hate to leave this colorful place. The schoolyard has been restful for me," said Mary.

"That's the trouble with some folks. They is never satisfied. And just look at all the foofaroo tucked inside that there wagon. Oooo-weee! Mercy, it will take a huge hut to hold all them goods!" The words came from Mrs. Fletcher, dressed in a clean white apron and long, full gingham skirt and blouse made from a flour sack. She was all smiles. "I had to come to thank the folks that raised those chilluns. Why, they put Mr. Fletcher on his feet again. I thank the Lord that the sun rose on this day and put the notion in your head to come to Nicodemus!" She embraced Ell.

Mary climbed off the wagon seat and shook Mrs. Fletcher's hand. "I'm Mary Irwin. That's my husband, Joe, and our oldest, Will. There was a lot of goings-on at your place? I hope my children didn't upset you. If they did I'm sorry."

"Don't say sorry. I praise the Lord for this upset! You might say it was them Splitlogs that caused this hallelujah day. Them boys are good at judging the mind-set of folks." She patted the tiny black dog held tightly in the crook of one arm.

Joe came forward and held out his hand. "I am glad to meet you, ma'am, and hope your husband recovers. Say—I'd like to buy some vegetables if you have some for sale."

"Oh, the Reverend Roundtree will give you plenty of greens. Too bad his pole beans ain't ready." She was looking from Joe to

Charlie. Charlie was edging up to pet the dog.

Joe said, "Point me in the right direction to this Reverend's place and I'd be mighty obliged."

"Straight up the dirt road. He has all his produce growing in the front yard. Say, you folks ain't got a dog tied up in there?" She pointed toward the wagon.

"No," said Joe. "We ain't had a dog lately. But we used to have one. Stayed outdoors mostly. The kids liked it."

"Somehow I knew," she said. "Sodbusters need a good dog. This one's mother's smart, runs from every cat in town. The male that stood up to her is the one chases racoons out of the town's garbage. Zach picked this here puppy, so it ain't the litter's runt either." She held the pup around the middle with her right hand and shoved it into Charlie's hands. It was black as a lump of coal, and not much larger than a good baking potato. "Hang on, son, it's lively."

Charlie held the pup close to his chest and put his hand on the soft, warm fur. He could feel the fast thumping of the pup's heart against the slower thumping of his own heart. It was a wonderful feeling. "Thank you!" said Charlie, and a tingling went up and down his back.

Joe cleared his throat. "A pup might not ride too well."

"If you feed it and let it get your smell, it'll get used to you soon enough," said Mrs. Fletcher, watching Charlie put his face down against the pup's dark fur. "Chilluns needs a dog. And you can train it to keep deer outen your cornfield, or hunt according to your preference. You can see it's a good mix, some Irish setter, some sheepdog, some racin' greyhound."

"Maybe you ought not give this dog away. I don't have a thing to give you in trade," said Joe, sadly rubbing his hands together.

"It's a present. Mister, I don't trade for no present."

"What if one of the children let it go? You can see it'd come running right back here," said Mary, but half wishing Joe would accept the present.

"That's no problem." Mrs. Fletcher took out a thick braided-cloth leash from her wide apron pocket and tied it around the pup's neck.

Charlie looked up and saw that Ell wanted to hold the little furry pup and that Will wouldn't be opposed to holding the end of that multicolored leash. Frank looked as if he thought the pup belonged to the family already.

Joe chuckled. "Mrs. Fletcher, to oppose you is like blowing against the wind."

Mary let out her breath and petted the tiny pup.

"Yes, so take it and keep your breath," said Mrs. Fletcher. Her dark eyes shone, then dimmed, and her body stiffened. "I want to ask you something. I need advice."

"Well, now," said Joe. "I don't know if—"

"Hear me out first," she said. "It was a heart-tearing sight to watch my man sicken and grow thin. But something happened before that. Maybe it was worse. This whole town died while we watched. Nicodemus was full of life and hope and good folk. Then the southwest winds came and seared the crops and gardens. Then the town turned sick and some of the folk moved out. The church was hardly filled come worship time." Mrs. Fletcher took a deep breath. "You think Mr. Fletcher's sickness was loneliness for a town filled with happy folks? Seven years ago we had five hundred souls and now there are less than two hundred. Mr. Fletcher helped to build this town for all those bright folks." She hesitated and looked from Mary to Joe, hoping that they understood what she was trying to ask. "Today is different. Today Mr. Fletcher got his head shook and an idea broke loose. Listen, he wants to welcome all folks that come through this here town. He wants to give them a restful place to stop, to eat, and to choose a souvenir to take away. He wants the settlers going West to come through here." She looked hopefully from Joe to Mary, who did not fully understand. "Folks might like my pressed prairie flowers, or the Reverend's collard greens, or something Mr. Fletcher carves from the post rock. What do you think? It was your chilluns that started this idea." She paused and saw for sure that Mary and Joe now understood.

Mary nodded and smiled. Joe said he thought it was a dandy idea. "Oh, ladies like flowers—all kinds. The settlers will need vegetables, they'd probably like blackberries and wild currants if you have them ready-picked. The word'll get around and you'll have wagons clattering here so thick you'll be bellyaching about the dust."

Mary said, "Women might look for quilts and dresses for their newborn babies." Mrs. Fletcher's eyes shone and she hugged Mary.

"Thank you, folks. That's my answer. I have to leave now—vespers." Everything was still for a moment like a silent prayer.

Mary suddenly had an idea of her own. "Could we—uh—we'd like to worship with you. If you think the puppy would stay quiet tied here in the wagon and if you wouldn't mind having us."

Mrs. Fletcher's face lighted up in the afternoon sunshine. She took Mary's arm and started walking toward town. Charlie tied the leash and Ell brought a pan of water for the pup, then all the other Irwins followed after the two women. They stopped in front of the exiguous Methodist church, built of Kansas limestone. Mrs. Fletcher pointed to the bell in the yard. Zach stood beside it with a rope, ready to pull the clapper. "It came from a steam locomotive," she said with no other explanation, because the bell began to clang loudly.

Inside they were seated on backless, wooden benches. The preacher noticed the newcomers and nodded. Charlie noticed the preacher's right cheek had a deep red scar in the form of an *X*. Charlie noticed the ugly scar before he saw that the man wore a white muslin shirt with shirring at its yoke and buckskin trousers and leather sandals. Charlie knew it was the Reverend Roundtree that Zach had talked about.

The inside walls of the church were whitewashed sod and post rock and shook with the hymns "lined" by Reverend Roundtree. The singing of all those rich voices reminded Charlie of honey pouring from delicate china pitchers into a fine milk-glass bowl.

During the sermon, impassioned amens rose again and again. The words rolled from Reverend Roundtree's mouth like the river pouring out of the hills in the spring, Charlie thought.

The sunflowers, goldenrod, and spiky yellow sage near the altar looked so bright that it could have been Easter Sunday.

There were candles everywhere. There was a large candle above the pulpit. There were no stained-glass windows, but there was a melodeon behind the pulpit. The organist, in a black coat and leather breeches, was skilled in pumping out soul-stirring tones by pushing air through the metal reed by the bellows, operated by his nimble bare feet.

Afterward the Irwin family shook hands with about everyone in town. Frank turned his hands over to see if any of the black had come off after shaking so many black hands. Zach teased him.

"Bless you," the Reverend told them.

"Much obliged," said Joe, who still wanted to purchase some fresh vegetables.

The Reverend hung on to Joe's hand as if reading his mind. "Mrs. Fletcher told me about your need for greens. Follow Zach to the end of the street. He'll get you a gunnysack full of collards, spinach, and lettuce." He saw Joe reach into his pocket as if to pull out a couple of bills to pay for the greens. "No, my friends, this is the Sabbath, we don't take money on the Sabbath. We give in joy and the joy comes back to us. Believe, my friend. You are always welcome in Nicodemus. Lord, go with this man and his family."

That warm summer evening the Irwins rolled across the prairie in the moonlight. They sang all the familiar gospel hymns together. After a couple of hours they stopped on a gravel bank of the Solomon River. Charlie said, "Is it some kind of miracle that the people of Nicodemus sing the same songs we sing? Maybe they thought we learned their songs real fast."

"No—I think they knew we worshiped the same," said Mary.

"Lookee at little Nicodemus, sound asleep on my lap," said Charlie, pointing to the curled-up black pup.

SEVEN

Homesteaders Union Association

For the next couple of days the Irwins made good time riding on the stage road. They forded Prairie Dog Creek and drove on through Colby until they came to the end of the railroad track. Then all there was for the eye to see was undulating plain covered with rich buffalo grass. A creek flowed through the middle of the bottom land and there were hardwoods growing beside the willows. Joe looked around and suddenly announced with a whoop, "This is it!"

Sparrows flittered and chickadees chirped. Squirrels ran across the trees.

Joe looked hard at this land where the weather could bring heavy winds, sleet or rain, or dust and drought. This land was the lure which meant poverty or prosperity, apathy or adventure, and repression or the freedom to develop one's own future. Joe found the three flat stones buried at the northwest corner of his section. "We're home!" he cried.

Charlie could see there were no forests to clear, no swampy places to drain, and the grassy vegetation would make easy plowing. The rocks and boulders could be piled at the edge of a field for a fence. There was a constant movement of air, the humidity was low.

First thing Mary looked for was the old soddy she remembered. It was dark all year long, with dirt from the walls and roof sifting, always sifting into everything. When there was rain there was mud on the floor. The beetles, roaches, spiders, and mites came out of the dirt. It was an ongoing battle to prove who were the inhabitants of the soddy. Mary could not find a sign of the old place. It seemed to have melted back into the land.

"That is no concern," consoled Joe. "We'll have a home better than the first. It will be cool in summer and snug in winter."

"A dirt house?" asked Ell, sulking in a corner of the wagon like a cat that's had its tail stepped on.

The pup jumped out and sniffed all around, then waited for Charlie to climb out of the wagon.

The next few days Joe went over what he remembered was his quarter section. He couldn't understand why the old soddy was missing or destroyed. "Ought to be something left to show where she stood," he said to himself.

"Pa, lookee here," said Charlie. "These stones might have been piled at the corner of the parcel—but they seem kicked loose and scattered. Could snow or water do that?"

"I don't think so," said Joe, examining the assortment of limestone. Some of the rock contained fossils of small worms, crinoids, and mollusks, showing that water had covered this land thousands of years ago. Some of the rock was a mass of tiny concretions, built up layer by layer around some small nucleus, looking like it was made of tiny round granules. Each granule grew as it was rolled by waves or currents. There was some marl, or stones rich in clay, and some containing silica in the form of chert. "These stones were collected by man, because there are several varieties here. They could be the stones I used on the old soddy. I can mark off our section from the corner with the three stones buried. We'll plant vinegar bottles upside down over stakes with the corner plot measurements inside each one. There'll be no question of property lines, nor ownership."

While Joe and Will worked on sighting the property corners and putting in marking stakes, Frank and Charlie scrounged the prairie for buffalo chips, sunflower stalks, and dried sticks from the willows and oaks along the creek bank. This was fuel for their mother's cooking fire.

The season was late for planting much of anything. Joe decided a barn should be built first. The family lived in the wagon. Some days Charlie went with his father and Will to use the breaking plow, which threw up the sod in parallel strips three to five inches thick.

One afternoon toward the end of July, Charlie was by the creek with his father building a slicker, a sled with pole runners. Joe wanted to use it to haul the fifty-pound chunks of sod up to the place he'd selected for a barn. A slicker could be pulled across the slippery prairie grasses. Nick was with Charlie for company. The pup grumbled low in its throat and became tense and its hair bristled. Charlie looked around to see if another animal were close by and he wished he'd brought his rope. He waved the pup back and moved to a clump of grass where his rifle lay. He stood still to listen. Someone called, "Hullo there, neighbor!"

Charlie called back and Nick began barking and jumping like a crazy animal. Charlie said, "Nick, hush! Down, boy!"

The pup stopped barking but stood, sniffing the air in front of its nose.

Charlie called to his father, who was chopping a slim oak for a pole, and a man came over the small rise. The stranger wiped his face with a strip of faded blue cloth. He was short, with a barrel chest, thick arms, and a bushy white mustache and beard. He carried a Winchester, wore a wide-brimmed felt hat over gray hair, a flannel shirt, blue denim pants, and heavy work boots.

"Jack Collins," he said, coming down off the rise.

Charlie thought Mr. Collins was probably out hunting. But a man who wandered around the prairie in the hot sun hoping to find game looked as crazy as the frantic pup. Charlie wanted to say something, but he only held out his hand and said, "Charlie Irwin, and here comes my pa, Joseph Irwin. Are we neighbors?"

"I would guess so. I have a homestead over near Shermanville. It was Barney Bronson told me you folks was here."

"I don't know a Bronson," said Joe frowning.

"Barney's a homesteader, like the rest of us. Knows everyone around for about four counties. Someone new comes in and he knows all about the family. He's our newspaper."

Nick sniffed the man and then lay down under a clump of tall grass. Charlie brought out the lard bucket packed with corn pone and hunks of roast rabbit. He took another bucket to the creek and dipped it full of water.

Mr. Collins drank the bucket half-empty and ate quickly everything Charlie passed him. He picked his teeth with a piece of dried grass stem.

Joe was eating and asked Collins if he were farming.

"Yup, same's everybody," Collins answered.

"What about this Bronson," asked Joe, digging the last piece of meat from the bucket.

"He was one of the first homesteaders to file a claim in these here parts," said Collins. "Everybody knows him. You will, too. Say, did ya know about them gol-durned land hunters jumping claims just to get the big fee? I call that plain unprincipled! We settlers were here first. We don't want to be robbed by those Johnny-come-latelies. Why, they was scared to come here when the land was vacant, 'cept for the buffalo and a few Injuns. I say we got to get ourselves organized."

It occurred to Joe to ask about what might have happened to his old soddy, but he said, "Did the cold weather drive a number of range cattle into the towns last winter?"

"Yup, some," Collins said. "There was a couple weeks when someone's cows huddled in the shelter of the general store and livery stable in Goodland last winter."

"If I get me a herd I'll have to get me some barbed wire or set posts at the corners of my barn and house so's the cattle won't rub hollows there."

Collins's head jerked up. "Say, that's what I come to say. I'll give you a hand with your building if you plan to start right away."

Charlie saw his father look pleased and shake Collins's hand. Collins stayed and helped Joe with the slicker. Charlie could see that he was cooperative and full of chatter. In addition to his farming, Collins and his three sons were bone gatherers. They had a crew of men and five teams that were hitched to wagons, and when the wagons were full of old buffalo bones they went to the Kansas–Pacific railhead about sixty miles east of their camp near Shermanville. The bones went to plants in the East, where they were pulverized into fertilizer for Pennsylvania and Ohio farmers. Collins was in northwest Kansas a couple of summers, not going farther south than five, six miles from Beaver Creek. He seemed to know everyone who homesteaded the area.

"I betcha' I've collected more than a thousand tons of bones, including buffalo, antelope, horse, but none them wild cows, their bones is too light to be worth the effort," said Collins. Slowly he added, "What do ya think? Want to join up?"

"Sure, I'd like to," Charlie said right away. "And maybe Frank could help out some, too. He's my younger brother."

Collins looked at Joe.

"What? Do I want to join your bone-hunting crew? No, thanks," said Joe.

"Look, Joseph, I was referring to protection. You join our organization and you can get help with problems of the claim contesters and them free-roaming herds you mentioned."

"I've not heard of such a group," said Joe suspiciously.

"That's another reason I'm here," said Collins. "Most of the cattlemen are organized and are offering five hundred dollars for evidence to convict a man of killing range cattle. You can see, with proper incentive, a man might turn in his neighbor. When drought hits him hard and his children cry for food, temptation is fierce. A man could butcher one of his own yearling for veal, sell some to friends, and suddenly find hisself accused."

Joe said something about personal freedom and not getting nosy with any neighbor's private business. "Every man has a responsibility to his neighbors as well as to himself," said Joe.

"Just my sentiments," said Collins. "Have you been notified by the Oberlin Land Office that someone's contesting this here claim of yours?"

"No!" Joe said immediately. "I've paid full price for my quarter section. I paid in seventy-nine. It's on the books. The Oberlin Land Office has got the record."

Charlie felt the muscles in the back of his neck go tense.

"Then you're safe—I suppose."

"Yes—what's to suppose?" asked Joe sharply.

"Well, you know Barney Bronson? He was county assessor in eighty-five."

Joe made no comment.

Charlie was trying to put things together, but there were pieces missing.

Finally Collins said mournfully, "Barney Bronson says he has proof that he was the first homesteader and lived in this here county five years. He came to Sherman County in eighty-one."

"Well, a man likes to draw attention to himself at times," said Joe, holding his temper. "I see no harm in that."

"If Bronson took a page out from that record book, leaving his record on the first page, it would seem that you have not paid up your claim, Joseph."

Charlie saw now how the pieces fit snug.

"You mean he would ask me for a fee to take off his contest?" Joe was showing annoyance. "Whole thing don't sound real neighborly."

Charlie watched Collins roll a cigarette.

"That's where the Homesteaders Union Association can be of service. We're having a meeting over to Art Stahm's dugout the fifteenth of August, starting eight o'clock. I'll show you where to find his place."

Collins found a sunflower stem and drew a crude map in the dirt. "You'll meet Bronson like I said. He's been invited to this same secret meeting."

The following day Collins sent his oldest son, Rob, to help Joe.

Joe staked off a plot of level land for the barn. Rob and Will cleared all of the growing material from the plot. Then Rob showed Will how to dry wild grape leaves and then crush and roll them in thin paper for a smoke. Charlie and Frank smoothed and pounded the cleared surface with a spade to form a hard earthen floor. By noon Collins brought his grasshopper plow to slice strips of sod from the earth easier and faster than Joe's breaking plow. The plow was harnessed to the workhorses, Suzie and Jed. Will and Rob chopped the strips into bricks. These were loaded on the slicker so that Flame, led by Charlie, pulled the sod bricks to the barn site, where Joe and Collins worked.

On the fifteenth of August, Joe asked Will to ride horseback with him to Art Stahm's dugout. Will begged off, saying that he'd promised Rob he'd go into Goodland to see what was happening in town. Charlie saw the disappointment on their father's face. "Pa, I'd like to go with you," said Charlie.

"Well, thanks, son, I think you are too young to join that association, but you can ride with me. I'm glad the moon's bright so we can watch for trail signs and talk at the same time."

Several men were there already when Joe and Charlie arrived. Collins introduced the Irwins to Art Stahm, a short man with piercing black eyes. His black hair was straight, below his ears, and he had a high forehead. He wore small steel-rimmed glasses. Stahm consulted his gold watch on a heavy chain every few minutes. Stahm introduced Joe to Barney Bronson.

He was not as Charlie had imagined. He was a big man, about the size of Charlie's father. He wore a buckskin shirt and buckskin breeches with moccasins on his feet. He was blond and blue-eyed. Bronson seemed surprised, almost startled, to meet Joe and Charlie Irwin, and his squinty blue eyes searched the one room, as though looking for a back door, though his head did not seem to move.

Charlie thought Bronson's face was much too pale for a farmer, more like the sickly look on the underbelly of a catfish. His feet in those thin-soled moccasins would be mighty sore walking over broken sod and clods of dirt and stones.

He was forced to sit in the only chair available between Joe and Charlie. He ignored Charlie, cleared his throat, and said to Joe, "Lived six years on the southwest four-fifteen, six-thirty-eight. Made my settlement the twentieth day of June, eighteen eighty-one." His watery blue eyes squinted at Joe's face.

Joe lowered his head, feeling embarrassed with such close scrutiny. "Made mine in seventy-nine," Joe said. "And I've got the carbon copy to prove it."

Now Joe watched and saw Bronson blanch like that same catfish overlong out of water.

Charlie wanted to shout "Hooray and hallelujah!" for his father.

The new candidates for the Homesteaders Union Association were led outside to wait for the preparations for their initiation. There were only six new members invited to join. Charlie was taken out of the dugout with the candidates and told he was to wait there until the initiation was all over. He had expected that, but he would have liked to see what went on in that secret part of the meeting. Joe winked at him, and he thought his father knew how he felt and on the way home might tell something. He sat by himself on the grass and stared at the moon glistening in the sky, which was salted with sparkling stars. He was close enough to hear the conversation of the men waiting to be initiated. He pondered why the conceited Bronson was invited to be in the HUA. Charlie had the feeling that his pa felt Bronson had something to do with the destruction of the old sod house and removal of the plot stakes. He wondered how his pa could feel comfortable around the deceitful man.

As a matter of fact, Joe was talking himself out of joining the Homesteaders Union Association when Collins came out and called Bronson back into the dugout as the first initiate. Bronson went inside and the door closed behind him.

"Hey," Joe said to Collins, who was still outside looking over the men. "I'm not feeling too good. Think I'll just get my horse and boy and we'll go on home. Sorry."

"Joseph," said Collins, coming to his side quickly and touching his hand lightly.

"It's Joe," said Joe irritably.

"Don't go, Joe," said Collins. "You don't seem to have a fever. Maybe just a little fright at this secrecy and oath business. It won't take long, not for you and these others anyway. For Bronson, yes—it might be longer." His voice was lowered.

Charlie could not help himself. He blurted out loud, "What's so special about a dude like that?"

"I thought you had it figured—you are quick with other things," Collins snapped. He was irritated that the kid spoke up.

"Figured what?" Joe answered. "That you settlers want a claim contester and cattle informant in your midst? What is this organization, a bunch of thieves and informants? I want no part of this!" Joe had let his anger show and started to leave, motioning for Charlie to follow. The other initiates were staring at them.

Collins grabbed Joe's arm. "Listen, we're in business to protect ourselves against men like that! If we take in a man that informs on his neighbors, we can scare him into secrecy. He'll know that we all know about his past deeds and we'd be the first to correct the situation if it happens again. This is a way of keeping him in line—on our side. Don't you see that?"

Charlie was dumbfounded. He could see the logic, but doubted if he could have figured it out for himself.

Joe looked at Collins, then at the other four men. They nodded in approval. Joe was not certain. He wanted to think. Collins shook his hand and left.

"There's no law enforcement to protect us," said one of the men.

"We settlers are defenseless alone," said another.

"I had to pay fifty dollars because I was five days late beginning improvements on my land. During those five days we had a blizzard, wind and snow. My God! No one could walk a straight path across the frozen ground, the wind came acrost so hard. It was Bronson turned me in for half my fee. We're not fond of him either," said a man with heavy shoulders, thick arms. He was short and stocky like Collins, and his broad face was bristled.

The fourth man, his brown eyes barely visible because of the way he squinted after years of farming against sun and wind and dust, said, "Stick with us, Joe. We need thoughtful men like you. And your kid's all right, too."

Collins came out of the dugout letting the light from inside make a broad fanlike pattern outside on the dirt and clumps of yellowed grass. Collins said, "Joseph—Joe Irwin, next." He stood next to the door trying hard to appear official.

Joe cleared his throat, touched the wide brim of his hat, looked at Charlie, and nodded that it was all right, and walked in behind Collins.

Charlie could see that the center of the room had been cleared except for a couple wooden crates stacked on top of one another so as to be waist high. They were covered with bleached, pure white flour sacks. Collins closed the wooden door.

Now Charlie saw why the other four men stayed huddled together; they were looking in the only window of the dugout where the heavy oiled paper had torn and left a good-sized hole. There was a trumpet vine growing over the side of the dugout and in front of the window, so that no one from inside could see those faces outside looking in. Charlie could hear Stahm read several oaths that his father was asked to repeat. The first being not to contest a neighbor's claim during his absence. Next not to tear down the house of a neighbor while he was away.

"Goddamnit!" said Joe. "Any man that knows me even the faintest knows I wouldn't do those things! Why do I have to swear to these things that are my nature anyway?"

The men outside murmured to one another. One came over and said to Charlie, "Your pa's a scrapper and stubborn to boot. You wanna see?"

Charlie pulled himself up from the grass and followed the man to the window. The men moved a little as Charlie climbed up on a stone. Then the heads behind Charlie adjusted so that they could all see what was going on. Charlie could hear them breathing close around him.

Stahm was looking at the dirt floor. His breath was coming in quick gasps. He said, "Damnit, just repeat after me, neighbor."

Joe's eyes fell to the homemade altar and he put his hands around the sides for support.

"Go on," Collins said to Stahm.

Other oaths were repeated that were strong reasons for settlers supporting the protective association. When Joe spoke, his voice thundered in the room. Charlie thought it was because his father had decided if the organization was good, he'd enter it wholeheartedly.

Joe was kneeling and putting his right hand on the open Bible that was on the white altar.

"Repeat after me," said Stahm, regarding Joe cautiously. "I do solemnly swear not to tell anything that may in any way lead owners of cattle, which may be running at large, contrary to law, and destroying the settlers' crops, to discover who has killed or crippled or in any way injured these same cattle, when driving them away from the crops or at any other time. If I do, then I shall expect this Homesteaders Union Association to use me thus."

At this crucial point a straw dummy in a red shirt and blue denim trousers, with a rope around its neck, was floated past Joe.

The straw dummy so startled Charlie that his knees buckled and he felt himself hit the side of the rock he stood on. His arm was scraped. One of the men behind him had an arm around his middle and stood him back on the rock. "Hanging's part of life. Better get used to it." Charlie felt squeamish and didn't want to look through the window. The stocky man with his face full of bristles put a steadying hand on Charlie's back. Charlie could hear the four men around him snickering. He looked up and saw that his father's face was white and he had his tongue clamped between his teeth. Charlie felt better seeing his father had been frightened by the hanging dummy also.

Bronson must have been frightened into secrecy that night, because Charlie never heard his father say to anyone that Bronson sold information for money after his initiation into the HUA. Charlie never asked, but he was certain the Irwins' paid-up claim was never contested.

EIGHT

House-raising

It took close to a month of slow, tedious work until, near the end of August, the Irwin barn was complete. One corner of the barn was kept clear as living quarters until the sod house was finished. Pieces of sod more than a foot thick, stacked on top of one another, made the barn sides. The roof was reinforced with split oak logs tied together with willow. Layers of sod went on top of the logs. There were no windows. For light Joe used a coal-oil lantern, or left the door open. The door was a wooden frame hung with thick deer hide. The four horses and cow were kept in crude stalls on one side along with a place for hay. Hay was the fresh-cut prairie grass. On the other side was a bin made of split logs for the oats Joe bought from Jack Collins.

The weather became rainy and Joe moved the horses and cow into the barn. Mary moved herself and Ell inside the barn at night. They spread comforters over the oats, wiggled down to make a bowl-shaped bed for themselves. The three boys and Joe slept in the wagon.

One day Mary told Joe that the thing she wanted most of all was a kitchen stove. She did not like to cook in a fireplace, nor over an open fire outdoors. Joe counted his money and one clear morning announced that he and the three boys were going into town, Goodland, for supplies. He went directly to the General Mercantile and bought the only Majestic cast-iron cookstove in the store. The clerk told Joe that stoves were brought by wagon from the town of Wallace. "Wallace gets 'em from the East by rail. Don't sell more'n two or three a year."

It took the clerk along with Joe and his sons to load the heavy iron range onto the wagon.

The clerk said, "Grease her well. Heat cures the grease into the metal, then she don't rust." Then he cautioned, "Ride easy. Cast iron's brittle and can crack if youse take to bouncing from rut to gulley."

Joe braced the blue-black pieces of flue pipe in front of the stove and drove as carefully as he knew how back over the prairie.

Mary's delight astonished everyone. As soon as the stove was set on the ground she put twigs inside the firebox and burned them to see how the stove heated up. She made biscuits in her griddle on top of the stove. She cooked them on one side, then on the other side. She heated a bucket of hot water for a bath and sent the boys to the creek to hunt wild plums or persimmons for a pie. That night she asked Joe to put the stove in the barn so she could bake and cook in any kind of weather.

Joe said, "I can't."

"Sure you can. Will and Charlie can help," she said. Her sunbonnet brim hid her disappointed face.

"But I ain't about to. There's dry grass in the barn. You don't want it to go up in a blaze from a spark out of the firebox?" asked Joe.

She said, "I'll cook outside in the clearing until the house is built. Charlie can fix the wagon-cover tarp over it for shade and to keep off the rain."

"I'll build the house next," said Joe, and he pulled Mary close against his chest. "It'll have real windows, not paper soaked in grease, and curtains at the windows and those fancy little vases to hold flowers for the sills."

Mary felt better knowing Joe understood she wanted to begin her domestic duties in a cheerful place.

Joe saw the smile flicker at the corner of Mary's mouth and her eyes light when she turned her face toward him.

"Can we have three bedrooms and a big kitchen?" she asked.

"Yep, if that's what you want."

Mary put her arms around Joe. "Don't let me get carried

away. It wouldn't do any good for you to get rich. I'd have you furnish my house with an inside well and fancy fixin's for furniture. Then I'd insist you get the latest plows and maybe another horse."

"And not an extra piece of meat hanging in the kitchen rafters?" cried Joe.

"Don't bellow! I'm just telling the truth, that we both know. Money seems to burn a hole in my pocket and in your pocket," Mary said with a sigh.

"You can't fault me for wanting to buy everything for you. You deserve the best I can give. I know coming out here was not an easy decision for you."

Mary tightened her arms around Joe. She put her face up for his tender kiss.

However, Joe did not build the house next. He and the boys built a sod chicken house. Joe said it was for Ell. Ell pouted the whole day it was going up. "Am I going to feed those stupid chickens and gather eggs?" she whined. "It's just another chore. I swear! The only thing those stupid chickens are good for is to use their flesh to draw poison from a snake bite!"

"Ell!" chided Charlie. "Nothing wrong with that! Think of all the chicken and dumplings and egg pie chickens are good for. I'll feed those chickens for you."

Ell's face changed. Her downturned mouth turned up. Her green eyes sparkled. She was jubilant. "Oh, Charlie, will you? I knew I could count on you. You always know how to make me happy. Oh, joy!"

"I'll fatten your chickens and sell 'em. I'll buy you books, so you can be the best teacher in the Sappa area," teased Charlie.

Ell admitted that Charlie had a way of taking the burden out of ordinary chores. "Charlie, I love you most," cooed Ell, "egg pie second."

Her words of flattery gave Charlie a warm glow. "It's just a way to get through the muddle of every day," he said and began singing "Nobody Knows the Trouble I've Seen" in a deep voice to make Ell laugh.

She sobered and looked demure. "I've been wondering if Pa's friend, Jack Collins, would send his children here if I started reading and writing lessons."

"Ask him," said Charlie. "But his boy Rob is too old for lessons."

"Charlie! If he wants to come for lessons, you can't stop him because of age. Besides, I kind of like the way he looks. He makes me feel good. He gives me tingles with his eyes."

"He gives me goose bumps," said Charlie.

"There you go—teasing me because I told you how I felt."

Ell did not have to wait long to talk with Jack Collins. He came on the first of September to collect the bones Charlie and Frank collected and paid them a few cents for their effort. He also brought a half carcass of deer. Behind him came Rob carrying a hammer, wedges, and squares. Then came a large, strapping woman carrying a pick and shovel. Behind her was a passel of younger children. Charlie counted two towheaded boys and three towheaded little girls.

"Time you started your house or you'll be in the dark barn all winter!" called Collins.

"Well, I've marked the space and cleared the ground of grass and roots," said Joe. "I was about to cut the sod. You don't think I'd let my family live in a barn in winter? Why, there ain't no windows!"

"Windows you gots to have. That's why we come in one of the bone wagons. It can haul more'n yours. I figure we go to Wallace for lumber for the frames and window glass while the others get started on the posts for the corners and roof supports and cutting plenty of sod," said Collins. "You can count on the HUAers coming for your house-raising."

"How far is this here Wallace?" asked Joe, remembering the Mercantile clerk mentioning the town.

"Maybe thirty, forty miles south. We ford the North Fork of the Smoky Hill River and get a view of the highest point in Kansas. Wallace's the only place I know where there's window glass. Your woman has her heart set on letting daylight shine in her place, just the same's my Cora here." Collins pointed to the large, coarse, yellow-haired woman.

Mary was helping Mrs. Collins put the pick and shovel against the chicken house and asking her to sit at the table under the canvas lean-to Charlie had built. Mary put a kettle of water on the stove for coffee and called Ell to stir up some cornmeal mush for the five little children. Rob spoke right up and said he'd like mush himself.

Ell looked at Rob. He was close to Will's age, twenty or twenty-one. He was built like his father and mother, broad-shouldered and short. His face was tanned and his hair almost cottony-white from sun bleaching. He never took his eyes off Ell.

Charlie thought Cora Collins looked robust enough to simmer down those young ones, but she paid no heed to them. They banged cups on the table and stood on the wooden benches Will had made. Charlie herded the five boisterous children out beside the barn to show them some rope tricks so that his mother and Cora Collins could talk. "You kids stop your racket or I'll tie you all together with this here rope," Charlie threatened. "Don't you have manners?" He swung his rope in a loop above their heads. They had never seen anything like that before. They watched in silence, their eyes wide, their mouths open.

Charlie was thinking that Cora Collins did not look like the kind of a woman most men would stare at more than once. She was so homely that even a horsefly wouldn't look at her twice. Charlie saw his father and Mr. Collins leave in the bone wagon and wished he'd asked to go along. He knew they'd be gone overnight because Cora Collins had quilts for her brood to stay here all night. "Guess I'm stuck with you chickens like some old mother hen," Charlie exploded out loud. The children thought he was funny and laughed. The children thought Charlie was wonderful when he found a short rope and showed each one how to spin it.

Ell called that the mush was ready. The children clustered around Charlie. He noticed that Rob followed Ell. Charlie thought it would serve Rob well if Ell spilled hot mush down his front when she turned too quickly. Then he'd run fast as a scalded cat.

Mary pulled the youngest Collins child on her lap. The little towheaded girl was not bashful. She sat contentedly. Mary fed her mush from a cup and a small wooden spoon. Charlie gave his mother a grateful look. He thought, if she'd take a couple more of these rowdy kids he wouldn't feel like he was being mauled by bear cubs. Charlie noticed that Cora Collins's eyes were orange-brown. His mother's were deep green in the morning light. Cora had freckles across her nose and under her eyes so that Charlie knew she neglected to wear her sunbonnet. Her forehead and cheeks were lightly tanned. She smiled at her boy Rob and opened her mouth.

"Mrs. Irwin—Mary—that was my own ma's name. Bless her soul. She'd shake a finger at me if she could see the offspring I've got and the dirt house I live in. But she's gone, so's I don't have to explain to her. I'm glad I have another woman to prattle on with. You know, I sometimes talk to Rob like I would with another woman. I get so lonely for company my age. We'll talk all day." Her eyes twinkled and her hands moved when she talked. "Say, I do envy you that kitchen range out here." She winked. "Your Charlie seems good with children. Your Will and Frank can get the tools lined up and maybe start some sod cutting while Rob and Ell take a couple horses to ride out and tell some of the HUAers about your house-raising. By tomorrow this place will be buzzing louder'n any hive pawed at by some brown bear."

Charlie frowned. So that was it. Cora Collins could sit and talk with his mother all day while he took care of the children and Ell went on horseback over the countryside with that bobcat, Rob. Well, he'd do something about that there notion. Charlie untangled himself from the tiny arms and legs of the children and went to Ell with a big smile on his face. "Sis, these kids want you to tell them a story and then they'd like to learn to write their names. You musta talked to Mr. Collins."

"Yes, I did. He was happy as a colt in an apple orchard."

"See, I told you he'd like the idea. So you show the kids what kind of schoolmarm you are. Rob and I will invite the settlers to the house-raising."

Rob was leaning against the wagon. He made one step forward and took Charlie's arm. "You've got it wrong, pal. School starts tomorrow. Today Ell and I ride out. We talk to the settlers. Didn't you hear Ma?"

Charlie growled. He didn't know what to say. He looked from Ell to his ma, and by that time a couple of the towheaded children were pulling at his trousers. He knew he'd lost the argument. Thus, he had to herd five little kids for the rest of the day. By afternoon Charlie tied all five children together in his rope and told them to see if anyone could get loose before Injuns came over the hills. He flopped down in the tall grass, closed his eyes for a short rest. Next thing he heard the hooves of horses clattering into the yard. The two horses, Suzie and Jed, were lathered as though they'd been run hard. Rob climbed down and went to the water bucket for a drink.

Ell said, "Charlie, if you cool out the horses, I'll untangle those kids for you." Her face shone with perspiration and pleasure. There was a smudge of dirt under one eye. The buttons on her dress were fastened wrong; there was an extra loop at the neck.

"What happened?" asked Charlie.

"Not much." Ell's eyes crinkled with joy. "Rob rode like a

gust of wind. I had to keep up. It was wonderful! I feel vibrant —full of life! Rob's different, like you said."

"Fix your dress before Ma sees it," said Charlie sharply.

"Oh—I undid it to feel the wind all over my body. You ought to try it. Oh, joy!" Ell sighed.

"Did he touch you?" asked Charlie, squinting against the sun, feeling a tightness in his belly.

"Charlie! That's evil! He didn't. But what if he did? Would you want to know how it felt?" She shivered and straightened her dress.

"Wash—wash your face," stuttered Charlie, feeling sweaty on the palms of his hands. "I'll take care of the horses. You untie those giggly kids. Be careful—you'll think an avalanche hit."

Charlie unsaddled the horses, brushed them with handfuls of wild grass, and turned them loose behind the barn in the little meadow.

After the supper dishes were washed and put away, Mary said to Charlie, "I've enjoyed this day. Did you and Ell enjoy the Collinses' young'uns?"

Charlie looked where Ell was holding Nick while Frank printed DOG with a stick in the dust so the children could imitate the letters. The youngest child had a minute-long attention span and left drawing in the dirt to pet the pup.

His mother went on. "I see Frank is interested in those young'uns. And look there, Will's found a friend in Rob. That's real nice."

Charlie knew that Rob and Will had their heads together talking about women and at the same time rolling cigarettes made of Rob's dried grape leaves.

Charlie nodded. He was not going to spoil his mother's good time with some foolish telltale stories or fleeting bad feelings he had about Rob Collins. The children had worn him down and he was glad when it was bedtime.

The four older boys slept in comforters in the wagon. The women and little children slept in the barn. Mary fixed a place in the oats for herself and Cora, then she lay comforters on the sweet, dry grass for Ell and the five little children.

Before daybreak Ell started a fire in the stove. Charlie got up and splashed cold water on his face and neck. He rinsed out his mouth with water two or three times and said, "My turn to milk Clover. But why'd you get up so early?"

"I want to wash my hair before all the settlers come," said Ell.

"Are many of them HUAers?" asked Charlie.

Ell said, "Most, I think." She carried the bucket of hot water into the barn, protecting her hands from the hot bail with a wad of rags.

Charlie sat on the wooden bench beside the stove a moment to warm himself and was startled when Rob sat beside him.

"She's something to look at." Rob was looking at the barn.

"You like our sod barn?" said Charlie, rubbing his eyes.

"Your sister, you dunce! Ever notice how she presses her lips together, but still there's a curve at the corners? Her braids caress her white shoulders when she dips rainwater from the barrel. Her eyes looked dark as India ink, but her skin is creamy as moonlight."

"You're cracked!" cried Charlie. "No one ever talked about Ell like that. She's only a girl! Besides, she was shivering under a heavy shawl while she poked sunflower stalks into the range. You couldn't see no skin. Jeems, you're daft."

Rob stood by the warm stove and stretched lazily. "I imagined, my friend." He smiled and looked at Charlie through pale cyanic-colored eyes.

Charlie snorted and said, "You've time for another hour's sleep. Better get it before the others wake up." He clanged the milk pail on the edge of the range for emphasis and went off to the barn. He left the deer-hide door hooked by a thong to a nail so he had some light inside as he milked the cow.

Charlie's mother and Cora were already dressed and babbling with Ell, who was sponging herself. Cora looked at the tiny stitching in Ell's white muslin drawers and camisole. This made Ell pleased because she'd done the sewing herself. Ell gave Cora a splash of her good-smelling rosewater, then she bent over a kettle of warm water with a cup of vinegar added. The kettle was on the milking stool.

"Ma, I need the stool if I'm to do the milking," said Charlie, feeling bored and silly standing around waiting for women, who could talk a donkey's hind leg off, to stop so that he could do his chores.

"Give your brother the stool. You can bend on your knees for that rinsing." Mary left to make biscuits in the first morning light.

Ell flipped her hair so that Charlie's shirt was splashed. "Hey," he said, "I don't want to smell like pickles!"

Ell laughed when Charlie ran his hands over the wetness on

his shirt. She gave him the stool and threatened to splash again. Charlie ran to the other side of the barn and was glad to sit himself under the cow. He had dipped a rag in the soapy water bucket to clean off Clover's udders. Ell called, "If the milk tastes like lye soap, it'll be your fault!"

Charlie rolled his eyes and made a funny face.

One of the little Collins girls climbed out of her warm comforter. "Can you do that to my hair?" she asked Ell.

"Mine, too?" came several other wide-awake children's shrill voices.

Ell was surprised at their eagerness. "Of course, as soon as I get the soap out of mine. How about baby Carrie?" The youngest nodded her towhead and picked straw from her long cotton dress, which she'd slept in.

Cora left to admire the cooking stove again and to help Mary.

Charlie concentrated on the squeeze and pull of milking when his eye caught a shadow by the door. It was Rob standing inside against the wall so that his face was clear in the bluish light of dawn. Charlie saw Rob's eyes move up and down. He watched Ell in her drawers and camisole. Charlie did not stop milking, but he worked in slow motion. He watched the expression on Rob's face and could tell when his eyes stopped along the edge of Ell's neckline, where the cleavage of her breasts was apparent under the camisole when she bent to wash the baby's hair. Charlie's breathing was shallow. The pull and squeeze rhythm of his hand became stronger. The cow switched her tail and stepped forward. Charlie hitched the stool forward and held the pail between his knees tighter.

Ell looked up with a start. She seemed to realize that Rob had watched her for some minutes. Speechless, she let her eyes fall from the top of his sun-bleached hair, over his tanned face with those sulky eyes and lips, over the gray cotton shirt to the gray denim trousers with threadbare knees, to the dusty boots that were laced over muscular legs.

"So? Do you like what you see?" Rob asked in a husky voice.

"Why are you here?" Ell asked, pulling the drying sheet around her shoulders and picking up the little girl to cover the front of her undergarments. Her eyes snapped with the reflection of the first hint of sunlight.

"Your ma sent me to say you should cut the primpin' and get out to see the crowd that's already here to help build your new house."

"She didn't!"

"Here, let me help you dry Carrie's hair. Shoo, outside, let the sunshine dry your hair," he called to the other children, and motioned with his hands as they went out the door. "Looks like your hair needs rubbing with the sheet." Rob reached to catch the end of the bath sheet and pull it away in his strong hands.

Charlie saw Ell's eyes widen, and instead of moving away she moved closer. She set Carrie on the floor. "Go outside with your brothers and sisters. The sun will dry your hair and make it shine," she said. Her voice was low in her chest. Outside the sun was beginning to rise, making the prairie awash in pale yellow light.

Ell stood still. Rob rubbed her hair and let his thigh touch Ell's thigh. Rob moved one hand down the sheet to Ell's shoulder, where it rested a moment, then began to creep downward until it rested full on her small breast. Charlie saw Rob's fingers curl. He heard Ell's breath draw in, but she did not move. Her eyes were closed and her face showed a sensuality Charlie'd never noticed. Rob's face had the same lustful quality around his full mouth. His body swayed and the hand cupping Ell's breast slipped inside her camisole.

Charlie could not take his eyes away. He saw Ell push herself against Rob. She moaned and pushed his hand tight up against her breast once again. His hand holding the bath sheet slipped to her shoulders, then around her waist.

Charlie's hands stopped pulling and squeezing; they were held tight between his knees. The milk pail was on the floor at his feet. He tried to pull his feet back and put his weight on them. His legs were soft as boiled macaroni. Charlie stood up. The stool scraped the floor.

Rob dropped the sheet. His heavy lids opened and the pale-blue circles stared coldly at Charlie. "Where the hell'd you come from?"

At first Charlie's mouth felt numb and he could not clear his befuddled mind to speak.

Rob said, "Get out of here. You're no better'n a sow bug." He lunged for Charlie, who ducked behind the cow.

Rob was determined that he was not going to let Charlie stand in the way of his desires. He'd see Ell later. He thought, let her stew awhile. Rob stalked out of the barn.

Charlie waited for Ell to pull her dress over her head, then went outside with her. She began to brush the children's fine hair, keeping her eyes down. Charlie was sure Ell was waiting for her heart to stop thumping. He knew he was waiting for his heart to slow down. He did not understand his flustered feeling. He wanted to strike out, to do something physical, hit Rob in the solar plexus, shake Ell until her eyes popped out. His breathing was deeper now and his hands shook. He took the pail of milk to the creek for cooling. He broke off a bunch of willow branches that were full-leaved to put over the top of the pail to keep insects and rodents out. When he got back to the wagon and the shade he'd rigged over the table with the wagon's canvas, he saw that Rob had been right. People were arriving for the house-raising. He poured himself a cup of scalding coffee.

Ell was fighting off the steam of passion by washing all the buckets and kettles she could find. She looked at Charlie and became flushed. She began to help Cora heft the half deer onto an oak spit held by a tripod over a fire pit. Cora said, "My dear, the little ones look pert with their hairs fresh-washed."

Some of the settlers brought puddings and casseroles. The men sought out Will and went out to cut bricks of sod. Charlie nudged Frank, who was sitting at the table. "Time for you and me to get to work."

Frank said he'd not finished all the biscuits he planned to eat, and he was not a slave waiting for orders from a master. Charlie left the table in a huff. Actually, he was not ready to face Rob while cutting sod. The thought of him reminded Charlie of a scruffy tomcat chasing a she cat in heat. Charlie decided he'd talk to Ell as soon as he could. He began to greet the newcomers. His mother admired and thanked the women for the food that was brought.

Sarah Melstrom explained her covered dish. "Mrs. Irwin, it's not my usual good quality. It's stewed rabbit and I had only a few scrawny onions and scraggly carrots to flesh it out."

Mary knew she meant it was her best-made dish of stewed rabbit. The food was each woman's finest. It was their way to show off their creative talents. It was their escape to color and variation from the drab, hard farm life. There was gooseberry pie, navy beans and noodles, custard pudding, clabbered milk, potato dumplings, and rhubarb cobbler.

Charlie shook hands with the bachelors and pointed them in the direction of the sod cutters. Jess Tracey, Wes Holmes, Frank Leslie Miner, and Art Wells came because of the anticipation of lots of good food.

Some families came in wagons, such as Wilt Clayton and his wife, Clara, and their three children, John and Kate Bray and their boy, Goy; Al and Sarah Melstrom and their little girl, Artie.

Mr. Bill Hill, a small, shy man, came by himself in a wagon. He brought a crock of persimmon beer and told Charlie that he was originally from Indiana, but had been in western Kansas for some time now.

Charlie was glad to take the crock to the creek to keep cool. He told Mr. Hill, "You sit down and have a cup of coffee or some creek water." When Charlie came back he said, "The day's turning hot. I doused my head in the creek." He slicked back his sandy hair, letting the water run down his neck. Hill was on his second cup of water.

Mr. Hill unbuttoned his shirt collar and rolled his sleeves. "I want to say something before I go to work."

"Maybe you should talk to Ma, or wait until Pa comes back from Wallace," said Charlie, who looked at Mr. Hill's dusty black shoes and dusty black suit. The jacket lying on the table was covered with hundreds of tiny seeds called sticktights. "I hope you're not a claim contester."

"Oh, no!" Mr. Hill ran his hand though his gray hair. "Some folks criticize my work, though. I brought the darkies to Kansas."

Charlie looked at Mr. Hill. "But you're not—not—"

"No, I'm not a darkie. But I'm human. I found a lawyer in Topeka, took him to Nicodemus, and together we set that town up on a lawful basis and let the citizens run it themselves. It's in a slump, but it will snap out of it when more southern darkies decide they can do well farming in Kansas."

"You founded that colorful town?" Charlie was astonished.

"I found those people were being soaked with fees for assistance in obtaining land and filing homestead papers. My lawyer friend and I cleared out the trouble in the Oberlin Land Office. We tar-and-feathered a young man named Bronson who was collecting those high fees."

Charlie's mouth fell open. "I met a Barney Bronson once. Dressed in buckskin pants."

"Same man. He's out of this country now. Went East to tell of his adventures in the Wild West. I heard he was mortally afraid of being lynched and hung not by citizens of Nicodemus but by white folks."

Charlie was stunned. He hardly felt the hot sun on his back drying his shirt and hair.

"How's your black dog?" asked Mr. Hill. "Mrs. Fletcher wants to know."

Charlie's breath exploded. "You know her—Zach—and his

pa? You know about Nick?"

Mr. Hill exploded with laughter. "Yes—it was the best story I'd heard in a long time. Unbelievable! But truth is stranger than fiction."

Charlie reached out to shake Mr. Hill's hand. "My pa says that, but I never knew what it meant until just now. Imagine that old man sleeping with my Henry rifle. Imagine me finding it in that place!" Charlie called the pup. "See. Nick's hardly a pup now. Doing fine. We couldn't do without that dog."

"I'll tell Mrs. Fletcher. Would your pa object if Matt Splitlog and Reverend Roundtree dug you folks a well?"

"Why would he do that?"

"Because Roundtree is a darky and Splitlog is a redskin."

"My pa went to Reverend Roundtree's church. Matt Splitlog is my friend. Jeems, who's to object? Are the other Splitlogs coming?" Charlie was already anticipating his welcoming of the three brothers.

"No, Mark and John are staying in Nicodemus to weave baskets or string beads for the settlers coming through. The town has a new industry—selling local crafts and homegrown edibles to settlers going West. Maybe it'll be a good-sized trading post in a couple of years."

"Pa and Ma will be pleased to see Reverend Roundtree again, and I want Pa to meet Matt. But I don't understand why they'd come all the way to Sappa country to dig a well."

"Son, it's a way of doing a kindness. Look at these people here today. Likely you've never met most."

Charlie nodded.

"Well, the next time you'll want to do some kindness, like help a new family build a house or barn, dig a well, pull a dumb cow out of a marsh," said Mr. Hill. "Some of this began with a kind-hearted young man and a rifle, you know."

"I didn't know it then," said Charlie.

"That's most commendable," said Mr. Hill. Then he looked shy again, as if he'd talked far too long. "I need to find a shovel or a pick."

"Mr. Hill," started Charlie. "You—you shouldn't work in Sunday trousers and those shoes, sir. Maybe we could talk with Ma and she'd find something of Pa's you could wear. My brother Will might have a pair of boots for you."

Mr. Hill winked. "See what I mean about kindness? I've already done most of my job. I'll make a couple of cuts with the shovel, then be on my way to tell my two friends to come dig your well."

Charlie opened his mouth, but Mr. Hill interrupted. "Don't fret, I'll see your mama before I go."

Mr. Hill carried the shovel when he went to talk to Mary. Charlie could see he was shy and had a hard time getting started, but once he got a conversation going he was all right. Charlie was sure his mother would tell Mr. Hill about what a hard worker Will was, that Frank was the baby, and that Ell was like Grandma Malinda and wanted to be a teacher and healer. Charlie went off to find Ell.

Going from the wagon to the barn, Charlie met two new arrivals, Otto Hurst and Marietta Roberts. Some of the women were cutting sod. The men loaded it on wagons and the slicker and hauled it to the area marked off for the house. Some of the boys spread fresh green cow manure on the hardened dirt floor. "Hey, what's that for?" asked Charlie, holding his nose.

"It's vile! It doesn't belong in a house. Who told you to do this?" shouted Ell, waving her arms and making a face.

One of the boys explained that when dried, cow dung would make a shiny, hard surface on the packed dirt and the smell would be gone in a few days.

"You'd better be right, or in a few days I'll find you and take you apart!" shouted Ell.

Some of the women were preparing more food over small fires or sitting on blankets in the shade of their wagons, tending young children or napping babies.

Charlie nodded to the women and called to Ell, "Hey, now you're talking like my sister!"

"Charlie, can you imagine a floor of cow pies?" She began to giggle.

"Listen, can you imagine Reverend Roundtree and Matt Splitlog coming to dig a well for Pa?"

"They are? Reverend Roundtree and one of those Injuns? Oh, my goodness! Gosh! What's going to happen next?" She sat with her back against a boulder.

Charlie sat on the bare ground, careful to avoid a prickly pear. He sifted the dust through his fingers, letting the wind carry it three, four yards away. "I'm not a fortune-teller, but if you don't stop leading on—being friendly with Rob Collins, you'll fix things so that you'll never be a teacher. How many kids does Mrs. Collins have?"

"Five," said Ell, wondering what Charlie was talking about.

"Six, counting Rob," corrected Charlie, "and the little ones in a chain, each year."

"Ya—poor Mrs. Collins, maybe she doesn't know what caused all them kids. She's not too smart, you know. But she's not Rob's ma. His ma came from some mail order Mr. Collins answered. She died of fright when a plague of grasshoppers caught her out in a field and started eating her clothes. The story actually frightened me—it must have been awful. Rob was four or five and saw it."

Charlie said, "Ell, you're not good for him. He's not good for you. Why, any girl that is nice to him will be"—Charlie bit his tongue, then decided to say it out loud—"with child before he even talks about marriage."

"Charlie! I'm not that kind!" Ell cried. "Why are you talking like this? Just because you saw Rob give me a hug and kiss me. I'm old enough for that!"

"Rob would have taken more if I had not stood up in the barn, and you know it. I think that's what makes you so angry."

Ell began to cry. "Charlie, he gives me shivers. I like the feel of them. I think of him near naked like those Injuns. It gives me a strange feeling and it frightens me, but I keep thinking anyway."

Charlie suggested, "Why don't you talk to Ma about your feeling."

"No! She wouldn't know anything about my feeling! I couldn't," sobbed Ell.

"Then promise me something. Will you?"

"I don't know."

"Promise me you'll not let Rob think of you as a girl who is easy, you know. And you won't let him touch you—put his hand where he wants, the rest of the time he's here."

"Oh, why not? Then after that?"

"Before that, you'll notice other boys and you'll compare them to creepy Rob. There's something not right with him. I swear!" said Charlie.

"I don't believe that!" said Ell.

"Because you won't let yourself believe. Just watch for a while and keep yourself busy, not in a lather so your eyes are clouded."

"Humph! You sure have some notions!" Ell got up and went to help their mother with the noon meal.

Some of the families came because they could remember when Joe and Mary Irwin were here before and no more than poor dirt farmers like themselves, but driven out by the dust and drought. And here they were back again! The women wanted to see what kind of furniture Mary brought this time, if she had embroidery on her nightdresses. They wanted to see with their own eyes what changes had taken place with the Irwins. When neighbors came to a house-raising, not many secrets were kept.

The men were interested in the mechanics of the house building. The back wall of the Irwins' house was cut out of a hill.

After the midday meal the men did not stand around but went right to work again. Mary asked Charlie to dig a trench in the ground to keep leftover food cool. Charlie dug a square hole about four by four feet. Mary lined it with clean, damp dishtowels. "This'll keep the food fresh for tomorrow," she said.

The evening meal was mostly navy beans, corn bread, and coffee. The men sat out on the wild grass and talked about trenching below the surface of the floor. That is cutting a narrow ditch all around the perimeter of the house so that they could start the walls from the trench with chunks of evenly cut prairie marble. The children were rolled into blankets under the wagons. Mary saw it was getting dark. She went to each family and to the bachelors, saying, "You better lay here for the night." She brought out her extra comforters and fixed places in the hay for some of the women and small children who were not already asleep or did not want to sleep out under the stars.

Charlie could see no moon, but the stars forming the constellations winked like cold firelight: Cassiopeia, the Big and Little Dipper, Sagittarius, and Scorpio. The stars looked as if they could be touched. The falling stars whooshed through the dark heavens with a sparkling trail and no sound. Charlie put out his hand and the next falling star seemed to fall through his fingers like water. When his hand grasped around it, nothing was there. The star vanished like so much smoke in the wind.

By noon the next day Joe and Collins were back with the dimension stuff, two by eight boards for rafters, window frames, and sills, a door frame, and three glass windows, a couple hundred pounds of hard coal for Joe's forge, and three painted china vases for Mary, one for each windowsill.

Reverend Roundtree and Matt Splitlog came in about the same time and helped unload the wagon. Charlie was glad to see his pa shake hands with Matt and hand him a forked branch. Matt walked over the area in front of and beside the house. Under the lea of the hill on the east side the stick he held in his two hands dropped, pointing to the very spot Matt said a well should be dug. He promised Joe water at about twenty or thirty feet. "If I'd been back of the house on the hill, might be forty feet."

Andy Melstrom, Al's brother, built a pulley, or windlass, using small poles and oak logs. His pony pulled the end of a rope just far enough to raise a bucket out of the well hole to be emptied. Then the pony backed up to lower the bucket again.

Charlie yelled down the well hole, "Can you men get to the top for your noon meal?"

"Oh, for certain," called Reverend Roundtree. "Bill Hill told us he left persimmon beer. I can climb out of anything for that!"

Ell poured milk for the small children and coffee for the women. Mary poured the beer for the men, who smacked their lips. Will and Rob pretended they were full-grown men and drank their share before going back to work on the well digging. Others put undressed V-notched logs at the corners of the house and laced the two-by-eight oak rafters with willow sticks to hold the sod. The cow dung was dry to Hurd Horton's touch. He was ready for the floor's final treatment. He went to his wagon and brought up a couple five-gallon cans of fresh cow's blood. He'd saved it after butchering for the Errington and Rich grocery store in Goodland. He called in a couple of the bachelors to grab a broom. Several brooms lay in the bed of his wagon, stained brown from previous floor paintings. The men swept off the excess cow dung. Les Miner called out, "How thick should this blood be spread!"

"Until it's all used up. Then wash the cans in the creek and pop 'em in my wagon over there. It'll be a nice floor!"

Miner was not sure about that. He'd never heard of putting blood on top of the dried cow dung. Art Wells, also working the floor, explained, "Blood on top of dried dung makes a packed dirt floor nearly impervious to water, besides giving it a rich dark color."

Ell brought a dipper and a pail of creek water to the men sweeping the coagulated blood over the entire floor. "I hate this place! This soddy'll smell like a barn or slaughterhouse! It's vile!"

"I have to agree, it smells like a wolf den now, but the best opinion here, this'll be one of the finest floors in Sappa Meadows." Miner smiled. He was a rangy young man in his mid-twenties. His hair was tawny, nearly the same color as Ell's. "I thought I was going to be putting on a roof, but here I am sweeping a floor. Might as well be wearing an apron."

This made Ell laugh. She poured water over Wells's hands

before she'd let him hold the dipper. He had a shock of unruly dark hair that covered his ears. "I feel like a bloody savage," he said.

Ell held a hand to her lips. "Sshh! There's a true Wyandot digging the well, and he becomes furious if you call him savage."

"Is that right?" asked Miner. His brown eyes looked her square in the face. He looked like someone who would treat everyone fair. Ell could see that he didn't look like he'd cut a man down with words just because he knew something about him. "The Wyandot a friend of yours?"

"Oh, yes. We met on the trail coming to Sappa Meadows." Her eyes twinkled merrily. "I think you've named our place! Sappa Meadows! I like it. What's your name?"

"Frank Leslie Miner."

"I'm Art Wells. We're pleased to meet such a pretty girl out in farming country."

Ell blinked her long eyelashes.

"Say, will you have supper with me?" asked Miner, surprising himself with his boldness.

"Why, sure, if you wash real good first." Ell pinched her nose and went off to take the water pail to other workers.

Miner and Wells double-scrubbed before sitting in the grass a little ways from the other men, waiting for Ell to bring her plate of boiled squash and cabbage and salt pork. "The boiled cabbage smell mixes right in with the odor of that floor," she said, tucking her long skirt underneath her black-stockinged legs.

"Believe me, in a couple of weeks the smell's gone and the floor's hard and shines pretty as a new penny." Wells had his tin plate nearly clean.

"I just hope." Ell sighed, picked at her cabbage. "I should have gone to the creek for some sourgrass for greens."

"Don't fret, this is good grub." Miner went back for seconds. Wells drank the juice from his plate. Miner came back and said, "Your folks have one of the best soddies I've seen. And look how good the grass grows out here in your meadow! Oats and wheat'll grow as well. You crochet or knit?"

"No," said Ell. "Is that important?"

"It is to me. So, you cook and read. What else?" Miner's eyes looked directly at her, so she blushed.

"That's the only reason you boys came here—to eat. How'd you know I read?"

"We seen you with the younguns, reading, writing, and making them sit still with stories. We worked quiet and heard them stories." Wells picked his teeth with a dried grass stem.

"Art! Don't tell our secrets! You know we didn't make any mistake coming for the food," said Miner.

"Want me to teach you to read and write?" Ell teased.

"Maybe I'm foolish to say this—but I already know," said Wells.

"I taught first graders in Chillicothe."

"Ya? Well, guess what I do," said Miner.

"I know you don't own a restaurant, because you'd eat all your profits."

"I'm a farmer, but I've worked in the silver mines in Colorado, Cripple Creek, and I've done books for the mining company. We had a Chinese cook, always made chop suey, stew with rice."

"I've never met a miner before," Ell said.

"So, now you've met Les Miner. I brought your pa a gift."

"For the housewarming?" Ell was surprised that a bachelor would think of such a thing. It was usually the women who brought gifts of food and small things for the new house.

"I brought some seed corn. It's special. It's named after the old man that first grew it in Kansas. Sherrod's White Dent. Wells gave me a couple handfuls of seed first. I've grown it two years," said Miner.

"I knew a man who grew it," said Wells, motioning for Charlie to bring his plate over and sit with the three of them. "Listen, this man had corn that was resistant to those gol-darned, pesky borers and grew three ears to each stalk."

"Maybe your pa and I can start something new in Kansas if we get good yields," said Miner.

"This is the second time Pa's been here. The drought of seventy-eight was too much and the winters were hard on Ma," said Ell.

Charlie set his plate on the grass. He was worn out from lifting huge sod blocks, but didn't want to admit that in front of anyone. "Was last winter as bad as some guys said?" he asked.

Wells was half-asleep with his arms around and his head on his knees. Rob Collins walked by and came back to sit down. Charlie picked up the empty tin plates and told Rob to take them to the women for washing. Rob scowled and looked at Ell. She was looking at Miner, who was saying, "I'll tell you something. It was called the Killer Blizzard and came the first of the year. There was wind, rain, and then it was twenty below and there was wind and snow. Until the end of January the temperature averaged between fifteen to thirty below. Lots of people froze to death and nearly all livestock died of cold or scarcity of feed. I found birds and jackrabbits frozen to death on my place."

Rob muttered, "Damn cold winter," and left with the dirty plates.

Charlie thought the account was fascinating. Ell thought maybe it was exaggerated, mostly she was interested with the rich timbre of Miner's voice.

Charlie said, "Jeems, that was cold! I hope our house keeps the wind out."

"That house is tight as a woodtick in a dog's tail," said Wells, stretching his legs out and rubbing his eyes. "Soddies are better than board houses out here. They'll hold up under a pile of snow, high winds, gully washer rains, and the moisture-eating hot suns."

"I'd have a puncheon floor if it were mine," said Ell. "Then I'd use a splint broom. Can't use nothing but a feather duster on a dirt floor—if you can stop holding your nose long enough."

"Aw, don't complain so danged much. Remember what I said. It will be fine, just give it time. I'm gonna leave that sack of seed with your pa. Thanks for the food," said Miner.

"You're welcome, Mr. Miner," said Ell.

"You ought to just call me Les," said Miner, pulling Wells to his feet. The boys waved and ambled off to work.

When the boys were out of hearing distance, Ell said to Charlie, "They're all right. But that one with tawny hair sure can talk."

Charlie inspected the progress at the well first thing after eating rhubarb pie for breakfast. He was surprised how much was done. Sand was reached at the floor of the deep hole. Split logs shored up the sides. His father had a rag tied around his head to keep perspiration from dripping into his eyes. The ugly scar in the form of an *X* on the side of the Reverend's face was crimson. Matt saw Charlie at the top of the hole. "Heave-ho! Here comes a bucket of sand." Andy Melstrom's pony pulled the rope and Melstrom emptied it on the pile of clay and sand. The pony backed up and the bucket was lowered. "We ought to strike water before noon," predicted Matt. "Charlie, get us more logs. Right away!"

Charlie found Art Wells and the two of them rolled half a dozen logs that were in a pile by the creek onto the slicker and pulled them up beside the house. "Hey!" yelled Charlie. "Pa and the guys in the well needs these split right away!"

"Keep your shirt on!" called Les Miner, climbing down from a window frame. Miner and Collins placed iron wedges at the right intervals and hit them with heavy sledgehammers until all six logs were split in less than twenty minutes. Charlie and Wells dragged the logs into place and one by one put them down the deep hole. Then Charlie lay on his belly for a moment to get a better look inside. He could see that the three men in the well had to move fast because one side was caving. Charlie motioned for Melstrom and Wells to have a look. Matt was wedging a log in place and oozing sand popped it flat on the floor.

"Gotta get this wet sand out of here," said the Reverend, who had taken his shirt off and hung it over the handle of a shovel not in use. "Clear the way! Coming up topside with a full bucket!"

Melstrom nearly tripped over Charlie as he got back to his pony to pull up the bucket. Two, three bucketfuls and the new log wedged into place. The three men on the bottom of the hole sighed with relief and began to wedge in more logs. Then they dug the sand from the bottom. Charlie moved out of the way, then decided to take one last look. The bucket was brimful and slowly coming up. He heard the rope snap, then saw the bucket tumble back into the hole. "Yowee!" he yelled when he heard the snap.

The strange cry was enough to cause Matt to look up and see the sun glint off the bucket's side, then nothing but the falling shadow. He darted to the middle of the hole and pushed the Reverend, who was doggedly digging with his head down, to the side where Joe was holding a log in place. Joe was smashed against the log and the jolt caused more sand to gush out from behind the barricade. The falling bucket missed the Reverend's head by inches.

"Hey, you up there! You all aiming to scare or score?" Reverend Roundtree hollered.

Charlie was holding his breath. "Jeems! It was an accident!"

"It was your yelling that alerted me—so thanks, my friend!" called Matt. He secured the bucket, refilled it, and sent it to the top while Joe and the Reverend pushed the logs upright and into place against the hydrostatic pressure of the wet, oozing sand.

Charlie stayed at the top with Melstrom and checked the rope at periodic intervals. It wouldn't do to have any more mishaps.

About noon the men at the bottom of the well had decided to abandon the wedging of the split wood. Water had begun to flow in from the bottom for good. The three men tried to get all the lumber away from the sides and let it rise to the top with the water. Melstrom and Charlie sent the bucket down for the small sticks and pieces of dimension Joe had used. Suddenly Joe called, "Matt, grab the rope! Let the damn wood float up! Tread water! Watch the wood!"

The water crept up fast. It was like bubbling brown porridge. Matt grabbed the rope, cut the bucket off, and heaved it with all his strength to the top of the hole. If Charlie had not caught the bucket in midair near the edge, it would have fallen back and sunk out of sight in that oozing thick brown water.

Matt slipped the rope loop he'd made over the Reverend's head and down under his arms. The Reverend moved up the side of the hole. The pony strained with the rope. Melstrom urged it on and dived to the edge of the hole when he saw the Reverend's hands clawing and pulling at the mud and rocks. The minute Reverend Roundtree was standing up, caked with mud and sticks and sand, a cheer came from the gathering crowd of women and children. "Hooray! Hooray!"

The rope disappeared again. Matt secured it around Joe, who clung to a log caught against the side. Before being pulled upward, Joe tugged and heaved to loosen the log. Wood left to rot in his well would contaminate his good water. When he was safe the cheers greeted him. Joe waved back, but did not keep his eyes on the group. He kneeled and put his face over the well to make certain that Matt had his head above water and the rope under his arms, ready to be lifted out. There were more cheers when Matt came over the edge.

Mary and Cora brought out the crock of leftover persimmon beer. Mary'd wrapped it in layers of newspaper to keep it cool for this momentous occasion. The night before she'd found the recipe printed on fine vellum paper waxed to the side of the crock so that it appeared at first to be a decoration.

> Mash and add 1 cup cornmeal to 1 full gal. washed ripe persimmons. Add 5 gals. water and 4 cups sugar. Let set until fruit rises (3 to 4 days). Strain and drink. Or bottle and seal. Liquid is fizzy and light-colored. Fill bottles only 2/3 full as it may be explosive if opened on a hot summer day.*

*Reprinted with permission of Ferne Shulton, from *Pioneer Comforts and Kitchen Remedies*.

Charlie helped take the logs and boards from the well by snaring them in a lasso loop. There was all of fifteen feet of water—more than Joe had hoped for. Joe had privately figured it would take him, with his three boys, all next spring to get the well dug. Now it was done and the remaining beer was the right touch to celebrate with.

When the beer was gone the well diggers went to the creek to wash off the mud. Charlie tied a tin cup to his rope and brought up a sample of the heavily sedimented well water. He knew it would be clear in a day or two. He found Ell and told her to try his sample.

"Charlie! It's full of gravel! I don't have a gizzard. I think you are trying to poison me!" Ell tossed the muddy water out and threw the cup at Charlie. "That water is so thick a snake could have been hiding in it!"

"Poisonous snakes float on water!" called Charlie.

NINE

Housewarming

Joe wanted to give these men something for their valuable labor and time. He looked at his house. The windows were already in the frames. The soddy was large, like he'd marked off, with enough space to divide into three bedrooms. The kitchen range was already against the wall, making that part look like a kitchen. Joe began to talk with Matt, the Reverend Roundtree, and Jack Collins. "I'd like to pay for this labor and time."

Collins said, "You couldn't hire any one of us to do this work. Not even for you. People here are proud. You have our friendship. You owe us your friendship. One day we'll call on you or your woman for something."

"That's no more than fair," said Joe. "But still I'd like to do something now."

Reverend Roundtree eyed the pile of hard coal Joe had brought in from Wallace. "You're a smith. Why don't you make something?"

Matt eyed the portable forge and the tools that lay in a heap on the ground near the chicken house. "A steel-bladed knife that holds its sharpness. Any man'd find that useful."

By afternoon Joe had the forge together and fired up. He selected a bar of steel and turned it over in his hands to make certain it was perfect for what he had in mind: a bowie knife, with the blade and hand guard all from the same metal piece. Joe agreed with Matt. A man in this country had use for a good bowie knife. Joe heated the metal a red-orange and hit the end lick after lick, shaping it just right with his hammer. Joe concentrated on making the blade. He wanted it to be his best work.

Not wanting to be outdone, Mary asked Charlie if he could help her make a splint broom from an old hickory pole she found in the wagon. "Ma, it'll take me until next week, if I find out how to make one. I've never seen it done in my life!" said Charlie, wondering why his mother had asked him to do this chore.

"Well, start now and use a sharp jackknife to hurry it," said his mother, pouring water from a pitcher into Nick's empty pan. "Seek out Reverend Roundtree."

"Does he have a jackknife?" asked Charlie.

"He has understanding and creativity," said Mary.

Charlie and Reverend Roundtree sat near Joe's portable forge and took turns shaving fine splits from the bottom of the pole up ten inches, removing the very heartwood, then shaving from ten inches above, down close to those at the bottom, turning the top splints down and tying them with wire.

"That'll make a woman's floor look bright and grateful. The splints are thin and soft enough to be used on a treated dirt floor, I believe," said the Reverend. "Where did this sharp, two-handled shaver come from?"

Charlie explained that it was from the cordwainer's set of tools that had once belonged to a grandfather he'd never known. "But some say I resemble him."

"That tells me he was a fine man," said the Reverend.

Joe was finished making the bowie knife. He was pleased. It was one of the finest he'd ever seen. The hand guard was smooth and straight. He made a handle out of a piece of cedar heartwood he found among a box of gear. He gouged his initials in the handle, then cleaned it out with a hot fine blade. He liked the balance and feel of the knife. He could see any one of the men around his place cutting the tops off a field of beets or turnips or harvesting corn or skinning out a deer or cleaning fish.

Will was working with some of the bachelors putting the stovepipe and chimney in place. Mary warned them not to scratch her floor.

Everything was completed before supper. The women decided everyone would eat outside even though the range was all ready to burn stove wood. They planned how they would use the remaining food. When that was over the women went to their wagons or reached into their pockets for a small remembrance to leave with Mary. This was customary. The men sat around on the gravel bar on the creek to wash and refresh themselves, and to wait for the women to put supper out.

Charlie sat around with Ell while she and Frank played school with the Collinses' young ones. He could not help but hear the chatter of the women and the good-time voice his mother had as she laughed and talked.

Effa Belless was sitting at the table under the canvas directly across from Mary. "You should have my recipe for good haying water," she said. "My ma made it all the time and took it to my pa's haying crew. Heat like today made their throats feel like they'd swallered slaked lime. This is it: You mix two cups of wild honey with a cup of cider vinegar, stir, and keep in a glass jar. Then add four teaspoons of that mix to every glass of water you put in the water tub for the field. You can crush in cinnamon or clove if you have any."

An old woman smiled broadly because she'd brought a tiny poke of cinnamon, and she hurriedly pulled it out of her apron pocket.

A couple of the women brought candles, one a tatting spool, another spice sachets and a piece of muslin home-dyed with bluebottle blooms and alum.

Mrs. Russel gave Mary something new, wrapped in fancy blue and white paper. It was store-bought soap that was so light it floated on water and was labeled boldly: IVORY.

Kate Bray brought a cough syrup bottle filled with rosewater and glycerin. Clara Clayton brought a white hen, which was put into the chicken house and given a plate of water and a handful of potato peelings.

Cora Collins gave Mary a cotton pound sugar sack full of tiny pearllike chive bulbs. "The leaves are the best thing for salads and you'll have lilac-colored flowers from them."

Mary said thank you over and over. "Thank you, chives will be in a garden close to the house early next spring."

Marietta Roberts told folklore stories. "A horseshoe hung in your chimney flue will protect that white hen from hawks."

Ell heard that and rummaged through Joe's boxes until she found an old horseshoe.

"Were any of your boys born on January first?" Sarah Melstrom asked.

"No," said Mary. "Will is closest, February 27th."

"Maybe—that's close enough. He should be lucky in raising cattle."

"He'll be glad to hear that," said Mary, giving Sarah a quick hug. "Charlie, go fetch the men. Let's eat before sundown so there'll be more time for dancing. Joe's going to play his fiddle tonight."

The women chattered like magpies as they brought out the food from the cooling trench and arranged it on the table. Some with small children fed them first so the babies would not be whiny when the men came to sit with them.

Charlie heard the men laugh, splash water, and run around snapping shirts or belts at one another. For three days they'd worked hard; now it was time for fun and relaxation. "Why did the farmer take his nose apart," asked Jess Tracey. "To see it run!" he whooped. "Here's another: Why did the farmer put a chair in the coffin? Do you give up? For rigor mortis to set in!" The men whooped.

After supper, while the women were doing the dishes and the men were tramping down the grass to make a smooth, slick place for dancing, Cora and the old woman who'd brought the poke of cinnamon put up horse blankets as temporary curtains between the rooms in the new soddy.

"It'll be nice for them to have a private place," said Cora.

"Nice," the old woman said with a laugh. "I guess we know what you think is nice with all them children you have. We've all had it. When winter comes, there'll be more of it."

Cora looked properly shocked, but she could not wait to tell Mary what the old woman had said so they could have a good laugh.

The sun moved quietly down below the horizon. Instantly there was a different light. It was a mix of cloud-reflected sunlight and early starlight. The golden glow reflected off each object it touched so that everything stood out as if giving off an inner luminescence. Each stem, blade of grass, stone, crack or abrasion, bird, beak, and feather was more defined than with the energy of pure daylight. The radiance that separated each thing from the whole object also seemed to fan out and unite everything with the eerie glow. The gray shadows darkened, people talked in hushed voices.

The mood was right for Mary and Joe to go over the threshold of the finished house first. After they were inside a few moments according to custom, the others went in quickly, bringing some piece of household goods, such as the cedar chest, rocking chair, a bundle of clothing. Some were disappointed about the meagerness of the furniture, but others nodded in quiet approval. Several men brought armloads of sweet, wild grass to put under the bedding until wooden bed frames could be made. By now the light was faded to dark gray and the twinkling stars were clearly visible. People's voices became bright and gay. They chattered like a flock of sparrows.

Joe beat a tin cup on the Majestic range for quiet. "My family and I thank every one of you, and to show our appreciation we'd like to give a gift to each of you." A murmur went through the crowd that sounded like a babbling brook right after a thunderstorm. Joe beat the cup on the range. "You and I know that's impossible, so I'd like to give each man a chance to have this brand-new bowie knife." He held the knife above his head so all could see. "Then some lucky lady will have a chance to own this splint broom." Mary held the broom high.

The murmur grew to a loud buzz like the wind in the tops of trees, and then there was a clapping of hands.

"I saw both of them there prizes being made this afternoon," someone said. "Joe's a right smart smith," said another. "My old lady'd like that swell broom."

Ell had paper slips with everyone's name. Charlie put the slips in his father's broad-brimmed hat. He took the hat to the middle of the crowd, stirred them a moment, then held the hat on the top of his head so he could not see inside. All the time he was talking to keep the crowd quiet and amused. "I'll tell you what I'm going to do! I'll get these papers mixed real good! The first name that is pulled out will be the proud owner of Pa's dandy present to you all—the all-purpose bowie knife, if he be a man!"

Someone joked, "And if *he* be a woman?"

Charlie answered, "Then that woman is the happy owner of the splint broom Ma made." Charlie looked over the crowd as he held the hat on the top of his head, adding to the anticipation. An idea popped into his head. "We have a genuine preacher here with us. Reverend Roundtree from Nicodemus! He will lead us in prayer, so everybody, bow your heads." Charlie nodded his head, nearly spilling the papers from the hat he held on top, toward the Reverend who was as astonished as the others. But Charlie saw the first look on the Reverend's face and knew everything was all right. The Reverend was pleased as a cat with cream. Some of the people had not noticed the Reverend's dark skin and now stood back as if awed or afraid of someone different.

Reverend Roundtree was used to public speaking. He picked up a wooden kitchen chair and stood on it so everyone could have a good look. People moved around from the back so that he faced everyone. The only noise was the scuffling of feet; people, for the most part, kept their mouths closed, waiting to see what would happen. They saw the Reverend's shirt was spotless, where it was caked with mud a few hours before. His trousers were clean and dry, but stiff from being dried by first being beaten on a large stone, then lying out in the hot sun. His boots were shiny from being polished with handfuls of cottonwood leaves. He smiled and the wide X-shaped scar on his cheek looked more like a cross. His hands raised and spread out, encompassing everyone in the room. He bowed his head. The people's nervous stirring quieted. "Oh, Lord, our Father in Heaven, we, Your chilluns, thank You for this here powerful feeling of friendship. We praise You! Oh, Lord, remember us the year round. Bless this house and all who enter it. We praise You! Hallelujah!" He raised his head and the people responded.

"Hallelujah!"

The room beams seemed to vibrate and dirt sift from the walls to the shiny dark floor. The Reverend put his arms down. "This is the best house-raisin' I've been to in my entire life. The fellowship is strong and the food is excellent. What we needs now is music. Mr. Irwin can play his fiddle and we'll sing 'The Old Rugged Cross.'"

Charlie took the hatful of little papers from his head. He saw that no one was standing back with awe or fear. In fact, when the Reverend had them sing "I'm Gwine to Alabamy," many were toe-tapping and hand-clapping. Charlie wondered if he could get back and have the drawing. It seemed people had now put that behind and were more eager to sing. It dawned on him this was what Colonel Johnson was saying when he told Charlie not to upstage him. Charlie motioned for the Reverend to step off the chair a moment. The people kept singing, "For to see my mammy—Ah."

Charlie said, "Don't upstage my drawing for the prize too long, cuz at midnight this house turns to a punkin."

The Reverend chuckled and winked at Charlie, then climbed back on the chair and sang with the people. Charlie sang so loud he could not hear the others. It felt good. When the song was over, Charlie moved in front of Reverend Roundtree. "I'll tell you what I'm going to do right now!" Charlie's voice boomed out around all the people. "The Reverend will reach into this hat I'm holding on the top of my head. He will give it one more good stirring. Then he will take out one slip of paper and open it." Charlie could feel the Reverend stirring the papers, and the room was still as snow falling into a moonlit river. Charlie moved to one side and looked up. The Reverend held a slip in his hand and his eyes were shut tight. "Open your eyes and read the name of the lucky winner!"

The Reverend looked at the paper and his black eyes grew wide, then they squinted down, as if he couldn't read the writing. His mouth formed a circle, then flattened out as he licked his lips. "The Lord, he is playing tricks on my eyesight!"

"What does the paper say?" someone shouted. "Let Charlie read it!" called another.

The Reverend handed the slip to Charlie, who nearly doubled over with laughter. "Folks, you saw that this here drawing was fair and square. Isn't that right?"

Everyone answered, "Yes!"

"Well, the name Reverend Roundtree pulled from my pa's hat is his own! The bowie knife goes to Reverend Roundtree!" Charlie turned and reached up and shook the Reverend's hand. The Reverend was all smiles. The crowd was all smiles and applause. Charlie felt a great relief, because he saw what the Reverend had at first imagined, that the crowd could have as easily turned and made wrongful accusations. Joe presented the knife in a leather case to the Reverend. Charlie felt the need to keep the momentum going. He climbed up on the chair.

"I need a lady volunteer to stir the papers and pull out another winner!" he called.

Cora Collins came forward and stirred with her whole fist. The people held their breath to see what would happen this time. Charlie held the hat up and bent so that Cora could just reach in. "Now, on this bit of paper is the name of a lady—"

"What if it's a man?" came a voice from the back.

"We'll draw again!" Charlie smiled. "On this paper may be the name of the lady who will have her floors shining with gratitude. She'll have a new splint broom!"

Cora held the slip of paper between her thumb and forefinger as her eyes moved over the crowd. "Cass Minney, Grandma Minney!" There was a buzzing in the crowd and a movement on the left side. Finally some of the people moved away so that Charlie could see the old grandmother who had brought the tiny poke of cinnamon. She was sound asleep in his ma's rocking chair.

Mary was beside the old woman, patting her hands and whispering in her ear. Her eyes flew open and her toothless gums parted.

"For me? Thank you! Mine? Why I've never won anything before!" Mary gave her a hug and laid the broom across her lap. Both women had watery eyes.

Cora whispered, "Praise the Lord! It couldn't have gone to a better lady!"

Charlie was back on the chair waving his arms. "There's dancing out on the prairie, and I know for a fact that my pa is playing the fiddle and Reverend Roundtree is calling the square dances!"

Charlie gave back his pa's hat and saw Matt smiling and talking with Jack Collins. They were both as happy as Charlie that the Reverend had won the bowie knife. Charlie was going to say something to the two men, until he saw Rob Collins sidle close to Ell, who carried a saltcellar.

"What's the salt for?" Rob asked. "You fixing some grub for your other men friends?" His eyes ran over the length of her.

Ell's green eyes locked with Rob's blue ones. "Some of us women that felt the need to make a wish sprinkled salt over our left shoulder," she said and turned her head away.

"Take a walk with me. You wished for me, didn't you?" Rob had a pleading in his voice. He leaned purposefully closer. Ell felt the goose pimples rise, but it was not all excitement. She felt anger. He'd looked at her like some prize filly he'd found and intended to break in. Such conceit! she thought.

Charlie wanted to step in and tell Rob to get lost, but he decided he ought to see if Ell was right first. She'd said she could take care of herself.

"Hell's fire, who'd miss us?" he insisted. "We could get to be real good friends."

Ell was not only angry, she was afraid Rob could make a scene and spoil this wonderful time for everyone. She decided to walk with him, staying near the square dance area.

Les Miner put his hand on Charlie's shoulder. "I've been looking for your sister. I'd like to dance with her. You seen where she went?"

"Sure," said Charlie. He had a feeling of relief. "She went outside, probably wanted to dance."

Miner hurried outside. He caught up to Ell. He saw that Rob walked with her, but chose to ignore him because he was known as a troublemaker in the area, used to making everything go his way.

"I'm glad the Reverend got your pa's knife. Course, I would have liked it," Miner said.

"Actually, the Reverend worked harder. He's still working, listen . . ." said Ell.

They could hear the Reverend calling, "Hunt your partners, and a do-si-do we'll go!"

"You be my partner?" said Miner

"I love to dance," said Ell. She looked at Rob.

"Go on—I can't dance. I'll wait," Rob said. "Then I'll take you for that walk."

"Thanks," said Ell. She turned away from Rob, but heard him cuss under his breath.

"Damnit, I'll have my way with you yet!"

"Nice the old woman got the broom. I like her, even when she's sleeping, better'n that pest, Rob. He's not likable in my book. Your folks are sure well liked. Nice thing to do. You know, the drawing. Makes folks feel appreciated."

Miner was talking close to Ell's ear. She enjoyed the tickling sensation his breath caused and she giggled.

"What if you'd won the broom?" she said.

"Well, I can't clean house any more'n I can sew lace on a collar. Anyway, that's woman's work. Don't you think so?"

"I think that's what most men would say. I'd say a person ought to do what he does best. For instance, if I can set a broken bone better'n you, then I ought to do that. If you can make lye soap better'n me, then you ought to do that."

Miner's brown eyes were flecked with yellow and reminded Ell of a friendly pup. "A little girl like you can set broken bones?"

"I can," she said matter-of-factly.

"Then your logic makes sense. Let's dance."

Everyone was dancing. Frank was hopping up and down with one of the Collinses' little girls. Charlie twirled baby Carrie around several times. She became dizzy and staggered around him giggling. He munched on a pocketful of dried apples. The smaller children held their hands out for pieces of apple. Once in a while Charlie danced around with a child sitting on his shoulder.

Rob was with Will when they heard of some of the men

cracking a couple of jugs of hard cider that were in the back of the Brays' wagon. The two of them joined the drinking until Rob noticed Ell sitting in the grass talking to Art Wells, while Miner went for eats.

"I've got some unfinished business," he said to Will, and ambled over to Ell. "You avoiding me?" he asked, smiling so that the lantern light near Joe and the Reverend glinted off a soft gold barely traceable mustache above his lip. "What have I done to deserve such treatment?" He was trying to be charming.

Ell knew she'd promised to walk with him and now wished she hadn't. "I'm not avoiding you," she said, but turning her head so as not to meet his gaze. "I have to be a good hostess and dance and talk with everybody. It's expected of a good neighbor."

"Be a good neighbor and take a short walk with me, then," he said.

There was no way out. She rolled her eyes skyward as if to say, I'd prefer not, but I must, after all, he worked on the soddy.

"I'll probably eat that corn pone Les is bringing for you!" called Wells.

"See, I said you bachelor boys eat everything in sight!" Ell called back teasingly.

"I'm not letting you go this time," said Rob. He took one of Ell's hands. "We'll go down by the creek and sit on the gravel bar. I'll show you my favorite constellation."

Twilight was long gone and the sky glittered with millions of silver stars. The air was still, bone-dry, and cool. An owl somewhere in a tree by the creek called. A whippoorwill called back. Ell did not take her hand back. She felt relaxed and fancied she could make the walk something enjoyable.

"See there in the western sky is Venus, a planet of love and beauty," he said.

She saw it bright and clear, low on the horizon.

They walked without speaking. Then Rob had his left arm around Ell's waist, and he moved in front of her and put his right arm across her shoulders and held her hard against himself, his left hand slipping down past the small of her back, resting on her buttock.

Ell gasped and she became alert. She pushed herself free and ran to the gravel bar. "Now show me your stars."

Rob was displeased he'd let her go so easily. "You'll like what I show you," he said dreamily.

Ell felt a curious warming in her midsection. She was inquisitive of what he'd show, but also, since the experience in the barn and talk with Charlie, she was fearful not knowing what liberties he might try.

"You can't be afraid of me?" he said roughly.

"You? What's there to be afraid of? Your parents are friends with mine," she said. "Thus, you must be honorable. What do you want me to see?"

"Honorable—right," he said. He felt suddenly off balance. No one had called him honorable before. "Why don't we just sit here and watch for falling stars? They look so close you can catch one. See the five stars in the shape of a chair? Know who sits there?" he asked. He lay back on the gravel to look up.

"That's the old Greek Goddess—my grandma told me," said Ell.

Rob turned and pulled on her arm. "I'm supposed to tell the answers." He laughed arrogantly.

She lost her balance as he pulled and she fell off the stone she sat on. Her legs flew out and her skirt billowed upward. She began to laugh and get up. It was an opportunity Rob would not let pass. He rolled to her, took her head between his large hands, and pressed his mouth to hers.

Ell felt his lips warm and hard as they moved against hers. His hands held her shoulders and one leg came across her thighs so that she could not move. She felt his tongue move against her lips, along with a tingling sensation that spread downward to her chest and to that strange place in her belly where the fire grew and spread wherever he touched her. She opened her mouth and his tongue darted between her lips. Ell pressed her tongue against his and her heart seemed to swell and beat faster. The wet kiss was a wonderful new sensation. Her hands grasped at his shoulders and curled around his neck.

Time was suspended. Rob's breathing was fast and he fumbled at the hooks and eyes on the front of her dress. His hands brushed against her breasts.

"Don't! Don't do this!" she whispered.

"One look! Ell, please!" he pleaded.

His words gave Ell a delicious shiver that roared down her back to that center fire. His hands worked on her camisole. Suddenly one hand slid under the garment and cupped her breast. Her whole chest was on fire. It was an eternity before her hands covered his and pushed them aside with astounding strength. She heard a twig snap. Her mind awakened and became alert. She heard shouts and footsteps, or was it her imagination?

Rob knew he could overpower her, and he desperately wanted to. But something in the back of his mind held him, either the look on her face, or the compliment she'd given when she said he was honorable. "Jesus Christ!" he whispered. "I just want to look. I won't hurt you. You'd feel good just showing me, I promise. Give me my way!"

"I can't!" she whispered. "Don't spoil this night. There's someone coming!" She twisted away and her fingers were clumsy as she put her clothing in order.

Rob swore again and moaned as he pulled himself away from her and stood up.

"I hear noises!" Ell felt ill at ease. She gave a stifled laugh and started back toward the dancers.

A rustle in the grass and a drunken roar of surprise caused both Ell and Rob to jump back. It was Will toting Charlie's Henry rifle. "I'm looking for a pal to do a little target practicing with me!" he shouted. "Hey—I've found him! Come on, Robby. I'll prove I can shoot better'n you." Will staggered out on the gravel bar. "I've three tomato cans for targets and a handful of shells."

Ell knew she'd run into trouble. Will was so shaky he couldn't hit the side of a barn.

Rob took one look at the rifle and his eyes gleamed. "Let me sight through once. You think we can see in this light? There's only half a moon up there."

"I'll put the cans on that big white rock. We'll see it. Who was that with you? You and one of the boys came out to skip flat stones in the creek or tell dirty jokes?" asked Will. "Or you scouting Injuns?"

Rob chuckled.

Ell was running so fast she had a stitch in her side. She stopped and bent over to ease the pain.

Charlie was coming down the path with his rope over his shoulder.

"Hey, Ell! I thought you were dancing. You see Will? He swiped my rifle and ran around bragging about what a good shot he is. I aim to rope him and bring him in before Pa finds out he's been in the hard cider. Jeems, I hope he doesn't fire that rifle."

Charlie didn't wait for an answer but ran on toward the creek.

He found Will and Rob setting up the empty tomato cans and swung the rope around his head a couple of times. Will must have heard the whir of the loop in the air, because he turned his head to look across the gravel bar just as the loop settled around his shoulders. The rifle clattered to the stones and Will yelled as though he'd been caught in a bobcat trap. Rob hid behind the big white rock, thinking they'd for sure been attacked by Injuns.

Charlie tied his end of the rope to an oak tree and went out to pick up his rifle. He kept beyond the distance of the rope length. He heard Will moaning and Rob breathing fast little shallow breaths. He picked up the rifle, wiped it off on his sleeve. Then he went to Will, who was lying on his face.

"Don't shoot!" cried Will. "You can have the gun!"

"Damn tootin', I can!" yelled Charlie. "And why'd you think I'd shoot you? I'm Charlie—your kid brother."

Will groaned again.

Charlie put a foot in the middle of Will's back. "Give me the shells you swiped, or I'll stomp on your back."

"Take the shells out of my right front pocket. Don't stomp on my back—I'll throw up. Oh, I'm not feeling so good."

Charlie took the shells and put them in his own pocket. He waited for Will to heave. Then they went back to the dancing and sat on the sidelines to watch. The little children were all asleep in wagons, or under wagons.

Ell was dancing with Miner. She spotted Charlie. "Let's tell my brother Charlie to get some water or coffee for Pa and Reverend Roundtree. They've been playing and hollering out dances for quite a while."

"Now, that's good thinking!" said Miner. "I'll go with Charlie and get me some salt pork wrapped in corn pone. Dancing gives me an appetite. You want some?"

"I can't eat anything more. I just want to dance. So hurry or I'll find your friend Art Wells to dance with," teased Ell.

They took both cold water and hot coffee to Joe and the Reverend. Joe asked Charlie to stay and sing a while so that the Reverend could rest his voice. Charlie not only sang, but also did a few rope tricks to entertain the crowd and give his pa a rest from fiddling.

Back with Ell, Miner said, "You know this is the most fun I've had since some of the boys gave a Welshman some likker and took his carbide lamp so's he thought he'd been poisoned and had gone blind."

"You didn't?" Ell giggled.

"No—but some other sport did. That Welshman came near

putting his teeth down the sport's throat when he found it was a joke."

Ell and Miner danced until the pearl-gray dawn appeared. Then Miner remembered he'd left a few chores at his place. He smiled, patted her hand, and hurried off to locate his horse. He turned and called, "See you sometime soon."

Ell waved and smiled. She realized she was tired and for the first time noticed most of the people had already left. Her mother and Cora Collins washed dishes inside the new sod house. Charlie dried and stacked them.

They could hear the last stragglers call out good-byes and the wagon wheels grind over gravel. There was singing in the distance as the wagons rolled down the two ruts called a road.

Jack Collins came in the house to say that he had all the little children rolled up in blankets and in the back of the wagon. It was now sunup and time to go on home. Cora wiped her hands, gave Mary a hug, and waited for Jack to shake Joe's hand. Then they were gone.

"That's everyone," said Joe with a sigh. "It's just us, the Irwins, and this land now."

"Someone ought to see if Rob Collins is still at the creek!" said Charlie.

"He's in the back of the wagon, dead to the world. As sound asleep as Will and Frank are on the hay back there in their room," said Joe.

Charlie went to the boys' bedroom and fell into his blankets, not bothering to remove more than his coiled rope. He was asleep instantly.

Ell took a candle to see where her blankets were in her bedroom and blew it out after curling up in a down quilt. She knew she'd sleep through the next day.

Mary arranged the comforters over the clean hay in her and Joe's bedroom. She pushed extra hay under Joe's place.

Joe's voice was quiet. "It is going to be a good home. The people are the best. My dear, look at that sun coming up through the window. You'll have to get some curtains up. Won't bother me now, though. I'll sleep all day."

"Me, too," Mary said with a sigh. "Those women are wonderful. I'm kind of looking forward to new settlers coming in. We'll have more parties."

"This was not only a party—it was work. Don't you know what a party can be like?"

She murmured, "I guess I do."

"I'll tell you what. I'll wake up at noon and if the younguns are still asleep and I feel more strength, I'll show you a party in the hay, Mrs. Irwin."

"I'm looking forward to it," she said with a smile curling her lips. She closed her eyes and was asleep.

TEN

Goodland, Kansas

Goodland grew from one soddy, which housed the Sherman County Development Company, to several hundred soddies from June to November 1887. The business buildings were lined side by side along both sides of a wide dirt road called Main Street. Several of the buildings were fronted with clapboard so they looked modern and permanent. The expensive, eight-thousand-dollar wooden courthouse was at the eastern end of the street. There were rumors that a future Rock Island Railroad line would run parallel with Main Street.

That fall a Grand Rally was planned by A. B. Montgomery, the secretary of the Sherman County Development Company, to show off Goodland as a rapid-growing, booming agricultural center. Montgomery had no idea that later he would be called the Father of Goodland. The Homesteaders Union Association put on a drive to name Goodland the Sherman county seat. It was opposed by a few businessmen who preferred the county seat to be Eustis, a town boasting of a sheriff and a jail, which Goodland lacked. Eustis was a mile northeast from Goodland.

On Friday, November 2, the Irwins attended the Grand Rally. Two brass bands played and A. B. Montgomery gave a speech about the humming town of Goodland. He had a gold watch in his vest pocket that was attached to one of the vest buttons by a gold chain. He looked at the watch frequently as he talked.

"I'd like a pocket watch," said Charlie.

"You have to be somebody big first," said Frank.

Joe looked at the boys, meaning that they should hush so that he could hear the speech.

Montgomery was saying that there might be as many as thirty-five hundred people in Goodland this day for the Grand Rally. When he sat down, there was a speech by a man who represented the opposing town, Eustis, for county seat. This man was Jesse Tait, editor of the Eustis paper, the *Dark Horse*.

"Let's go. I've heard enough," said Joe. "Eustis hasn't a snowball's chance in mid-July. By summer she'll move her main buildings over to Goodland. Eustis is as good as dead as a town even before the election."

They walked to the edge of town to see the horse-racing event.

"I've always wanted to race. Always," Frank said in a high-pitched voice.

Charlie knew that Frank could stick to any of the horses. "Pa, he's so small the horse won't feel a thing. If Frank digs his heels in the horse's sides and talks into its ear, he could have a winner."

Joe scowled, but told the horse owner, who wore a sheepskin jacket and a wide-brimmed hat, that Frank wanted to try out as a jockey.

Charlie saw Frank's eyes light up. Frank broke away to rub the legs of the black horse he'd chosen to ride in the first of the races.

Later the racehorse owner in the sheepskin jacket spoke to Joe, who'd come to see the finish of the races. "On horseback your kid is beautiful, agile, smooth as royal blood. He's like a little prince and we ought to pay him to ride for us." The man reached into his pocket and said to Frank, "Here's two bucks. You can ride for us anytime." The man put his hand on Joe's shoulder. "Your kid came in first on anything he rode. It must be a natural-born instinct. When he rode I saw him shift weight ever so slightly, had me worried, but as I watched I saw the horse slow down or speed up as the weight shift seemed to direct."

Frank smiled, blinked, and wrinkled his nose so that the freckles ran together like overfilled mud puddles, but Charlie felt the man overdid the flattery with Frank. Joe got close so that

Frank could hear him over the string band. "It's time to leave. I'm proud of you, son."

Still grinning, Frank raised his eyes toward his racehorse friend.

The morning of November 19, 1887, Les came after Charlie and Ell to go to the rally in Eustis.

After sampling the food at the K. P. Hall the three young people decided it was time to leave. The wind had come up and the clouds were the kind that can dump bushels of snow in an hour or two. Charlie was excited because he was sure he'd spotted Rob Collins's cotton-white head in the center of a bunch of boys. "Where there's Rob, there's trouble," he whispered to Miner.

Ell wanted to stay for the dance, but she didn't want to run into Rob, and she knew it would snow before they hit Sappa Meadows. Reluctantly she climbed into the wagon and pulled a quilt tight around her lap and saved some to wrap around Miner.

Charlie climbed into the back and wrapped himself in another quilt. He kept his face out of the wind and felt warm, contented, and sleepy. He was not sure he really cared whether Eustis or Goodland became the county seat. What did it matter? He didn't have to decide.

Miner looked ahead but he thought how beautiful Ell looked in the white shirtwaist with tiny tucks around the neckline and on top of the puffed sleeves. Her deep-green flannel skirt matched the color of her eyes and was tight-fitting at the waist, but had a wide ruffle at the bottom that swept the tops of her patent-leather shoes. Now her hands were resting in her brown cloth muff. Her brown coat fit snugly over her skirt. Mary's silver filigreed cameo brooch showed at her neck. The wispy, wild fringes of hair poked out around the edge of her wool cap and were blown tight against her face. Miner thought about touching one of those soft, quince-colored wisps. He looked back and saw that Charlie's eyes were closed. "Tired?" he whispered to Ell.

"A little," she said. "It's the constant wind."

"Either hot or cold," he said, putting his arm around her and holding the reins in the other hand.

The wind blew down Charlie's back. He pulled the quilt tighter. He looked up and was surprised to find his sister and his friend sitting close together. "Jeems!" he yelled. "Have you two chucked your senses or is it getting that cold out here?"

Miner's face turned crimson. He turned to look at Charlie.

"That's right. It must be way below freezing. And the wind's blowing so hard we couldn't hear each other unless we sat close."

"I didn't know you liked to talk!" Charlie yelled against the wind.

"Well—there's times, like when lots of people are around, I can't talk at all. But when I'm with good friends, like you, it's easier to say things. You know, some people make all the difference." Miner turned back and drew Ell even closer.

"I know. With some people I feel as out of place as a cow in the front room!" hollered Charlie. He adjusted the quilt up around his ears and again closed his eyes.

Ell whispered to Miner, "What do you see when you close your eyes?"

Miner was amused. He felt a warm glow in the pit of his stomach. "I see green eyes and shining, fawn-colored hair, a little pink nose."

Charlie's eyes flew open. He hooted. The wind carried Miner's words to the back of the wagon. "Sounds like you see the tabby cat in the barn! Want to know what I see with my eyes closed? I see a rope in a perfect loop floating above the clouds."

Ell turned so that she could see Charlie. She smiled and stuck out the tip of her tongue. "A rope is all you ever think about. If you went to a wedding, you'd have your rope over your shoulder."

Miner pulled back his arm and held the reins loosely in his hands. The horse plodded along the road, unheeding of the light snowflakes that dusted its back.

"Close your eyes, Ell, and tell us what you see," said Miner.

A deep sigh arose from the middle of Ell's chest. "I see firm, warm lips, a strong chin, rough as sandpaper." She ignored Charlie's laugh and looked toward Miner, her eyes crinkled half-closed.

Miner felt a warmth spread through his loins. This girl with the flashing green eyes could arouse a man with words as well as with the way she caused her eyes to glisten, her head to tilt, or her graceful body to move.

"Watch out," warned Charlie. "I heard Will say that half the men in Goodland are in love with Ell. I think she encourages them. You remember how that brain-sick Rob Collins acted when he saw the girl he thinks he's mad about hanging on to the arm of someone else?"

"Charlie, hush!" cautioned Ell.

Miner let the horse have more slack and hoped Charlie could

not see how he felt. He vowed that he'd never let Rob Collins, nor his ilk, have Ell. He was drawn to those flashing green eyes like a nail to a magnet. She was his girl. He could take care of her. The snowflakes were larger and coming in eddies with the wind gusts.

Suddenly Charlie knew that Miner was gathering courage to court his sister.

Ell spoke and her words were so unexpected that Charlie felt like he was hit with a sheet of ice. "I've thought of going back to Missouri because I miss teaching."

Charlie sucked in his breath and hoped no one heard the faint hiss of air going to his lungs over the howling wind. A dull ache throbbed in his chest. He knew his ma and pa would make a fuss. He'd miss Ell even if she was a girl. He didn't want her to leave. A family ought to stay together, he reasoned.

The snow made noiseless white swirls under the horse's hooves.

Miner was so startled he could not speak right away. Finally he said, "Have you thought of teaching around here?"

Charlie held his breath, knowing she'd taught the Collinses' little ones off and on.

"Yes," she said. "The Mennonites have a school for their own kind and Reverend Wallace and his wife have the settlers' school near Gandy. Frank goes there with mostly kids from the Gandy family. Then there's a Mr. Koon with a school in Shermanville. That's north eight or ten miles. There's no schoolhouse for me."

Charlie felt cold air creep across his shoulders and thought, so that's what she wants—her own schoolhouse. He hitched the quilt up some.

Miner had a momentary emptiness in his belly and his chest squeezed tight with a stabbing pain. It wasn't shyness, but some real physical infirmity now that made it an effort for him to talk. Miner was frightened. He'd never been weak or frail in his life. He thought a good belt of corn whiskey would loosen the cords in his neck. "Are you some kind of quitter?" he sputtered.

Ell pulled herself up so her back was straight. The snowflakes blowing against her long lashes made her blink. "I hate it! This wind and cold and then the wind and heat." Her eyes watered and spilled over so her cheeks were shiny wet. She found a handkerchief in her reticule and wiped her eyes.

Charlie's mind was numb and he could not think. He let the quilt slip so that he could hear better.

"You don't look too happy with the idea of leaving," said

Miner, breathing deep into the cold air, then saying quickly, "Try thinking of the wind that ripples and flashes the tall grasses or pushes the snow in swirls that look like froth on an ocean wave. Think of heat and drought causing the prairie grasses to grow roots as deep as a two-story house. That root-tangled soil is unfazed by most plows. That's why it makes such good sod brick. Have you ever thought of this country as beautiful with wine-colored grasses and a rainbow of wildflowers blooming like a granny's patchwork quilt? The groves of trees around creeks and springs are like cool, green islands of shade in summer. People here are like solid, country rock. They endure days of isolation, snowed in. They survive weeks of dehydration while under the summer glare. Their hearts are big. They'd do anything for a neighbor in trouble, and they always look for some excuse to have a party. There's never a locked door. Even the thieving land grabbers honor a man's home if it's being lived in. These folks find peace of mind on this prairie that they won't get from a mountain or forest. Mountains and forests make these folks suffocate. Sure, sometimes they get feisty, but it fades and everyone's friends. Stay and you'll see I'm right. Try to like this prairie a little. It grows on a person, I swear."

Charlie wanted to stand up and clap his hands and cheer. It was the best Kansas speech he'd heard. He turned to say so, but Miner was not paying Charlie any heed. His head was close to Ell's and she was saying something in a low whisper, which sounded like "I've had a sign."

"A sign?" repeated Miner.

"I found a stone with a hole in the center. The small end pointed to the east, like an arrowhead, in the direction of Missouri."

"Superstition? You run your life by meaningless signs?"

"Don't be sarcastic!" Ell pulled the quilt tighter around her throat. She brushed at her eyes with the back of her hand. "My grandmother taught me signs. She was wonderful. She could have read medicine if she'd had the chance. And she'd have been a famous medical doctor. Actually she was a well-known herb doctor."

Miner hardly thought before speaking. He was not playing a game, but he was fighting for something he desperately wanted. "Ell, you're the wonderful teacher here. You can be famous. Honest. You're smart with letters and numbers and wonderful working with little children." His throat ached. "And you learn fast. Your ma told me you learned to crochet and did some of them rugs at your place. They sure add a glory of color to the floor. I wish I had one for my place."

Ell's emerald eyes lighted with the praise. She relaxed. "I could make you one before I go."

Miner squinted down the nearly invisible road. He hoped the horse was on the road to the Irwin farm as he turned and looked at Ell. "Look, if you really wanted to leave—it seems to me that you'd be acting happy."

Ell's hand came out of her muff and went to her mouth and tears welled again in her eyes. She wiped her eyes and blew her nose, then sat perfectly still. She brushed Miner's arm when she put a hand back inside her muff. "Once I start crying or feeling sad, it's hard to stop."

Miner felt a tingling all the way through his coat and sweater sleeve. She looked at him and smiled and he saw the snowflakes melt off her rosy cheeks. Miner thought he was going to black out. It was a moment before he could breathe normal again.

"You're right," she said. "Honestly, I find the buffalo grass with patches of wildflowers a lovely sight. I care about prairie people like you." She took out her handkerchief and wiped her eyes with finality. "Truly, I like you."

Miner wanted to hug Ell. He wanted to hold her delicate pink face close to his, to feel her warm hand over his wind-chilled hand. He wanted to hear her soft voice rise and fall as the wind undulated in the yellow, dried grasses that were now covered with fluffy, white snow. He felt vibrant with joy. She cared about him. She really liked him.

Charlie couldn't take the silence. "Going around the coffeepot trying to find the handle will about cover the extent of Ell's travels to Missouri, I'd reckon." No one disagreed with him so he continued. "How come you live alone?"

"I guess you mean me," said Miner, stretching out his legs as if he had a cramp in each one. "Well, mainly, I ain't found anyone I want to live with." Now he paused. He wanted to say more. He was not sure the time was right. He squeezed his chin thinking that the longer he waited the more uncertain he was.

Charlie and Ell sat quiet, neither dared to breathe.

"Oh, you mean my folks," said Miner, hedging. "Pa was a Colorado miner and was shot over the Independence claim. Ma died of pneumonia the next winter."

Ell's hands went to her mouth. "I had no idea," she whispered.

"I never told you before."

She put her hand on his arm and left it there.

His heart pounded so hard he thought everyone could hear it. Then miraculously his mind cleared and he had a sudden idea about Ell's teaching. "The Wallaces teach mostly older kids and let them go in the fall and spring for harvesting and planting. Well, listen to this idea. You teach the young'uns and keep 'em in school all fall, winter, and spring until the weather gets hot and dry. You could really learn 'em with all that time. Forget Missouri. It's behind. Your life is here—with these little schoolkids and me."

Charlie let out his breath before he exploded. He wanted to climb up to the seat and shake Miner's hand.

Ell cried out in a funny, high-pitched voice, "My life with you?"

"Yes. You and me." Miner almost choked. He did not intend to say this. He'd wanted to think about it longer. He'd never really thought about having a wife. Why, early this morning a wife was the farthest thing from his mind. And there was a burr to his happiness. He was certain that Ell was the sort who needed more than a sod hut to decorate and keep clean from bedbugs, cockroaches, and rats. She was strong-minded and would have a say in what her man did and how his work would affect her. She needed challenge.

Ell was quiet as the wagon pulled up into the yard beside the Irwin soddy. She did not make a move to get out of the wagon. Miner's chest was tight with anxiousness and his heart beat with hope. He hoped Ell's hand still on his arm was a good sign.

Charlie was up folding his quilt. He nudged Miner. "We're home, old-timer." Charlie stamped his feet on the ground to shake out the stiffness and shake off the numbness. "Say, you want to stay at our place till this snow blows itself out?"

Miner was tempted. "Thanks." He was out of the wagon now, helping Ell climb down. "I'd best get back and feed my stock and get the wood inside before everything's hidden from sight. Look at those flakes coming down!"

Charlie folded the other blanket and left it on the seat of the wagon. Then he walked backward toward the soddy's front door. He grinned because he was sure neither Ell nor Miner saw him as they stood there holding hands, looking at each other as if they were statues. Ell moved first by putting her hands up to Miner's face. She kissed him full on the mouth, then broke away, and fled inside with Charlie.

Then and there Miner promised himself he'd talk to families

with small children ready for school around Goodland. And he'd build a one-room soddy for Ell to use as a school wherever she wanted it. He thought, by God, it's a good feeling doing something for another person. I'll get on this project right away. He climbed into the wagon, picked up the reins, and started his horse on a slow turn and then back down the lane to the main road. He whistled into the wind, enjoying the snappy bite of the blowing snow. There were swirling white sheets moving this way and that, depending on the wind gusts.

Ell hung her coat and muff on the wall peg and then stood in front of the wood-framed, oval mirror above the pie table. She smiled and put her fingers to her lips. She looked at one side of her face, then the other. She took off her bonnet and fluffed her hair around her face. Then she pulled out the silver combs and let it fall down her back. She held it up in a golden ponytail. Not yet satisfied, she let go so that it hung like a shawl. She tossed her head to shake the hair down her back like a long sheaf of wheat.

Joe was stirring some horse liniment he'd made. "What's the excitement in Eustis?"

Charlie was warming his feet by the kitchen range. "Not much. About the same as Goodland's." He inhaled the head-clearing camphor in the brown liniment mixture.

"The election's in three days. Then we'll know which place is *big,*" said Joe.

"Pa, we didn't stay for the dance because Charlie thought he saw Rob Collins," said Ell.

"Maybe he did." Joe looked at Charlie. "You scared of that Collins kid?"

"I don't know. He acts before he thinks—remember?"

"Rob's nothing but an immature rascal," said Joe. "If he's smart he'll grow up and forget about being a rascal."

"I'm glad we don't have rascal problems," called Mary from the bedroom, where she was putting a mustard plaster on Frank's congested chest. He had one of his winter colds again. "My heart aches for Cora Collins, raising all those children."

"What about us?" asked Charlie. "Do we make your heart ache?"

"You're not the same kind of rascals!" snapped Joe. Then he stepped over and put his hand on Charlie's shoulder. "Rely on your good sense. It'll get you through most situations." He poured liniment through a funnel into a brown glass gallon jug. Joe was a prodigiously huge man. Over six feet tall and weighing close to three hundred pounds. He gave confidence to anyone who was around him and assurance that nothing dire could happen if he were in charge.

Will had come into the soddy from the barn. He'd cut off a ham roast from the dressed deer hanging frozen from the rafters. "What if Goodland wins the election and is legally the county seat? Eustis will have to give up its files of county records to Goodland."

"Miner and me heard that Eustis has some people who will get a junction to forbid removal of those records. I thought *junction* was 'to join together,'" said Charlie. He pushed his hair from his eyes.

Will chuckled and Joe held up his hand. "Son, that's *in*junction. It means those people forbid anyone from Goodland taking those papers from Eustis."

"That doesn't sound right to me," said Mary, washing off the venison ham.

"'Tisn't. And I 'spect the HUAers will do something about it, even if we have to fight this gol-durned blizzard," said Joe.

"I wish I could go with you to vote," said Charlie.

"Les'll vote," said Ell.

"Sure, he'll vote for Goodland so that when it's the county seat, there has to be a school for little kids. Les knows a wonderful schoolmarm who'd love to teach them kids," said Charlie, dancing a little jig in front of Ell.

Ell's face went fiery red. "Charlie! You didn't have to listen to everything, then blab. That's sneaky!"

Joe held his hand up so she would stop yelling.

"The wind was pretty loud, maybe I didn't hear everything. But I saw everything. You kissed Les while I was trying to get the front latch unfastened."

Ell's mouth was open but no words were coming out.

Charlie halfway wished he hadn't spilled the beans about Ell's impetuous kiss. He tried to smooth it over. "Boy, I really liked what Les said about the prairie. He's smart, you know. I could love this land like he does." His eyes twinkled and he felt better.

Mary looked up from the range. "I'm glad Ell likes Les."

"Does that mean he's your sweetheart?" asked Will.

"Ma! Will! Charlie!" Ell was furious. "It's none of your concern—my likes and my friends!"

Joe wiped the liniment off his hands on a dishtowel. "But it's my business! I'm head of this here family! I'd like quiet! Ell is too young for sweethearts!"

The rest of the evening Joe watched his daughter from the corner of his eye. He could see that she was not a girl, but nearly a young woman and good-looking. She had a teasing quality about her that he'd never noticed before. He could see she was not too young for a sweetheart.

When they were all in bed, Mary snuggled close to Joe. She felt a great comfort being encircled by the enormous frame of her husband. She whispered, "Ell's been ready for courting ever since we came to Kansas. She is, what some say, ripe."

"My daughter called ripe?"

"I'm surprised you've not noticed how she attracts boys like honey attracts flies."

It was several minutes before Mary heard the soothing sounds of Joe's snoring.

For the next couple of days the Irwins watched the blizzard from their soddy's front windows. On the third day the low hills were visible against the pale blue sky. Joe, Will, and Charlie shoveled a path to the barn, taking turns. The cow was milked and Mary took warm water out to the stock for drinking right away before it froze. She added leftover pork bones to the hot mush she took to the dog, Nick. Joe had wild hay piled high in the barn. The cow and horses had their own stalls. Joe laid by staples, such as sugar, salt, flour, corn meal, salt pork, beans, vinegar, and yeast, on sod shelves in the barn to see them through the winter. The barn was good protection from snow and fierce winds.

Frank was getting over his chest cold and ready to go back to school. Mary suggested Will take Frank to school and go after him while the rest went to Goodland to vote for the county seat.

Will said he might just go to Eustis and vote. Joe nodded his head to let Will know it was a good idea.

Before the cold weather had come, Joe plowed a couple acres for his winter wheat. Going to Goodland on voting day, he stopped the horse and told Charlie to scrape through the snow to the frozen ground. To Joe's delight Charlie found delicate green blades piercing the soil. Charlie covered the hole to keep the tiny shoots warm and jumped into the wagon.

"I'm certain I can grow potatoes and vegetables to keep in a root cellar next winter and a half dozen acres more of winter wheat," said Joe, smiling at Mary.

"That will be nice to go with the bread, beans, and salt pork we have now," agreed Mary.

Joe drove directly to the courthouse. Joe went in to vote, leaving Mary, Ell, and Charlie in the wagon. Ell kept looking at the people going into the courthouse. Charlie knew she was looking for Miner.

Afterward the Irwins went to Marietta Roberts's Restaurant. Charlie and his father drank hot soup from two-handled cups. Mary asked advice about piecing together her quilt squares. Ell asked Marietta if she would help her sew a suitable schoolmarm's dress.

Marietta thought. She wiped her hands on her apron and sucked in her cheeks. She was a good-looking, middle-aged widow with brown hair braided and wound on her head coronet fashion. She was respected by everyone for her ambition, managing a restaurant and sewing. "I can order a soft brown wool for a jacket and skirt. Who's the schoolteacher?" Her eyes went from Ell to Mary.

"I am," said Ell proudly. "I'm going to be the first schoolteacher in Goodland when it's the official county seat."

"I admire your confidence and your politics," said Marietta. "Are you absolutely positive that Goodland will be Sherman County's seat?"

"Yes. I saw the sign. During the last blizzard, the snow blew toward Goodland and left Eustis bare," said Ell.

"Oh, land sakes! That always happens!" Marietta's dark eyes shone. "In winter the wind always blows that way."

Ell did not crack a smile. "The sign means people will move in the same direction, leaving Eustis."

Marietta's face creased with smile lines. She nodded her head. "Yes, we'll see. In the meantime I'll check on the price of the brown wool."

By midnight the votes were counted, and as Ell predicted, Goodland won. In the town guns and revolvers were shot, anvils pounded, as people celebrated. All that was needed now was for the county commissioners to canvass the vote and declare Goodland the permanent county seat. But next day, besides a thick snowfall to put a damper on more celebrations, an injunction was served on the county commissioners by the town of Eustis that enjoined them from canvassing the vote. The allegations were that no election notices were posted and that the ballots had been mixed together. Therefore everything was over, but the results were not official.

For the next several weeks Joe watched the newspapers carefully to find how the difficulties of the county seat would be resolved. There was no immediate resolution. The roads became icy and frozen.

Joe took Charlie on farrier rounds. One day, after Christmas, the axle on the wagon broke and had to be repaired on the spot in a sleet storm. Joe and Charlie sawed down a cottonwood. Charlie held the tree trunk steady while Joe used an ax and knife to whittle it down into the shape of an axle.

Joe read in the paper that Goodland would open its official post office on New Year's Day, 1888. Jim Warrington, one of Joe's HUA friends, was postmaster in the one-room soddy on Main Street. A stage would take the mail, once a week, to Wallace for sorting and bagging for the mail train.

On January second, posters appeared on barns and town buildings stating that Goodland was indeed the seat of Sherman County. Mary wrote a long letter to her folks in Chillicothe, but when it was finished no one could take it to the post office. Snow was falling and drifting deep against the soddy and barn. Roads were hidden for a week. Then the snow stopped and the wind seemed to increase and the temperature dropped to $-30°$ F.

Ten days later, when the weather moderated, Jack Collins came on horseback to announce a meeting of the HUAers in the Goodland Courthouse. To everyone's surprise, Goodland was not yet legally the county seat, because the town of Eustis had not officially registered its votes.

That same day Les came to the Irwin soddy to ask Will and Charlie to ride to Eustis with him. He explained that John Navert was the self-appointed sheriff for Goodland and he wanted someone to go to Eustis for those unregistered ballots. "Martin Tomblin, lawyer and president of the Goodland Town Company, believes Eustis is foot dragging, so he's offering two town lots and a couple hundred dollars in cash for those records. Rumor says George Benson has the records in a trunk in his basement."

Will was ready to go as soon as he heard there was money for the job. He said, "I heard Jack Collins tell Pa that Tomblin has rags soaked with turpentine wrapped around straw. Those turpentine balls can be torched and thrown on Benson's porch. That'll make Benson give us those records!"

Mary gasped and put her hand to her mouth.

Les said, "We're not taking any fire balls. We're taking Charlie with his gift of gab. He'll talk Benson or his wife into giving us the records."

Mary's hand came away from her mouth, but she clicked her tongue against her teeth to show her disapproval. She said, "If you have to go, dress warm, it's still freezing out there."

The boys wore woolen stockings inside their boots, two flannel shirts under sheepskin-lined coats, two pairs of woolen pants, and gloves inside woolen mittens. Charlie thought one flannel shirt was enough for him. Two were cumbersome when he put his lasso over his shoulder. He offered the flannel shirt to Les, who gladly put it on. They pulled their caps over their ears and told Mary they'd be back by noon.

She clamped her top teeth over her bottom lip so she wouldn't say anything. She knew she'd see the boys nearer suppertime.

Charlie held his scarf over his nose and bent over his horse for warmth. Les waved, saying they'd bring Joe back from the courthouse if the HUAers meeting was over.

They rode straight for Eustis, down the main street toward the Benson house. The house was clapboard with a wide wooden porch. The back part was the original old soddy. The boys hitched their horses to the gate post and went on the porch. Will took off his mitten and knocked with his glove on.

Mrs. Benson looked from the window and motioned them inside. "Don't stand out in that Arctic air. Come right on in," she said and closed the door quickly. "Are you boys on some errand?" Her blond hair was tucked under a cotton kerchief.

"Yes, we are," said Charlie. He looked around the room. "Is Mr. Benson home?"

"No, George is with Eustis's Mayor Dayton at the Sherman County Bank. I'll get you lads some hot tea. Put your feet next to the wood stove. Get warm before you go outside again. They say the weather's moderated, but it can't be more'n ten, fifteen degrees warmer. You can still freeze your toes. Did you want to see George?"

"That's all right. We really came for something," said Charlie. He sipped the hot tea, wondering how he was going to ask her for the voting records.

"I suspect George sent you. He mentioned that he wanted to store the voting records in a safe place at the bank." Mrs. Benson winked. "I'm glad to get shut of them myself."

"I can understand that," said Charlie.

She lighted a candle and the boys followed her to the basement. There was a lock on the trunk. Mrs. Benson said she didn't know where George kept the key. Les said that the trunk had to be opened right away. She nodded and went upstairs. The boys were in the dark. Charlie's teeth chattered and he was afraid to move. Mrs. Benson came back with the light and a hammer. Les hit the lock several hard blows and the clasp broke. Mrs. Benson took an armload of papers out. She divided it into two piles and shoved each pile in the front of Will's and Les's sheepskin coats. "You're too young to be carrying such valuable papers," she told Charlie.

He was exasperated and wanted to tell her he could take some of the papers.

"Here, I want you to take George's pipe to him. He forgot it this morning. Here's his tobacco pouch." She handed them to Charlie and patted the top of his head. Charlie nodded. He wanted to run out the front door.

Les put the teacups in the kitchen sink, then shook Mrs. Benson's hand and told her thank you. Will shook her hand and smiled.

Once the boys were out the door, they hurried to mount their horses. Charlie stopped to put the pipe and tobacco in one hand and pull his soggy scarf over his nose. Will and Les trotted down the street. As Charlie mounted he heard boots squeak the cold snow. A man turned in at the gate and looked up at Charlie.

"Say! That's my pipe!" he cried. "Why you little thief!" He grabbed Charlie's leg, pulled him off the horse, and tipped him over his shoulder.

"I'm not a thief!" yelled Charlie, waving his hands and kicking his feet.

"Sonny, I'm George Benson and that's my pipe in your fist!" Benson grabbed at the pipe and tobacco pouch and managed to shove them in the pocket of his coat and still hold on to Charlie, who thrashed about. "Stop fighting me!" yelled Benson.

Charlie was taken to the Eustis jail several blocks away. The deputy put him behind bars, then talked with Benson. Charlie hollered, "What about my horse! It's too cold to leave him standing out there!"

Benson said he'd bring the horse to the stable behind the jail. He added that he wasn't inhumane.

"I'm innocent," said Charlie. His bottom lip stuck out. "Do I get a trial?"

"Wait to see what the sheriff says," said the deputy, who was clean-shaven in contrast to George Benson, who had a full, coffee-colored beard.

Charlie was certain Benson did not know that Will and Les

were on their way to Goodland with the Eustis voting records, and he'd never tell.

"What were you doing with my pipe?" asked Benson, combing his fingers through his beard.

"I was bringing it to you," sniffed Charlie.

"Won't hurt to cool your heels awhile." Benson shook hands with the deputy and left.

"My heels are pretty near froze," said Charlie, pulling off his mittens and rubbing his gloved hands together. The jail was not heated. The only stove Charlie could see was a round potbelly in the office. The deputy closed the door to the office. Charlie was alone with a canvas cot, no mattress, no blanket, and a china pot with a top. He pounded on the vertical iron bars. "Hey, deputy! Don't I get lunch and a blanket? I'm freezing, you know!" He wished he had the second flannel shirt. He threw his rope under the cot.

The deputy opened the door. Charlie felt the warm air. "I got no orders 'cept stay in this here office and fill out my report," said the deputy, whose eyes were like raisins poked into a plump dough-face. "What's your name, occupation, and where you from?"

Charlie held on to the bars with gloved hands and said, "I'm John Brown, ask me again and I'll knock you down!"

"Don't give me that arkymalarky. Your name, I already know anyways. You look like one of Joe Irwin's boys."

"Charles Burton Irwin. I'm a rancher. I'm from out West."

"Are you guilty or not guilty?"

"What else have you?"

"That's all. Did you steal Benson's pipe and fight with him?"

"I'm mute."

"Kid, you got more guts than you could hang on a fence rail," said the deputy, scratching one pudgy cheek. "I'm writing on this report that you are to be hanged in the morning. I hope it will be a lesson to you ever after." The door slammed shut.

Charlie lost his appetite for lunch. He thought of hanging and his neck ached. There was no window. He lay down and thought of home and the cheerfulness of his mother and father. He knew his father was gruff, but it was because he cared for him. His mother would cry if he were hanged. His eyes watered and he rubbed them with his scarf, which was stiff with frost. He wondered when Will and Les discovered he wasn't following them. He sat up and hugged his knees to keep them from shaking.

He imagined Benson going home. He could almost hear him shouting at his wife. She'd cry. Hot tears slid down Charlie's face. He sniffed and ran his sleeve across his face. He remembered something his father once said: "Rely on good sense to get you through."

He heard a door slam and no more noises in the office. He had no idea how long he'd felt sorry for himself. His stomach growled. His heels kicked against his rope under the cot. He bent and picked up the rope and wound it around his fist and left elbow. He pushed his fist and rope through the cold bars. He sucked in his breath and his mouth turned up into a tiny smile. He twirled one end of the rope with his right hand. His hand was cold. He grunted and drew his hand close to a space between the bars and blew his warm breath toward it. His eyes were accustomed to the dark and he could make out the door to the office. He could not really see the doorknob, but he knew where it should be. He twirled the rope faster and let it fly out farther and farther until it hit the door with a *bonk* and the floor with a *swak*. The two sounds were as loud as a close clap of thunder.

Charlie pulled in the rope, coiled it, and twirled and tossed again and again and again. He was not shivering. He could feel the perspiration under his arms. Once the rope hung up on something, then slipped off. "Okay, catch this time!" he cried. The rope was caught! He gave it a tug and the loop cinched and held tight. "Here goes nuthin'," he said, and jerked hard. He knew he couldn't turn the knob, but if the latch didn't fit tight, he was sure it would spring open. He gave it another tug, pulling the rope taut against an iron bar. "A miracle!" he shouted as the door flew open and he felt the rush of warm air.

He saw the red twinkle of the banked fire in the potbellied stove. He tied his end of the rope to one of the horizontal bars. His hands ached and he could see his breath vapor in the air. He lay on the cot. After a while he was sure the air was warmer. His eyelids grew heavy.

He woke to find his neck had a kink and his feet were cold. He stood and stretched and wondered if it was morning. He pulled off his gloves, loosened his scarf, and pushed up his cap. He used the china pot. Minutes later there was ice on the chamberpot sides. His mouth tasted like he'd eaten something rotten. The fire was out in the potbellied stove. He heard noises.

Charlie half hoped it was not morning. He remembered the threat of hanging. The door opened and a man with brown hair slicked back with grease tossed a gray wool cap on the coat rack, then took off his sheepskin. The man whistled and poked inside the stove's fire box, put in kindling, and struck a match on the bottom of the top drawer of the desk. The man went out and came back with several hunks of cordwood. He dropped one in the fire box and the rest on the floor. He adjusted the damper. He turned and looked at Charlie. "Say, what are you doing here?" He looked startled.

Charlie could see light from a gray sky through the outer door. "Slowly freezing to death," he said.

"I wasn't informed of a prisoner. I'm Sheriff Albright." He picked up a paper from the desktop. "Aha, you're one of the Irwin boys—a rancher, this says. What are you doing here?" he repeated.

Charlie decided not to answer any more questions.

The sheriff examined the door and the rope attached to the knob. "This your work?"

Charlie's teeth chattered.

The sheriff pulled the rope off the knob and Charlie snaked it back between the bars. He drew in a deep breath and asked his own question. "Does that paper say anything about a hanging?"

"Nope. Not that I can make out." The sheriff's mouth turned up at the corners and his blue eyes twinkled. "I bet you Deputy Benn put you behind those bars! He gets a bang out of scaring kids. You're not old enough to be my prisoner."

Charlie did not mind being called young this time. He grinned.

"That must be your horse in the stable. Leave the blanket that's on its back and hightail it home, son. Whatever it was you did, don't do it again."

"Does that paper tell what I did?" Charlie put his bare hand on one of the iron bars. The skin stuck to the freezing metal. He pulled and some of the skin came off. Tears welled in his eyes. He sat to cradle his hands in his lap. He thought frozen skin hurt as much as burned skin.

"Someone wrote: Fighting and Stealing. But both are crossed out. I can't keep you here. Your conviction sheet is unsigned and invalid."

Charlie couldn't say a word. He let the tears fall in his cupped hands.

Suddenly there was a loud pounding at the outer door and there stood Will, Les, Jack Collins, and Joe grinning as big as mountain cats. "You had us worried. But you look all right!" shouted Joe.

"This kid a relative of yours?" The sheriff pointed to Les.

"Yes, in a way, a young brother," said Les.

"Young brothers are always in the way!" said the sheriff with a loud laugh.

"I'm his pa!" cried Joe. "He's done nuthin' to be in jail for!"

"I know that!" said the sheriff, getting up from his chair. He put cotton gloves on and unlocked the cell. "Say, you gents hear the news this afternoon? The city officials of this one-horse town wouldn't count the ballots, so their votes don't count. George Benson is breathing fire and fury because he kept those records at his place where no one could get 'em. Three little bitty kids took the ballots from his wife, hauled them to Goodland, and counted 'em. But it didn't count for much. Those ballots are worthless."

"Yup! We heard," said Jack Collins.

When they were outside Will told Charlie they didn't get a cent from Tomblin.

Money didn't seem important to Charlie. "What time is it?" he asked.

"Suppertime!" cried Les.

"I wasn't in jail overnight?" Charlie was dumbfounded. "I sure hope the new jail in Goodland has more than one wood stove. Honest, I might've froze if I didn't have my rope to open the office door."

Joe helped Charlie on his horse. He tossed the blanket on a pile of hay, then held his hand up. "Honest, anyone that tells Mary that Charlie spent the day in jail will get his tongue pulled through his nose!"

Les Miner later told the story of riding to Eustis, getting the voting records, and taking them to Goodland. "When me and Will got to Goodland, we counted the yeas and neas in the courthouse. Eustis voted 256 for Goodland and 106 for itself for county seat. The votes aren't worth anything and don't mean much, because even before they were counted, Goodland was finally made the official county seat."

The first election for Goodland's city officers was held on April 24, 1888. An HUAer, E. F. Murphy, was elected mayor for a salary of one hundred dollars per annum to be paid quarterly. Five new councilmen were elected. John McCune was the first police judge and J. W. Navert was elected sheriff.

Among the first ordinances for Goodland, as the county seat, was a poll tax. Businesses were required to have licenses. Activities that were prohibited included prostitution, games, gambling, fast riding and driving on the streets, riding wagons on sidewalks, and running of cattle or other domestic animals at large.

By spring Tait had his newspaper building and his loyalties moved to Goodland. On the seventeenth of May he wrote, "Goodland holds the prize."

Many businesses from Eustis were moved to Goodland. The small frame buildings were loaded on several wagon beds and moved by teams of horses. The sod buildings were taken down "brick by brick" and carried by wagons to Goodland, where they were quickly put back together. Tait wrote, "The buildings are moving so fast that our reporter has been unable to keep up with the exits."

On the last day of May, Tait wrote, "Our building made the trip from Eustis to Goodland without cracking the plastering or disturbing a brick on the chimney."

The county seat fight had occupied the news so long that now the editors had to find something new for readers of newspapers. The *Goodland News* stated, "Since the cruel county seat war is over, it is no picnic to fill a paper full of local news for the reader, and if we publish a chapter of the Bible now and then, you need not growl. It might be news to some of you anyway."*

Charlie thought of all the activities that had taken place during the last six months. His father called the events the "politics of growth." Charlie thought the events were more like growing pains. He decided that if he were ever a mayor or sheriff—and he had the certainty of youth that he could do anything he put his mind to—he'd be clear-headed in his thinking. He'd never falter in his duty. He'd make plans and see the job was carried out posthaste. He'd learned that decisions mattered. He'd never waste time with name calling, gun fighting, liquor drinking, or tobacco spitting.

He'd learned something about politics. If a person's viewpoint was defeated by a majority vote, it was unseemly to lick your wounds in public for all to see. If he were in a public office, he'd lick the wounds of defeat in private and at the same time figure out a way to see the situation for something good. Charlie told himself he'd never shilly-shally from one side to the other nor would he be wishy-washy and take the middle road. A man that straddles the fence could end up with a mighty sore crotch.

*Reprinted with permission of Betty Walker, from the Sherman County Historical Society, Goodland, Kansas.

ELEVEN

Wild Horses

At the onset of 1888 there was no railroad within Sherman County, Kansas. By spring of the same year people in the county had seen railroad survey teams with tripods and transits on pack horses or in wagons. The men carried measuring chains and left wooden stakes for the proposed railroad beds. A branch of the Rock Island, the Chicago, Kansas and Nebraska Railroad, ran a survey from Jansen, Nebraska, to Colorado Springs. Their proposed roadbed was staked out a half-mile south of Goodland's courthouse.

The federal government gave land grants to early railroad companies, who in turn sold their land grant to have money to build their rail line. As soon as Jesse Tait located his newspaper in Goodland, Joe went to see him. "I've talked to the HUAers, and they suggest that the county hold a special election to vote on selling a given amount of railroad bonds. If the election carries, then the railroad whose bonds are voted can issue and sell their bonds. The money from the sale of those bonds could be used to build us a railroad."

By the time the last spring snow melted, a special election to obtain permission to sell the CK and N bonds was over and had carried. The mud thawed and dried on the dirt roads. The fields were right for plowing. Will did not mind getting his hands dirty nor his shirts sweaty in the course of farming. He made no deliberate decisions for himself. His blocky shoulders were right for his short neck and large head. His dark eyes were full of fun, with no serious depth of an intellectual. Yet he was nobody's fool. He kept a written account of all that was spent and all that was earned on the farm. He was at times boisterous and animated, and once when asked if he'd work for the railroad construction gang, he nodded his head, saying, "I don't know where I'm going, but I'm on my way for sure." Thus events happened for Will with no before nor after thought.

Then one day Will gave the farm and farrier bookkeeping notes to Charlie and went to work for the railroad construction gang grading the ground west of Norton so that it was flat or banked at the correct angle. He made the railbed ready for the next workers with the black, creosoted ties and steel rails.

With his first paycheck Will bought Charlie a nickel-plated stem-winder and stem-setter watch. Charlie was overjoyed. However, he would not say yes to Will again concerning the use of his Henry rifle.

Next Will bought a couple bars of quality cast iron so that his father could forge new front-door hinges for the Irwin soddy. Then he bought himself a pair of mules to use pulling the road scraper used in construction of the railroad bed. Each of his mules cost him three times as much as the railroad company paid for those heavy gauge, steel scrapers, which were $7.25 up to $10.50, depending on whether they held three and a half, or five, or seven cubic feet of dirt.

The scraper's bit was controlled by the team driver, like Will. When the scraper was filled, it was flipped over to unload. Will fit right in with the other noisy workers, who continually yelled to their animals, "Gee, haw, whoa and giddyap!" and sang ribald songs. Some of the gang were foreigners, such as the frugal Mennonites from Russia, the hardworking Bohemians, called Bohunks, Irishmen, smelling of whiskey and tobacco and as anxious to spend their money as Will, and a few Welsh slate miners, whose voices rose and fell like singing birds. The pay was good, two dollars for a twelve-hour day. Thus, many homesteaders worked with their own teams of horses or mules. The workers stayed in tents in camps near the construction. Temporary stables were built for the work animals. As the work progressed the camps were moved.

On Friday, the 30th of March, 1888, fifty teams, with wagons filled with three sizes of scrapers, tents, bedding, cooking utensils, and gear belonging to the construction gang went down Goodland's Main Street like a holiday parade. The gang was going to make camp forty miles west of Goodland and work their way back east, moving tons of dirt along the survey until they met the remainder of the gang coming west from Norton. The two gangs planned to meet in Goodland by summer to join the two tracks into a single line. Goodlanders and homesteaders came out to watch the construction gang and its teams go through town. The *Goodland News* said, "It was the most substantial evidence of a railroad for this part of the country we have had, and gave the people both in town and country lots of encouragement."

The businessmen gave out cigars to the railroad workers. Tait's *Dark Horse* reported, "Every man in the outfit left town smoking and promising to be back by summer."

Goodland's Main Street was renamed the Boulevard. Before June was half over hitch racks were put up along both sides of the Boulevard.

While Will worked on building the railroad, Charlie helped his father on farrier rounds, traveling from farm to farm, repairing horseshoes, plows, or applying a little medical knowledge to the ailments of horses and other livestock or farm animals. Charlie often listened for the whistle of faraway trains and once in a while could see smoke against the eastern horizon on those rounds.

Charlie was now nearly six feet tall. Beside other boys his age he looked like a giant. His bright, brown eyes took in everything and his mind recorded every item. His mouth seemed small until he smiled, and then it stretched across the bottom of his face. He no longer dreamed of being as tall and strong as his brother Will; that goal was in plain sight.

Charlie was looking for a new goal. He was quick to learn from observation and experience. He knew the best goals were hard to attain. He'd seen his Grandmother Malinda fight for a goal of happiness, only to have loneliness consume and destroy her. He was aware of the backbreaking hours his folks spent just to keep food in their bellies and the dirt soddy halfway bearable. He saw his folks were serious about conforming to their values in life. They were so serious that Charlie could never let loose his true feelings in their presence. At times he'd like to yell and stamp his feet or call Frank a dumb crybaby. Other times he wanted to put his arms around Frank and tell him not to whine, things would get better. But Joe was gargantuan and gruff and formidable to Charlie. He felt uneasy doing anything outside of a narrow band of parental-acceptable behavior. Thus, he was never overly happy nor overly sad in front of his folks.

This was not to say Charlie did not let himself go on occasions. Most everyone knew he had a quick temper followed by quick contriteness. He could make sour-faced Frank laugh with his high exuberance. By the time he was thirteen or fourteen he'd concluded life was not to be scrimped and saved nor was it to be wasted. Life was to be used fully and enjoyed. Charlie surprised his father with the thoroughness of the accounts he kept in Will's farm and farrier notes. And he began keeping records of household bills, weather, including rainfall and hours of sunlight, and the amount of feed bought and used by the livestock. His mother said, "Don't you want to add to your notes how much water I use for cooking and washing?"

For pure joy Charlie liked racing on foot or riding fast on horseback. He outraced every boy his own age. Some said it was because his legs were so long, others said it was the length of his arms that propelled him like a windmill. He seemed to have charm and good manners so that people liked him. He seemed to enjoy carrying out his chores and never grumbled about cleaning out the barn, adding sweet-smelling hay to the stalls, brushing down the horses, or milking the cow. Next to people he liked horses. He liked their looks and their smell and to watch their gracefulness. When he was with people, he liked to exchange thoughts and was amazed at how much he learned or how differently others thought about some of the most common things.

Unbeknownst to Charlie his next goal was already in place. He was slowly confronting the conflicts that would fall in his way as he took over the leadership of the Irwin family. Already he'd decided he wanted the Irwin name to be important—mean something more than a sodbuster or dirt farmer. He seemed to realize that if he wanted something done, he had to get it started and nurse it along himself.

One day Charlie pointed out a little flat place, protected by hillocks on two sides. He and his father were returning home from doing some horseshoeing. "Pa, that would be just right for Ell's schoolhouse. The place is halfway between our place and Goodland."

A few days later Joe and Les Miner put up the one-room school soddy. Charlie told his father how the children would enjoy seeing sunshine or rain or wind clouds, so Joe bought two glass windows. Then Miner surprised everyone by putting in a cast-iron stove and three rows of poplar wood benches. Charlie gently reminded his father that the children would need an outhouse because they would spend the entire day at the school. He built a two-hole sod outhouse. At the same time Miner made Ell a desk, more like a rough-hewn table, and a chair, like a tall milking stool.

Youngsters, five to twelve, came to Miss Ell's School. Ell loved teaching and the children loved her. She understood their fantasies and readily entered into their make-believe play world. Ell was consistent when dealing with the children's lessons. The children's folks paid what they could for the schooling, from twenty-five cents to as much as a dollar a week. With the first month's money Ell bought a dozen slates. With the following month's salary she bought a set of seven volumes of the popular McGuffey's *Eclectic Readers*. She did not mention going to Missouri again.

At seventeen Ell was a beauty. Her skin was a clear rose-pink. She had slim legs, slender hips, and a shapely bosom. Her long lucent hair, once amber, was now more like a flaming sunset. Her bottle-green eyes shone with a come-hither look that promised unknown pleasures. Her nose was a perfect triangle and her mouth a wide, pleasant, upturned arc. Her voice was quiet, but she spoke with conviction, because she was well versed in the classics and newsprint of the times. She never hesitated to ask if there were some point she did not understand in any conversation. Her consistency fell apart when she dealt with men. Then she relied on her instinct.

Young and old men flocked around Ell. She spoke with cool politeness, but her eyes shone like liquid hot greenglass. She always smelled of fresh roses, even in winter. Intuitively she knew how to wear her homemade clothes so that with the slightest movement her figure showed off to perfection. However, she habitually laid her clothes on her bed or the floor or a chair rather than on the hooks her father had fastened into a board on the dirt wall.

Most of the men, including Les Miner, were in a constant state of excitement when near her. Rumor said she was Miner's girl. Still that did not detour the ogling and hopeful dreams of the other men. Another rumor said because Ell had spurned him, Rob Collins went to work in the Colorado coal mines so depressed that he no longer took an interest in the opposite sex.

Little Frank still used the cart he and Charlie rigged up to scrounge the prairie for old bones for Rob and Mr. Collins. Frank now took his collection to the Goodland Livery, where he was paid the rate of six dollars for a thousand pounds. The bones were stacked and held until the train would run through town and take them east to be crushed into fertilizer.

On one of the first warm afternoons of early spring, Charlie was beside the barn practicing rope spinning over his leg when Frank came up on the old, plodding Flame with the little cart full of bleached buffalo bones.

Frank's face was flushed and he was puffing for breath. "Charlie! Hundreds of horses! Wild! Down in the meadow. Maybe you could rope one. Wanna try?" He slid off the horse.

Charlie helped his young brother unhook the cart and put Flame in the barn, rub him down, and give the horse some oats. Then the two boys ran to the small meadow next to the creek.

They sat behind a clump of willows and looked in awe at the statuesque, magnificent horses silhouetted against the prairie sun quietly nibbling the grass between the sagebrush. At first scent of the unfamiliar humans the horses were skittish and ran from the low meadow, up the creek to a low rise, then out into the prairie. Charlie could not get close enough to put a loop around any of them. He and Frank marveled at their shaggy, thick coats and strong, straight legs. Charlie remembered he read somewhere that wild horses were not native. He told Frank they were from the Spanish Barb and Andalusian horses that were brought over by Spanish explorers in the early 1500s. "Some of those horses escaped or were left by the explorers and they began to live like wild animals, forming bands. The ones that survive are the strongest."

For the next two, three mornings Charlie came early. He sat alone against the clump of willows to watch the horses. There were plenty of stallions, but some mares stood around under the few trees by the creek. He noticed places where the grass was mashed close to the ground, as though the mares had come back to the meadow to sleep. Several mares looked as though they were ready to foal any time. He marveled how the mares, heavy with foal, could run and how graceful they seemed. Looking at them, he had a sense of freedom and toughness. He wanted to move closer, and as he crawled in the grass one of the stallions stopped grazing. Charlie felt the horse look right at him.

He meticulously examined and recorded times when the horses moved from one place to another. He never forgot his nickel-plated pocket watch, pencil, and notebook. Usually he brought leftover breakfast biscuits and bacon to munch on. Once he forgot. He stretched out on his stomach and nibbled the grass like a horse. He thought it was not unlike young dandelion greens his sister picked for spring salad. He found the horses grazed an hour after their first morning fill of water. Then they grouped together as though talking over their plans for the rest of the day. For two hours they grazed again. About midday they rested. At two o'clock they grazed again.

Before the sun went down, always about six o'clock, the herd went to the creek again to drink before finding their places for the night. The mares with foals preferred the tall grass against small rises in the earth where they could lay down and be sheltered from the wind. The stallions bunched together in a clearing or sought protection from a willow or alder clump. They did not lie down. He noticed half a dozen young stallions were pushed out of the main bunch. Each time they were ejected the young stallions moved closer to the mares as though looking them over for a possible mate.

Charlie learned that the wild horses generally drank most heavily early in the morning, at first sign of light. Then for about thirty or forty minutes the horses could not run fast. He found if he got up before sunup he could lasso one stallion. But the animal reared and pawed the air so that Charlie could not hold on to the rope. The next day he came back hoping to get the rope. He rode one of the workhorses and came up behind a group drinking their morning water. He edged them away and toward the small corral his father had made at the edge of the meadow. Often Joe kept the workhorses in this corral when he was using them in the fields. The workhorse whinnied and the stallions darted in all directions. Charlie was able to get one into the corral. He could not take the workhorse close to the wild one, which reared up and would bite.

Charlie had no idea how he was going to tame the horse. He had never talked to anyone about bronco-busting. He reasoned he had to tire the stallion, so he ran it around and around the corral by keeping the workhorse behind it. He was astonished at the stamina the wild horse had. After a week of running around and around each morning Charlie was about to ride close enough to throw a gunnysack full of heavy dirt onto the horse's back. He went wild. The sack of dirt was thrown off. Next day Charlie got the sack of dirt back on the horse. He wanted to strap it on. Only after another week could he do that. Charlie was lucky one morning and herded the stallion wearing his rope into the corral. The end of the rope was badly frayed, but he knew that could be mended. It was ten days before he could touch the rope. Slowly he loosened it and flung it off the animal's head. The rope touched the ears and the stallion reared back and darted against the side of the corral. Charlie ran to the opposite side and climbed over the fence. He wondered if he had enough patience to break these wild horses.

Joe had seen the wild bunch and after finding the first strange horse in the corral knew what Charlie was doing. He decided not to interfere and not to tell Mary, who would worry about her son's safety. Joe believed a person should depend on no one but himself; then he had no others to blame if things went wrong, and he learned to do the best job. Joe also believed in letting his children be free to make their own decisions. He knew children could stub their toes, but it was better to do that and end up with scraped knees during childhood than mollycoddling them so when it was time to leave home the adult children could not take care of themselves.

It never entered Charlie's mind that one of these wild horses might rear up, knock him over, step on him, or kick him. After days the horse with the bag of dirt on his back was glad to have Charlie undo the strap and put a saddle in its place. He thought he'd never get a bit in their mouths. Charlie cinched the saddle one morning, climbed on, and rode one of the horses around the barnyard. The horse was nervous, but it did not buck.

Charlie asked Frank to sit on the corral fence and time one lap around the barnyard. Frank was eager to hold Charlie's watch. He climbed the fence and held out his hand as Charlie rode by. The watch slipped as Frank grabbed. It fell to the ground. The horse stepped on it, breaking the glass and mutilating the face. Charlie was afraid to yell at Frank for fear the horse would become frightened. He pointed in the direction of the house. Frank climbed down, hung his head, and walked slowly. Charlie followed him halfway to the house. He talked in a normal tone as he patted the horse's neck. "You dumb cluck. Will bought me that watch because he used my Henry rifle. Now you broke it."

Charlie's mother saw him and called, "Where on earth did you get that big horse?"

"Out in the meadow. Ain't he a beauty? Want to see another I got?"

"Charlie Burton Irwin, come here this minute!" she called. She was dumbfounded. It was hard to believe Charlie had corralled and tamed two horses and no one knew until now.

Joe pretended to be astounded. He asked Charlie how many

horses he could break before summer.

"Maybe two, three more. That's all. It's nearly a full-time occupation. I have to get up early to work with them so I can do my regular chores during the day."

"How about if I work with you? Then you could have time to brush them and make them look good. I could sell each one for at least fifty bucks. We'd be rich," said Joe.

Together they brought in six more biting, fighting horses before the herd moved on to safer ground. Two of the horses were mares, one yellow, the other pure black, that had not yet foaled. Charlie was not sure how to tame the mares. His father scratched his head and decided a bag of dirt on their backs could not hurt. "But I'm half afraid to put the girth strap on."

"We could wait until they foal; maybe that'll make them gentle."

"Or scared to death," said Joe, scratching his head. "What do you think?"

"I'll put the strap on and not pull it tight," said Charlie. He talked to the horses and let them watch him with their wild, shy eyes.

Without saying anything to Charlie, Joe sold two of the stallions to the livery man. Charlie asked for the money. "I got the horses and broke them; the money is mine."

"I sold them for the best price I could get. This is a family. Everything goes to the head of the family to be used as I see best."

"But what do I get out of it?" Charlie was heartbroken. He'd worked hard with those horses and grown fond of them.

"You get a roof over your head. You get food in your belly. You get the finest education in the land on how to be self-sufficient," answered Joe.

In the middle of the night Charlie thought he heard horses whinnying. He grabbed for his pants and a candle and headed for the barn. On the way he called out to his father, "Pa, I'm going to check the mares." Charlie was still put out and thought his father might ignore him.

Joe was right behind him. He grabbed some bottles of antiseptic and rags and dipped a bucket of hot water from the laundry tub on the stove.

The yellow mare's ears were back and she was sweaty. She lay in the middle of a pile of hay. Charlie took off the girth strap. The colt came easily, feet first, then head and shoulders. Charlie went to the next stall to see the black mare. He took away the girth strap and her foal came just as easy. It was a black filly.

"That running free sure makes a horse strong," said Joe. "Take a look at those foals, up on wobbly legs already. See how straight the legs are."

Charlie thought they looked turned in at all angles. The yellow and white colt fell, then awkwardly stood up and nudged the mare to stand so he could nurse.

"No one has to tell him what to do."

"Just like the calves, or dogs or cats," said Joe matter-of-factly.

"Colts seem smarter. Can we keep these foals?"

"As long as they don't eat us to the gate of the poorhouse."

"Thanks, Pa." Charlie, still under the influence of the miracle of birth, wanted to put his arms around his father.

"Don't thank me, son. You did it. You brought them mares into the corral. I told you stallions would be best."

"Those mares will make good workhorses. Frank and me'll train the colt and filly. Maybe we'll make racers out of them. You can take 'em to the fair. Frank'll ride 'em. I'll pick up the bets." Charlie smiled just thinking about it.

"The sky's the limit with you," said Joe. "I guess your thinking can't bounce any higher than the sky. Let me tell you something. When your thinking does come down to hit the dust, keep it there. Don't get those highfalutin ideas stuck in your head. We're just common sodbusters. You'll have more than scraped knees. You'll have a nosebleed one of these days if you don't tone down your thinking. Did I say I wouldn't ever sell them foals?"

Charlie's heart hit the ground. He blew out the candle after making certain the mares and their foals were fine. He could not sleep. When the sky began to lighten to a dull gray, he fell asleep thinking how he could keep the colt and filly so he and Frank could train them.

In the morning his mother said, "I'm glad the wild stallions are gone. Your father has strung them out behind the farrier's wagon and taken them to the farmers along his route. He was sure he'd sell all of them. I thank God only the mares and their foals are left."

Charlie did not say anything. He went out to look at the foals and bring oats and water to the mares.

All spring Joe grumbled about the trouble the mares caused him. However, in the quiet night hours he whispered to Mary that he was so proud of Charlie and actually glad to have the extra mares. They would be strong horses to hitch to his plow next spring, if they weren't in foal again by that time.

Mary agreed. "You were able to buy seed potatoes and another plow because of the extra money Charlie's horses brought in."

Joe put his arm around her waist and pulled her close. "You think I'm too hard on him?"

"Charlie uses his head. He thinks before acting. You like that in a person. Why don't you tell him that? Giving advice is fine, but praise can go a long way," said Mary.

"I would give a brass-studded bridle if the others were like him. Will's so forgetful at times I wouldn't be surprised to hear he put his candle to bed and blew himself out. I hope to Saint Peter he remembers to feed his own mules a bite of oats once in a while," said Joe. "Let Charlie be, he's learning to get for himself."

Several days later Joe saw an advertisement in the *Sherman County News*. For forty cents in postage he could send for a nickel-plated stem-winder and stem-setter watch. He wrote for the watch. He put Charlie's name on the return address.

The weather warmed so that on Saturdays, Mary and Ell brought the chicken supper outdoors. The Irwins sat on quilts and ate with their hands, not letting plates and forks spoil the good flavor. Each talked about their week's adventures.

One suppertime near the end of May, Frank was not hungry. He was quiet and kept his hand against his left jaw. Ell noticed the jaw was swollen and guessed he had a sore tooth. She suggested oil of cloves to ease the pain. Frank shook his head. "Then chew on a piece of bull nettle root," she said. Frank would not open his mouth.

Joe rummaged through his farrier's tools for a pair of pliers, but Frank moaned and groaned so loud the tools were put out of sight.

Mary tried a warm, flannel rag on his jaw.

Charlie remembered reading an ad in the *Dark Horse* about a tooth extractor and rummaged through the old papers. "Listen to this," he said. "Dr. L. L. Shively, the magnetic tooth extractor and dentist, will be in Goodland May twenty-sixth through twenty-ninth. Fifty cents to have a tooth pulled, one dollar for difficult extractions, but watching is free. Prof. E. P. Lgarnger, the celebrated solo violinist, will give a Grand Concert during the work on the street; he is also business manager for Dr. Shively."

Joe got the wagon out early Saturday morning and gave Charlie a half dollar to pay the dentist. Mary fussed over a place in the back of the wagon where Frank could lie comfortably on a couple of quilts.

Prairie puccoons, with single white flowers and lobed leaves, stood out beside the roadway. Charlie knew that if he broke off a piece of the puccoon's root it would ooze red juice as if bleeding.

In Goodland Charlie found an empty hitch rack along the Boulevard and patted Frank's shoulder. "Come on. You gotta stand in that yonder line." Both boys noticed the violinist played louder whenever a patient yelled. When it was Frank's turn he hung back.

"Charlie, sit in the little canvas folding chair and see how it feels."

"I don't have a toothache."

"Go on. I want to know it's safe." Frank shoved Charlie so that he backed into the camp chair.

Dr. Shively was about thirty, with a pox-marked face, shaggy, oily hair, low forehead, and beaklike nose. He grabbed Charlie, pulled his chin down and looked inside his mouth. The dentist had to hold Charlie's face to one side because his beak nose was so long he could not move up for a close look. He spoke sparingly, took pliers from a bucket of rinse water, and began tapping the upper row of teeth. "Hurt?" he said after he'd tapped the lower teeth.

"It's—I'm not—"

"Tell him it's the last double tooth on the left, top row," Frank whispered.

"Uumm," said the dentist, leaving his hand in Charlie's mouth.

Charlie reached out for Frank. Frank pretended he could not see Charlie's hand waving. Charlie made a noise in his throat. The dentist took this as a sign that he had put the pliers over the aching tooth. His right knee lay across Charlie's lap. His left hand rested on Charlie's sweating forehead. Charlie's hands shot up and grabbed Shively's right arm.

"Hold tight, sonny!" yelled Shively.

There was a slight grating noise as the tooth pulled away from bone and flesh. Shively's knuckles were white. His muscles bulged in his upper arm with the pulling. Charlie's eyes watered and he salivated. Then everything came free and the healthy bicuspid was held up as a trophy with its long, triple root dripping red. It looked like the broken root of the white puccoon.

Shively handed Charlie a tin cup to dip into a bucket of clear cistern water. "Wrench," he said. "Fine specimen." He waved the tooth around for all nearby to see, then he cleaned the cavity with a swab of cotton dipped into tincture of opium. "Numbs the hurt."

Charlie's jaw hurt and his tongue continued to probe a hole large enough to hide a gold piece. He was angry. He let out a yell that would scare a tired work-bull off his bed ground. He grabbed for the bloody molar from the end of the pliers, let it roll to the center of his fist, and jabbed Shively with a fast upper cut to the chin.

"I had no hurt until you caused one!" he said. His eyes were squinted down against the glare of the sun off the rinse water. His eyes seemed to shoot sparks.

Shively stepped backward. He shook his head and grabbed for Charlie. "I don't want to fight. Just a dollar for that there tooth."

"A buck for a perfectly good tooth?" Charlie sputtered. His arms were pinned tight against his back by Shively so he couldn't move.

"Not an easy extraction," explained Shively, letting one of his big hands free to pick up the pliers. He brought the pliers close to his nose, which was close to Charlie's face.

Charlie heard violin music and someone singing "Darling Clementine."

Frank said, "Pay the man."

Charlie glared and began backing away. Shively put his hand close to Charlie's chest. Charlie could see the man's nostrils move in and out. He reached into his pocket, let go of the tooth, and felt the nickel-plated, stem-winder, stem-setter. The dentist's warm breath was on his face and his hand took hold of Charlie's shirt. Charlie's hand came from his pocket holding the precious watch. Shively held on to Charlie and tapped the watch with his pliers. "That old ticker work?"

"It's not old," said Charlie.

"I'll take it," said Shively, letting go the shirt and grabbing up the nickel-plated watch. He put it to his ear and smiled when he heard its loud ticking. He looked at the sun, then at the time. "About right." He motioned to his next customer to sit in the chair. Frank sat.

Charlie's jaw throbbed. He felt himself pushed to one side. He saw no one with sympathetic eyes. People stared ahead watching Shively pocket the shiny watch and open a black box that seemed to hold a thousand different teeth and a flat bottle. Shively nodded toward Frank, smiled, uncorked the bottle to let at least a three-finger measure trickle down his throat. He put the bottle back into the box, then picked up the bloody pliers, rinsed them, and wiped them on a piece of rag that might have been a lady's skirt at one time.

Frank pointed to his abcessed tooth. Before he could pull his finger away the tooth was out and Shively held it out for all to see. The violinist hadn't pulled the bow across the strings. Frank rinsed his mouth with water from the tin cup. The extraction site was dabbed with cotton and numbed.

"Four bits," said Shively.

Frank motioned for Charlie to pay. "Hardly hurt," he said, smiling. "Thanks."

"Thanks for nuthin'," mumbled Charlie, giving Frank the fifty-cent piece.

Frank stepped off the walk and took hold of Charlie's arm. "I'm glad you had yours done first. I wasn't scared. I didn't yell."

Charlie felt sick. He knew he ought to have known better than let Frank push him around. "That was a rotten trick. I won't let you forget that you owe me a new stem-winder."

"Let's go home," said Frank. His tongue probed the hole where his aching tooth had been.

On the third of July the first train of the Colorado, Kansas, and Nebraska, a branch of the Rock Island route, came whistling and clanging into Goodland. Frank and Charlie cleaned out the horse stalls, made sure there was plenty of water in the trough and oats in the feed bins. They could not hear the train, nor see its coal smoke.

The two boys went to the meadow where the horses grazed with the cow. Charlie ran to the creek and back several times as he had every day since the colt and filly had been born. He paced himself slow at first, then on the last run he pushed to go as fast as he could.

"What if the wild horses come back? Will the mares go with them?" asked Frank while Charlie stood bent over, breathing hard.

"Pa says they won't. He says the wild ones won't be back this year." Charlie panted. "I wish I had my watch to time my runs."

"Will you get more horses for Pa to sell next spring?" asked Frank.

"How do I know? Maybe they won't come back. We ought to start walking the colt and filly. Say, tomorrow you could find out how to train a horse for racing. Ask your racehorse friend. He'll be in town for the celebration."

Frank nodded, nuzzled the side of the filly's head, and went to the house with Charlie, saying, "We could name them Sunny and Tar Baby. I heard Pa call the mares Golden and Midnight."

The train that had come as far as the western outskirts of Goodland was a work train carrying wooden ties and rails necessary to complete the track. Will was there, and at the end of the day he and the other railroaders collected a free cigar with their pay.

The next day, the Fourth of July, Goodland was packed with people from all over who wanted to see the final piece of track put in, connecting Goodland with the East and the West.

Charlie kept looking for the black engine to come puffing down the tracks from the east. He saw only the cloudless sky. He heard the Coronet Band practicing behind the courthouse all morning. By noon the saloons became overcrowded, and the crowd grew on the wooden platform in front of the small depot.

Frank nudged Charlie and said excitedly, "I hear the whistle! Honest, I do!" He pointed toward Colby. "It's the Iron Horse coming!"

Charlie squinted. He could not be sure he saw smoke or clouds low on the rim of the blue sky. Then suddenly there were church bells clanging, men whistling, and rifles and pistols going off in the air. People were crowding the platform and spilling over close to the tracks. The train was coming. Charlie heard the wheels clinking and saw the gray puffs of smoke. He felt a tingling sensation crawl down his back and his heart beat faster.

People shouted and clapped and threw their arms around each other. Dogs barked and horses snorted and reared back as if they were going to break their tethers. Some men yelled at the group of boys close to the tracks. The boys paid no attention and ran to meet the engine as it came in slowly. The engineer waved. The boys scrambled over the cowcatcher and up inside the cab and out on the diamond-shaped smokestack. The engine puffed steam and the engineer blew the whistle and rang the bell for some minutes as the boys jumped down to the ground.

Railroad and city dignitaries along with the newspaper editors crowded around as Marcus A. Low, president of the CK and N Railroad, dressed in a dark suit and bow tie, his blond hair slicked back, shiny with perfumed mineral oil, pounded in the last spike to hold the final shining rail.

Mr. Low invited everyone to look inside the chair car to see the comfortable maroon-colored plush seats and sample ice water from tiny, folded paper cups.

Next Charlie wandered to the edge of town to watch the baseball game. Will was catcher because he was big and had long arms that could reach out for the ball, high or low. The railroaders lost to the Goodland team, and the Goodland team lost to the little town of Ruleton, ten miles west on the rail line.

Frank entered the horse races with the boy riders. He won his first race and from then on did not even place. His father took him aside when he saw the disappointment in the boy's eyes. He told him if he'd done his best, there was nothing to be ashamed of. But as he saw it, Frank kept his head too high and kicked the horse far too soon. "Don't get haughty, keep your head down, and pace your horse. Do some practicing at home."

They watched Charlie in the boys' footraces. Charlie hunkered his big shoulders down and bent his knees. He lost the first race and decided it was his boots that held him back. For the next race he wore only his wool socks and his pants. He made his long legs stretch way out. He won easily. Sweating happily, he pocketed his two-dollar prize money.

Ell and Les Miner asked Charlie to watch the parade led by the Coronet Band. So much dust was kicked up by the parade on that hot day, Mary and Joe took to one of the side streets to drink their fresh-bought lemonade. There was a display of a threshing machine. Joe looked the machine over carefully. He wanted one.

Frank asked his father for a nickel to ride the merry-go-round swing. There was a violinist who encouraged the passersby to try the thrilling ride. The advertisement said it "takes you once around the world and back to Goodland." One patient mule was its motive power.

In the evening there was a display of fireworks that caused the people to say "Ooooooo" and "Aaahhh!" In Goodland's opera house was a dance with music by the Coronet Band.

Charlie wasn't much interested in dancing with girls. Just shy of fourteen he felt a girl was about as insipid as oyster stew without oysters. He saw Frank talk to some racehorse owners and thought it best not to interrupt, so he wandered up and down the Boulevard and several side streets looking for his older brother, Will. The ice cream shop was busy and the saloons were well-lighted and busy. He found Will bending his elbow with some Chinese and Irish railroaders. Will saw Charlie and came out on the boardwalk.

"Nice night?" asked Will.

"Yep," agreed Charlie.

"Want to go looking for some female companionship?"

"Nope," said Charlie. "But I've heard if you go past the courthouse and down to the last soddy, it gets pretty interestin'. There's some Mexican girls and an Indian lady that board there with Miss Rose."

"Charlie, you son of a gun! You been there?" Will's eyes were round.

"Nope, but I heard some guys talkin'."

"If I had more money I'd buy another drink and maybe go there. You got any money I could borrow?"

"I got two dollars from the footrace. I'm saving it to buy another pocket watch."

"Another? Where's the one Pa got you?"

Charlie instantly wished he'd kept his mouth shut. "Well, I sort of lost it. Now, don't go telling Pa."

"Lend me your two bucks and I'll be quiet as an oyster about your watch when I'm with Pa."

Charlie wondered how he could get out of this trap he'd put himself into. He hadn't been too smart. He put his head in the air and tried to act like he couldn't be pushed around. "I reckon you've smelt out the wrong hound's butt this time."

Will put his arm around Charlie and his other hand in Charlie's pocket, taking out the two silver dollars. Will dropped his arm and gave a long, low chuckle. "You know, with me, you have about as much chance as a rabbit in a hound's mouth." Will walked slow and easy back into the saloon.

"Have a fine evening," Charlie said, and worked his tongue around in his mouth, then spit alongside the boardwalk. Why was it that he was so angry when his own brothers outsmarted him? he wondered. He took long, fat steps back to the opera house.

The *Dark Horse* published an article on Thursday, July 5, 1888, which stated, "Early on the morning of the Fourth, crowds began to assemble from all directions, and by eleven o'clock it was estimated that there were no less than five thousand people in and around the city. Many had been watching the progress in the building of the railroad and the approach of the Iron Horse, and today they would get to see the first passenger coach run into the city of Goodland."

On July 6 the *Sherman County Republican* printed a large cartoon of a rooster crowing with the headlines "HURRAH! HUR-

RAH!! HURRAH!!! COCK-A-DOODLE-DOO. Goodland connected to the outside world by Railroad and Telegraphic Lines. The first train arrived in Goodland on Tuesday July third. Following this grand achievement there was a mammoth Fourth of July celebration."

That fall Mary entered her currant jelly in the Sherman County Agricultural Association Fair and won a blue ribbon.

With six or seven other young ladies Ell entered the Lady Equestrians. Their horses were brushed and combed so the coats shone. Ell rode sidesaddle, so her green skirt showed off beautifully against the silky, red-chestnut coat of the horse she rode to teach school each day. As she approached the judges in the grandstand, she drew her green satin ribbons apart and took off her bonnet. Her long golden-red hair flew out along with the horse's mane and fine, brushed tail. The reddish colors meshed as one long streamer as she paraded by. Her green eyes crinkled, her mouth curled into a smile. The judges were on their feet applauding. One of them announced loudly, "Miss Ell wins first premium!"

Jim Gandy took first place in the boy riders' horse race and Frank took second. Charlie came in first in the footraces and also in the mule race, but he had to forfeit each award because it had been decided that only one member of a family could be a winner in the races. Frank had raced first. Fred Warren's long-eared mule was awarded first money and Art Wells was given first in the footraces.

Charlie was crushed. He could not figure how the judging could be more unfair. "Next year I'll enter under a different name, by jeems," he said to himself, but he knew he wouldn't. He wanted the Irwin name to be important, but also honorable.

On the way home from the fair Ell waved her bonnet in the air and announced to her family and the wide prairie, "In two years I'll be Mrs. Frank Leslie Miner. You can bet your last dollar on that."

Mary was all hugs and kisses with Ell.

Frank said, "It's time. Les is at our place so much, I already think of him as part of the family."

Joe said, "I like Miner all right, but two years is a long restraint on any man."

"Hush," said Mary. "Young people understand self-control these days."

Momentarily Charlie forgot about the unfairness of the county fair racing judges and thought about Miner as a member of the Irwin family. It sounded swell to him. He always liked Miner.

Two years later, in September 1890, the Irwin soddy was filled with activity in preparation for the forthcoming wedding, set for the eleventh. Charlie whitewashed the inside dirt walls, making the cockroaches scurry out of the sod to find new homes as he filled in holes and crevices. He was surprised by a three-foot bull snake that came through the ceiling over Will's bed. After a scramble with a spade he managed to chop the snake in half and throw the remains out onto the scrap heap at the side of the house. Serve Will right if I'd left the snake in his bed and pulled the comforter up over it, thought Charlie.

"Ma! Do you want the ceilings whitewashed?" he called.

"This place looks so clean and bright, I wonder why we never thought of doing this before," she said. "The light seems to come in from all over. Yes, do the ceilings. Oh, my, how bright and beautiful it is in here!"

Charlie had whitewash running down his arms and spattering on his face and down the wooden handle of the mop he used. When the job was complete, he pulled up the old newspapers that had protected the braided rugs, kitchen table, beds, and chairs from being covered with calcium hydroxide. He dumped the left-over solution out the front door, then seeing it stay in a puddle on the stone walk, he took a broom and tried to sweep the flat stepping stones clean.

"You've made the walkway white as if it were snow. I like it. Thanks," said Ell, shaking scraps of material and threads off her apron. She was making her wedding dress from muslin bleached white as a christening dress, with tucks and stitches so dainty they were nearly invisible. The front yoke was scalloped and had cutout designs embroidered on it and on the leg-o-mutton sleeves. Mary had splurged and purchased from Marietta Roberts a long piece of blue, changeable silk for the sash. Joe took Ell to town and bought her the finest pair of soft kid, high-button black shoes.

Will no longer worked on the railroad, but had bought himself a dozen head of white-faced, red Hereford cows and several hogs. He promised Ell he'd butcher a hog and roast it for her wedding-day feast.

Ell talked to the folks of her schoolchildren about delaying the beginning of school a few days after the wedding so that she and

Miner might have a short honeymoon. Everyone was pleased that she was going to continue teaching. "We'll start school on the fifteenth of September," she promised, and invited all the folks and children to her wedding. Many were the same good people who had come to the Irwin house-raising several years before.

Reverend J. C. Dana, from the Goodland Methodist Episcopal Church, was going to conduct the wedding ceremony. It was a time all would remember for many years. The sun shone and it seemed the everlasting wind had stopped just for this day.

Ell stayed in her bedroom with the flowered curtain pulled across the front until the ceremony began. It was bad luck to be seen by the groom until the wedding time. Her mother stayed with her, giving her last-minute advice and pushes and pulls to the wedding dress.

Miner was waiting in the boys' bedroom with Will to keep him company. Will was the best man. Charlie felt a tinge of disappointment and jealousy because he thought he was the best friend of Miner. Hadn't he been witness to their first kiss?

The smell of freshly ground and roasted mocha coffee was strong and delicious in the soddy. The soddy was decorated with wild asters and Queen Anne's lace in wide-mouth canning jars. Outside, Will's hog roasted on a thick, green sappling.

Reverend Dana brought out a mouth organ and blew a note. The guests hummed "Here Comes the Bride." Miner and Will hurried to the area near the front door where the airy white Queen Anne's lace was poked in little bunches all around the wooden frame. Joe, dressed in his best wool pants and dark wool jacket, mopped his face with his handkerchief and went back to the curtain to escort Ell to the doorway. Mary came out to stand with the women guests, her nose shining and her eyes brimming with tears.

"It's always this way at weddings, especially the first child's," consoled Cora Collins, who had tears spilling over her red cheeks. "This is the most beautiful part of a woman's life. See how she glows with heavenly light. I hope Mr. Miner knows what he's getting."

"A woman is the most precious thing in any man's life," agreed Granny Harris.

"Her light shines as pure as these white walls," said Nora Lewis.

"Ssshhh," said Mary.

The ceremony was short. Afterward the kitchen table was moved out into the yard along with quilts and blankets to serve as places for the guests to sit, visit, eat, and drink. The table held a large bowl of steaming boiled potatoes covered with thick sour cream, and a platter piled high with the roasted pork. The wedding cake was yellow, because the egg yolks had to be used, and filled with chewy raisins, and covered with icing that was syrup beat up with egg whites. The pot of coffee was emptied and more was made. The guests danced to the music of Bill Gandy's fiddle and Reverend Dana's mouth organ. Whiskey for the men was passed around in a jug after each dance. Each man who danced with the bride pinned a greenback onto her long, full white skirt.

Without warning the music and laughter stopped. Rob Collins stood in front of Ell. His shrill, drunken voice rang out, "If you're too good for me, you're too good for him. No one will have you when I'm done!" He pointed a revolver at Ell. His hand shook so that the end of the gun went from her face to the blue silk sash and back to her face.

"You're crazy!" shouted Miner, who was held back by several men.

Old Nick and the other dogs barked. Rob eyed the dogs for an instant, then his eyes flashed back to Miner. "No, I ain't. I know what I'm doing."

Jack Collins cried out, "You damned fool! I told you to stay away for good!"

Rob's pale blue eyes grew cold. "Nobody gives me orders. Don't move or I'll shoot. I mean it!" All the time his eyes were frozen on Ell. She stood rigid. The greenbacks on her skirt fluttered like leaves on a quaking aspen.

"I want some singing," ordered Rob. "Good singing at this here wedding and this here killing. This is a beginning and an ending. It starts shiny white and finishes dull black. Sing, damn you!"

No one moved. There was complete silence except for the buzz of the bees in Mary's hollyhocks. At the far side of the crowd, a hunched-over figure on a blue and green quilt gave a moan that grew into a kind of wail.

Charlie recognized his mother's cry and his mind worked fast. He saw everyone frozen as in a painting. Only Rob seemed alive as he jerked his body to spread his feet apart and thus brace himself, then his body swayed back and forth. Charlie started humming in time with the swaying. At first the sound was faint as though caught in his throat. The moaning from his mother was louder. His hands bunched. He didn't have his rope, but his fingers reached for it. No one else had a weapon. Weapons were left in wagons, saddlebags, or against the wall inside the soddy. Charlie visualized his rope on top of the bedroom bureau. Next to the bureau was his pole bed with the Henry rifle on two nails above it. He hummed louder and looked at the people. Frank's face was gray as smoke, Miner's face was ashen. His mother's wailing rose and fell. Charlie prayed and kept humming, hoping others would pick up the song. They sat numb as in the grip of some helpless spell.

Charlie saw Rob's look of contempt as he shifted his gaze from Ell to Miner for a short moment. Then he heard Reverend Dana humming and he nodded and moved his head ever so slightly trying to make others understand and join in. Several little children cried. Charlie looked at them and nodded. One watched him and began to hum, then others joined so that slowly, one by one, everyone was humming the old hymn "I Would Be True." Not a word was sung, nor said. Charlie was on his hands and knees. He inched backward slowly, keeping his eyes on Rob, who continued to rock back and forth. Rob had a smile on his face, as though enjoying the humming, but his eyes never blinked and his chest seemed to heave in and out with the swaying.

Charlie edged behind a couple of men, sat on his haunches, then rose behind the men and stood next to Will who was next to the soddy door. He passed Will as though he were invisible, pressed against the door frame and inched across the front of the open door, then took one step backward and was in the shadow inside the soddy. He did not feel perspiration trickle down his back. His throat was constricted and his humming came in pieces, similar to his breathing. He had to think fast. He found his rope and gripped the hard cords. Then he boosted himself to the bed and reached up to the wall for his Henry rifle. Nervously he fumbled in the bureau drawers for cartridges. When he came out the door into the sunlight he could not see Rob at all. He had to move so the sun was not in his eyes. Suddenly Rob yelled, "You're going to pay for everything!" Charlie froze, but the humming went on.

It seemed to Charlie that the crowd had inched away, leaving Rob more ground. Charlie held the rifle vertically against his back, out of Rob's sight. He moved past Will to the back of Rob. Beyond that thick, cotton-white head of hair he could see Ell's face, her mouth drawn tight, her eyes wide with fear.

Rob's shirt and trousers were buff-colored like a young buck. The thought passed through Charlie's head that to shoot him would be like shooting an animal. Charlie moved slow. He wanted a clear path between himself and Rob. When he was certain Rob could not see, he held the rifle up to his eye. Close by a woman gasped and scuttled sideways like a crab. That made several women look up and draw in their breath or shuffle their feet. Rob was alerted. He turned and was facing Charlie's rifle. "Oh, no, you don't!" Rob shouted. "You can't stop me!"

Charlie saw Miner move up behind Rob and pull Ell back into the crowd that was getting to its feet and moving away.

"You're out of your head," said Charlie. "This isn't really you, Rob."

"Shut your face, you overgrowed fly-roost."

"If you go through with your plan, you'll hang."

"Back away!" Rob's breathing was labored and sounded like the steam engine coming into Goodland.

"Listen to me." Charlie tried to keep the Henry on Rob. His mouth went dry as a parched field.

"You never learn, do you, Irwin? You're the same kind of crap as the rest of your tribe. I could blow your head off easy as a gopher's." Rob's short spurt of laughter held no mirth.

"Drop your gun," pleaded Charlie, moving closer. "You could kill someone."

"You son of a bitch, I could blow your brains out!" Rob moved from side to side as though the humming had not stopped. His shirt was stained with perspiration, his eyes were red-rimmed and his mouth twitched.

Charlie raised his right foot and stretched it out slowly in a long stride and pulled his arms out full length so that he pushed the muzzle of the rifle against Rob's left side.

Rob's face flushed, his cheeks grew full as the exhaled air rushed out. His arms flung up and outward as the shot rang out. His eyes bulged and he fell to the ground, holding his bleeding shoulder.

Charlie had not fired the Henry. He was shaking and thinking Rob shot himself. But Rob's weapon was leveled on Charlie, always. Holding on to the rifle, Charlie bent to pick up the discarded revolver. It was not warm and smelled of oil, not powder. He slipped on the safety and heard Rob moan.

Jack Collins peeled out of the crowd. "Son! I shot you! Forgive me!"

The crowd was surging forward and Collins looked at Charlie. "By Jesus, Charlie, you stood in my line of fire so long I thought I'd have to fire to get you to move." His voice cracked. He was down on hands and knees examining Rob's wound. "Better get you into town." To Charlie he said, "I don't know where he got that revolver, but get it out of sight."

Charlie had the revolver under his belt and felt inundated by the gaggle of voices. A passage opened so that Collins and Reverend Dana could carry Rob to the Collinses' wagon. Charlie felt his knees buckle, so he sat on the ground and put his head between his knees.

"That was a purty thing you did there, son." Charlie felt his father's hand on his shoulder and the swell of the words in his head. He looked up. "But why didn't you use your rope? You had us petrified with that rifle."

Charlie didn't feel like talking. He wanted to lean against his father's broad chest and feel the solidness of it as he had when he was small.

Miner took Charlie's hands and squeezed them hard. "I owe you, brother." Ell edged in and, with no concern for her wedding dress, sat on the ground beside Charlie and put her arms around him. He felt nearly smothered and had to push her away so he could get some air in his lungs. Then Will crowded down against him, saying in his ear, "You stupid bastard. You could have nailed him right there and no one would have blamed you."

Charlie didn't reply, but he gave Will a look that would have peeled bark off a tree.

The Collinses' wagon scraped gravel and drove off.

Mary had a damp flannel rag in her hand. She wiped Charlie's face and hands as if he were a small boy. "Come, son. Put the rifle away and have something to eat." She moved back to help the guests, who were again flocking around the table. The past tension gone, they talked and laughed in loud voices.

Frank brought Charlie a piece of wedding cake. Charlie smiled but pushed it aside. Someone passed the brown whiskey jug to him. Will coaxed, "Take a swallow, Charlie. It'll stiffen your legs and set your head on your shoulders."

"I do feel wobbly," admitted Charlie, and he took a drink, hoping his older brother was right. Then he took another and he did feel better. He got to his feet and walked easier. He gave the rifle to his father to put away. "Thanks, Pa. Put it above my bed. It ain't been fired, so no need to swab it out. And put this out of sight." He handed his father the revolver. It's the first time I ever gave Pa orders, he thought. He took the jug from Will and had a third drink and now felt much stronger after the liquid got past the place where it burned in his throat.

"Have more," teased Will. "Can't hurt. Hey, don't cry in the jug, it makes your drink weak."

Charlie forced a weak smile, wiped his eyes on his sleeve, and took another drink.

Charlie was not sure when all the guests left.

Ell and Miner fixed a place to stay overnight in the barn before they moved into Miner's place the next morning.

Some of the young people, railroad section crew, farmers, and cowboys from the county, came to the Irwin homestead about midnight, when they figured most everyone was asleep. They shivareed the newly married couple by banging on iron frying pans and kettles and blowing tin horns. The racket was so much, Mary got up and invited everyone inside for coffee and more wedding cake. That's what they wanted anyway.

It was not long before Ell and Miner came into the soddy fully dressed.

"Not in bed yet!" yelled one of the boys.

"We got dressed," said Miner sheepishly, his arm around Ell and his face beet-red, "as soon as we heard the horses come up the road."

"I bet it took longer to put your clothes on than take them off," another joked.

Charlie lay in bed and swore to himself. The room spun and he'd been up several times feeling like he was going to die, if not this night, tomorrow for sure. Once Will came to see if he wanted some coffee and made fun of him and his pale face in the candlelight. Frank slipped out of bed and came back in his underwear, munching cake. He'd picked out the raisins and offered those to Charlie.

"Go away," said Charlie. "Don't jump on the bed. Can't you see I'm not well?"

"Will says you have buck fever. Pa says you had too much whiskey. Which is it?"

"Frank, if you ever grow up and think about something besides eating and horses, you'll know." Charlie put his hands on his head to keep it from flying around the room like a balloon about to burst. His insides were tangled and tight. He vowed he'd never try whiskey again as long as he lived, at least not more than one or two swallows.

TWELVE

McGuckins

Charlie and Frank exercised the two foals, Sunny and Tar Baby, each morning. The foals pulled against their lead shank, eager to run.

Charlie said, "Frank, act like Pa! Let 'em know who's boss. Don't let 'em get away with nuthin'. Their life has to be in a narrow track." He seemed to know that with horses it did no good to lose one's temper nor to be rough. Consistent tough, but gentle, training was best.

The mares were strong, but the strain of pulling a plow or grubbing out roots and stones showed on each of them. They slowed down, tired easily, by the time they had heavier and slightly darker winter coats.

By spring the young horses' baby hair had shed. Sunny's lighter spots were gone and she was golden like her mother. Tar Baby stayed black as tar.

Charlie and Frank found training the young horses took all the patience they had along with a bucket of oats or a couple of carrots. During the morning hours the boys led Sunny and Tar Baby around and around the meadow by a lead rope attached to biteless head stalls. This walking helped the animals lose their nervousness at being restricted and held back.

"Keep 'em in a narrow track, like I said. Don't force them, or they'll get mean and ornery. But make sure they know you're in charge," repeated Charlie. He knew neither he nor Frank could make the horses do something they didn't want to do. Horses could be stubborn as mules. Charlie adjusted their halters so they would be used to having their heads handled, and he rubbed their ears so they wouldn't be balky when it came time to put on a bridle. Sunny and Tar Baby were walked or run until both boys were tuckered. Neither thought that was too much strain for the horses.

Charlie took one horse at a time and put an old bridle over its head. "You kinda' fool 'em into thinking it's a halter," he explained. "If the headpiece accidently touches their ears, they'll be ornerier than a rat-tailed horse in flytime." Charlie talked all the while Frank slipped the bit into each horse's mouth. "It's only a hunk of rubber. Won't hurt you none."

There were more weeks of patience to get the horses used to something on their backs, such as saddle and rider. Then months more of running. By the time Sunny and Tar Baby were two-year-olds they were well molded into racers. Crowds of yelling people didn't faze them. When Frank was in the saddle, sweeping his hand down over either horse's neck, it was running, body stretched out, ears cocked back flat against its head.

Nothing Frank could think of compared with sitting on a racing horse. Tar Baby's strides lengthened to a fast gallop and the rail whizzed by. Sunny pulled out so she looked almost long of body as she turned on the speed that thrilled Frank. "She's a flier," he said. "She can keep up with Tar Baby easy. You can bet your bottom dollar on either and be a winner. I'm sure."

Frank no longer rode other trainers' horses in the county fair races. He rode his own and showed others how to ride, to control a horse by getting a tight hold on its mouth, digging in with his heels, whispering soothingly in its ear, and always his hand and seat firm. His reputation as a first-class jockey and trainer had begun.

Charlie pulled in three, four more mustangs, gentled them, and sold them himself. He was not sure what he'd do with his money yet. Sometimes he thought of owning a horse ranch. Other times he thought of buying land. He was a consistent winner of the foot racing and rope spinning during the local fairs. He still loved the deliciously exciting feeling that applause from a crowd gave him. He was a keeper of the Irwin account books and he kept the notes on the two racehorses.

Again when winter came, Charlie insisted that the racers be

taken for daily gallops, even through mud and snow. He checked their legs. He had Will file the sharp edges on their teeth and look over their hooves for bruises or cracks. When there were signs of wear, Will shod the front feet. Will said with hind feet bare the racers were not apt to kick their front feet and cut the coronary band.

Will knew nearly as much as his father about veterinary medicine, so he now did most of the farrier's work. He planned to build a new soddy barn for his stock. He dreamed of being a dairy farmer. That way he wouldn't be constantly depending on weather for a decent growing season and good harvest as his father did.

Joe wanted a thresher to make harvesting easier and faster. Threshing machines weren't new, but their popularity was increasing. Finally, in the fall of 1892, Joe rented a McCormick Harvester. The machines were called binders and were pulled by four horses. The binder cut grain, gathered the stems into bundles, tied the bundles with twine, and left them on the field.

Joe left so many bundles that he had to ask Will, Charlie, and Frank to gather them up. The boys stood a dozen bundles on end to form a kind of tepee. The tepee was called a shock. Shocking the bundles kept the heads of grain off the ground. When the field was partly covered with the spread-out shocks, Mary came out to help with the harvest. She laid two bundles across the top of the shock to shed the rain and snow.

Mary sold her eggs and friers in town and added roasting ears for five cents a dozen.

Mary especially missed Ell. She would think of things to tell her about one of the farm animals or how fast the baby chicks were growing. Ell and Miner visited on Sundays and stayed for dinner. Then Mary was so happy to have them around, she forgot what she had saved to tell. "Oh, never mind," she'd say, smiling uncomfortably.

A Texas-born Farmers' Alliance movement took the place of the old Homesteaders Union Association. Joe wanted the alliance to back a movement for grain elevators and mills along the railroad tracks. "If we modernize, Goodland could be a permanent settlement," he said at one of the meetings.

A. B. Montgomery, secretary of the Sherman County Development Company, stood up, ran his finger between his collar and throat, smoothed his graying mustache, then said, "This summer's heat's about to suffocate me. Creeks and ponds are dry. Pastures will soon be scorched. With no crops, who needs a grain elevator? Half the wells in the county will go dry by midsummer. What Sherman County needs is a rainmaker!"

A finance committee was named, and before the meeting was over a fair amount of money was collected. Montgomery was elated. He decided the rainmaker would be in Goodland during the County Fair.

Joe was chairman of the committee to erect a temporary building according to the rainmaker's specifications. The building would house the rainmaking apparatus. Joe and his committee put together a twelve-by-fourteen foot, two-story, unpainted structure in a week. The ground floor had a single door, facing east, away from the prairie winds. The second story could be reached by a ladder and had a small window on all four sides. These windows were covered with black oilcloth. The plans called for a good-sized hole in the roof so that the mysterious gases that were supposed to produce the rain could rise and form clouds.

Charlie put waist-high stakes into the ground in a circle around the raw, wooden building. The stakes had metal eyes on top so that a rope could be threaded through. The rope was to keep curious people from harm when the rainmaking apparatus was revved up and to keep anyone from disrupting the operation. As compensation for putting up the stake and rope fence, Joe let Charlie walk around the fairgrounds.

He went to the paddock where Frank was going to race Tar Baby. On the way he watched a couple prizefighters, their bodies shining from sweat. He saw a man in a dirty white apron selling hunks of chocolate candy. Standing close to the fence he saw Frank hunkered close to the neck of Tar Baby, riding a length behind his opponent. "Keep an even pull on the bit!" he yelled.

An unfamiliar voice at Charlie's elbow said, "Look at them go! You like horses?"

Charlie looked down and saw a girl with brown hair, soft like good tanned suede, and clear, deep blue eyes. She was small-boned, less than five feet tall, and couldn't weigh a hundred pounds. Her pixielike quality distracted him and now the race was over. He hadn't seen Frank win and he was annoyed. "Yes. I aim to have a ranch full of horses one day."

Lightfooted, the girl ran along the fence, disappearing into the crowd that yelled "Atta boy! Frank Irwin! Champion Jockey of Sherman County!"

Frank came down the track leading Tar Baby. When he saw Charlie he said, "I won five dollars!"

Charlie was all smiles. "That's great! I get half, remember I helped train the horse and you owe me a stem-winder pocket watch." He climbed under the fence and helped Frank walk the horse to the paddock. He was cleaning Tar Baby's quivering nostrils when he heard the voice again.

"Is that your horse?" The voice was like wind sighing in the treetops, soft and melodious. It broke into Charlie's thoughts of rubbing the horse dry with the old rag Frank held out.

"Hey, what do you want?" Charlie looked down into wide, ink-blue, intelligent eyes. The girl must have ducked under the fence when he wasn't looking.

"Nothing. Just talk."

"You made me miss seeing my brother come over the finish line." He tried to sound put-out. His voice cracked.

The girl laughed, a lighthearted trilling sound, then she said, "It was a lovely sight. I'm sorry you didn't see it." Her eyes turned dark purple, like woods violets growing in the shade. "You going to the depot to see the rainmaker come in?"

"Nope. I'll see him when he gets to the fair."

"I'll see you." Her feet hardly touched the ground, she was that light.

An unusual warmth ran up Charlie's backbone to his neck and face. He felt a kind of elation. He was sure it was not because Frank was Champion Jockey of the county. He enjoyed the feeling but was puzzled by it. He looked at Frank, who was smiling and rubbing down the horse. "Winning the race makes you feel good, huh?" said Charlie.

"People are waving at me from the fence. Men tip their hats and women dip their parasols. I'm a celebrity!" said Frank.

Charlie looked at the flannel-gray clouds overhead. "Enjoy it because tomorrow this rainmaker's going to be a winner."

The next day the gray clouds were gone. The sun moved alone in the blue sky. Charlie thought about the rainmaker and wondered what he looked like. The Irwin family headed for the fairgrounds early. They didn't want to miss a thing.

There was already a crowd around the rainmaker's building. Joe told Mary about the hole in the ceiling of the second floor. Will and Frank went to check on the racehorses. Charlie moved close to the rope. He was curious how rain could be made. He looked around and thought most of the town had come to see also.

Staring at the rainmaker's building was a serious-looking couple with a dozen children huddled around their legs. The mother's face was smooth as porcelain, as though if she dared smile it would crack in a thousand pieces. Her gray dress buttoned high under her chin matched the gray poke bonnet where her brown hair was pushed nearly out of sight. The father was forbidding, with dark-brown hair and sideburns that met a broad beard and steely blue eyes.

Without meaning to, Charlie's eyes met the inquisitive blue eyes of one of the children. She stood on the outer edge of the family circumference. It was the pixielike girl who talked to Charlie at the fair yesterday. Her fine brown hair was blown around the impish set of her mouth and upturned nose. Her face glowed and her arms waved as she explained something to the younger brothers and sisters. She was the only one of this family wearing some color. The long blue flowered skirt swung around her ankles. Her black button shoes were scuffed on the toes. The other children were dressed in all black or gray to match their solemn folks. I wonder who they are? thought Charlie.

"Oh, look, that must be the McGuckins," said a woman to her husband, who was standing next to Charlie. "I heard they came from New York State, then Missouri's Livingston County, before coming here."

Charlie raised his head in their direction. He found that information startling and hard to believe. Then he wondered if the girl knew his Grandma and Grandpa Brassfield.

Mrs. McGuckin directed her eyes toward Charlie. He felt his toes curl. Then birdlike, she cocked her head and said, "This is the Lord's day, son. You are going to observe one of His miracles performed right here."

The rainmaker came out of the building wearing a black cape with a red satin lining and carrying a black cane. He had a black top hat and white duck breeches tucked into black alligator-skin boots. But this rainmaker resembled the medicine man, Colonel Johnson, of years back. He no longer wore ten-dollar gold pieces as buttons, and he had no mustache. But he still had that high belly up under his vest from which thundered a slow, deep voice. Charlie pushed on the rope to see if he could get a closer look.

"Colonel Johnson!" called Charlie. "Remember me and the Irwin Smithery?"

The rainmaker colored slightly pink and said, "The name's Dr. Melbourne, son." He moved closer to Charlie and Will. Both were more than six feet tall and together weighed more than three hundred and fifty pounds. Surprised, Dr. Melbourne took Charlie's hand. "Hell's brimstone!" he whispered.

"I'm the kid," said Charlie, grinning, pushing his hair out of his eyes.

"I don't recall a body as big as yours. But now I see the same alert brown eyes and mop of sandy hair. Jehoshaphat! You came to see my splendid performance. So, the show continues. I'll see you later."

Dr. Melbourne strutted about showing off his knowledge about rain. He told the people about the wind bringing in clouds. "It's a scientific fact that water is made from two colorless, tasteless, and odorless gases. They are called oxy-gin and hydry-gin. If lightning strikes a mixture of these gases—*wham! bam!* Water is formed. Therefore, if I can generate hydry-gin and let it get up into the atmosphere to mix with the oxy-gin there, and a wee spark or bit of lightning hits—zap! That's rain!"

A couple of men in work boots and overalls carried a ten-gallon, glass carboy filled with a clear, oily-looking liquid from a wagon on the street to the door facing east. Next they brought in a couple of long, foot-wide strips of corregated sheet metal. Melbourne opened the door so the things could be carried inside. He closed the door before Charlie had a good look inside. Then he came close to the rope and grasped the hands that were outstretched. "Folks, welcome, all of you. I'm grateful to be invited to your beautiful town. You know who I am, Dr. Melbourne, the well-known rainmaker from Australia."

People buzzed like bees in a meadow of alfalfa. Charlie saw his auburn hair was flecked with gray. He wore a huge gold ring with a diamond setting. "Are there alligators in Australia?" asked Charlie.

"Don't push on the rope. I'm not parading out here to answer questions."

"I had no idea you were in the business of making rain," said Charlie, following him around the rope fence.

He moved close to Charlie and whispered. "I'm in the business of making money. Are you interested, Your Honor? Then bend way down, Corporal, and come through the barricade. I could use some help." He looked up at the clear blue sky.

Charlie was on the other side of the rope in a second. He took a deep breath and stepped to one side of Melbourne, who shook his hand and turned to the crowd. "Folks, you wonder what a tall man can sense that the rest of us ordinary people cannot? Well, my friends, this young man, one of your very own citizens, is going to tell you when to expect rain. He's going to smell the clouds forming."

"What?" Charlie heard himself say.

"You know—test the crowd. Work their fancies, entertain."

"But I've never smelled clouds!"

"Don't matter. Sing that new song, 'Home on the Range.' You'll knock 'em over."

Charlie swallowed. "Tell me how you use the metal sheets?"

Melbourne took off his cape and flung it around Charlie's shoulders and pretended he was fastening the neck piece as he briefly described rainmaking. "I'm going inside," he nodded toward the temporary building, "and do my experiment. Pray for rain clouds! Talk to the folks. Sell my famous anodyne, used by the social set in Australia. Use your spiel!" He patted Charlie on the back. "My Lord, you sure grew big!" He disappeared inside the building.

Charlie gulped and turned his face up to the sky. "Ladies and gentlemen!" He wondered where Melbourne kept the anodyne. "You have seen the famous Dr. Melbourne from the home of kangaroos. At this very moment he's preparing the final stage of his experiment." Charlie moved from one foot to the other, not quite certain what to say next.

One of the men in work boots and overalls placed a wooden box full of little brown bottles beside him. The man went into the building without saying a word. Charlie held up a bottle and felt his heart flutter like a butterfly. "This tiny bottle contains Australian painkiller made from secret ingredients." Charlie waved his hands. He felt the air swish the cape around his ankles and billow it out around his sides. People were quiet. Their eyes were on him. He walked slowly along the inside of the rope as he'd seen Melbourne do. Then he saw her, the tiny, pert Miss McGuckin. He pretended he was talking only to her. He used some of Melbourne's exact words. "This medicine is used by the social set in Australia." He read from the label. "One bottle, two bits. Only twenty-five cents. This pain reliever acts in harmony with the laws of life so perfectly it cleanses the blood of all disease." He paused, giving Miss McGuckin a chance to think on his words. "Who'll be first to have this rare curative? Yes, ma'am, two bottles. You won't regret your purchase. Yes, sir, one. And one here!"

Charlie sold until the case was empty, and miraculously another full case appeared at his feet along with a cigar box for the loose change. He began to sing the first verse of "Home on the Range."

He looked skyward. No clouds except for a few beginning to form low on the northern horizon. He wondered what Melbourne was doing. He filled his hands with more brown bottles. He saw Ed Murphy, the railroad ticket agent, run through the crowd and stand in front of him. Murphy waved his green, celluloid eyeshade. "I've got to see the rainmaker quick!"

"He's doing his secret experiment. No one can see him," said Charlie.

"Son, we've been gettin' wires from towns all along the northern line into Nebraska! People are drowning!" He sputtered the words.

Charlie gasped. The crowd buzzed and rumors flew. Charlie held up his hands. "The depot's deluged with telegrams telling of thunderstorms and flash flooding, bridges washed out. I'm going to tell Dr. Melbourne to shut off his rain machine for today."

The crowd *aahh*ed in one breath, then began to talk in a buzz. "He created rain! He actually did! Rain to the north! Rain's needed here!"

Murphy was knocking on the door of the unpainted building. Melbourne came out and stood beside Charlie. He eased the cape off Charlie's back and winked. He called out, "I'm telling you what I'm going to do! I'm going to set up my secret apparatus tomorrow morning and bring rain here. I won't fail you! Glorious, quenching rain! Think about it! Pray about it."

Charlie was exhilarated. He shook Melbourne's hand and promised to see him in the morning.

When Charlie caught up with his folks, his father spoke first. "Back there you reminded me of the time you sold liniment for the medicine man. You were only a boy then—but now? It doesn't seem decent for a local boy to act like a sideshow barker, talking about manmade rain, singing and selling."

"Pa! Dr. Melbourne *is* Colonel Johnson. Didn't you see?"

"Blasphemy! Settlers and people of Goodland paid good money for Dr. Melbourne. They set hopes in him. What do you think they're sayin' right now about you selling Australian tonic? It don't set right!"

"I promised Dr. Melbourne I'd be back tomorrow."

There were certain rules in the Irwin family. One was never to break a promise.

Mary's voice was steady. "Chores, then if there's daylight, you can come to town. That's that."

Next morning Charlie was up at the first hint of light. He planned to work steady and be done by noon. There was not a cloud in the sky when Charlie saddled his horse and left for town without lunch.

"I expected you this morning," said Melbourne, his face dark.

"Well, yes—there were chores," said Charlie.

"Don't blot out your transgressions. Just sounds like your saddle slipped to me," said Melbourne. His two assistants looked at each other and laughed quietly. He told Charlie to follow him up the rickety stairs.

"My pa worked on this building," said Charlie.

"Slapped up this building, you mean. Now, pay attention, Your Highness, because if you know how this works you can talk to the folks with some intelligence. Made more anodyne last night. Couldn't get the right-sized bottles, so charge thirty cents for these."

"The labels say 'twenty-five cents.'"

"Costs to import from Australia. Tell folks what a bargain they're getting, Admiral. I'm speaking honest with you. Wouldn't unless I was offering you a position on my staff. You want to come with me? We'll make a fortune off this rain business. When it fizzles out, there's always another scheme or fad waiting for us. What do you say, partner?"

Charlie, in his wildest dreams, had not expected such an offer. he hesitated to give himself time to think.

"Speak up. You're full grown. Think of the advantages. You'll get out of this godforsaken town, see the country, meet important people. You'll be important. Your picture will be in newspapers."

This was persuasive stuff for an eighteen-year-old, son of a farmer and farrier. Charlie wanted to shake Melbourne's hand and tell him yes right there, but he continued looking at the bottles of painkiller that didn't come from Australia at all. Finally he reached out, took the rainmaker's hand, and said, "Thank you, Colonel Johnson." That was an unintentional slip. He was embarrassed. "I mean Dr. Melbourne."

"Well, you'll have to keep your wits about you. Names used

correctly are important. A name can change with an occupation. People relate your name to your occupation and residence. I'm Dr. Melbourne from Australia."

"Yes sir, I'm sorry."

"That's another thing. Don't apologize. Whatever you do, act as if that is the way you intended. Make it the other man's problem. He's the one that should be sorry."

"I'll learn," said Charlie.

"That's the right attitude, Mate!" He clapped Charlie on the back. He showed Charlie how acid was poured slowly from the carboy into a large granite pitcher that was already more than half full of water. It took the two assistants to do the pouring of the clear syruplike acid. Charlie heard rumblings as if the mixture were boiling in the pitcher. A mist rose from the surface. When the pitcher was full, Melbourne turned with a flourish and stood beside the metal sheet. "The dilute acid is poured over the zinc, which stands in a granite tub. All precaution is taken not to spill. See the black spots on the floor? Even dilute oil of vitriol burns wood, clothing, and skin."

Charlie moved back, spellbound. There was a great effervescence when the diluted acid came into contact with the zinc. The bubbles hissed and popped.

Melbourne pushed the oilcloth curtains aside. The crowd was growing outside. "The hydry-gin gas is bubbling and rising heavenward. Go tell the folks, Partisan. Make them believe in miracles."

Charlie backed down the rickety steps and opened the door. He wore a cream-colored coat with large pearl buttons and a wide-brimmed felt hat to match. Melbourne said he was a knockout in the outfit. Underneath he wore his muslin shirt, black wool pants, and black boots.

Charlie raised his hands as he'd seen preachers do when giving the benediction at the end of Sunday service. The crowd quieted. He moved slowly, looking at the people as he talked. He felt a bond with his audience, as if a thin string tied them together as he talked. He could feel the string tighten when the audience was attentive and slacken when restive.

He pointed to the steam rising from the opening in the upper story. "Similar to fog." The folks understood and nodded. "See clouds moving in from the north?" They were! A whole bank of light, fluffy, white clouds was blowing in. "I smell the rain coming. Get your umbrellas ready."

* * *

Two days into Dr. Melbourne's experiments, a breeze, softer than the others, brought the first splatters of rain. People moved together in little groups and watched the rolling thunderheads. The breeze multiplied into a driving wind. Lightning cracked and thunder roared and the rain poured. Folks held papers and scarves over their heads if they had no umbrella. Some moved for shelter in buggies and under blankets in wagons.

Charlie was left standing alone, soaked. The cream-colored coat and hat showed their shabbiness and stains. He backed against the building, waiting for someone to open the door. The wind gusted into driving rushes of cold air. A couple of running men stopped and waved to him as if giving thanks for the downpour. Charlie thought his father would be pleased. He wanted rain. He thought his mother might fix something special for him for supper. Then another thought struck him. He wouldn't be home for supper. The mental image of his mother's sad, gray-green eyes pulled on his heart. Then he thought, why can't I leave to make my own life? Ma and Pa can make out without me.

Finally one of the assistants opened the door and helped Charlie bring in the empty wooden cases. The assistant smiled when he saw how bedraggled Charlie looked. The rainmaking apparatus was downstairs against the wall. The granite tub caught the rain that pelted through the hole in the roof. Melbourne sat on an overturned case eating bread and cheese. Charlie sat beside him. He was honored and overwhelmed to be in the presence of a man who could control the forces of nature. "You did it! You deserve more than praise!"

"Money is all I ask for." Melbourne smiled and offered Charlie a piece of bread. Charlie took off the wet coat.

The rain stopped as quickly as it started.

Melbourne opened the door and said to Charlie. "Help load this gear into that wagon over there. Kiss the girls good-bye, Duke, we're on our way to Lincoln, Nebraska. Hitch your horse to the back of the wagon. We'll take it along so you won't get homesick."

Charlie thought he saw the pixielike McGuckin girl standing against the rope, watching him haul gear to the wagon. When he stopped to look again she was gone. He packed boxes, glass spoons, stirring rods, and beakers into a straw-filled barrel. The black stallions tied to the front of the wagon snorted as though eager to be moving on. Melbourne piled some lumber from the building into his wagon. The assistants pulled up the stakes holding the rope Charlie had strung. They rolled the rope and tucked it into the wagon beside the wooden stakes.

"My pa bought that rope," said Charlie.

"A good man. You're living proof, huh?" said Melbourne, then in a loud voice he said, "Come here! Hang your jacket up to dry properly. Pay attention to your costume. Your hat needs to be rounded out over a pot so it'll dry without streaking or shrinking." He handed Charlie a white, granite saucepan. "If your hat shrinks, we'd believe it was your head that swelled. Tee-hee!"

Charlie nodded and pulled the hat around the bottom of the saucepan and put it on top of the lumber. He laid the damp coat nearby. Melbourne had spoken to him the same way his mother spoke when he was forgetful. His folks had every right to speak up if he didn't please them. But if he were old enough to do a job, he was old enough to see for himself what had to be done. Maybe if he couldn't see what was considered important, the job wasn't for him. Drying an already scruffy coat and hat wasn't much to get riled about. He went back to the building to see if there were something else to go into the wagon. He went to find his horse. The girl was there beside the hitching post.

"I wiped off your horse and saddle. I didn't think you'd mind. Ma had a pile of rags in our wagon, so after I wiped our horses I just did yours. You look better without that dirty, cream-colored coat."

Charlie bit his lip. He knew he should tell her he was leaving. He felt horrid, like he was getting a stomachache. The words would not come out. He told her thanks and walked back to the wagon without his horse.

A. B. Montgomery shook hands with Dr. Melbourne and handed him a brown envelope. "Your expenses plus fee for bringing that lovely rainstorm. This morning there was not a cloud in the sky. I didn't think you could pull it off. But I'm a total believer now."

Dr. Melbourne grinned so his white teeth gleamed in the late sun. He pocketed the envelope, then shook hands with Montgomery.

"You might get more rain tomorrow, a kind of aftereffect. I sent waves of hydry-gin into the atmosphere, and some of it may not be used up."

"How'd you do that?" asked Charlie as Dr. Melbourne turned to leave.

"I use my head. Listen here. I watch the clouds and I follow the rivers and creeks and valleys and I move where it's most likely to rain."

Charlie was aghast. "But that's fraud!"

"Quiet there, don't get flooded with holy enthusiasm. I use my head and I read all the latest scientific books and papers I can get my hands on.

"If you're coming, tie your horse to the wagon, Your Highness."

Ed Murphy from the depot came to shake Melbourne's hand. "Watch this, my good man," Melbourne said out of the side of his mouth to Charlie. He extended his hand to shake Murphy's. "Say, Mr.—ah—"

"Murphy," whispered Charlie.

"Mr. Murphy, I thank you for warning me yesterday about the strength of my rainmaking." He clapped Murphy on the shoulder. "Here's something for you. Take this buckeye. I brought it all the way from Ohio. Carry it in your vest pocket, all your enemies become kind to you." He saw Murphy wore no vest. "Now, if you were to carry it in your lower pocket or a purse—" Melbourne hesitated just a moment.

"I don't carry no purse," Murphy said, and laughed. He pushed his eyeshade higher on his forehead.

"Oh, I know that, but if you were to give this to a friend that does, or just leave it in one of your lower pockets, you or she would expect prosperity," Melbourne said and winked.

The ticket agent's eyes lit up and he said, "Why, thank you a heap, my friend," and he hurried back to the depot.

Charlie almost doubled over with a spasm of laughter. "Say, how can you give someone almost nothing and make him so grateful for it?"

"Son, it's a funny thing about people. They like little surprise presents. Then they remember the times I make right moves. To the point, the times I made it rain. So, I build a decent reputation. This work depends primarily on reputation. It pays better than hawking salves and alteratives, but it don't hurt none to push that, too, if the folks have money to spend."

Charlie blinked. "You gave Mr. Murphy a worthless seed and he'll remember you for it?"

Melbourne sniffed and wiped the back of his hand across his nose. "Master Irwin, are you listening to me?"

"Oh, yes, sir, every word."

"Well, then, I must be speaking in Hindustani."

"Oh, no, sir, I understand your words. But I don't see—" Charlie was afraid he did see and he wanted to be certain.

"Let's see now. For helping me with this little experiment I want you to have this cork from the alkyhall bottle. Bottle's empty. I used the alkyhall in the last batch of anodyne you sold. Wait a minute, I'll carve your initials in it. Then, also, you may have one of these Australian anodynes. It cures anything from corns to laryngitis. Come now, get your horse and then hike yourself up in the back of the wagon, right next to that carboy. You'll have to tuck your legs in."

Charlie put the bottle of tonic in his front pocket and the cork in his other pocket and dug in the mud with his boot. He cleared his throat and wiped his hand across his eyes so he could see without squinting. "I"m not going. I've decided to be a famous rancher and raise horses. If you ever come by my place, stop in. I'll always be CBI like the initials on the cork." He reached out to shake hands with Melbourne.

Maybe Melbourne had kind of figured Charlie had other plans because he said, "Horses? You ever think about racehorses? Don't forget me, Senator. I could work the odds for you."

Charlie walked past the empty rainmaking building to his horse. He saw the girl standing by the wagonload of kids. She came toward him.

"Boy, that Doc Melbourne can chew the fat," he said.

"You seemed to be chewing some yourself."

"Well, I really owe him. I learned a lot about clouds and stuff."

She seemed kind of quiet and Charlie didn't know if he'd said something that hurt her feelings. Her eyes looked sad and faraway.

He reached in his pocket and took out a cork with his initials. "Here's a souvenir. It's the top to one of those big bottles Dr. Melbourne has for mixing his anodyne ingredients."

She rolled it around in her hand, smelled it, and looked at the neatly carved CBI.

"That's my initials," said Charlie. "Stands for Charles Burton Irwin."

Her blue eyes looked like spring violets. "Thank you. I'll keep it. My name's Etta Mae McGuckin."

"Say, one day maybe you could come to our place."

The violet eyes glittered and her mouth turned up into an

impish smile. "It is better manners if the boy goes to the girl's place."

"Well, I—I could come tomorrow. Does you pa need a plow sharpened or a horse shoed?"

"My pa asked yours yesterday to look at our dog. When he comes, come with him. I make good gooseberry pie." She looked toward her wagon. "Uh-oh, Pa is fixing to leave. Bye!"

"Pie! Good-bye!" The musical rhyme rang in his ears. He decided to give the bottle of anodyne to his pa and a handful of long, slim cattails he'd find in the slough to his ma. Supper would taste good.

In the weeks that followed, the pixielike girl stayed in Charlie's thoughts. He hauled wood from the creek banks, harvested wheat, stacked hay during good fall weather, and before the warm stove at night he repaired a harness or read from books Ell had left behind: Virgil, Thomas Gray, Hesiod, John Dryden. Frequently he looked in the fire box to the flickering flames and indulged in dreamy contemplations. He thought about Etta's brown hair, sky-blue eyes.

Charlie rode eagerly with his father on farrier rounds, hoping to stop at the McGuckin place. He watched young girls in town, seeking a certain toss of the head, a manner of skipping to cause the skirt to swing jauntily. When he could stand it no longer, he asked, "Pa, those new settlers—McGuckins—weren't you to do something at their place?"

"McGuckins? Oh, that was a hound dog with worms. A son-in-law sent word the dog died."

"What a shame. Shouldn't we look at their other animals?"

Joe looked up from polishing his fiddle. "Whatever for? I wasn't asked."

"To say we're sorry—about the dog?"

Amused, Joe said, "A dead dog?"

"We could go to church—see the McGuckins there." Charlie's heart thumped. He waited for the answer.

"If you feel the need to give condolence for a dog or to hear one of Reverend Dana's sermons on Hell's fire and damnation, go. You don't need me nor your ma. We've other things to do. Irwins and church don't seem to mix well. Stay here. Read the Bible. Take a walk by the creek, you'll feel the presence of the Lord. Think on it."

The next Sunday, Charlie sat in the back pew so he could see who came into church. The McGuckins came and took one complete pew for their brood. Charlie moved up. Etta smiled. She did not turn to look at Charlie, but he felt she knew he was there. Her cheeks were tanned and taut over the facial bones.

Mr. McGuckin surveyed his row of children. He said so Charlie could hear, "It's against the commandments to sing poplar songs like that 'Home on the Range.' But it's a mark in your favor to sing church hymns." His head turned farther, his eyes lingering on Charlie, uncertain and fiery.

For a moment Charlie held his breath. When it was time to sing, Charlie did his best. The sound came from deep inside his chest and resonated from his diaphragm to his palate.

The boy in front of him stopped swinging his legs, turned, and whispered, "What's your name?"

Charlie hummed the *amen*. "Charlie. What's yours?"

"Curly." The boy turned quickly and looked straight ahead. His father was inspecting the row of children from the corner of his eye.

Charlie studied the head of brown, curly hair, then bent forward and said quietly, "Tell your sister, Etta, I'd like to take her home."

Curly's back stiffened, but he did not turn.

Charlie's mind was elsewhere for the remainder of the service. The moment the benediction was over, he was on his feet. The McGuckins took their time getting out of the pew. The parents pressed their lips together as a sign they disapproved of the children's lingering. Each child took a long look at Charlie as though knowing by osmosis that he'd whispered to Curly. "I'm Walt," whispered the last child, who was barely in his teens. "Do you like Etta?"

"Maybe," whispered Charlie, feeling embarrassed.

"You can't take her home," Walt said, hardly moving his lips.

When Charlie was out the sanctuary door, the McGuckins were piling pellmell into their wagon. His heart beat fast. Momentarily he wished he'd said nothing to Curly or Walt. It wasn't any of their business. He then saw Etta. She smiled and waved. He pulled himself up straight and walked purposefully to the McGuckin wagon.

Mr. McGuckin's face was weathered, lined coarse by the action of wind, sun, and rain. He stood beside the wagon as his wife climbed, unaided, to the seat. His hands remained at his sides. He did not reach to take the hand Charlie proffered.

"Good day," said Charlie heartily.

"What is it you want?" said Mr. McGuckin tartly.

Charlie kept a friendly look on his face. "I came to ask permission to take Etta home in my wagon." He could feel perspiration on his palms evaporating, making his hands cold.

Mr. McGuckin's acerbity caused Charlie's shoulders to slump. He looked for Etta. She was helping the smaller children find places to sit comfortably. Mr. McGuckin was talking.

"It's the smart alecks like you, you know, that give young people a bad name these days. Singing popular songs. I haven't forgotten."

Charlie thought he heard some stifled giggles, then wasn't sure. Maybe it was the wind in the treetop. His heart sank. "I beg your pardon, sir. I will stay directly behind your wagon and let Etta out when we are at your gate." He could feel the clammy fingers of wind at the back of his neck.

"Don't beg my pardon. I don't allow Etta, nor any of my offspring, to ride in a whippersnapper's wagon." Mr. McGuckin climbed into his wagon, clicked his tongue, and at the same time picked up the reins. His two horses moved together in step, *clip-clop, clip-clop*.

Dumbfounded, Charlie stood rebuffed. Etta waved. He imagined tears in her violet eyes. Her gray bonnet hung down her back and the fine, brown silk threads of her hair shone in the sunlight.

"Be gone. You younker!" Mr. McGuckin called.

Charlie's head snapped up. He wanted to wave, but his hand wouldn't move. When the wagon was out of sight, except for the rolling ball of dust behind, he thought, why in blue blazes am I standing here? I'm a fool. Women! They are a nuisance, inconsistent, vexatious, an annoyance, a plague, sour gall, an effrontery to man's intelligence. He was thankful his brothers, Will and Frank, weren't around to tease him. He vowed he'd face this and all misfortunes with fortitude. He'd show those who knew him that he had integrity, high standards, and an appreciation of his fellow men.

Reverend Dana came across the churchyard to Charlie's side. "Doesn't take the congregation long to clear out these days."

"Is it against the Lord's commandments to sing popular songs?" asked Charlie.

"Not that I heard directly. So long's the singing's not accompanied by swearing and spirits." He looked at Charlie firmly. "You have a run-in with McGuckin?"

"No, sir!" Charlie was adamant. Then he added, "Not of my making."

"I suppose it's none of my business, but I'm going to warn

you that McGuckin is a stern, unyielding man. He's against and intolerant of any temptation, gambling, even laughing, it seems. In some ways he's been made sour because of the heap of acid in his life." He waited, then added, "Opposite side of the coin is your ma. She's soft-hearted, forgiving, tries to please. She sees a healing power in fun and laughter."

Charlie did not find the contrast pleasant, but felt forced to comment. "Life doesn't have to be a bitter pill. Does it?" Charlie walked toward his wagon. "I want mine to be an exciting adventure."

"Most get what they want. It's a matter of attitude. Keep the Lord's commandments, and do the best you can each day. See you next Sunday?"

"I can't say next Sunday for sure," said Charlie. "But I'll see you again for sure."

The ride home was pleasant. Charlie's mind was occupied with what he might have said to Mr. McGuckin. Jeems! He could have told him he'd outgrown the smart-aleck stage and never was a whippersnapper. He combed his brain for wise phrases he might have used. Mr. McGuckin was a fool, a shallow-brained, insensate eccentric.

Charlie was so deep in his exasperation that he hardly noticed and did not question the dark, quivering cloud coming straight for him, low on the road. When the strange cloud was nearer, his eyes widened. It appeared to be a brightly colored, shimmering swarm. It appeared to be thousands upon thousands of teeny-tiny orange, white, and black birds, all fluttering together. He stopped. When the fluttering creatures were closer, he recognized them. Butterflies! Then he was inundated with butterflies. Some lighted on his head, shoulders, and hands, on the horse's head and nose. The horse shivered and switched its tail. To Charlie this was a beautiful, wondrous sight, exciting. The insects fluttered their wings, then let the breeze carry them along before they flew again. Some rested on the alternate, lance-shaped leaves of the milkweeds. Some plants were covered with butterflies so that they looked like exotic, tropical flowers. The butterflies moved south and he wondered if they followed the call of the Canada geese. He estimated that the butterfly cloud was a mile long and half a mile wide; how deep he was not sure, maybe a few hundred feet.

There were stragglers long behind the main cloud. He got off the horse and examined a few on a milkweed. Their wings were ragged and torn. Poor creatures must have come a long way, he mused. Why? Where were they going? Why? Some Pied Piper calls in butterfly language. He climbed into the wagon, held up on the reins, staying dead still. He listened. He could hear nothing unusual, only the constant whooshing of the wind across the flat land.

Confidence in Melbourne's rainmaking ability was expressed the following spring when he was asked to produce crop rains in forty western counties at ten cents a cultivated acre. After his departure from Goodland, the Inter-State Artificial Rain Company was formed. The president was Ed Murphy. Martin Tomblin and A. B. Montgomery were directors. Montgomery went to Topeka for a charter and to visit with the attorney general about the irrigation laws applying to rainmaking. This company made a deal in Temple Texas to sell one of their rainmaking machines for fifty thousand dollars. In 1892 a man from Tulare, California, came to Ed Murphy to contract for rain.

That same year Dr. W. B. Swisher of Goodland chartered the Swisher Rain Company, which went to Texas and Mexico to operate. A third company was the Goodland Artificial Rain Company chartered with J. H. Stewart as president. That summer Dr. Melbourne returned to Kansas to produce half an inch of rain over six thousand square miles near Belleville for five hundred dollars.

A reporter for a Dodge City paper wrote: "If Kansans are gullible enough, and Providence helps the wizard out with one or two coincident wet spells, this is liable to prove a good thing for Melbourne, who, of course, is not in the business for his health."*

Winter came and summer, then winter again. The drought was broken.

During a conference on rainfall and irrigation held in Wichita, Kansas, during the summer of 1893, Mr. A. B. Montgomery gave a talk stating that he'd operated the Inter-State's rain machine three times during the spring growing season in Sherman County and as a result of sufficient rain there were one hundred thousand bushels of wheat produced. He ended his speech by pointing out that there was little wheat produced in any of the surrounding dry counties.

*Courtesy of the *Sherman County Historical Society Bulletin,* Goodland, Kansas, Vol. 5, No. 3, Jan. 1980, "The Rain Makers."

From March to August, Goodland's rain companies operated at various locations in Kansas and Nebraska. Each claimed credit for any rain that fell. However, by the first of September the rainmaking experiments slacked off and by the end of the month most experiments were canceled by the growing number of skeptics.

In Minden, Nebraska, a president of one of the Goodland rain companies was tied to a pole and treated to the fire hose by active doubters to show that president how a spray of water can easily be made with no prescribed mumbo jumbo and secret operations.

One warm afternoon in the summer of 1894, Les Miner ran into Rob Collins in the Mercantile in Goodland. Rob allowed as how he was back for good, looking for a job as hired hand. He asked Les if he were hiring. Les said his spread was not large enough.

Les noticed Rob's speech was slurred and his words slow. He supposed Rob had been drinking. Rob turned ugly and threatened Les for scorning him and not giving him a job. Rob said he'd kill Les the next time they met and it was a promise. He crossed his heart to show he was sincere.

Les tried to think of something to say, but couldn't. He noticed Rob was nervous and kept looking around at people who passed. No one looked at them. Les walked away, his knees watery.

Les didn't tell Ell. He didn't want to frighten her. He loved her so much he didn't want to do anything to hurt her. But he dreamed about running, running faster and faster so his chest was on fire and his legs ached. Rob was always a few steps behind him. Rob's feet went *bam, bam* on the wooden boardwalk. The dreams were worse than the real thing. In reality Rob never chased Les. Soon he was afraid to sleep for fear of dreaming that Rob caught him. He avoided Ell, he couldn't talk with her. One day he decided he had to hold on to his sanity. He had to talk to someone. "Let's go visit your folks. I want to talk with Charlie," he said.

"I hope you say more to him than you say to me," Ell said. "I know something's bothering you, but if you don't say, how can anyone help?" Tears ran down her cheeks. "You don't see me anymore. I could be dead," she sobbed. "What can Charlie do? We'll be squandering his time. He doesn't understand being married."

Les shifted uneasily at the kitchen table. "You wouldn't have said that if you knew as much as I."

"What makes you think I know nothing?" Ell sounded angry and sobbed harder.

"I hate fusses. Let's go see how your folks are making it." Les was stern. He got up and went out, saddled two horses, and waited for Ell. Her eyes were red. He rode ahead and said nothing.

Mary and Joe were delighted. "You don't come often enough to suit either of us," said Joe, taking Les aside to talk crops and land irrigation. He wanted to lay pipes from the Middle Fork of Sappa Creek to the small meadow.

Mary saw immediately that Ell had been weeping. She asked no questions, biding her time for the explanation. She busied herself making the meal. When the table was set and the platter of meatloaf, bowl of boiled potatoes, boiled green beans, jams, and biscuits were in place, she called, "Come, while it's hot!"

"Eat, we'll talk later," said Joe, munching steadily on meat and potatoes.

Will and Frank eyed Les, wondering exactly why he'd come this particular day. Charlie looked at Ell, who watched Les like a hawk, and knew there was more to this visit than farm talk.

"Why can't we talk while we eat?" asked Frank.

"Hush," said Mary. "Isn't it enough just to have these two at our table again?" She shook her head and fixed her eye on Frank for being so insensitive. "Leave things be."

"If leaving things be by ignoring them is so valuable, we ought to admire the ostrich with his head in the sand," said Will, pouring coffee into a saucer to cool it.

Mary cleared the plates away. Ell got up and took the serving bowls from the table. Les caught Charlie's eye. "Show me the latest wild bronco you've tamed."

Out in the meadow Les watched a black-maned red stallion munch the grass. He put his hand on Charlie's shoulder. "I have something to tell you. If I don't tell someone, I could blow wide open like a puffball in the hot sun. Rob Collins is around Goodland again." They sat on the grass, each chewing on a wild-rye stem. Les told Charlie about his meeting with Rob and the subsequent disquieting dreams. "I don't know why his threat bothers me, except I believe he would not hesitate to shoot me, or club me, or choke me to death. I married the girl he wanted. Truly, I don't believe he knows what love is. Not in the way most people feel."

Charlie was quiet for a long time. He stared at a fat bumblebee gathering yellow pollen on its legs from jimmyweed flowers.

"Well," said Les, "what can I do? I can't tell the sheriff. He'd think I was a cracked brain. Maybe I am. What do you think?" He bit the wild-rye in two.

"I think there's something else. You've kept the whole thing from Ell. She's your wife. If you can't tell her, you have no business telling someone else."

Les stood up.

Charlie's throat grew tight. "You say you love Ell. Then share everything." His words sounded brittle, unlike he intended.

"It would frighten her."

"Haven't you noticed? She's already frightened of something."

"It's because I've been such a bear to live with," Les flashed.

"There's something else. Something's got her bleary-eyed."

"I grind my teeth at night like I could eat the sights off my six-gun. She hates the sound."

Charlie looked up as something flashed at the top of the rise. "Sit down. She's coming over here."

"Why is she doing that?" Les said in a strangling voice.

"Maybe she'll tell us," said Charlie.

The wind blew Ell's hair like an amber-orange fan around her face. She was crying. She'd picked a bunch of milkweed flowers.

The flowers reminded Charlie of the time a couple years back when he'd found himself in the center of a cloud of butterflies.

"This is men's talk," said Charlie, "so dry your eyes and you can join us. I'll tell you about the time I saw a bunch of butterflies light on those pink and white flowers, completely covering them."

Ell smiled and dabbed at her face with a wadded handkerchief.

"Monarchs lay eggs on the milkweed. Grandma Malinda told me," she said, sounding like she had a head cold. She sat beside Les, facing Charlie. "I got the flowers for Ma's window vases. I came to talk."

"It's running in the family. Shoot. What's on your mind?" Charlie pretended to button his lips shut.

She took Les's hand in hers. "Don't tease. I'm scared to death. I didn't want to worry you about something that happened in town. But the more I thought about it, the more frightened I am. Remember when I went after the dress Marietta's making for me?"

"Is Miss Roberts ill?" asked Les.

"No, far worse. Rob Collins is back." She said it with finality, as if that event heralded a new era.

Charlie pushed the hair out of his eyes. "Jeems! Incredible! One guy with rats in the balcony affects two normal people so that they act addled. Did he chase you?"

Her eyes had a faraway look, misty. "Chase? He rushed at me headlong."

Les put his arms protectively around her and drew her against his chest.

"Don't squeeze so tight," she gasped. "I can't talk if I can't breathe."

"I could skin that snot-nose alive!" Les waved his hands and stood up. "I'll pull his picket pin!"

"Sit down. Hear Ell out. Blast it! I swear, when I'm married I'll listen to my wife before I jump up and go off half-cocked."

Les was indignant. "What do you know about marriage?"

"Nothing. Except I've noticed my folks. Their spats don't seem to mean much. More like funning each other. They respect each other. They like talking things out. I used to listen to them murmur after I should have been asleep, when I was little."

"I want to talk," Ell said quietly. "If I hold in any longer, I'll explode." Her voice rose. "I don't want to seem amiss. I'm frightened. My appetite's gone. I can't sleep!" She ended on a high crescendo.

"Start at the beginning. There'll be no interruptions. I promise." Charlie glared at Les.

Les sat down and took Ell's hand in his and said, "So, you went after your dress, then what?"

"Yes, then I go to the Mercantile for chalk for school. When I come out someone comes up behind me so quiet I never suspect. A voice says, 'Afternoon, Miss Ell. Permit me to sit in your wagon a few minutes. We'll talk old times.' My legs turn to tapioca. My mouth dries like parchment. I know without turning my head it's Rob. I get into the wagon and tell the horse 'Giddyap!' Rob moves in front of my horse. Honest. I can't believe my eyes. I pull the reins in to avoid him. He's quick and swerves this way and that, but always stays in front of my horse. I have to stop or run him down."

"You should have run the son-of-a-gun down!" snorted Les.

"Hush! We promised," reiterated Charlie.

"He jumps to the seat beside me. He's grinning and puffing.

He leans toward me and says in a loud voice, 'You're the feistiest but prettiest woman in the whole state of Kansas. Every man that looks at you is mad with desire. Me most of all.' I can tell his passion is up." Ell looks sideways at Les. "He's ready for—"

"My God! That reprobate!"

Charlie reached out a sweaty palm and touched Les. "Sshh!"

"Marietta and I played beauty parlor. Tinted talc is on my cheeks and berry juice on my lips. I do look fixed up. Rob leans near and I can tell he's had spirits. He's hesitant—gropes for words."

Les brightened and he nodded.

Charlie fixed him with his eyes. Then he sighed, relieved when Les was silent. Charlie breathed faster, waiting for Ell to continue.

"I accuse him of drinking and he says it is me that makes him dizzy with cravings. Then he says real quiet, in a monotone like this"—she makes her lips tight across her teeth—"'If I can't have my way with you, I'll fix you so that no other man can.' Oh, Lord, his eyes are fearful. They dart back and forth like blue steel buttons—cold and cruel."

Les shivered, but Ell went on.

"There's a bunch of settlers across from the Mercantile. I waved to them when I went into the store. I'm friendly. They wave back. Now out of the corner of my eye I can see those men gabbing and laughing. Rob inches closer. All of a sudden he's pressing his lips against mine. Right out in front of everyone, in broad daylight. His hand is on my—bosom. I feel it, tight." Ell stopped to catch her breath and look at Les and Charlie.

Les's mouth was open and his eyes were wide. His hands were clutched around his knees.

Charlie seemed to be studying his sister. He was mesmerized by her voice modulations. He sensed her words were more than a simple confession. The words were something tangibly intimate between a married couple. The words were bold and exciting to Charlie.

Ell went on. "I jerk the reins and my horse starts off. I scream and my horse trots. I slap the reins and break away from that—that maniac. The horse runs like a cat with its tail on fire, down the Boulevard, past the settlers, leaving a cloud of dust. Rob clutches the seat instead of me. He cusses. At the end of the Boulevard I turn the wagon around and drive into that dust cloud. Rob coughs. I pull up my foot and, honest to goodness, kick him in the side—hard. He loses his balance and falls into the street. I haul up the reins, stop. The settlers make a circle around Rob's body. Some laugh, from nervousness, because Rob doesn't move. One man asks if I gave him the bloody nose. Someone suggests they put him in my wagon and I take him to his place. I say no. I feel kind of faint. I don't want that man in my wagon under any circumstances. I lose my head and shout, 'Keep him away from me!' My head clears and I'm not going to faint even though my hands tremble."

Les took a deep breath and flexed his hands. He waited silently for his wife to continue.

Charlie was aware that some of the settlers hung around downtown to watch the ladies. He knew that one lady they watched was his sister because her features were good to look at, like fine-cut pink and white cameo. She was the respected schoolmarm of Sappa Valley. The men looked, but anyone who made an indecent advance was as welcome as a rattler in a chinchilla farm.

"My shout brings Rob around and he sits up, looking like he doesn't know what's happened. When he gets to his feet, those six settlers are after him, punching, pummeling, kicking, tripping. He gets more than a nosebleed. His face is so swollen his ma wouldn't know him. He sure can't see much when he limps off to the north part of town. He's a real pitiful sight."

Charlie detected a curious, savage joy in his sister's face. She'd enjoyed the fight for her honor. With a mere kick and a shout she'd rallied half a dozen men to defend her reputation. Justice was in her hands. She'd enjoyed that feeling of power.

Les was boiling. "If I see that man, I'll shoot him where he looks biggest! I swear it!"

Charlie rocked on his haunches and said softly, "Nobody's going to kill Rob. He'll destroy himself."

For a moment the three sat motionless. No one spoke. No one dared be first to break the spell those last words cast.

Les was the first to speak. He told his own latest experience with Rob, then hung his head. "I'm so ashamed I acted like a bear. Worrying about myself, I pretended to be protecting your peace of mind." He put his arms around Ell. "My God! You're shaking! We were both so scared we couldn't talk." He held her close.

She closed her eyes and held her face to Les. The kiss was sensual, born of the overwhelming relief flooding through them.

Charlie felt as though he were privy to the deepest emotion between a man and woman. He had a throbbing sensation in his abdomen where it joined his thighs. His legs would not move. His breathing was shallow and fast. He felt trapped in a swamp, not able to pick up his feet. He was able to choke down on himself and take a deep breath.

Ell and Les had broken apart, each visibly affected by the highly charged emotion. Ell looked at Charlie with eyes that shone. "What are we going to do?"

Charlie gulped. "Jeems, you know better than I."

Her eyes opened. "Think on it, Charlie. You brought us together. You listened to us. Now what?"

"Well, I'm thinking on it." He bunched his legs under his bottom and boosted himself upright. His legs tingled as though they'd been asleep. He walked around, clearing his head. "Have you some goal? What do you honestly think of farming?" He looked at Les.

Les's face colored as red as the setting sun. "All I know is farming and mining. But I've always wanted to work with ciphers. I keep my books so they balance from top to bottom, bottom to top, and sideways. I enjoy that and would like to do it full-time. But I figure it's too enjoyable to be my everyday job. Now, what has that got to do with this—this other stuff with Rob Collins?"

"I'm working on it." Charlie grinned, feeling now he was in control of his emotions. His breathing was easier.

Then Ell began to talk. "You know how scared I am? Some days I go away from my school soddy with this surge of fear that Rob is outside waiting. I carry a broken vinegar bottle. It's a weapon. I'm prepared to get him first. I daydream that my last living act is writing my name in blood on a slate. I write his name in my blood, so people know." Her voice cracked. "My heart pounds when I go to school and when I leave, when I go to town now, which is only once since the episode, because I forget what I am there for, and I have palpitations and have to come home."

"I haven't been for supplies," admitted Les.

"I know one thing." Her green eyes brightened. "Those men, the settlers, will fight for me. I can count on them."

"Sure, they're loyal to you. You represent their ideal. A decent woman is on a high pedestal. But if someday"—Charlie looked down at his hands—"Rob gets you to his place? Will the men think you are something out of their reach? So the question isn't, what can you do. It's, where do you go."

"Go? What are you thinking?" asked Ell.

Les got to his feet stiffly. "How about Colorado Springs? I've mined thereabouts. I could do it again."

Ell was quiet. Charlie knew she was thinking about her school. She thought of miners with bent rheumatic backs and sickly babies and women with cataracts. She pictured herself clearing, like magic, the cataracts with herbs, straightening the stiff backs with salves, and making the babies fat and healthy with teas. She could start another school. Her mind filled with fantastic expectations. Now her heart beat with this new anticipation and thankfulness. This suggestion gave both her and Les an honorable escape. "Yes," she said, "we'll move. I'd not let a maniac shame my family." Ell was not in the least ashamed of seizing this opportunity.

They ran back to the soddy. Before going inside Charlie caught up with Les and asked, "You ever hear of a homesteader called McGuckin?"

"Nope," said Les, "never did. Why? Is there someone in that family like this cotton-headed, cotton-mouthed character that has given Ell and me fits?"

"You're a goon. But I gotta thank you. You got me to thinking that no one, even a person's family, has the right to take happiness from another. For a couple years I've been knocking around like a blind dog in a meatmarket. No more. I'm going to call on that pixie, if she's not spoken for."

Ell giggled. "Pixie? A little person? Charlie, you're demented. You suppose it's from listening to your sister and brother-in-law?"

"I'll tell you one thing for sure," said Charlie, his eyes flashing. "I wouldn't marry a schoolteacher. I'll tell you the reason why. She makes a soup of polliwog tails and says it's raisin pie."

"That's vulgar and horrid!" yelled Ell, but she was laughing and some of her anxiousness was forgotten.

That evening Les explained to his father-in-law that he was about fed up with sporadic rains, crops dying in drought, dying with rust or rot, and he was seriously thinking of going back to Colorado and mining. He explained that he and Ell'd talked it over and she was eager to start a school for miners' kids and use her knowledge of herbs on those who were interested.

Ell told the news to Mary. "If mining turns out to be worse than farming, Les and I will be back to farm with you and Pa," she promised her mother. Mary was aware of the pine scent from incense in Ell's clothing and hair. The aromatic essence triggered a feeling of melancholy. "You two won't be back," predicted Mary with a catch in her voice. "Your husband is intelligent. He wants control over his life. Farming won't permit a man to control. Farming directs a man's actions." Her brown face was drawn. Her fingers drummed on the side of her rocker. She was a sparse woman, not well padded, as were so many settlers' wives. She wore her shawl even in summer to keep the constant wind off her parchmentlike skin. Her steps and hand movements had become jerky. At the end of busy days standing on her feet, she complained of swollen ankles. "I wish we'd divided the land among the boys. Maybe bought twice as much. Keep everyone together." Her voice sounded harsh. "Your pa thinks about it, but he never does anything. He leaves the doing to Will—who only does as he pleases."

Ell fell to her knees, put her head in her mother's lap. Mary continued her rocking back and forth in the chair. She patted Ell's hair. "You smell like a summer day, my dear. Send us letters."

"Yes, I will," said Ell quietly. A mist covered her eyes so that she could not see. She blinked and tears dropped to her mother's lap. "Oh, Ma, I will miss seeing all of you."

Mary's hands pressed down on her daughter's shoulders. Tears ran down her cheeks.

That night in bed Charlie tried to recount the day's emotional upheavals. He felt drained and empty. His mind could not hold one thought in front of another. He was asleep before he could recall his uncertainty about being drawn into Les's problems and his role in the solution.

The first few weeks after Ell and Les sold their land and were gone, Mary had to work to find strength to get out of bed mornings. A letter in Ell's handwriting and smelling like pine told her that Les had a job in a coal mine. They rented a one-room house and Ell tramped the foothills for herbs to treat lung disease. "I want not only to cure those men with the cough, but to prevent the others, mainly my dear Les, from getting sick. This is my mission. I'm fascinated with herbs that cure disease." Ell's letter was passed to each member of the family.

Men are fascinated with Ell as moths are fascinated by a flame, thought Charlie. Out loud he said, "We ought to send Ell a big bouquet of turnips for settling our minds about her welfare."

Frank snickered. "Do that and she'll carve your statue in butter."

The letter made Joe feel magnanimous. "Let's pack some grub and all go on rounds with me early tomorrow morning." Hopefully he looked toward his frail wife. "I'll stop wherever you want. You can pick sulfur flowers or anything to fill your window vases."

"I declare I'd have gone stir-crazy if I'd stayed home another day."

Next morning she hummed as she put bread, roast beef, and a jar of red-currant jelly in a basket. The air was cool, the sun bright, promising a warm summer day. "I'll fill a couple of jars with well water and I'm set."

Charlie added water to slick the front lock of his hair back into a pompadour. He teased, "Ma, I bet you'll talk the hide off the first cow you see." He was six feet four inches tall and weighed one hundred seventy pounds, so that he looked rangy at eighteen.

Mary gave him the cutoff sign and gave the picnic basket to Will to put in the back of the wagon. Will was near six feet and as dark as his father. His shoulders were broad and his hands large enough to pick up a watermelon in one. He weighed close to one hundred ninety pounds.

"Ma, you'll talk so fast we'll smell sulfur burning," teased Frank, helping his mother up to the wagon's seat beside his father. He was small for sixteen, not weighing more than a hundred pounds.

"You just wish you could listen to my intelligent newsworthy palavering instead of holding up the leg of some balky horse," said Mary, reaching up and pinching the back of Frank's thin arm.

"Hey, that hurts!" Frank cried."What'd I do?"

"That's just 'cuz I love you," said Mary, giggling. They rode in silence, enjoying the sunshine.

Frank clapped his hand over his mouth and pointed. A young girl ran across the front of a soddy. The girl seemed familiar, yet different. She was like the girl who had pestered Charlie at the county fair two summers back. He took his hand away and whistled low. "Cripes, we heading there?"

Joe chuckled, agreeing with his youngest son's taste in female pulchritude. "Yup. Name's Lewis." Joe brought the wagon up into the soddy's yard, helped Mary down, then rolled out the portable forge.

"Let the boys help you with that," scolded Mary under her breath.

"When I get so old that I can't lift my tools out of the wagon, then I'd better quit blacksmithing," snapped Joe.

Frank was out standing before the lissome girl, who had short brown hair, curly at the ends. The bangs were lifted off her forehead by the breeze. Her eyes were a startling violet-blue.

"Howdy. This the Lewis place?" asked Frank.

Charlie was taking the anvil from the back of the wagon and looking around for the stand to set it on when he heard her answer. It wasn't her words that made his knees turn to pudding, it was her melodious voice, like a bird singing for the joy of sunshine.

"Yes, did you folks come to see Ray? He said he had a couple horses needed new shoes."

"This is the friendly farrier's wagon," said Frank.

"I'll tell Ray the blacksmith's here." She ran lickety-split to the back of the soddy, then to the barn.

Charlie watched her skirt fly around her legs, like a big blue butterfly fluttering against the wind. His hand felt clammy as he ran a finger around his collar. She was like the pixie-girl who had now become a figment of his imagination and daydreams. He was reminded of his conversation with Ell and Les when he vowed to call at the farm of the McGuckins.

The lithe girl came back and showed Joe where to set up his forge and pointed to the man coming from the barn. He wore faded blue overalls, and his shirt was unbuttoned and on the outside. He pushed his blond hair back with a tanned hand. He shook hands with Joe, saying he'd been expecting him. Mr. Lewis did not seem much older than the rosy-cheeked girl.

Mary smiled and stepped forward. "I'm Mary Irwin."

Charlie thought he saw the girl catch her breath. "It's nice you came," she said. "We don't get much company."

"I came because the day was too beautiful to stay in a dark soddy. I'm going to spread a blanket under the poplar tree and do a little mending. I'd be pleased to have you sit with me."

"All right." The girl looked in the back of the wagon at the other blacksmithing apparatus. Charlie set the anvil down and came for the bag of coal. The girl put her hand over her mouth. "You lifted that anvil by yourself? I don't think I ever saw anyone that strong."

Charlie was catching his breath, letting his hands rest on the coal bag. He thought her voice sounded like fast, white rapids in a creek that was knee-deep with clear, cool water.

Suddenly she said, "Look there!" She pointed to a black and white, plump, big-headed, slim-tailed bird that deliberately impaled a field mouse on a hawthorn bush at the corner of the soddy.

Charlie looked closer and saw other dead mice wedged into a crotch of the same branch. The bird sensed someone near and flew close to the ground. With rapid wingbeats it sailed over the soddy and out of sight.

"What kind of bird hangs its food out like a man would hang a deer carcass?" Her eyes were near purple in the shade.

"That's a shrike. He generally comes in fall, tells us winter is near."

"That's silly, it's summer," said the girl.

"Birds can get mixed up. Like some people. Maybe it's a crazy bird." Charlie laughed, then his heart made a sudden leap. She had stepped closer and was looking up into his face.

"You are like Charlie. Charlie Irwin!"

"I know—I am! You're Etta. Etta Mae McGuckin!" Then he stopped suddenly and his heart fell to the ground. "Is that man your—your—" He couldn't say the word.

"You're crazy! Ray isn't my father. You don't remember much. Ray is my brother-in-law."

"Oh, jeems, I'm glad." Charlie held his hand out.

Her small hand was lost in his huge one. It was a few moments before she withdrew her hand and Charlie thought he was going to black out. His heart beat so hard he was certain everyone could hear. His whole hand tingled as if singed with a hot flame.

"I can tell you are all related, one family, because there is a resemblance that is common. You have your ma's hair and your pa's build and eyes." She was skipping beside Charlie to keep up.

"Ma, this is Etta Mae. I met her—two, three years ago, in Goodland."

"Well, what a coincidence. Sit on the blanket," said Mary, making room. "It's hot enough to sunburn a darky." She took off her sunbonnet, ran her fingers through her thin, damp hair. She noticed how pretty Etta was.

"I'll get you a dipper of water from the well," offered Etta.

"Nothing like sweet water to slake your thirst—we have a couple of jars of water in the wagon, but I'd rather have the cooler well water," said Mary, pulling darning cotton through the heel of a stocking.

Etta returned with the dipper full of water and a boy about five, dressed in overalls, barefoot, and hanging on to her skirt. "This is Jimmy. He's my sister's boy. I look after him so that

Kate can put up the corn and green beans without him underfoot; you know how it is with young'uns."

"What a handsome boy. I like yellow hair and blue eyes. I bet he'd like a handful of raisins." Mary got up and rummaged in the wagon and deep into the picnic basket and came out with a fist of dark raisins and dried prunes. "See the size of my little boys," joked Mary, pointing to Charlie firing up the forge. "I can't hold them on my lap at all."

"Do you want a little boy?" Jimmy asked.

"I'd like to hold one," she said.

Jimmy plunked down contentedly in Mary's lap and munched on the raisins and prunes.

Charlie came back, hardly able to take his eyes off Etta. He untied the horses that were munching at the thin, yellow grass. He pulled tools, liniment bottles from the wagon and carried them to the barn. He looked back and saw his mother and Etta both sewing and chatting. Jimmy had his head down on Mary's lap, asleep. The day was warm, but the breeze from the west kept the air comfortable.

About noon Charlie came back to the shade tree. "Sure is nice to sit in the shade where the air is cool for a while. Been working the forge all morning."

"You shoeing Ray's horses?" asked Etta.

"That's nearly done," said Charlie, stretching his muscular arms upward to relieve the cramped feeling. Then he was on his feet again and bringing the picnic basket to the blanket. He whistled. "Going to make a meat sandwich for Pa, Frank, and Will. I guess Ray'd like one, too. How about you?" He looked from Etta to Mary.

Etta spoke right up. "You wash up before you get food out."

"Of course," said Charlie, his face turning pink under the tan. "Where's the soap?"

"By the basin on the bench over there next to the front door."

Charlie poured well water in the basin and made a show of washing his hands as far as his elbows and then his face. He wet his hair and combed it back with his fingers, throwing the wash water out on the stubbled grass.

"Pass inspection?" He held his hands up.

Etta smiled and nodded. "Excuse me. I am so used to telling brothers and sisters and Jimmy what to do, I just talk that way without thinking."

"Oh, I understand how that is. I have a big brother that'd like to tell me what to do."

Mary said, "Make the sandwiches and don't talk so loud, you'll wake the baby."

"I'll take him to the house," said Etta apologetically.

"No, leave him be. He'll wake up if you move him. Anyway, it's cooler in this breeze." Mary leaned her back against the tree's trunk and ate the sandwich Charlie handed to her. She closed her eyes and rested.

Charlie whistled softly and put the bread away after he'd made himself a second jelly sandwich. "Say, we could dance before I go back to work." He whistled a little louder.

"I don't know how to dance."

"Come on, then, I'll show you. It'll come in handy when someone asks you to one of those Farmers' Alliance dances." He took her hand and put his arm around her waist. And he was not disappointed. His heart thumped. "You put your left hand on my shoulder and we'll be off on the right foot."

"No one'll ask me to a dance," she said sadly.

"Oh, yes. A girl as light on her feet as you." Her head hardly came to his shoulder. He picked her up, hands around her waist and danced around with her toes just skimming the dusty ground. She giggled. A soft bubbling sound. She didn't say anything. She listened carefully to Charlie's instructions and caught on quickly and was soon dancing the two-step as if she'd been doing it since first grade. Charlie lost all track of time. He could hold her all day.

She broke in on his whistling. "You don't think I'm clumsy?"

"Oh, no."

"You once thought I was a pest."

"Oh, I forgot about that. I don't seem to mind it now."

She laughed. "I told you I'm bossy. I guess you'd mind if I'd go overboard with telling you what to do. Kate and Ray sometimes poke fun at me and say I'm loutish."

"I'd never say that." Charlie dared hold her a little closer. He could hardly breathe, so he let up some.

The sun was three quarters across the sky when Kate came out of the soddy. She was taller than Etta, but she had the same kind of small-boned look and light-brown hair, which hung in two braids down her back. Her complexion was fair and clear and her eyes dark blue.

"Kate! Come meet the Irwins!" cried Etta.

Kate's mouth turned down at the sight of her sister dancing in the front yard. "You should be in the house. Look at you! Hair flying around and your sleeves pushed up, the neck of your dress unbuttoned. What is this?" She had not noticed Mary, who was awake and bouncing Jimmy on her knee in time to Charlie's whistling. "Oh, my!"

"Come and rest a spell. Etta says you were canning. Hard job but nice to have the vegetables when the snow is deep. I'm Mary Irwin and this is my middle son, Charlie." She patted the blanket again. "Sit, Mrs. Lewis. We're having a little fun. Helps forget the heat. You've been in that soddy cooking all day. Time to rest."

Kate started to take off her apron, then thought better of it. "First nap Jimmy's had in a week. How'd you do it?" Her eyes were suspicious.

Mary took it as a compliment and smiled. "After raising four of my own I just did what was natural. He ate some raisins, drank a little water, and listened to Charlie whistling tunes. I do believe I had a little nap myself and feel much refreshed for it."

"There's never been an afternoon party here. We don't sit on this stubble much. We stay in the house unless we're working in the fields or garden. I never thought of coming out here for the noon meal." Kate eyed the picnic basket and the jelly bread Mary was fixing for Jimmy. Mary made another quickly and handed it to Kate.

"You could invite them inside to wait for the men to be finished," said Etta. She looked at Charlie and blushed.

"Our pa would have a cat fit and step in it if he knew I left folks out in the yard," said Kate. "You should have told me." She spoke angrily to Etta.

"I left you so you could do the canning the way you like. Pa's not here to say what we do. Charlie will show you how easy it is to dance." Etta's eyes brightened.

Charlie took the hint and danced around with Jimmy, all the time whistling. Then he gingerly took Kate's hand and danced on the dusty ground, avoiding the dried grass because she, too, had bare feet. Kate was not as graceful as Etta, but Charlie was sure if she'd been moving around with her own husband, she'd be more relaxed and would soon forget herself and smile. He hummed a slow polka and took steps around the blanket. Kate got her feet mixed at first, then found the pattern and grinned with delight.

Mary hummed with Charlie and clapped her hands, and soon Jimmy and Etta were clapping in time.

Now Kate wished she'd come out of the house sooner. She drained the dipper of water that Charlie brought to her. She fanned her face. She said, "I'm sorry I was rude. I guess I was tired."

"Forget it," said Charlie. "Excuse me, I have to go back and see if Pa needs me."

Kate told Mary her family came all the way from Rochester, New York, by train to first live in Missouri, then western Kansas. "Pa told us to be sedate and never laugh overmuch or it'd make as many lines in the face as frowns. I've never liked it here much until today. You don't have as many lines as our ma. Maybe laughing isn't so bad." Kate was uncertain. "Pa does a lot of reading, but only from the Bible. I don't think he's read another book," said Kate.

"When I was in school he'd take books away from me, saying they weren't fit to read. I had to hide most everything I read," said Etta. "I keep my books here at Kate's now."

"How is one to know what goes on in the world if one doesn't read?" asked Mary, astonished.

Kate colored. "Pa's old-fashioned. And Ma goes along with him to keep peace." She looked at Jimmy, who sat quietly in Mary's lap. "For a long time I've known Pa's ways weren't all right." She looked at Etta. She'd said more than she intended and was confused. "It's disloyal for me to be talking this way. I'd better stop."

Joe and the three boys came to the front and began loading up the wagon.

Charlie said, "I hate to just dump out these hot coals in the forge. You want them for your cookstove?"

Kate brought out an iron skillet for the coals. Then Charlie loaded the forge and anvil into the wagon beside the other gear.

They washed in the basin by the front door. Joe shook hands with Ray Lewis and said, "I'll send one of the boys back for those chickens and potatoes next week. You can settle up the rest with him. It'll come to five dollars and thirty cents counting the treatment we gave your house cat for worms. Keep using the medicine once a day for two weeks. Cat'll be all right. Keep it away from the vegetable garden."

"Mighty obliged to all of you," said Lewis.

Charlie said, "I'll come next week. Maybe we'll dance again." He grinned at Kate and Etta.

Lewis shook his head and began to laugh. "I'm not exactly laughing at you, but I can't help it. A tall muscular fellow like you, with calluses and broken fingernails, work hands, showing girls how to dance. That beats all! You're not only tall, but smart." He wiped his watering eyes and shook hands with Charlie. "I'll look forward to seeing you."

Jimmy pulled on Mary's skirt. "I wish you could come, too."

"Sometimes wishes come true," said Mary, giving the youngster a hug.

Charlie climbed into the wagon and nodded to Etta. She looked exactly the way he'd imagined in his mind's eye for the past couple of years.

The following week Charlie eagerly hitched one of the mares to the empty spring wagon and drove to the Lewis farm to collect half a dozen laying hens and a sack of potatoes for part payment for farrier's work. Joe told him to collect the money if he could, and if not, sign an I.O.U. for more farm produce. "One of his yearling hogs comes to mind," suggested Joe.

As Charlie tied the mare to the Lewises' poplar tree his breathing came faster. It kept time with his beating heart. Kate opened the door to his knock and gave him a sly smile. Charlie felt something was amiss. His pulse quickened and he dismissed altogether the speech he'd prepared riding out to say to Etta. "Good morning. I'm here to collect on the farrier's work that was done last week."

"Ray has everything," said Kate.

She was pushed aside as Jimmy came roaring out the door, grabbing at Charlie's legs. "I knew you'd come!"

Charlie picked the child up and swung him to his shoulder and danced around in front of the house. "I can see the top of the barn!" Jimmy squealed.

"Where's your Aunt Etta?" asked Charlie, putting Jimmy down.

"She went home. Grandpa needed her to pick corn."

Charlie felt a lump in his throat.

Kate was back at the door. "Mr. Irwin, Ray is getting a crate for the hens and hog. Potatoes are out back in a gunnysack."

"I'll get it," said Charlie sharply.

"Wait a minute," said Kate. "Would it be an imposition to ask you to drive three miles up the road to Pa's place? We have a butter churn that belongs to Ma." Kate's voice was kind of trembly and her eyes looked at Charlie, uncertain.

"Yes! I mean, no! I'll take that churn up the road. Would you let Jimmy ride up and back? It's no trouble for me. Honest."

* * *

Jimmy pointed to a neat, rather large, but spare soddy. As Charlie pulled the wagon to the front he noticed a pile of bundled sunflower stalks and cattails, dried and tied. He guessed they were used as fuel or in an old rush light like his Grandma Malinda used to own.

Charlie whistled loudly as he lifted Jimmy from the wagon, hoping Etta was inside and would come out. His hands felt sweaty. He knocked. Mr. McGuckin opened the door. A frown spread across his lined face. He pushed his silver-rimmed eyeglasses back up his nose and looked Charlie over.

"I'm here, Grandpa!" called Jimmy.

McGuckin stepped aside to let Jimmy in, then stepped back as if blocking the entrance until he'd finished checking over Charlie.

Charlie could hear a gaggle of voices inside talking with Jimmy.

"I brought your butter churn from your son-in-law, Ray Lewis."

"Put the churn by the door. I don't intend to buy any of the foofaraw you're peddling, so keep right on moving. I never buy anything I don't need." McGuckin's gaze was fiery.

"Yes, sir," said Charlie. He thought, in two, three years the man hadn't changed. He wondered what was biting him. Charlie felt a tug of pity for someone who treated life with so much anger. "You're not obligated to pay me for bringing the churn to you." Charlie tried to be amicable. He set the churn by the front door and caught a glimpse of a lace curtain move through the one window in the front of the soddy. Then in another instant Etta was outside beside her father.

"Oh, it's you! Pa, this is Mr. Charlie Irwin. I told you about the good job he and his pa and brothers did at Kate and Ray's. Shoed the horses, remember? Maybe you'd like him to look at your horses?"

McGuckin didn't answer, he was running his hands over the butter churn, making certain it was not cracked or in any way mistreated.

"Come in. Ma will be glad to see you. We wondered who brought Jimmy—actually we thought Ray and Kate had come."

Charlie stepped inside and she closed the screen. "Pa's well meaning, you know. He doesn't like strangers. He says he has enough people to look after with all of us around." She pointed to the flock of children hovered around the kitchen table, watching. Two older boys were dishing up rice pudding for the younger children. "That's Curly and Walt," said Etta.

Charlie remembered Curly. The boy was now near five feet ten and filled out. His hair was still in dark ringlets, like a mop on his round head. The young man looked up with brown eyes and nodded to Charlie. He winked at Etta, which caused her to be flustered for a few seconds. The other young man called Walt had ordinary brown hair that hung below his ears. His eyes were deep, rich blue, like Etta's. "Have a seat. There's still plenty of pudding to go around."

"Thanks." Charlie slid into a space at the end of the near bench. He was next to Mrs. McGuckin at the foot of the table. The empty chair at the head he assumed belonged to Mr. McGuckin.

Mrs. McGuckin passed a clean bowl and spoon to Charlie. "Etta made us pudding," she said, tucking a stray, limp strand of brownish hair under her gray bonnet.

"How are you, Mrs. McGuckin?" said Charlie, holding out his hand.

She took a sip of tea.

Charlie brought his hand back. "My ma would send her greeting if she'd realized that I was going to come here. I brought the churn from Mr. and Mrs. Lewis. Jimmy rode up with me."

Mrs. McGuckin looked up. "Don't go yet. We thank you." She dipped her teaspoon into the tea and noisily sucked the spoon dry. This made Charlie once again think of his Grandma Malinda.

Charlie ate his pudding. He especially liked the raisins and cinnamon that Etta had added and told her so.

Mr. McGuckin came back to the table. The children sat still and fell silent. Mr. McGuckin said, "I had me a tannery business back in Rochester. Left it to get into farming. Had a revelation one morning, you know. The Lord said to me in a voice just as clear as your own, 'Brian McGuckin, you are appointed food supplier, henceforth.'"

The children's eyes were on Charlie.

"There's no disputing the call of the Lord. Sold my tannery and sought the place He wanted me to plow. Hit Missouri first. That wasn't it—nary a drop of rain the whole summer we was there."

"We *were* there," corrected Etta.

"We weren't there long," continued Mr. McGuckin. "We took

the train's daycoach and looked at all the places in Kansas. When the train stopped at Goodland, I knew this was where I'd been headed. It's just about the last town in Kansas of any account. The land was flat, needed no clearing. I found this place for a homestead, and just as I was moved in and got the roots grubbed out of the soil and the wheat coming along pretty good, this here rainmaker came and sent water. From that time forward there's been enough rain and my wheat's pure gold. The Lord smiled on me."

Charlie excused himself and said he had to get Jimmy home before sundown.

McGuckin put his gnarled hand on Charlie's arm. "The Lord has spoke to me a second time. You want to know what he said?"

"Has *spoken,*" corrected Etta again.

"Yes, sir. I was spoken to. He said I was to look up to Him as a lighthouse of salvation in the stormy sea."

Mrs. McGuckin put her spoon noisily into the teacup and gathered her skirt around her thighs. "It was the wind a-blowing in your head, Mr. McGuckin." She moved tight-lipped into a bedroom behind a flowered curtain.

Charlie was amused and turned to Etta, who had covered her face with her hand. She said she'd walk him to his wagon.

In the living room Charlie saw how white the curtain was against the window. Everything looked neat and clean. Then he saw the rush light in the corner. "My grandma had one of these in Missouri," he said. "She had a stand made out of cast iron. I guess my grandpa made it—maybe my pa, I don't know. She stripped rushes bare of the skin and left only the ridge at the back to keep the tender pith from spilling out. She tied a bunch of them together, about enough to make a bundle the size of my arm. The bunch was dipped in grease."

"Like this?" Etta showed him a bundle of oily rushes clamped to the holder in the black stand. Underneath was a pan to catch the drippings and ash. "Pa had a blacksmith make this in Missouri."

"Yes. When my pa hears about this, he'll have to come himself to see. He always teased my grandma, saying it was a lamp for the meaner sort, meaning the poor. My grandma was a notorious herbalist, so a rush light suited her."

Etta said in a confidential tone, leaning close to Charlie, "Ma doesn't like to hear Pa tell of his salvation or his callings by the Lord. She thinks he's a might tetched about that subject and leaves the room. She wasn't being rude to you."

"I didn't think much of it, except funny, humorous like," said Charlie. He looked down at Etta's soft, warm brown hair, which was pulled behind her ears and tied with a blue satin ribbon. She wore a flowered gingham dress. Charlie thought she was lovely.

Curly and Walt clattered away from the table bringing Jimmy with them. "This kid eats too much. You can take him home," teased Walt.

"If you ever need someone to help with the blacksmithing, remember me. I'd like to learn," said Curly.

"I'll tell Pa. If I decide to go west, you can take my place."

Suddenly Etta looked down-in-the-mouth. Charlie noticed and wondered if it was something he'd said.

"Etta, he's not going away tomorrow!" rumbled Curly. "Holy smoke, women take everything seriously."

"Ya," said Walt, "Etta ought to get married. She's tired of taking care of Ma's kids. That itinerant preacher's been getting up nerve to ask Pa if he can court her." Walt's eyes were bright and he looked over to Curly. "Isn't that right?"

"Yep," said Curly.

"What itinerant preacher?" asked Charlie.

"Brother Morton," said Walt. "He sets up a tent in the lot next to the courthouse. You ever gone?"

"Nope. Never heard of 'im," said Charlie.

Etta twisted her hands together and looked uncomfortable.

Suddenly Jimmy darted out the front door and climbed into the wagon.

Charlie wasn't far behind. He didn't want to look at Etta. His heart ached. He looked at the wagon's wheels and said more to himself, "I'm going to have to set this wagon wheel in the watering trough."

Jimmy looked over the side at the wheel.

Charlie explained. "Lookee there how the iron hoop is kind of loose."

Etta hunched down for a look. "Couldn't you take a piece of iron out and strap it back on? Then, if the wood swells, the iron is harder and holds the wood in."

"Hmmmm, never thought of that. That's a swell idea."

A breeze riffled Etta's hair. She turned her head and ran back into the soddy. Charlie jumped into the wagon's seat and squeezed his eyes down. Jimmy climbed to the seat beside him. "Etta likes you," he said.

"I hope so." Charlie was smiling. Then he opened his eyes and carefully threaded the reins through his fingers. His big, square hands with the long limber fingers were fastened to strong wrists. He thought about the day he'd have a team of his own and Etta'd sit up on the seat beside him. It would be hard to see any finger move as he threaded and climbed the reins. He began to whistle "Onward Christian Soldiers." Jimmy swung his feet in time. They passed a place where the bear smell was so strong Jimmy put his nose down against Charlie's chest. Charlie didn't bother to look around to see if the bear was near the road. He would take Jimmy home, then head on to his own home.

The hens flared at one another and cackled. The porker snuffled loudly and oinked at the flighty chickens. Charlie yelled, "Shut up! What do any of you know about real feelings, anyway?"

THIRTEEN

Etta Mae

On Sunday morning the weather was clear and warm. The wheat swayed in the breeze. The corn was ripe on the stalk. Charlie washed and shaved, and put on a clean shirt, his Sunday trousers, and black, ankle-high shoes. "Ma," he said, "I'm going to hear that tent preacher."

"What for?" asked Mary, starting morning biscuits.

"No reason. I just never heard one of those wandering, Bible-carrying men. You suppose I could take some of them biscuits, some cold beef, and a raisin pie in the picnic basket? If the service is overly long, I'll be hungry on the way home."

The tent was up when Charlie tied the reins to the tavern railing. He slowly ambled across the street to the vacant lot next to the courthouse. It felt warm inside the big tent, out of the wind. He thought it would feel warmer if all those wooden benches and folding chairs were filled with people. At the front was a wooden podium, scarred and scratched, as though it had seen a lot of Sunday services.

Charlie took a seat by himself toward the back so that he could see both front and back entrances and not miss Etta when she came in, but he'd told himself it was to see the preacher better when he came in.

He saw Etta, standing near the front with a black satin bonnet and a dress of dove-gray. Her eyes went over the congregation and stopped when she spotted Charlie. She turned and all Charlie could see was her back.

Brother Morton preached about the easy road to hell and damnation. He was a man in his fifties, bald except for a fringe of white hair over each ear. When he talked his white eyebrows moved like fuzzy caterpillars chasing one another. Surely Etta was not attracted to this man, thought Charlie. The more he watched, the funnier Brother Morton became. Charlie moved beside Ray, who stood and flexed his knees and moved up on his toes to keep from being drowsy.

"You believe I could bring Etta to your place after this show? I brought one of Ma's raisin pies," Charlie whispered, letting Jimmy climb on his lap.

"Depends."

"On what?"

"On her pa. He's been trying to get Brother Morton to court Etta."

Charlie felt his knees might buckle. Then what Walt and Curly said was true. He was astonished. "McGuckin couldn't do that! Just look how bizarre that man looks," Charlie said loudly.

People nearby said, "Sshushh."

"I'd say he was ridiculous for looks. Kate says he's a scaramouch. I don't know what that is, but it sounds good," Ray whispered.

Charlie didn't know what a scaramouch was either, but he was going to find out. "Why would McGuckin pick this man?"

"His nature, I suppose."

"I pray a man's nature's not all inherited," Charlie said, leaning close to Ray.

"Naw—Kate's not like her pa. Neither's Etta. If I hadn't married Kate, I'd probably have waited for Etta." He winked at a woman in a straw leghorn bonnet who shushed him.

Charlie bowed his head for the prayer and joined in the loud *amen*. When it was over he moved to the front with Ray, carrying Jimmy, who was sleeping. Etta and Kate were moving toward an exit, so Charlie put Jimmy in Ray's arms and followed after them.

Outside he could not find Etta and Kate. He looked up and down the hitching rails and saw McGuckin alone beside his wagon. Charlie walked toward him. He saw McGuckin lower a newspaper-covered jug, cork it, wipe his mouth on his sleeve, and push the jug under a gray blanket in the corner of the wagon.

"Good to see you again, Mr. McGuckin," said Charlie, holding out his hand.

"You spying on me?" McGuckin asked suspiciously.

"Oh, no, sir. I came to wish you a good morning and ask what an itinerant preacher has that Reverend Dana don't satisfy."

"I have no time for you. People who belittle Brother Morton are heathens. I have no use for you. I wish you a good riddance."

Charlie took a step back. He hadn't come to retreat. He stepped forward. "I ask a question and you answer like I was some kind of rubbish? Maybe it's not you answering, but the spirits from that jug." Charlie put his hands in his pockets to keep them from shaking.

"Oh—now it comes out. You came for a sip of my medicine, eh?" McGuckin leaned on his wagon box and reached under the gray blanket. Suddenly he stopped and looked up and down the street, then he uncorked the jug and took a long swig. "This here cost me a whole cartwheel. It's the best cough remedy a man can buy. The best I buy leastways. About cured my cough."

"Does Brother Morton brew spirits?" asked Charlie confidentially.

"It's a sideline. Only he once told me he made more on the spirits than he did on the collection plate." McGuckin laughed and offered Charlie a sip from the bottle. "Just try a little on your tongue. It'll make you appreciate Brother Morton's talents."

Charlie had the jug to his lips. He decided if this was the way to be friendly with McGuckin, he'd better go along this once anyway.

"Don't pour down too much, heathen. I need it. You ain't ailing like me. That medicine calms my nerves. Give it here."

Charlie swallowed and felt fire like a double-blade sword go down his throat. He sputtered and his eyes watered. He coughed and handed the jug back. He was reminded of being drunk as a fiddler's clerk at Ell's wedding and the sickening consequences. He'd made a vow never to feel that way again.

McGuckin took a long pull and chortled, "Say, heathen, you like my medicine?"

"Not overly much," said Charlie, thinking his breath was fiery.

"One more taste and the cough'll disappear. One more."

Charlie didn't want another taste. He wanted to talk with McGuckin about that Brother Morton. He looked around, wondering where the rest of the McGuckins were.

"They all went to get something to eat," said McGuckin, noticing Charlie look up and down the street. "Won't be back for a few minutes. Told 'em I weren't hungry, go without me."

"Say, is Brother Morton married?" Charlie tried to sound casual.

McGuckin flushed. "Told me he had a woman in Dodge, but ditched her. Wants someone to travel with him."

"Does he have anyone in mind?" Charlie felt like he was sawing off the branch he was sitting on.

"Never said. But I'm fixing to offer him a deal. He'd be like a personal physician to me. He'd be one of the family."

Charlie didn't want to hear any more. Those words depressed him so much that he drank a couple more rounds with McGuckin. He was not able to pull himself away.

McGuckin on the other hand was more friendly and put a hand on Charlie's shoulder. He began singing hymns. After three or four he looked up into Charlie's face and said, "My wife and children respect and obey me. I see to that. I'll never let them be touched by a heathen. Never, by cracky!"

Charlie was befuddled, but he knew he preferred singing better than hearing McGuckin's irksome rules, so he belted out a couple songs. Soon there was a crowd around the two men as they sang. Charlie grinned gloriously at the crowd. Then he saw Etta with her bonnet off and her hair shining in the sunlight. He wavered on his feet, pulled himself up straight, and sang something of his own, "Beautiful Etta Mae, on this lovely day, ride off with me, without delay!"

Charlie heard McGuckin growl and felt him touch his elbow. When he turned to look, McGuckin punched him square in the nose. Charlie caught his breath, lost sight of Etta, and balled up his fist to swing back at McGuckin.

McGuckin moved to the hitching rail to untie his team. Charlie's swing landed on the wagon box, making a loud retort as the board split. His right hand hurt something terrible. Skin was scraped off the knuckles. His nose bled. The crowd was quiet. Charlie stood out like a tall man at a funeral. Then Ray Lewis was beside him. "Better ride on home and forget the whole thing," he advised.

He felt lightheaded and dizzy sick. He didn't open his mouth. He heard the buzz of voices and the snickering and stifled laughter all around. He was the joke. He stumbled to his horse, grabbed the reins, and managed to get through the blur of faces and out onto the dusty road.

He was not far before that dizzy sickness climbed up from his stomach to his throat. He stopped and hung over the side of his horse. He was sick. His stomach squeezed and he gagged. Charlie shivered and wiped his mouth with a clean bandanna. When he got to a pond, he got off his horse and wet his bandanna so he could clean up. The cold water felt good on his face. He dabbed at his shirt and trousers. "Darn that cussed man," Charlie said out loud. But inside Charlie knew the whole stupid episode was his fault. He supposed Etta had seen what a fool he was. Ray Lewis was right. Forget it. For a second time in his life he vowed to leave strong spirits alone. He opened the picnic basket. The food that should have been so attractive sickened him. He heaved the raisin pie as far as he could into the tall weeds and followed with the biscuits and beef. The raucous crows cawed thanks. Charlie welcomed the cold bite of the wind.

In November, Joe asked Charlie to accompany him on farrier's rounds. "Before we get snow, better get the sleighs repaired." Gradually, over the last few years, Joe's hair had turned gray. Charlie was suddenly struck by the change. He was startled to see his father's huge calloused hands were not evenly tanned, but had a spattering of dark pigmented spots.

"Pa, you should let Will, Frank, and me do more of this work. We can, you know. Some afternoons, you stay in the house and keep Ma company. She'd like that."

Joe snapped, "If I sat in the house afternoons, your ma'd go around me like I was a swamp. The day I don't work is the day I can't justify my existence."

The last place on the rounds was Lewis's. Charlie and his father checked the livestock. Joe picked up the hind foot of the plow horse. He tapped the cracked hoof with his fist. "Better use tips on these brittle hooves. I'll work on this next round, in a week, ten days." He slapped the horse on the quarters and shook hands with Ray. "You owe me nothing for today, everything else looks good."

Before Joe had the wagon turned around and headed down the road, Jimmy ran out to greet Charlie. Joe was patient while Charlie danced around the wagon with Jimmy, then told him to let the boy go back inside or he'd catch his death in the icy wind.

"Etta's here," said Jimmy.

"Aw, well—she don't want to see me," said Charlie sadly. What more was there to say? Etta had other fish to fry.

"Afternoon," said Etta, pulling a thick woolen shawl tightly about her slim shoulders. "She *does* want to see you."

Charlie's jaw dropped.

She waited for him to collect himself.

"Afternoon to you," Charlie managed.

"My pa, Mr. McGuckin, has a cow that is ready to give birth, but it doesn't look right. He'd like to have you look at it, Mr. Irwin. Ray was to go check on it later if you didn't show up. Lucky you came."

She wasn't talking to Charlie, she was talking to his father.

"Hop in, son. We'll scoot right on to McGuckin's," said Joe.

Charlie nodded to Etta and started for the wagon.

"Uh—is it all right—uh, could Charlie stay here and maybe teach Jimmy some songs? On your way back you could stop for him."

"For the little tyke, Jimmy?" asked Joe, teasing. "Sure, I'll do that." He flicked the reins and called "Giddyap," leaving Charlie surprised.

"Let's go in. I'm cold," said Jimmy, taking Charlie's hand.

Kate greeted Charlie warmly and began to set cups for tea on the kitchen table. "Haven't seen you in town on Sunday lately," she said.

"That's right," said Charlie, stirring another teaspoonful of sugar in his tea and feeling his nose.

They laughed and Charlie knew he was out of the doghouse with Etta. He relaxed and enjoyed the tea. "Say, you wouldn't have a biscuit to go with this?"

Etta jumped up and brought a dishtowel full of biscuits to the table.

"Would you have some jelly?" asked Jimmy, his eyes gleaming as he looked toward Charlie.

When Kate picked up the teacups, Charlie said, "I know there's a reason for me being here. What is it?"

"It's about Pa," said Etta. "He's festering inside. He blames you for his mortification."

Charlie looked away. "He's right."

"But you don't understand. You had no way of knowing." Her face was sober, her eyes were inky-blue. "Pa's had this thing about drinking for a long time—maybe before I was born. Ma never said a word to us kids, but we knew he had spells. People talked about him and he left one job after another. He tried to run away from the problem. He got the tannery thinking he'd be so busy he'd not be tempted. But he couldn't handle it. The problems made him drink, and the more he drank the more problems. In Missouri he didn't have his own farm. He was a hired man and he was fired. That rubs salt into a wound for any man.

"Then he came here and took to religion. Ma was so pleased she even thanked Brother Morton once. All the time he was selling Pa spirits. Reverend Dana knew, but Ma ignored his hints. It was you that opened it up so we could see." Etta paused.

"That's not a high honor," said Charlie.

"Well, Pa agrees with that," said Kate. "There's some people that call him names, like *souse* and *pickle*. Some call out things like 'Where'd you find your nose paint now that Brother Morton's gone?'"

"Brother Morton's gone?" Charlie brightened.

"Oh, yes, right away. Three weeks ago. And good riddance. He gave me the creeps," said Etta.

"Listen, Pa sees you the cause of people laughing at him. He said if he lives to be a hundred, he'll remember it was you that humiliated him," said Kate.

"What do you want me to do? I could talk to him. Tell him people forget. They really do." Charlie could feel the wetness forming on his palms.

"He has a gun. You saw it in the house, over the mantel, a shotgun," said Etta. "Next time you see it, maybe it won't be over the mantel."

"No, he's not that foolish," said Charlie.

"We're not sure," said Ray. "We don't want you to take any chances. Keep clear of him. Let your pa or brothers go out to his place, but don't you go."

Tears ran down Etta's cheeks.

Kate took over. "What do you intend—what are your intentions?"

"With respect to what?" asked Charlie dumbly.

"My God," said Ray. "Etta's crying her heart out over you and you don't know. I thought you were smarter."

"Why I—I thought—I reckon I didn't think at all! Walt and Curly, they said—and Etta said that old knave of a preacher was so polite—and Mr. McGuckin said he was fixing to take him into the family—so naturally I thought—I'm a fool!" Charlie cried. "I made a stupid mess of everything!"

Etta's head was up and she was watching Charlie for some sign. Her small fists were clenched, her bosom moved up and down at the same time Charlie heard her breathe in and out. She wiped the tears away and more came.

Charlie felt numb, his mouth was dry. "I'm sorry," he mumbled.

She wanted him to say more, but her anger rose to shut off her patience. She slid off the bench and went blindly out of the soddy and up the road. Her shawl flapped madly in the breeze at her back.

Charlie went to the door, watched. She had her hands up to her face because she was crying.

"Go after her," said Ray quietly. "I'll talk with your pa when he comes back."

Charlie trailed after her. He knew Jimmy and the others were watching from the front window. He had a lump in his throat about as big as a crab apple, and he could not swallow it. He saw Etta stumble. She was such a little thing, stumbling up ahead and crying her heart out. She didn't deserve it. He should have told her how he felt. Now it was too late. Now she hated him. He tried running, then slackened his pace and just lumbered along.

She felt helpless. She'd not intended to let him see her cry. She was almost blind because of the tears. She had no idea he was behind her. She pulled her shawl up around her throat. She felt the day broken and lost. She was alone, her dreams were gone.

She kicked at the ruts in the dirt that was the road. She kicked a stone and it hurt, she stumbled. She tried to ignore the pain but it was great. She hobbled a few yards off the road and squatted in the tall weeds. A swarm of gnats flew above her. She'd upset their quiet. She put her face in her hands and cried. She sobbed. No one could see her—what did it matter?

Charlie stood over her. He did not know what to do. For a short moment he felt waves of cold and hot shame. His mind could think of only one thing. He bent and put his wide hand on her shoulder. Then he reached down gently with two hands and straightened her head so that she looked at him. She was tiny and delicate as a pale-pink spring beauty. He'd really never thought of her like this before. It gave him the tingly feeling. He felt exhilarated. He felt strong and sure and he slipped one arm around her.

Etta tried to break away and she might have slipped and fallen if he'd not held her. "Hold on, there," he said.

"Don't!" She pulled away and would not look at him again.

"You're not really hurt," he said. "Stand up and dry your eyes."

Etta stood, not looking at him. She dried her eyes on the edge of her soft blue skirt. She felt his strong hand and arms and knew she'd not try to pull away.

"That's better," he said. "You tripped on that big stone in the road back there, that's all."

He stepped away from her and she looked up.

Charlie was beyond thinking one way or another. He knew only that she was here and there was nothing that was important beyond that. "Etta, I love you." The words were uttered as something fresh from him, something not pondered over, or thought out. He reached to draw her in tenderly to the protective circle of his arms.

Her arms went around his waist as he pulled her close. As his lips touched hers he felt lifted right off his feet, in a way a man fording a stream hits the middle and unexpectedly runs into an undertow that lifts his feet right off the bottom, then sets him down gently before he has time to catch his breath.

Charlie straightened up. "If we do this often you'll need a stepping stool."

She giggled and put her arms around his waist and buried her face in his abdomen. Charlie didn't move. He looked at this slip of a girl that could cause such a powerful feeling in him. He felt good, a joyful all over feeling, and she knew how he felt, he was certain.

Her hair was fluffed out around her face. She smiled at Charlie. No matter what, she thought, it will always be like this. He'll smooth things out and mend the breaks. "We'd better go back," she said softly. "Your pa will be looking for you."

Then a shadow came across her face, a sadness. "What shall we do about my pa? Oh, Charlie!"

"Stop," he said. "Don't spoil this. We'll tell my pa and go one step at a time."

Joe's wagon was outside the barn. The forge was fired up and he was replacing the shoes and putting on tips on the brittle hooves of the old plow horse. They watched as he burnt the shoe in place, cooled it in the slack bucket, and nailed it on. Then he pushed a new pair of horseshoes into the center of the red-hot forge, and with his left arm over the bellows pole, he worked as though he had all the time in the world. The pumping came as naturally as his easy breathing. As his arm kind of floated up and down slowly with the pole Charlie thought of trout moving their fins to keep perfect balance when they seem to be resting on the bottom of a creek bed.

"You better let me talk to him," whispered Charlie.

"Well?" questioned Joe when he heard the whispering.

"Pa—we, Etta and I, are going to get married," blurted Charlie.

Joe's smile was broad and welcome. "Well, now, that's fine with me." He looked at Etta kind of dancing around Charlie. He liked her. She was pretty—no, lovely. Her kind of beauty was the lasting kind. She had a lot of spunk for a young thing. He liked that, too. "I think your mother would like to know about this, so be sure to tell her as soon as we get home." He went back to the horseshoes.

Etta could not hold her words a minute longer. "Look here, Charles Irwin, you never once asked me if I wanted to marry you. You assumed I'd want to. What makes you think—" Her eyes were flecked with reflections of sparks from the forge.

Charlie pulled her close to him, so that she stood under the crook of his outstretched arm and put his hand over her mouth.

"I'm as surprised as you, Pa. This morning I never thought about being married. This afternoon I think marriage is—is the natural thing to do," said Charlie.

"I'm not surprised," said his father laconically.

"Sunday, when you're not using the wagon, I'll go out and see Etta's pa. He'll give his blessing—he'll have to."

Etta was jumping up and down and waving her hands.

"If the young lady's not suffocated by then," said his father. "Let her say something, son."

Charlie took his hand from Etta's face. She took a deep breath.

"I thank you, Mr. Irwin. Between you and me I'd be pleased to be Charlie's wife—if he'd ask me." Etta was convulsed with giggles.

Charlie's heart leaped with joy. The words were like sweet birdsong on a warm spring morning. He tried to calm his emotions so that he was composed. "I just realized that I'd be far better off if I had you around. In fact, from now on I can't think of being without you. I can't see that being with me would be too hard on you. You'd probably get used to it. Will you be my wife, Etta?" Charlie stood as straight as he could, all six feet four inches.

She reached out her hands. "Oh, yes," she whispered.

Joe chuckled over the joy the two were having just play-talking. Then he interrupted. "I have to ask something. You are such a mite of a girl, how old are you?"

"I'll be nineteen on the twenty-third."

"Fine. Charlie's eighteen." Joe turned his back and pumped the forge.

"I'll always be older." Etta smiled smugly and put her arms around Charlie's waist.

That evening Joe said to Mary, "Horses and a good woman sure make a man go whistling, when he's young enough to pucker. Listen to Charlie a-humming and a-whistling even in his sleep."

"Pa, he's not asleep. Charlie's burning a candle. He's figuring how much of this place is his, or can be his, if he either pays or works for it. He's going to bring that darling Etta here to live. I'll have to fix the place up." Mary turned on her side and put her arms around Joe. "Those two'll make each other happy. I liked Etta the first I saw her."

"She's a gal that knows her own mind," said Joe, holding Mary close and thinking of all the joys and sadness a couple can have together.

When the McGuckins' wagon pulled up into their yard on Sunday, Charlie was standing beside his horse waiting. Mrs. McGuckin nodded. Curly and Walt said, "Good to see you." Etta took her bonnet off and let her hair hang loose as she helped the younger children from the wagon. Mr. McGuckin frowned and motioned for Walt and Curly to unhitch the team of horses.

Charlie started off gingerly. "Sir, I'd like to apologize for the way I behaved to you in town. I pray there'll be no permanent injury to you in this area. I've already told a number of folks it was my fault." He looked at the split board in the wagon. "It'll blow over. By spring people'll be gossiping about something else. I think you know I'm right." He was racking his brains for the right words to lead him to his purpose for being there.

"Who told you to think for me?" McGuckin said, brushing off his black wool trousers, smoothing the collar of his matching coat, and pulling his bowler hat to the middle of his forehead. He turned to Etta and said, "You look like the wrath of God. Put your bonnet on. What has come over you?"

"Oh, Pa! And Ma!" she cried twisting the bonnet's ribbons. "I'm—Charlie and I are getting married."

Charlie felt the breath go out of his lungs. He heard the tittering of the kids standing around gawking, their eyes wide and mouths open.

McGuckin looked as if he'd been hit by a bolt of lightning.

His voice was a monotone. "That's something. That's it. That's the worst piece of news I've ever heard in my life. That's not the end of this story. That's—" he began to sputter.

"Mr. McGuckin, I'm here to ask your permission to court Etta. I'd like Mrs. McGuckin's permission also." Charlie was sweating.

Mrs. McGuckin nodded her head the least bit and, keeping her gaze on her husband, said, "Come inside the soddy." Then to the staring kids she said, "Go on! Shoo!" She flapped her skirt as if she were scattering a bunch of chickens.

Charlie stood nervously with his wide-brimmed hat in his hand until Mrs. McGuckin indicated that he should sit on the bench next to the table. "I'll get a board and replace the one that's split on your wagon," he said.

"You're a blamed liar," said McGuckin between clenched teeth.

"I don't want to offend you, nor fight with you," said Charlie, looking directly at McGuckin.

"Looks like you have and you might," said McGuckin.

"I apologize."

"Damn that Brother Morton," said McGuckin under his breath. "He's pulled up his tent stakes and left. I can't settle this thing without my cough medicine."

"I haven't heard you cough once," said Mrs. McGuckin. "Don't pretend. We all know about that medicine. It's the devil's brew."

Charlie felt like he was in the middle of a hornet's nest. "Next week I'll bring Etta home from Sunday service in my wagon, or to her sister Kate's place. That'll give us a chance to talk."

Charlie looked at Mrs. McGuckin and thought he imagined a slight flicker of a smile. He kept his eyes on her. She took off her gray bonnet and fluffed out her thin, graying hair, in a way that reminded Charlie of Etta. To win this day meant everything to Charlie. He felt clumsy and unsure, but he had to continue. He moved one hand toward Mrs. McGuckin's hand that lay on the table, but he did not touch her. He lowered his voice so that everyone had to sit quiet to hear. "There's so much peacefulness in this valley. You notice it's dark green in summer where the clouds shade it and bright green where the sunshine strikes. That long, narrow road I came up is like two lines drawn through the gold side of a quilt my ma made once. The other side of that quilt was the same color as your rye field, green with rich brown patches of prairie soil.

"There's an excitement that comes sometimes so sudden you have no time to think about it. The thunder and lightning, the wind and snowdrifts as high as my head, the time the grasshoppers came in shimmering clouds that sounded like wind rushing through treetops and ate every green leaf and blade of grass in the meadow, the lone wild horse that wandered in and grazed with the regular bunch . . . these are little miracles." He pulled his hand back and folded it with the other on top of the table.

Mrs. McGuckin brushed her hand across her eyes. "Oh, my. That's beautiful. Let's have some tea." She got up and put several pinches of tea leaves from a tin can into the teakettle on the stove. Etta and some of the younger girls put cups on the table. Walt brought out an empty tomato can filled with spoons. He set it next to the sugar bowl.

McGuckin hit the side of his cup with his spoon for attention. "Shucks, that was only talk. Didn't mean a thing. How in Hades you expect to take care of my daughter? Is your old man going to give you his homestead or the farrier circuit? Oh, no! Wait, you sing—hell's bells, I almost forgot. You expect to sing in some tavern to collect enough money to keep a wife?" He was getting worked up. "I think you're tetched in the head. Maybe I should go after the sheriff or have you sent to that hospital in Denver that has only crazies." McGuckin was standing. "Your pa ought to have something to say about all this, I bet."

Charlie thought he was getting nowhere, except more and more exasperated. "My pa is not marrying your daughter. I am. Good day to you all." He was up and heading for the door, not looking back.

"Sit down, Mr. Irwin. Don't say it's a good day until I tell you it is a good day. We ain't finished."

"Brian, do be careful. Your face is red!" said Mrs. McGuckin.

Charlie wished he were out the door, on his way home. He'd had about all of this talk he wanted. "All right, what is it?"

"In my opinion you are shiftless, dirty, and ignorant. Look at the mud and dust on your shoes." McGuckin seemed pleased. As his anger came he felt he was outshining Charlie and he would soon have the boy completely cowed.

Charlie looked at his boots. He'd wiped them off with a damp rag only this morning, rubbed in grease, and polished with a wad of sheep's wool. "Like you said, that's just talk. Words with no backing don't mean a thing. Etta and I invite all of you to our wedding."

It became as noisy as an empty wagon on a hard-frozen road.

Everyone was talking at once. Etta got up and poured tea. She set the kettle down in front of her pa. "Listen, I have something to say! The wedding will be on the first day of January. Charlie and I are going to start at the beginning together. He's going to ask Reverend Dana to marry us."

"Amen," said Mrs. McGuckin. There were tears in her eyes.

"Don't tell me what you are going to do, Etta Mae McGuckin." McGuckin's face was purple with rage. "Irwins are heathens!"

Charlie hardly heard him; he wondered how this could end and his liking for McGuckin was wearing thin. His words came out slow. "I'm proud to be an Irwin. We are not held back by our pa, or our ma. If we make a mistake, they don't pretend like it wasn't ever done. They give advice if we ask, but they let us take the responsibility." The words astounded him. McGuckin was huddled against his wife. He had a hangdog droop to his shoulders. Slower yet, Charlie said, "Etta, get your things, I'll take you to your sister's place." He held out his hand.

"I'm ready." She put her hand in his and held on like a frightened child. Curly handed her the heavy wool shawl. "So long," he said.

Etta pulled one hand away from Charlie's waist and wiped the tears from her eyes. She was in the saddle behind Charlie. "You did fine," she said.

He didn't look back but his mouth turned up into a smile. "Look here, Miss McGuckin, you never once consulted with me about our wedding date nor the preacher. So what makes you think I want to be married in the Methodist Episcopal Church on New Year's Day?" His eyes sparkled.

"Would you rather wait until June?" Etta asked, giggled, and put her head against his broad back.

Charlie and Etta were married January 1, 1894, in the Methodist Episcopal Church of Goodland. Most everybody was there: Sheriff Navert and his wife, Martin Tomblin, Jesse Tait, Marietta Roberts, A. B. Montgomery, George Benson and his wife, several members of the Farmers' Alliance, Ell and Les, Curly and Walt McGuckin, Kate and Ray Lewis. Mr. and Mrs. McGuckin did not come.

Mary spent hours cleaning, straightening. She made the windows of the soddy shine by rubbing them with wadded newspapers. She baked three white cakes and put them together with white frosting. Ell made jars of mulled cider.

Etta and her sister Kate made the white wedding dress with mosquito-netting veil. Charlie gave Etta a bouquet of fresh violets that matched her eyes. He managed to get them by train from someplace. The place was his secret.

Etta was given away by her brothers Curly and Walt who made it to the church at the last moment. Etta was breathtaking in the layers of thin, meshlike marquisette of her wedding dress. She wore Ell's pearl necklace and borrowed Mary's silver, filigreed brooch and Kate's silver bracelet and blue petticoat. The blue petticoat she wore underneath her white muslin one.

During the ceremony Reverend Dana asked Charlie quietly if he had a ring. Charlie put a wide platinum circle on Etta's finger.

The weather was fair, but cold. The sun was covered by high clouds so that it looked like a white china plate. There was three, four inches of fresh snow on top of the foot of packed old snow. The roads were cleared, sleighs had packed the snow hard. After the ceremony people piled into sleighs and pulled fur robes high under their chins, ready for the ride to the Irwins' soddy for refreshments.

Ell asked Etta how she knew Charlie was the right man. Etta was quick to answer that she had heard if a girl counted the stars each night for nine nights, she'd dream of her future husband on the ninth night. "I dreamed of Charlie all nine nights!" Etta said. "And I tried something else. I wrote my full name on a paper, Etta Mae McGuckin. Under my name I wrote Charles Burton Irwin. I canceled out the matching letters in our names and said 'true' and 'false' to each uncanceled letter. My name ended true and Charlie's name ended true. That's proof enough!"

Ell was delighted with this petite girl who was Charlie's wife.

Frank and Will and Les threw rice, the fertility symbol, into the sleigh Joe drove that carried Etta and Charlie. Joe grumbled about all the good rice pudding going to waste. He paid for a room in the hotel in Goodland so that Etta and Charlie could be alone for a couple of days before they went to Colorado Springs for three days with Ell and Les.

FOURTEEN

Floyd Leslie

By 1895 Goodland was eight years old. Most every house in town was frame, but in the rural areas nearly every house was sod. Outhouses were behind all frame houses, soddies, and business houses. The streets in town were wide so that a horse-drawn wagon could easily turn around. The streets were dirt, dusty in the dry season, muddy in the wet season. Only the larger businesses had sidewalks, which were board planks.

Crops were good that year. Joe had a magnificent potato crop. Fall wheat averaged sixteen bushels to the acre and went for fifty cents a bushel. There was good competition for the grain among the three buying firms. Looking ahead in a practical way at the growing market for wheat, oats, rye, and corn, Editor Tait wrote in the *Dark Horse*: "It is ascertained that the chinch bug is subject to cholera and the disease is killing them out. We don't suppose this will make the least bit of difference, as next year we will have a cousin or uncle of the chinch bug come along and ruin more wheat than the first bug."

Etta and Charlie celebrated their first wedding anniversary by staying in bed until the sun was fully up. Etta was five months pregnant. "Remember the first time I bedded you?" whispered Charlie.

"My brothers and your brothers banged on pots they'd

sneaked from your ma's cupboard." Etta snuggled close to Charlie, putting a small foot across his muscular, hairy legs.

"Ya, they banged so loud we had to invite them in before the hotel threw us out. The more noise they made the more aroused you became. Oh, my dear, who could have guessed this tiny body of yours held all that wildfire. You were as eager as I." Charlie put his hand underneath her flannel nightgown and felt the turgid tips of her breasts. "You have everything I want." He could feel the tingling sensation start in his loins and grow into the warm urgent throbbing. "Come on, let's see if we can finish together. Oh, Etta, I'm ready. I'm big as a horse and need to be loved." His hand had moved between her legs.

"Charlie, I love you, I'm ready, easy, easy." She found it hard to say anything. His warm, hairy chest was against her face. What he was doing between her legs was marvelous. The sensation was so overwhelming and so pleasurable that she closed her eyes to all sight and her ears to all sound. She was lost as in a fog and she moved deeper and deeper into the mist. Her body took over and moved rhythmically on its own.

Charlie held himself back, letting the excitement build slowly. He held himself on his elbows, not letting all his weight rest on Etta. Making love to her gratified all his senses. He thought of her as a pixie that enchanted him. She brought him to this state of euphoria and at the pinnacle he exploded.

After breakfast Etta caught Will before he went out to check on his red-bodied, white-faced Herefords he'd bought with money from selling several of the mustangs. "I have to wash clothes today. I can't hang them outside, they'll be stiff in seconds. Please, could you string up a clothesline in the kitchen, near the stove?"

"What a bossy sister-in-law," joked Will. "You kissed Charlie and now he thinks he's the prince instead of the frog. Why doesn't he string up your clothesline and wet wash?"

"'Cause I think he went to meet your pa. Your ma keeps opening the door to look for him. He's gone half an hour and she worries."

Will nodded. He understood. The day was bone cold and the wind cut like a butcher knife.

"Frank, please go out and hang some gunnysacks on the chicken house for warmth. Wrap my shawl around your head and neck before you put your sheepskin on. Your ears could freeze white today," said Etta.

Frank took the shawl. "Where'd Pa go on a day like this?"

"Town, to get a couple sacks of oats and a barrel of salt pork. If you'd talked Will into butchering one of his beefs we wouldn't need the salt pork."

"Ah, geez, Etta. How'd I know Pa would get it in his head to go out today? I hope to God he wore two pairs of wool pants."

"I don't know, he left before I was up."

"Ya, you and Charlie stayed in the bed a long time this morning. What for?"

"Don't think about it. It's none of your business." She flushed and went to check on the clothesline.

"Does it hurt to do it, when you're—you're with child?" Frank had Etta's shawl around his head and shoulders.

"Frank R. Irwin, didn't your ma tell you anything?" snapped Etta. "Is it up to me to tell you about everything?" With a broom handle she stirred the boiling white clothes, which were in the tub on top of the stove.

"Pa says the more one knows, the more joy there is in life," answered Frank with a smirk on his face.

Mary parted the curtains that separated her and Joe's bedroom. "What's that? You want me for some explaining here?" Her long white hair was neatly twisted in a circle at the back of her neck and held with tortoiseshell combs and hairpins. Her hazel eyes were dull even after sleeping all night.

"You feeling all right today, Mary?" asked Etta. "We're getting the wash hung and keeping the wind out of the chicken house."

"I'm fine. Only I wish the swelling in my ankles would go down. Used to be after a night's rest they was fine, but look there, they look like two sticks of firewood instead of ankles." She held her skirts up for Etta to look.

"Stay off your feet and I'll rub them for you in a bit." Etta put the boiling white clothes in a tub of cold rinse water, then wrung out as much water as her small hands could manage.

"I could help you with that," said Mary.

"No. If they drip I'll get the mop."

"Smells like laundry soap in here," said Frank, going out the door with an armload of gunnysacks.

Charlie burst in the door. "Pa's coming up the road. He's with someone!"

Mary was looking out the window. "Who can that be? There's a horse tied behind our springboard."

Joe opened the front door. "I have a man, a woman, and a passel of kids. I'm sending them in where it's warm."

Charlie went out and put blankets on the Irwin horse and the strange, big-chested brown. He gave them a couple fistfuls of oats and some hay and cracked the surface of the well for a bucket of water. He rolled the barrel of pork to the woodshed next to the barn and put the sacks of oats inside the barn door as fast as he could manage. He was curious about the people his pa had brought home.

In the house Mary and Etta were feeding a boy, about four, and a girl, about five years old. "Where's the other kids," asked Etta.

"This is all, far's I know," said the strange woman. She was not much older than Etta, but she was taller. Her hair was yellow as sunflower petals and her eyes watery blue. "The mister probably called 'em a passel 'cause them two sound like a dozen kids when they take out after each other."

"They scrap, huh?" asked Charlie. He saw the boy kick the girl under the table when they ate.

The man was big-boned, tall, like Charlie, but weighed maybe thirty pounds more and was about fifteen years older. He had brown hair, a receding hairline, and a small mustache above his upper lip resembling the tip of a horse's tail. He held out his hand to Charlie and smiled so that the corners of the steely gray eyes crinkled. "Horn's the name, Tom Horn. I'm grateful for the shelter." Etta brought him and the yellow-haired woman a plate of potatoes and butter beans and bacon. "And the grub looks good. I'm hungry enough to eat a saddle blanket."

"Pa'd do that for anyone out in this cold. You looking for a homestead for your family?"

"Not my family. I ran into 'em down the road a piece. They were walking, but not sure where they was heading. She hasn't mentioned her old man once since we been moving north. Didn't know where we were until we met your pa. Too cold to be lost." Horn stopped to concentrate on eating.

Later, after supper, Charlie saw that Horn was a gentleman around women and that he instinctively knew to talk politics with Joe, horses with Frank, cattle with Will, and roping with Charlie. Horn noticed the Henry rifle Charlie had finally laid on two pegs in the wall beside the door. "You ever been to Mexico?" Horn asked Charlie, looking over the rifle.

"Nope, not yet," said Charlie.

"This here piece reminds me when I was living with Apaches and all I had was a short forty-four rimfire Henry and a bowie knife. You want to know what happened to my Henry? I'll tell you in a word: lost. Yes, sir, I lost it. You ever hear of the earthquake of eighty-seven? Well, sir, we were headed for the town of Bavispe, which was shaken down to its foundation. I was leading about fifty Apache scouts for Captain Emmet Crawford of the Third Cavalry. We had half a dozen pack trains. We bivouacked amidst the earthquake rubble of Bavispe. The pack mules and horses and rifles were stolen by smugglers who'd sell everything in the States. I chased two smugglers with my bowie knife, slashed them both so that more than likely they bled to death. When I got everything back together I couldn't find my Henry rifle. To this day I don't know if one of those smugglers took it or one of my Apache scouts. There was some rumor that Geronimo came into possession of a rimfire Henry. We passed Tupper's Battleground on the Sierra Madre when a storm made everything so dark we could hardly see from one cutbank to the next. Then the hail came. It was so cold I can feel it now. Waugh! It was over in a few minutes, leaving a regular torrent running in the bottom of the ravine. We were looking for Geronimo and his renegades. I wanted to get Geronimo back to San Carlos so bad I could taste it. I'd do anything."

Charlie had never heard anyone talk about the adventures of being a scout before. He was spellbound. Horn was a talker who knew how to use his voice and face to attract an audience. Charlie watched how he used his hands, then how his face changed expression as he talked. The man is good-looking, even though he is getting bald and has a nose so large he could store a small dog in it, Charlie thought.

"You've had some experiences," said Will. "So what are you doing in the prairie country?"

"I'm getting away from all the killing. I saw Captain Crawford and some of my closest friends killed and scalped by hostiles. I even saw a man half et by a bear." He looked up to see if the ladies were listening, but they were all in the bedroom getting the children to sleep. "He was the worst used-up man I ever saw. The cavalry surgeon couldn't do anything. He was crushed in every bone and bitten in every muscle. The man was a sheepherder. Some of the men in the sheep camp allowed as how the bear had been eating their sheep and got tired of mutton and when it came on a hog it decided to have a mess of that. Ha Ha." Horn laughed, holding his sides.

None of the Irwins laughed. Charlie looked pale and had cold chills. Frank held his stomach and looked ill.

"Well, I've been deputy sheriff of Yavapair, and Gila County. I won a prize on the Fourth of July at Globe, near the San Carlos Reservation, for tying down a steer. There was a county rivalry among cowboys from all over the territory as to who was the quickest man at that business. I won the prize at the Territorial Fair in Phoenix a couple of weeks later," Horn said with a swagger. "I won it in forty-nine and one half seconds. The Pinkerton National Detective Agency at Denver wrote to me stating that they wanted me to work for them. Well, I never did really like the work with Pinkertons, so I'm headed for Wyoming and work with the Swan Land and Cattle Company as a range detective."

Charlie noticed how Horn started a story and became sidetracked and told several things before getting back to the intended story. He decided maybe that was because the man had seen and done so many things. He longed for the cold weather to break so that he could ask this Horn fellow to demonstrate his roping ability.

Will and Frank gave up their beds for the yellow-haired woman, Plucky, and her two children and slept with Horn under piles of quilts on the hay in the barn.

Horn liked to talk after supper each evening. Charlie wondered if the talking wasn't too braggy. The stories didn't always tie together well. Will and Frank enjoyed the stories immensely. Charlie noticed that Horn's piercing gray eyes sometimes seemed to look past his listeners and into some distant land where he lived in his imaginings or rambling.

Mary and Etta seemed to revel in taking care of Plucky and her two children. Etta was thankful that she no longer suffered from the incapacitating sickness and the overwhelming desire to run outdoors to get away from the smell of cooking, which had been nauseating. The day after the big January thaw Horn announced that he would be leaving the next day if the warm weather held. He offered Will twelve dollars for old Flame, who was now a swaybacked nag and a beloved family pet. Will was loath to part with the horse, even though he knew he'd never be offered more.

"I was told by Apaches there are Sioux up north and they'll take half of everything I have. Figured if I have two horses, I could give them your old nag. A man is crippled as a bird without wings if he's without his own horse. Twelve bucks is more'n the horse's worth. Taking it off your hands now saves you a lot of extra oats and hay," said Horn.

"It's yours." There were tears in Will's eyes. "You taking Plucky?"

"You can see there's only two things I'm afraid of—a decent woman and being left without a horse."

Plucky told Etta that she'd just as soon stay around Goodland, if there was a place she and her two young'uns could stay. Etta said Plucky might live with Marietta Roberts.

The temperature fell during the night; snow fell also. The wind made drifts like small sand dunes against the west side of the soddy and barn, against cottonwoods and hillocks.

Charlie couldn't sleep. He heard noises, probably the wind blowing, but they kept him awake. As soon as it was light he was up. He tucked the quilts around Etta so she could sleep longer.

Then Charlie had a crazy idea. He thought he'd take Sunny for a short ride on the thin patches of snow, skirting around the drifts before everyone was up. He knew he could get a tongue lashing. Then he decided he was master of his own destiny, old enough to make his own decisions. Let Frank be angry when I get back. He'll get over it. Then he saw the picture of Will and Plucky cuddled up in the barn and chuckled, sighed, and felt real good.

Quietly he took the saddle and horse out of the barn, letting the dog, Nick, out at the same time. The dog began to jump and yip around in the snow. "Sshh!" warned Charlie. "You'll have everyone awake asking questions before I leave." He shut Nick back in the barn. The dog squealed and whined and scratched at the door a few seconds, then was quiet.

Now Charlie noticed in the brighter morning light that snow was trampled around the barn door. He didn't dwell on it, thinking it was himself and Nick and Sunny that had trampled most of it. He snugged up the saddle so it wouldn't slip and rode toward the creek and out onto the settlers' road in the direction of Ruleton, a little town not more than ten miles from Goodland. The air was sharp and his sheepskin and wool cap hardly enough. The thin early morning clouds were gone and the fading stars hung so low it seemed he could touch them. Charlie tucked his nose deep into the front of his coat and pulled the horse around the drifts. He let his mind wander and thought of expanding the farm, maybe building a soddy for him and Etta and the baby, somewhere creekside of the Sappa. There was the place in front of his eyes, the little meadow with its two protecting hills on the northwestern side. The cottonwood skeletons swayed in the wind.

Charlie turned for home, ready to do the morning chores. He stopped and gazed one last moment at a wisp of haze against the sky, trailing out more like smoke than clouds. Must be fog rising from the Sappa, he thought.

Then his thoughts crystallized. The Sappa is mostly frozen. The air is sharp and dry. He bent his head to think better and saw prints around his pony's hooves. On closer inspection he found the front left foot of the prints turned in exactly like old Flame's! Charlie did not wait to ponder if Sunny could go through the drifts. He pulled the collar up on his coat to keep his ears warmer. Ice cracked as Sunny walked across the frozen marshland when he was nearer the creek. He pushed his mittened hands under his armpits a few moments. When he came around the hills he could easily follow the tracks of two horses. Flame was following a man on horseback.

It had to be Horn. Charlie saw the pinprick of firelight at the base of the west hill. And he thought he saw someone move against the snow-covered hill. "Hello! Hello, over there!" he called, and waited for an answer, watching his steamy breath flow away and disappear. He only heard the snuffling of Sunny. The horse was not used to carrying a load in such cold weather.

Charlie and the horse continued to move across the meadow. Charlie couldn't figure Horn. It was too cold for anyone to be traveling far. He was welcome at the Irwin soddy. Why hadn't he stayed? The land seemed still except for the fire. Charlie wondered where Horn had found the wood so far from the creek. Then he saw the bundles of dried sunflower stalks tied with familiar twine. "Pa," he called, "is that you?" His legs were so cold they felt like numb chair legs. He slid out of the saddle and awkwardly jumped up and down. When he broke through the snow crust he sank to his knees. His feet began to tingle and ache. "Jeems!" he said under his breath. "What's going on?" Around the fire were large dark patches that faded out to a blood red, then a pink in the snow. Charlie's stomach tightened.

The horse lay in the snow. Charlie looked away and smelled the hunk of thigh meat sizzling on a tripod over the flames. The man stirred and jumped up. His eyes rolled and the bloody comforter slipped to the hard-packed snow. The horse's belly was slit where all the entrails were removed and the blood drained out. The entrails were in a frozen heap behind the horse. Charlie could not speak. He breathed deeply to quiet the wave of nausea that swept over him.

"Go back!" Horn yelled. "This is my business!"

Charlie was immobile. Old Flame was like a large empty pouch. It was impossible.

"Why?" he whispered.

"The horse was old. Couldn't take the bitter cold. I left you good money for it." Horn went back to the protective carcass and sat on the blood-stained comforter. He hugged his knees. "Soon's this nag died I knew what I had to do. Pack the meat in the hide and use that to trade the Sioux. It was too cold to skin the animal out, so I did enough to keep me warm for the night with the thought of completing the job in the morning. Had to build me a fire or the damn wolves'd be here by the time I closed my eyes."

Charlie looked at Horn and felt anger and disgust, but it was mixed with sadness for the old beloved horse. His hands clenched and he could not feel the ache in his feet anymore. He swallowed, trying to push aside the lump of ice. "Mr. Horn, you were sheltered and fed at our place. This was no time to set out anywhere."

Horn fingered the leather binocular case that hung across his chest. The case was open and be brought out a roll of paper money from it. He counted out eight bucks and handed them to Charlie. "Horse worth twenty bucks to you? I left your brother twelve. Here's the difference."

Horn had shoved his wide-brimmed hat back on his head and Charlie could see his hard glasslike gray eyes in the firelight. Those eyes were as cold as the ice under his boots.

Charlie took the eight dollars and put them in his sheepskin's pocket. "Wyoming's a big place. Don't get lost," said Charlie.

Horn nodded and glanced ever so slightly toward his big-chested hunter tethered to a small scrub oak.

"We're friends now, huh? I'll run across your trail again. We'll trade roping tricks. Give my thanks to your ma and that sweet wife of yours. Someday you can tell me how you managed to lasso such a wonderful little lady. And a word about that Plucky; she's one of them widows whose greatest need's to have her weeds plowed under."

Charlie held the reins and led Sunny across the meadow and out to the settlers' road not looking back. His mind whirled. The sky was cold gray by the time he brought Sunny to the barn. The minute he opened the door, Nick began barking again. "You knew Horn had left and tried to tell me," said Charlie with a sigh. "I saw the signs and ignored them. Darn!"

Frank sat up and rubbed his eyes. Will sat up and brushed the sunflower-yellow hair from his chest. He smiled at Charlie and shrugged his shoulders. "She came in last night to get something from Horn that belonged to her. I thought it was the binoculars. But Horn grabbed them from her like they were some heirloom of his. Cuffed her on the face, knocked her down. Geez, I had to put her in a pile of quilts to keep him off of her."

Plucky was awake, pulling a quilt up around her bare shoulders. She smiled at Will and said in a husky voice, "Don't worry about me. Don't think unkindly about Tom Horn. He brought me and my kids here alive. I give him credit. He can survive most anywhere."

Frank was watching Will and Plucky. He crawled out of his blankets and brushed the straw from his pants and shirt, which he'd left on for warmth. "Geez, it's too cold to sleep in the wherewithall," he murmured. "You two must be out of your tree!" His eyes stayed on Will and Plucky. "Where's Mr. Horn?"

"He's gone. He needed to get over into Wyoming for that job," said Charlie.

Around Saint Valentine's Day, Etta told Charlie that she could feel the baby inside her move. "Now I know he's in there," she said happily. "He's more active in the evenings, when I first go to bed. That's when he wants to play."

"Just like his pa, huh?" chuckled Charlie. "What'll we name him? How about Joe Marvin after Pa?"

"Or Brian, after my pa?" Etta giggled. Then she was serious. "I really like the name Leslie. You know, after Les Miner," said Etta, snuggling against Charlie, letting him put his wide hand over her belly to feel the baby move a tiny arm or leg.

The ground stayed snow-covered during all of February and March. Then the chinook winds came and melted the snow almost overnight. The ground was wet and soggy, hard to plow. Joe was afraid the hot weather would come suddenly and burn out all the corn and wheat seed. He said, "Farming is as unpredictable as weather." He spent hours checking the tiny green shoots of wheat. By mid-April the stems began to elongate fast.

The day he discovered the rosettelike leaves developing near the ground he sang all the way home. When he found two or three nodes, the thickened swellings on the stems, he danced around the table and played his fiddle after supper. "The crops will be good this year! It's no crime to celebrate good fortune!"

Mary stayed calm. The only time for true celebration was at

harvest time. But she did enjoy seeing Joe in such fine spirits and told Charlie that if her ankles weren't so swelled up she'd get right up and dance with him. Her arthritis had flared up again during the spring, causing her legs to ache, and her hands had deep burning sensations when she clenched them.

Charlie and Frank spaded the kitchen garden for their mother. The turned-over earth dried out faster. Mary and Etta put in seeds of pole beans, squash, peas, beets, turnips, lettuce, and watermelon.

Etta held her hands under her distended abdomen and said, "I think my watermelon is about to drop any moment. It gets heavier every day."

"You have a couple more weeks," said Mary. "I'll write to Ell today. She'll be the best help you ever saw."

"My own ma could come," said Etta.

"Child, we'd both like that. But she's all those young'uns of her own to care for. Besides, you think your pa would let her come?"

Etta's face fell. "I guess not. Pa thinks I married into irreligious heathens." She added, "I'm sorry."

"Land sakes, after meeting the Splitlogs, I don't know what heathens are," said Mary hastily.

"You don't know what heathens are—?" whispered Etta.

"That's right. Those 'uncivilized' men practiced the Golden Rule like it was meant to be practiced. Someday I would like to shake their mother's hand. It's the mother that teaches values. Motherhood is a responsibility. I'm telling you, Indians are not all heathens," said Mary, "and no Irwin is a heathen either!"

One afternoon Mary and Etta weeded the kitchen garden, then brought the kitchen chairs outside so they could rest and enjoy the warm sunshine. The willows along the creek were lush with soft, green leaves. The few oaks had long, caterpillarlike, greenish-yellow blossoms that fell at the base of the tree in thick carpets. The Indian grass out on the prairie was knee-high; by midsummer it would be eight feet. The prairie was rich with wildflowers, yellow sawthistles, purple phlox, and white starlike flowers. A marsh hawk skimmed silently over the waving green grass toward the meadow and creek beyond. The land seemed an extension of the soddy and the people who lived there. Etta wiped the yellow pollen from her black high-button shoes with the hem of her long skirt. "I have to take these phlox inside. Flowers bring beauty to the darkest of corners," she said.

"The air smells like rain," said Mary, and she looked at the sky. "I thought so. See that dark cloud coming in from the southwest? There's lightning in it." The cloud was tinged with purple, the outer edges a bilious yellow.

Charlie herded the cows into the meadow and helped Will and Frank bring the horses up to the barn. "Boy, that's going to be some storm," he said. The new green blades undulated as a churning green sea.

"Hear those chickens squawking," said Frank, coming into the yard.

"Yup. Reminds me of Plucky's kids," said Will.

"How's she doing?" asked Charlie, carrying Etta's chair into the soddy.

Will took his mother's chair. "She's fine. Got her own soddy off the Boulevard. She's working for Len Ching. You know, that Celestial across from Marietta's. She waits tables and does a good job serving up Chinese noodles with sweet and sour pork."

"I hoped she'd stay with Marietta," said Mary with a sigh. "Would have been good for those children. Given them something solid to hang on to. Oh, well."

Charlie put his arm around his mother and led her into the soddy. Outside the gathering clouds were rumbling. Charlie and his mother went to the door. The chickens were quiet and the buzzing of the flies stopped. The air was heavy with moisture, but dead still. Off to the west the sulfurous-edged clouds moved toward the center of the sky, over the soddy. Suddenly the wind rushed in as if to fill a vacuum. The rushing sounded like a great fall of water. Mary clung to Charlie.

Etta was bewildered and grabbed out to hang on to something. She clung to Will. Frank moved against Etta and she slipped a protective arm around his waist.

Charlie felt the wind against his eyes and had to half-close them. The chicken house floated upward to push against the hillside. The barn's roof lifted up and slid down seemingly in slow motion, to the very spot the chicken house was. Charlie felt a tingling on his arms, but was unaware it was dust and dirt blown against his skin.

The Irwins huddled together, under the door frame, hardly breathing, until rain pelted the ground and the outside light changed from an eerie saffron to the familiar gray of a rainy day. With the first rain came marble-sized hail.

"Thank God, the house is still here!" cried Mary.

Etta put kettles and pots under the leaking roof on the kitchen side of the soddy. "Wind must of pulled a lot of sod off the top.

But that can be fixed." Her breathing was labored.

"I gotta sit down, my legs are wobbly," sobbed Mary. "Oh, my God! Where's Pa?" Color drained from her face. Her now moss-green eyes were wide. "Lord-a-mercy!" she cried. "Where is Joseph?"

"He's here!" Joe's voice yelled back. He climbed from behind the kitchen range. "Looks like a tornado hit us!" He was dripping wet, grinning.

Everyone began to talk. Joe never saw the chicken house and barn blowing away. The wind was not so bad in the wheatfield if he bent low to the ground. It was the rain and hail that sent him to hightail it for home, where he found the kitchen side peeled off like someone took hold of the top and tore downward.

In the midst of noise and confusion no one standing in the door frame had seen the gaping hole behind the Majestic range. Joe came into the soddy through that hole and ducked behind the stove for protection.

Joe and Charlie tried to close off the huge gaping hole by pinning up a couple of horse blankets and some gunnysacks.

Not until the next morning did the rain let up enough so anyone could go out to see the damage. Joe's voice quivered. "Looks like this family has to shore up a lot. All the wheat and corn's gone. Garden's a worse mess than if a herd of deer had spent the night there. Hail beat it to death. Killed everything!" He held his hands out. "Hell's bells! There's plenty of time to repair the house and build a new roof for the barn."

Mary looked around. Tears streamed down her face. "The chicken house!"

"I'll fix that, too," said Joe, putting his arm around his wife. For a few moments they clung to each other.

"We'll all get started right away. Won't be like we have to cut out a bunch of sod blocks. We just have to find out where they fit and put them back," said Charlie. He tried to keep his mother from seeing that some of the chickens were crushed to death under the heavy blocks of sod. There were no live chickens in sight. "When the chicken house is done, we'll get you a broody hen or two and you can hatch some chicks. We'll start your garden right away. Seeds'll sprout fast in warmer weather."

Will found one of the workhorses with a wooden plank in its neck. It was dead. The mustangs were all right. Their hay was soaked. Etta tried to bend over and carry the damp hay out where it could dry.

Charlie spoke sharply, "Don't do that! I hear you puff with the least little exertion. Jeems, if my belly were that big, I'd set and give orders. You write a letter to Ell. Someone's bound to go into town in the next few days. Ell ought to be getting here or else the baby will come and she'll miss using her mumbo jumbo."

Etta put her hand in the middle of her back and smiled gratefully. "I'll sit."

Will and Charlie went to town the next day. They found the Goodland Post Office damaged but open for business. The barber shop next door was blown down. The Mercantile had no roof and was damaged by rain and the rough handling of the goods. They stared unbelievingly at Len Ching's. The Chinese restaurant was boarded up—closed.

"Let's see if Plucky and those kids are all right!" cried Will. They hurried the team to the little soddy off the Boulevard. The land was as bare as if it had never existed. No one seemed to know where Plucky and the Celestial had gone, until they met Martin Tomblin. He said, "You'll never believe this. That Len Ching got Reverend Dana out of bed to marry 'em. Ching took his new bride to Ruleton to open a restaurant. Can you beat that story? A blond woman with two white-haired brats marrying a noodle-eating man?"

Will was tight-lipped, staring off into space.

The two Irwins bought dimension wood and nails from John Foster's lumber yard, then drove out to Swarts's Ice House. Mary wanted one hundred pounds of ice to keep the milk and some of her cooked things fresh for a few days.

"I know it's an extravagance," Mary had told Will. "But it'll be nice also to have for Etta. Her time's any day and chipped ice in a glass of water would go down easy with her."

Joe never wanted to be called stingy. He had called out, "Get two hundred pounds for good measure!"

There were others who were wiped out of their money crop that spring. However, Joe had his portable forge. Right away he began the farrier rounds. He bartered his work for last year's potatoes, scantlings, gunnysacks, or anything he thought useful. That year the settlers had little money and even less material goods to barter, yet their horses needed treatment and their farm equipment needed repairs. The Irwin family was certain to get along.

Next to the last day in April 1895, Etta could not sleep early in the morning. She got up and put a couple sticks of wood into the range to heat water for a cup of tea.

Ell, who had arrived a few days before, stirred on her cot near the stove. "You all right?"

"My back aches and I can't sleep. I was thinking of my own ma biting on a peeled sassafras stick and pulling on rags tied to the bed so her knuckles were white. Will I be like that when my time comes?"

Ell got out of bed and pulled a quilt around her flannel nightgown. She put her hand gently on Etta's bulging belly. "Dropped a lot in the two days I've been here."

"Maybe it's just colic. I have a kind of pushing up here." She used her hands to show a tightness in her belly. "It comes and goes."

"Tell me when it comes," said Ell, leaving her hand on Etta's belly.

Etta gritted her teeth and waved her hand.

"Contractions," said Ell. "Maybe today we'll have a new Irwin."

"Today?" asked Etta, her pixie face pink from the heat of the range. "I'm not ready. It's way too early to wake the menfolk. They'll be cranky."

"If this is the day, you can't put it off. Ready or not, the baby comes." Ell went to one of the curtained bedroom areas and called out, "Men! This is the day you have been waiting for. The moon is in the fourth quarter and right for second planting. Get that seed corn that's in the barn and the wheat Les sent. Get it in the ground. You might have a crop or two yet."

Mary was up before the men, her hair combed and a fresh apron over her dress. Black stockings were pulled to her knees, rolled, and knotted so they'd stay up. She wore her black high-button shoes, but did not have them buttoned over the ankles. "Ankles swelled even in the morning now," she complained. Then her face brightened and she hugged her daughter. "Ell, you married a good man. One that would send seed to Pa is all right. Your pa's been brokenhearted about losing his crops. This'll get him busy and he'll forget the troubles. Thank you. Thank you."

"Ma, when Etta wrote about that wind and hail, I knew what we had to do. Pa always said the family should stick together. So Les and I are doing our part."

Mary's eyes misted. "You sound like your grandma Malinda."

"Maybe I really am her. She loved life. She might have come back and taken over my soul. Go sit with Etta at the table. She's got some pains this morning." Ell half-believed she might be a reincarnation of Malinda Irwin.

"You're as daft as I remembered," said Charlie, pulling Ell's apron strings. "What do you think of my wife? She just pretending she's going to have a baby so she won't have to weed the garden?"

"Are we going to plow those fields again to put in more seed?" asked Frank, coming out of his bedroom to pull on his boots.

"You're as whiny as I remember," said Ell.

"If I'm going out for all day, I'm taking some bacon and biscuits," said Will. "Otherwise I'll starve."

"Me, too," agreed Charlie.

"I'll put together enough for all of you, including your pa," said Etta, bending over to ease a contraction.

When Ell saw the biscuits and bacon Etta had put in a dishtowel, she yelled, "Don't you men touch that! You'll get cramps from eating food handled by a birthin' woman. Throw it out! Here, Ma, you wrap up this bread and give them some pork rinds."

"Throw away good food! Come on, sis," said Charlie, rolling his eyes upward. "Is Les prepared for all this waste you conjur up?" He took the biscuits and bacon out the door, all the time surreptitiously munching on a good thick piece of fried bacon. He called to the old black dog. "Here, Nick, better than stewed squirrel this morning."

The dog got up slowly, almost blind now, and smelled the salty meat. Its head lifted so that Charlie scratched behind the ears. "You can have it all if you don't drool on me," he said, putting the food on the dirt between the dog's front paws. He wiped his hands on his denim pants and found the sack of dried corn and sack of wheat Ell had brought. He put one on each shoulder, met his father in the front yard. "Get the team and the plow," he said. Then, thinking suddenly why he was going out at daybreak, he put the grain sacks on the ground and ran back inside. "I just want to say something to my wife," he said to Ell. Etta sat on the edge of the cot Ell had slept in. "I wanted to tell you—uh—have a good birth day."

Ell and Mary put their hands over their mouths to suppress their giggles and turned their backs on the couple.

"I love you," whispered Etta.

"When it's over you can have Marietta Roberts make you any kind of new dress you want. Have it all silk if you want. The meadowlarks are singing outside. I'll leave the door open so's you can hear when I'm gone." He kissed Etta lightly on the forehead and tasted the salt from her dampness.

"How do you like the name Floyd Leslie?" she called as he left. Charlie gave no indication he'd heard.

He picked up the sacks of seed and headed out toward the field. Not seeing the others ahead of him, he looked back and saw them standing around the door of the barn. "Come on! Shake a leg!" he called.

"In a minute!" yelled Will. "We have a piece of work to do here first."

Charlie stalked over to the barn. "Frank get caught in a bear trap that was lying around?" He smirked.

"Old Nick is dead," said Joe sadly. "You feed him them rations Ell said to throw out?"

"I did."

"See, here on the floor, Nick throwed up most of what was et. Then looks like he just laid down and died." Joe's eyes watered.

"How could you be so stupid!" cried Frank. "You heard Ell say throw them things out. For chrissake!"

"That's a bunch of superstitious hogwash," said Charlie.

"It happened though," said Will, shaking his head.

"Ya," admitted Charlie, "the dog was awful slow coming to get breakfast. I think Nick was ailing then, but I was so wrapped up in having a baby I didn't notice anything else much."

"Charlie, take Nick in a gunnysack and bury the remains on top of the little hogback next to the first field Frank and Will are going to plow. I'll take your sacks of seed," said Joe.

"Pa, why me?" Charlie's heart was on the ground.

"You saw Nick last. Nick counted on you and you let him down. You ignored the signs." Joe's lip trembled.

Charlie grabbed the shovel and gunnysack. His eyes clouded with water. He was consumed with rage and grief. He dropped on his knees in the dirt and shoveled the dog's bodily remains into the coarse bag.

All the time he dug the grave he felt strong pains in his belly. His insides pulled together. He plunged the gunnysack into the hole and filled dirt in over the top. He stopped to wipe perspiration and tears from his face. The perspiration stung his eyes. His belly ached and he hunkered over the fresh-dug earth. He pulled out his bandanna from his back pocket and a three-inch hunk of withered root fell out. "Son of a gun," he said, picking up the twisted root. He thought, that sister of mine beats all. Who else would do such a thing. He waved the root in the air and detected a faint sweet odor of sweet flag, or calamus. How'd she suppose

I could make tea from this out in the field? Maybe she thought I'd just take a nip out of it. He put the root in his mouth and sucked on it, then took a small bite and chewed it. All the time he was hunched down to ease the pain in his gut. He straightened to put his bandanna back in his pocket. He felt better. "That's the fastest thing in the world for a bellyache," he said aloud. "I guess Ell knew I'd munch on that spoiled bacon." Then he laughed, thinking he was getting as superstitious as Ell.

Joe and his three boys worked all day plowing and reworking the fields and planting. On the way back to the barn in the twilight Joe said, "Tomorrow we'll go out with the farrier's wagon."

"Not me," said Frank. "I'm bushed."

When they were in sight of the soddy, Charlie ran, not thinking of being tired. The door was closed, but he rushed in and stood a moment, feeling a blast of heat from the range. "It's hot enough in here to bake a batch of cinnamon rolls!"

"Sshh!" said Ell. "Can't you see your wife has had a busy day and is asleep? She drank a quart of stinkweed tea."

"When will she wake up?" asked Charlie. "I want to ask her something."

"Maybe tomorrow morning. What do you want to ask her?"

"A baby? Do we have a baby?"

Ell could not hold back her mirth. "Look at Ma sitting in the rocker. She's holding her first grandson."

"Jeems! A boy. Let me see him." Charlie bent over the blanketed bundle in his mother's lap. The little red-faced thing waved its fists in the air nervously and opened its mouth and howled. "That's Floyd Leslie!" he cried, so excited he could hardly stand still. "Oh, Pa ought to see him. The newest Irwin cub."

"Go wash your hands and you can hold him," said Mary. "He's yours, you know." There were tears in her eyes.

That reminded Charlie of the real sadness, and he said, "Old Nick died this morning. I buried him on the knoll in front of the first cornfield."

"Birth and death are a pair," whispered Ell.

FIFTEEN

Summer Days

The railroad roundhouse at Goodland originally had ten stalls for engine repairs and was now adding more. This stone-and-brick structure was located three hundred yards north of the tracks and a little west of the Boulevard, not far from the frame depot, which was at the foot of Broadway and the Boulevard. Inside the depot was a beanery, or dining room specializing in baked beans and bean soup, that was constantly busy with road-house workers.

Mr. Henry H. Auer built a small, frame restaurant near the depot, hoping to take in some of the roundhouse business. He specialized in sandwiches and fast service. When his business did not flourish as he had anticipated, he decided to sell. The June 21 issue of the *Goodland News* stated, "The buyers took immediate possession, and while the invoice was going on, they 'set up' cider, lemonade, and cigars free to everybody that came in. After the invoice was completed they found that they did not have enough to settle and the trade was declared off, leaving Auer to foot the bill for the free entertainment."

Before June was over, screen doors were put up by most everyone in town to avoid the flies.

Joe put a screen door on the front of his soddy so that Mary could leave the front door open for air and keep out flies and other bugs.

Before she left, Ell suggested that the bedroom walls and ceilings be covered with gunnysacks, then with colored voile. "It would keep dirt and dust and bugs from sifting into beds and clothing."

"What'd happen when there's another tornado and the roof blew off?" asked Mary. "The voile would be ruined. On the other hand, if I had a beautifully decorated soddy it'd look like I was acting uppity. I can't do that. Flowers in my windowsill vases is decoration enough. And I can change that color with each season."

Etta was amazed at the fuss made over baby Floyd even after Ell went back to Colorado Springs. The baby was treated like a prince. The moment he cried, Mary picked him up. "I love having a baby in my house again," she said. She rocked the baby and let Etta do the baking and canning. After supper she sat in the same rocker and sewed a comforter or flannel gown for the baby. Etta's mother had had a baby almost every year and no one thought much about making a fuss.

Etta had not seen her folks since before she was married. A couple of times Mary suggested she and Charlie take the baby to the McGuckins. Etta made excuses.

During the Fourth of July celebration in Goodland, Charlie talked with Ray Lewis. McGuckin had a dog that ran afoul of a porcupine. "He needs a salve of permanganate of potash and lard to keep infection down," said Charlie.

"You and Etta take a jar out to him. I'll pay for it," said Ray.

Etta was nervous. She would have backed out in a second if Charlie had hinted at an excuse. She bathed the baby and dressed him in a flannel diaper, belly band, and flannel shirt. The day was warm. "At least all the kids will be glad to see us," said Etta with a sigh.

Mr. McGuckin said little the whole time. Mrs. McGuckin brought out gooseberry pie and coffee. She held Floyd so that Etta could eat. Etta said the coffee must have boiled all morning, it was that strong.

Mr. McGuckin said, "There ain't no strong coffee, there's only weak people." He looked at Charlie.

Charlie thought he was going to clout him about not having the baby baptized yet. He didn't.

Etta's brothers Curly and Walt sat next to Charlie. The flies came through holes in the screen door. The smaller children ran around with open hands or folded newspapers swatting and grabbing and yelling.

"Horses hate the flies, too," said Curly.

"Mix a concoction of equal parts pine tar and lard and smear it on the horses," said Charlie. "It's messy and smelly, so it keeps the horseflies, deerflies, mosquitoes, and gnats away."

"I'd put it on myself," said Walt, slapping at the flies settling on his bare arms.

Etta looked at the broken screen. "You have an old rag or some cotton lint?"

One of her little sisters brought out a pillowcase full of cotton scraps. Etta showed her how to make little wads and fill the holes in the screen. "Walt'll put pine tar on those little balls and no more pesky flies," said Etta.

"Do the Irwins do that?" asked the child, called Hannah.

"No, their screen is not broken," said Etta. Etta put her arms around the little girl and kissed her. "See if you can talk Ma and Pa into bringing you and the other kids for a visit. You'd like the Irwins."

"They're heathens and eat worms."

"That's not true! Who told you that?" Etta was steamed.

"Pa," whispered Hannah. "Don't get mad. I didn't believe him. I like Charlie. Your baby smells good."

Etta couldn't think of anything to say. She thought, one can count on Pa to plant an untrue idea. Despite herself, however, she was stirred by the feeling of her own mother's arms around her. Mrs. McGuckin said, under her breath, "Come back again."

Charlie held his breath, then bent and kissed Mrs. McGuckin's sallow cheek. "We'd be mighty pleased if you, Mr. McGuckin, and the kids would come to Sunday dinner—after service."

Etta was surprised, but pleased. "We could have a picnic in the meadow."

The children sang out, "Oh, let's go!"

Etta and Charlie looked at Mr. McGuckin, sitting at the kitchen table.

McGuckin looked with surprise at Charlie. "Me and my missus and the brood will think about coming to your place on Sunday. It'll be a chance to talk with your pa about your boldness, impudence, and how your manhood's distended your hide. If he's as wise as you say, he'll see that I judge from the strength of truth, even though I'm a weak man without my tonic."

Charlie sighed and stood, holding out his hand to shake

McGuckin's. He did not feel lighthearted, but he did not feel downcast. He thought, I'll tell Ma to fix thunder and lightning stewed down to a fine poison for McGuckin on Sunday.

Out in the yard Curly said, "Don't let Pa fool you. He's not weak from no tonic, he spent all yesterday putting his M brand on his yearling calves. He's worn out from that. Ma watches him with an eagle's eye so he can't touch spirits. It chafes him. Don't count on him and Ma coming to your place. Walt and me will be there. Count on it."

Etta relaxed when they stopped at Ray and Kate's place to let Jimmy hold baby Floyd. On the way home they stopped in town to get a newspaper for Joe and pick up mail from the post office. There was only a single letter to Mary from Joe's oldest sister, Elizabeth.

On the high-centered, twin-rutted road toward Sappa Meadows, Charlie pulled up on the reins and stopped the horse. "Look at all the columbines. Let's get some for Ma's window vases."

"That's why I love you," said Etta. "You're always thinking what others would like." She spread a blanket in the shade of the wagon box and carefully laid the sleeping baby on it. She took off her shoes and stockings and ran barefoot through the prairie grass colored with scarlet columbines, pink and white clover, and tall purple gentian.

Charlie tied the reins to the wagon's seat, dropped to the ground, and felt all the earlier tension drain away. He chased a scared rabbit and called to Etta, who was nearly hidden in the tall grass, "We're cavorting like fat ponies in high oats."

"Your running's a mighty miration, I mean gyration," teased Etta. "Look, here's a game trail by this little creek." She pointed to the shiny, fresh deer droppings and the many dry gray-green ones that had wintered under the snow.

Charlie put his arm around his wife and smelled the fresh soaplike odor of her hair and clothes. He held his breath and listened. A male grouse was drumming. It started slow and rapidly increased the tattoo, announcing that it had staked its claim to a piece of land. Charlie pointed so that Etta, too, saw it standing on a chalky stone, beating its powerful wings to cause the air to rush into a vacuum created by this beating. "Put, put, put, put-put-put-ut-ut-urrrr." The grouse vanished and Charlie sat on the chalk stone, took his boots off, and stretched his legs. He felt the warmth rise through his feet. The stone was in an area of white rock that was crisscrossed with ancient marine coral. It reflected the sun. Ahead was a dip in the terrain with a large bare place that would hold a quantity of rainwater, but was now flat and dry with a lacework of cracks. A redwinged blackbird balanced on the tip of a scrub willow growing in the middle of the tiny creek. It flashed scarlet and yellow epaulets and with a clear flutelike sound sang a short song.

Charlie took a deep breath and felt the tingling sensation flow from the pit of his stomach to all parts of his body. He half-closed his eyes in order to sharpen his view of the gentle rolling hills of deep green, blue, and wine surrounding him, and above, the clear blue of the sky. The sun seemed to focus on this spot, on him. It was his place. This earth was a part of him. He again squinted his eyes. He could see the line of trees that grew along the Middle Fork of Sappa Creek. To the left he saw the Irwin soddy tucked up against another rise of land. He looked in the direction of Goodland and only imagined he could see its buildings lined along a wide road. To the right, which was southwest, the land seemed completely flat, only the grass waving under the push of the wind and the patient horse munching the rich grass at its feet and the baby content to sleep in the wagon's shade after being bounced from one relative to another. To the west there was a gathering haze between the blue and green. This grayness seemed to mesh both sky and land so that neither was distinguishable. It made Charlie wonder what was beyond.

Without a clear break in his musings he was aware of the wind whipping Etta's blue cotton skirt and lifting her hair in little peaks. She, too, was looking, her hand on her forehead, shading her eyes. Again he was acutely aware of the smell of fresh laundry soap still minutely entangled in her clothes, and like hearing the various instruments in full orchestra, he also smelled the sweet coumarin from the bruised wild dropseed grass as he crushed it with bare feet, the bitter scent of daisies, and the sweet nectar of the clover. These blended in a huge satisfying fullness. He sat down, pulling Etta with him, and watched a bee moving from one flower to another. He moved his hands over the grasses, uncovering little bugs, grasshoppers, ants, and mites, busy with daily chores, living there next to his earth. Charlie was filled with gladness that he was here at this moment on this dynamic land. "My dear, I love you," said Charlie, lying back with Etta across his chest.

"I shall always love you," Etta said, kissing him full on the mouth. She thought, when there is love, one puts all else aside—

parents, brothers and sisters, children. After that one doesn't think at all, but uses the senses. One feels, smells, listens, tastes, and looks. Love is a banquet. Love is rapture, ecstasy, intoxication, an orgy. She felt Charlie's hands on her, heating her flesh with fire. She smelled his smoky perspiration, the dry alkaline chalk rock and spicy crushed grass. She heard his quick breathing and the beating of his powerful heart. She tasted the saltiness of his skin. She saw his beautiful brown shoulders and chest with the curling brown hairs. Her eyes closed. Love is a gorge with steep heights blocking out everything but the narrow pass. She was as eager as he. She forgot everything except the complete enjoyment of the shared sensual pleasure.

When she opened her eyes, the tall grasses and the red and yellow columbines swayed against the deep-blue sky.

Charlie buttoned his trousers and helped Etta straighten her clothes. His eyes sparkled. "What would your pa say to that!"

Etta giggled and it sounded like water gurgling over a rock wall.

"I think he would be envious. Oh, oh, I hear what our baby is saying." Etta flew back to the quilt. Floyd waved arms and legs and cried with sucking sounds. "He's hungry." She curled her feet under her and sat with a straight back to nurse her child. Her breasts were swollen and already sticky with milk as a result of the lovemaking.

Charlie had nearly forgotten about the letter posted from Atchison, Kansas, for his mother. He went out to the empty wagon for it. When he came back, Etta whispered, "Where's the columbine?" They both laughed at the private joke.

When Charlie handed the letter to his mother, he sobered. The handwriting was small and pinched. He had a feeling this day was suddenly coming to an end.

Mary went to the coal-oil lamp to see better. "Wonder why your sister wrote to me?" she asked Joe. "You suppose she's coming for a visit?"

"Why now?" said Joe, putting down his newspaper.

Mary finished reading the letter and came back to her rocking chair. Her voice was flat with no emotion. "My ma and pa are gone. Ma last year and Pa this."

Joe moved his chair next to her.

"Your sister, Elizabeth, she's the one wrote this letter to me. The boys buried Ma in the yard under that big old shagbark hickory—not in the town cemetery like Old Charles and Malinda. She went to a church supper and ate some homemade sausage."

"What about Riley?" asked Joe.

"He was chopping wood in the heat and just sat down to rest, and when he keeled over no one could get him going again. I can't believe they're gone."

"Was he put in beside Rachel?"

"Yes, under the shagbark." Mary wiped her eyes with her handkerchief.

"I can see it now," said Joe. "That was the place Rachel and Riley liked to sit in summer and sip cold tea. Remember that?"

"Yes," said Mary. "Laura, my oldest sister, and her husband are going to move back there. My two brothers are still on the farm with their families. That's a big place. Always has been. There's at least three hundred acres, maybe more now, if the boys have started homesteading the adjacent land. They ought to."

"I suppose your brothers have a pretty big herd of cattle by now—they were always good at luring in strays and fixing their brand on 'em. A man hears stories about his in-laws."

"Joe, they're your in-laws," she said sharply.

"Out-laws," he corrected. "Your brothers, leastways."

Mary sat back, thinking of the farm and of Chillicothe, the fields, the cattle, the dusty roads, the heat of summer, the ice-cold of winter. Her ma and her pa were gone. She could see the barns, henhouse, haycocks, meadowlarks, sleds on the snow-slick hills.

Charlie, Will, and Frank were quiet with their own memories of their grandmother and grandfather Brassfield. It would be summer in Chillicothe. The bittersweet would be twining up the trees, the sunny places would be brilliant with orange trumpet weed, and there'd be nettles and beggar's-lice. Charlie could hear his grandmother Rachel's voice calling for him to wipe the dust off his feet and to put his rope away before he caught one of her setting hens with it. He thought, soon's Floyd is old enough I'll show him how to use a rope. He went outside to the barn, found his old rope, and began to twirl it. He was pleased at what he could still do. Ought to do more of this every day, he thought. Then he heard his mother and father talking outside. His father said, "Would you like to go back again?"

"Yes," said his mother quickly, then, "No—Joe, I'm not sure."

Charlie went to the barn door and saw them sitting up on the wagon's seat. His mother had her hands in her lap and her shoulders drooped.

His father was looking out over the prairie. "You could go to visit your sisters and two brothers," he said. "You could take the stage to the Kansas Pacific Railroad Station at Oakley. With what I got from blacksmithing, there'd be nothing to stop you."

What he got blacksmithing was chickens and hogs, potatoes and canned goods, thought Charlie.

"Do you think they'd be glad to see me? Maybe I could take Etta and Floyd with me. I could show off my grandson."

Charlie's father pulled his arm off the back of the seat and turned slightly so that he could see Mary's face. "Truthfully, I'd like to see you right here. Mary, dear, it wasn't either of your brothers nor any of your sisters who wrote to you. Any one of them could have, last year and this year."

The sun was low in the sky. Charlie shivered. His mother did not look at his father. She said, "Maybe they didn't know where to send a letter. Maybe they were too busy getting everything straightened out—afterward."

"And maybe they was too busy arguing about who was to get what and if they didn't have to figure you in—well, there'd be more for them. I like it here, without no one asking me to lend them money they never intend to pay back. Without no one to know about my horsethieving and cattle rustling brothers-in-law, and laughing behind my back when I pretend I don't know what they're talking about. But if it would ease your mind and make you feel better, I ain't the one to tell you to stay here. I'll take you and Etta and Floyd to the train in town tomorrow."

Charlie took a deep breath. He never knew all this. When he was smaller, life was much simpler. He began to appreciate what his mother and father were feeling. Then he thought, I'd never really appreciate this if I weren't married. Etta makes all the difference. Etta going to Chillicothe? Is this true?

"Well, yes," said his mother, "that's right. I'll think on it."

They went back into the house. Charlie hung up his rope and went in to take care of Floyd while Etta and his mother prepared supper. No one said a word about Chillicothe.

Joe stayed far over on his side of the bed and Mary was far over on her side. She could not sleep. She knew that as a child she'd loved her parents. As she grew older her ma's shrill voice and her pa's sticky fingers when it came to cattle always irritated her. Riley's attitude had always been, easy come, easy go, and his sons lived just this side of the law. Their rule was, never get caught red-handed. Well, they'd never had any big scrapes with the law. So maybe they were all right now. They'd certainly be glad to see her and baby Floyd. They'd be surprised, too. She'd like to see a proper kind of town with boardwalks up and down all the streets for a change and real frame houses. "I could visit my old friends and talk to women who have wallpaper on their walls, instead of newspaper or gunny material covering dirt. I could talk about furniture and curtains and they wouldn't think I was trying to be snobbish."

Joe said, "Is that really so important, my dear?"

"Yes, sometimes it is."

Joe got up and pushed aside the bedroom curtain and went out the front door.

Mary could feel the west wind coming inside the soddy and hoped that Joe would close the door when he came back. Her head ached, her legs ached, her ankles were puffy, and she felt miserable.

He shut the door when he came in. "Think I'll dig potatoes tomorrow. Charlie and the boys can begin to pick the corn. You know, I'm thinking of letting Charlie run the farm and divide up proceeds between the Irwin men." In the back of his mind he was thinking Charlie might add another quarter section or two until eventually they had a whole section of land. This pleased Joe. "Charlie's a married man now and he can take the added responsibility."

"Charlie's always taken on more responsibility," said Mary.

"Yup, with only five years of real school, he knows more than most grown men I've met. He's good at figures and at sizing up a good horse as well as men." Then a burr caught in Joe's throat. Will might be furious with Charlie in charge. Then maybe not. Will had never shown any inclination to being tied to a farm. It wasn't that he was scared of work; he'd do his share if motivated; if not he'd lie down beside the biggest kind of job and go to sleep. Frank was not good with figures. He knew horses and that was about all. Frank did not understand men and business, he was too easily swayed. He had no convictions that were his own. He believed what anyone told him. "I'm sure glad Charlie's bride is that slip of a girl called Etta. She brings a lot of cheer and good sense to this place."

Mary rolled over and smoothed out the quilts. "Etta and I are going to can the beans from the garden tomorrow. We should have done it day before yesterday. We'll snip some marigolds for the window vases."

Joe sat up on the edge of the bed hardly breathing, afraid to move or to speak.

"You see, if you don't stand in the way of my going back," said Mary, looking down the quilts to where her feet made tiny mounds, "I'd rather stay here more than anything."

Etta's brothers, Curly and Walt, came in time for the Sunday dinner. Their hair was coated with fine dust the wagon wheels had kicked up. Walt coaxed a dog out of the wagon. The dog's legs were thin as telegraph wire.

Charlie was out in the yard in a moment, shaking hands with the McGuckin boys, a pleased smile across his face. "Come in. We're all at the table."

"First," said Walt, "we'd like to give you and Ettie a late wedding present, this here greyhound dog."

Charlie stared. He could not believe that they'd bring him such a gift. "Is it good for herding cows or for chasing deer out of the corn?" He patted the greyhound on the small head and scratched behind its ears, then persuaded it to lie in the shade of a currant bush.

"We thought we owed you something," said Curly. "You know we never stayed around to give you and Ettie a shivaree, and before we could think of anything you up and had a baby."

"What he's saying is that we went to Abilene to buy cattle for Pa," said Walt.

Charlie grinned. "You bought a dog in Abilene?" His grin grew wider.

"It's a racing dog!" whooped Curly. "It's the latest sport! We made some money in Abilene betting on dog races. We remembered the rumor that Goodland's going to sponsor a coursing club!"

"This lean-looking hound has such a small face it looks like a dime's worth of dog meat," Charlie scoffed.

Etta came out and examined the funny-looking dog. "You boys have the dumbest idea of what wedding presents are all about. I swan!"

"This is serious," said Curly. "Tait's going to print something in the paper about Goodland being host for dog races. Charlie, you train your dog and we'll take bets on him!"

"I never heard any rumors, but I'll read the papers more

closely. Thanks for the doggonest present I ever got," Charlie said, and held his sides laughing. "You boys going to help the critter?"

"Dog's yours now," said Curly, brushing the dust out of his hair.

Everybody went inside to eat. The greyhound sniffed at the tether Charlie had put around its neck and tied to the base of the prickery currant bush. The dog was white with black ears and huge black spots on its back, which looked as if somebody had spilled pine tar on it. After dinner Mary went out to see the new dog. "Let Joe see it. He knows something that'll help its legs." She picked up a front paw and the dog pulled it back. When she pulled the hind legs out the legs twitched and the dog growled.

"Get a bucket of hot water and some washing soda. Make a solution to dip the legs in," said Joe, sitting beside the dog. He estimated it weighed about seventy pounds. He said it wasn't skinny, it was built that way, slim, streamlined. He pointed out that its head was narrow and its ears thrown back and folded, its chest was deep. The hind thighs were wide and muscular.

"You can call it Lightning," suggested Walt.

The dog was quiet. Its head was between its paws. Its eyes were closed, but its ears twitched once in a while.

Walt explained. "You should have seen us coming out of Abilene. We were riding horseback ahead of it and it chased us. Of course, way back, there was some rubes chasing it and hollering, 'Come back Alex!' That *was* its name, Alexander. But that dog had no intention of going back. It wanted to be with us."

Etta gasped and said, "Sounds suspicious. You swipe that dog?"

"Aw, Ettie," said Curly, his eyes twinkling and his voice syrupy, "you don't have to say that. Every man looks out for hisself. If an opportunity arises he steps in and makes the best of the situation."

"Amen!" said Will, looking over the dog.

"We all have standards," said Frank, hunkering down to pet the dog.

"Honestly, how'd you get this dog?" Etta made her voice stern.

Walt pursed his lips and looked heavenward. "We already said. Haven't you heard, never look a gift dog in the mouth?" He held his finger up so Etta wouldn't butt in. "We're glad you married Charlie. He isn't asking a lot of questions about your gift. This breed of dog is royalty. Curly and me heard that the ancient Egyptians were partial to this breed. Henry the Eighth had all his noblemen rear and train greyhounds."

"Doesn't look gray to me," said Charlie.

Walt smiled and continued, "To get a greyhound to run you have to get it to chase a rabbit or something that moves. The eyes are sharp but the nose is dead. It can't smell."

"It's skinny as a lightning bolt," said Charlie.

"Has good muscles. Notice how its hocks are well back? Gives it leverage for running," said Joe.

"I know that," said Curly. "Never feed it raw catfish. There's flukes in fish."

"I can feed this here dog. You watch." Joe went back inside, slamming the screen.

Charlie nudged Lightning to its feet and dipped each leg into a bucket of warm washing-soda solution. "Guess I do this three, four times a day for a while. Then I'll start walking it around the yard. If it does all right I'll start some runs."

"Like I said, rabbit chases are best," said Walt.

Joe brought out a tin plate with several beef marrow bones and a liberal spooning of gravy from the dinner biscuits. Lightning's tail came up and moved in a semicircle. Its dark eyes were bright and expectant. The women went inside to wash the dishes. Charlie chewed on a timothy stem and watched Lightning eye the dish for several seconds before licking one of the bones. Then it took a bone in its mouth and slowly moved it to the shade of the house. When it finished cracking the bone, it rested its head between its front paws, licked its lips, yawned, and closed its eyes.

"Honestly, Lightning doesn't look like much of a racer to me," said Charlie.

At the end of two weeks' care Lightning's legs were healed. Each morning, at dawn, Charlie and Etta ran the dog. Then it was given a mix of boiled squirrel and gravy. One morning Charlie suggested taking Lightning out to the meadow, where rabbits burrowed under grass. With much keener vision than smell, Lightning flushed out a rabbit within minutes. It ran until the rabbit was far ahead, then it cut across to intercept it. Etta was so astonished and pleased at this showing of great intellect. She skinned the rabbit the dog brought back, stewed it, and served it to the dog that afternoon.

* * *

Early in August, 1895, Tait had a two-column article in the *Dark Horse* about the Goodland Coursing Club, which was following the rules and constitution of the American Coursing Club. So far there were ten local members.

Charlie went to town and had a talk with the club's president, Bill Walker, who owned a black greyhound named Amorita. Charlie joined the club and was told that Goodland was to be the national meeting place of the famous Kenmore Coursing Club. "People from several states will be here in mid-October," said Walker, scratching his blunt nose. "Rules will be printed in all the papers. The race will be held eight miles southeast of town. The sheriff and two deputies will control the crowds."

News of the large amount of winnings to be given away was in all the local papers and even in Denver and St. Louis papers. Many out-of-towners came to Goodland that fall to see or participate in the dog races. The first race began on the seventeenth of October. The crowd formed the shape of a crescent and moved ahead when signaled by a racing marshal. At the center of the crescent a man on foot, called the slipper, led the two dogs that raced first. Rhea, the white greyhound, belonged to Frank Robinson, and Sherman was John Jordan's dog.

Rhea and Sherman were fastened together with a spring collar. Charlie stood to one side, with Lightning on a leash, with the other men who had dogs that would race this first day. A man let a rabbit out of a wire cage. The rabbit jumped into the track where the short grass made it easy to run. The crowd stood still. Not a word was spoken. No one wanted to frighten the rabbit off the track into the weeds. As soon as the rabbit was eighty to a hundred yards away, in a straight line with the dogs, the leashes were slipped from the spring collar. The dogs were free to run.

Charlie held tight to Lightning until it was his turn. No one but the judge and the dogs' owners were allowed to follow the pair of racing dogs up the track. At the end of the course was a finish line drawn deep in the dirt. The rabbit was then forced to run into the tall grass where the dogs could not see its movement. Then the dogs slowed and stopped. Rhea had won. The next pair of dogs were put in the slip and the crowd moved forward again watching for a rabbit to be let loose, run the course then hop into the trampled tall grass.

Once in a while a dog caught a rabbit. A good race dog would not bite the quarry, but would hold it gently and on command from its owner let the rabbit go. The next day the winners of the previous day's races were put on the program and run off in the same manner. By doing this the card was reduced until only two dogs remained. They raced to decide the first- and second-place winners. When Lightning won the first day Charlie felt on top of the world. "We need posters on the telegraph poles about dog racing," he said to Etta. "Our dog has as much chance to be a final winner as any. I want everyone to come to see Lightning."

But the second day Charlie was concerned about Lightning. The dog's legs were holding up, but its muscles twitched. It was getting tired. Rabbits were getting scarce. The ones that did hop onto the course were fast. Excitement ran high making the dogs nervous.

Some men with racing hounds had come in from Denver by train. These men were friends of a man who brought some fresh rabbits in wire cages from Colorado Springs. The men from Denver had four dogs that they wanted to enter in the races.

Judge Mulcaster had to make a quick decision. He didn't want a fight to break out, so he told the Denver men that the first race would be between two of their dogs, followed by a second race between their other two dogs. The two winners would be allowed to run against the winners of the previous day's race.

Before the fourth race Van Hummell, a doctor from Kansas City, told Charlie he was going to check on his dogs and the men handling them. Charlie nodded, but was so interested in the race he didn't see him leave. Van Hummell's dogs were tied with others to a poplar tree waiting their turn. Van Hummell petted his dogs. They all lay quietly, almost asleep, at the base of the tree.

One of the Denver men carried a paper bag smelling like decaying melon rinds. Van Hummell wrinkled his nose and thought it was trash from some picnic. But when the Denver man came back in front of the tree the bag appeared empty. He nodded to Van Hummell and went back into the crowd.

Van Hummell stepped around the tree and saw scattered garbage and an empty trash can overturned. In the middle of the damp, moldy mess were melon rinds mixed with scraps of bacon. The dogs were gorging themselves. Van Hummell called to his handlers. "None of this mess, not even the trash can, was here ten minutes ago. I swear it," said one of the handlers.

Van Hummell was so indignant he told both his handlers to find their own rail fare home. With his dogs on leashes trotting behind him, he looked for owners of the remaining dogs.

Charlie untied Lightning, who licked at the bacon rinds. The dog's eyes were half closed as if it wanted to sleep in the shade. Van Hummell told Charlie what he suspected. "It's not proof, but it's mighty suspicious. Those Denver men want our dogs out of the race." Then he went to the judges with his complaint. Charlie followed, pulling Lightning after him. "Those men ought to be disbarred. They came late anyway," he said.

"Only if you can prove conclusively they fed garbage to your dog," said Mulcaster. "It's possible you didn't notice the trash can by the tree when you tied your dog."

"Darn tootin' I didn't!" exploded Charlie. "It was brought in about fifteen minutes ago!"

"Did you see it brought in?" asked Mulcaster with raised eyebrows.

All day the decisions of the judges were a disappointment to Charlie. A fast St. Louis dog, called Chloe, was out of the races early because it remained standing a few seconds before directly pursuing the rabbit. It was given no points. In the third race Walker's dog, Amorita, was defeated by a dog from Cripple Creek because of poor slips by Ralph Taylor of Denver. Likewise, Lightning failed to win because of poor slips, despite the fact that the hound held the rabbit in its teeth and bent it in a right angle for the kill, which was worth at least two points in anybody's book. Two cowdogs from Colorado Springs won over local greyhounds of championship form.

Van Hummell suggested Goodland not invite the Kenmore Club for a national meeting again. Lightning seemed to hold his head down and it limped. Deep down Charlie knew the dog's legs were weak. Lightning never would be a winner.

Charlie noticed a group of men talking. He recognized one of the Denver men. He meandered over beside the group. Lightning stayed close to his side. "You Denver boys put on a mighty fine race," he said. "I congratulate you."

"Thanks," said the man he'd recognized. "Looks like Colorado's cowdogs won over some of your locals." He pointed a sharp fingernail at Lightning. "It looks like a champion—but fate had her way, so it's a loser." The man smiled a sickly grin.

"You boys sure know how to make winners. Thanks for coming to Goodland," said Charlie.

"Maybe the race will be in Denver next year. We'll tie your dog's ears together again," he said, and laughed. "We'll outrun any dog from this rainmaking burgh."

The innuendo about Goodland's rainmaking efforts several years ago was not lost on Charlie. The man was bad-mouthing Goodland. Charlie gritted his teeth and tried to keep his mind on what he'd come to do. "You boys can understand my predicament. I've lost some money. That is, Lightning, my hound and I, are flat broke after entering a few of these races. Entrance fees, you know."

Someone said snidely, "You don't look like you're starving."

Charlie felt like lashing out. He bit his tongue. "I have a young wife. She doesn't understand gambling and racing."

"Let her grow up," said another with a snicker.

"You're right, my friend," said Charlie. "Look at that hound. She loves that dog. She used to get up before daylight and bathe its feet. Then bathe them two, three times during the day. She still walks it regularly. When it had ticks she put hot wax on them and pulled them off. She fed it balls of butter and bicarb of soda for a sour stomach. Can you believe this? She thought it was constipated and gave it an enema of soap and water."

"After that it ran good?" asked the Denver man with a wink.

"It's a winner!" said Charlie with a straight face. "My wife calls it a treasure. It was a wedding gift from her brothers. Those fellows paid a lot for it. It was a thoroughbred and a champion in the East."

Someone slapped Charlie on the back as if to say, the dog must be worth something. "You got papers on your hound?"

"Not me," said Charlie. "But maybe my brothers-in-law do. Who knows? They were secretive to me about how valuable that dog is—I think they told my wife everything. You boys married? Well, you know how it is with in-laws—no trust."

The man nodded, understanding perfectly.

"Have a drink, pal. Make you feel better." One of the men took a half-full flask from his hip pocket.

Charlie turned it down and passed it along to the man next to him. The sky clouded over and the day darkened. Lightning lay at Charlie's feet. "Thrashers ask a high price nowadays," complained Charlie, keeping his voice low and mournful. "A dollar a day and you have to watch them all the time."

"You a farmer?" one of the men asked.

"You are right, again. But it's not all sunshine and roses. I can tell you. There are crooks. Like those thrashers," said Charlie. "Oh, I should hold my tongue among friends."

"Oh—well, we all understand." The bottle was emptied and another came from somewhere and made the rounds. Charlie simply passed it on to the man next to him. By now the line of dark clouds was almost overheard. He moved his feet and acted as if he were getting ready to leave. He bent to pet Lightning.

"Don't go, not just yet. Say, how would you like to sell me your dog?" This was the man from Denver. He was called Jack and his black hair was oily, as if he'd put grease on it that morning.

"Well—I never thought of selling," said Charlie, acting surprised. "It would be hard to go home without the hound. The wife, you know." He laughed nervously.

"But if you're broke, you could use some money. I'm thinking of offering you fifty dollars for that sleepy-looking hound." The man rubbed Lightning's ears.

Lightning stiffened, laid its ears back, and growled low in its throat. "Hush!" Charlie's voice was deep and curt. The dog became quiet and relaxed. Charlie noted that the man saw how well it obeyed. "I would never give it away for that! I'm sure it cost more, much more when it was purchased with papers and all."

The sky looked like rain. A strong breeze came up. Lightning had its nose in the direction of the wind.

Jack balanced on his toes, then back down on his heels for a few minutes as if in deep thought. "If I offer something like seventy-five dollars, would you respond to that?"

Charlie stood a moment, rubbing his upper lip with forefinger and thumb. He could feel the stubble of his whiskers beginning. His voice was unhurried, "Nope. I couldn't. Not at that price. This here is a genuine thoroughbred. It's worth twice as much, if not more. Guess I'd better be going before I get caught in a downpour."

Jack pulled the brim of his felt hat low over his face as the first few drops of rain hit the dust. "I'll give you a hundred and fifty smackers for that hound and not a cent more, thoroughbred or no."

Charlie got a tingling feeling in his chest and the top of his mouth started to go dry. "There were two days of entry fees that were taken from my pocket. Twenty dollars each day."

"Yes, I can understand how you'd feel losing that." Annoyed, Jack reached deep into his pants' pocket. "Twenty and another twenty—" Then he counted out one hundred and fifty dollars and held them out toward Charlie's face. The money smelled like tobacco.

Charlie blinked once, slowly raised his hand, and at the same time held out Lightning's lead rope. "You've got yourself the best greyhound in Sherman County, Jack. Good luck in Denver." Charlie scratched Lightning behind the ears and patted its head. "So long."

Jack smiled and looked pleased.

Charlie felt like he was going to burst. He kept his face forward and his head up. He felt the splatters of rain. It was about ten minutes before he got into the wagon.

"I think you'd better get this old buckboard home before we are all wet as frogs in swamp water," said Charlie.

Frank asked, "Where's Lightning? What's the matter, Charlie? Are you crying or is it the rain?"

"I don't know if I'm laughing or crying," admitted Charlie, "but I sold that hound to one of those Denver fellows. I hope it was the fellow who dumped garbage and threw the race. I cleaned him for a hundred and ninety dollars!"

The wagon moved. Charlie sat back, closed his eyes. His whole face relaxed.

"Wow! One hundred and ninety bucks! I heard that Denver crowd was tough as whang leather," said Will, handling the horses. "How'd you do it?"

"I don't really know. Kept my temper. Let the guy talk. I pretended I was Colonel Johnson, then Dr. Melbourne. Honest!"

"You can buy an honest-to-God thoroughbred greyhound," said Frank.

"Not on your life!" said Charlie. "I'm finished with dogs. I'm going to get Ma a new oilcloth for the kitchen table and Pa some of those new rust-resistant corn seeds. The rest I'm saving."

"You could divide the rest with your brothers. We could have a whale of a good time," said Will.

"The rest is for Etta." Charlie watched the jagged streaks of lightning. "Let's move! Someone up there's fixin' to pull the cork!"

SIXTEEN

Colorado Springs, Colorado

Will was restless that fall. He made several trips to the little farming town of Ruleton, west of Goodland. Twice he took Frank on the pretext of checking out some Herefords that were for sale. They came home with hangovers instead of Herefords.

It was a cold, pale October morning when Will and Charlie went out to clean the barn. The lush prairie grass lay dry and yellow underfoot. Above, the weak, icy-white sun displayed a white ring. Charlie took the shovel and scooped a black pile of manure out the door. Will scraped manure and hay from the floor into a pile with a hoe.

A gloomy day for a lowly chore, thought Charlie. The barn and soddy seemed pitifully shabby. The wind gusts blew little spirals of dust around the barn door and rattled the faded weed stalks on the roof of sod.

"Wouldn't you be smart to look somewhere besides Ruleton for those Herefords you have your heart set on?" asked Charlie.

Will looked up from his mucking hoe. His eyes, fixed on something outside the barn door, were quiescent.

"What's the matter?" scowled Charlie. "You run out of money?"

Will closed his eyes, drew a weary breath, then opened them.

"No, it's not money, nor cows that's on my mind. It's a girl."

Charlie's leather glove slipped on the shovel handle. "Jeems! What's so unusual about that? You've had girls on your mind for years, lots of girls."

"That's just it, lots of them. Remember that dance Frank and I went to in Ruleton? I wasn't in Ruleton for a dance. I wanted to find Plucky. She's gone—moved—disappeared."

Charlie shifted first one foot then the other. "You want to tell me about the dance?"

Will settled on an old wooden crate. The hoe rested against his knee. He pulled off his gloves and rolled a cigarette, put it in his mouth, struck a match on his thumbnail, and inhaled deeply. He picked a speck of tobacco off his tongue. "Charlie, I'm going to tell you something. I want you to keep it under your hat."

The blue smoke hit Charlie's face. He liked the aroma, but his eyes watered, so he moved to see Will better. "You in some kind of trouble?" He felt his stomach tighten and anger rise in his throat.

"Not yet."

Charlie saw red. "Not yet? Sounds like trouble around the corner! There's enough trouble keeping this farm solvent without you bringing more problems. You know how Ma and Pa have their heart and soul tied up in this seedy place. They believed it would make them free. But look at them! They're slaves to this land! You bring in your problems and you tie them tighter to the land."

Will stared straight ahead through the gray daylight. "I thought you loved this land."

"I do. But I know what capricious weather does. I'm thinking of keeping a record on rainfall, frost, snow, sun, temperature. Maybe that will give us some reason for planting certain crops at certain times. It's irony that Pa was the one who told me knowledge is freedom."

Will looked exasperated. "What I have to say is not related to irony or to some figures you want to keep in a ledger. Maybe I won't tell you. I'll work it out myself."

Charlie leaned forward. "Start at the beginning."

"I will, but don't interrupt with some fool remark that has no bearing on the subject." He stepped on his cigarette and pushed it with his boot against a pile of manure. Charlie nodded, wishing Will would get on with his story. Will was old enough to take his own responsibility, to be master of his own actions.

"I always wondered if I'd ever get involved with a female. I only took Sam Oldum's sister to the dance because Frank had set it up."

Charlie squatted down on his haunches and leaned against the door frame. He closed his eyes and hoped Will wouldn't take too long to tell about his female problems. Charlie thanked the Almighty God he was married.

"Sam Oldum's sister was pretty and nice enough, but there was this other girl, Arnold Rick's sister, who attracted me. I admit I had a couple drinks before the dance, but only to bolster my depressed state. This Margaret Rick is like Etta. She's blond and easily riled. Small, agile, blue eyes, and giggly."

Charlie was thinking of Etta's sweet smile and her gay chatter that was like the tinkling of a silver bell.

"After the dance I persuaded Arnold Rick to take Sam Oldum's sister home and I took his sister home. Her folks are plain homesteaders like ours. The drought and cold winter nearly wiped them out, same as us. I got to talking with her pa and one thing led to another. Remember the first time Frank and I went to Colorado Springs to see Ell and Les? Margaret went with us to have her earache cured." He rolled another cigarette.

"This girl, Margaret? She went where?" Charlie asked.

"To Ell's place. She was wide-eyed, like a kid, when she saw the mountains and the pines."

"Frank was with you?"

"Yes."

"What did he think about taking some girl to Ell's?"

"Well, he knew we were taking her so that Ell could cure the earache, so he didn't say much."

"And Ell, what did she think?"

"She liked Margaret right away," he lied. "It was her idea that we get married."

"Married!" Charlie jumped and the shovel clattered to his feet.

"Ell said I could be in a lot of trouble. Margaret is fifteen." Will gave him a look so full of meaning that he froze.

"Ell signed the marriage certificate. Margaret's Ma can sign underneath if she wants."

Charlie's knees thawed to water. "Her folks don't know? You've been married since July? Why didn't you bring her here? Earache? What about an earache?" Charlie became so wound up that his questions ran faster than a nickel-plated wristwatch.

"Margaret had an earache. Nothing cured it. So I told her pa about this famous herb doctor I knew in Colorado." Will smiled wanly.

"Why would her pa let you and Frank take her anywhere? He didn't know you that well."

Will looked embarrassed. "Mr. Rick thought Frank and I were rich ranchers. That man is too dumb to roll rocks down a steep hill. I doubt he can write his name. He and his wife were honored to have Frank and me take their ailing daughter on the train, at our own expense, to have a noted herb woman treat her."

Charlie was livid. This was his older brother; eight years older. "I can't believe you!" Charlie raised his hands and let them drop at his sides.

Will was contrite. "We took care of that girl. When we brought her home her earache was cured."

"If she's pregnant, the secret won't be kept long."

"Oh, you think you know everything." Will got up and stood opposite Charlie against the door frame. "That's the sour note." Then he brightened. "Ell's tea cured her earache. I could take her to Colorado on the pretext of a further examination. Ell certainly has something for pregnancy. Hasn't she?" He glowed, believing he'd solved the problem. "I'll use coitus interruptus until Ell fixes Margaret up with something, just in case. It will work out. There's no big problem. Thanks, Charlie, talking to you helped a lot. See, I know some things Pa never told me."

"Don't thank me yet. Your problem is still there, multiplying. You have a wife and I am led to believe you've *known* her more than once."

"Charlie, say it! I've fucked her. And it was good every time."

Wind roared between the barn and the soddy, and dirty gray clouds rolled across the halfhearted sun. Snow swirled through the open door like confetti.

Charlie put his big hand on Will's arm. His voice was grave. "Don't make this worse by being an ignoramus. You go after her now! You talk to her ma and pa. Tell them how much you care for their lovely daughter and what a good husband you'll be. Stay near the truth."

"I can't. They think I'm a rich rancher. How can I tell them I live with my folks? I'll be the laughingstock of the whole Rick family."

Charlie saw defeat in Will's stare.

"When Margaret is here with us, Ma, Pa, Etta, baby Floyd,

Frank, and you, she'll know you're all right. She'll forget about money rich and feel love rich."

"I don't know."

"You won't know until you try—run the experiment. Go get Margaret and bring her home. You want me to go with you?"

Will shook his head and began to finish the mucking job. "I've thought of something else. There's not one smithery that Frank and I could find in Colorado Springs. You know how Ma wants the family together? Well, I could open up a blacksmith shop in Colorado Springs, and if it's a success you could bring everyone there." Will smiled at Charlie's stern face.

"Let's work out one thing at a time. First on the list is this barn," said Charlie. "Second on the list is your wife."

The raw wind pushed leaden clouds across the stale October sky. The ground was white. The cottonwood trees at the creek's bank were bare. Their leaves were buried under the snow. Their sap was cut off at the roots.

Charlie stood at the window breathing the warm stagnant air of the soddy, wishing he could fling open the door and find the prairie green and fertile and the air sweet with the aromatic smell of blossoms. To see Will bring his wife home on horseback, bundled in a blanket so that only her eyes and nose showed, was a shame. He felt hot tears in his eyes for the girl his brother had so scurrilously taken in and wedded. At the far end of the road, where it met the sky, he saw the riders thump heels against the horse's ribs and the horse trot faster. Charlie grabbed the door and ducked outside. He waved both arms and whistled between his teeth. Will gave one long, shrill whistle back. Charlie hurried inside.

"Etta! Ma and Pa! They're here! Will and his bride!"

Etta was first to greet them. Will jumped off the horse and pulled the willowy girl off as though she were as light as a corn-husk doll in a blanket. He pushed back his hat and said, "This used to be Margaret Rick, but now she's Mrs. William Irwin."

Margaret's face turned red as she folded the blanket and handed it to Etta. Her deep-blue eyes were veiled in apprehension and her hands trembled. Long blond hair flowed around her shoulders.

Etta put her arms around Margaret. "Welcome to the Irwin clan. We are glad Will brought you home."

"I thought this was a big cattle spread," said Margaret. "I had no idea it was only a soddy." There were tears of disappointment in her eyes.

"Well, one day we'll have an Irwin ranch," said Etta brightly. "Come, I'll show you around. You want to wash?"

She was introduced and Etta took her to the bedroom.

Mary looked at Will. "Son, she's a baby. You brought home a baby bride. Be gentle. It's a wonder her ma let her go. What's happening to boys and girls these days? They're grown before their time."

"Ma, her folks know you'll take care of her. I told them how you fuss over us."

Mary glowed with his flattery, but she wasn't fooled. "I only fuss over babies. Didn't Frank come home with you?"

"Yes, but when we got to the branch in the road, he didn't turn toward the soddy. I bet my last dollar he went to tell some of the boys to hold a shivaree tonight," said Will.

She got to her feet unsteadily and shuffled to the kitchen shelves. "I'll be making coffee cakes."

Margaret came out with her long ecru-colored hair in pigtails and a comforter wrapped around the long nightdress Etta had put on her to keep her warm. She sat in Will's lap like a sleepy child.

"You like sugar in hot tea, honeybun?"

She snuggled against Will's chest and nodded yes to his question. Her dark eyes had blue shadows around them so they looked even larger.

Etta put water in the teakettle and wood in the fire box. She got raisins off the shelf for Mary.

Charlie thought, Margaret looks like she's going to suck her thumb. Baby Floyd cried. He excused himself and went to change the baby and bring him out for Margaret to see. "Guess you want supper, huh?" He fed Floyd bits of biscuit left over from the noon meal. The boy reached his chubby hand for more, at the same time Margaret took a whole biscuit for herself.

Charlie and Etta put Will and Margaret in their room. They piled quilts on the kitchen floor near the range for themselves.

"How many nights'll we sleep here?" groused Charlie.

"Sshh! In the spring you'll help Will build an addition. Make it big. If Frank gets married he'll want a room of his own."

The boys came on horseback and someone brought a buggy. They beat on kettles with wooden spoons and whistled. Etta tried to hush them when they came inside, but it was no use. They were bound to give Will and his bride a memorable shivaree.

Frank and Curley took Margaret out to the buggy on the pretense of showing her something new. Will ran after them with his shirt-tail flapping, but it was too late. They were back in thirty minutes. Frank called out, "Will, your missus is all right! Walt spun around on the ice down in the meadow a couple of times! Scared her half to death! Ha! Ha!"

"I'd be petrified!" Etta said to Charlie.

The remainder of the winter was mild. Charlie went with his father to the Farmers' Alliance meetings and heard men discuss the possibility of an overabundance of destructive insects in the spring. One settler suggested bringing in harmless insects that would destroy the harmful ones. "Ladybugs eat aphids. That's a scientific fact."

During March 1896 the weather became surprisingly warm. Joe and his boys planted wheat, corn, and oats before the dry weather began. Charlie plowed a kitchen garden at the side of the soddy. Mary's ankles ached so that Etta planted the garden.

By May it was obvious Joe's wheat crop was infected with the red spores of leaf rust. He discussed the disease with the three boys and finally, with a sinking heart, torched his wheat fields so that they were black smudges on the dry earth. Other farmers were forced to do the same. Some even went so far as to hunt out patches of the meadow rue, which was the alternative host for the rust. They burned the patches of rue, hoping to control the rust.

Another scourge hit the farmers during the summer. The fishy smell of stinking smut was carried by the wind from some fields where the kernels of grain were replaced with the black spores the farmers called smut balls. The Turkey Red wheat brought to Kansas by the Mennonites in 1874 was wonderfully drought-resistant and hardy, but was not immune to the rust and smut that flourished during a time of high humidity and thick morning dew.

"I don't know which smells worse," said Joe, "the blackened fields of stubble or the mildew in the damp earth of the soddies."

When Charlie went to town he heard talk about jointworms, chinch bugs, aphids, grasshoppers, and corn borers.

"Looks like the worst year yet," he told his father. "I hear many settlers are selling for any price or leaving everything to go West and start over or to go to relatives in the East." He felt a deep fatigue and lassitude come over him.

His father said, "Son, we could always get by in years past doing farrier work. But this time no folks have anything to pay for my work." He turned his face away from Charlie.

Charlie reached out to his father. "Pa, I'm going to send Will and Frank to Colorado Springs to look for a building to house the new Irwin Smithery. We can read the signs of poverty as well as anyone. We're not going to pray for something that won't happen. We're going to start over in another place." Inside his chest he felt his heart nearly stop, waiting for his father to say something.

The shoulders slumped as his father pulled out a faded bandanna and blew his nose. "It's hard to believe," he whispered, "but you're right." His head bowed. "Your ma will cry when she hears. Be prepared for that. But it won't all be sadness for leaving. She'll have some joy seeing her children in one place. The family will be together." Again, he blew his nose.

Charlie felt anger rise to his throat because life was so formidable.

A week later, night was fading away and Charlie was aware the crickets' chirp had begun. He knew the temperature was rising, because the chirp was increasing. He lay quietly marking off fifteen seconds on his pocket watch held in a ray of light coming through the curtains across the front window. He counted the number of chirps in fifteen seconds and added the number thirty-eight. Three times he checked the number. He put his hand on Etta's shoulder, "Etta, it's eighty outside right now, six in the morning. Think what the temperature'll be by noon."

"Did you get up and look at the thermometer, Charlie Irwin?" mumbled Etta, still groggy from sleeping in the summer heat.

"No, but I'm right. I've been working this out for a couple of weeks. Go check for me and you'll see I'm right." He was up, pulling on his trousers. "One thing I'll like about moving—maybe we'll get our own bedroom. It's not decent for a man to sleep on the floor in front of the open door in summer and in front of the kitchen range in winter."

Etta rolled out the other side of the quilts, slipped into her gingham dress, and ran to the kitchen wall, where the mercury thermometer hung beside the calendar from the Farmers and Merchants Bank.

"This reads eighty-two." She folded up a quilt and threw it at Charlie. "What you going to do with all those figures and measurements you keep in your ledger when we move?"

"Well, Miss Smarty, I'll do a couple of things. First I'll tell Mr. Tait down at the *Dark Horse* how to measure the temperature if he can count the chirps of the cricket fast enough, and he can print it in his paper. Then those folks without thermometers will know exactly how hot it is."

"Or cold," put in Etta.

"Then I'll keep my record and make some kind of graph for the rainfall and temperature and give it to the Farmers' Alliance before we leave, or mail it to them. Maybe I'll keep some records somewhere else, too. You see, I can do things with figures besides—"

"Charlie! You wouldn't, not now! Sshh! The others will be getting up! Stop teasing!"

"Once you said you'd do anything for me," said Charlie, putting his boots on.

"I meant it. I will, but I get to choose the time and place." Etta's face shone with perspiration.

Charlie bent and kissed her cheek. "Salty."

"Mum, mum," gurgled baby Floyd.

"This little boy made a lake out of his crib." Etta fussed over the baby. "Here, hold him. I'm going to take the sheet to the line to dry." She went outside.

Charlie let his boy hold on to a chair. He could walk if there was something to hold on to. Charlie folded the quilts, put yesterday's biscuits on the table, along with tin cups and plates, and built a small fire in the range to boil coffee.

Etta flew inside, letting the screen bang. "They're coming! They're bringing a herd of something—mustangs!"

Charlie could hear the hoofbeats echoing against the low hills. He looked out the screen. "Not mustangs. Those are scrub cattle! No! Yearling calves!"

"How many?"

"Jeems! Looks like a couple dozen! What if those boys spent money on cows instead of a smithery? Gol-durn! I'll skin them both so's Ma won't know them from fresh rawhide. Excuse me!"

The others got up to see what was going on.

"It's Frank and Will!" cried Mary, clapping her hands. "Why, they've a whole herd of calves. We're not in the beef or dairy business. Are we?"

Margaret ran out barefoot to meet Will, not bothering to put a wrapper over her nightdress.

The men on horseback waved their hats and called in duet, "Yahoo! Look what we brought for you!"

Will was first to jump from his horse. The yearling calves milled around the yard, bawling.

"Those are some sweet dogies," said Will. "We found them

out in the bluestem west of Ruleton. Nobody was around. So we figured someone was working ahead of a roundup. But we hadn't seen anyone behind. We figured someone ditched them, and if no one claimed them on the way home they were ours. None carry a brand." He was breathless.

"Soon's I get something to eat, we'll take them to the meadow and under half crop their ears so's they'll match Will's Herefords." Frank pulled his gear from the back of his horse.

Charlie took the horses to the barn. When he came back everyone was at the kitchen table. Charlie poured himself a cup of coffee, moved away from the hot stove. He felt uneasy. He was glad to see his brothers, but all those calves made him nervous.

Joe stood, one gnarled hand on Frank's shoulder. He looked across the table at Will, who had Margaret on his lap. His right hand raised and shook. No one spoke. Then with the ferocity of an angry bull Joe roared. "Get those calves off my land! They ain't legit! Someone'll spread the word if they ain't done it already. I suspect we'll see Goodland's new sheriff before sundown." He lowered his hand and sat down slowly. His mouth was set in a straight line.

"Oh, no!" cried Margaret. "Say it ain't so. Tell us those cows weren't rustled."

Will's face was white. He dropped his head against Margaret's shoulder.

Joe released his hand from Frank's shoulder. Frank sprang up. "I'm taking those calves to the meadow."

"Eat your biscuits," said Charlie. "Pa and me have something to talk over." He motioned for his father to step outside.

"Pa and I," murmured Etta, nursing Floyd. Suddenly she clapped a hand over her mouth, put the baby in Mary's lap, and went out to the well, where Charlie and Joe were talking.

Charlie and Joe on horseback herded the noisy calves away from the house, across the field of lespedeza blooms, to the settlers' road. Neither man said a word. Charlie saw the droop to his father's shoulders and felt a constriction around his heart.

When one calf bawled for its mother, the others started. When one calf farted, the others followed.

They rode past Ray Lewis's place, staying several hundred yards on the far side of the road. When they reached McGuckin's place, their clothes were wet with perspiration, and dust streaked their faces. Charlie reined in his horse and put his hand out for his father to stop. The calves continued. "Let them get over in the pasture, off the road some, into the little dip of land," said Charlie. "I'll go along now and see they all stay together."

"I don't know about Etta's idea," said Joe, uneasylike. "That girl's got spunk, but her pa's got a temper." Charlie waved. Joe sat woodenly and watched his son edge the calves into the gully. When Charlie came back he pushed his hat back on his head and looked surreptitiously toward the McGuckin yard. Everything was quiet.

Charlie fanned himself with his hat. "Glad that's done," he whispered.

"You think McGuckin'll keep those strays? Or will he report them to the sheriff?" asked his father.

"I guess we'll see," said Charlie. "Let's head home before the folks are up and about."

When they were passing Lewis's again far out in the field, away from the road, his father said, "Thanks, Charlie. You and Etta got us out of a tough spot."

Charlie smiled. "I hope the boys learned something."

"Darn tootin', they did. I had a mind to let Will and Margaret stay in the soddy, so's he could raise his cows, while the rest of us went to Colorado. But I've changed my mind. We'll stay together and keep an eye on everybody."

"I'd rather be the watcher than watched," said Charlie.

Midmorning the next day the newly elected sheriff, John McCune, rode into the Irwins' yard.

Will was telling about the building next to the Antlers Hotel that he and Frank had signed for in Colorado Springs. "I have the deed in my other shirt pocket. Jeez, I hope Margaret hasn't washed it yet." He went to the bedroom and brought out the deed.

"Etta's done all that child's washing," said Mary, not unkindly but bluntly.

Margaret was staring dreamily out the screen door and saw the glint of the sheriff's silver star. She flung her arms around Will and cried, "Will! Oh, Will! He's come for you!"

"What do you suppose McCune wants?" Will looked as innocent as possible and motioned for Etta to take Margaret to the bedroom.

"He's going to ask about Will's sticky rope!" sobbed Margaret. "He'll take Will away. I'll have to go home and admit I married a rustler. Boo-hoo!"

"Hush!" glowered Etta, dropping a diaper in Margaret's lap.

Margaret wiped her face and looked sulky.

Sheriff McCune must have heard Margaret's wailing because the first thing he said through the screen to Joe was, "Everything all right here, Mr. Irwin?"

Charlie stood by his father and studied McCune's face through the screen. He was clean-shaven, with a large, straight nose. His thick red hair was drawn back behind his ears and held in place with petroleum jelly. His mouth was large, not indicating a great deal of sensitivity. His chin was round with a cleft, leading Charlie to believe that he was unwavering, and this was confirmed by his wide-set brown eyes which looked out with patience.

"Yes, sir. Just fine. Will got himself a new bride and she's not used to seeing roaches and mice come out of the walls of the soddy like the rest of us. Sometimes fusses a lot about it." His upper lip trembled slightly as if agitated by some inner ferment.

"I know the type, high-strung and easily overwrought. My own wife was that way for the first year we were married"—McCune looked at Will shyly—"until we had our first baby." Then he added, "Children settle a woman."

Charlie knew he'd seen Etta take baby Floyd and follow Margaret into the bedroom. He wondered when McCune was going to state his reason for being out in Sappa Meadows. Charlie was cautious, but not discourteous. "Come in. Coffee's on the stove."

"Heard you folks were selling your place and heading West." McCune sipped the coffee carefully so he wouldn't burn his tongue. "It's a shame to lose good folks like you."

Charlie was certain he meant what he said, so he pointed to the envelope on the kitchen windowsill. "That's the deed to a building in Colorado Springs that's the future Irwin Smithery."

McCune's eyes roamed around the soddy and finally settled on Charlie. "Some Farmers' Alliance men found McGuckin with two dozen calves that don't suck his cows. McGuckin says they ain't his, but he's going to keep them because he knows where they come from."

Frank backed away against the wall.

Will opened his mouth and started, "Why, that dirty damn—"

"Hey! Remember McGuckin is my father-in-law," said Charlie, feeling like he was in a house of cards that would suddenly collapse about his shoulders.

"Sure, but he don't come over here," said Joe. "That man has a notion that the Irwins ain't religious enough. He hasn't even been to see his daughter since the wedding a year and a half ago.

Can you imagine not wanting to see your grandson? Don't you think this eats on him?" Joe's face was red except for two small white spots in the middle of each cheek. His white beard twitched against his chest. "It'd please him to see a son of mine have his good character sullied. It's a mean thing to do when we was fixing to move because the land don't provide enough."

McCune wiped his face with his handkerchief. "This hot spell ought to break soon. It's got us all on edge." He turned and looked at Frank, who sat in the darkest corner of the room. "Where were you yesterday morning?"

Frank was startled and let out a loud burst of air. "Why, early yesterday morning Will and I left the town of Kanorado. Charlie told you we'd bought a building in Colorado Springs."

"Oh, yes." McCune's hands balled and then relaxed. "You were expecting your boys home yesterday?" he asked Joe.

"Well," Joe cleared his throat. "Charlie and Etta, his wife, were looking out the window for them."

Charlie heard his mother's rocking chair. *Crick-crack, crick-crack.* She was sewing, holding the cloth close to her face when she pushed the needle through. He thought of the crickets and what he was going to tell Mr. Tait about how to determine the temperature.

"It was warm yesterday, I figured about eighty near dawn. Pa and I went out on the farrier's route before the noon heat could sap our strength. We saw some calves on McGuckin's place. I think they're truly his. The talk from him is just from jealousy and should be ignored." Charlie stared at McCune's sweat-stained boots.

McCune stretched out his hand cordially to Joe. "I think you're right. I'll tell McGuckin to quit bellyaching and get those calves branded in the morning. Thanks for the coffee." He got up and went out to his horse, which was switching its tail to keep the flies off. "Heartbreaking to see so many fields burned black on account of the rust. You have a buyer for the place?"

Joe nodded. "Yup, some dude from Topeka talked with Tomblin at the bank and Tomblin sent him out here. Wants possession next week, when his wife and kids come out by railroad."

"You've a lot of packing to do. Don't envy your missus. You know women usually have to make all the decisions about what and how to crate things." He paused. "Say, I'm sorry I troubled you. My hunch was right. You folks have no use for a couple dozen young cows. Well, good luck." He rode off in a cloud of dust.

Joe came inside, sat down. Charlie could see he didn't want to speak, but felt he must. His eyes looked misted. He ran his hand through his white hair and motioned for Frank to get up out of the corner and sit at the table beside Will. "I don't believe you boys are stupid. But you knew those were rustled calves. The Alliance men could have hanged you for bringing them here. Now, get this straight. Irwins pay for what they get one way or another. If we ever start a ranch, it'll be with cattle that are paid for!"

The two wagons were packed tight with goods the Irwins had accumulated. Mary's eyes were red. She had so many memories. The old soddy seemed a part of her. Somehow it seemed strange that, with such a momentous change taking place in her life, the summer should continue hot, the prairie grass should blow dry and yellow, and the willows along the edge of the creek should be bright green as she always remembered.

Joe drew a blue bandanna from his hip pocket and dabbed at his mustache. "I could use some of that winter wind, cold as blazes, right now."

"Well, we're on our way!" exclaimed Charlie. "To a town of eleven thousand souls. That's bigger than Goodland."

"It'll be twice the size in another five years," said Will. "Coal mining and gold mining make use of horses. We'll have plenty of shoeing jobs."

Joe nodded. He'd made a fair deal on this Kansas homestead, sold the steel plow and workhorses for twice as much as they'd cost him. He'd made good money on the mustangs, too. Joe clicked his tongue and the four-horse team started slow at first. The women rode in the wagon. The three boys were on horseback, and one milk cow was tied to the back of the wagon.

Joe followed the Colorado, Rock Island, and Pacific Railroad tracks. The rounded contours of prairie land leveled off toward the horizon. Every gully and blowout was hollowed out by the wind and faced the same direction, south. Once they stopped for a midday meal beside a tiny stream whose thick Indian grass crossed over the clear band of water.

They forded creeks and shallow rivers, camped outside such towns as Burlington, Bovine, Limon. Then the land began to swell upward and there were dark evergreen forests. They no longer rode through patches of purple tasseled Scotch thistle and the annoying devil's claw, with seeds that clung to everything that moved and touched them. Joe moved the wagon fast through patches of locoweed before the fresh cow would have a chance to put its head down to try the succulent-looking green plants with violet, cream, or white flowers.

Etta found the pink wild rose blossoms and wanted to take a couple "stalks" to plant beside their new house. Margaret brought in a pale lavender columbine she found by a stream. Will had to send her back for the water bucket she was to fill. "Are you so slow-witted you forgot to bring up water for the supper?"

Her eyes filled with tears. Mary called her to spread the quilt for the table. "Child, dry your eyes. Find a sugar sack and each noon stop, hunt the sunflower stalks that rattle in the breeze. Put the seeds in your sack. We'll have a flower garden."

At night the full moon brought howls from coyotes and wolves. There were fireflies winking in the sage and bats swooping out of the trees over the campfire.

One day four wagons retreating eastward passed. Charlie saw that the strangers looked tired and defeated. Joe stopped to tell them "hello." The man driving one of the wagons called, "Man, you go too far west and the rock mountains have a wind so fierce it pushes trees to one side so they are stunted. Nary a grass is able to take root in the rock. I'm warning ya, turn back."

Another called out, "Howdy to you all. The West is country better left to Injuns and mountain goats."

One of the women looked at Etta holding baby Floyd and shook her head to and fro. "Buried our Laddie two days ago. If you want to see your boy growd, turn back."

"We're not going through no rock mountains!" snapped Joe. "And if we did, we'd use an Injun for a guide." He banged the front of the wagon box.

Toward evening the team pulled the wagon over a rolling ridge that was so gentle it was hardly noticeable, yet at the summit there was a panoramic view of a spruce forest and blue mountains. The dark green looked cool and inviting. The wagon wheels screeched as they rolled along the brown sandy loam past the sagebrush and juniper and into the shadowy lane with its canopy of dark branches covered with lacy patterns of thin green splinters against a gray-blue sky. The aroma of resin was strong as a breeze whispered through the tufted spindles. Daylight dimmed and a few log houses passed with lance-leafed cottonwoods growing by the back-door creek.

"Shouldn't we make camp before night?" asked Mary.

The horses plodded on the road made soft with layers of brown needles. Ahead were yellow lights, more wooden houses, and amazing gaslights along the main street.

"We're here!" shouted Will. "Now to find a little place numbered five-thirty on a street named South Nevada."

The plank house did not look little with a newly built porch on three sides. Les came out, the light behind making him look dark and muscular. "Yo! Who's there?" he called.

The wagon rocked to a halt and Joe shouted, "It's the Irwin clan here to camp on your new veranda!"

Ell was out in a second, grasping first one then the other, a smile at her mouth, tears streaming down her cheeks.

Charlie and Joe were more than pleased with the building Will and Frank had found next to the Antlers Hotel. It was sturdy wood, rainproof, and could easily be converted to a blacksmith shop.

During the warm days of August, Joe and his three boys fitted out the smithery and advertised for business. The women looked at frame houses the family might buy or rent. There were not many. The town was booming.

A week passed. At the end of August they looked at a house on West Huerfano Street, number 116. "It's too small," said Margaret with a pout.

"I wish it weren't locked, so we could go inside," said Etta. "I think it's bigger than it looks." She held her hands against the side of her face and looked inside. "It's not far from the smithery."

"Maybe the men could add a couple rooms to the back," suggested Mary, sitting on the steps to rest her legs. "It looks clean."

"It's a doll's house," said Margaret, refusing to look inside.

That night Charlie said, "We'll stretch the house to fit all of us. Tomorrow I'll go to the register of deeds and see if we can buy it."

"The Irwin hibernacle!" said Ell, clapping her hands. "I'll help you buy furniture."

Joe cautiously conserved the money he had from the sale of the Kansas homestead and livestock, but Ell told him he could buy furnishings cheap from the part of town called Little Lunnon.

Many Englishmen came to this part of Colorado Springs to work in the mines. When a mine closed they moved to another mining town in Colorado. Because money was necessary to move, the Englishmen sold family heirlooms for a song. "You have to buy fast, because when the English decide to slip out, there are others from that country who slip in to buy the house and snatch up the extra household goods. At his job, Les hears about who is moving because of a mine closure. He will tell us when the next Englishman is moving," explained Ell.

"Sounds like this place is built on slippery waxed paper," commented Charlie.

Etta and Mary divided the two large bedrooms with yellow chintz curtains and put matching curtains at the windows. Margaret had been a great help putting on wallpaper with a yellow rose pattern to go with the chintz. Etta and Margaret calcimined the other rooms in the house. Mary sat in her rocker and held baby Floyd. With Ell's help they bought mahogany dressers, brass candlesticks, and canopy beds. However, Margaret chose an Empire bed, solid head and footboard, with an eagle's head carving. Mary found a large mirror with beveled edges for her own bedroom and a low four-post bed for Frank. Etta liked the banister-backed chairs with rush seats to go with an elegant Hepplewhite plain wood table.

When the family was settled, Etta told Charlie that she had a secret which couldn't be kept much longer. "We are going to have another child, a playmate for little Floyd."

"When?" he asked, wide-eyed.

"Before Christmas."

"I've been so busy at the smithery I never thought—I never noticed—I—" he stuttered.

"You never noticed the morning sickness before we left Sappa Meadows."

He held her close, cradling her face in his huge hands. "That's wonderful news. Are you sure you've not worked too hard?" He kissed her upturned face, eyes, nose, and mouth.

"No, what I couldn't do, I had Margaret to help."

"But she's incompetent. Jeems, she can't do anything!" he cried.

"She's learning. It's that she never did anything at home. She'll grow up. Be patient. She thinks Will is the king."

Charlie said he'd wait and see. "In the meantime Pa can make a new trundle bed for Floyd so the newest member can have the crib."

"You think of the perfect things. Floyd will have new furniture same as us. Thank you, Charlie."

"Honestly, it's you who does the right thing, dear. A new business, a new house, a new baby."

Pikes Peak attracted eastern tourists. The railroad brought them to the heart of the city. The same railroad ran behind the smithery. It stopped at the Antlers Hotel for the convenience of invalids who came for the clear mountain air and pure mineral springwater and grand mountain views for a few weeks. The Chicago, Rock Island, and Pacific Railway had its western terminal and roundhouse at Colorado Springs. The CRI & P publicized the area as a "Scenic Wonderland and Health Resort." Physicians praised the dry air and bright sunshine, and established several tubercular sanitariums.

From the beginning Etta felt at home, as if this were the kind of place she'd dreamed about. Cottonwood trees were planted twenty years before along the streets and in the parks. The trees were irrigated by ditches along the streets. In summer petunias, marigolds, moss roses, and even vegetables grew in profusion along the borders. Anyone could use the ditch water for washing, just for the taking, but clear, cold drinking water was sold in the streets by the barrel for twenty-five cents.

The city had recently recovered from the silver panic followed by the gold strikes at Cripple Creek to the west, over the mountains. The gold strikes caused the city to become a lively industrial center with several ore-reduction mills, railroad shops, millworkers, and miners, who came to town on horseback and eventually needed a blacksmith's services. The Irwin Blacksmith Shop thrived.

Etta and Margaret joined the fashionable afternoon promenade to the post office, hoping to hear from relatives in Kansas. They learned to play croquet on the hard ground behind the house. Baby Floyd was walking alone and had cut his first teeth.

The Irwin family had a Thanksgiving dinner without the usual roast hens from Mary's flock. Charlie brought home a goose and Les brought several wild ducks. After supper they sang hymns and the songs they remembered from childhood. Joe brought in the trundle bed for Floyd, and Charlie gave Etta a joint stool. This was a stool to sit on and rock the crib. The stool's legs could be removed so that it could be suspended on a frame with heavy steel springs to rock back and forth.

On the eighth of December Ell was called in. Etta was in labor for twelve hours. Charlie stayed by her bedside, held her hands, and kept a cool cloth on her head.

"It shouldn't take this long," she repeated over and over.

"Boys are obstinate," Charlie said to reassure her.

Their second child was a girl, healthy and pink, with a fringe of light fuzz on her head.

Charlie had decided on the name Joe for the new baby.

"You'll have to use Pa's name another time," said Ell.

Etta's face was moist with perspiration and her eyes half-closed when she answered. "It's best to use things when you have them. The baby will be named Joella."

Mary was rocking outside the bedroom and had heard the name through the curtain. She smiled to herself, well pleased with the choice. "I always liked the name Mildred," she called out.

"That's the baby's name, Joella Mildred," said Etta. Her eyes were deep violet and in another minute closed with sleep.

After Etta's second baby was born, Charlie always came home from the blacksmith shop for supper. On the other hand, Will occasionally worked late or stopped at the corner saloon after closing up the shop. It blazed with tin lamp reflectors hung on the walls and smelled of unbathed bodies. Some evenings he walked to the south side of Colorado Avenue to visit the bars and dance halls and came home long after supper, smelling of murky smoke and sweet cloying spirits.

Margaret never scolded her husband, but at night when he lay beside her she searched his face for an answer that never seemed to come.

To Will his time was something personal and needed no explanation nor discussion. He felt it was not gentlemanly to take his wife to the places he enjoyed going to. It would be wrong in his thinking to take Margaret to the Spiritual Wheel, which was a speakeasy equipped with a revolving disk on which a customer left twenty-five cents and was given a glass of liquor from the barkeeper, who was hidden out of sight behind a gaudily painted partition. Will had the notion that his wife needed the protection of home, like a child. He knew she'd be cared for by Etta and his folks. She'd remained innocent and pure, requiring only his love and approbation from time to time when he found it convenient.

Margaret had changed from the sweet, clinging child Will had married in Ruleton. There she was gullible enough to believe he was a big cattle rancher running a huge spread near Goodland. Now she'd learned people were not always what they pretended. She was an apt pupil for Etta's lessons in home canning, milking the cow and making cheese, cooking, and keeping a house and babies neat and clean, with time left for marketing, shopping, or playing cards or croquet.

During the winter Mary seldom went outside. The cold air caused her joints to stiffen and her ears to ache. She sat around the living room potbellied wood stove on Etta's joint stool and rocked the baby.

One morning during a February snow Margaret and Etta were washing clothes and pinned them up to dry on a line strung in the kitchen. Floyd was playing with wooden blocks, Mary and Joella were dozing. Etta noticed a slight thickening around Margaret's slim waist and asked, without malice, but with a sister's curiosity, "So, when can we expect another addition to the Irwin family?"

Margaret seemed surprised and did not immediately answer. When she found her tongue, she seemed confused. "Addition? What do you mean? Am I adding additional pounds? It's the cream and mashed potatoes. I enjoy cooking and eating. I never ate as well home with my ma and pa. How about you?"

"Margaret, I meant you might be in a family way. You and Will want children, don't you?"

"Will hasn't said. He doesn't say much. He goes to work, comes home mostly when I'm sleeping. He works hard at the blacksmith shop."

"Of course he does. He works as hard as Grandpa Joe, Frank, or Charlie."

"Harder!" said Margaret, stamping her foot.

"Well, maybe. Joe's not so young and it's difficult for him to get around, so he depends more on his boys. He's put Charlie in charge of the bookkeeping. Charlie kept track of all that at the Sappa Meadows place. I was wondering if we couldn't do some of the bookwork at home. Help the men out. What do you think?"

Margaret had paid no attention to the last few words. She pulled a clothespin out of her mouth and flung a wet petticoat on the line. "Will's the oldest, so it makes sense for him to be in charge. Tell me this: Why does your frigging Charlie take over like he's the big cheese?"

Etta was astounded. Her mouth gaped open. She could not believe her ears.

"And what's more," Margaret went on, cursing fluently, her face red with anger, "you boss me. You tell me to do this and don't do that, pick up this, put down that, feed the babies, feed the milk cow, fetch ditch water, take a bath. I don't like someone telling me when to take a bath or wash my hair. I don't want someone telling me how to stir the strawberry jam and pour it into scalded jars."

Etta gasped and shouted, "Hooray! You're standing up for yourself. Now, I like that!"

Margaret puffed, "I'm no fool. I want to know why Will is being pushed out of the blacksmith shop."

"Pushed out? Who told you that?" Etta was perplexed.

"Will told me. Said he was told to leave a few times, so he went out to talk with some friends. That's why he was home late."

"Oh, my!" Etta felt her face burn. She wondered what she was to say to this young girl who was in the process of becoming a wife fighting for not only her rights but those of her husband. She felt guilty because she understood what was taking place. Etta saw from the corner of her eye that Margaret was moving close. "I'm going to tell you because you'll find out anyway. Your husband spends more time in the speakeasy than he spends at the blacksmith shop. At times he's come to work at noon staggering and shaking from bottle fever. He couldn't shoe a horse all fuzzled like that. Charlie tried to hide Will from his pa by sending him home early. But Joe's not a fool. He told Will to leave the spirits alone or he'd be looking for a job on his own," Etta said. Her heart thumped and her face burned.

Margaret began to cry. "Damn you," she said. "I half-suspected." The rest of the morning she shuffled from one chore to the next, sniffling.

"I don't think gloominess is so good for your growing baby," said Etta, glancing at Margaret's thickening waist again.

"I'm not in a family way!" snapped Margaret. "Don't you go spreading such rumors." Her smile was mildly triumphant. She dried her eyes and sat in a chair with a pan of potatoes to peel in her lap.

"Margaret, it's no crime. It's bound to happen. Just caught you off guard, that's all. It won't be bad. You can grow up with your young one. Will likes children."

Margaret relapsed into silence.

"Will's sister will do the midwifery. You like her."

"She's called to the wealthy stone homes, sometimes to Little Lunnon?" said Margaret.

"Yes, and she goes to the tin huts and canvas tents of the miners. She's a medicine woman and treats each patient with the same compassion."

"Could she tell me if I am or if I'm not in a family way?" She was disconsolate.

"I'm certain Ell could do that." Etta's face brightened. "Let's get the lunch, and while the babies are napping with Mary to watch them, we'll go for a walk in the snow and call on Mrs. Les Miner."

Margaret's reddened eyes widened, then crinkled at the corners. "A baby could explain why I've been feeling kind of poorly and never wanting to get out of bed in the mornings."

From several pertinent questions about Margaret's monthly periods and the onset of the squeamish feelings, Ell judiciously announced that Margaret was two months along in her first pregnancy and she could expect a baby by mid-October. She served warm blackberry wine with sassafras sticks in translucent porcelain cups with saucers to match.

Then Ell showed them where she'd placed the antique mirror in her bedroom. Margaret gasped at the floor-length lace curtains framed by curtains of wine velvet that were held back by twisted silk cords. "I let the daylight in or close it out so that it is like night in here." She demonstrated by loosening the cords.

That same evening in their bedroom, Margaret told Will she was in a family way and that because of his inclination toward spirits, Charlie was in charge of the blacksmith books.

A Pandora's box was opened.

"Etta ought to mind her own business!" stormed Will. "And you have no business discussing me with her!" He faced Margaret and lurched forward with clenched fists.

Margaret climbed across the Empire bed. "Don't lay a hand on me when your mind is muzzy."

Will swung across the bed. Margaret slid away.

"Please," she said, "calm down. You're acting like a bully."

Will came across the end of the bed. Margaret crouched in the corner a minute, then scooted across the bed again.

"Don't hit me!" she cried. "I don't want the baby hurt! Stop!"

Will was infuriated and lashed out at Margaret's hands that protected her face. He struck her chin and her head hit the headboard.

"Please don't hurt me," she whispered through a fat purple lip.

Will's gorge was up and he saw only the ugly purple lip—the swollen lower lip. Everything else was a shadowy gray scrim.

When his eyes and head cleared his mother was pulling at his shirt, crying for him to halt. He was hanging on to Margaret's long hair and beating her head against the eagle's-head carving.

Margaret's face was ashen, her lip was twice its normal size, and her jaw was red and shiny. Her eyes were closed.

Mary pushed Will, who was shaking, aside and put a cold damp cloth on Margaret's head. She murmured, "Poor child, poor child" as Margaret came around.

"Why did you hit me?" Margaret asked Will, who had tears running down his face.

"I'm sorry," he said mechanically.

"You dirty devil!" Margaret climbed off the bed and went to the living room with Mary.

Two nights later Will came home carrying a pint bottle of whiskey. He lurched for the leather chair, ignoring those seated at the supper table. He was near six feet tall and his legs stretched far out in the room. His eyes sparkled in the light from the kerosene lamp.

"I don't give a damn what you think. This is my life," he said, tipping the bottle to his lips. "I go out each morning to earn a living for a wife, who does what all women do, gossips. But you know what she wants to do? She wants to walk along the street pushing a baby buggy with the town's society women, showing off her stylish clothes. My wife has class."

Joe said, "Put the bottle down, son. That's nothing but rotgut that'll ruin your liver."

"Ho! I'm no one's fool. I know you favor my teetotaler brother. I'm sick and tired of getting my pay from my own pa. I aim to do something on my own. I'm hightailing it out of this outfit."

Mary had her head buried in her hands. Margaret was staring past Will, as though she saw something on the opposite wall. Frank's face was white as milk glass. Etta slipped her hand in Charlie's.

Joe said, "Son—no one is asking you to leave. Think of your responsibilities to your wife and to your regular customers at the smithery and then to yourself. I'd say you have only one or two outstanding faults. First, you are not overzealous in any work, second you imbibe, as we have recently witnessed, to the point of belligerence. Your chief virtue is amiability. The decision of what to do in the future is yours." Joe's whiskers trembled against his chest as he settled his back against the slats of his chair.

To Will, who was used to making his own decisions, but not taking into account the consideration of others, this viewpoint brought obligations. To accuse him of being at fault was unfair. A man's life was his own to live his own way. If someone, even his father, blamed him for something that didn't follow expectations, well, that wasn't his problem—it was his father's for interfering with his life. His eyes lifted to his father's face, an immobile mask with piercing dark eye slits. Those eyes cut to the quick. He knew he'd leave.

"I won't be working for the Irwin Blacksmith Shop!"

The following morning, with great composure, Will asked for his back pay. Despite the ankle-deep snow and galelike wind he moved Margaret into a rented tin hovel at the coal mining Timberline Camp.

In the afternoon Mary had a "spell" while ironing on the board placed over the backs of two chairs. She put the flatiron back on the stove and clutched at her chest.

"Everyone's upset," excused Etta, getting a cup of hot tea for Mary. "Relax. The ironing will keep."

Mary talked in a monotone. "Remember when you used to run and then complain of a side ache? I feel like that. Only the pain's in my chest. It's like a wet leather thong drying and getting tighter under my arms. It must be this cold weather. This house is drafty."

Suddenly the teacup and saucer fell to the floor and Mary looked straight ahead. She didn't say another word. It was as if she never felt the hot tea that spilled across her lap. Etta put her to bed, then cleaned up the tea and broken china. Mary slept all day and part of the next. When she got up she seemed good as new.

"I just had a spell. It was nothing, forget it," she said.

Because she seemed perfectly well, everyone took her advice and forgot the incident.

The wind growled outside and the windows rattled. The windows were beautifully decorated with frost scenes of some primitive forest with tall, lacy ferns. A braided rug was put across the bottom of the two doors leading outside to keep the icy fingers of cold air from seeping in. The rug also kept the powdery snow from sifting in.

"If we were at Sappa Meadows I'd have this kitchen floor packed with a couple of bushels of cattail down and a braided rug over top," said Mary. "These days my legs ache to the very marrow." Her pinched face looked at Charlie, dressed with two pairs of wool socks and two pairs of wool pants, ready for the walk to the blacksmith shop.

"Ma, if you were as tall as me, you'd find all the heat up near the ceiling. Keeps my head warm, while my knees and feet freeze."

He kissed his wife and patted his mother's graying head. He left for the smithery, saying, "Either Frank or I will be back at noon for our lunch. No time this morning. Have it ready, all right?"

Etta, nursing Joella, nodded.

"Of course, she will," said Mary.

The day was March 4, 1897. Etta baked bread while the baby slept. Mary was good at keeping Floyd out of mischief. She taught him finger games and nursery rhymes. The two-year-old was the light of her life.

Etta, seeing everything was under control inside, put on her black overshoes, coat, scarf, wool cap, and mittens. She went out the back to the little shed to feed the milk cow and see that it had water. It was warm in the shed because of the animal's body heat. She gave the cow more hay and cracked the ice on the water trough. Coming back she noticed how the air pierced, then numbed her skin. The snow under her feet squeaked as she walked. There were drifts of snow against the west side of the house and shed.

Back inside she blew on her fingers before taking off the overshoes. She heard Joella crying and looked up. Mary was lying in a heap on the floor and Floyd was beside her with the flour sifter she'd left on the kitchen table. Flour was everywhere. Floyd was grinning up at her, turning the handle with his chubby fingers. "Mama. Sleep." He sifted flour over his grandmother.

Etta threw off her wraps and knelt on the floor, pulling Floyd to her lap. "Mary! Grandma Mary! What is it?" Etta's eyes were wide and she gently patted the cool cheeks of her mother-in-law, Mary. "She—she doesn't hear me." Suddenly she realized that Mary might not hear ever again. She was holding Floyd so tight he was crying. Etta put him in his bed and went back to Mary. She did not hear the babies crying. She put her arms around Mary and shook her. "Wake up! Wake up!" Mary stared back at her with open eyes, her jaw slack.

Charlie opened the back door and saw Etta's wraps thrown in a heap on the floor and in the next moment saw her crouched down beside his mother.

Tears streamed down Etta's face and dropped into the flour, making tiny puffs like dust. "She's only fifty-two," Etta whispered. "I was outside. I wasn't with her. Why then?"

Charlie's breath came quick and sharp. "Help me put her on

the bed and get this damn flour off her face and arms. It makes her look so—so dead white." He sobbed.

The next days blurred together for Charlie and Etta. Charlie remembered the wooden coffin his pa made at the shop. He wouldn't let anyone help. He closed the shop.

Ell and Etta washed Mary's body and put her best dress on over her good corset and petticoats. Who took care of the babies, Charlie could not recall. But he remembered the frozen clods of earth as they hit the lid of the pine coffin with the single rose carved in the top. Joe and his children stood huddled under the cold blue sky, bound together for strength, comfort, and warmth. Ell asked the Baptist minister, whose two babies she'd delivered, to give the final service at the cemetery. There were no comforting friends. The Irwins had not been in Colorado Springs long enough to have close friends. Mary Irwin's death was barely noted in the local newspapers. However, her death left a hole too large to mend easily in the hearts of her husband and children.

For months afterward Joe could not talk about Mary without his voice cracking or tears filling his eyes. Charlie often was wakened at night to the soft sobs of Etta. He held her close and was himself comforted. Then, quiet themselves, they'd hear the still softer rhythmical sounds from Joe's room. It was a sighing—as quiet as a summer breeze whispering in the treetops, or a cat walking through the tall prairie grass. "Poor, poor Pa," Charlie'd whisper, "he loved Ma more than his right arm. We have to help him mend his broken heart."

Etta answered by pulling Charlie's arm tighter around herself and murmuring, "Will doesn't help by staying away and ignoring his father. He and Margaret didn't even come to the cemetery."

"We all know that," said Charlie with a tightness in his voice, "but we know in our hearts that Will needs us, maybe more than we need him. Wait, have patience, he'll come around. Ma used to say patience is a virtue seldom found in woman and never found in man. We'll have patience, even though it's a virtue few people are willing to wait to develop."

SEVENTEEN

Cheyenne, Wyoming

As soon as the weather warmed, Charlie took the family to the summit of Pikes Peak on the cog railroad. He was enchanted with the scenery. There were grotesque rock masses of red sandstone, huge upthrusts of gypsum, a cave where winds howled constantly, crannies where doves and swallows nested, sentinel timberline pines with rough, gray, weathered bark, dwarfed, gnarled limbs, snow-bent and grotesque.

Charlie was more and more convinced that he was not going to spend his entire career in a dark smithery. He dreamed of prairie land edged with scallops of blue mountains and fringed with green pines. He imagined herds of graceful horses in meadows feeding upon acres of nutritious wild hay.

In the evenings Joe read the newspapers from front to back. Once he commented to Charlie about all the newcomers moving into Colorado Springs. "I never know what language a man's going to use when I greet him at the shop. With all this riffraff coming in to work, there'll be more miners than anything. A paintbox mix of people, those miners are: black, white, red, and yellow."

Etta laughed and reminded Joe that not so long ago they were newcomers.

Charlie reminded him that the smithery business was making

more now than it ever had just because of that paintbox of people.

"We have a good business. The Irwin name is well known. I don't want to go back to starve-to-death farming, a sod house, and past hardships. I don't mind saying good morning to anyone, as long as I can work on his horse and see the color of his money," said Charlie.

Joe folded the newspaper. "Son, just once before I die, I'd like to grow me a good crop of rust-free wheat." Then with a gleam in his eye he said, "Speaking of different people, there's a certain bohunk widow woman who brings her horses to the shop. I thought I understood her meaning, but she was way ahead of me. You know the one. She uses Pozzoni's powder on her face to make it white. Well, by jimminy, she asked me to her place for dinner."

Charlie's eyes widened. "Pa, she probably liked the way you talk. She's probably lonely. You don't have to ask my permission to go out and enjoy yourself."

The next couple of evenings Joe was quiet, saying nothing about his widow friend. Finally Charlie asked, "Did you have a good time Sunday afternoon at that widow woman's house? She cook good?"

Joe cleared his throat. "Well, I told you she's way ahead of me. She knows each move before I make it. I was touched by her kindness to have me to dinner. She's as good a cook as Etta. So, I leaned over—wagh! At my age I should have known better!"

Charlie's eyes lit up and his mouth curved into a smile. "Yes?"

"Pshaw, I reached out to pat her hand. She held on like a calf with lockjaw. I told her she was a passable cook. She told me that I not only warmed her hand, but her heart."

Charlie put his hand over his mouth to suppress a chuckle.

"So then I lost my head and kissed her cheek."

"What did she do?"

"She gave me a peck on the lips and said that I was certainly not cold yet."

"And you said?" urged Charlie.

"And I said that both me and my little daughter-in-law were looking for someone like her to cook, keep my socks clean, and if she wanted to come over twice a week, it'd be fine with us. We'd pay her fair and square."

Charlie burst into laughter.

"It's not so funny when you think it over," snapped Joe. "That's not what she wanted me to say. I insulted a good customer." He paused, looked up at Charlie, and began to laugh. "Oh, well, what the hell, there's others where that one came from." Joe took out his clean, faded bandanna and wiped his eyes. "Customers I need. I don't need, nor want, another woman to call my own. One was enough to last me a lifetime."

Charlie understood his father. He meant that Mary was the only woman in his life and there could never be a replacement as long as he lived.

In August, Charlie took his father and Frank to the thoroughbred and quarter horse racing at Pikes Peak Meadows. After that Frank could hardly be kept at the smithery. The excitement of the track, the horses expending all their energy in a graceful run, pulled at his imagination.

The first of October brought snow to whiten the mountaintops. Two, three days later snowflakes, large as goose feathers, fell on the valley, settled, and melted. A week later Margaret came down the damp hillside by horseback, eleven miles from the Timberline Camp to Ell's place on South Nevada Street. Inside Ell's place, out of the frosty wind, Margaret caught her breath at the sight of the sunlight that came through the parlor window and reflected from dozens of little glass prisms hanging from the ceiling.

"It's the latest thing," said Ell. "It's like having bits of sunshine in the house." She wore a dark-green cashmere basque that looked like it came from Paris. Margaret felt like a yokel in her heavy cotton shirtwaist and long pleated pant-skirt she'd worn for horseback riding. "I've become fascinated with collecting antiques," said Ell. "Come see a most unusual thing in my bedroom."

On a Sheraton candlestand was a glass globe filled with water, which concentrated the light of candles behind it, then threw the light out on a spot of roses in the patterned rug.

"Oh my! I could look at the light from the globe all day," said Margaret, holding her hands on the top of her skirt where it protruded out like a round boulder on a hillside. "It's a hundred times more beautiful than the view from my kitchen window, which is nothing but a lot of black coal dust." She sat on the feather mattress of the four-poster bed and sank to her hips. "I'm big as a house!" she cried. "That's why I'm here. It's past the fifteenth of October with no sign the baby is ready to sample the Colorado air."

"Lay back so I can see if the baby has dropped," said Ell, gently pushing and probing. "You haven't long to wait. Stay here. I'll send word to Will."

On the nineteenth of October 1897, Margaret had the most beautiful baby girl Ell had ever seen. Margaret named the child Gladys Laye. For two weeks Ell kept a bag of asafetida tied around mother's and baby's necks to keep germs away. Ell gave Margaret teas and infusions laced with castor oil and condensed milk.

The day Ell was certain Margaret could care for her baby girl herself, she put on a feathered toque that matched the green cashmere bodice of her dress. She helped Margaret into a rented Wood Bros. buggy. Les came out of the house wearing corduroy trousers tucked into high-laced boots and a corduroy coat at the same time. Margaret asked how her horse was going to get back to the Timberline Camp. Les answered, "I'm riding your horse. You don't think I'd let two women and a baby ride alone up to that mining camp, do you?"

Margaret had to laugh. "I rode down from that camp alone."

Before returning the Wood Bros. buggy the next day Ell and Les went to see the Irwins.

"Margaret's baby is like a play doll, she's so perfect," said Ell.

"Will held the baby like it was fine Wedgwood. A baby will be good for them," said Les, giving Ell a secret, longing look.

Ell gave him an arch smile, which he translated to mean that she was not ready for such responsibility, especially not while diphtheria was sweeping the mining camps.

The first real winter storm came in November, leaving several inches of snow. From then until spring, storm succeeded storm, freezing, thawing on rooftops, drifting against fences and into coulees. There were glorious, short intervals of sun, which melted and compacted the snow. The house was always warm, with kitchen range and parlor stove going full blast.

Etta bought fresh meat from Antelope Jim's Market. Jim called his meat beef, but customers knew it was usually deer, elk, or antelope. Etta enjoyed living in town. She joined the Fortnightly Club and heard the latest literature discussed. The club ladies met in the Antlers Hotel next to the Irwin Blacksmith Shop. In the hotel lobby modern electric bulbs replaced candles in the tin lamp reflectors, which were shoulder high on the walls. Electric lamps were on the tables where coffee and cakes were served.

In the spring the children gathered wild strawberries on the stony hillsides. In summer the family spent weekends on the side of Cheyenne Mountain with gallon pails tied around their waists so they could use two hands to pick wild currants, chokecherries, and wild plums.

Before noon on the twenty-fifth of September, Etta had her third child. Ell again helped with the delivery at home. Charlie named the infant Pauline Lorraine and gave out cigars to customers at the blacksmith shop. He grinned and asked one of his customers if he liked music. The customer was a little surprised by Charlie's question, but told him, yes, he liked music. Charlie grinned more, handed the man a cigar, and said, "Here's a band."

Charlie didn't smoke, but the baby's easy birth was an occasion for celebration. He put a cigar in his mouth, bit off one end, and lit the other end. He began shoeing a big Percheron, a draft horse, belonging to the city's fire department. Charlie moved the cigar from one side of his mouth to the other. He took the horse's back left foot in his large hands, braced the hoof against his aproned hip so he could file a rough spot. He inhaled slowly to make the tip of the cigar glow. He blew out the smoke, feeling its warmth and a bitter burning sensation in his throat and mouth. All of a sudden the horse jerked.

Charlie grabbed on to the hoof. At the same time he shifted the cigar so that some of the hot ash fell on the horse's leg. Again the big horse jerked. This time the hoof flew out of Charlie's grasp. The horse turned sideways. The movement was so fast Charlie didn't have time to think about stepping back. The horse raised its leg and kicked. The edge of the hoof hit Charlie squarely between the eyes.

Everything went black and quiet for a moment. Charlie lay flat on his back. When he came to he was bewildered for a moment. He put his hand to his forehead and he could feel no pain, but his fingers traced a deep crescent or half-moon indentation between his eyes. As his fingers continued to move over the impression, the numbness faded and was replaced by a deep throbbing ache. The wound now stung like he'd been hit with a white-hot poker. Without warning the wound began to bleed profusely.

Charlie sat up and bent his head. He was stunned at the sight of blood dripping and felt faint. He heard the swish of the horse's tail and felt a surge of rage that brought him to his feet. The lightheadedness was replaced with the rush of anger for the horse that knocked him to the floor and caused his head to throb unmercifully. His hands were balled into tight fists. He knew what a swift kick from a horse could do to a man. He'd seen men who were never the same after being kicked by a spooked horse. Those men suffered from blindness, paralysis, slurred speech, absentmindedness, or worse, he'd seen one man die from a hard blow by a horse's hoof in his father's smithery in Missouri.

Charlie gingerly felt his forehead again. His head throbbed and felt like he'd been beaten with a giant sledgehammer. His hand was covered with sticky, bright-red blood. Slowly, because each step jarred his head, he walked unsteadily around to the front of the big Percheron. The horse now seemed to be waiting patiently for Charlie to finish the shoeing job. Charlie looked at the black head of the horse, took a deep breath, stepped back an arm's length, squeezed his right fist down as much as possible, let out one booming, rafter-rattling cry, and hit the horse between the eyes with all the strength he could muster.

The horse's legs folded like an overused camp cot's. The jughead horse lay on its side at Charlie's unsteady feet.

Frank and Joe heard the bloodcurdling cry and felt the building tremble when the horse fell. They ran to see what was happening to Charlie.

Charlie held his bandanna to his pulsating forehead. He saw his brother and father from the corner of his eye, which he could not take off the stunned horse. "I killed him!" he cried.

"That's unbelievable!" said Joe. He stared at the prone horse in astonishment.

Frank's face was pale. "Why?" he squeaked.

"Because that blasted gol-durned beast gave me a huge headache!"

"The horse is really out cold, unconscious!" said Joe, hardly able to believe what his eyes told him. He could not believe his middle son possessed enough strength to knock out a big draft horse. "Oh, my God! Let me look at your head! There's a chunk of skin hanging down like an open door."

"It flaps when you move!" cried Frank, looking pale green.

"Hold still!" said Joe. "I'll get that skin in place and wrap a clean rag around your head. That'll hold it in place." Joe rummaged around on one of the shelves and came back with part of an old pillowcase, which he ripped into strips. "It'll heal together in a couple of days. Bend over a little more. I'll dab a little turpentine—Hold your head up!"

The pain was excruciating. Charlie barely heard his father speak. His knees sagged. Blackness closed out everything once again. He lay sprawled on the plank floor. He heard his father call from somewhere far off. The inside of his head seemed to twirl. He opened his eyes and saw Joe and Frank peering down at him anxiously.

"Come on, sit up!" called Joe. Joe's strong arms were under Charlie's arms, lifting him forward. The gray mist melted away and his father's voice was clear. "Drink! Frank'll get you more water. Do you feel all right? Is your eyesight clear? Answer me, son!"

He did feel better. The dizziness disappeared, but the enormous throbbing in his head was there. Cautiously he felt the bands of torn pillowcase that were pulled tight and smooth around his head. Joe could heal a wound as well as most men who called themselves doctors. What worried Charlie was the comatose horse lying on the floor with myriad flies buzzing and crawling over it.

"Will I owe the fire department for one horse?" moaned Charlie, looking at the limp form on the floor.

"I'll get the damned knothead back on its feet before someone from the fire department comes. Don't worry about that horse. It's not hurting as much as you," said Joe. His hands massaged behind the horse's ears and back of its head. The ears twitched. Joe moved away fast. He called for Charlie to move away. "When the horse raises its head and gets up, no telling what it'll do! I hope it doesn't go crazy!"

Charlie stood with his father and Frank outside the door. The horse whinnied, shook its great head, and got to its feet. It shook its head once again and then seemed to wait for someone to lead it to one of the stalls in back. Cautiously Joe led the horse. It seemed gentle enough and not the least crazy. He gave it water and fresh hay and came back to tell his boys that the horse seemed better off than Charlie.

"I'm heading home. Enough has happened today," said Charlie.

Frank said, "Remind me never to start a fight with you. You have power! A man that can knock out a horse with one blow—that's really something!"

"Aw, don't worry. I'll never hit a man like that," said Charlie, holding his head. "What man would kick me as hard as that blamed horse!"

From mid-August until the end of October 1898, most everyone was talking about the dense meteor showers that were visible each night. Some said the earth was passing through the tail of a comet. Others claimed that the falling stars were a warning of some disaster to hit the earth, such as floods, storms, earthquakes, or volcanic eruptions. Charlie heard some men at the blacksmith shop say the meteors were the result of so much gunpowder burned in the atmosphere during the Spanish-American War.

Several evenings Charlie and Etta stood in back of their house in the pitch dark to see the hundreds of meteor trails, like silver streaks in the night. "I'd like to see the full sky, out on the prairie, where it's not hidden by mountains," said Charlie. "I bet it's a spectacle."

Etta understood what he meant, but she'd been observant herself. "Charlie, you wouldn't see more shooting stars. Just notice how they all seem to come from a well-defined band."

Her astute remark pleased Charlie. "If I were to find a ranch that was in a remote area, far from a town, you'd be a wonderful teacher for our children."

It was high praise, but Etta did not reply. She really liked living in the city. She'd dreamed of sending her children to the school in Colorado Springs. While they were in school learning, she'd read, join a women's club, sew, and learn to play the piano —when she talked Charlie into buying a piano.

Joe would not let Charlie go back to work until all the swelling was down and the discoloration on his forehead faded. Charlie enjoyed being nursed back to his former robust health for a few days, then he became bored with so much idleness. He read newspapers and farm journals. Toward the end of his recuperation he took several short trips by horseback to look over the grazing land in eastern Colorado. He was restless to get back to an active life, but he knew he did not look forward to the dark smithery.

His dream for a horse ranch drove him to look over the dry farmlands, the outcroppings of sandstone, shale, and limestone. The Colorado prairie grass seemed good, and he imagined several hundred head of cattle grazing along the flat high plains and broad rolling prairies that met the foothills of the magnificent Rocky Mountains. The only thing that held him back was the profitability of having the sole smithery in the city of Colorado Springs. It was impossible and foolish to pull up stakes and leave a money-making concern.

Etta listened but she did not share his enthusiasm for this desolate, open prairie land. She loved the security of the blue mountains.

Charlie was back in the blacksmith shop, doing nothing but

handling the money and bartered transactions for the first few weeks. He took notice of the amount of money each week that went into the First National Bank. He was marking some of the money in his mind for down payment on the dream ranch. He even went without new leather boots and a new wide-brimmed felt hat. Frank and Joe could not understand Charlie's self-inflicted parsimony and thought it a residue left in his mind due to the kick in the head.

When the bandages were removed, the head wound was healing well. But it was still a noticeable red crescent between his eyes. Charlie would carry this crescent-shaped scar for the rest of his life.

In the spring of 1899 there was a minor boom in the gold- and silver-mining business. The railroad brought carload after carload of black powder through Colorado Springs to be used in blasting the mines. Many times these boxcars were left on a siding behind the Antlers Hotel and the Irwin Blacksmith Shop until the mining companies sent a wagon out to collect their share of the powder.

Four-year-old Floyd played in the cinder piles near the tracks. Etta watched him constantly so that he'd not wander onto the tracks nor around the boxcars in demurrage on the siding.

Ell and Les came often to visit. Les sat at the kitchen table with Charlie, Joe, and Frank and talked about his accounting business at the mine, then listened to the Irwin men tell how Joe wanted to build on to the blacksmith shop, make it twice as big, and take on two more men. "I sure wish Will would come back," said Joe with a sigh. "There's a place waiting for him right here. A family should stay together."

Ell and Etta went to the parlor to talk women talk. Ell said that Will was working hard, staying sober, and doing well at the coal mine. Margaret was again wearing clothes as big as a circus tent, which was proof of her impending motherhood and also proof that Will spent time at home in the evenings.

Etta showed Ell the new dress she was making to wear to the Fortnightly Club meeting. It was brown pongee with a lighter brown taffeta petticoat.

In August, Ell came to visit in a carriage. She wore a changeable taffeta dress with a full-brimmed, royal-blue hat with matching willow plume on the top of her reddish pompadour. "It was too warm to walk," she explained. "I came to tell you that Margaret stayed only ten days at my place after she had her baby boy."

Etta was pleased Margaret had a boy. "What did she name him?"

"Will did the naming. The baby is called Charles Marvin."

When Joe was told about the new baby, he was most pleased. His middle name was Marvin and his father's name was Charles. "Will's still a member of the family. He let us know where his feelings really are when he named my new grandson. My God, I'd like to see those babies."

Before summer's end Charlie showed his father the smithery's account books and how much money he was giving Frank. "I believe we should raise Frank's salary. Maybe yours and mine. We can afford it."

Joe drew himself up and squinted his farsighted eyes into slits to see better. He studied the pages of the ledger intently. Then he waved his quaking hand through the air. "Hell's fire! I knew we were well off—but this much frightens me. Rich men come to an unhappy end. This can't last! Certainly raise everyone's salary by ten percent and hire someone to build a couple bedrooms on the back of the house. The way you and Etta are adding to the population, it's become a regular nursery."

The next morning Charlie woke with a strange premonition that something was about to happen. He climbed out of bed and checked on his three sleeping children. The house was quiet and his footfalls sounded as loud as the clang on the anvil in the shop. He added kindling to the kitchen range, restarted the fire, boiled a pot of water, and made coffee. Still he was uneasy. He stirred condensed milk and honey into his coffee and complained because there would be no fresh milk until the cow was milked that evening. He decided he was unsettled because of more rumors of another miners' strike.

Miners were a rough breed of men. Even when working they were never satisfied. They always wanted higher wages. Several times they threatened the mine managers with pickaxes. Some of the miners came to town armed.

Charlie finished his coffee and wondered if he weren't borrowing trouble. He went out the back door, holding the screen so it would not slam and waken the others. The first hint of dawn was coming into the eastern sky, reddening the mountain peaks.

It was a wondrous sight and thrilled Charlie. He took several breaths of crisp morning air. Then he went inside, dressed, and walked to the blacksmith shop.

He rubbed some of the smudge off the shop's back window

and opened the back door to give more light inside. He stood looking at the rows on rows of boxcars loaded with black powder waiting to be sent up to Canon City or Coaldale or Cripple Creek. If there's a strike, they'll be here indefinitely, he thought. He stepped outside. The door slammed. Charlie looked at the door. No, it was open. His eyes raised toward the line of boxcars and saw them silhouetted against the sunlight that was moving ever downward from the top of the mountain to the floor of the valleys. Maybe someone shot a pistol, he thought.

With no warning there was another loud, sharp crack. Then a bright, yellow-white light flashed, followed by a thundering boom. Charlie was out in the field behind the blacksmith shop trying to locate the origin of the light that was followed by orange sparks and more deep booms. Rocks and sticks of wood flew through the air and hit gardens and roofs. Charlie felt the earth under his feet vibrate, giving a rocking sensation like a powerful rock slippage during an earthquake. The next shock seemed to roll through his chest. From the corner of his eye he saw the back half of the hotel next door sway back and forth, then split wide open. He turned and fell to his knees with his hands over his head to avoid being hit with flying splinters. When he looked up, the back door of the shop was off the sheet-iron hinges he'd made. It lay in a pile of cinders Floyd played in. Over on the tracks he saw long branches of yellow flames engulfing several boxcars, more explosions, and sparks filling the sky like red shooting stars. "Fire! Fire!" he yelled.

He never recalled running home. But he found himself in the backyard holding Floyd and Joella. Etta held baby Pauline, comforting her cries, "Hush-a-bye-baby-hush. Sshhush."

Frank ran to the yard in time to see billows of heavy smoke roll from the railroad yards. The rising sun was red through the black pall that spread over the sky. He was speechless, his legs leaden.

Joe came from the house waving his pants and boots. His white hair and beard were awry and his legs pathetically scrawny beneath his flannel nightshirt. "What in Sam Hill's going on?" he shouted. "Where are those blasted cannons? We're being attacked! This here is a siege! Take cover!"

Charlie put Floyd in Frank's arms and grabbed his father's arm. "There's no war, Pa! It's the black powder on the railroad siding! The shop is flat. The Antlers is unrecognizable." Tears streamed down his face. He saw the sagging roofs, blown-out windows, and collapsed eastern walls of houses next to his.

"Looks like a ninety-mile-an-hour gale hit!" blubbered Frank, finding his tongue. "Look at my bedroom, you can see everything. The wall is completely gone!"

There were several more explosions, then more sparks and flames and black smoke. The three children were screaming.

Joe ran to the front of the house; his pants were on, but he was still waving his boots. "Get the shotgun! We'll hold 'em off!"

"Please don't say that," called Charlie. "It's not a war." He wiped his eyes and saw that Frank and Etta were also crying.

"We're not alone. Look at the places across the street," said Charlie in a hushed tone. "Jeems, people are going to need help."

The city's fire engine drawn by two big Percherons raced down the street and around the corner to the freight yard. Bells clanged and wheels screeched. Mothers called their children, dogs barked, chickens cackled, horses snorted, people ran along the street carrying blankets, books, kettles, lamps. One man carried an ax. There were half a dozen men with buckets of water from the irrigation ditches along the street. They splashed the water over the outside walls of their houses to keep the sparks that the wind carried out over the city from starting a conflagration. The ditches soon became mud holes.

Charlie told his father to get dressed and go with him to the area of the shop. He grabbed Frank's arm. "Let Etta take care of the children. They'll be all right here. People are trapped in the hotel. We gotta help!" Frank ran whimpering toward the hotel.

Joe was the last to leave. He gathered his wits and realized what had happened. He went through the house and made certain it was structurally sound for Etta to stay there with the children. "Honey, just don't go back in the two back bedrooms, mine and Frank's. We'll have to shim them up tight later. If it looks bad, keep the kids outside. Lots of broken window glass. Maybe move some of the furniture out. Oh, hell, forget that!" he shouted. "Come see for yourself what's happened to the side of your room. We're damn lucky you took them babies outside."

Etta left Joella with Floyd and carried Pauline in her arms back inside to see what Joe was talking about. There were splinters and plaster over everything. In the back the roof was half-gone and the outside wall all gone. The beds and dressers were crushed under the weight of two-by-fours and ceiling plaster. Then Etta looked in her room, which was crowded with the big double bed and Joella's crib and the old wicker bassinet.

The crib was smashed against the large bed. When she saw the bassinet in shreds, the little wooden pieces, small as matchsticks, scattered all over the room, her heart shattered. She sobbed into the baby's blanket she was holding around Pauline. Joe tried to comfort her. "There, there, Ettie. Don't take it so hard. It was just a basket. Other stuff, costing a lot more, is busted. The main thing is we're all right. Ettie, don't cry." He put his big arms around her quivering shoulders.

It wasn't the cost. That baby bassinet was a kind of link to Etta's family, to her past. Her sister Kate had given it to her when Floyd was born. Etta'd slept in the little basket herself, as had her brothers and sisters and Kate's Jimmy and her own Floyd and Joella. Now it was in smithereens. She could not stop crying. Her whole world seemed shattered. Then suddenly she remembered that all of Joe's possessions were under sticks of wood, bits of tar paper, crushed, broken, maybe torn to shreds. She looked up and said, "Yes, the Lord has power to destroy, but He's compassionate. Look, we're all safe."

"You'd best check on Floyd before you say any more, Honey," said Joe with a crooked grin. "That boy can get into more trouble in five minutes than an orphan girl in a poker game, if you know what I mean."

He was right. Floyd had left Joella alone, without shoes. He'd filled the baby shoes with dust, threw them in the air, yelling, "Boom!" and watched the dust slip out like long puffs of smoke. To Floyd, the dust bombs were like the billows of smoke coming over the treetops from the railroad tracks. He laughed, ran back and forth throwing the dust bombs. Joella crawled in the dirt, coughing as she breathed the dust in the air.

Etta grabbed Floyd, dusted his clothes, hung on to him as she shook out the baby shoes, and let the stream of salty, stinging tears run down her cheeks. When the tears ran dry she sat on the ground with her arms around her three children. She rocked herself from side to side.

Joe came out to the back carrying the Henry rifle. The sight of the gun frightened Etta. "You're not taking that gun to the shop?"

"No! I found it under a battered bureau drawer when I was hunting a clean shirt in all the mess. I'm giving it to you to keep handy. This rifle'll stop any of them miners that get an idea they can loot our place and—who knows what else they'll think of." He closed his mouth. He handed the rifle to Etta.

She took it and was surprised at the smooth coolness of the barrel. When she looked up Joe was gone.

She thought, I don't know how to use a gun. I can't shoot. I can't go around carrying a gun and a baby. She took the rifle inside. "Floyd, you look after the girls. Don't let them crawl out of your sight."

His little face was tear-streaked and sober. "Yes, Mama."

Etta moved clothing and bedding from the broken side of the house to the untouched side. She looked out the back several times to check on the children. They sat still and watched the sky.

The orange streamers of fire were being contained in the freight yards, but there were sparks that rose and were blown toward the city like tiny red meteors that turned to cold ash before landing.

Etta propped up the broken crib with chunks of stove wood. She brought Pauline inside and put her in the crib. A neighbor woman startled Etta. She'd come to ask how things were. She told Etta that closer to town the houses were nearly all destroyed by the blasts. "In town the Antlers Hotel and your man's blacksmith shop were flattened. I come to say I'm sorry, Missus Irwin."

Etta nodded. She'd guessed as much about the blacksmith shop.

Etta and the neighbor woman made hot coffee and biscuits for their less fortunate neighbors whose homes were splintered to the ground. She sent the men to town to work with Charlie, clearing away debris to find those crying for help. Charlie sent them back to Etta when he felt they needed a rest. After feeding a dozen people supper of sow belly, more coffee, and biscuits, Etta brought the crib inside and set it up in the parlor. She put Floyd and Joella to sleep bundled in comforters on the floor. She invited homeless women, strangers with their children, to come rest in her home.

One man came to the back door about midnight. "Missus Irwin, I came because your man sent me. I'd go home, but I have no home. I'm looking for my wife and little girl." The man held his cloth cap between his hands.

"Come with me," said Etta. He stood in the doorway to the parlor and tears spilled over his chin when he saw that his wife and child were sound asleep wrapped in a quilt on the floor. Etta gave a dishtowel filled with fresh biscuits for Charlie, Frank, and Joe to the man after he'd rested an hour.

"Your man is quite a leader," he said. He put his fingers to his lips. "Listen, hear those explosions? I'm warning you, Missus, they'll be coming here before daylight. The sheriff deputized men to dynamite those buildings and houses that are unsafe. It's said some of the dynamiters enjoy their work overmuch and destroy more than necessary."

Other men came for a short rest, then went back to take orders from Charlie, who had taken charge of the rescue squad at the Antlers Hotel. One told Etta, "Charlie Irwin is some organizer. He has a brigade set up to clear sticks and slabs off every place he hears the slightest noise. He's even set up overturned wagons and caught a runaway team of horses."

Another said, "It's a pleasure to work with your man. He's saved half a dozen lives this night, ma'am."

"Ja," agreed a big Swede, warming his hands around a hot tin cup of coffee. "He's a powerful son of a gun. He lifts the wood beam off a man's back. That beam held up the second story of a house. That's some man!"

Etta could hear the dynamiters coming closer. She guessed they were miners with blasting caps and sticks of dynamite. She decided to rest a moment herself and sat in the low sewing rocker she'd pulled to the kitchen. She laid the Henry rifle across her lap before closing her eyes. She told herself she'd never use it, nor need it, but she felt safer in case a dynamiter strayed into the neighborhood.

It was still dark when Charlie came to the back steps and into the back door. He had only his pants and boots on. He'd given away his hat and corduroy coat and flannel shirt. His face and chest were streaked with dust, soot, and sweat.

Etta's eyes snapped open. It was pitch dark. She imagined she saw two half-naked hairy men standing over her. She smelled their sweaty bodies. She pointed the nozzle of the rifle barrel at chest level. "Get out!" she screamed. "Get out! I'll blast you to pieces! We're off limits to dynamiters."

Charlie's voice came from the dark, calm as a barrel of rainwater: "Dear, put the gun down. I'm your Charlie. I'm tired. I doubt I could swallow a rifle's iron pellet. Don't shoot—please."

Etta put the rifle back on her lap. Tears ran down her cheeks.

Charlie moved the rifle to the corner and smiled. "Two things you did wrong. You left the safety on and the dang thing isn't loaded. One thing you did right. You scared the pea soup outa' me. If I'd been any other man, I'd have hightailed it out of here faster than it takes a snake to lick up a fly."

Frank and Joe came home about the time the women and children left by twos and threes, thinking more clearly with the morning light, now able to collect their valuables from the scattered debris that was once a home.

A two-block area in the center of downtown Colorado Springs was demolished and on either side of that area other buildings and homes were badly damaged.

The Irwin horses kept in the stalls behind the shop were gone. The stalls had vanished and the shop was in scantlings. The heart of Colorado Springs was on the ground. But Charlie Irwin made the people pick up their spirit and start over. He gave them hope. Each day Charlie, his brother Frank, and his father, Joe, went out to help people clean up and begin rebuilding. Charlie talked to W. S. Stratton, the mining district's famous millionaire, who lived in a modest home on North Weber Street. "The citizens need money to rebuild. If they stay they'll be the backbone of the city. Loan the folks money, and in six months the women will be hanging up blankets on the line to air, beating carpets, and washing windows. In a year you'll have every one of the loans paid in full, earned some interest, and the everlasting regard of those citizens."

Stratton, suffering from a kidney ailment, was not sure it was wise for him to do such a thing as lend money like a bank.

"Then set up a trust fund that people can borrow from," suggested Charlie.

"You are one heck of a salesman for a cause you believe in," said Stratton. "I'll set up a fund at the First National, and anyone in need can go there for an interest-free loan. But the loan will have to be repaid within three years."

"Fair enough!" shouted Charlie, shaking the white-haired man's hand.

The city of Colorado Springs was twice the size it was when Charlie and his family moved there a few years ago, going from twelve thousand to twenty-three thousand people. His father often complained that all the people moving into the city stifled him. Frank went to the racetrack at Pikes Peak Meadows and longed for racehorses, or a trotter that pulled one of those little carts, or sulkies. There was no place in town where he could raise horses. It was against the city's health inspector's rules now to have chickens in the backyard. The Irwin family was forced to get rid of their cow. Charlie decided to put the family quarrels to rest and took the cow to Timberline for Will and Margaret and their two small children. He did not stay long because the children had a colicky influenza that was sweeping the Timberline community.

Six weeks after the powder blast Charlie announced at the supper table that he'd decided not to rebuild the blacksmith shop. He said he had a plan to move to the eastern part of the state where Joe could grow rust-resistant wheat and Frank could raise horses. "If there is a strike at the coal mines, I think Will might come with us. He was so glad to get our milk cow. He even talked about having a dairy herd of his own and selling milk to the city. He could sell milk to any number of little towns no matter where we went, if that's what he wants."

Etta stood up, stopped nursing Pauline, fastened her shirtwaist, put the baby over her shoulder, and patted the tiny back. "Charlie, we all know what everyone wants to do, but what is it you want to do? Are you moving to a place where you can do what you want? It's good to think of others, Charlie, but what of yourself?"

Charlie's mouth hung open. He looked around and saw that his father and Frank were smiling. "Well, what's the matter with you? Don't you want to go to see someplace new?"

"What do you think of eastern Colorado's prairie?" asked Joe.

"Well, it's like Kansas. It's all dryland farming," said Charlie.

"We know what that's like," said Frank. "So what about Nebraska or Wyoming? Yeah, Wyoming, that's where that fellow Tom Horn was headed."

"Ell told me most all of Colorado's homesteaded," said Etta. "Couldn't we find somewhere near a city that has lots of space? Space for a ranch."

"Etta, you willing to take the kids and move to a ranch?" asked Joe.

"If it's close to a city or town where there's a school. Everyone knows I like it here. But here there's mining and no room for a ranch."

"How much do we have in the bank?" asked Frank.

"Well," said Charlie, hesitating, "not as much as we had. Seems the black powder wiped some of the money out. We have three thousand dollars."

"What do you mean!" cried Frank. "We had a hell of a lot of money saved!" He glared at Charlie.

"I gave a couple hundred to Tom Henry's widow and another hundred to Jeb Stahl's son to buy more sheepdogs. He had a lot killed by the blast. There were some who were too proud to take a loan from W. S. Stratton. They needed something to get them started, so I gave them a little, sort of anonymous."

"You spent—you gave away our money without asking?" cried Frank.

"There wasn't time to ask. I'll take it from my pay. I keep good books," said Charlie. "Listen, the Lord gave me a nudge at the right time for those folks who were dead broke with no way to rebuild. I was so gol-durned thankful that none of my family was hurt. I wanted to help those unlucky bums." The palms of his hands were perspiring.

"As I see it, we were saved for some reason. You going to fault Charlie on his kindness?" Joe stared at Frank until he put his head down. Then he looked at Charlie. "The Irwins have strong backs. We can do anything we put our minds and hearts to." His eyes were liquid, soft, and gentle. He dug his fists in both eyes and sniffed once.

Etta was amazed. She knew nothing about this charitable giveaway her man conducted. At first she was like Frank and even opened her mouth to give Charlie a good scolding. The more she thought about it, the more she bit her tongue. She saw Charlie in a different light. He seemed pleased. The whole affair seemed to greatly please him. He really enjoyed telling how some of the people reacted to finding an envelope with money under their front door.

Charlie was a big man, six feet four inches tall. He weighed close to two hundred pounds. He ducked his head to go into an ordinary door frame. His heart is as big as all outdoors, Etta thought. How small I'd be to try to change him. Smaller than I am already.

She was still tiny like a pixie, just barely five feet high and weighing one hundred pounds. "Let's go north to Wyoming. Someplace we've not been. If there's not enough money to buy a ranch, we'll homestead. You men can be cowboys. Learn how others run their ranches." She felt exaltation in her heart. She was ready to start over.

"I could do odd jobs, like blacksmithing, until we get our feet on the ground," said Joe. "I'd look over the land and get me a quarter of a section to homestead and grow me some rust-resistant wheat." His eyes crinkled. "I remember Horn. He was going to work for a Swan Land and Cattle Company somewheres near Laramie or Cheyenne. I always thought that was a peculiar name. Let's go find out if there's such a place as Swan Land. By cracky, let's go before there's a big row between employers and miners—started by labor leaders. Look at it this way: With more people using the railroads, the individual mines getting their own blacksmith for the mules, where is our business going to be?"

"You're saying it's a good time for some bohunk to buy the land where our shop was? Maybe he'll put in a grocery store. We'll shore up this house good and tight and get her sold," said Frank. "We gonna take a vote on where to head, before someone reneges? Charlie wants a ranch, Pa wants wheat, Etta wants a school, and I want racehorses."

"Keep Will in mind with cattle," reminded Charlie.

The vote was unanimous for Wyoming. The state was unknown and new and therefore held mystery and excitement. Joe's face was flushed. "I feel like I did when we first set out for Kansas. That was unknown territory to me and your ma." His eyes were watery.

Etta went over and kissed his cheek. Then she kissed Frank on the cheek and Charlie on the mouth. "I reckon we'd better plan, because once we get there, there's no turning back."

The last morning meal in the repaired, repainted frame house was not a real pleasure for anyone. The three children were fussy. Etta wished they'd left without eating. She kept going over lists in her mind, making certain she packed all the necessities for the children.

Charlie felt perhaps he'd forgotten something. Some last-minute signature on the land or house deed. Joe was weary and short-tempered. The night before he'd visited Mary's grave with a handful of blue harebells and columbine. Before that he'd gone early in the morning to tell Ell and Les good-bye and then for the first time found his way on horseback to Will and Margaret's place. Will was not home. Margaret was overjoyed and woke both her recuperating children to see their grandfather. Before he left, Margaret cried with her arms tight around his neck. "I hope Will and me can follow soon," she sobbed.

Frank was depressed and getting cold feet. He said he was not certain about going to a place he knew nothing about.

With a wagon and newly bought team of two horses, the Irwin family headed north along the railroad tracks. The atmosphere was so clear that hills and mountains that were far away seemed near. At night the stars shone so brilliantly they looked within reach. The Irwins met section gangs along the Denver and Rio Grande Western Railway replacing ties. The shining rails ran in silver ribbons for miles; block signals raised or lowered their wooden arms. Etta and the children put Indian paintbrush, fireweed, and columbine in a jar of water to decorate the supper table, which was a quilt on the ground.

Charlie whistled at the picketpin gophers that sat motionless on the black ties. Floyd pointed to huge hawks that feasted on dead rabbits or sat watchful on the peaked roofs of the deserted tarpaper shacks that dotted the prairie alongside dry creek banks. They saw the Castle Rock and Denver with clusters of boxcar houses with the smell of boiling cabbage. They passed frame houses squatting near tall water tanks along the tracks. They passed sand-washed flats, deeply-gouged arroyos, belts of pine and birch, small creeks in meadows outlined by willows, reddish-orange with sap, sunflowers, rabbitbrush, red and yellow wild currants. In the distance they saw snow-covered peaks. During the day they saw shy deer and curious antelope. By twilight they saw coyotes shaded with gray, black, and tan.

The Irwins traveled through the fertile valleys of the Cache la Poudre and South Platte rivers after leaving the northern Colorado coal fields and experienced a sudden electrical storm. Everyone huddled inside the wagon and feared washing away when the rain came in a deluge of water, wind, thunder, and lightning. The horses stood with their heads down, water washing over their hooves and lapping at their knees.

Joe explained to Floyd why the railroad tracks were built high on a levee in the flat country. "A cloudburst can't wash the tracks out. Look at us—water up to the wagon hubs. The track is clear of water."

"What if we get in trouble, Grandpa Joe? There's no one to help." The youngster peeked out the front of the wagon and saw nothing but sagebrush flats peppered by huge waterdrops coming so fast that they ran together in long, thin streams of water.

"Why, we'd wait for the next train or use the standard distress signal of three shots," explained Joe, putting a hand on Charlie's Henry rifle. It was wrapped in a canvas case Etta had made.

"Could I pull the trigger?" asked Floyd. His eyes were wide and shining.

"We don't need help. Not unless it gets wet enough to bog a snipe," said Joe.

By evening the rain stopped, leaving the pungent odor of greasewood. The next day they came into dry range country, where the wind set tumbleweeds bounding along beside the wagon for miles. The wagon passed a string of settlements with shoddy stores, more like trading posts, but no saloons nor gambling halls that had filled the speculative townsites in the coalfield district.

The wagon went by thousands of Herefords and Shorthorns grazing on the open range. Crossing the Colorado border into Wyoming they passed more white-faced cattle grazing freely. They were passing through ranchlands belonging to Francis E. Warren, a senator from Wyoming. Charlie was unaware that this grazing land belonged to anyone, let alone a U. S. Senator.

The brown rolling hills were broken once in a while by weathered rocky outcroppings. One gray sandstone outcrop was carved by the constant wind and fierce cloudbursts into a high-walled corral. Joe pulled back on the reins so that he could look at this naturally formed fort. The eastern slope was protected by the rocky terrain; the west slope had thick growths of underbrush along a creek.

Charlie said, "I bet my boots that this was the sight of many Indian battles, and maybe even bandits holed up here, out of sight of lawmen."

Floyd asked to explore the eighty- by thirty-foot fort. Etta, fascinated by the looks of the natural fortress, said this was the place to have the noon meal, "out of the wind."

As Charlie ate a lunch of biscuits washed down with creek water, he imagined the battles that might have been fought, staining the gray rock walls blood red. He said he was ready to look over the town of Cheyenne before going over the broad plain that gently sloped to meet the Laramie Mountains to the west. Cheyenne was laid out parallel with the Union Pacific Railroad and the streets diagonal to the four directions.

Joe left Etta, the children, and Frank on Crow Creek to make camp while he and Charlie set out on foot for town. They located the newspaper office of the *Wyoming State Tribune-Leader,* asked about land for sale in the area. The Irwin men were advised to move out twenty, thirty miles from town and homestead.

Charlie knew Etta would like Cheyenne with its ten thousand people, cement sidewalks, and electric lights. Joe found that Cheyenne was really the capital of a vast cattle-ranching area. Many of the ranches were owned by Europeans, many deals made "by the book," and range detectives were hired to safeguard the stockmen's interests. Cheyenne was made state capital nine years before, and its gold-domed capitol building cost the enormous sum of one hundred and fifty thousand dollars.

They turned to leave the newspaper office, and a young reporter got up from his desk and waved a piece of paper. "I forgot to mention there's a quarter section on Horse Creek that has a couple of buildings. Frank Sinon's place. He wants to sell—move back East. I think you could get it reasonable. Land around there is available for homesteading. It's maybe forty-five miles out."

Charlie shook his head. "We want something not too far from town."

"You don't want anything close to town—too expensive. Lots that were a hundred and fifty dollars ten, fifteen years ago are now twenty-five hundred dollars. Go on out and look this place over. Go to Horse Creek, then a little way east to Meriden, and you're there. Look for a bunkhouse made from railroad ties. You can't miss it!"

Joe drove the wagon north on a dirt road until they came to the creek that fit the description of Horse Creek. He turned up the two-rut road to the east and passed a couple log buildings, close together. He and Charlie decided that could be Meriden. They saw the house made of ties and knew they were on the right road. The place was deserted except for flocks of crows. A ridge of bare hills rose far away in front of the broad acres of rolling grassland. Behind was a ridge of pine.

Etta and the children looked in the windows of the cabin and explored the outbuildings. There was no stone fireplace in the cabin, which was rectangular, about twelve by fifteen feet, built by notching the ties and fitting them one above the other at the corners. The joints between the ties were battened with wood chips over which a chinking of mud or clay mixed with dried hay was daubed. There was no foundation. Earth was banked around the base to keep out the cold and wind.

The roof was made of rough slabs covered by rough wooden shingles. The front of the cabin had a door in the center and a small window on one side, of the barn-sash type; that is, a single sash with four small panes, hung on hinges to open out. There were no windows or doors on the north, which was common practice in the windswept open country and also in places where snowfall was heavy and slow to melt, but there was a door off to one side with a window opposite on the south.

The stovepipe rising from the back of the black, potbellied iron stove was collared by a piece of sheet iron and projected above the roof. There was an attic or loft in the bunkhouse with a window on the south side. Frank, Joe, and Floyd could easily sleep in the loft. There were four beds against the walls built of rough lumber and fitted with springs made of rawhide. Etta saw only two chairs at the crude table. The cowhide on the seats was cracked, but could be easily replaced. On the wall near the stove she saw two Happy Jack lanterns, made from tin syrup cans and lit by candles.

The men tramped through the tall grass to see how many rabbits they could scare, while they daydreamed about the heads of cattle or horses they could raise on such a fine place. Portions of the land were overgrazed stubble, as though the previous owner had many more cattle than the land was able to sustain.

Charlie knew this was the place he'd dreamed about. The Irwins camped three days by the cabin. Frank spent most of the daylight sitting on the edge of the corral fence looking over at the creek. He hoped to see mustangs come in for water. Joe went through the makeshift barn and knew what he'd do to repair and enlarge the building. He knew where he'd put an icehouse, blacksmith shed, toolshed, and chicken coop.

Going past Cheyenne, Etta had seen the old brick and stone homes, many with stables and chicken coops in their back yards. There were cottonwoods and poplars giving shade to the houses. Her heart was set on one of those houses in town. However, for now she saw that the ranch land had great possibilities for the Irwin men, so she kept her mouth shut.

On the third day Joe went to town on horseback with a checkbook in his pocket. No one expected him back until the next day.

"As soon as Pa has everything in order I'm going to homestead some parcels of land," said Charlie. "Here's my idea. All of us are going to sign homestead papers, me, Frank, Pa, and you, Etta, for quarter sections. That'll make a whole additional section. That'll make us ranchers!" Charlie was excited.

"If Will and Margaret were to move here, there'd be six of us homesteading," said Etta, caught up in Charlie's excitement.

Charlie was thinking of the layout and what could be done with all the land. "Too bad Floyd and the babies aren't old enough to homestead," he joked.

"We'll need an official brand for our stock to show our ownership," said Frank. "Can we do that? How about an *I* in a circle or an *I* in a diamond shape? Pa can make the branding iron when he gets some tools. And you can do the branding, Charlie."

"You'll learn too, Frank," said Charlie.

Joe was back before midnight, tired but triumphant. "I got the whole one hundred and sixty acres for about two dollars an acre.

There's money left to buy a thrasher, fix up the barn, get some stock, and build a blacksmith shed."

"What about a house and extra food and clothing?" asked Etta. "Maybe if we'd first build a small place on one of the other quarter sections we could talk Will and Margaret into coming."

Joe munched on some warmed-over fried potatoes and hot coffee. "Listen, there are some real big ranches around here, run by real cattle barons, mostly Englishmen and Scotchmen—eight to ten sections. You want to compete with them? You thinking that big?" Joe was laughing. "What's this about other quarter sections?"

"We're going to homestead as much as we can," said Charlie. "If Will and Margaret come out, why, we'd have six extra quarters."

Etta sat up in her blankets. "That's it! That's the symbol for the ranch. That's our stock brand. Can't you see? Why six! Y6! Have the Y's tail make the 6!"

"I'll go to the courthouse and register our brand. No one else can use it. We'll officially be ranchers!" cried Charlie.

That fall before the first snow the Irwin men refurbished the barn and bought several dozen head of broad-shouldered Texas Shorthorns, and Joe planted several acres of winter wheat. Etta scrubbed and scoured the bunkhouse with lye, and scraped and polished the stove. She made curtains from bleached flour sacks. As soon as they could get back to town, the four adult Irwins signed for homesteading rights on four quarter sections northeast of the main ranch. Etta began writing a series of letters to Margaret, hoping to entice her and Will to Wyoming.

> While the newspapers are filled with stories of the Spanish-American War and Battle for Manila Bay, it will surprise you to know that a gentleman named Elmer Lovejoy, living nearby in Laramie, owns a bicycle shop and made a horseless carriage. Honest. Charlie is going to take us all to see the machine as soon as the snow melts. If you were here you could come with us. I'm convinced we'll be seeing these machines on our roads. They travel at twelve miles an hour.

In another letter to Margaret, Etta wrote glowing words about the city of Cheyenne.

This city has a three-story train depot with a tower that is a landmark for anyone coming into town. There is a fountain, with a series of levels of water, for horses or dogs.

Fort Russell is a permanent military post here, with about twenty-seven buildings. It's quite a sight to see the infantry parading, knowing some of the troops are going to Cuba.

We have a two-story city hall and jail and a state capitol building, whose dome is covered with gold leaf and patterned after our national Capitol in Washington. There are seven churches. Three of them on opposite corners, which is called Church Corner. We have a hospital, whose first building was constructed by a Dr. Graham and a *Dr. Irwin*. No relation, Joe says. The first high school in this territory was built in Cheyenne.

A month later she sent another letter.

Margaret, you would love the celebration that takes place in late September called Frontier Days. At noon cannons are fired at the fort and all the churches ring their bells and the engines in the railroad yards blow their whistles. Citizens fire shotguns, rifles, and pistols in the air. The streets are decorated with red, white, and blue paper ribbons. The fair is officially opened. The ladies who sit close to the open arena raise and point parasols toward steers or broncos that come too close to the fence, so the animals always turn in another direction. This is a wonderful sight. Before this festival there is a fair where ladies exhibit baked goods and needlework, even babies are judged for most beautiful and cutest. Your little Gladys could easily win the first, and I believe your Charles would win the second category.

Margaret sent a reply.

Will has added a dozen more dairy cows to the one you folks gave us. We sell milk and butter to miners around here. It's a good living. The children are growing up fast and have not taken the diphtheria nor whooping cough.

W. S. Stratton, Charlie's wealthy friend, is rumored to be ill, some kidney trouble, and going to Carlsbad for the mineral-water treatments. He went to London, taking his private physician, to sell the Independence silver mine to some outfit there. They say he got eleven million dollars. I can't count that high!

Etta continued to entice Margaret and Will away from Colorado Springs, with the hope they'd soon come to live in Wyoming on homestead land adjacent to the main Y6 Ranch.

The sport for men here is horseback riding and horseracing. There are shooting matches and picnics in public parks. Noted performers stop here on their way to San Francisco. You and I could go to the theater.

Andrew Carnegie offered Cheyenne $50,000 toward a free public library. Besides telegraphs there are telephones in the newspaper buildings. Water and electricity are in the city's houses. It's all real modern. Charlie says you can have a telephone when you come out to homestead, if wires are strung out this way. He's sure they will be.

In order to buy all of the lumber and other equipment the ranch needed, Charlie and Frank had to hire out as cowboys on the nearby ranches. Thus they began asking about jobs. Joe, Etta, and the children were to be left on the ranch. Joe built a new outhouse. Etta closed up the chinks with mud reinforced with straw inside and outside the house. Joe put up plank, one-room shacks on the homestead land.

Charlie heard at the Stock Growers National Bank in Cheyenne that the Union Stock Yards National Bank in Omaha was looking for a man to herd beef cattle from Omaha to the Pine Ridge Indian Reservation in southwestern South Dakota. Charlie knew this was something he could do, the job paid well, and he could quit at any time.

What he did not know was that the United States Government had promised the Sioux in 1882 twenty-five thousand cows and a thousand bulls if the adult, male Sioux would sign a paper giving away fourteen thousand square miles of land. The government sent a man as interpreter, who had once been a missionary, to the Sioux in order to get as many signatures as possible. This man not only told those in the Pine Ridge Reservation, but all in the Great Sioux Reservation, that if the men failed to sign the agreement, the Sioux would lose rations and annuities. He had boys as young as seven years old mark an X beside their name to obtain the necessary three-fourths of the adult male signatures. It was not until the summer of 1889 that a final agreement was signed that took lands from the Great Sioux Reservation and in turn promised payment in cash and cattle to the individual reservations: Park Ridge, Rosebud, Red Cloud, Lower Brulé, Crow Creek, Cheyenne River, and Standing Rock. Then the government began delivering the cattle in large herds in 1899.

Charlie needed a letter of recommendation for the job of foreman of the cattle outfit. He thought of the men he knew in Colorado, General William Palmer, promoter of the Denver and Rio Grande Western Railroad, and W. S. Stratton. These two men knew Charlie as a fine blacksmith, but not as a man who could ride horseback all day herding cattle. Then he remembered he already had a letter given him by his Farmers' Alliance friend, Marty Robinson, who had been a dryland farmer and was now a real estate broker. Robinson gave Charlie the letter the day the Irwins left Goodland. Charlie dug through the *Irwin Important Papers* and finally found what he wanted.

July 18, 1896

To whom it may concern:

I take pleasure in recommending Chas. Irwin Esq., a young gentleman whom I have known for a number of years, as a horseman in way of driving and taking care of horses. He is considered an expert in this locality. Sober, honest, industrious, and willing to work, he enjoys the confidence and good will of all with whom he had been associated with here. Anyone in need of such a man would do well by employing him.

Yours, etc.,*
M. Robinson

Charlie took the Union Pacific train from Cheyenne to Omaha as soon as the spring thaw began. From the Union Stock Yards National Bank, he was sent to the C. J. Hysham & Co., Beef Contractors. Suddenly he found himself in charge of twenty-five hundred second-grade scrub cows and one hundred scrub bulls bound for the Pine Ridge Sioux Indian Reservation. He was foreman for nine cowboys and a cook with a chuck wagon.

Day after day the eleven men ate dust and tried to prevent

*Original letter from the Charles M. Bennett Collection, Scottsdale, Arizona.

stampedes as they rounded up straying animals. Each night they ate beans, bacon, and biscuits and drank boiling-hot coffee that was strong enough to float a boiled egg. In the twilight one of the cowboys plucked the strings of his banjo and another played his mouth organ while the rest, led by Charlie, sang sad songs, mostly about lost love or the cruel cowboy life. The men used their own language: calling biscuits "hot rocks"; tobacco, "makings"; a skunk, "a nice kitty"; a saddle, "a rig"; cooties, "seam squirrels"; stealing, "yamping."

Often when the evening air was still and sultry, jagged lightning blinked back and forth between rolls of dark clouds that built up in the southwest. When the clouds disappeared, the dark sky was full of star-bright twinkles that looked to be as small as pinpricks or as large as a balled fist. Other times the entire night sky was blacked out and there was no light except from the reddish glow of the campfire. When the fire went dead, there was pitch blackness and night sounds of the high, fast chirps of crickets and cicadas in the grass and sage.

Charlie noted the temperature in his record book by counting the short, shrill sounds of the crickets. The nights it rained the men sought cover in ponchos and ducked under the chuck wagon. Next morning they ate cold biscuits and beans under deafening wind and rain, mounted up, herded their cattle through muck and swollen creeks. Usually by afternoon the sun beat down from the cloudless sky. Then the air was hot and humid.

At Pine Ridge, Charlie was shocked. He could not believe the appalling conditions the Sioux were expected to live in and call home. Three rows of a couple dozen one-room, unpainted frame houses looked like they'd come from the poorest section of some shantytown. On the roofs, shingles were askew and missing.

A breeze brought a swirl of dust past Charlie, who was on foot, having picketed his horse in front of the sutler's store. The dust devil sailed between two sagging, gray houses to a skin tepee, where it broke up. The dust blew against the tepee flap just as it was raised. Charlie saw an old man hunched down, come out, straighten up stiffly, and walk across the bare earth toward him. The man's dark skin was tough and wrinkled. His clothing was shabby, a rolled red cloth held his stringy gray hair back from his face, which was shrunken so that his nose seemed much too large. His eyes were deep-seated, dark, and bright.

Charlie lowered his head and wandered a little ways away pretending not to see the old man. He didn't have the heart to face a fellow human that was forced to live in such squalor. He walked silently past women with loose-fitting cotton dresses and children in faded flannel shirts and patched Levi's, barefoot. He could not bring himself to look directly at any of these people. For some reason he could not explain he didn't want the people to think him a nosy white man, trying to ease his conscience by being a do-gooder and bringing them this large herd of cattle. Here he was a businessman, and he'd brought these people scrub cattle for their meat and hides. It was the scrub cattle that really bothered him. These people saw what he brought them. They knew. It made Charlie feel second-class. He vowed to talk with his boss in Omaha and ask for a decent herd next time.

Finally his natural friendliness won out and he began to talk with some men and boys. When the old man came into the group, he shook his hand, sensing that he was venerated by the others because of age and experience. "I have never been here before," explained Charlie. "I was hired to leave that big herd of cattle for your people. Some are poor and need to be slaughtered right away, cut up for making stew. Others you might want to use for breeding."

The old man nodded; his facial expression showed little. "You are welcome." He held his hand out again.

Charlie seemed to know instinctively that it was not mannerly to strike up a conversation with the women or girls without first being introduced or having had a long friendship.

The loose skin on the old man's cheeks moved up and down. "I have not told you my name. You have not told me yours."

"Oh, I'm sorry about that. I'm Charlie Irwin, C. B. Irwin from Cheyenne, Wyoming."

"I'm Red Cloud," said the old man simply.

For a moment Charlie was stunned. He knew full well that a Red Cloud had fought against General Custer. That in 1876 Red Cloud had advised his Oglalas not to go anywhere with the Sioux that followed Crazy Horse. The other men were smiling. Charlie knew this old man could certainly be Red Cloud. He estimated the old man's age to be between seventy-five and eighty. He'd learned somewhere in his early schooling that in the fall of 1822, there was an unusually large, blazing star illuminating the western sky with a red glow in the black of the night. Or had he heard that story recently when discussing the unusually dense showing of meteorites last summer? "I heard that seventy-seven years ago a great warrior gave his name to a newly born son. On the night of the birth there was a red, glowing ball of fire in the sky. The name of the father and son was Red Cloud."

The old man looked up at Charlie. "A red cloud at night impresses all who see it. My own son is called Jack Red Cloud." He was pleased that this white man had heard how he got his name.

One of the men whispered something to the old man. The others continued smiling, saying nothing, but waiting for the old one to take the lead, as was their custom. Red Cloud said, "Years back there was an agent here called Dr. James Irwin. Is he your father?"

It was Charlie's turn to laugh. "No, sir. I never heard of your agent, Dr. James Irwin. My father is Joe Irwin and he's the best blacksmith I know."

Red Cloud looked pleased. He told Charlie that he had a quarrel with Dr. Irwin about sending too many of their own supplies to Chief Crazy Horse. For questioning the rights of Crazy Horse, Red Cloud was ousted as chief of the Oglala Sioux. "But what is there to life if a man cannot state his feeling as freely as the whippoorwill or argue with another like the frogs around a pond at night? You are understanding, not like the other Irwin."

Later Charlie learned from the present agent that Dr. Irwin's wife, Sarah, wrote the life history of that old Shoshone woman, Sacajawea, who accompanied Lewis and Clark to the West Coast. Before the Irwins were transferred from the Wind River Reservation to Pine Ridge, fate intervened. There was a fire in their office and the handwritten papers and other important documents went up in smoke.

Charlie turned down the invitation to spend the night at the agent's frame house. He stayed with his men and slept next to the creek, in sight of skin tents of the Sioux. This way he showed preference for neither the government men nor the Sioux. The Sioux were quick to note that these white men stayed "on the fence," or halfway between the white and red man. Red Cloud said, "Our friend prefers the sighs of the wind drifting over the creek, for he knows all things share the same breath, the beasts, trees, men."

Charlie saw that the Sioux were crowded in the single-room houses, as several families were assigned to each house. He estimated there were approximately six thousand Oglalas living on the Pine Ridge Reservation, though not in the village of Pine Ridge itself. There were about twenty-five hundred grown men. A crier was sent out to bring the men in to claim his cow or bull. This one animal per adult man was to be the beginning of a larger herd for each man according to the government order. No account was given to how many adult men were in each family, or whether the family had access to water, grazing land, or hay.

In the morning Charlie was appalled to see women scrape green mold off a slab of bacon and drop it into a boiling pot of water. No one had taught them how to slice and fry bacon, nor to cut the rind away with the mold. The men preferred the lightweight, comfortable moccasins their women made to the thick-soled, heavy, ill-fitting black boots they were forced to wear. These boots were the same footwear given to the U.S. infantrymen. They were made at the military prison at Fort Leavenworth, Kansas, from coarse leather. The uppers were fastened to the sole by brass screws. Rights and lefts were indistinguishable, they were usually oversized, and the square toes did not conform to the foot's shape. Some of the children had coughing sickness, tuberculosis, because they were forced by the agent to live in close quarters and not allowed to move on horseback across the land. While Charlie was there, a young woman died in childbirth because of lack of sanitation on the part of the reservation doctor, who came late. This lack of heartfelt caring seemed bitterly cruel and tragic. But it was a hopeless situation forced on people who had little authority to do anything for themselves and who had centuries of tradition of doing everything for themselves.

Charlie talked to his nine cowboys and the cook, Salty, about staying over an extra day to meet with the Indians who came in for their single cow or bull. "We'll talk to them about winter care for the animals. They're not used to looking out for stock. We'll teach them the use of the bulls and cows to add young ones to the herd. Maybe I'll have time to tell them how to breed horses to use on roundups, separating cattle from the main herd, or bringing in a bunch-quitter."

"The Injuns'll be sick and tired of sitting on their cans listening to all that palavering!" yelled one of the cowboys. "They barely tolerate taking words from the agent now."

"You're right," agreed Charlie. "Salty, you think you can fix enough coffee, with lots of sugar, for—oh—maybe two thousand Indians? They'll listen if there's eats afterward—same as the rest of us."

Salty's head shook from side to side. His round face looked sad with his mouth turned down. His hands were thrown out in front of his chest. "I can't boil water fast enough to keep up with that kind of crowd for one thing, and there's not enough tin cups in the chuck wagon for another."

"No problem," said Charlie, full of confidence. He pushed his hair off his forehead and put his big brimmed hat on to hold the hair in place. "I'll talk to the old gentleman, Red Cloud, so he'll spread the word for the Sioux to bring their own cups. The agency'll loan you a couple washtubs to boil water in and give you extra coffee and sugar."

"Swell," said Salty. "I can manage, then."

Charlie pushed his hat up a little on his forehead. "The rest of us are showing those men how to let their cattle graze and how to round up and cut one or two for butchering—can we do that?"

The cowboys nodded their approval. "Hell, yes."

Charlie went off toward the agency office singing to himself, knowing he could convince the government men to let him borrow a couple washtubs. The coffee and sugar would naturally come next.

"I'll bet you boys a good lariat them Injuns make a feast of roast beef out of the cow we butcher for demonstration. Kiyi! This'll be a regular party," yelped Salty, dancing around.

When it was time to demonstrate cutting out a couple of the cows from the herd grazing in the wide pasture in front of the little shacks, Charlie had Red Cloud appoint a dozen men to come in on horseback. They would follow Charlie and his men on horseback. Suddenly one of the Indians came close, touched Charlie's arm, nodded for him and his men to keep their horses quiet. The man, dressed in wool pants and flannel shirt, but barefoot, held a butcher knife between his teeth. The men mounted behind him had bows and arrows in their hands. The man with the butcher knife made his horse spurt out ahead, and he ran neck and neck with a frightened cow. Suddenly he hung low in the saddle. In the next instant several more of the Sioux followed, their long hair flying. Twelve men on horseback went pell-mell into the herd of milling cattle. Twelve cows lay dead on the dusty pasture. Before anyone could blink, twelve more men climbed on the horses and were out hunting a cow or bull to bring down. There was so much *kiyi*ing and jumping up and down, no one paid any attention to Charlie, who ran around like a chicken with its head cut off, trying to get the killing stopped. Then before Charlie could get to one of the cows to bring back for a butchering demonstration, women of all sizes and shapes swarmed around the dead animals in the field, sang a high-pitched tremolo, flashed wooden-handled butcher knives in the sun, cut the hides down the back, exposed the red meat.

In three quarters of an hour several dozen cows were skinned, cut up into pieces, and brought to drying racks beside the tepees for more slicing. Old women built fires in pits they dug quickly on the parade ground. Stewpots appeared with boiling water ready for the hunks of red meat. Other women hung strips of thin meat for jerky or pemmican on the spindly-looking racks of willow sticks. Nothing was wasted. The fat was put aside to render down when the fires were low. Bones and hooves were kept for marrow and gelatin, and then ground into a flourlike meal.

Charlie knew the Sioux had bested him and he was impressed. The agent was stymied. "The Sioux did more, faster, better than I've ever seen. Why? Because a bunch of dumb cowboys put ants in their pants—gave them enthusiasm? Mark my words, it won't last. Next time you're here, those people'll be the same, indifferent, indolent primitives you first saw," he said.

"So, then we'll have more festivities and your Indians'll perk up. They need motivation—something they can relate to their old ways—not oppression. Did you see those fellows ride their ponies? Jeems, it was wonderful," Charlie said.

"I'll admit it was a beautiful sight, seeing those men hang low so only their feet show. They haven't done that before that I've seen," said the agent.

"Why not have some horse races for the men—sewing bees for the women? They'll like that. They'll like you."

The agent shook hands with Charlie and said, "I'll have to do it on my own. Washington sends us no orders like that!"

Charlie laughed. "Rules, huh? Man makes them. Man breaks them."

"Hell, you could work with these people better than I," the agent said with a smile, wiping the sweat from his face with a bandanna.

Charlie went to say good-bye to old Red Cloud. The old man thought his men had played a good joke on Charlie and his cowboys by beating them to the slaughter and showing how fast the Oglala women could butcher a few dozen cows. "Easier than buffalo." Red Cloud laughed and assured Charlie that the women knew how to use every bit of the hide for moccasins, leather boxes, or bags. "What they don't need, they sell to the whites for a dollar and a half a hide and convince them it's genuine buffalo skin."

Charlie grinned all the way back to Omaha, thinking about how he thought he was so smart, wanting to show the Sioux how to butcher a cow.

Later he told Etta about his first trip to the reservation, ending with, "Those people have butchered animals long before you and

I were gleams in our fathers' eyes. Was I stupid for thinking I could show them a thing or two? You bet! They worked over those cows so fast it'd make your head spin. My dear, you could learn something from those women," he said with a chuckle. "I sure learned from those men riding horseback."

EIGHTEEN

Francis E. Warren

Before the year was over, Charlie was sent to the Pine Ridge Reservation twice more. Then C. J. Hysham sent him to Fort Yates, North Dakota, and the Standing Rock Reservation. Charlie was foreman of the outfit taking beef cattle to these Hunkpapa Sioux. He brought lemon drops for the children and packets of needles for the women, who used them for sewing the tiny colored seed beads they used for decoration on leather goods. He brought the men tobacco and cigarette papers.

Charlie became friendly with George H. Bingucheimer, Indian agent at Standing Rock. This agent was fiercely individualistic, honest, and forthright. He was short compared to Charlie and had a black brush-type mustache across his upper lip. His office and sleeping quarters were a one-room log cabin, similar to the houses built for the Indians by the government. Charlie enjoyed sitting with the agent in one of the several wooden chairs under a poplar tree in front of the office.

Bingucheimer said that twenty years before, Sitting Bull had advised his people at Standing Rock not to sign white men's papers. Sitting Bull'd seen the Sioux's land shrink each time "white chiefs let Sioux chiefs touch the pen." Because none of the Indians could read, they had no idea what they were asked to sign. It was the old story about the Sioux cajoled out of fourteen thousand square miles of land in the Black Hills. After Sitting Bull's death the Hunkpapas left Standing Rock. Some went south to Pine Ridge for Red Cloud's protection, but most were forced by U.S. soldiers to move to the Wounded Knee camp, where horses, guns, land, and lives were taken. Finally, Bingucheimer explained, the Hunkpapas left Red Cloud's Sioux and were re-admitted to the Standing Rock Reservation.

"There must have been a lot of Indians moving around Horse Creek, where my father has his ranch," said Charlie, "because I've found several arrowheads on high ground, above Horse Creek."

"Horse Creek!" said Bingucheimer excitedly. "Horse Creek, close to the Nebraska border?"

"Yes, that's it. Why do you ask?"

Bingucheimer could not wait to tell Charlie about the Horse Creek Treaty that took place fifty years before.

"Colonel David D. Mitchell, a Virginia fur trader who fought in the Mexican War, was superintendent of all the western Indian country in 1851."

"That's a little before my time, but my father was born in 1846 and he remembers people that were fur traders," said Charlie, leaning back so he had his chair resting on two back legs.

"Well, Mitchell, along with the first western Indian agent, Tom Fitzpatrick, supported a general peace treaty between the U.S. Government and all the Plains Indians. Mitchell and Fitzpatrick promised the Indians gifts if they'd come to Fort Laramie on the North Platte to discuss peace and justice."

"As the crow flies, Fort Laramie's not more than thirty miles from our ranch," said Charlie.

"Ten thousand Indians came," said Bingucheimer, using his hands as he spoke. "The gathering was so large it had to be moved to the meadow at the mouth of Horse Creek, thirty-five miles downstream from Fort Laramie."

"I know right where that is," said Charlie. His brown eyes were wide with surprise and interest.

"This was the largest assembly of American Indians ever held before or since," said Bingucheimer.

The next time Charlie took beef cattle to the Hunkpapa at Standing Rock, he went to some trouble to bring better than scrub animals. Bingucheimer was impressed with Charlie's compassion for the Indians.

"Say, how did the treaty work out?" Charlie asked. "Did the

government keep its word and give the Indians fifty thousand dollars' worth of goods every year for fifty years?"

"No. Peace prevailed and all went well until 1854, when some hungry Sioux butchered a poor immigrant's cow. Two officers at Fort Laramie sent an army detachment to arrest the Sioux, instead of the usual punishment, withholding goods of equal value at the next Sioux annuity distribution and paying the immigrant for his loss. The Sioux was scared to death."

"Agitated as a June bug," said Charlie.

"Ya. He resisted arrest and the historical Grattan Massacre was the result."

"Next time I come around you can tell me about that massacre," said Charlie.

"I'll tell you now that there was no more fifty thousand spent on goods for the Indians. From then on there were other bloody confrontations between Indians and whites, Indians and Indians. Now, half a century later, the Indians are on reservations and wards of the government. They depend on people like you, C.B., to bring them decent cattle for meat and hides."

Before the big November snowfall Charlie learned that all the cattle owed to the Sioux reservations by the U.S. Government had been delivered. Charlie was out of a job. He was disappointed there would be no more history lessons from the Indian agent at Standing Rock.

Another disappointment waited for him at the Y6 ranch. His father had built a substantial shed for his blacksmith shop. He spent a lot of money for new tools. Frank continually complained about the new shed. He said that the space could have been put to better use if the shop were built onto the barn. Also, he resented the money his father spent, saying it could have been better spent on a couple of new saddles which Frank wanted.

Instead of helping his father in the blacksmith shop or working in the barn, Frank spent whole days at Frank Meanea's Saddle Shop in Cheyenne. The two-story, brick building on West Seventeenth Street had a huge salesroom in front and a well-equipped workshop in the back with more than twenty leather workers. Frank looked over saddles priced from twenty-five dollars to fifty-five dollars, pack saddles at eight dollars. Twelve-foot long bullwhips sold for three dollars and fifty cents, quirts for seventy-five cents to two dollars. Frank looked longingly at the leather collars and cuffs from fifty cents to three dollars. He itched to spend money. When he found his father would not pay him for the days he spent away from the ranch, he was really angry.

"Geez, Pa! I need gear for my horse. I need to get other horses and saddles for them."

"Frank, keeping horses, buying saddles, brings no income, unless you actually sell them for more than you paid for them. Also, you get income for gear and more horses if you spend your time working," Joe said.

"I don't like to work in the blacksmith shop. I like to work with horses and I don't have much to work with," wailed Frank.

Joe exploded. "Dadburn it, son! You are the whiniest person I ever heard. I thought when you were growd you'd stop crying and bellyaching. But for once't I was wrong. You go out and work with the horses, rub 'em down, brush 'em, feed 'em, anything, but don't complain about me spending my money. If you want money to spend, get your own. Another thing, stop complaining about the weather, the way Etta makes gravy, the location of the smithery, the bitter taste of my coffee."

Frank was stunned. "I only thought you could put a pinch of salt in the coffeepot, Pa, that's all."

"See, that's what I'm talking about! If you want something done, do it!" shouted Joe.

Frank went into the house, rolled up a couple of his flannel shirts, some wool pants, Levi's, boots, bandannas, and underwear in two, three blankets and left without saying good-bye or when he'd be back.

Joe found out Frank was working for a dollar a day and a place in the bunkhouse as a ranch hand for an aristocratic fellow from the East named John Coble. "It's west of here at the Iron Mountain Ranch."

"I'm heartsick that you two quarreled," said Charlie. "That kind of thing pushes the family apart." He waved his hands.

"You know I believe in keeping the family together," said Joe, "but truthfully, it's been quiet since Frank's been gone. Now that I know he's not far away and earning an honest dollar, I don't fret about him. So leave him be. Don't go bringing him back in a hurry."

That evening Charlie heard more disquieting words from Etta while she mended. "I'm tired of being isolated, not seeing another woman for weeks. I miss the city. I miss being close to town. What's to become of our children? Floyd will grow up knowing nothing but cows, horses, and blacksmithing. I want him to read and write. While you were gone I read him Edwin

Markham's poem 'The Man With the Hoe,' and he can repeat the first four lines by heart. Our son is smart. The little girls need a place to wear nice dresses, and they should live in a modern house with indoor plumbing." Etta rubbed her eyes and looked at Charlie.

Now even Etta was against him. She might have stopped to think how he felt with no job, Frank gone, and Pa glad of it. A gray mist covered Charlie's eyes, his bottom lip trembled, and he held back his rage and disappointment. He sat down next to the potbellied, sheet-metal heater. "Are our young ones angry with me also?" His words were sarcastic.

"They missed you. We all did. In a way I'm glad your job taking cattle to the Indians is over. Now, don't get some lame-brained idea about rushing off to Bonanza Creek or to Alaska because gold's been discovered there. We want you to settle down and work here."

Charlie was bone-weary and at a loss for poetical words befitting this delicate crisis. Jeems, women had a way of making a man feel like the worst ogre in the world. "I wrote to you. Didn't you get my letters?" He was afraid she'd ask about the many letters he thought about, but didn't write.

"Only two. I wore them out with rereading." She drew herself up.

"I'll find something to do close by. I'm going to look around as soon as I get caught up on my sleep. You can count on that."

He saw her hands reach out as she pushed her chair closer to him. Her lithe figure moved beneath the full-skirted cotton dress. Her eyes were icy-blue. Her fingers were cold and pressed hard into his palms. He was always a little startled at the strength she possessed.

"I am counting! Actions count more than words." She pulled her hands back and raised her shoulders in a shrug. Her mouth was a straight line.

Charlie rubbed his palms together and began to tell her of his own longings on the trail between Omaha and Pine Ridge and Standing Rock. He told of his fatigue, being in the saddle all day, eating dust or hunkering down in a rain slicker. With pathos he told the terrible difficulty the Sioux were going through, converting thousands of years of living close to the earth to being clothed and force-fed by the whites' customs.

Etta listened intently, and he saw her mouth grow sad, her eyes grow soft violet and liquid. "My heart goes out to those people. In a roundabout way I know how they feel, uprooted from their homeland and dependent on strangers. I came from a family that had more rules than yours. Really, I didn't know how to think for myself when I was first married. I expected you to tell me when to wash my hair. At least I speak your language."

Charlie was astounded. He'd thought Etta was the black sheep of her family—the one who spoke out of turn, who acted and thought for herself.

"It wasn't so much that I was trying to be different than the others or embarrass my folks. I have always been curious and need to have that curiosity satisfied." Color flowed together in her cheeks until just under her wide eyes two small, bright-red spots blazed.

"You are the most curiously intelligent woman I know." He smiled as though to keep the talk from going sour. He stood up and held his arms out. Without hesitation she put her mending on the floor and was out of her sewing chair, standing close against him. Charlie thought that women need a lot of assurance and a lot of love. He bent down and kissed her forehead, then her lips. "Oh, dear, I missed you so much. You are my best friend."

Tears streamed down her face. "Charlie," she whispered, "I have an idea I'd like to be a friend to those Indian women."

The idea surprised him. "Well, that's possible—who knows the future? Would you relish living on a reservation with the Sioux? One of the agents said I could do his job better than he."

"Charlie Irwin!" Etta pulled away and stood on her toes so that she'd seem taller. "I've been telling you I would like to live in town, not on a reservation in South Dakota. I've been telling you our children should go to real school in a real town." She dropped to her normal height, but kept her head high. Her eyes sparked like sapphires. "You could blacksmith in town and occasionally come out to the ranch to check on everything."

Charlie now felt giddy from lack of sleep and the complexities of all this emotional upheaval. "I'm sorry, Etta! We can't do anything until we get the ranch paid for and homesteaded. Besides, none of the young ones are ready for school yet. If you want to teach Floyd poetry, go ahead. But in the meantime this is our home. This is where you and the kids stay."

"I suppose you think I can live anywhere, just so that you have a job that brings in money to save for a new barn and horses."

Jeems! How did I get back into this? thought Charlie.

"Dear, I'll start a ranch house right after the barn is finished. Maybe I'll get you indoor plumbing. I'll find a ranch job close by—better yet, I'll look for one where a man's wife can cook for the hands." He waited for the blow. He expected Etta to lambaste him severely for such a thought.

To his surprise she sank into the sewing chair and burst into tears. "Oh, Charlie!" she cried. "That would work out just right. Will and Margaret are coming. They'll need the ranch house. You understood after all!"

Charlie was on one knee beside her. "Certainly I understand." He looked at her tenderly, wondering if he understood anything at all.

She put her arms around his waist. His hand went around her neck. They seemed to float together in a pocket of weightlessness.

Joe coughed and they sprang apart. Charlie saw her face turn red to mask the fiery spots in her cheeks, and her breasts rose and fell unevenly. He felt his face turn hot and a vein in his neck throb.

"We're just going to bed," he said. "I'm not waiting for supper."

"That's what I came to say. With the little tykes asleep there's no need to make a hot supper. I'll just find myself some cold meat and biscuits, maybe an apple. We'll talk more in the morning." Joe laughed heartily and fanned himself with the newspaper.

Charlie felt like he, too, needed fanning. It was a grand feeling. He glanced at Etta, who was busy rolling darning floss on a spool, her eyes averted. He was so glad he'd married her. She could make him hot and flustered even after three children. Well, he knew what to do when she acted like that, moving close, and pressing herself against him. He said, "Come, Mrs. Irwin," in a hearty voice.

"Yes, sir," she whispered, her hand slipping into his, "I'm ready."

The next morning he left early to look for work on several of the nearest ranches. In his pocket were two letters of recommendation. One was from his friend, the Indian agent, George Bingucheimer, and the other was from the Hysham & Co., Beef Contractors. Everyone was cordial, but no one had need of an extra hired hand.

Charlie told himself he could not go back to Etta without some kind of a job. He rode his horse all the way into Cheyenne. He stopped to look at the bulletin board in Frank Meanea's Saddle

Shop. Often a rancher pinned a slip of paper to the board, stating he was looking for a hired hand or that he had cattle or hogs to sell reasonably.

"Looking for something, mister?" The man who spoke was almost as tall as Charlie. His rich dark hair, parted in the middle, grew over his collar in the back. He had large ears that stood away from his head and deep brown eyes and an oblong face that looked distinguished. His mustache turned up at the corners above his mouth and was much lighter than his hair.

"A job," said Charlie simply.

"Ever do any anvil clanging? Blacksmithing?" asked the man.

"Yes, sir, I've done my share," Charlie said with a shrug.

"Come work for me." The man smiled and his face brightened.

"I'm Charles Burton Irwin and new here." From the first clutch of hands Charlie felt this man knew more and could do more than he.

"You'll double as my blacksmith and horse wrangler."

"But you know nothing about me," protested Charlie. "How do you know I can tell a horseshoe from a crowbar? I have a couple letters of introduction here in my pocket." Charlie took out his letters and handed them to the man.

"Do you know who I am?" The man had a fresh, bright look. He read Charlie's letters quickly.

"No, sir." Charlie shook his head and took his letters back, refolding them so they would fit in his pocket.

"You're probably the only one in this town that can say that! I'm Francis E. Warren, ex-governor of the Territory of Wyoming and presently senator of Wyoming." He made a wry face as if making fun of the titles. "My spread is called the Lodgepole Ranch and it's south of Cheyenne."

"Do you need a cook and dishwasher?" asked Charlie anxiously.

"Nope. Have one called Bobcat, who also doubles as horse wrangler."

Charlie could not turn the job down. He would just have to make Etta understand that until there was enough money, he'd have to work away from the Y6.

That winter Charlie was able to get to the Y6 once or twice a month. Whenever the weather permitted, he helped Joe put up one-room pine-slab shacks on the homestead property. The inside was finished with tar paper held down by laths fastened by shingle nails in tin disks. Since the shacks would be used only in the warm months, they were also covered on the outside with tar paper and laths. The slabs on the roof were covered with tar paper, with one-third to one-fourth pitch to shed snow in winter. Since these shacks were not accredited toward improvements on a homestead, a barn was usually the next substantial structure that was built. Charlie also began to long to have Will and Margaret come to Wyoming to help build barns and homestead the Irwin land.

Charlie's first job for Senator Warren, whose livestock company was one of the largest outfits in Wyoming, was to make proper iron hinges for all the corral gates. He had no idea that more than eighty years later, some of those same hand-forged hinges would still be in use. Warren was impressed with the work of his latest, young hired hand. He liked the way Charlie handled horses and the men he worked with. Often Warren worked in the blacksmith shop with Charlie, so they became good friends. Charlie began to learn the ranching business. From Warren he learned that a lot of the beef from Cheyenne was not sent out in boxcars to the east on the hoof, but butchered into quarters and shipped in refrigerator cars.

"That meat arrives in good shape," assured Warren. "Charlie, you're years behind the times. Some buyer sent beef quarters as far as France for their army during the Franco-Prussian War. Ranchers out here are modern. That's why I have a telephone in the ranch house. Saves me going to town to check if my supplies are in. I can stay here and talk to a shopkeeper, the freight agent at the Union Pacific, or someone in the capitol building."

Another time Warren told Charlie that business in Cheyenne had been rocky during the 1880 to 1890 decade. "Morton Post's bank closed its doors in 1888; the same year, because of overexpanded cattle business, the Union Cattle Company went bankrupt. The year before that one of the largest ranches in the area went bankrupt, the Swan Land and Cattle Company."

Charlie drew in his breath. And didn't say anything for a few minutes. Warren believed that Charlie wanted to know more about what was taking place in the state.

"I was governor from 1885 until 1886, after Thomas Moonlight served in that office. He was a Kansas Democrat appointed by President Cleveland. Not one of the stockmen in Cheyenne liked Moonlight, because he was out to break up the big ranches. So when President Harrison appointed me to take Governor Moonlight's place, I couldn't refuse. Wyoming became a state and I resigned when I thought things were back on an even keel and the Republicans could run things for a while. I went back to ranching."

In a matter of a few weeks Charlie was made top cowhand. Warren had told him about the Johnson County War. "The cattlemen imported gunmen from Texas to kill cattle rustlers. But the rustlers became so bold, they were only stopped by federal troops."

Charlie was surprised. He'd never heard of all this going on while he was growing up.

"The whole thing is summed up in a recent copy of the *Denver Times,*" said Warren. "I'll get it so you can read it. It will help you understand how the cattlemen around here feel about rustlers and about local lawmen."

The article was written by Frank Benton, a Colorado-Wyoming cattleman who began his career as a cowboy, then as a settler with a little bunch of cattle in Johnson County, Wyoming. Charlie lay on his bunk bed and read by the light of a flickering kerosene lantern. He was appalled at that.

> . . . Well, these cattle rustlers kept getting worse and more powerful, till they finally elected a rustler sheriff, and it became impossible to convict a cow thief, no matter if he was caught red-handed in the act. . . .*

By the time winter was over Charlie was Warren's assistant foreman over a dozen cowhands. Charlie's job was to go to Texas to pick up five hundred head of Shorthorns at a ranch between the New Mexico border and Amarillo. This was the first time he'd been down in the semiarid rangeland. The hot scythelike, southern winds that tore through a man were similar to the winds he'd felt across the prairie in the Kansas summers. At the Texas ranch Charlie asked if he and his crew could sleep in the bunkhouse out of the constant wind once before starting back north. The ranch hands were glad for a few extra dollars and made the arrangements. Charlie and his cowboys were to sleep during the day so that the regular hands had their usual use of the bunkhouse at night. This worked out until the ranch hands complained that Charlie and his cowboys sang all through the night waiting for daylight.

"It's worse than the coyotes!" one man cried.

"Aw, shucks," said Charlie, who could see the humorous side

*Courtesy Charles M. Bennett Collection, Scottsdale, Arizona.

to most things. "That there was the coyotes who came to serenade us. Everytime Bobcat here plays his Jew's harp, the coyotes pick up on the chorus and yodel."

Charlie and his men found themselves heading back for Wyoming in the dark, right after supper. They hurried the Shorthorns through the desert, swam rivers, and pushed on to a dry camp. By morning's first light they followed a windswept trail to a stream twenty-five or thirty miles away. The lead steer always instinctively moved out ahead, away from the billowing dust kicked up by the rest of the herd. On each flank rode a cowboy.

The leaders moved faster when they smelled water. Then came the other cowboys on horseback with the pack horses stringing behind. The mess wagon had a shabby canvas tarp over the top and was drawn by four mules. The wagon driver swung the wagon upstream and unhitched the team, which went to the water to drink their fill. The cattle and horses also stood in the water to drink. Dinner was prepared. The fording was done in the morning at sunup. Whenever Charlie came upon a lush green meadow, he was as eager as the cattle to mill around on the grass. The cows, steers, and heifers were fat. This was a quality herd.

Dodge was one main business street running parallel to the Sante Fe Railroad tracks. The most active business was done in the saloons. The city reminded Charlie of Abilene, Kansas. There was a hotel at the end of the street, Cox's Hotel, but the cowboys would rather sleep in their blankets under the stars than inside on a lousy mattress. The cook loaded his mess wagon at York, Parker, and Draper's store, which was in the center of the beer parlors and gambling houses. Charlie's outfit moved on to Denver, then on to Cheyenne.

About mid-September, Warren came out to the bunkhouse one evening and asked Charlie to come into the ranch house. The two men sat at the kitchen table sipping hot coffee with thick cream and sugar. Warren finally said what was on his mind. "Charlie, I want you to go to the upcoming celebration in town, the Frontier Days. Dress in your best red shirt and Levi's and polish your boots. This is some kind of annual exhibition our town is becoming well known for, and I want you to see it. So, you and I are taking the day off. Two of my friends, Warren Richardson, from the Union Pacific Railroad, and Colonel Slack, ink-slinger on the Cheyenne *Sun Leader,* came up with this idea for the celebration. The first Frontier Days was in 1897, three years ago. Richardson had the Union Pacific put on excursion trains with special rates.

Red, white, and blue bunting and the Stars and Stripes decorate all business buildings. People wear Frontier badges. The excitement is highest at the fairgrounds."

"Yes, I've read about the upcoming happening in the papers. Seems to be a big event," said Charlie. "Last year my wife and father took our children. I was out of town. They especially enjoyed the sham battle by troops from Fort Russell."

"That's why I'm asking you," said Warren, not waiting for Charlie to say more, "you're no imitation. Actually, you're a politician—oh, not in a derogatory sense, but meaning you are a statesman who seizes opportunities. You have aspirations and an underlying set of decent principles. You're enthusiastic. Would you believe I used to think my hired hands, from foreman on down, were muttonheads? You've changed those men or opened my eyes. C.B., you get the best from people, because you expect it, you dwell on their good qualities. The dust and barnyard manure that is in everyday life does not cling to you. I specifically remember you saying, 'The country is so beautiful,' after you brought in the Shorthorns. 'The mesquite is in bloom so that the desert is patched with scrambled-egg yellow, against the rain-fed green.' You also said, 'The oleanders grow as trees in Amarillo, perfuming the air with pink, white, and purple flowers.' I know what Amarillo looks like—dirty, dusty, squally brats, yapping dogs, conniving Mexicans. Not once did you complain about the wind nor rain, the thickheaded cows nor the cantankerous men."

Charlie swallowed all the coffee in his cup. He didn't know how to react. He wondered why Senator Warren was telling him this, but he didn't have to wonder long.

"I'm taking you with me because you don't drink."

"I don't condemn a man if he does," said Charlie.

"Befuddles the brain."

"Sometimes a man needs something to help him unwind."

"Get on a horse and ride a piece."

Charlie nodded. It wouldn't do to argue that a man was not always where he could get on a horse.

"I have another, more important reason for your company tomorrow," said Warren. "I want you to meet some friends. Actually, I'd like them to meet you. Ever think about entering politics? You're on the ranchers' side as much as I. You could start off small at first, get your feet wet, run for mayor of Cheyenne." Warren had a terse, direct manner of speaking, always to the point.

Charlie twirled his spoon on the table. He was flattered and surprised. This was a field he'd never thought about. He hadn't yet learned the ranching business. He couldn't leave one field unfinished and jump to another. Even Etta would frown. "As mayor of Cheyenne I'd stress justice and decency. But there's a big drawback having me as mayor. I'm not a native of Wyoming. I've just begun to learn ranching. I'm not prepared to fight publicly. That doesn't mean I'm indecent nor unmanly. I'm truthful and showing respect for your idea. When I'm better prepared, I'll consider your offer."

"All right—think about it. But what do you mean 'prepared to fight'?"

"Oh, that's one of those secrets of life. It's a rule. You know, some men feel it's a sign of weakness to be courteous, to show kindness, to protect the weak, respect women, be gentle with animals. We know that's just and decent. A man can uphold just and decent ideas so long as he's prepared to fight for them. When he fights hard enough, he earns the respect of his opponents."

It was Senator Warren's turn to be surprised.

"You are even more of a statesman than I'd suspected. Meet me here after breakfast tomorrow," he said. After that he described the half-mile race staged for the previous year's Frontier Days celebration. "It was a delight. The contestants rode a quarter of a mile on horseback, dismounted, turned their coats inside out, remounted, rode an eighth of a mile, dismounted, lighted cigars and put up their umbrellas, mounted, and rode in carrying umbrellas and smoking cigars." He told about the reenactment of the first election in Wyoming, an imitation lynching, a pioneer wedding, a fake Indian attack on an immigrant train, and stagecoach holdups, that the audience enjoyed.

That evening Charlie washed a yard-square, solid-red neckerchief in soapy water, then soaked it in salt water and vinegar for half the night so that the color would never run. In the morning he waited in the kitchen of the ranch house. He wore a clean red shirt and blue Levi's. His boots were fresh-polished and his neckerchief was knotted in the back of his neck.

Warren came down the back stairs whistling. The horse had been hitched to the buggy. Warren stepped up, brushed off the seat board with his tan calfskin gloves that matched his trousers and jacket. He sat and picked up the reins, waiting for Charlie to get in. "Let's go! Giddyap!"

All the way into town they did not talk much. Charlie began to sing. Senator Warren looked sideways at him, then his eyes twinkled and he sang with Charlie, "Barbara Allen," "Git Along,

Little Dogies," "The Red River Valley," "The Old Chisholm Trail." The two men went back through the same songs until they spotted the dome of the capitol far ahead above the center of the road.

"So, you sing to unwind," said Warren.

"I spin a rope to relax. It is physical and leaves my mind free to wander if I'm not trying out a new loop," said Charlie.

"Exactly," said Warren.

The town was overflowing with people in a festive mood. There were long streamers hung to hitching posts and the lamp poles. Warren stopped in front of the Cheyenne Club. This huge two-story brick building had a wide veranda around two sides facing Seventeenth and Warren. It had a mansard roof and out front nineteen hitching posts.

"We'll freshen up here," said Warren.

They went inside to use the rest room. Charlie instantly thought of Etta and knew she'd have taken great delight in the huge porcelain bathtub. He washed his hands at the porcelain bowl and dried them on a rough, snow-white linen towel. He rolled his sleeves down, buttoned them, straightened his neckerchief, slicked down his hair with his hands, using his long fingers for a comb. He surveyed his looks in the wall mirror and added water to his hands and combed his hair again. He noticed that his forehead, which was always shaded by a hat, was pale compared to his clean-shaved cheeks and chin.

Warren took him to the lounge on the main floor. First he showed him a picture of two bulls which had two six-shooter holes near the bottom. One bull was lying down next to twin trees, a bullet hole in its front left tibia. The other bull was standing and the second hole was in the ground, below the left front hoof. "This was painted by a man by name of Nesker about fifteen years ago. He called it 'Paul Potter's Bulls.' Those holes bored by a six-shooter were made by the hand of John C. Coble."

"He isn't a very good shot with a forty-five. At least if an oil painting is his target," remarked Charlie.

"Well, John thought the painting was a travesty on Wyoming livestock. In an inebriated state he pulled out his gun and defaced this beautiful painting."

"I kind of agree with the man—the bulls are scrawny and look malnourished," said Charlie.

"Well, he was suspended from the club and later resigned. One day you'll meet him. Actually, he's a fine, dignified, honorable man."

Charlie knew he'd heard of Mr. Coble from somewhere, but at that moment he could not remember where. He was looking at pictures of horses, and Bierstadt's engraving titled "In the Heart of the Bighorns" when Warren broke in on his thought.

"Phil Dater was one of the first presidents of the club, then came Charles Campbell. He's a splendid Scotch-Canadian, solid and conservative. A dozen years ago he had trouble because of the terrible winter of eighty-seven. In his more prosperous days he ranched with Johnnie Gordon, whom we call the Wyoming poet; he's an irrigation expert. Worked on a land project on Horse Creek not far from your ranch."

Warren took Charlie on a quick tour, showing him the billiard room, card room, reading room with *Harper's Weekly* and *Monthly*, the *New York World*, the *Spirit of the Times*, the *Boston Sunday Herald*, and the *New York Daily Graphic*. The kitchen and wine cellar, stocked with Geisler champagne, St. Cruz rum, Zinfandel claret, Old Tom gin and Red Dog whiskey, were in the basement. Charlie's head was still reeling from the beauty of the washroom. On the stairway they passed a large, broad-shouldered man, who was slightly bald, but his bushy straw-colored eyebrows seemed to make up for the loss of hair on his head.

"John, I want you to meet my friend and foreman, C. B. Irwin—John Clay." Then, turning to Charlie, Warren said, "Clay is going to put the Swan Land back on her feet." Then back at Clay he said, "We're on our way to the festivities. Come with us."

"All right, come on up to my room. I'd like to put on a more suitable shirt. More like yours," he pointed to Charlie. He was dressed in a black suit with a vest and tie and white shirt. His accent was Scotch. He was well educated, self-confident, and pleasant.

The room on the second floor was furnished with a hand-carved walnut bed, marble-topped dresser and commode, and a ceiling-high walnut wardrobe. The fireplace was topped with a marble mantel inscribed with Shakespearean quotations. The wine-red carpet was thick, rich wool, matching the brocaded satin and velvet drapes. Charlie could not believe anything could be so luxurious. Later he learned that membership was limited to fifty men, initiation fee was fifty dollars, and dues were thirty dollars a year. The rules were strict, no profanity, no drunkenness, no fighting, no cheating at cards, no smoking of pipes, no betting, and no games on Sunday. Many of the members were cattle barons, who spent summers in Cheyenne and winters in

Europe. The club was in bad financial shape, mostly because of the 1887 losses sustained by the members, so that bond holders on the building had to accept twenty cents on the dollar. The building had been taken over by the Club of Cheyenne and in a few years more would be known as the Cheyenne Industrial Club.

John Clay joined the two men. He wore a red flannel shirt and stiff, new Levi's. "We'll walk," said Clay. "Pioneer Park is not far."

No admission was charged to the fairgrounds, but the uncovered bleacher seats were fifteen cents and grandstand seats were thirty-five cents. They took seats in the grandstand after some pushing and jostling through the crowd. They were four rows up from the judges' stand. Here Charlie was introduced to E. A. Slack, the editor of the *Sun Leader*. He was six feet one and weighed two hundred and thirty pounds. Warren told Charlie that the man used a sledgehammer when he wrote an editorial. "That man reminds me of you with his tremendous willpower, indomitable energy, and high personal character."

Charlie learned that John Clay had been president of the Wyoming Stock Growers Association from 1890 to 1895, when he was introduced to W. C. Irvine, the present president. Irvine was a big man with large penetrating brown eyes, a big nose, and a cigar constantly in his left hand.

Warren leaned over and told the men to hush and watch the show. "Charlie here could be a contestant if I'd given him more than a day off. Charlie can do anything he sets his mind to. He could be mayor."

"Only if there is trick roping and the others are really poor," said Charlie with a laugh, "and the mayor thing is a little far-fetched for now."

The rodeo seemed to attract the most shouts and applause from the audience. Suddenly Charlie thought how much Frank would enjoy this event. Then came the steer roping, which caught Charlie's interest. The steer was given a one-hundred-foot start on the roper. Five-year-old steers were used. The first man's rope snapped when he made the "trip and bust." Hugh McPhee of Cheyenne made a record time of forty seconds to rope, bust, tie his steer, and remount his horse. Charlie's hands were sweaty. He could feel his own rope slide, tighten, slide again as he imagined himself roping a five-year-old steer.

After the roping contest Warren waved to a man in a dark-brown shirt and light-tan trousers and a round face under a wide-brimmed hat. "Governor Richards, I want you to meet a friend of mine."

Richards excused himself and came up the plank seats. He shook hands with Warren as if they were old friends. "This is the best Frontier Days so far. I can't wait until the bucking horses come out. I've got my money on Thad Sowder, the cowboy who won the championship this year in Denver."

Warren put his hand on Richards's shoulder. "This is C. B. Irwin. One day we'll be hearing more of his name—mark my words. He's a good Republican already and just the kind of man we need in the office of mayor or House of Representatives." Charlie shook hands with DeForest Richards, noting that he seemed short of breath and his face was flushed. He wondered if the man was nervous or embarrassed around Senator Warren or ill.

The bucking-horse contest was announced and the men sat down.

"People really go for this event," said Warren.

"Why's that?" asked Charlie.

"Violence, son. People are not so far down from the trees that they don't enjoy blood-and-guts violence."

"I've heard a lot about Buffalo Bill Cody. He puts on a similar show? Mostly entertainment."

"Certainly, that's what this is. Buffalo Bill found what people would pay for. That's an entertainer. Our boys from the West entertain by doing what they do on ranches every day." Warren winked. "Most every day, anyway. The townspeople eat it up and cheer for the fellows they know. The easterners never saw anything like it, plus they get a chance to see some of the most beautiful country in the world."

"I feel the same way about the western prairie and mountains. It's hard for me to stay in the blacksmith shed all day," said Charlie.

"I have a daughter, Franny, in an eastern school. She writes that those folks think we still fight red men and eat buffalo and tame rattlesnakes. It's her first time with easterners and females at Wellesley."

"Was she raised on the ranch, sir?"

"Of course. She's an excellent horsewoman. She likes any kind of outdoor thing, hiking, camping. You and your wife must meet her."

"If she's a girl with her own mind, Etta will take to her right off." Charlie had to talk above the applause of the crowd because the bronc riders were lining up and the broncs were being pushed forward. Suddenly he drew in his breath. He recognized Frank among the bronc riders. He felt anger rise in his throat. He took a deep breath and saw that his reaction was foolish. Frank was on his own. He could do anything he pleased. He remembered that earlier he'd thought how much Frank would enjoy this horse show. Soon he felt some kind of pride that Frank had found out what was going on in town and had joined in the affairs. He concentrated on the event and nearly forgot the man he'd come with. Charlie stomped and clapped and yelled encouragement to all the contestants and especially to Frank, who tried desperately to stay on the saddle, but was thrown to the dust. Frank was game. He scrambled to his feet and took the option of remounting his animal for a second attempt.

The horses were saddled in the arena for everyone to watch as the rider and his assistants handled the animal. The assistants quickly pulled off the saddle as Frank held his horse by a rope attached to its halter. One of the assistants tied a blind over the horse's eyes. Another fellow grabbed the horse's ears, twisting them to cause enough discomfort to distract the nervous horse's attention from the feel of a new saddle that was being carefully placed on its back. Frank gave the rope to one of his assistants and tightened the cinch to his liking. Then he climbed in the saddle and nodded for the blindfold to be removed and the rope dropped. The bucking began. Frank raked the sides of the animal once with his spurs and the horse reared its head high, then lowered its head and reared its back. Frank could not ride this bucking horse to a standstill. He was once again thrown in the dirt. The crowd yelled and applauded and called for him to try again. He walked slowly to the side of the arena. Charlie thought he detected a limp in the right leg. He sighed with relief. At least his brother was still in one piece and able to walk away. He'd not placed in the event, but he was not hurt.

The next rider, Thad Sowder, had the crowd standing. He remained several minutes on his outlaw, or bucking horse. Then for a moment it seemed the man threw both hands down in front to grab onto the saddle.

Warren yelled, "Did you see that! Sowder grabbed leather!"

Sowder was still on his wildly thrashing horse, hanging on to the saddle horn with one hand now. He continued to ride until the horse came to a standstill, wheezing loudly.

The crowd was yelling.

Warren said, "A decision in favor of that young man is unfair to the other contestants."

Charlie was learning. He had not known that this balancing act was to be done with one hand only; using two hands at any time was enough to disqualify a rider.

"There may be some truth to the rumor that a decision was made in advance of this contest." Warren stamped his foot.

"Can the townfolk disqualify dishonest judges?" asked Charlie.

"Maybe. What this town needs is a good manager of the whole fair. Henry Altman is chairman this year, but he also has a ranch to look after. What they need is a manager of the fair that will look after the cowboys, horses, and steers. C.B., you could do that! By golly, you could!" said Warren in his abrupt, disarming way.

"Oh, whoa back. I'm still learning. Remember? I'm the new kid in town. Give me some time."

"This is the time to start," said Warren.

NINETEEN

Johnnie Gordon

By spring Charlie often went into the kitchen when the supper dishes were finished and the others were in the bunkhouse playing cards. He enjoyed drinking coffee and talking with Warren. One rainy evening he was feeling particularly blue because he missed Etta and the children terribly. He wished there were some way they could live near him. He felt as miserable as the weather looked and took his time stirring the cream and sugar into his coffee. "Hope my wife and kids are all right. This rain could have them flooded out, and I'd never know about it for a couple of days." Charlie looked anxiously at Warren.

"Reminds me of that blizzard in January. The darn thing kept us storm-stayed three days. Remember how we worried about the dumb calves in the meadow?" Warren smiled. He drank his hot, steaming coffee gingerly, blowing before sipping.

"How could I forget? I couldn't see ten feet ahead when I went to the meadow. Those calves were calm as all get out, chomping on the hay we'd spread for them down in a little snow-filled gully. Above their heads the snow was blown about by a sixty-mile-an-hour gale. Out of the gully the cold cut like a thousand knives. Not even the toughest bronc could face that wind for long. I had to face away even with a wool scarf over my face and hunch over like an old man to walk. But those calves were safe."

Warren put down his coffee cup. "How'd your father come through the storm? Did he lose any animals?"

"Pa didn't lose any cows. His herd's small and he kept a stack of hay for them under a cutbank that protected the herd from the wind. Then, too, his cows are Shorthorns and skinny. They take the cold and wind better than some others."

Warren lifted his cup and looked across the steaming liquid to Charlie. "So—I'd guess your wife is doing just fine during this rainy season. Your father will look after things. We always have a bad rainy spell every spring. Then the weather can get cold again —maybe for two or three days and snow. That's the worst. Wet, heavy spring snow can take a herd down to nothing if they're caught in it. I heard Johnnie Gordon, a Scotchman with the broad *a* dialect, lives north on Horse Creek, right next to your pa's Y6, had bad luck with the January blizzard."

"I remember him," said Charlie. "Asked him if he needed someone to help get his hay in. Gordon said, 'Aye, be brief, I have a living to make. I have not a cent for you to take.' I chuckled over his manner of speech all the way to Cheyenne. That was the same day you hired me. He's not the only one who had bad luck. I heard the Two Bar had calves caught in wire fences. The calves stood against the fence and didn't move. Froze to death. They fell, making mounds of cattle. There was nothing visible but a couple heads when the snow drifted over them. Must have been a mess to get rid of those stinking carcasses when the snow melted," said Charlie, holding his cup for more coffee.

"Smelt stronger than a wolf den when everything thawed. That's one reason I don't like barbed-wire fences. Even Gordon feels the same. He said, 'Barbed wire has its abuses and its uses.' Now, here's an enigma. One day those rotten carcasses smell so powerful, you can't get on the lee side. Then the very next day they've mostly disappeared. Probably wolves, other scavengers, like crows and buzzards. Just when you think you can't stand the mess, it's almost gone. That reminds me of something Gordon said the last time I saw him. He seems to have changed his mind about hiring help. He wanted to know if I could recommend a good hired hand for him. He's in dire need of a foreman. He wants to take down his fence and put up some trees in his meadow before next spring storm hits." Warren watched Charlie's face. "You want to work for Gordon? He's our Wyoming poet and chief storyteller. You and your family could be together." Warren smiled as Charlie seemed to relax. Warren laced his hands behind his head and cracked his knuckles. "Gordon also needs a cook. There's a ranch house. You and your family could live there."

Charlie smiled back. He got up and looked out the window. The rain seemed to be easing up. He felt suddenly cheerful. "Thanks a lot! I'll sure miss you though, Senator. Let's keep in touch."

The two men shook hands. Warren was immediately sorry he'd told Charlie about the foreman's job at Gordon's L5 ranch. He'd lose one of the best men he'd ever had. In his heart he'd known Charlie wouldn't stay with him forever. Charlie was quick to learn, easy to get along with, patient with men and animals, and could do the work of two men.

Charlie was sorry to leave his good friend, but he also knew he'd not stay on the Warren Lodgepole Ranch forever. Next morning he tied his gear onto the back of his saddle and rode home to tell Etta the good news. On the way he stopped at the L5 on Horse Creek to look at the ranch house, where he and his family would be staying.

The house sat firmly on a foundation of wide logs. Its sides were unpainted, weathered silver-gray logs, chinked with white plaster. The roof was gray shingles, steep to ward off snow. Built against the east wall, sheltered from the winds was a shed, more like an enclosed lean-to. Charlie supposed dry wood could be stored in there and venison could be hung and cured, frozen in winter so thin slices could be cut off to fry with breakfast biscuits.

What a delicious sizzling a beefsteak can make on a hot stove! Charlie's mouth watered. When the weather is steely cold and the morning's sun is just a faint orange glow in the east, inside there's warmth and Etta looking after the first meal. Reluctantly he pulled away from his daydreaming and knocked on the open door of the shed. There was no answer, so he went inside the shed and knocked on the back door. It was instantly opened by a wiry man of medium height. His hair was yellow-white and reached to his collar. He had long sideburns that partially covered his ears like muffs. The rest of his face was clean-shaven. "Ah, Mr. Charles Irwin. I've been looking for you ever since I told Francis Warren I need a foreman. You come to work for me, I'll see you get a fair fee."

Charlie could not help himself. He laughed softly. "Yes, I'll take your job. I understand you want a fence removed and trees put in right away and you want a cook. I'll do the trees, my wife will cook."

The men shook hands. Charlie said he'd be back first thing in the morning to begin.

Gordon said, "You'll occupy this house. I'll move to the bunkhouse. I fired four cowboys, couldn't stand their noise. Lost most of my cattle. They were winter killed. All that's left is a pile of hides." Gordon's mouth turned down, and Charlie thought he saw a tear in the corner of the clear blue eyes.

When he left the L5, Charlie noticed the large square box in the creek. He looked inside and saw himself in miniature against a background of deep blue. There was a bucket and dipper tied to the box. It was an ingenious way to dam up the creek into a well of ready water. Along the south part of the yard was the bunkhouse and privy. Charlie noticed a dip in the land beyond and thought it would be ideal for a barn or other sheds and a corral in the center.

Etta was washing clothes in front of the stove. She used a round zinc tub and washboard and homemade lye soap. The tub was perched on a wide board laid between two wooden chairs. At her feet was another tub containing cold rinse water, already full of soaped, scrubbed, and wrung clothes.

Charlie burst into the door, shouting, "We're together! No more separations!" He hugged Etta, feeling her wet hands warm and sudsy on the back of his neck. He lifted her off her feet and swung her around.

"I wish someone had done this to me when I was a kid," she squealed. "What will the children think if they see us?"

"My dear, they'll think I should swing them around next." He put her down and told her the news. "I'm not going to miss the best of life anymore—you and the kids."

Joe had seen his son come up the lane. He left his wood chopping, gathered up the three children, who were feeding the chickens or chasing them to see if they would fly. "Come, your pa's home. Let's see what he has to say."

The two little girls, now two and four years old, climbed into Charlie's lap. Floyd, six years old, dragged a clothesline rope behind him and began to roll it up. "Pa, I put a loop around the rooster today," he said proudly.

"Did I ever tell you what my grandma Rachel did to me for lassoing one of her best laying hens? It's best you practice on bushes and stumps. I'll set up a couple fence posts for that purpose when we get to the L5." Charlie's eyes danced.

"Pa, stumps don't move," said Floyd. "I'm ready for roping moving objects."

"I think I saw some cats around Mr. Gordon's bunkhouse," said Charlie. "Now, get your clothes in a pile so we can pack them in the wagon."

"What about Grandpa Joe?" asked Joella.

"Oh, don't worry about me, child. The L5's not more than four miles from the southwest corner of the Y6. Besides, I have news of my own. Will is bringing his family out as soon as he can find a buyer for his dairy herd."

"Margaret didn't write a word to me!" cried Etta. "I've been writing to her ever since we got here."

"It paid off," said Joe. "Will thinks cattle grow fatter and faster here than anywhere on earth. You accomplished what you set out to do—convince them to join us. They're acoming!"

Etta bit her tongue. Joe was right. Actually, it would be good to have Margaret here. Her face lighted up. "Everybody has good news. I have some news myself. If I don't say anything you'll find out soon enough." Suddenly she became shy and thought maybe she should have waited to tell Charlie when they were alone.

Joe saw her face turn pink and her eyes drop. "Honey, you tell Charlie. I already figured it out when you didn't run fast as an antelope after this here grandson of mine. Write to Ell, so's she can come when it's time." Joe cleared his throat and punched Charlie's upper arm. "Musta been some Christmas Eve you spent here. Nice Christmas present you left," he whispered.

"Pa!" said Charlie, himself turning red. Then he turned to Etta, who was smiling. "When?"

"Early October. I'm about three months gone."

"And you're emptying those tubs by yourself?" He was looking at the washtubs of water.

"Oh, I dip the water out with a bucket like I always do until there's only a little in the bottom before I take the tub outside to dump." Now Etta laughed and looked up. Her laughter sounded like the rippling of the creek behind the ranch house on the L5, bubbly and clear.

Charlie helped Etta rinse, wring, and hang the remaining clothes. He emptied the tubs and set them up against the back of the house.

"I get the wash done twice as fast this way. You're going to be a big help from now on," said Etta.

"Oh, no, just for a few months," Charlie teased.

Etta could not believe the room there was in the two-bedroom cabin Mr. Gordon had built. She especially liked the hot-water reservoir at the back of the kitchen range. There was a heater in the sitting room and doors hung on the openings to the bedrooms, which could be closed off in winter. There was a front door, which was hardly ever used. Outside the front door Etta planted blue-flowering morning glories and forget-me-nots. Gordon said they reminded him of the heather in the old country.

Charlie and Gordon dug cottonwoods from the banks of Horse Creek and planted them on the northeast side of the meadow. The meadow was filled with yellow, red, and lavender wildflowers. Looking at it from a little rise of earth behind the privy, it looked like a patchwork quilt. Gordon's handful of skinny cows would soon grow fat munching this mixture of grasses and green shoots and multicolored flowers.

The final snowstorm in April was a deluge of wet flakes covering everything with a six- to eight-inch blanket quickly. Charlie spread hay on top of the snow for the cattle that stood close to the six-foot-high, freshly planted boxwoods and cottonwoods. "The more hay the fewer hides," said Gordon. While the snow melted into the ground, Charlie and Mr. Gordon went over the L5's books. Charlie was determined to put the ranch in the black as soon as possible. He liked this honest, well-educated, gallant man.

"I expect much and get little," said Gordon. "Maybe if I expect little, I'll get a great deal."

Charlie suggested that they raise Herefords instead of Shorthorns. "I've noticed that the Shorthorns develop tuberculosis easily. It may be some delicacy in their inheritance. Anyway, no use accumulating a lot of veterinary bills." Charlie asked Mr. Gordon to run his few cattle with those of the Y6 so they could be worked as one herd until roundup time, or time to brand or time to sell to packing houses. "Running with Pa's herd may increase yours and his more rapidly. I'm going to have to figure some way of building up your cattle herd. It takes money to buy calves," said Charlie with a sigh, "and your barrel's empty. We gotta close the spigot."

Gordon's blue eyes brightened. "C.B., you go to the upcoming meeting of the Wyoming Stock Growers' Association as my representative. Aye, Senator Warren will be there and some others you might or should know. Though times be bad, this man will thrive, for he has the will to strive."

Charlie had no idea what he was getting into when he went to the meeting in Cheyenne's opera house. The men were seated on wooden folding chairs in the basement banquet room, which was a large rectangular box painted white inside. Charlie first looked at the large, framed pictures on the four walls. They were oils done by contemporary artists, some garish with color, others subdued, a scene along the Chugwater, elk in the canyon of the North Platte, a cattle roundup near Medicine Bow, and snow on the Laramie Peaks. The stockgrowers had no prepared talks. Anyone could get up and say what was on his mind. There were not only cattlemen present, but railroaders, packers, National Forest rangers, and a couple sheep growers, who pretty much kept to themselves.

Charlie could tell from the talks that the railroaders were courting the stockmen's business, hoping for a marriage between ranchers and the freight business.

When Judge Joseph M. Carey, with white sideburns and a white beard, blue eyes, and a nearly bald head, stood up, the whispering stopped. He spoke of preserving the range, especially from overgrazing by both cattle and sheep. He had a fair grasp of how the cattlemen hated the sheep grazing on cattle pastures. He was fluent and was not intimidated nor stampeded by questions from cowboys and ranchers.

Another man got up, adjusted his silver-framed spectacles, and spoke about mavericks, the stray, unbranded animal.

This law that mavericks were the property of the state was new to Charlie. He sat up and listened intently to the rest of the talks.

After the meeting he found Senator Warren talking with Richardson from the Union Pacific. Most of the other participants, a colorful variety of people, ranchers, cowboys, railroad men, the governor of Colorado, meat packers from Chicago and Omaha, feed station and stockyard managers, and men hunting jobs, went across the street to Hank Murphy's Saloon.

Warren was talking about the upcoming meeting of the newly formed Consolidated Cattle Growers' Association, which was to be in St. Louis. "I intend to go and will keep you gentlemen informed of anything new." He also said that he'd heard one of the large ranchers in Montana, Conrad Kohrs, had to dispose of fifty or sixty head of cattle because of turberculosis.

"I been watching the Herefords on Gordon's ranch. The ones that made it through the winter seem like tough, rugged animals. I've advised Gordon to breed them with the few Shorthorns my pa has," said Charlie.

"I'm going to try the same thing," said Warren. "Might eradicate tuberculosis altogether. See, you know as much about cattle as any of us."

"I want to know who is handling the meeting in St. Louis. The Union Pacific was asked, but turned the honor down," said Richardson.

"Oh, some commission firm, Hunter, Evans, and Company. They work for the meat packers," said Warren. "Notice of the meeting came from them."

At the beginning of summer Charlie ran into Senator Warren again. He was buying supplies in Cheyenne. He asked the senator how much the state wanted for mavericks and how the money should be paid.

"As I understand the law, it is clear that the money should be sent to Governor Richards, who then distributes it throughout the state for the benefit of cattlemen. You have some mavericks, C.B.?"

"Well, there are some listed on Johnnie Gordon's books. We ran across some two-year-old steers, unmarked, in the Coad draw, brought them back to Gordon's place. I talked to Mark Coad about them, and together we decided to let Gordon have them, because his winter losses were greatest. I want to know who to pay for those nine steers."

"Have you got the L5 brand on them?" asked Warren.

"Yup, did that after talking with Coad."

"Fine, you've done right for that old poet. The law has to do with roundups. A foreman is supposed to sell all the mavericks to the highest bidder. In your case, no one bid, except Gordon, and he set no price. The bidder puts his brand and/or ear slit on the cattle. Now, if you sent a check to Governor Richards for maverick steers, he'd be so shocked he'd believe you were plumb weak north of your ears—so would I."

They walked across the street and stood under the red and white striped awning shading the window at the Tivoli. Charlie wanted to ask Warren about the meeting in St. Louis, but Warren spoke first. "Let's go in and have a cup of coffee. I want to tell you about the St. Louis meeting."

The Tivoli was a bar and restaurant where organ music was

played most afternoons at four. There were ladies sipping tea at several of the tables.

"Counting numbers of people, that meeting in St. Louis was huge; counting its success, depends on where you come from. Let me explain," said Warren.

"C.B., these Texas cattle aren't ready for the rich pastures of Wyoming or Montana; they have to come up the trail and gradually get used to them. Besides, many have tick fever. I was so disgusted. Those southern ranchers believe in the motto, let the buyer beware. Those men had the audacity to hold up banners during the meetings and pass out paper fliers—all containing one word: *Trail*," said Warren.

"So, they're serious about cutting a wide track from top to bottom of our country? Leaving a scar on the belly of Mother Earth, my friend Red Cloud would say." Charlie felt scorn rise and constrict his throat. He pushed back a lock of sandy-brown hair. "They'll destroy pastures and watering holes. Northerners'll carry shotguns!"

"The Texas cowboys looked for a fight. The northerners said they'd put up fences, charge for crossing their ranchlands and using their watering holes. We held caucuses, argued for a day and a half, until the Texans backed away from the conflagration of our fiery words. Then the southerners turned right around and proudly pointed out that they voted for William Jennings Bryan because he was against cutting a canal through the Isthmus of Panama. They thought that would make us feel better. Can't they see the two cuts are entirely different? That's an example of pure woolly-headed thinking. It turned my stomach."

"Our vice-president, Teddy Roosevelt, lived on a ranch in Dakota Territory. Don't Texans know that? Every cattleman I know is a Republican. Jeems, haven't Texans heard of conservation?" said Charlie.

"They're overstocked. Waste is a way of life," said Warren.

"I hope a wide cattle trail comes to nothing. In another year the Texans will ship stock by rail and vote Republican. It's the only way to go. I wouldn't go on another trail drive—not for all the Shorthorns in Texas!" said Charlie.

Both men laughed heartily.

By the end of July, Will and Margaret, their two children, and their household goods had come by rail to Denver, then north to Cheyenne. They were enthusiastically welcomed by the Irwins. Their baggage and belongings were deposited at the Y6, but everyone stopped at the L5, where Etta had prepared a huge ranch dinner. Joe came in just as Charlie was introducing Johnnie Gordon and the hired hands to his brother and sister-in-law. No one was more surprised than Charlie to see his brother Frank standing with Joe. Frank looked wonderful. "I heard Will was coming here. I wanted to welcome him," Frank said.

Etta seated everyone around the large dining table, which was lighted with lanterns hung from the walls. The children were seated in the kitchen, with Floyd at the head of the small table to look after the smaller children.

There was beefsteak, slabs of baked salmon (from a can), mashed potatoes and milk gravy, wilted lettuce with vinegar and oil, baking powder biscuits and fresh butter, apple pie and coffee for dessert. Everyone spoke and laughed at the same time. The men talked about irrigation. "A little water and the hand of industry moves," said Gordon. Next they discussed the settlers who were moving in close to the ranches. One of the cowboys said, "Settlers are handy with the rope and carry a lightweight branding iron inside their boot. Mavericks will be a thing of the past, same as dinosaurs." Margaret and Etta talked below the men's deep voices and carried on talk about their children.

After dinner the men went to the sitting room. The children were allowed to go outside and play with the kittens. Margaret and Etta cleared the table and washed and dried and stacked the dishes and scrubbed the pots and pans. The dishwater was thrown out the back door on the morning glory vines. The children were called inside while the men went out to look around and get Will somewhat acquainted with ranching in Wyoming. Johnnie Gordon was delighted to show off his new barn and horses and cattle in the near pasture. Frank talked about the settlers who were bringing sheep into cattle country. He was all in favor of sending the herders farther north, into Canada. "Sheep graze the grass so short there's nothing left. Besides, where sheep have been, cattle won't feed, 'cuz they hate the smell of wool and sheep turds."

Charlie told about all the wild turkeys he'd seen on the corral railing early in the morning. The big birds came in to feed on grain that'd fallen from the horses' mouth bags the day before.

Charlie thought Will had become a hail-fellow-well-met, with a breezy nature. He seemed to be an optimist, coated with a humorous varnish, with a twinkle in his eye so that one never knew if he was putting a story over or not.

Will said, "I sold my three dozen black and white Holstein milk cows for forty dollars apiece, and with what I'd saved from working the coal mines, I come here pretty well-heeled. I've got my eye on buying a hundred and fifty Herefords, yearlings, as soon as possible."

Gordon told him to be sure to feed them plenty of hay during the winter. "The more hay, the fewer hides," he repeated to Will. "Better to sell live cattle than the hide. Winters make or break a man here."

With a straight face Will said, "I bucked a couple big snows while mining the Timberline. Once after a chinook the boss sent me to Colorado Springs for supplies. I loaded my packhorse with a dozen quarts of whiskey and a big gunnysack full of bread. When he saw that load, the boss was really disgusted and he yelled, 'How in tarnation we gonna use up all that durned bread?'"

Before dark Charlie hitched two horses to the spring wagon and took his father, Will, Margaret, and little Gladys and Charles to the Y6. Joe had cleaned the ranch house and fixed the loft for the children. They were delighted to sleep *upstairs* with their Grandpa Joe. Will and Margaret shared the big bed built against the wall, with leather lacings stretched tight across the bottom. Will dreamed of a great herd of white-faced cattle getting fat and sleek on the rich Wyoming grasses. Margaret had visions of riding horseback, visiting with Etta, and learning to sew.

Long after the cowboys had gone to the bunkhouse and Etta and the children had gone to bed, Charlie, Frank, and Johnnie Gordon were up exchanging yarns, telling their thoughts about the Wyoming cowboys.

"The boys I work with on Coble's Iron Mountain Ranch are a devil-may-care lot," said Frank, "roystering, gambling, revolver-heeled, brazen, light-fingered, with a touch of bravado that's really appealing. But there's one who's almost shy. That loner, Tom Horn, is at the IM. Remember when—"

"I know what you mean," interrupted Gordon. "In a herd cowpunchers are mean, but individually they are good workers, genuinely sincere. To know some is an inspiration, to trade with some is an education. If you let any one of them bluff you, your discipline is shot to hell. And those boys move from one outfit to another, free as the wind. Theirs is a kind of nomadic life on the plains."

"Well, I've found that the foreman cannot ever be wrong. That's why everyone wants to be foreman," said Charlie. "That fellow, Horn, he doesn't want to be foreman?"

"No, no," said Frank.

"If a foreman doesn't make money for his employer, his services drop rapidly in value," Charlie went on. "Same as being mayor of a town. You gotta keep the town solvent."

Gordon said he couldn't agree more. It was well after sunup the next day when Frank saddled up and rode off toward Cheyenne and then across the Pole Mountain Road to the IM ranch, where he worked as hard as any other cowboy. He was a born horseback rider. His legs fit the saddle so he had complete control of his horse. As he rode out across the prairie he hummed "Git Along, Little Dogies."

Johnnie Gordon was pleased to have Etta and the children living in his ranch house. He liked to take six-year-old Floyd to the corral when the cowboys were breaking in a new bronc. One morning he told Etta that there were two broncs being broken. "C.B. found one horse down by the wide place in Horse Creek. The other horse must have come back to the drinking hole hoping to find his friend. C.B. got the second horse this morning. They're in the corral together. I have more horses on this ranch than I've bought outright. C.B. and you, ma'am, have brought life back to this place. I'll sell those horses and buy Herefords."

"Oh, Mr. Gordon, let Charlie sell them for you. He can sell duck-down jackets to Mexican cowboys in the middle of a heat wave," said Etta. Her laughter bubbled up to match the rippling of the creek.

Gordon nodded, knowing that Charlie could get better quality and three or four more cows for the strong, beautiful horses than he. Charlie was a master at bargaining. "Let your son come to the corral. He'd enjoy seeing two broncs tamed."

Etta agreed. She and four-year-old Joella and two-year-old Pauline would pick the wild currants she'd seen on the bank of Horse Creek behind the house. The men would enjoy currant jelly on their biscuits.

"Don't let Floyd get in the way. Watch him with his rope. You know he pulled Tom, the cat, out of the cottonwood yesterday. The dog chased Tom up the tree and Floyd chased the dog," called Etta.

Right away Floyd surprised Gordon and the two cowboys by climbing on the back of someone's horse from his high perch on the corral railing to ride around the outside. The boy hung on to the horse's mane and waved with his other hand. A wide grin spread across his tanned face.

"That kid is something," said one of the cowboys.

"He'll be a top-notch rider one day for sure," said the other cowboy.

"I can see it now, a big poster reading FLOYD IRWIN, BOY BRONC RIDER! at the Cheyenne Frontier Days," said the first cowboy, wiping his face on his red bandanna.

Gordon yelled, "Ki-yi-yippy! Ki-yi-yippy-yea!"

Floyd smiled broadly with all the attention. He swung his rope while riding the horse and caught the corral gate post. Gordon sucked in his breath. He thought the boy was going to be pulled from the horse. He wasn't; the horse stopped just in time. Gordon ran and pulled the boy off. "Go back to the house, where you'll be safe, and stay until we get these horses broke. My God, it's a wonder you weren't bucked off or pulled off with your own rope." He sat the boy on the ground and gave him a gentle shove toward the house. "Your father would never forgive me if something happened to you on one of those horses. Don't put your rope around the neck of any of the laying hens either, you hear me, buddy? Your mother'd scalp me for that." Floyd turned and waved as he trudged to the house. He wore boots and Levi's, same as the men. As he got close to the house, he swung his rope around his head and let it land over the head and front paws of the sleeping dog. The dog began to yip and bark loudly. It danced here and there trying to get the rope off. Floyd laughed, tripped, and the dog ran away with the rope trailing behind. Luckily Etta had come from behind the house to investigate the commotion.

"Son, get that rope off the dog. It could choke if the rope ever caught on something. Bring the rope to me. I'll put it up so the animals will be safe for one day at least."

Floyd stomped inside, growling to himself. "Now I suppose I gotta work my numbers?"

"That's right—school time for you and no berry-picking time for me," said Etta.

At the end of August all ranch work came to a halt. It was time for the annual Frontier Days celebration between Tuesday, August 28, and Saturday, September 1. Charlie volunteered to be on the entertainment committee along with Warren Richardson. He was in town every day for a week prior to the festivities. By Tuesday the city of Cheyenne was crowded, and still people poured in on every incoming train and stage. The first excursion train from Denver came in Tuesday morning, met by a large throng and a band. Other bands were stationed at street corners giving concerts. Many settlers came in to spend the morning buying supplies and the afternoon going to the fake shows. The favorite was Bosco the Snake Eater. Cowboys and ranch people also seemed to take a morbid interest in Bosco's handling of the snakes and taking one in his mouth to eat every once in a while.

Charlie stayed in town at the Industrial Club with Johnnie Gordon. Etta and the children came to town for the sights in a wagon with Joe, Will and Margaret, and their two youngsters. The children were wide-eyed seeing vendors up and down the street with brightly decorated canes, tin horns, megaphones, balloons, badges, and flags. The adults were surprised at how quickly these items were sold out.

Blind beggars and other mendicants were plying for money here and there throughout the crowds. Restaurants were packed to the hilt. Etta and Margaret were glad they'd brought picnic baskets, because both overheard visitors say they had been in the city all morning and could not find a place to obtain a meal. The saloons and gambling houses also had long lines of people waiting outside for their turns to get inside.

By eleven o'clock Joe and Will led their group to the shuttle so that they would have a good seat to see the afternoon's events. A streetcar packed to the doors left the Cheyenne depot at 12:15 p.m. for Pioneer Park. When it arrived at the park, the grandstand was already half-full and the bleachers were filling fast. The Irwins had tickets in the grandstand. Sitting high, they could see the roads leading to the park dotted with people, on horseback, on wheels, or on foot. Clouds of choking dust were raised by all the travel, and those on the roads came into the park with their clothes all the same color, alkali gray. The streetcars were run every fifteen minutes by courtesy of the Union Pacific until the last event was staged.

The sports were to start at two o'clock. Owing to the difficulty of getting some judges and officials to the Frontier show on time, the first sport was delayed for about half an hour. Floyd, Joella, and Gladys yelled along with some of the impatient spectators, "You'll have to hurry!" Joe stamped his feet and joined the children's cries. Etta and Margaret tried to hush them.

The first event was the cow-pony race for a half-mile. The purse was sixty dollars to be divided, first place, forty-five dollars, second place, nine dollars, and third place, six dollars. All of the entries were required to carry a hundred and eighty pounds or more. C. E. Thornburg riding Charles Hirsig's horse, Bumskie, won.

Next was the running half-mile, free-for-all, catch weights, with a similar purse. The horses would not line up properly at first. After half a dozen false starts, the horses were allowed to go over seventy-five yards of track. Bob Hilton won on Hirsig's Johnnie J.

The cow ponies ridden by ladies attracted more attention and enthusiasm than any other event besides the wild-horse riding. The distance was half a mile and the purse was twenty-five dollars for first place, fifteen for second, and ten for third. All of the ladies wore divided skirts, and several were rigged up in typical cowgirl style with bandannas around their necks and wide-brimmed hats on their heads. When the horses began racing, the people in the grandstand and bleachers rose as one in their excitement. Etta and Margaret yelled as the ladies rode in reckless fashion and kept everyone breathless by the chances they took.

"Oh, I'd like to wear one of those getups and ride a cow pony like that!" yelled Margaret. "You think I could do it?"

"Of course you can," said Etta. "Look on the program—one of the riders is a Mrs. B. Michaels, and another Mrs. Clara McGhee."

"I mean do you think Will would permit it?" said Margaret.

"Ask him," said Etta.

"I don't care what you do. If you want to do something, go ahead," said Will, not really paying attention to his wife's request, but watching two ladies' horses come down the stretch neck and neck. Fourteen-year-old Jennie Pawson's horse won by a nose. The ovation was thunderous as the good-looking, lithe girl rode to the judges' stand.

The two-mile relay race was interesting to everyone. Each cowboy rider was provided with four horses and rode half a mile on each. At the end of each heat he dismounted, changed his saddle to the next horse, mounted, and rode the next half. There were three entries: Frank Irwin, using horses jointly owned by himself and his brother, Charlie; C. E. Thornburg, using Charles Hirsig's horses; and S. Shirley, riding horses provided by the Richardson brothers.

To the embarrassment of Etta, Floyd stood up and yelled, "Hello there, Uncle Frank!"

Frank waved toward the grandstand. Floyd beamed and waved back. People around Floyd hissed, "Sit down, young fella, so we can see." Etta quickly pulled him down and gave him a fierce scowl.

The three bunches of horses were stationed at intervals of one hundred yards along the track to avoid confusion in changing saddles. In the first heat Frank came under the wire first, but almost lost his head to C. E. Thornburg, who was much quicker at changing saddles. In the second and third heats Frank came in first, and he won the fourth half by fifty yards. Joe clapped harder and longer than everyone around him, saying, "That cowboy's my youngest son!"

When the wild-horse race was called, the crowd had a real sample of wild life in the woolly West. The animals for the contest were provided mostly by the entrants. None of the horses were familiar to the feel of a rope with a cowboy on the other end of it. The distance of the race was half a mile, no hobbling or tying-down of stirrups was allowed. Each rider was given one assistant to help him saddle and bridle his animal. The purse of one hundred dollars was divided into three moneys. The fun began when the first horse was taken from the corral and continued until after the winner of the race had been across the line for some time. Eight riders and eight horses were taken with some difficulty before the judges' stand with saddles and bridles lying on the ground beside them. At the signal the men laid on the leather.

"There's Uncle Charlie!" squealed little Gladys. All eyes turned to Charlie, who was in the middle of the track in front of the grandstand in a grand melee of flying heels and heads, pitching, rearing, biting, kicking horses, and dodging men. The first man to mount, Otto Plaga, was up in less than a minute. His horse gave an exhibition of the real thing in cussedness. Plaga's belt caught on the pommel of the saddle, causing him to be thrown, but he quickly remounted, and soon after his horse settled down to run. The other riders had their share of trouble. The mounts persisted in bucking all the way around the half-mile. Charlie's horse insisted on turning and coming back to the grandstand to give another show of fancy pitching before bucking him to the ground. Cowboy clowns diverted the wild horse so Charlie could hobble to safety. One of the horses could not be saddled at all and finally broke the rope that held it and escaped. The horse was pursued by a crowd of whooping cowboys. Jack Dolan, from Pine Bluffs, won the race; Otta Plaga, from Sybille, came in second; and W. H. LaPash, from Cheyenne, was third.

The program of sports was closed that evening by a realistic imitation of a frontier stagecoach held up by Indians and rescued by the cavalry. This show had been Charlie's idea. Six government mules from Fort Russell were hitched to a cumbersome old

Deadwood coach. A big load of pioneers, who were actually cowboys and cowgirls, completed the equipment. The Indians carried out their part of the holdup in dead earnest. The cavalry had some difficulty in persuading them that a good thing could be carried too far.

As soon as possible after the holdup the crowds came back to Cheyenne for their supper and the open-air ball or the French ball.

Etta was too tired to stay, so she, Charlie, and Joe took all five children back to the wagons to sleep. Will and Margaret stayed for the open-air ball. A large canvas enclosure had been erected that was crowded to capacity by eight-thirty that evening. At that time a vaudeville performance was given, and when it was over the dancing continued until midnight. The weather was excellent for open-air entertainment.

Next afternoon at the Pioneer Park there was Indian foot racing, then Indian horse racing, and bronco riding.

Today Frank was ready to ride John Coble's wild bronco, Steamboat. The horse did not squeal or neigh like other horses, but roared with a loud honking, similar to the low, growling hoots of a steamboat in foggy waters. The horse was pulled in wild on the 1901 spring roundup. It was jet-black with two rear and one front white stocking feet. The fourth foot was coal black. Some cowboys believed that the horse was somehow injured during the gelding process so that his voice was ever after low and hoarse. Others said it was because he was injured when someone tried to pull him with a rope around his neck. Actually he was brought in from the Laramie Mountains by Frank Foss. Foss branded and castrated Steamboat and in doing so let the horse strike its head against the side of a large rock half out of the ground in the corral, breaking a bone in its nose. Foss saw the bone poking out and told Sam Moore to trim the bone. Moore tapped the protruding bone with a fingernail, then, with a pair of snippers usually used on barbed wire, he trimmed the bone so that it was flush with the horse's nostril. "All is well," Moore said. But all was not well. The horse had a strange, loud whistle as it breathed. Jimmy Danks said it sounded like a steamboat. So that became its name.

Steamboat was one of those horses that could never be broken; he was always a bucking bronco. He was destined to become a legend—more famous than most of the men that rode him. The wild and nervous horse was led out into the arena and walked to the front of the grandstand. The crowd roared and whistled as it sensed the power this horse would show in his jumps. Steamboat was blindfolded and seemed to quiet down some. He stood with his feet spread wide as the saddle was put over his back and seemed to squat slightly when the cinch was tightened. Charlie eared down the horse, by holding his head down and pulling on his ears, so that Frank could get in the saddle. Will talked gently to the twitching horse, and when he saw Frank was firmly saddled he nodded to Charlie, who let go the ears and whipped off the blindfold. The two brothers jumped back to the arena railing as Steamboat exploded into long crooked jumps. The crowd gasped as he sunfished and seemed to turn in midair. Suddenly Frank lurched too far to the right. His foot held in the stirrup only a fraction of a second, but long enough to send his body swinging like a pendulum under Steamboat's body. The crowd gasped.

Frank automatically stiffened his body and passed smoothly underneath the horse, but he was kicked by flying hooves before he cleared. This was the single event that established Steamboat's ongoing reputation as a wild bronc. Frank held his head afterward and complained of a headache for a week. Charlie wanted more than anything else to own the wild bronc from the first moment he'd heard its terrifying, wheezing whistle. He'd seen Danks trying to break it. The horse was stubborn and when Danks thought it was halter broke and took it out of the corral to a nearby flat, he found it was a bucker. Steamboat had a special way of throwing himself around with a twist, forelegs going south, hindlegs going north. Danks never could stay on his back. He told Coble, "I can't teach that gol-darned horse a blamed thing."

Coble told him to turn the horse out, as there was no time to fool with a damn bucking horse. Coble wanted to give the horse to the Elks Lodge in Cheyenne. He thought it might be used as a "goat" in their initiation rites or keep the grass around their hall cropped close to the ground. The lodge never took the horse after several members saw it buck Frank off its back to its belly, then the hard ground. Charlie had never been sorry that he later bought Steamboat from Coble.

In the next event Duncan Clark did some fine work in the fancy cattle roping and won a one-hundred-dollar purse. Charlie watched this event carefully. He felt he could give Clark some competition and promised himself he'd enter the steer-roping contest the next year or so.

Charlie recognized the cowboy, Tom Horn, by his mustache and cool, gray eyes. Horn had a group of bronco busters and fancy cattle ropers with him from the IM Ranch. Horn's group won first honors in their riding and roping contests.

Charlie went over and shook hands with Horn. He was in a good mood and said he certainly did remember Charlie. He also said he'd seen Frank, who worked with the same outfit as he, the IM.

"I've never ridden in a roundup with your kid brother, but I understand he's a decent cowpuncher, if he ain't crying about the food, thin blankets in the bunkhouse, and no advance pay. I'll tell you one thing. He sure has guts when he's riding that black outlaw pony called Steamboat. I admired that show!" said Horn. Then he talked Charlie into entering the very next event. A novel contest that Charlie admitted he set up himself. It was called the Rough Riding contest in which men acted as horses. Each man bore upon his back a rider and tried to dislodge his burden. Charlie was one of the horses and Leonard Lynch was his rider. Duncan Clark was a horse with DeWitt Irving as his rider. There were three other horses and riders.

Charlie and his rider, Lynch, won this contest. Charlie did well as the "horse," giving the best stunts, giving out a bunch of high and lofty bucks, a snaky, weaving motion. Lynch did well as the rider, looking like he was lost overboard in a choppy sea. But he hung on like a government postage stamp. He wore a pink shirt and pair of white chaps that were beauties.

Then occurred the most exciting event of that Saturday afternoon. The notorious Pearl Ward and a Denver girl, Buckskin Jimmie, had an altercation over a yellow band around Pearl's hat. "A yellow ribbon brings bad luck to any kind of contest. Not only that, it shows you are chicken-hearted with a yellow streak." There was a fierce fistfight. "Take off that band!" continued Buckskin Jimmie.

"I won't and you can't make me," answered Pearl, who was large, athletic, good-looking, and dressed in bright colors. She swung out with a right fist, then a left on the other's chin. The police interfered and removed the girls amid much cheering and applause. After the ladies' cow-pony race there was a reconciliation and both girls agreed to give an exhibition of fancy riding at the City Park on Sunday afternoon.

A week later at the L5 ranch a couple of the cowboys were training a new cutting horse for the fall roundup. Floyd was back on the top rail, watching. When the training was ended, one of the boys took Floyd in the saddle with him. "Come on, let's you and me see how this horse works, cowboy."

"Yup," said Floyd, "let's see." He put his rope around the saddle horn.

They rode out across the rocky field strewn with green and yellow grass and small yellow cactus flowers growing in clumps. Some cattle were grazing in the open field and some near Horse Creek.

"You see that little white-faced dogie?" asked the cowboy, pointing straight ahead. "We'll get that pretty little heifer away from the herd. Hang on. Here we go!"

Floyd held to the pommel. He watched as the chosen cow dodged and shifted suddenly. The freshly trained horse was ready, as if he knew exactly what the cow was going to do next. His ears worked to and fro, making Floyd laugh. The horse's eyes seemed to flash in the sunlight, and he seemed to be enjoying every minute as much as Floyd. The horse had the cow in the corral in no time. The next cow they worked out was not so easy, and it had no intention of being put into the corral except by ropes. Floyd found that when a cow is determined to duck and twist out of the way, there is little a cutting horse can do with it but run right alongside, turning and spinning as the cow does. The boy gritted his teeth, hung on to the saddle horn, and watched the cow move in a snaky line as it spun. The horse dashed back and forth, kicked up dust on one direction, reared backward, and then fell forward like it was shot from a cannon. Then the horse got behind the cow and rushed it into the enclosure. Floyd relaxed, held up one small hand, and yelled, "Hey—nice going! I'm going to be a steer roper!"

"You bet," said the cowboy, looking played-out himself.

By the first of October, 1901, Ell was at the L5 to help Etta through the delivery of her fourth child. All Ell could talk about was the assassination of President McKinley.

"Why would the president meet his assassin, Leon Czolgosz, in Buffalo, New York?" she asked one evening after supper.

"Why, dinna you understand? That is where the Pan American Exposition was in progress and the president went to see what was there," answered Johnnie Gordon pragmatically, leaning his chair back on two legs one evening after supper. "There is no need to worry. The country has a fine leader in Theodore Roosevelt. This country will have the Panama Canal built and guarantee its neutrality."

"What about those territories we gained from the Spanish-American War? There might be trouble there," said Ell. "Anarchy seems to be a way of life for some these days. I don't want to raise a child during these uncertain times."

Etta gasped in surprise and looked sharply at Ell. "You don't really mean that."

"But I do," said Ell. "There's going to be a war involving more than just little Spanish-speaking countries. The Americans will be involved in a global dispute because of all this unrest by those who wish to dominate. An anarchist doesn't believe in government or laws, but he wants to rule. It's a topsy-turvy mess. It's a convoluted way to reason. I'd like to see an end to it, but I don't." She threw her hands up in the air and let them drop in her lap. "It's no place for a woman of my temperament to raise children." Ell did not raise her eyes to Etta.

"Aye, aye, dear lady, where is your faith? Roosevelt sees all the problems. He'll provide more military training for the United States officers in due course. He's heard severe criticism of the army's performance in that Spanish-American War," said Gordon. "If this country is well prepared there won't be a confrontation; at least if there is, the United States will come out the winner. Dinna wonder why people fear things that are different? They fear ideas, they are suspicious of people that look and behave differently."

Etta cleared the table, washed the dishes, and put the three children to bed. When she came back, Ell, Gordon, and Charlie were still sitting around the table with the kerosene lamp lit in the center. They were talking about men who were different. Gordon was talking in general terms when Etta joined them again.

"Love is perennial, but crime is constant," said the Wyoming poet.

"So that the ranchers are easy prey for theft when their property is scattered all over the county. There are men who are eager to take advantage of low-priced beef and ask no questions about its origin," said Charlie.

"Aye, it's nigh impossible to convict a cattle rustler. Juries are nearly always composed of people who are on the side of the poor settler or underdog as rustlers are sometimes portrayed. We ranchers are villains, even though we may be broke and owing for the cattle we raise."

"Why are ranchers villains? Seems to me you could work together, ranchers and settlers and farmers," said Ell.

"Ranchers came to this area first, and we have something the latecomers want. We have the land they prefer, even though there's plenty still available for homesteading, as C.B. has discovered and is taking advantage of—say, he'll probably have you apply for a quarter section before you return to Colorado. He's smart, you know. He's homesteading in a kind of checkerboard pattern so no one will want those unclaimed sections surrounded by his property, then he can run his cattle over twice as much land," said Gordon, relighting his pipe and laughing and enjoying the pleasant fellowship.

"I never should tell you my plans," chided Charlie, putting a couple chunks of wood in the range to keep the chill off the kitchen as they talked. "If you hear I'm running for mayor of Cheyenne, don't believe it. I've changed my mind."

"Let me tell you about a case that involves me and that fellow, Tom Horn," said Gordon, settling in his chair. "He was hired as a range detective by the Swan Land and Cattle Company—a large consortium, owning several ranches in the area, and all run from corporate headquarters in Edinburgh, Scotland. Horn is different. He's half-Indian and half-French, according to him, and a natural-born sleuth, according to me. He can stalk as quiet as a cat or come out in the open and fight tooth and nail like a man and take the medicine if he loses. He was with General Miles, hunting Apaches, he's run train robbers into the arm of the law, he's a western man, living on the banks of the Rio Grande, deserts of Arizona, prairies of Montana, and now the banks of the Chugwater and Sybille. I don't understand him. He doesn't like living in any kind of house, and a road is useless to him. He can slip into canyons, getting to his destination faster than most by means known only to himself. He has a constitution of iron and the mind of a fox."

Charlie interrupted. "Years ago I lived on the Middle Fork of the Sappa, on a farm, with my folks. One winter a man stopped off at our place with a woman and several kids. The man was Tom Horn. He bought an old horse of ours and took off in the middle of night—one of the coldest nights of the year. I was a curious kid, and as soon as I found he'd gone by himself, I tracked him. I found him holed up in a ravine using the carcass of that old horse to keep from freezing to death. I was astonished."

"That's the same Horn as works for Ora Haley, mainly at the Two Bar and now and again for John Coble at the IM. He knows all the ways of the Apaches. He and Geronimo were thicker than ticks on a hound dog."

Etta set coffee cups on the table and brought in fresh hot coffee and cream and sugar. "He sounds like an interesting character."

"You'll probably hear stories about him yourself. He's a loner, but he also likes to spin tall tales. People love to retell Horn's stories."

"I enjoy listening to your brogue, Mr. Gordon," said Ell huskily.

"Well, this story I'm going to tell isn't short, so there'll be much listening enjoyment," chuckled Gordon, relighting his pipe with a match.

"Jack Madden was a settler who had hauled a wagon load of beef into Laramie every couple of weeks. That Irish chap's stock was two cows and a couple unbranded yearlings he'd lured into his corral. The ranchers knew what he was doing, getting rich butchering someone else's steers. The hides never showed a brand, but they were most often cut strange so as to leave out the mark. He always said that was the way the Irish skinned out an animal, to placate the little people, you know, the elves and such. The sheriff at Laramie said no one could pin a thing on the man unless he could be caught in the act and a brand on a piece of hide could be produced.

"Horn knew that and he also knew that the local juries aren't worth the powder to blow them into perdition." Here Gordon, the gentleman, stopped and nodded toward the ladies.

"I certainly appreciate your high regard for women's sensitivity," said Ell, fluttering her eyelashes.

Gordon beamed and continued. "Last November I was up in the middle of the night, excuse me, can't always hold my water, and I saw Horn riding through my pasture, his Winchester by his side, a blanket behind his saddle. He wore overshoes and an overcoat and carried field glasses. I heard two or three days later that he walked into the office of the Swan and spoke to his boss, Alexander Swan. Nobody had heard him ride up nor walk into that office. Swan, sitting on a chair tipped against the wall, knew that Horn would not spill what was on his mind right off, so he talked about the ranch gossip. A cowboy gossipping can say less but talk longer than any living creature I know. Horn sat against the wall, down on his haunches, and finally he told about his detective work. He'd watched Madden, his wife, and a cowhand, Hugh Dorson, drive a slew of cattle to the Madden pasture. This was no regular roundup, just a gentle nudge up a gully where those cattle were quietly grazing. Since all of the Swan cattle were used to free running, they could be moved easily from one pasture to another where the grass was thick.

"Horn is thorough. He not only watched Madden's pasture,

but he kept an eye on the log shack. Out in the hills there are no curtains on windows and Horn saw that when Madden was doing chores outside, Dorson was inside kissing Mrs. Madden. Each night a cow was cut out from the herd in the pasture and enticed up to the barn door by a pile of fresh hay. The cow was shot, lifted by block and tackle inside the barn. It was butchered and packed into the wagon.

"Alex Swan told Horn to cut his gossip tongue and stay away from drink, but to go to Laramie and find out who was buying Madden's beef. Horn did what he was told, and he also picked up the hide that had been disposed of by Dorson in a little draw behind Madden's place. A horseshoe brand was on the hide. Horn kept the stiff cowhide hidden in the bunkhouse on the IM. After a couple of weeks he added to the hide a dozen patches of hide all with the horseshoe brand. Suddenly one afternoon the boys at one of Swan's ranches noticed that they had another slew of newly weaned calves missing. Horn was told. He took off like a scalded rabbit down the valley past the cottonwood, whose yellow leaves were dropping. He skirted the main road to the Chug. There was no movement of man nor cattle along the Sybille. Horn circled wide around ranch houses and kept his eye peeled for men on horseback or moving cattle herds. He saw nothing, so circled back, finishing the biscuit and bacon rind he carried in his pockets.

"At the Two Bar ranch he unsaddled his horse and took it into the barn. He ate supper, picked up a couple of men, harnessed a team to a wagon, and saddled a couple of horses. The men spread out, rode fifteen miles in two hours. Then, over an embankment they saw a little creek and beyond it was a meadow with a hundred grazing cattle, and there, sheltered by a hill from the southwest winds, was the Madden log shack and barn. Horn took the lead, his Winchester in his right hand. Near the barn he halted and raised his hand for the others to stop. They waited for Horn to go hunched down inside the barn. There was some yelling and a sharp scream and the double doors swung wide open. The boys didn't wait now, they rushed in and found Horn covering Madden with his rifle. Behind Madden was a half-skinned cow, and Madden's wife holding a lantern so that the men could see to butcher."

Etta was wide-eyed with attention. Ell kept her velvet-green eyes on Gordon as though he were the only other person in the room.

Charlie, caught up in this dramatic moment, waved his hands

and said excitedly, "I can just see Horn standing there with his trusty Winchester raised to his shoulder, and the rustler startled, crouching with his bloody knife lowered against the corpse, and his wife, standing like a statue, her dress bloodied and her eyes galvanized in the light of the lamp."

Gordon shook his finger in Charlie's direction. "Aye, but you dinna know the wife wore a yellow rain slicker to protect her dress." Gordon's eyes glistened. "One of the cowboys used his head. He took the lamp and set it outside, far away from the barn. Another tied Madden's hands together behind him. Madden's wife tongue lashed that cowboy with strong, unladylike language until his ears were burned. Horn, with savage stoicism, took the raging woman to the house, which was no more than a poor, one-room log shack. Inside two children lay sleeping on a grimy blanket on the floor. Horn took Madden in the wagon to the Cheyenne sheriff, along with the damning evidence of that bloody, half-skinned cow sporting the horseshoe brand of the Swan outfit.

"Next morning the deputy sheriff went out to the shack and brought Mrs. Madden and the children into Cheyenne for questioning. Then they were released to go back to that dirty, rundown hovel. Madden had to stay in jail to await trial. Of course, he didn't admit he had enough money for his bail. His lawyer took the mortgage on his meager ranch and the effects left in the log house and barn as payment for his fee.

"Hugh Dorson stayed at the Madden place to look after his own interests. Even the severed branch grows again. Life went on. Madden's trial was three months later. I was on the jury."

"I'd bet my last dollar you were jury foreman, Mr. Gordon. Anyone with your intellectual capacity and understanding of people should be," said Ell, licking her lips, ready to say more.

"Sis, you have more wind than a bull going uphill. Let Gordon do the storytelling," said Charlie.

Ell smiled sweetly at Charlie. Then she smiled more sweetly at Gordon. "I can hardly wait to hear the whole story. I love to listen to your voice."

"The case was stretched out over two days and made all the papers. It could have been over in two hours. During the trial the two innocent children held hands and smiled. The judge had more sympathy than justice. Horace was right when he said, 'A jest, a smile, often decides the highest matters better than seriousness.' In his final speech Madden's lawyer said nothing of cattle rustling, only of unculpable children forced by strangers, who could never understand their plight, to attend a trial about matters they could not understand. The lawyer argued that the big ranchers were starving out the little ranchers. He said the big Swan company, in fact, was a foreign company that dared to invade the state of Wyoming. Using that line of reasoning, the lawyer, a pettifogger, reasoned that there could be no crime stealing from foreigners who had no business in the United States anyway. It was all horse sh—horse manure, wet hay. The jury went out late in the afternoon. I can tell you I dinna know what to do. I was sick in my heart. The crime was plain as the brand on the cowhide. The judge went home for supper and about eight in the evening returned.

"I told the other jurors that if they dinna convict, worse things may happen. I told them all ranchers would be losers. As soon as the judge returned I, foreman of the jury, sent word we were ready to report. You know how news spreads? There was a huge crowd inside the courtroom that night to hear the verdict. Our report was that the Maddens were guilty.

"The judge gave Madden a little talk and sentenced him for three years. Mrs. Madden was let off free to raise those two innocent children. Dorson celebrated by going on a three-day drinking spree, which landed him in jail the fourth day."

"What a good story about Wyoming law," said Ell. "I expected a lynching. Honest."

"But that's not the end of my story. The deputy sheriff, an easygoing lad, did not tie the hands of Madden, the prisoner. Remember there was a crowd in the courtroom and a large number of settlers outside in the hall. When the prisoner passed the settlers, an argument broke out between two roughly dressed farmers who acted drunk. The deputy's attention was sidetracked. The prisoner pulled away and went pell-mell down the stairs, out to the main floor. The deputy came to his senses and charged lickety-split after him, but one of the farmers fell in his path so that the deputy went flat on his face. Madden was out on the street, mounted a waiting horse, and rode out of sight.

"A search was started. But no one was prepared to hunt a man at night. Someone tried sending a telegraph message to Chugwater to keep an eye peeled for Madden, but no one answered at the station. Some of the crowd went to Hank Murphy's Saloon to oil their throats and loosen their tongues before they decided how to conduct a search. Horn said something like this to Alex Swan that night: 'Difficulties cause the average man to leave off what he has begun, but a true man does not slacken in carrying out what he has begun. Although obstacles may tower a thousandfold I will succeed in finding the prisoner.' Most of us went home disgusted.

"Next morning the *Cheyenne Leader* carried the whole sordid story of Madden's escape. In time it was about forgotten. An offer of a thousand dollars for his return had been made, but no one claimed it. Some thought Madden teamed up with the Hole in the Wall gang. It was rumored that after a couple of months Mrs. Madden, the two children, and Hugh Dorson left for Laramie. There they took a train headed for Washington or Oregon Territory. Of course the lawyer got the farm, the horses, and the cattle, selling them at a premium to some unsuspecting neighbor."

"Which shows people do what they have to according to their own standards," said Ell, reaching out her hand to touch Gordon. "Marriage can be like a horse with a broken leg. You shoot it, but that don't fix the leg. What happened to Mrs. Madden? I think she's got spunk. Dorson and Madden don't amount to spit in the river."

Charlie frowned at his sister for flirting with old Gordon. Etta poured more hot coffee.

"Now comes more about our friend Horn," said Gordon, keeping the tension high so the women would stay for the end of his story. "One day I met Horn in the Tivoli, where he'd been drinking beer. He wanted to talk. He told me he'd heard of a plot to find Madden. He didn't think anything about it because he himself had looked everywhere he could think of, even going back to the log shack once in a while. But not long after he was riding the Swan line, hunting stray cattle, and he came past the Madden shack. He remembered about the plot, so he tethered his horse and went up to look at the deserted place one last time. But it wasn't deserted; someone was inside.

"Madden was at the rickety kitchen table with his head in his hands. He wasn't armed, so Horn sat across from him and asked what he was doing. The man seemed dazed. 'I'm looking for my wife and kids,' he said. Horn tried to tell him they had gone long ago and it was useless to look for them. 'Old Hugh Dorson's looking after them,' Horn said. That angered Madden and he kicked at the table legs and the wall of the shack, making it tremble as bad as an earthquake. Horn tried to get Madden to go into Cheyenne with him, but he refused. Horn said he'd send someone for him. The man raved and ranted, so Horn left. A couple of days later Horn said he went back to take the man some grub and again talk him into forgetting his wife and kids and going to Cheyenne. He was certain Madden wasn't rustling cattle any longer and thought the most the sheriff would do was credit Horn with bringing back a fugitive and then let the man go. Horn would pick up an easy thousand dollars.

"When Horn got to the cabin, everything seemed deathly still. Only the buzzing of those big green horseflies could be heard with the rushing of the creek water. There was no horse, no saddle, no bridle in the barn. Inside the shack the smell was so nauseous and thick he could cut it with a knife. He found Madden lying on a cot. His gray wool blanket snugged around his chest was dark with dried blood. His revolver lay beside him. Horn said there was no doubt in his mind what had happened. He felt sick at his stomach and he went outside for a gulp of fresh, clean air. He told me he grabbed some dead wood and, without really thinking about what he was doing, piled it inside the open door, lit a match, and numbly saw it flare up into orange flames. He turned, got on his horse, and rode away, not looking back as the whole dry shack caught fire." Gordon sighed and closed his eyes.

Ell sighed. Her eyes did not leave Gordon. Her hand fluttered like an aspen leaf against her blanched throat. "I'll never have kids."

"Jeems, the man lost the reward money. He let it go up in smoke," said Charlie. "He drinks locoweed in his coffee."

"Charlie!" said Etta sharply. "Maybe the man had another goal, other than making money."

"You can be the judge of that," whispered Gordon. He continued in a low voice. "Horn's face was like a mask when he told me the last part of Madden's story. Then all of a sudden something in his face slipped or fell away. I saw a hint of softness. Horn's chin quivered and his eyes were not steely, but liquid, like deep, still water. He muttered. His voice was barely audible. 'That Madden was a dirty rustler, a jailbreaker, but he'd suffered plenty for his crimes. He didn't commit suicide—not really. He was murdered. You know who killed him? I killed him. I told him his wife and kids were with his cowhand, a man he'd trusted. I didn't lay a hand on him, nor point a gun at him. But I put that forty-five slug in his heart, as sure as I'm sitting here drinking beer.' Then his eyes glassed up and his face became brittle again. It was a moment to be remembered. A moment that rarely happens. It stirred my heart. To this day I can see that enigmatic man gaze over my head as if watching something far beyond vision. For just a fraction of a second he'd held himself for my inspection. I was honored beyond words. Horn's hard and thorny as cactus, but there's a soft place deep inside. He only acts cold-blooded as a rattler with a chill."

Six days later, October 6, 1901, Ell asked Charlie to take the three children to Margaret at the Y6 after breakfast. "Etta is having contractions."

Charlie looked in the bedroom before leaving. "I saw you up this morning looking perfectly fine. You sure this is the day?"

"I've had three others. I'd say I'm birthwise." She smiled and grabbed the rags tied to the rung at the head of the bed. She gritted her teeth and grimaced. A low growl grew into a scream that slashed the air.

"Wait! I'll be right back!" called Charlie. He pushed Floyd and the two little girls out the front door. He buttoned the children's coats and pulled their wool caps down below their ears as he boosted each one up in the wagon.

"What's the matter with Mama?" asked Joella. "Is she sick?"

"You dumb bunny. She's having a baby," said Floyd.

"How?" asked Joella. "You said she already had one in her tummy."

Charlie hitched the horse to the wagon and wondered how his six-year-old son was going to unravel Joella's tangled thoughts.

"The baby's coming out. That's why we have to go visit cousin Gladys and Charles." Floyd was practical.

Pauline began to cry. "I wanna stay with Mama!"

"You can't," said Floyd. "Don't act like a baby, because today you grow up. There's a new little baby coming to our house." He sat with his back straight and held the reins until Charlie jumped up into the wagon.

"A noodle baby?" asked Joella, incredulous.

Floyd turned and looked at his sister like she was a hair in his soup.

The sun was bright all day, but the wind blew in clouds by late afternoon. Charlie stayed in the barn and brushed the horses after he'd cleaned out the stalls. He checked over their shoes and mended two of them with the meager blacksmith equipment Gordon had. "I'll get Pa to look over all your horses in the spring. He's one of the best farriers you've ever seen."

Gordon nodded. "C.B., why don't you go up to the house and see how things are coming. You go from one thing to another here, and your thoughts are not on what you're doing. Look, there's a hole in your shirt, where a spark lit. You didn't even see it. Aye, go, lad."

Charlie didn't need coaxing. Inside, he drank a cup of coffee and sat at the kitchen table, hesitant to barge into the bedroom. He could hear Ell talking to his wife.

"I don't know what we are going to do if this baby doesn't come by night. I'll have to send all the boys to the Y6 for supper. What'll Margaret say about that?" Ell laughed.

Etta said something. Charlie couldn't hear because she muttered and groaned. Charlie was no longer hesitant. His wife was in pain, and he wanted to be there to make her feel better.

He saw Ell bending over at the foot of the bed. There were newspapers spread out over the bed where Etta lay. Then he saw Ell's hands move in like the pincers on a lobster. They were red and held tight and rocked back and forth. The top of the baby's head emerged, the hands were out of sight, but the arms rocked gently and skillfully, and one tiny shoulder emerged, then the other slipped into view. Suddenly a wormlike tiny being was in her bloody hands. Charlie could hardly breathe. He didn't move. Ell laid the ugly, glistening creature on the newspapers between Etta's legs and cut the dark cord. She bound it quickly and neatly with a thin strip of torn cloth. She held the baby up to the light from the window. The wormlike being had arms and legs and it cried. The sky beyond was streaked with wide red gashes. Charlie could not tell if the infant was a girl or a boy.

Ell was sponging the baby's face with mineral oil. She wrapped it in a clean rag. Charlie wanted to tell her to wash the rest of the baby. He opened his mouth, his throat was dry. He closed his mouth, and his hands doubled into fists at his sides. Ell was hovering over Etta. She was whispering in staccato bursts, "Bear down! The afterbirth! Atta girl! Good work!"

Etta gasped, then lay quiet, breathing easier, rhythmically, as if asleep. Ell looked up, but said nothing to Charlie standing in the doorway. She did not rouse Etta but packed a wad of cloth between her legs, cleared away the red, soggy papers, and walked past Charlie to put them in the kitchen range to burn. Ell went back to the newborn, cleaning it thoroughly with warm water and mineral oil. She wrapped the baby in a clean, flannel square and laid it in the little wooden bed Joe made for Floyd. The baby was really not so bad-looking.

Charlie began to rock on his feet. He was going to see Etta, to hold her hand and tell her everything was fine. Her face was as white as the bed sheet.

Ell got between Charlie and Etta. She was efficient and knew exactly what had to be done next. She knew that Etta was pale from loss of blood. She looked in her black medical bag on the dresser, took out a darning needle, threaded it with catgut that was being softened in a pan of hot oil on the back of the range. She bent over Etta and deftly sewed a couple stitches in the torn, soft tissue, pulling tight, but not puckering the edges. She pushed the packing back in place and bound it securely.

Etta awoke and feebly felt her midsection. "Where's my baby?"

Charlie was thinking, I'll tell her to name the baby Frank, after my baby brother. Pa's so proud of him. He's finally growing up and going to amount to something. He can sure ride a horse.

"The baby's right here," said Ell. "What are you going to call this cotton-headed little girl?"

Etta reached up for the bundle. "Let me look first," she said softly.

Charlie knelt beside the bed. "This is Frankie," he said.

"Frances is better," Etta murmured.

"She certainly took her sweet time coming," said Ell, sitting in the rocking chair. "I'd say this one is as stubborn as any Texas mule. As far as babies are concerned, I'd call it quits."

TWENTY

John Coble

Three days after her fourth baby's birth, Etta lay in bed watching through the window as the sky slowly became darker. Before supper Ell brought in the baby to nurse. Suddenly Etta could wait no longer. She was bursting with curiosity. "Please, tell me what you mean that you'll never have kids? You love kids. Kids love you."

Ell looked startled. The outside light was a pearly gray. She started to pull the curtain.

"No, don't shut out the twilight and don't turn on the lamp. Talk to me." Etta was propped up by pillows in white, muslin cases. The baby took short audible breaths as it nursed and a tiny fist lay warm against Etta's breast.

"I can't talk about it. I never should have said anything. I talked during a weak moment," said Ell. "Of course, Les and I want—wanted children. It's unfair. It's so hard." Tears filled her eyes and she brushed them away with a corner of her apron.

"Go on—just say it. Tell me. You'll feel better. A woman with your special talents . . . all the medical knowledge you have . . . the compassion, the caring for others . . . you shouldn't be troubled with hard problems. Come on, what's the matter?" Etta put the sucking baby on her other breast. A drop of blue-white milk rolled across the baby's chin. Her vigorous nursing ceased, and she slept.

"Promise you won't say a word to Charlie?" Ell twisted a button on the front of her dress until it lay in her hand.

"Promise, cross my heart, hope to die," said Etta.

"Well—here goes. Les had the mumps when we moved to Colorado Springs. Both sides of his face swelled so he looked like a jack-o'-lantern. His earlobes bent in right angles. He said he felt worse than a calf with the slobbers. I was a young, heartless sap. I teased him, saying I'd married a kid, not a man." Her voice caught. She waited a few minutes before continuing. She began to twist another button, then suddenly stopped and held her hands together.

Etta could see the outline of Ell's face and figure in the deepening gray light. She was a beauty, with a flawless face, deep, green eyes and long lashes, a straight narrow nose above a full mouth that turned up into the most alluring smile, a long slim neck that met strong shoulders. There were dimples beneath those shoulders in the back, especially when her arms swung backward. Charlie and the children had the same kind of dimples. Etta thought them beautiful, a delightful Irwin trait.

Ell was not a simple person, but she had a way of taking the complications out of others' lives and setting their minds at rest. Her hands were warm. Her hands were cool. Whatever the need, Ell could satisfy. She was good with the elderly, her peers, or children.

Etta thought about how old Johnnie Gordon was positively smitten by Ell. But Ell knew her place and how to handle feelings. All the Irwin children loved their Aunt Ell, who named the meadow flowers, let caterpillars crawl in her hand. She ran and sang with the children, but at the same time kept their high spirits in check.

"Then I was embarrassed, disgraced. I was shamed. I could tell no one. I thought it was my fault, that I should have known of some powerful root or bark that could bring him back to normal. I was angry and hurt. I shut Les out. I was scared to death." She pushed a bracelet around and around her wrist. "I was bitter. I thought only of myself, being deprived of sex. Not deprived of love because Les does love me. Marriage is more than sex. But at first I could think of nothing else. I had a home, companionship, understanding, compassion, clothes, the good life, but I was deprived—there were no good times in bed."

"Deprived of sex, no good times? What do you mean?" asked Etta, conscious of the baby's breathing, the laughter of the three children playing outside in the dark. In her mind she saw the three children bundled against the cold, and she imagined Ell in a flannel nightgown, woolen stockings on her feet. A sudden catch contracted the muscles in her chest.

Ell pressed her hand to her forehead. "When Les recovered he couldn't perform—he couldn't—he wanted to—and I wanted to. Oh, God, I wanted to!" Ell sobbed into her hands. Finally she dried her eyes and looked away from the sleeping baby.

"You love him?"

"Yes, I do love him. But I'm bitter. I can't understand why almighty God let this happen to us. Etta, we were perfect together and ecstatically happy. Now making love is as useless as putting a milk bucket under a bull or tits on a boar pig."

Etta wanted to laugh, but something held her back. She said, "Bitterness has added color to your language, for sure. Poor Ell. Poor Les. I'm so sorry. You both must have been humiliated and sick in your hearts."

"I felt deeply hurt. Me, who always had been a healer. I couldn't heal the one I loved most. I was blinded by self-pity. The thought of no sex forever was excruciating. Sex, to me, was a kind of power. Now I had no power over the most important person in my life. Thus, Les was not the only one left impotent. Life was rough as a cob." Her tears started up again.

Etta reached out for her sister-in-law's hand. "You can't fight something like that with tears. Les is still the same person with all the decent attributes you saw when you first knew him. Sex isn't everything. Charlie says, 'If you can't flee, go with the flow.'"

"That's easy for you to say. You don't know what it's like. I tried potions, lotions, massages, sitz baths, magic words and gestures, even prayer. When nothing worked on Les, I was angry, then sad. I felt inadequate and inferior. You have no idea the mortification I went through."

"You're right, I don't know, but I'm not ignorant. Stress enriches life, and you're letting stress ravage yours."

Ell looked surprised. She thought she was telling Etta all her feelings. She thought Etta would understand, not criticize. Tears washed her face. She got up from the rocking chair and went to the window, looking out on the yellowed grass where the children were throwing wood chips at a tomato-can target.

Etta held out the sleeping baby. "Please put her back in the crib." She felt empty without the child in her arms, more vulnerable.

"Why? Why is it so hard for me to deal with?" asked Ell.

"No one knows how to react in a situation until the time comes. Each person is an individual. What did Les do?"

"He took one of the rooms upstairs. He goes to work at his accountant's office every day. He comes home in the evening and eats supper with the men patients I look after. He takes care of my bookkeeping. He advises me about the health-care business. We go out to the latest plays. He is like a wonderful man courting his lady friend. We hold hands."

"Some of the most famous men, Plato, Leonardo da Vinci, Michelangelo—"

"That doesn't make me feel any better—they were homosexuals, not geldings."

"Ell, Les is not a gelding! My God! He's, he's—listen, I don't think it's fair to make a judgment, to put a name on it, except impotent."

Ell twisted her bracelet around.

"Everything you loved about him, except that one ability, is still there."

"Yes, you're right. I know that."

"You know he suffers. You admit you've been selfish and indulgent in self-pity. He'd change if he could. Don't you suppose it's been really hard for him to accept the truth?"

"He knows what he is," said Ell, sighing.

"Do *you* know what he is?" asked Etta.

"Well, he's a man. He's suffered. He's kind, tolerant, and responsible. He's unhappy. He's married and wants to stay with me. He knows his obligations. He's a man with a handicap," she said without hesitation.

"He's more of a man than some we've both seen," added Etta.

"Honest, I can't imagine myself married to any other—yet there's this big gap in my life. I miss sex. I like sex. Is that terribly wrong?"

"I'm surprised at my own feeling. I don't think it's wrong at all. Talk it over with Les. Let him know you love him. Tell him of being unsatisfied, unfulfilled. Every problem has a solution when you think rationally. Your marriage is like a horse with a broken leg."

Ell hesitated then had to smile. "How's that?"

"You shoot it—you haven't fixed the leg."

Neither young woman spoke for a while. Then each looked

up. Ell spoke first. "I have my patients to look after, babies are born, children break bones, get diphtheria, adults have TB, dropsy. Did you know mostly men come to stay at my health spa for rest, hydrotherapy, herbal teas, lotion massages?" Her face brightened. "When those men leave me, I want them to feel a whole lot better. It just dawned on me that I'm going to do whatever I can to make them feel their best. You know what I mean?"

Etta's eyes widened. She put a hand to her mouth.

"Les and I will share everything, except bed. I'll make him happy in other ways. But there's no reason why we both must suffer forever, and by God I won't. I should have thought of that before."

"What about children?" asked Etta, her heart pounding hard.

"Children?" she asked sadly. "I'll come to play with yours and Will's. My men will pay well for what I know about certain plants and human cycles. I'll not be embarrassed by a pregnancy that ties me to some strange man."

Again Etta was shocked by her sister-in-law. She didn't say a word for a moment. Then she ventured, "I wonder what your grandma Malinda would say if she knew? What would she say about using contraceptive knowledge for—uh—you and your men patients to—uh—to have an affair with no intense devotion or attachment. It's—it's sinful. You wouldn't. You are really joking, just to see what I'd say. Aren't you? Your grandmother would be scandalized. She'd say you are bringing a hornet's nest about your ears."

Ell brushed her hand over her silken, strawberry-blond hair. She smiled. "She'd understand. She always said, 'A person does what he has to do. Life is short. Live it thoroughly. Don't keep your head in a sack.'"

There was more silence. Etta had tears in her eyes. "I'm so sorry for you and Les. This is hard to believe. My feelings are all mixed together. It's like looking in the looking glass and suddenly seeing a face you don't recognize. I can't believe what I've heard."

"Look at it this way. There must be others that have had such a problem. Grandma Malinda used to say, 'There's nothing new under the sun when it comes to men and women together.' I'm lucky—Les and I love each other, even if that love is on a different plane nowadays. I'm beginning to think of him not as my Adonis, but as my mentor." She took a deep breath. "Well, little Etta, you know what kind of sister-in-law you have."

Etta pointed to the kitchen. The children were banging on the door to come inside. "I think they're cold. They've been out a long time."

"I'm coming, you little coyotes," called Ell. She let the children in and helped them hang up their coats, caps, scarves, and mittens. Pauline had only one mitten.

"The dog took it," said Joella. "I think he ate it, so no use going to look for it."

That logic made Ell laugh. "Joella thinks like me."

Etta said, "Oh, please, don't tell me that—not today."

Pauline put a cold, chubby hand on the baby's face and instantly the baby woke crying. Ell picked her up and rocked her back and forth in her arms. "Hush-a-bye, sweet Frances—Sweet Frances, what middle name do you have that will last a lifetime—bittersweet lifetime?"

"You give her a middle name," called Etta. "Make it melodic, something unusual. Name the baby before you leave us."

"Get supper first," said Floyd. "Want me to lasso a chicken?"

Two days later Etta was out of bed, doing the easy household chores. Ell was packing her suitcase. She was about ready for Charlie to take her to the Cheyenne depot so she could take the Union Pacific train to Denver, then the Denver and Rio Grande to Colorado Springs. The three older children were watching their aunt Ell.

"Are you going to wake baby Frances to say good-bye?" asked Joella, tossing her long blond hair about her shoulders.

Ell took up the baby and held her high in the air. "I'm going to give her a good-bye kiss even if she isn't awake. And we're going to have a naming ceremony before I leave."

The children gathered around, wondering what their fun-loving aunt would do next. Etta followed them to the sitting room.

"Is this a big ceremony? Should I tell Pa to come in?" asked Floyd.

"No, no, it's just us. Now, watch and listen." Holding the baby in a flannel blanket, Ell twirled around three times and held the baby away from her dark wool dress so she wouldn't be covered with white flannel fuzz when she boarded the train. She looked at the floor and whispered to the children, "Can you see them? All the little people have gathered with us to hear your baby sister's full name."

"Little people? Like the ones Mr. Gordon talks about?" asked Floyd, showing some doubt after looking at the bare floor.

"They live outdoors, but come in for special occasions, usually making themselves invisible to unbelievers. Mr. Gordon told me the most melodic and lovely name he knew. It was his mother's name, Gwendolyn. I do believe it is a favorite among the little people. Ooops!" Ell pulled three-year-old Pauline back beside Floyd. "You almost tripped on one little person. Here's the genuine ceremony: I name this wee lamb, Frances Gwendolyn." She handed the baby to Etta.

"A cup of tea to seal the name giving," said Ell, putting cups on the kitchen table and motioning for everyone to come sit.

"There's no time," said Etta. "Charlie will be in any minute calling, 'All aboard for the depot!'"

"There's time," said Ell. "Charlie needs a hot drink before setting out for Cheyenne. Look out that window. Lazy snowflakes are beginning to fall."

The Irwin-Gordon fall roundup of 1901 brought in more than a hundred unbranded steers, cows, and heifers. Charlie surmised that the animals were caught in a coulee in the area where most of the Irwin cattle range during the winter. They were out of sight so were never found by their rightful owners and probably written off their books by now.

"I don't have any intention of some damned line rider seeing us outlined against the sky or squatting over a lonely campfire with a bunch of mixed, unbranded cattle nearby," said Will. "Let's get these scrawny critters over to the Y6 and slap a brand on them pronto."

"All right. Let's move them out now," said Charlie.

"Afterward, you think we could make one more roundup to see what more we find?" asked Will.

"Nope. We have our own cattle and then some. Don't be greedy."

"Aw, Charlie, if I'm going to raise beef cattle I have to have a sizable herd. I'm not going to run a cattle ranch like some female chicken farm," said Will as he rode around the bunched-up herd, careful not to frighten a skittish cow by talking too loudly or lighting up a cigarette where the cow could see the bright flame or smell the smoke. In the Y6 pasture Will, Charlie, and Johnnie Gordon sorted out the unmarked animals after they had sorted the Y6 brands from the L5.

Will took the young, unmarked cattle for the Y6 brand. Charlie took the rest for Gordon's L5 brand.

Gordon was stunned. He could not believe that anyone would share their cattle herd with him, even if the animals were rangy, wild beasts.

"Listen, boss, I don't think anyone with an ounce of pride would claim them scrawny things right now," said Charlie. "But you and I know that a winter with our main herd, some spring fattening on rich, green grass, and they'll be something fine to sell those Chicago packers. You'll be in the black on your books."

Johnnie Gordon shook his head. He was still amazed. This foreman, C.B. Irwin, had a heart as big as a grandfather bull buffalo. "You're right. Where is my pride? Those scrubs are so thin we'll have to wrap them in extra cowhide to keep them together. But if they fatten up during the spring, I'll sell them. I'm thinking if our Hereford bulls breed with those skinny Shorthorn cows, we'll have something more worthwhile by spring. C.B., thanks for everything." Then he stopped as though something else was on his mind and he didn't know how to say it. "Uh—I'm so curious, I have to ask this. Why did your delightful sister want to know my mother's name—she's been dead six years."

Charlie burst into a fit of laughter. "No offense, sir, but this is the honest truth. Our youngest baby was just given your dear mother's name as her middle name. Didn't Etta tell you? My sister wanted to honor you, and she didn't want you to feel she was in any way—uh—flirting, but that is something she does quite naturally."

"C.B., I was taken by your sister. She impressed me as a competent woman—and intelligent. She honored me. Why, I am flattered. You and your family have wrapped yourselves around my little finger."

"If that's the case, sir, then you get another honor."

"What's that?"

"Put the ear crops on these steers and cows as soon as Will and I get them branded." Charlie chuckled heartily.

Gordon nodded and moseyed off to the barn to sharpen his knife on the revolving, round cement block. He pumped the contraption like a bicycle and lay the knife blade against the spinning cement.

Charlie hired a local rancher's wife, Dora Miller, to come help Etta with the cooking and cleaning for a few weeks. A cot was placed in the children's room for Mrs. Miller, who was glad to have a change from cooking for her man, two boys, and a schoolteacher who rented a room at the Miller place. She said Miss Kimmell, the teacher, would cook, but save the cleaning at her house until she returned. Mrs. Miller was a large woman, with powerful arms and legs, strong shoulders and back, and large breasts. She knew what had to be done and went right to doing it. She peeled potatoes, fried the beefsteaks, and made gravy. She couldn't understand why anyone might want something else for supper. She scrubbed the floors, but could not understand why Etta wanted the window curtains washed and ironed. She was impressed with the books on the shelves in the sitting room and even more surprised to see Floyd read.

"I taught him," said Etta proudly. "He really needs to go to school with a trained teacher."

Mrs. Miller said, "My boys ain't much interested in school, although they're interested in the schoolteacher. Her name is Miss Glendolene Kimmell. My, oh, my, she has the most unusual eyes you ever saw, big and brown and kind of fish-shaped. I told my man, James, 'I think she's oriental somewhere in her background,' he says, 'Those Celestials have all the looks, but they're too small-boned for any kind of work, except book reading.' I used to think she had the loveliest name until I heard what you named your youngest. Say, *Gwendolyn* and *Glendolene* are alike. You know our schoolmarm?"

"No," said Etta, checking the bread she was baking. "Baby Frances was named for Mr. Gordon's mother."

"I had three strapping boys, but never a little girl." Mrs. Miller looked longingly at Joella and Pauline sitting at the kitchen table, stringing macaroni on cord to see who could make the longer chain. "Girls are sweet and docile. I believe they even smell different, like clover honey. Boys smell like cow pies right from the start. Don't you agree?"

During the winter of 1901 Etta had a letter from her sister, Kate. She wrote how their mother and father had sold the Kansas farm and moved with all the young ones to Tonkawa, Oklahoma. Mr. McGuckin found the town needed a Baptist minister. Immediately he found his calling. In a few months he rallied the congregation into donating time, money, and materials for the construction of the First Baptist Church in Tonkawa. The news made Etta feel good. To Charlie she said, "Ma must be so proud. She's always wanted Pa to do something that would be uplifting. Ma never did like living on a farm; she wanted to be citified. I know how she felt, because I miss living in town. I heard some of the ranchers have a house in town for their wives and children to stay in while the young ones go to school. In summer they're all back together on the ranch. Sounds nice. What do you think?"

"I think it takes money," said Charlie. "My dear, there's nothing I wouldn't do for you. First let's get Gordon on his feet, then we'll start saving—"

"You mean we haven't saved anything yet? Where has the money gone?"

"You know."

"No, I don't know. Tell me."

"Well, I sent some to Will and Margaret so they could have enough for their fare here. Then I paid the Wyoming Stock Growers' Association two dollars a head for the unbranded stock we found in the fall roundup. I know Warren told me to forget it, but there were more than a dozen head and I didn't want anyone accusing us of burning rawhide that don't belong to us. We picked up a lot of unclaimed stock, others were just too lazy to hunt for them, or they were gathered by someone working ahead of the roundup. Anyway, they're paid for fair and square. Alice Smith, the association's secretary, said I was the first to get a bill of sale for unbranded stock."

"Charlie, you bought stock for your brother Will and for Gordon, both?"

"Why not? Keeps us out of trouble and they'll each make money on them. Will says he'll put his money on the Y6 books."

"We'll never have enough to get a house in town and send Floyd to school!" Etta cried.

"I said there's nothing I won't do for you. Be patient," said Charlie.

"I hope that Floyd isn't sixteen by then," said Etta with a laugh. The sound was harsh. "Maybe I'll send him to a one-room ranch school."

"There's none close, unless we start our own," said Charlie. "Just have more faith in me. I'll get you what you want soon enough. There's always a way if we don't play leapfrog with a unicorn."

"Charlie, you say funny things." Etta laughed. This time it was a melodious sound. "I can't stay angry with you." She put her arms around his waist and drew him close. "I love you so much. I don't really begrudge Gordon nor Will a few scrubby cattle. After all, I have you and four children who all, like you, have dimples in their backs."

There was a foot of snow on the ground and it wasn't yet Thanksgiving. Etta and Dora, as they now called Mrs. Miller, had cleaned the cupboards and were dusting the books on the shelves. Etta told Dora about her desire to send the children to the school in Cheyenne. "I want them to have the best education possible. If we can't live in Cheyenne, I suppose your Miss Kimmell is good."

"Miss Kimmell is no bigger than you are, Missus Irwin. I'm sure she's fine as a schoolmarm. One of the cowboys from over at the Iron Mountain Ranch is sweet on her."

"Charlie's brother Frank works there, at the IM. It's not him that is courting your schoolmarm, is it?" Etta teased.

"Oh, no. It's another cowboy, Tom Horn. A big man, about as tall as your Charlie, and he wears this little mustache across his upper lip. It looks like a piece of deer moss. He tells her how to be firm with those big kids, especially the Nickell kids. They need discipline."

"Why's that?"

"Missus Irwin, I could write a book on that there subject. Didn't you read the papers about Willie Nickell's shooting last summer, July eighteenth to be exact?"

"No, I don't remember anything like that. Did this Willie shoot well?"

"Oh, don't say that. He didn't do no shooting. He was shot. That overgrown thirteen-year-old was dry-gulched, let me tell you." Dora set her dustcloth down. Tears streamed down her face like a rainstorm hitting the side of a craggy cliff. "Oh, Lord, if you don't know nothing, I have to start way back. So much has happened. You won't believe how people can be—mean—heartless." Her eyes were red and puffy. She blew her nose on a rag she kept in her apron pocket. "Kels Nickell and his dumpy wife, Mary, had a nerve to blame my husband, James, for the shooting of that boy. I'll swear, whoever asks, that James was home, sick with a headache built for a horse, the day of the killing. James, himself, told John Coble he stayed to home that day. Coble came out to ask what we all knew about that trouble."

"Mr. Coble?" asked Etta.

"You know that fine-looking gentleman?"

"No, but I've heard of him. Charlie's brother works for him, like I said."

"Ya, I guess most everyone has worked for him once. He raises mostly horses. Sells them back East as polo ponies. It was ten years ago when Kels Nickell went to John Coble's ranch to accuse him of letting the IM cattle graze in his sheep pastures. Nickell got into an argument with Coble's foreman, George

Cross. Cross told Nickell that it was more like Nickell's sheep trespassing onto the IM pasture. Everyone knows cattle won't graze where sheeps've been. Anyway, there was a frightful scrap. John Coble tried to break it up. A more honorable man I never met. Nickell has the morals of a hydrophoby skunk. He jumped Coble like a roadrunner on a rattler and ran his knife into Coble's stomach—twice.

"Cross brought Nickell into town to the sheriff. Then took Coble to Doc Maynard's place. This was in the *Cheyenne Daily Leader*. I can remember James reading it to me as if it were yesterday. It was hot as ashes in Hades that day. I guess we all learned Nickell has a short fuse. Poor John Coble carries a couple of ugly scars on his stomach to prove Nickell's temper."

"Dora, that's a horrid story, an awful way to settle a dispute." Etta felt unsettled.

"Well, missus, it was that same devil, Kels Nickell, that caused James to shoot Baby Brother. Honest." Tears again streamed down Dora's face.

"Dora, you don't have to tell me this. It's too painful. Let's wash the floor," said Etta, fascinated yet repulsed by the violence in these people's lives.

"You know, now that I've started, it's better that I finish," Dora said, and wiped her eyes on the hem of her dress. "Kels was one of the first ones in these parts to have the gall to raise sheep in cattle country. Right off, them sheep grazed over on our place, as well as over on Coble's and others. James went to Nickell and told him nice to keep the sheep out of our cow pasture. Kels paid no attention. He said, 'Mister Miller, I think you're full of horse manure.' So James started carrying a rifle and swore he'd shoot every sheep he found on our place."

"Oh, I don't like guns. Did you stop him—your James?"

"Oh, no, ma'am. I don't tell my man what to do, that ain't safe. Only a fool argues with a mule. Early this spring, when there was snow on the north side of the hills and in the gully, James took our precious four-year-old, Baby Brother, out target shooting. Actually, they went looking for sheep. I don't know if they found any, but the gun'd been shot. James cleaned the rifle and showed Baby Brother how to look inside the barrel to see the crud that needed wiping out. James swears he checked and got all the shells out. But he was wrong. Accidentally he let the hammer slam back just as Baby Brother walked up to have a look into that barrel." Her shoulders hunched forward and she sobbed, with her hands over her face. Then she looked up and said, "That was the blackest day of my life so far. That .30-.30 shell smashed into Baby Brother something fearful. He never knew what hit him." She let the tears slide down her cheeks unchecked. "It was Nickell's fault for having sheep in the first place!"

"Oh, my, Dora, I'm so sorry," comforted Etta. "But it's wrong to blame someone else for our mistakes no matter how terrible."

"Missus Irwin, James wouldn't have had that gun unless he was after sheep, and that's what killed Baby Brother. I swear to God, I can't feel any kindness toward the Nickells. Neither does James and our two boys."

Etta gasped. "Dora, don't say that! What about this Willie Nickell that's dead? His mother has a broken heart same as you."

"Oh—on that fateful morning the kid, little Willie, was dressed in his pa's hat and rain slicker on account of the drizzly weather. Folks say he was going to bring back a sheepherder who'd left his pa's ranch the day before. I guess Mr. Nickell had a change of heart and decided to hire the herder and sent the boy to bring him back. Willie brought his horse to the gate, climbed down, and removed the wire loops from the post, took his horse through, and before he could put the loops back he was shot twice. The thirteen-year-old son of Mary and Kels Nickell shot! Now they know what grief is!"

"Oh, my! Who would do such a thing? Who?" repeated Etta.

"Someone who hates sheep. So most any of the ranchers, I'd say. But it don't make no difference; the boy was mistaken for his pa. Remember he was wearing his pa's hat and slicker and riding his pa's big brown horse and the morning light was gray with rain and clouds."

Etta wondered why she was held spellbound by Dora's gruesome talk. She told herself she'd not repeat a word of it to Charlie, but she also knew she'd tell him every word.

Dora could not be stopped. Her mouth was like a windup toy; it chattered until the spring lost its tension. "James and our two boys were taken by the sheriff to Cheyenne. They were asked a lot of questions; stupid, James said, but nobody could prove anything. James wasn't the least bit scared, but the boys were petrified. The varmint Nickell was shot in the arm not more than a week after James and the boys came back from Cheyenne." Dora snickered. "I think Nickell was going to the barn with his little girl at his side to milk his cows. Musta' scared the stuffing out of the little girl to see her daddy curl up, grovel in the dust, because he was shot. And to make matters worse, a couple days afterward some of Nickell's sheep were clubbed to death."

"That poor man!" cried Etta.

"No, he ain't. He buys sheep for two dollars, grazes them for a year, and sells them for ten. He makes money faster than the cattlemen. I can't make myself feel sorry for a man that's lucky he wasn't killed same as his son, Willie, and of course our Baby Brother. The man's well off, if you think how he blamed near ruined me."

"Ruined you?"

"Yes, ma'am. I'm a woman, but I don't want no more children, no more. Children are more heartache than joy. They do as they please, not as you say, and they curse you more times than they praise you. But you love 'em. You don't want one killed. When Baby Brother died, I was no good for nuthin' for weeks."

Etta felt out of sorts by Dora's attitude. She began to scrub the floor herself. Dora began to get the noon meal. Each was quiet with her own thoughts.

During the meal, Dora, who hadn't been to many homes besides her own, and was a bit unsteady about her manners, happened to pour buttermilk in her coffee instead of cream.

"I'll get you another cup of coffee," said Etta quietly. "You're still upset from me letting you talk this morning. It's my fault."

"Oh, no, don't go to any bother for me." Dora blew on the curdled mixture. "I often use buttermilk in my coffee. It gives it a tart flavor."

No one said a word. The cowhands kept their faces steady.

After the men had eaten and left for additional chores, Etta put Joella and Pauline down for afternoon naps. Floyd was allowed to go down to the corral with the men. Etta sat in the rocking chair to nurse the baby, and Dora heated water to wash the dishes.

Dora broke the stillness. "I was afraid your mister was going to ask me why I was talking instead of working this morning." She gave Etta a glance.

"Charlie wouldn't criticize you. He'd leave that to me."

"If he'd asked me I was going to tell him I was working until I got hurt. You see, I was fixing the noon meal and I slipped on the bar of lye soap left on the floor from the scrubbing and wrenched my knee." Dora leered, without a suggestion of a smile.

Etta laughed. "You wouldn't?"

"Yes, I would, but I didn't have time to practice the limp. Say, I've been wondering. Does the mister want another?" She was drying the pewter flatware and nodding toward baby Frances.

"Charlie's good with children," said Etta. "Yes, I think he'd like another boy."

"I knew a family once had five children; three boys, then a girl, then another boy. They was named Matthew, Mark, Luke, Ann, John. You know, most men don't want the consequences. That's a fact. All they want is the fun of acting like bulls. Most are that way. Maybe yours is an exception. An exception is somebody who don't follow the ordinary rules. That fellow Horn don't follow ordinary ways. He told me he left home when he was only fourteen on account of a whipping his pa gave him that laid him in bed for a week." Her eyes squinted and she seemed to wink to the right. "He's sweet on our schoolmarm, Miss Glendolene Myrtle Kimmell—comes to see her. My boys August and Victor have calf eyes for her, but she don't have time for them. I think she likes older men. Tom Horn is ten, fifteen years older than your man. Ah, he's good to look at. He's about six feet two, broad-shouldered, deep-chested, not an ounce of superfluous flesh, with muscles of steel, straight as an Indian, with just a suggestion of a swing or swagger. He might be hard-featured except for his full lips. His eyes don't flinch and can stare anyone down. He's always polite and good-natured. Mr. Coble thinks he's one of the finest cowboys in the country. When he was at our place, he told us about his getting up on the ridge pole of the corral gate and dropping down to the bare back of a bronco as it came out. He had no saddle or bridle, nothing to hold him on except his spurs. That's a wild ride!"

"Tom Horn must be someone important in these parts. Mr. Gordon told a story about him bringing in a rustler."

"Important? I don't know anyone important. Horn's a cowboy with a wonderful shot. He can stoop down while riding a horse, pick up a stone or can, throw it in the air, and hit it once or twice before it falls to the ground. The Indians are said to be afraid of him because he's so quick on the trigger. James sees him riding the line once in a while, looking for sheep or cattle grazing outside their own territory. If he saw someone suspicious, someone moving cattle or burning out brands, he'd have the drop on them. He works for John Coble, who got Nannie E. Steele to nurse him back to health when he came to these parts from the Spanish-American War with malignant fever. Mrs. Steele lives about a mile from the Nickell ranch."

Etta's mind was in a whirl. She could hardly wait for evening to tell Charlie all the things Dora Miller talked about.

* * *

"Women spread stories faster than jam on bread. I swear there's not as much in the newspaper. Did Dora say anything else about Tom Horn? We'll know more about his life than he does himself, if Dora Miller continues to prattle. What else did she say?"

"I've told you every bit." Etta snuggled closer to Charlie. "No, I haven't. I just thought of something else." She giggled and her laughter was like the ringing of tiny silver bells. "She said men are fun-loving bulls."

"Why, that woman talks about everything! I bet she could talk a donkey's hind leg off. Doesn't she ever work!" cried Charlie.

"Sshh! You'll waken the children. Or worse—Dora will hear you. She sleeps with the bedroom door open, just to hear what goes on at night. Floyd told me she snores." Etta giggled again. "I think Floyd will be glad when she's gone and not sharing the children's room."

"I agree with Floyd. The minute you feel strong enough to scrub the floor alone I'll take her home," whispered Charlie, punching his pillow into a ball under his head.

"I scrubbed it myself today," said Etta.

Next morning Dora surprised Etta by saying, "Tom Horn is being questioned about Willie Nickell's death. I'm telling you this for your own good. Most settlers and farmers don't like anything about the big ranchers, including their cowhands. James told me they are looking for something suspicious about Horn, maybe that pins him to the Willie Nickell shooting. 'Horn's as good as any and better than some,' said James. Horn's not new to the law. He was deputy for three Arizona sheriffs, he has no love for sheep men, and even you said he's known for getting rustlers out of the territory. When I get home I'm going to tell James what you said yesterday about him in the company of a rustler. It'll make the case against Horn more air tight. Lock him up for murder." Her voice took a bitter vindictive quality. Etta did not like it. Dora's face was white and her mouth was a tight slash. "I hate the sound of ba-a-a-ing sheep and the smell of sheep dung. But, then, I don't have much use for those swanky big ranchers."

Etta gasped and almost dropped the flatiron. She laid the damp gingham curtain on the board and felt the steam rise against her face as she ran the iron over the material. "Maybe we shouldn't talk so much. This whole thing is awfully confusing to me. In some ways it sounds like a family feud."

"Forgive me, Missus Irwin, I didn't mean you, nor your man.

After all, C.B.'s only a foreman. He doesn't run his own place nor belong to the association where the big ranchers are. You've been nice to me and we are friends.

"John Coble's a big rancher. Our schoolmarm told me he comes from a wealthy Pennsylvania family and came out West rather than accept an appointment at the Naval Academy. Can you believe that? He started the Frontier Land and Cattle Company with a hoity-toity Irishman, a Sir, if you please, Horace Plunkett. But the two were wiped out in the horrible winter of eighty-six and eighty-seven. The Irishman went back to Ireland to be some kind of politician, and Coble moved to the Iron Mountain region to start a horse ranch. I think he took in a lot of them wild horses and broke them for his herd. You can do that if you've lost most of your money."

Etta continued to iron, breathing deeply of the hot, moist steam, as if it would stiffen her backbone. "Dora, I have some good news for you."

"Oh, I could use some of that," said Dora, smiling.

"Charlie—Mr. Irwin—is going to give you your pay tonight after supper."

"God bless him. I can use all the money I can get my hands on."

"And he's going to take you back to your family. I'll miss you, but see, I can do lots of work myself now and still look after the children. Floyd can help with some of the lesser chores, like bringing in kindling and setting the table."

Dora looked dumbfounded. "You don't want me no more?"

"Your work is finished. I'm sure your husband and sons will be glad to have you back. Even the schoolmarm will be glad to let you do the cooking," said Etta. "Laws, you were a help to me. You can tell your family that. The cowboys here spoke about the good meals you prepared."

"It was your biscuits, Missus Irwin. But I'll tell James what you said anyways. I've never been away before. My boys, Vic and Gussie, will be happy to see me back. You've been real nice. I hate to leave these pretty girls of yours. Maybe you'll come to visit me."

"Of course," said Etta, feeling an overwhelming fatigue. She wished supper were finished and Charlie were hitching up the wagon to take Dora Miller home.

A week after Frances was born, Frank came to the L5 ranch to borrow Charlie's Henry rifle. "I want to go elk hunting. If I get one, I'll send a roast to you for your supper." Charlie agreed. He thought Frank looked good. He was a little taller and still thin, his face was tanned, and his eyes sparkled.

"The foreman, Duncan Clark, is leaving the IM for Montana. I bet you could take his place," Frank told Charlie.

"I'm here until after spring roundup. I want to be sure Johnnie Gordon is back on his feet."

"Couldn't Will look in on him once in a while? Will could go on roundup with him. My boss, Coble, built a new ranch house. Etta and the kids would like it. The bunks are upstairs on the second floor right now. He's going to build a bunkhouse in the spring. Want me to tell him you'd like the job?"

"What about Pa, doing all the blacksmithing by himself?" asked Charlie.

"Will's there. Mr. Coble has horses, not a lot of dumb cattle. What do you say?" Frank tied the rifle behind his saddle. "Remember those wild horses we broke back in Kansas? You always said you wanted a horse ranch."

"I'll think about it, then this weekend if I've decided in favor of the job and it's still open, I'll ride over to the IM. I'd like to see your spread anyway. Been hearing a lot about John Coble."

"He talks a little funny, but you'll like him," said Frank, letting his horse carry him out to the road near Gordon's place.

Charlie first talked with Etta. She was in favor of the move if there was a raise in pay for Charlie and if there was a one-room ranch school close by for Floyd. Then he talked with his father. "If it's an opportunity, go, son. Don't worry about me. Will and I'll work on this place until you come back and run it yourself." Will promised to help Gordon with his spring roundup. "Maybe you could get a day or two off and come with us," suggested Will. "Then you could be sure Gordon got the right cattle."

"That sounds all right," said Charlie. "Now I have to talk with Gordon."

Gordon surprised Charlie by saying that he himself was contemplating a change. "I've found a fellow by the name of Hunter who wants to buy my place. He's looked at my books and seems satisfied that I have plenty of cattle. To meet Hunter was an inspiration, to make a deal with him is an education. He has some ideas about irrigation."

Charlie said, "Show me an irrigator and I'll show you a worker."

"Couldn't have said it better myself," said Gordon, smiling. "T. B. Hicks at the First National Bank said Hunter had a ranch called TY on the Chugwater in the early days, and now he raises

Herefords on Crow Creek, eight or ten miles from Cheyenne, so he knows what he's doing."

"What are you doing, sir?" asked Charlie.

"I'm going to visit the old country. I think I'll jump on the bread wagon and loaf with the rest of the bundles."

"I'll miss you. Etta and the kids will miss you," said Charlie.

"C.B., the love of your fellow man is the best monument that you can leave behind. If you'll miss me because we were friends, it's enough for me. I know I'll never forget your generosity and kindness. I often see you at work and say to myself, 'My God, there goes a man!'"

"You'll give me a bad attack of swelled head," said Charlie with a chuckle, reaching out to shake Gordon's hand.

"I do have some advice for you, C.B. Don't try to be the Napoleon of the West, but when you get hold of a good thing, freeze on to it. I want you to write to me. I'll leave the address. Write on one side of the paper and both sides of the subject. This country is turning a corner. There's going to be some interesting happenings. More irrigation, more industrialization."

John Coble reminded Charlie of a banty rooster. He was hardly more than five and a half feet tall. He was a neat dresser. His hair was tinted with coal black and neatly cut. He had a short, trim mustache across his upper lip. He spoke with a clipped, aristocratic, eastern accent and used his hands for emphasis. Johnnie Gordon told Charlie that Coble was one of the best cattlemen in Laramie County. Gordon sought out Coble and told him that C. B. Irwin was the most competent foreman he'd seen since coming to Wyoming twenty years ago.

Charlie went on horseback to the Iron Mountain Ranch to seek out the foreman's job. It was an all-day trip. Coble acted surprised to see him, although he'd expected him since talking with Gordon the week before.

Coble waved his arms around, saying, "I daresay, the job is yours, Mr. Irwin. The ranch house is ready for your wife and children to move in immediately. I don't live here at the ranch. I come to help with roundups, branding, breaking the wild horses, and right now I'm working on the new bunkhouse off and on. In the meantime, the cowhands bunk upstairs in the ranch house."

Charlie was grateful for the job and shook Coble's hand. He said, "Thank you. I'll bring Etta and the kids over next week with all our gear."

"Sounds good to me. We're ready for the fall roundup. I've

got to move four hundred cows and steers and about half as many heifers from their summer grazing in yonder mountains to the low meadowlands in the foothills. It's your job to cut out the three-year-olds and take them to the stockyards while they're fat. A hard winter is a killer for cattle. Gordon told me you saved his herd." Coble's brown eyes drilled into Charlie.

Charlie didn't flinch. "Yes, sir. We put a thin, ratty-looking herd on some summer grass, and they're fat and healthy enough for anyone's book."

Etta felt blue whenever she thought of leaving the L5. She'd begun to think of the ranch house as home, mainly because Frances was born there.

The Irwin family occupied the first floor of Mr. Coble's new log house. The entire second story was one large room where all the ranch hands, including Frank, bunked on cots placed side by side. There was a bathroom inside the large wooden house. That is what it was for, bathing. One huge porcelain tub with claw feet sat on oversize bricks. There were galvanized tins used for wash-tubs in the room. Hot water from the kitchen range was carried in buckets to the tubs, and cold well water was used to cool the bathwater to the desired temperature. On Saturday nights there was standing room only while the cowboys waited for their baths. On the average, three to four men could bathe in the same water before it was carried out and the full buckets of water tossed off the back steps. Then fresh hot and cold water was carried in.

Etta made it a policy to keep herself and the children out of the way during the Saturday night baths. She and the children bathed in a washtub in front of the kitchen range during midday, when she could close and bolt the kitchen door.

Etta did all the cooking at the ranch house when the cowboys and chuck-wagon cook were gone. She cooked for the hands left behind to make repairs and do the blacksmith work, while the others were on the roundup.

One morning Floyd slammed the kitchen door and called for his mother, "Ma, I have something to tell you!"

"I'm changing the baby's diaper. Come into the bedroom," she said.

"Ma, the cowboy Mrs. Miller thinks should be locked up for murder is in Pa's crew, one of his hired hands on the roundup." Floyd was breathless.

"What are you talking about? Tell me from the beginning and go slow," said Etta, with a safety pin held between her teeth.

"You know, Tom Horn."

"Floyd, that was a lot of grownup talk you heard between me and Dora Miller."

"Ma, I heard Mr. Coble tell Pa the name of the men who were going on the roundup. He said, 'Tom Horn,' then said, with his hand over his mouth, 'Don't believe rumors, Horn is a good man. He's a square shooter and would never shoot a boy. Rustlers and sheep men respect him, but would sure like to see him move to Montana.'"

"Floyd, you must not listen to adults talking. You carry tales, and that is gossiping. Find your pencil. We'll work on your sums while it's quiet in the house. Go sit beside Joella at the kitchen table. She's writing out the numbers."

"Oh, Ma! I wish I'd fed the horses the sugar lumps in my pocket instead of coming to tell you some news. Oh, crap! Double crap!"

Floyd slid into the chair beside his sister and took one of her pencils, which made her yell.

Etta stood behind her son with a wet washcloth and a bar of yellow soap. She rubbed the cloth on the soap and tilted Floyd's head back.

"I'm washing your mouth of those foul words. Think before you speak," she said quietly, holding Floyd's head firm while she swished the washcloth in and out of his mouth.

Floyd's eyes watered, but he did not whimper nor cry out. Joella watched with a gleam in her eyes. She held the indelible pencil tip against her tongue, making a large purple dot.

Charlie leaned out from his horse to shake hands with the men John Coble introduced. Horn was last and was about as Charlie remembered, a trim mustache, receding hairline to his brown hair, and eyes that pierced through a man like an ice pick jabbed into a block of ice. He was more than six feet tall and weighed over two hundred pounds. He rode a large-chested, sleek brown horse he called E.W. His voice was soft and clear so that Charlie could hear him talk to the horse, but underneath was the sharpness Charlie remembered.

"Horn, you old horse thief! Remember when you bunked at the Irwin place in Kansas, Middle Sappa Creek, you bought an old horse and used its hide for a lean-to?"

Horn pulled out a small sack of tobacco and roll of papers. He rolled a cigarette, all the time looking at Charlie with clear, cold eyes. "Don't ever call me a thief, mister. I remember the episode. That was a lifetime ago."

"You were on your way out to Wyoming, going to work for Swan Land as a range detective or something," continued Charlie. "Is there good money in that?"

Horn took a long pull on the cigarette, glanced at his boss, Coble. "You talk a lot. I'm cowboying, and that's all that's your business."

"Take it easy," said Coble. "I never realized you two met. I guess it was before Horn worked for John Clay or Ora Haley."

Charlie laughed. "All right, past is past."

"You're growed some since the last time I saw you, Charlie. You've got Mr. Coble calling you C.B., so I guess you changed your name since the last time I saw you."

Charlie shook hands with Horn and said, "You call me Mr. Irwin, when you work for me."

John Coble told Charlie that Horn was a good worker and didn't irritate the others with a lot of nonsense talk or any fool practical jokes, as some men were prone to do.

The third night out on the roundup, before getting into their bedrolls, a couple of the men had Jew's harp matches. A tall blond rangy kid, Jim Danks, took the winnings. Then Charlie saw his opportunity and challenged John Coble to a roping contest. "I just got a twenty-dollar bill that says no one can even rope a decent second to me. And if we can get a competent set of judges out of this outfit, I'll wager more because I know I'm tops."

Coble never had one of his foremen challenge him before. He could rope a steer or a horse as well as anyone; therefore, he decided to go along with the challenge.

"Too bad Duncan Clark ain't here," said one of the cowboys. "He was one of the best ropers I ever seen."

Horn stepped forward. "You boys know that I can rope; my bunch of ropers won at the Frontier Days fair. I'll be judge."

"I've seen every Frontier Days fair Cheyenne has ever had. I'll be an impartial judge," said Slim Burke, the range cook. "With me judging there won't be any trouble, because cussing a cook's as risky as branding a mule's tail."

"You boys get your ropes warmed up. Maybe some fancy tricks first, then some calf-roping. See who can bring one down and tie it faster," said Clayton Danks, Jim's brother.

"Suits me fine," said Charlie, pushing his wide-brimmed hat

back on his head. He grinned at his brother Frank, who sat on his bedroll. Frank wondered what had come over Charlie to dare the ranch manager to match rope juggling. Charlie knew what he was doing. He knew that he was the new boy in the neighborhood and he had to prove himself as soon as possible so that the men would respect and obey him.

John Coble already had his calf-rope in his hand. It ran about twenty-five feet in length, and one end was whipped tight to prevent unraveling. An eye was fixed at the other end through which the rope was run through to make the loop. This was the honda.

Charlie checked over his rope. He had rewrapped the honda the previous night, so he knew it was smooth and tight.

Coble began to cast his rope from his hands so that it whirled before it touched the ground. The centrifugal force of the loop distended it so that it was open in midair as it revolved. The friction of the spoke, or free end, against the honda prevented the loop from closing. Coble stood with his feet slightly apart, body bent forward at the waist, then he threw the right hand in counterclockwise direction slightly away from his body, and at the same time released the loop with both hands and held the guiding spoke with the right-hand fingers. He did a flat loop, wedding ring, then a big loop, over his head and around his body. A couple of the boys whistled, the others clapped. Coble was egged on so he made a big loop and stepped in, stepped out, and passed it around his body.

Charlie bit his bottom lip. He was surprised. His new boss, a short man, but strong, was good with his rope. Charlie was impressed and wished he'd done some practicing while on the trail for old man Gordon. Now, here I am, he thought, foreman of another outfit and I have to prove myself. Well—here goes—nothing.

The cowboys chattered about the skills of John Coble. Charlie stood on a flat piece of ground, placed his feet just right, and began a spin just over the ground. A good flat spin, getting into the rhythm of the spin so that he could give just enough push with his spinning hand to keep the loop out without overdoing it. He well remembered the hours of wasted time he'd spent in untangling rope when he first started and when he could not keep the rope dilated and clear of the ground. Charlie began humming. He was hardly aware of the faces before him. He brought the rope up and did the butterfly, a figure eight with a small loop, humming in time to the spinning rope. Then he did the zigzag and ocean wave. If the men were cheering or clapping he was unaware. His concentration was strong. He brought the loop back to his right side by a series of butterflies, and then carried the spinning to the left across his front and over his shoulder so that it rolled gracefully and like a rigid wheel down to the opposite side, then he came down into a butterfly and went into the over-the-spoke trick. He brought the loop between his two hands in such a way that it fell in front of the rope, then caught it afterward with a butterfly.

Horn realized at once how hard this trick was to perform and whistled loudly. Someone told him that the judge should shut up and not influence the voting of the men.

Charlie rolled the loop over his left leg, which was held out straight before him. His hand let go and caught the spoke on the opposite side as the loop fell. He finished off with the rolling butterfly, where the spinning loop was thrown up and over.

Charlie was still humming, and the noise sounded like the drone of hive bees, getting louder and louder, then falling back and becoming so quiet it was almost inaudible, then gradually rising in a crescendo once again until the droning was so loud it seemed the air was in constant vibration. When the last rolling butterfly was complete, the rope went limp and the droning stopped abruptly and Charlie, now sweating profusely, bowed and stood with a big grin on his face.

"Son of a gun!" yelled John Coble. "This man has to enter the fairs. Wow! That was the most beautiful thing I've ever seen."

"Wait a darned minute!" yelled Horn. "We haven't seen the roping yet. Let's see you pull in one of the young ones—a calf!"

Charlie wiped his face with his kerchief and mounted up beside Coble, who was already on his horse. They rode out beside the herd of grazing cattle in the moonlight. The dampness on his skin cooled him quickly and Charlie began to shiver. Coble was first to cast and caught his calf by the two front feet and threw it heavily. Before it could rise, Coble had dismounted and grabbed the hind feet and wrapped a short rope around them. While Coble was standing beside his calf, Charlie looked for a likely place to make his cast. Coble's horse had stuck to the ground but now moved its hind feet around a little. The calf must have seen and it lashed out, pulling loose its hind feet.

Charlie was afraid it would frighten the other animals and start a stampede. Luckily Coble had seen to it that the animal was away from the main herd.

Charlie rode around slowly until he found a calf standing

alone close to some brush. The mother was ten, twelve yards away lying down, but watching. Charlie swung. He talked softly so not to frighten the mother, who was now standing on her feet, but not alarmed enough to bellow or run.

Charlie brought his calf all tied tight and proper over his shoulder so that the boys could have a good look.

"Mr. Coble had his calf wrapped up on my count of four. Mr. Irwin had his tied on my count of five, but it is still tied. You can see it's tied because Mr. Irwin brought it over here on his shoulder for us to examine." Horn could hardly keep his voice controlled.

"Charlie," said Frank in a funny squeaky voice, "you don't have to bring the animal in. That's not in the rules!"

"My God, he's carrying that animal!" cried Jim Danks. "That's a strong man!"

"Hey!" yelled Charlie. "Hold on there!"

Coble and Horn were laughing and pounding each other on the back. Coble pulled out a wad of money, but put it back in his hip pocket.

"I thought Mr. Irwin won both contests," said Jim Danks.

Slim Burke said, "Sit tight and watch."

A pockmarked man rose and walked in his peculiar horseman's gait to the edge of the camp firelight, then ambled back again while the men were bantering and dickering about who had won the show. "Looks like rain," he said. "That ring around the moon always brings rain."

No one seemed interested in preparing for wet weather, so he brought out his bedroll and placed it under a small pine tree that had thick branches on only one side. It was out of the wind and somewhat sheltered from any driving rain, should one come.

Horn asked, "Mr. Coble, how much were you counting on paying anyone that could skunk you with roping tricks?"

"I was promised a cool twenty and decided to add a ten to that," said Coble, with a jolly look to his face.

Charlie looked half-sick. "You boys mean I have to pay this —rotten snake in the grass thirty dollars? That's a month's pay for a good cowboy. You know I won fair and square. What's the matter with your eyes? They crossed?"

"What's the matter with you, Mr. Irwin?" asked Coble. "Don't you have the cash?"

"You'll get your money," snapped Charlie. "But now it's bedtime with us." He felt a little put out with John Coble and wondered where things began to go wrong. He decided it was best if he acted like a proper foreman and thought the incident out alone. "Frank Irwin and Slim Burke are the first guard men. We'll point the herd on a due southerly course and point them up that little divide in the morning. Now get to bed, everybody. We'll come out of this high pastureland tomorrow."

Horn and Burke were talking, and Charlie spoke sharply to both men. "Get to bed, Horn. Get on your horse, Burke."

"We just want to say that as judges for tonight's contest we made a hell of a mistake. It is the new foreman that wins the pot. How about it, boys? Do you all agree?" said Burke.

There were hoots and hollers and shouting with agreement. Coble glared at Horn and Burke, then at Charlie, and handed over his wad of three ten-dollar bills. "I didn't think I'd ever have to let loose of that," he said with a sigh.

"But you knew you didn't win. Your horse moved. Your calf broke out of the pigging string. And you didn't speak up to say so," said Charlie, almost in a whisper. "What kind of impression you think that made on your men? You want them to think you're some kind of weasel?"

Coble turned pale in the firelight. "I'm the boss. No one talks to me like that!" Coble edged toward Charlie. Several of the boys dropped their blankets and were on top of Coble in a second. They held him pinned to the ground. Charlie pulled the men away and helped Coble to his feet.

"I'm sorry about that. I hope you aren't hurt, sir," said Charlie. He turned to the men, who were grinning from ear to ear. "Mr. Coble is the boss and if he wants to punch me he can. If he gives me an order I don't think is right, I'll tell him—if he can show me the merit, I'll follow, but you boys don't argue. Follow orders. Understand?"

There were more hoots and hollers. Coble grabbed Charlie's hand. "I say C. B. Irwin passed the initiation. He's a top-grade foreman. Welcome to the IM. From now on you're in charge of these cowboys. They saw firsthand how you react in a squeeze and how you feel about fair play and discipline. You have our respect."

Charlie's mouth hung open. "My own brother didn't warn me. I ought to wring his neck." He closed his mouth and his eyes glinted in the tiny firelight. Then he said, "I'm sorry I called Mr. Coble a rotten snake in the grass. Actually, right now he's more like a puffed-up frog in a cream can."

Coble waved his arms and bent over in a fancy bow. The cowboys whistled.

* * *

Charlie noticed that most of the men were asleep with their feet pointed toward the dead fire when Frank woke him. Frank said, "Wake up, ol' C.B. and take hold. You're on guard. Slim is calling Coble out."

Charlie groaned and sat up, ready to take his turn.

Frank said, "If you expect to follow the trail, you'll have to learn to sleep fast. Just look at all those smooth white feet; you'd think someone would sleep with his boots on. I guess no one expects Indians to attack."

Charlie poured himself a cup of strong coffee from the graniteware pot sitting on a stone beside the fire. "Coffee's as cold as I am," he said.

On guard Charlie sang to keep awake and to keep the cattle settled. As the two men went around and met, Charlie said, "Is it true Horn is sweet on a round-faced, almond-eyed wench that teaches at the Iron Mountain School?"

The next meeting, Coble said, "Keep a closed mouth, but that's the one. She's smooth to get him. Miller boys came to the ranch to invite him to a supper that she prepared."

Charlie said, "Hope he didn't spill his coffee."

Coble turned back in the saddle and added, "Nope, but he confessed to me that he felt like his collar was too tight."

Coble began whistling and Charlie picked up the rhythm and sang softly. The cows were all bedded down and content to chew their cud.

Then Charlie said, "You have a girl, Mr. Coble?"

Coble answered, "Yes, I do. She is lovely. Wears lavender and reminds me of heather. But I wonder how she feels about me."

Charlie heard Coble sigh as their horses slowly walked past each other. Charlie said, "She invite you to her place?"

"Once or twice," said Coble, slowing his horse. "She showed me her girlhood pictures in an album held together with a big silver lock, like my five-dollar belt buckle."

"That's your answer," said Charlie as they passed by once again. "Could I send my seven-year-old boy to that Iron Mountain School?"

"Certainly. Lots of the ranch kids go. But if he were mine, I'd let him go to the school in Cheyenne," said Coble.

"You and my wife," said Charlie.

When they met again, Coble spoke first. "You don't want your son to be a gristle-headed, barnyard yokel who never stops at the back door to scrape the manure off his boots. Boys need proper training. Don't let him become like the Nickell kids or even the Miller boys."

"I'll think about it and save my pay for the proper school," said Charlie. "You can't force a woman, and she has to think the whole idea is her own." Charlie sang his way past the fire, climbed down from his horse, and gently told Burke that it was time to get up and get more than coffee hot for the boys. A thin line of light was noticeable in the eastern sky. The wind had come up, and the stars were hidden by clouds. By noon there was a steady drizzle and a grayish fog over everything.

The creeks ran bankful, and two or three times they crossed over a small, fast-running creek. The cattle always stopped to drink and the boys had to prod them on.

"What if another spread ran their herd up here for the winter?" Charlie asked Coble.

"That's impossible. We just cut out what does not belong to us when we come back for ours or bring them all in and cut them out as we pass their ranches. Don't worry, by summer you'll know all the brands between here and Medicine Bow."

"Ever run into any Indians?"

Coble laughed. "Nope. They're all on the reservations, my friend."

Charlie told Coble about his experience with the Sioux at Pine Ridge.

"Poor devils, I say."

"You'd change your mind if you ever saw a Sioux riding a good horse."

That night the rain stopped and the moon stood nearly full in the sky. The men did not complain. Their slickers had protected them some, but most slept between blankets and all had a cold supper because dry wood could not be found. The next day was clear. They were back to the meadow, which was protected on three sides by shallow rocky walls and bordered on the fourth side by a small creek so that none of the cows would wander far away. They had picked up a dozen unmarked cows, which were held by a rope and branded while Charlie marked their ears for the IM. Also in the herd were two dark-coated buffalo cows with a young one apiece.

"Leave them be," said Coble. "By spring they may still be here, showing these domesticated beasts where the grass is best."

Etta had sizzling hot steaks and mashed potatoes for the cowboys' dinner, along with milk gravy and biscuits and string beans and raisin pie.

"You feed too good," warned Burke, "and the IM ranch will pick up every stray cowboy that goes through this country."

Etta smiled. She knew what the men appreciated.

TWENTY-ONE

Fire at Iron Mountain

Many a night after the cows were milked and fed and the chores completed, the cowboys sat at the big oak dining table and swapped yarns or played solo, a game similar to bridge, except that one successful bidder alone took on the others, or cribbage, pegging out the scores, fifteen-two, fifteen-four, fifteen-six, or poker, long after Etta cleared off the table. Etta often put a kettle of oatmeal on the back of the stove to simmer all night and be ready for the next morning's breakfast of biscuits, gravy, thin-sliced steaks, fried eggs, thick oatmeal with salt and pepper and fresh butter or thick cream and sugar. Of course there was always the hot black coffee.

Charlie looked forward to the evenings around the table. He kept his mouth shut and let the others talk. He loved to hear the exploits the cowboys bragged about. Most were only half-true.

Horn was that way. He loved telling about how good he was with his Winchester, how he could site a coyote, or even a man, at five, six hundred yards and hit the target midway between the eyes.

"I heard you have a kind of signature or trademark," Charlie said to Horn one evening. "Some say you leave a rock under the head of your victims whether they be man or beast."

Horn colored, rubbed his hands together, cleared his throat, and said, "Boys, if you believe that, you can believe that tomorrow the sky will be green and the grass blue." His eyes seemed to be deep gray with a never-ending bottom, like a deep pit.

Later that evening Charlie and Etta talked quietly. "It's some craziness when neighbor is pitted against neighbor, brother against brother," said Charlie. "Everyone suspects everyone else in this Nickell affair."

"Maybe it's because the papers print a little here, a little there all the time, so's it's even in the big eastern papers," said Etta.

"That's coming from Joe LeFors. He's a tinhorn deputy marshal who thinks if he can pin a murder on some unsuspecting man, he'll get himself a big promotion, even go into politics, have any position in the state he wants."

"I don't like it. It's ugly. Isn't there something I can do?"

"Squelch every rumor. Think in straight lines. Throw cold water on anything that looks like fire," said Charlie.

All the talk about guns and hitting targets reminded Etta that Frank had borrowed Charlie's rifle. "I don't remember Frank bringing the old Henry back after he brought in the dressed venison."

"Sure, he brought it back. It's on the bedroom closet shelf. Go look," said Charlie.

She did and found the rifle. "I feel ashamed of myself. I just don't want Frank to be seen with a gun and have someone accuse him of something he didn't do. Oh, Charlie, times are terrible. Everyone who carries a gun is a suspect."

"That includes about every dadburned rancher in Wyoming!" Charlie's voice boomed out.

Charlie was surprised at the work his father and Will had done to the ranch house on the Y6, a twelve-room, two-story place. Out back was the bunkhouse. The closet, as Joe called the outhouse, was built to one end of the icehouse, about twenty yards from the kitchen door. Will laughed when he showed Charlie, saying that Margaret still had the children using chamber pots because she didn't want to bundle them in coats, hats, and scarves each time they had to go. Not far from the back door was the water pump. Beyond the bunkhouse was the smithy and carpenter shed with all of Joe's tools. East of the huge barn was the chicken house, wagon shed, granary, corrals, and cattle sheds. Charlie suddenly wanted to start work on his own ranch so bad he could taste it.

"I'm coming back here with Etta and the kids just as soon as I can buy some good horseflesh," promised Charlie. "The time will be here soon, you'll see."

Joe's hair was white, but he seemed just as quick and agile as before. He and Charlie rode horseback out to where Bear Creek ran into Horse Creek. The ground was clear of snow in many places where the wind had blown it away. Ahead the hills looked like the long backbone of some prehistoric monster. "That's all ours." Joe waved his arm in a wide arc. "See there, that hill at the end of the range, soft and rounded? I call it Round Top. It's my favorite. It seems to me a sentinel, looking over this here land, a place from where the winds are born and come howling from that round top out across the flat plain. One day I left my bedroom window open and that wind blew everything out the door but my mattress!"

"Frank and I want to come over here on our days off and bring in some wild horses. We'll tame them and bring them in to use as broncos for this year's Frontier Days. What do you think, Pa?"

"I think, do it. But be sure you get paid for the use of your stock," said Joe. "You should watch Margaret ride that big yellow horse she calls Old Gold. She has the fancy notion that she might enter the cow-pony race during the Frontier Days celebration. What do you think about that?"

"I think it's fine. She's trying to prove to herself that she can live on a ranch. She also wants to prove to everyone else that she is as good or better than these other ranch girls."

"What will Etta think?" asked Joe, dubious about his daughter-in-law entering a horse race. "Is she inclined to this modern notion that women can do everything a man can do?"

"Pa, Etta believes in initiative and teamwork. I would guess that when Etta learns Margaret is ready to enter the race, she'll help."

The moon came up, a partial globe at the edge of the horizon. It floated over the dark curtain of night like a split pumpkin rind. It sent down enough reflected light so that Charlie easily followed the roads back to the IM ranch. Charlie thought of Margaret and Etta. They were like blond and brunette sisters. Etta strait-laced as a fine calfskin shoe, usually, and Margaret flirty as an Abilene dance hall girl, at times.

The snow flew around the first of December. There was no letup for a week. When it was finished, the snow was as high as the first-floor windows. The men were kept busy hauling hay out to the cows and horses.

Floyd rode horseback to the one-room schoolhouse. He liked

the schoolmarm, Miss Kimmell. She let the boys chop the firewood and have footraces and rope-spinning contests. There were five boys and eight girls, giving the school the unlucky number of thirteen pupils. For two, three days Floyd could not get to the schoolhouse. Then the winds came and blew harder than usual, making eight- to ten-foot drifts against the house and barn. The roads were generally blown clear of snow.

Etta and Charlie invited Will, Margaret, their children, and Joe to the IM ranch house for Christmas day. Nothing marred the festivities. Everyone, including the ranch hands, enjoyed the dinner of roast pork, beefsteaks, mashed potatoes, gravy, biscuits, canned tomatoes, applesauce, mince pie, pound cake, whipped cream, and coffee.

During the meal Floyd asked, "Why does Ma say, 'Clean your plate before dessert'? If I were a mother, I'd let my boy eat dessert first, then if he still had room, try the other stuff. What if there's a fire while we're eating dinner? We'd have to run out before the best part. If I were boss—I'd make a rule for dessert first." This sense of priority endeared him to his sisters and cousins.

The new year of 1902 was cold and the snow continued to fall so that there were drifts deeper than three feet where protected from wind.

Charlie made sleds for the three older children from the wooden crates the two-dozen canned tomatoes and peaches were packed in when bought from the Union Mercantile. For metal runners that were slick and fast on the snow, he used barrel hoops fastened to long blocks of wood. Etta often went sledding with the children after supper if the baby was sleeping. Charlie talked with the cowboys. Some, such as Jim and Clayton Danks, John Ryan, and Dan Thor, stayed year-round; others came and went with the seasons, working north in summer and south in winter. Tom Horn stayed, but one day told Charlie he was thinking of moving to Montana.

One evening, about the middle of January, Etta was out in the back of the ranch house with Floyd, Joella, and Pauline romping in the snow. She threw snowballs and jumped on Floyd's sled. She let snowflakes melt on her tongue and laughed when her face was wet. She whooped and yelled with her children, pulling each up the small hill. She showed them how to make "angels" in the snow by lying full length on a pristine spot and moving arms from their sides up to their heads for "wings." She had each child put his sled against the back wall of the house before going inside.

Charlie thought that when Etta laughed and played in the snow she was like a precocious child herself. He was sure a stranger would not be able to say for certain she was the mother. She had more life and happiness in her tiny body than any two farm women he'd seen come into Cheyenne for supplies. Etta's cheeks were red as apples and matched the children's.

Inside, where it was warm, she put two chunks of split wood into the fire box of the kitchen range and a pan of milk on top for making hot chocolate. She took her own wraps off. Then she helped the children remove their coats, leggings, scarves, mittens, and overshoes.

"Ma, I want to pass around the cocoa cups," said five-year-old Joella. "I won't spill."

"Girls always want to do this or that," complained Floyd, a year older. "Boy, I'd give Joella whereat. When I hit her with a snowball, she cried. I wish her tears had froze, on her nose, so it glowed like a rose—"

"Floyd, stop!" said Etta sharply. "You put soda crackers on each saucer." She reached into the cupboard for the box of crackers.

"Floyd, you can pour the cocoa," said Joella with generosity.

After their cocoa was finished the children were sent to bed. Each called good night to the cowboys, who were also enjoying the cocoa and crackers.

Etta rinsed off saucers and washed cups and the cocoa pan. Charlie munched on crackers while tucking the children in their beds.

Eventually the cowboys, tired of talk, climbed the stairs to their beds. Etta turned out all but one coal-oil lamp. This last lamp she carried into her and Charlie's bedroom.

"Listen to that wind blow. It's become stronger in the last hour. I've a notion to wear two pairs of underwear and two pairs of socks to keep warm," said Charlie.

The baby began to fret. Etta pulled the crib next to her bed and changed the flannelette diaper, and sat on the bed to nurse her.

Charlie lay back in bed and watched his pixie wife sway back and forth, rocking Frances back to sleep. Charlie lifted his eyes and looked about the familiar room, then something in the doorway stopped his glancing. There young Floyd stood in his long-johns.

Charlie sat up. "You all right, son?"

"I don't like the wind. It sounds like crying. It's blowing smoke from the fireplace back into the house. Smell it?"

"Aw, you're dreaming. Come sit on the bed with me. We'll sing a song while your mother feeds the baby."

Floyd ran across the room and flung himself into his father's lap. Charlie wrapped the dark-haired, slender boy in his big red flannel shirt and softly sang "The Old Rugged Cross." Etta laid the sleeping Frances back in her crib and thought of putting the old pink shawl over the crib blankets. She decided the baby was warm enough. Besides, the floor was too cold to walk on with bare feet, even as far as the closet for the shawl.

The bedrooms were not heated. Charlie carried Floyd to his room off the kitchen. It was meant to be a pantry, but there were not enough hands at the ranch yet to have use for that many stores. Everything could be kept in the kitchen's cupboards, drawers, and bins. Floyd had an iron cot, painted white. He'd asked for that when he saw the cowboys slept in white iron cots upstairs. "I don't want none of sissy feather beds," he'd told his mother. The stairs leading to the cowboys' second floor were outside Floyd's room.

Five-year-old Joella and three-year-old Pauline had thick feather mattresses in the small bedroom down the hall from Charlie and Etta. On the dresser was a pitcher of water and china bowl for washing. Joella's chore was to put fresh water in the pitchers each day. The old unused water was put in the bucket on the back of the stove for dishwater.

"Thank goodness, the cows and horses are close by this winter, with stacks of hay," said Charlie, sliding back into bed. "My feet are ice."

"I know, that's why I moved way over here," said Etta, giggling.

"Hope it doesn't snow tonight. Cows are so dumb, they won't find the hay if it's covered up, even if they walk over it."

"Can't snow, the clouds are high," said Etta. "In the spring could we rent a couple rooms in Cheyenne so that I could move in with the children, then Floyd could go to school? Please, Charlie?"

"You'd leave me here? Who'd cook? Who'd warm my feet?"

"Slim Burke'll come back. He can cook. You don't eat anything but biscuits and gravy, mashed potatoes and beef, and canned peaches. Anyone can fix that. A couple of rocks heated in the fireplace and wrapped in a flannel towel will warm your feet."

"You're hard-hearted, dear. I'd miss you and the kids."

"When you come to town for supplies, or some meeting, you could stay over with me and the kids."

"Couldn't you teach Floyd yourself, just a while longer? Is it that important that he go to school?"

"I bet you that your brother, Will, lets Margaret stay in town with her kids while they are old enough to be in school."

"Ah, green-eyed jealous," said Charlie, moving closer to Etta. "Margaret won't move to town and you know it. She likes the ranch and the horses. She'll send her kids to a one-room school like we have for the Iron Mountain district."

"Jealous? Not of Margaret. She rides horses with the cowboys. She wears divided skirts. I'd really like a house in town so I could dress up once in a while."

"My ma felt that way. Maybe that's why Pa frowns when he sees Margaret climb on a horse bareback and race around the pasture. But Pa likes Margaret. He told me not long ago how good she was taking care of the ranch house and that her cooking has improved. Once you told me you didn't think she could cook even if she set a haystack on fire."

"Oh, Charlie, I remember. That wasn't nice of me. I like Margaret. But still, it's unladylike to ride a horse all day and let the housework go and those kids shift for themselves. I suppose she lets Joe do the cleaning and chase after those two kids."

"Don't be so sharp-tongued," said Charlie.

"I remember when they were married. Margaret was just a child. Not bad-looking, really pretty, but she had so much to learn. I guess she's learned."

"We Irwins know how to find good women," said Charlie, half-asleep.

"I'll make ice cream tomorrow. Floyd can help turn the freezer crank. We'll use icicles from the eaves, so you won't have to go to the ice house." Etta waited for Charlie to notice she'd changed the subject. She heard only his even breathing of sleep. She listened to the short breaths of the sleeping Frances. Soon Etta was asleep.

After midnight the wind blew hard. Fine snow was picked up and moved around against the base of hillocks and buildings. It blew off the flat ground, exposing gray, dead grass. Charlie woke, listened to the howling wind, then gently as possible took his one hundred ninety pounds out of the bed. He didn't want to disturb Etta. The floor was like walking on an iceberg. He scratched his broad chest and listened again. The wind was blowing a gale, screaming around house corners. He pulled on his pants and shirt, wrapped himself in an old blue robe, but still could not stop shivering. He padded out to the sitting room. There was something in the cold air he could not quite identify. He smelled the cold ashes of the fireplace and thought of Floyd thinking the wind blew smoke back inside the house. His nostrils retained the smoky smell of the ashes. He went into the kitchen and lit a coal-oil lamp left on the table. Carrying the lamp he checked to see if Floyd was well covered. Of course he was. Charlie continued along the icy floor to the girls' room.

He looked beyond the half-opened door and chuckled. Joella was sleeping with a wide, pink hair ribbon perched on top of her head. Pauline was snuggled so far down in her covers that it was hard to see her soft, straight brown hair. Satisfied that everyone was all right he went back to the kitchen. Then on some impulse he took the lamp up the wooden stairs. He sniffed the warmer air at the top. The warmth felt good, especially around his legs.

He pushed the door wide open, kept the lantern behind him so as not to waken the cowboys. A table was against the far wall, where the men sometimes played cards or talked before going to bed. The room was stuffy. Charlie thought, six men sleeping can't be enough warm bodies to make the room feel this close. Or can it? Heat rises. The soles of his feet felt warm. He put the low-glowing lamp on the table and bent to feel the floor. He heard John Ryan snore. The floor was warm. That's not right, reasoned Charlie. He ran his eyes over the rough floor planking. Some of the cracks between the boards were wide enough to sweep in all the mud and dirt these men could bring up on their boots. He felt the floor again and moved closer to the wall by the table. There was a blackened pie tin with several old cigarette butts. Charlie wrinkled his nose. He was tempted to dump the mess. A smelly cigarette butt could go down some of the cracks between floor boards easily.

Charlie wondered if the men ever lost anything—like a jackknife or coins or pocket comb—down the wide cracks. His eye caught something by his foot—a gray-blue wispy tail. He sniffed smoke. Yes, smoke, and it shouldn't be there! He stayed on his hands and knees and smelled along another wide crack. His nostrils felt the sting of acrid smoke and the floor was hot on his knees, right through his two pairs of underwear. His mind could not believe what his eyes and nose told him. He crawled to the far side of the room and found that also unusually warm. Then out of one of the wider cracks came a tiny, thin finger of red flame and his brain knew.

He scrambled to his feet yelling, "Men! Fire! Get out! Fire! The house is on fire! Get up!"

The Danks brothers were up first. Charlie stood by the cots, calling urgently, "Move quickly. There's a fire under the floor boards!" His eyes betrayed his terror.

All six men pulled on Levi's, shirts, grabbed boots, blankets, angora chaps, sheepskin coats, a saddle, a .30-.30 Winchester, anything they saw of value. None were fully awake, but all fully aware of the danger. Orange flame rippled like liquid waves. Charlie dumped the water from the pitchers on the floor and followed them down the stairs.

Clayton Danks went after Floyd. Charlie ran to waken the girls, thinking he'd take them in to Etta.

Neil Clark grabbed Charlie's arms. "You get the missus and the baby. I'll get the children. Jimmy'll get the payroll and books."

Charlie took his sheepskin coat and cap from the hook. He picked up Floyd's boots and his own.

"We'll get pails of water and drown it," said Charlie, going after Etta. He talked to himself. "I'll get an ax and open a hole in the floor. We'll drown her good." He caught a flash of Floyd wrapped in a woolen blanket, carrying a lantern, and a pile of dishes, going out the back door with John Ryan.

Etta rushed to put her coat over her nightdress and overshoes on her stockinged feet. She picked up Frances and went to the closet for the big, pink woolen shawl to wrap around the baby, who had on only a diaper shirt and a long cotton nightdress.

When everyone was standing outdoors, shivering, Charlie yelled, "Why aren't the pails by the water pump? We need to get water on that upstairs floor. Come on!"

Clark took the bucket of warm water off the back of the kitchen stove and ran upstairs. His blue robe flapped around his legs beneath his coat. Frank went into the back shed for a broad-blade ax and a couple of hand axes. Etta dropped the baby in Joella's lap. Joella sat on the back steps as if still asleep, the pink ribbon still in her hair.

"Hold Frannie while Floyd and I pump water!"

Etta grabbed a bucket where several hung on nails at the back of the house. The wind tore at her hair and pulled Floyd's blanket open.

She yelled, "Pull the fool thing closed and don't get wet! I'll pin the blanket so's you can work easier." Quickly she pulled two big safety pins from her coat pocket and tugged at Floyd's blanket.

"Ain't that something pretty," said Floyd, pointing to the flames that were licking out of the east top-floor window. Yellow sap oozed from the pine frames and the lapping flames roared and snapped.

"Take the water inside to the men!" Etta screamed. She put another bucket under the spigot and worked the pump. Her heart was pounding. She was afraid the water would freeze and the pump would go dry. "Fire is the most ugly something on the prairie," she said. She then yelled at Frank, "Hey, drop those axes and take this water upstairs! Don't spill! I know it's heavy, but you can do it!"

"Hey, I'm not six years old!" Frank yelled back.

One of the Danks brothers ran out of the house with an armload of yesterday's baked bread and some kitchen knives. He put it all on a blanket near the bunkhouse, then went to help Floyd carry a water bucket.

Etta pumped water as fast as she could, keeping the buckets filled as they were brought back. She glanced at Joella huddled over the baby and at Pauline huddled against Joella for protection from the wind.

Suddenly the men came pell-mell out of the house, each carrying something—books, a chair, an iron griddle, a clock, a lard bucket, a can of coffee. Charlie held Floyd. He yelled, "We gotta let her go! It's hot enough to singe the feathers off a chicken at the top of the stairs. When the stairs go, the whole place'll go fast. I got the Henry rifle, I'm going back for the baby's crib and your clothes. That's all!"

"Oh, no!" Etta shrieked and grabbed Charlie's arm. "What if the ceiling falls? You'd be trapped. Frannie can sleep anywhere. My clothes aren't important." Etta began to laugh hysterically. She couldn't help herself. The men stared at her. She pointed. "Look what Joella has in her lap. Her big hand mirror! Oh, that is so funny!"

"Lookit Pauline!" cried Floyd. "She's hugging her pillow."

The boys chuckled and looked at the items they'd brought out.

Etta was adamant. No one else should go inside the burning house. "If I can leave my mother's silver brooch," she said softly, sobbing, "which means a lot to me—you can leave the rest of the things. Nothing is worth getting burned for."

Charlie grabbed a bucket and shoved it toward Etta. "We gotta save something for Mr. Coble! Throw water on that half-done bunkhouse, and the barn. Move! Watch out for the hot ash and sparks! Floyd, take your sisters inside the bunkhouse out of this blamed wind!"

"I thank Mr. Coble for putting a roof on the bunkhouse last weekend," said Etta.

"We shoulda' moved in half-furnished or not. Then this wouldn't have happened," said Clayton Danks, grabbing a full bucket of water, passing it to his brother, who passed it on to Frank, who got it to Neil Clark, who threw it on the bunkhouse roof and sides.

After about thirty minutes the line shifted so that the men were closer to the barn. Charlie had a ladder against the barn's side so that he could scramble up and down as the buckets were passed to him.

"Water turns to ice the minute it splashes out," Charlie panted. "But keep it coming!"

Suddenly everything was bright. Brighter than if the northern lights were on full power. The outdoors was lit up like arc lights. The ranch house was a jack-o'-lantern, then it burst into flames from top to bottom.

"Watch the sparks!" repeated Charlie. "Stay away from the house! It's a goner! You can't save her. Save the barn and the bunkhouse."

The men continued to throw water on the bunkhouse roof and the barn walls.

A couple hours later Clark was at the water pump. The handle froze and would not move up and down. "Oh, hell! Fill the buckets with snow and spread on the barn's roof!"

Charlie yelled, "Snow won't stay, the wind'll blow it off! What blamed luck! Kick those burning boards in a pile. We'll melt the snow!"

"Missus Irwin, you go inside the bunkhouse with the children," said Jim Danks.

"But—I can help. Charlie needs—" sputtered Etta, not used to being told what to do.

"Sure, you're needed. But not out here, freezing your a—arms. Go inside and look after the kids."

Etta went. How good it felt inside the half-finished bunkhouse, out of the piercing wind. She heard Joella and Pauline crying softly. "No crying," she said gently. "I'll find a lamp and we'll look around here. I know the men brought blankets somewhere."

"We're sitting on them," sobbed Joella. "And here's the lamps."

"I sat on the bread," said Pauline. Her voice quivered.

Etta lit the lamp from matches in her coat pocket. She thought of the waste of good matches with all the flames outside. She found the round-bellied iron stove and made certain by feeling that it had a pipe connected from the stove to a hole in the ceiling before she broke up an old wood crate and put it in the stove. Here's hoping snow's not packed in the chimney, she thought as she held a thick splinter in the lamp flame. When the fire was blazing, she went outside to bring Floyd in to warm up a bit. "Bring a bucket of clean snow," she said. "I found a sack of sugar and some coffee."

Floyd was not happy staying inside with the women. But he was so sleepy his eyes would hardly stay open. Beside the stove he felt warm and relaxed.

Etta fixed the girls a place to sleep between big sacks of flour and grain that were stored in the bunkhouse. The baby was cradled on a pile of clean hay between two grain sacks lined with a thick quilt. Frances hardly wakened during all the yelling and commotion.

Frank came in for warmth, found some cups and bowls someone had saved from the house. He poured himself steaming coffee. "Goddamn it's cold as hell working with freezing snow water in this bitchy wind." He glanced at Etta and said, "Sorry, I thought you went outside."

"Don't you ever talk that way in front of the girls, nor Floyd either," she snapped.

"I don't have any mittens. My hands are frostbitten," he whined, and held his hands clutched together.

Etta looked at his hands under the yellow kerosene lamp, hoping they weren't frozen. She looked around the long room, bent, and pulled Floyd's boots off. The child was so exhausted he did not open his eyes as his mother took his socks off. He slept with his head on a sack of flour, his back toward the stove. Etta flung the socks toward Frank. "Wear these, but bring them back when you're done. Floyd will need them tomorrow."

"Thanks, Et." Frank rushed from the bunkhouse, his hands in the black wool stockings.

Charlie and Jimmy Danks came in next for coffee.

"I put a lot of sugar in for you," said Etta.

"Don't apologize. It's the best I've had," said Charlie, smacking his lips. "Wind takes heat right out of a body." He sat on the floor with his back against the wall.

Jimmy said, "Yep, fans the flames and blows the snow. My face gets hot and my feet freeze."

"How in blue blazes did this inferno start, Jimmy?" asked Charlie, so tired he could hardly hold his cup of coffee.

"You suspect me?" asked Jimmy, his soot-streaked face peering up into Charlie's.

Charlie looked down and stared a few seconds, resting. His mind was slowly warming up. "You are the one that smokes like a Bessemer converter. A cigarette butt or two pushed between cracks in that floor keeps the room neat, but if those butts are not stone cold—they could smolder for hours, then all of a sudden flare up." Charlie closed his eyes.

"Occasionally I empty the pie tin down those cracks before we hit the hay. Last night we played cards a spell and I got rid of the stinky butts when we finished. You think—maybe—oh, God! It is possible!" His eyes bulged out in terror.

"I don't see another explanation," said Charlie, opening his eyes. "I know you didn't deliberately set fire to the ranch house. Drink your coffee. Go back out there and keep your mouth shut. Don't be a sap. No one set this fire on purpose. It was fate."

Disheartened, the two men went out the door not looking back. Each knew that Etta would not breathe a word of what she'd heard.

Clayton Danks and Neil Clark came in next for their coffee. "This hot coffee has enough sugar to give me the energy I need to climb to the top of that gol-darn barn once more if I have to," said young Clark. "Did you see the wind catch that firebrand and carry it clean over the barn's roof? I used two buckets of snow to get those small fires out caused by flying sparks. Wind blows on top of that barn like it was the highest peak of the Himalayas."

Etta filled their cups twice.

"With your cheeks red and your hair blown around your face—well, it reminds me of a Greek goddess I once saw in a book," said Clark.

"Oh, go on!" said Etta.

"Yes, ma'am."

"Thanks," said Danks. "We'll be in again before dawn." He put his cup on the floor and his arm on Clark's shoulder. "You've a lot of nerve to practice being Romeo with the boss's wife."

Clark turned to Etta before he ducked out the door. "Who expected the night to be like this when we enjoyed cocoa in the kitchen—ages ago, ma'am."

Etta smiled. She felt like crying. John Coble's new ranch house was gone. The men could manage in the unfinished bunkhouse. She and the children would have to go to the Y6 and live with Joe and Will and Margaret.

Neil Clark came back inside. "I just want to say that come morning, I'll milk the cows so your little ones'll have fresh milk."

"That's thoughtful. But it's my job to do the milking. I reckon I can still do it." Etta decided she liked this gallant young man who practiced his courting talk on her.

"You work hard. I'm going to suggest to Mr. Irwin that we take turns with the milking. Women should be admired and looked at."

"Mr. Clark—thank you. I suspect you are rehearsing those words to use on some young lady in Cheyenne." Etta wiped her eyes and smiled.

"In Laramie," Clark said, and went outside.

Thor and Ryan came for coffee and a short rest, then found strength to go out again. Etta watched through the window. She saw the men dump snow on flaming sticks blown near the barn. Then she saw the men turn in unison as a chorus line and her eyes followed theirs. The house roof fell in slow motion and at the same time the second floor pitched crazily sideways and fell into the first floor with a muffled boom and a deafening roar. Sparks flew outward in the shape of a fan with the wind. The roar of the flames was resounding, even inside the bunkhouse. The windows shook as if the air were rent by thunder. When the burning slacked off, the house stood as a skeleton, blackened bare bones with the inside gutted. Only the carbonized first floor walls stood. Then suddenly they, too, were eaten fast by thick yellow tongues that licked out as far as they were stretched by the wind. The skeleton was gone. Only ghostly gray smoke was left. The men came into the bunkhouse one by one. Their faces were dirty from soot and shadowy beards. Two men had burns on their hands. Charlie thought his hands were frostbitten. He had piled snow around the burning house to keep the lower flames and debris contained and not blown from there halfway across the prairie. Frank kept moaning that his feet were blocks of ice.

No one took his coat off.

Jimmy Danks stood beside Charlie. Everyone could see he

was so tired that he could hardly put his hand out to shake Charlie's. "Mr. Irwin, we all thank you for getting us out of there. We'd have burnt when that hellfire broke loose. We'd never woke up soon enough to get to them stairs. Nobody's noticed, but you're a hero."

"Charlie's a person like the rest of us. He did what was called for. I'd have jumped out the window if Charlie hadn't come upstairs," said Frank, who was on the floor with his back against the wall, closing his eyes.

"And broken your head as wide open as any breakfast egg," grinned Charlie, who was utterly exhausted. Everything seemed to go slower than normal. "Tomorrow we have to talk about what we are going to say to John Coble," he said, stretching out on the floor next to the sacks of grain. He held his aching hands in a bucket of melted snow water. He had to grit down on his teeth to keep from crying out, the pain was so bad.

Etta helped Frank put his feet into another bucket of snow water. In a few minutes tears were running down his face. "My God, my feet feel like they're on fire."

"I'm so tired my tongue's hanging out a foot and about forty inches," said Clayton Danks.

Etta knew the men were hurting because of fatigue, frostbite, and burns. She blurted out something she'd heard her own mother say once to her brothers. "Put your warm hands over your ears and hum softly to take the pain away."

Charlie hummed for ten, twelve minutes, then fell asleep. The others tried. Frank pulled his feet from the bucket and slept. He woke and hummed and slept again. Etta put the pink wool shawl around his feet. The others had rolled into the blankets. Etta found a blanket and lay close to Charlie after turning the lamp out. Charlie saw sparks jump from dying embers of the house behind his closed eyelids. It seemed morning came only minutes later. The wind had died down. White clouds ran across the pale-blue sky, their underside planed flat by the wind. A golden glow spread out in long spokes from the horizon as the sun emerged. The air was clear and dry and cold. The blackened snow and charcoal-rectangle remains of the IM ranch house were leftovers from a garish nightmare.

Charlie was stiff in every muscle. He crawled to the window and looked out in the cold, blue dawn. He smelled his clothes strong with smoke and felt a sickness rise from deep within his stomach. He thought if daybreak was so special, it should be scheduled at a more convenient hour.

Yesterday there was a beautiful, useful ranch house. Today's light showed nothing. Worse than nothing. Something that was a blackened mess, that had to be cleaned and scraped away.

All knew John Coble's heart would break. He'd taken such delight in building the ranch house with all the comforts one could desire. He was a bachelor who relied on female advice. Etta guessed that he, along with Neil Clark, was looking for a feminine partner. She thought that Mr. Coble, with his eastern accent, ruddy complexion, and neat attire, was attractive to women. She dreaded the moment he would come to see the ruins of his ranch house. She felt she could never again look at his face without crying. His ranch house had suited her better than any place she'd lived. To her it was not losing a piece of valuable property as it would be to Mr. Coble. To her it was losing a protective shelter, an outer layer that was comfortable and safe as well as decorative.

The snow glistened with the brightening golden light of sunrise as the sun's orb cleared the earth's edge. Millions of glittering crystals almost too brilliant to look at greeted Etta through the soot-stained window.

The children wakened. Etta gave them each a small hunk of bread torn from a loaf that was still warm from being next to Pauline as she slept.

"I'm sure stove up," said Clayton Danks with a laugh. He went out and chopped hunks of meat with a hatchet from the beef that hung in the barn loft. He brought the meat back in a bucket. Etta thanked him and added snow to the bucket before putting it on the back of the stove to simmer. "I'll see what else I can find," said Danks. In twenty minutes he was back with spoons, enameled plates, and a couple of kettles. All were sooty black and smelled of acrid smoke.

"Laws, the scrubbing I'll have to do," said Etta with a sigh.

Danks look disappointed.

"Oh, I don't mind," Etta said quickly. "I'll scrub them and it'll save eating with our fingers." She made her petticoats into dishtowels, washcloths, and diapers.

After breakfast of bread, sweet coffee, and milk the men decided to sort through the ashes, pick out whatever was usable, and store it in the barn. Jimmy Danks hauled all usable logs to one side and chopped some for firewood.

"I hope we find more buckets or kettles for milk," said Clark. "There doesn't seem to be enough for cleaning, cooking, and milking."

"Could we freeze the milk and keep it like blocks of ice?" asked Etta.

"You sure think good, besides looking good," said Clark.

The noon meal was stewed beef and fresh milk. Afterward Charlie and Jimmy Thor rode for Bosler to find Mr. Coble.

Floyd found his stockings under Frank's blanket. He dressed in boots, underwear, and a wool blanket and went out to help the men sift through the ashes and charred remains of the house.

"If you find Mama's silver brooch, put it in your pocket and bring it to me," said Floyd.

Before dark Charlie and Jimmy Thor were back. Their horses were loaded with food supplies along with several faded, threadbare shirts and Levi's. Charlie called out so that even those in the barn could hear, "Mr. Coble's coming here day after tomorrow! He wants to rebuild!" In the meantime they were all to carry on from the bunkhouse as best they could. John Coble said he'd sell beef cattle to raise money to rebuild.

After supper of more stewed beef and bread and some canned peaches Floyd dug deep into his pocket and pulled out Etta's silver brooch. The clasp was melted against the back. "Neil found it," said Floyd.

Etta knew it was silly to be sentimental about a silver brooch, but she could not stop the tears that slid down her face. "My mama gave it to me when I was married. It belonged to her mama," she explained to Floyd. "I'm not crying because I'm sad. These are happy tears."

The men watched the children pass the delicate filigreed pin among themselves as though they'd never seen it before. Finally Floyd said, "I'd like you to wear it."

Etta pinned the brooch to the neck of her nightgown with a safety pin. In the gray twilight the burnished silver looked beautifully fine, dainty—exquisite.

Neil Clark said, "Go for a walk, ma'am, before it is too dark to see. Look in the barn and see all the stuff we saved. Me and the men'll have the dishes done when you get back—the snow water's boiling already. Mr. Irwin, go with her."

Etta had her coat and scarf on before anyone could change his mind.

Charlie was embarrassed by the attention Etta caused by being tearful over a sentimental brooch. He was glad to get outdoors. He breathed deeply of the cold air and felt better. He locked hands with Etta.

"What does that runt, Neil Clark, think he is, running the

foreman and his wife out in the cold?" Charlie growled. He tucked Etta's arm under his own.

"I like him," said Etta. Her voice was warm and rolling like a tiny creek meandering through a meadow in spring.

"I was about to tell you the same. He's right, you know. You've worked as hard as any of the men. You and the kids are going to Cheyenne. I'm going to get a house in town for you."

Etta stopped walking. She couldn't talk. Her throat constricted and squeezed more tears from her eyes.

"Don't cry, dear. I thought about a house in Cheyenne all the way to and from Bosler. Don't say we can't afford it, because I thought about that, too. I'm going to stay here, working for Mr. Coble until he builds a new ranch house and things are going all right for him, then I'm going to work with Pa and Will on the Y6. It's time I started raising my own horses. That's what we came to Cheyenne for—horses."

Etta had her arms around Charlie's wide waist. Her tears spilled on his sheepskin.

"I sure hope those tears are for happiness," he said with his arms around her shoulders.

Etta looked up and smiled. "The children and I will stay at the Y6 until we find a place in town. I can raise chickens and add to our savings." Her throat was open and she wanted to talk.

"Don't count on chickens. We're going to find that place in town right away. Mr. Coble told me about one that's for sale."

Etta felt Charlie's belt buckle press against her breast. "What did Mr. Coble say about the fire?"

"First he was mighty relieved that no one was hurt. He knew the wind was blowing like fury. He suggested a couple of sparks might have left the chimney and hit the roof, or even spit out the fireplace when we were all in bed. I let him talk. He said, 'I've the best bunch there ever was at Iron Mountain. We'll rebuild the house just the way she was.'"

Etta turned and looked at the blackened remains. The only things that could be identified were the kitchen range, tangled iron from the sleeping cots and bedsteads, and the stone fireplace. The sight made her feel half-sick. She turned away to sort out her thoughts quickly. When she took Charlie's hand and looked up into his face her eyes were bright. "That's wonderful! Not the fire, but Mr. Coble and Cheyenne. There's something to look forward to. That old saying is true. Heaven is right next to hell."

A week later Etta sat in the kitchen of the Y6 ranch house to read the papers Joe had brought in from Cheyenne. She was holding baby Frances on her lap. The *Cheyenne Daily Leader* attracted her attention with bold headlines: LOCAL COWBOY CONFESSES KILLING WILLIE NICKELL. She read that Tom Horn was arrested on Monday, January 13, 1902, in the lobby of the Inter-Ocean Hotel in Cheyenne.

The paper said Horn confessed the killing of Willie Nickell to Deputy U.S. Marshal Joe LeFors. Even Etta could figure out that Horn walked into a deliberately set trap. Horn went to see LeFors about the job in Montana. He and LeFors had a couple friendly drinks while talking about the Montana job. Then LeFors began asking Horn about the Willie Nickell killing.

All the time they were talking and LeFors was being so friendly, the court stenographer, Charles Ohnhaus, was in the next room with his ear to the crack in the door, taking shorthand notes! Etta felt her mouth become dry. LeFors had indeed set a trap for Horn.

"It's so unfair!" cried Etta angrily.

"LeFors is desperate," said Joe. "He wants someone to pin the Nickell killing on. And Etta, you're for sure all growed up when you notice life's mostly unfair."

Etta said, "Grandpa Joe, I wonder when Miss Kimmell's coming back? Rumor has it the schoolhouse is closed tight. I wonder if she would lie to give Tom an alibi if he needed one?"

Joe chuckled and said, "Etta, it's none of your business. But I'd guess she would. She's in love with Horn."

Her eyes glistened. "I'd lie for Charlie. But I know positively he'd never commit murder."

"Horn has an alibi. He was in Laramie the day Willie Nickell was shot. People saw him there that evening."

Etta read on. A few moments later she looked up again. Joe could tell she was steaming. Her words sounded like the hissing of boiling water. "You and I and everyone else knows Tom exaggerates when he's likkered. He'll tell how he captured every cattle rustler in the country single-handed. Remember his story about bringing in Geronimo? That's just talk! Now read! Right here! LeFors says Tom bragged about the shot he made at the Nickell boy. 'It was the best shot I ever made, and the dirtiest trick I ever done.' Tom uses better grammar. He's say 'ever did.' I know I have an ear for language." She was so agitated she wouldn't let Joe open his mouth. "Look at this! It says Tom told LeFors the reason there were no footprints around the Nickell gate was because he did the job barefoot! Laws! What boasting!

No one can run around without boots on that cactus- and rock-lined ground. If he were barefoot his feet'd be cut. I know his feet weren't cut. You want to know how I know?"

Joe was curious to hear what Etta had to say.

"Dora Miller told me. She saw Tom and Miss Kimmell in Miss Kimmell's room at Miller's. Dora thought Tom'd left the night before, but instead he'd stayed and in Miss Kimmell's bed." Etta's face was pink. "Dora told me that Tom had big white feet that were smooth as a baby's bottom." Etta wiped her face with her apron and didn't look at Joe. "Well—women see those things. Dora never mentioned if Tom's feet were cut or bruised. She'd have noticed that. She saw his feet not more'n two days after he got back from Laramie. She said they were white and smooth." She rested her elbows on the table.

Joe blinked and cleared his throat. "Etta! Don't go repeating that. You're a married woman!"

"Dora told me. She's married. Being married makes it easier to tell. Do you suppose I could get Dora to tell the sheriff about Tom's big smooth feet?"

Joe stared at his daughter-in-law trying to remain calm, when all the time he was breaking up with laughter at her description of a man's naked feet. "What if the Miller kid is the culprit? Do you suppose Dora Miller's going to testify about Horn's baby-bottom feet?"

TWENTY-TWO

Frontier Days

Charlie told Etta that there was an unwritten story in the Tom Horn–Willie Nickell affair. "It's about the cattle barons versus the sheepherders and homesteaders."

Horn's preliminary hearing came eleven days after he was arrested in the Inter-Ocean Hotel. Rumors ran rampant. No one expected Horn would stay in jail nor be convicted for this crime.

Charlie went to town for supplies once a week on orders from Mr. Coble. Then he went to the county jail. He and Horn sang or talked about many subjects. One day they'd sing all the ballads they could remember. Another day they commiserated with each other about how the country was changing.

The house in Cheyenne that John Coble suggested to Charlie was on a large triangular lot. The right angle was bordered by Eddie and Twenty-eighth avenues. The long side was along Randall. The white clapboard house faced Eddie. When that avenue was later renamed the full address became 2712 Pioneer Avenue. There was a full porch supported by pillars. Inside Etta liked the living room with its wide windows facing the front tree-lined street. Charlie liked the dining room because it was large enough to hold a desk and chair at one end. "I'll keep all the books and papers for the Y6 here. I'll manage the Y6 the way Pa expects and this will be my office." He tried to speak in a calm, slow voice.

Etta was busy examining the two bedrooms, with bath between, which were along the north side of the dining room. Beyond the dining room was the good-sized kitchen with the third bedroom, and a pantry was built along the north side. Going out the back door, Charlie and Etta discovered an L-shaped building. The short side was east, behind the kitchen, and contained a bunkhouse that could sleep six men easily. The long side was north of the house and held six horse stalls and three storage rooms, one for coal, one for horse feed, and the third a tack room, for saddles, horse medicine, etc. Between the house and the L-shaped "barn" was a wide space to work the horses. Behind the barn's storage room were corrals. Behind the bunkhouse was a neat stack of baled hay.

Etta could see right off that she didn't have to coax Charlie to buy this place. He'd already decided it was the place for her and the children. He'd decided he could spend weekends here getting caught up on the book work and working any special horses he might acquire. "The children can walk from here to the Central School."

"Come on, let's go downtown to get the papers on this place," said Charlie. "It's a necessity, not a luxury."

"I'll wait right here on the front porch steps until you come back," said Etta. "I'm going to decide where to plant trees for shade and flowers for color and joy."

"But there's snow covering the yard." Charlie bent to kiss Etta.

"I can see the green grass in my mind's eye."

Charlie waved, climbed into the wagon, and snapped the lines so that the horse trotted toward Cheyenne's business district.

Etta walked around the house and barn half a dozen times, tramping down the snow, imagining what it would be like with the children running around inside and outside.

In two days Etta and the children were moved into the house. On the second day Etta admitted to Charlie that the place was "more than I anticipated even in my wildest dreams."

Charlie went back to the IM as foreman. Floyd was enrolled in the Central School's second grade.

The school was a large brick structure with a yard enclosed by an open fence of round, iron railing. Floyd was impressed by the method of dispensing water during recess. Someone had installed two large rectangular tanks with iron drinking cups chained to the front. "Girls drink from the tank on their side of the playground and boys from the tank on their side," he explained to his mother. "Someone must drain the tanks at night and fill them in the day, or during this cold weather the water would freeze and split the tanks."

Etta nodded agreement. She was sure not many six-and-a-half-year-olds would be that astute. As she hugged him, she gave thanks to God for letting Floyd go to a proper school. She didn't want him to go to a one-room school again, not even the way she had to in New York State years ago, when most of the pupils were McGuckins, her brothers and sisters. She was pleased that the pupils were separated into different rooms according to their grade. What Floyd does is his responsibility and no sister will come home and tattle on his behavior, she thought. That's the way school should be.

One weekend in the spring, before the snow was completely gone, Charlie came home and made an announcement. "I'm going to have a meeting here tomorrow morning. A couple of the ranchers want to come here and discuss the changes that are taking place."

"Who's coming and what changes?" asked Etta.

"John Coble for one is coming and John Clay and Ora Haley. Some of the big ranches are going to break up. They want to talk about putting fences around their pastures—to keep the sheep out."

"Those men are big ranchers—why would they want to come here, instead of the Industrial Club or the Inter-Ocean Hotel, and talk about such things?" Etta clattered the breakfast dishes.

"You should be flattered. They want to see this place. I suspect John Coble wants to see the children. I think he misses having them at the IM Ranch. I know he misses your cooking, dear."

"That's flattery. I want the truth!"

"I have told you all I know. Mr. Coble asked if they couldn't meet here on Sunday morning."

"What if I decided to go to church and take the kids?"

"They'd have to wait until you got back to see you and the kids."

"Charlie, there's one thing wrong."

"No, dear, it's all right. The men will meet here and see all the work you've put into making curtains and decorating this house. They'll be impressed."

Etta scowled. "That's it. What's wrong is the house!"

"I don't understand." Charlie was confused. "There's a living room, a dining room, three bedrooms, a pantry, a big front veranda, a bunkhouse for cowboys who come to town, and six horse stalls—"

"See—most of the decorating has been getting things for the bunkhouse or fixing up the barn. Things you want. Look at the dining room! A desk and chair and papers, but no table with chairs to match!"

Charlie's eyes darted to the dining room. "I told you that was to be my office. There's plenty of room for my desk in there."

Etta wiped her hands on her apron and strode to the dining room. "It's—it's bare! Really, Charlie, you can't have those older, respected ranchmen meet in a place with no furniture. What would they tell their friends? 'Etta Irwin is only a farmer's daughter and her house proves it.'" She was breathless.

Charlie was stupefied. He'd never given it a thought. Etta wanted her house to look as nice and well furnished as any other well-to-do ranch wife living in town. Charlie loved Etta more than life itself. He loved to watch her putter in the kitchen, fly around like a mother hen getting the four children dressed in the morning, send Floyd off to school and the others out to play. Etta always hugged Floyd and at the same time felt under his coat for the hidden lariat. At six years old Floyd was only interested in juggling his rope. It was a hemp lariat Charlie'd bought him and then shown him how to remove the kinks and make it pliable by stretching it between trees. Charlie had shown Floyd how to make the rope waterproof by greasing it with petroleum jelly and equal parts of melted paraffin. Etta scolded them both for spilling hot wax on the kitchen floor.

Etta was small, lean as a whip, wiry. She was vivacious. Charlie could rest his arm on the top of her silky brown hair. "So, that's what this caterwauling is about. This house is not enough; you want furniture and clutter!"

Etta turned and glowered at Charlie. "I do not want clutter! I want good furniture! Someday you are going to be a big rancher, and how you live and entertain is as important as what you do on your ranch."

Charlie stepped back and pushed the hair off his forehead. His brown eyes shone. "I'm not manager of the Y6 yet. My pa is. I am only the foreman at Mr. Coble's IM. But you're right about one thing. I'm going to be big. I'm going to be well known around Cheyenne! I aim to be as important as John Coble, John

Clay, or Ora Haley! Maybe more important, maybe I'll run for public office someday!"

Five-year-old Joella went out on the porch, slamming the front door behind her. Three-year-old Pauline stood next to the front window sucking her thumb and watching her sister. Frances cried out from her crib in the bedroom.

Charlie and Etta paid no attention to the children. They glared at each other.

"You tell your friends to hold their meeting in the Industrial Club until I can get my house furnished properly to have guests." Etta waved her arms around the bare room.

"We can't meet at the club, I'm not a member. Not yet!"

"The others are!" she snapped. "If they need you at this meeting, you can be their guest!" Etta's face was stormy and her eyes glinted like chips of ice.

"Confound it! John Coble's not allowed in the club! Something about him taking a couple shots at a painting—Paul Potter's bull—I told you that story."

Etta's eyebrows went up.

Charlie went on. "Tomorrow morning we're going to have three men here for a meeting. We'll sit around the kitchen table. I suppose they think if some of the larger ranches break up they'll be bought out by sheep men. We're all so against sheep we wouldn't even ride through a flock with a wool shirt on."

For a moment Etta was silent as though gathering more steam. "You act as though the way the house looks doesn't matter. Charlie, it does matter, just as much as how I look or how you look. Do you think all I know is what I learned on that dryland Kansas farm?"

"I think you are jealous. You watched me spend money on the bunkhouse for new cots and blankets and on the barn, and now you think it's only fair I spend some on the house."

Etta was astonished at his words. She blinked. She knew Charlie had dreams of being one of the largest horse breeders in Wyoming. She wanted to do everything she could to see his dream fulfilled. When she married Charlie she knew there would be disagreements, yet she was sure, with understanding and love, the quarrels would dissolve. Etta believed in dealing with everyday affairs in a practical, straightforward way.

Charlie was a dreamer and believed in an idealistic scheme of things. He thought everyone was his friend and in business matters the ranchers all worked together. He wondered if Etta didn't secretly applaud the inferno that took the IM ranch house. When they first came to Wyoming, she'd had her eye on one house or another in town. Had she used Floyd as the excuse to get a house in town? She always said Floyd and the girls had to have the best schooling available. He couldn't argue with that. He wanted the same thing.

"I'm not asking you to spend a lot of money. You can get something on sale at the Cheyenne Furniture. In the long run having a nice place to entertain or hold meetings will make you money. We can invite Senator Warren for supper. Charlie, someday you'll be invited to the Governor's Ball because of your influence on ranching. I know it as well as I know Joella will be in first grade next fall. Look in yesterday's paper. See if there is a ranch auction. We could get a dining room set cheap at an auction. Let's—"

Charlie had a hard time controlling his voice. "Etta, you don't have to buy someone's used furniture. Do you think I can't afford to get the things my wife wants?"

"Charlie, I don't have my head in the sand. I know what it took to get this house. I'm—"

"My wife is going to want for nothing!"

"I want you to let me finish a sentence!"

Charlie's eyes opened wide. His mouth was open, then it was closed and his lips were pressed tight. He turned to the closet for his overcoat and stalked from the house.

Etta was afraid she'd cry if she called out to Charlie. She looked out the window where Pauline was standing. She saw Joella in a coat half-buttoned, a wool cap pulled over her blond hair and no overshoes nor mittens. The child was sliding on a piece of old oilcloth down the front steps into the snowbank beside the walk. Etta saw Charlie bend down to say something to Joella and lay the oilcloth over the porch railing, then turn her toward the front door, pointing to her wet shoes. Then he walked toward town, pulling his muffler up around his ears.

Etta ran out and grabbed Joella. "Young lady, don't ever go out without your overshoes and mittens!" she cried. "You'll freeze!"

At lunchtime Charlie was not home, but a horse-drawn wagon stopped in front of the house. Two delivery boys came to the door. One said there was a dining room table and six chairs in the wagon for Mrs. C. B. Irwin.

Etta was so surprised, her first inclination was to tell the delivery boys they'd made a mistake. The driver showed her Charlie's signed note for the furniture, and she knew it was no mistake.

She showed them where to put the mahogany table and chairs.

That evening she served supper on the table covered with a carefully ironed bedsheet. "My dear," said Charlie, "this room looks like a real dining room. Before tomorrow morning bake some of your delicious cinnamon rolls for our three guests."

Etta was not smiling. She was breathing hard. "Charlie, I'm more than grateful, but you can see I have no proper cloth for the table."

"I don't see that." He went to the coat closet and handed her a large package from the Cheyenne Merc.

Puzzled, Etta took the box and said, "What's inside?"

"Your tablecloth, Mrs. Irwin."

When the three men arrived, Etta had the cinnamon rolls baked and on the dining room table with cups of hot coffee. She used the delicate Haviland china Ell had given her when they lived in Colorado Springs. Etta had fresh cream, butter, strawberry jam, honey, and white and brown sugar.

John Clay said he'd longed for brown sugar in his coffee ever since leaving Edinburgh. Ora Haley said he'd never tasted such good cinnamon rolls, and John Coble kept his mouth full so he couldn't say anything until Etta came to clear the dishes away and the men could have their meeting.

"This is a lovely room. You have wonderful taste. I just noticed that the lace curtains and the tablecloth match," said Coble.

Etta smiled broadly and touched Charlie's shoulder as she left with the dishes on an enameled tray.

"When we leave here it will be like this meeting and conversation never took place, you understand?" said John Clay, pulling at the lobe of one ear.

"Yes, sir," Charlie said. He was going to listen carefully. He was grateful to Etta for taking the children outside. He knew these three men were probably about the most important ranchers in southeastern Wyoming. To have them meet at his place was indeed an honor.

Charlie knew about the range conflicts that were discussed first. There was no secret that the cattlemen claimed the grazing land was theirs. They had been in the territory first. The newcomers, small ranchers, sheepmen claimed there were no legal rights because of prior use and the free public grazing lands were for anyone. The cattlemen were frustrated because the small settlers were becoming more numerous and many helped themselves to the beef of the larger operators. Many accused rustlers were turned loose because of lack of evidence or sympathy for the accused and his family. It was well known that property in both cattle and horses was nonexistent in the minds of the small settlers. Coble, Clay, and Haley wanted no range war like the Johnson County war, but they wanted to explore what could be done to keep the rights of the cattlemen protected by the law. By afternoon they had decided to hire Tom Horn to ride protection for their ranges and pay him as much as the Montanan offered.

"Horn was credited but never arrested for the 1895 murders of two local small homesteaders living near Horse Creek in the Laramie Mountains," said Haley. "He's in jail now and I for one think he's been framed. By George, when he's out and riding the line again for us, he'll sure enough scare the damned sheepherders off!" He lit the cigar he'd been chewing.

"So, we agree to hire him to ride the line as soon as he's free," said Coble. "That's it. All we want for him to do is ride the pasture lines between the Sybille and Chugwater creeks. That territory is big enough to keep him out several nights a month. His reputation will be our success in preventing any more thievery, changing cattle brands, and ignorance of our property boundaries. Sounds good."

The three men shook hands. They shook hands with Charlie. "Thanks, C.B., for giving us a place to meet where we don't raise a lot of questions. Remember, we weren't ever here. You didn't hear anything." Coble spoke in a whisper. "No one's to know Horn's working for three ranches."

The spring brought electrical storms, whirlwinds, hail, and cloudbursts. Then came the hot summer winds from the southwest. Traveling on horseback half a day from the IM ranch to Cheyenne, Charlie brushed passed the willows, reddish brown with sap, that lined the tiny streams. The roadway was fringed with yellow sunflowers and rabbit brush. He and Frank had brought in more wild horses that spring. Charlie was going to send a wire to the office of the Denver Festival of Mountain and Plain and offer to supply them with a dozen bucking horses that year.

During the two-day Frontier Days celebration of 1902, Etta looked after her own four children plus Margaret's boy and girl. She sat with the children in the grandstand.

Margaret entered the ladies' cow-pony race riding her favorite horse, Old Gold. She wore a white divided skirt and a red silk blouse that she'd sewn on Etta's machine. The Irwin children sat on the edge of the wood plank to see Margaret.

She won in fifty-two seconds for the half-mile race. Jennie Pawson in a green shirt was second.

Etta stood and cheered.

Then came the wild bronco race, and Frank Irwin, delicate in appearance but tough as sisal, won the fifty-dollar purse.

One event fascinated them beyond belief. There were fifteen Shoshone braves with ten squaws all the way from the Wind River Reservation, near Fort Washakie, who came out on their favorite ponies, all saddleless, some with rope bridles, some with hackamores, some absolutely bare. All of these Shoshones, in beautiful colored regalia, lined up before the judges' stand. The flag was brought up and dashed downward. The race was on! The ponies were lashed with quirts in order to move them closer to the front. In several cases the long legs of the Indian riders encircled the bodies of the ponies. This race was for a purse of twenty dollars, the winner to receive fifteen, the second best three, and the third two.

Yellow Calf, the Shoshone chief, dressed in jeans, tattered buckskin jacket, and a black wide-brimmed hat with a high round crown, had the best horse, and came under the wire an easy winner. Yellow Calf was not satisfied with the promise of his winnings by the judges and wanted his money as soon as he'd earned it. So before he or his fellow buckskin-jacketed Shoshone contestants dismounted, they were paid in silver dollars.

Next, half a dozen Shoshone braves, with long braids hanging down their chests, came out to the center of the arena and performed a corn dance, or reasonable facsimile. Two of the breechclouted near-naked men, their bodies glistening with goose grease in the sun, beat their hands on taut buffalo-skin drums. The other four danced the heel-toe step and wailed in an eerie, high-pitched keening that seemed to penetrate the innermost soul of all the listeners. The four dancing Shoshones were dressed in decorated breechclouts, moccasins, and beautiful white doeskin shirts, which they believed showed their thankfulness to the Great Spirit for a bountiful corn crop.

The next event was the squaw race, with ten participants. The women were dressed in doeskin tunics that were beaded on the yoke and sleeves and fringed at the bottom. They wore high-top moccasins that reached their knees, which were beaded along the sides and on the tops. The women had only a beaded band or thong tied around the forehead to the back of their heads to keep their hair out of their eyes. When the winner, My Goose, was announced, her husband, Yellow Calf, came to collect the silver dollars.

Charlie, as foreman of the IM spread, had Slim Burke take the chuck wagon out to the fairgrounds and do the cooking for his cowboys who participated in the two days of events. The men slept in the bunkhouse at Charlie's place on Eddie Avenue. Rumor spread fast that C. B. Irwin was a square foreman, one who treated his men well. At suppertime men from other outfits stopped by the chuck wagon that was inside the gate at Frontier Park, to seek out Charlie and ask for a job at the IM that fall.

Charlie already had a reputation for being a strict foreman, but one who never played favorites with his men. Everyone who worked for Mr. C. B. Irwin had to consistently follow the same rules.

In the evening, when the park was deserted except for the livestock and the night watchmen, the Irwin family was with the rest of the merrymakers on the crowded streets, watching the masqueraders and listening to the bands on various downtown corners. There were French balls, cakewalks, and clog dancing. The streets had been scraped, rolled, and covered with canvas for easy outdoor dancing.

Etta carried Frances, who was asleep. The other children were becoming tired and whiny.

"Let's take the children home," suggested Margaret. "After all, I have to get some sleep, too, because tomorrow afternoon after the last show I am to have my picture taken for the paper. Honestly, I was almost afraid to enter the race. I thought I was not strong enough, my horse not ready. And now, suddenly it's over and I'm to have my picture taken so people will know who I am."

"And who are you?" asked Etta gently.

Margaret was carrying three-year-old Charles and holding the hand of five-year-old Gladys. "I'm Margaret Irwin, mother of these two children, Will Irwin's wife, and somewhere in between a person who likes horses and loves to ride. That's not too complicated, is it?"

"Oh, no!" said Etta, boosting Frances to a more comfortable position on her shoulder. "It is exactly what I expected. But I will tell you something in confidence. See these houses with the lights shining out their windows and their closeness to their neighbors? That is what I like. I like my house in town."

"You don't like the ranch?" Margaret was surprised.

"I like it only because Charlie likes it. Charlie is going to come back to the ranch and raise horses. Supplying the horses for the Denver festivities and for this Frontier Days has filled him with enthusiasm for getting back to the Y6."

"Does Charlie know you prefer town?" asked Margaret softly.

"No, I don't suppose he does, but the Lord knows I've given him enough hints. There's the old saying, there's none so deaf than those who won't hear. He won't listen to me. He loves the outdoors, the sunshine, the fresh air, the smell of dust and barnyards, the rippling muscles of a horse running in the pasture, or the knotted muscles of a horse ready to explode as it bucks skyward. I love Charlie more than anything. So I'll manage, and now I have these four children to keep me running from morning until night." Her laugh was lighthearted.

The women put the children to bed and then sat down to talk until the men came in.

"Do you remember when Will first brought me to the soddy in Kansas?" asked Margaret.

"We called you Will's Baby then. The roles seem to be changed now. You baby Will along with your children. He never objects. He likes being pampered," said Etta. "You're the grown-up, Margaret."

Next afternoon Margaret was back in the arena on Old Gold and won the silver loving cup. And late in the afternoon Charlie took Floyd to see the tented exhibition titled "Buffalo Bill."

Buffalo Bill Cody sat regally on the back of a golden palomino. His long yellow hair flowed out from a tooled, leather headband. His performers tumbled and vaulted from one horse to another, spinning around in midair. Afterward Floyd stood in front of the big top and tugged on Charlie's sleeve. "Pa, I'm going to be a roper and trick rider."

"It's hard work, son. Takes practice, every day," said Charlie.

At Charlie's elbow a clear voice said, "The important thing is publicity. Let me present myself. I am the one and only Buffalo Bill."

The man was as tall as Charlie, his face was tanned. His beard matched his long yellow hair and his eyes were as blue as turquoise. Charlie introduced himself and pointed to Floyd saying, "My son."

Buffalo Bill shook hands with Charlie and looked down at Floyd. "Start out with ten tricks. Practice until you never make a mistake. Hire a photographer to take action shots. Send the shots to state fairs, circuses, anywhere that might hire a trick rider.

Wear silk shirts and sparkles, work where the trick can be seen by the whole audience. When you are five years older, come see me. What's your name, son? I never forget a face nor a name."

"Floyd Leslie Irwin, trick roper and rider, sir." Floyd held out his hand.

Charlie gulped.

"Aahh, that's good! Publicize yourself! If you can't believe you're good, who will? Get your name and picture everywhere." Buffalo bent down to put his hand on Floyd's arm. The buckskin fringe on his coat tickled Floyd's nose. "I'll hire you by the tricks you can perform. I'll feature the stunts that are most spectacular. Don't you forget me, Master Floyd Irwin." He shook Floyd's hand.

Most Wyoming cowboys were not overly impressed with Buffalo Bill's trick riders and ropers. They were too familiar with this type of entertainment and most of them could do the stunts he and his performers featured. Charlie wasn't impressed either and vowed that if Floyd performed it would be with new and exciting tricks. What impressed Charlie was the rush of memories and the similarity between his old friend Colonel Johnson and Buffalo Bill. There was a flashy grandeur that was charming—almost enchanting.

The final attraction was an old-fashioned stage holdup by the Indians and a rescue by the cowboys. The stagecoach pulled out and the Indians on spotted ponies ran *kiyi*-ing after it. The Indians were in breechclouts and moccasins and daubed with colored paints and goose grease. In a few minutes the Indians were overtaken by a bunch of cowboys. A noisy, fierce battle ensued and the Indians were defeated. The firing of blanks from the revolvers did not stop until the stagecoach reached the grandstand. Then the audience saw old Chief Yellow Calf and his son stealthily coming behind. Two cowboys swung their lassos and captured father and son. They were hauled up on the cowboys' horses and trotted off to the other side of the arena amid loud applause from the crowd.

Floyd stayed close to Charlie to watch the cowboys pick up their gear after the final act. With ropes hanging from the horns of their saddles and their revolvers in holsters at their hips, they looked like desperados in broad-brimmed hats and angora chaps. In reality, most cowboys were courteous, quiet, and unpretentious, with hearts as big as the broad cattle range that extended from horizon to horizon. Actually their gun was as innocent as their rope. It was ready for an emergency when nothing else would do.

Charlie jostled his way through the crowd to get to the corrals and tend to the animals. The fence was wrapped in orange and black crepe paper, same as most of the buildings and many homes in town were decorated with twists and streamers in the colors of this year's Frontier Days, orange and black. Charlie felt empty all of a sudden. The celebration was anticipated for months and was now nothing but memories. He smiled to himself. All fall and winter he and his family and the cowboys would retell stories about this year's Frontier Days events clear up until time for next year's events.

TWENTY-THREE

Hanging of Tom Horn

That fall Charlie made numerous trips to Cheyenne to see Etta and the children. Both Floyd and Joella were in school. Charlie also came to town to attend Tom Horn's trial. He thought it was the thing to do. He was foreman of the outfit Horn worked for. Traveling on horseback Charlie noticed the small gullies held splashes of red and yellow wild currant and the rosebushes were yellowing. The hillsides were bright with frost-touched golden aspens. He spotted herons in the small creeks and flocks of crows flapping to distant rookeries. He noticed the pungent odor of greasewood and the scent of pine and newly cut alfalfa and native hay. He loved these sights and smells.

Tom Horn's trial began on October 10, 1902. There were more than a hundred witnesses, and the case hit every major newspaper in the West from St. Louis to San Francisco. The courtroom had standing room only during the entire two-week proceeding.

On October 24, 1902, the verdict was in. Tom Horn was guilty and was to hang on January 9, 1903, between 10 A.M. and 3 P.M.

One cattleman commented, "Cheyenne juries ain't worth the powder to blow them into hell." Another said, "When a man ain't good for anything else, he is just right to set on a jury."

Horn's attorneys filed a motion for a new trial in the district court. Judge Scott refused. Appeals were made. A petition of error was filed and a stay of execution was granted, but no new trial.

The winter was hard and feed for cattle and game was covered with hard-packed snow on the range. Before Christmas, Charlie heard rumors of a plot to blow up the jail and set Horn free. He did not believe them. Then dynamite was found concealed in the snow outside the brick wall of the courthouse and a piece of lead pipe was found in Horn's pants leg.

Warm summer winds blew over the prairies sending Russian thistle bounding across the flats and hollows. The stretch of buck fences could be seen for miles; the snow fences seemed to lead nowhere. The air was so clear that mountains far away seemed close, and the stars shone so brilliantly they looked within reach.

Early Sunday morning, August 10, 1903, Tom Horn and a man, Jim McCloud, also on death row, escaped. Horn grabbed a Belgian-made revolver from the sheriff's office as he ran out. He went through the alley, away from the direction in which McCloud rode off on horseback. On the lot across the street from the courthouse was a small carnival. Horn stood close to the merry-go-round and tried to remove the safety on the revolver. He was nervous and anxious. The safety would not slide front or back or either side. It was jammed or locked! He ran over a pile of dirt just as the merry-go-round operator tackled him. Deputy Dick Proctor told him to walk back to the courthouse or else he would fire his six-shooter into his back. Horn felt the muzzle of the gun and walked. It was humiliating to walk in front of the large crowd that had come from various church services and gathered in front of the courthouse, curious to get a glimpse of the jailbreakers. "I hope to heaven McCloud got away," said Horn.

However, McCloud was also being escorted to the courthouse not far behind Horn.

The sun was bright in a cloudless sky that Sunday. Etta walked serenely to church with the four children. Coming home she overheard the buzzing excitement in people's voices as they retold how Tom Horn had attempted to escape. She could hardly wait to tell Charlie, who was at home gathering his gear to ride back to the IM ranch.

* * *

Charlie, on horseback, made a little detour going past the courthouse on his way out of Cheyenne. He noticed a crowd in front of the Inter-Ocean Hotel across from the Union Pacific Depot. He stopped and listened.

The attempted jailbreak gave strength to plenty of gossip in the streets of Cheyenne.

The governor ordered armed soldiers to patrol Cheyenne's streets. A Gatling gun was mounted in the entrance to the Laramie County Courthouse and Jail. A deputy sheriff and guard were at every window. An arc light near the courthouse burning night and day was added to reinforce discouragement of any rumored attack or attempted jailbreak.

A week later John Coble asked Charlie to ride up to the Miller Ranch. He was certain young Victor Miller had shot Willie Nickell and wanted Charlie to convince Miller to make a clean confession.

Coble said, "I've had word from Al Bristol. He used to work for me. Good man. He's always been trustworthy. Bristol said he once caught Victor Miller skulking around the IM's horses in the Wall Rock pasture. The kid climbed over the fence and was near one of my special bred racers. Bristol grabbed the kid by the back of his collar. The kid admitted he was stealing the horse. Bristol growled and scared the kid right down to his toenails. He told Bristol it was he who shot Willie Nickell twice in the back and it was he who put a flat rock under Willie's head, the way he'd heard Horn had done to a couple of cattle rustlers. Said he'd do it again because he hated the whole Nickell outfit. Said old man Nickell had sheep pellets for brains."

"Why, that little cold-blooded son-of-gun!" cried Charlie.

Coble lowered his voice a trifle so that Charlie had to lean forward to hear all he said. "Bristol said he took the kid into Cheyenne for a talk with an attorney, Walter Stoll. The kid was so scared his mouth kept going dry and he shook the whole time. Remember the kid had been in jail not long before on account of shooting old man Nickell in the elbow?"

"He was let go on insufficient evidence," said Charlie.

"Right. Bristol knew Stoll would do nothing about the attempted horse theft, it was his word against the kid's, but he wanted the attorney to take down the kid's murder confession."

Charlie's eyes brightened. "That would be a lucky break for Tom Horn. Sad for the poor kid, though."

"Well, when Bristol took the kid to Cheyenne, the kid denied even being at the Rock Wall pasture. He said he was in Cheyenne the day Willie Nickell was murdered. He even signed an affidavit saying so. It was his word against Bristol's. And for reasons of his own, Stoll believed the two-faced kid."

"You want me to go to the Miller place and get Victor to go back into Cheyenne and confess?" Charlie was dubious.

Coble laughed and said, "C.B., I know your ability to talk a man into most anything. Remember this is going to get an innocent man out of jail. Tom Horn did not shoot Willie Nickell!" Coble's voice went up. He leaned over and put his hand on Charlie's arm. "I want you to tell Victor that you have word that the Cheyenne law officers are on their way out to arrest him. Tell him the best thing to do is to go quietly to town and confess. That way it'll be much easier on himself and his family." Coble paused and looked at Charlie.

Charlie felt his heart pounding fast. This was not the kind of job he wanted to do for his boss. "Mr. Coble, Victor isn't going to do anything I say. Look here, you are the honored, upright, honest, big-time rancher. He'd be more likely to do as you suggest."

Coble turned red, then smiled and picked at the dried grass beside the ranch house step. "I would do it, but I'm taking a lady friend, a special schoolmarm, to Denver, for a performance by Lillie Langtry."

Charlie rolled his eyes. "I didn't know you were courting."

Coble smiled and said, "I know I can count on you, C.B." He shook Charlie's hand, picked up the tether line, mounted his horse, and trotted down the dusty road.

Coble's visit soured Charlie for any kind of work for a week. His mind whirled with thoughts. He never liked to be obligated to anyone, especially someone he worked for. Obligations meant trouble. If he went to the Miller place, one of those boys might have a shotgun aimed on him. They could accuse him of being there to steal horses or rustle cattle. With no outside witnesses he'd be jail bait himself.

Finally Charlie decided to take Neil Clark with him. Neil Clark, blond and raw-boned, was just about the best horseman Charlie had known. The two men rode across the prairie that was filled with *dog towns*. The white-tailed, prairie dogs burrowed holes in the earth for miles in all directions. Each burrow entrance was surrounded by a ring of earth, and as the two horsemen approached they saw the prairie dogs sit on top of the mounds, barking the alarm in a voice similar to a yappy little dog. The prickly pear cactus was flowering, yellow, tinged with a thin line of red on the edge. They rode past black sage with its dull green leaves and oily, pungent aroma. Along the creek bottoms the wild plum and chokecherry were ripe.

The Miller ranch was one of the few that was completely fenced. Dora Miller was out in the yard. She wore her husband's big, black, rubber overshoes. When she walked, the unfastened buckles scraped against each other. She wore a man's red flannel shirt over her long cotton dress. She looked as if she'd pulled a cow out of quicksand. The mud-encrusted cow was tied to a skinny aspen. The cow's legs were spraddled. Its tail was up and it bawled so loud no one could hear himself speak.

"Howdy, ma'am!" Charlie yelled, riding in close. "Your place looks mighty fine!" He tried to sound cheerful. "I could use an extra hand and wondered if your boy, Victor, would be interested! I'd like to talk with him!"

"Oh, no! Vic's in Wheatland doing work for Mr. Clay! But I do wish he'd skeedaddle home and do something about this blamed cow!" Then she recognized Charlie and put her hand to her mouth. Taking her hand away she asked, "Mr. Irwin, there's no trouble, is there?"

Keeping Clark behind him, Charlie said, "Dora, what kind of trouble do you mean?"

"Well—well, you see—you know there are some who'd like to see poor Vic, or my husband, James, in jail in place of that hired killer, Tom Horn! The schoolmarm, Miss Kimmell, she moved away, swore to Sheriff Smalley that James and both our boys were here the morning Willie Nickell was shot!" The cow stopped bellowing. "That schoolmarm was sweet on Tom Horn. You know that. He was with her here more'n once when we was all in town." Her eyes were bright and she tried to smooth her tangled hair.

Charlie wondered why she said this to him. It was something women would gossip about. He nodded and winked. "I guess you could say they were sweethearts."

"More." Dora touched Charlie's leg. "I could tell every time he was here. I kept her room straight and washed them sheets."

Charlie felt his ears burn. He thought that Dora Miller was lonely and that was why she was running at the mouth.

"I heard that schoolmarm warn Tom about Joe LeFors, the peace officer. She told him LeFors had something up his sleeve. Tom wasn't scared of no man and paid her words no heed. So—he's the one in trouble. Isn't he?"

"His trouble seems to be sitting around in jail getting pale and letting his muscle turn soft on account of some weasel who's too chicken to tell the truth." Charlie watched Dora's face.

She looked straight ahead at the sad-looking cow and blinked once or twice. A vein in her forehead throbbed. A nerve spasm made one shoulder twitch. "The Lord takes His own revenge on all critters." She was looking at the cow that had begun bawling again.

Charlie yelled, "I'll put my faith in the Lord anytime!" He tipped his hat and nodded.

Charlie and Clark rode out to the Chugwater Creek with the intention of following it up to Wheatland, hoping to intercept Victor. Charlie knew Dora didn't want him looking for Victor, even though she had not come out and said so. Going to Wheatland was an all-day trip.

They were lucky and found the boy at John Clay's place. Charlie left young Clark to talk ranching with Clay, while he took Victor out behind the barn and repeated the arrest story. He urged Victor to ride into Cheyenne with him and confess before the officers came after him.

"Son, it would be a terrible sin for an innocent man to suffer and be punished for a crime he didn't commit. For a crime that you, yourself, already confessed to. If you don't tell the authorities now, but continue to lie, think how it will weigh on your conscience forever. You'll never be rid of it. It will follow you around and burn like fire and brimstone in your brain. Who really shot Willie Nickell?"

Victor looked pale. Charlie hoped the boy was not going to be sick. "No man has been hanged in Wyoming for the past ten years. And because you won't talk, a man is going to hang."

Victor licked his lips. "Ma told me what would happen if I ever again told anyone I shot Willie. Willie was scum! No better'n his sheep-raising pa. I ain't guilty. If I say I am, my pa will think I'm a yellow-livered skunk. I ain't that! So, like I said, I ain't guilty of nuthin'. I intend to go home, even if there are a dozen law men after me!" He paused and licked his lips again. "I didn't sign nuthin' saying I locked horns with Al Bristol! There's no proof I even talked with him. It's his word against mine. I signed a paper saying I was in Cheyenne when Willie was shot and that I was never at the Rock Wall." Victor was shaking and his face was as white as birch bark. His tongue kept moving and licking his lips, same as his ma's had. "I wasn't there. Must have been some other rustler Bristol talked with. He doesn't really know me. He could have thought it was me."

Charlie had heard enough excuses. He grabbed the boy's arm. His hand fit all around. He squeezed hard. "Did I say anything about Al Bristol and the pasture at Rock Wall?" Charlie's brown eyes had orange flecks, like tiny flames reflecting in them.

"No—I guess not," Victor stammered and kept his head down. A sudden breeze blew his hat to the ground. Charlie thought he saw tears before the boy's hair fell over the pale blue eyes.

Charlie's voice was gruff. "Put your hat on, keep your hair back so you can see me."

Victor pulled his arm free and grabbed his hat. "You hurt my arm bad."

"Your conscience hurts worse, doesn't it? Get on your horse and ride with me straight to Cheyenne and confess. Save your poor ma and your pa, too, an untold amount of grief and heartache." Charlie grabbed the boy's arm again, increased the pressure, and waited for an answer.

Victor looked at Charlie, opened his thin mouth, blinked his watery, pale, fishlike eyes. Charlie could see beads of sweat on his forehead and feel the muscle spasms in his thin arm. He let up on the pressure, expecting the boy to answer in the affirmative.

Instead Victor proved his agility by jerking fast downward, stomping on the top of Charlie's instep and hitting him in the belly with his small, balled fist. He ran out of the barnyard before Charlie could gasp a good-sized breath. Charlie watched Victor mount his horse and ride off without looking backward.

John Clay looked up. "Something sure put lightning in that kid's feet!"

It is a fact that during Tom Horn's riding of the line the stealing of calves practically ceased. But during his twenty-two months in jail, murders and more sheep killings took place. In July 1902, one hundred and fifty armed men stopped fifteen herds of sheep, destroyed two thousand head and scattered the rest, killed one herder and drove out the others. In February 1903 a gang of masked men killed Bill Minnick and two hundred of his sheep. In March, seven masked men tied up a herder, burned his wagon, killed his horses and five hundred sheep. In July, National Guardsmen restored order in Thermopolis, where sheepmen threatened to lynch a man suspected of the murder of Minnick. Most of the perpetrators of these crimes were not found and brought to trial. If they stood trial, they were not convicted.

Some of the witnesses dared not testify, nor counsel dare to plead, because of fear for their lives. Horn was in jail nearly two years and roughly fifty murders were committed in Wyoming then, with no convictions.

It is ironic but true that if Horn were a rustler, he would not be spending his time in jail. The area's cattle thieves regarded Horn as their enemy and they wanted him removed, just as they, along with the big cattle ranchers, wanted Nickell, the area's first sheep herder, out of the country.

It became a common saying on the streets of Cheyenne, "Show me a cattleman who is against Tom Horn, and I will show you a rustler!"

Charlie was upset. He told Etta about talking with Victor Miller on John Clay's ranch.

Etta looked pensive. Charlie liked that little-girl look. She put her hand on Charlie's arm. He liked the feeling of her warmth through his shirtsleeve. "Let's say Tom Horn had nothing to do with Willie Nickell, and Victor Miller nor his pa didn't either—who, then?" said Etta.

"It's a mystery to me! Maybe someone from the outside. I don't know. All I know is this thing has me on edge. I like Tom. I fear the wrong man will hang. Tom is a scapegoat. Tom is so confident that the murderer will step forward and give himself up that he's not worried. Not even nervous." Charlie looked up. "I have a gut feeling that someone could write a letter to the governor saying he was the true murderer and the governor would ignore it."

"Charlie, don't look so down-in-the-mouth. You tried. Forget Victor Miller. Maybe Mr. Coble will think of something else. I heard Coble's personally responsible for hiring the best legal defense for Tom that could be found in the state, Judge Lacey, and District Attorney T. E. Burke. Certainly they will defend Tom. You don't have to worry. So don't take your feelings out on the cowboys."

He got up and she got up and stood on her toes. He bent down and kissed her. "Dear, this whole legal thing has me stymied. Next week I'm going to take another gunnysack of horsehair to Tom for his rope making."

"Try to be more sociable than a rotten tooth." Etta kissed him again.

"Ya! I'll see you in a couple of weeks when me and the boys come in town for Frontier Days." His voice became soft and gentle. "I couldn't live without seeing you and the kids." He gave her a squeeze and went for his coat and hat.

In September the streets of Cheyenne were decorated with orange and black crepe paper streamers for the annual Frontier Days celebration. Thousands of visitors and residents of Cheyenne again thrilled to the cowboys bouncing across the arena on whirling, frothing, wide-eyed cayuses, or racing long-horned steers from the Y6 ranch neck and neck, flying into the air and landing in the dust. The newspapers ignored Tom Horn for a week.

Charlie entered the steer-roping contest. He didn't even come in third. Frank won the quarter-mile horse race. Margaret won the ladies' half-mile race. The Irwin family was beginning to earn a fine reputation among cowhands and cattlemen all around Cheyenne.

A week later Charlie's team of horses and wagon kicked up a fog of dust that floated above the potholed, graveled highway leading into Cheyenne. The dust drifted downwind until it settled on lupines, lespedezas, umbrellalike blooms of the wild buck-wheat, and autumn goldenrod. Charlie barely saw the gray powder on the petals of roadside sunflowers and blades of yucca. His eyes took in the whole spectrum of wildflowers, the tall bluestem grass and the dust all combined. He heard distant cow-bells. The songbirds had already gone away. He thought it was good to see the open space, where the earth met the sky. It soothed his mind.

The air before sunup was crisp. Charlie's breath condensed into wispy fog and so did the breath from the loping horses. Charlie wore his wide-brimmed hat, a sheep's-wool-lined jacket, muffler, gloves, wool trousers, and boots. He glanced at the translucent gray sky. He knew it would turn a tremulous red against the low clouds, as if announcing the coming of a cool, clear blue dawn.

Charlie was on his way into Cheyenne for the ranch supplies. After the wagon was loaded he planned to have lunch with Etta and the children, then go to the county jail for a visit with Horn. He was going to take Horn another gunnysack of horsehair.

Horn had on soft leather slippers. Charlie wondered if he missed wearing boots. Horn's faded blue flannel shirt was clean and so were his brown trousers. His hair had been freshly trimmed and so had his mustache. His face and hands were deathly white, faded from lack of sunshine. "It'll sure feel good to sleep in the hills with the stars overhead once again. Charlie, if anything happens—did anyone think to take my thirty-thirty

Winchester out of Coble's place during the fire?"

"Hey! So, it's yours? Frank put it in the IM bunkhouse. Nobody claimed it. Coble said it wasn't his. Jeems! I should have known! I guess we didn't save your bedroll and field glasses." Suddenly Charlie felt melancholy.

"You and Coble are the only ones who have been in to see me. After I finish braiding all this horsehair I'm going to write some letters. Maybe I'll send you one. If you go fishing send me one that weighs five or six pounds. I'm hungry for fish. Charlie, if anything happens—that Winchester—it's your rifle."

"Hey! What's going to happen? You have the best lawyers in the state. You'll be out before spring roundup," said Charlie.

"Maybe—I keep thinking I could have been killed in that stupid break me and McCloud staged. I was lucky. Luck can run dry, you know."

"Do you know the song the cowboys are singing now?" Charlie wanted to cheer up his friend. "*Life's Railway To Heaven*?"

"No. Do you?" asked Horn.

"Yes. I'll teach you." Charlie sang the sentimental song in his full tenor voice.

Life is like a mountain railroad, with an engineer that's brave;
We must make the run successful, from the cradle to the grave;
Watch the curves, the fills, the tunnels; never falter, never quail;
Keep your hand upon the throttle, and your eye upon the rail.

Chorus:

Blessed Savior, Thou wilt guide us till we reach that blissful shore,
Where the angels wait to join us, in Thy praise forever more.

You will roll up grades of trial; you will cross the bridge of strife;
See that Christ is your conductor, on this lightning train of life;
Always mindful of obstructions, do your duty, never fail;
Keep your hand upon the throttle, and your eye upon the rail.

You will often find obstructions; look for storms of wind
and rain;
On a fill, or curve, or trestle, they will almost ditch your
train;
Put your trust alone in Jesus; never falter, never fail;
Keep your hand upon the throttle, and your eye upon the
rail.

As you roll across the trestle, spanning Jordan's swelling
tide,
You behold the Union Depot, into which your train will
glide;
There you'll meet the Superintendent, God the Father, God
the Son,
With the hearty, joyous plaudit, "Weary pilgrim, welcome
home."*

"If the governor commutes the sentence to life imprisonment, they'll move me by train from here to the state penitentiary in Rawlins. I'll be like a caged bear. There's only one way out. I'm going for it," Horn whispered.

Charlie saw Horn's intensely piercing dark, almost black, eyes turn liquid, like deep, still water on a moonless night. Charlie whispered, "You planning another escape, my friend?"

While Charlie was out of town, his sister, Ell, from Colorado Springs, had come to visit Etta and the children, as she did every year about this time.

Etta was amazed that Ell's silky, long hair was no longer the color of honey, but a soft apricot-orange. The braid encircling her head was like a bright, double halo that complimented her sea-green eyes. Ell smelled erotically musky. She wore multicolored beads like a rainbow around her neck. The brown, slim, pongee dress daringly showed her ankles below the tiny flounce when she got off the train. Her high-heels were covered with an apricot-orange-colored silk. Her silk stockings matched.

The redcap, who recognized beauty, carried her bags and hatbox inside the depot, then asked if he could fetch her a drink of

*Reprinted with permission from: Tom Horn, *Life of Tom Horn,* New York; Jingle Bob Brand, Crown Publishers Inc., 1977 [James Horan], 1904 [John Coble], p. 310.

water. The men on the depot's sidewalk stopped to look at this striking, sensual young woman.

"If you are going to help me with commonplace chores, we'd better go home before some gentleman makes a pass," whispered Etta, giggling.

Ell's voice came loud from deep inside her throat. "Yes. Isn't it marvelous how attentive men are? I love it. Does Charlie treat you right?" Her lashes brushed her cheeks when she blinked, which she did a lot.

"Charlie—is just Charlie. I love him. He's old-fashioned. You know, he believes women are complementary to men—a secure comfort men can depend on." Etta leaned near Ell. "Confidentially, he'd be embarrassed with the attention you attract."

"Here's a secret to think about. Mattie Silks was my heroine." Ell had a throaty laugh.

"Mattie?" Etta was puzzled. Ell's perfume suddenly smelled cloyingly sweet.

"A wealthy jezebel."

"Honest?" Etta was glad Charlie was not home. He'd not only be embarrassed, he'd be shocked.

Etta felt a twinge of jealousy because Ell looked lovely even while mopping the kitchen floor. She wore floor-length flowered skirts, crisp, white blouses, and rainbow twists of beads. Ell was not only beautiful, she was also competent. She papered the bedrooms and sewed curtains while Etta prepared meals and looked after the children. Floyd and Joella got chicken pox. When they were nearly well, Pauline and Frances got chicken pox. Then all four had pinkeye. No one thought to call a doctor. Etta waited and if there was no continuing soaring fever, she knew they'd be well soon. Ell applied herb lotions and fed the children bark and root infusions that she said stopped inflammation and fever.

Baby Frances fascinated Ell with an ability to get into cupboards and closets before she was missed. She crawled faster than most toddlers walked. Pauline delighted Ell by watching over Frances like a mother hen. Joella confided in her aunt Ell what the other girls wore to school and what was in their lunch pails, what boys she liked best. Floyd confessed to Ell that he wanted to spend weekends on the Y6 with Grandpa Joe. "I can juggle my rope there without Ma's nagging."

By the middle of October the sun had changed color. It was no longer a great golden globe. As the winter approached, the sun turned to a ball of plasma that was like white-hot silver radiating through the gray clouds. The yellow fluttering leaves of cottonwood and willows had fallen on the creek banks. The wind was cold.

Etta and Ell had canned garden corn, string beans, and tomatoes.

Coble had asked Charlie and Frank to take petitions all over the state for signatures asking the governor to commute Horn's sentence. Coble paid the men's expenses. Everyone in the state had heard of Tom Horn and the murder of Willie Nickell. There were few who believed Horn a desperado or criminal. Charlie and Frank crisscrossed the state from Sheridan to Rock Springs, from Jackson Hole to Casper. They rode the train and hired horses to get signatures from businessmen, churchmen, ordinary citizens, cattle ranchers, sheep ranchers, and thousands of cowboys. The large ranchers were invariably on the side of Horn's innocence and glad to sign. Many added an extra note: "When T.H. was free there was fewer rustlers." "Squatters are the crooks." "Small settlers steal our cattle. Horn can stop the stealing." "Horn's a straight shooter." "Horn wouldn't shoot a kid in the back."

Frank and Charlie avoided the small settlers, as these folks believed Horn guilty of some crime, maybe not the one in question, but something in the past. They were afraid of Tom Horn.

Charlie and Frank had thousands of names and began to feel good about this mission. Back in Cheyenne they filled up on Etta's cooking.

"Dear, can you guess how many greasy spoons we've seen?" said Charlie.

Etta teased, "I can tell by looking. Frank used to be so skinny a strong wind would lift him; now he'll give his horse a swayback. And you, Charlie, will have to get your belt lengthened and send out for special-made pants."

This year Ell had an added mission to her visit. She asked Charlie for money to invest in her earth medicines. "I'm going to be an apothecary and dispense only natural medicines. You know I've always wanted to do this."

"What does Les think?" said Charlie, sipping coffee.

"Oh, pooh—Les thinks I've not quite grown up. He won't allow me another cent to spend on some exciting new herbs from Mexico. Why, some of the teas I make from Mexican yams are as good for animals as for people. A friend was sick with consumption and coughing all the time. He got relief from a tea I made him from yam peelings. Another time I bathed the back of this same friend's collie dog, where it got gouged on some barbed wire. The wound healed clean as morning dew."

Charlie snorted and shook his head. "I'm a skeptic, same as Les. But that don't mean I don't believe in teas. Remember how Grandma Malinda knew a plant for most any sickness—but she stayed in her own backyard. She didn't go off to Mexico. I'd say Les has good sense not letting you spend his money on some fool sweet potatoes. Grow your own. That's a darn sight cheaper."

Ell turned from Charlie and looked at her brother Frank. She smiled and seemed as expectant as a sparrow watching a wormhole. "You can stop watching me like I have a pocketful of money. I'm plumb broke." Frank pushed his chair away from the dining table.

Etta pulled the children away from their father and uncle so that the two men could deliver their precious petitions to the acting governor, Fenimore Chatterton, who'd taken the job when DeForest Richards died. Charlie and Frank left the house with high hopes that the petitions would convey the message that the ranchers of some account were all in favor of letting Horn go free. Horn cherished life; he lived by the old range code. It was against his grain to dry-gulch a thirteen-year-old kid.

Charlie felt a kind of awe as he hitched his horse to the post and walked up the wide concrete steps of the gold-domed capitol building. He was surprised to see men from the Wyoming National Guard stationed at the entrance. One of the guards stood in front of the door. "What is your business?" He held his rifle across his midsection to block the entrance.

"We have something for the governor. Mr. John Coble telephoned that we were coming," said Charlie. He was astonished that the capitol building was protected. "What's happening? What's the security for?"

"The governor's life has been threatened." The guard took the petitions and asked Charlie and Frank to open their coats. When it was clear that the two men carried no weapons, the petitions were given back and the door opened. There was another guard at the door to the governor's office. Again the men were searched before they could go inside. By now Charlie was keyed up. He had a fleeting suspicion that the governor was overreactive.

"Brace yourself, we might have a hard sell here," Charlie whispered to Frank.

Fenimore Chatterton was a portly gentleman with a broad mouth and nose and tiny, raisinlike eyes. He seemed inflexible.

Charlie did his best. He complimented the governor on the beautiful scenes of Wyoming in the paintings on his office walls. He talked to him about fly-fishing, which was the governor's favorite sport. He talked about how the people of Wyoming believed in the governor, how the constituency regarded him as a fine, upstanding, empathetic representative of their values. "Those people never questioned your integrity, sir. The good people all over the state know you'll do what they desire most. Do you believe in capital punishment, sir?" asked Charlie.

Governor Chatterton took the pages of legal paper with the thousands of signatures, but he would not look them over while Charlie and Frank were sitting in front of his massive oak desk. He said, "No, personally I do not believe in capital punishment. You may tell your fellow cattlemen that a proper hearing has been given Mr. Thomas Horn and the recommendation of the jury must be taken under the law. Good day, gentlemen."

In the foyer Frank whispered, "It seems he's made up his mind. Never interfere with nothing what don't bother him none." A smile spread across his face. "Charlie, you could—"

"Oh, no! Don't even think it. Frank, we've done our part. That governor doesn't believe in capital punishment personally, he said so, but he does politically," said Charlie. He felt let down, deflated as a worn-out bellows.

"Maybe Mr. Coble'll think of something."

"It's too late. Forget it, Frank. If this thing went some other way, someone else would be hanged. Some people won't be satisfied until they have a hanging."

"I need a drink," said Frank. "I'm drier than an empty water barrel."

"Forget that, too," said Charlie. "We're heading out to the IM and getting back to work. Jeems, that Chatterton is pigheaded! I truly believe someone has got to him, paid him off, and scared him to death."

Frank said, "Suppose the governor takes time to look over those petitions and wants to contact us. Maybe we ought to stay in town overnight."

"You're right. Let's go home. Etta'll make us dinner."

For the following week Charlie's mind was in a torment. He couldn't stand to stay in the IM bunkhouse; it was stuffy and he couldn't breathe. He couldn't stand the barn; it was dark and dusty. He couldn't stand the blacksmith shed; it was hot and uncomfortable. The sunshine was too bright. The breeze was too strong. The air too cold.

He wondered if Horn was actually being railroaded. Or was Horn keeping his mouth closed to protect someone? Who?

Charlie was upset. He decided he had to talk with the cattle barons. If Horn was innocent, he should be freed. If there was more than a slight doubt about his innocence, maybe he should be given life in the pen, but not hanged on such trumped-up, flimsy evidence as LeFors's interview. And Charlie had a plan.

"If Horn's sentence is commuted so that he gets off, fine. But if the sentence is changed to life in prison, it's worse than hanging for Horn. Life in the Rawlins penitentiary'll kill him," said Charlie.

Everyone nodded. Their faces were clouded and dark. "There's a chance Horn will get life," Charlie continued. "He'll be put on the westbound U.P. for the state penitentiary in Rawlins. That train leaves Cheyenne in early evening when it's still light. By the time the train hits Medicine Bow, it's dark. We'll have Horn's horse ready, saddled, and carrying his gear. When the train comes through, we'll cause some commotion, stage a train robbery, anything to divert attention, so that Horn can be taken off. He'll get on his horse and head south to Mexico. I'm sure we can pull it off."

"C.B. Irwin!" sputtered Coble. "Why didn't you tell us of this scheme sooner! We'll have to think about this and work out the details."

Charlie went out to see his father. Joe's back seemed to have a permanent curve, like a scythe. His hair was snow-white. His face and arms and hands were tanned. The skin looked like wrinkled parchment flecked with liver spots. Charlie knew Joe would never admit he was slowing down, but Charlie saw how slow he walked and how he'd get caught up in story telling and forget all about blacksmithing or mending corral fences.

"Son, when you coming to stay at the Y6? I can do the work all right, but I don't have the head for thinking that you have," said Joe shaking Charlie's hand. "A family ought to stay together."

"I know, Pa. I'll give it some serious thought," said Charlie, feeling relieved that Joe didn't suspect there'd been talk of buying off Governor Chatterton and stopping a U.P. train in order to get Tom Horn off and on his escape route to Mexico.

* * *

When John Coble came out to the IM ranch to see how the new house was coming along, Charlie put down hammer and nails and spoke first. "Mr. Coble, my father is on the Y6 ranch over yonder on Horse Creek by hisself. It's quite a job for a man his age. I have an obligation to my father. The house is about done here. I've enjoyed working for you. What I'm trying to say is that I want your permission and good wishes to leave as soon as I can. Neil Clark would make a good foreman. Honestly, I mean no offense. I'm looking forward to being my own boss."

"I admire a man that wants to look after his family," said Coble. He extended his hand and spoke softly. "I'm depressed about our friend in the Laramie County jail. The governor hasn't done a thing. I hope he doesn't wait until the day of the hanging to commute the sentence and ship him to Rawlins."

"There's plenty of time. Everything's ready. All I need is the word," said Charlie.

On the 19th of November, 1903, Charlie came in from the Irwin Y6 ranch on horseback. The day was clear and cold. There was a fine, crystalline snow blowing across the prairie. He was surprised to see so many wagons and strange horses tied to the hitching posts in town and strangers walking the streets.

"Hey!" he called to Etta. "You see all those people in town?"

She came out from the kitchen and hugged Charlie, then let him take off his mackinaw and wool cap and muffler. "It's barbaric! I can understand friends of Horn's coming to town, like yourself, but not all these eastern newspapermen and just curious people. It's like selling souvenirs at a funeral. It's a circus. Perfectly decent people coming for a hanging! There's something black, wicked, and perverse in human nature."

"Not in you," said Charlie nipping her ear.

Etta grumbled some about not having room for all the horses. Actually there was plenty of room in the six stalls alongside the house.

After supper Charlie did not go to town with Frank and the cowboys. He did not drink and he did not want to get mixed up with the crowd and the carnival mood. He felt half-sick. His dinner sat heavy on his stomach and he kept wondering how his friend Horn felt. Charlie didn't want to attend tomorrow's hanging. But it was something he had to do. He had to show his respect and friendship for Horn. He had to say his last farewell.

There was a large knot in his stomach. His throat also had a lump that seemed to rub against the larger one.

Floyd coaxed Charlie into going outside a moment to see his latest rope trick. The temperature was near freezing. With a quick wrist movement Floyd brought the loop up, over, and around in front. Then with a rotary motion he let go with one hand and the loop slipped over Charlie's head and shoulders, caught his arms at his sides, and pulled tight around his middle.

"Gottcha!" squealed eight-year-old Floyd.

Charlie growled, then had to laugh. The trick brought back a rush of memories of his own boyhood. He felt better. Then he saw a movement through the bunkhouse window that caught his eye. At first he thought it was only Frank and the other cowboys playing cards around the kerosene lamp in the center of the table. He looked at his pocket watch as Floyd rewound the rope and ran for the warmth of the house. He thought the boys had come back from town early. Then he saw the red dress. Ell was sitting in the midst of the men, a cigarette in her mouth, dealing the cards. Everyone was laughing, having a good time.

He told himself it was not the gambling that bothered him. He enjoyed gambling himself. It was not the cigarette. Ell could do as she pleased. It was the sight of a woman, in a slinky, red dress in the bunkhouse on this particular night. A woman playing cards in a bunkhouse was thought by most ranchers to be bad luck.

That night before he went to sleep he told Etta that he'd called the depot and arranged for Ell's train ticket. "It has to be used first thing in the morning. I'll give her some money for those Mexican herbs she came for!"

Next morning Etta noticed that the men picked at the biscuits. She wondered if it were because their vivacious card-playing partner had taken the five A.M. southbound to Colorado or the impending unlucky hanging that left them quiet as featherdusters.

More snow fell during the night. The air was crisp. The wind blew from the northwest. Horn's lawyers were appealing to the governor at that very moment for a complete pardon or a commutation of the sentence.

"An appeal for a new trial on the ground that the verdict was contrary to the evidence, contrary to law, and was not sustained by sufficient evidence was overruled. Therefore this hanging goes on as scheduled." The governor refused to interfere, no matter how logical the lawyers sounded, no matter how emotional the lawyers became.

The men that left Charlie Irwin's home were subdued as they huddled inside sheepskins and walked quickly in the cold air. Their boots made the snow squeak.

At dawn the funeral bell at St. Mary's Cathedral rang for a long, tense five minutes. Charlie and Frank and their friends walked close together toward the courthouse.

Frank spoke softly, "Jeez, look at all the guards. Over there, on top of the jail's roof, see the rapid-firing guns?"

Sheriff Smalley handed Charlie an envelope, which he opened and read:

Cheyenne, Wyo.
November 20, 1903

John C. Coble, Esq.,
Cheyenne, Wyo.

As you have just requested, I will tell all my knowledge of everything I know in regard to the killing of the Nickell boy.

The day I laid over at Miller's ranch, he asked me to do so, so that I could meet Billy McDonald.

Billy McDonald came up and Miller and I met him up the creek, above Miller's house. Billy opened the conversation by saying that he and Miller were going to kill off the Nickell outfit and wanted me to go in on it. They said that Underwood and Jordon would pay me.

Miller and McDonald said they would do the work. I refused to have anything to do with them, as I was not interested in any way. McDonald said that the sheep were then on Coble's land and I got on my horse and went up to see, and they were not on Coble's land.

I promised to stay all night again at Miller's, as McDonald said he would come up again next morning.

He came back next morning and asked me if I still felt the same as I did the day before, and I told him I did.

"Well," he said, "we have made up our minds to wipe up the whole Nickell outfit."

I got on my horse and left, and went on about my business. I went on as John Brae and Otto Plaga said I did, and on to the ranch, where I got in on Saturday. I heard there of the boy being killed. I felt I was well out of the mix up.

I was over in that part of the country six weeks or two

COURTESY BETTY STEELE, LITTLETON, COLORADO.

Etta Mae McGuckin,
eighteen years old.

COURTESY CHARLES M. BENNETT, SCOTTSDALE, ARIZONA.

Charles Burton Irwin.

COURTESY M. C. PARKER COLLECTION, GOODLAND, KANSAS.

Kenmore Coursing Club group, 1895. C. B. Irwin is in front with a spotted dog. Frank Irwin, well-known jockey, is on the left on a horse. The building in the background is the Sherman County Courthouse in Goodland, Kansas.

IRWIN BROS.
CHEYENNE FRONTIER DAYS
WILDWEST SHOW

CHEYENNE, WYO. 19

Opinions expressed by prominent people:

President Roosevelt: "Saw the show twice in 1904 and 1912—best in the world."

President Taft: "Nothing like it; best I ever saw; worth going miles to witness."

U. S. Senator F. E. Warren: "Best show on earth."

A. R. Cory, Sec'y State Fair Ass'n, Des Moines: "Broke our attendance records in 1912; cowboys and cowgirls the real thing."

W. R. Miller, Sec'y Nebraska State Fair: "Gate receipts in 1912 biggest ever; something doing every minute."

Chas. Pickins, Prest. Ak-Sar-Ben, Omaha: "Have seen them all for 45 years, but the Irwin Bros. Show is the best yet."

References:
E. W. Stone, Cashier Citizens National Bank, the First National Bank, and the Stockgrowers National Bank, Cheyenne, Wyo.

We own and operate the famous Ranch, and carry champions in every line in the Wild West show business.

Business stationery used by C. B. Irwin.

COURTESY CHARLES M. BENNETT, SCOTTSDALE, ARIZONA.

COPYRIGHT J. E. STIMSON, COURTESY DR. J. S. PALEN, CHEYENNE, WYOMING, AND THE AMERICAN HERITAGE CENTER, LARAMIE, WYOMING.

C. B. Irwin roping an unruly steer, 1906. This picture appeared in the December 1925 *National Geographic*, page 624.

Clayton Danks in angora chaps, and the famous bucking bronc, Steamboat.

COURTESY CHARLES M. BENNETT, SCOTTSDALE, ARIZONA, AND THE CARNEGIE BRANCH LIBRARY FOR LOCAL HISTORY, BOULDER HISTORICAL SOCIETY COLLECTION.

Charlie and Etta Irwin's children.
Floyd, *top; left to right:* Joella, Frances, and Pauline, about 1908.

COURTESY CHARLES M. BENNETT, SCOTTSDALE, ARIZONA.

Left to right: Teddy Roosevelt, Buffalo Bill, Charles Hirsig, and Charlie Irwin, Cheyenne Frontier Days, August 28, 1910.

COURTESY DR. J. S. PALEN, CHEYENNE, WYOMING.

Joseph Marvin Irwin, Charlie's father, and William H. Irwin, Charlie's brother, about 1910.

COURTESY DR. J. S. PALEN, CHEYENNE, WYOMING.

C. B. Irwin and Charles Hirsig driving a buffalo team during a Frontier Days celebration, about 1910.

COURTESY CHARLES M. BENNETT, SCOTTSDALE, ARIZONA.

ROUTE CARD

Irwin Bros. Wild West Show

June	15-16	Cheyenne, Wyo.
"	17	Sidney, Neb.
"	18-19-20	Alliance, Neb.
"	21	En Route.
"	22	Broken Bow, Neb.
"	23	York, Neb.
"	24	Fairbury, Neb.
"	25	Red Cloud, Neb.
"	26	Hastings, Neb.
"	27	Holdredge, Neb.
"	28	En Route.
"	29	Sterling, Col.
"	30	Ft. Morgan, Col.
July	1	En Route.
July	2-3-4	Ft. Collins, Col.
July	5	En Route.

OFFICIAL ROUTE CARD
—OF THE—

Irwin Bros. Real Wild West Show

Season 1914

Elko, Nevda,	July 13th
Winnemucca, Nevada,	July 14th
Lovelock, Nevada,	July 15th
Reno, Nevada,	July 16th
Enroute	July 17th
"	July 18th
Colfax, California,	July 19th, 20th and 21st
Roseville, California,	July 22nd
Sacramento, California,	July 23rd
San Francisco, California,	July 24th, 25th, 26th, 27th, 28th and 29th

AL. FAIRBROTHER,
Mail Superintendent.

COURTESY DR. J. S. PALEN, CHEYENNE, WYOMING.

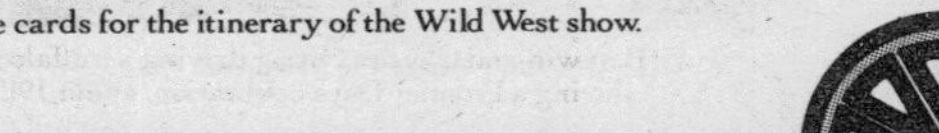

Route cards for the itinerary of the Wild West show.

COURTESY WYOMING STATE ARCHIVES, MUSEUMS, AND HISTORICAL DEPARTMENT, CHEYENNE, WYOMING.

Left to right: Frances, Pauline, and Joella Irwin, 1914. The three girls have the same saddles, bits, and headstalls on their horses.

COURTESY CHARLES M. BENNETT, SCOTTSDALE, ARIZONA.

Charlie Irwin in the New York Stampede, 1916.

Irwin Bros. Cheyenne Frontier Days

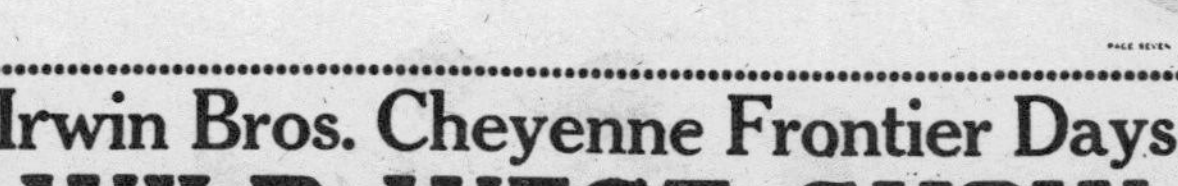

CHEYENNE

JUNE 14

LET'S GO!!

"Prairie Rose" Henderson

The famous band of SIOUX INDIANS from Pine Ridge, including Chiefs "Makes Enemy" and "Chase in the Morning."

SPECIAL EXCURSION RATES
ONE and ONE-THIRD FARE from all points in Wyoming on Union Pacific Ry. Lowest ever given any attraction.

Cool, Clean Comfortable Seats for 10,000 People

TWO BIG BANDS

FRANK CARTER
World's Champion Broncho Buster—Winner of Contest at Cheyenne 1912

PAULINE IRWIN
Winner of Ladies' Relay at Cheyenne 1912

"SCOUT" MAISH
Champion Roper of the World. Winner 1912 Frontier contest.

JOELLA IRWIN
Winner of Ladies' Relay at Cheyenne 1911

Gladys Irwin
FINEST HORSEWOMAN IN THE WEST. Will compete with her mother for arena honors.

"Cheyenne"
The only educated Texas Long Horn in the world.

TWO PERFORMANCES
Afternoon at 2—Evening at 8—Doors open one hour before big show begins.

FLOYD IRWIN AND "MONTANA JACK"
In new and novel exhibitions of TEAM, TRICK and FANCY ROPING

Clayton Danks
TWICE WINNER OF THE WORLD'S CHAMPIONSHIP AT CHEYENNE

BIG SIDE SHOW
Containing the NEWEST and CLEANEST Attractions Ever Displayed Under Canvas.

FRANK C. MILLER, CHAMPION RIFLE AND PISTOL SHOT.

FLOYD IRWIN
NEW TRICK RIDING and ROPING FEATURES

Mrs. W. H. Irwin
TWICE CHAMPION LADY RIDER AT FRONTIER
Will again enter the arena after many years retirement.

Mrs. Clayton Danks
Winner of Ladies' Championship in 1909

SCOTTY and PETE
ONLY TRAINED BUFFALO IN EXISTENCE

"MONTANA JACK" RAY
The Most Sensational Trick Rider in Any Land

Fanny Sperry Steele
CHAMPION LADY BRONCHO BUSTER at "STAMPEDE" at CALGARY, 1912

"Old Steamboat," "Teddy Roosevelt," "Aeroplane," "Senator Warren," "Young Steamboat," "Silver City," "Whizzer," "Biplane," "Nevada Kid," "Bill Taft," "Archbishop," "Wildcat," "Gin Fizz," "Cheyenne Red Bird," "Laramie Plains Red Bird," "Red Sandy," "Miller's Kid," "Hot Shot," "Woodrow Wilson," "War Paint." ALL THE OLD OUTLAWS AND ABOUT FORTY NEW ONES.

30—CARLOADS OF THE BEST WILD WEST FEATURES IN THE WORLD—30

Two Performances
Afternoon at 2 Evening at 8
Doors Open One Hour before Big Show Commences

Monster Street Spectacle
Biggest Ever Seen in Cheyenne—AT NOON
DON'T MISS IT

IRWIN BROTHERS CHEYENNE FRONTIER DAYS WILD WEST SHOW travels in the most superbly equipped train of any traveling show in this country--Electric lighted throughout, beautifully decorated coaches, palace horse cars, etc.

An advertisement for the Irwin Bros. Cheyenne Frontier Days Wild West Show.
The Wyoming Tribune, Saturday, June 7, 1913, p. 7.

COURTESY CHARLES M. BENNETT, SCOTTSDALE, ARIZONA.

Floyd Irwin on his horse, Fashion, in front of the Sioux camp outside Frontier Park in Cheyenne, Wyoming.

COURTESY CHARLES M. BENNETT, SCOTTSDALE, ARIZONA.

Buddy Sterling in the driver's seat and Roy Kivett. Sterling took care of Will Rogers' polo ponies. Kivett was raised as a member of the Irwin family.

C. B. Irwin (*left*) and the Baron de Rothschild of France, standing beside the Buick touring car and Model T Ford.

COURTESY CHARLES M. BENNETT, SCOTTSDALE, ARIZONA.

The Wyoming State Board of Child and Animal Protection

Know all Men by these Presents, That I, F. R. Dildine President of *The Wyoming State Board of Child and Animal Protection,* being thereunto duly authorized by the Board of Directors of said Board, do hereby appoint and commission Charles B. Irwin of Cheyenne, County of Laramie and State of Wyoming, an *Officer of said Board for the State of Wyoming.*

It is the duty of said Officer to familiarize himself with the laws under which he shall act; to investigate all cases of cruelty to animals, or neglect or abuse of children, coming within his notice; to take whatever action in each case shall best secure the prevention and punishment of cruelty to animals and wrongs to children; to utilize every opportunity to create humane sentiment, and to discharge his duty as an officer of the law and of this Board impartially and fearlessly.

He shall furnish a report of his work to the said Board whenever it shall be called for. He shall have no power to contract debts or incur liabilities for the said Board. He shall remain in office until his successor shall have been appointed, or this commission revoked.

This commission shall be his authority to act for the said Board in all matters herein specified.

Given at the office of *The State Board of Child and Animal Protection,* at Cheyenne, Wyoming, this 4th day of June, A. D. 1918.

Witness my hand and the seal of the Board.

F. R. Dildine
President

ATTEST: L. B. Bartlett
Secretary

E. H. Burke

Charlie was given his commission and star as an officer of the Wyoming Humane Society and State Board of Child and Animal Protection in 1918 and remained an officer for the rest of his life.

COURTESY CHARLES M. BENNETT, SCOTTSDALE, ARIZONA.

COURTESY DR. J. S. PALEN, CHEYENNE, WYOMING.

Frontier Days Parade on 17th and Capitol Avenue, Cheyenne, in the early 1920s.

COURTESY CHARLES M. BENNETT, SCOTTSDALE, ARIZONA

Fire at the Tia Juana Racetrack in Mexico in 1924. All the barns on this side of the railroad tracks were destroyed.

Left to right: Pablo Martinez, a famous jockey, Will Rogers, and C. B. Irwin.

COURTESY CHARLES M. BENNETT, SCOTTSDALE, ARIZONA.

General "Black Jack" Pershing (*left*) and Charlie Irwin.

COURTESY CHARLES M. BENNETT, SCOTTSDALE, ARIZONA.

Douglas Fairbanks, Sr. (*left*), and Charlie Irwin.

Chief Red Cloud and Charlie Irwin with three Sioux women.

GENERAL HEADQUARTERS
AMERICAN EXPEDITIONARY FORCES

France, April 18, 1919.

PERSONAL

Mr. C. B. Irwin,
Cheyenne, Wyoming.

My dear Charley:

I have received your letter of January 1st, and am pleased to know that you are getting on well and thank you for the newspaper clipping which you enclosed.

With reference to your inquiry regarding certain members of this Expedition, it is learned with deep regret that the men you mention met with misfortune in the honorable discharge of their duties, fighting in a noble cause, and I ask that in conveying the following to the respective families, you express my sincere sympathy at their loss.

Private Sidney McIntosh, 122953, 96th Company, 6th Marines, was reported on July 22, 1918, wounded in action, severe, between June 2nd and 10th, and his death was reported February 9, 1919. He was buried in American Battle Area Cemetery in Commune of Bouresches, Department of the Aisne, grave No. 34, marked with a cross. The exact date of Private McIntosh's death and burial, unfortunately, are not available.

As to W. C. Irvine's boy, Flying Squadron, Canadian Forces; records of the American Statistical Section with the British show a Van Renssaler V. Irvine, 43 Squadron Royal Air Force, missing in action since July 29th. This case is now in the hands of the American Statistical Section with the British to determine the status of this soldier.

Relative to John Hay's boy, of Rock Springs, Wyoming: Records show that Sergeant Archibald L. Hay, 2260716, Company G, 362nd Infantry, was killed in action September 29th and that he was buried October 1st, one kilometer south of Epionville, Cemetery No. 1. Sergeant Hay's grave is marked with a cross.

Reply to your letter has been delayed awaiting additional information regarding Mr. Irvine's boy, but nothing further having been learned to date, I am sending this on now and will communicate anything additional immediately upon its receipt.

With best wishes, believe me, as always,

Very sincerely yours,

John J Pershing.

A personal letter to C. B. Irwin from General John Pershing.

C. B. Irwin with jockey E. Taplin on Bonnie Kay at the Agua Caliente track in Tia Juana, Mexico, 1930.

Flood at the Y6 ranch, 1935.

Pine Ridge, South Dakota.
April 3. 1934.

Dear Mrs. Pauline Sawyer:

I am writing this letter to tell you how sorry we felt for my good friend Mr. Charles B. Irwin's death. All the Indians who made good friends with your Dad. Mr. Irwin. felt pretty bad. I know I never will find a better man like Mr. Irwin again. The sioux Indins will miss him pretty bad. We thought we was going to see him again this year. but I guess we will never see him again any more.

I will always remember Mr. C. B. Irwin like the day I last saw him.

I am hoping you will answer me right away and tell me about Mr. Charles B. Irwin's death. I am anxious to hear about it. The Indians who knew Mr. Irwin lost a good man.

I remain a friend of Mr. Charles B. Irwin and family.

Mr. Charles Yellow Boy.
Pine Rid ge,
South Dakota.

The above letter to Charlie's middle daughter, Pauline, from one of the Sioux, meant a great deal to the Irwin family.

months later and saw both McDonald and Miller, and they were laughing and blowing to me about running and shooting the sheep of Nickell. I told them I did not want to hear of it at all, for I could see that McDonald wanted to tell me the whole scheme. They both gave me the laugh and said I was suspicioned of the whole thing. I knew there was some suspicion against me, but did not pay the attention to it that I should.

That is all there is to it so far as I know. . . . All that supposed confession in the United States marshal's office was prearranged, and everything that was sworn to by those fellows was a lie, made up before I came to Cheyenne. Of course, there was talk of the killing of the boy, but LaFors did all of it. I did not even make an admission, but allowed LaFors to make some insinuations.

Ohnahaus, LaFors and Snow . . . all swore to lies to fit the case.

Your name was not mentioned in the marshal's office.

This is the truth, as I am going to die in ten minutes.

Thanking you for your kindness and continued goodness to me, I am

Sincerely yours,
Tom Horn*

"What are you going to do with that?" asked Frank. "It's Coble's and you read it!"

"I figure it was given to me for some reason. Wait." He recognized George Evans of the *Cheyenne State Leader* and John Thompson of the *Wyoming Tribune*. He showed them the letter and urged, "Make it fast. You gotta get this in the paper and out on the streets before the hanging. A couple of hours at most."

The next two hours were tense. Charlie walked into the outside courtyard and nodded toward Thompson. Thompson shook his head and pointed his thumbs down. Charlie's heart sank to the ground. There had not been time enough to get an extra or even a flier printed before this execution. Oh, double jeems! thought Charlie. A man's life is cut off, thrown away for lack of time! For not moving fast enough!

*Reprinted with permission from: Tom Horn, *Life of Tom Horn*, New York, New York; Jingle Bob Brand, Crown Publishers, Inc, 1977. James D. Horan; 1904, John Coble, pp.283–4.

The men stayed inside the courthouse where it was warm until they were given tiny white ribbons to wear in their lapel and led out to the courtyard. Two companies of the Wyoming National Guard surrounded the courthouse. There were ten armed men around the jail itself. No one was allowed to be on the streets near the courthouse while the hanging was taking place. The governor wanted no attack against the jail to get the doomed Horn out.

Deputy Proctor stepped up to the gallows' platform and in a loud voice began to point out how they were designed by Cheyenne's architect, James P. Julian.

"My stomach's in knots," whispered Frank.

Charlie flexed his knees and breathed deeply the needlelike near-freezing air.

Deputy Proctor paused and looked at the open door of the cell leading to the platform. "All right, we're ready now."

Horn stood up and looked at the cross beam. He was pale from his long confinement in jail.

Charlie's stomach contracted. He swallowed and was acutely aware of his neck muscles. He felt dizzy. His head throbbed.

"Lost his tan," murmured Frank, "and he looks thin."

Horn walked out and seemed to tower above even those men on the second tier of the platform. He was well over six feet tall. His features were sharp and clean. He had a neat, small mustache on his upper lip that was brown and matched his thinning hair. He had on flat, leather slippers, dark trousers, a brown corduroy vest, and a yellow and white striped, soft silk shirt. The collar of the shirt was unbuttoned, showing a red scar on Horn's neck. He brushed cigarette ashes off his vest and glanced back at his carefully made cot where he'd left a braided horsehair hackamore, not yet finished. Horn sighed audibly. Then, chin up, he walked twelve steps, handed his cigarette to the *Wyoming State Tribune*'s John Thompson, and stopped on the side of the gallows' platform. He looked at the group of sheriffs and said to Ed Smalley, "What a scared-looking lot of lawmen. What's making them shiver? Is it the cold this twentieth of November, 1903, or is it fright for what they are to see?" His eyes were squeezed down hard and penetrating. Suddenly his face softened. "Hello there, Charlie."

"Hello, Tom," said Charlie, having a hard time keeping his teeth from chattering as the wind came up sharp and biting.

"You and Frank sing me one of your songs. You can do that?"

"Oh—sure," said Charlie. His knees trembled. "Frank and

I'll sing." He cleared his throat and began to hum. Frank swallowed hard before taking up the tune, "Life's Railway to Heaven." Charlie could not look at Tom, nor at Frank, as he sang the popular hymn. His voice had more than the usual amount of vibrato. After the first verse the words came out somewhat easier, steadier. Their voices carried deep and now unbroken over the entire courtyard. ". . . never falter, never quail . . . Keep your hand upon the throttle and your eye upon the rail."

As the two men sang in their rich tenor voices, Ed Proctor fitted the straps that held Horn's arms and legs. Charlie could feel perspiration gather under his arms and in the middle of his back. Tears streamed unchecked down his face. He could not see that there was not a dry eye among any of the men, except for Tom Horn himself. The song was over, Charlie mopped his face with his handkerchief, and the courtyard was deathly still. A light snow was falling.

The leg straps pulled Horn's legs together and he nearly lost his balance. In a jesting tone Horn said, "Seems to me you birds might steady me. I might tip over." Sheriff Smalley and Joe Cahill held his arms, supported him, while his knees and feet were bound together.

Proctor fixed the noose, formed with a knot of thirteen wraps. Cahill pulled the black cap over Horn's head. In a loud voice Proctor asked, "Tom, are you ready?"

Without a moment's hesitation came the reply, "Yes."

Sheriff Smalley sobbed and put his arm over his face, and turned his back toward Horn.

"You can't be losing your nerve, Ed?" said Horn through the black hood.

Cahill and Proctor lifted Horn onto the trapdoor. The only sound was the hissing of rushing water underneath Horn's feet.

Charlie thought the sound of the water went on and on. The gurgling heightened the tense feeling of doom. Charlie could not hold back his heaving sobs. Then suddenly, without warning, the trapdoor divided with a loud crash and Horn's body swung between two halves of the door. The force of Horn's weight on a four-inch by four-inch rod, supporting the door, pressed on a spring. The spring acted on a hydraulic valve which opened and let water run from a container. When the container's equilibrium was upset, water spilled out, tripped a weight, and the trapdoor fell open and Horn hanged himself. There were two, three spasmodic quiverings, then the body went limp in the frigid air.

Thompson of the *Wyoming State Tribune* was first to break the tension. "He was hanged at eleven-o-four. Thirty-one seconds since he was on that damn door! He's fallen nearly four feet!"

Everyone knew after Proctor's explanation of the device that the drop could not be longer, because the full weight of the body would rip the head off.

Charlie let the breath out of his burning lungs. It was an explosive sound of hot, pent-up air.

BOOK II

TWENTY-FOUR

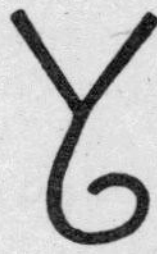

Theodore Roosevelt

Charlie began to bring his favorite horses to town and leave them there, in the barn, with store-bought high-protein grain feed. It was Floyd's job to walk the horses around the block two or three times each morning before school.

When each of the three girls turned six, they, too, were expected to walk the horses. Joella was first to make use of the big tree stump on the corner north from the house. She'd lead the particular horse she was exercising to the stump, climb on top of the stump, then hoist herself onto the horse's back. She grinned and kicked her heels against the horse's side as she rode at a gallop several times around the block.

Floyd invariably scolded her. "Jo, the horse is supposed to exercise by hisself, not with a load on its back! If Pa knew he'd wup you good."

Joella acted as if she never heard.

When in town, away from the Y6, Charlie took time to be with his children. He played horse with the younger ones, letting them ride on his back around the living room and through the bedrooms. He bounced Frances on his foot and sang. Sometimes Joella sang, delighting him. At the same time she'd put her little hands on her waist and dance around the room like some professional entertainer. One weekend he came home and found Floyd braiding a horsehair rope. "You're just like my grown-up cowboys," he said.

"Pa, if I had some chewing tobacco, I'd be a real cowboy," said Floyd.

"I'll get you all the *tobacco* you need to chew, cowboy," said Charlie, filling the boy's pockets with dried prunes from a jar in the kitchen. "When you ride in the saddle all day you need to stock up on prunes. Every true cowboy has a supply of this *tobacco*. Chew all you want. But don't chew that other junk, it makes your teeth brown."

"Pa, can I chew tobacco?" asked Joella.

"Certainly, sis," said Charlie, filling the little girl's overall pockets with prunes. "But young lady, don't you ever let me catch you chewing anything else, nor smoking cigarettes. Some women like to do that, you know. Makes them think they are just as good as a man. Makes them feel real smart. They look real dumb."

"I'd want to be smart," said Pauline, who was five years old.

Charlie sat down on the floor with his children around him. "All of you are smart," he said. "But let me tell you it is not smart to do some things. None of you want brown teeth nor to smell like a coal-burning engine."

Joella moved close to her father and put her arm around one of his knees. "Pa, what would you do if I chewed real tobacco?" Her soft, blue eyes sparkled like fast water in sunlight.

"I'd tan you with a hairbrush and wash your mouth out with yellow soap."

"Ugh, I hate the taste of soap," said Floyd, closing his eyes tight and sticking out his tongue.

"Me, too," said Pauline.

Later, when Joella and Floyd were in the barn feeding oats to the horses, Joella elbowed Floyd. "Have you never tried tobacco?"

"Nope," he said, filling a bucket with water from a hose.

"One of the cowboys would give you some if you asked."

"So what! Jo, don't you remember what Pa said?"

"Yes. But I was just wondering why cowboys like it if it's so bad."

Etta called them for supper. "Don't wear overalls at the supper table. Joella, put on a dress," said Etta.

"Oh, Ma," said Joella, sticking out her tongue at Floyd, who could always wear overalls or pants to the table.

That evening Charlie announced that he'd told Frank, some of the other cowboys from Iron Mountain, and his own cowboys at the Y6 about the sale of cavalry horses at Fort Russell the following day.

"Wish I didn't have to go to school. Then I'd go, too," said Floyd.

"If I buy any horses you can look them over," promised Charlie.

Charlie bought several horses. Frank, egged on by some cowboys, tested one he'd bought by getting on bareback and swinging his rope overhead a couple of times. The horse bucked. Frank somersaulted and landed spread eagle on the ground with a broken arm.

President Theodore Roosevelt was touring the Southwest. The secretaries of the Cheyenne Spanish-American War veterans and the Cheyenne Grand Army of the Republic sent him a telegram inviting him for their Memorial Day festivities and to deliver the Memorial Day address. The whole town of Cheyenne was pleased when Roosevelt sent a telegram accepting.

John Coble rode over to the Y6 to ask Charlie to organize some of the local ranch boys into a small rodeo show for the President at Pioneer Park on the Monday after Memorial Day. "You're the only one I know that won't panic on such short notice. I've talked with Senator Warren about Roosevelt's love of the outdoors, and he suggested that we have someone meet the President's special train at Laramie with horses on the morning of May thirtieth. Then the whole party can ride horseback into Cheyenne. Can you supply the horses and organize such a delegation to meet the President?"

Charlie took the President and party of local ranch managers through Cheyenne Pass to the head of Telephone Canyon, then to Pole Mountain Road, which was called Happy Jack Road by the locals. They went through a stretch of hills that were covered with carpets of wildflowers—yellow and lavender shooting stars, red Indian paintbrush, and tall, purple fireweed, their blossoms vivid against the lush, green prairie grass and gray, jagged rocks. The serviceberry was redolent with masses of white blossoms and the creek banks thick with wild roses from pure white to deep red scenting the air.

The President's party rode through a forest reserve, where there were lodgepole pines, tall and straight against the sky, up one hundred feet.

Senator Warren, John Coble, Ora Haley, and Charlie were the official escort for President Roosevelt. From the crest of a hill the men could see the faint blue, snowcapped Colorado mountains that lay sixty miles to the south. Coming down to a thick aspen grove they rode alongside Pole Mountain Creek, which was clear and cold. Roosevelt was first to suggest they stop for a drink of water. The men scooped the water up in their hats and drank thirstily. They let the horses drink and hurried on because the deer flies, gnats, and mosquitoes were a great annoyance.

Senator Warren said, "If we're lucky we'll see an elk or deer or antelope, maybe a moose, black bear, ring-necked pheasant, or prairie chickens."

Roosevelt asked, "Are you troubled with wood ticks?"

Warren said, "We can search for them and pull them off, but the sheep are most troubled in this area."

Rocky Mountain spotted fever, sometimes fatal, was caused by an organism carried by the wood ticks.

"I believe I saw rainbow trout in a quiet pool along the opposite bank of the creek," said Roosevelt.

"I'm sure you saw rainbows. We're going to pass Crystal Lake, which you'll see down in a small valley. There's excellent trout fishing there."

The party arrived at Van Tassell's Islay Ranch in time for lunch at 12:45 P.M. Lunch was a cup of bouillon, pan-sized rainbow trout, new potatoes, wilted lettuce, and deep-dish home-canned huckleberry pie with cream. When they mounted and set out again, rocks, pines, mountain peaks, and open spaces alternated in their view.

The road wound downward out of the hills. There were huge gray sandstones, weathered round, exposed on the emerald-green, grassy hill. Yellow and gray-green lichen covered the south side of the rocks.

In the rolling fields cattle were grazing. There were prairie dogs who scurried to their burrows as the men on horseback went by.

They noticed that the wild hay seemed greener and less infested with sage and bull thistles than closer to Laramie. Looking back was a good view of the rocky Laramie Mountain peaks. The wind was strong and blew dust from the road around the horses and riders, so they quickly moved on, leaving the huge clouds of dust behind them.

Closer to Cheyenne the dark green aromatic sagebrush with

tufted stems grew close to the roadsides, and here also were sweet cactus, small plants resting close to the sandy soil. This fifty-six mile trek ended as the party entered Fort Russell amid a twenty-one gun salute by the Thirteenth Field Artillery. Roosevelt visited the commander of the fort for nearly an hour. Everyone was fed in the officers' mess hall. After dinner Roosevelt mounted his horse once again and headed for the outdoor speaker's stand at Fifteenth and Carey streets in Cheyenne. He was introduced by Senator Warren at seven o'clock and gave a thirty-minute Memorial Day address. Senator Warren took the President to the Industrial Club, where he was given lodging for the night.

The following afternoon the special Wild West rodeo was staged at Pioneer Park for the President. Most of Charlie's cowboys were on hand to demonstrate bronc riding. Charlie let Floyd, who was eight years old, give a short demonstration of his trick roping.

At first the boy was nervous. Then when everything went the way he'd rehearsed, he gained confidence and wanted to stay and run through his routine once again. A group of ranchers came from Douglas, Wyoming, to give Roosevelt a gift of a Western horse called Rag-a-lon. Roosevelt shook Floyd's hand and confided that he didn't know what he was to do with a Western horse, but he'd sure like to take it to Washington, D.C.

"My pa can take care of that for you," said Floyd. "He'll get your horse shipped anywhere. My pa can do anything."

"I'll talk to him," said Roosevelt.

"I'll get your horse on a special boxcar and head him out to Washington, D.C.," promised Charlie.

Warren put one hand on the President's shoulder, the other on Charlie's shoulder. "When the rodeo is over you're coming to my ranch for beans and barbecue."

"You bet," said the President.

"I couldn't keep Etta away," said Charlie. "First I have to think of some way to pay for shipping a horse to Washington."

"Then go out there and show us how you rope a steer, but don't break your fool neck!" said Warren. Charlie inched his way down the grandstand to the registration table next to the judges' stand.

By this time Charlie had half-talked himself out of his crazy idea of roping and branding a steer. He was not dressed in his old Levi's and work shirt. He had on his suit and a clean, starched, white cotton dress shirt and a tie. He removed the tie and put it in his coat pocket. Fate took charge of his next few moments. His coat and vest hung on the corral fence.

He lined up with the other cowboys when his name was called. Charlie had no time to daydream before it was his turn. He was on his own horse, Custer, his favorite horse, a roan with white legs. Charlie swung the mainline as far as possible. The loop was around the steer's horns in a moment. Charlie left his horse and with a short rope tied the legs of the steer. The steer squealed and made a lot of noise. Charlie pulled a piece of hide from his back pocket that he had been handed as he mounted his horse. Someone handed him a red-hot brand. He laid the skin on the flank of the steer and put the brand on the piece of old hide. The burning of the hair on the dead skin burned Charlie's nose, and he handed the hot iron back to his helper. Charlie raised his hat, untied the steer, and mounted his horse.

The cowboy, after Charlie branded his steer, untied him, and rode him about twenty feet before getting back on his horse to the howling and hooting of the crowd.

Then the official announcement came: "Winner of the steer roping, C. B. Irwin, with the Y6 ranch! The purse is two hundred fifty dollars in gold dust, donated by the Cheyenne *Tribune*. Irwin takes one hundred and fifty dollars, Guy Holt, second place winner, takes seventy-five dollars, and third place—"

Charlie didn't hear the rest. He wiped his face with his handkerchief, took off his hat and ran his fingers through his thick sandy hair, and put the hat on before the hair fell down in his eyes again. He wiped his boots off on the backs of his pants' legs, then brushed off his pants. He put his vest on and buttoned it, then rolled down his shirtsleeves and buttoned them. Casually he walked to the judges' stand.

"Congratulations! Being late didn't hurt your luck!" said the man who'd signed him in.

"Thank you," said Charlie, grinning. "Say, you fellows invited to Senator Warren's place for supper?"

"You bet!" said the man. "All the cattle barons and Cheyenne bigwigs'll be there." He handed Charlie a certificate and note to pick up his winnings at the Stock Growers National Bank.

"I'll see you then," said Charlie.

By the time Charlie was back in the grandstand, everyone was on his feet. Senator Carey was shaking hands with President Roosevelt and Senator Warren.

"Who is it that's going to see that my gift horse, Rag-a-lon, is taken to the railroad and loaded into a boxcar properly?"

"I am, sir," said Charlie, reaching out his hand. "Did you think I'd forgotten?"

"Well, no, but I thought you'd found more excitement in roping steers. Can't say I blame you, son."

Senator Warren was shaking his head and chuckling over Charlie's inability to find the right words. He said, "Go get that horse settled, C.B. I'll tell the President you entered that fool contest to pay the freight on his horse. No—better yet—you tell him at my barbecue. Your wife will be interested in hearing about your escapade also, I bet."

Etta was in a dither when Charlie came home. "I've been wondering where you've been. The Wild West show's been over quite a while."

"I took the President's gift horse to the station and had a boxcar made up so it could be shipped to the White House. Guess someone will build a barn for it. The President said he'd ride it each morning for exercise, his and the horse's."

"Tell me about him," said Etta.

"Well, you mean the horse or the President?" said Charlie. "Honestly, I know what you mean," Charlie said. "The man is large. Looks like the outdoor type. He is kind and I imagine the life of any party. His fun and vitality are contagious. You'll like him. He looks like a typical British ranch manager. He's big, burly, and well dressed in a gray business suit with vest and coat and black riding boots. He smokes cigars. When he talks he bites off every word quick, like he was eating the most delicious beefsteak. Nice man, not a bit pompous. The guests invited to Senator Warren's barbecue this evening were asked to come by horseback. So, I'm going to change my clothes. I roped a steer during the show. I won first prize. Don't ask for the money. I spent it."

Etta could not help but laugh. Charlie was going to change his good suit that he'd worn while performing in the rodeo. "I guess you can wear most anything," she said.

He washed and changed to a pair of twill pants and a red shirt and dark blue neckerchief. He polished his boots. Etta wore her navy silk riding skirt, which was actually wide legs, but hung together appearing as a beautiful long skirt. She wore her high-collared, white lace shirt and her rose-colored crocheted wool shawl. She tied an extra woolen blanket to the back of her saddle in case it was chilly when they rode the thirteen miles from the Warren Ranch north, back to town.

Etta got an early supper for the children. She and Charlie rode horses that were kept at the Irwin barn in town. They took the Terry Ranch Road, which was two tracks in the dirt. They noticed horseback riders ahead and behind. Delicate shooting stars and bluebells grew amidst the meadow grass between cottonwoods along the creek. In one section the brick-red Indian paintbrush was thick. Etta slowed and dismounted. She made a small bouquet of wildflowers. Charlie teased her when she remounted and arranged her flowers into a little nosegay. "Since when do women take flowers to men? Warren will think you've gone unhinged."

However, Senator Warren was quite touched with the gift of colorful, dainty wildflowers. He told Etta she was the first woman to bring him flowers. "When my wife was living, she liked the big splashy things like dahlias, oriental poppies. Frankly, I prefer the smaller, wild varieties and I see you do also. I think Indian paintbrush is my all-time favorite. How about you?"

"I like the wood violets," said Etta. "These blooms will be cheerful on your kitchen windowsill. While Charlie is seeing to the horses, I'll take them to the kitchen and find a glass of water for them."

"Splendid! Thank you," said Warren, patting Etta's hand.

She went in the front door of the ranch house and saw a half-dozen little knots of people standing around the dining room table. In the kitchen she introduced herself to the ranch cook and the cowboy hands who were helping with this special dinner. "Any of you seen the President?" asked Etta as she placed the flowers in a small blue glass sugar bowl.

"Nope," said the cook.

Roosevelt shook hands and asked the Chattertons something about their home in Cheyenne. He then said to Etta, "I saw you take flowers to the kitchen. Bring them out to the dining table for our enjoyment. The Indian paintbrush is a favorite of mine."

For a moment Etta was without words. However, when she saw Senator Warren smiling, she said, "You know, they are Senator Warren's favorite also. I'll be right back."

The sprightly colored little bouquet of wildflowers in the clear, blue glass sugar bowl was a spot of lovely brightness on the stark white dinner table and a fine source for talk of remembered family picnics and hikes. Roosevelt told of the many buttercups and even wild strawberry blossoms he'd seen along the Pole Mountain Road two days ago. Charlie spoke of the rare moccasin flowers he'd found on the roundups in the Laramie Mountains.

"I love this country. It makes me feel alive," said Mrs. Chatterton, her eyes going from Charlie to Senator Warren to the President.

When dinner was over the men went to the parlor to smoke cigars, pipes, cigarettes and to talk. The women went outside to the porch. Etta and Mrs. Chatterton moved among the one hundred and fifty lawn guests. They shook hands and spoke with as many as they could.

"We came to see the President," some said. "Is he coming out?"

"Just be patient," said Etta with a smile. "He'll be out as soon as he wipes the barbecue sauce from his chin."

"This was a wonderful meal," most agreed.

Etta left Mrs. Chatterton talking with the editor of the *Wyoming State Tribune* about the barbequed steaks, beans, potato salad, sourdough biscuits, strawberries, and vanilla ice cream.

She stood in the doorway of the parlor, coughed once, then in a quiet voice said, "Mr. President, there are many lawn guests under the canvas awning who would certainly like to shake your hand when you have a moment."

Roosevelt stood up, straightened his coat and tie. "Thank you, of course I'll take a few moments." As he walked by Etta he said, "And I'll take a few of the flowers of the land so they will see I appreciate the natural beauty."

He took the sugar bowl of wildflowers in his big hands and went out on the front lawn. People swooped on him and he held them back by pinching off a single blossom and passing it out here and there. He told the people the name of the flower and reminded them that they lived on the best land possible in this great country.

Inside Charlie looked about the big parlor and saw he was the only one not smoking. No one else seemed to notice. Charlie thought, all these men are in high places because they worked and seized opportunities. But their parents were farmers, or tradesmen, or blacksmiths like my own pa. They really pulled themselves up by their bootstraps. Now where do they go from here? What will their sons and daughters do?

Governor Chatterton came over to Charlie. He took Charlie's

elbow and guided him toward the porch, where there were now few people. "I've been meaning to tell you that I was impressed with the plea you and your brother made in my office on behalf of Tom Horn."

"Not impressed enough, though," Charlie said sadly.

"I've come to believe Horn was framed and died in place of one, maybe two others," said Chatterton.

Charlie was astonished. He stuttered, "You—you could have held off on the hanging until you got more—more facts. A man's life depended on your belief. With that kind of power you have to be dead sure before making a decision."

"You would make a poor lawyer, C.B. Nothing is black or white, right or wrong. A man should never regret. The winds of fate cannot be quelled. They blow with the times and constantly, with no slack. What I decide today may be different from the way I'll decide tomorrow." The governor stretched out his hand toward Charlie.

Charlie hesitated, then took the governor's small hand in his large one. "Your Honor, I heartily disagree. You and I have control. We can put up a wind break. We can build a windmill. So we change that wind or make use of it. We listen to what it says and are not ruled by whims of fate." Charlie adjusted his string tie. "Man was given brains and he is derelict if he doesn't use them or takes the easy road." Charlie pulled his hand away, then nodded as the governor strolled away.

Charlie wandered around the lawn alone for a while trying to cool down, then found Etta. They told Senator Warren what a wonderful party he'd had.

"Let's get together again," said Warren. "Don't wait until the President comes to Cheyenne again, though." He put his arm around Etta. "The party went well because of you. You are the one that made everyone feel at home." His eyes turned soft and he spoke in a lower tone. "My daughter has played hostess for me in Washington, when she's not in school. She'd have her eyes opened watching how unassuming and gracious you are. Frankie's coming here at Christmas. I'll have you come meet her." There were tears in his eyes. He took out his handkerchief and quickly wiped his face.

Etta was deeply moved by his kindness and knew that he felt a profound loneliness since his wife had died. Etta sensed that was why he spent most of his time in Washington, instead of on his beloved ranch in Wyoming.

"We'll come," Etta promised, "if you and your Frankie will come to our house in town for one of Charlie's ranch-cured hams."

"It's a deal. We'll be together soon then. You know I've always kind of regretted sending Charlie to that poet, Johnnie Gordon."

"Oh, never regret," said Etta. "But make amends." She laughed. "You started Charlie in the ranch business. Look where he is now—raising horses on the Y6. Charlie's never been happier. That's success."

Senator Warren bent and kissed Etta on the cheek.

She blushed.

Charlie chuckled. "Invite Mr. Roosevelt back. I'll have another Wild West show, bigger and better."

"I will, if you'll do rope tricks from horseback," teased Warren.

"Oh, no!" cried Etta. "Charlie's brother Frank has a broken arm for doing one of those foolhardy tricks. I don't want Charlie laid up. I'll tell you a secret: A sick man's worse than tending a sick child." She giggled and it was such a nice merry sound that Charlie knew she was teasing. However, in a pleasant way she was saying she didn't want Charlie hurt.

"Thanks to both of you, good friends," called Warren as Charlie and Etta went out to the hitching rails to get their horses.

"What nice people we met at Warren's place," said Etta, wrapping the warm blanket over her shawl before Charlie helped her into the saddle. "I am glad we are here, not in Kansas, or even Colorado. This is your place, Charlie. You fit in with these people."

"Seems Senator Warren and I have always been friends," said Charlie with a sigh. "We think alike. And he kind of reminds me of Pa. If Pa had had a chance for an education, he'd be like Warren—a senator."

"I should go out to see old Joe and Will and Margaret and those children real soon," said Etta.

"You can do it while Frank is laid up. He can stay with the kids," suggested Charlie.

"Joe would like to see our kids," said Etta.

Charlie buttoned his coat to keep the chilly night air out as they trotted along the dusty road.

"So, I'll bring Pa home with us for a few days. The change will do him good."

Joe spent a week with Etta in town, but was eager to get back to the ranch. As soon as Frank was better he went back to the IM. That summer Etta and the children spent much time at the Y6.

Will built more stalls for the growing string of racehorses Charlie and Frank purchased from owners in Chicago and Omaha. The barn was enlarged so that more cows could be brought in for milking. Will planted alfalfa in the upper meadow and hired Arnold and Johnny Rick, Margaret's brothers, as cowboys. Each of the Rick brothers filed for a section of land in the upper meadow area as a part of the Y6 ranch.

Margaret won the Frontier Days Ladies' Relay Race and brought to the ranch a seventeen-inch-high trophy with a scrollwork pedestal. The cup and handles were solid silver and engraved with: MARGARET RICK IRWIN, AUGUST 30,1904.

Margaret was so enthusiastic she entered the state fair in Douglas, Wyoming, in October. Again she won the ladies' relay race and came home all smiles with another silver loving cup engraved with her name and dated, October 3, 4, 5, 6, 1904. When she saw Etta she said, "I love it when the wind blows through my hair and the horse runs and there's only green grass and blue sky to see. That's peace and serenity."

"Peace and serenity is when I sew or when I cook a big meal for the family," said Etta. "I only ride a horse to get from one place to another."

Just before Thanksgiving Charlie talked to W. E. Lawrence, Livestock Agent for the Union Pacific. He was resigning to take over some business of his own and wondered if Charlie would like to take the livestock agent job. "The work is not enough for full-time, so you could do it and keep busy at your ranch," Bill Lawrence said.

Charlie stroked the ears of Lawrence's cocker spaniel, tipped his hat, and headed for the depot to see his friend Warren Richardson. The men shook hands and Charlie said he'd like to have the job as Livestock Agent.

Etta was ecstatic. "Now you'll spend more time in town. You have an office with this new job?" she asked.

"I might," Charlie said. "I don't know if I have the job yet."

Etta hugged Charlie as if she didn't want to let him go. "You have it, I'm certain. I'm so proud of you. It'll be like a second honeymoon."

"I like that last thought about the honeymoon," said Charlie, chuckling.

Charlie's first job as Livestock Agent for the Union Pacific was to ride the train from Cheyenne to Laramie to make himself known to the Union Pacific people. He had the whole state of Wyoming along the Union Pacific line as his territory and was sure he could see that all the prominent stockmen shipped their stock to market on the U.P.

Charlie spent two, three days each week on the railroad and the rest of the time at the ranch. He always helped his father with the repair jobs. Joe was as healthy and as spry as Charlie could remember. Joe was a doer and restless and bored when he was not making, fixing, or mending something. In the smithy he was as competent as ever. His workmanship had always been superior. He was always contemptuous of poor, sloppy work, but he had a kindness and understanding for anyone who did his best. He longed for all of his children to be home on the ranch with him. Joe would rather have a party at the ranch house than go out to another ranch for a party or for a supper. He was disappointed that Etta would not stay on the ranch year-round.

After Thanksgiving Etta and Charlie received a handwritten invitation from Senator Warren to have supper at his ranch and meet his daughter.

Frankie Warren was a brunette with a trim figure and jolly sense of humor. She and Charlie got along just fine.

"Whenever there is some mischief discovered at Wellesley," said Frankie, laughing, "the housemothers get together and ask, 'Where was Frances Warren?' "

Etta brought Senator Warren a bunch of dried chives, thyme, and sage to use as seasonings in cooking. "I am making it a habit to always bring a bouquet to your place." Her eyes sparkled. "Didn't the President fairly ruin that first bouquet I brought, pulling all the flowers off?"

"Well, yes, but you'd be surprised how many people have a pressed flower in their family Bible that the President of the United States gave to them," said Warren. Then he called out the back door, "Jack, come inside now and meet my friends! Jack!"

A tall, intelligent-looking man with a crooked grin and gangly arms came inside and stood beside Warren. "Yes, sir," he said. "I'm here." He wore a U.S. Army captain's uniform and his hair was gray at the temples.

"Etta, I want you to meet Captain Jack Pershing. This is Etta Irwin; she's like a breath of spring no matter what the season," said Warren.

Etta reached out to shake hands. She noticed that the man's face seemed tired except whenever he looked over at Frankie Warren. Then his face lit up like a lantern, making the hollows under his cheekbones appear deeper and darker.

"Have you been ill?" asked Etta cautiously.

"I was in the Philippines four years ago and was quite ill, but I'm feeling fine now," he said.

"How long are you going to stay in this wonderful country?" she asked.

"Can you keep a secret?" His brown eyes fairly flashed from under his eyebrows.

Etta looked around and saw that Charlie was talking with Warren's daughter. "Of course," she said, noticing that Warren, standing in the center of the room grinning, looked like the coyote who had just cleaned out the rabbit den. "What's happening around here?"

Captain Pershing said in a whisper, "I'm staying long enough to marry that enticing creature." His eyes glanced at Frances. "Then we are going to Tokyo together."

"How exciting," breathed Etta.

"Captain, where are you from?" Charlie asked. Charlie was slightly taller than Pershing, who was broad-shouldered, with regular, but not handsome, features, and he had sunken, searching eyes.

"Manila. Rather the long way around, first to England, where I found those people knew nothing of their own soldiers fighting against the Boers in South Africa. I saw the Suez Canal, the Indian Ocean, and the Straits of Malacca. I arrived in Manila aboard the hospital ship *Missouri*. Ironic, I was born in a little place, Laclede, Missouri."

"Oh!" Charlie nearly exploded. "I remember you! My pa knew yours. Well—I'll be—" Charlie had his arm around the captain's shoulder and they were exchanging tales about Missouri, farming, and blacksmithing. Both were talking at once. Both were totally oblivious to anyone else in the room.

Charlie sat down and paused for a breath.

Jack Pershing sat on the big leather footstool beside Frankie and studied Charlie and Etta for a few moments. Finally he said, "I see why the senator said you two were wonderful people. I can size up a man in about ten minutes and know what he's like under stress in about thirty minutes. Both of you pass muster."

"I'm certainly glad for that," said Etta with a laugh.

"Why don't you come to our place in town for Christmas supper? All of you," she added. "We aren't half talked out yet and you can meet Charlie's pa. He'd never forgive us if there was someone from Missouri here and he didn't get to meet him."

"Oh, we'll come," said Frankie. "I wouldn't want to miss it, because who knows when Jack and I will be in Wyoming again. I'm eager to meet those children, and if there are horses around, I'll race with them."

"I want to see that," said Jack Pershing.

"I hope the winter stays as open as this," said Charlie, looking across the Warren ranch at the yellow grass exposed on the little hilltops and all along the south sides of the hills and gullies.

Etta brought their coats from the bedroom."We'll see you by four o'clock on the twenty-fifth. Merry Christmas!" she called.

Frankie waved until Etta and Charlie could see her no longer.

"I'm glad we rode out in the buggy," said Charlie. "That wind is cold coming down from the northwest." He tucked the blanket tighter about Etta and himself as he sent the horse down the road toward Cheyenne. Those two ruts were like cement when it was dry, but like sponge in the rainy season.

The spruce tree touched the living room ceiling and smelled of fresh resin. It was left bare until Christmas Eve, when Joe, Will, Margaret, little Charles, and Gladys came in from the Y6 to help the family celebrate Christmas. Frank came in later from the Iron Mountain ranch, and then everyone added bits of tinsel and delicate colored ornaments to the tree as Etta handed them out. The children danced around with paper chains they'd made at school.

"Hang those right there!" Charlie called out in his booming voice, making the children squeal with delight.

At the tips of the branches were fastened little brass holders for the tiny, slim white candles. Charlie lit a dozen of the candles and gathered the children around him on the floor while Etta and Margaret went to the kitchen to make hot chocolate. Joe, Will, and Frank sat beside the circle of children, each with his own thoughts.

Charlie read from the pages of a worn book. The same book Joe had read from each Christmas when Charlie was a boy. "'Twas the night before Christmas and all through the house," he began.

The children watched his face with fascination because he

made motions with his eyes and nose. Once in a while he raised a hand near his face for emphasis, so the story was near real to them. When it was over they lingered, reluctant to break the spell. Etta waved her hands, fluttering them around the children. They knew she was motioning them toward the bedrooms. Each child felt certain he would never fall asleep, but stay fully conscious to see when Santa Claus made his visit. Floyd had talked to the cowboys about Santa Claus and so was aware that his father left toys under the Christmas tree. But he liked the myth so well himself that he did not tell any of the other children that Santa Claus was only pretend.

Etta was first out of bed in the morning. She rekindled the fire in the living room stove and put more wood in the kitchen range. She mixed pancake batter.

Little Frances was up. She rubbed her eyes and pushed her cotton-white hair out of her face. "Ma, did Santa Claus come?"

"Come on! Let's look!" called Floyd, followed by the other children in their nightclothes.

"First, get dressed and have breakfast," said Etta. "By then everyone will be up and join in the fun."

"Oh, you always say that," said Floyd, sighing. He and little Charles went out to the bunkhouse behind the kitchen, where they had slept along with their Uncle Frank and Grandpa Joe.

"Have Joella comb your hair after you are dressed and your teeth are brushed," Etta said to Frances.

"You always say that!" called Joella, so everyone laughed.

Margaret and Will and Charlie were up sitting at the kitchen table waiting for the others coming one by one.

"I hope I get a ten-gallon hat and a rope," said little Charles, who was five years old.

"I think you got something for a boy, like mittens, or pajamas. I saw your toe poking out of those you wore last night. Wouldn't you like a set of wooden blocks?" asked Frank, lighting up a cigarette after his first sip of black coffee.

"Uncle Frank! I don't need that stuff. I'm a cowboy!" said Charles in a huff.

"That's just the way Floyd used to talk," said Etta, laughing as she put a stack of pancakes on the boys' plates. "Land sakes, is that all boys ever think of, horses, cattle, ropes, saddles, and ten-gallon hats?"

Pauline came in with a clean dress, buttoned wrong in front, but her straight brown hair was combed, her long black stockings were pulled up but not fastened to her garter belt, and her black high-top shoes were not buttoned. Margaret fastened the stockings and buttoned the dress and shoes.

Gladys came in holding the big white tabby cat.

"Does Kitty know it's Chrisum?" asked Frances.

"You give her a treat so she'll know. Put this sausage in her bowl and after it's gone we'll give her some cream," said Etta.

No one was allowed to go to the living room to see the tree complete with all the gifts around the bottom and all the candles lit until all had finished their breakfast.

"This is the best sausage we've had from the ranch," said Charlie, taking several from the serving platter. "Have some more," he said, passing the platter to Floyd. "Eat now, you don't know for sure when the next meal is coming."

"Pa, I'm finished. I'm ready to go to the living room," said Floyd.

After an agonizing wait for the children they were permitted to troop into the living room and sit in a semicircle on the floor around the tree. Even the adults sat on the floor, where they could see the expressions on the children's faces when each gift was opened.

Both Floyd and little Charles received wide-brimmed hats and a rope. Little Charles's rope was not much more than a short twelve-foot clothesline, but it was a cowboy rope as far as he was concerned. Floyd's rope was a good twenty feet of tight twisted hemp that could be used for trick roping or putting over a fence post or slow calf. The rope was three-eighths of an inch in diameter and braided into what was called sash cord so the loop was more pliable and the rope less likely to curl.

Charlie guessed that Floyd would be out roping anything in sight, and little Charles would stick as tight as a tick to a dog to his cousin while trying the same tricks with his shorter rope.

Charlie had his own philosophy for buying gifts for his family. If one thing was good, two were better, and three or more were best. He had new Stetsons for his two brothers and his father and the best rope money could buy for each one. Each of the little girls had a new doll. The dolls were all alike, with china heads, eyes that opened and closed, and cloth bodies, and dressed in long white lawn baby dresses, pink knit booties, and bonnets. Each child received a ten-dollar gold piece.

Charlie gave Etta and Margaret a bottle of Shalimar perfume.

Etta had sent to Denver for a white silk shirt for Charlie with his initials across the pocket under the Y6 symbol, all embroidered deep red.

After the gifts were opened and the children sent outside to exercise the horses, Joe and Frank got together to talk about picking up some wild horses and breaking them to work on the ranch. Frank described how John Coble added new horses to his stock each spring that way, and most were strong and excellent workhorses when broken.

Will and Margaret cleaned up wrapping paper and added more wood to the stove. Etta went to the kitchen to prepare ham and other fixings for the Christmas supper. Charlie followed her with his hands behind his back.

"I have—something—a surprise for you, dear." Charlie was almost as tongue-tied as he was when he'd first met Etta. His eyes sparkled and a grin cut across the bottom of his face.

"Oh, Charlie, let me see," Etta sang and skipped two, three steps toward him, wiping her hands on her apron. "With you every day is Christmas. I love you more each year." Her eyes danced. She slipped off the red ribbon from a tiny square white box. Inside were a pair of diamond earrings. "Oh!" she cried with delight. "How beautiful!" Then she sobered. "Charlie, these are expensive. The money should go into the ranch, not something frivolous like diamonds. Grandpa Joe and Frank are talking about breaking more wild horses. I wonder if you ought to start breeding good workhorses, or even racers, whatever you want. Maybe John Coble's done some breeding. You could find out."

"My dear, put on the earrings. You won't need lights in a room when you wear those shiners. Let me worry about the ranch and horses. I wouldn't buy these if I couldn't have paid cash. My, you look beautiful. There's plenty of women that can't look so nice, you know."

She held her face up for his kiss. Then said, "There's plenty that won't be eating as well as we this Christmas." She twitched her nose and smelled something burning. "Oh, Charlie, the ham glaze is burning!" she cried.

"See, you stick to the cooking and I'll stick to the ranching." Charlie let her go and laughed.

After pouring the honey-colored glaze over the ham Etta pushed the roasting pan into the oven. "What do you think of Captain Pershing?"

"I like him. I'm glad he's coming with Warren and his daughter for supper tonight. He's a person who keeps his personal feelings to himself. I guess that makes him a good soldier. He's what you'd call self-reliant. He doesn't trust others, only himself. But I did see when he looked at Frankie he lost all his toughness.

He and the senator seem to get along well. You know, I believe it is he and Frankie who have eyes for each other."

Etta was smiling and could hardly keep from interrupting when Charlie was talking. "I think you should not talk about it, but keep your ears open, you might hear something, and I won't have to tell you that Captain Pershing told me right off his feelings."

"Dear—you know! The senator told me it was a secret, not yet announced. Pershing and Frankie are to be married. Don't say a word now." Charlie was chuckling.

Etta put her arms around Charlie's waist and gave him a big hug before shooing him from the kitchen.

Charlie had been right. His pa thoroughly enjoyed talking with Captain Pershing all evening. Joe told stories about his younger days as a farrier in Missouri. He told stories Frank, Will, Charlie, and Jack Pershing had never heard involving Jack's father, Fletcher.

Joe went into the bunkhouse and came back with his fiddle. He played a couple tunes for the children to dance to, then settled down so that the adults could sing Christmas songs with his accompaniment. Frankie and Jack Pershing sang "Yonder Comes My True Love," then both blushed something fierce, so that everyone laughed. The children were sent off to bed, but the singing continued until the last log in the living room stove burned down to a few bright coals.

Etta brought out a quilt for Warren, Frankie, and Pershing to put over their laps on the way home.

"It's turned windy and that can cut right through. Don't worry about returning it soon. When you happen to be in town you can drop it by," Etta told Warren.

Jack Pershing put his arm across Etta's shoulders and said, "I'm certain to be back from Tokyo soon. I'll see you again then."

No one had any idea it would be a decade before he spoke to Charlie again.

TWENTY-FIVE

Y6

Fourth of July

The Y6 ranch was divided into an upper and lower section. The upper section was a wide prairie meadow, which was ideal for growing wheat and hay. During winter the wind swept over the gently undulating land, leaving it barren. The snow drifted into gullies, gorges, and hollows and piled ten to twelve feet high at the base of the rocky hills. These hills were a long chainlike formation to the south, which from a distance looked like the backbone of some ancient amphibian.

The lower ranch was a long valley of great beauty, sloping down from both the south and north to meet Horse Creek at the fertile bottom. Horse Creek sparkled and rippled alongside the two-story ranch house and nourished the fast-growing poplar trees that lined its banks. In summer the poplar leaves seemed to Charlie to mimic the sparkling creek. They quivered in the breeze, glinting with highlights of sun on their dark tops and light undersides.

One huge cottonwood shaded the front yard. It was unfazed by the blazing sun, searing winds, or subzero winter air. In midsummer the crisp, yellowed grass of the yard was covered with soft cotton tassels that whitened the ground with a snow-white rug. The air was filled with thousands of white fuzzies that looked like dry snowflakes to Charlie. To Will the cottonwood tassels were a great annoyance. The dry snow or cottony fluff together with the dry dusty earth caused his eyes to redden, his throat to itch, and his nose to run.

East of the ranch house the creek ran beside the long, flat meadow, which was lush with rich, wild grass in summer and used as a holding pasture in winter because hay could easily be brought to the stock. Joe and Will built corrals and stock pens on parts of the meadow.

Looking east from the front porch of the ranch house one could see the long backbone of the divide in the distance. At the western end was a high domed formation, so ancient that its sides were no longer steep cutbanks as most of the other rocky hills in the chain. The huge dome was called Round Top.

On the north side of the ranch house, in the meadow, was a corral for breaking the wild horses. Frank claimed this was his favorite place on the whole ranch.

The house and attendant buildings were in the center of the lower valley. Eventually the whole Y6 area would cover twenty-three thousand acres.

Will knew cattle and farming better than most men, but he was not a leader. He gave sketchy instructions and blew up when his hired hands failed to correctly interpret the orders. Charlie was the leader. He found money to buy new stock. He decided when, where, and to whom to sell. He went out of his way to become acquainted with Louis Swift, the Chicago meat packer, and J. O. Armour, the Omaha meat packer. He became friendly with Updikes of the Updike Coal Company and had a standing order for coal for the Y6's blacksmith shop. He was friends with George Brandeis, owner of the big department store in Omaha where he bought all his Stetson hats, boots, and sheep-lined jackets.

For Christmas, Charlie not only bought dolls for the girls, but surprised everyone when he ordered an upright Clayton piano from Detroit for the house in town. Etta taught the three girls to play.

John Coble was married. His bride wore a long, lavender lace dress. Etta and Charlie held the reception at their house in town. Etta played the piano and everyone gathered around and sang the latest songs, then they rode wagons to the ranch for some dancing with gramophone music in the large upstairs ballroom.

On the first of March the Wyoming newspapers carried an article about an act of Congress that opened up fifteen million acres of land in the Shoshone Indian Wind River Reservation for settlement and entry under the Homestead Act.

That reminded Charlie that it was time for the Irwin family to homestead more land in the Horse Creek area. "People will come into Wyoming by the droves when they get the word about the Wind River land, and you can bet your lace underwear some will drift this way. Why, we can't have people coming in and breaking up our upper and lower ranch." One weekend he saw Frank in Cheyenne and tried to get him to come to work on the Y6 and build a house on a new section. "Come on, homestead it for a year so we can add it to the Y6 spread," urged Charlie.

"Too bad Frank isn't married," Will joked. "He could have his old lady file for another section, then we'd have some six or eight sections completely boxed in. Good grazing land in the center."

The second week in March was bitterly cold and snowy. A spring snowstorm might be short, but it is harsh for cattle that are thin and for rangy horses that are weakened by scant food. Will and Joe and Charlie found more than a dozen cattle apiece that had failed to live through the late blizzard. The men stripped off the hide and brought it back to the ranch to cure. The hide would bring two to five dollars.

The carcass was sometimes brought in to feed to the ranch dogs, but usually left out in the open, where wolves, coyotes, and vultures could quickly clean it up. Sometimes Charlie put a large piece of the meat close to a well-hidden trap. This would also offset the loss of the cow or steer with a winter pelt and bounty money. Wolves and coyotes were deadly pests. They were killers to cattlemen and sheepherders in the West during this time. During a spring blizzard or hard winter wolves and coyotes invariably prowled around the weakened stock, going out after the weaker ones that lagged behind the main herd. Many times Charlie shot into the middle of a wolf pack with his Henry rifle to scatter the animals so they could not gang up on a skinny steer or hollow-eyed horse. It was the law of the West that if a spring blizzard did not take the weaker animals, the stronger carnivores would.

After the weather cleared, Frank visited the Y6 to see how the stock had fared. He was full of disaster stories from the Iron Mountain ranch and others close by. He saw the rows of hides Charlie had spread on the corral fence in back of the barn and said, "Hope you spread them hides out, not overlapping each other. They need the air to help them dry properly." He waved his hands to show what he meant.

"You think my head is so hollow I have to talk with my hands to keep away the echo?" chuckled Charlie. "I know how to dry out hides proper. You know I got past the flyleaf of my first-grade primer."

Frank smiled and scratched his ear. He looked at Joe and his face turned red as chokecherries in July. "I'm going to ask for next week off. We don't have so much to do yet—it's not quite time for roundup."

"What are you going to take time off for, son? That's a crazy thing to do," said Joe. "I thought you wanted to save as much money as possible to buy horses. You're not mixed up with the wrong crowd, are you? Going somewhere to look for a pile of fast money? 'Cause if you are, none of us will visit you in the hoosegow."

"My God, Pa! Don't you trust me?"

"Tell me you're going to enter some Wild West show or rodeo," said Charlie, putting his arm around Frank's slight shoulders.

"Say, can't a man have some time off without being charged with robbing a bank or entering a rodeo, jeeze. I need some time to myself. I'm going to Colorado Springs."

Now Joe looked brighter. His face was browned, but it took on a rosy glow. "You going to see Ell and Les? Oh, boy, I'd like to go with you."

"Me, too," said Will. "How about it? Why don't we all go and spend two or three days? Make it a kind of family reunion. It'd give Ell a surprise!"

"Hey!" said Frank loudly. "I want to go by myself! Crap! I wish I hadn't said anything. Now I suppose I have to tell you. I'm getting married."

Charlie's mouth fell open. Joe and Will didn't move. They stood like statues staring at Frank.

"It's the Patterson girl, Clara Belle. She lives with her ma in Cheyenne. Remember her pa died a couple winters ago up on the Chugwater, caught in a snowstorm bringing his cattle out on a roundup."

"I remember," said Will. "He and his horse broke through ice a mile below where the Chugwater comes out of the Laramie River. You got your eye on that girl or the ranch?" he teased.

"Must be the girl. Her ma sold the ranch. She prefers living in town," said Frank, recovering from his embarrassment. "Clara Belle wants to be married next to Pikes Peak."

Will nudged Charlie and laughed. "Wonder what that means?

Frank's girl wants to spend her honeymoon in the shadow of Pikes Peak. I could say something funny about that! Something earthy! Frank, you taking the train or going by horseback to Colorado? Just keep in mind that a cowboy who makes love on horseback doesn't get much of a ride."

"Shut your face," said Frank. "It's just that she's never seen Pikes Peak."

"Like I said—something else could be implied by your words!" hooted Will.

Charlie entered in the fun of teasing his younger brother. "Cowboys who make love on a hillside are not on the level!"

"Listen, keep your mouths buttoned. Don't say things like that in front of Clara Belle. She's—she's young and sensitive," said Frank, his face taking on the red color of half-ripe chokecherries again.

"Son," said Joe, striving to change the subject, "if Les Miner has any good-looking horses he wants to trade or sell, make him a deal. We could have the horses shipped to Cheyenne by boxcar, especially since Charlie's livestock agent."

"I'll think about that," said Frank.

"Hey, this Clara Belle, would she—will you buy that section near Bear Creek that borders on the one Will got in Margaret's name?" asked Charlie. "It's a dandy place to winter horses. Good grass, plenty of washes and gullies for shelter."

"I'll think about that, too, if you lend me the money," said Frank. Then in a whiny, questioning voice he asked, "Charlie, will you visit Mrs. Patterson when you go to Cheyenne?"

"She's not going to be my mother-in-law. Put starch in your backbone, little brother, and go yourself."

"Charlie, that woman makes me feel helpless as a frozen snake. But she knows all about you. She has a high opinion of you. She knows you were friendly with Teddy Roosevelt and worked for Senator Warren. She's impressed by that stuff."

Charlie smiled.

Frank said, "I've thought she tolerates me because I'm C. B. Irwin's brother. Talk to her, Charlie. Impress her with the Irwin family. Take Etta with you. Etta knows how to talk to other women real good."

The others were looking at Frank not knowing if they should laugh out loud or take it as seriously as Frank was making the visit sound. Frank looked from one to the other. He said, "Don't you want me to get married? Why the long faces? All of you guys got married. Why not me?"

"It's the fact that none of us suspected. You've been courting—going to town and seeing one special girl—and we never suspected," said Charlie.

"Hell, we'll get used to the idea," said Will.

"You and your bride can't live in the bunkhouse at Coble's ranch. Bring her here. Etta and Margaret will fix her up with a room, and you can ride over to the Y6 on your day off," suggested Joe.

"We'd better tell Etta and Margaret," said Charlie. "They'd never forgive us if we kept this secret."

Frank and Clara Belle were married on March 13, 1905, in Colorado Springs. The wedding did not go as smoothly as they had planned. When the couple went to the Colorado Springs county clerk's office for their marriage license, the request was turned down because the pretty blond, blue-eyed Clara Belle was underage, only seventeen years old, and her home address was in Wyoming. They were stunned. Frank thought about writing a letter to Clara Belle's mother. But to get written permission from her would take several days by mail. Then he had a better idea. Ell had a telephone. Frank called the Union Pacific depot in Cheyenne and asked for C. B. Irwin. Charlie was in Warren Richardson's office.

"Charlie, you gotta make that visit to Mrs. Patterson today!" shouted Frank. "Tell her to write a letter giving her permission for Clara Belle to marry me, sign it, and be sure she has her signature notarized! Send that letter to me, in care of Ell, PDQ!"

Charlie went to see Mrs. Patterson, who was a good-sized woman with ice-blue eyes, a face like rising bread dough, and light brown hair with even waves made by a curling iron. Mrs. Patterson puckered her mouth to the size of a wrinkled raisin when Charlie introduced himself. "Hmm, you are taller, more ruddy, than your brother. I prefer big men, myself."

Charlie explained that he needed her written permission for her daughter to marry his brother. He reassured her that Clara Belle was fine at his sister's place in Colorado Springs. "No, ma'am, my sister does not have a little, bitty house. She has plenty of room to put them up in—uh—separate bedrooms until they are properly married. The wedding cannot take place until you send a letter giving your consent."

Mrs. Patterson questioned Charlie thoroughly to make certain he was not single. "I told Clara Belle to find an older man, one that was settled and was making some money. I did not mention cowboys who are skinny and bowlegged."

"Mrs. Patterson, my brother is very fond of your daughter. He would be terribly disappointed if he had to send Clara Belle back on the next train because you would not write a simple letter." He hesitated a moment while Mrs. Patterson squeezed her raisin mouth with thumb and forefinger. "What if your daughter refused to come home, but preferred to live in some cheap hotel with my brother? Of course my brother wouldn't think of such a thing, but—"

"Yes, well, you must know Clara Belle has a stubborn streak." She put on fragile silver-rimmed glasses, went to a roll-top desk, and wrote for several minutes. She folded the letter.

"Don't seal the envelope, Mrs. Patterson, but come to the bank with me and we'll have Charles Hirsig notarize your signature so there can be no argument that you wrote those words."

"I signed my name. That is me, the mother of Clara Belle," said Mrs. Patterson stubbornly.

"I know that, but people in Colorado Springs don't know that. The minister who will marry my brother and your daughter doesn't know you."

"A minister?"

"Well, if they have a church wedding, there will be a minister."

"A church wedding! Frank told me the Irwins did everything in a big way. Oh, my, he meant it. You suppose the *Tribune* would run a story about the wedding?"

"I wouldn't be surprised," said Charlie, crossing his fingers behind his back. "Let's go to the bank."

Mrs. Patterson used three hankies at the bank, showing Mr. Hirsig how much she was going to miss her daughter.

Charlie shook Hirsig's hand and hurried out of the bank before Mrs. Patterson could tell anyone else about the big church wedding her daughter was having and the fabulously expensive honeymoon in a resort hotel near Pike's Peak. The woman made Charlie embarrassed, she was so effusive. Outside the bank Mrs. Patterson allowed as how she'd forgotten her notarized letter inside.

"You wait right here. I'll get it in a jiffy," said Charlie.

Hirsig had it ready. "I knew you'd be back," he said. Then he laughed heartily. "Your brother getting married in Colorado Springs? It's colder than a mother-in-law's kiss out there in March!"

"You don't say!" answered Charlie, putting the letter in his inside coat pocket.

He walked Mrs. Patterson home. Told her he could not stay for a nice cup of hot tea. He had to get back to his office right away. Then he promised her he'd talk to his friends at the *Tribune* and make certain they'd print a story about Clara Belle's and Frank's wedding.

Charlie bit his tongue, hated himself, and put the letter on the U.P.'s mail car in the afternoon, and by the next morning Frank had it in his hands. He and Clara Belle were married by the justice of the peace. Ell and Les Miner stood with them. The newlyweds stayed in one of the furnished rooms upstairs at Ell's place for three days, coming out only for an occasional meal and call of nature. Miner went back to his accounting job and rented one-room apartment. About six months before, he'd moved out of the big house. He told Ell it changed their relationship not one iota. He came to see her every day to give advice and support. He continued to keep her account books in order. She made two, three times as much money as he.

"The sky's the limit at my place," said Ell, the second evening at the supper table.

"Good, we won't go any higher than the sky," said Frank, hugging Clara, who was in a long baby-blue silk see-through nightie.

"Honey, you'd better put on a robe. My men patients are staring at you," whispered Ell to Clara Belle. Ell's green eyes twinkled with amusement along with disapproval.

"Mrs. Miner, I'm not the least bit cold," said Clara Belle naively, sitting so close to Frank they looked like Siamese twins attached at the hip.

Ell handed Clara Belle one of her own satin housecoats. "Wear this whenever you come downstairs. Now, give my men a chance to cool off."

Ell heard the low sighs and twitters as Clara Belle slipped into the robe, which smelled like sandalwood.

Ell winked and fluttered like a butterfly among her patients, coaxing them to eat what was on their plates, then selecting some for the massage and others for sunbathing, and the rest for leisurely sitz baths.

It was obvious that the men all adored Ell. They looked at her with the same kind of calf eyes that Frank used to look at Clara Belle. Whatever the patient's problems, Ell took care of them, soothed them, and nursed them back to health. At the end of their treatment, which was nothing more than a balanced diet, herb teas, fresh air, exercise, plenty of sleep, and no outside worries, many men were reluctant to leave. Ell became their queen mother. She kept them not only in good health, but in a kind of euphoric continuous sexual excitement, with her sensual incense and perfumes, by bodily enjoyment of warm bathing, massages with fragrant oils and pleasant surroundings, kind words, and soft pleasureful touching. As quickly as possible Ell shooed Clara Belle back upstairs. She realized her patients watched the young baby-faced wife of her brother instead of herself. Ell repeated a nonsense nursery rhyme to Clara Belle, "If a body met a body in a bag of beans, can a body tell a body what a body means?"

Clara Belle bent double with laughter. Ell closed the door behind Clara Belle and Frank and blew them a silent kiss through the door.

"Now that's settled and out of the way, what are you going to do next?" asked a handsome, dark, wavy-haired patient who had been chosen for a massage. His liquid, brown eyes were rimmed with long dark lashes.

Ell smiled and ran her hands down her hips, feeling the soft smooth material of her pongee dress. "What can you handle," she said huskily.

"Women, like glass, with care," was his throaty answer.

After Charlie had taken Frank's telephone call in Richardson's office, he realized how much more businesslike he could have been with Mrs. Patterson if he'd had his own office. He could have called her on the telephone, he thought—if she had a telephone.

Later on, the same afternoon he'd mailed the letter, he took Floyd to Frank Meanea's Saddle Shop to look around some, hear what was going on in town, and mainly to check out his own thoughts.

Floyd saw a couple of saddles he liked. "That's good taste," Meanea said to Floyd. "I'm making a couple of dozen like that for the Canadian Northwest Mounted Police. If you want to see, come into the back workshop. You, too, C.B. I want to show you the tooling on the saddle I'm making for George Eastman, you know, the Kodak man. I need some advice. You men think he'd like the back of the saddle with a little more roll to it?"

Floyd answered before Charlie had finished studying the saddle. "Yes, sir. He would. See like this, so his foot can slide off easier when he dismounts in a hurry."

Charlie grinned and said, "Meanea, you can call it your Cheyenne roll cantle."

"Yes, sir, Cheyenne cantle," said Floyd, mimicking his father.

Meanea looked at Floyd. "You understand saddles, young one. You going to ride a bronc at Frontier this year?"

"Not this year. But I'll be there on a saddled horse with my rope tricks. Want to see a good trick?"

Meanea moved close to Floyd in a hurry. "No! Not inside here. Someday, outside, son."

Charlie shook his head at Floyd and scowled, then he looked at Meanea. "Frank, I'm Livestock Agent for the U.P. and I don't have an office. I go in and look through papers and mail, but I have to use Richardson's office. It's not very dignified for me. In fact, it's embarrassing and I like Richardson, but I can't seem to complain to him."

"Charlie, go over there and look around. Find an office that has some space, a place for a desk and a swivel chair. Then tell Richardson you are moving to that empty desk unless there is some objection." Meanea put his hand on Charlie's arm. "It's the first time you've admitted you had a hard time doing anything. It's nice to know you're like the rest of us poor souls."

Charlie shook Meanea's hand warmly. He'd found the advice he'd needed. He knew he should have thought of it himself, but sometimes a man couldn't see the forest for the trees. He and Floyd walked to the depot and into Richardson's office. Charlie told Floyd to look, but not say anything. Floyd understood his father was working out a deal. "Say, there's this old oak desk in the freight office that nobody seems to be using. I could take all my papers there, and it would be a dandy place for me to work two, three days a week."

Richardson's mouth flew open. "C.B., I was waiting for the right time to mention the same thing to you. I didn't want you to think I was throwing you out of my office."

Charlie had a big smile as he and Floyd walked home. A brisk wind was at their backs. Charlie felt he'd accomplished a few things that day. He talked Mrs. Patterson into writing a letter, and he got a new office with his own desk and swivel chair. He was happy.

Next morning he was up before Etta. The kitchen was warm when she came in her slippers and nightdress, her hair combed neatly. "Charlie, you tossed and turned last night. I thought you were worried about something on the ranch. But look at you this morning. You're all dressed up in your good suit and a smile on your face. What's going on?"

"Dear, I wanted to leave before you could ask, because I wanted to get it all fixed up and official before I showed you."

"Oh, tell me. Is it a surprise?" she pleaded.

"Might be. But it's not simple."

"Is it more complicated than that new theory—relativity—thought up by that professor, what's his name, Albert Einstein?" Etta pretended to pout a moment, then said, "If it's something you are going to buy for a surprise—I'd like more than anything a bunch of live violets and that gramophone recording by Enrico Caruso."

"Woman! It's only March. Snow could start again anytime. How can I get violets? I could get the moon as easily. The gramophone record, maybe I can find that. I'll stop by Arp's Hardware and see."

"Charlie!" squealed Etta. "Actually, I want to know what it is that you really have on your mind. What did you and Floyd do in town?"

"I went to the depot."

"Did someone special come in?"

"Nope. I checked my business mail. I'm Livestock Agent."

"All right, go on. But hurry back because I want to know what this surprise is about." She pushed him out the front door. She remembered his felt hat and ran after him with it in her hand.

Charlie chuckled all the way to the U.P. depot and his new office because little Etta had run outside after him in only her flannel night dress and was so intent on giving him the hat and so worked up about his surprise that she never noticed.

Etta knew that Charlie always enjoyed surprises. He was impulsive, although his hunches were good. She, on the other hand, tended to ponder for some time and plan what she wanted to do for days ahead of time and always to talk it over with Charlie, or at least with another member of the family, with Margaret, or Joe or Will or with Frank. Etta did not think it was appropriate to ask advice from someone not in the family.

When the three older children were on their way to school, she dressed and sat at the kitchen table and held three-year-old Frances on her lap and read the little girl three stories from a cloth book. She dressed the baby and sat her on the kitchen floor with a stack of baking pans and some big spoons. Etta began her morning sweeping and dusting and bed making.

Just before noon Charlie was back. He was exuberant. "My dear, you'll like it!"

"What do you have!" she called from the kitchen. "Charlie, please tell me! Is it a gold mine? A prize horse? A disease?"

"None of those. I got a new desk and a swivel chair from the U.P. for my new office. Now I can work there two, three days a week. I'll get people to ship their stock for Wild West shows and rodeos on the U.P. I'll bring in all sorts of business by having my own office. It's just perfect. Richardson asked how I'd like to have his swivel chair to go with the desk. Said he was more comfortable in a straight chair. He took that swivel chair and put it in front of my new desk. Nice man!"

Etta looked at him and her mouth went slack. "I thought it was something exciting. Something monumental."

"This is! Don't you see? Oh, dear—I forgot—" Charlie had his coat and hat on and slammed the door behind him. Before an hour had gone he was back with the Caruso gramophone recording under his arm.

When Frank and Clara Belle came back from Colorado Springs, it was time for the roundups. Clara Belle lived in the main ranch house at the Y6 for a few weeks. Now everyone hoped more than ever that Frank would come full-time to work on the Y6.

"I have to work the spring roundup for John Coble, then I'll see what looks best," he said.

"Come home to the Y6," said Joe. "Then all my boys will be together. One family—like God intended us to live."

The last day in March, early in the morning Charlie, Will, and ten-year-old Floyd and a dozen other ranchers and cowboys headed southeast toward the backbone of rock and windblown pines that made up the chain of rugged hills. The men divided into groups of three or four. Will, Charlie, and Floyd circled Round Top.

They found cattle bunched up in the shallow gullies where feed had been left. Eventually the animals were to be herded to the big Y6 Guerney pasture. There a maternity ward was available in a crude log shed beside one of the corrals. The cows that appeared near delivery were brought there first for shelter. Their birthing was usually easy with little complications.

Floyd rode off to the next shallow indentation in the earth at the foot of Round Top and found a lone steer lying at the edge of a stream of fast-flowing snow melt. The steer had gnawed on a few tender, yellow willow stems, but it was thin and weak. Floyd climbed down from his horse. He took a high grip on the steer's tail and tried pulling it up. Once up, it stood, but it looked like the slightest breeze would blow it down in a second. Floyd opened his pocketknife and cut handfuls of dried grass and willow branches. He left them in front of the steer.

At noontime beside the chuck wagon Floyd told his father how he'd lifted up the heavy, staggering steer. Charlie was pleased. "There's a slim chance it'll be down when you go back to it. If it's down, the odds are it's too far gone to save. If it hasn't eaten, it won't make it back to the Guerney pasture with the others. So, we'll come back later and get his hide."

Floyd looked disappointed. Charlie had told his son the worst that could happen so he would be prepared and not get his hopes up too high, but when he saw the long face on Floyd, he added, "If that baby eats and rests tonight, you can bring it into the main herd tomorrow morning. I bet it'll make it."

Floyd was up at the first hint of dawn. He brought the thin steer into camp and put it with the L5 cattle pointing to the L5 brand on its side. Colin Hunter, who now owned Johnny Gordon's L5 outfit, saw Floyd and said, "Thanks a bunch, kid. That's sure a down-and-outer, but he'll fatten up before the summer's over. I owe you."

Floyd smiled back and felt good. He knew that Hunter meant he'd done him a favor by saving the thin steer. The word *thanks* was reward enough for Floyd.

The weather stayed clear so that the cowboys slept wrapped in blankets on the ground. Charlie told Floyd to sleep under the chuck wagon, but the boy edged over with the men, not wanting to be left out or pampered in any way.

At mealtime on the range no milk, cream, or butter was used. Charlie always thought of one of Johnnie Gordon's favorite sayings: "In the American West there are more cows and less butter, more rivers and less water, and you can look farther and see less, than in any other country in the world."

Ranchers and cowboys could read "sign" about as well as Indians and trappers a generation before them. They watched the direction of the wind and movement of clouds to predict the weather. A flight of a black crow followed by another crow coming from the same point told them that there was a dead carcass below. If there were no more crows, it was assumed the carcass was small as a rabbit or weasel. If there were more crows than one following the first, it meant the carcass was as large as a dead cow or deer.

As the spring progressed several more roundups were organized and slowly the cowboys sent the cattle and horses drifting back to their home ranges. With every roundup Charlie's herd was increased with the cattle and horses that were picked up with no brands and no obvious mothers that claimed them. The Y6 was the ranch where the roundup originated, and so, in Charlie's logic, where the unclaimed livestock remained.

Etta would not permit Floyd to go on another roundup until the Easter holiday from school.

During the Easter roundup Floyd asked his father about his first horseback ride. Charlie told Floyd he was six weeks old and wrapped in a Navaho blanket, tied to the back of a saddle. "I took you with me to bring in some stray cattle because you cried all morning with colic and nearly drove your mother berserk. I took you out so she could get some rest. With me you didn't peep, but went to sleep. Your ma never quite forgave me." He chuckled and rode away to talk to Will about cutting out the Y6 cattle from the large herd that had just come into the Guerney pasture. The cattle cut out were put in smaller herds under the care of the cowboys of their owner. This was continued until the whole herd was cut or divided and cattle under the same brand separated from other brands. Horses were specially trained for this work.

Will rode into the herd and one by one found those with the Y6 brand. He rode behind each Y6 animal and, with careful manipulation of the movement of his horse, forced the animal through the bunched, milling, bawling animals to the edge, then with dexterous movements he inched closer to the animal, then it began to run away from the herd. Charlie rode up and drove the animal to the Y6 group in a corral. Other cowboys moved in and out of the herd until the cattle were separated. At times a cowboy used a long whip with a short handle to help with the cutting out. The whip also helped to drive the stragglers back into the herd when they were on the trail. As on previous roundups, the various outfits eventually drove their herds into the corrals or branding pens. Branding began the next day.

The men were up at dawn with their bedrolls picked up and breakfast under their belts. The herds in the corrals were fairly small so the animals would not crowd one another. The calves were lassoed one at a time. The roper dragged it to the fire. Cowboys worked in pairs. One man flanked or tailed the calf, then threw it down on one side. The other man put his knee on the calf's neck. His left hand pulled the top front leg back and up, so that the knee of the calf was bent. His right hand pulled the nose of the calf up and he held it tight, angled to the left with his knee still on the neck. Thus the head was held fairly secure. The flanker sat down and with one hand pulled the top hind leg back and put his foot against the calf's bottom hind leg, just above the back. With his other hand he held the tail taut. Then Charlie put the red-hot branding iron, fresh from the fire, on the calf's left hip long enough to scorch the brand in the flesh. At the same time Will vaccinated the calf against cowpox and with his sharpened knife earmarked it with the Irwin mark, a half crop on both the right and left ear. Then, if it was male, Will moved to the back of the calf. The flanker had the back legs held down tight as Will cut the testicles and dropped them in a tin bucket. He wiped pine tar dip over the cut to keep the flies out. Then the calf was released, to go off crying for its mother. By then another calf was roped and brought bawling to the branding fire and the whole procedure repeated. When the full-grown cattle were branded, the men on horseback generally roped all four feet of the animal to hold it tight.

Floyd watched for a while. He coiled his rope, smoothing out each loop, laying the loops one atop the other until the noose was on the top coil so it could not tangle whenever he made his throw. He saw a stray calf outside the corral and thought if he took good aim he could pick up the hind legs and get the animal inside the corral. He looked around and saw that everyone was busy. Even the chuck wagon was closed. The huge dishpan was hung upside down on the wagon top. Dishtowels hung out to dry on a rope pegged into the ground. The cook was working the branding iron for some outfit. Floyd began to whistle by blowing air between his front teeth, making a hissing sound. He looked at other calves in the corral, then his eyes went back to the little Hereford with the full white face against the fence. He never thought to check the gate on the corral. He rode his horse close to the calf and began pacing it around the outside of the corral. Suddenly the calf caught sight of Floyd's horse and shot out at a fast pace. Floyd spurred his horse and swung his rope in a loop high overhead. When he was neck and neck with the calf, he drew in his breath and made his throw. The rope looped through the air and settled around the calf's neck. Floyd breathed out and moved his horse close beside the corral fence and made a fast flip offside so that the rope went around the calf's left hip. He remembered to run his horse at right angles so that the rope suddenly became tight as he slipped the noose over the saddle horn, pulling his fingers away quickly so they would not be caught and snapped off. He swung his leg over the back of his saddle, felt the horse falter slightly, then steady itself; he saw the calf had tripped and fallen to the ground, causing a puff of dust to rise. The calf remained on its side, breathless. Floyd kept the rope taut with his left hand as he jumped down to the ground. He pulled the pigging string from his pocket, caught the calf's hooves and tied the two hind ones with one of the front. He straightened up just in time to avoid being hit head-on by another calf that had run frantically from the parted corral gate. He went for the fence and hoisted himself on the top rung in order to catch his breath and to keep out of the path of more milling calves. His horse faced the down calf, backed a step or two to keep the rope tight.

A bawling calf stupidly ran into the taut rope and pawed at the earth, not having sense enough to back up and away from the rope. Another calf ran into the downed animal, stepping on its neck in a panic to move away. Floyd could see he had made trouble for the calf he'd roped and for his horse, who was holding the rope tight.

Charlie handed the hot branding iron to someone near and ran to the corral to see what all the commotion was about. Seconds later Colin Hunter was beside him. "Better get that critter up before it's trampled to death," said Hunter in his strong Highland brogue. His red hair ruffled in the wind. "We'll keep the other calves diverted and head them back into the corral."

Floyd slid off the fence.

"Untie the pigging string and slip the rope off. Then get back onto your horse!" yelled Hunter.

Floyd had seen the dark look on his father's face as he slid to the ground. He pushed his wide-brimmed hat back a little on his forehead so he could see better and untied the string, put it into his pocket, pulled the rope free and clear of the calf, and let out a sigh of relief. He nudged the calf with his boot to get it on its feet just as a calf hit him broadside with its hind thigh. The calf he'd nudged was up and running, but Floyd tasted dust. He felt the second calf's hind foot in his back as it tried to get over him.

Hunter was over the corral fence and pulling Floyd up and over as fast as he could. Charlie was hollering and moving the calves back into the corral by quickly moving alongside each one until it went inside the gate. When the last calf was inside and Hunter had closed the gate, Charlie yelled at Floyd. "You want to get yourself killed? I'll keep that rope until I think you can handle it! Now get on your horse and ride all the way back to the ranch. Go!"

"But, Pa!"

"Go!" Charlie's arm shot out, pointing to the direction of the main ranch house.

The cowboys didn't say a word. Most of them could remember when they had first tried to rope a calf or steer, and their sympathies lay on the side of young Floyd.

"Should've left him lay so he could get bruised up a little," Charlie snapped at Colin Hunter. "Then he wouldn't forget."

"Your lad will remember," said Hunter, smiling. His blue eyes twinkled like bright flax flowers in the sunlight. "He actually did a good fast job on that calf. I was watching him. In a couple years he'll have us all outclassed."

The garden was plowed and planted in early May. Etta went out to the ranch to plant the vegetable garden on a warm weekend. She took all the children with her. Floyd never wanted to come back to town for school after he'd been at the ranch. Charlie plowed and planted his potato patch. When the ranch gardens were planted and Charlie was busy putting in wheat and alfalfa, Etta planted a garden outside the kitchen door of the house in Cheyenne. This town garden not only had vegetables, but it had gooseberry bushes, a currant bush, rhubarb plants and flowers, zinnias, cosmos, marigolds, nasturtiums and pansies. When school was out Etta let the children spend the summer at the ranch. She helped cook at the ranch and only stayed in town overnight with Charlie when he came in to take care of his Union Pacific office work. Charlie enjoyed summers at the ranch, breaking the wild broncs and having weekend picnics with his family and nearby ranch families. Sometimes they had horse races and bucking-bronc contests between cowboys of local ranchers. Charlie was always the master of ceremonies, calling names and events in his booming voice.

"Floyd! Floyd Leslie Irwin!" Charlie snapped. Then muttered, "Where is that boy?" He opened the back screen to the ranch house and called, "Floyd, come here!"

This was the Fourth of July. Nearby ranchers, their families, and cowboys were expected at the Y6 ranch any moment. The women would bring food to add to that Etta already had out on the table under the cottonwood in the front yard. The men were expected to bring a favorite horse, a rope, and a shotgun. They would race and compete in a roping contest and a shooting match. The contests took place several times during the day.

The Fourth of July at the Irwin ranch had become an annual affair. It was not only a celebration of Independence Day, but also a celebration of the summer season's first harvest of the local home-grown watermelons. The cowboys held a contest to see who could eat the most watermelon in a given amount of time and another to see who could spit the flat, black seeds farthest.

Charlie looked for Floyd to bring in a big chunk of ice from the ice house for Etta's lemonade. "I can't find that boy anywhere," complained Charlie.

"I thought he was sitting on the back porch with Joella," said Will, twisting the end of his cigarette and lighting it. "Kids sure want to grow up fast these days. Your Joella wants to sample everything, including my cigarette."

"Don't let her! It's Floyd I want right now. I saw all of them, including your two, Gladys and Charles, not more than ten minutes ago." He'd seen Floyd in a clean checkered shirt, Levi's, and polished boots, cutting himself a piece of warm cake just out of the oven before Etta had time to ice it. He'd thought, if the girls did that, Etta'd skin them alive. She lets Floyd get away with murder. He remembered the girls were sent outside with the white tablecloth. They were in pastel dresses with long sleeves, long white stockings. Their hair was combed and their faces shiny clean under the brims of sunbonnets. Etta insisted her girls wear bonnets in the sunshine so their skin stayed pink and white. A bronze tan and freckles were considered hickish and seen only on the children of the poorest families and squatters. Charlie remembered Joella's long golden braids hung over her shoulders, the ends curled, they were so tight.

"I saw all of them chatting and wandering off toward the blacksmith shed," said Etta, peeling skins off boiled potatoes so that she could make salad. "I hope they stay clean until the guests arrive."

Charlie gave Etta a quick peck on the top of her head and went out the back door. His boots clicked noisily across the porch and down the steps. His face was dark above his red flannel shirt.

He heard the faint singsong voices of his children. He heard the dog bark. He sighed and his face lightened. He loved his family more than anything he could think of, especially his only son, the rope juggler. The sun rose and set in the boy, who was nearly perfect in Charlie's eyes, because Charlie would guide and mold him into perfection. He would not pamper his son, but he would teach him to be a real man, someone with courage and guts.

Nearer the shed Charlie heard sounds of crying. He scowled. "Floyd! What's happened?"

Joella was out into the sunlight first. She was holding her head with both hands. Her bonnet was pushed down on her back. She held out one of her hands. Clutched in her fist was a long golden braid, swinging in the breeze like a scalplock. She sobbed, "Pa —Pa, I didn't do anything. Not one darned thing. Floyd just whacked it off." Tears flowed down her cheeks like the floodgates were stuck on open.

Charlie was stunned. Joella looked crazily unsymmetrical. One side of her head was adorned with a long yellow pigtail and the other was covered with short, uneven strawlike stubble.

Charlie's heart sank to the ground. His mouth felt like it was full of dry cotton fuzz.

Floyd came from the shed holding the steel-handled tin snips in one hand and his rope in the other. His head was down so that Charlie could not see his frightened brown eyes. Behind Floyd stood the other two girls; their heads were down and they were crying. Frances had a thumb in her mouth. The other fist was smearing tears across her face. "I told Floyd he'd get a whupping," she sobbed.

Pauline heaved a broken sigh, wiped her face on her sleeve, and told Frances to hush or they'd all get a whipping. The cousins, eight-year-old Gladys and six-year-old Charles, blinked in the sunlight.

Charlie scowled, pushing his eyebrows together, making his face look dark and fierce. "Why, son? Why'd you cut your sister's hair?"

Floyd's bottom lip trembled. He clamped his upper teeth over his lip.

"Look at me, son!" said Charlie, swatting a huge horsefly buzzing near his face. "Talk! We can see what you've done. You've not only hurt Joella, but your mother. How many times have I said, 'Think before you act'?" Charlie could feel his breath coming in short gasps.

Floyd gritted his teeth, trying not to cry. Then he blurted out, "Oh, Pa! You can thrash me to kingdom come. I only did what Jo wanted. She pestered me until I felt like I had a shirt full of fleas. She wouldn't stop asking what it felt like. I told her there was nothing to it."

Joella began to cry out loud.

"To what?" asked Charlie.

"You know, Jo always wants to know what everything is like. Every time I have my hair cut she asks if it hurts. It's tiresome. Today, after Ma trimmed my hair, she asked again. I got cross as a bear and said I'd show her it didn't hurt. Hair has no feeling. She should know that! Girls are bubbleheads!"

Joella clutched her head and groaned.

"You're wrong. It hurt. Your sister is crying. I'm upset," Charlie growled and clenched his fists. "Your ma is going to be hurt." He took the tin snips from Floyd and put them on the bench inside the cool, dark shed. Outside he momentarily squinted in the bright light. "You kids, except Floyd, go to the house. Don't cry." He took out his handkerchief and gave it to Joella, saying, "Hair grows. Tell your mother to even it up; if she can't, Aunt Margaret will."

"I look a fright," Joella sobbed into the handkerchief. She ran to catch up with the younger girls.

Charlie stepped back into the shed and pulled a thick leather strap from a nail on the wall. He took Floyd's arm and could feel the boy was frightened. "Turn around and bend over." He pulled the strap back over his head, then pulled it through the air so that it made the fricative sound *whsst!* Then the strap landed on Floyd's backside, *thmk!*

Charlie knew that his son would not utter a sound. He was as gritty as cornmeal. "You could have let me talk to Joella. I would have answered her question so she wouldn't annoy you."

"I didn't think of that," said Floyd. "I only wanted to be rid of her and those saucy braided ropes of hair. That's the truth!"

Charlie knew that Floyd told the truth. "Stand up straight!" said Charlie. "Go wash your face in the pump and let me talk to your mother. Being strictly truthful with women is at times a luxury a man can't afford."

Floyd rubbed his stinging backside. He didn't understand his father. "What do you mean?"

"Grown women don't see yellow braids as saucy ropes. They see virtue in everything about their children. Animal mothers are the same way. It's in a mother's constitution." Charlie slapped the leather strap in the dust, causing Floyd to cough and rub his eyes until they were red.

Floyd listened but was not sure he understood how his ma would be hurt by Joella's haircut and at the same time hurt by the thrashing he'd taken from his pa. He watched his father's chin as the words clipped past his teeth. Floyd knew his father was still angry.

"I'll go away. Then Ma won't see me and you won't have to give me a hiding with the strap. I'll ride my horse into Cheyenne and hang around Meanea's. Maybe I'll get a job somewhere—like Montana, Miles City."

Charlie drew in his breath indignantly. "No! Jeems! The only place you are going is to the icehouse. Get a big chunk of ice, wash the straw off before you drop it in your mother's lemonade bucket. Then, if you've cooled down, join our Fourth of July doings. Bring your rope. Somebody might like to see how your twirling's improved."

Floyd flung his rope over his shoulder, turned, and walked sullenly away.

"Look alive! Hurry with the ice!" called Charlie. He unclinched his hands as a phrase his own father had said to him as a boy came to mind: "Make a virtue of necessity to do or accept with an agreeable attitude that which must be done or accepted anyway."

Etta was astonished at first when she saw Joella with one of her lovely golden braids held in her hand like a long, fat, silken caterpillar. Then she was heartbroken as she snipped off the remaining braid and evened out the short haircut. Joella cried until Margaret found a pink ribbon and tied it around the wisps of blond hair.

By the time Charlie got back to the house, Joella had a mournful smile on her face. Etta was furious with Floyd and said she hoped Charlie had tanned him good.

"I gave him a whipping and I talked to him. He went after the ice," said Charlie. "Now, don't worry, I didn't whip him too hard, just enough to knock a little sense in his head. Jeems! Fourth of July and he pulls a trick like that. The most unpredictable thing in the world next to women and wild broncs is kids."

"Charlie! Don't talk like that, not in front of Joella!" said Etta. "Tell her how lovely she looks. Different, but she's still pretty."

Charlie thought his oldest daughter looked even more delicate with short hair bouncing over her ears. The look in her eyes was childlike and trustful. Yet there was a disquieting curiosity that made Charlie's heart throb and his stomach sink.

Floyd brought in the ice, but disappeared again. Etta thought he might have gone to his room to sulk. The rest of the day seemed to go smoothly. The front yard was filled with ranchers, their families, and cowboys. Charlie roasted a whole hog in a pit most of the afternoon. The moment it was tender and well done, dinner was served. Etta was certain that there would be leftover pork for a week, but the cowboys proved her wrong. They ate as though they'd been starved the past week.

Watermelons were cooled in Horse Creek. The children had a seed-spitting contest. Joella spit seeds farthest and was given a new red bandanna. Now she acted as though her hair had always been short. She'd about forgotten the long braids that were lying in an empty shoe box on Etta's dresser.

Charlie showed off a few rope tricks. He ran footraces with the cowboys and ranchers, *kiyi*-ing like an Indian and generally coming in first. He rode out on his favorite horse, Custer, and challenged the men to a horse race down in the pasture. He came back singing at the top of his lungs, "Alfalfa Hay."

Joella and seven-year-old Pauline raced their cow ponies with some of the other girls near their age. Joella always managed to come in first. After dinner she asked, "Where's Boots?" using the name the cowboys used for her brother.

"I saw him in the meadow, back of the barn, alongside Horse Creek, swinging his rope," said one of the cowboys.

"He ought to be back joining in the fun," said Joella, swinging her head so that her hair bounced like newly formed cornsilk.

"Hey, I smell smoke! Burning hay!" yelled another cowboy, waving a slice of watermelon.

Joella smelled it and pointed to the cloud of dark smoke coming over the far side of the barn. Charlie and the men ran toward the barn, each hoping it was not on fire. Charlie's mind was sorting out the location of pails and buckets that could be dipped into Horse Creek for water. At the back of the barn the men stopped. A haystack was on fire. Floyd was frantically beating the flames with his shirt.

"Stand back, son! Let her go!" yelled Charlie.

Floyd looked up, then slowly moved back among the cowboys and watched the fire wave long flags of red toward the blue, cloudless sky. Billows of dirty gray smoke rolled across the barn and over the meadow, dispersing against the sky. Soon everyone was standing in little excited groups, pointing to sparks that started small fires around the outer periphery of the haystack. Joe and Charlie each had a shovel. They spread dust and dirt on the flames. Others formed a bucket brigade to pour water on the smoldering haystack.

Floyd tried to avoid his father. Charlie called out orders in his booming voice so that the fire was safely quelled in a short time. Charlie then sent the people back for more food and dancing. "Come here, son!" he called to Floyd, who stood several yards away. Floyd made an apologetic cough as he came toward his father. "Tell me how it happened," said Charlie.

Charlie could see the tears in his son's eyes and the struggle he was having to keep them from spilling over onto his cheeks. Floyd opened his mouth and tried to speak. At first the words were caught inside his throat. Finally he was able to say, "Pa, I—I went to cool down. Like you said."

"A burning haystack isn't my idea of cool," said Charlie.

"Pa, don't be mad. I won't do it again. I promise." Floyd's cheeks trembled and his arms twitched.

"Do what?"

"I rolled up a cigarette and tried to smoke it. I got a little dizzy and lay by the haystack for a while. When I opened my eyes I couldn't find that fag, but the hay was burning. I—I tried to smother it." He held up his shirt, a pathetic-looking piece of checked navy blue flannel, scorched and singed with large ragged holes and tiny pinprick holes that were ringed in black.

Charlie pressed his fingers to his forehead. "Where'd you get the makings? The cowboys? I'll have their hide!"

"Uncle Will said all cowboys smoke or chew and it couldn't hurt nothing," said Floyd.

"I forbid it!" shouted Charlie. "I swear, you don't hear me!" His cheeks were flushed.

"Yes." Floyd blinked his naive brown eyes. "I heard you. I don't want brown teeth. But Uncle Will doesn't have brown teeth."

Charlie looked at his son with surprise. "What does Will know? He never disciplines his children. They can grow as wild as mountain goats, for all he cares. Give me the tobacco and papers he gave you."

Floyd reached into his pants pocket. "Here, Pa. Please don't be mad."

"Go back with the others, but no dinner for you. Nothing to eat all day."

Floyd tried to say something, but in his disappointment and alarm he could not get a word out. He was embarrassed and kicked his toes in the dust as he went off toward the ranch house leaving his shirt behind, but his rope was swinging from his shoulder.

A few minutes later Etta came from the house and spoke with Charlie. "What happened to Floyd. Why is he sick?"

Charlie shook his head. "He's all right. Let him be. He is learning to grow up. I hope he makes it."

The evening was cool and beautiful. Joe brought out his fiddle and there was square dancing as Charlie made the calls. The stars came out and seemed within fingertips' reach.

Joella went inside, knocked on Floyd's door. He didn't answer so she pushed the door open. He was on the bed staring at the ceiling. She gave him two thick slices of bread. He ate one, stuffing big bites into his mouth and swallowing little pieces. Joella sat on the edge of the bed. "You smell like smoke," she said.

After a while he said, "Remember the cigarette makings Uncle Will gave to you? I took them. But I never tattled. I never told Pa you gave them to me. I said Uncle Will gave them to me."

Joella shrugged her shoulders. Her face was pale in the dark room. Her eyes were yellow-green, catlike. "Humph! I don't remember anyone giving me anything today, except a lousy haircut."

TWENTY-SIX

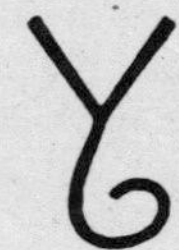

Champions

In the summer of 1905 Charlie took first place in the Elk's-sponsored rodeo in Laramie, winning a silver-trimmed saddle. He was voted the most popular cowboy in the state of Wyoming and promised himself that he would be the champion steer roper in the state one day.

He and Frank took Floyd when they went to Canon City, Colorado, with their rodeo and Wild West show. The difference between a Wild West show and a rodeo in those days was small. Charlie paid all the entry fees for his performers, but split their winnings. He continued to use the Pine Ridge Sioux with permission from the Department of Interior's Indian Field Service Office.

Floyd sat with a couple of Sioux youngsters and watched his Uncle Frank win the five-eighths of a mile dash on Honest Jon and the quarter-mile dash on a black horse called Billie Mason. One of the Sioux boys asked Floyd to join in their dance.

"I don't know how to dance Injun," said Floyd.

"Sure you do," said the boy, his black eyes glinting. "Come on, pardner, follow me and whoop it up. Make noise. That's what the people like."

"Hey, I'm no redskin," protested Floyd. "I'm a rancher and horse rider."

"I don't see you riding no bronc, pard. Take that hat off and put on these here feathers. Hunker over, shuffle along, holler loud—here we go!"

Floyd felt top heavy with the eagle-feather headdress that someone snugged down on his head. He stood straight. A brown hand pushed on his neck so that he had to bend over as they moved out to the center of the arena to perform. "I'm John Red Cloud," whispered the boy in front of Floyd. "Who are you, pale eyes?"

"Floyd Boots Irwin," said Floyd. He stomped his boots against the ground, causing a dust cloud to follow him.

The boy behind said, "Hey, Boots! Cut that out! Next time wear moccasins or go barefoot!"

"Good idea!" said Floyd, moving from side to side with the beat of the tom-toms. "I never can get these boots on till I've worn 'em for a while!" There was a lot of *tee-hee*ing along the line of Sioux dancers. Afterward Floyd sat against the fence with his new friends to watch the next event. John took the headdress off Floyd and shoved his cowboy hat toward him.

"You ever make big loops with that rope hanging 'round your neck?"

"Want to see?" Floyd stood and laid his hat on the ground as an audience of Sioux boys gathered around. He swung a wide loop over his head, a vertical one at his side. While twirling he picked up his hat and set it on his head, then stepped inside the loop as it went around. Suddenly the rope went slack. Floyd looked up into his father's scowling face.

"Stop! Don't make a fool show yourself, unless you're on the program!"

None of the Sioux boys said a word. They moved back to the fence and sat down. Floyd felt his face become hot. He followed the others to the fence, then nodded to Charlie. John moved beside Floyd. "That your pa? He's a big man with us." John's eyes were wide.

They watched Thad Sowder wearing a bright yellow shirt ride the outlaw, Whistler. That horse turned somersaults, landed on its back with Sowder underneath. The crowd stood, silent. Sowder was twice champion bronc rider of the world, but this day he couldn't get up off the ground.

"Is he dead?" asked John.

"My pa'll get him on his feet," said Floyd with confidence.

Charlie waved his hat so that people would listen. "Ladies and gentlemen!" He hollered. "One of our boys is having some bad luck. Maybe he'll have to have his arm in a sling. A couple of my boys'll pass the hat. Reach deep into your pockets!" Charlie reached into his own pocket and put a couple of bills into his hat. He motioned to Floyd and John. "Take the hat to the grandstand."

The boys collected one hundred twelve dollars for Sowder, a tribute to his great athletic ability.

Afterward, when Floyd again leaned against the fence, he saw a gray cloud rolling in. "It's going to rain!"

John disappeared and was back in a couple of minutes. "My pa says no," said John. "Wait and see."

The wind came up in quick gusts. Some of the onlookers brought out their umbrellas in preparation for rain. Billy Carver and his wife gave an exhibition of rope throwing, then came the roping and branding of calves. Some of the calves gave the cowboys a merry chase.

Charlie on horseback jumped over six barrels side by side, winning the barrel race. In the last event Pete Burns was thrown by a wild horse and had to be carried off the field. Floyd and his friend John passed Charlie's hat for a collection. Fifty-seven dollars were collected to help pay Burns's medical expenses.

Rain never materialized. Floyd said, "We both have okay pas." The boys shook hands.

"We're plenty good friends," agreed John.

A couple days later Charlie, Frank, and Floyd were in Denver with their rodeo. Charlie talked Frank out of borrowing fifteen hundred dollars to buy a couple racehorses. Then on an impulse Charlie said he'd like to go to Chillicothe. He was successful in getting the Missouri Good Roads Convention to sponsor his show at the local fairgrounds. The paper in Chillicothe carried the following report:

> Buffalo Bill's efforts in this same direction are but a kindergarten in comparison. It was a carnival of champions. A more polite party of ladies and gentlemen never came to Chillicothe than these performers. During the entire week they were courted and dined by the best people of our city and everybody regrets their departure.*

All the time Charlie was reminded of when he'd first learned about working a crowd in Chillicothe with Colonel Johnson. The

*Courtesy Charles M. Bennett Collection, Scottsdale, Arizona.

old vacant lot now held rows of houses, all alike. Graham's covered bridge was gone. When the show closed Charlie was ready to move on to St. Louis, Chicago, Kansas City, Salina, Omaha, and Goodland.

The first moment back home Charlie called to Etta, "Come see what I brought you!"

Etta came from the kitchen wiping her hands on her apron. "Oh, Charlie! Violets! My favorite! Thank you. I'm so glad to have you and Floyd back home."

Charlie pointed to the front door where Curly and Walter McGuckin stood grinning and turning their hats around and around in their hands. "They've been working for me in the rodeo," said Charlie grinning.

Tears came to Etta's eyes and a lump formed in her throat. She couldn't say anything.

"Sis! You look just the same. Tiny and short!" cried Curly.

"Say, we didn't bring no greyhound with us. Are you a mite disappointed?" asked Walt. Then he laughed.

Charlie gave her his white pocket handkerchief to wipe the tears.

"We've seen some terrific rodeos," said Curly. "But Charlie here has the winner."

"That's right! We've seen Hagenbeck, Forespaw, Miller's 101, Ringling, and Buffalo Bill in Chillicothe," said Walt.

"You've seen Buffalo Bill?" asked Etta. "Charlie knows Mr. Cody. Town of Cody's named for him. He made big land investments in Sheridan and the Big Horn Basin that brought in lots of admiration." She clicked her tongue. "But he lost some admirers when he tried to divorce his wife in Cheyenne to marry some young English actress. Some even gossip about his first wife trying to poison him and how they wouldn't walk across the street to see him. I feel kind of sorry for him."

Charlie said, "You saw Ringling? Did you see that gol-durned outfit run by steam that goes round and round under a painted canvas?"

"Sure," said Curly. "Cost me a nickel to ride on a wooden horse, goat, sheep, or elk. All the time the animals go around, music comes from a steam-run calliope. I liked it."

Charlie slapped his leg and said, "The kids around here weren't much impressed. They're used to riding the real thing, so a wooden horse or whatever don't impress 'em."

"Doesn't impress them," corrected Etta.

* * *

A few days later Charlie noticed an old, unused freight car standing on the siding beyond the depot. He asked around and found that the car was unfit to haul stock. He asked if he could buy it.

"What do you have in mind for that old boxcar?" asked his friend Richardson. "You must have some scheme up your sleeve."

"I do! I'm going to have my own cookhouse at the fairgrounds."

"C.B., if you can move that boxcar off the tracks, you'd do the railroad a favor."

Charlie didn't take long to get some men to hitch ropes to the boxcar and move it near where he kept his horses on the fairgrounds. "I believe I'll look for another old boxcar and bring it here for a barn," he told Etta. It didn't take him long to find one that the U.P. was glad to let him have and get it off their demurrage list. Now Charlie had a cookhouse with a wood-burning range, tubs for water, a countertop for food preparation, an icebox, and two rows of long tables. The other boxcar was outfitted with stalls for horses and steers, racks along one side to hang saddles, ropes, and other gear.

The Frontier Days committee decided in 1906 that major rodeo events would have winners on the basis of an average of all performances instead of the best single bucking horse ride or the best single steer-roping event.

Joella was the youngest girl in the ladies' relay race and came in second. She was not the least dejected, but stood in front of the grandstand, waved her hat, smiled, and danced a little two-step. The crowd gave her a standing ovation when Charlie announced that she was ten years old and competed with ladies twice her age.

That year a startling event took place in Wyoming. Bill Pickett, a handsome Cherokee Negro from Taylor, Texas, threw a steer to the ground and held it there with his teeth. Charlie could not believe his eyes as he watched the man go after a wild-eyed, stomping, dust-flinging steer. The man was as agile as a ballet dancer as he crouched under the steer's breast, turned, and without even using his hands sank his powerful, white teeth into the underlip of the beast, pushed his shoulder against the steer's neck to slowly bend the neck backward. The steer trembled, its legs wobbled, and it sank to the ground. Bill Pickett was an instant hero. The applause was thunderous and lasted a full ten minutes.

Charlie felt a tingling sensation go up his back as the steer-roping event was announced. This was the day he was going to be champion steer roper, he decided. Two steers had to be roped, one after another, and the average time was the official time for each roper. Ten men were in the contest.

Charlie was relieved when the first, W. H. Garrett, in skin-tight blue denims, roped his steers in an average of 1:22⅘ seconds. Mike Schoncey made two of the best throws Charlie had seen, but he could not keep his animals down, so he did not make the time. The third man, Wills, completed his work in forty-one seconds flat. That was two seconds better than the world record and five seconds faster than the Frontier Days' record made by Hugh McPhee in 1900.

Charlie watched each man, studied his technique, then determined how he could throw to cut the time shorter by a few seconds. His eyes stung from the dust kicked up in the arena. His nostrils burned from the particles of dung in the air. His head ached from excitement and tension. The moment he looked down at his white shirt he felt better. The losers wore yellow shirts. There it was as plain as a reflection from a mirror. Yellow was bad luck!

Charlie flexed his legs and arms, mounted his favorite horse, a roan called Custer. He settled tight in the saddle and felt his stomach muscles clench, let go, then relax. He blinked his eyes and felt the rough braid of his rope and knew it coiled perfectly. He was ready, so his arm went up high in the air as the first steer was let out from the corral. The steer ran like crazy. Charlie gritted his teeth, swung, and roped the animal by the horns. He kept it down easily and made the tie. He breathed fast and hard. He did not hear the audience cheer. He mounted his horse, made his rope ready to swing again.

The *Denver Republican*'s headlines for August 17, 1906, were: CHAMPION ROPER OF THE WORLD—C. B. IRWIN OF CHEYENNE. The paper stated:

> Then came the spectacular performance of C. B. Irwin, the retention of the Wyoming championship, and the gaining of the world's championship by a Wyomingite. Compelled to run his animal fully three times the distance that was covered by Wills a few minutes ago. Irwin made a perfect cast and stunning throw, and despite the fact that his steer struggled against the tie, tied in 38⅕. The ap-

> plause following the announcement of Irwin's world's record partook of the nature of an ovation for the good-natured big roper.*

Charlie was ecstatic. He felt the joyful pumping of his heart. His head was clear and he waved his hat toward the crowd. The applause was almost deafening and seemed to go on and on.

Charlie's world record for steer roping held for six years. In 1911 it was broken when the head start for the steer was shortened from one hundred to sixty feet. Today the steers at Frontier Days are given a thirty-foot start. At some rodeos now there is only a ten-foot start. Therefore, Charlie's time made in 1906 would top most of the steer roping time made even today if the headstart were lengthened back to one hundred feet.

A year later on the eighteenth of September, Charlie was having supper in town with Etta and the children. Afterward Etta sat next to him while he sang songs as Joella played the piano. They were both proud of the quick way Joella learned, with minimum practice. She had a good ear for music and could play any popular tune without seeing the music.

Then Etta remembered and got up to find the newspaper. "Listen to this!" She read:

> "Sheriff Sheffner of Natrona County passed through Cheyenne yesterday en route from Laramie to Casper with the two Irwin brothers in custody. The prisoners are suspected of being the men who recently held up the saloon of D. A. Robertson at Casper and robbed the gambling department of $2,150. They were arrested in Laramie, where the elder had gone to answer a charge of horse stealing and the younger to appear as a witness in his brother's behalf."†

Charlie felt like he'd been kicked in the stomach. Joella stopped playing the piano. "Did Uncle Frank and Uncle Will steal horses and rob a saloon?" Her emerald eyes were wide.

Charlie had to lean over with his head between his knees. He couldn't think straight.

"Shush!" Etta said. "This is family business and doesn't go

*Courtesy Charles M. Bennett Collection, Scottsdale, Arizona.
†Courtesy Dr. J.S. Palen Collection, Cheyenne, Wyoming.

out of the house. Do you understand? It is all right to know, but not right to tell."

"I hear you," said Joella. "But how many people read the paper?"

Charlie took the paper from Etta to read himself. He found it hard to focus his eyes on the headline, TAKES IRWINS TO CASPER JAIL.

"Frank's wife is expecting and Will's just had baby Gene—poor things," said Etta. Then she held up her head. "I remember reading last week about bandits who held up a saloon in the heart of the business district in Casper, about noon. That doesn't sound like Frank and Will."

"What about the horse stealing?" groaned Charlie.

"Yes, but look here," Etta had her finger on the words. "The paper says one witness thinks the bandits were only youngsters on a lark. Frank and Will are no kids."

All night Charlie tossed and turned. He was up early in the morning. "I'm going to call Sheriff Sheffner in Casper. I'll use the U.P.'s phone. I can get through faster. Central'll think it's official business."

"Do you want sausage and eggs before you go?" asked Etta.

"Can't eat." He put on his coat and hat and walked to the depot. He hoped the air would clear the fuzziness in his head.

"What are the charges on my two brothers?" He talked so loud the sheriff had to hold the receiver away from his ear.

"Who are you?" asked Sheffner in a quiet voice.

"I'm C. B. Irwin, manager of the Y6 Ranch, northeast of Cheyenne, and livestock agent for the U.P."

"Oho, it's an honor to be speaking with you, sir! You're the famous steer roper! Are your brothers from Laramie?" asked Sheffner.

"No, but they've been to Laramie."

"The older kid stole a horse from behind the post office. Caught red-handed by the postmaster."

Charlie rubbed his temples. "You say kid. About how old would you guess?"

"About twenty. The younger one sixteen or seventeen, hardly shaving. Are they your brothers? If so, they aren't champions."

"No, sir! My brothers are twice as old, hardly kids anymore. Thanks a whole bunch!" Charlie let out his breath. He could hear the sheriff let out a hoot before he hung up. The morning sunshine never felt better to Charlie and he was hungry as a bear. Before starting to work he went back home for breakfast.

* * *

Everything went smoothly for Charlie until the end of the summer, 1907, when iron-willed David H. Moffat came to Cheyenne to solicit money for his broad-gauge railroad that would cross the northern mountain ranges in Colorado. He'd built a railroad from Denver to Hot Sulphur Springs and wanted it to go farther west through the mountains to the northwestern plains. He was aware of the huge grazing land west of Denver, the vegetable farms, wheat ranches, rivers for irrigation and hydroelectric power, rich coal beds with potential power for manufacturing. He saw growth for the inland city of Denver if it were on the main line of a transcontinental railroad.

Of course, the Union Pacific was against Moffat expanding his road into western Colorado. Money he sought had dried up the moment he explained that building in the mountains meant steep grades, snow storms blocking the road for weeks, unless tunnels were blasted through the rock. Moffat was stubborn, middle-aged, with a thick head of brown hair, graying at the temples. His eyes were bright and he gave a dynamic speech appealing for funds from the Union Pacific officials in Cheyenne.

Charlie and Richardson smiled at the audacity of a man asking a competing railroad to finance his plans. Richardson said, "Moffat's a politician, cagey."

Charlie said, "If he manages to get a line through the mountains, more ranchers would ship or buy stock to or from the west coast. That would cut the U.P.'s business."

"That's the very reason the U.P.'s going to buy that little spur from Walcott to Saratoga. They'll probably complete the spur through to Encampment to get the mining business," said Richardson. "I agree, there's no reason to negotiate with a man who wants our money and then competes with us. If he doesn't want to cooperate and lower freight rates and make good connections with the U.P.'s main lines, I say give him competition," said Richardson.

Richardson was about the same age as Charlie, not as tall, but his hair was the same sandy color. Together they looked like brothers. They argued like brothers who were close and fond of each other.

A week after David Moffat had been in Cheyenne, Richardson came to Charlie's office. "Headquarters wants you and me to make contact with all the stockmen we can find between Walcott and Hot Sulphur Springs, the North Park area, the valley west of the Medicine Bow Range."

Charlie pushed the hair from his eyes. "Warren, I suggested we talk to those same stockmen two years ago. I said so a week ago. I said we ought to get them to ship on the U.P., especially now that we have the Saratoga and Encampment Valley Railroad almost built to the Colorado border."

"Somebody heard you. We are to talk stockmen into using the new road, then transfer to the main road at Walcott."

"We're going to give Moffat some competition!" said Charlie.

"We're taking a trip. Charles Ware, general superintendent, sent a wire. Read it." Richardson reached into his shirt pocket. "We leave before the fall blizzards hit the passes."

Charlie read once, then twice, then grinned. "Quit spitting on the handle. I'm ready to go across the Continental Divide."

In two days they were on the Union Pacific heading out of Laramie for Walcott. They carried what local cowboys called "war bags," instead of a regular grip or suitcase. War bags were bedrolls with woolen blankets, mackinaws, wool shirts, and pants. Each wore boots and a wide-brimmed hat. Their instructions were to get horses in Walcott, then ride south across the Divide at Willow Creek Pass, a distance of more than two hundred miles overland to Hot Sulphur Springs.

The Medicine Bow River was clear and shallow, the birch pale yellow. Snow fences made from slashings, sometimes in double or triple rows, lined the track. Near Walcott the land became flat, chalk-white, sprinkled with dusty, lavender sagebrush. Walcott had wide streets filled with wagons and horses. More freight was handled there than at any other Union Pacific station between Omaha and Ogden. Mine and smelter machinery, coal, and building materials came in for the development of the Grand Encampment copper mines. The men left the train to look for horses.

The livery man was impressed that U.P. men were going to rent his horses to impress stockmen of the benefits of their line rather than the Moffat Road with higher rates. "Yes, sir, get stockmen to use the new shortline. The U.P.'ll need two trains to hold all the stock and two banks to hold all the money."

In the warm September sunshine the two men followed the tracks south. The picket-pin gophers sat motionless beside the sagebrush as the horses passed. In late afternoon the chugging coal-fed locomotive came up out of the valley, which was called a park, hauling half a dozen boxcars and as many flatbed cars with long bars of smeltered copper. They spent the first night beside the railroad's building crew. They moved out before daybreak. Wherever there was a herder's shack or any sign of habitation they stopped and talked with the stockmen.

In Saratoga they stayed at the Hotel Wolf and next morning they were seeking out ranchers' cabins, which were usually round logs with mud chinking. Twice they passed sandstone ledges that held rocks piled in slender shafts, six to eight feet tall. The sheepherders built the silent sentinels, talked to them as if they were men when days or nights were lonely. Charlie thought the monuments looked like tall men silhouetted against the sky.

Near creeks the men wore bandannas tied around their heads under their hats for protection against the swarms of mosquitoes and gnats. Along the creek banks they found other examples of sheepherders' art in aspen and cottonwood trunks. The herders carved elaborate pictures, many of the fair sex, in the bark of the trees to pass the time during long summer days. One evening Richardson said, "C.B., the nights are colder. We saw only one rancher today. We have to go faster before the weather declines or we'll have to get out of here on snowshoes."

"I've thought about that," said Charlie. "We could get fliers made at Encampment. Leave some at the post office, take the rest to other little towns, put them in stores. When the ranchers go to town for supplies they'll see that the U.P. will give them a better rate than Moffat."

"Fliers?" Richardson sounded puzzled. "Headquarters never mentioned that."

"So what! U.P. guarantees to discount livestock freight rates." Charlie wrote the words high in the air.

Richardson scratched the stubble on his face. "It's not bad. It'll reinforce the ranchers we already talked to and get some we missed."

Once they saw a flock of more than a hundred prairie chickens waddle and half fly out of the way. Next they saw a drove of several dozen antelope, and Richardson got a buck that lagged behind the rest with his rifle. The meat was a good change from beans and bacon.

One morning they woke to find a thin layer of powder snow had fallen during the night. While hunting for dry wood to build a fire, Charlie suddenly held his hands down by his side, palms out behind, signifying for Richardson to stop. Charlie whispered, "Poor devils! Look down there!"

Both men crouched together and saw what looked like Indians huddled against the white ground.

"None of them move," whispered Richardson. He stood up

and held his hand above his eyes to get a better look. He began to laugh. "Charlie! Your Indians are tree stumps!"

Charlie's face turned scarlet as the chokecherry leaves. "I'm embarrassed, but I feel a lot better!"

The two men guffawed over the mistake until their sides ached.

One of the herders said he knew a rail line was coming south because of the number of crossties floating down the North Platte River toward Encampment.

At Encampment they put their bedrolls next to the tents of the railroad surveying crew. In the morning they rode past the ore smelter. It was a huge, sprawling, gray wood structure. A sixteen-mile aerial tramway, longest in the world, came from the copper mines in the mountains. They had one hundred fliers made at the *Grand Encampment Herald* and charged them to the U.P. RR.

"C.B., I'm going to put a couple fliers in tramway buckets. They'll get to the stockmen working the mines!" Richardson was enthusiastic.

Tents, log cabins, tar-paper shacks scarified the hills half a mile in every direction. The outhouses amused both men. They were sturdy frame shacks built on a cribbed-up log base. The silolike buildings were as high as fifteen feet, with a door opening halfway up the laddered front. The tall structures were necessary because of the deep, drifting snows in winter.

Going across a steep grade, Charlie saw that the winds and early snow had forced fallen tamarack needles into gullies, so that there were deep piles, several hundred yards long. No plants grew from under this layer of orange-brown needles because the turpentinelike aromatics destroyed all other seedlings. Charlie called to Richardson: "I'm going to have some fun! I'm going to slide down the ravine on those needles! It'll be same as a toboggan on snow!"

"C.B., you're nuts!" cried Richardson, staying on his horse.

Charlie found a piece of butcher's paper that was around their bacon. He tore off a big hunk, folded it in two, and sat on it. He waved and hollered and dug his boots into the needles to give himself a push. He waved again, hung on to the paper, and sailed down the gulley.

Richardson led Charlie's horse down the hill. "Cripes!" he said, pushing his hat higher on his forehead. "I've just witnessed the damndest show-off in the West! Charlie, you have a mind as sharp as the north wind, the strength of Paul Bunyon's blue ox, and a fun-loving streak down your back about the size of a sixteen-year-old."

They contacted four ranchers that day, and by night saw the terrain become rocky and again the sagebrush dotted the land. Here and there were tiny lakes where there was usually a sheepherder in a lean-to guarding his small winter flock, or a cowboy lineman checking out the cattle that grazed on the meadows.

The day they hit Willow Creek Pass, which was more than ninety-five hundred feet above sea level, they found the creeks running muddy. "Must be raining along the Divide," said Charlie.

Here the aspen had lost their leaves and the willows were yellowed sticks. When the rain hit, it was stinging cold. The two men stopped under a rock overhang. Charlie hunted for dry wood. They drank strong coffee and ate hard, chewy beans with their salty meat. Both spoke about the good antelope meat that was long gone because they left a large rump roast with the Encampment newspaper man who made the fliers quickly. They rode through several canyons when the rain let up. Charlie was relieved when they were out of the canyons. He had visions of the creeks suddenly swelling and gushing in a flash flood across their path where there was nowhere to escape.

They saw the hillsides covered with pines. A trail ran past a jitney sawmill run by a rancher and his two sons. The mill cut the bark off four sides of a log. The slabs were used for shacks, snow fences, or cross ties. Cross ties were treated with zinc chloride. The process was called burnitizing, and hardened the wood. The ties were dipped into creosote for waterproofing and insectproofing. Charlie made notes on this process to add to his final report to U.P. Headquarters.

They rode along a small creek and found the hillsides covered with grass instead of trees. There were surveyors' markers and about a mile of railroad bed cut alongside a hill. "Must be close to Hot Sulphur Springs," said Richardson.

There was no depot in town, which disappointed the men. On one of the sidings next to the main line were empty boxcars to be exchanged for loaded ones to be sent back to Denver. They rode their horses cautiously around the railroad work camp. "If anyone asks, we're looking for a job," said Richardson out of the side of his mouth. "For God's sake don't let on that we work for the U.P." No one paid any attention to the two men on horseback.

Charlie and Richardson ate supper in one of the saloons located across the creek that ran through the heart of the town. They learned that the railroad crew's communication with the main office was by the telegraph linesman, who used a handcar to travel the tracks. The handcar was thrown off the tracks a few days before by renegades who'd left the construction crew because of some grievance. The railroad men in their work overalls were armed, prepared for anything.

The next morning after sleeping in a clapboard hotel they went into the General Store for more grub, mainly hardtack. Richardson warned Charlie to keep a low profile. "We only talk to the ranchers. U.P. spells *enemy* to anyone working for Moffat's Road. Maybe we can find someone who can telegraph a message to headquarters and let them know we're here and heading back. Time to head home, I'm running out of cash."

The men had left their rifles with the bartender where they'd eaten breakfast and headed for the railroad tracks where Charlie had seen a telegraph linesman in a handcar. "Let me do the talking," said Charlie when he spotted the handcar coming down the track.

He walked slowly down the middle of the track until the linesman waved to him. He waved back and hoped the man would stop. He cupped his hands around his mouth and yelled, "Say! I'm in a bit of a fix!" The linesman stopped. Charlie explained, "I have to send a message up north and don't know exactly how."

"North, where?" asked the linesman, wiping his hands on his overalls.

"Cheyenne."

"I can do that. I just tap into Denver and then it goes up to Cheyenne. Both you boys in some kind of jam?" The linesman put his hand on the rifle that was in the handcar.

"No jam. We aren't even armed. Or maybe that's trouble," said Charlie, keeping his eyes on the rifle. "We're short on cash just now."

"Who's the message for?"

"Well—uh—let's see—send it to the superintendent of the Union Pacific in Cheyenne. The message is only three words—on way home, then sign that WR and CBI."

"That some kind of code?" The linesman picked up his rifle and put it over his shoulder.

"Oh, no, sir. Ah—I'll pay for your trouble. Will a dollar be all right?" Charlie said with a smile.

The linesman took the dollar and asked for the initials again.

He wrote them in a notebook he took from his pocket. "You boys live in Cheyenne? You sent here by the U.P. to look over Moffat's enterprise? We heard some fellers were on their way over the Snowy Range." His eyes became small and beady. His mustache was coarse and yellow. It quivered. "If they're important, we'll get 'em when they get here."

Charlie could hear Richardson's breathing. Slowly Richardson pointed to his boots. "Do railroaders ride horseback? These are cowboy boots, friend. We don't walk far in them." Then a grin spread across his face. "We're sending a message to our ma, so she won't worry. Superintendent happens to be an old family acquaintance and knows the quickest way to reach her."

"Mothers worry," said the linesman, chewing a corner of his mustache. "They figure it's a duty, no matter how grown the children be." He made a clucking sound with his tongue on the roof of his mouth. "Say, this time of the year could be dangerous going on horseback across the Divide. The Snowy Range is white. Sell your saddles and horses, buy yourselves tickets on the Moffat Road to Denver, then go on to Cheyenne. Save yourselves a heap of trouble and your poor ol' ma more worry. I can get you on the train in Hot Sulphur Springs. Comes in once a day, usually a couple of boxcars this time of year. Should have seen the length of the train when the ranchers were shipping stock to Denver—ten, twelve cars every day."

Charlie stared at the tracks and wondered how he was going to get out of this without arousing any suspicion.

"You looking at how Moffat's gang laid them tracks?" asked the linesman. "They're safe. Best-laid tracks in the West. Track walkers out once a week checking."

"Get many passengers from here?" asked Charlie.

"A few. You want to ship your horses to Denver? I'll let you ride with them," said the linesman.

"That part about the horses is a new thought. We have to think about it," said Richardson, twisting the ends of the bandanna he wore and startling Charlie.

For several seconds there was silence. Then Charlie looked up at the linesman and said, "Much obliged for all your trouble. Send the message. We'll see you later about taking the train to Denver. What'd you say the going rate is?"

"I can get you two brothers on a boxcar full of stock for ten dollars apiece. You give me the money."

Richardson let out a little puff of air. "Well—well, we have to sell those saddles first." He began walking backward toward Hot

Sulphur Springs. "Then we can sell our horses and have some money."

The linesman shifted his rifle and called after the two men, who were walking fast hitting every other tie with each step. "I've been known to track a bear through running water!"

Charlie waved and said, "Keep walking along the tracks. If we move off he'll think we're running from him. He knows we aren't armed, so he's not sure about that dumb story about our poor ma. You couldn't keep your mouth shut, could you?"

Richardson grinned. "Let's move out. We don't want to start a railroad war. You pay the livery man. I'll get our rifles."

Charlie saddled the horses and made sure the war bags and supplies and finally the rifles were fastened securely behind the saddles. They rode over the rattly wooden bridge in the center of town and headed west around the high barren hills, staying close to the dark rocks. About three miles out of town they headed northeast, hoping to hit Willow Creek before nightfall.

"No one's following us," said Charlie with a laugh. "I guess we're not so important."

Richardson said, "Headquarters'll say we're important. We've seen more than fifty ranchers and left fliers all over. We're champions! Our next job is to get through the snow over the pass."

In two days they had left their spent horses with a sheepherder and were making their way on snowshoes. More than two weeks later they were standing in the depot at Walcott waiting for the train to take them to Cheyenne.

The *Cheyenne Leader* and *Denver Republican* published glowing stories of the two U.P. men crossing the Divide on horseback and returning on snowshoes after reminding all ranchers in the vicinity to ship by U.P., which guaranteed lower rates. Charlie and Richardson were heroes at the railroad headquarters. All winter they repeated the stories about their trip through North Park.

The U.P. had a noticeable increase in freight coming out of and into northern Colorado by midsummer.

One afternoon Charlie was in Meanea's Saddlery telling Meanea that the U.P. ought to give him and Richardson an increase in salary for all the trouble they went to locating those isolated ranchers. "Worst walk in the world. Snowshoes hurt my back and legs, not to mention my feet," said Charlie.

A stranger came into the store. His hair was unkempt and his shirttail hung out. He smiled and said he wanted Frank Meanea to make him one of those special kind of Cheyenne roll saddles. "I heard about them in Montana and I came to get me one," he said with a big smile.

"It'll cost you thirty-five dollars," said Meanea.

"Hey! Do I look like I'm made of goddamn money? That's damn robbery!" The stranger smiled when he swore. "My wife'd have a fit if she knew I paid that much for a goddamn saddle. But I gotta have it. I never saw anything so purty."

Charlie looked the man over and decided he had an honest smile. He thought he was just temporarily down on his luck. "Let Meanea make your saddle, stranger. In the meantime come home with me. My wife is one of the best cooks in town," said Charlie.

"You bet, I'll come if I can bring my friend." The stranger pointed to another man, who was smiling at the other end of the counter. I call him the Cherokee Kid. He's champion rope twirler of the West."

Charlie swallowed and reached his hand across the counter. "Pleased to meet you. I'm sure my wife can find enough fixings for two extras at the table."

The man called Cherokee Kid was slender, with an extra-long body, which maybe accounted for his shirttail being out in back. Some men just naturally go around in a kind of untidy state, thought Charlie. Cherokee Kid's hair was straight and dark like an Indian's and hung down over his forehead. He looked up at Charlie with a kind of sheepish look. "This here is my pal, Charlie Russell. It's like some magnetic force brought us together. I'm a roper from Oklahoma and he's a painter—he draws—from Montana. We don't see each other much. We just happened to come to Cheyenne at the same time. You say supper's hot? Let's go."

While Etta was adding more potatoes and onions to the beef stew, Floyd was looking over the Cherokee Kid. "Pa says you twirl a rope."

"By golly, you want to see some champeen twirling right now?" asked Cherokee Kid.

"There's no time for rope demonstrations," said Charlie, pointing to a chair so Floyd would sit down.

"I just wanna see if this dude's better than he looks," whispered Floyd.

Charlie muttered and cleared his throat. "My son fancies himself a trick roper. After supper we'll trade roping secrets. I've got me a pasture four miles from town. Right now I have some of the finest horses in Wyoming out there."

The three men began to talk about horses. Floyd thought they looked like losers. He couldn't believe that Cherokee Kid ever had much more than a rawhide rope between his fingers.

"Something wrong with a man who don't like a horse," said Cherokee Kid. "The 101 Ranch in Oklahoma has the best horses in that territory."

"Nice of you to ask us to your place," said Russell.

Etta heard them talking and smiled. She knew Charlie was enjoying himself talking with new folks. Charlie was so generous that he'd share dinner or his pay with anyone in need.

When they came into the dining room, the taller came forward and held out his hand. Etta smiled, her cheeks pink from the heat of the cookstove. "I'm Etta Irwin, Charlie's wife. You've met our boy, Floyd, and these are our girls, Joella, Pauline, and Frances."

"I'm Charlie Russell from Great Falls, Montana, and this here is Cherokee Kid on account of he's part Injun. Shucks, his real name is just Will—Will Rogers. We're mighty grateful to you and your husband. Delicious smells! I'm starved!"

On closer inspection Etta saw that their clothing was rumpled, but not dirty. Russell had interesting hands with long fingers, like a musician, and the nails were clean, which was unusual for a cowboy. Rogers brushed a lock of dark hair from his forehead, only to have it slide back. He had friendly eyes. He nodded toward the three girls in their freshly starched pastel dresses for company dinner.

"Say, these fillies are the purtiest things I've seen since the miniature pony I had as a kid. Pure white, it was, dainty, just like little girls."

Etta was flattered. "There's plenty to eat. We have a garden at the ranch."

"Ranch?" asked Russell.

"Forty-five miles northeast," said Charlie. "If you want to have a look, I'll take you out in the morning. I could use a couple extra hands right now anyway."

"Well, we—ah, well—" Russell stuttered and turned red.

Etta came to the rescue. She put a hand on Russell's arm. "It's all right. Charlie needs help since one of his cowboys got snookered into the annual snipe hunt. Charlie, tell them that funny story." She seated herself and began passing bowls and platters.

Charlie chuckled and his eyes sparkled. "There was this greenhorn kid who came out to the ranch for a job. I could tell he wasn't much over twenty and he was hungry as a horse. We fed him and sent him out with some fencing nails to fasten up barbed wire that had come off during the winter. On Saturday it rained and the cowboys sat around the bunkhouse telling tales about the whistling marmots, the streaking emu, and the snipe. Some joker suggested the snipe hunt. This poor sap was so green he didn't seem to have ever heard of snipe." Charlie stopped and tilted his head toward the two guests. "Of course, you have snipe in Montana and Oklahoma?"

Rogers didn't blink an eye. "No, never heard of them. What happened?"

"Well, so the boys told this greenhorn how snipe hunting was done and made sure he understood he was to stand by the fence and wait for the snipe to sneak into his open gunnysack. The next day was one of those windy, bitter April ones, and someone offered the kid his new Pendelton jacket. Someone else noticed his boots had holes in the soles, so he gave him his brand-new pair to wear for the hunt. A cowboy gave him a kerchief and a new hat so he'd be warm. The cowboys all felt a tiny pang of pity sending this poor kid out into the cold to hold the sack for the snipe to crawl in. However, their excitement about a snipe hunt was greater than their feeling of pity, you can bet your own boots on that.

"They figured he'd be out an hour and then come sheepishly back to the bunkhouse, ready to admit he didn't see a thing, holding the empty sack. After he'd gone they all had a good laugh and began a game of Seven-Up.

"When this fool wasn't back in two hours they began to talk about him and feel a mite edgy about him out in the cold wind for so long. Two cowboys decided to go out and bring him in. When they got to where he was holding the sack, only the sack was left—that boy walked off with a brand-new set of duds!"

Etta laughed, saying that each time she heard the story it was funnier.

Russell held his sides. Rogers wiped tears from his eyes and said, "There's nothing that impresses the ordinary cowboy like a cowboy that ain't ordinary. By golly, I'll tell that story over and over!"

After they finished eating, Charlie took his two new friends out to his Four-Mile pasture, where they looked over his horses. Floyd brought his rope along and gave it to Rogers. Floyd was sure the man couldn't twirl any better than baby Frances.

Rogers whistled, let a small loop grow large over his head, and began to talk as he handled the rope. "There was this man called Texas Jack over in London who offered fifty pounds to anyone who could do the same rope trick he did. I asked him for a job and he asked me what I could do. I showed him something common back in Oklahoma, the Big Crinoline, which was the same trick he did, but I didn't know that. He gave me the job. Then I found out about his trick. And because no one in Texas Jack's show could collect the reward for doing his trick as well or better than he, I didn't get the reward money."

"You were left holding the bag—in London?" Floyd's eyes were large as he watched the expert way Rogers was twirling the rope.

"Rogers!" hollered Charlie. "Now, I recall hearing about a Will Rogers, a trick roper in Colonel Mulhall's Wild West Show, 101 ranch. I pictured you wearing a brand-new silk shirt and tight pants and long hair, like—Buffalo Bill. But lookit here! Jeems, it's a good thing I found you. Both you fellows have to spend time at the ranch. Get some food into you, get a little work under your belt and some clothes that fit you. Yes, sir, it's good I ran across you both."

The three men laughed and talked as if they had been old friends for years. Floyd tried to keep up with the conversation, but all he could understand was that Rogers was some kind of cowboy performer and Russell a cowboy who'd rather paint.

"Barn at the ranch needs painting," Floyd said.

Rogers chuckled and put his hand on Floyd's shoulder. When they came back to the house on horseback, they found Joella playing the piano.

Rogers said, "Move over a bit," and he began to play. At first it was slow and soft, then he went into a raucous ragtime beat. His face glowed. He played a folk song and sang the words. Then Etta and Charlie were singing with him and soon everyone was crowded around the piano having a wonderful time. Floyd's rope slipped from his shoulder. He bent to pick it up and noticed Russell was not singing, but sitting in a corner. He was drawing on the back of an envelope a picture of everyone's face as he sang. His long supple fingers held the soft lead pencil so that the tip seemed almost to be his index finger. He brushed the lines to catch the right expression.

Charlie put the men up in the bunkhouse behind the big house and the next day took them out to the Y6. He put them both to work plowing the potato patch, picking peas, and mending fences. Charlie worked with them, telling stories and singing. On Saturday Etta and the children came out. Floyd took his rope to Rogers, who said, "I used to have a hundred-foot cotton rope.

Imagine how heavy that was when I got that Big Crinoline loop wide open. I had to build up plenty of muscle to keep that up in the air. Let me see what you can do."

Floyd did his best to top Rogers with big loops, the Butterfly, and Ocean Waves. Rogers was impressed and said, "You're the first boy I ever saw who could lasso the tail off a blowfly."

Floyd grinned.

After three, four days of work Russell said it was time he went to town and picked up his saddle and headed back to Montana.

"Time for me to vamoose, too," said Rogers.

"I gave you a job cowboying for me. Now you want your pay and you want to leave? Where is your feeling of responsibility? There's more to be done; for instance, when are you going to paint the barn doors?"

"Paint, C.B.? I can't paint," said Rogers. "Let Russell paint and you and I go out with the kids and have a horse race." He pushed his small-brimmed hat back on his head.

"The three of us will paint," said Charlie, "because Etta said those barn doors are a fright. She could hold out the feed until the job's finished."

"Your wife's tiny as a kitten. You're big as a bobcat. She tells you what to do? Holy-moley!" chortled Rogers.

"Show us the bucket of red paint and a couple of brushes. We can paint if it means we can eat!" said Russell.

In front of the barn several cowboys stood holding one side of the huge double doors. "We're fixing to saw off the bottom of this side so it closes," said one cowboy. "We'll do this before you paint."

"Good idea," agreed Charlie.

They went to the toolshed, where there was a huge saw in an iron frame mounted on four wheels. They tried to move it out of the shed. They heaved and pushed and pulled. Nothing moved, not even the wheels.

Charlie wandered over to see what was taking so long. "I've never seen such weaklings as they raise nowadays," he said, and picked up one end of the saw and pulled it off the wheels and carried it outside. "Now bring the wheels out. Turn them sideways so they make it past the doorway. That's it!"

When the sawing was done, Joe checked the hinges and found them still strong. "Put the door up. All that baby needs is paint."

Rogers, Russell, and Charlie worked, laughing and singing. They came in for lunch with red barn paint on their clothes, specks on their faces and in their hair. Etta smiled. She knew they were all three having the best time.

"Say, Etta," said Rogers, "do you have any other color paint besides this red?"

"In the toolshed, next to the blacksmith shed, are paint cans. You going to do some touch-up work?"

"That's it! Touch up some places," said Rogers with a wink.

"Don't come around until we're done," said Charlie. "Women and kids around a paint job can spoil everything."

Joe was working in the blacksmith shed when Russell and Rogers came crowding inside looking for paint. Joe called out, "Say, you young fellers looking for the liniment?"

"Mr. Irwin, we're looking for paint," explained Russell.

"Next door in the toolshed. Look behind the anvil. Don't step behind this here horse or you'll get kicked and get a worse scar between your eyes than Charlie!"

The two men brought out several cans of various colors.

When supper was about half ready, Etta went out on the back porch to rest a moment. She could see the men standing off from the barn door, kind of admiring their work. She thought, if they come up now they can use turpentine and get the paint washed off before supper. I'll just mosey down and tell them. She could see them all grinning as she came nearer.

"Well, dear, how do you like it? A masterpiece, huh?" asked Charlie. The other men looked pleased as punch. Etta thought they all looked like schoolboys who'd been caught smoking behind the outhouse.

She looked at the door. She blinked and stared. She swallowed. There was a sudden sharp pain in her midsection. The huge double barn door was painted red, the color of the barn, but on top of that red background was a picture of a bull standing on its hind legs pawing at the air in front of it. The bull's head was held high in the air. The proud animal was more than three times normal size. Its eyes looked at Etta no matter where she moved. As hard as she tried to keep her gaze on the bull's magnificent face, something, as strong as a magnet on iron filings, brought her eyes in line with the lower half of the bull's anatomy. She felt riveted and her face turned crimson. Finally she willed herself the courage to close her eyes, turn, and face the three men. The minute her tongue loosened her eyes flew open and she saw Charlie convulsed with laughter.

"It's vulgar—and—tacky! Women and children pass by this barn every day! This is a ranch. We all know about animals, but to have one drawn here with a—a feature that stands out—

strikes out at the viewer—a feature three times normal size—is—is offensive!" She could feel her heart beating rapidly and her breathing come in short gasps. The painting was so lifelike she could imagine the bull itself blowing its hot breath in a loud snort and leaping away from the door.

"You'll get used to it," burst out Charlie.

Rogers grinned with friendly amusement. "Ma'am, there's glory in a healthy bull. What I'm saying—it can't be offending. We put a lot of work on this here door to make it authentic and one of a kind."

Etta sniffed. "Paint it out!" She clenched her hands into small fists.

Russell looked up, incredulous, dumbfounded by the absurdity of her suggestion. "Mrs. Irwin, look at it this way, no one in all of Wyoming, nor Montana, has such a wondrous, goddamned thing on their barn door. Why, if my wife, Nancy, knew about this here painting, she'd have the door off its hinges in a minute and ship it to New York to put in some big damned gallery where all the easterners could marvel at it." He hit the door a good whack with the palm of his hand. Then he saw that his hand was red and he'd left a hand print. "I put my mark of approval on the whole thing!"

"That's where the approval should go, along with the bull—to New York!" cried Etta. She grabbed at a paint brush.

"Oh, no!" cried Charlie. "Don't mess with this! We'll take care of it! Go back and finish getting supper."

When she left Russell said, "It'll be a goddamned, pitiful, castrated steer on that door!"

"I told you it was so good that it looked like it'd pounce on the first cow that ambled by," snorted Rogers.

"Let's ask Pa what he thinks," said Charlie.

Joe liked it. "It's the best gol-darned mirage I've ever seen!" he said. Joe brought Will and a couple of the cowboys over to see. They all thought it was an aristocratic bull. "He will sure liven up each day when we see him out here just rearing to go like that," said Will. "I'm glad Etta saw it first. Margaret would have taken an ax to the doors."

"Well, now we have to perform the docking operation," said Charlie.

"I'll geld this beautiful beast with one helluva sweep of goddamned turpentine," said Russell dramatically. He poured the turpentine on his paint rag and swung his arm out against the bull. "There, it's done."

"It still looks like the champeen bull," said Rogers with a sigh. "It's the best painting we three ever did together."

Rogers stayed a week after Russell left the ranch so he, too, could go back home with a Cheyenne saddle of his own. Charlie went to see Dr. Henneberry because he thought he was gaining weight.

The doctor laughed and said, "You're healthy as a horse. You eat well, so get a little more exercise and don't worry. A man who's six foot four, with a frame like yours, can easily carry two hundred, two hundred and fifty pounds. In my opinion you're not overweight."

At the ranch Charlie rode one of the racehorses for half an hour before breakfast. In town he went out to the Four Mile pasture and rode bareback for thirty minutes before breakfast. One day during breakfast he told Etta he was going to spend a day or so in Denver on business, not to worry, he'd be home as soon as possible. He left on the Union Pacific, but came home driving his first automobile, a shiny, black and silver Colburn.

The Colburn was built in Denver, patterned after the French Renault, with the radiator behind the hood. It was a four-door with a canvas top that could be lowered. Charlie had the top lowered all the way home. It took him nearly a full day to drive twenty miles an hour from Denver to Cheyenne. He stopped to talk with anyone who wanted to look over his new automobile. One man asked if he'd looked at Elmer Lovejoy's balloon-tired contraption in Laramie. Another said he'd read in the *Laramie Boomerang* that there were about a hundred and twenty different automobile manufacturers in this country, this year. "I doubt if one of these machines can drag a plow as well as my two old workhorses," said a man on horseback. "Hey, mister, don't panic my cows with all that speed!" cried a farmer driving five milk cows to pasture. Charlie waved and felt wonderful.

At the ranch he raced the Colburn against some of the fastest horses. Generally the horses won. In November, Frank and Clara Belle had a baby girl, named Maxine Eleanor. Charlie drove to town, picked up Etta in the Colburn, and drove the few blocks to see Clara Belle and the new baby.

When the dirt and gravel roads lay under a blanket of snow, the prized Colburn sat on blocks of cordwood behind the big, closed barn door, as impotent as the castrated bull on the front. Charlie took the battery out, the tires off, and stored them, to

Etta's great consternation, in the kitchen pantry in town, where it was warm.

There was a popular argument going on among ranchers that winter about which horse was faster and possessed more stamina, the Western bronc or the thoroughbred Arabian. "Listen to this!" Charlie called to Etta one evening as she dried the dishes, "The editors of the *Denver Post,* Bonfils and Tammen, are arguing that Arabians are hot bloods and our broncs are cold bloods."

"Are they saying Arabians are faster?" asked Etta, taking off her apron and sitting on the davenport beside Charlie.

"Yes! Those galoots are just full of wet hay! Anybody with any sense at all knows Western broncs are fast and tough. Horses raised on prairie grass are the best in the world!"

"Charlie! You're prejudiced!" Etta patted his hand.

"Of course not! I know!" He gave her a quick peck on the cheek.

On the eighth of January, 1908, the *Denver Post* announced that the paper was going to underwrite a long-distance race between Arabians and Western broncs, the Great Endurance Race. The route would backtrack the old Overland Trail, run parallel with the U.P. tracks. Charlie immediately called the U.P.'s headquarters in Omaha and suggested that the railroad might like to donate prize money and boxcars to carry horses to the starting point in Evanston, in the southwest corner of Wyoming. Then he called the *Denver Post* and talked to the sports editor, Otto C. Floto.

Charlie volunteered to drive Floto in his Colburn over the race course, from Evanston, northeast to the Green River, east to Rawlins and Medicine Bow, south to Laramie, southeast to Cheyenne, then due south to Denver. "We could set up rest stations about fifty miles apart for the racers. At each station the rider's horse could be checked by a veterinarian and two humane society officials, who could decide if a horse was still in condition to continue the race."

"C.B., now you're thinking!" Floto hollered into the phone. "I believe there should be no rules or restrictions on kinds of saddles or equipment, except each rider and his gear should weigh at least one hundred sixty pounds! What do you think?"

"I think, just before the race, on the twenty-sixth of May, there could be a chartered U.P. train leaving Denver, which could carry entrants and their horses. Any remaining entrants could be picked up at various stops along the way," said Charlie.

Floto told Charlie there was to be a prize of three hundred dollars in gold dust for the man whose horse completed the race in the best shape.

Charlie drove his Colburn to Denver on Monday so that he could help load the horses into U.P. boxcars. He also drove his Colburn up the broad ramp and into one of the boxcars. He carried his hemp rope over his shoulder in case it was needed to bring in a reluctant horse. He talked with Frank "Dode" Wykert from Severance, Colorado, a contestant, whose horse's breeding was listed as "unknown." Charlie saw it was really an ordinary cow pony whose legs looked granite hard. "What you feed this baby?"

"Small on hay, heavy on oats, exercise every day for more than a month now," said Wykert. "Horse's name's Sam."

"Hey, you one of them judges?" asked another contestant, Jack Smith, who came in from New Mexico with a coal-black, half-breed horse called Dick Turpin.

"Nope. I'm just going to see that the Denver newspaper gets its story by getting to each check point in time to have a reporter interview the first man coming in."

By six A.M. in Denver the next morning everyone was aboard the special train and on their way to Cheyenne. Charlie had bought two leather caps with flaps to cover the ears and fastened under the chin. He had bought two pairs of goggles. He gave a cap and pair of goggles to Floto.

Floto laughed and said, "Thanks, C.B., but we're not in an automobile race. It's a horse race. We'll look like a couple of loonies wearing these!"

"We'll need 'em if the wind kicks up when we drive through the Red Desert. You won't laugh when they keep our ears from aching and our eyes from smarting," said Charlie.

The *Denver Post* U.P. Special was dubbed the Pony Express. It picked up entrants all day and a few at night along the route. Many towns staged a gala celebration as the train pulled in. No one got much sleep because of singing, usually led by Charlie, and some pranksters. Around midnight someone set off a string of railroad fuses. The red glow lit up the center aisle of one of the chaircars for more than three quarters of an hour. "If I'd just boarded this train I'd think it was on fire!" cried Charlie. He left his seat and went to do some talking with the conductor and brakeman.

The three huddled together in the vestibule between the chaircar and boxcar. Charlie pulled two stocking caps from his suit coat pocket and a couple of colored bandannas. "Don't cover your eyes!" he yelled at the conductor. "Jeems! Make this look like the real, honest thing! It ought to look like the holdup's been planned for a long time—like we know what we're doing." Charlie put his hand over his mouth to surpress a big laugh. "Watch through the window, when I pull out a paper cup for a drink of water, you come busting into the coach yelling and *kiyi*-ing as if you mean business. Ask Davis to put his gold wedding ring and his pocket watch into your hat. That'll serve him right for his bad singing." Charlie's eyes twinkled and he felt a prickling of excitement go up his back as they planned the prank.

"If I use my official cap to collect the loot, those fellows'll believe we swiped the clothing off the train officials and dumped them overboard. What a lark!" The conductor tried to smother his laugh.

"Don't act nervous, just act like you've pulled off jobs like this before," snickered Charlie, opening the door into the coach. He felt the welcome blast of warm air. He rolled the black serge railroad coats along with his suit coat and hoisted them on to the wire rack above his seat. He sat down for a moment, then murmured something about being warm and need of ice water. He took a breath and grabbed a flat, triangular white paper cup out of the slot. Two men appeared from the vestibule, wearing stocking caps pulled low over their foreheads and bandannas tied around their noses and mouths. They pushed past Charlie, knocking the water from his hand.

"Hey, watch what you're doing!" yelled Charlie. "Who do you think you are?"

"The Bunkum Brothers!" yelled the brakeman. "This is a holdup!"

"Bunkums?" someone asked. "Train robbers?" "Oh, Lord!" "I never dreamt this'd happen!"

The brakeman held what appeared to be a pistol. He waved the gun over his head. "Anyone moves, I fire! I'm a crack shot—known for shooting glass balls out of the air in Texas."

The conductor's cap and brakeman's cap were filling up with gold rings and chains and leather wallets.

Charlie's hand covered his mouth to hide his grin. The conductor was beside him. "You there! Ya, you, fatso, stand up!"

"Don't call me that!" yelled Charlie, half mad at his friend. "Why should I have to stand, no one else did?" He kept his seat.

"I want your belt. That there buckle is part gold, part silver. I fancy it for my own!"

"Now, wait one minute!" hollered Charlie. "You want me to lose my pants besides an expensive E. A. Logan buckle?"

"Yup!" The conductor held out his hand.

Charlie whipped off his belt and flung it like one would use a rope on a runaway steer. The conductor lunged and the belt fell over his arm. Charlie's pants slipped and he grabbed for them. "You won't get away with this!"

"Fellas, I saw the initials CBI on this gent's underwear!" hooted the conductor. "Write that down, Mr. Reporter, for the *Denver Post*. C. B. Irwin lost his pants between Cheyenne and Evanston."

"How'd you know that man was C. B. Irwin?" shouted Wykert. "You know anyone else in this coach?"

"Does a dog sniff a tree?" hollered the brakeman, turning toward the vestibule, trying to hide his snickers.

Charlie was grinning. He could not hold his laughter in. His sides hurt. He called the two men back so that most everyone knew it had all been a practical joke. The rest of the early morning was spent sorting out gold rings, watches, money clips, and wallets. When everyone had their valuables back, there was a rousing applause as the pent-up emotion was let loose. Charlie was the champion prankster and no one would soon forget this train ride.

The train pulled into Evanston at six in the morning and the ground was white from snow flurries. Charlie looked up and down the depot platform for the final entrant. There were to be thirteen cold bloods and twelve hot bloods. Then Charlie saw the lean man, built like a jockey, riding his big-boned, smoky-brown bronc coming across the tracks. He went to the edge of the wooden platform. "You, Charles Workman!" he called. The horse stepped over the tracks and around the ties as if it were the natural thing to do. Its muscles seemed steel hard. This was the only horse entered in the race from Wyoming. Charlie liked it right away.

"I'm Workman and this is Teddy. We've walked from Cody to join you gents!"

Charlie's mouth fell open. It was three hundred miles from Cody to Evanston. He closed his mouth and nodded approval. He was suddenly pleased this man and horse were the sole entrants from Wyoming. Looks like a winner, he thought, and reached up to shake Workman's hand. He showed him where to take his horse for a rubdown and feed. He introduced Workman to some of the other entrants and said, "There's something in Wyoming's air that makes a man a man and a horse a horse!"

There was a rest period of two days in Evanston so that riders and horses could become acquainted. The townspeople did all they could to make the men comfortable and even entertained them with a band concert, baseball game, boxing match, barbecue, and a grand parade with Charlie Irwin in the lead in his black and silver Colburn.

At six A.M. on May thirtieth, inspection and roll call were complete. The horses were lined up across Front Street. Wyoming's governor read the racing rules and called, "On your mark! Get set! Go!" The horses and their riders loped off on the five-hundred-mile trek to Denver amid shouting and shotgun firing. At the edge of town Teddy began to buck. Three times Workman brought the horse into line with some well-placed flicks of a quirt. Finally they were off, trailing the other riders.

Charlie and Floto climbed into the Colburn. Charlie drove past the business places facing the Union Pacific station until they were out among rolling hills and green dairy lands. Both men put on their leather caps and goggles. Floto wrote notes on a thick pad of lined paper and confided that he'd put money on Wykert and his horse, Sam.

"I'm going to put my money on Workman," said Charlie.

They crossed the Green River on a pole bridge at Black's Fork and were surrounded by sagebrush flats. It was forty-seven miles to Carter, the first checking station. Charlie and Floto sat in the Colburn arguing who'd come in first. It was Workman. The next checking station was Granger. Workman was first at four in the afternoon. Charlie smiled and waved his cap. Eight minutes later Jack Smith and Charlie Trew came in joking together. The horses were taken care of at the local livery and the men had a light meal with Charlie and Floto. Floto noted for his paper that each rider drank two glasses of milk, then they were on horseback again. One of the riders conceded that he was out of his range and pulled out of the race.

"Wykert's not pushing. He's saving the speed for the end," said Floto.

"That's an opinion. You have to write facts for your newspaper," said Charlie.

Otto C. Floto was a former bill poster and saloon man. He was an internationally known authority on boxing and wrestling and a small-circus owner. He hung on to the side of the Colburn when Charlie drove across a railroad bridge. "This is worse than a galloping horse!" he yelled.

"Hang on to your teeth!" called Charlie, gunning the four-wheeled monster in a series of tiny hops that seemed to shake every bone and every bolt.

"If a train comes we'll both check out! I think I hear one coming!" Floto could not relax until they thundered over the last tie and kicked up bits of cinders from under the tires.

Charlie grinned and enjoyed every minute. He stopped to inspect tires and underpinnings and was satisfied everything was as good as new. He spied a scorpion coming across the road, cranked the car in a hurry, and climbed inside. Floto made a sketch of Castle Rock rising a thousand feet above the Green River. Charlie heard the magpies talk to one another from the greasewood and mesquite.

At the Green River station Jack Smith's horse had cramps and colic. The inspection officials agreed that the horse should not go on. Workman, Trew, Charlie, and Floto slept at Green River and started out early in the morning.

During the day the heat was fierce and the constant wind blew dust and grit into their faces. Charlie carried cans of water, which he left at intervals along the race route through the desert. Each time he stopped, Floto got out and wiped the dust from the windshield.

"I hope this grit stays out of the pistons and thingamabobs in the gasoline carriage," said Floto. "I'd hate for your machine to die and leave me with no phone line to my newspaper. This race is being followed by fans all over the country, probably Europe, too."

The days were hot, but the nights near freezing. Charlie worried about keeping gasoline in the Colburn. In Rock Springs he bought two extra cans of gas and put them on the floor of the backseat. The two men turned their backs to the wind and ate lunch sitting on the running board. Perspiration gathered and trickled down the furrow of their backs. Charlie sang "Alfalfa Hay."

"I wish I'd never volunteered to cover this race," said Floto.

"It's a chance of a lifetime," said Charlie. "This race will go down in history. I don't want to miss a thing in my lifetime."

"Stop!" yelled Floto. He got out of the Colburn and ran to the front. He picked up a big rock and slid half under the radiator.

Charlie sat up straight. "Don't slam that rock against my automobile!"

"I gotta have water! All the cans are back alongside the road! I'll perish without water!" cried Floto.

"It's the hot sun and ham in the sandwiches." Charlie was out of the Colburn and grabbing at Floto's feet to pull him away from the automobile. "Radiator water'll kill you! I'll kill you if you make a hole! Get ahold of yourself!" Charlie left Floto in the middle of the gravel road and ran back to the Colburn. In a minute he was back. "Here drink this." He handed his friend a half empty jar of tomatoes. "At least we know what's in that juice." He helped Floto to his feet. Floto began to laugh, splashing tomato juice with every step. "By God, C.B., this is real life!"

"I wouldn't miss it!" cried Charlie. "Now, write for the *Denver Post* how I saved you from dying of thirst. Etta will get a boot out of reading that piece about her canned tomatoes."

Float groaned, wiped his face and shirt with his handkerchief, and climbed back inside the Colburn. He was quiet for the next couple of days as he wrote copious notes, not only about the condition of the men and horses at every checkpoint but also about the weather and land through the Red Desert.

At Bitter Creek, Charlie noticed Trew's thoroughbred suffered from bruised feet. No one at the checkpoint said anything about it. Charlie could tell Trew was worried. "Come on," he said, "we'll go to the livery for some pine tar, swab those hooves good, and wrap them with strips of leather and tie it all up with gunnysack."

Trew was skeptical. He asked the veterinarian at the checking station and was told there was nothing in the rules said such treatment was forbidden. Charlie found leather and tar and gunnysacks and gave the stable boy two silver dollars for all of it. They went to work making shoes for the horse, which was called Archie. "When these wear out, you ought to be in Cheyenne," said Charlie. "You'll be out of the rocky country by then."

"Thanks heaps," said Trew, riding off on his prancing Archie.

"I thought you bet on Workman," said Floto, scratching his head.

"The man and horse needed help," said Charlie. "Are you watching Wykert? He's pushing his blue roan and it's taking the push like it's born to race."

"I told you he was a winner!" gloated Floto.

They filled more water cans at Barrel Springs Station, which was no more than a wide spot in the road where a fifty-gallon whisky barrel was set in the ground around the ice-cold, sweet spring water. Around the spring were gray weathered relics of old wagons from another age and under the surface dust were Indian spear points. The morning sunlight made the Red Desert hills and gullies change colors depending on what direction the automobile headed. By mid-morning the Colburn was in Wamsutter, which marked the end of the Red Desert. Four more horses were out of the race.

Floto wanted to hang around Wamsutter to talk to the racers as they came in one by one. Next morning nearly everyone in town was out to wave the remaining racers on and wish them good luck. Charlie and Floto ate a big breakfast, letting the men on horseback get a good start, as this was the gradual approach to the Continental Divide. Not far out of town Charlie stopped the Colburn, rolled up the canvas top, to wait out the driving hailstorm.

Here the Divide came so gradually that neither man could tell where the highest point lay. Coming down on the eastern side they saw a long line of broken hills and outcrops of gray sandstone and curved stone fences erected long ago to hide hunters of antelope so they could shoot arrows at close range. By noon Charlie and Floto were talking to Workman in Rawlins. Workman said he'd lost the road during the hailstorm. "I followed the railroad tracks until I hit the road again. Shucks, I didn't lose more'n, a couple hours. My horse wasn't worried at all." He never admitted thirst, hunger, or fatigue. He tipped his hat and rode off.

"The man is driven by an invisible motor," said Charlie.

"I can't put that in the paper. I have to print what I see," said Floto. "What I'm going to say to the boss in Denver is that the racers are strung over fifty miles of the course."

"Be sure to add that coming last at a leisurely pace is your favorite man, Dode Wykert. Not pushing his horse, but not letting up."

"I can tell you admire that man even if he is from Colorado. He knows how to pace his horse," said Floto, writing as he talked.

In Elmo a track walker said that some ditch rider in gum boots deliberately gave Workman wrong directions for the race route. "Someone wants the man from Wyoming out of the race," said the U.P. track walker.

"Why?" asked Charlie.

"Maybe someone's got big money laid on one of the other men, like someone from Colorado. Where's the *Denver Post* located?"

"Hey! I resent that!" yelled Floto. He reached for the door handle.

Charlie held him back and said between clenched teeth, "Don't raise cain. The fellow just gave you information. Write it in your report." Charlie tipped his goggles to the track walker and drove on. "Snow gets deep around here. In winter trains are held up two, three days," said Charlie to calm Floto. "Someone ought to build snowsheds over the tracks. I'll tell headquarters about my idea."

On the fifth day they were in Medicine Bow. The riders stood around the checking station shaking hands and wishing each other "the best of luck," then they rode out together.

"See you all in Laramie!" Floto shouted. Charlie squeezed the air horn. They stayed behind to have a good night's sleep.

Wykert made Medicine Bow by mid-morning. He didn't seem disturbed that he was several dozen miles behind the others. "Maybe I'll take a nap on the prairie tonight, but it'll be short. I'll catch up in Laramie," he said.

"Hope he's right," said Floto. "I'm betting on him."

They followed the horses past the Never Summer Range, Rock River, Lookout and Copper Lake, crossed the Laramie River and added water to the Colburn's radiator in Bosler, and gasoline to its tank. Charlie bought a loaf of bread and a quart of milk.

"Don't drink all the milk!" cried Floto with his mouth full of bread. "I gotta wash this down." He took several gulps. "Reminds me of when I was a kid and I ate bread and milk. Always put sugar on it."

They hit Laramie at sunset. They were tired and went right to the hotel. Charlie could well imagine how tired the horseback riders and their horses were. Wykert had not caught up by morning and now no one believed that he would be in time to leave with the crowd. But when they were all finished with breakfast, Wykert was waiting.

Charlie noticed a subtle change. None of the riders was smiling. No one yelled, "Hello stranger!" When they mounted their horses, no one trotted around to shake the others' hands. When they left Laramie none of the riders waved at Charlie and Floto, not even Trew, whose horse's feet were still wrapped in leather strips, although the gunnysack was worn away. The riders did not stay in a bunch and talk for the first mile or so. Each man rode alone, watching his own horse and setting his own pace.

Charlie and Floto passed the riders near Tie Siding. Charlie tooted the horn, but the riders kept their eyes down and ignored the men in the Colburn.

Charlie began to again feel a twinge of excitement as they neared Cheyenne with red, white, and blue bunting along the streets. To his surprise Wykert came into town first, escorted by the governor. The sheriff escorted the next rider, who was Workman, looking about played out.

Charlie waved to Senator Warren, who was on a horse. "What do you think of the endurance these men and horses are showing?"

"Unbelievable," said Warren.

Floto left the automobile and went to the checking station to find that there were four broncs and one thoroughbred still in the race. He tried to interview the men as they came in. None wanted to say much, nor speculate which horse was in the best shape.

The racing officials made arrangements for local horsemen and Charlie's Colburn to escort the riders all the way to Denver. Workman asked Charlie to see that he was awake by midnight so he could be on his way. "Six hours' rest ought to leave Teddy and me fresh as bridegrooms."

"You can't see the road at night without a full moon," objected Charlie. "You'll lose your way again."

"I'll see it," said Workman.

Not long after midnight Workman was riding Teddy out of Cheyenne. Charlie and Floto were up pacing him with the Colburn. Etta had tried to keep them resting at the house until dawn, but the two men would not admit they were as tired as they looked. A mile out of Cheyenne, Charlie handed Floto a huge sack.

"What's this?" he asked.

"It's flour," said Charlie. "Lean out the window and sift it on the road. We're going to ride ahead of Workman and leave a trail he can see in this pitch dark. Don't worry, it'll help the others, too."

At Ault a huge bonfire lighted the Section Road. Workman arrived first. Rollo Means on Jay Bird was second and Wykert on Sam was third. Someone pushed coffee and sandwiches at Wykert and said, "Beat the son of a gun from Wyoming!" The reception was the same at Eaton, since Wykert had lived in that area for much of his life.

In Greeley the horse ridden by Means was so spent it sank to the ground the minute it stood still. The veterinarian took it out of the race.

Coming out of Brighton, Charlie noticed that the two front riders were slowing down, walking their horses. He mentioned the fact to Floto. "You're right! It's Workman and Wykert side by side! That's the only way to save the lives of their horses!"

"It's going to end in a tie," said Charlie. "They're both winners."

Charlie nearly jumped out of his automobile when he drove outside of Denver, where sticks of dynamite were set off to indicate the racers were on their way. It was two o'clock in the morning.

Five miles from the edge of town the two front contestants ran beside their horses. Charlie could see they were going on nothing but willpower. Suddenly Wykert mounted Sam and attempted to pass Workman, knocking him off his feet. Workman scrambled up. Wykert crossed the finish line first at 2:33 A.M. Workman came running in, leading his horse a close second later.

The judges ruled that Wykert pushed Workman down. Because he had failed to act in a gentlemanly manner the Great Endurance Race ended in a tie for first place. Twenty-five thousand people shouted their congratulations.

Charlie wanted to shout about the great amount of strength in these two men and their horses. He wanted to put his arms around both men and tell them he was proud to have witnessed such a race with more stamina than he thought existed.

Floto had his arm around Charlie hollering in his ear. "You called the finish way back there! How'd you know the judges would see it the same way? Double champions, two men, two horses, both Western broncs!"

Charlie grinned. "Otto, you know I don't drink! But you buy something and let me have a sip!"

At home with Etta, Charlie mused about waiting hours for the men on horseback to come into the various checking stations. Charlie guessed that he could have made the five hundred twenty-three miles by automobile in two and a half to three days. It had taken the fastest Western broncs seven days.

Etta grinned and said, "With time and man's creativity, distance may shrink faster than a pair of wool socks in hot water."

TWENTY-SEVEN

Roy Kivett

This was a happy family with Charlie the acknowledged titular head of the entire Y6 spread. It seemed that no matter how much Charlie worked or exercised, he continued slowly to gain girth around his middle. Some say that he suffered a thyroid disorder; others say it was a love of good food. No matter what, his energy continued. He got up at four-thirty every morning, winter and summer. He worked with his horses on the Four Mile pasture. In winter he was in his U.P. office every morning at 8 A.M. He saw to it that Will and the cattle were making a good profit. He worried about Will's drinking and told Will that if he didn't stop, he'd give the monthly paycheck to Margaret.

Old Joe wouldn't give up the blacksmith work to a younger man. He made a plate to hold the battery firm in Charlie's Colburn as it bounced over the deep dirt ruts and graveled wagon roads.

Etta, with her delicate beauty, love of nature, gentle spirit, endless patience, and deep understanding, was a leveling agent for the Irwins. Her days were busy to overflowing with children and the guests Charlie brought to the ranch in summer or to the house in town in winter. Everyone loved her. She was reserved, yet she had wit and charm. She was a good listener, but when she spoke she went right to the point. She was the perfect mate for her self-confident, jolly, gentle, strict husband. The meals she served were simple but bountiful, making up in plain fun, bubbly conversation for the absence of intoxicating drink. There were a few guests who were boorish enough to ask for drinks, but quietly and unobtrusively Etta explained that Charlie didn't imbibe in alcoholic spirits, therefore, there was none to be had in his house.

In later years this policy changed. Charlie stored good liquors from Mexico in the cellar of the ranch house for guests who liked a little nip before supper or before retiring. Charlie was always the perfect host. Once in a while Charlie would light a cigar along with a guest, but after a few moments he'd lay it down. Whenever a friend offered him a cigar, he took it out of courtesy to his friend. His favorite expression to his hired hands was, "The man who doesn't smoke can have his horse saddled, his breakfast eaten, and be three miles down the road, while the man who smokes is rolling his cigarettes, finishing his breakfast, and taking his time. That man never gets caught up. Remember this, never eat breakfast too long, 'cause there's always someone who wants to nail your boots to the floor."

When the children were young, their life was not different from the lives of other Wyoming ranch children. They lived in town to attend school in fall and winter; in spring and summer there were ranch chores and roundups and preparation for Wild West shows and local rodeos. No one viewed such a life as filled with romance or adventure. It was the same for Roy Kivett, a skinny scrap of a boy about seven years old that Charlie had found living by his wits along the Union Pacific Railroad in Salt Lake City. Charlie brought the homeless boy to the Y6 and raised him right along with his own children. When Charlie taught Floyd and Roy to skin out a cow, he also had the three girls beside him. Frances and Roy were hardly old enough to hold a butcher knife. "Look here," he said, "you never know what your circumstances will be. You might have to do this one day when you're alone, just to survive. Better to learn now the easy way, than later and make a mess of it."

When all the children, except Roy, came down with measles, Charlie took him to Albuquerque with the Wild West show. On the way home they changed trains in Denver. Charlie took his Colburn from one of the boxcars, put aviator caps and goggles on Roy and himself, and announced to all those standing around the depot that they were going to break the last record of two hours and twenty-five minutes for an automobile to go from Denver to

Cheyenne. Charlie and Roy made the one-hundred-eight-mile trip in two hours and five minutes, easily breaking the record. The local paper carried this line:

> He is a record breaker, Charlie is, whether it's a hoss or an auto, it must have the speed and the bottom to it or it's no good.*

Roy never let Charlie out of his sight when they were together. This big, exciting man was everything and more that the boy had dreamed of for a father.

Charlie scolded any child who went out for a horseback ride and did not carry a small hammer, nails, string, and wire cutters. "If I ever catch you going out without material to mend fences or take care of a cow mired in a mud hole, I'll make you do kitchen duty for a week." Then he would teach the children a popular cowboy song, no matter if it were a bit ribald.

None of the children minded kitchen duty with Etta, however. She was even-tempered and taught them poetry or read to them from the classics or sang Baptist hymns as they worked. Etta was soothing.

Charlie was explosive. To be with him was to stay alert. There was no subject he could not talk about. It seemed there was nothing he did not know. He watched, listened, and learned constantly from everything and everybody around him. He told stories of cattle thieves, Indians, tracking deer, elk, brown bear, antelope, skinning out porcupine and badger, eating it roasted or raw.

Joe played checkers and cribbage with the children. The boys especially asked their Grandpa Joe to tell about the Civil War, the Spanish-American War, fighting Indians, and pioneers moving to the Far West. The girls begged for stories about their Grandma Mary and how she lived in a sod house.

The main ranch house was decorated with the heads of wild game on the walls, especially in Charlie's den. There were framed, original illustrations done by their old friend Charlie Russell and a more recent friend, who came to the Y6 for relaxation, Edwin Borein. The kitchen table and benches had been made by Joe.

The trunk at the foot of the huge bed where Charlie and Etta slept at the ranch was brought from Rochester, New York, when

*Courtesy Charles M. Bennett Collection, Scottsdale, Arizona.

Etta came west with her parents. The hall mirror, without a crack or mar, also came from Rochester and was sent to Etta by her sister, Kate, when their folks passed away.

The bearskin rug in the boys' room was from the animal that Charlie tracked for more than a month before he got near enough to shoot it. The bear came to the chicken yard and took one chicken each night for a dozen times. The horsehide on the floor of the girls' room was from one of Charlie's favorite workhorses. Once it had been wild in the Medicine Bow Range. In the cellar were saddles used by Charlie, Joe, or Floyd, or whoever was the ranch foreman. Several were elaborately tooled; they were prizes from county fairs and local rodeos won by members of the Irwin family. Everything in the ranch house seemed to have a story behind it.

The children loved the blacksmith shop with its hundreds of tools, cool, dark interior, sound of bellows, clanging of the anvil, and Joe's breathy whistling as he shod a horse. Inside this shed were more saddles and harnesses, bells, cinches, bright saddle blankets.

All the children learned to climb the cottonwood tree that stood with protective branches between the house and barn. When they were older and more daring, they climbed the cottonwoods that grew along the bank of Horse Creek. They all learned to swim in the wide place in the creek. Charlie took each child at the age of three or four and dropped him into the quiet, deep pool under the cottonwoods and overhanging willows.

Floyd learned immediately to paddle arms and legs toward the nearest shore, as though he'd learned the art of swimming in his bath as an infant. Joella and Pauline both sputtered each time they were dunked, but by the end of a summer they were shooting through the quiet water like a pair of pale frogs and laughing and shouting whenever Charlie caught them in his strong arms as they splashed past him. Frances learned as quickly as Floyd and told Charlie it was easy, just like Johnny Red Cloud had told her. "Breathe out slow and relax, then move your arms and kick like hell." Frances learned there were some words a lady did not repeat, unless she was prepared to taste the bitter, slippery yellow soap her mother made.

Roy was eight when he learned to swim. He stood on the bank and shivered until Charlie gently pushed him into the water. Charlie tried to show the skinny little boy how to keep his head up by treading water, but he seemed to possess lead in his head as his bottom came to the surface and his feet tread air. In desperation Charlie gave Roy to Floyd and the three girls one afternoon. "Don't come in for supper, not one of you, until Roy has gone across the creek at least three times by himself." Then Charlie stomped his big hulk back up to the barn to find something to keep him busy the rest of the afternoon.

Suppertime came and the children were not at the table. Charlie explained to Etta what he'd done.

"That poor, dear child!" she cried. "He's down there shivering and his lips are blue as grapes. You want those children to stay at the creek all night? It's cold at night, especially in a wet bathing suit."

"They'll learn it's the air that makes them cold and it feels warmer in the water," grumbled Charlie. "Honestly, I thought they'd be back by now."

"I'll go and check," suggested Etta, feeling almost naked herself without the children surrounding her and Charlie at the table.

"They'll be back any moment. Eat your supper. I'll help with the dishes." Charlie moved his chair so he could see out the window past the cottonwood a little better.

Before the dishes were done, Etta gave the dishcloth to Charlie and hurried down to the swimming hole to see what was keeping the children from coming home for supper.

Charlie heard her run up the back steps to the porch and come in letting the door slam. She was out of breath. Her eyes were wide. "Charlie! The kids are all up in trees and Two-Bits is chasing the coyotes away!"

Charlie's mind whirled. He instinctively reached for the Henry rifle on the wall by the back door. "Find the shells," he called, and ran down the steps holding the gun shoulder high and away from his body.

She found the box of shells in the pantry and put them in her apron pocket and ran after Charlie. "Buddy told me to bring you fast," she repeated several times, using her pet name for Floyd.

Floyd, Joella, and Frances were in the cottonwood on the barn side of the creek. Pauline and Roy were in a smaller cottonwood across the swimming hole.

"Why aren't you all on the same side of the creek?" hollered Charlie.

"Pa, we swum here and couldn't get back because Two-Bits was swimming back and forth to chase the coyotes away. Floyd yelled at us until we all climbed the trees. Then he told us not to move until you came to get us."

"I don't hear Two-Bits yapping anymore," said Floyd. "You

think he finished off those coyotes, or—"

"Come on down," said Etta. "Nothing is going to hurt you. Your pa has his rifle."

Floyd and Joella were down in a minute standing beside Charlie. Etta helped Frances jump from the last branch into her arms. The little girl's teeth were chattering and she snuggled in her mother's arms for warmth. Charlie took his shirt off and gave it to Joella.

"You three scoot up to the house and get some clothes on while we get the other two over to this side," said Charlie to the three shivering youngsters.

"You two all right?" called Etta.

"Yes, Ma," called Pauline. "We're coming down now. My leg's asleep."

"Rub it before you start down," said Etta. "Roy, are you coming?"

"Yes, dear." Roy called Etta by the name he'd heard Charlie use. "Here I come." Roy fell out of the tree with a thud.

"Oh, are you hurt?" called Etta.

"No, dear. My arms are a little stiff, that's all."

"The water's warm," said Charlie gently. "Get in and come on over here so you can get supper now."

"I can't," whimpered Pauline. "I cut my foot and it hurts when I walk."

"Swim, don't walk," said Charlie. "Hop to the edge and fall into the water."

"Yes, Pa," she said in a quivering voice.

Etta wanted to swim out and get both children in her arms and bring them back. Charlie blocked her. "They'll be all right. They have to learn to overcome everyday difficulties. Don't spoil them by helping," he whispered. "We're with them. They know that."

There was a splash and Pauline was thrashing the water and slowly moving toward Charlie and Etta. Etta had her apron off. She handed Charlie the box of shells, which he put in his pocket. As soon as Pauline came out of the water Etta put her apron around the child's shoulders. "Run to the house and get warm," she said.

"No, Ma, I can't," said the girl. Water ran from her hair in tiny rivulets that shone in the long slanting sunlight. "I have to wait for Roy. He has to swim over and back to make three times. He's only gone once."

"Oh, no," said Charlie under his breath. "Roy, come on over, just drop into the water, you'll almost float over. Come on, son, you can do it," he coaxed.

"I have a side ache," said Roy.

"Breathe deep, the side ache will go away," said Etta, breathing deep herself to show him how.

"If this water were ice I'd just slide across," said Roy. "If you throw me an ax, I'll chop a log that will fall acrost and I'll walk over."

"I can see you're brave and can think of some good solutions, but swimming is the easiest and faster than anything," said Charlie. "Come on, wade in and stretch out, kick your feet, you'll get here."

"I'm not afraid," said Roy, his voice sounding choky.

"We know that," said Charlie.

Etta was pulling and tugging something under her skirt. Her petticoat dropped around her feet. "I have an underskirt to wrap around you," she called.

"What if my side aches while I'm swimming?" he called.

"It won't," said Charlie. "Think about what biscuits and roast beef will taste like."

Charlie could see that Roy was crying, but trying to brush the tears away with his fists.

"Oh, don't c—" began Pauline.

"Oh, don't catch a fish as you come over," called Charlie. "We have plenty of meat for supper."

"I'm coming. Here I am in the water. Watch me!" Roy was splashing but his feet were not off the bottom. He was hopping on one foot, and suddenly he was thrashing like an eggbeater.

Charlie was on the edge of the bank calling encouragement. "Fine! Keep it up. You're moving fast. You've made it!"

Etta ran beside Roy and draped the cotton petticoat around his clammy shoulders.

Roy pushed the petticoat away. "Hold it, dear," he said to Etta. "I'm going to swim across the creek to show you I'm no chicken. What's for dessert?"

Etta was startled. "Tapioca, your favorite." Roy's body flashed in the last sunlight that filtered through the cottonwood's leaves, and thousands of water droplets flew out in a wide circle as his body hit the edge of the placid swimming hole. The splash drenched Charlie and Etta and mixed with the tears on Etta's face.

"My dear, he's going to try for three times—no, four, he has to come back. Jeems! The kid's changing for the better."

Pauline said, "I told you. Roy knows he has to do it." She snuggled close to Etta. "Ma, he's afraid. He doesn't like water."

Etta wiped her face with her petticoat. "He'll change. He'll be out here every day after this." Roy's arms moved out over his head and down through the water. He was swimming like Floyd had shown him over and over.

Charlie cupped his hands around his mouth and yelled, "Roy, turn and come back here. That's right. You're swimming for sure!" He turned to Etta, his face beaming. "Look how straight he keeps his legs. His arms come up and over. His head moves down and over. Perfect!" Charlie ran to the edge to grasp Roy's hand. His shoes were in the water.

Roy sputtered and coughed and wiped the water from his face. He panted breathlessly and jumped up and down. He couldn't stand still. Finally he said, "I did it, didn't I?"

Charlie clasped the boy to his thigh. "You're a swimmer all right! You're better than a trout. When we have swimming races some Sunday, you'll be a winner. Son of a gun. Here, wrap this around yourself," he handed Roy the petticoat, "then run up to the house with Pauline. Your supper's waiting. Mother and I want to watch the sun set."

"I did four laps. That means I can have two desserts!" called Roy. His feet ran over rocks and twigs, immune to the hurt.

"Two desserts!" called Etta, laying her head against Charlie's damp chest, letting tears slide down her cheeks. After a few moments she looked up. "Roy's become one of the family. Love makes the world go around."

Charlie lifted her off her feet and held her in his arms. He kissed her eyelids and her mouth before letting her feet touch the ground. "You are the most wonderful woman a man could have."

Etta kept her eyes on his face. They flashed in the last golden rays of sunshine. "Don't forget the wonderful children. Roy's one of them today. Love makes our world go around."

Charlie pulled Etta close. "My dear, it's change, not love, that makes the world go around. Love is what keeps it populated."

Next morning Charlie found the dog, Two-Bits, in a hollow bounded on two sides by green and red shale. Charlie's stomach pinched. He'd miss that old hound dog. The dog never had a chance with the coyotes, it was torn limb from limb. Gently he turned the bloody carcass over; he swallowed and held his breath. The dog's face was slashed and torn. One eye hung by dried tissue. The other eye was covered with ants so it looked like a black, quivery tumor. Charlie let his breath out with a gush. He was angry with the coyotes and at the same time he was overcome with gratefulness to the dog who'd lured the wolflike creatures away from his children. "You dumb dog! You gave your life for those kids! Oh, my, I can't even rub your ears and tell you thanks." Tears filled his eyes. He went back to the toolshed for a shovel and buried the dog in the hollow. He placed the colored shale in a mound over the top of the shallow grave so that the coyotes would not further destroy the dead dog.

By afternoon Charlie had enough courage to tell the children how Two-Bits had enticed the coyotes away from the swimming hole and had lost his life. Floyd turned his back and rubbed his fists into his eyes. "I hate coyotes," said Joella. "Me, too," said Pauline. "If one comes at me again, I'll pull its jaws apart with my bare hands," said Roy. Frances put her arms around Floyd's waist and sobbed. "Coyotes ate Two-Bits. Why?"

"It's instinct," said Floyd, giving his little sister his neckerchief to wipe her eyes. "They'd eat you or me."

Charlie explained that coyotes killed because they were hungry. "But they didn't touch you kids because you had sense enough to climb the cottonwoods."

"Oh, eecks!" cried Roy. "They're cannibals. They eat their own kind! Bullies!" He hopped around on one foot, then the other, and swung his fists in the air fighting the unseen enemy.

Charlie pulled Roy against his leg and told him to calm down and listen. "You used to go behind Etta's back into the pantry, stuff hunks of bread and bacon into your pockets. You knew it was wrong, but you remembered when you were hungry all the time. You were protecting against that terrible empty feeling." Roy relaxed. Charlie went on. "Same with those coyotes. They didn't eat all of Two-Bits, but they killed the dog as a protection against their starvation."

"That's sickening, Pa!" yelled Pauline. "Roy's not at all like a coyote!"

Charlie tried to make the children understand what he had in mind. "You can figure. That's an advantage over animals. You can figure ways to get around a coyote, to get rid of one. You can use your head."

"Two-Bits figured how to get those devils out of our hair. He was like us!" cried Roy.

"You kids stayed calm and figured out what the next move was going to be. You figured how to protect yourselves. That's the best kind of survival. Two-Bits got the coyotes in a hollow, then couldn't protect himself."

"Pa, we weren't calm and unafraid. We were screaming, scared to death. We ran around like crazy. Then all of a sudden I saw those pink tongues and yellow eyes coming closer and I knew Roy and Noonie wouldn't run fast enough, or they'd trip. There wasn't anything else to do. They had to shinny up a tree. I yelled and can't remember if I climbed first or last," said Floyd.

"Buddy yelled just like you, Pa. He sounded calm. We were so scared we did what he said. Only Noonie kept crying and Two-Bits was barking," said Pauline, who called Frances their "new little baby" when she was born. Pauline's words sounded more like "noodle baby," which was eventually shortened by the children to "Noonie."

"I wasn't crying. I hollered just like you," said Frances to her sister.

For the remainder of the summer Charlie and his foreman kept a continuous watch for coyotes around the ranch. They shot six and by fall, when no more came around, the men decided they had the entire pack or at least had scared the rest off.

Etta and Charlie gave their children the freedom to explore their surroundings and their emotions. They gave each child understanding, respect, and advice. They taught them respect for all people and wild creatures. They expected to get back integrity and honor. "Never equivocate," advised Charlie. "It is easier to tell the truth. Tell it right away. That is honorable. If you did wrong, take your punishment like a man."

"I'm never going to take anything like a man!" cried Joella, combing out her blond hair so that the breeze caught the ends and they looked like some exotic, filmy cobweb floating in the air.

Charlie put a hand over his mouth to cover a smile. "That's good. Hold up your head, stiffen your backbone, tell the truth at all times. Tell it without tears and no made-up excuses."

The small things Etta and Charlie both tended to overlook. They never discouraged the excursions that the children spontaneously took to gather collections of rocks with a band of quartz running through in beautiful patterns, butterflies, grasshoppers, or minnows in a bucket.

Clara Belle showed Floyd how to use a straight pin, running it through the insect's soft thorax and pinning it to the bottom of an empty cigar box for safe keeping and later admiration or study.

The Irwin children made collections of bird feathers, pressed flowers, and spent shotgun shells. They collected dried cow dung for battles between boys and girls or their cousins. The children defended one another, always remembering that Two-Bits had spent his life in their defense.

Charlie taught them not to be shoved around, walked on, or forgotten. "Stick up for what you know is right and what you believe in. Speak up. It's not a sin to be different. It's a sin not to do anything. It's not a sin to be wrong, but it's a sin not to correct that wrong. It's not a sin to be gentle or tender. It's a sin to hurt another human being because you fail to understand his situation. Never hurt anyone for money or personal gain. That is mean and shows a revengeful spirit. That's the way of a coward. Look for justice, not revenge."

Etta taught the children compassion and tolerance. She told them, "You can't build character and courage by taking away the other fellow's initiative." There were moments when she believed the children ignored her advice and followed some kind of barbaric code they had forged for themselves. But as they grew older she realized it was the children's way of protecting themselves against some of the more stringent demands of adults. Therefore, she tried to soften her expectations and see things from the child's perspective. "If you want to be somebody, never say that you can't do something."

Roy and Charlie were alike in some ways. Both put on a big show of being self-assured. With each it was only a front for their inadequacies. Etta understood them better than anyone. She knew that Charlie always regretted that he'd not completed high school. Roy regretted that he'd not had a proper bringing up until he came to live with Charlie and Etta. He also regretted that his last name was Kivett, not Irwin. Charlie and Roy were both more intelligent than most.

Charlie was mostly self-taught in the field of book learning. He knew more literature, Shakespeare, Chaucer, history, politics, and current events than most. He could carry on a conversation with anyone. Roy didn't have to read Shakespeare and Chaucer to learn human nature; he'd experienced the vagaries firsthand. Once he'd learned to read and attended school, he read and learned more about horses and automobiles than most youngsters his age. He tried hard to please. To him the worst sin would be for Etta and Charlie to find him a disappointment. Charlie also tried to please. He didn't want Etta or his children to find him lacking in strength, physical nor moral.

The summer Roy was nine Charlie took him to the Western

Festival in Encampment. Charlie was asked to furnish the livestock along with a couple buffalo and some cowboys for the program. Charlie talked Frank into going with a few of his racehorses and Floyd into going to demonstrate some trick riding.

The spur line ran twice a day from Walcott to Encampment. Since the U.P. had built that line, the little mining town of Encampment, Wyoming, was called the Pittsburgh of the West.

The copper bubble had burst. Copper went from twenty cents a pound to thirteen cents. Many of the little mining boomtowns were closing.

Charlie took two boxcars of livestock into Encampment. Floyd and Roy rode in the boxcars with the rest of the cowboys. Frank sat across from Charlie in the daycoach and said, "That there Roy's like a lightning rod. He draws trouble."

"He's like most any kid now that dreams of being a cowboy, owning a silver-trimmed saddle, riding a palomino, and joining a mounted posse." Roy was no longer a skinny little punk. He had bright blue eyes and dark hair that hung over his forehead. He'd developed a strong back and shoulders for his age, and he was still full of cussedness, which Charlie tried to overlook.

Roy pestered Frank into letting him ride in one of the horse races. When he didn't place, Frank said, "Get off my horse and take your sunny face somewhere else. I'll cool the horse out myself."

"Pa says sunshine makes a desert," said Roy, laughing, "and I'm not that dry."

"Ya, well, you've more smoke than a wet wood fire. Try racing one of those cow ponies. That's more your style."

Roy left Frank to watch Floyd take first in the cow-pony race. "I wanted to ride one of those ponies," said Roy. "You know I could."

"Sure, kid," said Floyd. "Why don't you show this crowd what you can do riding bareback?"

Floyd brought a little cream-colored pony out of the corral. Roy didn't hesitate climbing up and waving Floyd away. "Tell Pa to announce me, doing some trick riding!" he yelled.

Floyd laughed and let the youngster go.

Charlie saw Roy on the pony and called out in his booming voice, "Ladies and gentlemen, this is the youngest trick rider this side of the Mississippi and the other side also. Roy Kivett on Daredevil!" He waved his big Stetson hat. Roy smiled from ear to ear as the crowd of four thousand people, more than had ever been in the entire town, even in its booming days, cheered and applauded for the courageous, talented youngster who did tricks on a bareback horse like a Comanche Indian.

Charlie couldn't have been more pleased and told Roy, "Son, you keep that up and you'll be better than Floyd. I'll put you in a Wild West show."

"Gee, you mean it?"

"Sure as you're a foot high," said Charlie, who looked like a giant beside the boy.

"You know, I could ride one of them broncs and never let sky show between his back and my backside. Just let me at one of them buckers. I'll show you how good I am!"

"Oh, no! Not until you get a little more heft to your body," said Charlie. "You stay away from the broncs. Even Floyd don't ride them."

But before Charlie could say, "Get down from there!" Roy was up on the back of a snorting black bronc. He held on to the mane with his right hand and the stamping old Humdinger kicked open the corral gate and dived for the center of the arena. The cowboy tending the gate gasped and stared open-mouthed.

Floyd closed his eyes and said out loud, "My Lord, that kid'll kill himself and Pa will kill me deader than a can of corned beef if I don't get him off old Humdinger." He opened his eyes and saw his father in the arena on his big white horse. Floyd grabbed one of the assistant's horses. Two of the assistants were dressed as clowns, and their job was to divert a horse from a man that had fallen to the ground. "That's my kid brother!" yelled Floyd.

Charlie motioned for him to come slowly. Humdinger kicked its front legs and kept its head down. Roy bounced all over the back of the animal. His right hand held tight to the mane, his mouth was open as if he were yelling, but no sound came out, his face was white as lime dust. Charlie and Floyd tried to get on either side of the bronc, to pen it in so that it would stop sunfishing long enough for them to get Roy off its back before he fell to the ground and was trampled. Floyd jerked at the youngster and pulled him over in front of him on the saddle. Then between the two horses the bronc was led back to the corral.

The crowd was hushed and on its feet. Roy looked at the grandstand and waved his hand. The crowd exploded into one long whoop, then *kiyi*ed and hollered for the brave youngster who'd dared to ride the notorious bronc. Roy stretched out and waved with both hands.

"Sit tight!" hissed Floyd.

Roy bent low before the crowd in a bow on one side, then the other.

"You brat! The cinch on this saddle won't hold and we'll both end up in the dirt. Sit still, you dumb bunny!" Floyd tried to put one arm around Roy to keep him from throwing his weight over the side of the horse in another bow; as he did so the horse turned and the saddle swung downward. Floyd kicked his toes from the stirrups and landed in the dirt on his back. He clutched Roy to his chest to soften the blow for him. The horse straddled the two boys then walked away following the antics of the two clowns that led it over to the side and to one of the corral gates.

Roy rolled over and found Floyd knocked out cold. "Buddy, wake up!" he yelled, and pounded on Floyd's chest with both fists, tears streaming down his eyes. Charlie pulled Roy away. Floyd was carried on a blanket, one cowboy at each corner, to the first-aid station under the flimsy grandstand.

Charlie saw what Floyd had done and approved. When Floyd was conscious, he found it painful on the right side under his arm to breathe. "Probably cracked a rib. Possibly Roy did that to you when he beat on you like you were some rawhide drum."

"Spank him," said Floyd with a wince, putting his hand on his hurting side.

"You just shut your mouth, Buddy," said Roy. "I rode as well as anyone. I didn't fall off Humdinger, did I?"

"No," said Charlie, "but in another thirty seconds you would have and your brains would be scrambled with dust."

Later Floyd sat on the rickety bleachers resting, watching the show, talking with Roy. "You don't tie your boot laces right. Here, let me show you."

"Yeah! I can take care of them myself. They stay put, don't they? You just think you're smart because your name is Irwin. Boots, Buddy, Floyd Leslie Irwin!"

"Is that your big pain? You want to be called Irwin?"

"Who wouldn't!" said the boy, looking longingly at Floyd with eyes as blue as robins' eggs. "The Irwins and their horses carry off practically all of the prizes in all the rodeos and Wild West shows."

"Why don't you tell Pa your gripe. He'll understand how you feel," said Floyd, breathing deeply to see how much air he could take before his side hurt. "Roy Kivett Irwin—doesn't sound too bad, not bad for a shrimp like you. Roy K. Irwin!"

"Shut up!" screamed Roy. "You don't have to tell the world until I see how the old man feels."

"Don't you call Pa an old man," advised Floyd.

Charlie took top prize in the roping contest, Hugh Clark was second, and Frank third. During the bucking contest Hugh Clark found it difficult to stay on his mount, Sabile, a tall sorrel. The horse began to plunge and took directions from the horse Roy had ridden, that is, kept its head down. Before Clark could get himself tight in the seat, he was tossed in a graceful loop over the sorrel's head. Luckily he was not hurt. First prize went to Frank Wilcox, who rode Steamboat but was eventually bucked off. Second prize went to Louis Guntz, who rode one of the Irwin broncs called Black Knight, and was eventually thrown to the ground in forty-five seconds.

The trio of Hugh Clark and Frank and Charlie Irwin won the potato race.

In the evening there was a prizefight between Kid Gilson of Denver and Charles Williams of Encampment. The ring was a wooden platform built outdoors with a rope waist-high all around. Williams was knocked down three times in the third round, and the referee stopped the fight. The decision went to Gilson.

For a week afterward Roy went around the ranch with his fists doubled and in front of his chest as he danced before an imaginary opponent. Finally Charlie took him by surprise and popped him gently in the solar plexus.

"Ooofff!" said Roy as he sank to his knees. "I didn't expect you to do that. I was just bluffing. I thought any old man'd know that, fatso!"

"Don't you ever call me an old man nor fatso again!" said Charlie emphatically. "If I even hear you said those words behind my back, you'll get more than the wind knocked out of you. I'll kick your tail until your nose bleeds. Understand? You call me Pa or Mr. Irwin, because that's my name. Do I go around calling you a rat face?"

Roy looked sheepish and hurt. "No, sir, Pa. I'd knock your block off if you did."

"Well, that's exactly what you looked like to me the day I asked you to be part of my family."

Roy stared straight ahead. His breathing was settling down, so he dared to raise his blue eyes. "Mr. Irwin—Pa. I've been thinking."

"I'm not sure if that's good or bad," said Charlie, smiling. He helped Roy to his feet. "Come on, let's sit on the side of the water trough and you tell me what you think."

Roy hesitated, looked up at Charlie, then thought it best to blurt his thoughts quickly and wait for the worst. "I'd like for you to say I was part of your family, not just act like it."

"Didn't I just do that?"

"No, you don't call me Irwin. I want to be Roy Kivett Irwin."

That took Charlie by surprise. Charlie thought, This poor tyke doesn't even know who he is. Jeems, it's hard to grow up, especially when you get a bum start.

"Pa, I'm not bluffing," said Roy.

"I know. Life's like poker. When you find out you're bluffing into a pat hand, you quit bluffing. So, from this day forward, you'll be Roy Kivett Irwin."

Roy's face shone, then darkened. "How'll I know?"

Charlie thought fast. "Today you'll have to take my word for it. But when you see the program for the Frontier Days celebration, it will read: 'Roy Kivett Irwin, trick and fancy riding.'"

"Thanks, Pa!" Roy grabbed Charlie around the waist as far as he could reach and hugged.

Charlie felt a wonderful tingling go up his spine, making his mouth turn into a huge grin. He put his hands on the boy's shoulders. "That's the way it should be, son," he said, brushing the hair away from the boy's eyes. "Say, you think you got enough hair in your eyes, you can see almost nothing? How about getting Etta to cut that hair sometime today?"

"You'd let a woman cut your hair?"

"Yep. And she does a fine job. Can't you tell?"

"Yep. I sure can. I'll tell her to do mine." Roy was smiling.

"Ask her if she will, son. Don't tell anyone to do anything. Makes 'em get their back up quicker'n lightning. Especially if they are female."

Roy nodded and bolted off for the ranch house. Charlie felt good. After Frontier Days I ought to take that kid target practicing, he thought. He could learn to shoot the old Henry.

Not long after that when Charlie was at his U.P. office, Richardson told him about a meeting to be held in Saratoga. "All the bigwigs are coming, and some prospective customers for the railroad."

The lodge at the mineral springs had been reserved for this meeting with Carl Gray, president of the Union Pacific; S. R. Toucey, superintendent; Charles Ware, general manager; and meat packers, Swift and Armour; coal seller, Updike; the department store owner, Brandeis; and others who had seldom shipped goods on the railroad.

"You and I are going," Richardson went on, "to discuss the possibility of shipping more meat, either packed in airtight cans or in refrigerated cars. There has to be a better way for shipping beef, mutton, and lamb than on the hoof. We'll talk about shipping raw wool to a factory in Omaha, or make it into clean yarn first. That could mean a yarn factory in Saratoga."

The train came into Saratoga at four in the morning. By the time it was daylight most of the town knew that Charlie Irwin was there. A clipping from the local paper read in part:

> . . . when Charlie Irwin comes to town there's somethin' doin'. He's the boy who can give out more hearty handshakes, and more pleasant greetings, than any two-legged animal this side of the Continental Divide . . . He came in at 4 o'clock Saturday morning with a U.P. special, private car and diner accompanied by a gang of railroad officials and millionaires and at exactly ten minutes past 4 o'clock every man, woman, and child in the town knew that "Charlie" was here. And you can bet your last dollar that he don't have to go round to the back door for a handout in this town. He's "value received," he is; whether he had any "chips" in the game or not.*

About mid-morning Charlie gave the men at the meeting a surprise. He decided that the discussion and meeting was over as far as he was concerned. The men had talked over the important points and Charlie knew he could get more business for the railroad if he saw some of the local stockmen. He began to pass the word that all the sheepherders and cattlemen were invited to dinner at the Hot Mineral Springs Hotel. Then he went back to the hotel and told the cooks to prepare for another fifty to seventy-five more guests. Then he found Carl Gray and told him about his idea. "Invite the men that are going to give the railroad all their business. They'll think there's no other railroad as good at the U.P.," said Charlie.

"I like your idea," said Gray, pushing his glasses up on his nose, "but it's too late to put it into action. Believe me, if I'd thought of this earlier we'd have all those sheep men at our sup-

*Courtesy Charles M. Bennett Collection, Scottsdale, Arizona.

per table tonight. Their thoughts would be most helpful."

"I knew you'd feel that way," said Charlie. "You'll meet with those men tonight, sir."

Gray's face turned white. "But the cooks aren't prepared to feed such a large crowd."

"The kitchen help's getting in more food right now. It's all taken care of. Don't worry about a thing. Your name will be linked with the U.P. forever and this will be one of the outstanding events in that link."

At first Gray was angry that Charlie had taken the meeting into his own hands, but later he came to thank Charlie for his foresight and quick thinking. Charlie meant no offense. His mind was quick. He saw no reason to sit around waiting for things to happen by themselves.

In 1908 the Frontier Days celebration was moved from Pioneer Park, between Cosgriff and Twenty-eighth, to a new park on city property, a mile north of town, that was much larger and had more modern physical facilities. This was called Frontier Park and cost twenty thousand dollars. The grandstand had a roof and was double-decked, with a seating capacity of twenty-eight hundred persons, private seating for nine hundred, and bleachers for four thousand. An electric trolley was built with a spur going to Frontier Park. Charlie moved his two boxcars to the new park and not only supplied the stock and many of the cowboy participants, but he entered his Colburn in the two-hundred-mile automobile race. The race was held on a new five-mile track built for motorcycle and auto racing. The other automobiles that participated were a Stanley Steamer, National, Buick, Thomas Flyer, Hupmobile, and Apperson Jack Rabbit. The Jack Rabbit won in two hours, fifty-eight minutes, and twenty-eight seconds.

Clayton Danks, Charlie's foreman, won the bronc riders' contest riding Steamboat without spurs. Spurs were outlawed by order of the Humane Society. Charlie saddled a buffalo and asked for volunteers to ride it, offering anyone fifty dollars if he'd stay on longer than sixty seconds. This became one of the popular events in future Frontier Days and a real challenge to the cowboys. Roy's name appeared in the program like Charlie had promised, and Roy had the crowd on their feet applauding wildly after his trick riding performance.

That fall Charlie made a shooting range alongside the hollow where Two-Bits was buried. He got half a dozen bales of hay and stacked two together, three bales high. Joella opened up a cardboard box and drew a huge bull's-eye in the center with red and white paint. After a couple weeks' practice Charlie let Roy shoot right along with the cowboys on Sundays. At first Roy was teased, but soon there were good wagers made on his ability to hit the center. When no one was around, Roy dug through the hay and dirt for the brass castings. He used them for whistles by blowing gently across the top.

When Floyd was fifteen he became interested in the racehorses his Uncle Frank trained. Frank raced in Denver and Oklahoma City for three furlongs (one furlong was one eighth of a mile) or half a mile with quarter horses or non-thoroughbreds. Thoroughbreds were not barred during that time, but there were not many of them that competed in the short distances. Frank and Charlie jointly owned a good quarter horse, called Sam F., which they entered in the quarter mile, three furlongs, and half a mile.

While at the Wild West shows with his stock Charlie began to look around for good sprinters. When they were his, he shipped them to the Y6 and Frank bred them to the thoroughbred sires. Charlie felt this would keep Frank off the bottle and in shape as a jockey. He had no inkling that he himself would ever be in the racing business where the big money lay.

These were the years the farmers and lumbermen in Wyoming and Colorado talked not of the hot summer or hard winter but of the pine bark beetle. The entire Northwest seemed to be infested with this insect. The best way to destroy this killer of pine trees was to remove the bark of an infested tree to kill the larvae by exposure to air. Charlie suggested to the Wyoming farmers to scorch the bark of infested trees before the insect girdled it. Mild scorching saved about half the trees.

The adult beetle entered the bark, made long narrow tunnels in the living inner bark, and laid eggs. The eggs hatched into grubs that ate the cambium layer. By the following year the needles turned brown and the tree was dead.

A blacksmith in Berwin, Nebraska, went up in his homemade balloon, which flipped over at three thousand feet, dropping the man five hundred and fifty miles east of Berwin.

"Blacksmiths weren't meant to fly through the air," said Joe when he read the paper.

In the same newspaper was an account of President Theodore Roosevelt completing a ninety-eight-mile, seventeen-hour ride by horseback from the White House, which he called the bully pulpit, to Warrenton, Virginia, and back to prove it wasn't unreasonable to require Army officers to make a ninety-eight-mile ride in three days as a test of physical fitness. He'd ordered all officers to make a similar ride if they wished to retain their rank.

"That man doesn't want his life in a narrow track," said Joe to Etta. "He's like Charlie. They both believe life's not meant to be an oyster. When any living thing stops growing it dies. They're always growing, in girth and intellect. I'm not sure either one wants to make a lot of money, which is the great cause for so many men these days. Teddy Roosevelt and our Charlie want something else; I think it's glory."

"Glory?" repeated Etta. "That's a new thought to me. And you can bet I'd never have thought to compare Charlie with the President of our country." She laughed and put her arms around Joe, who was white-haired and slightly stoop-shouldered from spending so many years over the anvil, striking red-hot iron.

That year the artificially colored teas from China were refused shipment into the United States. Also at the same time the inspectors of the pure food board of the Department of Agriculture found horse meat being sold as beef.

All ranchers, like Charlie, who sold good beef, were greatly upset with this vile practice because horse meat always undersold the beef. Charlie was elated when he read in the *Chicago Daily Farmers and Drovers Journal* that the selling of horse meat for human consumption was finally outlawed.

TWENTY-EIGHT

Grandpa Rick

That summer the new president William Howard Taft came to the Frontier Days celebration. He ate supper at the Irwin cookhouse and told Charlie, "It's the real thing, next to living in the Old West. It's the best I ever saw." Taft was a man not as tall as Charlie but just as broad of shoulder. His brown hair was thinning, and his thick eyebrows and handlebar mustache were strawlike. His hands were as wide as a tin for panning gold. His feet were small for a man his size, making him look sodden, as if he didn't take much exercise and ate too much.

Charlie offered to take the President to Albuquerque, New Mexico, for the cowboys' tournament. Taft refused, saying he had to help his friend Teddy Roosevelt campaign as leader of the Bull Moose party. Charlie took Frank and three of their race-horses, several bucking broncs, half a dozen steers, and Hugh McPhee, Duncan Clark, and Billy Wiley.

Frank was jockey and their horse, Billy Mason, broke the track record in the three-quarter mile race. Charlie took fourth in a forty-entry steer-roping contest and won a match from the champion roper of Arizona, winning two hundred dollars.

When Charlie was back in town, he settled Etta in the house in Cheyenne and saw the children all back in school, then he packed his grip and told Etta he was going to Rock Springs. Because he was Livestock Agent for the U.P., he was to oversee the Sweetwater County stockmen ship one hundred and fifty boxcars of cattle to the eastern markets. The shipment was a tremendous boost for the U.P. Railroad and all the credit went to Charlie Irwin. After the cattle were loaded, there was a short ceremony of recognition of the U.P. officials. Charlie was given a new wide-brimmed Stetson that was light-gray felt, with a rattlesnake skin band and a bullrider creased crown. He waved the hat high to show it off to the crowd, then gave a little talk. "I thank the U.P. officials who honored me with this beautiful gift. I'll get a lot of mileage out of a Stetson like this. I'll tell you something, these hats are made from the fur shaved off rabbits. The Stetson people need thousands of rabbits; they'll use French rabbits, Belgian rabbits, Australian rabbits, besides good American rabbits. It takes about eight ounces of fur to make one Stetson. That's about the size of a grapefruit. That ball of fur is shaped and stiffened with blasts of steam. Those steam jets beat any steam engine you've seen. Fur and steam are the chief ingredients that go into a fine hat like this. When it's shaped, it's buffed, powdered, sanded, dried, banded, decorated, and put into a hat box. Cowboys know just what kind of hat they want and they can work over a couple of dozen before one suits them. That's because a good hat'll last twenty-five years. Many a hat has fed water to a favorite horse and it's still tough as shoe leather. A Stetson is like a good woman, it gets better with age." Charlie put his new hat on his head and made sure it was at a slant low over his eyes and high in the back to keep it from blowing off. He waved as the crowd of U.P. officials and cattle ranchers applauded. No one had expected him to make a real speech. He'd surprised everyone with what he knew about the making of a Stetson.

When Charlie got back to the ranch he was surprised to find his father sitting at the kitchen table, picking his teeth while the blacksmith work piled up. "What's wrong, Pa?"

"Nothing, Charlie. Can't a man take the load off his feet without something being the matter?"

"You can tell me. I'm not going to blow my top just 'cause you aren't shoeing horses, making hinges, or sweeping out the shop. I can get one of the cowhands to do that. Something's worrying you. What is it?"

"Son, it's old man Rick, you know, old John, Margaret's pa. He was here visiting. He didn't look so good. He sits down after walking a dozen steps. He sleeps sitting up in that old stuffed leather chair on the back porch."

"Is Margaret worried about her pa?" asked Charlie.

"Son, she don't say much to me about it. But anyone can watch her around the old codger. She hovers over him like a fool mother hen."

"Margaret'll look after her pa. He's been living with her and Will for two, three years now. You think someone ought to go check on him before winter sets in, just to be sure he's all right?"

"Yep, that's what I'm thinking. If you could spare me for a few days, I'd like to go to Will's place over near Albin. There's not many of us old-timers left. It wouldn't hurt none if we looked in on each other. I have a hunch that old John come out here to see how I was doing, and it kind of set him back when he found out I was as spry as ever." Joe tapped his feet.

"Me and Etta and the kids are going to Overland Park in Denver this weekend. Duncan Clark can do the blacksmithing; you go on to Will's place. Take the wagon and a load of potatoes, some carrots and onions, too. Hey, when you come back, bring Will with you to help us thrash the wheat."

"Praise the Lord! You read my mind, son!" shouted Joe, running his fingers through his white beard. The beard was stained yellow at the sides where the chewing tobacco dribbled from the corners of Joe's mouth.

On Saturday morning at Overland Park, Charlie's three girls put on a magnificent program of rope twirling.

Charlie felt the tingling go down his shoulders and into his belly. He smiled. He was proud of his children. Suddenly he thought how much little Pauline looked like Etta. Even Floyd had a stance that reminded him of Etta. His eyes moved to the youngest, Frances. She didn't hold her head to one side like Etta. No, jeems! She was like himself. He glanced at Joella, her hand moved slightly along the rope; she was losing the rhythm. Charlie held his breath. No—she was all right. Joella looked so much like his sister, Ell, that it made him shiver. Funny, he thought, how families can never deny their members.

Then Floyd and Roy did a rope exhibition. Roy had become a real trooper and smiled all through his performance. They all wore red satin shirts with a white Y6 on the back.

Charlie brought Clayton Danks, Sam Scoville, and Elton Perry along to ride the broncs on Saturday and Sunday afternoon. Danks won first prize at the end of the celebration, which was five hundred dollars in gold dust for his bronco-busting rides. The same time the year before he'd been first at the Calgary Stampede in Canada. On Sunday, Scoville rode Steamboat and he could not stay on the leaping, twisting outlaw. It seemed no one could. Steamboat had become as well known as any of the Irwin Y6 cowboys. Steamboat was known as the star performer of their Wild West shows and rodeos. Elton Perry fell from his bucking horse, Two-Step, and hurt his leg. Charlie felt let down. He wanted his men to be top winners, but realistically he knew it could not always happen. When Charlie took cowboys from the Y6 to these Wild West shows, he paid their railroad fare (they usually rode in the stock cars), food, and entrance fees. Whatever they won they divided fifty-fifty with Charlie because it was his show and his stock they used. When Perry was hurt, Charlie passed his new broad-brimmed Stetson among the people in the grandstand and collected eighty-nine dollars for him. The doctor at the park felt the break, decided it was clean and sharp, so he wrapped the ankle with a strip of leather over two flat, thin three-inch-wide boards and told Perry to come to his office after the show on Sunday. The doctor gave Perry a pair of crutches and asked in exchange for half of Perry's part of the collection, twenty-two dollars and twenty-five cents.

When the last show was over Charlie helped his cowboys load up the horses. He'd taken Laura T. M. and Blumenthal with the thought of letting Frank and Floyd race them, but the races were postponed until the following weekend. Frank was disappointed and sore. He found a bottle of whiskey. Charlie exercised the two horses before taking them to the boxcar, where he reread a sign posted on a nearby tree trunk: HORSE RACING NEXT SATURDAY AFTERNOON. OVERLAND PARK. DENVER ELKS SPONSORS.

Suddenly he had an idea. He led the racers to a nearby livery.

"Mister, them horses yours?" asked the liveryman.

"Yes, sir," said Charlie.

"Say, if you don't mind me asking, how much you pay for that one?" He pointed to Laura T. M.

Charlie told and the man whistled. "Say, you could talk the socks off a banker if what you say is correct. I seen them horses run here at Overland, maybe a year ago. I never forget a horse. That one"—he pointed—"brought big money to Durnell and Gates in California. You gonna run 'em there?"

"Might," said Charlie. "For now I want you to keep 'em here with feed and water and a boy to exercise 'em every morning. I'll be back at the end of a week. Here's a five-dollar bill to begin with. You'll get more if you treat 'em right."

"Yes, sir!" The money was in the liveryman's pocket before Charlie could blink. "That's the prettiest matching pair I've seen in an age."

"Write these two in the Elks' Saturday races under the name of C. B. Irwin. I-R-W-I-N. Can you do that?"

"No problem. You got the entry fee, mister?"

Charlie gave the man another five-dollar bill. "I'll settle everything when I get back. Meanwhile, you got these two horses."

"Well, I swan! Thanks, mister." The liveryman whistled.

Charlie went back to the railroad siding across from the arena and park. He helped his cowboys load up the animals in the stock cars. He told Clayton Danks to make certain the animals had water. "The ride to Cheyenne ain't long. You and the men eat at the beanery, then go on to the ranch. Leave the animals at the Four-Mile pasture."

"What should we do with your brother? You want him to ride with the stock or in a daycoach?" asked Danks. "He's been drinking whiskey like a cowboy jilted by his best gal."

"Take him with you and don't let him lap up a thing, not even water. Get him to sleep it off. Jeems, he's worse than a stupid kid. Make sure he gets to his place on the ranch. Don't leave him to his own devices in Cheyenne."

"Mr. Irwin," Scoville interrupted, "ain't there supposed to be only two hands to a stock car? We got six men in here and more in the other."

"You boys got free rides to the doings in Denver," snapped Charlie. "Listen, I'm taking Mrs. Irwin and my kids to visit my sister in Colorado Springs a few days. You men take care of things at the Y6. You've got free rides to Cheyenne."

Perry hobbled past, laid his crutches inside the first boxcar, and hitched himself up and inside.

"Perry, throw away them crutches before I get back," said Charlie.

"Aw, Mr. Irwin . . ." started Perry. Charlie slammed the double doors of the stock car shut and walked away toward the depot, where he'd left Etta and the five youngsters.

"Are we gonna ride the caboose?" asked Roy.

"Son, we're going to take the southbound out of here for Colorado Springs," said Charlie, smiling at Etta. "Surprise, my dear. I think we need a few days' vacation."

His words had the effect he'd wished for. Etta opened her

mouth but could not speak at first. "We're going to see your sister? For real?"

"Yes, why not?" he said as calmly as possible. "I've been thinking that we are closer to her now than we are in Cheyenne. We ought to go south and see how the Miners are doing."

"We're going to see Aunt Ell!" squealed Joella with glee so the other children could hear.

"I remember Aunt Ell. The one that wears big hats with feathers and stuff," said Floyd. "She knows every kind of tea in the world and what kind of ache or pain it can cure."

"She some kind of lady doctor?" asked Roy.

"She doctors men, too," said Floyd emphatically.

Etta took the children into the beanery at the side of the Denver depot while waiting for the southbound U.P. "Vegetable soup with those round oyster crackers for the children and myself," she said. "Mr. Irwin will tell you what he wants."

"I want the roast beef sandwich with mashed potatoes and hot gravy," said Charlie.

"I'm so hungry my tapeworm near died," said Floyd, acting as though he were near fainting from his hunger.

"I'm so hungry my stomach thinks my throat's cut," said Roy, giggling because he said something that equaled Floyd's pronouncement on hunger.

"Boys, eat your soup. Cool it with the crackers. I believe I can hear our train coming into the station," said Etta, trying hard to eat the hot soup as quickly as possible.

"I don't hear anything," said Frances.

"Noonie, did you hear Ma? Close your mouth and eat!" ordered Joella, calling Frances by her baby name.

"I can still see the train with the yellow stock cars," said Pauline, her eyes round. "How can another train come in?"

"Eat and watch," said Charlie, cutting his roast beef with his knife in his right hand, fork in left, and like a Canadian he ate the first piece of meat from the fork in his left land. "The southbound will pull in on those tracks nearest us, next to the northbound. Here she comes, look at that steam!"

The train wheezed and chugged and tooted through billowing steam as it pulled to a stop. Etta finished her soup, stood up, and told Floyd and Joella to pick up the satchels and go out to stand beside the yellow daycoach with the red letters. She wiped the faces of the younger three children and sent them out to stand with the first two. She turned to Charlie, who was ordering coffee. "The train will not wait," she said softly.

"Dear, let me finish my supper," he said. "Enjoy your coffee."

The coffee was too hot to drink. Etta watched Charlie pour his coffee into the saucer to cool then drink it. She was much too fastidious to do such a thing herself. She stubbornly held her cup and saucer, gingerly putting her lips to the hot cup once in a while to test the temperature. The conductor came into the beanery and called "All aboard for Colorado Springs!"

Charlie paid the bill and motioned for Etta to finish her coffee. Her eyes went to the hot cup and back to Charlie, then back to the counter, where she wanted to place the cup and saucer.

A man, a total stranger, seated at the counter near Etta, said so that only she could hear, "Ma'am, you can have mine, it has been blowed and saucered." He passed his cup and saucer up to her and took hers in exchange. Gratefully she gulped it down, smiled, and hurried out the door beside Charlie.

Charlie helped Etta up the steps into the coach, then lifted the younger children up and waited for the others to scramble after the little ones. Charlie hesitated as the brakeman came by, then he himself bent over to inspect the tie rods. The brakeman laughed, "Say, I can always tell when I have a good blacksmith aboard. He always checks the welding. It'll hold, never worry about the U.P."

Charlie stood up, his face flushed. "C. B. Irwin." He held his hand out. "I'm the U.P. Livestock Agent." He gave the brakeman his card.

"Well, you going to be on this train for business?"

"I have the wife and family along," said Charlie, chortling. "This is mostly pleasure."

"Have a pleasant trip, Mr. Irwin. Does the conductor know you're on the train?"

"I don't suppose so," said Charlie.

"Hey, Bert!" called the brakeman. "This is the U.P.'s Livestock Agent. What'd you say your name was?"

"C. B. Irwin," said Charlie, shaking hands with the conductor. "Say, Bert, the wife and kids're on the daycoach. Looks crowded. 'Spose you can fix it so's we can all sit together?"

"Sure thing," said the conductor. "Follow me." He waved his signal to the engineer after he picked up the single step he'd placed on the wooden platform so it was easier to climb the train steps, then called a final "All aboard!" and swung up the steps. Charlie was directly behind him as the train lurched forward, creaking and rumbling and blowing steam with a long deep-throated *too-oot.* The conductor stepped in front of Charlie and closed the bottom half of the door across the back of the coach and put the yellow step stool down in front of the door. Charlie followed him through the open coach door, past the drinking fountain, its tank freshly filled with ice, past the rest rooms and smoking room, down the aisle to the red plush seat where Etta and Frances sat. There was a gray-haired gentleman in the seat behind Etta, and Roy sat beside him. The conductor talked to the gentleman and pointed to an unoccupied seat halfway up the coach on the opposite side where the other three children were headed. The man nodded, pulled his suitcase from under the seat, and moved up.

Charlie motioned for the three children to come back. The conductor flipped Etta's red velvet seat backward so that now there was a double seat for part of the family. The seat across the aisle was occupied by a thin man in a tan suit reading the newspaper with a magnifying glass. The conductor pointed to Floyd, still standing in the aisle, then to the man in the forward seat who had just moved. The man put the glass in his breast pocket, put his newspaper under one arm and his briefcase under the other, and moved forward. Floyd, Joella, and Roy hurried to the seat across from the double one. Roy managed to wiggle around the other two and sit by the window.

"There you are, Mr. Irwin. You and the missus will be comfortable and can keep an eye on the children," said the conductor. "We U.P. men take care of each other."

Charlie shook his hand, gave the conductor the tickets, and after they'd been punched, Charlie put the stubs in his hatband. "You go back to Cheyenne on the northbound train?" asked Charlie.

"That's my run, Colorado Springs to Cheyenne. I stay all night in one town then take the next train back, north one day, south the next," said the conductor.

"You take on ice, coal, and water in Denver?"

"Mostly ice and water. Sometimes I get sandwiches from the beanery. Folks get hungry riding the daycoach."

"How long you stop in Denver when you're heading north?" asked Charlie, squinting his eyes, thinking about the sign on the tree trunk.

"Oh, not long, 'bout thirty minutes."

"If you have to take on coal?"

"An hour at the most, then we're behind schedule."

"I see," said Charlie with a smile, crossing his hands in front of himself and lacing the fingers in a satisfied manner across his stomach.

Etta understood right away when Ell made an excuse for Les not being home. "He's so tied up with his bookkeeping. And now he's sent out of town. He'll hate to miss you," she said, motioning frantically with her hands behind her back. Etta saw, from the corner of her eye, a young fellow come out of the back bedroom with no shirt on, only the suspenders of his pants over his underwear. He nodded sleepily, went to the kitchen for a cup of tea, saying, "Three cheers, hon, you got some clover honey!"

"Who's that man?" asked Charlie.

"A—uh, a friend—a cousin—of Les's. His name's Marty. He's here to rest. He's a logger. Wants to set up a sawmill of his own."

"Les has a cousin that's a logger?" asked Charlie. "He never told me."

"Marty has asthma. He came here to try the curative effects of herbs." Ell followed after the children, who'd gone into the kitchen to look over Marty and the food and drink that was available.

"We'd all like tea," said Joella, acting as spokeswoman. "Aunt Ell, train sandwiches are dry as pages in an arithmetic workbook."

Marty rubbed the stubble on his face. "Hon, you didn't tell me all these folks was coming or I mighta' washed and shaved."

Ell seemed flustered as she introduced Charlie and Etta and the children. She stopped with Roy, looking at Charlie to supply his name and history. She pulled the sash of her blue silk wrapper tight about her narrow waist and at the same time pulled Roy close against her. "This adorable little boy was an urchin, but now he's an Irwin." She laughed, forcing the sound high in the back of her throat.

Roy bristled and pulled away. "What's that smell?" he cried. His eyes were wide. "Somebody's dead!"

Charlie understood immediately. He stepped forward and touched his sister's arm. "Don't be alarmed. Come here, son. You smell flowers—hundreds of flowers?"

Roy nodded. His body was stiff, but his hands twitched.

"That's perfume. Ladies like to smell like flowers. They think it makes them attractive," said Charlie.

"Oh, ya? Flowers go with funerals, and they ain't attractive to me." He stayed next to Charlie.

"Why, he's a little savage," whispered Ell, winking at Etta. "You have a lot of training with that one."

"He learns quickly," said Etta softly. "You see his nose is keen as a bear's on a trail for honey. And you'll soon discover that he hears like a jackrabbit and sees like a hawk."

Marty was still rubbing the stubble on his chin. He cleared his throat. "Besides this grizzly cub"—he pointed to Roy—"hon, you didn't tell me you had good-looking relatives. The cub and I'll chop kindling for the cookstove. You'll need a big pot of son-of-a-bitch stew."

Once again Ell looked flustered. Marty chuckled and looked at Etta. "This gal puts just about anything she finds in the pantry in that stew. The boys here sure smack their lips at mealtime. I was the one that gave her the recipe. We had a cook at a logging camp in Idaho that made it better'n anyone. We'd snag us a brown bear or maybe a moose or buffalo. These animals have innards that are sweet on account of they're herbivorous, eat greens. The animal was bled and slit on the belly side, from chin to tail."

The children were listening, their mouths shut, their eyes on Marty.

"I don't believe Ell uses your recipe at all," said Etta. "And it's not appropriate for children." Her mouth snapped shut.

"Well, now I'm telling facts, ma'am. I believe children should be told the truth, not mollycoddled and sheltered. The real world is not Santy Claus, you know."

Etta stiffened.

Charlie let out a sigh. "What about that kindling?"

"I can chop wood," said Floyd, following Marty and Roy out the back door.

"That man's uncouth," said Etta.

"He's not like that at all," said Ell. "He was just—just trying to impress you. He was showing off in a way."

Charlie ran a finger under the bandanna around his neck. "Sis, I should have known better. I showed off by coming unexpectedly. We don't have to stay. If you don't have room for all of us—I mean—"

"Charlie! There's always room here at 530 South Nevada for you and Etta and your kids. Relatives stick together. Remember when Pa told us that? Come on, there's two extra bedrooms upstairs, one for the boys and one for the girls. You and Etta don't mind sleeping apart?" She winked. "If it's a hardship I'll fix you a place on the sunporch. Tell me more about how you decided to keep Roy, and how is Pa?" She brought out clean white sheets from the wall cupboard. Etta helped make the beds. Charlie and the girls went back to the kitchen for tea. The water was boiling. Charlie and Joella looked in the cupboards but found no tea leaves.

"I'm going to put lots of honey in my hot water," said Pauline. "It tastes like cough syrup."

When Ell and Etta came into the kitchen, Charlie said, "How can you feed anyone? There's nothing to eat or drink in your cupboards. Sis, what's the matter? You need help?"

"Oh, Charlie, I love you. You'd help out any down-and-outer. You haven't changed. Look, push that panel, higher."

The wall panel swung open like a door. Behind it was a pantry.

"Oh, jeems! A secret cupboard!" shouted Charlie.

"Les built it for me. If the patients sleepwalk, they don't end up having a midnight snack and eating something not on their diet."

"It's a wonder that Les puts up with this nonsense. It's midday and you're still in a bathrobe. Les lives one place and you live here. This isn't natural. I feel unsettled." Charlie looked around the pantry.

"Here are the teas. If they were bears they'd bite you," said Ell. "How about horsemint tea, quiets an upset stomach?"

"No, I'm going out to talk with that—that Marty fellow to settle my mind," said Charlie, leaving the back door standing open.

Ell's eyes shone deep luminous green. She put a pinch of tea in a small square of cheesecloth and tied it. She placed it in Pauline's cup. She made more for the others, then sat down and put her head on Etta's shoulder. "You told Charlie about Les?"

"Yes, I told him. I can't keep anything from Charlie," said Etta. "It's hard for him to believe. He thinks two people that are married ought to live together. He knows you are a healer and thinks you can heal Les's problem. I told him that mumps are unusual for a grown man, and the consequences can't be healed. He says Les loves you and needs to be with you."

"Les loves me. That's right. He comes here a couple times a month. It used to be every day. We've worked this out. We've talked about it and he understands my needs."

"Hey, Aunt Ell, there's a bee wing in the honey!" cried Frances.

"Oh, Little Noonie, that's just part of the honey. It won't hurt you. I get it unstrained, so that it has all the richness of pollen and waxy comb. Close your eyes and stir it in your tea, sip. When you open your eyes the wing will be gone like magic. It will leave you with giggles all day long."

"Tell me about Les," said Etta.

"You kids stay at the kitchen table with your teacups," said Ell, leading Etta out onto the sunporch. She wore blue satin high heels that matched her silk wrapper. She pointed to the wicker chairs and Etta sat down, balancing her teacup on her knee. "He keeps busy. He lives in an apartment above his office. He's an accountant for a couple of the mines. He built the sunporch for me this spring. He likes to sit out here in the evenings before he leaves. He waits until the patients are in their rooms, then we sit on the love seat. He runs his fingers through my hair and his hands go over my body. He doesn't say a word. I've let him, but I don't like it. There's no sense to it. It's not a game that can be finished. I still cry when he's gone. The only way I can get over it is to keep busy with my patients, nursing them back to health. That keeps me sane and gives me happiness."

"So, what about this Marty? Is he more than a patient?" asked Etta, feeling bold.

"I'm quite fond of him. He gave me these." She pushed her flaming hair back so that Etta saw the emeralds in Ell's pierced ears.

"They are beautiful," breathed Etta. "They must have cost him a fortune."

"Logging is a lucrative business. He appreciates what I do for him. I like presents."

"How long will he stay?" asked Etta.

"I don't really know. Until he finds his belly doesn't hurt when it's empty. Until his wife finds out where he is. Until he's tired of my routine."

"There've been others?" asked Etta, her palms feeling sweaty.

"I grow quite fond of some of my patients. There's one now, I call Dick, who came in a Model T Ford, so I know he's well off. He likes me to massage his back. He asked me what I liked best. I told him matched saltwater pearls." She put her hand over her mouth and let her green eyes twinkle. "I bet you he brings me a present—a pearl necklace. I have perfumes—French perfumes.

They were presents. I'll give you a bottle to take home. Surprise Charlie." She ran her hand around her waist as if to see if her flimsy wrapper was closed. She smelled like lilacs.

"No, he always buys me Shalimar. I like that. Anyway, think how Roy might act." Etta giggled, then sobered. "Don't you ever long to have children?"

"I used to. Not so much now. I think of the men as my children. It's fate, kismet. If I'd known Les would get mumps, I'd have married him anyway. He's the most handsome man I know. He'd never leave me if the tables were turned. I'd let him have a mistress. Don't look so shocked. It's human nature. Les knows a lot of important people. If I want anything, he can arrange for it, no matter what it is. I'm going to have a mud bath and pool in the back. He has the plans already drawn up for it. This place is going to be a famous sanitarium one day. Grandma Malinda'd be proud of what I can do with herbs and roots and massaging with my hands. There's more than one way to skin a cat, to heal a man, to find happiness."

"Charlie'd like to see Les. Where is he?" asked Etta.

"He's inspecting mines. It's part of his job as accountant. It's something new. He told me it was something about keeping the mines safer, shoring them up with cedar timbers. He makes certain there's enough shoring."

"You two used to make such a nice-looking couple," said Etta, wiping tears from her eyes.

"We still do," said Ell. "Don't be dramatic. Try being pragmatic. Think: This is life. It's not all bad, not all good, but it's all right."

On Friday, Marty had packed his belongings, paid Ell for the health treatments. Roy reported to Floyd that he saw Marty hug Ell for a long time. Ell was crying when Marty said, "So long, kid. I'll see you around."

"I guess that cousin's gone, but she's got another cousin. He's blond and he has that Ford we pretended to drive. Boy, your aunt sure knows how to pick the men. She could teach my old lady a thing or two."

"Forget your old lady," said Floyd. "She didn't want you. You're with us now and this is your aunt Ell's house."

The boys quickly forgot Cousin Marty and his stew. They had heard Charlie say that Henry Ford intended to "put America on wheels," so they hung around the new patient Ell called Cousin Dick.

Cousin Dick spent his spare time waxing and polishing his

brand new Model T, which he parked behind the woodshed. The boys made faces and laughed at the reflection of their silliness in the shiny black doors.

Cousin Dick frowned when the boys touched his automobile. He was tall, with a small behind, a flat belly, and a narrow waist. He was a peroxide blond.

Once when Cousin Dick was having his daily massage, Roy and Floyd took turns pretending to drive around the vacant lot. They made loud whirring noises deep in their throats as they bounced on the black leather seats.

"You think we could get *our* cousin Dick to give us a ride?" asked Roy. "I'm going to ask him to let me drive if he'll crank the starter."

Dick turned the boys down. He said he was in no mood to drive around on corduroy streets. "And stay away from my automobile. I'll cut your fingers off if you touch it!"

"Jeez! Would he?" asked Roy.

"I don't know, let's ask Pa," said Floyd.

They found Charlie in the kitchen pantry looking for coffee and biscuit makings. All he could find was chicory, and he made a bitter tasting pseudo-coffee and a face each time he took a drink. "I'm longing for bacon and eggs and biscuits," he told the boys. "I think we better go home. You kids need to get to school."

"We can put up with tea and brown bread. I think Dick is going to show us how his Model T runs," said Floyd.

"Yeah, if he don't cut our hands off first," said Roy.

"What?" asked Charlie.

"Oh, he said we couldn't touch his automobile or he'd cut our fingers off. You think his car goes fast?"

"Let's see," said Charlie, going out the back door behind the woodshed where the car was parked. "You boys get in and I'll crank."

"You got the key?" asked Roy.

"No, but I don't need one." He undid the latches for the hood and examined the wires for a few minutes. Roy leaned forward and watched through the glass windshield. Charlie twisted two wires together.

"Boy, our pa knows everything," said Roy.

Charlie cranked the car and it sputtered, then backfired. He tried again and it began to purr like a big mountain lion. He climbed in and adjusted the choke, put his hand on the throttle, pulled down on the gas lever, and pulled across the alley into a field. He drove around the perimeter of the field once, then yelled, "Hang on to your false teeth!" He pushed the gas lever to the floorboard and waved his hand. The car bumped and bounced across the ruts and ridges and rocks and gopher holes. Floyd and Roy yelled and seemed to fly around in their seats. Then the car jerked and almost flung Roy into the front seat between Charlie and Floyd. Floyd hung onto the flat dashboard. Charlie had his arm outside hanging on to the door. The car stopped and the motor died. The front wheels were up against several large boulders. From the corner of his eye Charlie saw several people come around the woodshed and across the field. A tall, thin blond man led the pack. He carried a kitchen butcher knife.

"Jeems!" yelled Charlie. "You people ought to get these rocks out of this field. They could kill someone or knock a wheel off an automobile. Luckily I stopped in time. This is a nice set of wheels."

Dick's face was livid. His lips trembled and his hands shook. "You drove my car!"

"Is it yours?" asked Charlie, staying calm as he could. "You are to be congratulated. You know good machines."

"I told you brats to stay away!" He whirled the butcher knife around his head.

"Better give me that knife. You might cut your own throat," said Charlie. "Here, give me a hand now and we'll get your auto back against the woodshed."

Dick didn't lift a hand. "How'd you start this thing? I have the key."

"Well, it's that kind of knowledge that makes me so valuable," said Charlie, grinning. "I will bet you six bits that your key won't start this baby."

"You're on." Dick climbed in the seat and put the key in the ignition. "You mind cranking!" he yelled at Charlie, who'd handed the knife to Ell, who took it back into the house. Charlie cranked and nothing happened.

"What's wrong with that automobile?" asked Joella.

"It's a good thing I'm here," said Charlie. "Otherwise it'd cost more than six bits to have it repaired." He opened the hood and fiddled with the wires, noticing that the two he'd twisted together had come apart. He put them back as they were originally. He put the hood down and locked it. "I bet you another six bits it starts on the first crank," said Charlie with a laugh.

"It's a bet!" cried Dick. "You've broken my machine. You're going to pay for this!"

"Turn the ignition!" yelled Charlie. He cranked, pulling hard so that the crescent scar between his eyes shone silvery in the sunlight. "Choke her! All right, now put her in reverse and bring her up alongside the woodshed!" Charlie waved his arms and got the onlookers to move out of the way. "I bet I had that machine going forty miles an hour." He grinned at Etta. "Took the breath away from Floyd and Roy. They felt like we was flying."

"You *were* flying," corrected Etta.

"That's what I said. That automobile goes faster than my Colburn."

Dick was coming toward Charlie. His long legs covered a lot of ground fast. "I understand you are Miss Ell's brother. That don't cut any ice with me. If you're not gone by the next train out, you're going to die of throat trouble."

"You got a rope, mister?" asked Charlie. "Because I can run a loop in a rope faster'n you can say hydrophoby skunk."

Frances and Pauline began to cry. Joella put her arms around the two little girls. "You'd better say something to that man," she said to her aunt Ell. Ell put her hand on Dick's back and whispered something to him. One of the other men whistled. "Come on, we'll go inside and I'll play my Valentino records," said Ell, walking carefully on the ground so that she would not break a heel of her white pumps. She wore a peach-colored chiffon blouse and a white pleated skirt. Her hair was done in a large bun at the nape of her neck. The emerald earrings matched her flashing eyes.

At suppertime Etta announced that they were leaving Saturday morning.

"I'll get Dick to drive you to the depot," said Ell.

In the morning Charlie smiled at Dick as he came out of the kitchen. Dick held his head high and pushed past Charlie without a word. "Hey, where's the fire?" asked Charlie.

"I'm due for a sunbath," said Dick, not looking back.

Charlie headed for the sunporch, where Etta and Ell sat. "Where are the kids?" he asked. Etta wore a blue flowered dress. Ell had on a pale-yellow silk dress with a low-cut bodice and a belt that rode her hips.

"Oh, they're twirling the ropes I use for a clothesline. They're giving a regular Wild West show out in the back field. That Floyd is talented—he twirls a rope like you, Charlie. His stance is just like you."

"Well—who taught him?" said Charlie, feeling proud. "Where do your patients sunbathe?"

"Oh, in the back, behind the Virginia creeper fence cover. I schedule that for the tuberculosis patients particularly. Charlie, it helps."

"Yeah, nude?"

"How else?"

"My kids are out there and coming in right past there! Jeems! What kind of place is this?"

"Mercy, I'll go after them," said Etta. "Those men will cover up if I walk past. Humpfh!" She stalked out like a mother bear separated from her cubs. She was ready to fight anyone in the trail between her and the children.

"I guess you aren't going back with a very good impression," said Ell. "I'm sorry about that and sorry Les wasn't here." She rested her chin in a cupped hand. "Charlie, are you superstitious?"

"No! Of course not! I have only one thing that I think is bad luck and that is wearing yellow. I won't let any of my cowboys wear a yellow shirt." He stopped and stared at Ell's dress.

She laughed. "Is there anything else?"

"No—oh, well, peacocks. You know, they are bad luck, according to the Pine Ridge Sioux. If you own peacocks, someone in the family is bound to die, they say. Is that what you mean?"

"Not exactly. I dream a lot. In the dreams Grandma Malinda talks to me. She offers suggestions about treating my patients. Sometimes I feel she's right here, in this house watching over me."

"Sis, that's imagination. That's because you need Les here taking care of you," said Charlie, forgetting his anger with Dick and the nude men. This was his sister and she was lonely. "Hire some lady to cook for your men and come see us. Bring Les. It'd be good for both of you."

"Listen to me, Charlie. I'm serious. Last night Malinda warned me about something. She said, 'Joella's going to break her father's heart first.' Why'd she say that?"

"How the heck would I know? I don't go in for that hocus-pocus. Did you tell Etta?"

"No, I didn't want to frighten her. Joella's very pretty, you know. Some of the men here watch her."

"Oh, come on. She's just a child, barely fourteen. She's not even attracted to men. She climbs trees and swings a rope. She treats the cowboys like brothers. She arm wrestles with them and sometimes wins. She plays poker and wins. Dreams don't mean a thing. Do they?"

"I dreamt that you buried an old man in the snow. Is Pa all right?"

"He's just fine. And I've never buried anyone in the snow. Sis, don't dwell on those thoughts. That's depressing. It's sick. It's not good for you. Take care of yourself. Give me Les's telephone number. I'm going to call him when he's back."

"You know I make more money than Les? He comes here and makes all the additions to the house and never asks me to pay for a thing."

"I have a lot of respect for him. I always did. I guess life isn't always what we anticipate when we're young. And there's no sense in crying about it. We'd better get our suitcases down here. The train leaves midmorning for the north."

Dick and Ell rode in the front seat. She wore a white dress and a choker of matched pearls. She had Roy on her lap. "You smell like roses. I could learn to like perfume," he said. Charlie and Etta were in the back seat. Charlie held Pauline, Etta held Frances, and Floyd and Joella sat on the leather grips. Dick said little. Ell told him to drive past the Antlers Hotel. Charlie could hardly believe it had been rebuilt and looked so magnificent. There were two hundred rooms. It was a handsome brick structure with indoor plumbing.

At the depot Dick parked his car, got out, and put the Irwins' baggage on the platform. Charlie shook his hand. Ell held Etta's hand and they both cried a little. The children got out and stood by the suitcases. Dick got into the car, tipped his hat to Etta, told Floyd he could crank the starter, and leaned over to say something to Ell above the putt, putt, purr, purr of the motor.

Ell leaned out her side and waved. "We're going to the Zoo Park! Wish you'd stay longer. Come with us!" The tires spun out small gravel as Dick backed and turned and sped off in a cloud of dust.

"He didn't wait for us!" cried Pauline. "I'd like to go up to that Pikes Peak and see the animals with Cousin Dick."

"He gave me this," said Floyd. In his hand was the dollar fifty Dick owed Charlie for the bets they'd made. Charlie let his son keep the money. "Buy yourself a sandwich and remember the fun we had when we borrowed a *cousin's* automobile."

"I'll remember mountains with frosting on their tops," said Frances.

"I like the way Aunt Ell fixed my hair and showed me how to curl my eyelashes," said Joella. "I'm going to be just like her when I'm married."

Etta sucked in her breath. Charlie looked at his wife sharply so she would not say a word.

"When you write you can tell her I found cousin Marty's snoose. Remember he looked all over the woodshed for it?" Roy held up a small round red and yellow can. He spit on the railroad ties for emphasis.

"Give that to me!" hollered Charlie.

"Mr. Irwin, Pa, I didn't know you like snoose!" cried Roy.

"It's time to get away from here," said Charlie between tight lips.

"Charlie, don't get yourself riled," said Etta. "Your sister wanted to give me a bottle of genuine Parisian perfume. One of her patients gave it to her."

"Some of those men are more than patients," said Charlie, looking down at his wife. "They're no better'n gigolos. My sister takes expensive gifts from them. You know that Dick gave her the pearls she wore?"

"I thought they looked nice on her," said Etta. "You know Les can't give her everything since he had the mumps. So they have an understanding. They make the most of the situation."

"My dear! The point is, she's my sister! I have a sister that—that buys love. It's vulgar when I say it."

"Don't be dramatic! She always enjoyed taking care of others. In her way she still loves Les. And I believe he worships the ground she walks on. It's their life. We have our own problems."

"Etta, she's family and I'm responsible," said Charlie.

He felt the vibration of the train on the platform and looked to see it slowing down as it approached.

Just then there was a toot-toot and everyone looked toward the road. Dick drove past with Ell leaning out the window waving as they boarded the train.

"Jeems, he's a show-off," murmured Charlie.

"Well, I'm glad to have you back with us," said the conductor Charlie recognized as the man, called Bert, who rode the southbound train a week ago. He waved toward the automobile that drove in a wide circle. "Miss Ell's out early."

"You know her?" asked Charlie.

"Oh, yes, she has quite a reputation here. A fine herbalist and healer, among other things. Some claim she has a foreknowledge of things to come. All I know is that she's one of the most beautiful women I've ever seen."

Charlie led the way into the coach and settled everyone close together. The train moved slowly away from the station, and

Charlie could see the stream of dust left by the automobile as it bounded along the road trying to keep up with the train. Finally it was left behind. "Stupid fool, trying to race a train," mumbled Charlie.

The conductor came through the coach to punch tickets. He nudged Charlie and said under his breath, "Say, you been treated by Miss Ell?" and his face broke out into a big grin.

Charlie looked the conductor square in the eye and said so that Etta could hear, "I took my wife and children to visit at her place. She's my only sister. Her talents may be a delight to some folks, but we love her because she's family. She has a husband who's one of the state's most astute mine inspectors. He's a crackerjack accountant and knows cattle better'n most ranchers. He's so good he looks at me as if I'm some dude. And I've been ranching since ninety-seven."

Etta kicked Charlie in the shin. Charlie got up and sat with the conductor until they came to Denver. They laughed and exchanged ranching stories, not once mentioning Ell nor her husband, Les.

The moment the train's brakes squeaked, Charlie knew they were pulling into Denver. Charlie looked at his watch. He told Etta to stay on the train with the children, and if he didn't get back not to worry, he had some business to attend to and he'd be on the very next northbound train into Cheyenne. She believed him, never dreaming that he was thinking of the two sprinters he'd tied up at the nearby livery last week.

He talked to the conductor out on the platform. The children hovered around the window watching him. "Better have a look under there for a hotbox," he said, pointing under the daycoach. "Is there some way to get word out to Overland Park from here?" He looked at the ticket office, where there was a telephone.

"Mr. Irwin, you go into the depot and tell the ticket agent I sent you."

Charlie hurried. Inside he explained that he wanted someone to call Overland Park to hold the races. "Make sure a matched pair is entered in the name of C. B. Irwin."

"You need a couple of jockeys?" asked the ticket agent.

"My land, I forgot about that. I need to rent a couple uniforms. Tell 'em that when you call." He ran back on the train and told Floyd and Joella to come with him. The three of them started off at more of a trot than a walk. Charlie waved at a passing black Hupmobile. The driver waved back, thinking it was somebody he should know. A block beyond the driver realized that he did not know the man and youngsters on the run. He backed toward them.

Charlie yelled in his booming voice, "Sir, can you take us to the livery? The one close to Overland Park?" He pushed Floyd and Joella into the backseat and climbed next to the driver, handing him two dollars.

"You're good as there," said the man, who had a brown brushlike mustache.

Charlie turned around to look at Floyd and Joella. "You're my jockeys. We're going to race Laura T. M. and Blumenthal. Can you put all that hair under a jockey hat?" he asked Joella.

"Yes, Pa. Give me your bandanna. I'll tie it up and put the hat on top. I don't have a riding skirt."

"You're going to wear what I can get, jodhpurs, boots, and a shirt."

"Pa, where am I going to change?" said Joella.

"Stand behind Floyd. Act nonchalant and dress fast. The ticket agent said we had twenty-three minutes before the race."

Charlie gave the driver his card and hustled Floyd and Joella out of the livery stable. Charlie paid the liveryman, who could hardly believe Charlie was going to enter today's race with so short a lead time. "You been exercising these horses?" Charlie asked.

"Yes, sir," said the liveryman.

"Then everything's fine!" said Charlie.

He got the horses to the track on time, checked to see that the entrance fee was paid, and saw them lined up against a wide rubber band, which was a new kind of starting fence. Floyd was standing in the stirrups and looked ready to go. Joella looked like her racing silks were too small. The shirt pulled her shoulders together in front. He hoped that the boots didn't pinch her feet overly much. The horses looked in good condition. The flag came down and the wide elastic band was lifted. The horses' first leap into the race seemed to carry them right on to the finishing line. Charlie had not calmed down from getting the horses in on time and finding a seat near the judges' stand. The race was over. Charlie was breathing hard. Laura T. M. and Blumenthal had hit the finish line together, nose to nose. Floyd and Joella had kept their heads well up. Charlie collected his winnings, four hundred dollars. He went back in the tack room. "Jo and Floyd, hurry it up."

"Yes, sir," said Floyd, not able to hide his excitement as he handed his borrowed silks to a jockey, whose eyes nearly popped out of his head as Joella slipped into a petticoat and skirt, pulled on her long black stockings and put on her shoes, then handed him the boots and silks. "I didn't stretch it too badly in the wrong places," she said, and winked.

Charlie gave the boy a five-dollar bill. "Thanks for letting us borrow your clothing for the race."

Charlie left the saddles on the two horses and led them away from the arena. When he was well down the road, he let Floyd and Joella ride. He trotted along behind to the depot where the train was still waiting, taking on water. He took the horses to the stock car next to the caboose. He beat on one of the doors. "Open up. Railroad stock agent out here."

Immediately the door opened and a couple weary cowboys blinked in the sunlight. "Lower the ramp and get these into the car—you've got room?"

"Well, there's four horses in here, going to Laramie."

"Fine, take these two and cool them out as soon as you get them inside," said Charlie.

"Mister, did you push them this hard just to get them on the train?"

"No, you galoots, they just won the quarter mile, a tie at Overland Park. They paid a double purse. Get 'em in quick and walk 'em around slowly."

The horses went up the platform and would have walked right through the other side if it had not been closed. Charlie chuckled about that.

"When we get to Cheyenne, get these two out for me. See if you can earn your pay."

"Pay? Oh, sir, we will," the two hands said together.

Floyd and Joella could hardly wait to get back on the train to tell about their thrilling experience.

Etta had kept the three children quiet with ham sandwiches. Roy complained loudest that they were only two pieces of bread with a piece of ham that was so thin it had only one side. "Where's the jam, and butter, and pickles?" he asked.

Pauline and Frances pulled the crust off their bread and stuffed it in their pockets to feed birds when they got home. Etta looked relieved when she saw Charlie. Then a second look and a whiff of the horsey smell from Floyd and Joella made her look more thoroughly. Charlie smiled. He beamed. He took a bit of Roy's bread and swallowed before saying a word. Floyd and Joella were sweaty and disheveled, but their eyes were sparkling.

"We were the jocks and Pa won!" said Joella. "It all happened so fast I can hardly believe it's over. Oh, what fun we had!"

"Go wash up and comb your hair. Then tell us," said Etta. "Clean the bottoms of your shoes. Good heavens! You smell like a barn!"

The Irwin family had made quite a commotion on the coach and everyone was looking their way. Charlie looked around. "I'm making an announcement and everyone listen."

Several passengers from the forward coach came back to see what was going on.

"I own two wonderful sprinters and they just took first in the first race at this afternoon's meet. They tied. That was a first for Overland. I have been to the track. The racers are on this train's stock car. Now we're ready to go! All aboard!"

Just then the train's whistle blew two long blasts and the train lurched forward.

The conductor was grinning. "Boy, I heard the good news. Came over the phone in the ticket agent's office. I've never known anyone to get off the train, run his horses, win, and get back on. This is some day. I'll never forget it, nor you, Mr. C. B. Irwin. Oh, there was no hotbox on this coach, but the brakeman checked the forward coach and found one. Had to cool it before we could go on. Thanks to you." He tipped his hat.

Charlie smiled. That hotbox had given him the extra time he needed.

The passengers stood up and clapped when Floyd and Joella came back from the washrooms with their faces looking scrubbed and shiny and their hair combed neatly. Only the lurching train kept them from continuing with the applause.

Charlie felt wonderful.

Etta was embarrassed. Everyone stared at the Irwins for the rest of the trip home. That made her terribly self-conscious.

The weather turned chilly the day after they returned. A day or two later there was a skiff of snow on the lower pastures and in the yard of the ranch house. Charlie hunched his neck deeper into his mackinaw and hoped that it wouldn't snow so much that he couldn't get Etta and the children back into town before school Monday morning.

That evening Joe came in with the wagon and one horse from Will's place. He'd stayed longer than Charlie expected. He thought, maybe his father really enjoyed his visit with old man Rick, so what does it matter? Joe's face was pinched and seemed to have no color.

"Listen to that wind scream," Joe said finally. "I came home because old Rick is dead. We got to get him buried before the ground freezes solid more than a few feet down."

"Tomorrow we'll go to Rick's place," said Charlie. "The kids'll miss a couple more days of school. Well, so what. They're smart."

In the morning Charlie told the cook, Bertha, to fix "bacon and eggs, biscuits and gravy and hash browns, and your good coffee. This will be the best breakfast I've had in a week."

After breakfast Etta called the children into the kitchen. "You all know Aunt Margaret. Well, her pa's dead. You know, old Mr. Rick. Your father and I and Floyd are going to go to be with Margaret. She is sad right now, same as you'd be if something happened to your pa."

"Why is Buddy going?" asked Joella.

"He will be needed to help dig the frozen ground," answered Etta. "Joella, you are oldest. You are going to take care of the children. Bertha will do the cooking and help out when needed. But all of you know how to take care of yourselves, so we needn't worry. There are books to read, catalogs to cut paper dolls from, wood to whittle, and leather to braid."

"I thought we had to go to school in Cheyenne," said Roy.

"Death does not wait for everything to be settled and easy," said Etta. "Roy, you're the man of the family at the main ranch house. If you need help, you can go to the bunkhouse and see Clayton Danks, or one of the other cowboys."

"Can we use the team of Pete and Repeat and the wagon if there's a need?" asked Joella.

"Yes, of course. We're going to Will's in the Colburn. There'll be no trouble here. Will there?"

"No, Mama," said Pauline. "We'll listen for the sound of the Colburn coming back. You're not going away forever like old Grandpa Rick?"

"Oh, no, honey." Etta was on her hands and knees hugging the child.

The ground was frozen and so the Colburn had no trouble going over the fields of stubble straight to the upper ranch. All the way Joe sat huddled against the isinglass window in the back and didn't say anything. Floyd tried to bring his thoughts to the present with descriptions of Aunt Ell.

"Boy, she's pretty. Gramps, is she really older'n Pa? She don't look like it. She wears pure silk wrappers in the morning, once a pale blue silk dress for noon, and a black dress with sparkly stones around her neck for night. She makes her lips red. She fixed up Joella once. They were clowning around the way girls do. Aunt Ell let us put as much honey in our tea as we wanted. Roy had a cup of honey with two teaspoons of tea. He had to eat it with a spoon. She never once scolded."

When they got to Will's place, they found him so fortified with rum that he didn't realize the weather was near zero outdoors. "Did you tell Frank?" Charlie asked him.

"Oh, I had one of the hands go after him. He'll be back around suppertime." Will spoke each word carefully as though he were reciting in a school play.

"What about a preacher? Is there someone in Albin?" asked Charlie.

"I'll telephone," said Will.

"Where's your telephone?" asked Floyd. "No one told me you had one. Uncle Frank hasn't got one."

Will pulled himself erect from the easy chair he was in. "Frank's a skinflint. Won't get his wife a tele-ma-bob, a tele-fum. My brother Frank's tighter'n a Scotch lass on a cold night."

"Come on, get your shovels. We got work before supper. If it ain't done now, we'll not be able to get into the ground by tomorrow. It's cold enough to make a polar bear hunt cover," said Charlie, handing Will a sheep-lined coat. He touched his father's shoulder, "Pa, you want to stay here with Margaret?"

Joe shook his head, no. He'd rather be out in the freezing cold than shirking his duty to his old friend.

Will took another swig from the bottle on the table and passed it over to Floyd before Charlie could see. Floyd nearly choked on the burning, brown liquid.

"Why'd you drink that hot stuff, Uncle Will?" There were tears in Floyd's eyes. "It'll burn out your insides. Wow! It left a trail of fire down my throat!"

Joe looked at his grandson. "Don't touch spirits, my boy. Them's the Devil's own drink. Makes you lose your senses. You'll act plumb crazy and never remember at all."

Will was laughing as he went out into the cold night. He grabbed Floyd's arm. "But it sure makes working easier."

Etta and Margaret sat at the kitchen table. They each had a cup of hot tea, but they weren't drinking. Etta sensed Margaret was thinking something but not saying it. Finally Margaret said, "Joe and I were sitting on the bed talking to him. I was sitting next to him and he laid his head on my shoulder and rocked back and forth for a few moments. Just the way I used to do to him when I was a little girl."

Etta and Margaret let the tears run down their faces. They held hands across the table.

"We could hear this funny noise in his throat, like he was having a hard time breathing. Joe moved around so that he could help hold him up. The two old men hung on to each other. They didn't say a word. They just hung on in a long embrace. Then Joe let Pa's head rest against my shoulder again. Joe rubbed Pa's back. Pa closed his eyes and died."

Etta moved her chair to the other side of the table so that she could put her arms around Margaret. They both cried.

Then Margaret wiped her eyes with her apron and said, "I was always scared of death. I wasn't around when Mama died. This was peaceful. It wasn't scary, nor gruesome. Pa died close to people that loved him."

"Well," said Etta, wiping her eyes. "My oldest sister died and I used to feel she was still alive. Like she knew what I was doing and still shared part of my life. There were days when I thought of Hattie constantly and one day I was startled to find I'd not thought about her for several days. Life is stronger than death. In the end it is most important."

Frank came in when supper was over. He and Will ate huddled around the kitchen stove to get warm. Then Frank helped himself to Will's bottle. Next Frank and Will got to telling stories no one understood, but the two of them thought they were hilarious and laughed together until tears came to their eyes. The rest of the family bedded down. Joe slept in John Rick's bed, with Frank. Charlie and Floyd slept in the living room next to the heater. They wrapped themselves in heavy quilts.

"Pa," whispered Floyd. "Where's Grandpa Rick? Tonight I heard Cousin Gladys say he was all boxed up."

"He's in a long pine box laying stretched out full. He looks like he's sleeping, but there's no life left. That's gone. Gone to the Maker—to Heaven," whispered Charlie. He thought about what Ell had said about burying an old man in the snow.

"Where's the box?"

"Outside beside the house where it's cool. Your grandpa Joe made that box. He's quite a man, you know that? For an old man he can do twice as much as most cowboys today."

"It's cold outside. Is—is Grandpa Rick frozen?"

"I suppose so. Won't hurt him none, though."

"Look, it's snowing." Floyd was sitting up looking out the window. "It'll bury Grandpa Rick."

"Good thing we got the grave dug. Looks like the weather'll be bad tomorrow," said Charlie. He went to the window and looked into the falling white snowflakes. Everything looked the same white color. They could barely see the windmill, the blades seemed to barely turn. The water in the wooden trough had a layer of ice that was fast collecting a thick layer of snow.

"Pa," said Floyd, "what if the preacher can't get here?"

"Don't worry, son. We're not the first family to bury a loved one without a preacher. Grandpa Joe knows what to do. Long ago he used to go to people's homes and give them a hellfire and damnation sermon to think about the rest of the week. When I was your age, I guess younger really, there weren't many trained preachers. People make do with what they have. People build their own beliefs and way of doing things the way it's best for them. Our ranch was built that way. The old Y6'll be yours one day to carry on the way you think best."

"I hope I'll be as smart as you." Floyd put his hand in Charlie's. "Could I—could we see where the box is?" His teeth chattered.

Barefoot, they walked outside to the corner of the house and Charlie pointed to the white mound.

"Oh. Pa!" Floyd's voice was unsteady. He felt a lump in his throat that pressed on the huge knot that formed in his stomach. His eyes blurred, and he tried to take a deep breath and reset his clenched teeth, but the cold seared his lungs. He slipped his hand out of his father's and went back toward the open door.

"The cold preserves the body," whispered Charlie. "Just before old Rick is put into the ground the womenfolk will want to have one last look."

"No! Not me!" blurted Floyd, barging into the blast of heat inside the house and pulling the door shut tight.

In the morning Margaret and Etta were the first ones up. Margaret brought baby Gene to the kitchen and gave him a bottle of warm milk after she tied him to the kitchen chair with one of her dishtowels.

Etta made biscuits and fried the sausage. "The snow is tapering off," she said. "The road is covered. Can't tell where it turns to go over the wooden bridge on the creek."

Soon the others were in the kitchen, seated around the table or standing with a cup of hot coffee in their hands.

Will looked bleary-eyed and said he couldn't think until he'd poured rum into his coffee.

"You'll never feel clear-headed if you keep adding rum to your blood," said Charlie.

Frank took the bottle from Will, added rum to his coffee, and said, "Takes the chill out of a burying day. Will's wife didn't nag him, so Charlie, button your lip."

"Don't start anything this day of all days," Etta cautioned Charlie. "Don't answer. Hold your tongue."

Joe scowled and tapped the table with his spoon. "When the women have the dishes done, we'll start the burying. I'll do the praying and preaching, the rest of you do the singing."

"It's too cold out there to sing a note," complained Frank. "The cows are giving icicles."

Margaret told her boy Charles, who was now called Sharkey, to finish clearing the table. She had an idea. "Where's Aunt Etta?"

"She's dressing baby Gene," said Sharkey, swallowing a mouthful of sausage.

Margaret found Etta and Gladys playing peekaboo with the baby, who was nearly three years old. "Put Gene in the crib with blocks to play with. I want you to help me take the Victrola out on the porch. We'll play my daddy's favorite song, 'Come, All Ye Faithful,' while he's being buried. Gladys, get your coat on. You can do the winding for your grandpa."

The snow had stopped. Everyone was bundled in warm coats and hats and scarves, boots and mittens. Etta swept the front porch, then helped Margaret carry the walnut, upright Victrola outside.

Will took a couple steps into the snow. It was knee-deep. "Let's hurry with this show. I've hay to get to my cattle. Frank and Charlie, I'd like your help with the wagon and team. We'll take the wagon load of hay to the cattle I have up at the upper ranch. Those up around Round Top and the hills will have to fend for themselves. I'm not going that far in this snow."

Joe put his fingers to his lips so everyone would hush. Charlie and Frank had waded out to the row of pine trees that served as a windbreak. They brushed the snow off the piece of old kitchen linoleum they'd laid over the hole that was dug the day before. Charlie yelled for someone to bring him a broom. Sharkey was coming out of the house, so he ducked in and got the broom. He plowed through the light snow, dragging the broom to his uncle Charlie.

"That's it, make a wide path so the ladies can come out here when it's time. I'll sweep a wide space around this here grave so we can stand at the edge. Jeems!" He swept into the pile of earth that had come out of the hole. "I gotta get this cleared off, too."

"You can start the music," said Joe. "We'll sing with the Victrola."

Gladys turned the handle, but it was hard to turn in the cold. Floyd tried to help her. The four men had to use a pick ax to get the pine box loose. It was frozen solid to the ground. They carried it to the front porch. Charlie pried the lid up so that all could view the body.

Joe began to sing with the Victrola music; Charlie and the others joined in as they formed a circle around the open coffin.

Floyd said to Gladys, "Don't look. It'll give you nightmares. Stop turning the handle! It's wound up enough!"

Gladys had looked at her grandfather's corpse before Floyd had warned her. She turned white as a winding sheet and slipped to her knees.

"My God, she's fainted!" yelled Frank. "Somebody get her inside quick before she freezes to death lying there on the porch!"

Charlie scooped Gladys up in his arms and took her inside. When he came out, he said she was fine and would look after the baby. "Turn the record over so we can sing 'The Old Rugged Cross,'" he told Floyd.

Floyd looked up to see his father and could not keep his eyes off old Grandpa Rick. Snow had sifted inside and lay in thick lines on the arms of his black suit.

Charlie kept singing, but bent down to close the box. The hinges squeaked in the cold.

"He looks good," said Will, then went on singing.

"No one looks good dead," answered Charlie.

Floyd stopped the Victrola, turned the record over, and waited for his grandfather.

Joe cleared his throat and began. "I see by this here family Bible that this man's name was not John Joseph Rick, as we all believed, but Julian Joseph Rick." His eyes watered and he wiped across them with leather gloves. "The Lord has enlightened us this day of J. J. Rick's burial. I carved his name, John, on the lid, but it's all right. I think he must have preferred that name. So, now we say farewell to this friend and relative. He was a husband, a father, a grandfather, and my good friend." Joe repeated the twenty-third Psalm from memory.

The four men lifted the pine coffin and carried it through the broken path to the foot of the pines. Charlie called over his shoulder, "Start the Victrola!"

With lasso ropes at either end they lowered the box inside the ground to the music of "Come All Ye Faithful." Charlie loosened the mound of earth with the pick and the others shoveled the frozen clods into the hole on top of the pine box.

Margaret and Etta clung to each other, shivering with the cold, afraid to cry and have frozen tears. The tools were put away, and the women pushed and pulled and shoved and tugged, but had the Victrola back in the house before the pale gray sky with no visible sunshine let loose with millions of big lazy snowflakes. In an hour the wind was up and the snowflakes were smaller and more compact.

Back at the Y6, fourteen-year-old Joella made hats from the scraps of material Etta kept in a large flour sack. She chattered and was happy sewing hats for Pauline, Frances, and Roy. She promised each they could be fashion models if they'd wear the hats to school. Bertha, the cook, smiled and thanked God that Joella had found something to keep the children busy during this terrible snowstorm.

"Bertie," said Joella. "You have to wear one of these hats to church on Sunday, so that you, too, can be a model."

TWENTY-NINE

Y6

Pablo Martinez

The Y6 ranch was on the southern side of a great depression in the plateau of east-central Wyoming, which was once the bed of an ancient lake. The valley was the southern part of the fertile Goshen Hole, named for a Frenchman, Gosche, who trapped in the area during the mid-1800s. Eastward the valley was bounded by high, pitted, and eroded mountainous bluffs. The faded tan bluffs resembled a long, gigantic fortress or the lengthy backbone of some monstrous dinosaurian beast. At the southern end, standing alone, was Round Top, the huge dome-shaped hill. The chalky dome supported sage, prairie grasses, and an occasional greasewood on its lower slopes. Farther up were wind-stunted lodgepole pines with soft green feathery tops and large-trunked, weathered cedars with grayish loose, stringy bark. The huge old cedar trunks were furrowed with deep, rounded ridges. Their bases looked like flaring buttresses. It took hundreds of years of struggle for this tough, hardwood tree to grow on the sides of the windswept bluffs.

Early pioneers recognized the decay-proof, insect-proof properties of these ancient cedars and built their rough-hewn log cabins from the twisted, aromatic wood. The wood was unaffected by hot sun, hard winds, pelting rains, or freezing snows.

Round Top that held the roots of the tenacious cedars and

lodgepole pines was a magnificent thing to Charlie. It rose abruptly from the edge of the valley floor and gave him a sense of uplift. He was conscious of man's inner strength, the rhythm of life, birth, and death, but the dominant spirit of man always triumphed. That spiritual strength was like the rounded mountain bluff, so much a part of the species that it had outlived generation after generation of plants and animals.

Often he had ridden horseback to the middle of the eastern pastureland and gazed at the high rounded dome in the moonlight. It shone with the light of the moon reflecting off its pale chalky surface with an incandescence of silver. During the day Round Top reflected all colors of the rainbow: in early morning it was red, orange, and yellow; by noon it showed the green of its vegetation; in the soft light of late afternoon it was blue-indigo and in the twilight violet. Never was it dark or hidden from sight; even in the wildest blizzards Charlie could make out Round Top's ghostly outline against the pale sky and between the flying streaks of snowflakes.

Charlie felt Round Top was his. He owned its land because it was on his homestead section. He did not own it as something to be possessed but as something to measure himself against. Early in his life at the Y6 he'd found that neither horse nor man could climb the steep sides unless multiple switchbacks and hairpin turns were executed. Charlie found what he thought was an old game trail that led him to the top with his horse slipping and sliding at the turns. When he finally stood on the high, flat ground he knew he'd not used a game trail, but a path used long ago by men of an ancient race. The ground was strewn with chips of translucent white quartz. There were half a dozen circles of stones, undisturbed, resembling the oval pattern of tepees. Charlie was sure the stones were once used to keep the tepee skirts pinned to the sandstone during high winds. He found evidence of mining with rock wedges and hammers for the transparent crystals that lay in the sandstone. The quartz fractured in a smooth curve, leaving sharp edges; ideal for large or small spear points.

Charlie found several rounded pits that contained layers of the white transparent flakes. Each pit was large enough for a single man to sit inside, out of the constant wind, and work at making his spear points. Charlie eased himself inside a pit and folded his legs in front of him. He picked up a handful of discarded chips that were slightly curved and thin. His eyes looked over the edge of the pit, where he saw a ring of thousands of arrowheads, a few stone ax heads and choppers. This was a regular assembly line for manufacturing weapons, he thought. Inside the tepee rings he found bifaced cleavers, scrapers, grinding stones, and knives. In one large pit he found bones, thousands of bones, deer, antelope, rabbit bones just under the soil's surface.

From the top of Round Top, Charlie could see over the whole valley, as far as the snowcapped Laramie Mountain peaks to the west and to the spot of dark green, which was certainly trees in the town of Cheyenne.

Several times each year Charlie rode to the high plateau of Round Top. There was peace. The only sound was the wind blowing through the stunted pines and cedars, but it was warm crouched inside an earthen pit. The mountaintop gave him a good safe feeling.

He could look out and see the Y6 ranch house, barn, bunkhouse, and outbuildings. He could see the log house and the windmill at the upper ranch. He saw the cattle bunched together in the pasture and wondered if they'd found a spring.

It had been a long time since Charlie had ridden out to Round Top. He'd watched it all winter and when spring came decided he'd pay the little mountain a visit.

As he rode his horse across the lush green fast-growing spring grass, he looked up the line of chalk bluffs called the Divide because the hills divided the upper ranch from the grazing land. In front of the Divide was a circular but flat bluff. This bluff was about the same size as Round Top, but weathering had cut the top off. It stood out from the main range. Charlie had not paid much attention to this bluff before, but this day in 1910 he was drawn to it like a rustler to an extra cinch ring. The sides were steep. His horse could not climb to the top even using a series of switchbacks. Charlie rode around the circumference and was about ready to give up and go back to the ranch house when he discovered steps or wedges dug into the rock up the backside.

He knew he'd found something none of the old-timers knew about. His heart beat with excitement as he tethered his horse under the shade of a greasewood. He pulled himself up from one foothold to another. He knew he dare not slip as there was no brush nor vegetation to grab alongside the footholds in the rock. He kept his body flat against the wall. Moving his bare hands on the chalky rock made them feel dry and stiff. He wondered who had been the last man before himself to go to the top of this bluff. He stopped a moment, took off his hat and held it against the sky, and looked up. The footholds were set equidistant and comfortable for a man to grab into with his hands and his toes. He turned a little and saw behind him the soft-looking pines near the Divide. He knew that was an illusion. The pines were not soft. The two green needles clasped together were stiff as toothpicks. The lodgepoles were all about the same size. Charlie knew the similarity in size was because at one time there must have been a fire in the area. The egg-shaped lodgepole cones were sealed until a forest fire opened them like an exploding puffball to release their seeds. Many had a curve in the main trunk at the same level where the weight of one winter's snowfall bent them as saplings. Charlie came back to the effort of climbing to the top. Awkwardly he pushed his hair back out of his eyes and put his hat on. Then he pulled himself up and up, careful not to hit any sharp outthrust with an arm or a leg. He could feel the perspiration run down his back and the wind ruffle his shirt, keeping it dry. At the last foothold he pulled with all the strength left in his powerful shoulders and brought his body up over the edge of the cliff.

The first thing he did was stand up and look out over the opposite edge. He ignored the spear points and flakes, walked around the earthen pits until he could look out over the edge of this truncated mound. He could see the bright green lines of willow that lined Horse Creek, Little Horse Creek, and Bear Creek. From here he could see the whole valley. He could look back and see the line of chalky mountains that had resembled a giant backbone from the valley. Off to his right he spied a tannish formation that resembled a boat—a steamboat. "That's Steamboat Rock!" he said aloud. He was exuberant with the name, thinking of his world-famous, wild, bucking horse with the name Steamboat.

Above him low clouds moved against the mountains. The wind became stronger and a chill mist saturated the clear air. Charlie blinked and looked north where he recognized Bear Mountain, ten, fifteen miles north of Bear Creek, which, from the valley, looked like a giant sleeping black bear. From Bear Mountain east was a wide gap. That was where Bear Creek broke away from Horse Creek. North of LeGrange was a chalk mountain that connected with the Divide. This chalk mountain was called Sixty-six. Charlie recalled the story old Colin Hunter, who'd been born in Fowle's Wester, Scotland, in 1848, told his father shortly after buying the L5 and Horse Creek Cattle Company from Johnnie Gordon.

"Sixty-seven westward-bound men, women, and children in a wagon train stopped against that particular chalk mountain as shelter against the wind and heavy rain. When the rain let up, skulking Indians saw their flickering campfires and no doubt watched the women dip water from the creek. More whites coming into the red man's land meant less land and less game. So the Indians attacked at dawn. They killed sixty-six people, leaving a redheaded six-year-old boy. The Indians had never seen red hair before so believed the boy to be something special. He was given to the chief, who'd lost a son the same age from the mountain coughing sickness the winter before. The boy was raised as an Oglala Sioux and never again heard from."*

A peculiar oppressive feeling crept over Charlie. The sky overhead was swirling with heavy, gray clouds. The mist was gone, but the sunlight from the cloud's edge gave a sulfurous tinge to the valley. He followed the ribbon of chartreuse, which was willows, along Horse Creek. He saw the white clapboard house, the barn, and outbuildings of the Hunter Ranch. Suddenly he recalled that Hunter's son James had died in 1906, almost causing the death of old Colin. His son Tom had taken over the ranch with the help of a foreman from Aberegale, Wales, Alfred Scoon. Al Scoon made trips to Europe with horses for the Arbuckle Coffee Company from Fred Boice's Po horse ranch on Pole Mountain Creek about twenty miles west of Cheyenne.

Charlie took the bandanna from his neck and wiped the perspiration from his face. The wind was full of moisture and did not dry the mist left on the rocks and pine branches. His eyes followed the straight line of an open ditch that came from Horse Creek into the big pasture beside the Hunter barn. The ditch looked like a metallic band of olive-green. It was made to irrigate all of Gordon's pastureland. However, the price of digging such a long trench and keeping it open became exorbitant so was eventually named Gordon's Folly, mainly because the pastureland didn't need extra water.

A small narrow strip of Gordon's land was sold to the Coad Brothers, John F. and Mark M., themselves Irish immigrants. The brothers built their ranch on Horse Creek at Meriden and formed the Maple Grove Land and Livestock Company two miles over the hills from the Y6 ranch.

Charlie clearly remembered his father talking to Hunter about an agreement the Coad brothers made with John Iliff, a cattle

*Story told by Irvin Joe Petsch, Y6 Ranch, Cheyenne, Wyoming, 1984.

baron from Colorado. All the land south of the Union Pacific tracks was to be Iliff's range and all north of that line was to be the Coads'.

Charlie chuckled to himself because the two outfits were dealing in property that belonged to neither. Much of that land was owned by homesteaders like the Irwins or it was in public domain, or land bought by the U.P. for construction of their transcontinental system. The Coads acted as though the land were legally all theirs and let their cattle graze over the entire region. Not long ago one of the brothers suffered a heartbreaking loss. Mark had been shot while in Cheyenne by some restaurant worker who went loco with a loaded .45.

When Charlie had bought the land four miles out of Cheyenne, which he called his Four-Mile pasture, from Johnny Gordon, Mark Coad had made a fuss, claiming that the land belonged to him through an agreement with Iliff. Since Mark's death there'd been no more contesting the ownership of the Four-Mile property. John Coad was not as aggressive, nor high-handed, as his brother.

Charlie breathed deeply, finding the soft moist air somehow cloying to his nostrils and not sharp and sweet as the clear dry air he'd always found on Round Top. He guessed it was just the day and looked out over the pastures which seemed to be more mossy-looking in the light from the cloud-covered sun. He saw the necessity store and thought he could make out the gasoline pumps at Dan Donahue's in Meriden. Dan married an Englishwoman, Kate Richardson. She always wore a wool cap, saying the constant wind in the valley was too much for her sensitive ears. Dan had a funny sense of humor. He'd ask an acquaintance if he knew Fat Burns in Lagrange. Invariably the answer was "no." "Well," answered Dan, "of course fat burns in Lagrange, it does everywhere." Whenever the conversation got too deep for him, he'd say, "Well, Horse Creek's still running," or "Hold the phone." Drunk, Dan could throw the knotted end of a rope through the rope's loop straighter than anyone. Sober he couldn't rope a fence post.

Charlie followed the dull silver strip that was the gravel road past the Sand Hills and to the right he saw Ray Burkholder's sod house. The only sod house in the valley. The roof was cedar shakes and the inside walls smooth as any plaster and whitewashed so that everything looked as clean as the hospital in Cheyenne. Then Charlie watched the grazing cattle and the horses, looking smaller than red ants. He was sure he saw Floyd and Joella racing in the pasture behind the Y6 barn. Why, from this broken mound he could see everything that happened in the valley. He looked over to Round Top and somehow knew there had been communication from there to here ages ago. There were smoke signals or sun shining on bits of shiny quartz like mirrors, or at night, fires built in the open. The hair on the back of his neck seemed to bristle. The presence of these ancients seemed somehow very close. Charlie tried to shrug off the feeling. He remembered telling Ell he was not superstitious. Ghosts are the figment of an overactive imagination, he told himself, and laughed to ease the tension.

Now he noticed the pits at his feet. Most of them were blackened and larger than those on Round Top. They had a fire in the center to keep at least two men warm, thought Charlie. He kicked at the arrowheads at the edge of a pit. They were in a little pile. So, this was the lookout. Lookout Mountain. Round Top was the munitions plant. The Indians guarded this valley from enemies encroaching to hunt game or steal horses from the camps that were probably along Horse Creek and Bear Creek. He slid inside one of the large pits. He got some of the blackened dirt on his shirt. The pit was warm inside, the wind blew across the top. Charlie imagined he could smell a warm sweaty body next to himself. The smell was mingled with fresh horse manure and urine. He scrambled out of the pit, into the open breeze, and felt better.

Jeems, he thought, those Indians knew everything that went on in this valley, the slightest movement of their own people, the other tribes that came for a visit or for the sport of horse stealing, the movement of the whites through this land. Maybe from this very point warriors were told of the wagon train where sixty-six people were massacred! The tribe that held the mountains had the power. But the Indians are gone and I am here, thought Charlie. This is my place. I can pass it on to my son, and so on. He heard the rumble of thunder. He looked up and saw a jagged flash of pink lightning and the thunder came immediately, vibrating the earth beneath his feet. A chill ran up his back. The feeling on this mountain was menacing and cruel. The feeling on Round Top had always been benign, peaceful, calm. Was he feeling the attitude of those former owners of this land? Was there one large tribe? Or were there two different tribes, one the manufacturers of arrows and the others the warriors? With a start he saw the logic in this dual arrangement. Man was an enigma, peace-loving and at another instant dark and cruel. He rubbed his hands together and smudged the blackness. He rubbed the moist dirt on his pants. He was oppressed and wanted off this Lookout Mountain. He was disturbed with this feeling of something nonexistent, yet so real as a vivid remembered dream. He did not like the antagonistic vibrations that seemed to be released by his presence. He looked through the open foliage of a scrawny pine and felt the cold drops of rain on his face. He stepped out into an open place and took off his hat, letting the water fall on his head. He turned and saw the blue sky, the color of his faded denim pants behind the clouds that were scudding over the Divide. The rain came down harder, soaking his shirt. The wind rose and the water stung his face so that he had to look down. Then he saw the larger stones and cedar logs around the pits and guessed the Indians had used brush or skins to cover the pits in case of rain or snow. The wind screamed through the twisted, tormented pines and the sound set Charlie's nerves on edge. He was going to leave the minute the rain let up. As soon as the thought was formed in his head, the sun flashed out warm and yellow from behind the low black clouds that followed the line of hills and were now nearly midway to Bear Mountain. Charlie looked for a rainbow. He saw nothing, and was sure if he'd been on Round Top the rainbow would have been clearly visible.

He backed over the edge of the chalky rock and moved his feet down slowly to find the toeholds for his boots. His hand felt along the rocky ledge and he lay his body along the rock so that it embraced the mountain. His breath caught in his throat, and he could not still the pounding of his heart. One hand slipped on a wet rock and he braced himself against the side of the bluff, but felt his foot slide downward. "Oh, my! Don't let me slide!" he prayed. "If I miss the toeholds there's nothing else to hold me!"

His arm scraped against an outthrust, but he didn't feel the pain of the skin being removed. A large rock broke loose from the wet soil and rolled against his right arm, pinning him to the cliff momentarily. He'd heard a crack as the rock hit, but he dismissed it, concentrating all his senses on moving slowly and deliberately.

His feet swung free and dangled against the rock. In his mind he saw his rope tied to the saddle horn. "Oh, no!" he cried. "I've lost my senses!" He knew he should never go anywhere without his rope. Then his right foot slipped into a pocket of rock as though guided there by some unseen force. He closed his eyes and breathed a sigh of relief. His right arm relaxed and lay loose against the wall of the cliff. His left hand gripped the edge of a high toehold. The rock on his right arm rolled free and tumbled against his shoulder, then bounced away. It made a terrific racket as it hit against rock and broke other fragments free to fall after it. Finally it hit the slippery grass and sagebrush and slid to a stop against two close growing greasewoods. His right arm throbbed.

Charlie's heart was beating fast and loud, but he was still. He lowered his right foot and felt for another foothold and found it. Slowly, painfully, he lowered himself, hugging the side of the bluff. Now he was far enough down where his hand could hold on to the notches. His right arm was bleeding, but that didn't bother him. He concentrated on moving another foot, then his hand, gripping tightly. Momentarily he thought if those unknown Indians had a chance to watch him, they'd be rolling on the ground with laughter at his clumsiness. His knees cramped and he waited a moment until he could bend the left one and hunt another notch. Then he loosened his hand and lowered it alongside the other, found the foothold, and put his left hand in the lower notch that was about waist-high. He bent his other knee and moved on down, concentrating on his movements, each one as deliberate as he could manage. Suddenly he slipped. He could not hold on to the rocks. He fell on his right arm.

He did not go to his horse right away but lay on the scree in the sunshine breathing hard, resting, waiting until he could relax his arms and legs and back and neck. Finally he moved his right arm and cried out in pain. He knew immediately that the rock had broken the bone. He'd heard the snap that sounded different from rock hitting against rock, but he'd concentrated so hard on moving his arm and legs that he'd blocked out the meaning of the sound and the pain. Oh, the pain was awful now. He held his arm to his chest. On horseback each bounce was misery as it jounced his arm. He tried making a sling from his bandanna and holding his arm against his shirt. Once he thought he was going to pass out. He was cold, but sweating like he was in a sauna. He shivered and that hurt his arm. He took his hat off and let the wind ruffle his hair and dry the sweat off his forehead. He creased the top of his hat and put it on, picked up the reins, and gritted his teeth. To ride across the valley toward home seemed to take forever. Twice Charlie was afraid he'd fall off the horse. He ached from head to foot.

Joe saw him ride into the yard and knew instantly something

was wrong. He ran out the front door. Charlie's shirt was torn and there was dried blood on the right sleeve and on the front where he'd held his arm against his chest. The bandanna sling was crusty with blood. His denims were muddy and in tatters, and his boots were muddy and scuffed. He leaned against the horse and smiled. "How'd you like to drive the Colburn, Pa?"

"Son, you know them wheels scare me, almost as much as they scare the horses. Say, did your horse throw and drag you? If it did I'll shoot it!"

"Pa, save your ammunition. I slipped off that measly mesa in front of the Divide."

"What were you doing there?"

"Just exploring the land. I have a broken arm. Drive me to town in the Colburn. I need a doc to set it."

"Come inside and sit. I can see you're pale as the moon on a cold winter night. I don't want you fainting out here."

"Pa! I don't want no horse doctor working on me!" yelled Charlie.

"What's wrong with horse doctors? I've set more bones in dogs than horses. This is the only time I approve of dousing a man with spirits. Looks like you could use a belt or two."

"Pa!" Charlie was in pain as Joe ripped the shirt from his arm.

"I'll clean this up with a little turpentine," said Joe.

"No, you won't!" wailed Charlie, trying to get out of the kitchen chair.

"Son, you're in no shape to be fighting me. First I'll soak it in hot water, so stop your bellering."

Joe poured two fingers of whiskey in a water glass, then laced it with a good slug of laudanum he used to calm a hurt dog or cat. "Drink that. It'll ease the pain."

Charlie took a big swallow. It scalded his throat. He coughed.

The pain was excruciating. He held his arm against his chest and rocked back and forth while tears ran down his cheeks. The throbbing in his arm calmed and was nearly tolerable. Charlie drank the remainder of the fiery liquid. In a few minutes his head seemed to be floating away from his body.

Joe cleaned the scraped and broken arm with a white rag and steaming water. Charlie felt little pain. He smiled. Then he heard Joe's voice from far away saying, "The damn thing's in place, but if I let up on it, it'll pop out again!"

Charlie was lying on his back on the kitchen floor. He could not think clearly. Joe had yanked his arm to put the bone fragments together and the pain had brought Charlie back to consciousness. "Use my belt," he mumbled.

Joe had whittled kindling into flat splints.

By daylight Charlie was up stretching his legs trying to get the kinks and soreness out. His head ached and his thoughts were filtered through a mesh of damp cobwebs. His broken arm throbbed. He drank black coffee with Joe and the cowboys.

"You were sleeping in the corner when we came in for supper," said Jimmy Danks. "Joe told us you were sleeping it off!"

"It's hard to believe you actually tied one on!" teased Frank.

"You men know damn well I don't drink," growled Charlie. "I fell off that mesa in front of the Divide. Honest. Maybe I was pushed off by the ghosts of some angry Indians who used to spy on this here valley because it was theirs." When the words were out, he knew he'd talked too much.

"Ha, ha! I think you fell off your horse," said Joe. "None of us believe in Injun ghosts."

"Maybe a doc in town ought to look at my arm," said Charlie.

"He'd say I did a good job, son," said Joe, putting his thumbs in his waistband.

Charlie didn't see a doctor in town. He stayed at the Y6 until the stiffness and ache were out of his muscles. By then the bone had begun to knit and the abrasions were well scabbed.

That spring he went on the roundup, but depended on his cowboys and two brothers to do most of the work. They brought the cattle out from the hidden clefts at the base of the hills, working all the way around Round Top. The Irwin crew with neighboring ranchers, Tom Hunter, Teeq Kirkbride, John Coad, and Lon Davies, were to bring the cattle to the upper ranch, where they would be sorted and branded.

Charles Hirsig, a rancher and banker, was invited to the roundup. Charlie wanted to show Hirsig the extent of the Irwin cattle and horse holdings because he was going to ask Hirsig to put up some money and be co-owner of the Wild West show. While sitting around for his arm to heal, Charlie had thought of ideas for enlarging the show.

During each roundup the men herded in a bunch of elk and several buffalo that grazed with the domesticated stock. "Look," Charlie explained to Hirsig, "imagine Floyd hitching a couple of them buffalo the men bring in to a prairie schooner and driving around the arena. Won't people love that! You bet their silver spurs they will!"

"Sure," agreed Hirsig. "But C.B., you don't need my money to buy buffalo, they come free."

"Your money will buy the prairie schooner," said Charlie, showing Hirsig the corrals where the stock would be sorted and branded.

"How do you keep your animals from getting grass tetanus, you know, cramps, from eating the fast-growing spring grass?" asked Hirsig. "I have trouble with that every spring."

"My pa worried about the same thing. You notice none of your stock gets cramps in the summer?"

"That's right."

"Pa has the idea that spring grass grows so fast it lacks something that the summer grass takes time out to pick up from the soil. Once a week, in winter, Pa loads hay on sleds and takes it out to the pastures. The stock that gets to the hay never get cramps."

"Your old man study that somewhere? Go to an agricultural college?" Hirsig was impressed with Charlie's father.

Charlie chuckled. "No, I don't believe he went as far as I did in formal school. Pa has more practical knowledge than most because he observes. He's always talking about cause and effect."

Hirsig was impressed with the strong legs and sleekness of the horses that were being brought in from the canyons and deep arroyos and put in the fenced paddocks. Charlie admitted that it was his idea to let the horses run free all winter where the hills made a natural barrier. "I believe if a horse has bad legs, the cold and constant movement as it grazes for dried grasses is the best remedy in the world to make the legs strong. I can see the effect. The horses come home with rock-hard leg muscles, strong lungs, no parasites, nor saddle and cinch sores."

Hirsig was impressed.

Near Lookout Mountain the roundup crew found tents and a couple tar-paper, settlers' shacks. Frank pointed out the land was legally Y6 and those people had no business there. He was for going straight up and telling those squatters to get out.

Charlie was equally angry. He walked back and forth for some moments. Suddenly he stopped. "When I was on the top of Lookout I saw a herd of horses yonder, behind the mountain, behind the hills. I assumed they were wild."

"What if they belong to those squatters?" asked Hirsig.

"When I saw the horses, the squatters hadn't moved in yet, or I'd have seen their camp. Frank, you and a couple of the men round up those horses if they are unbranded."

Hirsig held up his hand. "Wait a minute. What if those squatters rounded up those horses, even if they are mavericks. The horses belong to those men in the shacks. Anything unbranded goes to the man who takes the trouble to bring it in. C.B., you'd be working ahead of those fellows' roundup. That's rustling!" Hirsig's face was dark and stern.

"Naw! You know me better than that! I'm no rustler! Those folks are squatters. They're the ones doing something illegal. I'll get their poor, dumb beasts back to them. It might take a few weeks. But be patient and watch me!"

Frank, Tom Hunter, and one of Charlie's cowboys brought in a dozen horses from behind the rocky hills beyond Lookout Mountain. They trailed wide and came out by Round Top, avoiding the squatters' camp. The horses were a sad, scruffy lot, looking like they'd been driven for miles before being allowed to graze at all.

Charlie took the horses to a meadow close to the main ranch and let them graze undisturbed several weeks. Then one fine spring day he asked Joe if the splints could be removed from his arm that itched worse than prickly heat.

"Not yet. That's the new skin growing that makes it itch. Try to set your mind on something important, son," said Joe.

"It's time for me to talk to them squatters," said Charlie.

Charlie circled their camp several times before going close. "Howdy. You men been here long?" he called.

"Long enough for someone to steal our horses," grumbled a man who looked like he'd never seen a razor nor a haircut.

"Say, that's too bad," said Charlie. "You plan on staying here long?"

"We'd move out tomorrow if we had them horses. Don't like rustlers' country. You come from around here, stranger?"

"Yep. This is my spread. Called the Y6. You happen to see any of my horses in the hills? They're branded on the right hip."

"Nope, haven't seen any brands. Our horses were clear, no brands."

"If I see them, I'll let you know. There's good creek water off to the north a ways. Say, I have a few horses I could spare. Course, you'd have to pay for them."

"How much?" asked another man, also with whiskers and wearing faded overalls and a red flannel shirt.

"Well, let's see, I've had to feed them and see they stay healthy. The going price for a good workhorse is seventy-five dollars."

"We don't need no workhorses, unless we bring in womenfolk to farm." The first man cackled as though that were a joke.

"Well, I can see you men want to bargain," said Charlie cautiously, not getting down off his horse. "For a riding horse, how about fifty dollars?"

"Man, you think we just come from a paying gold mine in Colorado?"

"No, I don't know where you come from," said Charlie. "And I'm not going to ask. That's your business." He could see the man in the red shirt relax a little. A couple more men came out of the tents and stood behind the first two. They don't look like they have a dollar among them, thought Charlie. "Well, these are horses I don't really need and they eat too much anyway. Thirty-five dollars apiece for half a dozen. They were wild, but they've all been broke to a saddle."

"Twenty-five and we'll take ten if you can spare that many," said the first man.

"That's a lot of horses," said Charlie. "I'm not sure I can spare that many and the price is a holdup."

"You come back tomorrow with the horses and you'll see the money," said a sawed-off-looking man who had tousled blond hair.

Charlie smiled, waved his hat, and turned to leave. When the camp was out of sight, he began singing "Alfalfa Hay."

Next day he brought six of the dozen horses that belonged to the squatters. They'd been brushed until their coats shone, fattened out a little, and the Y6 brand on the right hip was plain as a man's reflection in a clear creek. Several men came out of the ramshackle shacks and a couple from the tents to inspect the horses. Finally the man in the red shirt gave Charlie a hundred and fifty dollars in greenbacks. "You got about four more like this?" asked the man.

"Might have. You want them?" asked Charlie.

"Ya. We've decided to move on. No woman likes to live out here by these high hills. The wind screams like a bunch of Injuns doing a war dance at night."

"Wait here. I'll be back before sunset. I have to ask my brothers if they can let loose four more of their herd," said Charlie, chewing on a piece of gamma grass. "You men dodging the law?" asked Charlie quietly.

"Who says?" one of the men asked.

"No one, I was just curious. Ain't had no squatters on my land before. I like horses and don't fancy you riding so fast on these I took care of that they have to kick the rabbits out of their way."

"Won't be your worry, 'cause we'll own 'em," said the man in the faded overalls.

"You fellows got enough greenbacks to buy four more horses?" asked Charlie.

"We're rich enough to be called mister," said the short one.

Charlie rode back to the upper ranch, where he'd left the other six horses. He picked out the sleekest and fattest four and rode back to the squatters. The tents were down and packed on the back of the first string of horses.

"We're leavin' the cabins," said one of the men, pointing to the shacks.

Charlie shrugged as though he couldn't care less.

"We want a bill of sale in case anyone asks where we got these horses," said another.

Charlie pulled a piece of paper out of his pocket. "This says you bought six horses for twenty-five dollars apiece and four for thirty-five dollars apiece from me, C. B. Irwin of the Y6."

"Let me see that," said the man in the flannel shirt. "Thirty-five dollars!"

Charlie moved away from the camp taking the four horses. He stopped, saw the men huddled together. He put his hand on his rope. He wasn't armed and he did not know what these men might try. He didn't want to be without a rope again. Breaking an arm was one thing, but being bushwhacked by a bunch of squatters was another. The rope was the best defense he knew of. "I might have swung my rope at those red-skinned ghosts on Lookout," he said out loud. All of a sudden he felt the hair on the back of his neck rise as if someone were staring at him from behind. He turned and the short fellow was holding out a handful of bills, grinning. Charlie pulled his horse up closer, reached down, counted one hundred forty dollars. "Yep! We're even, mister," he said tipping his hat.

On Monday, with his arm still in a sling, the ache completely gone, but the itching worse than a horde of mosquitoes, Charlie went back to Cheyenne and his office in the depot. He figured it was time the Union Pacific had an annual special train running from Denver to Cheyenne and from Omaha to Cheyenne and back again for the Frontier Days celebration, which was becoming well-known nationwide. People from all over the United States were coming to Cheyenne for the annual Western festivities.

Charlie spoke of his idea about the special trains to Warren Richardson. Richardson was negative. "C.B., you're always thinking of something creative. Nobody on the Union Pacific would want a once a year run, no matter where it terminated or began. Railroads are conservative."

But before the summer heated up, Charlie's plan was being discussed in every office on the U.P. Wheels began to turn that would make his idea a reality for the upcoming Frontier Days. The fact that Charlie was responsible for the idea and original plans was lost in the shuffle, but that didn't bother Charlie, because during the middle of this spring he'd been appointed to the National Convention of Fair Boards to represent the Cheyenne Frontier Days celebrations.

By the Fourth of July it was known that ex-President Roosevelt was back from a hunting expedition in Africa and was coming to Cheyenne for the purpose of asking ranchers and state farmers and miners to save the dwindling herds of buffalo. It had been estimated that there were only fifteen hundred head of buffalo left in the United States. Roosevelt was in Montana urging those people to do the same and to think about setting up some kind of game preserve, where the buffalo could be protected. As a member of the National Convention of Fair Boards, Charlie wrote to his friend Teddy Roosevelt, saying he'd heard he was coming to Cheyenne, and suggesting he come for the Frontier Days festivities. Charlie hoped this annual celebration would not be too tame for a man who was more active than most, who believed every man ought to rise like a sky-rocket and sail with the stars, and who laughed loudly at his own jokes.

Roosevelt's special train came in from Montana in the morning of Friday, the twenty-sixth of August. He was in the lead automobile that paraded around Cheyenne shortly after his arrival. With him were several senators, Governor Bryant B. Brooks, and E. W. Stone, Chairman of the Frontier Committee. Next came an automobile carrying James R. Garfield, former Secretary of the Interior, now Roosevelt's private secretary, Frank Harper, and several other editors and publishers. Riding in Charlie's Colburn were his old friends, Senator Warren, F. G. Bonfils of the *Denver Post*, C. E. Kern of the Associated Press, H. F. Griffin of the *New York Sun*, and G. C. Hill, the *Sun*'s Washington correspondent. This year, as in the years past when Charlie had supplied most of the stock for the arena program, he was master of ceremonies, riding a white palomino called Wathal and announcing each act in his deep, booming voice through a megaphone.

Charlie was amused as the men in his automobile talked about President Taft's request to have guns at all the forts in the Northwest discharged at 8:00 A.M. daily, in the hope of bringing rain. At this time the entire Northwest was under a blanket of smoke from forest fires near Wallace and Mullan, Idaho, Spokane and Newport, Washington, and Big Fork, Montana. Already as many as two hundred and five forestry employees, settlers, and loggers were killed by the fires. Incoming ships in the Pacific reported that the smoke hampered navigation. Even here, in Cheyenne, the sun appeared as a giant red ball because of the smoky haze in the air.

Senator Warren said that the U.S. Navy wanted to fire all their guns simultaneously each morning, but the U.S. Army chiefs refused to go along with the plan.

"I agree with the Army officers," said Charlie, recalling his own experience with Colonel Johnson, alias Dr. Melbourne, the rainmaker. "The firing of guns won't cause rain, no more than some hocus-pocus rainmaker. The Army would be wiser to send aeroplanes over the forest fires, sprinkling loads of sand or pulverized asbestos to smother the flames. The Army needs to get its heads together and figure something, because there'll be more fires as more people move West."

Bonfils looked up from his note-taking. "C.B., may I quote in the *Post* what you just said?"

"Certainly, you've quoted me before. Make sure it's accurate this time." Charlie tipped his hat at the ladies in long lawn dresses, who carried matching parasols. Ahead he saw Roosevelt wave his black slouch hat and people along the sidewalk wave small flags and take snapshots.

Roosevelt was taken to the Inter-Ocean Hotel for a short rest. Then the three automobiles left for the Industrial Club, where a reviewing stand had been set up in the shade of the poplar trees. The club's porch was reserved for representatives of the press.

Charlie and E. W. Stone sat on the raw, wooden slabs of the

reviewing stand with the ex-President and his party.

Great crowds formed along the sides of the street to watch the Frontier Days parade. First a squadron of the Ninth Cavalry marched by amid cheers and much flag waving. Then came a squadron of mounted police, followed by marching soldiers from Fort Russell. Next were one hundred and fifty Sioux Indians in colored headdresses, tunics, leggings, and moccasins.

Two days later the *Cheyenne Sunday State Leader* reported on its front page:

> . . . the braves waving their lances and blankets frantically to the accompaniment of their war whoops, while the squaws threw kisses at Colonel Roosevelt as they passed the reviewing stand.*

A long line of cowboys and cowgirls on horseback came by, all waving. Charlie recognized Floyd and Roy and his three girls and waved vigorously. Several cowboys yelled together, "Hello there, C.B.!"

Then came the colorful clowns, cutting up and dancing with huge floppy shoes. One called, "Hi, Teddy!" That brought laughter from the crowd. A gleaming new, red, motorized fire wagon drove past slowly. The driver waved his red fire hat before the reviewing stand as the crowd applauded.

Just before Roosevelt had come to town, Charlie and his cowboys brought in the finest steers and bucking horses and four buffalo for the celebration. Charlie could always be depended upon to have an adequate supply of show animals to fulfill his contract. He brought Mac, the Y6's summer cook, to the Irwin boxcar cookhouse at Frontier Park with great supplies of beefsteaks, fresh vegetables and fruit, white enamel dishes, stainless steel kettles, and silverware.

Each year the Irwin cookhouse at Frontier Days became more famous. There were two long tables, one for family and guests, the other for cowboys and workers. The same good food was served at each table. All during the Frontier Days, Roosevelt, state officials, Cheyenne officials, railroad officials, bankers, representatives of the press, and big ranchers ate with Charlie and his family. At the cowboys' table there was always more than one down-and-outer. These were men who'd come to Cheyenne look-

*Courtesy Charles M. Bennett Collection, Scottsdale, Arizona.

ing for work, with nowhere to go, no money for a decent meal. Charlie never turned a man away. He was known as the champion of the underdog, the untutored, the naive. He was a friend to all, rich or poor, old or young, red or white.

Charlie was full of energy. He was always on the move. Halfway through his meal he'd leave his table and sit with the cowboys. He had a genuine love for human beings and could ease any man's burdens, let him laugh or cry on his huge shoulder. It was believed that C. B. Irwin could solve any problem man or beast could dream of.

Charlie would not tolerate a shirker. He paid decent wages for his hands, but if a man would not pull his own weight or put in a full day's work, he was given his wages and sent on his way.

The morning before the first day of the Frontier Days the roof of Charlie's cookhouse was thick with hemp ropes the cowboys had laid out to dry in the morning sun. When the sun hit the tin roof, the dew evaporated to thin vapor streams like wisps of silver-gray filaments rising to join the feathery tufts of high cirrus clouds.

When the rope was dry, every cowboy who valued his rope hooked one end over a large hook at the base of the Y6 boxcar barn. He fastened the other end of his rope to his saddle horn, then stretched it out as tight as it would go to take the kinks out. Invariably Charlie had to remind the eager cowboys not to hook more than one rope at a time on to the large hooks in the barn or certainly the whole danged barn would fall down.

Two boys argued who'd hook his rope first and had drawn a crowd as they tried to settle the argument in a fistfight. Charlie pulled the men apart with his good left arm, hoping they wouldn't hit the right arm that was still in a sling. "Come to the cookhouse for breakfast," he said. "Your differences will evaporate with biscuits and gravy and strong coffee under your belt."

Roosevelt asked what Charlie did if the boys would not stop fighting. Charlie replied, "When that situation arises I hope I can think of something."

"Tell you what. I'll send you a couple pairs of boxing gloves," said Roosevelt with a chuckle, spearing an extra sausage to go with his scrambled eggs, hash browns, biscuits and gravy, and thick strips of bacon.

On the last day's opening ceremony Charlie knew what would appeal to the crowd. He had the Ninth Cavalry Band play the National Anthem, and while the twenty-five thousand spectators were on their feet Teddy Roosevelt mounted Charlie's white palomino and cantered around the arena's rim.

Charlie handed Roosevelt the bullhorn so that he could make a final plea to save the mighty buffalo, the symbol of a free land.

Roosevelt said, "Of the twenty million or more buffalo that roamed over the West, only a few remain today. Today, you saw four of the magnificent beasts that are being kept healthy by C. B. Irwin. I propose that we have a game reserve for the buffalo in this state's Yellowstone National Park. These animals will be fully protected from hunters." The crowd's response was positive. They were aware that over a period of twenty years the animal had become almost extinct. Roosevelt went on, "The buffalo were the trailmakers of the West. In wintertime they went south to get feed more easily. In spring they returned north. They traveled across the country in single file. These great, heavy animals made trails, which, once seen, can never be forgotten. They grazed in massive herds moving from one feeding ground to another. They ate the short buffalo grass, growing in patches in rich soil. That grass grows to about two inches, and when walking on it one feels as if he were on a deep carpet. This grass is very rich and fattening. I believe C.B.'s cattle follow the few buffalo in this area to feed on buffalo grass. I propose we save what is left of these animals so that our children and grandchildren will know what the red men depended on for food, fuel, shelter, and clothing." The crowd stood and waved their tiny American flags, which were fastened to small sticks.

"Speaking of rich and fattening"—he rubbed his protruding midsection—"my friend C. B. Irwin has the finest meals in his cookhouse I have ever tasted. If everyone in Wyoming eats like that it is no wonder her cowboys have such stamina!" Charlie bent over in a low bow and waved his hat. The crowd went wild. Roosevelt was not finished. "I wish to express to the people of Cheyenne my appreciation of these last fifty-two hours. If Wyoming and her neighboring states breed the kind of men I have seen and met here, your Uncle Sam can be certain he has a cavalry ready-made. I congratulate all the participants in this great show of Western sports. I thank C. B. Irwin, who arranged these shows that are so satisfying. This is the greatest portrayal of early Western days I've ever seen! Whenever I mount a horse after this I will remember the gentlemen who can stick to a saddle no matter where the horse is. Personally, though, I like my horse to do things horizontally rather than vertically!"

The wildest broncs in the Irwin string were used in the last day's bronc-riding contests. Clayton Danks, who had won the title Champion Bronc Rider of the World in Denver, gave a beautiful performance on Archbishop, until the horse's endurance wore out the rider and Danks was thrown from the saddle. Danks got up and limped to the sidelines.

Charlie passed his Stetson, urged the crowd to dig into their pockets to help a fellow cowboy who was wounded. Everyone knew that a man who broke a leg or arm or rib needed doctor's care. Cowboys never saved enough to pay huge doctor bills.

Then the previous year's Frontier Days champion, Dick Stanley, rode a horse called Rocking Chair. This wild, Irwin outlaw bucked hard and caused Stanley to pull leather, that is, to grip the saddle with both his hands. He was out of the contest. Hugh Clark, another former champion, came to an embarrassing grief while riding a horse Charlie had named Teddy Roosevelt, in honor of his friend. Clark was thrown in front of the grandstand, but was not injured. Sam Scoville rode Denver, a runaway bucker. He held on beautifully. In the finals Scoville rode Aeroplane and had the crowd on its feet whistling as the horse hung its head in submission. There was little doubt that the rider was champion for that year.

Between events Charlie had a special way with a crowd. He could make them sing for the sheer joy of watching the gracefulness of a running horse and a beautiful girl astride that horse in the relay races. He could make the crowd tense and excited watching the outcome of a steer-roping contest. He could make the crowd angry and sad with a story of some Sioux who was bilked out of his meager savings by betting on a favorite horse or playing the plum-pit game with a couple cheating cowboys behind his cookhouse. People dug into their pockets and filled Charlie's Stetson so that the bilked Indian invariably received two or three times as much as he lost.

When the show ended, Roosevelt was driven by carriage, which waited by the arena gate, to his train at the depot on the other side of town. Then Roosevelt stood on the rear platform of the train and waved his hat and bowed for as long as people could see him.

Back at the fairgrounds there was a letdown feeling. Everyone had such a good time, but now everyone had to go back to their usual way of life. There had been parties in many hotel rooms, and parties on the special trains run by the U.P. from Denver and from Omaha. Those people who had berths on Pullman cars used them as overnight accommodations. Many people made reservations for the following year on those now annual, special trains.

Of course there was drinking, which led to fights among the more rowdy cowboys. Once in a while a hotel bar chair or two were broken, a wall or ceiling shot into, but the damage was always well paid for, usually by an advance from a kind-hearted rancher, so there was no resentment against the intense energy of the cowboys. The old expression, "It was a bad night," meant that there had been a good fight.

Charlie helped clean up the cookhouse and the barn so that they could be closed and used the following year. He made sure the horses were cooled out and rubbed down before being given water and fresh oats. If there were any down-and-outers left, Charlie put them to work. The horses and steers had to be moved to the Four Mile pasture for grazing along with the buffalo for temporary holding. Eventually the stock was taken back to the Guerney Pasture area on the Y6. He'd tell the cowboys to bring all the stock to the ranch and have an old-fashioned picnic. When they made it to the ranch and the stock was put to pasture, he'd say, "First you gotta put in a little honest work and build me a fence around the triangle pasture or finish putting up the poles on the sides of my new corral. Then we can have a good feed! Come on, smile! There's always a good time at the Y6!"

Actually, no one minded doing work for C. B. Irwin, because they knew the food would be the best there was and there might be a dance that evening in the front yard with old Joe playing his fiddle.

In all these things that Charlie did and planned to do, there was one thing that was different from the thoughts of the other ranchers in the southeastern part of Wyoming. This was horse racing.

Rodeoing and the Wild West shows were not an everyday thing, but they were not completely unusual. People were familiar with Buffalo Bill, and the Miller Brothers' 101 Wild West Shows. The Miller Brothers ran a respectable ranch in Oklahoma. But a rancher raising racehorses was something different.

Charlie was farsighted enough to see what horse racing could do for a man who was really interested. Perhaps he saw the potential when he raised racehorses with his brother, Frank. Perhaps when he had a taste of racing a greyhound. Perhaps when he bought the trotter, Annawill, for Frank to race.

Nine years before, Frank had entered Annawill in the harness races at Denver's Overland Park. People that bet didn't seem to favor her, even after she won the first heat at two minutes, thirteen and a quarter seconds. Later Annawill went into a final race with four to one odds. She won in two minutes, twelve and a half seconds and Charlie got a two-thousand-dollar purse.

Charlie knew he had to start somewhere in order to be known as a horse racer. Thus, after establishing recognition for his ability to train and raise trotters, with Frank as the jockey, he moved on to quarter horses. He began training one or two horses at a time to run the quarter mile. These horses had to be fast sprinters. He began running matched races, first the one in Denver with Laura T. M. and Blumenthal, his own horses. Then he ran matched races with a horse he called Sam F. Sam F. turned out to be one of the fastest sprinters that ever lived.

After the Frontier Days celebration Charlie took Sam F. to Denver and entered him in several three-furlong races. He won every one. Then he decided to try the horse in a half-mile race in Oklahoma City. These races were generally for quarter horses or non-thoroughbreds.

In Oklahoma City, Charlie boasted, "My Sam F. can beat any horse at a quarter, most of them at three furlongs, and a few of them at a half-mile." He sat behind the judges' stand to watch Frank ride Sam F. in a quarter-mile race. The horse won easily. Charlie had put Sam F. in the three-quarter-mile race, which was to be last on the program. The owner of the track told him it couldn't be done.

"Is there a law at this track against running the same horse twice?" questioned Charlie.

"No," said the man, who smoked a small brown pipe with a carved bowl. Charlie noticed two entwined snakes on the bowl and thought they looked like the man's eyebrows. The man squinted in the sunlight as he faced Charlie. "I know there are some who change the name of their horses and run them again, but you don't have the decency to change his name. You boldly put him in two races. There must be something wrong with that."

"If you have no rule against it and I tell you I'm not pulling a fast one, how about letting me run my horse in both races?"

"A horse can't take that kind of treatment!" shouted the man, bobbing his head around on his skinny neck.

"Of course it can," said Charlie calmly. "My horses are so keyed up after a quarter-of-a-mile race, they could go for a full mile right away and win."

"All right. Run your horse, mister. If he wins both races, I'll personally double both purses."

Charlie smiled and nodded agreement. He'd neglected to tell

Frank, afraid he'd be so overconfident that he'd become over-eager and blow away both races.

Frank was as eager as Charlie to win the purse on the first race. He didn't spend any time in the tack room, where he changed to the red and white silks of the Y6. Sam F. reared back on his hind legs and shot out like a bolt of lightning, winning the first race. Laura T. M. and Blumenthal placed in the money, even though they did not take first in their races.

When it was time to line up the jockeys for the last race, Charlie found Frank now in the tack room sitting on the floor, with his back against the wall. An empty gin bottle lay on the floor.

"Hey, who's been feeding this jockey booze?" Charlie yelled.

"He feed hisself." The answer came from a skinny Mexican boy, with enormous brown eyes peering from under long, straight black hair. "He have that rotgut stashed under street clothes." The boy did not smile, but looked at Charlie sympathetically. "My father sleep all the same. My mother find another father, and another, and another. *¡Caramba!*"

Charlie swore under his breath. "That man is a jockey and his horse race is coming up!" Charlie kicked at the bottle. It rolled against the brick wall and broke.

"You want another jockey?" asked the boy matter-of-factly.

"No! I want this bum to sober up!" yelled Charlie. "Jeems, why?"

The boy took his dirty white cotton shirt off. He dropped it on the floor and reached over to put Frank's hat on his head. "We all the same size. See? The lash also fits in my hand."

Charlie watched, helpless, as the youngster held the whip with a looped lash and red and white ribbons fluttering from the handle. Then the boy bent over Frank and unbuttoned his satin shirt, slipped it off, and buttoned it on himself, tucked it in his dirty white cotton pants, pulled the cotton rope belt tighter, and bent to tuck the pants into the tops of his own brown boots. When he stood up, he winked at Charlie. "Show me the jock's ride. What horse?"

Charlie blinked. He could not believe what he saw nor what he heard. "You ride my horse? How old are you? We can't change jockeys just like this. What about the overnight? The overnight sheet listing horses and their jockeys has been out for twenty-four hours, kid!"

"You want to win?"

"Take that outfit off!" sputtered Charlie. "Have you ever been on a horse in your life?"

"Sí, mister. All my life I want to be a jockey. Today I am one." The boy grinned broadly and ducked out the door of the tack room. He lined up with the other jockeys. No one said a word to him.

Charlie started to run out and grab the boy. Then he slowed down. Even if Sam F. came in last he'd be in the race; the entrance fee was already paid. So, let him go, thought Charlie. Let him be in a race. He'll never want to ride again. It'll scare the Mexican hot sauce right out of him.

Charlie squared his shoulders and went out to his seat. He'd noticed that Sam F. was already saddled in the paddock and the judge called, "Jockey up!" The paddock judge was calling out numbers and getting the jockeys on their mounts. Charlie watched the little Mexican kid. When his number was called, he stepped forward. The pony boy brought Sam F. over for him to mount. The pony boys led the horses and jockeys to the front of the stands, then to the starting post by means of a strap. Charlie's heart thumped.

He knew that Sam F. was a good live mount with Frank on him, but now this kid needed more weight. He estimated the kid's weight to be close to a hundred pounds, Frank's weight was between one fifteen and one eighteen. Charlie's heart sank to the bottom of his stomach. He crossed his fingers. He hoped the stewards didn't remember what Frank looked like. He prayed that they didn't examine the riders. He was half-afraid to watch the race. He glanced quickly at Sam F. and noticed the kid bent low, talking in the horse's ear. The horse walked calmly to its post position. The kid's rump was up in the air, but his feet were tucked firmly in the stirrups. The flag went down and the race was on!

Charlie felt like he couldn't breathe. The horses made it past the quarter pole and the next! Charlie sat up straight. That kid used push. He pushed on the horse with his hands, he moved with the horse! He was looking good! But he was taking the overland route, racing wide around the track as if he were afraid of the other horses. Charlie squinted his eyes. I think the kid is afraid of the other jockeys, he said to himself. Look at him ride that horse! "Go, boy, go!" he shouted. The third post was gone and Sam F. was crowding over a little now toward the center of the track. Charlie saw the kid lay his head between Sam F.'s ears.

Sam F. pushed his legs a trifle harder and hit the finish line a good head before any other! Charlie sat down and felt as if all the air had been knocked out of him. Then he saw SAM F. in huge, white chalk letters on the board. He had not been a favorite and paid off six to one.

The purses were paid to the owners and Charlie collected double five hundred dollars for the first and last race and the rest of his earnings for his other sprinters that showed. He wanted to take his horses to the railroad and get them in their stock car as soon as possible—before he let himself kick Frank from here to kingdom come. Charlie watched the young hot walkers cooling the horses and found it hard to wait for the jockeys to change into street clothes. He hoped Frank was sober enough now to change. He wondered if the Mexican kid would come to see him or if he was completely rewarded by riding a horse to the finish line. Riding a winner, Charlie reminded himself. He owed the Mexican kid. He felt a tug on his suit coat.

"We did O.K.," said the Mexican kid. "Your boy is dressed. Here, I bring his colors. I was proud to wear them."

Charlie took the shirt, hat, and stick, which were folded together in a neat roll. "I owe you," said Charlie. "Thanks, *hombre*. You think you can handle this?" He peeled off ten five-dollar bills from his wad of greenbacks and handed them to the boy.

"Thanks, *señor*. Now it is I that owe you. You want me to ride again, another time and another time? Your boy might run away, then you have me."

"Listen, kid, he—that jock in there is not my boy. He's my fool brother. And you can't stay with me. I'm taking my horses and my jock and leaving for Cheyenne tonight."

"Cheyenne fine. I like it there. My father, he is no more. My mother dead since last year. I am Pablo Martinez. I am jockey for the Y6. I can read some. I am smart, all right?"

"You're Mexican."

"Born in Mexico, *sí*. Been in California most of time since father go. Now I hang out with your outfit."

"No! I don't think so. Thanks, anyway." Charlie saw the steward and track owner coming toward him. He swallowed and felt his heart sink. "Beat it, kid!" he hissed under his breath.

The steward reached out his hand. "Congratulations, Mr. Irwin. I hear you finally got the best of Wes here. Made him pay up double because your horse won twice the same day. No rule against that—but now you've done it, it'll catch on at all tracks and be as hard to control as a ringer."

"I'll bet there's a rule within a year," said the owner with confidence.

"I'll bet against that with you," said Charlie, putting out his hand so they could shake on the bet. The owner drew back a couple of steps.

"Oh, no! Goddamnit! I don't really mean that! I'm not laying out more money for you! Mr. Irwin, it was a pleasure having you at my track, but I don't really want to see you soon again."

The steward laughed out loud. "Say," he said out of the corner of his mouth to Charlie, "I heard your jockey keeps his weight down by staying on a liquid diet. Now, I have a theory about that. Your horse runs fast to get away from the jock's hot breath. We don't allow liquor among the jockeys here. No drinking and riding. If you or any of your outfit set foot on our track again, you'll be suspended and fined. Understand?"

"Yes, sir, I do." Charlie motioned to Frank, who was lounging at the door of the tack room, listening to the conversation.

Charlie moved off, ready to pick up his saddle and other gear as quickly as possible.

"Why, that dirty, lousy fart!" said Frank. "I never drank and rode!"

"You drank and slept," said Charlie. "You don't know what happened. Get those horses and we'll shove out right away, before you find your teeth down your throat."

They brought the horses and gear to the empty stock car on the railroad siding. Charlie found the sickle in the car and cut grass at the side of the tracks. He carried it inside the car for the horses. "It's a little dry, boys and girls, but it'll do until I can get some oats." He filled an old bucket with water from a spigot in the yards and replenished the tubs in the car. "Frank, I've a notion to let you ride all the way back to Cheyenne with the horses."

"Forget it. I had only a little drink. Then I fell asleep. You shoulda' woke me up."

"Look around. How'd you like to stay here? I'm mad enough to just go off and leave you in Oklahoma. This is a dust bowl."

"Leave Clara Belle and our baby to take care of themselves? You're crazy, Charlie. I'm the best jockey you have. You couldn't race horses without me."

"Why is it that every time things seem to be going well for me, either you or Will, someone in the family, breaks it up?

Jeems! And you know something else? Clara Belle doesn't deserve you!" Charlie spit the words out. He could feel his blood boil.

The stock car was picked up by the Atchison, Topeka, and Santa Fe going north. It would be transferred several times until it hit the U.P. line for Cheyenne. When the train stopped in Wichita, Charlie got off the coach and went back to his stock car to make sure the animals were all right. He hoped to find some hay around the yards that he could put in the car. He pounded on the double sliding door. It opened and he climbed in, looked about quickly. Everything looked fine. There were several broken bales of hay already in front of the horses. The water looked clean. Charlie wondered if Frank got out at Enid and got some hay. Frank was asleep against the side of the car. Charlie thought that was strange, and before he could check around more he heard a familiar voice.

"Well, things look O.K., huh, mister?" said the Mexican kid.

Charlie nearly jumped off the edge of the boxcar. "Kid, how'd you get in here?"

"Same as you. I go through the door."

THIRTY

Barney Oldfield

In the spring of 1911, Harry P. Hynds suggested to Charlie that the office at the front of the Plains Hotel was too public for him, but someone like Charlie might like to rent the space. Hynds had come to Cheyenne as a blacksmith. He was great friends with Joe. Charlie suspected that Joe had told Hynds that he needed more space for his livestock agent business than he had at the U.P.'s freight office. Hynds had financed the newly built Plains Hotel and intended it to be the best hotel in town. It was across the street from the Union Pacific depot and in the heart of Cheyenne, on the northwest corner of Sixteenth Street and Central Avenue.

The hotel's lobby contained highly polished cedar furniture. On the colored leather upholstered chairs were handpainted Western scenes. On the walls were typical Western mountain and prairie scenes. Some of the pictures were framed with shiny cedar, others were framed with woven strips of leather cut in the shape of Wyoming cattle brands.

Charlie inspected the office. It was just what he wanted. He had a telephone installed and hired himself a secretary named Jane. Jane took care of writing letters and telephone calls and saw to it that plenty of stock was shipped on the Union Pacific. During the spring and summer Charlie traveled with the Irwin Bros.

Wild West Show. He was now booking his shows farther west, into Idaho, Washington, Oregon, California, and Canada besides Colorado, Nebraska, and northern Wyoming.

After the spring roundup Margaret had a fourth child, a girl named Juanita Helen. Ell came to stay at the upper ranch house with Margaret several days before the baby arrived. When Ell came, Will decided there was someone to look after his wife and children, so he went north to Montana to purchase beef cattle.

Ell was not fond of living in a ranch house isolated from the luxuries of town. When she was certain Margaret could manage alone, she went back to her health spa in Colorado Springs.

Charlie felt some embarrassment when he brought Ell to the depot to catch the southbound train. He introduced her to several of his railroad friends. She flirted brazenly with each one. Her black silk dress was skin-tight, low-necked, and accented with gaudy jewelry. Her perfume was sensuously pleasing and men were drawn to her faster than deer to salt. Charlie was actually relieved when her train pulled out of the station.

"Too bad your sister couldn't stay longer," said one of Charlie's friends. "She sure don't mind showing off her fetlocks." He winked and slapped Charlie on the back.

Charlie took the five children and Etta on the train to Nevada and California during July. Old Joe was left to look after the ranch. The children performed in the Wild West show in Elko, Winnemucca, Lovelock, and Reno, then they traveled to Colfax, Roseville, Sacramento, San Francisco, and San Bernardino. In San Bernardino Charlie met Barney Oldfield.

During this time the automobile industry used auto racing as an important part of its advertising. The large companies made special racers and found fearless men to drive them. Barney Oldfield was a kind of daredevil young man who became famous for his automobile racing.

Charlie sat on the edge of the grandstand seat watching a man chomp on a cigar while he raced an automobile a half-mile in a contest with Lincoln Beachey and his Curtiss biplane.

Charlie loved any kind of race. He understood showmanship. He understood people. As he watched the man with the cigar seated in an automobile race against the biplane, Charlie thought how Elmer Lovejoy in Laramie had once told him it was undignified to resort to cheap, tawdry commercialism. "People know a good product when they see one. Automobiles will sell themselves."

Charlie told Lovejoy not to look down his nose at a little

entertainment. "That's good salesmanship. Give people a chance to see your product in action. Your wife buys a new spring hat because she sees advertisements in the newspaper. She's convinced she has to have a new hat. Selling automobiles is the same."

Two years later Elmer Lovejoy closed his garage and barely had enough money to pay creditors.

Charlie could feel the excitement of the crowd as they watched the race between automobile and aeroplane. He stood up to see the driver of the automobile better. He thought, People are hungry for horseless carriages, like this one, with no kidney-breaking bounce. His Wild West show parade couldn't top this for exciting salesmanship. He thought how the audience loved the roar of the cylinders, loved the excitement of the brightly painted automobile and biplane, even the clothing worn by the drivers. It was like the excitement at horse races. The tension built up by the sound of the beating of the hooves on the track, the color and physical appearance of the horses, the colorful splash of the jockeys' silks. It was man against man, man against beast, and man against machines. It was entertainment. It was commercial. It was a living for whoever wanted to join in the show.

The sun moved to the center of the hazy, blue California sky and the Curtiss biplane won the race. Charlie moved down onto the track. He elbowed his way through the crowd. He grabbed the arms of the automobile driver. "Shake it off, you'll win next time. Say, if that biplane wouldn't scare the tar out of a thoroughbred, I'd like to have a horse race with it. I have a horse called Sam F. that could beat a flying machine in a half-mile contest."

"Say, man, could your Sam F. beat me in a 140-horsepower Christi? I doubt it." Oldfield moved his cigar from one side of his mouth to the other. "Bring that horse on and we'll see."

"I can't do that, I have a Wild West show to put on. But I could fit in a race tomorrow afternoon. I'm going to put on a matched race with a couple thoroughbreds that have never been in a race outside of Wyoming."

"Well, I wish you more luck than I had, my friend. I'm going to Detroit this afternoon to look over some new designs. I promise to see you again before the year's out. Maybe we'll meet at another racetrack—that's fate, you know."

"Mr. uh—uh—what new design?" asked Charlie.

"Mr. Berner Eli Oldfield, Barney's the name." He stuck out his hand, and Charlie shook it warmly. "Electric headlights instead of the acetylene generator and Prest-O-Lite tank."

"Here's my card," said Charlie, pulling one out of his suit's breast pocket. "Can you stay for some of the show?"

"If I race to the train depot," said Oldfield with a laugh.

Charlie and his family were back in Cheyenne by the time Clara Belle had her second baby near the end of July that summer. The baby was a girl, named Louise Adelaide. Etta sent a wire to Ell to come right away. She delivered the baby with no complications. She fed Clara Belle a tonic concoction of ergot and reserpine made from ground roots, leaves, and grain. Clara Belle was on her feet in a week and tending to the care of her children and the housework in the little house in Cheyenne. Ell told her the tonic was something she'd learned from the famous lung specialist, Dr. Gerald Webb. By now Nevada Avenue in Colorado Springs was lined with convalescent homes for people with lung diseases and a hospital called Glockner, which was surrounded by invalids' tents. Ell took in lungers, charging less than the hospital, but she also took patients suffering from other ailments. She explained that she never mentioned the diseases of her patients, mainly because people had such a great fear of the lungers.

When Etta permitted her children to see their newest cousin, the children were more interested in the stories Ell told than the baby Louise. Ell told Floyd and Roy their rope tricks were so spectacular that the act would soon be showing in New York City's Madison Square Garden. She praised the piano-playing ability of Joella, Pauline, and Frances, saying that they were each one good enough to study abroad, in London, if Charlie would only let them go. "Joella, in two or three years your voice will be equally as good as the noted singing beauty, Lillie Langtry," she said. Then not to leave Clara Belle's four-year-old Maxine out she said, "Maxine, you learn to ride a pony. One day you'll be the champion lady relay rider." The children loved their flamboyant, easy-talking aunt.

Ell insisted on staying through the Frontier Days activities, which took place on the twenty-third to the twenty-sixth of August. Charlie, always embarrassed to introduce Ell to anyone, finally took her to the ranch to meet the new cowboys and see their father. Ell seemed to strip a person bare, touch every muscle in the shoulders, buttocks, and thighs, judge body weight and sexual ability with one penetrating look. She gave Joe an affectionate hug, but knew before her hands grasped across his back that he'd not lost one ounce of good, solid weight and that he was extraordinarily well for a man sixty-five years old.

"How's Les?" shouted Joe, pulling away.

"Pa, aren't you happy to see me?" asked Ell. Her green eyes filled with water.

He studied his only daughter, standing straight, sure of herself, her head held high, her neck slim and white, her breasts like twin peaks rising against the gauzy, soft material of her shirtwaist, her belly flat and her legs slim, ending with her feet in black, high-heeled pumps. "Take off those silly stilts. Get a pair of boots on! I'll show you around the place. Me and Roy and a new fellow, Pablo, done a lot since you were here this spring. And you have to see Will and Margaret's little Juanita—why, she turns over and looks me square in the eye. Grown from a polliwog to a frog."

Charlie breathed a sigh of relief and let his father take Ell around the ranch and show her off to the new boys. He found a pair of Etta's boots for her to wear.

"These are snug," said Ell, pulling on the round-toed boots with the heart-shaped inlay.

"That's good, they match your skirt," said Charlie. The minute the words were out, he wished he'd bitten his tongue.

"Sarcasm doesn't become you," said Ell softly. She touched Charlie's cheek and fluttered her eyes at him. He inhaled the most wonderful scent, like a spring morning when all the flowers were in bloom at one time.

Inside the barn Joe called, "Pablo, come here, I want you to meet C.B.'s sister. My grown daughter."

Pablo was portioning out fresh hay for the horses that were in the stalls. He was small and quick and darted under a pure black horse and came up alongside Joe.

"Pablo Martinez. He's going to be the best jockey in Wyoming," said Joe.

Surrounded by the smell of horses, leather, fresh hay, and dust, Ell brushed her hand across her eyes as if to see better in the smoky light of the barn. She moved so that her red hair was caught in the sunbeam coming through the open door.

"Best jock in the world, beautiful *señorita,*" said Martinez, his white teeth flashing against his dark face. His eyes were wide, admiring Ell appreciatively. She smiled back and held out her hand. He held it momentarily, gently, as if it were made of fine china. His small agile body made him look like a boy of not more than twelve, but his eyes were those of a man seeing a gorgeous woman.

In the corral at the side of the barn was a tall, well-built man, maybe ten years younger than Ell, and half a head taller. He wore a navy blue shirt, open at the throat, showing a healthy tan and a red silk neckerchief knotted at the side. He had on black twill trousers that clung tightly to his slim hips; around his waist was a tooled leather belt studded with silver conchos. His boots were brown leather, custom-made, and polished. He wore a black, narrow-brimmed hat at a jaunty angle. He seemed out of place, too neat, almost like a dude, standing in the center of the corral throwing his seventy-foot-long rope at a blue-gray pony.

"Tom Mix. He's learning to make a forty-foot reach with that rope," said Joe. "Tom's here temporarily. One of those Miller brothers from that 101 Ranch near Ponca City, Oklahoma, left him here for Charlie to shape up into some kind of rope twirler," said Joe. Then under his breath he added, "You can see he's too pretty for a cowboy. I believe he'd get lost in an acre meadow. He's so slow he'd freeze to death before turning around to come in out of a hard frost."

Mix said, "Pleased to meet you," and bowed.

Ell was intrigued with this big handsome man. "I'm Joe Irwin's daughter." She shaded her eyes against the sun.

"You are the prettiest thing I've seen on this here ranch next to Old Blue." He pointed to the horse, and smiled.

Ell immediately took a liking to the man. She could feel his male energy spark the air like electricity.

That afternoon Charlie told her that Colonel Joseph C. Miller had seen Floyd ride a horse and do trick roping in Denver. He was impressed and wanted someone to do the same for the 101 Real Wild West Show that he and his brothers were producing. Joe Miller wanted this Tom Mix person to be their trick rider and roper. However, his brother, Colonel Zack Miller, didn't think Tom Mix was much of a cowboy, because he was so uncoordinated that he could not sit on his horse and twirl his rope at the same time. Zack Miller told Charlie that the man had become one of those celluloid cowboys doing a little for William Selig, in Chicago, owner of the Selig Polyscope Company, which made motion pictures of the West.

Ell went out beside the barn to watch Tom Mix practice roping while riding his horse. She could see that he tried to get his eye, hand, and legs to react together as a team. When he stopped to rewind his rope, she could see he was also a dreamer. His eyes became languid, as though their spirit were turned inward. He swayed in the saddle and began to let his twirling rope out so that the noose encircled his body; now it included the body of his horse. He let the noose grow so that he could have encircled two other horses, one on each side.

Ell could not hold back. "Now ride, go around the corral full speed! Keep the rope twirling!"

He let the long rope slide through his hands. His hand was above his head, the loop circled the knees of his horse. She clapped her hands. Suddenly he looked up and his eyes were alive and sparkling. The rope fell in a heap.

"Oh, damn! Well, excuse me, ma'am. This thing is more than I can learn. Your brother wants me to get out in the middle of the arena during those Frontier Days goings-on and do this body spin on my horse. He said he'll have his two boys on each side of me so the spin has to be with about forty feet of this rope. If my horse has to run he'll get tangled in my rope and we'll be treated to an instantaneous, violent, spectacular bust in a cloud of dust! I don't look forward to being thrown in the dirt!" He looked at his clean shirt and trousers.

Ell laughed softly. "How long do you work out?"

"Every afternoon. In the mornings I mend corral fences, or clear the brush around the creek, or exercise the horses. After the noon meal your brother watches me and gives me pointers for about an hour, then I'm on my own to perfect whatever is wrong. And you, what do you do?"

Ell was taken off guard. "Well, I—I came to Cheyenne to deliver a healthy baby girl to my sister-in-law and brother Frank. Then I decided to stay for the Frontier festivities before going home to my patients in Colorado Springs."

"Aha, the home of the Simmons' Cog Train." Mix climbed from his horse and came to the fence. "You're a lady doc?"

Ell felt warm all over. She hadn't felt this way since she was a young girl. Since the three Indian brothers on the way to Kansas. She laughed and leaned forward over the fence. He put his hands on her shoulders. "Yes, I heal the sick in body, heart, and mind."

"Whoa! You'll fall head over heels right at my feet."

"Would that upset you?"

"Pshaw, no, all the women do that when they're near me." His words were more jocular than conceited. He smelled like sweat and horse and leather.

"I don't want to be so ordinary." She tried to keep her voice steady. "Would it hurt if we took a walk, maybe go over to the creek and see what you've done there to clear out the brush? I hope you haven't cut out any of the huckleberry bushes."

"I don't know what they look like. I guess you'd better show me." He left his rope on top of the snubbing post and walked his pony into the first stall of the barn. When they'd walked out of sight of the ranch house, Mix said, "Lordy, it's hot! You mind if I take off my wool shirt?"

"No, of course not." Ell felt her pulse quickening in her throat. His muscles rippled in the sun and made a fire in the pit of her stomach. She wondered if he knew how she felt. She told herself she was foolish. She'd seen many men naked from the waist up—from the waist down, too, for that matter. Why should she be worked up about this one? He was better-looking than most and had a casual, boyish way about him that told Ell he was not an amateur around women. "What do you think of the Y6 spread?"

Mix pointed a long index finger toward the slightly rolling land. "Looks and feels a lot like Oklahoma, but greener. I grew up in Pennsylvania. Never dreamed about Wyoming. Instead I dreamed about mountains and lumberjacks. Mountains gave me security."

He'd been to school as far as the fourth grade. His father dragged logs from the woods with a team of horses to lumber mills near Hick's Run. When he was twelve he shot himself in the leg with a single-shot pistol while target practicing with a friend. "I rode the old workhorses bareback and the mules, too. Once I rode a horse into the barn door I never thought I was too tall to clear and was knocked off into a pile of hay." That discouraged him from riding for a while, but he took up roping. When he was fourteen he went out to the stockyards near home, tied one end of his rope around his waist, and roped a bull with the loop. The bull was stronger than the boy, who had brought the end of the rope from his waist, keeping it taut, around the rear side of his right thigh, leaning backward to act as a snubbing post himself. He was dragged, cut, and bruised before being rescued. His mother thought he was a big devil, preferring football or baseball to helping in his father's work. When war was declared against Spain, Mix enlisted in Washington, D.C., lying about his age. Two years later he re-enlisted because of the Boer War and on one of his furloughs he was married, but he said the marriage didn't last.

Ell thought he was still married. His words seemed to confirm her suspicions.

Some months later he decided not to go back to his wife nor the U.S. Artillery. He was a deserter, but there was never a warrant for his arrest. He admitted that he ran scared for several years and didn't give out much information about his past. He thought the Army might be looking for him. He attended the St. Louis World's Fair as a drum major of the Oklahoma Cavalry Band, even though he was no musician nor in the militia. But his dark, good looks were most attractive to ladies. There he met Will Rogers. After that he kind of drifted around doing odd jobs—bartending, part-time ranch hand—then he joined the Cowboy Brigade in Omaha, Nebraska, traveled by train to Washington, D.C., for the celebration of the inauguration of President Theodore Roosevelt's second term. It was not long after that when he went to work for the Miller brothers. "And then that brings me here," ended Mix. He lay in the sun and mounded up soil between his fingers.

"Do you ever think of getting married again?" asked Ell.

"Oh, I was married again. Didn't last. She didn't like the idea of being married to a cowboy who had no desire to settle down and raise a bunch of kids."

"Well, one day you'll settle down. Maybe become a rancher?"

Mix rolled over, brushed the soil off his hands, put his head on his folded shirt, and rolled a cigarette. "Would you go for a walk with me again before the Frontier thing? Maybe tell me how I've improved and how good I am at roping and riding?"

"The day before you go to Cheyenne, I will. You ought to be good enough so I can say so without telling a lie by then."

He put on his shirt, undid his belt buckle, and tucked his shirt into his pants. Ell watched his big hands push against his hips. She closed her eyes and wondered what those hands would feel like against her own hips.

A few days later Ell was standing by the corral fence watching Mix twirl his big loop around the legs of his horse. She waved her straw hat in the air. "I think you have it, but make the horse walk or turn in circles."

The rope dropped and crumpled like a dead snake. "If I'm going to do this on a horse I have to keep it still. C.B. and I decided that this morning. I can't do two things at once." He rolled up his rope. "But I can do one at a time and do just as well as the next guy." He stuck his chin out and looked at her with narrowed eyes. "Tell me I looked good."

"Of course, you looked good. But to be tops you have to do better than the next guy."

He struck back: "I done more than most guys. I've made a couple films for Bill Selig. When they're released you'll say, 'I knew that fellow. Hotzigity, he was good!' "

Ell laughed, feeling light-headed and suddenly foolishly young. "Yes, hotzigity! Let's go wading in the creek."

This time he told her more than he'd ever told anyone else about his life. He'd been interested in Colonel Mulhall's daughter, Lucille, the Champion Cowgirl of the Mulhall Wild West Show. But old Colonel Mulhall didn't approve of a no-account cowboy that earned fifteen dollars a month working for the Millers. He said Mix was so muddle-headed he didn't know dung from wild honey, and Miller ran him off to C. B. Irwin to learn trick roping.

How pleasant it felt to put their bare feet into the creek. Ell found huckleberries and filled her hat with fat, sweet dusky blue fruit. "I'm glad you didn't get these bushes. Notice what the leaves look like so if Charlie sends you out here to clear brush again, you'll not cut them."

He looked, but he was not sure he could tell one leaf or one plant from another. Ell told him to look for the big purple-blue berries. He asked her what if they'd all been picked. She held her sides and laughed, then splashed water on him. "I don't know if you are a real dumb cluck or smart like a fox."

"I'm cagey as a mountain cat," he said, pulling her over against his wide chest so that she was caught in his arms. She smelled her own perfume mixed with the strong masculine scent of his sweat. His silver belt buckle rubbed against her stomach. She could feel his hands run up the back of her head and sweep out the combs and pins from her long golden red hair. The fire spread from her loins throughout her body. It was a pent-up passion that completely surprised her. It rushed out inundating her so that she was not able to struggle away from the horse-and-leather smell of his hands, his hot breath and fiery lips full against her mouth, nor struggle from the aching pressure of his knee widening the V between her thighs. As a kind of dreamy mirage from her childhood, she saw the three, near-naked brown bodies of the Indians, with their hair in braids, except one who had his braids stuck to the top of his head with daubs of mud. Her straw hat fell to the grass and she could hear the voice from long ago telling her not to stay in the prairie sun too long without a bonnet. And suddenly the picture changed. It was a wild-eyed, sunburned, cotton-headed boy named Rob that was crowding down on her with hot, hard lips. His tongue broke through her lips and moved its exploratory tip against her teeth. Their tongues met and pressed. She could feel his hands move down to her hips and press her closer to him so that she could feel his maleness swell with a life of its own. Her breathing was fast. This was her dream. This was what she wanted, what she needed. Her whole being was aflame, crying out.

When she cried, he pulled away. His dark eyes stared into hers questioningly. "What the—?" His voice was choked, far away.

She heard her voice as if detached from her electrified body, calm and logical. "No, not here. It's not right for the others, for Pa, or Charlie and the kids. This is their place, not mine."

Afterward she was not sure why she'd let him pull away nor why she'd spoken up with that excuse. She guessed she had more willpower than she'd imagined, or somewhere in the back of her mind she remembered the way Charlie'd looked at her when he caught her playing poker in the bunkhouse with some of the boys; then he'd sent her home. She didn't want to be sent home. She was a grown woman, able to determine her own fate.

During the Frontier Days activities Ell mingled with the cowboys and cowgirls, trying to stay close to the girls who were going to perform their rope tricks. When Floyd and Roy performed, she was the first to stand up and clap. When Tom Mix performed his body-spin, his horse, old Blue, stood still. Floyd and Roy sat on their horses on either side of him, and he spun that loop out to encircle all three horses. The crowd gave him a huge applause, but Ell held her head down. She knew that Mix should have been doing the trick from the back of a horse going full speed if he were more than just a handsome face.

Charlie was out in the ring announcing the events over his bullhorn. He trotted on his horse around the arena singing in his booming voice "Good-bye, Old Paint" and "Alfalfa Hay." Everyone knew he was proud of his two boys and his three girls, especially little Frances, who did her rope tricks from the back of Blondie, the show steer.

On Sunday morning Charlie and the whole family, including most of the cowboys, were back at the arena to take the animals back to the ranch, or over to the Four-Mile pasture, to close up the cookhouse and barn. Etta, Ell, and the girls helped the cook clean the cookhouse, stack the wooden tables and benches against the walls, sweep out and make certain the white, enameled dishes were all covered over with fresh dishtowels. When it was finished, Etta said she was going to the house to rest.

"Mama, could we go swimming?" asked Joella. "Aunt Ell could take us girls to Lion's Park."

Because the horses were loaded with saddles and other gear for the ranch, Ell took Charlie's Colburn. "Anyone want to go swimming?" she called.

She was surprised when Tom Mix sauntered over, looking like he'd just stepped out of Harrington's Men's Furnishings in Cheyenne.

"I'll go to be with you, adorable lady," Mix said. "Come on, tell me my rope tricks were spectacular. The best you ever saw."

"To say that would be a lie," said Ell. "I've seen better from my nephew, Floyd. But don't look so sad. You were a sensation with the ladies. They love your style, your tight pants, your firm jaw, your good looks."

"Oh, that's what I want to hear. Say, you and I going swimming alone?" He put his big, brown hand over hers on the edge of the automobile. "Because if we are, I'll show you where I was shot in the leg, if you'll show me—"

"Hush," said Ell. "My three nieces are coming. Say, you don't look like you've been cleaning anybody's barn." She looked over his immaculate attire. He didn't even look like he'd worked up a good sweat doing his rope tricks. Nothing was out of place, not a lock of dark hair, nor the colorful neckerchief which lay against the deep red of his flannel shirt. He smiled, showing off his beautiful, even, white teeth. "Climb in the backseat," she said. "Your smile is really infectious, like the plague, and just about as dangerous."

Etta had outfitted her girls with dresses to their knees, cotton pantaloons to match, and long black stockings for swimming. As the girls scrambled out of the automobile and ran to the sandy edge of the man-made lake, Ell slipped out of the loose-fitting smock and dashed after the girls. Mix sat on the sand to take off his boots. Then he waded, and the bottoms of his twill trousers got wet. He was looking at Ell, who wore the latest in Parisian bathing wear, a skimpy black suit, no sleeves, a very short skirt and black stockings, which she'd rolled just below her knees.

"My God, you'll be arrested!" he called. "Baby, there's not enough material in your outfit to dust a fiddle!"

"Don't tell my father!" squealed Ell, playfully throwing water on him.

"Hey, wait until I get my shirt and hat off, at least." He ran for shore and tossed down his hat and tore off his neckerchief and shirt, folding them before laying each under his hat.

The girls were good swimmers. Mix could not swim. When they splashed him, he ran for shore.

Finally, when they were sunning on the shore, he rolled up his trouser leg and showed Ell the big scar on his leg. "I got shot in a big skirmish in Puerto Rico in 1898. I was with the Fourth Artillery Regiment."

"I thought you shot yourself when you were twelve," said Ell, snickering. "Let me look at that nasty scar." She felt his leg with her sensitive fingers and ran her thumbs over the deep pit, a purple scar. She pressed around the tibia and closed her eyes. "Flex your foot once or twice," she said. He did. She opened her eyes and asked him if what she'd done hurt at all.

"Nope, just my feelings because you didn't move your hands higher up on my leg. Truthfully, it hurts before any rainstorm. I'm every bit as good as them Apaches in Oklahoma at predicting weather."

"The bullet is still in your leg," Ell said.

"You're crazy! Oh, Jesus, that's what I get for fooling around with a lady medicine man. There's no bullet in that leg."

However, Ell's words proved to be true. About six years later the leg began to act up and give him trouble. The bullet was located and surgically removed.

But this afternoon he told all the girls who were crowded around him on the sandy beach in Lion's Park how he'd broken his other leg the year before. He was with the Miller Brothers' 101 Wild West Show and didn't have his faithful horse, Old Blue, with him to enter a roping contest in Oklahoma City. So he borrowed one of the 101's horses and entered the rodeo. The horse bucked just as he roped his steer and he was dragged in the dirt. His leg was broken and he was hospitalized. He told one of the stable boys to take the horse to the nearest ranch and gave the boy a ten-dollar bill for the job. The boy left the horse with Zack Mulhall. By the time Mix was out of the hospital, the horse was gone. The Miller Brothers sued him for embezzlement and his bond was set at a thousand dollars. He couldn't pay it and finally convinced the Miller Brothers that losing the horse was not his fault. They took him back and said he could pay for the horse by continuing to work for them. He guessed that was why they never increased his pay from fifteen dollars a month, room and board. "Hey, it's lucky I'm here. Your brother"—he looked at the younger girls—"your father, pays me thirty dollars a month. I think I'm drawing two salaries, one from the Y6 and one from the 101."

Joella put her first and third fingers in her mouth and gave a shrill whistle. Then said, "You lucky son of a gun."

"You bet. Look how hard you work around here," said Pauline.

"To tell the truth I'm thinking of doing some more motion pictures," said Mix casually. "I did one called *The Range Rider* last year, and before I came out here Selig shot *Back to the Primitive* with me riding Old Blue."

"Is that really true?" asked Frances, edging closer and looking up into Mix's face.

"Have I ever lied to you, little princess? Last year I made a couple others. Haven't you heard of *Up San Juan Hill, Briton and Boer* or *Millionaire Cowboy*? They're all mine. I'd like to work for William Fox next. That man finds the good-looking leading ladies."

"I guess the Star hasn't heard of your shows yet. Maybe they've been at the Lyric, but I haven't heard of any movie stars named Tom Mix!" Frances rolled over in the sand giggling.

Ell glanced at Mix. He winked and the sun glinted off his straight, white teeth. Suddenly she could not picture this man wrestling calves at a branding fire, notching their ears, castrating the male calves, or keeping the irons hot and handing them to the brander. She could not see him taking the kicks and thrashing of the calves that always went for the groin, until the cowboy learned to wrestle tough and dirty. He wanted the glory, but he didn't have the self-discipline for the constant practice that gave a man skill, agility, strong arms, muscles in the shoulders, tough, calloused hands.

Mix slipped one hand around her thin waist. She felt his eyes peeling away her skimpy bathing suit, then stripping each of her stockings down past her ankles. His eyes gave her goose bumps and she did not trust herself to look long into his face. She was not certain now that his story about being in picture shows was no more than hot air.

The next morning Ell left on the early southbound train for Colorado Springs. She'd begun to hanker for the gratifying feeling of working with a pale, debilitated patient until he was sunbrowned and full of energy. Ell would have been in the middle of the excitement that took place in the afternoon had she stayed a few hours longer. A couple cowboys from the Warren Ranch, south of Cheyenne, found a blue-colored pony lying dead beside the road, hit sometime in the night by a passing automobile.

The Warren hands asked around and finally found that the horse belonged to one of Charlie Irwin's men. Someone called Charlie at home in Cheyenne, and from the description Charlie was certain it was Tom Mix's horse. He asked Mix what he'd done with Old Blue. "You send your horse back to the Y6? After your performance Saturday what did you do with your horse? On Sunday when we cleaned up, where was your horse?"

"I don't remember, sir. I handed the reins to some of the cowboys after my roping performance. I don't know if I saw him on Sunday."

"I can't remember seeing much of you!" hollered Charlie.

"I went to Lion's Park with the girls, sir," said Mix defensively.

"You didn't see that your horse had water and grain?" asked Charlie, dumbfounded.

"I figured the other boys would see to that."

Charlie was a whale of a man, with a deep, booming, resonant voice. He stood six feet four inches tall and weighed at least two hundred and twenty pounds. He had an owlish look as he peered down at Mix. "I want you to know that your excuse is so weak and lamebrained that I believe it! You let your horse wander off because you were so bent on looking pretty for the crowd and impressing the females. Man, I'm sending you back to those three colonels, the Miller brothers, because I can't teach you a thing!"

Mix looked stunned.

"I don't think you have the nerve nor the skill to stick in the saddle on a salty, raring, busting bronc while you perform rope tricks. All you'll be known for is the wide body spin. You'd better get some diamond-studded spurs, white boots, and a white, western-cut dress suit, as it suits your style and the crowd will expect fancy dress if they don't get he-man action! And look around for another horse!"

After Charlie gave him a tongue-lashing he took Mix to bury the horse beside the road in a patch of big, beautiful white blossoming bull thistles. Charlie piled the grave with rocks, and Mix touched away his tears with a silk neckerchief. Charlie sat beside the road to rest and saw a discarded, flat board. On the front he gouged out the words OLD BLUE, THE BEST COW PONY THAT EVER PULLED A ROPE with his pocketknife. He tossed the board to Mix, who sat with his head in his hands. "You got your tack hammer and nails in your pocket?" asked Charlie. "Put this here on a post so you'll be able to find your poor, old horse."

Mix put his hands in his pockets and then held them out flat. "I don't have nails nor a hammer."

"Jeems, man, I'm right, you'll never be a cussed cowboy! Never leave the bunkhouse without nails, hammer, knife, and lasso in your possession. Even my girls know that and don't have to be told twice when they're at the ranch! Here, use mine."

When the marker was up, Charlie grunted with satisfaction.

The two men got into Charlie's Colburn and chugged back to the house in town. Before getting out of the car Charlie told Tom Mix to collect his gear and take the next train south that connected with the Santa Fe and headed for Ponca City and the Miller 101 Ranch. "I'll buy your ticket," said Charlie. "Just get out of here and don't come back."

Charlie made more money supplying stock to the Frontier Days festivities. One day before school began he came home to surprise Etta with a brand-new automobile, an Overland. It was larger than the Colburn and did not need to be cranked before starting.

At this time Charlie had all the children at the ranch mending corral fences and even helping with the butchering. Charlie was certain everything they could learn to do on their own on the ranch would make his children mature and self-sufficient and independent.

Pablo Martinez lived in the bunkhouse with the cowboys. Etta thought he ought to go to school. "Charlie, that boy acts like he knows nothing. Watch him around the yard, he's the clumsiest kid I've ever seen."

Charlie had to agree. "I saw Pablo pounding barbed wire on a fence post yesterday, and he hit his thumb more times than the nail. Floyd ended up getting the wire attached to the post for him. But did you ever notice how he stands around and smiles and nods his head, no matter if I speak gently or if I yell my head off at him? He's the grinningest kid I've seen. Bunkhouse boys call him Kid Mex."

"He needs to be able to read and write," said Etta.

"I'll tell you what I'm going to do," teased Charlie. He picked up Etta and swung her around two, three times before he set her feet on the floor. "I don't think Pablo'd learn so much in school. He'd frustrate the sawdust out of any schoolmarm."

Etta put up her hand and began to object.

"Now, wait just a minute until I'm finished," said Charlie. "I suggest that Pablo stay at the ranch this winter and work with my father some more. There's another side to the kid. You ever watch him on a horse?"

Etta's eyes lit up. "He hunkers down close to the horse's ears and seems to talk to it. He puts his arms around the critter's neck. He seems to know what the horse is going to do before it even does it. When that boy is on the back of a horse, he's part of it. It's uncanny, but I swear it's true." She laughed and looked up at Charlie to see what he was going to say.

"Maybe we shouldn't laugh at him. I believe he's going to be one of my best jockeys. Don't say a word, but he's better than Frank." Charlie put his arms around Etta, enfolding her. "Joe will teach him to read and write, on those long winter evenings when they both would rather be on horseback. Joe can teach him how to braid a horsehair rope or repair a saddle or bridle, and at the same time work in some English reading and writing."

"Charlie, you are a genius! That'll be good for both of them." Etta gave him a squeeze. "I already saw Joe showing Pablo how to use the telephone. He had him speak the numbers in English over and over."

"So, that's taken care of. I'm going to have the kids dig some potatoes and carrots. I'll get some squash and load it up in the back of the Overland and take it to that orphanage at Torrington. I heard their farm was plumb washed out when the North Platte flooded last spring. They could use a little help going into winter." Charlie went out the back door.

Suddenly Etta was on the screened back porch, listening. She called to Charlie, "Are you leaving already? Why'd you turn your car motor on?"

Charlie looked around. "What is that sound? It's not the wind."

Etta was outside beside Charlie. "It's a motor of some kind." She walked to the front of the house and opened the front gate, went through the wrought-iron archway in the front yard, and stood in the middle of the dirt road. "Charlie, come quick. We're going to have company. Look at that cloud of dust. Look at that beautiful red automobile. Who can that be, for heaven's sake?"

Charlie took his hat off and rolled the brim back to the sides. He began to chuckle deep inside his chest. "Jeems, he meant every word he said. I'd almost forgotten, but not him. Dear, that's my old friend, Barney Oldfield. I met him in San Bernardino. You remember, the man who raced against the Curtiss biplane? I bet you my good Heiser saddle it's him."

"It's *he*," corrected Etta.

"That's what I said. Who else would drive like chain lightning with a link snapped?"

The red automobile came to a halt on the south side of the archway. The dust rolled across the yard. Etta fanned at it with the hem of her apron. The driver got out. He was chewing on the end of a large cigar. First thing he reached for Etta's hand.

"I'd have been here a lot sooner had I known you were this good-looking," he said. He gripped her small hand and his tanned face crinkled into a jolly smile. "I drove all the way up here from Denver. I scared more than a dozen horses clean off the road. Hey, the first person I asked in Cheyenne told me how to get here. Guess you're about as popular as I am! Hope your popularity runs to fixing good eats. My belly button's rubbing against my backbone, I'm so hungry."

"You're Barney Oldfield!" Etta liked him right away. "You're the one to first drive an automobile sixty miles an hour on a circular track. You two talk and I'll get you some fixings as fast as a lamb can shake its tail."

"Don't talk about sheep, even baby sheep, on this ranch, dear." Charlie gave Etta a mocking look as she hurried around the house and into the back door.

"Did you drive that red devil all the way from California?" asked Charlie.

"No," said Oldfield with a laugh. "I picked this up in Denver. It's a Pierce Arrow. I am being exploited to focus attention on National Highways, and of course the automobile company finds it's good advertisement. After I show off around Cheyenne tomorrow, I'm driving to Chicago."

Charlie looked under the hood and inspected the six-cylinder, forty-eight horsepower touring car. He thought it was the most beautiful piece of metal he'd seen.

"I know it'll go faster than my old Colburn, and probably than my new Overland. But I have quarter horses that are fast as a tornado." Charlie grinned.

"Precisely why I came. You said something about a race that day we first met. So, let's see if this Pierce Arrow gas-burner can go faster than your speediest hay-burner racehorse."

"Let's go!" yelled Charlie, feeling the excitement well up inside his chest. Inside the barn he found Martinez brushing one of the horses. "You think Sam F. can outrun an automobile?"

"Sí," said Martinez, pulling his shirt sleeves down and fastening the buttons at his wrists.

"What makes you think that?" asked Oldfield.

"He's got the heart of a racer. He's fit and likes nothing better than to get his legs going round and round."

"Saddle him in a jiffy!" cried Charlie.

"But shouldn't I walk him around some before starting to run?" asked Martinez softly, not wanting to embarrass Charlie in front of his guest.

"Of course, don't talk, just move. Hurry up!" Charlie instructed Martinez to take Sam F. out into the flat pasture and when he was ready to run to raise his hand so that Mr. Oldfield could step on the gas pedal and line up wheel to toe.

Martinez nodded. He kept the horse close to the fence, motioning for Oldfield to keep his automobile away from the horse while he was warming up.

Martinez stared in astonishment at the red Pierce Arrow; however, in a few moments his full attention was on the horse. Charlie got in the car with Oldfield. They rode around one end of the field. Pablo motioned for them to come a little closer, and he trotted the horse alongside the automobile. Suddenly Martinez held his hand out, a signal to stop and line up.

"We'll go a mile," said Charlie. "That's two times around the pasture. I'll move my hand down when the race is on. Get ready!"

"I'm looking for the signal," said Martinez, grinning. Charlie could see that the boy's muscles were tense, holding the horse back until time to let loose. Charlie walked back to the car and got in. Oldfield seemed relaxed behind the wheel. He was smiling. A fresh cigar was in his mouth. This was some fun he'd planned all the way from Denver.

Inside the ranch house dinner was on the table. Everyone looked around for Charlie, Martinez, and Oldfield.

"I left the boy brushing down the horses," said Joe. "He ain't there now. Everything's left like he just up and walked out. I'm going to have to give him a piece of my mind. Kids and cowboys don't take responsibility like they used to."

"He's probably inspecting that red and silver automobile in the front yard," said Etta.

"Inspecting, hell," said Floyd. "Pa's out in the field with the automobile and Pablo's on Sam F. They're having a winner-takes-all race!"

Etta looked at Floyd. Floyd bit his tongue. He'd forgotten

himself. In the bunkhouse he could talk with the men and use any kind of language, but in the house, especially if ladies were present, no one was permitted to use foul language. Charlie made no exceptions to that rule.

"Jesus! I'd like to see that goddamned machine," said Roy, thinking that if Floyd could get away with "man talk," he could.

Etta first pulled Floyd then Roy off their chairs by an ear and headed them toward the kitchen. The girls and cowboys around the table began to snicker.

"Continue with the meal," said Etta. "These boys of mine have something to be washed out of their mouths before they can eat."

"I hope she never catches me swearing," said fifteen-year-old Joella, passing a bowl of buttered noodles around the table. The men said nothing. They began to pass food, then kept their mouths full of green beans, roast beef, mashed potatoes and gravy, noodles, or hot biscuits with honey.

Floyd and Roy came back with their faces scrubbed shiny pink. Their smiles were wiped off and neither was hungry.

"Mama," said ten-year-old Frances, "Roy and Floyd don't eat."

"That's their choice," said her mother stiff-lipped. "By breakfast time they will have their appetites back."

At sundown Charlie, Oldfield, and Martinez were still out in the field. Etta began to worry. She knew that Charlie didn't like to be chased after and worried about as though he were some shiftless kid. So she waited all through the meal. The girls helped Etta and the cook with the dishes, and when everyone was out of the kitchen, she went out to the screened porch and out the back door. The cowboys had the lanterns lit in the bunkhouse. Then she heard the deep, familiar singing of "Alfalfa Hay." She walked out toward the field and her eyes grew accustomed to the early evening dusky light. She saw Charlie sitting in one of the racing sulkies that Frank used for his harness races. Annawill was pulling the light, two-wheeled carriage. The horse looked as though it had been in a race. It plodded along as if it were worn out.

Behind the sulky came Sam F., plodding along with Martinez on top in the saddle.

"Don't you worry none, Mrs. Irwin, we've cooled the horses out. I'll feed them and make sure they don't drink overmuch. I'm sorry I missed supper," said Martinez.

Etta was somewhat appeased, but not totally so. "It is good of you to think of the horses. But Mr. Oldfield was starving when he arrived, and you've kept him here six hours past then. He'll be so weak he won't be able to walk inside the kitchen." Then she heard the deep droning of the motor, like a thousand bees homing in on their hive, as the Pierce Arrow came rolling up out of a little dip in the field. The electric headlights were on. She shielded her eyes with her hands from the unnatural brightness. The horses sputtered and stamped their front feet. Sam F. began to paw the air. Martinez spoke gently in his ear and calmed him right away. Oldfield put the automobile in neutral and turned the motor off. He got out and walked over to Etta. Before she could flash him a quick searching look, he put his hand out and barely touched her shoulder, then his hand dropped to his side.

"That was the most fun I've had in a long, long time. Your man, C.B., is a wonderful person. He knows how to get the most and the best from life." Oldfield's face was incredibly joyful and luminous. His eyes, under bushy eyebrows, were earnest and warm.

Charlie was out of the sulky. His face glowed. "Is dinner ready, dear?"

"Ready and over. But there's plenty in the warming oven for three hungry men," she said with affectionate amusement.

"Bravo! That's what our mouths are watering for!" hollered Charlie.

"Then come in before you waste away to nothing." Etta saw the Mexican boy heading for the barn with Sam F. in tow. "Charlie, bring Pablo with you. Someone else from the bunkhouse can take care of the horses and put the sulky in the shed. He's as tired and hungry as you are."

Charlie nodded, then sprinted after Martinez. Oldfield turned the lights off his red automobile and waited by the bunkhouse for Charlie.

When Charlie came back with his arm around Martinez, he stopped beside the bunkhouse and yelled, "Floyd! Come out here, please!"

The door opened. "Take those two horses to the barn and put all that gear away. Thanks." He noticed that Floyd had a handful of cards. "You playing poker? Here, take an extra five dollars."

Floyd looked startled. "Well, I—Gee, thanks, Pa." Then he looked a little sheepish. "I'm going to clean everyone out with this hand. So, I'll get the horses in a minute!"

Charlie grabbed back the five-dollar bill. "No minute! We all know what happened to Tom Mix's horse when he got busy with something else!" he yelled with rugged bluntness. "Hey, Roy! You come here and do a job for me!" He waved the five-dollar bill. "Maybe this'll help keep you in the men's game."

Roy said, "You want me to rub down the horses, or what? Maybe I should see if I can rope 'em and ride 'em bareback?"

"Forget this!" Charlie grabbed for the five-dollar bill, put it in his pocket and snorted. "I don't like smart talk either. Don't ride either of those horses bareback, or I'll tan your hide so hot you'll grow horsehair where it'll never see the light of day! Both you boys get out to the field and act like cowboys!"

Martinez was following Etta into the kitchen with his arms flying like windmills to relieve the tension from holding the reins for the last few hours. Talking excitedly, so that he lapsed into part English and part Spanish, Martinez explained to Etta that Sam F. could run faster than the red automobile if the ground was uneven, but the automobile ran faster than Annawill, especially when Charlie added his weight to the sulky. He laughed.

Etta laughed with Martinez as she piled his plate high with roast beef and mashed potatoes.

Charlie and Oldfield were on the back porch and had overheard some of the conversation. "Hey, no wisecracks about my weight!" said Charlie jovially. "Barney ain't so light either."

"He *isn't* lightweight," said Etta.

"I said that. He isn't no featherweight. Barney rode the sulky, too. Then I drove his Pierce Arrow. What a smooth automobile! I won that race. But he doesn't owe me a thing, 'cause he won the first race. It's lucky 'cause I bet the ranch!"

"Well, I'd have let that horse run flat out, but I was afraid I'd turn over, flip upside down, get weeds in my hair, maybe break a wheel off that little sulky. Then I knew I'd have to face your tongue-lashing, C.B. I don't want that!" teased Oldfield.

"It would have been a leg you'd broken, if you wrecked that sulky. I bet the danged thing cost half as much as your automobile," said Charlie. "Listen, if I had a Pierce Arrow, I could run across my pastures pulling a wagonload of hay to all the stock, even up in the Guerney pasture. I could turn on the headlights and run around my fields at night, if I couldn't sleep. Wouldn't Tom Hunter come running over here then to see what I was up to?" Charlie danced around the table before he sat down.

Etta drank a cup of coffee while the men ate. When they were quiet with full mouths, she said, "If I know Charlie, there will be a day coming when he'll come into the house, either here or in

Cheyenne, and call out, 'Come quick, dear, see something brand-new!' It'll be a big red Pierce Arrow!"

"Yippi!" cried Martinez with a mouth full of hot mashed potatoes and gravy.

"Charlie has a new Overland," Etta said. "Did he show you?"

"Can't kick up much dust in a lumbering old crate like that," said Oldfield. "But I can't deny an Overland is roomy. It'll carry all your supplies from town."

"So, Charlie had a workhorse in mind when he bought that automobile. But what's creeping into his head right now? I'll tell you, a red Pierce Arrow," said Etta, her eyes twinkling.

"Amen," said Charlie, dismissing the subject. "Barney, don't hog the green beans. Pablo and I have tapeworms screaming for fodder."

Oldfield sent Charlie two pairs of boxing gloves. At the ranch, one night after supper, Charlie took all the cowboys to the bunkhouse and showed them where he hung the boxing gloves on a nail. "From now on if there's any arguments or disputes, there'll be no fistfights. Use the mitts. When you're tired of punching each other, shake hands and call a truce. All boxing takes place outside the bunkhouse, rain, snow, or shine. That's the rules. Any questions?"

"Ya," said Jack Ray, nicknamed Montana Jack. "I want to know what happens if the dinner bell rings and I'm not over my arguing?"

"Well," said Charlie, "you can skip dinner or both of you come and eat and settle what's left afterward."

One morning after Christmas a severe blizzard developed. Snow swirled down to a depth of six inches an hour. Drifts were high as the windows on the Cheyenne storefronts by noon. No one seemed to be going out of the Plains Hotel as Charlie was working. Several people came in out of the storm. When he came out of his office for lunch he noticed a peculiar-looking woman sitting in one of the large leather chairs in the lobby. She wore a wool parka, men's work boots, and leather mittens. Her eyes were dark with gray circles underneath. Her face was blue-white, thin, and pinched.

"Excuse me, ma'am, may I help you?" asked Charlie.

It appeared to take a terrible effort for the woman to speak. "Listen," she said in a hoarse whisper, "I'm on my way to

Denver. Just let me rest a few minutes and I'll be going again."

"You can't go out in weather like this," said Charlie.

"This is nothing. I've been through worse. Just leave me be." She slouched down in the chair and closed her eyes.

Charlie talked with his secretary, Jane, a widow woman who did not look her forty years. "See what you can find out about that woman."

Charlie watched as Jane sat beside the woman and talked to her so softly he could not hear. The woman seemed to be worn out. Her eyes were barely open, but she talked to Jane. The talk was short, the woman could not keep her eyes open. She slept.

"She's somebody all right," said Jane, nodding her head so hard the hair wound into a tight knot in the back wobbled. "She married a man, Robley Edwards, who's in the Kansas penitentiary for bad-check forgery. When she discovered that meant there was no money coming in, she left home, changed her name, and ended up in Shoshoni, Wyoming. A few weeks ago some idiots bet her that she was too soft to walk to Denver through a blinding blizzard. Those stupid people told her they'd mail her winnings to the Denver post office, general delivery. That poor woman was hungry for money, so she took the bets, along with a couple belts of whiskey, and started out. She's this far."

"We can't let her go back out there. It's rough as a cob. Snow's three feet if it's an inch." Charlie took off his reading glasses and shuffled through a stack of papers. "I'll tell you what. She talked with you, so ask her to lunch. We'll get her some hot soup and crackers and then decide what to do. No woman's going out in that storm by herself!"

Jane had the woman by the hand. "You can't sleep in the lobby. My boss and I will take you to the dining room. After you eat we'll figure something out." The woman was sitting upright, and she'd pulled the big leather mittens off. Jane said, "Put your wraps in the office."

Charlie found it hard to believe that a woman's desire for money was so great that she'd risk her life for it.

Seated at a table with a snow-white cloth Charlie ordered vegetable soup, hot tea, and soda crackers for each of them.

The woman's blond hair hung in matted strings as if it'd not seen soap and water for months. Her hands were red, the skin rough, the nails long, yellow, and broken. She wore an oversize, dirty gray sweater buttoned to the neck and a man's pair of black wool pants tucked into the tops of her heavy boots. She was skinnier than a wet weasel.

"What's that smell?" asked Charlie.

Jane sniffed and looked around.

The woman said matter-of-factly, "It's these boots. They're rubbed with skunk oil to keep out the wet." Her soup was gone and she was eating soda crackers as if she were trying to pad out her belly. "If I can get my man out of jail with the money, it will be worth it. If not, I just let myself die."

"Hey, don't talk that way!" cried Charlie. "Don't go bitter in the mouth and run away from troubles. We're going to help."

"Ya? Well, put my head east and leave my boots on," she said. "Why would people I don't know do something for me, Arizona Owens? You want something from me?" Suspiciously she pushed back her chair, scraping the floor. She broke a handful of crackers into her teacup, poured hot water over them, and ate quickly. "No one, not even those I worked for in Shoshoni, gave me a free meal."

Charlie motioned to the waiter, "Fred, wrap a loaf of bread and some of that cheddar cheese you serve with apple pie in a paper. Bring it here. Yes, I'll pay for it."

When Arizona Owens had the bread and cheese under her arm, Jane said, "This is hard for me to say, but if you'd like to come home with me tonight, you are welcome. I don't usually take anyone home, you see."

"Oh, no, thanks, I'm leaving. I feel better. I'm going to get that money. Nobody's going to stop me doing that. It's a free country, I have my rights."

"Look here, Missus Owens, or whoever you are, think what you're saying. As I see it, your husband is the weak one of the team and you're the one with all the strength. You can't strengthen the weak by weakening the strong. That's common sense."

"Don't bad-mouth my man, mister. You don't know nuthin' about him. Not like I do."

Charlie looked out the window. The snow was coming down fast at a forty-five degree angle, and the wind made a whining sound as it blew past. "My wife'd fix you somewhere at our place, if you don't mind kids. We have four, uh—five, and two of my brother's staying here in town for school. But there's room. All you'd need is a cot. This is murderous weather. You'll freeze out there!"

"Actually, it doesn't make much difference one way or t'other. There'll be no mourners." Arizona Owens got up from her chair, hung on to the bread and cheese, and bolted from Charlie's office. She grabbed her outer clothing and looked wild-eyed at Jane, who came right after her. Jane felt it was her duty to keep the woman inside, then her mind clicked. The poor thing hasn't eaten for a day or so and she ate so fast, she's ill. Jane pointed to the ladies' rest room and the woman raced inside.

Charlie sat down at his desk, wiped his hand across his forehead, fingering the white, crescent scar between his eyes. "We'd better keep her here." He left the door open so that they could see when she came from the rest room. For half an hour Charlie and Jane said nothing, but neither could work. They shuffled papers and wished the telephone would ring. Finally Jane said, "Mr. Irwin, I'm going to check on that poor soul."

Charlie nodded. Jane was back in a minute. "She's gone! The window's open—snow's blowing in and it's freezing in there. She must be crazy!" Jane went back to pull down the rest room window.

Months later the *Sunday State Leader* carried a story on the second page that caused Charlie to whistle. "Etta, read this. It's a story about the same woman who wandered into the Plains last winter during the blizzard."

Etta nodded and took the paper.

"It says she won her bet. She made it to Denver. But read the end, she's taken an overdose of laudanum. She doesn't want to live, because she has no money to pay all her debts. I wonder what she did with her winnings," said Charlie.

"That paper says she fought the police surgeon, who wanted to give her an antidote. She doesn't want to do anything but die. That's pitiful. She must have suffered so much." Etta's eyes were soft and liquid.

"I don't know why this makes me feel bad—shaken—but it does. How can a person be so down and out that life has no joy? This is terrible. Someone's pulled her down to the bottom floor with no thought of her feeling or sensitivity. I don't know whether to blame her no-good husband or those morons in Shoshoni who waged that bet with her. Oh, dear, people are inhuman."

"Charlie, she has nothing to do with you. A stranger comes in, you take her to lunch, and she runs out. Forget her." Etta tried to comfort him.

"I should have found her a job. That would have kept her in

Cheyenne and given her a good life. She'd be well today. I didn't even try. Maybe if I contact the woman she's been living with in Denver. Look, the paper gave her name, Kathleen, no, Katherine Young. I'll send some money for her burial, at least keep her out of the potter's cemetery. That's the least I can do. It's a tragedy."

Etta got up and went to sit beside Charlie on the davenport. She put her arms around him as far as they'd reach. "Charlie, honest, you're not obligated to even do that much. But that's a kindness you could do."

"Yes, I'm going to do it," said Charlie. His eyes were closed and he was visualizing the emaciated young woman with the matted, blond hair, who might have been good-looking if she'd washed and put on some decent clothes. He sighed a deep, sad expulsion of air.

"Look at this same paper," said Etta, trying hard to find something to cheer Charlie. "A goat in Lusk chewed on a box of matches in a bunkhouse and set it on fire. Three saddles and all the cowboys' clothing were burned. Now, that's a tragedy."

"Let me see that," said Charlie. Then he said, "Here's another story about a fire destroying several tons of hay and a pile of corral poles on a ranch in Casper. Here's something about an electrical storm near Valley View, killed some cattle, and a man was chased by a female bear after he fired some birdshot at it. Say, that's kind of funny." He laughed. "If you think of these tragedies in the right way, maybe some people cause their own problems."

"I believe that," said Etta, holding Charlie's hand.

"Let me unfold the paper, woman." He chuckled. "Here's a piece about a Chinaman who made a bunch of small private rooms in his restaurant and got a booming business. Made money hand over foot. But his money-making was in violation of a city law that says no screen or curtains between tables in a restaurant. Now that poor, wily Celestial has to go to court and explain his actions."

"What did he do that was so wrong?" asked Etta.

Charlie guffawed. "My dear wife, you are innocent! The law was passed so that spooning among the younger folk might be regulated."

"Oho," she said, rolling her eyes, understanding right away.

At that moment Floyd came into the ranch house by the back screen door, followed by Roy. Roy held the branding iron high above his head. "If this were hot, I'd leave the Y6 mark on your thigh permanently, Buddy. Don't ever call me those names again!

If I hear you said them behind my back, I'll knock the wind out of you, put your head in a sack tied around your neck. Understand? You call me Roy or Mr. Irwin, because that's my name. Did I ever call you dog face?" He stopped, looked at the adults, and his face turned red. He put the branding iron down on the back porch and came into the kitchen, his feet shuffling. "I'm sorry," he said contritely. "Buddy called me names and I ran after him without thinking. I wouldn't really hit him."

"Yes, you would have," said Floyd, still panting. "You meant to hit me."

Roy turned his luminous blue eyes toward Etta. "Dear, wouldn't blood rush to my head if I stood on it?"

"I suppose it would," she said, hoping the fuss had ended.

"Well, I'm standing on my feet; why don't it rush to them?"

Floyd answered, "Because your feet ain't empty."

"You—you—Injun!" yelled Roy, waving his arms around.

Charlie stood in the kitchen doorway. Roy stood like a statue. Floyd didn't move. "That's right, look at me!" bellowed Charlie. "I'm bigger than both you together. Shake hands and call a truce, or I'll see that your heads are put together by my bare hands. If children were not so weak, fathers and mothers could not be so strong."

"Goddamn that little runt," whispered Floyd.

Charlie heard him and said, "Out to the barn for a whipping."

Floyd stuck his tongue out deliberately at Roy and left, slamming the screen door behind him.

Etta took a step toward Roy and he backed off. "Son," she said, "you are going to have to stop this scrapping. Now, don't cry, no one hurt you. I don't want to know who started the name calling. Take that branding iron off of the porch and hang it up in its proper place. Then you go to my kitchen garden and pick a mess of green peas for supper. When you come in, sit in my kitchen chair and shell them, every one. Think what it would be like without Floyd around here. Deep down you'll discover you'd miss him."

"What you gonna do to the darling boy I'd miss?" asked Roy, all ready to dart out the back door.

Charlie stepped across the kitchen. "That is not your affair. Go, before I get the belt out!" He put his hand on the long leather belt around his waist.

Roy slammed the door. Charlie drank a dipperful of water at the kitchen sink. Etta laid her hand on his arm. "Don't whip Roy nor Buddy. Talk to them. They understand. Boys need to learn to control their temper. Those are tantrums they must overcome, and a whipping will only make the boys flare up and raise fits to you."

"Floyd is older. He knows better than to tease Roy. He does it every chance he gets, because he knows it gets a rise out of the kid. In my opinion a whipping will put a stop to that. At this stage he'll understand a whipping better than talk."

"You won't whip my son," said Etta. "Reason with him."

"I'll take my belt to him, then I'll reason with him," said Charlie firmly.

"No! You won't lay a hand on him!" sobbed Etta.

"My dear, if you won't be quiet, I'll throw you out the window."

For a moment Etta was quiet, but her fingers worked nervously, twisting the jabot attached to the bodice of her dress. Her face was white and her lips straight and thin. "That will be just fine. Then I will take the children and leave you. If you lay a hand on me in anger, I'll not stay."

Charlie was dumbfounded. His mouth fell open. "I didn't mean it to sound that way. I would never do a thing to hurt you. I'd never think of striking you. You are my life, my reason for living."

"You said you'd throw me out the window." Her lips pressed together. "I'll leave before you can do that."

"My dear! You would never leave me. Would you?" He stared at his petite wife, who never moved back a step and who didn't blink an eye. Something caught in his throat. He couldn't talk. His nose seemed to close and he felt he was under water suffocating. He blinked and tears ran down his cheeks. He sat down and pulled a red bandanna from his pocket and blew his nose. He felt his innards constrict and a pounding started in his head.

Etta did not move.

Charlie put his head down in his hands, and he felt the hot tears. He was sobbing like a baby. He never realized that Etta would walk out on him. He was shocked, stunned. The thought cut through him cleaner than a knife and more deeply. He loved her more than anything. He loved her more than life itself. He could not fathom how she could say she'd leave. How could she ever take the children, his pride and joy, and leave? It was inconceivable. Charlie was crushed. The hurt permeated his whole body. He shook and was unable to think.

Etta could not watch. It broke her heart to see Charlie this way. Slowly she walked out the back door and found herself in the barn. "Buddy," she called softly.

"Ya," answered Floyd. "Where's Pa? I expected him and a good tanning."

"I came to talk to you. Come where I can see you."

When Floyd moved toward the light coming through the door, she could see that he'd been crying. His eyes were red and swollen. His hair was wet with perspiration.

"The Irwins are all blessed with strong feelings. I am talking about tempers. To get along with those you love and those you might have to work for when you are a man, that temper must be controlled. If you don't try now, it will get out of hand. You'll end up hurting Roy or one of your sisters. You might even use your fists on your pa or me. Buddy, look at me. Do you understand what I'm saying?"

"Yes, I understand, Ma," said Floyd. "Is Pa belting Roy? That kid deserves it and you ought to wash his mouth out with soap."

"Roy is out in the hot sun picking peas for the supper table. Your pa is weeping. He is broken-hearted because he, too, lost control of his temper. He threatened to throw me out the window."

"Ma! He wouldn't dare! Out the window! He wouldn't do that to you. Not you, Ma. I'll punch some sense into him for even threatening you! Why, his cinch is getting frayed. That makes me madder than a drunk squaw."

"Don't say that," said Etta. "Pa won't do anything. He's remorseful for having said anything. I lost my temper and told him I'd take the children and leave. It broke his heart."

"You wouldn't. I wouldn't go."

"Get the hoe and shovel. Clean out the barn before supper."

"But Ma, I cleaned it last night!" cried Floyd, trying to make his mother see the illogic in her request. "Give me something else to do. I could go help Grandpa Joe in the smithy."

"Clean the barn first." Etta left the barn not looking back, but listening to the scrape, scrape sound of Floyd's hoe. She brushed a bluebottle fly off the back of her hand. In the kitchen she put water in a cooking pot and added a couple chunks of wood to the fire box. She picked out a dozen large potatoes from the bin and put them in the sink. She poured a basin of water for washing and began paring them and cutting them in quarters for boiling. Her head ached.

THIRTY-ONE

Y6

The Iron-jawed Butterfly

The weekend before the new year Charlie took his family to the ranch. Joe smiled from ear to ear when he had Charlie, Etta, and the children at the ranch. Etta would have liked staying in town, but she knew it was important for the children to be with their grandfather and for Charlie to check the winter activities at the Y6. The first morning Charlie was out of bed before dawn. He smelled bacon sizzling in a pan downstairs.

Etta was up. Charlie tucked his shirt inside his pants and pulled on his boots. In the upstairs hall he stopped to look inside the big north room. He walked to the window and looked out over the pasture across the road from the front yard. A thin blanket of snow covered everything. He couldn't see Round Top. Something was hopping along the road. Charlie didn't look twice. He thought it was the dog. The air began to fill with big lazy snowflakes. He moved back and bumped into one of half a dozen cots in the room. He thought that the cowboys who bunked up here in the summer could just as well stay in the bunkhouse, if he'd build another room onto it. Then he and Joe could partition this room, that was large enough to hold a dance for all of Torrington, and make bedrooms for each of the girls.

Downstairs, Etta heard a banging, opened the back door, and saw a boy about twelve who was covered with snow. "Did you roll down the ravine?" she asked, then pulled the youngster inside out of the cold wind and swirly snowflakes.

"No, ma'am—I mean yes, ma'am. I got off my horse halfway between here and Meriden to tighten the cinch strap. When I pulled myself back up, she bucked me off. She was on her way back to Donahue's hay pile at Meriden when I last saw her. I said heck and came on. I have the mail for Mr. C. B. Irwin."

"Child, you mean Mr. Joe Irwin. You stopped at Meriden and picked up Grandpa Joe's mail."

"No. I come from Cheyenne."

"Child, you rode all the way from Cheyenne just to bring Mr. Irwin's mail?"

"Yes, ma'am. I heard Mr. Irwin say that he wished the mail left at his office could be forwarded to the ranch."

Etta looked at him crosswise.

"Well, you see, I wasn't doing anything but sitting in one of those leather chairs in the lobby of the Plains when I heard him say those words. Yesterday I wasn't doing nothing so I told the lady at Mr. Irwin's big desk, in his office at the Plains, that I'd bring his mail out to him. She gave me a dollar. I left early this morning." The boy smiled and wiped the water from his face that was beginning to melt off his wool cap.

"Charlie! Charlie, come see what this young man has brought you!" called Etta. She helped the boy take off his snow-caked wraps. She put him in her rocking chair close to the stove so he could warm up. She shook his thawing, snowy wraps on the back porch, then hung them on the clothesline behind the stove.

"I saw something coming up the road," said Charlie. "It walked with a hitch and a limp, sort of like our old ranch dog, or a snowman hippy-hopping. I couldn't believe a snowman was walking along the road. I thought it was the old dog and kind of forgot about the fact that it could be a real live person."

The boy smiled and pointed to the mail on the kitchen table.

"Thanks, son. Let's see what's in all these envelopes."

The boy continued to smile, squeezing the freckles together at the corners of his mouth. He pushed his brown hair out of his eyes and watched Charlie. He seemed about to say something, then decided against it.

"Dear, give this young man something hot to drink, some bread and butter to stick to his ribs," said Charlie, taking the letters back to his study.

Etta gave the boy hot cocoa made with thick cream, and bread with butter and currant jelly. "You live in Cheyenne?"

"With my folks."

"What's your name?"

"Arthur."

"Arthur what?"

"Arthur H. Burmister."

Charlie was back in the kitchen. "I'd like some of that cocoa with my toast and bacon and eggs," he said. He put his breakfast plate on the kitchen counter and began to eat. Then he looked at the boy and chuckled. "Son, I'd call you Hippy by the way you limped up here."

The boy hung his head. "Got thrown from my horse. Nothing's broken."

"So, that happens to lots of cowboys. Your friends call you Art?"

"I don't have friends. We've not been here long."

"Nobody at school?" asked Charlie, looking over the edge of his white enameled plate.

"Sometimes after school I hang around the Plains. You know, just to see who comes and goes. Once I saw President Taft, and the bronco buster, Thad Sowder, and Bill Pickett." The boy's eyes brightened and he bent forward in the chair. Charlie noticed the palms of his hands were red, probably from letting a hemp rope slide when he should have held on for dear life.

Charlie gave the boy he called Hippy a horse to ride down the snowy road to Meriden. "Leave my horse with old man Donahue, pick up yours from beside the haystack. Oh, better give Donahue this to pay for the hay he'll say your horse ate and for what mine will eat." He pulled out fifty cents from his pocket, then he pulled out two silver dollars and put them in the boy's other hand. "For coming all the way out with my mail. I appreciate it. Thanks, Hippy, maybe I'll see you in the Plains someday."

Etta handed Hippy his dry wraps and watched him follow Charlie out to the barn. She thought that the youngster had something else on his mind, but for some reason didn't find this the right time to say anything. Might be his horse knocked it out of him. I'll bet he finds some excuse to come back again.

That same morning Charlie began to measure the big room upstairs to see where he'd build the partitions. He went to the bunkhouse with his father, and they measured where another room could be added.

"I could sleep out in the bunkhouse with the boys," said Joe.

"No, no, you'd better stay in your room in the ranch house, Pa. Unless going up and down those stairs is too much for you."

"Of course stairs don't bother me none," scoffed Joe.

When the snow let up Charlie sent Roy out to mend the corral fence in the sand pasture across the road. "Don't use it often, but if we want it in a hurry, we'd want it solid so that no wild horses could walk their way out."

Roy had all the tools in his pockets and his rope over his arm. He brought a little red roan from the barn and swung his leg up and started out of the yard.

"Hey!" yelled Charlie. "Where do you think you're going with no saddle on that horse! Come back here!"

"Pa, I'm not going to be gone long. Why do I have to go to all that extra work?"

"That's lazy talk. I told you once before not to ride bareback. Jeems! You're going to grow horsehair on your behind for sure. Now get saddled up proper and do the mending job proper. No corner cutting. You hear?"

"Yes, sir!" called Roy, going back to the barn for the saddle blanket and the saddle.

Several days after that Roy was upstairs alone in Joella's room. He had his pants down and was looking in the long mirror on Joella's wall.

Joella, not expecting anyone in her room, jumped when she saw him exposing himself before her mirror. "Cripes! What are you doing, you little creep?"

"Looking to see if I had red horsehair."

Joella giggled. "Did Pa tell you that old story about growing horsehair if you rode bareback?"

"Don't laugh. I've seen some of the cowboys and it's a fact—there's hair." His voice dropped to a whisper and he pulled up his pants.

Joella watched him and was not sure what it was that she felt. Her hands were sweaty. Her heart pounded and her head felt queer.

She felt a warmth in her loins that was nice.

Roy missed little. Sensing a change in Joella's mood he cocked his head to one side and said, "I've seen you ride bareback." His eyes were partially closed as if he were remembering what he'd seen. He licked his lips. "Let's see if you have horsehair. I bet you've got it."

Joella felt her legs weaken like soft bacon rind. The funny warm spot in her middle spread. Blood rushed to her cheeks. She struck her hand out to smack Roy on his face, then dropped it to her side. She could feel herself breathing like she'd been walking uphill. "You're the one that's going to get it if you don't get out of my room. Your rump will sting like a brier scratch cleaned with turpentine. Get out! I'll scream and Pa'll find you here!"

"We could go to the hayloft," whispered Roy.

Joella thought her insides were going to explode. She didn't know what was the matter with her. She really wanted Roy to stay so she could explore this queer feeling. She wanted to ask him if he felt the same. Then she decided he wouldn't understand, he was just a little kid.

"I'd never go to the hayloft with a runt like you. Besides I have better things to do. Now, get out, so I can change to a clean dress for supper." She rummaged around her dress rack, which was a wooden pole held in loops of rope nailed to the ceiling. The whole thing was covered with a flowered drape or curtain. There was a shelf behind the rod that held dresses, where underwear and other clean garments were kept. There were no closets in the bedrooms.

Roy ran out down the hall and to the room he shared with Floyd. If the truth were known, he wanted to be like Floyd, to look like him physically, to ride a horse like him, to spin a rope like him, and to have Charlie announce at the Wild West shows that he, Roy Irwin, was his son and the world's best cowboy, like he did for Floyd.

That evening at supper Roy winked when he was close to Joella, who hung her head and hoped no one saw her flaming neck and cheeks. Joella felt the queerness in her stomach and decided it was a feeling she liked.

Next morning Joella cleared the breakfast table. This was the last day they were going to be at the ranch until summer. School began the following day. Charlie was taking everybody back to town in the Overland.

Roy came in from mucking out the barn. He wanted a hot cup of coffee. No one else was around the kitchen. The other girls and Etta were up in their rooms packing. Roy said in a singsong sarcastic manner, "The purtier the gal the worse coffee she makes."

"What does that mean?" said Joella. "The coffee is good or bad?"

"You're purtie."

She exploded. "I hope my coffee scorches your voice box, stunts your growth, and burns all the hair off your upper lip!"

Roy's reply was fast. "My horsehair, too?"

Joella dropped the dishes in the sink. It was lucky for her that they were enamelware or most would have broken. Her hands were unsteady and the queer feeling was there spreading down her legs and making her belly hot.

That spring Charlie had several thousand fliers made, advertising IRWIN BROS. CHEYENNE FRONTIER DAYS WILD WEST SHOW. He liked the name. It told what his show was really all about. After all, it was the Irwin Y6 ranch that supplied cowboys and the stock for Cheyenne's Frontier Days. Thus, to incorporate the Frontier Days name defined the greatness of his wonderful, traveling show. It was better than the old Buffalo Bill's Wild West Show and Congress of Rough Riders. Why, the Irwin Brothers' show was better than the well-known 101 Wild West show from Ponca City, Oklahoma, even after the 101 show joined forces with Colonel Zach Mulhall. Adding the words, *Cheyenne Frontier Days* to the show's name was just what it needed to indicate the authentic Western flavor, thought Charlie. It was a logical outcome of his work with the Cheyenne festivities. Charlie was an entrepreneur. He was proud of the new name, which told audiences where his show originated. He'd heard rumors that Buffalo Bill had changed the name of his fleabitten Wild West show to the Buffalo Bill Exposition of Frontier Days and the Passing of the West. And that old codger, Buffalo Bill Cody, had tried to make some kind of contact with Otto Floto about some kind of merger with the Floto Circus.

"We not only need these new fliers," Charlie explained to his banker and business partner, Charles Hirsig, "we need something to excite the crowds, to keep them enthusiastic about our show."

"You have some tricks up your sleeve?" asked Hirsig.

"Last winter when Will Rogers stopped at the ranch for a few days' rest, he told me about a trick that he pulled at the St. Louis World's Fair. I bet we could do something similar." Charlie hoped Hirsig would like the idea, which had just that minute occurred to him.

"What kind of trick?" asked Hirsig.

"Here's the idea. During one of the Ponca City 101 shows, Will Rogers saw a runaway steer from the Mulhall corral break loose and run up toward the grandstand seats. The crowd was in chaos. But Will kept his head and ran into the stands swinging his rope. He got the steer around the back feet and dragged the bellowing, pawing animal down the aisle by its tail. Will was an instant hero. That story got a lot of publicity. In the spring the

Mulhall bunch went to Madison Square Garden in New York and let a steer loose on purpose by pushing it through a rope fence near the grandstand. Again Will Rogers dashed into the stands with his rope swinging. He caught it around the neck and slid the poor animal back under the rope and into the arena while the crowd cheered. The master of ceremonies asked Will why he took the steer out of the grandstand. 'Because he doesn't have a ticket,' called Will."

"You want to do that?" asked Hirsig, skeptical.

"Sure, but when the action starts, I'll tell you what I'll do. Me and some of the boys'll get up a bet that one of my cowboys can handle the situation in a given amount of time. Most people will think us crazy and will bet that no one could possibly get the animal out in less than two minutes. Floyd'll rope the steer with the help of his horse before there's any damage and beat the allotted time. We'll make money on that show, I'll bet you a new Stetson on it," said Charlie, talking fast and letting his eyes sparkle.

"That's a wonderful idea! C.B., you're a genius!" shouted Hirsig, slapping his thigh. "I should have known you'd be creative and use Will Rogers's idea to bring in something exciting for the public."

"Well, I know it isn't exactly my idea. I know I borrowed it from Will Rogers." Charlie smiled. "But it sounds good enough for me to use."

Then Charlie had another idea. He took the U.P. to Denver, where he met with one of the advance men for the Sells Circus. He talked about having the circus and his Wild West show perform together. Charlie figured working a town together would be mutually beneficial to both shows. He wanted his new fliers to appear on telegraph poles, telephone poles, sides of barns, and stores, alongside those of the circus. After checking with his manager the advance man assured Charlie by letter that the posters would appear together and when his circus was cleared to perform in a town, the Wild West show would have the same clearance.

That spring Charlie had portable seats built that could be carried on a railroad boxcar. The frames for these grandstand seats were like huge A's, with slots to slide green painted boards into. Charlie then made certain that the new grandstand seats, tents, and other paraphernalia would all fit into one or two boxcars. In other boxcars he carried the show animals, horses, steers, buffalo, fourteen to each car, with plenty of fresh hay. In those cars he put the roustabouts who looked after the animals, put together the grandstand seats, drove in tent stakes, stretched ropes for the tents. There were supposed to be two men to a stock car. Charlie nearly always carried no less than half a dozen to each car. The performers, cowboys, rode in the daycoaches. Charlie and his family rode in a private car at the end of the train. He was Livestock Agent and entitled to a private car, if it was not being used by some other U.P. official. Charlie was always generous with complimentary passes to his Wild West shows, giving them out in advance to the town officials where they played and to all the railroad people, officials to redcaps.

The first show after the children were out of school was scheduled for Spokane, Washington. A young man, Chester Byers, was hired by Charlie to do some spectacular roping tricks. He also was hired to work over the roping tricks of Floyd and the girls. Charlie knew a good roper when he saw one. Byers could swing a wide rope around five mounted horses standing side by side. Another new man Charlie had hired was the well-known performer, Frank Miller, the crack shot. Miller threw cans of tomatoes into the air and shot them full of holes before they hit the ground. Of course part of the excitement was spraying the crowd with tomato juice. This was an old trick and Charlie thought it was still interesting enough to continue.

The first event began with Frances in a red bolero, white satin shirt with spangles, and pants with angora chaps, riding a big brown horse and carrying a big American flag. The four- or five-piece band played "The Star-Spangled Banner." The crowd stood with their hands over their hearts as the flag passed and the band played. The whole crew, cowboys, cowgirls, clowns, Indians, all riding horseback, paraded by. The minute the band stopped, the people clapped and cheered.

Then came the bucking horses and riders, the cowboy races, some trick riding featuring Floyd, and roping with Floyd, Byers, Roy, and the three Irwin girls, then the crack-shot performance and the cowgirl races.

The three Irwin girls and several local Spokane girls were in the first race. Ten-year-old Frances rode a horse called The Senator, Joella rode Toby Gray, and Pauline rode Baby Sister. Joella had her hair combed out so that it hung long, blond, and beautiful. Pauline's dark hair was pulled behind her ears; her eyes were huge, dark, and shining, her features were even and flawless for a thirteen-year-old. Her wide-brimmed hat was in her hands ready to be placed on her head. Frances had her hip-length blond hair pulled back so that with her hat on her head, only her bangs showed from the front.

Joella said loud enough for only her sisters to hear, "I'm going to win this race."

"I just wish for once you'd not be so cocky and think you can win every race you're in. I hope one of the locals beats you," said Pauline, who boosted Frances up on The Senator.

"Yep, I'd like to win,"' said Frances, moving around in her saddle so she felt secure on the horse.

The girls lined up their horses and a few seconds later the race had begun. Frances leaned over and whispered in The Senator's ear, "Come on, come on, hurry!" Then she stretched her small hand, which held a little riding crop, back behind the saddle and just touched the back of the horse. The Senator ran faster, trying to get away from whatever had touched its back. Frances was bent low, whispering in the horse's ear as they crossed the finish line. Frances and The Senator were first by a half a length. Already at the age of ten she knew the subtle tricks of racing. She'd watched her Uncle Frank and Pablo Martinez. Pablo'd watched her from the starting line. It was against the rules to hit the horse on the flanks. What she'd done with the riding crop was legal. A touch of the riding crop on the horse's back was not against the rules and could make a horse run a little faster.

The crowd's ovation was tremendous. Frances Irwin was the youngest cowgirl competing in the arena. Her first prize was a spectacular, huge, pink satin Gibson-girl hat with long black plumes. The breeze caused the plumes to flutter as if hundreds of butterflies were on bare, willowy branches. Frances removed her tan, broad-brimmed cowboy hat, put on the fancy pink and black hat, and looked up at the audience. The applause thundered. The young equestrian was not only beautiful and charming, but she was a skilled athlete. From that day forward she was a favorite with the Wild West and rodeo enthusiasts.

Frances was buoyed by the crowd. That day, all the practice, hard work, even exercising the horses before school, was worth the effort. She felt wonderful. The earth under her feet vibrated as the crowd stomped. The air pulsated with cheers. Her face lit up like a Christmas candle as the cameraman from the *Spokesman Review* said, "Smile, honey, smile!"

She felt as though she were going to burst into tears at any moment. She smiled and was aware of a sudden relief. The race was over. Her smile broadened as water welled up in her eyes, making them sparkle.

"Perfect!" said the cameraman.

"Let me try your hat, just once," begged Joella. "Let's see what the cowboys think of it."

Frances ran to the paddock where the horses were kept. The plumes of the big hat trailed out behind like streaming, shimmering pennants in a Royal Neighbors' parade. She called back, "No, never!" The hat was her prize. She didn't care a fig what the boys thought. Boys were in the same category as lizards and stinkbugs. She was going to take her lovely hat home and hang it on the dresser post beside the mirror. She'd look at it every morning and every night and remember the indescribable satisfaction she had winning it. She'd let no one touch her first prize.

As usual the last event of the Wild West show was the enactment of some dramatic Western event, such as a horse-thief act, buffalo hunt, or cowboy-Indian battle. This time there was an Indian attack on a covered wagon. Lee Gray, one of Charlie's cowboys, drove the team of six oxen. Eva McGuckin, one of Etta's sisters, took the part of the pioneer mother; Frank Miller, the crack shot, was the father. Frances and her cousin, Gladys, were the children riding in the covered wagon heading for the center of the arena. The wagon stopped and the father climbed down off the seat. He began to pound stakes in the ground to hang the cooking kettles on. The mother pretended to prepare the supper. The two children were sent off with a bucket to get water.

Opposite the grandstand seats, on the other side of the arena, was a row of tents, railroad coaches on a siding, housing animals and actors and performers, and some circus equipment. In front of the tents were several Indian tepees, which the spotlight played on so that the audience could see Henry Makes Enemy, one of the Sioux, crouched down in front of a tepee, get up, tiptoe to the back of the covered wagon, and fire several shots. Of course they were blanks. The noise brought out other Sioux from the tepees. The two girls with the water bucket ran for help.

The girls ran to the back of the arena, where there was now no light. In the spotlight, they came back to the wagon riding horseback behind a couple of cowboys. Behind these riders were half a dozen or more cowboys on horseback. But by the time they got to the wagon, the Indians had doused the cheesecloth top with coal oil and set it on fire. This was the part the Sioux performers liked best. It had been their idea. Etta was afraid of fire, but they'd promised her it could never get out of hand. They knew big C. B. Irwin would see to that.

The cowboys circled the burning wagon, poured the big bucket of water over the flaming cover, doused out the fire. The Indians *kiyi*ed, hollered, and danced around the wagon, making a big show. The cowboys waved their rifles and chased the Indians away. The audience loved the whole pageant.

When the crowd had departed, the performers piled into the mess tent for supper. Ten or twelve tables were lined up and everyone ate with their own group. The circus people ate together, the Indians ate together, the roustabouts ate together, the Irwin family and their cowboys and cowgirls ate together.

While eating, Charlie told Floyd that he had not played to the audience during the evening performance. "Son, people like it when you wave your hat and look at them. Smile at them. Don't keep your head down. What's the matter with you?"

"Oh, Pa, don't chew me out in front of everyone. Not now!" Floyd looked over at the circus performers, hoping they couldn't hear the loud, booming voice of his father. His eyes searched over the female bareback riders and tight-wire walkers.

Charlie followed his son's gaze and decided Floyd was just letting his eyes wander over the pretty girls. "Pay attention to me. I want you to get Roy on one of the buffalo at our next town. Let them ride around the arena a couple of times. Then you get on your horse and go after them as though the buffalo is loose and can't be stopped. Rope the buffalo and bring them to a halt. The crowd will love it."

"Pa, I know what you want me to do. But I don't want to go out there and make an ass of myself in front of a lot of people by roping a buffalo that is as tame as a pet dog. I'll go out and do some rope tricks and at the same time do some trick riding on my horse. You go out with Roy when he gets on one of those dumb buffalo. You don't mind being in those stupid sack races, so I guess you won't mind wearin' a gaudy clown suit and standing in front of a running buffalo to stop it. The crowd'll eat it up."

Charlie stood up, reached for Floyd, upset his glass of water, and yelled, "That is no way to talk to your father!"

Floyd ducked, slid off his wooden folding chair, and ran out of the mess tent. Charlie was at his heels hollering, "I want my son to show me more respect! All right, Floyd! If you don't want to do something, fine, tell me! But don't make fun of any job!"

Charlie stopped to catch his breath and to see where Floyd was headed. It was night and he let his eyes become accustomed to the dark.

Floyd ran across the way to the Indian tepees. He ran with his head down and almost ran into John Brooks, the Indian interpreter. "Whoa, there! Slow down," said Brooks, grabbing Floyd.

Floyd was wild-eyed and gasping. "I gotta see your wife! Quick, let me inside the tepee."

Inside the tepee Floyd grabbed the hand of a brown-skinned, attractive young Sioux woman. A lighted coal-oil lantern hung by a leather thong on one of the poles. "Emma, hide me. Please, hide me before Pa whips the living daylights out of me in front of the whole crew."

Emma looked around; she looked out the tepee flap. Her husband was standing quietly with his hands behind his back, an unlit cigarette in his mouth. He was watching Charlie on a white horse, looking here and there, for something—or someone—in the dark.

An owl hooted from somewhere in the trees by the tracks and a bat flew around the top of the tepee in ever tightening circles until finally it darted off high above the tepee poles and into the night.

Emma dropped the flap with a low guttural noise in her throat. "All right, White Papoose, get down on your knees." She threw a red and blue blanket over Floyd. Brooks came inside and sat beside his wife on the red and blue blanket.

Floyd wondered how long he could brace himself under that blanket, which smelled a little like it had been wrapped around a dead deer carcass. The weight on his back dug his knees and elbows into the dirt.

There was a scratching at the tepee flap. Emma got up to see who it was. Charlie said, "Good evening. Finished your supper early, I see. I'm looking for my son, Floyd. You see him anywhere?"

"Nope, Mr. Irwin, we don't see no boy around here. Do you?"

Charlie dropped the reins of his horse and looked inside the tepee.

"How's that pretty little squaw of yours?" asked Emma. "She brought us smoked salmon from a market in town. It was all right. Tell her we ate all of it, then licked our fingers."

Charlie smiled. "I'll tell Etta you send your thanks. If you see Floyd, send him to our Pullman car. I want a talk with him."

John and Emma Brooks nodded. The unlit cigarette still dangled from Brooks's lips.

As soon as Charlie was out of sight, Emma told her husband to get up. She pulled the blanket from Floyd and shook her finger at his face. "You hightail it to your place! Be there when your papa comes in. Unless you want a leather strap across that skinny backside." She pulled her own leather belt from her waist and cracked it in the air above Floyd's head with a fast flick of her wrist.

Floyd darted out of the tepee as if he'd been shot from a cannon. He crept around to the back side of the tepee in preparation for a quick dash to the Pullman car. He heard the Brookses laughing.

In the shadow of circus equipment Charlie saw his son run from the Brookses' tepee, then across the stubble field to the tracks. He never said a word about it. He knew John and Emma Brooks had used their best judgment. In their way they'd kept Charlie from beating the daylights out of his son, and they'd sent his son back home where he belonged. Charlie was grateful.

Charlie stayed hidden to ponder the problems of fatherhood. He'd found that it was easier to give advice to others than to follow the same advice himself. It was hardest to use good judgment when it came to his own family. He took off his hat and scratched his head, pushed his hair out of his eyes, and replaced the hat. He shrugged and led his horse from the shadows. Raising children properly was harder than trying to find hair on a frog.

That evening when the midway was closed, six huge, rough, and hearty men, dressed in loose-fitting shirts and tight pants and fancy leather boots, sought out Charlie. They did not speak much English. One man gave Charlie a printed card:

Horseback riders par excellence

Captain Geogi	Prince Willikow
Prince Luke	Prince Emily
Tephon	Isheah

Russian Cossacks for Hire for Public Entertainment

Charlie put the card in his pocket and took the burly men out to the corral. "You men ride with or without saddles?" he asked.

Captain Geogi, the only one with a scarlet sash around his waist, nodded his head up and down then from side to side. Charlie decided he meant they'd ride either way. He brought out six of the race horses and watched the thick-necked, wide-shouldered men line them up in the open field.

Geogi grunted and motioned for Charlie to come closer. He curled the four fingers on each hand and pulled his thumbs underneath to form circles. He held the circles to his eyes like eyeglasses or binoculars. Charlie nodded, knowing that meant to watch closely. "Don't ride far! It's already dark!" Charlie's voice boomed.

Geogi grinned and his teeth made a white line in the blue night light. The six men mounted the horses without saddles and were off racing down the field. Charlie stood open-mouthed. He could hear the clopping of the hooves, smell the crushed grass and stirred dust, then suddenly a line of six horses came close. Not a man was sitting on the back of a horse—they were under the horses, hanging on to sashes that were pulled across the horses' backs. Charlie heard a muffled grunt and in unison the men were up and standing on the horses, the colored sashes somehow looped around their mounts' necks. Again when they came pounding out of the darkness, not a man was to be seen, yet Charlie was certain all six were lying on the far side of each horse, out of sight except for the colored sash pulled tight around the middle of every horse. Charlie caught the invigorating smell of the warm animals, mixed with it the tangy odor of men working themselves into a good sweat. Next the men exchanged horses, jumping from the back of one to another. Charlie clapped and hollered, "Bravo! You're hired for the next show! We go to Canada!"

They stopped and pulled up in a straight line in front of Charlie and yelled in unison, "Umpa!" They dismounted, patted their mounts and began to walk them around slowly to cool out. Charlie was more than impressed. He walked beside their leader, Geogi. "You stay with the cowboys in the boxcars. Understand? You eat at my cooktent. Understand?"

Geogi rubbed his belly and laughed deeply. He shook hands with Charlie. Charlie felt like his hand was in a vise. He pointed to the cooktent. The men nodded as Charlie went to get the cook to get out any leftovers for the six newcomers. Then he told Floyd that he would be in charge of placing the Cossacks' performance between the trick shooter and trick ropers.

He phoned Charlie Hirsig about these magnificent horsemen.

"C.B., hire them! Sounds like a wonderful act. Something few people have seen. How did they find you?"

"I have no idea, unless they were with some circus and were somehow left behind. I can't understand much they say."

"That's not important. Give them a place to sleep, feed them, and keep those colored sashes clean and in good repair. Watch Floyd, he'll be wanting to do those daredevil tricks! Our show'll make money this season!"

Charlie hung up and could imagine Hirsig rubbing his hands together.

From Spokane the Irwin Bros. Wild West show went by train to Calgary, a ranching town on the prairie of southern Alberta, Canada.

Slim, eager, blond-haired Chester Byers was with the show demonstrating his rope tricks and working with all of the Irwin children, including Roy. Tiny, agile, dark-complexioned Martinez was featured as Kid Mex, on the program. He came in first in most cowboy horse races. Charlie began making some money by betting on the horses Martinez rode. He raised the jockey's salary and told Etta that he was sure Martinez could ride any old nag and make it look good in a race.

The Russian Cossacks were a hit with all audiences. The men were accepted as part of Charlie's crew. No one ever found out where they'd come from.

Pauline, Joella, and their cousin Gladys entered the girls' relay race. Charlie would not let Frances enter that year. He told her, "Next year you can compete in the relay." During a relay race, girls now changed not only horses but saddles as well. The Irwin girls were short and one of the roustabouts had to toss a wooden crate to them so that they could step on the crate, throw the saddle up on the horse, tighten the cinch, and throw their leg over the saddle. Joella came in first in this race in Calgary, beating a horse called Sammy's Glory that had not been beaten in a relay race before. Pauline came in third.

Joella won a silver medallion and was proclaimed the Best All-Around Cowgirl in the World. Charlie was all smiles and strutted around the Calgary arena, getting the crowd to sing with him the "Old Cowman's Appeal."

"Let cattle rub my tombstone round,
And coyotes mourn their kin;
Let horses come and paw my mound,
But don't you fence me in!"

Etta was pleased. She could not make up her mind whether to laugh or cry. Finally she borrowed one of Charlie's large white handkerchiefs.

Joella took off her wide-brimmed hat, tossed her golden hair about her slim shoulders, waved to the crowd, and blew them kisses. Someone handed her a rope, which she twirled for a minute; then she saw Roy with a rope over his shoulder. She crooked her finger and, when he was close, twirled her rope around him, lifted his rope from his shoulder and before he could grab it back or call her a "thieving, doe-eyed packrat," she was twirling two ropes and the crowd was on its feet applauding and whistling up a storm. Then, as a bit of frosting on the cake, she motioned for Floyd to come out with his rope. Floyd strutted out, thinking he'd perform beside his sister. He began to twirl his rope, and looked up at the crowd and grinned. He was about to skip through the vertical loop when Joella reached over and, as smooth as if it had been practiced, was twirling three ropes. The crowd erupted into a standing ovation.

Afterward she admitted to Floyd and to Roy that she and twenty-five-year-old Chester Byers got up at five o'clock in the morning, while they were on the road. Byers made her work with the rope until her arms were ready to drop off. "Chet made me set my teeth and spin my rope every way he could think of. He never seemed to become tired. Said he learned how to conserve his energy when he worked in South America."

Byers taught Joella the trick of using three ropes. She admitted that it was not as hard as it looked. "But I'm not going to show anyone else how to keep the ropes separate, twirling in opposite directions, not for any price. This is going to be my trick. Chet gave it to me."

The show was in Pendleton, Oregon, for their roundup celebration. Tom Mix was there at the same time. He rode a bucking bronc and was thrown to the dirt in about two seconds. Charlie went over to the railing where the cowboys stood in little groups so that he could say hello to Mix. By the time Charlie elbowed his way through the knots of cowboys, Mix had disappeared. Mix never did come by to greet Charlie or other members of the family. Once Joella walked over where she thought she saw him talking to a couple Oregon cowboys, but he saw her and slipped away.

After entertaining another half-dozen towns in Oregon and Washington, Charlie closed his Wild West show for the winter.

He and Etta were invited to Wyoming Governor J. M. Carey's Inauguration Ball in the rotunda of the capitol building in Cheyenne. Charlie wanted to look his best, so he went to Denver to have a tuxedo custom-made. Etta made herself a long cream-colored, satin gown. They drove to the ball in Charlie's Overland. Afterward Etta said it was something she'd always remember. Everyone was dressed in their finest so that it was next to impossible to recognize them unless she talked with them for a few moments. The food was so fancy that Etta said she could not pronounce half of what was on the long tables and no knife nor fork touched it. People ate with their fingers!

That winter the weather was mild and spring came early. The show horses were brought from the ranch to the Four-Mile pasture. Four or five horses at a time were brought in to the stalls in back of the Cheyenne house. Charlie gave the four children his annual talk about exercising the horses each morning before school. The Irwin house was a mile from what they called the pump house. The four children galloped the horses to the pump house and back each morning before school.

With the early spring weather came thoughts of the season's Wild West show. Charlie took Floyd to the ranch each weekend so that the two of them could look over steers, horses, and buffalo they might use in the show. They brushed, currycombed the animals so their fur glistened. They taped the ankles of the racehorses. Charlie decided to again work with the Sells Circus. They were first going into Nebraska and then South and North Dakota and to Canada. Father and son mulled over whether to have hog races as something different and in the end settled on goat races.

Charlie bought half a dozen Angora goats from a sheep herder who'd imported some from Canada a few years back, thinking he'd make some money on selling mohair. These goats had soft, silky, cream-colored hair that covered even their legs with close-matted ringlets. Charlie was told that if he didn't shear his goats in the spring, they'd drop the curly fleece naturally before summer. Underneath would be a fine crop of short white hairs.

Floyd was in charge of training the goats in the art of running. Floyd graduated from high school that spring. No boy was happier to get out of the stuffy classroom. It was heaven to shuck off all thought of homework and be able to spend the days outdoors paying full attention to ranching. As soon as I can I'm going to spend all my time on the ranch, thought Floyd. I'm going to let Roy take over the show work. Full-time ranching is what I want.

Charlie bought a bright red Pierce Arrow automobile, similar to the one Barney Oldfield had at the ranch. While Charlie was in town Floyd took the Pierce Arrow out to the level field across the road. He drove slowly, enjoying the sound of the motor. He intended to drive it right back and park it in the yard. Suddenly he felt a jolt and some bumps. He stopped and got out and was met by two of the Angora goats. Their lop ears twitched and their twisted horns were lowered for another assault on the big, red monster. "You've dented Pa's new car!"

It took Floyd a while to get the goats back inside the corral and mend the fence they'd butted and broken. He was nervous and uneasy the rest of the day. During supper he kept his head down, avoiding his father.

Finally Charlie said, "Something bothering you, son?"

Floyd murmured, "No, it's not much."

"I hope you got the goats back in the corral. I noticed two out in the field this morning," said Charlie.

Floyd felt a lump the size of an egg in his throat. He could hardly talk. "They're back. The fence is mended." His hands were sweaty and his stomach turned squeamish so he could not eat.

"Did any of you see what those buttin' billies did to my new Pierce Arrow? There's a long dent in the side and scratches on the front and back, worse than if I'd driven through Horse Creek where all the boulders and sticker bushes are. There's red paint on the horns of two of them. I'm so mad I could have roast goat for all three meals tomorrow!"

Floyd looked up. Charlie's face was dark and stern, but there were flecks of light in his eyes. His hands were relaxed, on top of the table, not clenched into tight fists.

Floyd took a deep breath. "I'd saw the horns off those feisty creatures! They butted me while I was getting them inside the corral."

Joe made a noise in this throat and put a napkin to his face.

"You all right, Grandpa?" asked Floyd.

"Of course I am," said Joe, reaching for another slab of corned beef. "It's you I'm worried about. Just look at that long gash on your arm. That's it, push up your sleeve and look. Them goats is fierce. I saw you workin' with 'em. That'll infect if you don't wash it and put something—iodine—on it."

Floyd stared at his grandfather. They'd been together when Floyd had gouged himself on some barbed wire. "Did you forget—"

"Heavens, no! I didn't forget nuthin'! Once my own daddy said to me, 'A lie is an abomination unto the Lord and a very present help in trouble.'"

Charlie made a funny noise in his throat and put his hand over his mouth.

Joe's eyes squeezed together, making little furrows at the corners. His hands were on his round stomach, which moved up and down with laughter.

The laugher was infectious. Soon everyone was laughing. Floyd excused himself. He rolled under the Pierce Arrow trying to figure how he could pound the dents out of the door. Take the door off, he decided. Then he'd have to see if he could find some paint in the shed that would match Pierce Arrow red. He'd touch up the scratches and rub 'em down with linseed oil.

Floyd went out with the ranchers on the spring roundup. He circled Round Top, driving stray cows to the main flock. He was happy and content. Moving farther along the range of hills, Floyd went behind the truncated hill and felt his heart drop. There were half a dozen steer dead, mostly eaten by coyotes, ravens, and crows. The animals had been caught by some cedar downfall, probably in a snowstorm. They'd been without food, and the snow had frozen on their nostrils and mouths, making them unable to even swallow snow for moisture. When their nostrils closed from freezing, they smothered.

"I felt like the devil looking at those piles of bones and rotting hide," Floyd told Charlie.

Charlie understood. "That's the way it is around old Lookout. I believe that high mesa is surrounded with the spirits of some vengeful Indian tribe. I never do feel good around there. But Round Top is just the opposite. She stands for all that's good. I sing whenever I go near her."

"I did exactly that!" said Floyd, putting his hand up on his father's shoulder.

The shows went well that year, no heavy rains to wash them out or cause delays in the booking dates. They were in Grand Forks, North Dakota, ready to move on to Winnipeg, Manitoba, Canada. First the circus and Wild West show played a couple of the small towns along the route, making only one-day stands.

After each of his performances Floyd hurried over to the big circus tent to watch the high-wire performers. He was especially intrigued with a small, dark-haired girl with sparkling black eyes. She held a big brass ring attached to a rope or cable in her mouth and was lifted off the ground. High above the crowd she spun and flew back and forth in the most graceful fashion. She wore a scanty costume with gauzy, pink material between the open sleeves and her waist. She appeared to be some exotic butterfly, floating near the tent top. No amount of height seemed to bother her. Her controlled athletic ability and fragile beauty fascinated Floyd. He could not imagine a girl having that much strength in her teeth and jaw to dangle and dance through the air for five or six minutes.

One morning Floyd watched the rehearsal for an afternoon show. When the petite, dark-haired girl stood on the ground, Floyd clapped loudly and whistled, then yelled, "Bravo, bravo for the Iron-jawed Butterfly!"

She smiled at Floyd sitting on the bottom board of the blue-painted grandstand. "Would you like to try?" she asked with an amused expression. "It's really not hard—no trick."

"Well, uh, I—" stammered Floyd, turning red as a Dakota sunset.

"Maybe you'd rather try the high-wire. See, the net's under it now. That's harder. You get soft-soled shoes and I'll show you."

"Where am I to get soft shoes?" said Floyd with a laugh. He felt a tingle go up his spine. Her teeth were even and white.

"How about from your Injun friends," she said matter-of-factly.

"You are sharp as a toad-jabber," kidded Floyd. "Your folks in this here circus?" She had a dimple in each cheek when she smiled.

"No." She blinked and turned her head away. Floyd saw the teardrop underneath her long, dark lashes. "I never knew my father. My mother had to work. I was raised by Aunt Ed and Uncle Ann."

"Aunt Ed? Uncle Ann?" questioned Floyd.

"Yes, I've always called them that."

Her voice rippled with a giggle. "They have the high-wire act. They said I was a natural for the butterfly act because when I was a baby everything went into my mouth. I'd clamp down on all that stuff and not let go." Her eyes sparkled. "You're not so bad with the trick horseback riding and trick roping."

"You've watched my act?" Floyd felt the perspiration run down the middle of his back.

"Yes. I've seen all of you. Your whole family. I like the way your dad takes over. He comes into the arena and he has 'Top Dog' written across his forehead. I mean, anyone can tell that whatever he says goes. He's the man in charge."

Floyd nodded. His father was exactly like that. That's why he was so successful managing the Wild West show and keeping all the cowboys and cowgirls and other performers in line.

"I like the way your oldest sister rides and plays to the audience. She understands show business. Aunt Ed told me to keep my eye on her and I'd learn a few tricks."

"Come on—truthfully, what's this Aunt Ed and Uncle Ann business? You are funning to see if I'd pick up on it?"

"No, honest. I told you. That's their names, Aunt Edith and Uncle Andrew. It's my name too."

"Edith Andrew?"

"No, silly, Edith. Edith Stumph." She giggled and pressed her fingers to her forehead.

"So, you are Miss Silly Edith Stumph?"

"Diddely-dee-dee!" She clapped her hands with delight. "You're the silly one. But I like you." She made a ferocious face, grabbed Floyd's hat, and set it on the back of her head.

Floyd seized his hat and held her hands. "So, tell me, did you learn any tricks from my sister, Joella?"

"I learned to look directly at the audience. Keep my eyes on them all the time and smile. They want to know that you enjoy entertaining them. You do that. So does your little brother. He's kind of cute. He has a pointy nose so his face kind of reminds me of a fox."

"Roy's not really my brother. He's—uh—kind of like you. We kinda' adopted him. Pa tells us how to work the audience before we go into the arena. I don't know where he learned. Just picked it up, I guess." He felt exhilarated and wanted to prolong the feeling. "Come have supper at our table tonight."

"The Wild West and circus people don't mix!" she exclaimed.

"Well, why not, Dee Dee?" Floyd felt his face turn warm as he realized that he'd given her a name. He stuttered, "I—I mean, Edie."

"I like what you said first," she said quietly. "Call me Dee Dee."

"I'll watch for you at suppertime," he said. He started out the back entrance, then turned. "See ya, Dee Dee."

Floyd went to the railroad siding where the Wild West show's cars were. Some of the roustabouts were sitting on the grass playing cards on an old gray blanket. Floyd said howdy and swung up two steps at a time into the Pullman car. Etta was in a double seat with costumes spread out over the cushions. She was sponging clean and mending the girls' show outfits.

"Ma, I want to wear my white satin shirt, the elastic rhinestone arm bands, and my straw hat this afternoon."

"Why, Bud, why all the fuss for a small town? Wait until we get to Winnipeg. You know your pa told some of the Indians they could have the day off."

"Oh, Jeez, Ma! The more practice we have doing a show the better we'll be. I'd like to have a good practice wearing my best outfit."

Etta sighed and patted the hand of her eldest. "I suppose one day won't hurt. All right."

"I'm going to walk around the midway with the Wandering Minstrel and do a couple of easy rope tricks. Kind of advertise the show. I need to dress for that. Or—here's another idea—I could ride Blondie; that white steer would look good with my white suit—the crowd would love it."

Now Etta was laughing. "Lord, have mercy! Bud, what has gotten into you? Just two days ago you said that it didn't matter how one was dressed, that the audience understood a good roper no matter what he had on." She rolled her eyes toward the ceiling and put her hands on her hips. "Here's my idea: You hold up the cards for Cleo the Brain, in the sideshow. Let him guess what's printed on the other side." She smiled smugly.

"Ma, you're teasing. Cleo's smart. He sits on a chair every afternoon, evenings in the big towns. When people ask him questions about railroads or state capitals, he knows the answer. He knows every state, every capital, all the railroads and rivers in this country."

"But son, that's the point. He doesn't know anything else. A genius in one tiny field. Of course the crowd doesn't know that. They only ask him questions he can answer. Why, yesterday Uncle Curly found Cleo wandering around the midway. Cleo looked lost and when Uncle Curly asked him where he thought he was going, Cleo said, 'I can't find the cookhouse. Who moved the goddamn thing?'" Etta put her hand to her mouth and laughed hard.

Floyd stared at her. "Ma, I never heard you swear before! Pa wouldn't like it!"

"Well, that's what Cleo said. It's part of the story. You're old enough to understand that women, even your mother, aren't celluloid dolls to be kept on a closet shelf."

"But you're a lady, everyone knows that."

Etta's lips quivered. A tear appeared at the corner of one eye. "Thank you, son. I'll remember and be more careful with my tongue."

Floyd looked away. "Ya, I guess Cleo's a strange guy. He doesn't fit anywhere but in the circus."

Etta dabbed at her eyes with a white hankie from her skirt pocket. "I'll tell you about the strange guy. It's that little man with the glass blower's jug. You know that big glass jug he has with the doll inside? On top is a rubber hose. The jug's sealed and the doll stays on the top until someone blows hard on the hose and puts the doll on the bottom. Would you pay a dime to blow on a hose that's been blown on by thousands before you?"

"Not me!"

"Sure are lots that do."

"The midway with all the sideshow stuff is like a carnival. Sells ought to stick just to his circus with animals and the performers, like tight-rope walkers and the Butterfly. You ever see the Butterfly, Ma? The girl with the iron-jaw? She's wonderful. Is it true that the circus performers look down on the cowboys and cowgirls and that us Wild West performers look down on the circus people? We never eat at the same tables?"

"I never thought about that." Etta sat down and moved some of the clothing aside so that Floyd could sit beside her. "I kind of like the circus people myself. For instance, the two black cannibals, Gene and Roy. Whenever I walk past their booth on the midway, they always say, 'Good evening,' or 'Good afternoon, Mrs. Irwin.' Then they go back to their act, pretending to eat raw meat and those green rubber garter snakes. I get kind of tickled when people gasp and turn pale. Gene is one of the nicest fellows there is. He's a comic and Roy is a straight man. Don't you like the way they have their hair all shaved off except for the round spot as big as a silver dollar right on top of their heads?" She giggled and the sound was like a gentle wind blowing through quaking aspen leaves. "That was Gene's idea."

Floyd leaned toward his mother and slipped his arm across the back of the seat. "Ma, what would you think if some of the circus people ate at our supper table?"

"Wouldn't hurt. Might be nice to get to know them. Bud, you know anyone over there?"

Floyd's face turned crimson. He brushed his hair out of his eyes and he hoped his mother didn't notice that he'd gasped a little on hearing her question. "Yep. I think you'd like them. I sure hope Pa and the girls do."

"Don't you worry. If I do, they all will. You want to wear your satin shirt to supper?"

"Sure, I do."

THIRTY-TWO

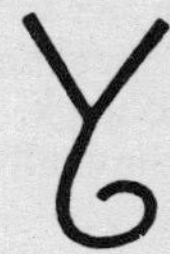

Irwin Bros. Real Wild West Show

Several days later, in the Winnipeg sunshine, Charlie walked along the midway. The matinee was over. Now was the break, a three- or four-hour lull, before the hustle and bustle of an evening performance. The midway looked forlorn. He saw drunken roughies sleeping their binge off in the grass, roustabouts whiling away their time playing cards, and several half-starved stray dogs wandering about.

Charlie stopped by the Pullman car on the siding for Etta. The night before they'd decided to go to town to buy wool shirts or sweaters for the three girls and Floyd and Roy. Etta told Charlie how she admired the towners' colorful sweaters. "The minute the sun goes down here the air becomes chilly. After trick roping, horseback riding, the kids' muscles need to be kept warm so they don't tighten nor ache."

"What about the rest of our performers?" asked Charlie. "Those people have muscles same as our kids. That's it! Dear, you're brilliant! Sweaters for the whole crew. Red sweaters so you can sew a white Y6 on the back. That's a wonderful idea." He picked up Etta and began to dance around.

Etta sputtered and stuttered and tried to pry herself loose. "Ch-Charlie! It's—It's no, it's not a good idea. The red sweaters, yes, but not the Y6. Yes, you bring stock from the Y6 ranch, but the performers come from all over. Look, there's Montana Jack, the Russian Cossacks—Charlie Hirsig's your partner. He has his own brand."

Charlie exhaled and it sounded like air rushing out of a balloon. "Yes, of course, you're right. But still, red sweaters for everyone. Huh? It's such a good idea. It's good for morale. You know, brings everyone close together. The common bond." His voice was getting louder than the whir of the grasshopper wings and the sharp *crack-crack* of their jumping legs rubbing together in the tall, dried grass near the track.

"Charlie, think. Can the show afford sweaters for everyone?" asked Etta.

"Of course. I'll tell you what I'll do." His voice bellowed. "I'll run the goat race two, three times. After the first race the crowd'll know the number of the goat that comes in first. They'll bet on that one to come in first again, or they'll bet on the one that comes in second. You and I know goats. They're damn—excuse me—so darn unpredictable. We'll make enough money off those bets to pay for our sweaters!"

"Why people enjoy seeing goats with whiny bleating, pinched faces, sour smells, and nervous twitches run around a sawdust track is a mystery to me," she said, holding her nose.

Charlie pulled Etta close to his chest and encircled her with his arms and huge hands. He buried his face in her soft, shiny hair. "Sure, you know. It's the excitement of uncertainty. Each race is different. If there is a bet, even fifty cents, the race is even more exciting, because someone's going to win. Everyone is sure he has as much chance to win as the next guy."

Etta let out a little squeak.

"I know it's not true, but the bettors don't pay attention to facts."

Uptown Charlie nudged Etta to look at a billboard advertisement in front of a show house stating: BACK TO THE PRIMITIVE—STARRING KATHLYN WILLIAMS, CHARLES CLARY, AND TOM MIX. FILMED IN FLORIDA.

Etta squealed with surprise. "Oh, oh, it's Tom! He's playacting!"

They looked over the large black and white photograph on the ad. Mix wore the typical outfit of the white hunter braving the dangers of jungle life. There was a photo of Mix saving Kathlyn's life by wrestling, bare-handed, an attacking leopard.

"Hard to believe the hero didn't trip over the jungle cat and get himself mauled. When he was with us, he was clumsy as a blind bear climbing up a bramble slope. He'd put the saddle on the wrong horse!" said Charlie.

"It's his good looks that overcome his handicaps," said Etta, laughing merrily. "That's his secret talent. He's learned not to stand in his own light."

Charlie took Etta's hand. "Let's see if Canadian sweaters are made of Angora goat's wool. If I find those billy goats of mine carry a fortune in their long curly hair, I'll have them sheared slick as a billiard ball. Goats aren't my favorite animal. They're close to sheep on my list."

Charlie could not make up his mind between red wool shirts and red wool sweaters. Finally Etta asked the clerk if he could deliver a hundred shirts of various sizes to the town's arena.

"No, ma'am, we don't even have that many flannel shirts in the warehouse. But if you'd take these sweaters, we could deliver today. We're overstocked. Been overstocked for a while, no one in town wants an all-red sweater. I could even give you a good price on a hundred," said the clerk, holding a bulky-knit sweater out for Etta to examine.

She slipped into the sweater and paraded around in front of Charlie.

"You have one that will fit me?" asked Charlie, jokingly.

"No, sir, but I can have one made up by tomorrow morning," said the clerk, taking a tape measure from his pocket and stretching it across Charlie's shoulders. He whistled, wrote a figure down on the back of an envelope he'd pulled from his pocket. "How many this size, sir?"

"One, and my wife will tell you how many of the size she has and how many regular mediums and larges. If you deliver the whole shebang to the Pullman car out there on the siding next to the arena right after breakfast, I'll give you the rest of your money." Charlie took a roll of bills from his pocket and peeled off two twenty-dollar bills.

The clerk went to the counter, put the tip of the pencil in his mouth, then made more notations on the back of the envelope as Etta talked with him.

Next morning after breakfast the store clerk came by in a Model T truck with half a dozen large brown paper bundles containing the sweaters. Charlie looked over the bill.

"I thought the order was for one hundred sweaters. This says one hundred and one!"

"Oh, yes, sir. But it took two to make one for—for your large frame," said the clerk. He pursed his lips together, then said defensively, "My wife put your sweater together from two of the large ones."

Etta had already opened a couple of the packages. "She did a beautiful job. Pay him right away, Charlie."

Charlie put on his sweater. It had a rolled or shawl collar and pearl-white buttons. He buttoned the front and put his hands in the two front pockets along the waist band. "Fits like it was made for me," he said with a laugh. "Boy, I can't wait until I give these out."

"I'm sure you carny people will like the bright color. People in town prefer more muted tones, the grays and tans," said the clerk, getting into the truck.

Charlie glared back and was ready to say something about calling cowboys names when he felt Etta put something into his hand.

"Give the gentleman two complimentary tickets for tonight's show," she said, adding under her breath, "You'll catch more flies with honey than vinegar."

Charlie gave the sweaters out to all of his crew, from the top performers down to the roustabouts and animal handlers when they came into the cooktent for the noon meal. Everyone was surprised and delighted. With all the crew in the same kind of sweater, it was easy to tell the Wild West people from the circus people. The red sweaters drew the Wild West people close together that summer, like a big, boisterous family.

That evening before the main Wild West events, Charlie walked along the midway to make certain everything was running smoothly and to count the number of tip, or people that were in line for tickets for the main Wild West show. The merry-go-round and Ferris wheel spun invitingly, pumping out canned music that could be heard above the sound of happy voices and laughter. The bright lights winked, adding to the gaiety. The voice of a pitchman rose above the noise as Charlie moved close to the ticket booth: "Say, there! Tell you what I'm gonna do!"

Charlie chuckled to himself as he saw the marks moving closer to see what the spiel was all about. Charlie walked hurriedly past the bally in front of the circus girlie show, which was called a "Revue." He heard someone call out, "Hi there, Mr. Irwin! Going to be a nice evening! Huh?"

He waved to one of the girls. She smiled and swayed her hips in his direction. He chuckled. It was all part of her act. She looked pretty enough now, but an hour before not many would take a second look as she went to her rundown railroad car to put on makeup, a rhinestone-spangled bra and flimsy harem pants.

The talker spieled, "Gentlemen! This show ain't for women nor children," and Charlie shook his head in agreement. Then in contrast he thought of the slim, dark-haired girl his son brought to the Irwin supper table a couple of nights before. Floyd called her the Iron-jawed Butterfly, and later, Dee Dee. She was embarrassed when the cowboys whistled. She was almost too shy to eat. So, Floyd was seventeen. That was old enough to be interested in girls. Charlie never imagined his son would be attracted to a circus performer. Yet, why not? She was an entertainer, same as anyone in the Wild West show.

Charlie thought there was something appealing about Dee Dee. She didn't seem as brazen as some of the other circus performers. Then he thought of something one of the Sells men had said: "Don't ever say nothin' bad about a circus woman—she may be one of the family next year." Charlie laughed to himself.

Floyd, wearing his new red sweater unbuttoned and flapping around his arms, came running through the crowd. His face was pale and sober. "Pa! Come quick! The high-voltage cables are sparking!"

"Go tell the men to turn off the generator," said Charlie calmly. He followed close behind Floyd. "I'm coming with you! Let's hurry!" Nearing the cable he could see white sparks shooting into the blackness, like Fourth-of-July sparklers. Now Charlie ran beside Floyd. Together they shouted, "Turn off the generator!" He ran toward the sparks. He could hear excited voices and knew they were his cowboys and roustabouts; he'd left the tip, or crowd, behind.

Charlie sent one of his men, a patch, to talk to Winnipeg's policemen, who had come to see what the large gathering was doing on the back lot of the circus and Wild West show. The patch was a man chosen to be a kind of liaison between the show and the town's policemen. Charlie was kneeling down beside the cable. "Bring me a light! A match, a candle, anything!" he shouted. The lights were off. It was dark as the insides of a black bear. Charlie and a couple of the roustabouts cut the thick cable and stripped the rubber and cloth from the wires. They felt the wires. It was hard to see anything in the feeble candlelight. "I can't find my nose with both hands," complained one roustabout. "Bring that flickering flame closer. You don't have to singe my eyebrows!"

The men examined the wire by feel and found a break. They

twisted the wires back together and patched the cable with nearly a full roll of black tape. Charlie handed the coal-oil lamp to one of the men and said, "Turn the juice on!" He moved back along the midway, thankful that only one generator was out of commission for a short time, and glad that it was the lights for the Wild West show that were out, because the show was not due to start for another thirty minutes. However, the tip were already beginning to line up for their tickets. He passed the cannibal pen and saw the two black men inside on all fours, snarling and tugging at a raw chicken; the crowd was open-mouthed and fascinated. All of a sudden one of the blacks stood up and attempted to climb out of the sturdy pen he was in. The crowd backed away, screaming. Then, when nothing happened, they inched back to see the two "Cannibals from Borneo." The black man called Gene stood up, the crowd surged backward once again. The man called out, "Get the lights fixed, Mr. Irwin?"

Charlie yelled back, "Certainly did. You gonna eat that chicken without hot pepper sauce?"

"Yes, sir. I'll eat it sure as Master Floyd's found hisself a little iron-jawed filly!" Gene called back.

The crowd began to hiss and point at the talking cannibal. Gene swung the raw, plucked chicken around his head, growled deep in his chest, and rolled his eyes. In those few magic seconds the crowd seemed to forget and saw only two, untamed, savage men tearing apart a raw chicken into bite-size pieces.

Floyd tugged at Charlie's sleeve. "Pa, the lights to the Wild West show are on the blink again. Show goes on in fifteen minutes!"

"Jeems. I hope this doesn't start a clem. We don't need any kind of fuss. We don't need town rowdies coming in all lickered up looking for excitement nor exercise." Charlie shrugged his big shoulders and headed back to the generator.

"A couple of the roustabouts are rigging up some star candles. The Indians are rigging up pine-pitch torches. Everybody's trying to help in case we can't get the generator going," said Floyd.

Some of the men were hunkered around the ailing generator. "Trouble's not in the cable, Mr. Irwin. This generator just up and died." Charlie saw the candle boards and pitch torches and nodded his approval.

"I guess before there was electricity, this kind of light satisfied an audience. So let's make the most of it tonight. At least our show will be lit different from the circus show." He suggested the roustabouts build "chandeliers" for the center pole of his big top.

They nailed together wide lath boards with holes, where they stuck plain white candles. Four of these boards hung on the center pole. It only took Charlie a few moments as master of ceremonies standing in the center to move away from the center pole and the chandeliers because the wax dripped on anything underneath. Charlie kept the sides of the big tent down because the breeze made the torches smoke or go out.

That evening's performance was smoky anyway. Floyd did tricks riding on the back of a horse. Martinez rode standing backward on Blondie, the steer. Most of the audience thought the steer was a horse with a crown of horns. Charlie could hear coughing and see the ladies wipe their eyes with white handkerchiefs because of the smoke. The audience clapped loudly for the last act, but Charlie had the feeling it was not for his show, but because the people were leaving for fresher air. Charlie held his hands high and made a startling announcement: "Ladies and gentlemen, because of circumstances beyond our control we resorted to a lighting system used a generation ago, and because you were such a wonderful audience, I'm buying out all the seats in the circus tent for this evening's performance. You may go directly there from here and see one complete circus show for free, compliments of the Irwin Brothers Cheyenne Frontier Days Wild West Shows."

Now there was a wild ovation with whistling and stomping of feet.

Charlie called out, "Thank you! Thank you!" But it was doubtful anyone heard him.

As soon as the Wild West big top was empty, Charlie sent the patch to seek out Mr. Sells to say that Charlie was buying every seat in the circus big top for that evening's performance. Charlie made certain all torches were extinguished and the hardened wax was shoveled out of the sawdust, which covered the circular arena. He and Etta went to see the circus along with the rest of the excited crowd. The air was sharp and she was glad the children had sweaters.

Floyd's eyes were glued on the Iron-jawed Butterfly, who wore pink spangled tights and leotard. She twisted and turned in the air, always looking straight ahead, not daring to smile for fear of losing her tight-toothed grip on the big brass ring. She spun around and around, then let herself unwind. The audience applauded wildly. Floyd stood up and whistled. He yelled, "Bravo, Dee Dee!"

Joella whispered, "Sit down, Bud. Oh, boy, you smell like

you've been sitting on the wrong side of a bonfire."

"Hush," warned Etta. "All members of the Irwin Wild West Show can be identified by their smoky smell this night."

"Ha!" Floyd glared at Joella. "A stinking dog never smells itself."

"Ma, Floyd called me a dog!" cried Joella, looking insulted.

"I said hush," repeated Etta, looking straight ahead. "Be as quiet as that little Butterfly girl."

Floyd was still standing. He waved his arms.

Joella continued to complain. "Look, Ma, Bud acts like one of the joeys. If he had a white face, he could go right down there with the rest of the clowns. He could ride on one of those elephants. At least people could see him perform here. Gad, those pine-pitch torches the Indians made for the Wild West show were smoky!"

"The trouble with you is that you think no one saw you perform with all that smoke. You're jealous of me because people recognize I'm a trick rider." Floyd sneered and snapped his fingers. "Did you wish some towner'd think you a good-looker and send you an invite for dinner or somethin'?"

"You've a big mouth and calluses from patting your own back!" snapped Joella, swishing her yellow hair about her shoulders.

"Hey! Stop that kind of talk," said Charlie. He looked at Etta and hoped she'd put a stop to the children's fussing.

Etta was entranced with the wisp of a girl twirling like a lacy pink butterfly above the center of the arena, and paid no attention to what was being said.

The next act was on the high wire and the Iron-jawed Butterfly performed again. She walked across the wire with a parasol held high above her head. She smiled. The Amazing Stumphs—Floyd knew it was Aunt Ed and Uncle Ann—met her halfway across the wire. She balanced herself on one shoulder of each of them while they clung to the wire with feet in soft shoes. The girl twisted and turned so she faced the opposite side of the arena. She waved.

Etta held her breath. Charlie clapped loudly. The three girls cheered. Floyd smiled smugly. He was quiet as a tree full of owls.

Charlie was getting ready for bed when there was a loud pounding on the door of the Pullman car. "I'll go," said Charlie, getting back into his pants. "Probably one of the cowboys needing to borrow ten dollars so he can stay in a lousy poker game."

It was one of the cowboys. "Mr. Irwin, I'm sorry to bother, sir, but the depot, over yonder, sent word that there's a telephone call for you from Cheyenne."

"Jeems, I hope it's not bad news!" said Charlie. "I'll be back as soon as I can, dear."

It was his partner, Charles Hirsig, in Cheyenne, saying, "C.B., I couldn't get you when the show was in progress, so I waited until now. I got wind of some news I thought you'd want to hear right away."

"What's so important that couldn't wait until morning?" shouted Charlie.

"I heard that the Sells brothers are merging with the Floto Circus."

"So what! You could have called Otto Floto at the *Denver Post* to check that out. Use my name. He and I are friends since the Endurance Race."

"Charlie, listen to me. Sells is going to throw out a lot of duplication of equipment, mainly because theirs is not as new as what Floto has. If you play your cards right, you can get a calliope for a song. Then our Wild West show won't have to tag along with a circus. We can be on our own. Be nice to the circus people."

Charlie guffawed. "Hirsig, you sound as eager as a stud at the snortin' pole. What's changed your mind? Used to be you didn't like circus people. You said they were worse than gypsies."

"I still feel that way. But I won't be working with them. You get along with all kinds of people." Hirsig paused.

"When's the merger?" asked Charlie.

"In a day or two."

"Sells didn't say a word to me. And I bought out his entire house tonight."

"You what?" Hirsig's voice cracked.

"Well, it's a long story, but we made a big hit with the towners."

"How much did that cost us? Close to a thousand dollars?"

"Don't worry about it. The goodwill it bought more than makes up for the cost."

"C.B., what's going on? Tell me. I'm your partner, remember?"

"I didn't forget. Floyd's learning the Russian Drag from those six cossacks we hired in Spokane. He's damn good slinging his body under a horse and riding pell-mell down the track, then pulling himself upright again. First he falls off the back of his horse, hangs down backward with his head about six or eight inches from the horse's hooves. The horse runs full speed, then Floyd pulls himself up with straps hooked on to the saddle and stands up in the saddle. It's really something. I made him put a double cinch on his saddle for safety. I bet you he's the first American to do the Russian Drag."

"See that Floyd's cautious and don't break his fool neck," warned Hirsig. "Remember when I told you to hire those god-damned Russians? I said no American ought to perform such a dangerous, daredevil feat."

"Sure, I remember. But you know boys. They try new things—take chances—nothing happens to 'em. It's part of growing. Maybe you'd like to know those cossacks are a wild bunch. I had to get two of them out of a local bar a couple of days ago. They don't understand a word of English and thought some fool cow-boy'd insulted one of them. They were hell-bent for pounding the cowboy right through the floor. Now I send three men, roust-abouts or cowboys, to be with them at all times. We can't afford to have them acting like animals—they might attack a woman in broad daylight on one of the streets. Say, speaking of affording—I bought everyone a red sweater—gets cold in the evenings this far north. Don't worry, they're all paid for. This thing about the Sells brothers must be just a rumor. I haven't heard a thing and I keep my ear to the ground."

"C.B., have you thought that they don't want everybody and his cat knowing about their merger? Ringling could come along and buy one or the other out."

"Or both," said Charlie. "But Ringling don't want to fool around with small outfits like Sells and Floto. You go back to bed. In the morning I'll see what I can find out."

Hirsig didn't hang up. He hesitated just a moment, "C.B., as partners, I think you ought not treat my news lightly."

"Ya, all right. Thanks for telling me. In the morning I'll see what I can find out," said Charlie, yawning, noticing the ghostly deep-blue light out the window when the moon came out from under a cloud.

"We wouldn't need to hire a brass band if we had a calliope—save us a lot of money. Be nice to have circus cars, with colorful pictures painted on the sides to ship our stock in—be good ad-vertisement."

"Okay. I'll talk to you in a few days," said Charlie.

"A few days? You call me in the morning or maybe I ought to

look around for another partner!" yelled Hirsig. "This is serious."

"Who else has horses, steers, buffalo, and people who can ride all three?" asked Charlie calmly.

"Buffalo Bill Cody—the Miller Brothers' 101 Ranch!" snapped Hirsig.

"Irwin Brothers' show shines like a beacon over all the land compared to the dying glowworm shine of either of those shows you mentioned. Besides, you have to stick with me. I understand your money coming in from selling polo ponies to that rich easterner, William Rockefeller, has about dried up."

"Where'd you hear that?" shouted Hirsig. "Hurry up and tell me, this telephone call is costing me my right arm."

"Old Bill Rockefeller's breeding his own horses. He's selling the colts as polo ponies to all his friends," Charlie chuckled.

Hirsig growled and hung up the receiver.

Etta was brushing her hair. "What was that about?"

"Hirsig said the Sellses are merging with Floto and maybe we could buy some circus equipment cheap."

"That sounds grand," said Etta. "The show could use a couple circus wagons, for horses and steers, and more bleacher seats."

"I thought so myself," admitted Charlie. "But a partner ought to have sense enough to call me earlier, or wait until morning. Jeems! Even if he does own half the property, he's a pain in the a—ankle. I'd rather run my own Wild West show!"

In the narrow lower berth Etta lay close to Charlie. She could feel his heart pound and his back stiffen. She heard Floyd and Roy whispering in the upper berth. Across the aisle the girls slept, Joella in the top and the younger girls in the bottom berth. At the other end of the car a berth was made up for the porter and cook. Etta thought she heard Frances sneeze. Etta put her arm around Charlie and said, "With the income from the Wild West show and supplying stock to Cheyenne's Frontier Days, you could find enough money to buy out Charlie Hirsig. He's not depending on the income from this operation. He makes a good deal selling polo ponies to his Rockefeller friend in New York."

"Yes. I've been thinking about that. I'm going to sleep now. I'll decide soon enough. Jeems! It's true! I've made enough to own my own outfit. My own Wild West show! Maybe I'll buy out Frank. He doesn't contribute so much anymore. And I can't depend on him. I wonder what Clara Belle says to him about his drinking?"

"That's between them. Not any of your business." Etta loosened her hold around Charlie's chest. "But I know what I'd say."

* * *

The next morning was taken up with packing to get the show animals and equipment into boxcars so it could head out to Calgary. Everyone was in high spirits, the show was on the move again, the crew eagerly anticipated new towns. Winnipeg had been a disappointment at first. It was a town of ranchers. They had not been impressed by this first Wild West show to perform for their entertainment by cowboys and cowgirls from the U.S. The Canadians felt that what cowboys or girls did south of their border was no different from what they did every day. Then the generator and electrical cable went on the fritz and Charlie gave out free tickets to the circus. After that fateful night the crowds were tremendous. That was the best public relations move Charlie made so far. The Irwin Brothers Wild West show was known from then on as fair and square among towners in Canada and the U.S.

On the way to Calgary, Charlie's train stopped in several small towns for a few short stands, a matinee in one place and a tented-up evening show in another. During the short stands Charlie trotted Steamboat around the ring, letting the bucking horse snort, honk, and rare up on his hind legs a couple of times. Then he called out to the audience, "Who is brave enough to give me five dollars to ride this bronc, whose forelegs go one way and hind-legs the opposite way? The horse is part Morgan. Comes from well-bred stock." He paused so that the crowd could look over the coal-black horse with two white hind legs and one white foreleg. Then he said, "That's a lucky white spot in the middle of its forehead. If you stay on the horse, I'll give you ten dollars! Who's game? Of course you want to earn an easy ten bucks! Give me five and I'll give you ten if you stick tight as a burr for one minute. That's only sixty seconds!"

More than a dozen cowboys poured out of the audience in each small town, but not one was able to stay on Steamboat's back for a minute. The horse worked terrific jolts in between his twisting and turning. Most riders could only take one or two of those poundings. Steamboat was called King of the Hurricane Deck.

Charlie made Steamboat the champion of all his bucking-bronc rodeo events. This twisting, sunfishing bronc was known worldwide.

This time in Calgary, before the second day was over, Charlie had decided not to stay the full week. The six Russian Cossacks were in a street fight and it took half a dozen of his cowboys to settle things. The Cossacks were big, burly young men, with wide, dark mustaches and beards. Their hair was long and tied with strips of thin leather bands. They spoke Russian to each other. To make themselves understood among others, they spoke a few words of broken English and used vivid facial expressions, hand and body movements. The six men were each near six feet tall, muscular, agile as boxers, and graceful as ballet dancers. While riding, their heads moved slowly but constantly, so that their dark, penetrating eyes took in everything as they whizzed past.

After the Cossacks' street fight Charlie had to pay for three broken windows, one bent street lamp, and a smashed fire hydrant. He was afraid there'd be more fistfights and his American crew would be the losers on Canadian soil. The show's reputation as being fair and square could be turned inside out if the Cossacks vented their pent-up energy in more fistfights.

After supper on that second day in Calgary, Charlie called his friend Charlie Hirsig. "Hey, Sells denied the rumor of merging with Floto. Maybe you ought to call Otto Floto in Denver. See what he says. By the way, I'm pulling out of Calgary tomorrow morning. Show tonight is final. This is a dirty town and could be an expensive town if I have to pay for more broken windows." He told about the fight.

"C.B., you can't. What about the route card?" said Hirsig.

Charlie imagined Hirsig's eyes closing and his mouth drawing together into small folds. "The names of those towns are just on paper. Paper's not permanent. So who says I have to follow the route card? When a place is unpleasant, no matter whose fault it is, I'm leaving. We're headed for Lethbridge, then to Shelby and Great Falls, Montana."

Hirsig became angry. Charlie could imagine him pounding the wall beside the telephone with his fist. "That's a dirty thing to do, C.B. You send me the revised itinerary. I have to know where you are."

"Stay calm. I will," said Charlie, hanging up the receiver. He shook his head and sighed. He was glad he'd not said anything about buying Hirsig's share of the Wild West show. Charlie believed business negotiations were better done when the negotiators were in a good mood. A laugh decides important events better than a growl.

While talking to the arena people Charlie found out that Tom Mix had been there in the spring, sometime in March. Mix was with a man who knew horses inside out, Guy Weadick. The two men had staged a rodeo for the local cowboys and were so successful that Calgary ranchers and city officials were in favor of it being an annual affair, something like Cheyenne's Frontier Days, but called the Calgary Stampede. Charlie was dumbfounded. He grinned and admitted he'd figured Tom Mix all wrong. "Why, I'd have voted for that dude to be a loser when it came to cowboying; now he's proved me all wet by teaming up with a top winner."

Before leaving Calgary, Charlie bought a large thoroughbred horse from one of the Canadians at the arena. The horse was named Frank Lubbock. Charlie liked its looks and could not wait to enter it in the races around Cheyenne.

Joella, Pauline, Frances, Margaret, Gladys, Clayton Danks's wife, Marie, and Etta's youngest sister, Eva McGuckin, were ready to enter the ladies' horse races in Lethbridge, Alberta, Canada. Before the race Charlie made a big show of lining up the seven girls so the crowd could see that the U.S. grew its share of pulchritude. He called off each name in his booming voice, which seemed to cause the grandstand to vibrate. When he stood beside Joella she whispered, "Pa, I don't feel like racing today. I have a darned head cold. Do I have to race?"

That surprised Charlie. "Honey, your horse could outrun the racer Buffalo Bill. You'll be today's winner. The people will love you. Get out there and do your stuff!"

Joella hung her head and nodded.

"Smile!" called Charlie. All the girls looked around the stands and smiled.

As the girls left to get on their horses, Charlie saw Pauline and Gladys whispering. He walked between them so they stopped. "Just today, hold back on your horses. It's Joella's turn to win. She's feeling blue over something or other. Let's perk her up," he said.

Everything went just fine with the cowgirls' half-mile race and Charlie was about to relax. Suddenly he jerked his head up. There was Gladys coming around from the back stretch, passing everyone right in front of the grandstand. Pauline was right behind her, Joella was third. Charlie leaned way over the grandstand rail and yelled to Gladys, "Hold your horse! Hold him back!"

Gladys saw Charlie from the corner of her eye and remembered what he'd said. She pulled on the reins and her horse instantly jumped the arena fence separating the track from the front of the grandstand. Pauline's horse followed, jumping the fence right behind Gladys. Then Joella's horse followed the first two.

The crowd gasped, then laughed and stamped their feet and applauded as Margaret came in first, Marie Danks second, Eva McGuckin third, and Frances came trotting in last.

Charlie glared at Gladys, who sat on her horse on the wrong side of the arena fence. Pauline brought her horse close to the fence and called through, "Pa, it wasn't Gladys's fault. When she pulled back her horse went over the railing." She could not hold back her giggles. "You have to admit it was funny to see me and Joella's horse follow behind Gladys as if we were playing Follow-the-Leader."

Gladys began to laugh, but Joella was in tears.

"Pa, you promised I'd win," she wailed.

"Honey, you can't always win," said Charlie. "Look at the funny side, the way Gladys and Pauline do. I can't believe Gladys made her horse jump that fence on purpose."

"I do!" Joella moved her head up and down sassily and walked away, leading her horse in front of a line of cowboys who clapped and whistled at the pretty blond-haired girl parading in front of them.

Charlie moved quickly to the finish line, helped Margaret down from her horse, shook hands with Marie and Eva, and took all three to the center of the arena. He told the crowd that Margaret was an old-timer in the ladies' half-mile races and one of the top U.S. lady riders. He introduced Marie Danks as a champion rider who'd ridden with Buffalo Bill's show for several years, and he introduced Eva McGuckin as a newcomer who showed tremendous promise. Eva had never won a race before and she beamed brighter than a polished coal-oil lantern.

Charlie was thinking that in a couple of days the girls would all get a good laugh over the incident when he heard laughter coming from the group of cowboys. Eva was walking past the cowboys who were talking to Joella and must have lost her balance or tripped on something, because she fell flat on her face in the dust. Joella laughed loud, tossed her long yellow hair about her shoulders, and flashed her eyes at the guffawing boys.

Charlie sauntered over, his thumbs tucked into his belt loops. "What kind of men are you? The lady may be hurt. Help her to her feet. If you work for me, pick up your pay and collect your belongings. You no longer work for me!" The laughter stopped.

Eva got to her feet, brushed herself off, and smoothed her short brown hair. She felt her freckled, pug nose and decided it was not broken. "I'm all right. I must have tripped over my own clumsy feet. You know how awkward I am."

"You tripped over someone's foot," he said, glaring at Joella and noticing that all the cowboys he could see were strangers, probably from around Lethbridge. "Go sit in the stands, or take care of your horses, you—you clowns!" yelled Charlie. He waved his arms and the young men scattered, not even glancing back at Joella.

One cowboy was heard asking another, "Who's that giant with the loud voice?"

The other answered, "You fool! That's *her* old man. The famous C. B. Irwin!"

Before going back to Cheyenne after playing Great Falls, Charlie took the show to Helena, Butte, and Billings, Montana. He'd heard that Buffalo Bill Cody had made a cleaning in Billings.

The show train pulled in early in the afternoon and the cowboys decided that they had enough time to visit a nearby tavern before unloading and setting up equipment. Charlie told them he was against the visit in the first place and in the second place they had only an hour before he expected each one to be back setting up for the evening show.

The local coal miners finished work and came to the same tavern for a drink. When they saw all the strangers sitting around the tables laughing and joking, they assumed that these men had come to take their jobs. They jumped Charlie's cowboys. Most of the miners were Europeans and spoke as little English as the Cossacks. It was a free-for-all. Fists flew, glass broke, chairs and tables fell. Someone called Charlie and when he saw the scene he thought there was going to be bloody murder. He moved to the middle of the fracas and shouted, "Grab your hats and leave!" No one seemed to hear him. The miners yelled in gibberish and the cowboys swore. He held one of the miners in front of himself like a shield and shouted, "Get out of here!" He let the man go and eased himself toward the door, shoving two cowboys in front of him. "Get to the depot and get us an engine with an engineer, a brakeman, and fireman pronto!" he cried. He went back inside and could not believe what he saw. The miners were swinging chairs against his cowboys' heads, slamming the cowboys against the wall, trying to break their noses. He pushed his way toward a couple of miners and held them by their coat collars. He let them know he was stronger than they by hitting their heads together. Someone hit Charlie from behind with a bottle. The room spun. Charlie grabbed the nearest object, a stovepipe that rattled and sagged. He blinked and managed to stay on his feet. "Train leaves in five minutes!" he yelled. "Any one still here is on his own!"

At that moment two Cossacks, Tephon and Luke, came into the tavern. Seeing the skirmish, they smiled from ear to ear. They shouted in their native tongue and began pushing the cowboys toward the door one by one. The other four Cossacks stood outside with clenched fists waiting for the miners to retreat. Whenever one came out the door he was tackled and put aside like cordwood. In less than ten minutes Charlie had the bruised and battered cowboys and grinning Cossacks scrambling toward the railroad siding.

Charlie and the Sioux women applied iodine and bandages, thankful no bones were broken, although several cowboys had teeth missing. The men, animals, and equipment were reloaded. From the depot Charlie called the Billings' mayor and canceled the Wild West show's week-long engagement. Then he called Hirsig in Cheyenne to say he was bringing the crew home. Hirsig said, "C.B., I'm sorry. Come to Cheyenne, there's no trouble here. I'll see if I can get us booked at Frontier Park as soon as you arrive. We'll give a two-day show for the people in Cheyenne."

"Can you do that?" asked Charlie. "It's almost Frontier time. Maybe you'd better check with the chairman of the Frontier Committeemen. Will he permit a show so close to the daddy of 'em all?"

"I'll have the park rented by the time you get back. It'll take your mind off the fight with those miners in Billings. So, look forward to a show in your own home town." Hirsig hung up.

Charlie wondered if Hirsig could actually rent the park by himself. On all other deals they each had to sign the agreement papers because they were partners.

A few days later Charlie and the show crew were in Cheyenne. The days were warm, the sky cloudless. People were glad to see Charlie back in town and shook his hand when they met him on the street. Hirsig had rented Frontier Park for Saturday and Sunday, posted colored fliers advertising the IRWIN BROS. CHEYENNE FRONTIER DAYS WILD WEST SHOW on every telephone and telegraph pole in town.

On Saturday afternoon Charlie was walking over to the cookhouse for lunch with Floyd and Roy. He told them they looked better and better performing their roping tricks. "Instead of having Chester Byers teach you how to hold a rope, one of these days you'll be the teacher for some kid with a burning desire to be the country's best trick roper."

"Poor, stupid kid." Roy grinned.

A skinny youngster, about twelve years old, was kicking up dust as he ran toward Charlie. "Mr. Irwin! Wait! I want to talk to you!"

Charlie recognized the boy as Arthur Burmister. He turned to Floyd and Roy. "You two go on, but leave me some greens and cream pie." Then he looked at the boy, who was standing as straight as he could in front of Charlie and trying to catch his breath so he could talk.

"Hippy! You delivering my mail?" Charlie squinted into the sun.

"No, Mr. Irwin, I came to ask for a job. I'm at Little Horse Pickerton Ranch right now. My folks moved somewheres south. I just can't stand it until I get a job with you on this here show."

"Now, wait a minute. I can't hire you. You haven't finished school yet."

"Aw, to hell with school," said Hippy.

"I haven't a vacancy for you," said Charlie.

"Back there, during that last practice race, I saw you let one of your cowboys go because he raked the sides of his horse. I could take his place. I can ride anything. I'm gentle with animals. Just try me." The boy's face drew together in a frown, then his eyes opened a little wider as he said, "I already told Pickerton I was coming to your show and hire on. I've taken all my gear out of his bunkhouse."

Charlie looked at the puny kid he'd named Hippy and thought a few moments. "I'll give you a job riding the buffalo." He was sure the kid would back off. He didn't.

"By God, I'll ride your buffalo."

That evening, while the rest of the show was going on, Charlie was busy putting Hippy Burmister up on a buffalo with a saddle. The buffalo was headed toward the middle of the arena with the skinny kid. It gave one kick with its hind legs and Hippy was snapped off into the dirt. He got up grinning. Charlie put the saddle on one of the bulls and boosted Hippy into the seat and headed the bull to the center of the arena. The bull began to kick up dust, making Charlie cough. Hippy stayed on a few seconds then was tossed off onto the ground, and the bull was herded hurriedly back into its pen by the arena clowns. Hippy was up in a flash, waving to the crowd. He smiled and bowed to the grandstand. He turned to the bleachers and smiled and bowed.

Charlie motioned for Hippy to come back to the line of cowboys.

"How'd I do, Mr. Irwin? I stayed on pretty good, huh?"

"Listen, son," said Charlie. "You've got guts and that's something in my book. So, you're hired to ride buffalo. But don't forget, in the fall and winter when the work slacks off, you go to school. Stay in the bunkhouse. Ride a horse to Albin for school every morning."

"Yes, sir. Thanks lots, Mr. Irwin. I'll never forget this."

"I won't either," said Charlie with a laugh.

Monday morning Charlie was in his office at the Plains Hotel. He had a telephone call from Clyde Watts, the district court commissioner. Watts explained that the Cheyenne's office of mayor and some of the business section people were fearful that the Irwin Bros. Wild West Show might diminish the attendance to the upcoming Cheyenne Frontier Days program. Watts said he was sending Charlie a letter stating that henceforth Mr. Irwin and Mr. Hirsig were prohibited, by a city injunction, from using or taking from the city of Cheyenne any horses, riders, or equipment or anything that might be used in the Cheyenne Frontier Days. He cited the contract Hirsig had signed with the city of Cheyenne. "That contract states you will not use any of the stock and equipment for thirty days or less before the Frontier Days show. You put on a show over the past weekend and it is now exactly two weeks before the upcoming big celebration. That is a breach of contract, Mr. Irwin."

Charlie was stunned. His mouth was so dry he could not speak. His stomach was pulled together in one huge knot. He thought for a moment he might black out. "Jeems!" he finally blurted. "Why didn't someone tell me? I never signed such an agreement. Hirsig and I are partners!"

"I know nothing of that. The letter is in the mail, Mr. Irwin."

Charlie heard the receiver fall into the hook. His hands were sweaty and he could not think straight. How could this have happened? He remembered seeing Clyde Watts at the Sunday show. There was no hint that the businesspeople were troubled. Saturday was a big day for their business and the local restaurants did well on Sunday. Charlie sat still and began to remember questioning Hirsig about checking with the mayor and the Frontier Days committeemen. Hirsig said, "Don't worry, everything's taken care of." Charlie picked up the telephone receiver and called Hirsig.

Charlie Hirsig seemed furious. He couldn't understand why

the town was so troubled by having a Wild West show performed on a weekend when nothing else was going on. "I can remember when Pawnee Bill, Buffalo Bill Cody, the Miller Brothers' 101, and lots of smaller outfits rented the park any time they wanted and put on their shows. Sometimes they were a week before or a week after the big Frontier Days. Jesus, it didn't matter; if there were enough cowboys to enter the contests, there was a show. This town has always had that kind of entertainment. No one ever worried about them taking away attendance from the Frontier Days affair. What's in their damn craw? Sure, I signed an agreement. But that was only a formality so we could rent the park. Lots of organizations use the park."

Charlie tried to explain that actually the other shows had never performed less than a month before the Frontier Days celebration.

"Remember I told you to check. Stone—did you talk with him? You paid the rent for the park—but those fellows don't give a hoot what the place is used for. I could have checked. I had a feeling, a hunch, there could be trouble and I ignored it."

"C.B., this here is a free country. It's our equipment, our stock, and our crew. So—we can damn well have our show! What difference does it make if some of the same stock and stuff is used for Frontier Days! When the park people rent to us that means we can use Frontier Park for what we have in mind. It's ours for the time we've paid for! I rented the park for us. They took our money!"

"I hear you." Charlie wiped his sleeve across his face. "You signed a contract. I never saw that paper! You never told me about it! Now we've broken that contract and now Clyde Watts means business. That's all there is to it," said Charlie. He could hear Hirsig breathing. "I can't take the Wild West show out of town."

"How'll we make a profit?" asked Hirsig. "If the show can't go out of town, I quit. You no longer have the financial support from my half of the show. I'm getting out. C.B., did you hear me?"

Charlie took the receiver from his ear and looked at it a moment. What had happened in the last half hour? he thought. Things were falling apart. This was not the way he'd envisioned Hirsig getting out of the partnership. This was emotional, not the logical kind of a business deal Charlie preferred. He pushed the receiver against his ear. "You mean you're pulling out and taking your half of the equipment? I want to see the contract you signed with the city."

"You will. I'm selling it all to you, C.B. I'm liquidating. I'm putting all my funds into my ranch. I'm washing my hands of your Wild West outfit. And I'm not letting Clyde Watts tell me what to do and when to do it!"

"For your information, I believe Clyde Watts just told you when to sell out to your partner," said Charlie. His eyes watered and he rubbed each one with a fist.

"If I were you I wouldn't furnish stock to Frontier Days anymore. I wouldn't give the Frontier people the satisfaction of thinking you needed them. Who do they think they are? They act as if they're the big mucky-mucks. They act like those thugs, the union miners, pushing your cowboys around in Billings."

"Okay! So, where are those Russian Cossacks who'll get me out of something I never should have walked into in the first place?" Charlie jerked his bandanna from his neck and wiped the perspiration from his face.

"That's your problem," said Hirsig.

"What?"

"You should have asked me about the contract in the first place."

"You should have told me you had one. Both of us should have signed it. We were partners!" Charlie could feel the walnut-sized lump in his throat. He tried to get rid of it by swallowing. It would not go away. "I'll wrestle with it," he said. "Come to my office this week as soon as you make a list of the assets you want me to take off your hands. We'll come to an agreement on the worth of your half of the show." He hesitated a moment, then added, "You could've told me you needed money for your ranch. We might've worked something out better than this breakup."

"Ya, I suppose so. C.B., let me tell you now, if you hear a rumor about me hiring Eddie McCarty as foreman of my spread, forget it. Eddie McCarty doesn't know the first thing about caring for stock, he's just a bronc rider and steer roper."

Charlie could not eat. He could not sleep. He tossed and turned and thought constantly about his partnership with his friend Hirsig and where it had gone wrong. He heard the rumor about Eddie McCarty going to work on Hirsig's ranch. McCarty would make a good foreman. Charlie thought maybe Hirsig needed money to pay McCarty's salary. But a man who worked at a bank besides managing a ranch couldn't be broke. The rumor also said McCarty was in debt to Hirsig. McCarty had borrowed plenty so he could buy horses and steers to supply the Frontier Days with stock. Why would McCarty do that? thought Charlie. He knows I've always supplied the Frontier Days celebration with my stock. For several days he discounted the last part of the rumor, thinking that a bronc rider couldn't know much about caring for stock and moving animals from one place to another safely. Then it dawned on him that McCarty was a fast talker. He was from Cheyenne and could easily talk Hirsig into a deal while Charlie was out traveling around the country with his Wild West show. Hirsig never could keep his mouth shut about the money that could be made supplying stock to local rodeo events. Charlie supposed he'd talked in front of McCarty. Maybe McCarty wanted in on the partnership. Hirsig must have known Charlie would be against taking in another man, so he set up a way to dissolve the partnership. He signed a contract with the city of Cheyenne and bet that Charlie would break it. Charlie could see Hirsig telling the mayor what to put in the contract.

Charlie chided himself for thinking the worst of his partner, especially when he didn't know the facts. Finally he told Etta he was going to buy out Hirsig's share of the Wild West show.

He talked to Will about the show. Will said he was not interested in the show anymore, and he also wanted out of the Irwin brothers' half. He said he'd rather stay at the ranch and look after the cattle. He said, "C.B., go ahead, travel all over the country during the summer. I'll stay here and look after Pa. He's not as spry as he used to be, or have you noticed?"

Charlie felt the barbed remark, but bit his tongue and said nothing.

"If my wife and kids want to ride horses in your shows, I don't object," said Will. "You pay 'em same as you pay the other performers."

Charlie talked to Frank about the show. Frank wanted to stay and continue as a jockey. "That's the only thing that gets me off this ranch to see what's happening in other damn towns. I heard Eddie McCarty is going to sell some nice racehorses at Frontier Days. Lend me a couple hundred dollars. I've a mind to buy some. All right?"

"No!" bellowed Charlie. "I'm not loaning you money to give to a crooked bronc rider who muscled in on my territory. Only thing I'd give you for McCarty is a load of buckshot!"

By the end of the week Charlie had settled with his brother Will for the steers he had for the show. He'd settled with Hirsig with a cashier's check from Hirsig's bank. Now Charlie owned all the equipment and stock for the show, except for Frank's horses. Charlie was reminded of one of his grandma Malinda's sayings: "Life is made up of twin tragedies; not to get what the heart desires and to get what the heart desires."

A week before the opening of the 1912 Frontier Days show Charlie had a call at his office from Otto Floto in Denver. The Floto Circus had bought out the Sells Circus, and then because of later financial difficulty merged with the Ringling Brothers, Barnum and Bailey Circus. "Charlie, you interested in buying any of our excess circus equipment? We've got a lot of things lying around here in boxcars in the freight yard. Most is old and needs paint. You can have it for a song. Wanna come down and have a look?"

"I'll come," said Charlie.

Charlie felt good. He spent the rest of the afternoon designing a new flier for his show, changing the name to: THE IRWIN BROS. REAL CHEYENNE WILD WEST SHOW, and adding THE GREATEST WILD WEST SHOW IN THE WORLD.

Charlie went to Denver and bought a couple show wagons that could be put on a railroad flatbed, a hundred boards for bleacher seats, some canvas for a couple of big tops, a bandwagon, and a calliope for a song, like Floto promised. For the first time in ten days Charlie felt the old enthusiasm coming back. He'd have enough new equipment to take a show on the road, if he felt so inclined.

When school was over in the spring of 1913, Charlie already had an advance man out booking various towns along the Union Pacific route. On June 9, 1913, while the show was in Alliance, Nebraska, Charlie received another injunction. This time it forbade him to use the words *Cheyenne* or *Cheyenne Frontier Days* on posters and fliers connected with his show.

Charlie found this last injunction hard to take. He'd spoken to the mayor of Cheyenne and the outgoing chairman of the Frontier Days Committee, E. W. Stone, and the new chairman, Fred Hofmann. Not one of the three men had objected to the new name of the Irwin Brothers' Wild West show. No one had seemed to believe using the name of Cheyenne would be a matter of concern. Hofmann told Charlie that using the name of Cheyenne would be "dandy advertisement for the city and bring people in from all parts of the country to see the now famous Cheyenne Frontier Days show." Charlie had met with Clyde Watts and explained that he had enough equipment to leave what was needed for the Frontier Days behind in his barn at the park, and he'd use only the newly acquired equipment for the traveling show. Then he proceeded to talk Watts into letting him use the same horses and steers, goats, buffalo, and other animals for all his shows, pointing out how expensive it would be to duplicate the livestock and actually how absurd to own two sets of bucking horses, steers, and buffalo. Watts understood, saying, "Mr. Irwin, that would be like asking a man to own two automobiles, one to use in town, the other to use in the country. No one would do that."

Charlie was still a member of the Wyoming Fair Board and still represented the Cheyenne celebration on the National Convention of Fair Boards. He could still have his own show at Frontier Days, but he could not rent his stock to anyone in the celebration. He wondered if the present injunction had come from those people. In his mind he went over his activities. How he'd used his position as stock agent on the railroad to run the Union Pacific special excursion cars from Denver to Omaha to Cheyenne at the time of the Frontier Days, so that huge crowds could enjoy the celebration. He'd shaped rodeos in these Cheyenne shows that later became a pattern for rodeos in the little towns up and down the Union Pacific line. He'd worked for safer conditions for the cowboys riding the bucking horses and humanitarian rules when it came to caring for the horses and other livestock. Charlie could not figure why some people waited until the very last minute to serve him with these injunctions. He could have, would have, left out the name of Cheyenne in his show title if anyone had explained to him why he should. When he'd talked with anyone on the fair board, they'd said, "Oh, C.B., it's all right. Don't worry. We know you'll be the best advertisement our town ever had. People in Canada know about Cheyenne mainly because you showed them a fantastic show. You showed those Canadians what the American cowboys are most adept at—fair dealing."

Charlie felt betrayed when he found that Buffalo Bill, who was even accused in the Cheyenne newspapers of lying about the number and quality of events in his show and charging more for general admission or some special shows than his fliers advertised, was not asked to remove *Frontier Days* from the title of his *Exposition*.

Charlie decided that there were some men that were naturally small and mean-minded. He took his own time to do away with the name *Cheyenne* and finally called his show The Irwin Bros.

Real Wild West Show, which complied with the order of the court injunction.

Charlie retained the words *Cheyenne Frontier Days* on his letterhead. After all, the settlement forbade him from using those three words on his posters and fliers; it said nothing about stationery.

Charlie tried not to show Etta his disappointment in the people running things in Cheyenne. He knew she was hurt. She was most hurt and Charlie felt most betrayed when they found Eddie McCarty landed the Frontier Days contract to supply the stock. Charlie tried to comfort her, saying, "Aw, when things blow over in a couple years, I'll have the contract back." For now Charlie tried not to show he was broken-hearted over people he'd held in high regard and trusted.

An ordinary man might walk away from all the problems Charlie had and spend more time at the office or on the ranch doing the same tedious things day after day. But not Charlie. He might change directions, but he never let his life become humdrum. He carried out what he'd begun, surmounting the obstacles one by one. He knew in a couple years he would again be supplying the stock for the Frontier Days festivities.

Etta did not believe in keeping the family problems from the children. They celebrated good times together, and they rallied around each other in the bad times.

Floyd was eighteen, Joella, seventeen, Pauline, fifteen, and Frances and Roy, twelve. The children were all old enough to know happiness and sadness and share it with the family. Thus, when Charlie had money, the children knew and enjoyed new clothes or toys; when Charlie was broke, the children knew and didn't ask for frivolous things, such as a new house in Cheyenne. Sharing the adults' joys and disappointments was Etta's way of teaching her children that life was not a continuous, straight, happy line, but in fact was a series of jagged peaks and valleys.

While the show was in Alliance, Nebraska, Charlie ran a parade down the main street every day. He used the calliope and show wagons in the parade. Music from the steam calliope could be heard three, four blocks away and brought the children out to follow as if it were the Pied Piper. Charlie had his signs repainted overnight, and people hardly realized he'd changed the name of his show. They were more interested in the parades and exciting events.

The newly hired Hippy Burmister had the time of his life

riding an old scruffy buffalo in the parades down Alliance's Main Street. When Hippy was fairly certain he was not going to be thrown off his buffalo, he'd wave to the crowd in the same fashion Charlie waved with his big hat. "Watch me in the show tonight!" he'd call out. "I'm going to have a saddle on one of these old bisons and I'll show you some riding like you've never seen before! Come to the show of shows!" The people waved back, smiled, and in the evenings came to the show.

On the last night in Alliance, Hippy asked Clayton Danks to check the cinch on the buffalo's saddle. "I don't want it to slip and find me riding with my head near the belly of that buffalo and close to its back hooves."

"Kid, I'll do better than that," said Danks. "Look at this here program. See, here's your name. You're going to ride old Steamboat."

"That means I've graduated from buffalo?" asked the boy, who didn't know of Steamboat, the most famous outlaw horse in the country.

Charlie was standing at one side listening, and he burst out with a roaring laugh when he saw Hippy's face drop to the ground at the mention of him riding a bucking horse.

"Oh, sir," Hippy's voice quavered, "I can't do that. I don't weigh much, sir. And a horse can toss me off like a cotton blanket."

Again Charlie laughed as he walked to where the two were talking. "Hippy, you told me you wanted to work here. If that's true, then you do the jobs assigned like everyone else. This is no crybaby outfit. You take your obligations like a man if you work for me. No excuses. Do the job to the best of your ability."

Charlie winked at Danks.

"Oh, I will, Mr. Irwin. Don't worry about me," said Hippy in a small, shaky voice.

"The arena here is only seventy-five feet wide and one hundred fifty feet long. I don't think old Steamboat will buck much. He's used to a much larger arena to kick his legs out," said Charlie, hardly able to keep his face straight. "And if you fall, there are clowns to pick you up. You must know clowns are some of our most talented cowboys."

Hippy was bucked off in the first ten seconds. But he was dry-eyed and back beside Charlie and Danks smiling. "That windmill wasn't long in gettin' rid of me," he said, watching the others laugh.

* * *

Charlie contacted the Department of Interior's Indian Field Service Office and again asked for official permission for the Sioux to accompany his shows for the summer. Each Indian received a specified salary for one or two dancing events, about the same as the usual salary for cowboys; those days, thirty dollars a month. Indians were also entitled to an additional bonus if they rode horses or steers in the show or performed in the last event, the Indian attack on a covered wagon.

Charlie had the calliope painted bright red and yellow. One of the cowboys played the keyboard, sending out songs through a series of steam whistles between the major events of his Wild West show. Charlie mixed rodeoing with his Wild West exhibitions in small-town stopovers, where merchants awarded prizes. Floyd and the three girls became known for their trick and fancy roping. Sometimes rope tricks were performed while one of the girl performers was mounted on the back of a horse, but Frances did her rope tricks mounted on the back of the longhorn steer named Blondie.

Charlie hired nationally known performers, such as Montana Jack, the man who could spin three ropes at once; Rose Wenger, a seasoned trick rider; Vera McGinnis, another excellent trick rider; and Lucille Mulhall, the outstanding lady steer roper. Charlie hired Marie Danks, Fanny Sperry, and Jane Bernoudy as trick and fancy ropers. Prairie Rose Henderson worked for Charlie as a lady bronc rider. Charlie gave them a salary and paid their expenses. When the performers became rodeo entrants, Charlie paid their entrance fees and split their earnings. This was profitable for the performers and for Charlie. The Irwin entrants in most rodeo contests placed first, second, or third in all the events they participated in.

Fifty Indians from the Pine Ridge Agency pitched tepees near the railroad siding; the roustabouts rolled in blankets under the stars or slept in the boxcars with the cowboys on the siding. The cowgirls and women performers were put up in the best hotel in the town along with Charlie's family, or in the Pullman sleeping car with the family. Whenever the weather was miserable and Charlie had a roll of money in his pocket, he would treat all his people to a hotel, so that no one had to sleep in the rain or a snowstorm.

When Charlie put on a show at any town the hundred or so animals, which included horses, steers, buffalo, elk, and goats, were put into a corral, which was built by roustabouts or the Indians.

The Irwin Bros. Real Wild West Show was a huge success wherever it went. The star of the show was unique, making this Wild West show different from all others. The star was not one of the famous persons; it was the wild, whirling dervish, none other than the bucking horse Steamboat.

In 1913 the show went to Pendleton, Oregon, Ellensburg, Washington, and Boise, Idaho. But Charlie stopped at many small towns in between, mixing rodeoing with his Wild West show. On August twentieth to the twenty-third, Irwin Bros. Real Wild West Show was back in Cheyenne for the Frontier Days festivities. Charlie did not have the stock contract, but he put on his own show.

A week later Charlie took the show wagons, calliope, cowboys, and cowgirls to Fort Collins, Colorado, and put on his Wild West show, which was sponsored by the Elks, and rodeo, which was sponsored by the town's merchants.

Charlie told Joella that she could ride the thoroughbred racehorse, Toby Gray, in the quarter-mile race. Joella was radiant. She knew that Toby Gray was the fastest quarter-mile racer in the rodeo stock. She went immediately to a group of cowboys who were limbering up their lariats to tell them the good news.

She had become a tease and outrageous flirt. Charlie saw how the young men showed off in his daughter's presence by twirling their ropes and smiling broadly.

"You're a sure winner!" said one of the cowboys. "I'll make my bet on you!" said another. "You're the best-looking gal that ever rode a horse!"

Joella beamed. She really enjoyed being a tease and flirting.

Her cousin Gladys was going to ride a horse called Buffalo Bill. Pauline was to ride a sorrel horse called Rondo. Charlie knew that Buffalo Bill could beat the other two horses if the race went half a mile, but in a fast short race, Toby Gray with Joella had the best chance.

When Charlie stood in front of the grandstand and announced the cowgirls' race, he looked and sounded like the showman his reputation had created. He always flashed a huge smile, cracked a joke, or sang a short song. Then he roared out the next event so that everyone paid attention.

"Ladies and gentlemen! You see three beautiful girls mounted on their horses ready for the quarter-mile race. Two of the girls are sisters, the other is a cousin. They are heated rivals. In fact, each girl has such a fierce desire to win that this desire will contribute to the danger as each tries to gain that little edge.

Ladies and gentlemen! I have seen these three lovely girls in the heat of a race. The outside rider might crowd against the rider on the inside, take one graceful foot out of the stirrup, and shove it under the dainty foot of the inside rider. Timed just right this will push the rider and horse over the fence to be eliminated from the race. So keep your eyes peeled! Watch closely to see if any of these beautiful girls crowds in just a little to get another horse off stride and hit the other rider's foot at the right moment. Of course it's dangerous! But not outlawed!"

Charlie knew his speech would stir up the audience and keep up their attentiveness during the race. He also knew that he explained exactly what might take place. His girls knew these tactics. The girls knew the tactics were dangerous, but an accepted maneuver in the sport of horse racing between ladies.

The girls came down the home stretch. Joella was in the lead as Charlie had predicted. She rode in the middle a half a length in front of the two horses beside her. Gladys was on the outside, Pauline on the inside. Gladys looked up and over toward Pauline. The look was almost imperceptible. Charlie had not missed it, though. Gladys looked as though she were going to use her quirt, a short whip, on Buffalo Bill's flank so that he'd move faster. In a split instant Charlie saw Gladys reach back. Instead of whipping her own horse she hit Joella's bottom just as she rose out of the saddle. The movement was fast, but enough to throw the horse off stride. Pauline won the race, with Gladys coming in second. Joella was the loser. The rest of the day Pauline and Gladys looked like cats that had found the cream. Joella didn't say a word because she knew if she'd thought of using her quirt on either of the other girls, she'd have done the same thing.

Charlie wondered how many other people in the stands saw that quick, sly wrist movement. He guessed hardly anyone, even after he'd told them some devilment could go on in the ladies' races.

On September 20, a month after the Frontier Days show, Charlie rented the Cheyenne arena and produced his own magnificent Wild West show and rodeo, which now included a calliope. This was a last celebration before the cold weather set in. Cowboys and cowgirls from all over the Northwest came to participate in the contests.

Charlie did not deny that he was doing this show out of spite. He said to himself, if the Cheyenne city fathers can put restrictions on me, I'll show them I can still use their arena and have my own show and it can be something wonderful. Two days after his show closed, boasting a record attendance, he received a letter from the chairman of the Frontier Days Committee, Fred Hofmann, stating that the fair committee had decided to ban the use of Charlie's supply of animals, equipment, and men for future annual Frontier Days, but he could remain in the arena to announce his own shows if they were booked. The animal and equipment contract would stay with Eddie McCarty, the bronc rider and steer roper from Bear Creek, north of Cheyenne.

Charlie laid the letter aside. He could not think. He could not speak. The walnut-sized lump in his throat had grown to the size of an orange. His mouth was dry and he could not swallow. He felt his heart pound and imagined himself beaten to a pulp. Charlie found it hard to blame any one but himself. This was a difficult lesson that vindictiveness is always the wrong road to follow.

Walking down the street in Cheyenne, Charlie imagined he was disgraced and everyone knew of his folly with the Wild West show contract.

Etta did her best to bring Charlie out of his depression. When she read in the paper about a rodeo being staged in Salt Lake City in mid-October, she showed the ad to Charlie. "Take all the kids and some of your best horses. Go to Salt Lake. No one gives a whip about your problems here, but you magnify them so that you are beginning to imagine things. In Salt Lake everyone thinks you are terrific. Go on, show them that they are correct."

Floyd and Roy were glad for another chance to show off their rope tricks before winter. The girls, including cousin Gladys, were happy with another weekend away from books, the piano, voice lessons, and mundane chores.

Etta stayed home, knowing that Charlie had to bring himself out of his terrible depression, and without her, he would push himself harder.

Charlie took a couple of his and Frank's thoroughbreds, including the horse, Frank Lubbock, that he'd bought in Calgary. Frank Lubbock was entered in the mile-and-a-quarter race at Agricultural Park. McBeth was the jockey as Frank Lubbock won the Turf Exchange handicap in the fast time of 2:10. This was the best time made on a half-mile track in a mile and a quarter race. Charlie had hired jockey McBeth in Salt Lake City because he'd been unsure of this racehorse. He'd left his best jockey, Martinez, back on the ranch. The Cheyenne *Tribune* grudgingly stated that even though the horse was well known to local horsemen and a favorite at the August Frontier Days races, it was hardly thought that it would be a real world-record beater.

Joella made a bet with a couple of the Salt Lake cowboys that her horse, Toby Gray, could beat any of theirs. On the last day of the rodeo she convinced Charlie that she could be in a race with those cowboys. Charlie felt apprehensive about this one. But Joella had been so moody and as changeable as a chameleon that he was willing to do most anything to see her in a cheerful smile. He looked at the young cowboys she was going to race against. He hoped she would be able to take care of herself. Charlie found it impossible to eat his lunch, because he was truly worried about this race he'd let Joella talk him into. Charlie wished Etta were there to talk to their eldest and best-looking daughter. Etta would know what to say. Charlie tried to warn her about any tricks the boys might try, but she was too keyed up to listen. She smiled, but he could tell the words ran right over her head. He gave up, gave her a hug, and patted her shoulder. He suddenly wished he had a rabbit's foot or something to give her for good luck. He remembered the Sioux carried bluejay feathers for good fortune. He wondered where he could find such a feather. He spotted the hats on the young cowboys' heads. Of course! In the hatband of these cowboys there was bound to be a jay feather. He went among the boys looking over their hatbands. Finally he found a small blue and white feather. "May I have that," he asked the cowboy.

"What for, pops?"

"I am Mr. Irwin, to you, and I want it for luck."

"Sure, one feather, what's the diff? That your kid who's racin' with us? She's a gutsy filly."

"Yes, she is. Thanks for the feather."

The cowboy saluted and went back to the conversation with his comrades.

Charlie found Joella and told her to put the feather in a pocket or in her own hatband for luck.

"Thanks, Pa. I'll need it. Hope it works." She gave him a hug.

The race was between five boys and Joella. It was the longer, half-mile race. Charlie was worried that Toby Gray would not last that long. He looked at the horses carefully. He saw someone press in toward Joella, but they were all bunched up at the start and he decided it was nothing. Joella was hunkered over, her head against the horse's ears. Toby Gray had not lost his stride. The last stretch was the time to watch carefully. Joella looked grim and determined. She was riding neck and neck with a horse that looked like it might spurt ahead and come in first. Ever so slightly Joella swerved against the other horse. Charlie could not see what took place, but he thought she had put her foot out and hit the bottom of the other rider's foot because he moved away toward the rail and Joella sprinted forward, overtaking the horse in the lead and winning the race. The crowd went wild with cheers.

Charlie hurried out to help her off the horse. "What's the matter? Stand up straight and smile," he whispered.

"I can't. My big toe is broken, I think," she grimaced.

"You broke it when you struck that fellow's instep!"

Joella grinned and tears were in her eyes as she held back another second, then walked out on her own and waved to the crowd.

Walking off the track Joella said, "Pa, did you see that guy hit me on the first stretch? He must have had a lead slug in his toe."

"Someone moved close to you. Is that when?"

She nodded. "I waited until I could get him back. Ooo-ouch!" She smiled and threw kisses to the crowd. She took the silver loving cup that was presented and smiled as her picture was taken.

Charlie helped her to the tack room, where he tightly wrapped the toe and told her it would heal just fine. "Don't put any weight on it. Guess you'll have to walk without your boot. Can you manage?"

"Yep," said Joella. "You know I can. I did all right today, huh, Pa? We really feel good about today?"

"You bet we do!" said Charlie.

THIRTY-THREE

Heartache

In the fall of 1913 the capitol building in Cheyenne was the scene of heated debates that brought Senator Warren back from Washington, D.C., fearing that the Democrats would take over the House of Representatives in Wyoming. The Republicans had a majority of thirty to twenty-seven in the House. Two of those Republicans were then induced to change their party affiliation with the promise that one of them would be appointed speaker. The House was then controlled by the Democrats, twenty-nine to twenty-eight. A young man named Martin Luther Pratt became the appointed speaker.

One morning after two weeks of shouting, charges, counter-charges, lies, counterlies, deceptions, falsehoods, and equivocations between both parties, Speaker Pratt came into the House chamber and found a Democratic speaker pro tem at the rostrum. He bolted up to the speaker's platform, grabbed the man by the shirt collar, and threw him off the platform, saying, "This is my place!"

Pratt rubbed his hands together as though dusting them off. He looked around at his new Democratic friends, then at some of his old Republican friends. With deliberation he stepped over the prone body of the speaker pro tem, stood in front of the rostrum, and announced in a loud, clear voice that from henceforth he would again be affiliated with the Republicans and he would also continue to act as speaker as had been promised him. "Fie on the deceitful Democrats! I'm fed up with their conniving plots!"

There were shouts of "Traitor!" "Double-crosser!" from the angry Democrats.

Charlie was in the hall outside the House chamber for the purpose of lobbying for higher Union Pacific freight rates that morning. He could not believe what he heard. The shouting and stomping was so violent that the floor under his feet shook. He opened one of the closed double doors and heard someone cry out, "The speaker pro tem's out like a light—cold. Get water!" Then there was silence. A fly buzzed around Charlie's head. He ignored it. Stepping inside the room he saw the speaker pro tem sit up. He was lifted to his feet by two men and moved away from Pratt. His arms were held so he couldn't lash out. His face was red. He shouted, "Up with Democrats! Down with Pratt and Republicans!" The two men hustled him from the room.

Then there was pandemonium. Every man was out of his chair, shouting at his neighbors. Papers and books flew through the air. Chairs were knocked over as men attacked each other with fists. Charlie moved back out of the door just as two men bumped through. He imagined the whole melee moving to the hall and out into the street. He moved down the hall to the office of Governor Joseph M. Carey and went inside without knocking.

"Sir!" he called past the secretary. "There's a fight in the House chambers! If you don't lend your authority"—Charlie took a deep breath—"you'll have to call out the National Guard!"

"What's this?" Governor Carey smoothed his small mustache and looked up with deep blue eyes to the giant of a man in front of him. Noise from the House became louder and more raucous. "Are you saying it's some kind of battle?"

"No, sir. It's a skirmish. Someone could get hurt."

"Who sent you?"

"Nobody." Charlie stepped around the big mahogany desk and took the governor by the arm and trundled him past the astonished secretary and down the hall to the House chamber. All the time Charlie talked softly. He told Carey to get up on the speaker's platform and take care of things. Pound the gavel. Stop the rioting. "Young Pratt'll move. Soon as he sees you enter the room, he'll step aside."

"Good Lord, man! Listen to the clamor. Aren't you frightened?"

"No, sir, not for myself."

"I can't go in there. Republicans will cut me to pieces!"

"Sir, you're the governor of the state of Wyoming. You have the authority. You have the power. You could stop a runaway steam engine and not suffer a scratch." Charlie led Carey straight to the speaker's platform, by elbowing his way through the groups of people. The room was noisier than a calf corral.

White-faced and nervous, young Pratt, gripping the podium, stared glassy-eyed at the approaching Carey. His mouth was closed as though his voice box was out of order. Charlie gave Pratt a nudge with his hip, and he let go the podium and stood to one side as helpless as a dummy with his hands cut off. Several Republicans did their best to shield Pratt from flying fists and kicking feet of two overheated Democrats with perspiring faces.

Charlie put the gavel in Carey's hand. "Pound it! Hard! Attract attention! Talk sense!" Charlie shouted above the racket. He shouldered his way down among the stormy groups of men, trying to break them apart. He wanted to separate the two factions to different sides of the room. "Quiet! The governor's here! The governor's speaking!" He spoke out loud as he forced himself between fighters. How long it took to bring any kind of order, Charlie had no idea. Several times he was punched and kicked. Men glared at each other, then at him. Finally he looked up and saw most of the Democrats on one side and Republicans on the other side of the room. "Jeems," he whispered to himself, "looks like a tornado's hit!"

Governor Carey was pounding the gavel as though he were an automaton. Charlie went back up beside him. "Sir, say something."

"What?"

"Anything. You'll think of something appropriate."

Carey wiped his face with a white handkerchief, then shook one clenched fist at both sides of the chamber, which was a shambles with overturned chairs, papers, books, pens, and pencils scattered on the floor where they'd been torn and broken under sliding, stomping, unheeding feet. "I'm sickened and disgusted with political infighting!" Carey's voice was loud, high-pitched and shaky. "Fisticuffs for grown men? It's un-American!" Now his voice steadied and settled down to a lower pitch. "Take a look at yourselves, at your colleagues. You're educated. You boast that communication is your forte. Yet this morning you turned to boxing and wrestling. I'm ashamed of all of you." Then he called upon the young politician, Pratt, to decide on his allegiance and to meet that night with the leadership of the two major parties, resolve differences, and present the conclusions to him the following day. His voice was clear and strong.

Before that notorious day was finished, every member of the legislative session knew big Charlie Irwin was a friend of Wyoming's favorite Republican, Senator Warren, and a peacemaker for the Democratic governor, Joseph Carey. Every member of the legislature was truly thankful for Charlie's large, powerful presence, quietly quelling the heat of a battle that might have grown into a full-blown riot.

In December, Charlie and Etta received another invitation to Governor Joseph Carey's Inaugural Ball. Etta made herself a new gown from blue silk. Charlie thought she looked more beautiful than ever. He marveled that this tiny woman with the enormous sparkling eyes in the little elfin face could make him so happy.

"What would you like for Christmas?" he asked.

"A new house, Charlie. Build one here. Tear down this one, which has a leaky roof, rattly windows, and heaven knows what else; let's build a new house, with a big kitchen and a bedroom for everyone." She looked at him. "What do you think? Is this the right time to ask for so much?"

He gave her a hug. "You ask for anything you want. You know it's yours. As soon as I have the money we'll work on plans for a new house."

A week before the Governor's Ball, Etta received a letter from Ray Lewis, her brother-in-law, saying her sister Kate had pneumonia and there was no one at home to look after Kate nor the younger children because Ray now worked full-time in his farm-equipment store. Etta made the only decision possible. That evening she told Charlie she was going to Kansas to look after Kate.

"Who'll I take to the Governor's Ball?" asked Charlie.

"Take Joella," said Etta impulsively. "Yes. It'll be a real education for a seventeen-year-old. She'll be thrilled. You'll enjoy the dance and seeing your friends. Now, don't look so sad. I won't be gone more than a week—two at the most. As soon as Kate is on her feet I'll come back home."

"Jeems, I'll miss you," said Charlie.

Joella reworked the blue silk dress so that it fit her. And several days in a row, when she came home from high school, she ran to her room to try on the long dress with the tight-fitting waist and graceful flaring, gored skirt. She took out a few stitches and added others here and there around the waist. "I wish Ma were here," she told Charlie.

"I hope that you've finished working on that dress by the time the ball is here," said Charlie. He thought Joella was so excited about going to the grand affair that she was nervous about how the dress would look. "You look almost as pretty as your mother. Your yellow hair is just the right color for that blue silk. Sets off the dress just the way your blond hair sets off your blue eyes."

"Oh, Pa! You say that because I belong to you." Then she said something that surprised Charlie. "I don't want to belong to just some boy. I don't want to get married."

Charlie laid his newspaper aside and pulled Joella onto his lap. "Baby, when the right man comes along, you'll change your tune."

Joella buried her face in his neck for an instant like she did when she was a little girl needing comforting. Then her back stiffened and Charlie heard her stifle a little cry as she pushed herself away and back on her feet. "I doubt it, because the right man might not want to marry me."

"Oh, what's all this jingo? You and marriage are a long ways off. You've other things to think about right now. How about going to the kitchen and helping Pauline with the supper?"

"I will in a minute. I want to play the piano a while. Maybe that will make me feel better." Joella wiped a tear from her eye and began to play Christmas carols.

"That will make us all feel good," called Charlie. "You play and I'll help Pauline." Charlie thought how much Joella was like his sister, Ell. She was so good-looking. One day she'd have some man wrapped around her little finger. My goodness, he thought, women are the movers and shakers behind every poor male on earth. Mothers, sisters, wives, and daughters can train us like dogs. They hold out the hoop, say jump, and we jump every time. In the kitchen he stirred the boiling potatoes and began to sing, "God Rest Ye Merry Gentlemen." Pauline and Frances sang with him. He opened the back door and called Roy and Floyd inside. They were twirling their ropes. "Soup's on!"

"I'm going back to the ranch this weekend," said Floyd. "Roy wants to go with me. Can someone bring him back on Sunday so he won't miss school?"

"Oh, let's see—" Charlie began to think out loud.

"Let me go with them," said Joella suddenly. "I could bring Roy back Sunday. I'll help the cook this weekend."

Charlie had a forkful of roast beef in midair. He held it there like a statue. Joella had never liked the ranch much in the winter. She was like her mother in that respect. Why'd she change her mind? What about the ball? She couldn't have forgotten that. She was wearing the long blue silk dress. "Take the ball gown off and put on a regular dress," he said. He wished Etta were home. There was something in the air he couldn't put his finger on. He put the beef in his mouth and while chewing looked at the other children. Nothing seemed amiss. Frances was telling Roy about some kids chasing a dog at school. Roy stuck his tongue out at Pauline because she didn't pass him the gravy soon enough.

"You do that again and I'll paint your tongue with horse liniment," said Charlie, shaking a finger at Roy.

"Oh, Pa, it's just that she's a poor excuse for a sister. I ask her to help me learn to twirl two ropes, and she won't let me use her rope. How can a guy learn anything when the girls are afraid he'll know more than they?"

"Is that true?" Charlie looked at Pauline. She was quiet. She reminded Charlie of Etta when she was sober. Pauline was sober and levelheaded more often than not. She didn't have the spontaneous vivaciousness her mother possessed.

"Yes, Pa. It's my rope and Roy can get another if he wants to twirl two loops at one time. You tell us to be responsible for our own things."

"That's right. Roy, looks like you're going to have to earn a new rope. You go to the ranch this weekend, help Martinez and the men take hay to the horses wintering on the Guerney pasture. Work a couple days and I'll give you regular cowboy's pay. When you have enough money, you can go to Meanea's and get another lasso."

"Yeah! Thanks, Pa." Roy stuck his tongue out at Pauline.

Charlie was up from his chair in a second. He took Roy to the kitchen and poured black liniment on his tongue while he held Roy's hands behind his back. At first Roy refused to open his mouth, but Charlie pushed the youngster's arms up toward his shoulders and when it hurt Roy yelled, "Ouuch!" and Charlie was there with the bitter, sharp-tasting medicine. "You are not going with Floyd to the ranch this weekend. You are going to stay home and help me around the house. We'll scrub the kitchen floor and maybe wash some windows inside."

"Oh, heck! I'm no sissy. Scrubbing floors is for girls."

"I'm no sissy, either. We are working together this weekend. You'll get paid, so quit bellyachin'."

On Friday, Joella moped over breakfast and said she didn't want to go to school. "I must be getting something. I feel sick to my stomach."

"Honey, go back to bed," said Charlie, picking up the breakfast dishes and piling them into the sink. Floyd saddled one of the horses they kept in town and headed out for the ranch. There were two, three inches of snow on the ground, but the sun was out and the air did not seem cold unless one were out on the flats in the wind.

On Saturday, Joella suggested that fifteen-year-old Pauline go to the Governor's Ball. "Pa, I can fix the dress for her, easy, just shorten the skirt."

"You don't feel any better?"

"No. It's the flu. It's going around."

"You sure you can sew on the dress all right?" Charlie was not sure what to do for his oldest daughter. Helplessly he'd watched her get up from the table and fly into the bathroom. He'd put his hand on her forehead, but felt no fever. She felt cold and clammy. "I think I'll call a doctor. Maybe it's flu and maybe not."

"Oh, Pa, don't call a doctor. I'll be all right in a couple of days. Ma never calls the doctor for flu."

He thought about it and decided she was right. He let the two girls fuss over the party dress. Jeems, I hope Pauline doesn't come down with influenza by tonight, or me come down with it.

Pauline checked with her father several times to make certain it would be all right if she went in place of Joella.

"Of course—don't make such a big deal out of it. There is one thing—the one that goes has to write a long letter to her mother telling all about it." He went to the closet to check his navy-blue business suit, then decided his tuxedo in the brown paper cleaner's bag was better.

"I can write," said Pauline. "Probably better than Joella. She has a bad case of the gags right now. Hope I don't get what she's got."

"I was thinking the same thing. Say, you think you could press this suit for me while I look for my black patent-leather shoes? It's been in the bag since last year. Your mother would want us to look real nice."

On Sunday, Joella came to the kitchen in a blue robe and wanted to know about the dance. Who was there and what everyone wore.

Pauline was still excited about the wonderful affair and told everything she could think of. No one seemed to notice that Joella didn't eat breakfast nor lunch, except Charlie, and he told her she'd get well faster if she'd eat. Charlie and Roy cleaned the kitchen and worked on the windows. Listless, Joella played the piano, Frances sang, and Pauline wrote a long letter to her mother.

By midweek Joella seemed no better. Charlie was determined to call a doctor. "Doctor Henneberry will just have a quick look and maybe give you something that will make you feel better right away."

Joella shrugged her shoulders. Her face seemed drawn and Charlie was sure now that she'd lost weight. "I don't need a doctor. Ma will be home in a couple of days. I'll probably be better by the time she gets home."

Joella was wrong. Etta did not come home in a couple of days. They had a letter from her on Friday saying that Kate was not out of the woods yet, and she'd decided to stay another week. "I love all of you. Take good care of each other until I'm back," she wrote.

Charlie said, "Oh, darn!" On the weekdays he'd sent the children to school and gone to his office at the Plains Hotel, but all the time he worried about Joella. Just when he thought she was getting better, he'd coax her to eat something and a few minutes later she'd run for the bathroom. He told his secretary that he thought Joella had stomach trouble, maybe ulcers. "The kid's so stubborn—she won't see a doctor."

His secretary nodded her head sympathetically. "Kids these days think they know it all. Good thing nature heals most things with time. You Irwins are strong. Just look at yourself," and she laughed.

Charlie thought about writing a letter to Etta, telling her about Joella. Maybe she'd write back telling him what to do. Maybe she'd come home. Of course that wouldn't be fair. She had to take care of her sister, and he had to take care of Joella. Friday before coming home from work he bought Roy a new rope and Floyd a silver belt buckle. Then he went to the jewelry store and bought three silver bangle bracelets for the girls and a pair of cameo earrings for Etta.

"Oh, you didn't forget my birthday!" squealed Joella. "I love it. Oh, Pa, it's beautiful." She danced around as though she'd never been ill.

The other girls were just as impressed with their gifts. "When Joella has a birthday, we all get presents. That's all right. Floyd and Ma will be surprised when they come home," said Frances.

Roy went outside to try twirling a rope in each hand. "I'll be good in next year's Frontier Days," he said.

Pauline baked a cake for supper. The cake made Joella ill. She ran white as a sheet, gagging, for the bathroom.

Charlie knocked on the bathroom door. "I want you to go to bed. You made yourself sick by jumping around with your new bracelet. No more jumping around."

"Uumm," said Joella. "Don't worry, Pa. I'll be all right. I promise you."

Charlie thought he heard her crying, but he was not sure.

By Monday the snow was deep and crusty. Joella said she felt well enough to go back to school. This was her last year and she didn't want to miss more days than necessary. Charlie let her go, thinking that if she got her mind off herself maybe she'd get well quicker. There were dark circles under her wide, green eyes.

There was another letter from Etta. "I'll be home in a week for sure," she wrote. "Kate sends her thanks for your prayers. I thank Pauline for her description of the Governor's Ball. Too bad you were sick, Joella. But I'm sure with your father's good care you are well now. I miss all of you and love you heaps."

Charlie longed for Etta to come home. The past three weeks had been the longest he could remember. He feared she wouldn't be home by Christmas. He came home from the office early, sat in the easy chair, and closed his eyes for a short rest. In his imagination he saw saw-tooth hills at the edge of the upper ranch. At the front end was Round Top like the head of some ancient giant asleep, covered with a white fluffy blanket. The foot of Lookout Mountain reminded Charlie how humans cleaved to one another, pulling the very life from some.

He opened his eyes in time to see Roy scampering around from the front of the house to the back door. So school was out. The rest did him good, put his mind at ease. So what was he worried about? Maybe he'd take the kids to the ranch for the weekend. He opened the back door. The girls ran in behind Roy. Joella scampered up and threw snow down Roy's neck. Before he could say a cuss word, she said, "I'll race you. Saddle up a pair of horses. Pick the one you want to ride."

It didn't take Roy long to change to an old pair of trousers and run out to the stalls.

Charlie grinned to himself and settled back to his chair to read the *Chicago Daily Farmers and Drovers Journal*. He felt better than he had since Etta'd left. She'd be home in a week. Things were in good shape. Joella's dysentery was better. She didn't eat better than a bird, but her appetite would return.

After supper the children settled down to their homework without being told. Charlie was pleased. They'd learned he meant for work to be done without nagging. Before bedtime Roy came in. "Say, I've been thinking about Grandpa Joe. If Floyd don't put some cedar shakes on the roof of his blacksmith shop, I'll do it."

"That's a good thought. How'd you like to go to the ranch this weekend?"

"You bet I would! Yipee!" Roy went off to bed happy.

The thought of his father left at the ranch during the winter always made Charlie feel somewhat guilty for not bringing him to town. Still, sixty-six wasn't so old, and Grandpa Joe was no cripple. He had more vigor than some men of thirty-eight. Margaret and Will were there to look after him. Joe loved the ranch and would not have been happy living in town. Charlie checked the dampers on the kitchen and living room wood stoves before going to bed himself.

He saw a light under Joella's bedroom door. He knocked. "You still doing homework, honey?"

"Yes, Pa. I'm about done. Don't worry."

"I'm glad you're all better. Your ma's coming home in a week."

"I'll be all right by then."

Charlie walked slowly to bed. Something caught in his throat. Joella's reply was somehow strange. He expected her to say something about being glad or happy Aunt Kate was better. He sat on the bed and noticed that his hands were gripping the tops of his legs, like the foot of the hill grabbing at the land. He shook his head and decided he was lonely without his dear, sweet Etta, and his imagination was overactive.

In the middle of the night Charlie woke up. He'd heard the wind moaning around the corners of the house. No, it was a soft sniffling coming from Joella's room. He climbed out of bed, rummaged around for his robe and slippers. Finally he turned on the light to find them.

"Honey, what is it?" he whispered close to her door.

"Oh, Pa—it's nothing. I—I just don't feel too good."

He went in and saw her curled in a tight little ball, holding her knees under her chin, lying on her side. In the dark he could see the quilts kicked to the foot of the bed.

"That dysentery and vomiting come back?"

"Yes," she sobbed.

"Don't cry. Stay home from school tomorrow. One more day won't hurt."

"Oh, go away! Leave me alone! Why'd you come in my room anyway? Don't snoop!"

Charlie patted her head, again noticing there was no fever, only a kind of cold sweat with this disease.

He went back to bed. A queasy feeling was in the bottom of his stomach. He wondered where he'd seen anything like this before. He thought of all the strange illnesses the cows and horses had, then fell asleep. In the morning he got everyone, except Joella, off to school. Roy left without his sheep-lined coat, and Charlie called him back. "A red wool sweater's not enough on a cold, windy day. You'll be an icicle before you turn the corner."

"I just wanted to show the guys I could take it—take the wind and not shiver," said Roy.

"You can't. They can't. So don't try to be foolish. The wind comes across that prairie colder than a witch's caress. No mortal plays games with freezing wind. Hurry or you'll be late!"

The pale sunlight filtered into the kitchen windows as Charlie put a pot of coffee on the roaring hot kitchen range. He could hear Joella prowling around her bedroom and the bathroom. Then he heard a sob and muffled groan.

"What's she crying for today," he said out loud. He went into her room. There was blood on the flannel sheets. She'd pulled them together and put a quilt over the top, but Charlie had thrown the bed open for some reason and he'd seen. Then he thought, I'd better not say anything. She'll clean it up. It's her period and she didn't take care of herself. No wonder she was out of sorts last night. Jeems, he wished Etta were home to handle this. What did he know about female troubles?

He saw the spots of blood Joella left as she traipsed from bed to bathroom. He swore under his breath. "Damn bloody mess." Then out loud he said, "You all right, honey?"

"Pa! Oh, Pa!" cried Joella. "It's my insides! They're coming out! I'm dying!"

"I'm coming in!"

She was on the floor lying on her side with her legs drawn up under her chin. Her white nightdress was red around her feet. Suddenly she hugged her knees and cried out in pain. When it passed Charlie asked where the pain came from. Joella stretched her legs slowly and rubbed her rounded belly. Tears ran down her cheeks.

Charlie knelt on the floor. He put his hand on her belly and felt the tightness of her muscles through the flannel, then the subsidence of the contraction, and the muscles relaxed a little.

Joella watched her father with wide, frightened eyes.

He moved his big hand and said gruffly, "Get in the bathtub!" He was not surprised at what he'd found. The clues had been there for weeks. He'd read all the clues, but he'd not let his mind put them together. He'd known ever since the Governor's Ball that his oldest daughter was pregnant, but he wouldn't, couldn't admit it. He went to the kitchen, found the butcher knife and a couple clean, white dishtowels. He grabbed the teakettle from the range.

Joella screamed when she saw her father standing above her with a butcher knife in his hand.

"Who did this to you?" He was furious. His brown eyes were hard as flint. His voice was loud and steady. "I'll rip him open like a gutted coyote!"

"No one. I did it myself. I don't know who!" Joella grabbed her knees. She groaned deep in her throat. An animal sound, guttural. Then she relaxed and let the tears roll over her face. "Pa, it's a bad period. Started this morning."

"This isn't ordinary cramps. You think I haven't seen enough animals to know what pregnant is? And I watched your aunt Ell working with your mother." He put the kettle on the floor beside the dishtowels and pushed on her belly with the next contraction.

Joella tried to wriggle from his big hands, but he held her. "Stop that. You have a job to do. Can't back out, no matter how you try. Get the job done and over with. When did it happen?" Charlie felt hot, burning shame. Someone. Some stupid, hot-assed cowboy had taken his beautiful girl-child into the bushes. Who did he think he was? What right had he?

"I don't know! Honest!" Her hands were at her sides in tight balls, opening and closing, clawing at the porcelain tub.

"Who is the father? Tell me!" His fury was combined with a feeling of protective tenderness for his beautiful daughter made grotesque and ugly by the pain of the uterine spasm that knotted all her muscles. Bright red blood stained her nightgown. Charlie pulled the gown out of the way, above her thighs as her blood-streaked legs stiffened and her back arched. She made a deep guttural sound that rose to a high crescendo, then diminished and was abruptly cut off as she lay limp for a few seconds.

"You might as well say. I'll find out who you've been with if I have to ask every boy in high school." His voice was less harsh, more conciliatory. He wiped some of the blood from her legs with a dishtowel soaked in hot water from the teakettle. He used both of his strong hands to massage and push downward when the next spasms came.

Joella did not answer her father's questions. Her mind was far away, locked in a primordial struggle between new life and death.

Charlie could feel the trickle of perspiration run down the middle of his back. He wiped his forehead with the back of his hand. He'd seen dozens of cows and mares in the birthing process. He was adept at helping and soothing the mother. But this delivery was different. The mother was more precious, more delicate, more exasperating than anything he'd experienced. He wiped Joella's face, pushing her hair back behind her ears. She breathed through her mouth. There were dark blue-green circles under her eyes. Her tongue darted out to lick her lips. Her nostrils flared. Her hands clenched and unclenched the slippery sides of the tub. The short fingernails made a fragile pecking noise on the porcelain. Charlie's stomach pinched together, and for a moment he thought he was going to be sick. He pushed gently on her belly and stroked her sides. The fetus came inch by inch. It was small, a caricature, red and purple, no fingernails, no eyelashes, no breath. It was a boy, stillborn, not fully developed. Charlie left the bloody mass near the drain waiting for the afterbirth to be discharged. Joella's face was drained of all color. Her skin appeared transparent as though a touch would puncture it. She moaned with each shallow breath.

When the spongy afterbirth was expelled, Charlie pushed it against the fetus and wrapped the whole bloody mess in the *Drovers Journal*, then in a dishtowel. He laid the package on the floor and began cleaning his daughter, who lay quietly with her eyes closed, as if in a trance. When the teakettle water was gone he ran tepid water from the bathtub faucet and found that method much easier. He picked up the butcher knife and wondered why he'd brought it to the bathroom.

Suddenly he felt the hairs rise on the back of his neck and a chill run down his back as if he were being watched. He looked up. Three children in nightclothes were standing in the doorway, their hands over their mouths, their eyes wide with fright.

"Go away until I'm finished!" shouted Charlie. "It's none of your business!"

Horrified Charlie saw that the children did not move. He

began to pull himself up. One leg was cramped and he waited an instant before thrusting it under and pushing himself to his feet. In that instant Pauline yelled, "Oh, no, Pa! Don't! It's murder!"

Charlie dropped the knife and looked at his bloody hands. "Jeems, forgive me! It's your sister. She's—she's—" His voice broke and tears streamed down his face.

"You used the butcher knife on her!" screamed Roy.

"Oh, Pa! Papa!" Frances covered her whole face with her hands.

"No, no!" Charlie wiped his hands on a damp dishtowel. "No! I'm—I'm—Jo's had a miscarriage."

"Miscarriage? What's that?" asked Roy timidly. He held one arm protectingly in front of the girls.

"She was pregnant and the baby came too soon." Charlie felt exhausted, too tired to explain.

"The knife?" asked Roy. "Did you use it on the baby?"

"I didn't use it. I thought I was going to cut the cord or something. There's nothing to cut—it's dead. We gotta bury it."

Joella moaned as she tried to pull one leg up. Charlie saw that she was still hemorrhaging. "Frances, more dishtowels. Pauline, get a clean nightdress."

Charlie packed several towels between Joella's legs. "How am I going to keep the pads in place?" he said half to himself.

"Pa, make a triangle and tie one towel like a diaper," whispered Pauline.

While Charlie worked over Joella, Pauline put cold water in a washtub and dumped in the soiled nightgown and towels to soak.

"Her bedclothes need soaking, too," said Charlie. "Get clean sheets, Roy, and we'll put this girl to bed. Then we'd better talk."

Roy did his best to make up the bed, all the time crying because Charlie said the baby was dead.

Charlie piled quilts on top of Joella, who was still pale and cold. Her breathing seemed regular. He was afraid to leave her. He sat in the chair beside the bed and motioned for the three children to come sit on the floor. Gray light of dawn made the room shadowy. "This night was a trial," he said. "I don't know how to explain it to you. It is hard for me to believe what has happened. I had no idea Joella was—was pregnant." Charlie stopped and looked at the tear-stained faces looking up at him. "What is there to say." He sighed. "Maybe I knew, when she was vomiting, but I didn't know for sure. I didn't believe it would happen to us. Not to one of my girls."

"I know a girl who had to quit school and there was a lot of talk—" said Pauline. "Joella's not like her."

"No one better talk about Joella," said Frances, "even if she was bad."

"That's right. There'll be no talk. Nothing goes out of this house. It's our secret. If your mother found out, it would break her heart. She'd rather die than have anything happen to one of her girls."

"Or boys," said Roy.

"Are we going to school?" asked Frances.

"Yes, we are and we're going to act like a family," said Pauline.

"I'm not going to let any boy touch me," said Frances, scooting over and hugging Charlie's leg. "Jeems, we were scared."

"Watch your stupid tongue," said Roy.

Charlie bent and put his arm around Frances. "No one is going to say anything to anyone. You hear?

"All right, let's get breakfast and be on time for school." Charlie watched the three children get up. He was so weary. He felt he was ninety-nine years old.

It was midmorning when Charlie woke. He felt stiff in every joint. Joella was still asleep. Her forehead was no longer cold, but her face was pale and her hands dry. The house was quiet. The children had washed their dishes before going to school. Charlie drank some bitter coffee. He took the small white bundle from under the washbasin in the bathroom and went out on the back porch. The bundle felt soggy. He laid it down and went back for his heavy jacket. He found an ax in the woodshed. Tears ran down his cheeks. He laid the damp bundle on a wide piece of bark, then went into the house and brought out the butcher knife. He wondered how he was going to dig a hole in the frozen ground. He looked for something besides the ax in the woodshed. The floor was covered with wood chips and bark and splinters of wood. Next to the back wall he scraped an area down to the bare earth. The ground was hard as rock. He began scraping around the chopping block. He put his powerful arms around the big tree trunk and moved it a couple feet. The earth was cold, but not frozen solid. He cut out a hole with the ax about eighteen inches down and a foot in diameter. He stopped. He thought of Etta. She wanted a new house. He'd get her a new house, one with a big kitchen and bedrooms for everyone. A new house, right here. Tear down the old house and build a new one. They'd have to stay at the ranch while the new one was being built. The builders would dig out a new foundation. They'd find the bundle and see the tiny bones. His breath caught. He scooped up a handful of kindling and carried the bundle on the piece of bark back to the kitchen. He pushed the bark into the range's fire box and forced the bundle inside, then put the kindling on top. He lit a newspaper and shoved it under the kindling. He let it blaze up some before putting the lid on. Then he left the lid partly off so that air could get into the fire box. There was smoke and a sizzling sound as steam poured out of the bundle along with smoke. Charlie opened the damper and when the smell of burning cloth was strong, he closed the lid.

Charlie scrubbed the bathtub with yellow soap. Then he scrubbed the bathroom floor.

At noon Joella was still asleep. Charlie was not hungry. His chest felt tight and he was certain his heart was crushed into a thousand pieces. He put another stick of wood in the range's firebox, noticing that the ash and carbonized wood pulsated as it glowed. Pulsated like the beating of a tiny heart.

Then the thought of a tiny grandchild, a boy, struck him. He staggered back from the stove and clamped his teeth together. I can't think that way, he said to himself. I have to remember that the baby was born dead, too small to live anyway, a folly. The episode can't be thought about. I can't tell Etta because it would devastate her, break her apart. And I can't repeat what I've done, what Joella's done, because it would destroy everything. There'd be rumors, whisperings, innuendos, then slanders and insinuations. I can't let that happen to Etta, to Joella and the kids. I have to protect my family—and myself. Yes, I admit that! Myself!

He sat in Etta's kitchen rocking chair, looking at the stove, but not seeing it. He tried to rehearse what he'd say to Joella. But he knew he'd blurt out what was on his mind and not be gentle. He blamed himself, then Etta and Joella, then himself. He promised God he'd pay more attention to the feelings and emotions of his children, if He'd heal Joella—before Etta came home.

About two o'clock Charlie shoved the cold, gray ash from the range into the fire bucket. He dared not breathe on the ash or it flew everywhere like tiny, shadowy ghosts. He shook the grate, making a jangling noise that seemed loud and jarring. He carried the ashes out to the woodshed and put them in the bottom of the hole along with the butcher knife. I'll say I lost the knife if anyone asks, he thought. I don't want to look at that thing again. The pitiful pile of ashes covered the knife, the cold, sandy earth covered the ashes. Charlie stomped the earth and pulled the chopping block to its original position in the middle of the woodshed. He got down on his hands and knees and pushed the wood chips and bits of bark around so it seemed nothing had been disturbed. He rubbed the dirt off the ax with a piece of bark and struck the ax into a hunk of cordwood. His hands were cold. He blew on them. In the house he washed with warm water and yellow soap.

Joella held the fresh flannel sheets tight under her chin. Her eyes were open, green and liquid like strong horehound tea. Charlie sat on the edge of the bed. "Young lady, I've been thinking how selfish you've been."

She blinked and raised her head. Her eyes became young and fresh-looking as evergreen.

"You never shared your feeling with me nor your mother."

"You had so much to do. And Ma's so—so fastidious. Don't tell her. Don't go to school and ask questions. Please. It was none of those boys." She put her hand out, touching Charlie's arm.

"Who?" He wondered why he insisted on an answer to that question. What difference did it make? Joella was all right. She was much wiser—but all right. "Boys? More than one?" Charlie choked. His throat burned.

"Yes. But I didn't think—"

"Didn't think is right! My land! You could have talked to us about your feelings. We'd understand. We'd help. What are parents for? You're no orphan! You shut us out. Why?"

"I don't know. I was afraid. I've been sick for three months. I thought I had something terrible—like poliomyelitis. I rode horseback to keep from getting paralyzed. But when I'd missed two periods—I knew what I had." Her voice was a husky whisper.

"Who?" repeated Charlie. "Honey, you might as well tell."

"In Grand Forks, remember we had to wait there before going to Winnipeg. I ran around with the cowboys. We had fun. They weren't insipid, like those town boys at school. Pa, you know what I mean?"

"Yes, the cowboys are usually older. They're on their own, no one to answer to except their boss, who doesn't give a hang what's done on time off." Charlie was going to be as honest as he could.

"We were all friends. They included me. We played poker. I lost and had to—well, you know. The winner took me. It wasn't so terrible. Don't look that way! In Winnipeg—the same thing, then Calgary. It's like everybody does it. I didn't want to be different. I didn't want to be chicken."

"Oh, my word!" Charlie buried his face in his hands. "I never suspected a thing. Your mother had no idea."

"Ma? I told you—she's so prissy. Take a bath every day, keep your hair clean, wear a dress in the grandstand. That kind of thing. How could I say anything to her about playing poker, let alone please poker? Aunt Ell, I could have talked with her."

Charlie blanched. He waited a few seconds so that he could speak calmly. "You must have known it wasn't right. You could have tried to talk with us. You never tried. You deliberately, without thought of the consequences, did what you wanted. You never thought about the people who care most about you."

"But—" She waved one hand in the air. "You've always told us kids to think for ourselves."

"You admitted you didn't think. And that's what I believe. You knew what you were doing. You've seen your share of bulls and stallions mount females, then come the calves and foals. It's all one and the same, humans, animals, sex. The only difference is that humans learn to control their actions. Humans say no when the time is unripe. Young lady, it's over. Finished. Put your hand down and listen. You are not going to tell your mother, Aunt Ell, Grandpa Joe, no one. None of your aunts or uncles and no words to your brothers or sisters. Understand?"

Joella nodded her head. Her green eyes shone like deep well water.

"You'll act as though nothing took place, three, four months ago, or last night. You got over your sickness. You are grown now with a shameful experience, a lesson, under your belt. You'll remember that no decent person has fun at the expense of loved ones. You won't make that mistake again. Forget the cowboys and moon-eyed flirting. Your backbone is a steel rod. You walk away from any compromising situation. Don't expose your reputation to any suspicion. Know what I'm saying?"

"Yes, Pa. I know." Her eyes filled with tears and spilled out the corners of her eyes and ran through her hair to her ears before she took the handkerchief Charlie held out.

"You finish school, then you can work as my secretary. This alley-cat business is over! Right now! Today!"

Joella nodded and closed her eyes. Her face looked serene and untroubled. She was a beautiful seventeen-year-old. Charlie's eyes watered and a wrenching sob came from deep within his chest. His hand shook as he pulled the quilt up around her shoulders.

Etta was smiling and crying at the same time when Charlie met her at the depot. The whir of the old windmill that pumped water for the train station was loud in the sharp winter wind.

"Charlie, I'm so glad to be back home with you and the children, where our problems are small. At least we can talk about them. Kate and Ray haven't had it so easy. They can't even talk about finances without one or the other getting riled."

Charlie took her gloved hand in his and put it in his overcoat pocket along with his big mittened hand. "Jeems, I can't tell you how much you were missed," he said. "Here, I'll carry your grip. The Pierce Arrow's over there. I brought it because I thought you'd see it from the coach window and know I was here to meet you."

"I knew, without seeing the automobile," said Etta. "Say, I'd almost forgotten how cold it is in Cheyenne. That wind is fierce."

"Wasn't it windy in Kansas?"

"Only when I went outside to hang wash on the line." She laughed and held the skirt of her fur coat up so she could slip into the front seat of the automobile.

Charlie drove around Frontier Park so that Etta could have a look at the colorful show wagons lined up next to the fence beside the Irwin cookhouse and narrow barn. Crusty snow hung over the roof edges.

"They look like gingerbread houses with icing," said Etta.

"Yup, everything's a piece of cake here in Cheyenne," said Charlie.

On March 26, 1914, Charlie signed and mailed a contract with the Spokane Interstate Fair Board. The contract stated that he was under an obligation to put on a Wild West show "equal or better in every respect to the show put on in 1913."

It was up to Charlie to furnish all the people and animals, and pay freight and feed for people and animals. This meant ten carloads of livestock, or about one hundred twenty-five head, and one hundred people, besides the show equipment and paraphernalia, including the calliope.

On signing the contract Charlie also agreed not to put on his show within two hundred miles of Spokane before the date of that town's exhibition. Charlie was to receive one thousand dollars at the end of each day's exhibition and twelve hundred dollars at the end of the sixth day's performance. He was to receive all the excess of fifteen thousand dollars of the gate receipts to a maximum of twenty thousand dollars and half of everything above that amount. The Spokane Fair Board agreed to furnish electric lighting for the performances.

Etta and Frank's wife, Clara Belle, made all new costumes for the performers as soon as the Spokane contract was signed and mailed. They sewed white duck pants for the boys and duck jodhpurs or white satin split riding skirts for the girls. Etta did not think it was ladylike for girls to wear pants. She made skirts for them to put on before and after they rode. "The Irwin girls are always ladies," she said more than once. It was true, the Irwin girls were always neat and clean, not always the most expensively dressed cowgirls, nor the flashiest. The performers wore red satin shirts with a white Y6 on the back, and ordinary brown leather boots. None were encouraged to have those gaudy yellow dyed leather uppers nor those boots that were two tones, yellow and blue or black and red.

Charlie was superstitious about yellow, saying no performer of his would be allowed to wear that color, it was bad luck. Tom Horn was hanged wearing a yellow shirt.

In Spokane, Charlie announced that he would give twenty-five dollars to anyone who could ride his famous bucking horse, Steamboat. No one had ever been able to stay on Steamboat's back, except Dick Stanley, and that day was rainy and the track deep with mud. Steamboat could not get his feet out of the muck to make a decent jump.

The last day in Spokane was rainy. Everyone wore his or her yellow slicker. The audience stayed under their umbrellas and cardboard boxes until the last event was over, then hurried from the stands. Joella helped Floyd bring the horses into the corral after the show. Roy and Frances were inside the tack room packing all the satin costumes in trunks. Charlie went out to help the men get the animals into the stock cars. Etta was already on the train, hanging up her coat where it would dry. Suddenly Charlie spotted Pauline in a slicker and boots helping one of the cowboys get the bucking horses into a stock car. The cowboy was fearless Charley Johnson, slim, curly-haired, towheaded, with beautiful soft gray eyes, good-looking, who rode all the bucking horses.

"You going to ride this car with the horses?" Charlie asked Johnson.

Johnson pushed his hat back so his face got wet and shiny. "Yes, sir. Aw—Mr. Irwin—I want to say, I'm sorry I didn't ride old Steamboat today. I might have stayed on. By golly, that horse has everything you could want in a bucking horse, speed, crooked jumps, and when he hits the ground the rider gets his jolts. Some can't eat for a week after being thrown by him."

"Yup. He's my show stopper." Charlie grinned. "The trick is to keep a bucking horse's head up—the higher the better."

"Pa," interrupted Pauline, "could I ride the stock car? There's just Johnson and Johnny Rick in this car."

"Why'd you want to ride a smelly stock car? Well, suit yourself. You got Steamboat in there?"

"Yes."

"Make sure he has plenty of water and hay. If you have some animals that need cooling out, don't let them drink too much; rub them down with hay if you've nothing else."

"I know, Pa, and thanks," said Pauline, closing and latching the sliding door.

When everything was loaded Charlie waved the lantern he carried so that the engineer could see, then hoisted himself up into the vestibule of the Pullman car just as the train pulled out of the siding.

Floyd explained to Roy how people walked the high wire, and Etta handed towels to anyone who wanted to dry his or her hair. Rainwater swirled against the windows and looked like the rapids of the Kootenai River they were passing.

"Where's Pauline?" asked Etta. "Good grief, we've gone without her!"

"No, dear, she's in the stock car with the bucking horses," said Charlie, wiping the rainwater from his face.

"Did you make her ride there because of something she did? Poor child."

"As a matter of fact, she asked to ride there. She'll be a little whiffy on the lee side when we next see her," said Charlie with a laugh.

Joella looked up. "Pa, I'll bet my cowboy hat that gray-eyed Dane or Swede, whatever he is anyway, Charley Johnson, is on the same car."

"Charley Johnson? That good-looking young man?" asked Etta.

"She's kinda sweet on him. Maybe you ought to talk to her," said Joella.

"I said 'yes' without thinking," said Charlie with a sigh. "I've a mind to stop the train and get her out of there."

"Who's with them?" asked Etta.

"Johnny Rick," said Charlie, his stomach cramping and his mouth going dry.

"Oh, it's all right," said Etta. "They're both nice boys. They'll take care of Pauline."

"How will the bronc riders take care of the boss's daughter, I want to know?" said Charlie, sighing.

"I'll have a talk with Pauline. You're right, it isn't ladylike for her to ride the stock cars. I'll see she won't do it again," said Etta, picking up the towels and folding each one too carefully. "Don't worry. The boys are both gentlemen."

I've heard that before, thought Charlie, keeping his mouth shut.

A couple days later Etta told Charlie she'd had a talk with Pauline. "She understood that it didn't look good for her to ride the stock cars with the cowboys. She didn't say much, but I'm sure she understood. Then I smelled something like smoke. I asked her point blank if she'd been smoking. She said she'd been in the bunkhouse and the boys were. I took that opportunity to tell her that you'd be awfully disappointed if she or any of the other girls took up that dreadful habit. Charlie, I've seen some of the other cowgirls puffing the weed. I think it's the fad these days. I told her she'd get brown teeth. She told me she knew for a fact her fingers would get brown, but not her teeth."

"Temptations are everywhere for young people these days," said Charlie. "When we were young there weren't half of the exciting things available. I never thought it'd be hard raising children. I guess I thought they just grew into well-behaved adults. Makes one think, doesn't it? I hope ours turn out all right. I think my pa blames himself because Frank and Will drink."

"Grandpa Joe doesn't say much about it," said Etta. "But I know he's thankful Bud and none of our girls drink—spirits, he calls liquor."

"Yep. Me, too. I'm going to spend some time with Pa at the ranch this summer before Frontier Days," said Charlie.

"Then don't worry about the girls. I'll take care of them. Charlie, you have plenty to think about." Etta gave Charlie a hug. Then she said, "Charlie, if Pauline has her heart set on Charley Johnson, I may sign the papers for her. You know Frank married Clara Belle when she was about the same age. Her mother signed for her. That marriage has worked out pretty good."

Charlie felt like he'd been hit in the chest with a lead pipe.

"Dear, she's a baby—only fifteen. What does she know about—marriage?"

Etta put her small hand on Charlie's huge one. She looked at him with unflinching eyes. "Girls learn fast these days. Our girls have traveled more than most, seen more. They know their own minds. Pauline likes Charley Johnson. You like him? They'll both stay here on the ranch. Pauline'll finish school in Albin. She promised and Johnson agrees. You want to talk to them?"

"I don't know. Seems she was a little tyke yesterday, hardly big enough to ride a horse. What's the hurry? What's happening?"

"Nothing's happened, Charlie. Don't be angry. I had to ask—to see how you felt." Etta watched Charlie twist a button on his shirt. "I think we ought to let them get married," she said softly.

Charlie thought about Johnson. What did he know about the boy? Johnson's father had been in a couple Western films, same as Tom Mix. Johnson was handsome enough to be in silent films himself. Charlie wondered why Johnson hadn't followed in the footsteps of his father. Why'd he start cowboying? Pauline was the quiet one. Why, he hardly knew his middle daughter. She was sweet on Charley Johnson. Things moved too fast. He wanted to put the brakes on. He couldn't.

Pauline and Charley Johnson were married in town by a justice of the peace. Charlie in a three-piece blue serge suit and Etta in the shortened, blue silk ball dress stood with them. Johnson wore a tan suit and looked uncomfortable. Pauline wore a white lace dress with matching parasol and long gloves and looked lovely, young, and innocent.

Etta spent the rest of the summer at the ranch. Charlie and Joe cleaned out the blacksmith shop. Roy shingled the shop's roof.

On Sunday a month before the Frontier Days celebration in Cheyenne, Charlie called a couple of the neighboring ranchers, their families, and cowboys to his place. They'd have a Frontier Days rehearsal with horse racing, trick roping, and anything else they wanted to compete in. Frank and his family came to the ranch for the festivities. Joe said the day was perfect with all the family together again.

Monday morning Clara Belle packed her things so she and her two little girls could go back to Cheyenne. Frank asked to take them in the Pierce Arrow.

Seconds later he came into the kitchen yelling like a banshee.

"Louise spilled her nursing bottle on my good Pendleton shirt! I paid a month's wages for that! Clara Belle, get this kid out of my sight!"

Clara Belle picked up the crying three-year-old. She tried to dab at Frank's shirt with a wet dishtowel. "Stand still," she said.

"Woman, you gotta have some respect for my things. Keep that kid away or I'll shove that nipple up her nose like a rubber hose!"

Etta took the baby and told Frank not to talk to his wife that way. "A woman is one of the sweetest things a man can have. You've no call to treat your wife and children like dirt. Thank your stars for the good things Clara Belle does for you. On top of that she loves you. Grow up, Frank."

Frank looked down at Etta rocking the baby in her kitchen rocker. His eyes were dark and smoky. He pivoted on his heel and went through the back door, letting it slam shut. He walked out to the barn.

"He's been drinking again," said Clara Belle. "He promised to stop, but it's hard for him."

In ten minutes he was back. "Where's Charlie?" he said, as though he had something important on his mind.

"Right here," said Charlie, putting a coffee cup on the table. "You want some coffee before you drive my automobile to town?"

"How fast will it go?" asked Frank.

"Aw, don't slam the gas pedal to the floorboard, Frank. It's not a racehorse, you know." Charlie half-wished he'd not said Frank could drive the automobile.

"How fast will it get to town? We gotta get Charley Johnson there!" Frank pounded his fist on the table.

"What's wrong with Johnson?" asked Etta.

"I hit him!" Frank's hands were shaking.

"You knock him down?" asked Charlie.

"No, Lord, he was already down. Down on Pauline!"

"What?" Charlie grabbed Frank's arm. "Tell me from the beginning."

"I said I caught them both with their pants down in the hayloft. That's what!"

Louise began to cry and Etta rocked faster. Clara Belle sucked in her breath and put her hand over her mouth.

"Frank, why didn't you leave them alone. They're married!" yelled Charlie. He felt his blood begin to boil.

"No one told me they was married," sniffed Frank.

"Yes, we did," said Clara Belle. "You didn't listen. You were too busy looking for your booze bottle. Pauline and Charley Johnson are married. Did you hear that?"

"She was naked as a baby rat and he had his shotguns off. Guess what they were doing? I hit him on the back of the head with a crowbar. God, Pauline nearly scratched my eye out. Look there." He turned his face. Charlie saw three long red lines running from his left eye to his chin. "She said I was a Peeping Tom. Jesus, that girl is precocious."

Charlie could feel his breath coming in, going out. His thoughts swirled together. He steadied himself against the kitchen table, then said, "Let's go!" Frank followed him out the back door still jibbering about letting hired hands take advantage of the boss's daughter.

Pauline had her dress on and a sunbonnet was tied under her chin. Johnson's pants were on, but he was stretched out on his back.

Charlie bent, touched Johnson's forehead. It was warm. Carefully Charlie turned the boy's head and saw blood oozing from a shallow gouge. The blow left a lump nearly as large as Charlie's fist.

"I knocked him out cold, huh?" said Frank, leaning against a two-by-four railing in the loft.

Charlie nodded, "Uhuh." He smelled the sweet, dusty hay, then something else, something that caught his breath, like chlorine bleach. He moved the limp legs that covered the thick, whitish semen on the floorboards under a skimpy layer of hay.

Pauline knelt beside him. "Pa, he's all right? Isn't he?"

"I don't know, baby. We're taking him to town. Go tell your mother."

Johnson was breathing, but he wasn't moving.

"What was up came down, huh?" leered Frank.

"Shut up, you little weasel!" cried Charlie. "You had no call to come snooping up here and smack the kid on the head. Hang on to that leg! Let's get him down the stairs and into the car."

Charley Johnson lay in the backseat. Pauline sat on the floor holding her arms over him; her tears fell on his chest. He never opened his eyes from the ranch all the way into Cheyenne's St. Johns Hospital. Pauline told the admitting nurse she was Johnson's wife. Two orderlies took a cart to the automobile and brought Johnson inside.

The nurse raised her eyebrows. "Your age, Mrs. Johnson?"

"Fifteen."

"Look, her age ain't gonna help that kid right now," said Frank. "Leave her alone. Can't you see she's scared to death?"

"Hush," said Charlie.

The nurse showed them to the waiting room. "The doctor will come back in a little while."

Charlie slumped beside Pauline on a leather couch. He felt helpless. Frank noisily paged through an old newspaper.

Dr. Henneberry came in and went right up to Charlie. "C.B., that cowboy of yours was in a terrible fight. What's the story?" He smoothed down his dark wavy hair and pushed up his horn-rimmed glasses.

"Hit with a damn crowbar," muttered Frank.

"Hit in the worst possible place," said the doctor. "If he'd been hit on the forehead he'd be awake and talking. We'll wait and see what happens. I stitched the cut. The bleeding's stopped."

Charlie stood up, shook his hand. "Thanks."

"I've seen prizefighters get a blow to the back of the skull—never regain consciousness. I hope that's not the story of your young cowboy." He pushed his glasses up again.

Charlie's mouth was dry as dust. His eyes watered. "He's my son-in-law." Charlie's throat constricted. He watched Pauline's hands slide off the couch. Her legs folded underneath as she slid off onto the floor as limp as a rag doll.

Charlie had her on the couch in a second. The doctor came back with a vial of smelling salts and waved it under her nose.

"The floor came right up to my face," said Pauline, coming to.

"You fainted," said Frank, rattling his paper.

"Good thing it wasn't Pa that fainted." She half-laughed. "You couldn't have lifted him to the couch."

"I'm going out for some air," said Frank.

"Let's go back to the ranch. You can come back tomorrow," said Charlie.

"Pa, I'm going to stay at the house in town. You and Uncle Frank go back to the ranch."

"Baby, are you sure—"

"Yes. I want to be close to Charley."

Charlie found Frank in the bar at the Inter-Ocean Hotel. He slurred his words and lurched when getting into the automobile, trying to close the door before his right leg was inside. He yelled,

"Wait for me, Charlie. You're in such a goddamned hurry, you'd leave some of me out in the street!"

"It's a wonder Charley Johnson isn't dead," said Charlie. "And it's your doing. Frank, stop drinking before you do kill someone or yourself."

First thing Etta asked was, "How is he?"

"He's hurt bad. Pauline's staying in town."

"I thought she would." Etta led Charlie to their bedroom and closed the door. They could hear Frank banging around in the kitchen. "Charley Johnson is the handsomest cowboy we've had. If Lillie Langtry were young today, she would take him on the road with her in that special railroad car."

Charlie held Etta's face in his big burly hands. "Dear, Lillie traveled with her mother."

"Her mother would love Charley Johnson. But it's Pauline who loves him. Really, how is she?"

"It takes the two of us to raise the kids. You taught her to be a lady. I hope I taught her to be strong. Doc Henneberry said if the kid doesn't come out of the coma soon—it's wait and see. I don't think he knows what to expect. I'm ashamed to say I felt like crying and she passed out."

Etta lay on the bed with her arms around Charlie and his arms around her. She could not hold back her tears.

A week after Johnson was hurt, Charlie was scheduled to take his Wild West show to Colorado Springs. Grandpa Joe asked to go with Charlie so that he could visit Ell. "I'd sure like to see that girl of mine. I'd like to see what kind of place she has and maybe try some of that health food and mineral water. Couldn't hurt this backache I've had for a year."

Pauline assured Etta it was fine if all the family went to Colorado Springs. She'd send a wire if there was any change in Johnson's condition. Etta was torn between going to look after the other children and staying in Cheyenne to be with Pauline. In the end Clara Belle said she'd look after Pauline so Etta could go.

Charlie hired a taxi to take the family from the show wagon at the railroad siding to Ell's place. He was surprised at the changes in town. He rang Ell's front doorbell, noticing the flowers encircling the base of the pines in the front yard. The house looked like it had a fresh coat of white paint. A young man in a dark suit and snow-white shirt and white tie answered the bell. Charlie gaped a moment at the man, then said, "We came to see Mrs. Miner."

"Who is calling, sir?"

"Her family. This is her family—" Then Charlie saw Ell coming down the curving staircase. She wore a long black taffeta dress. Her orange-tinted hair was piled high. She wore rouge and lip paint. Her dark eyelashes swept upward in an arc. A long strand of multicolored beads was looped three times around her throat. Charlie drew in his breath. Ell was a gorgeous woman. At the same time she was bizarre. He'd almost forgotten how different his sister was from the ordinary town and ranch ladies he was used to seeing.

Ell paused a moment by a small pie-crust table of mahogany against the wall. Marks of the carving tool showed plainly along the edges of the crust. She touched the white vase on the table, and for an instant it looked as though she were going to rearrange the silk flowers; instead she looked up and smiled.

"My word! I didn't expect you! Come in! Come in! You look so good!" She moved from one to the other with hugs and little pecks that were kisses. When she came to Joella she ran her hands down her niece's slim body and twisted the long golden hair into a rope that she held to the top of her head. Joella stood still as a model. Suddenly Ell undid the cameo pin from the ruffles at her throat and pinned it on Joella's white blouse.

"Thank you," said Joella, hardly able to believe the cameo was hers.

"Welcome. Welcome everyone. What a surprise!" She spoke with the young man in the dark suit, and in a few moments he was back with a silver tray containing little cakes and tea.

"This is made from sea kelp." She pointed to a cake and handed it to her father. "Pa, it'll make your skin glow and give you libido."

Joe laughed heartily. "That's why I'm here." Then he leaned back in the plush, Queen Anne armchair to look around the front room with its priceless antique furniture.

Charlie was half-afraid to taste sea-kelp cake until he noticed that Etta and the girls didn't hesitate to take seconds. Floyd and Roy were drinking the tea as if it were pure springwater. Joe was beaming as he watched his only daughter. In his eyes, except for that unnatural carroty hair, she was the spitting image of his mother, Malinda.

Charlie wanted to leave his father and get the children out of Ell's place as soon as possible. He could see that the tea and cakes made everyone feel good. Ell's personality charmed them. Also he saw that the young man who acted like a housemaid adored Ell and would do anything she asked, even though she was at least ten, twelve years his senior.

"Where's Les?" asked Joe.

"He's working. Ever since the mine strikes he's been keeping books for some real estate men on Bennett Avenue. You have no idea how terrible those strikes have been. It was unsafe to walk down the street. Scrums hit anyone. Sometimes a timberman would pull the timber out of place so rock fell and broke a miner's neck. Others who didn't go along with the union men had their legs broken. Mother Jones was here. She's a feisty labor organizer and advocates birth control. She's about as tiny as Etta and her voice is as booming as Charlie's. She rallied the men to join the union by yelling 'Unions forever!' up and down Broadmoor. I thought I could hear her way out here. It was rumored that if she'd stayed longer, General Chase and his cavalry men would ride her down, along with the women following behind her. Chase calls her 'the most dangerous woman in America.'"

"Nothing about that in the Cheyenne papers," said Charlie.

"Well, it's not so bad now that the strikes are about ended. Land sakes, I hope the conditions in the mines and how the men are paid improve."

"Pauline's in Cheyenne," said Frances. "She's married."

"Yes, your mother wrote me. Isn't she lucky? Let me know when she's expecting. I'd dearly love to deliver her child."

Charlie thought, Part of my sister's charm is that she never finds fault. She's adjusted to the fact that people are weak, egotistic, and selfish. She overlooks those faults and sees the good in everyone. Or she makes use of those human weaknesses. He clenched his fists. That's it, she uses people's frailties. His collar felt tight. He undid the top button.

Ell put hands on Floyd's and Roy's shoulders. "You two tigers go over there and listen to my new Victrola records. Jo, you and Frances go out into the garden and gather some flowers."

"Flowers, this time of year?" gasped Etta.

"Heavens, yes. Come to the kitchen and look out the window, rows and rows of chrysanthemums. One of my boys, aw, men, has a real green thumb. I love what he's done to the back. Isn't it beautiful?" She gave Frances a pair of dainty shears and a basket. "Cut anything you like, sugars." When the girls were gone, she said, "His name is Steve. He's a cousin, I tell everyone."

"Must be a cousin on Les's side," said Charlie.

"Naturally. Oh, if there's anything you want just tell Josh," she pointed to the young man in the suit who had brought the silver tray to the kitchen. "I'm not jealous. I share my goodies." Ell winked at Etta.

Etta turned crimson. "Thanks, my needs are few. Anyway, we aren't staying long. Charlie's running a parade downtown at two-thirty and a Wild West show tonight. Did he tell you, Grandpa Joe wants to stay a while?"

"No." Ell stepped back and looked into the front room where Joe was listening to the Victrola. "He's aged. The rheumatism is bothering him. Poor Pa. I'll try to cheer him. Oh, my, his color is bad. He always worried about horses and cows and that darned blacksmith shop and never gave a thought about himself. Makes me feel old to look at him."

There were tears in her eyes when she went out to sit beside Joe. She motioned for the boys to keep the Victrola quiet. "Charlie, go with the boys on the front porch. You can play darts." Then she took her father's hands in hers and kissed them. "Pa, I'm so glad you came to be with me a while."

"Well, I knew my daughter ran a sanitarium, a place a person can recuperate, but I didn't know it was so grand."

"Well, it helps my patients get better. A few of them have coughing sickness contracted from the mines, some have drinking problems." Then softly she said, "How's Will and Frank?"

"Oh, they're fine. Each with a family to look after, so I don't see them much. I don't see you so much. So I came here. You think you can do something about the pain in my back?"

Etta watched as Ell put her arms around her father and laid her head against his cheek. "We'll work together, Pa. There's a room upstairs that looks out on the garden. And there's mud baths that all my rheumatism patients swear by for healing powers. You'll eat good here, fresh things. We'll use nature to heal. Nature doesn't like things out of order."

Josh took Joe's battered suitcase up the winding stairs. Joe followed, trying to act spry, but his legs trembled on the last few steps. Ell noticed the shaking and shortness of breath.

"I don't remember the staircase railing being so fancy," said Etta.

"Les had it made for me for last Christmas. And those," she pointed to the several desks and escritoires and the grandfather clock, "were presents from the boys. Oh, a cousin I had last year was a marvelous musician, wrote music. He gave me that." She pointed to the upright piano in the dining room. "He used to play while the patients ate. We all miss him. He went back East to get his works published."

The girls came in with the basket loaded with flowers. Ell gave each a hug. "Thank you, *mes chéries*," she said laughing. "Here, wipe the flower juice off your hands, then put it in your pocket." She gave Frances an exquisite, lace handkerchief with multicolored embroidery.

Frances put it in her pocket. It was too pretty to wipe with.

The clock struck two. Ell kissed them and said to Charlie, "Go before Pa comes back down. Remember him with coal-black hair and smiling eyes. Write me. I'll write you. Maybe I'll send some of my boys to see your show tonight—so play the audience to the hilt! My God, I love you all!" She stood on the porch and waved as they got into the taxi that was waiting. "Charlie, you're a high roller now—taxi that waits, huh!" She laughed deep in her throat.

At the railroad siding the parade was lined up, ready to go. Charlie walked around a little to loosen up his legs, then climbed to the back of the ivory-white palomino, Wathal. He handed his coat down to Etta. Clayton Danks handed him a white coat with gold braid on the shoulders. "You look like a colonel in that, C.B."

"Yep," said Charlie. "You're looking at Colonel Irwin, manager of the greatest Wild West show on earth." Immediately he thought of Colonel Johnson and his golden palomino.

The girls were on horses, Floyd swung his rope, and Roy rode the huge yellow steer, Blondie. Someone had put brass balls on the tips of the steer's horns.

Charlie waved his broad-brimmed hat and started down the street, leading the show wagons and prancing horses, cowgirls and cowboys. "Smile, this is a pee raid!"

"I wish he wouldn't say that," said Etta under her breath, paying the taxi driver, who was in no hurry to leave.

From Colorado Springs, Charlie took the show to Elko and Reno, Nevada, Colfax, Roseville, Sacramento, California. He wanted to go to Washington State and Idaho, but Etta reminded him that Frances was missing school.

The winter passed without incident. Johnson was well enough to go on the spring roundup and bring in several new, wild horses. Joella went to work at the Plains Hotel as Charlie's secretary. Floyd began to take over the responsibilities of the ranch so that Charlie could work at his railroad job as Livestock Agent and manage the Wild West show, which was becoming famous in all the western states.

Near the end of July, Charlie began to hold weekend contests at the Y6 ranch in preparation for the upcoming celebration of Frontier Days in Cheyenne. Charlie had a wild, bucking horse called Theodore Roosevelt that was becoming almost as famous as Steamboat at these annual affairs. He had a standing bet with the cowboys that anyone who could ride either horse would get twenty-five dollars. Charley Johnson rode Theodore Roosevelt and pocketed twenty-five dollars with a grin from ear to ear. Charlie had never been happier. He gave out money right and left to the winners of the various contests he thought up.

Monday morning he was back in Cheyenne ordering new saddles from some of the catalogs that Meanea had in the store. He wanted to surprise the three girls with saddles all alike, fancy ones with lots of silver and tooled roses. He picked out a saddle for Johnson, a new one for Floyd and Roy. Then he thought of Pablo Martinez and Hippy Burmister. "My land, I could go broke buying saddles," he told Frank Meanea. "Well, what else is money for, except to spend. It can't make a man happy to hoard it."

When he went to his office Joella handed him a telegram addressed to Colonel C. B. Irwin, Proprietor of the Irwin Bros. Real Wild West Show.

Telegrams bothered him. They were a portent to some impending disaster, similar to wearing yellow, in Charlie's mind. His hand shook when he opened the seal. It was from Ell.

PAPA DIED JULY 27, 1914

"Grandpa Joe's dead."

Joella blinked as tears slid down her face. "I can't imagine him not being alive."

"Yes, he's always been around. We'll miss him." Charlie put his suit coat on and went home.

"Poor old Pa, no one was with him!" Charlie said to Etta, whose eyes turned red and watery.

"Don't say that, Charlie. Both Grandpa Joe and Ell knew what the future held. Really, you and I did, too. That's why he went to her. She has a way with people. You have to admit it. She makes a person feel good about himself. We can criticize the life she leads, but what about an awful lot of people she makes happy?"

"There's Les."

"Charlie, that's unfair. Les loves her. He gives her anything she wants—all that he can. She's still married to him, isn't she?"

"I hope Pa didn't ask much about her 'cousins.'" He went to the kitchen for a drink of water. "I know he wants to be buried against that mountain next to Ma there in Colorado Springs. What else is going to happen?"

"This is life, Charlie," said Etta. "People live, people die."

"I loved that old man. I never told him."

"He knew."

Colorado Springs was hot and dry the day of the funeral. There was a short service for the family at the First Baptist Church. At the cemetery near Pikes Peak were several dozen men dressed in spotless black suits, white shirts, white ties. They were Ell's patients from her sanitarium. They were the men well enough to be outdoors, the men that had known and liked Grandpa Joe.

Will and Frank were there with their families. Charlie congratulated himself because he'd kept Frank out of the taverns before the funeral. However, he'd forgotten that Will might need the same kind of close watching.

Will waited on the church steps until everyone was inside, then he went back down the street to a nearby tavern.

At the cemetery Gladys whispered to Joella, "My daddy's one of Grandpa Joe's kids, why isn't he here?"

"Maybe there wasn't room in Pa's car," said Joella.

"Uncle Will's drunk as a skunk," said Roy. "I saw Pa and Uncle Frank talking to him when we got out of church. He told Pa he'd just waited in that bar down the street. Pa said, 'Waiting like a sponge in a full water glass.' And Uncle Will made a face and said he'd go back to where he was, the company was better."

"Your pa thinks he's the big cheese," said Gladys. "My daddy's as good as yours. He ought to be here. Your pa should have made him come. My daddy loved Grandpa Joe as much as yours." Gladys's lip quivered. "Aunt Ell's here with all those men and no one says a thing about that. Even her husband smiles at her!"

"Shut your mouth," said Joella. "This is no place to squabble, you stupid little twerp!"

Gladys told Joella she had no business calling her names and stalked off to stand with her mother, two brothers, and little sister during the prayers and lowering of the casket.

Charlie led the hymn singing. Then it was over. Everyone

walked slowly to the waiting automobiles. Charlie caught up with Les, who had his arm around Ell. Les was tan and smelled of shaving lotion. Les said to Charlie, "Slow, but sure, we're filling this family plot. For a long time there was only Mary Margaret, but now there's Joe beside her. Not so long ago we were building a soddy in Kansas. Huh? So, it won't be long before Ell and I'll be planted out here."

"That's morbid," said Ell behind her black lace veil.

"I wouldn't mind being buried here," said Frank, coming up from behind. "Resting at the foot of these mountains is about as close to paradise as I'll ever get. Looks better than that flat, windswept, burying grounds in Cheyenne."

"One day some city fathers will plant pines and shrubs in Cheyenne and it won't be so barren," said Etta, catching Charlie's arm. "I intend to be buried there. Cheyenne's home."

"I'll stay beside Etta," said Charlie.

"Let's all go to my place and talk until it's time to take you to the train," suggested Ell.

Josh brought out the silver tray with glasses of wine and cheese. The children went out to the porch to sit with Will, who was drinking hot, black coffee.

"What do you think of the situation in Tampico Bay?" Charlie wanted to talk about something besides death to Les, whom he admired and had not seen in many years.

"Well, you heard of the German ship unloading munitions at Veracruz? The U.S. and Mexico asked the South Americans to mediate or else Wilson's going to send soldiers to take Veracruz," said Les, sipping the heavy red wine. "And someone is going to get rich selling horses to the U.S. Army. Horses are needed badly in Mexico. I'd get in the business if I didn't have other things to do. You could do it, Charlie. Round up those wild broncs, leave a saddle on them for a day or two. They'd be broke enough to sell to the Army."

"What's the Army paying for broncs?" asked Frank.

"A hundred to a hundred and a quarter a head," said Les, rolling a cigarette.

Frank whistled. "Charlie, you and I could round up a couple hundred head. We could make a quarter of a million!" Frank licked his lips as though he could taste the money already.

THIRTY-FOUR

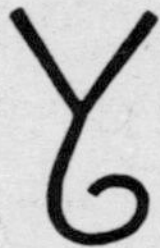

Steamboat

"You plan to be an herb healer like Aunt Ell?" Floyd asked Joella.

"I wouldn't mind. Say, you have any empty liniment bottles in the barn? Ma gave me some cold cream jars."

"That smelly salve really any good?"

"Want to try some? Heals cuts and scratches."

"Personally I think you ought to stick to answering the telephone and keeping Pa's books at the ranch and at the railroad office. Design ladies' hats in your spare time."

When Charlie came downstairs for breakfast, he was in a hurry. "No time for a lot of talk. I've all the boys lined up that want to go on this fall roundup, even taking some cowboys from the Hunter and Coad ranches."

"How about taking me instead of Uncle Frank?" asked Floyd.

"Bringing in wild horses is dangerous. It takes a special talent as a horse handler. If you want to try, come on. Tell your uncle Frank to help Pablo exercise the horses and work out the thoroughbreds while we're gone. He won't put up much fuss if you tell him you're giving him the easier job."

Charlie was glad Floyd had asked to go. He was one of the best horseback and rope men he knew. Rounding up a bunch of wild horses was a dangerous undertaking. At first Charlie thought he could not be paid enough, but after talking to Les Miner he figured a hundred to a hundred and twenty-five dollars a head was a good beginning.

When Charlie asked men from nearby ranches to join in the wild horse roundup no one turned him down. C. B. Irwin was generous, had the best cookwagon chow in the area, and was entertainment of the highest caliber. He'd sing "Alfalfa Hay," "Barbara Allen," or "Blue-Tailed Fly," tell of adventures on a cattle drive, the Endurance Race, going from Encampment across the Continental Divide in snow, or demonstrate his bucking horse, Steamboat, throwing off a seasoned bronc rider. Charlie had listeners near tears with a melancholy song, wide-eyed with terror from a macabre Indian tale, or rolling on the ground, holding their sides from a funny cowboy joke.

Men and women who knew Charlie loved and respected him. Others may have thought him high-handed when he demanded and got a good day's work from his hands or when he demanded that he be addressed as Mr. Irwin. He believed it was denigrating for anyone to say he was beef plumb to the hocks or fat in the middle and poor on both ends or call him names like Pops, Fatso, or Lard Bucket. He'd wrapped a bullwhip around more than one man for saying, "Gain another twenty pounds and you can join a sideshow." Charlie had principles. He never permitted drinking on the job; this eventually caused an irreconcilable rift between himself and his brothers. He never permitted the use of foul language around women.

Twenty cowboys and cattlemen rode over the prairie toward the Chugwater where there was a meadow wild horses generally grazed. Five, six miles from the meadow was a rocky box canyon where the men would do their best to herd the wild horses. Contrary to a towner's opinion, the wild horses were scruffy, inbred, and fat. The goal was to chase the horses around that box canyon without losing a single one, but tiring them so that they could be driven back to the corrals on the Y6 if nothing spooked them.

The second day out the men had more than a hundred wild horses in the box canyon. In the evening they ate steaks, baked potatoes, green beans, baking powder biscuits, deep-dish apple pie, and strong, scalding-hot coffee. Next morning Charlie sat atop his horse and hollered for the Hunter and Coad men to take out the horses that happened to have their brands. Once in a while the ranchers' horses put out for winter pasture ended up staying with the wild bunch. These horses would not come back in the regular spring roundup, so it was wise to bring them in now. As each rancher cut out his branded horses, Charlie pointed out the wild, unbranded ones he could also have. Charlie ended up with the most horses. No one complained. They all made extra money and had a wonderful time.

Tom Hunter asked Charlie if they'd be going out for the wild broncs in the spring.

Charlie said, "We'll go when we figure we need a new barn, new hay mower, or our missus wants one of those wringer wash machines."

Mark Coad said, "You gonna sell all them horses of yours to the Army Remount?"

Charlie said, "I was thinking of trying to mate one of my thoroughbred mares with one. Maybe get a decent racehorse. Racing is going to be a big thing, you know."

"That's a lot of hogwash, C.B.," said John Coad. He had his sheepskin-lined coat tied around his waist. "Horse racing will never amount to a hill of beans in this country. Americans like rodeos and circus ponies, that's about it."

"Oh, yeah? I'll make you a wager, the price of one of those wild broncs," said Charlie with a big belly laugh.

Floyd called on Martinez, Burmister, and other hands to help brush and comb the wild horses in Y6 corrals, so they'd appear sleek and beautiful for the Army Remount inspector and buyer. They shipped the horses from Burns. "It's a durn site closer than going to Cheyenne," said Charlie. He had obtained clearance from the Union Pacific to load or unload stock from that small town north of Cheyenne. That fall Charlie sold fifty half-tamed horses to the U.S. Army Remount for one hundred and ten dollars apiece. Etta mentioned that the money would make a good-sized nest egg for a new house.

A month later, on the thirteenth of October, Charlie and his crew of cowboys and Indians were in Salt Lake City to stage their last Wild West show of the season.

Charley Johnson, who appeared to be recuperating just fine, was with the show crew. Charlie's three girls and Will's Gladys rode in the ladies' relay races. Roy did a spectacular job of trick roping. Afterward Charlie was so proud he brought the boy to the middle of the arena and introduced him once again to the applauding crowd. "Roy Kivett Irwin, ladies and gentlemen! One of this nation's outstanding trick ropers. There's not a rope trick that's been invented that this young man doesn't know. Anyone have a request?"

"Do the Butterfly once more!" came the first request. "Big

Flat Loop!" "Skin in and out!" "Ocean Wave!" "Twirl two ropes, opposite directions!"

There seemed to be nothing Roy could not do. He pushed his hat back, like Will Rogers, grinned, and pointed to Charlie. "That's my old man! He taught me all I know!"

Charlie still on his horse, bent down, scooped up Roy, and stood him behind the saddle. He rode around the arena, waving his hat to the cheering audience and yelling in his resounding voice, "Roy! Roy! He's our boy!" Roy never peeled the grin off his face, even when Charlie turned and rode through dust the horse kicked up.

The last feature event was riding the bucking horses. As usual Charlie offered twenty-five dollars to anyone who could ride Teddy Roosevelt, which was a beautiful, strawberry roan and a mean spinner. When that horse was in the arena with a screaming crowd on two sides, it kicked, sunfished, then spun so fast the rider became dizzy and fell off. Today nobody from the crowd volunteered to ride Teddy Roosevelt, so one of Charlie's cowboys, Paul Hansen, stepped forward. Hansen had tried to ride old Steamboat more times than any of the other riders of Charlie's Wild West show, so he figured he had plenty of experience. Hansen bet Clayton Danks that he could use his short quirt on Teddy Roosevelt three times while he was spinning around and kicking his hind legs and still ride him.

The horse was led out into the open arena. Floyd eared him down while Roy blindfolded his eyes so that Hansen could mount up. Floyd let the ears go at the same time Roy pulled the blindfold off. The horse trotted a half-dozen steps, snorted, and stood still. The boys could see Hansen looking puzzled, then the horse began to turn around, spinning faster and faster. Hansen hit the horse once, twice, then it was Hansen who hit the ground.

He was taken out of the arena by a couple of baggy-suited clowns. Teddy Roosevelt was led away between two other horses ridden by Y6 cowboys.

Charlie hardly had time to think about the first time that horse was used in an arena. It was when President Teddy Roosevelt was a guest at the Frontier Days.

The most famous and the crowd's favorite bucking horse, Steamboat, was brought out next. Charlie paraded the horse in front of the grandstand, leading him behind his own horse.

"Ladies and gentlemen! I bring to you the King of Buckers! This great jet-black gelding with two rear and one front stockinged feet! You all know his history! If the ground is dry and the contest fair, there's not a man that can, nor has, stayed on his back for long! Ladies and gentlemen! I present—STEAMBOAT!"

Charlie waved his big Stetson around as he showed off the horse, hoping that he'd not take a notion to kick up his hind legs when he heard the roar of the crowd. Charlie smelled the arena dust, thickly laced with old and fresh manure; he was aware of the cheering crowd, the noise heightened by stomping feet. Charlie recalled how he first came to own this wonderful old horse over a dozen years ago.

Charlie made the same offer of twenty-five dollars to anyone who could ride Steamboat to a standstill.

Steamboat snorted and twitched his tail nervously. Roy came out and blindfolded him. He stood still as the saddle was hoisted up on his back. His feet spread apart as Floyd grabbed each of his ears and pulled downward.

Right away a cowboy came forward to ride the horse. The man was Harry Bowles from Salt Lake City. He was a cowhand who worked on a local ranch. He was big and muscular, with rich, dark skin, black eyes and straight, black hair. He looked like a local Indian, broad-shouldered and slim, but he did not have the slightly almond shape to his eyes and he had a snub nose. Bowles walked with the cockiness of a man who knew that he was a good horseman.

"Check the cinch strap," said Floyd.

"Been riding since I was a kid about five," said Bowles with a clipped speech that sounded Indian. He felt the strap and nodded.

Before he could swing his leg up and over the horse, Floyd asked, "You part Ute? If you are, you ought to meet some of the Sioux that work with the show. They're from Pine Ridge. Fine people."

"Nope. I ain't Injun," said Bowles, tightening the chin strap of his wide-brimmed black hat. "I'm English and Eyetalian. But you was close. I was raised by Ute."

Roy asked, "You an orphan?"

"S'pose so. My pappy died in a mine cave-in. My mammy froze to death looking for him. At least that's what Muddy Feet told me. Her man, Gusher, found me sleepin' in a packin' crate my pappy called home. Raised me with their own passel o'kids."

"You never went to school?" asked Roy, whose arms were getting tired holding the blindfold.

Bowles laughed. "Can't write my own name. Can you believe that?"

Floyd nudged Roy and whispered, "Roy, get on with the bucking contest. Can't you tell when someone's feeding you a line? Don't swallow that bait."

Bowles went on. "And I got me the prettiest little Ute woman you ever did see. You boys want to meet her sisters?" He was on the horse.

"No, thanks," said Floyd, then he nodded to Roy, the sign to pull off the blindfold.

Roy jerked off the black cloth. "Look at him buck!" he shouted, running for the fence. "Old Steamboat didn't like being held down so long!"

"That poor sucker won't stick long!" yelled Floyd, climbing the fence.

Steamboat danced. He stood on his hind feet so that his back was nearly perpendicular with the ground. Then he hit the ground like a rock bouncing down a cliff, kicked up his back feet, and swayed back and forth, enough to make the rider seasick. Steamboat always moved to the center of the field, away from the noise of the crowd. Two cowboys dressed as clowns were mounted, ready to herd the horse quickly into the corral when the rider was thrown. Steamboat dodged those two horses with long crooked jumps and was in the center of the arena when he slowed a little. Everyone could see that gave Bowles a chance to breathe and get set for more bucking and sunfishing. He was pushing Bowles from his head to his tail. Bowles tried to save himself by riding on his spurs rather than the grip of his legs. He held the hackamore rope in his left hand and decided to change hands, all the while keeping his loose hand above his head. Suddenly his yellow silk shirt ballooned. He was in the air, coming down, helpless. He hit the dirt, knocking out his breath. Immediately Bowles was pulled to the side of the arena into a pile of alfalfa, out of the way of the horse, which was pawing at the air in front. The clowns brought their horses on either side of Steamboat while he was still moving around trying to swap ends. One man grabbed the hackamore rope and the other moved his horse close to the other side, and they held on to Steamboat as he was led to the corral.

That day Harry Bowles was given the honors for riding Steamboat because he'd stayed on his horse longer than any of the other men on their bucking horses. Bowles was ecstatic. He danced around like a Ute and *kiyi*ed to the crowd.

In the tack room he offered Roy and Floyd a drink from the flask of whiskey he fished out of his gear. Charlie saw him tip the bottle to his mouth, and he moved into the tack room, his head nearly touching the doorway and his big body touching the sides of the door. "Look, Bowles, here's the twenty-five bucks I owe you. Now, clear out! Don't let me hear of you offering booze to any of my men again. You hear?"

"Of course I hear ya, Blubber-gut," sneered Bowles, snatching the paper money.

There was not a twitter, nor a sound of chaps moving against pants, nor leather against leather. The room was dead quiet. All eyes were on Charlie.

Charlie's face was dark, his eyes narrowed; he took one step forward away from the door. "Don't call me that again." Charlie's huge hand reached out and grabbed Bowles's silk shirt at the shoulder. "My name is Mr. Irwin to you. You rode my horse today. You did a fair job, but you gouged him unmercifully in the sides with your spurs. So, I want you to go out there and put pine tar in those cuts so the screw worms won't move in. What do you say, Mr. Bowles?"

Charlie moved his other arm across Bowles's throat, pushing his chin upward so that he had to look into Charlie's face.

"I say, yes, sir—Mr. Irwin."

"Fine. Then get going!" Charlie moved all the way inside the tack room so that Bowles could slip past him, which he quickly did.

Charlie let out his pent-up breath and glared at Floyd and Roy. "You boys ought to know better than take a drink on a track. You've seen how men behave under the influence of spirits, losing control of their arms and legs and not remembering what they say or do. If I catch you drinking before or during a show or race, neither will sit on a horse for six months. Now, what do you say?"

Simultaneously the boys said, "Yes, sir—Mr. Irwin."

"Oh, get out there and cool out the horses and get them loaded into the stock cars before that incoming storm hits."

"What storm?" asked Roy outside. "All I feel is wind."

"Look at the dark clouds boiling over there," said Floyd. "Looks like something's coming. Everything looks kind of yellow."

The wind gusts became stronger and the temperature dropped fast. As the boys worked they saw lightning coming from the clouds in the southwest.

"Why didn't you tell Pa we didn't take a drink from Bowles's bottle?" asked Roy.

"Hey, Pa knew we didn't drink. He was standing in the doorway all the time. He just wanted to give us his speech," said Floyd, punching Roy in the back.

"Criminantly! It's a good thing I didn't touch that flask!" said Roy.

"Did you want to?"

"Ya, sort of."

The horses whinnied. Steamboat snorted and began to rear up on his front legs as the thunder rumbled louder. A couple of times Steamboat sideswiped other horses and scared them so they scrambled to the other side of the corral. Steamboat jumped in his crooked manner as the lightning came closer, blinking on and off like some huge electric light. He banged into the side of the corral, acting as though someone had put a flank cinch on him. Floyd talked to him in a calm, soothing tone, but still he edged against the corral. He lunged hard, raked his side against the barbed wire, which was strung between the two top poles of the fence. Then the horse seemed to go crazy as he reared around and raked the other side deeply. The sky flashed with light, and thunder rumbled loudly at the same time.

"Holy geez!" screamed Roy. "Look at the sides of Steamboat! They're shiny wet!"

"Must be the pine tar Bowles daubed him with. He was sure free with the stuff!" called Floyd, loading horses into boxcars.

"Don't go near him. That horse is berserk! He'll kick you! Knock you down! Step on you! Get out of the way!" Roy was so excited that he climbed the fence and flung himself on the outside of the corral. The rain came in sheets with the gusts of wind. It blew the men's slickers close around their legs, and the horses' tails fanned out like tattered flags.

"Gee whiz! Help me get the rest of the horses loaded. Then we'll saddle up and try to get Steamboat calm enough to go all the way up the ramp and into the car, where he can't see the lightning. I hate this storm." Water ran down Floyd's face, making it hard for him to see.

Then the hail came, stinging where it hit face and hands, bouncing high when it hit the ground. The lightning seemed to fade and grow weaker. The thunder's rumble took longer and was less clamorous. The rain came back, spitting in large drops. The horses were loaded into the dry cars.

Steamboat snorted and drooled foam but otherwise was quiet between two other bucking horses. Floyd was ready to drop out of the boxcar to help the other dripping-wet cowboys load the steers, buffalo, and goats. He sneezed from the dusty hay that the horses stirred up with their feet and nosed around to munch.

Roy hollered, "You still there? Get Pa! Hurry!"

"What's the matter?" said Floyd.

"Don't ask, just get Pa!" Roy's voice sounded panicky.

Charlie was in a boxcar several cars beyond, wiping down one horse, then another with an old rag. He looked up and grinned. "Well, I'm glad you didn't melt in that downpour."

"Roy needs help. I think it's Steamboat. That horse went wild during the storm," said Floyd.

"He still bucking?"

"No, wheezing a lot, but standing quiet."

"Worst bucker in the West," said Charlie with a laugh. "Probably lathered up some. Check the rowel marks."

"I thought Bowles did."

"Let's go see." They hitched themselves out of one stock car and up into the other. The ramp had been pulled inside. Sharkey, Will's son, held a lantern so Roy could examine Steamboat's wounds. Roy's hands were red with blood. Both sides of the horse were oozing badly.

"Pa, there's no tar over the spur rakings," said Roy quietly. "And the rips are long and deep on both sides. From barbed wire."

Charlie's heart went to his mouth. The boxcar seemed steamy and close. The brakeman swung his lantern outside the boxcar. Then called inside, "You fellows want to close your door? It's all aboard!"

"No! No!" yelled Charlie. "Wait up! We want to check out a horse first. Please!"

"Hurry it up, Mr. Irwin. It's a flood out here!" said the brakeman, swinging the lantern so the engineer could see there was a delay.

Charlie ducked back beside Steamboat. The horse was not putting his nose into the hay. He'd drunk water. He looked like he wanted to lay down. "Stay on your feet, Old Man," soothed Charlie. "More than spurs raked those sides."

"Pa," said Floyd, "he bucked against the corral fence whenever the thunder was loud and the lightning bright. Me and Roy couldn't get near him. He jumped in that crazy way and turned end over end against the barbed wire."

"Oh, no," said Charlie deep in his chest. "I've never seen a horse cut to ribbons like this and no way to stop the bleeding."

No one spoke. The munching of hay and slurping of water

was loud. Finally Roy said, "Damn Bowles for not using pine tar!"

"Never mind, son, tar wouldn't help all the wire cuts."

Sharkey tried to hold the lantern steady. "Is he going to be all right? Is there something that can be done?" Sharkey was white.

"I don't know," said Charlie sadly. "We don't have clean-enough rags, nor enough water to wash him down. Let the blood clean out his cuts. Jeems, I hope he's not losing as much as it looks."

The dark-red blood oozed down under the hay. The hay seemed to be floating in black shimmering puddles.

"I'll be right back," said Charlie, hoisting his big frame over the side of the stock car. He waved to the conductor and brakeman, then ran to the last car. He told them he was riding in the stock car. He was back in less than two minutes after he'd seen that all the doors were slid closed on every boxcar but one. He waved to the brakeman, who signaled with his lantern to the engineer. The men hurried onto the slowly moving, steam-hissing train. Charlie closed the last boxcar door and went back to Steamboat, who was wheezing and snorting. His legs were wide, braced against the motion of the moving train.

Floyd and Roy sat with their backs to the side of the car, where they could see all of the dozen horses. Sharkey brought the water barrel close by so that Steamboat could have what was left. On the opposite side sat Bob Lee, Johnny Rick, and Paul Hansen. Their tanned faces were upturned as though seeking help from a higher source. Bob Lee held his hands together. The thumb of his left hand was missing, cut off quick and clean by a dally rope. The men were hushed, no one suggested a game of blackjack, nor let loose with the latest dirty joke they'd heard from some cowboy at the Salt Lake arena that day. The only sounds were the whir of the wheels on the track, the click, click from the breaks in the track. The flies buzzed and crawled on the horse dung, flew to the backs of the damp horses, and then flew around the men looking for a place to land. The horses all snorted and farted. Charlie talked softly to old Steamboat. That horse wheezed like a worn-out accordion as it breathed.

In Denver, Charlie wired ahead, so that a veterinarian waited at the depot in Cheyenne. The middle of the night was pitch black. The rain there had let up. The air smelled fresh.

Charlie watched closely as the gray-haired veterinarian nodded and sighed as he looked over Steamboat. Charlie wondered when he'd be ready to talk. He patted and probed and examined the eyes, ears, and throat of the weak horse. Finally he said, "Mr. Irwin, it don't look to me like there's a Chinaman's chance in hell to save this horse. Best thing, shoot him quick and save him the agony of gangrene, lockjaw, and screw worms. See how those cuts are swollen? That's blood poisoning. Rusty wire, no doubt."

Charlie could not answer right away. His heart fell to the ground and his tongue dried up. Steamboat was special to him. He'd performed most everywhere in the West. Steamboat was Charlie's whole show. The horse was the heart, the character of the Wild West. People came from all over just to see Steamboat.

Charlie shook hands with the vet. "I understand. It's a bitter pill. Oh, man, I love that horse." He choked and felt his eyes swim.

Floyd stood beside his father. "Pa, we know what has to be done. Are we going to take him back to the ranch?"

"Son, we're taking him to Frontier Park." It was something Charlie said on impulse. But the more he thought about it, the better it sounded. He instructed the cowboys to take the animals to the Four-Mile pasture and to stay at the bunkhouse in Cheyenne until morning. "Etta knows you're coming, probably has the coffee hot." Then he turned to the boys he'd been riding with and said, "There's a couple shovels in the stock car ahead of this. Get them. Go to Frontier Park. Dig a hole as big as a horse in front of the grandstand. Go now. If we wait until morning, word will be out and Frontier Park will be out. Keep what you're doing under your hats. Keep out of sight. Roy and Floyd lead the horse—go slow, don't let him die before you get to the park, or you'll end up carrying that old bronc."

"Pa, aren't you coming?" asked Roy.

"I'll catch up." Charlie looked at the boys lined up about ready to leave for the park—Sharkey, Hansen, Lee, Ricks, and his two boys, Roy and Floyd. He thought they looked as bad as he felt at the thought of shooting this magnificent animal. He'd be with the horse in its last moments. "I'm going to get a rifle. I'll come back in my pickup and meet you about the time you hit the park gates. Like I said, don't alert half the town with what we're doing. No *kiyi*ing. Keep your yaps shut."

"Yes, sir, Mr. Irwin. We all understand," said Bob Lee.

All the way home Charlie thought about the Henry rifle hanging on the wall in the den. Walking up the front steps, he saw the light in the kitchen. He hurried in to Etta.

"Where are the others?" she questioned.

"They're coming." It was hard to tell her that Steamboat had to be shot. "I'm the one to do it," he said. "I'm going to use Tom Horn's Winchester." The words were out of his mouth before he hardly realized what he'd said. All the time, until just now, he'd been thinking of the old Henry rifle. Tom Horn's rifle seemed suddenly more appropriate. "Bowles, the last man to ride Steamboat, wore a yellow shirt, same as Horn."

Etta did not understand what a yellow shirt had to do with shooting old Steamboat. She didn't ask Charlie. He was buried in his own thoughts as he left the house.

By the time Charlie got to Frontier Park, all the clouds had moved eastward and the night sky was bright with low-hanging stars. The half moon was well on its way to the western horizon. Charlie pulled the pickup beside the high iron gate. He got out, ducked under the chain, and hurried toward the grandstand.

Sharkey whispered loudly, "A horse would have been a lot more quiet than that damn Model T you drove up here. It snorts louder than Steamboat ever did."

Someone said, "Sshh!"

A hole that looked like the basement for a good-sized house was already dug. The tailings made a hill six feet tall and about ten or twelve feet in diameter. Charlie stared at the hole.

Hansen said, "The rain softened the ground. We didn't have any trouble digging."

In front of some temporary grandstand seats Roy stood over Steamboat, who was lying on the ground. The horse's breathing was shallow and made less sound than the wind through the wooden stands. Charlie stood beside the dying horse a few moments. Then he sat on his haunches, put his arm over Steamboat's neck, and said, "I brought that rifle Tom Horn gave me. It's better than the old Henry. Why, Horn's kind of a legend. But you've been a legend ever since my brother Frank rode you in 1902. You sunfished so bad that Frank went over your right side with his right foot catching the stirrup. He hung like a pendulum under your belly. But Frank was smart. He stiffened and passed all the way under. Then you got smart and your hind hoof kicked him before he got clear. Gave Frank a headache. Gave you a champion's reputation. So long, old friend. This day is October 14, 1914." Charlie motioned for Roy to move and he stepped back five or six paces, put the Winchester to his shoulder, aimed at the magnificent black head, pulled back. The single crack was loud, clean as any shot could be.

"Right between the eyes," Johnny Ricks whispered as the horse seemed to crumple and pull its legs in.

"Finish up!" snapped Charlie. He inhaled deeply, smelling the wet earth. He heard the sound of the clods hitting the solid horse-flesh. Some of the extra dirt was spread over the spot behind the stands where Steamboat had lain and made the ground bloody. This was stomped and smoothed. Charlie took the bandanna from around his neck and flicked the topsoil back and forth so no unusual marks were visible.

It took far less time to fill the hole than dig it. Charlie was humming "Good-bye, Old Paint." He was thinking the hole had been big enough to bury a boxcar. The earth was tramped on over and over. Charlie laughed at the sight of seven people stomping the ground like a bunch of red men doing a rain dance. The laughing made his eyes water and tears ran down his cheeks.

"Pa, don't," said Roy. "You'll have us all crying like a bunch of old women and babies. Come on, walk around here some more. The center humps up like that old root cellar behind the Hunter place."

When the ground was even and smooth, Floyd said, "No one will ever know where Steamboat's buried but us seven. It's our secret."

Charlie laid the rifle on an old piece of burlap in the bed of his pickup truck, started the engine. It wheezed, sputtered, roared, and backfired once, twice, then settled down to a steady roar. He waved and drove home.

Etta had extra blankets in the bunkhouse and in Floyd's room so everyone would have a place to sleep, even if it was on the floor.

Charlie washed up, climbed into bed next to Etta. He could not sleep. He heard the men come in one by one. He tried to imagine his Wild West show without the Bucking King, Old Steamboat.

"Nothing lives forever," whispered Etta. "Perhaps it's best that Steamboat died before he became old, tired, and docile. This way he'll always be famous as the wildest bucking bronc that ever lived. You'll never replace him, but you'll find other horses that will be outstanding in the bucking contest. You already have Teddy Roosevelt and there's Yellow Fever."

"I'd like to see a statue of Steamboat somewhere in Frontier Park," said Charlie."Wouldn't that be something?"

"A picture on the wall of the cookhouse would suit me," said Etta with a sigh, staying close to Charlie.

"I'm going to miss that horse. Why, I'd like to go like he did. I'd like to check out before I'm old and grouchy and incompetent. I'd like people to remember me as useful, energetic, and interesting." A shudder passed through his body.

"Don't talk that way. I don't want to think of ever being without you. I couldn't stand it. I'd die of heartbreak and loneliness."

Charlie lifted Etta's arm, turned to face her, and put her arm back around his shoulder. "Don't you worry. I'm not going anywhere for a while." He changed the subject. "That's the first time I ever used Tom's rifle. Tomorrow I'm going to clean it, put it in the gun case beside the old Henry. I'm not going to use it again."

"Yes, put this night behind you. Think ahead now." Then Etta asked where Steamboat was buried.

"I'm not saying a word. Don't go pumping the boys, because they'll not tell a thing. It's done. Like you said, nothing lasts forever. The deed is dead." He closed his eyes and could see Steamboat sunfishing and spinning as Bowles raked his sides. "The son of a gun wore a yellow shirt! Why didn't I make him take it off?"

"You said that once before," said Etta. "Why?"

"Tom was hanged in a yellow shirt. It's bad luck. I've never seen a man wear a yellow shirt and have anything but bad luck."

"You are so logical most of the time, but you fall back on cowboy superstitions once in a while. It surprises me."

"What superstitions?"

"Like Floyd wearing the same pair of wool socks in his boots every time he twirls a rope before a crowd. He says it keeps his rope from kinking. Some of the boys carry a rabbit's foot or wear a certain bandanna tied a certain way before they're to be in a relay. Joella always piles her long hair up under her hat. She says she won her first race that way and it's worked for the others she's won."

"Oh, fiddle, that's comfort, not superstition," scoffed Charlie. "Suddenly I'm so tired. Can't we talk tomorrow?"

"Tell me first, where did you bury Steamboat? Frontier Park?"

Charlie turned back, stretched out his long legs. "I'm not talking now nor tomorrow. It's done and over with."

"I guessed, didn't I?" Etta whispered, and smiled in the dark as she heard Charlie's even breathing.

During the month of November Charlie began to make plans for the coming season's Wild West show. He hired a military band, consisting of six musicians. He decided to stage a quadrille on horseback, using his three girls, Will's girl, Gladys, and

Frank's oldest girl, Maxine. Maxine was seven and she could be billed as "the youngest cowgirl in the West." Charlie remembered how the audience fell in love with Frances when she was only nine and rode in the girls' relay. He'd use four cowboys from the Y6 and Floyd on horseback to complete the quadrille. He became so enthusiastic that he called the ranch and told Floyd to come home so they could talk over some other changes in the program.

"Geez, Pa! A dance on horseback can't be so exciting. People want something that moves, fast and exciting," said Floyd. "You have to keep the people interested with events that are creative and daring."

"What do you suggest?" said Charlie.

"Let's get Frank Miller again, the champion crack shot. Have Miller shoot darts into a board around the outline of one of the girls. Have Joella, dressed in a skimpy costume that sparkles, stand against a board that resembles a bull's-eye or a big door. Miller could ride by bareback on a steer and shoot the arrows, ping, ping, ping, right around her. That's thrilling and different."

"Son, people come to see the Irwin Brothers because it's the Wild West, not a circus. Here's an idea: How about having a pony express ride with the Montana Earl and Scout Maish. Afterward Maish can give his demonstration of bulldogging. Remember he was Champion Steer Thrower of the World at the Winnipeg Stampede last year? I'll write to them and at the same time write to Bee Ho Gray to do some extra fancy roping for us next year."

"Pa, what about my roping? Isn't that fancy enough? That military band can play and I'll do some fast loops standing on the ground, then jump on my horse and stand up, kneel, stand on my head, all the time twirling my rope. People will love that."

"Bee Ho Gray wrote and asked for a job. He said Will Rogers told him I'd take him."

"Well, then, what can I say? You don't really need my advice, do you?" said Floyd.

"Sure I do. Tell me what you think about a horse race between a cowboy, cowgirl, and an Indian. Roy, Frances, and John Red Cloud can make that a good event. Then maybe a good, fast cowboy and Indian pony race. And the fast, fancy riding of the Russian Cossacks. They went to spend the winter somewhere in Colorado, but they'll be with me next spring."

"Pa, let me ride with them and learn to crack a long bullwhip like those Cossacks can."

"Floyd, I've already written to the Australian, Jack Morrissey, who's a champion whip cracker and shot, and he wrote back saying he'd be with our show."

"Well, I still get to trick ride with the identical, black Arabian horses in that old Liberty Act, or have you written to someone else to do it?"

"Son, certainly you can do that event."

Floyd waved his arms when he talked. "The band'll play a waltz and I'll get those six stallions to dance up on their hind legs all at the same time. Then I'll get the two mares to put their front feet up on high stools, and the gelding, the one with the little white on his nose and under his eyes, he'll put his head down and kind of look like he's trying to stand on his head. Not too graceful—but people will go for it. Won't they?" Floyd looked at Charlie, wanting his father to agree with him. Floyd wanted to be able to make his own decisions, be creative, and have his father praise him for his showmanship abilities. Floyd learned fast. Usually he made mistakes only once. He had a good sense of timing when he worked an act and knew intuitively what was a crowd pleaser.

"Sure, and we'll have a pushball game between cowboys and Indians."

"Pa, that's old hat."

"You can try the bucking-horse competition."

"Pa, I believe I could stay on every bucking horse you've got."

"Don't be too cocky," cautioned Charlie. "That's when you'll be dragged in the dust right in front of the grandstand. Let's have a forty-niners scene. Have the miners in a covered wagon and have the Indians attack."

"Yeah! The Indian attack never seems to get old. Can I be an Indian this year? Just for kicks, Pa?"

"Floyd, that's wrong! Your ma wouldn't like that and you know it. Be yourself!"

"Be myself? I just ask for some little thing and you yell at me. I want to give the show some flash. You asked for my advice. But you don't listen to me. I should have stayed at the ranch!"

"That does it!" shouted Charlie. "I know what I'm doing. I've been in the business long enough to know what people prefer." Charlie thought his son was stubborn, overconfident. He thought Floyd wanted to take over, tell him what to do, not exchange ideas as Charlie had anticipated.

"Pa, I know you think you do. But there are things you could be doing that no one else has yet tried. Then your show would be so much better. Now people compare it with Buffalo Bill or the 101 Ranch show. When you bought the calliope that helped, and the show wagons. Listen, I could get some of the old Sells-Floto people to advise you with new and colorful costumes."

Charlie felt his blood heat up. "Costumes? Did I ask for help with costumes? Your mother and Aunt Margaret do fine in that area." He did his best to hold his temper. He took a deep breath. "I could use some advice about the program layouts. What do you think about running in what President Taft said: 'It's the real thing, the best show I ever saw,' and what Teddy Roosevelt said to me, 'C.B., I saw your show twice, in 1904 and 1910—it is the best in the world.' That's good advertisement."

"Pa, I don't care what you put in the programs. I want the show to glitter. If it were mine—"

"The show moves. There's something doing every minute."

"You're right. But you need to modernize. Make something different from year to year. Keep up the interest. It's done that way in the circus. For instance, one season an elephant act is the main show, next something with trained dogs, then trained cockatoos."

Charlie saw red. He waved his hands. "Stop! I'm not having a bird act in a Wild West show. Are you lamebrained?"

"No, but—"

"No *buts!* Just leave me alone so I can think. Get out of here! I don't want to hear any more."

"Geez! You don't have to yell. I heard you. I'm leaving."

Charlie heard the front door slam and settled down to work out the front cover for the 1915 Wild West program. Sparkle, yes, he thought, Floyd's right, this year's program ought to be different, attract more interest, sparkle. The Irwin brothers have the best show in the country, even Teddy Roosevelt thought so. I have to keep it the best. That's my responsibility.

That evening before supper Etta asked Pauline to check the cowboys' quarters to see where Floyd was. Charlie went out to check the horses, thinking he might have taken one and gone back to the ranch. Floyd seemed to like it better at the ranch than in town. No one seemed to know where Floyd had gone. He'd not taken a horse. After supper Charlie cranked the phone and called the ranch. Floyd had not yet shown up.

Etta became uneasy. "Did you say something to him?" she asked Charlie.

"No, not really. Oh, well, we had a difference of opinion on how the show acts should be presented. It wasn't a big difference. He wanted to be an Indian in the covered wagon attack. I thought that was a ridiculous idea. I knew you wouldn't approve. He talked about trained elephants, dogs, and birds. I made fun of him and said we weren't managing a circus. I told him to leave me alone so I could do my own thinking."

Etta's eyes were wide with accusation. "He left? Oh, Heaven help us! Where would a nineteen-year-old take himself?"

"To the circus," said Joella, who'd not said a word all through supper.

Etta cried. She did the chores from habit. Her mind was elsewhere trying to imagine where Floyd would go. Each morning as always she dressed in fresh underclothing, put on the whalebone corset, laced both sides, pulled on her silk stockings carefully and slipped her feet into black shoes with medium heels. She wore a silk slip and clean, starched and freshly ironed house dress. Before leaving the bedroom each morning her hair was combed and in place. She never went around the house with a bedwrap or bathrobe like Ell.

Charlie lied. He told Etta he was sure Floyd would be back any day. He was sober and said few words, even at the office. He'd have given anything to have Floyd back. He went over and over what he could remember of their conversation. At first he justified his feelings and his shouting at Floyd. Finally he admitted he was a little harsh and didn't listen to Floyd's ideas, and they weren't so bad either. Would Floyd run off to the circus? Charlie thought about that for several days. He remembered the schoolboy's crush Floyd had on that cute little girl, the high-wire walker, the Iron-jawed Butterfly. It was cold in Cheyenne; the circus would be somewhere south.

Charlie and Etta clung to each other at night. The girls missed Floyd and his happy-go-lucky attitude. Roy seemed lost without an older brother and tried his best to make the girls laugh and to do everything Charlie asked, but otherwise he was totally ignored. He withdrew into a shell of quiet brooding.

At the end of a month Charlie and Etta received a postcard from Saratoga, Florida. "Caught the last act of the Sells-Floto in Ellensburg, Washington. Moved into winter camp. Been hired as a trick and fancy horse rider. They like my ideas here. Don't forget me. Yours, Floyd."

Tears streamed down Etta's face so that she could hardly make out the picture on the front of the card. It was a Sells-Floto show wagon. She also remembered the tiny, dark-haired Iron-jawed

Butterfly and wondered if Joella knew more than she said a few weeks ago when she mentioned the circus. She asked Joella, who could only say that she was certain Floyd was happy. "Ma, why don't you write to Aunt Ell. She sometimes knows things when no one else does."

Ell wrote back saying almost the same thing Joella had said. "Bud's happy. You'll have him home before Christmas and you'll be thankful for the stranger that's coming."

Etta laughed, then cried, and called to see if Margaret or Clara Belle were expecting. "Maybe it's Ell herself."

"Ma," said Joella, "a stranger coming does not have to mean someone is expecting."

"Mothers always think a new stranger means a baby's in the oven," said Etta, laughing for the first time in weeks. "Besides, Ell's been right about other things. She said her three brothers would each have four children."

"Frank and Clara Belle have two," said Joella.

"Give them time," said Etta.

Charlie looked at his wife and daughter. He rolled his eyes upward. "You know Ell. She likes to play physician and spiritual helper to every Tom, Dick, and Harry."

That winter was rough, even for southeastern Wyoming. Snow fell incessantly and the wind drifted it onto roads and against fences. Ranchers had a hard time keeping hay out in the open for their stock that huddled under the shelter of hillocks or shallow rock caves or in gullies and canyons. Charlie spent three, four days each week at the ranch. This is where he missed Floyd most. At nineteen Floyd could run the ranch almost as well as Charlie. He always knew what needed to be done and what men could do each job best.

Each day Etta watched the mail for another postcard from Floyd. She began to live one day at a time. Afraid to think beyond each present day. She hoped the next news from Floyd would be good, but she was afraid to get her hopes too high. The lump in her throat seemed to be permanent. She suffered from constant heartburn and indigestion. When the girls played on the piano or sang a song Floyd had sung, it brought tears to her eyes. She cried cooking bacon because it was a favorite of Floyd's. She cried when Charlie exercised the horses. The sight of a lasso would bring tears to her eyes.

Mid-December Charlie was in town straightening the papers on his desk. Joella said, "Phone call from Elko, Nevada. I think it's Elsie Coble."

"What's she in Nevada for? She and John went to California."

Elsie Coble was so choked up she could hardly talk. "I wanted you to be the first in Cheyenne to know, C.B." Then she cried.

"Elsie, what is it? Take your time. Then tell me," said Charlie.

"John—it's John. He's dead. Pneumonia." She sniffed and blew her nose. "Sorry. I'll be all right."

"I thought you were in California," said Charlie.

"We were, but John was out here to buy a ranch between the Diamond and Ruby mountains. I brought the children out to see the new ranch. The three girls are devastated, but little John's only two. He doesn't know what's happened. I'm bringing John back to Cheyenne. Oh, C.B., it's going to be so lonely without him."

"You want Etta to come out and help with the children for a week or so?" asked Charlie.

"No, no, we'll manage. I—I just don't know what to do with the ranches."

"If you want me to talk with Charlie Hirsig, a banker here in Cheyenne who knew John and knew about his business deals—"

"Oh, please have him call me when I get back to Cheyenne. Give Etta and the children my love."

"Yes, yes, I will. Take care," said Charlie, hanging up the receiver. He put his head in his hands. He could hear the wind howling outside and Joella typing inside. He wondered what life was all about. Irascible John Coble was only fifty-five and he had everything he wanted, a beautiful wife, children, money in the bank. Then one day, without warning, he was staring at the sky, but seeing nothing. What's life anyway? It falls apart like the flowers on a fresh grave. Life is vibrant and whole, then something touches it and it falls apart. One chance with something that is so fragile is hardly fair. Charlie got up and went outside. He thought, It's hard to cry in the cold. I'm freezing out here. He went inside.

Joella looked up questioningly, so Charlie told her about Elsie Coble's news. "It can happen to anyone. It could happen to me. I'm only thirty-nine."

Joella's green eyes widened. "I've always believed that's why you live like you do."

"Like what?"

"You put the most into life, into what you do now."

"You mean, you see me living each day as if it were the last?"

"No, Pa. You keep your eye on the future by living fully in the present. You are generous with the future by giving your all to the present."

Charlie arched his eyebrows. "That's deep. I'll think on it."

The next day Charlie saw Hirsig. It was the first time he'd talked to him since they'd dissolved their partnership. He told Hirsig to call Elsie Coble, then told him he needed to borrow money because he was going to build a new house for Etta.

"What's that address?" asked Hirsig, businesslike.

"You know, Pioneer Avenue."

"Why don't you build the garage first? Three-car garage is really something." Hirsig whistled. "You think you're one of those English barons that come out here to manage a ranch?"

"Come on, I have three cars. Maybe I'll get another one and leave it at the ranch. This is the only life I'm going to have. I'm going to make the most of it. I want to borrow five hundred dollars."

"I said you could. But I want a mortgage on your present house."

"All right, it's done."

"Show me the plans for that garage again," said Hirsig.

Charlie pulled a folded paper from his inside coat pocket.

"A garage with a second story? Isn't that unusual?"

"That's going to hold cots for my hired hands. It's the new bunkhouse. When the men come to town for Frontier Days, they'll have a place to stay. Hotels are full and the barn in the park is no place for a couple dozen men along with a couple dozen horses."

Hirsig went to his files and pulled out a form. "Sign here, C.B., and I'll give you cash. You take your time about paying this back, we're old friends."

Charlie smiled. "Ya, you want that three percent interest."

Charlie and Joella locked the office at five. Charlie was eager to go home and tell Etta about the loan. "As soon as this weather breaks I'll start. Most of the lumber work can be done by the time we get a January thaw, then the cement can be poured."

"I hope Ma is as excited as you are," said Joella.

"She will be, because when the garage is done, I'll borrow on it and start building her new house," said Charlie.

Coming up the walk they noticed all the lights in the house seemed to be on.

"You think Ma's cleaning house?" said Joella.

Suddenly the front door opened and Roy piled out in front of

Pauline and Frances. "Floyd's back!"

"Oh, thank goodness!" cried Charlie, and ran up the front steps. He rushed past Etta and there was his son, standing in the dining room, hands in his pockets, as if he'd just come in from riding his horse around the block. "Hello, son. How's everything?" said Charlie, his eyes watering. His heart thumped. The lump in his throat could not be swallowed. Floyd seemed taller, his smile broader. His face was tan. He seemed older.

"It's swell to be home." Floyd took his hands from his pockets, and Charlie pulled his son to his chest. He could not hold back the tears.

Etta stood just inside the room with the girls. Her face was shiny wet, but she was smiling. "Charlie, Charlie, there's someone else that needs a hug! Don't forget Floyd's wife."

Standing beside Etta and the girls was a small, dark-haired nervous-looking child. She was thin and wiry, with a snub nose and brown eyes under thick brows. The cleft in her chin moved up and down when she spoke.

"I'm glad to meet ya. Floyd's told me so much about his family. It feels like I've been here before."

"You're the Iron-jawed Butterfly!" cried Charlie. "Ell was right. Home before Christmas and a stranger!"

"This is Dee Dee," said Floyd. "We've been married a couple weeks."

Charlie gave the tiny girl a bear hug. He thought of the first time he saw Etta and how tiny, like a pixie, she, too, had seemed.

"Come out to the woodshed and see what we brought you," Dee Dee whispered.

"I hope it isn't a Christmas tree," said Charlie. "I don't think I'd like one of those Florida palms."

"No, it's birds for the ranch. Floyd bought them," Dee Dee said, leading the way to the woodshed.

Charlie smelled them the minute the door was opened. In a shipping crate were three peacocks and in another, identical crate, were three peahens. Charlie put his hand to his face. He felt half-faint. Etta and the girls were ooing and ahing about how pretty they were. Roy stood by Floyd, smiling from ear to ear, just glad to see him home. Charlie looked at Dee Dee. She was smiling like it was the most natural thing in the world to bring a gift like this.

"Why? Why did you bring these here?" he asked.

"They are beautiful, maybe we could use them in the show," said Floyd, putting his arm around Dee Dee.

Charlie could think of nothing to say, but to repeat the words Chief Red Cloud had once told him about peacocks. "They bring a violent death to anyone who owns them. Plenty bad luck."

"Pa, that's superstition. You don't believe what old Red Cloud said. Do you?"

"Well, some people see things different from the rest of us," said Charlie, thinking about his sister, Ell, and her forecasting.

"I'll take care of them out at the ranch. Dee Dee and I are going out tomorrow. We want to stay there."

"That's the best news I've had in weeks," said Charlie.

THIRTY-FIVE

John Red Cloud

Before the summer's Wild West show went on the road, Charlie went to Lusk, on Niobrara Creek, north of Fort Laramie to buy a couple outlaw horses from Charlie McGinnis. I-Be-Dam was a true show horse, a blue pinto, with a couple of small patches of white on his back and an ugly white face, with a pink nose and one dead eye, or so-called glass eye. Lightning Creek was I-Be-Dam's mate, a sorrel with four white stockinged legs. Now he felt more confident that he had some interesting bucking horses. Of course none could take the place of Steamboat, but these had the outlaw's spirit and would make the bucking contest interesting.

In the spring Charlie told Etta that she'd either have to move to the ranch or to the top floor of the hip-roofed garage while he tore down the house in preparation for the new one. Etta had a couple of the cowboys store most of the furniture in the three-car garage; the rest went upstairs, where Etta and the children moved until the new house was complete. There were three bedrooms, one bath, a kitchen, a dining room, and a big living room. It was enough for Etta and the children.

Spring was cold and the snow lay on the lawns and alongside the streets longer than usual. Charlie began taking Etta to the Cheyenne Opera House on Saturday evenings. They saw Johnnie and Della Pringle, the Georgia Minstrels, Sarah Bernhardt, Otis

Skinner, Valeska Suratt, and Paderewski. On Sunday afternoons the girls saw matinees of the Armin Stock Players, the Arlington Comedians and the Spooner Dramatic Company with the latest plays, such as *Uncle Tom's Cabin*. They saw and heard John Philip Sousa and his band.

Whenever Charlie and Etta or the children went out, they dressed in the latest fashions. Charlie felt no expense was too much for clothes. He was making more money and had more people on his payroll than any rodeo producer had before this time. Charlie sent to Chicago for monogrammed shirts and tailored suits. He was a large man, and looking neat and well-groomed meant that he had specially tailored clothes. He wore a gray or brown Western-style felt hat with his suits, but for the rodeos and Wild West shows he wore a white, wide-brimmed Stetson made specially for him, and bought by Etta, from the Brandeis Department Store in Omaha.

Etta ordered clothes for herself and the girls from B. Altman's or Marshall Field's in Chicago. Most of the boys' clothing came from Brandeis.

One Saturday afternoon before the program at the opera house, Charlie took the family to the Plains Hotel for dinner. He had Dee Dee sit next to him so that he could point out all his friends who were eating at the tables in the large dining room. Before his dinner was brought in he stood up and waved his brown hat in the air, then called, "Oh, Mr. Kuykendall, how are you? I want you to meet our new daughter-in-law." Mr. Kuykendall smiled and nodded his head, then Charlie said in a whisper to Dee Dee, "His pa was secretary of the Stock Association of Laramie County."

Dee Dee smiled and kept her hands together in her lap.

Etta felt like crawling under the table each time he stood up and waved his hat at someone. Finally she said, "Charlie, don't do that anymore. You are embarrassing me and the children. Your dinner's here, eat it before it congeals on your plate."

At that moment Pauline hiccuped. Charlie stared at her and she turned red. "I'm sorry, pardon me," she whispered, and hiccuped once more. The other children laughed.

Charlie reached over and patted her hand. "It's all right, honey. When Charley Johnson dresses up in some new clothes, we'll come here again and I'll show him off. But you gotta get him to get new things. He can afford it. I pay you and him the same as I do all the other hands. He's had those boots three, four years. They're a disgrace."

Pauline burst into tears.

Charlie wished he'd kept his mouth shut. "I'll buy the boots, if he tells me the size."

Etta put her hand on Charlie's arm. "Hush."

"What did I say?" Charlie looked helpless. He wished women could be realistic. He liked Johnson, but he wanted him to take some pride in his looks.

Etta passed Pauline a glass of ice water. Then she looked around the table. "Everyone go ahead and eat. I'm going to say a few words to Charlie." She faced Charlie. "It's hard for Pauline to watch Dee Dee and Bud. She remembers when Johnson was bright and fun to be with. Ever since he came back from the hospital, he's been different."

"Looks the same to me. Even wears the same clothes," said Charlie, cutting his beefsteak.

"He's not happy-go-lucky, the way he was. He's more sullen. He's mad at the world. He picks fights in the bunkhouse. I'll bet he's worn those boxing gloves more than any other cowboy you have. Right now he's blowing on his harmonica instead of coming with his wife."

"Sometimes a man just likes to be alone." Charlie looked at Pauline, who had her head down and her hand on her fork, but she was not eating.

"Alone and drunk," whispered Pauline.

"Drunk?" said Charlie. "Johnson drinking while he's working for me?"

"He gets headaches and he says it helps," said Pauline. "Sometimes he doesn't remember I'm his wife. He treats me like the boss's daughter, something to look at and tease, but not touch. I love him. But I don't know what to do or say to him anymore." She wiped her eyes.

Charlie cut off another piece of beefsteak, put mashed potatoes on top of it, then put it in his mouth. "Yeah, well let me talk to him tomorrow. Honey, those headaches are his problem, not you."

"Everyone eat," said Etta again. "Dad will take care of Johnson, so no need to worry one iota. Let's talk about the new picture show, *The Birth of a Nation*. We'll go when it comes to the Lyric."

"We ought to celebrate Floyd's twentieth birthday with a party," said Joella. "Go to the show."

"I'd rather stay at the ranch and have a barbecue," said Floyd. "A horse race, a footrace, maybe a sack race or two."

Charlie's face lit up. "Sure! We'll invite all the neighbors. There's a fence that's been down since that last wet, heavy snowfall. We'll have a contest to see who can put up the posts and string up the tightest wire in an hour. Maybe I'll get some of those logs I have at the ranch sawed, too, while we're at it. A sawing contest. Yes, sir! We'll have a swell birthday party!"

Not only were there thick beefsteaks at Floyd's party, but stacks of fresh cutthroat trout from Horse Creek that Dee Dee and Pauline had caught the day before. "I don't know if it's more fun eating or more fun fishing," said Dee Dee, her dimple bobbing up and down.

"Don't you miss the circus?" asked Pauline.

"Oh, sure, but I'm going to learn to do acrobatics from the back of a horse. Floyd said I could be in the Wild West show with him. You can't be a tight-rope walker forever, you know." She giggled. "Did you ever see a gray-haired tight-rope walker?"

During the party there was laughter and funning everywhere, except in the bunkhouse, where Johnson sat alone, playing sad tunes on his harmonica. Two or three times Pauline went in to sit with the good-looking blond fellow. "Pa says if your head aches, come on out and he'll give you some coffee with something he gives the horses. Says you'll feel better right away," she said once.

"He's right, this headache's built for a horse. But I'm not going out there with all them folks. I'd feel as out of place as a pig in a pawnshop."

She put her arms around him, and he said, "If your paw knew you were hugging the hired help, he'd clobber the both of us. Now, get out of here and leave me be."

Outside Floyd had Martinez by the water spigot holding a bucket to be filled. Somehow Floyd managed to fasten Martinez's belt to the spigot, and on the pretext of unfastening it he tied Martinez's hands behind his back. The wet and miserable Mexican boy kicked and stomped his feet in the mud. Floyd thought it was a good prank. "Kid Mex, if you were on horseback, you'd know how to get out of trouble, but with two feet on the ground your mind doesn't operate!" Floyd teased.

A laughing crowd formed around Martinez and Floyd until Charlie scattered them, scolded Floyd, and let Martinez loose and told him to get some dry pants on. He stayed in the bunkhouse the rest of the day, singing as Johnson played the harmonica. Etta took two enameled plates heaped high with steak and fish, baked potatoes, green beans, wilted lettuce salad, biscuits, and cups of coffee. She stopped and gasped after opening the door to leave. "Come and see this. It's something you've never seen before."

Johnson hesitated, but Martinez knew Mrs. Irwin wouldn't trick him, so he got up off his bunk and followed her out the door. He motioned for Johnson to come quick. Dee Dee walked barefoot on the top platform of the windmill. She stretched her arms out as though catching the breeze and walked all the way around the outside board next to the fluttering blades, yet she was not hit by one.

"Lordamercy! That child's like a cat. She can walk anyplace!" said Etta. "I suppose she could hang on to one of the blades and go round and round without getting dizzy."

"She's crazy," said Martinez.

"That's a sight, all right," agreed Johnson.

The shooting stars and buttercups were in bloom at the base of the windmill. The more Martinez looked at them the wider grew his smile.

"You thinking about the Wild West show this summer?" asked Etta.

"Sí, and those flowers, their colors remind me of my mother's kitchen in Mexico. Drying red peppers and yellow squashes, green dill and silver sage."

"What did she look like?" asked Etta. She'd never heard Martinez talk about his home before.

"No, I don't remember her. Sometimes I pretend you remind me of her." Momentarily his big, black eyes were filled with sadness.

High above, Dee Dee climbed down the windmill, hand over hand, balancing and holding on with her bare feet, not unlike a monkey.

"Señora with the iron muscles," said Martinez with admiration. "Me and Señor Floyd will put a rope with an iron ring through a pulley. She can clamp her teeth into the ring, and we can pull the rope up so she'll fly through the air."

"No, you don't! Don't even think about it!" said Etta.

Charlie had begun to lead a little group of cowboys and cowgirls in singing some of the latest songs. Pauline stood beside Johnson. They made a beautiful couple. He slim and blond. She slim and dark. His blue eyes were blue as the forget-me-nots in the meadow. Her brown eyes were like the huge brown centers in the sunflowers. She tugged gently on his arm. "Come with me, I have something to tell you. A surprise."

Johnson looked at his wife with his eyelids lowered. "I s'pose

I have to. Your pa made it clear that I should do as you say."

"Don't talk like that. Come with me because you want to."

Charlie watched the two wander off, following the creek, into the cottonwoods. He began to sing louder than before as more people gathered around, holding hands and swaying back and forth.

Pauline sat down beside Johnson on a warm sandy bank. She drew the handsome head down to her face. "I love you, Charley," she whispered. "I want us to be like we were before! Remember the happiness?"

"Before what?" He could not remember Uncle Frank coming into the barn with a crowbar. Pauline had told him over and over. Charlie told him that is what caused the headaches. But still he could not remember. Sometimes in the middle of the night he sat up in bed and laughed out loud. No one would hit him with a crowbar. He was sure he'd fallen off a horse. He could not remember getting married. At night he'd say to himself, So, if I married the boss's daughter, I'm lucky. But there's this terrible headache. So what good is luck?

Pauline thought he was so handsome, it was hard to believe he'd changed so much in the last couple of months. Sometimes his actions were strange and frightening. "Please pay attention." She wanted him to understand her words. "You are not the only one who is not the same as when we got married." She watched his eyes.

He wondered what she was talking about.

"We were always alone. But we're not going to be alone for long. We're going to have a baby. I'm—I'm going to have your baby."

"A baby!" Johnson shouted. His eyes darted back and forth. He stood up. "You are going to have a baby? You aren't old enough! You're a baby yourself."

"Sit down beside me," said Pauline. "Don't yell. Someone could hear you above Pa's singing."

"What did he—your pa, say about this—baby?"

"Sshh, he doesn't know. If I tell him, he might not let me finish school this spring and he won't let me go with the show for sure."

"You want to go with the show?"

"You know I do. I always go. I'm part of the show, the girls' relay race, the trick roping, the covered-wagon scene."

"I'm going to stay and work on this ranch. I can break the wild horses that are brought in on the spring roundup."

"Charley, that's already been done. You did that job. Oh, drat! Give me a cigarette. I could sure use something right now."

He pulled out the makings and rolled one for her and one for himself.

"I'm telling you that you are the father of my baby. How does that make you feel?" she said.

"Look, honey, I've never been a father."

"Look, honey, you will be."

"I don't want to be a father. So don't talk to me like that. You talk all the time and it makes my head hurt. Cheeze and crackers, tie down your nose. It sticks up too far in the air!"

"You're like a fantail yourself—wild, with your own thoughts. I can't get through to you. I love you and I want us to be a family. Think about that. Try thinking back why you were in the hospital. When that's worked out maybe the headaches will stop."

Pauline's eyes were brimmed with tears. She tried to hold them in by not blinking. A fly buzzed by and she blinked so the tears ran down her cheeks. She scrubbed at them with the backs of her hands. She smiled at Johnson. He smiled back and said, "I do like you and I like your pa."

She walked back alone and stood at the edge of the singing group. Joella came up alongside. "I never noticed before," she whispered, "but you gotta quit eating so many biscuits and gravy. You're getting fat!"

Pauline laughed. She couldn't help herself. "It's baby fat!"

"You've had a smoke. I can smell it!" Joella squealed. "You got some makings? We could go behind the barn. Say, baby fat—you mean?"

"Sshh—Johnson has the makings. Come on, over by the creek."

"Don't let Pa see us—he'd skin us alive!"

Charlie did not find out about the girls smoking right away, but several nights after Floyd's party Etta told him she suspected Pauline was pregnant.

"Jeems! Thank goodness she's finished with high school in May. Say, I was counting on her for the show this summer. Couldn't she put it off a little while, so she could do the relay races?"

"Let her ride in the parades. Take Charley Johnson and let him do some roping, or bronc riding."

"You think that will unscramble his brains?" said Charlie.

"Only time will do that, according to Dr. Henneberry. 'Wait and see,' he says."

"We've had our share of troubles lately," said Etta.

"Yup, it's a stage. Kids thinking for themselves and not thinking the way we'd want them to right off. I suspect we did the same to our parents."

"It's not just the children. Haven't you noticed Frank and Will? Back to the drinking again. I wonder if Frank ought to go out with the show this summer. He ought to stay and take care of his family. Clara Belle's pregnant."

"Another mouth to feed ought to settle him. I'm going to ask Clara Belle if we can take Maxine out with us this summer," said Charlie. "She looks cute on those big horses in the parade. You and the girls can look after her. We'll take Gladys and Sharkey; you think Gene wants to come?"

"I'm not running a nursery," said Etta. "But I'll look after them because they're family."

"I love you more than anything—always will," said Charlie, putting his arm around her.

The girls and Floyd rode the six Arabian horses in all the parades that summer. It was a good, safe place for Pauline to ride. Sometimes Dee Dee rode with Floyd. They rode one of the black stallions and had him kneel right on the sidewalk curb. The people cheered. Pauline and Maxine rode the black mares, Joella and Frances rode the black stallions. Gladys rode the gelding that had patches, like freckles of white around the nose and under the eyes. Once in a while Gladys would turn halfway around to see how Pauline was doing and she'd put her hand on the back hip of her gelding. In St. Paul the gelding kicked its back feet and nearly dumped Gladys. The onlookers loved it. After getting over her surprise Gladys tried it again with the same results. She'd found a new trick for her horse.

A couple of blocks farther up the street there was a peddler with a pushcart who followed dangerously close behind Gladys. Pauline moved her horse up beside Gladys. The girls talked about the man who got into their parade and followed so closely behind the horses. They thought he had a lot of nerve. They turned and glanced at him. He looked up and smiled. The girls could see he carried fruit, polished red apples, oranges, bananas, and pears. They heard him call out his wares, trying to sell to those watching the parade. Pauline leaned over and said, "Gladys, why don't you pat that gelding on the hip?"

Gladys smiled and nodded and eased over a little and put her hand on the back of the gelding she'd named Sioux, just as the peddler was smiling up at her. The horse kicked up its back feet, fruit flew high in the air. The peddler pulled his cart to the curb. He was white with fright. He could not chase after the fruit, nor stop the youngsters that darted in and out of the parade for apples or oranges.

"That peddler won't bother another parade," said Pauline. All day the girls giggled about the flying fruit.

Charlie bought a white shetland pony in Minneapolis. He had Charley Johnson dress up in a clown outfit and ride the pony. During the evening performance the pony turned its head back and took a nip at Johnson's leg. This made Johnson angry, so he laid his quirt on the horse's head and jumped off over the head. Johnson meant to land on his feet, but he fell flat on the ground. The horse went after him and caught him by the seat of his pants. The horse shook him hard. The crowd laughed up a storm. This was the funniest sight they'd seen. When the show was over, Johnson was livid with rage. "That horse made a fool of me!"

"Oh, come on. You were the star. People loved your act," soothed Charlie. "You want to do that tomorrow. It gets a tremendous hand."

"Honest?" asked Johnson.

"As honest as any yamper who'd steal my ten-gallon hat," said Charlie, eyeballing the hat Johnson picked up and put on his head.

"Oh, I'm sorry, sir. I thought it was mine," apologized Johnson.

"You knew it was mine," snapped Charlie. "What happened to your own hat?"

"Damn little white horse chewed it." Then he looked at Charlie and grinned. "Damn, if you ain't built like Pauline, fat in the middle and skinny on both ends."

"Johnson, you are referring to your wife, who is expecting, and to me, your father-in-law. You won't call either of us fat again!"

"But, sir, both of you wear shirts as big as a circus tent."

"Johnson! That's not funny!" yelled Charlie. He grabbed Johnson's multicolored shirt. "Would you like for me to say you act full grown in body only?"

"No, sir—no, Colonel Irwin. I savvy." He looked at Charlie, whose face was dark and whose eyes glowered. "I do understand. Don't make fun of me and I won't make fun of you."

Charlie thought to himself that there was some progress. Johnson was going to come along eventually. Patience was what he and Pauline had to have.

He noticed the wind had begun to blow. He was outside the tent watching dust, dirt, and papers swirl upward, then drop back to be picked up again. Roy and a couple cowboys and roustabouts were busy fastening the big tents down, because it looked like a big blow and possibly a rain was coming. The horses and animals were being moved out into a makeshift corral by Floyd. Charlie told Johnson to go help. "Take that asinine clown outfit off first though!" he advised loudly.

The moment the words were out, something cracked like a rifle report. Charlie stopped inside the tent to see what was going on. The side of the big tent caved in partway and rippled in the wind, then sagged toward the dirt floor. Charlie heard Floyd yell, "Vamoose!" Then he saw that Floyd was pulling Custer, the roan horse Charlie always rode when roping steers. He was pulling the horse away from the cave-in. The horse was hard to manage. It was spooked. It was plumb crackle-brained, kicking its hind feet and sashaying from side to side, showing clearly the thick sprinkling of white hairs in its hide.

Charlie held one side of the tent's entrance, making the exit larger. "Floyd, over here! Outside! Get Custer out! Come on, son!"

A jagged streak of lightning broke the sky and a strong gust of wind roared across the midway. Floyd led the frantic horse toward the opening just as the whole tent heaved and collapsed. Floyd was standing beside his father. The wind blew dust and a spray of rain in their faces. Neither said a word, but began pulling canvas and tangled ropes away so that the horse would not smother. The horse was down on its side. The instant the covering was lifted, it was up on its front feet. Charlie's heart soared with relief, like a lark flying heavenward on a bright spring day. The reddish-brown horse reared up on its hind feet, making an effort to cry. Its mouth was wide open. It faltered, made a gurgling sound, and dropped. A tent stake was driven through its neck. It could not make a sound. Suddenly blood spurted out both sides of its neck.

"He's gone," said Charlie with a gasp, as though the wind had knocked his voice out. "Custer's gone."

"Pa, it was the last horse I had to put in the corral," said Floyd softly. "I'm sorry."

"Let's get the tent rolled up before she blows away!" shouted

Charlie. "Hey! Over here!" He motioned to Johnson. "No time to get out of the clown suit, huh? Strike the tents! All of them!" Charlie disappeared. Then suddenly he was back.

Charlie gave Floyd a roll of greenbacks and asked him to take the body of Custer to the address on a piece of paper. "Leave the carcass in the man's backyard. He knows what to do with it."

"I'll go when this storm blows over."

"You'll go now! I made an effort to call this man on the telephone and said you'd be there right away. The Humane Society, city officials, and police will raise holy Ned with us if they find out we have a dead horse on the lot."

"But, Pa, it's raining cats and dogs."

"Harness a team of horses with a drag. Build the drag if you have to. But get the horse out of here now!" Charlie hollered.

The Wild West show moved on to Des Moines, then to Omaha, Lincoln, and Grand Island, where it played simultaneously with the Sells-Floto Circus. Dee Dee performed as the Iron-jawed Butterfly, causing Floyd to marvel all over again at his tiny wife's acrobatic ability. Two or three days in a row he rode a circus elephant down the midway just to see if his father would get huffy and scold him, saying that no cowboy would be caught dead on one of those huge beasts.

Charlie didn't say a word. He was wondering if maybe Floyd hadn't been right all along. The Wild West show needed a change of pace—some new acts. It occurred to Charlie that he might get hold of a brown bear, train it to do tricks.

He talked it over with Etta one night in Holdrege, Nebraska. She gave her wholehearted approval to the trained bear idea as long as she did not have to feed nor curry the dumb thing. "There's something I've meant to ask," she said, snuggling up against Charlie. "What did you do with Custer? Was he buried somewhere along the midway in Minneapolis?"

"That's not even a good guess," said Charlie in a mysterious tone. "You want to use another guess? I'll give you three guesses, then I'll tell you."

"You sold him to a glue factory." She giggled.

"That's cruel and wrong."

"You sold him for dog meat."

"That's a sick thought and wrong. This shows you don't really know me very well. I left Custer's remains in charge of a taxidermist in Minneapolis. He'll send the tanned hide, with that beautiful red and white head attached, to Cheyenne. I'm going to keep that beautiful horsehair robe on the floor of the den at the ranch house."

"Oh, yes! That's just like you! The hide will go with the antelope and deer hides already in the den and the buffalo head above the fireplace. Put Custer's hide in front of the bookcases, it'll look grand."

Charlie grinned. "Exactly what I had in mind."

Two nights later Etta and Charlie were helping to pack up after the last show in Holdrege. It was near midnight. Etta was keeping a sharp eye on Pauline so that she would not lift anything heavy. Over and over she'd told Johnson to take good care of her, but she was not sure he'd remember. Pauline was folding costumes with one of the young Sioux women, Mary Best Britches. Etta joined them.

Mary said to Etta, "Some of us have been talking. We'd like to take you and the mister into our tribe. You are one of us. You treat us like your family."

"That is the nicest thing that has been said about Charlie and me in a long time. Mr. Irwin and I would be honored to be Oglala Sioux."

"So then, we'll make the honor in Fort Morgan, Colorado. Something to think about for next week."

"Oh my, is it ever!" said Etta, smiling with Mary and laughing at Pauline, who had stopped work completely.

"Remember the time your son ran away and your man looked all over the Sioux camp for him? The interpreter's wife, Emma, hid Boots plenty good." Mary tee-heed and slapped her thigh several times.

"You call Floyd 'Boots'?" asked Etta.

"Sure thing. He's Boots. Good name for your boy. You ever see him without boots on? Maybe he sleeps in his boots." She laughed.

Pauline held her hand protectingly over her protruding belly and laughed. Etta laughed so hard she had to hold her sides.

"Boots and John Red Cloud are like brothers," said Mary, wiping her watering eyes. "You see, all of us enjoy being in the Charlie Irwin Wild West show and rodeos. It's the best thing to look forward to while we wait out winter at Pine Ridge."

"Tell me, did John have to go to school on the reservation?" asked Pauline.

"Oh, sure. All the children do now. But it's shameful. They don't learn the hunts, nor to value war honors, nor tanning of hides. They don't learn painting or sewing with shells, quills or seed beads, no basket-making or pottery, not even spear points. They learn words—to read from books and write on paper. They do sums and take-aways. They sing—not songs of the Sioux, but something else with an elephant music maker, the piano. It's nice, but not the same as the old ways."

"I'd like to learn painting and sewing with beads," said Pauline.

"I can show you," said Mary, her eyes sparkling. "When you are little mother, you will have time to sit with the baby and paint and sew. Then you show me how to make my mark on paper."

"Didn't John or one of the others who went to school show you?" asked Etta.

"Naw, too busy. You know how it is with young persons. John, he would rather be with horses."

The women went back to their work of folding the costumes and putting them into trunks and huge wicker baskets.

At the same time Floyd and John Red Cloud, grandson of the old Chief Red Cloud, were leading a string of four show horses to an open boxcar on the siding. John was on horseback, in the middle of the track, waiting for Floyd, who was on foot, to lower the ramp so the horses could walk into the boxcar.

A switch engine was backing up. The engineer had orders to pick up the cars on the siding. He was looking over his shoulder, coasting slowly, in order to couple with the first boxcar. Then he would move forward after the track was switched. It was dark enough to slow down a bat, but not that engine. Looking over his shoulder, the engineer never saw John on horseback in the middle of the track. When John heard the engine's rumble, he looked up, the back end was dark, he didn't know how close it was. He yelled, "Watch out!"

By the time Floyd looked up the noise of the engine and the confusion of the horses drowned out John's cry. John moved off the center of the tracks, chased the horses into a thicket, kicked his heels into the sides of his mount, galloped close beside Floyd, dived off his horse. He shoved Floyd out of the way of the half-lowered ramp and the boxcar. John had no time to move his own sprawled leg off the track. The wheels of the boxcar suddenly rolled backward, instantly cutting off John's foot.

John let out a bloodcurdling cry. Floyd rolled his friend down the embankment to a flat rocky shelf, ripped up his own shirt for a tourniquet to stop the blood spurting from the stump.

John was unconscious. Floyd pushed him close to the backside of the rock shelf, made certain his breathing was even and his pulse not thready. Then he stood up and yelled, "Someone! Get a doctor! Quick, someone get a doctor!"

Roy was locking up one of the show wagons when he heard the cry. He ran along the railroad embankment. "What's the matter?"

"John, he's hurt! John Red Cloud! Hurt bad!"

"There's a doctor on Main Street. I saw the sign. I'll get him. Pray he lives behind or above his office." Roy found John's horse and was gone.

Floyd sat crouched against the rock. He was drenched in perspiration. Several cowboys came down the embankment to see what was going on. One ran to get Charlie out of his berth in the Pullman car.

Heaving to catch his breath and still button his shirt, Charlie yelled, "That boy have anything broken?"

"Yes! Yes!" sobbed Floyd. "His foot! It's gone! Pa, he saved my life! My God, there's blood all over!"

Charlie looked at the battered, raw stump that was left of John's right leg. "Cut clean below the knee," Charlie talked to himself. "This boy needs a doctor." He looked up and leaned away from the rock. "What's that I hear in the brush?"

"The horses we were taking to the boxcar. When the switch engine moved in, they scattered. Everything happened so fast. Damn, I didn't see the lights. It was coming backward. If it weren't for John I'd—uh—I'd not be here talking to you. He dived off his horse, pushed me away from the loading ramp. Trouble is, his foot fell on the track."

John groaned and tried to sit up. Charlie was beside him, holding him down with his powerful arms. "Don't move. We'll get a doctor."

"Roy went for one," said Floyd, putting his head between his knees to shake off the dizzy feeling.

"Son, get out there and round up those fool horses," said Charlie, knowing that for Floyd to be busy was the best thing right now.

After what seemed an age to Charlie, the doctor came stumbling behind Roy down the hillside to the rock ledge. The doctor grumbled about being called out of bed past midnight to take care of a goddamned thieving redskin. "Somebody's going to pay for this!" he cried.

"Take care of the boy like you would any other human being!" bellowed Charlie. "We'll put him on one of those horses coming out of the brush yonder. Bring him to your place so's you can get some light to see him proper. I'll pay, whatever it takes."

"Yes," said the doctor, trudging back up the hill to the tracks. "Bring the patient along."

Charlie went along with the doctor and watched him cauterize John's leg with an alcohol lamp to stop the bleeding. Then the flesh was cleaned with boracic acid and lysol. Once Charlie had to go outside to get some air. Floyd, Roy, and half a dozen cowboys were hanging around the front of the office, waiting to see if John was going to be all right.

"Come on, you men look gray as sop," said Charlie. "John's going to be all right." He went back inside.

"If you're going to pay for this, the boy can sleep here. It's better not to move him again. If you take him with you now, I won't guarantee anything."

"I'll pay," said Charlie, taking a roll of paper bills from his pocket.

Outside Charlie explained that the doctor would care for John all night, but in the morning he'd be ready to put on the train. "Any of you men think to tell the Sioux what happened?"

"Not me," said Roy.

"I'll talk to them," said Floyd. "Pa, I'm going back for the foot. I know it sounds grisly, but John's relatives might want to have some kind of ceremony over it. You know Indians."

"Suit yourself," said Charlie.

Floyd hung around, hoping someone would speak up and say they'd go with him. No one did.

Roy said, "You afraid of coyotes? When they start howling to each other, just think of them as prairie lawyers arguing loud with one another."

Floyd nodded and shuffled his feet back and forth. Roy became a little bolder. "Say, how you going to carry that dead foot with the moccasin still on it? You could use an old Wild West poster to wrap around it. Seems appropriate."

"Roy! You're running at the mouth," said Charlie. "Floyd will do what he thinks best."

Floyd turned to go and burped loudly.

"Control yourself better'n that," said Roy. "My God, a dead leg ain't nuthing. Let me tell you about the time I was with a bunch of them Comanches."

"Stop!" yelled Hippy Burmister. "That's my story. There's this dried flesh dropping off of the skeletons of dead Indians that are up on racks in that poplar grove in Oklahoma. The dried flesh dropped on whoever passed beneath that treetop cemetery. The smell of the oversweet resin on those sick-yellow leaves was enough to make a person puke. Don't tell someone else's story, you hear? Button your lip like Mr. Irwin told you."

Floyd left. He didn't want to hear more. His shirttail flapped where he'd shortened it by tearing off strips for the tourniquet.

Charlie put his hand on Burmister's shoulder. "That gory story of yours didn't help Floyd. Enough has happened for one night. Time to turn in."

"It's morning, Pa," said Roy.

"Don't contradict me, son. Hit the hay!"

The cars were coupled and ready to move to the main track. The engineer was gone and the Pullman car was dark when Charlie climbed the steps and went into the vestibule. He stopped at the lower berth where Dee Dee slept. He spoke quietly, "Dee Dee, Floyd'll be in a little later. He'll tell you about what happened. Don't worry, he's just fine." He waited a few seconds until he heard the small voice.

"Yes, Mr. Irwin, thanks."

Charlie slipped out of his shirt and pants and climbed into the berth in his underwear. Etta was wide awake. "What's going on?"

"Sshh," he said. "No need to wake everybody. John Red Cloud saved Floyd's life by shoving him out of the way of a switch engine that ran backward with no lights. John's leg was cut off at the calf. Floyd is over at the Indian camp now. John is with a doctor in town. He'll be all right. We'll go after him with a small wagon tomorrow. How about letting John stay in one of our beds a couple of days? I'll sleep in the daycoach with the boys, or in one of the stock cars."

Etta could not control herself. She giggled.

"There's nothing funny about what happened," growled Charlie.

"Yes, there is. Just the thought of you trying to curl up in a short, narrow, daycoach seat is funny. Listen, I'll get Roy's berth fixed for John and let Roy sleep with you. I'll sleep on the seat." She giggled again.

"Jeems, I am so proud of both John and Floyd tonight. Floyd took that dead foot to the Indians and told them how John saved his life."

"Floyd picked up a dead foot!" squealed Etta. "Oh, mercy!"

Charlie turned over with a grunt and soon began to snore.

* * *

At the end of the parade in Fort Morgan, Mary Best Britches pulled on Etta's skirt. "Get your man and come quick. Now you become Sioux, kin to us."

"You still want to do this, even after John's accident?" asked Etta.

"You bet your bottom dollar. More now. The boys shared blood and death. You will see part of John buried."

"You folks been carrying around that old dead foot?" asked Etta.

"Saving it for this important time," said Mary, grinning.

Etta shivered and felt the color drain from her cheeks.

Mary touched Etta's chilly, pale face. "Use some paint. Look nice for the occasion. The Sioux will all be looking at you."

Etta nodded and went to find Charlie. "I'm sorry. I forgot to tell you about this ceremony," she apologized.

Charlie shrugged and put on his wide-brimmed white hat and led the way to the Indians' tents. Inside a large tepee were gathered about fifty male Sioux. Outside in a semicircle were an equal number of women and children. Someone was beating a drum and several others were chanting. Charlie thought they might be behind the tepee.

Charlie and Etta were led with the sun, in a clockwise manner, to the place of honor between the fire pit and the back of the tepee. They sat cross-legged in front of a small pile of sage. "I'll never get up," whispered Charlie. Etta kept her face straightforward, looking at the knees of the Indian men. "My good suit pants will get dirty," whispered Charlie. Etta ignored him.

Little Committee, a short, dark Oglala with beaver fur braided in his hair, spread a red bandanna on the ground and thumped Charlie on the back. "You old son of a gun, how can you be a Sioux if you worry about dirt on your pants?" All the men in the tepee seemed to smile at the same time.

Etta was not sure if the men were amused or kind of put out by Charlie's complaining. No one offered to spread anything under her skirt, nor protect her silk stockings, and she was going to keep her mouth shut tight. The air in the tepee became close and she could smell the sage in front of her mixed with the smell of horses, leather, and sweat.

Little Committee lifted several stalks of the sage and passed it to the four corners of the earth, then to the heavens and back to the earth, slowly and gracefully, almost like a dance. The men were passing a long pipe, made from an animal leg bone. Sinew had been pulled around and around the bone to keep it from cracking. Etta knew the tobacco in the pipe was kinnikinnick root and the dried, crushed inner bark of the red willow. The smell was sweet when it burned. But the smoke made Etta's eyes water, and she was afraid she might disgrace herself by coughing. She held her throat tight, bowed her head, and looked at the little pile of dried sage. There was a hole or dish made in the earth under the sage. She bent forward to see better. In that shallow dish was the foot with a worn moccasin and part of a brown corduroy trouser leg covering the ankle. A shudder went through Etta as she realized it was the severed foot of John Red Cloud right there in front of her, so close she could reach out and touch it.

Suddenly a deep resonant voice said, "We bury this dead flesh. We bring in new flesh." A man threw a handful of dust into the hole. Several other men came up and let handfuls of dust sift into the hole. Charlie sneezed. The man standing in front of him glared and hissed. Etta put her handkerchief in front of her nose and continued to hold her throat tight. The man in an ancient leather tunic with bright-colored paintings on the front and back motioned for Charlie to stand.

Charlie uncrossed his legs. Then he pushed with his hands and tried to get up easily. It was hard for a man who was six feet four inches tall and weighed two hundred and seventy-five pounds to get to his feet quickly. When he was standing and the smiles on the faces of the nearby men were wiped off, someone else said, "You will be known as Cheyenne Charlie among us." He pronounced it "Shai-en-na," with an accent of long breathing on the second syllable.

The man added more dust to the shallow hole until the foot was completely covered. He picked up the remaining sage and moved aside as several men with feathers tied in their braids tamped the earth with moccasined feet. Then the earth was smoothed out with the sage so that there was no evidence that a hole had ever been dug. The man in the tunic stood in front of Etta and said, "You will be known as Okla-howlan, Good Mother." The drum beat faster and the chanting became "Ho! Ka! Hey!" The men reached out and touched each other. Etta touched Charlie's hand. The pipe was passed to Charlie. He felt the heat in the stem. He tried not to think how many others had put it to their lips. He drew in slowly and felt the smoke bite his tongue; he took one last draw and felt the smoke hit the back of his throat. He gasped, passed the pipe quickly to Etta. "What you burning in here? It tastes like goat droppings!"

Etta was stunned and embarrassed. She could feel her cheeks

burn. She kept her head down. Suddenly the pipe was snatched away from her hands. She was a woman and not important enough to seal her name to the tribe with a smoke. Moreover her name was sealed at the same time her man smoked the sacred pipe. She looked up. Little Committee said, "Cheyenne Charlie, you have good taste. Your tongue speaks true. You drew smoke from burning willow, horse dung, and marmot fur." There was an uproar of "tee-hee."

Etta smiled. Her feelings were not hurt in the least when the pipe was passed over her head and around to the rest of the men.

The men parted so that Charlie and Etta could move with the sun, clockwise, to the open tepee flap. Outside the women were chattering like bluejays. They held out white, graniteware cups from Charlie's cook tent. "Hot coffee with sugar," said Mary Best Britches, grinning at Etta, "Okla-howlan. *Okla* means people or person. *How* means good, fine, honorable. *Lan* means here, now. Your name is Nice Person Here, Good Mother."

Etta smiled. She breathed the fresh air and felt fine. "Thank you. Thank all of you. I am happy to be in your family."

"Where's John?" asked Charlie. "I saw him on crutches this morning."

"He's having his uncle make a leg from the trunk of a small tree. His uncle will rub the tree with grease and wax until it feels like human skin," said Charles Yellow Boy, who wore a forehead band made from kit-fox jawbones.

"Didn't he come to my naming ceremony?" Charlie sounded disappointed.

"He was first to smoke the pipe, his uncle next," said Yellow Boy. "He said you'd make a leather contraption to hold the new wooden leg on if we told you about it."

Charlie was impressed with the way that he was told to invent some kind of fastening for the wooden peg leg. He put his arm across Yellow Boy's shoulder. "My mind tells me that John is going to have a new name. I'm going to call him Peg Leg."

"Ho! Ka! Hey!" sang Yellow Boy. "Cheyenne Charlie one fine man."

Charlie drank two cups of coffee and said he hoped that the regular cook brewed it because he would not trust a Sioux with such a hot, black concoction. "You people would have frog legs and lizard eyes in it for sure!"

Yellow Boy pounded Charlie on the back and ran off to tell his friends what Charlie had said about the women's cooking.

"In the old days a naming ceremony would mean a big feast

afterward," said a Sioux dressed like any other cowboy in a red flannel shirt, blue Levi's, boots with heels, and a brown felt, wide-brimmed hat.

Charlie knew that he was apologizing in his way for not having biscuits and meat to go with the coffee.

"For supper tonight, after the big show, we'll have beef stew and raisin pie to celebrate this naming business," said Charlie. "I'm not sure where the cook can get a cow, but I'll find a meat man that has just butchered one somewhere around town."

"Cheyenne Charlie's looking for a slow elk," the man called out, and there was more chattering and twittering in the crowd. Charlie had shown his appreciation of being made one of them because he was going to supply the feast himself, like the old days.

The last stop that summer was in Sheridan, Wyoming, for their annual Stampede. Pauline begged to enter the women's relay race. "Please, Pa! It'll be my last race before the baby comes. Nothing'll happen. I swear, no one will know. I'm not that big yet!"

Charlie put his arm around his middle daughter, nearly seventeen, finished with high school, and one of the best lady relay racers in the country. "I won't let anything happen to you. If I thought it was safe I'd let you go. I know what you're going to say, that nowadays the girls don't change saddles, only horses. But you'd have to run, grab the horn on a new saddle, get that horse racing as fast as you could, have him flying, then slow down some, climb off, and run to grab another horn. It's hard work, think how we'd feel if you fell or tripped."

"But that's where skill comes in. I won't fall or trip."

"The three Irwin girls in the relay will be your cousin, Gladys, and your sisters, Joella and Frances. Did you know that Lucille Mulhall will be in the race?"

"Oh, Pa, now I know I gotta race. We have to show her the Irwin girls are best. She's tough to beat. I heard she took second in a steer-roping in Garden City, Kansas, twenty-nine seconds!"

"You didn't hear all of it. She set a world's record in Winnipeg. Roped and tied a steer in twenty-three and three quarters seconds. That's a champion. So, the Irwin girls have to be in top form. No one seven months pregnant is going to run in our relay."

"Pa, I'd better talk with the girls. Be sure to let them use the fastest horses we have. Every little thing will help. Have you heard anything about the speed of the Mulhall horses?"

"Only that they have some top trick horses and a couple of good buckers for the bronco contest. I don't know about their racehorses, but consider them the best."

"We've always won in the women's relay. We have to keep up our reputation," said Pauline.

"Then talk to the three girls, watch them work out. Give them your ideas. Criticize when they aren't doing right."

Pauline told the girls that they would have to make every second count. There was a rumor that Lucille Mulhall was going to use local thoroughbred colts that were young and fast. The Irwin girls practiced changing horses, becoming firmly seated in half a second, so that the cowboys who held the horses would let go fast.

The afternoon of the race everyone was keyed up. "What if I can't get pulled up on my horse quick enough?" said Frances with a sigh.

"You have to. Don't even think any other way!" shouted Pauline. "Being your trainer is more nerve-wracking than if I were going out there to ride!"

The grandstand was packed. People from all over wanted to see the World's Champion Lady Steer Roper riding local colts.

Gladys, Joella, and Frances came out in red satin shirts, with the white Y6 stitched on the back, and white jodhpur britches, not skirts as was usual for women riders. The Irwin horses stood quiet, their coats brushed to a sleek shininess. An astute observer would notice that their feet were never still. These Irwin horses were used to running. The starting gun went off. The four girls ran their horses close together. They dismounted in front of the grandstand after going once around the track. There was some juggling and hurrying as each girl dismounted and ran to the next horse, grabbed the horn, pulled herself into the saddle, and was off again. Lucille was in the lead. She'd grabbed the horn and started her horse running before she was fully seated. By the time they were again in front of the grandstand, the Irwin girls had caught up with Lucille, her hair flying. She wore a skirt, not jodhpurs, that billowed.

The crowd cheered. Charlie and Pauline had their arms around each other. Etta bit her lip. The Mulhall girl left a second time ahead of the Irwin girls, and the third time she was way out front on a young colt that was as fast as any in the Irwin string. The horse was not only fast, but nervous, and the handler had some problems keeping him in place so that Lucille could grab the saddle horn firmly. She swung from her second horse and ran for this restless one. The Irwin girls came in and dismounted, ran to their third horses.

The crowd yelled and roared with excitement.

Lucille grabbed the horn, the horse began to run. Her body was not seated in the saddle, the wind blew through her skirt and maybe spooked the horse. She did not have a firm grip on the horn and consequently did not have full control over the horse. There was a marking post on the side of the track every sixteenth of a mile. As Lucille went past the third marking post, she was too close to the inside and her knee hit the post. One hand went to the mane of the horse and she clung for dear life.

The Irwin girls saw there was something wrong with the way Lucille was riding her horse. It was running without control. Charlie and Pauline had both seen Lucille's knee between the side of the horse and the marking post and guessed that she'd scraped hard. Lucille was a game performer and hung on. Her head stayed down close to the horse's head. She won the race by the length of her horse. But the horse did not stop. It took half a stretch to catch him and let Lucille know she'd won. The minute she was pulled from the horse, she fainted.

Joella placed second and Gladys was third. Frances was more worried about Lucille than she was about coming in last. "Let's see what happened!"

The Mulhall handlers would not let the three girls near where Lucille lay stretched out on a grandstand seat. One of the handlers told Frances that Lucille's kneecap was out of place and crushed. Frances could see Lucille's face was pale, and she guessed she wouldn't want to talk anyway. The girls waited until the handlers carried Lucille off the track and stood with the crowd, cheering.

Charlie rode out to the center field on horseback and sang into a megaphone, "For She's a Jolly Good Trouper."

Later Pauline gave some advice to the three girls. "No matter how much you want to win, never take shortcuts. Follow the rules, don't take wild chances. Sure, Lucille Mulhall won, but she paid a terrible price to show she was better than the Irwin girls."

Charlie sent a telegram to Lucille's father, Colonel Zach Mulhall, saying what a courageous daughter he had and the whole Irwin family hoped for her speedy recovery.

* * *

Before the Frontier Days celebration Charlie settled Etta, Joella, and Frances temporarily in the top of the new garage in town. Everyone else went to the ranch. Charlie was ready to have plans drawn for Etta's new house. The old white house had been taken down, board by board, the ground smoothed so one could not tell exactly where it had stood.

The quartermaster at Fort D. A. Russell told Charlie that some of the cavalry horses the Army bought would be sent to the U.S. troops on the Mexican border. "Wouldn't surprise me if we'd start sending horses overseas. The state of Wyoming sent flour to the Belgians when the Germans nearly took over their country last year. So horses could be sent next. Not many people worrying that Austria declared war on Serbia, but mark my words, if the British get involved in any way, the United States will be dragged into a European war."

"You talking about the Germans sinking the *Lusitania*?" asked Charlie. "That's going to drag American bankers into a lending program for England and France. We're a peaceable nation and enjoying a rise in prosperity at present. The English can take care of the Germans. I believe Henry Ford has the right idea; send a peace ship to Norway to negotiate an end to the European scrap."

"You're far too optimistic, C.B. Keep bringing in horses; the U.S. Cavalry will be prepared," said the quartermaster.

Charlie intended to bring in to the U.S. Army Remount as many wild horses as he could; the money was good. Suddenly he decided to put in a Delco power unit in the basement of the ranch house and string in the electrical wiring. "I could have electric lights in the barn during the evening milking." The money in Charlie's pocket was not half enough for a Delco generator. But that didn't stop Charlie. He decided he'd borrow the money and pay it back each time he brought in more horses for the U.S. Army Remount.

The first Monday morning in July was warm. The lawns in Cheyenne were green, as homeowners watered each evening. Cicadas strummed in the trees. Chipmunks lived in woodpiles or under porches and scurried in the yards foraging food. Red squirrels raced in the high branches of maple trees and chattered fiercely when Charlie walked under the trees. They seemed to be scolding him with a long-drawn-out churring. He imagined he'd react the same if someone invaded his property and grinned approvingly at the squirrels' chiding bravado.

Charlie had in his shirt pocket a piece of paper with the exact amount of money he wanted to borrow from the Stock Growers National Bank. When he stepped inside the bank, the first thing he heard was the whirring of the high ceiling fans. Charlie went to a teller and asked to see Charlie Hirsig. He was taken to an office with another ceiling fan and told to sit beside the desk. In a few moments his old friend Hirsig came in wearing a black suit and starched white shirt. Hirsig's face was red.

"If you just unbutton that top collar button you could breath easier," suggested Charlie. He leaned over the desk. "I've been a customer of this bank for a dozen years at least. Now I want to expand my ranch, and I need some cash."

"In other words, C.B., the Wild West show is not doing terribly well since I'm no longer there to keep you out of trouble. You're not as liquid as you would like to be."

Charlie squirmed, bit his tongue, and said, "I want to borrow about three thousand dollars."

"What will you use for collateral?" Hirsig sat up straight, giving an air of great dignity. "Stocks—bonds?"

"How about cattle?"

"Mmm—C.B., you realize each head must be counted and tabulated. And if you default on your loan the bank will sell your cattle and retain the proceeds."

"Certainly, I understand that. If you come to count my cattle, wear something else."

Hirsig looked at Charlie in such a way that Charlie wondered if his friend had any other clothes. "Hirsig, I'm sorry, when you get out to the ranch, I'll find something for you to wear. Floyd's about your size. I guess you spend so much time in the bank, you don't have time to go out on horseback and just look at the sky."

Hirsig's face turned a shade redder. "An officer of the bank does not make small property assessments. One of our bright young tellers will look over your stock. He will charge you for his time and automobile gasoline."

"I might have him do a little work for me to make up the charge. And if he does a good job, I might ask him to stay and enjoy supper at my place."

Hirsig swallowed and that seemed to cause his eyes to pop out a little.

Charlie stood up, shook Hirsig's hand, and then removed his own tie and undid the top button on his shirt. "Aahh—I feel so much better," he breathed. "I can talk decently now."

"Tomorrow, at noon, Mr. Ruben Carey will look over your cattle. You realize that you need a couple thousand head to borrow three thousand dollars."

"That's no problem," said Charlie. However, in his own mind he could see there were only about a thousand head at the ranch. "Send your man out, I'll be happy to oblige."

"Good day, then, C.B.," said Hirsig, doing his best to remain calm and formal with Charlie.

The next day at noon Charlie met the young man, Ruben Carey, coming up the road to the ranch house. A cloud of dust rolled out behind his Model T Ford and spread across the field in front of the ranch house. Carey said he was no relation to Wyoming's Governor Joseph M. Carey. "Then," said Charlie, "I can tell you what our Federal District Judge T. Blake Kennedy said about our governor. 'He's possessed of a peculiarly vindictive disposition and temperament oft-time akin to a schoolgirl.' So you see why I asked if you were related. I don't relish working with anyone who might have inherited a vindictive nature."

The young man was about five years older than Floyd and must have taken Hirsig's advice because he came in fresh, stiff Levi's, a red flannel shirt, and pointy-toed boots.

"You like to ride a horse out to the pasture to see my Herefords?" asked Charlie, knowing full well most of the cattle belonged to his brother, Will.

"If you show me where to go, we could drive in my car," said Carey, looking around to see if there was a road of any sort that led to some pasture nearby.

"Well," Charlie said with a chuckle, "tell you what. I'll take you out in my old pickup truck. Save your car from going over the rocks. If you see any cows along the way, you count them first."

Carey stepped onto the running board and got into the pickup's seat next to Charlie. Charlie grinned and started the motor. Then he pulled away from the side of the house so fast a mass of dust rolled across the top of the pickup and settled into every crack and crevice. Charlie felt the grittiness between his teeth. He drove down a narrow, two-rutted dirt road, making hairpin turns around little sandhills. He hung his left hand out the side of the car and pounded a drum beat on the side of the pickup. The pickup sprayed so much dirt and sand that Carey could not have seen a cow unless it stood directly in front of the pickup.

Charlie headed for the top of a gentle rise close to Round Top. When he stopped he pointed close to Round Top, where some of his cowboys had rounded up a bunch of cattle. Carey slapped some of the dust from his clothing and, with a red bandanna that matched his shirt, wiped off his dull, chalky-looking boots. He then took a pencil and notepad from his shirt pocket, wet the end of the pencil in his mouth, and poised it above the pad ready to write the number of cattle he was counting. Finally he said, "Could the men spread the cattle out a little, Mr. Irwin? They're hard to count when they're bunched up."

"Sure thing," said Charlie taking off his hat, dusting it off, redoing the crease in the crown, waving to the cowboys below, and wiping his face with his handkerchief.

The cowboys strung out the cattle and waited for Charlie's next signal.

"That's only eleven hundred and twenty head, Mr. Irwin. Didn't Mr. Hirsig tell you there was to be at least two thousand head in order to secure a loan for three thousand dollars?"

"Of course he did. He's a proper businessman, same as you." Charlie took a couple of hammers and some nails from the back of the pickup. He waved them in the air. "This won't take long," he said. "Give me a hand here with this fence. The boys are so busy with the cattle they don't have time to keep the rails on tight. That's it, hold the top rail steady. Put the nail right there so it goes into the post. Hit hard. I'll get this one over here. When you get finished, give me the high sign and we'll head on up to the upper ranch."

The cowboys below waved their hats and took off down the other side of the rise. When they were out of sight, they cut out those steers that were most easily recognizable and then drove the main bunch around to the upper ranch, where three, four other hands were waiting to help with the counting.

Carey wiped the perspiration from his face and hollered, "I've used up all my nails, Mr. Irwin! The section looks pretty strong to me!"

They put the tools in the back of the pickup, and Charlie drove over little hills, down into a couple small sandy washes, and finally came out to another good pastureland. There, directly in front of the pickup, was a large herd of steers milling around waiting to be tallied in Carey's notebook.

"There's nine hundred even in this group," said Carey. "Mr. Irwin, you qualify for your loan."

Back at the ranch Charlie and Carey brushed out more dust, washed their hands and faces at the water pump, and went inside to the dining room, where the cowboys were already seated at the table. Carey had never seen so much food in his life. It tasted delicious.

"Have another piece of apple cobbler," insisted Charlie after the cowboys left for the bunkhouse and evening chores, "and tell me more about your work at the bank. You like that indoor work, huh?"

"Well—" started Carey.

"Well," said Charlie, "if you ever want more fun, come on out to my ranch. I'll put you to work, then we'll have another big feed like this. Out here there's plenty of things to do, real work for a man. You can work for Mr. Hirsig during the week, but on weekends come on out here. You'll never regret it. Why, in a couple weekends you'll be riding horseback all the way out to Round Top and back. Some hill, huh? Notice how it makes a person feel good just to look at it?"

Carey never did realize that he'd counted the same bunch of cattle twice. Every once in a while he did go out to the ranch and help Charlie with fence mending and widening irrigation ditches, and each time he thought the food was the best he'd ever had.

Without telling Etta, Charlie used the loan and bought a couple new racing horses, paid for the Delco, put a new roof on the barn, and paid Frank's and Will's gambling debts. Then his conscience troubled him when he couldn't pay the architect for the plans for her new house. He wanted only the best for Etta, who was his leveling force. Charlie knew he'd get the money to pay the architect and pay back the loan as soon as the Frontier Days celebration was over. Suddenly he wanted to buy something for Etta. Something nice. Real pearl earrings. She'd be really surprised.

Charlie went back to the Stock Growers National Bank and asked to see Charlie Hirsig.

"C.B.! You come in to pay up on your loan?" Hirsig was still red in the face and his collar button was still fastened tight under his bow tie.

"No, I've come back to borrow a small sum. I need it to buy Etta a birthday gift. You know how it is with women. They like you to remember birthdays and anniversaries. It means a lot to them. You know Etta. She's the best."

"How much are you seeking?"

"Only two hundred dollars. You can send that smart young man, Ruben Carey, out to the ranch. He might assess the barn or some of the outbuildings."

"C.B., I'm doing this for Etta," said Hirsig, never cracking his face with a smile. "I'll send Carey. He's our finest assessor. Can't fool him."

Two days later Ruben Carey was at the ranch. He had his pencil and notepad out. He moistened the pencil in his mouth and looked at the barn, the blacksmith shop, and bunkhouse.

"Mr. Irwin, this is all much more valuable than the two hundred dollars that you wish to borrow. There must be something else that is worth only two hundred dollars." He was looking at the hay filling the barn's loft.

"All right, how about hay?" asked Charlie. "Come on out here and take a look." Charlie took him in the pickup, past the big irrigation ditch, and down the road to the big pasture that was split by Horse Creek. Charlie waved his hand at the hay that was stacked in neat piles on both sides of Horse Creek. "That's a lot of hay there. Couldn't fit it all in the barn. You can see that."

Carey wet his pencil and began to count the haystacks on this side of the creek and then up and down the draw on the other side of the creek.

Charlie neglected to tell Carey that only the hay on this side of Horse Creek belonged to him. All the hay on the other side was on the Coad Draw and belonged to John Coad.

Carey made four marks and crossed them to make a group of five. He did this a couple dozen times, then cleared his throat and said, "I think this ought to cover your loan, Mr. Irwin. I'll make out the papers, and next time you're in town you can have a check for two hundred dollars."

Charlie grinned and asked Carey how'd he like to go fishing. They spent the rest of the afternoon catching fish for the evening's supper. "Say, you going to charge me for looking at the hay and for the gasoline you used coming out here?" Charlie asked Carey at suppertime.

"Naw, I couldn't do that to you, Mr. Irwin. I always have such a good time out here, and you have the best grub in the state. I'd just rather be on a more friendly basis rather than strictly business."

THIRTY-SIX

General John Pershing

The day was bright hot. Charlie was on the roof of the ranch house laying down tar paper and new shingles. Frank was peeling off the curled, sun-cured cedar pieces, throwing them down to the grass below like dry, gray scales. Etta was in the house making lemonade. Clara Belle sorted out baby garments. Her girls, Maxine and Louise, played with their dolls on the screened-in back porch.

"Pauline, I can't give you all the baby clothes I have," said Clara Belle. "I've a confession. I'm going to have a baby of my own the end of October."

"And you never said a word," said Pauline. "I should have guessed. You haven't been riding horseback in an age."

"Mercy, babies are going to be popular this year," said Etta.

"I wouldn't mind another girl, but Frank wants a boy," said Clara Belle.

Frank wanted off the hot roof. He thought about the women inside, where it was cool. "Say, Charlie, you think I can go down and cool off? I'm about to drown in my own sweat."

"Frank, stay here. We'll be finished with this whole side in a little while, then we'll both go down and get something to drink," said Charlie, shifting the nails he held in his mouth so that he could talk.

"I could use a drink. I'm drier than a wooden leg. I'm drier than these sunbaked old shingles. Say, how much it cost you to build that seventy by thirty foot, two-story, three-car garage monstrosity in town?"

"About twelve thousand dollars, after I put in a bathroom, kitchen, bedroom, and living room upstairs. You know Etta has to live there until I can save enough to build a red brick house like she wants." Charlie sighed, put his hands against his back, and straightened up for a moment. "To get what you want isn't cheap anymore."

"I should say not!" Frank whistled, rolled his eyes heavenward. "That's the biggest hip-roofed, part-garage, part-barn ever built in Cheyenne. What's Etta say, you spending all that money?"

"She doesn't say anything. I used some of her new-house money and borrowed the rest. When she asked for a bathroom on the second floor"—he shrugged—"I got her a bathroom. Jeems, I hope to god she doesn't expect me to build the brick house this summer. I figure if I put it off, I'll get a couple of the loans paid and the nest egg back in savings by spring. Frank, don't go saying anything to Clara Belle. You know women. They'll start yapping and someone will spill the beans about me spending house money on a barn or new roof. Etta'll raise Cain."

"Huhuh. Charlie, does she know you bought those racehorses?" Frank shook his hammer toward Charlie.

"Yep. I had to tell Etta about them. But, hey, I bought her genuine pearl earrings to kind of ease the deal. She saw that I got something, but I got her something. She went hog-wild over the earrings. Women sure like to look pretty. Hey, you ought to get something special for Clara Belle."

"Wouldn't hurt if I got off this goddamned roof. I'm sweating like a racehorse," said Frank. "Charlie, I could black out, fall twelve feet to the ground, and bust my head clean open."

"Then you'd have a headache and feel like that poor kid, Charley Johnson."

"Hey, that's not fair to bring him into this conversation," whined Frank.

"I meant to bring him in," said Charlie. "Frank, I want Johnson to try the hot mineral springs in Saratoga, you know, on the North Platte. How about you donating seventy-five dollars? I'll match it and send him for two weeks."

"Hell, Charlie, I can't give away money without asking Clara Belle." Frank's mouth twitched and his eyes became round and beady. He hunted around for a nail that had slipped between tar paper and shingles. Charlie was reminded of a ferret.

"Don't you feel the least little bit of responsibility toward Johnson's condition?"

"Let's get off this hot roof before I'm fried crisp," said Frank, blowing on his hands to cool the palms. "This tar paper's like the top of a cookstove."

"You promise to match my seventy-five dollars?" said Charlie with a grin.

"Why, you—you dirty jackass! Where's the goddamned ladder?" Frank looked over the side of the house.

Charlie cupped his hands and hollered, "Floyd! Oh, Floyd! Set that danged ladder up against this side of the house! Must have slid into your ma's flowerbed."

Floyd came out of the barn running, put up the ladder, said, "Criminantly, you don't have to work in this heat!" and went back to the barn.

Frank went into the house and in a few minutes came back with two glasses of iced lemonade. Charlie sat next to Frank on a bench under the cottonwood tree. Frank set his glass down and reached into his pocket. He gave Charlie a roll of greenbacks.

Charlie counted the paper money, put it in his wallet, and said, "I hear it's nice in Saratoga. Minerals from a hot-water spring made a hard rim around one of the bathing places, so it's like a huge bowl. Indians call it a Devil's punchbowl. It's in a kind of park with cedars, spruce, some paintbrush, and wild columbine. Buffalo and elk graze there."

"Well, what I heard was that Injuns come in wagons and on ponies and camp for days, swimming in that hot stinking water or lying around on sulfurous mud banks. Christ, if Johnson enjoys bathing with Injuns, he can have it."

"Frank, how about you and me going after some more wild broncs? We can sell them to the Army at Fort D. A. Russell. Won't cost us a thing, only men to break them," said Charlie.

"When the weather changes. I hate to work in this heat." He wiped his face. "Say, Charlie, there's something I've been meaning to ask. What do you know about that first lieutenant Joella's been seen with?"

Charlie was caught off guard. He had no idea Joella was seeing anyone, especially one of those Army men from Fort Russell. He took out his bandanna and wiped the perspiration from his face.

Frank's eyes were squeezed down so that they were small, shiny black slits. Those narrow slits looked like hard obsidian after a rain. Charlie noticed that Frank's nose was thin and pointed, like a rat's. Frank opened his mouth, and it reminded Charlie of a black pit rimmed with glowing embers. "I've seen her exercising the horses up and down Pioneer. He's in his first lieutenant's uniform riding beside her."

"Frank, Joella's nineteen, good-looking. Why wouldn't young men be interested?"

"This one grins like a jackass eating cactus."

"What do you mean by that crack?" Charlie suddenly wondered if he weren't oversensitive about Joella being seen with a young man.

"That oldest girl of yours drives men crackle-brained. Her flirting reminds me of your sister, Ell."

"Ell is your sister, too, Frank."

"I don't think of her that way anymore," said Frank, with a churlishness. "When she comes to town, she stays at your place. She visits mine."

"You're the cracked one," said Charlie. "There's more room at my place." Then he thought of Joella resembling Ell. They both had a special faraway look and an aromatic fragrance that was both fascinating and intriguing to men. Charlie couldn't explain what happened, but when either woman talked to a man, be he young, old, handsome, or unattractive, she made him feel as if he were the most important person on the map. Charlie promised himself he'd ask Joella about this Army fellow if he heard any other rumors.

Several days later Charlie had finished roofing the ranch house and was back in Cheyenne with his family for Frontier Days. New rules were set down this year by Charlie's' committeemen working with the Humane Society so that (1) no shoulder nor other unnecessary spurring was allowed in horse races or bronc contests, and the saddle had to be "slick" saddle, with no more than a fifteen-inch swell; (2) bulldoggers were given three minutes to down a steer; (3) steer ropers had to catch the steer by the horns, never include a foot in the loop. They could have two trials, but each no longer than ninety seconds; (4) ladies' relay horses had to be saddled by a male attendant; and (5) there were separate judges for arena events and track events.

Charlie arranged for six special trains to come in from Denver, including a trainload of Shriners to stop off, who were headed to their convention on the West Coast, and a special train for businessmen from Omaha to visit the Cheyenne celebration and swell the crowd of thousands.

Charlie's outlaw horse Yellow Fever became an instant star when no cowboy could ride him during the three days of the show. The *Cheyenne Tribune* reported, "Yellow Fever—what a name—how suggestive of dread disaster—what a horse—legitimate successor to Old Steamboat—dread destroyer of riding reputations—"*

Joella won the ladies' relay race and received a standing ovation, special music from the Ninth Cavalry band, a purse of five hundred dollars, and a two-hundred-and-fifty-dollar saddle.

On the final night the Sioux staged a mock warpath, with feathers, paint, whoops, and decorated ponies. They waved tomahawks and stirred up dust from Frontier Park to the town's business section. They *kiyi*ed and danced on foot and horseback. Some went through hotel lobbies, others through the crowds in the streets, causing wild disorder.

Joella asked her father if she and a friend, Lieutenant Jones, could take the old Deadwood Cheyenne stagecoach and the four-horse team out to bring in all the cavorting Sioux that were on foot. "We'll bring them back to the tepee camp."

"You and a friend want to bring those rascals back here?" Charlie couldn't believe his ears. That could be a job rounding up nearly four dozen frolicking red men. It had to be done before any trouble erupted and the local police or a couple men from the Burns Detective Agency, that also patrolled Cheyenne's streets, took them to jail for disorderly conduct. Or Charlie would be socked with the fine.

"Yes, I want to take Lieutenant Deeke Jones so that he can feel and smell the flavor of our celebration. Pa, you'd like him." Joella held her head to one side. Her eyes sparkled.

"Bring the young man over to the cookhouse," said Charlie.

She came back with a clean-cut, dark-haired young man, in Army uniform. Lieutenant Jones reached out to shake Charlie's hand.

"Can you drive a team of horses attached to a stagecoach that's full of brawling Indians?" asked Charlie.

"Yes, sir, I believe so," answered Jones, crisp and clear. "Jo and I are going to get ice-cream cones for all the Indians who will

*Courtesy Charles M. Bennett Collection, Scottsdale, Arizona.

come with us. We'd be glad to have you and Mrs. Irwin come along, sir."

"It's pandemonium in town!" said Charlie, laughing. "A man would be foolish to take his wife. But if you think you can handle my daughter, four horses, and a whooping bunch of Indians, more power to you." Charlie handed Jones a pair of leather gloves. "Keep your hands from blistering."

Joella had her mother's arm and they went outside the cookhouse. "Ma, I want a home wedding. I'll make my own dress."

Etta's hand flew to her mouth. Slowly she removed it and said, "You want to marry the Army lieutenant?"

"Yes, more than anything."

"You hardly know him."

"Ma, he's taken me for dinner two, three times, when you've all been at the ranch, and I had to stay in town to work in Pa's office. Pa's giving Deeke his gloves. He's going to be hitching up the team in a minute. That's a sure sign Pa approves."

"I need time to think—get used to the idea," said Etta.

"Oh, Ma, you're a doll," said Joella.

Lieutenant Deeke Jones spent a month's pay on ice-cream cones, but the Indians were back in their tepees before the police or detective agency had a chance to arrest a one. Charlie told Etta that Joella's young man had won his approval.

The next few days went so fast there was no time for Etta to think. Clara Belle sprung a surprise wedding shower for Joella on Monday. Tuesday Charlie and Frank brought in fifty head of barely broken wild broncs and sold them to the Army Remount at Fort Russell. Charlie went straight downtown to the real estate office. He put his money on the counter, saying he wanted to buy the vacant brick house on the corner of Twenty-eighth and Pioneer. This red brick had a sun-porch he liked.

Before Cheyenne Days, Etta told Charlie that the red brick on the corner, across the street from her old, torn-down house, was exactly like the one she'd always dreamed about. She hoped the plans he was having made were like that.

"There are no plans," admitted Charlie. "I spent the house money fixing up the ranch. All I have is money from selling the wild broncs."

"I guessed as much," said Etta sadly. Then her mouth turned up into a smile and her eyes shone. "The red brick across the street is a sign then."

"What kind of sign is an empty house?" asked Charlie, relieved that Etta didn't go into a tirade about his spending her house money.

"A sign that we can live there. The big barn can be used for barn and garage and bunkhouse. You can put up a couple corrals where you took the house down. Joella wants to be married at home. What do you think?" She was breathless waiting for his answer.

He cleared his throat and reasoned that it was far better economically to buy a house already built than to build a new one. "I think Joella's young man is all right. She'll marry him no matter what we say. So, I say let's have them marry in our red brick house at 402 West Twenty-eighth."

Joella and First Lieutenant Deeke Jones were married on Thursday, July 29, 1915.

After the ceremony Charlie caught Jones looking at Joella with his calflike brown eyes. It was more adoration than Charlie could take. He went to Etta, who was smiling, wiping her eyes, saying to Dee Dee and Pauline that she was not in any way sad—her tears were of happiness for Joella. However, if she'd been completely truthful, she'd have admitted she was fearful Lieutenant Jones was going to take Joella away from Cheyenne.

Joella was the most beautiful bride Etta had seen. She wore a wide-brimmed white lace hat with a long, pink satin streamer down the back of her long golden hair. Her dress was white with a pink yoke, marquisette. It had a short train and was tucked in at the waist. She and Pauline had worked day and night on the dress while Etta and Frances moved furniture from the second story of the barn to the red brick house.

At the reception the dining table was laid out with smoked turkey, ham, jellies, dainty slices of bread, sweet butter, cookies, wedding cake, tea, and coffee. Etta made certain that the round-faced, blond Methodist minister, who'd performed the wedding ceremony, was served first.

Ell, who'd surprised the family by coming in on the Thursday morning train, looked almost like a bride herself in a long lavender satin dress. She tucked a stray strawberry-blond curl into the group of curls over her left ear and discreetly offered the Reverend some Irish whiskey from a small bottle in her large purse, for his coffee. The Reverend smiled appreciatively and winked slyly, holding out his cup. Soon he was laughing at Charlie's ranching stories.

Dee Dee whispered to Ell. "Let me try some of that medicine

in my coffee." Ell, looking like the cat who'd swallowed the canary, poured a nip into Dee Dee's cup. It was not long before Dee Dee lined up all the straight-backed chairs, took off her shoes, hitched up her long, pink silk dress, and walked across the backs of the chairs as gracefully as if they were laid end to end on solid flooring. Not a single chair tipped or jiggled. Dee Dee's cheeks were flushed and she smiled. Everyone clapped at her sporting agility and urged her to try it again.

Instantly Charlie saw Joella's mouth turn down into a tiny pout. He put his arm around her and said loudly to Pauline, "Honey, play a couple waltzes on the piano. I'm going to have the first dance with the bride."

Pauline was glad to sit at the piano. Joella was all smiles. She gave her father a kiss when he took her into his arms. They danced lightly all around the dining room, into the living room, and back. Then others were dancing. Charlie put Joella into the arms of her adoring husband. "She's all yours, son. Take good care."

"Yes, sir, Mr. Irwin, always. Ah, even if I'm transferred out to California," said Lieutenant Deeke Jones.

Three weeks later Etta sent another wire to Ell in Colorado Springs. "Pauline due any time. Come, if possible."

Ell came in time to deliver Pauline's baby girl, Etta Elizabeth, on August twenty-fourth.

When the baby was born, Charlie and Johnson were on the road with the Wild West show. They didn't know if the baby was a boy or a girl. Etta's wire to Charlie in Red Bluff, California, read PAULINE AND BABY DOING FINE.

Three days after baby Betts's birth, Ell said to Pauline, "Your child has such a good set of lungs, she'll be known as Cheyenne's town crier. You'd better nurse her. Put something in her mouth!"

Pauline sat up in the bed and took the squalling flannel bundle. She rocked as she nursed the baby. "Aunt Ell, you're sure she'll get enough milk today? Maybe we ought to use a bottle."

"Your milk ought to be coming on good by now," said Ell.

"Oooo—I know—it hurts."

"Pauline—relax, honey. Nursing is something a woman is supposed to enjoy, like sex."

"Is Pa taking Charley to Saratoga as soon as they come back from California?"

"No, he'll come to see your baby first. I bet he can't wait. His first grandchild."

"Charley's anxious to see her, too," said Pauline. "Pa will bring him to town, won't he?"

"Of course. Your father understands how you feel. That man has more kindness in his little finger than most have in both arms," said Ell.

"Ya, but he sure yells sometimes."

"Well, he knows what's right and fair. He thinks everyone else does also, so he yells when people disappoint him."

The baby had fallen asleep, her tiny pink fingers curled into little balls. Pauline held the baby over her shoulder and patted her gently. "I'm glad she's a girl. Pa wanted a grandson. I hope he's not disappointed!"

"When he sees her he'll change his mind. He has a boy he adores," said Ell. "He has Floyd."

"Two," corrected Pauline. "There's Roy. That kid adores Pa. He wanted to be an Irwin more than anything."

"Sad, sad," said Ell, almost to herself. "That boy is going down Floyd's path."

"That's true. Roy acts like Floyd on purpose. When you see them together, they walk alike. Pa loves those two guys." Pauline sighed. "Aunt Ell, I try to love my guy." She laid the baby in her lap and fastened the top of her nightgown.

"Kind of rough living with a man who ignores you, huh?" Ell brought a chair up close to the bed and sat down.

Tears welled up in Pauline's eyes. "You can't know how lonely it is when your man acts like you aren't around. Charley used to be so wonderful. We wanted to be together all the time. I couldn't keep my hands off him. But since the accident he doesn't hardly talk. He mostly snaps. Flies off the handle if things don't go his way."

"I do know what you mean. Wilbert's the same. Why, I got a letter yesterday, and he said I should come back to Colorado Springs because he misses me."

"Wilbert? Misses you?"

"Well, you've never met him. He's one of Les's cousins. He came to my spa two months ago. Wants me to run off to California with him. He's blond and long-legged, about like that preacher that married Joella and Deeke." She closed her eyes and ran her hands across her breasts and up and down her sides. "That man knows how to take care of a woman." She opened her eyes and smiled. Then she took the hairpins from her reddish-blond hair, combed, rebraided, and wound it in a halo around her head, pinning the ends securely.

"You might have brought Wilbert with you," said Pauline.

"Then you'd see your father have a fit and step in it."

"What about Les? What would he do?"

"Well, he wouldn't put it in the papers. He and I have an understanding. He takes care of me and his accounting business. He comes to see me once a month, does my books, and banking. I cook his favorite supper, hash browns, fried chicken, biscuits, honey, and strong coffee. We talk over old times and the present. We have a couple of laughs. He never criticizes, but he advises well. Hell—why am I beating around the bush? You're old enough to know we haven't slept together for years—not since he had mumps. We have a great respect for each other, if not much else."

Pauline's eyes were glassy and wide open; so was her mouth. "Ma never told me all that."

"Why should she? You had no need to know."

"But knowing sure explains a lot." Pauline patted the baby's head gently, fingering the fine hair. She hesitated, then said, "I want to tell you something. I don't like Charley to come near me. He used to be clean—like, take a bath every night. Now he doesn't go near water. He smells like a buck Indian in a sweat bath. He used to drink coffee with cream and sugar, now it's black. He used to ride a horse with some control, now he rides like wicked fury. He's impatient. If I don't answer some question right away, he ignores me the rest of the day. Sometimes I catch him staring at me like I was some kind of sideshow."

"What are you going to do if he doesn't get better?"

Pauline looked at the baby and the tears spilled over and ran down her cheeks. "I try hard not to think about that."

"There are some times when a woman does not have to stay married," Ell said gently.

"Aunt Ell!" Pauline cried. "A wife has to stand by her husband, no matter what! Marriage vows are to be respected! You respected yours!"

"Does Charley ever get so angry that he—uh—roughs you up?"

"You mean beat me? Yes. Once he yelled and came at me with a pitchfork when I asked him to put on a clean shirt. Another time he told me to take my clothes off. We were in the barn. He told me to piss in his pocket. I ran to the ranch house. That night he pounded on me."

"A wife doesn't have to take that stuff. You loved the other Charley. Do you love this Charley?"

"I'm so confused, because both Charleys look the same. Good God! He's so handsome. But now his actions are vile. I hate his actions."

"If Joella moved to California, you'll be your pa's secretary?" asked Ell.

"How'd you know? I'd love to work in Pa's office. Ma would take care of Betts."

The next day Ell went back to Colorado Springs.

Johnson wasn't much impressed with his first short visit with his daughter. He said to Pauline, "All babies look alike to me, kind of red and squirmy. If her looks improve, let me know."

Charlie was pleased with the baby. He said he thought she'd be as good a horsewoman as her mother. He was glad that Pauline had given her daughter the name, Etta Elizabeth.

Charlie came in from the Wild West show's tour of California. He took Charley Johnson to the mineral springs at Saratoga, Wyoming, with the intention of leaving him there under the care of the hotel doctor for two weeks.

The next day Charlie was in his shirtsleeves, sorting papers that had collected on his desk in the Plains Hotel. Joella was living in an apartment close to Fort Russell with her husband. Every day since her short honeymoon in Denver, Joella had been back at work as her father's secretary. Today she was filling out orders for moving steers to Chicago and sheep to Omaha. The telephone rang. It was the ticket agent at the U.P. station. He wanted to talk to Charlie, he told Joella. "Tell C.B. there's a wire here from San Francisco sent by General John Pershing."

Joella put her hand over the phone mouthpiece and said, "Some kind of wire from General Pershing to you."

Charlie got up to answer the phone. "C.B., you want to come over and get this wire or should I read it to you?"

"Read it, I'll come get it later," said Charlie. "Wonder if the general is coming to Cheyenne? I thought he was in El Paso, chasing Pancho Villa."

The ticket agent read the wire. It was brief. It stated that General Pershing's wife, Frankie, and their three little girls, Helen, Anne, and Mary, had died of asphyxiation in a fire at the Presidio. General Pershing requested that Charlie come to San Francisco without delay to accompany the four bodies back to Cheyenne for burial.

"Oh, no!" moaned Charlie. "That poor man! And I think he has a little boy!"

"C.B., is there anything I can do," came the ticket agent's voice over the phone.

"No, no, thanks. I'll take care of everything." Charlie slumped down in his chair, put his elbows on his desk, and buried his face in his hands.

Joella looked up. "Pa, what's the matter? Are you ill?"

"No, yes—get me a glass of water." He blew his nose in a bandanna-size handkerchief. "Can you take care of things for a week?"

"Of course. What about General Pershing?"

"He's lost his wife and three daughters. I'm going to make arrangements for their burial in Lakeview Cemetery."

"Senator Warren's daughter? All the children?"

"Yes, that's the one. He mentioned the three little girls, nothing about his son. Maybe the boy's all right. Poor child—sad, sad."

During the three days and nights on the train Charlie could only think of John Pershing's tragedy.

The undertaker's parlor was at Geary and Divisadero streets. Charlie set his brown leather grip inside the door of the chapel. He first saw Pershing leaning against a man who was introduced a few moments later as Frank Helm. Charlie sat next to Pershing, whose face was gray and his eyes bloodshot as though he'd not slept for several nights. Charlie put his arms around his old friend and didn't say a word. No words seemed appropriate. No words could describe the deep sadness Charlie felt nor console the devastation that was in Pershing's heart. Pershing sobbed unabashed against Charlie's huge, solid chest. Afterward Pershing knelt between his wife's and daughters' caskets. It was the last time he'd be with his wife and daughters. His shoulders shook and his hands caressed the caskets' white casing.

Charlie made arrangements for Pershing's sister in El Paso to come for his six-year-old son, Warren. He tried to coax Pershing to come back to Cheyenne with him. "You can stay at our new place in town."

"No thanks." Pershing's voice took on a glacial, formal, military tone. "You take care of the burial. I've been ordered by President Wilson to capture Pancho Villa. I dare not refuse. I must go to Mexico!"

Charlie felt Pershing grip his arm like a vise.

The caskets were boarded on a baggage car in San Francisco. Hundreds of floral sprays were kept on the snow-white caskets. Charlie rode the daycoach.

When the train stopped in Reno he went out for some air. He was surprised to see a plain brown casket loaded into the Pershing baggage car.

"Belongs to that lady getting on your daycoach," said the baggage man.

When the train left the station Charlie said, "Excuse me, ma'am. I couldn't help noticing that you got on with a—"

"Do I know you?" asked the woman, moving her silver-framed spectacles up onto her forehead and wiping her eyes.

"No—but we're on a similar mission," said Charlie in a hushed tone. "I'm Charles Irwin. My wife and family live in Cheyenne."

"I hope it's not your wife." She patted her gray, marcelled hair.

"No, ma'am, the wife and three little girls of a good friend."

Her eyes widened. "I heard General Black Jack Pershing lost his wife and daughters. My son—I'm taking him for burial in the family plot in Iowa."

"Oh, I'm truly sorry. Would you—would you take your dinner with me?"

"I have two pieces of fried chicken and a bread and butter sandwich, but I'd be glad to share. You look like you are used to eating." There was a twinkle in her eye behind the somber look.

Charlie explained that he wanted to take her to the dining car. Afterward, he made certain she ate in the dining car and he tipped one of the porters to find a Pullman berth for her and put all the cost on his U.P. bill. He found she'd spent her savings on the casket and trip to Reno and back. He took his hat in his hand and walked through the entire length of the train collecting money for her before she awoke the next morning.

"You can complete your sad duty without financial worry," Charlie explained.

"Mr. Irwin, how in the world can I thank you?" she said.

"Send me a Christmas card. I'll show it to my wife so she'll know you were the nice lady who offered to share her chicken dinner with me."

"Pshaw! Mr. Irwin, you tell your wife she has the nicest man I've ever met." The lady's eyes sparkled and her mouth turned up into a delightful smile.

In Cheyenne, Charlie made arrangements for burial of the three caskets in Lakeview Cemetery. He also gave the drawings that Pershing had made to a stone mason in Laramie, so that the headstones would be according to Pershing's specifications.

The first mild day in January, Charlie and Etta went out to the cemetery to see how the markers looked. "Look at the size! Oh, Charlie, no need to ever get anything even half that size for me. A sweet-smelling pine beside my grave will suffice."

"You are going to live forever," said Charlie, holding his tiny wife close. "Dear, I can't imagine life without you. You are the best part of me."

"Yes, I feel exactly the same. Charlie, you are so precious to me. That day I was shattered to bits because I thought you were going off with that rainmaker. Remember? Good old days—that was a terrible old day! My heart jumped clean to my throat. I thought you were the most handsome boy in Kansas."

"You suppose some divine being is watching over us? Pershing believed something like that. He also believed that what happens is God's will."

"I don't know about God's will," said Etta. "I do know that some people make their own tragedy and one must get over sorrow or it will break you. That poor man, John Pershing. How he loved his family and why it had to end, it's hard to answer." She snuggled closer inside Charlie's arms. Not far away they found John Coble's grave and stood beside it quietly a few moments.

"Death is the worst thing to happen to those left living," whispered Charlie. "Let's go home. I feel so blue out here. I don't think a person ever gets over the loss of someone they love. The missing person leaves a big hole in a living person's heart."

THIRTY-SEVEN

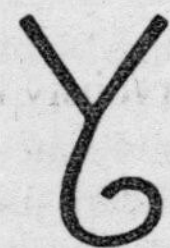

The White Masked Bandit

On the ninth of February, 1916, the news traveled fast up and down the Wyoming telegraph lines that "the eastbound Oregon-Washington Limited was held up between Green River and Rock Springs." This was train No. 18, a crack unit of the Union Pacific and the Oregon Short Line. The last train robbery on the Union Pacific had been sixteen years ago, when there'd been a holdup on an express car at Wilcox, Wyoming.

No one had any idea who today's bandit was. He'd worn a white, silk handkerchief over the bottom half of his face, hid under the back platform of the observation car, Portland Rose, until the train was out of sight of the Green River station. Then he climbed over the brass railing, kicked snow off his big, paddle feet, pushed open the rear door. The rear brakeman felt the cold air on the back of his neck. He jumped up, felt the muzzle of a gun in his back, and heard the quiet-spoken words, "Put your hands up."

The lone passenger in the observation car, a woman, screamed.

"Sit where you are and nobody's going to hurt you, lady," said the bandit softly. He pushed the brakeman toward the smoking compartment, parted the heavy green curtains, and said, "Everyone, get your hands up." The brakeman thought this was some sort of prank and laughed. No one moved. The bandit spoke in a loud, sharp voice, "Hands up, I said!" He pointed the gun, a small .32 pocket weapon, at the ceiling. One shot was enough to get five pairs of hands up.

The porter had been asleep in the forward end of the car in the barber chair. He'd heard the shot and slid with his eyes wide open to the aisle.

The bandit thumped him in the chest and told him to walk ahead with his cap in his hand. "You're taking the collection."

The bandit's hand went nervously in and out of his pocket and finally pulled out another gun. He pushed aside the smoking compartment's curtains again and waved the second gun at the brakeman. "Empty your pockets!" Money and gold watches went into the porter's hat.

One man put in several crisp five-dollar bills and some change. "That's all the money I got in the world," he said.

"Here's a dollar for your next grub," said the bandit, handing him back a cartwheel.

The woman had her valuables in her lap waiting for the bandit to come get them.

"I don't rob ladies nor children," he said, and pushed the porter ahead of him into the next car that was a Pullman. The bandit told the porter to stand by the door. He stuck one of the guns in the back of the Pullman porter. "Pull the curtains aside on the berths that have men inside. Do it! Then hold out your cap!"

The porter shook and his teeth chattered but he pulled the curtains aside. The startled men emptied their wallets. The bandit went to the next vestibule, pushing the porter ahead of him. In the vestibule the bandit pocketed the money. The porter pulled out the change in his pocket and nervously handed it to the bandit.

"Keep that," said the bandit. "Stand at the door in this next sleeping car."

When the bandit entered the next car, a conductor entered from the opposite end. He watched the bandit pushing the porter ahead, open several berths, thrust in the porter's cap, and bring it out. The conductor pulled the emergency cord.

The sparks flew against the tracks as the wheels screamed and slowed down. The bandit pushed ahead of the porter, flew back through the Pullman car. A woman yelled, "Please don't take my money. I haven't much."

The bandit looked back and smiled. "I don't take from women." He opened the rear door of the observation car and jumped over the side of the railing into the snow. There were snow fences all along the hillside. When the train finally came to a stop, no one was in sight and no foot tracks could be found in the dark, only places where heavy snow had rolled into the gullies. The wind would kick the snow back over any tracks. The temperature was well below zero. A slivered glass gun lay broken against the rail; the colored, round candies that were inside were spilled on the tie and some lay in the cold, frozen cinders.

"Some little kid's plaything," said the brakeman, kicking the broken glass roughly aside.

In Rock Springs there was a lot of talk that night about the man who'd robbed the eastbound train. The conductor sent a wire to William Jeffers, general superintendent of the Union Pacific in Omaha, the U.P.'s headquarters, saying that a bandit had held up passengers on No. 18 for fifty-two dollars and thirty-five cents. The porters were certain that the man was not more than thirty years old, more likely in his late twenties. He was at least six feet tall and weighed about one hundred seventy-five pounds. He had dark-brown hair, hazel to brown eyes, a large mouth, and high cheekbones. "Did you see how big his feet were?" asked the brakeman. "I'd bet his shoes were a size eleven!"

"And his hands, they were awful big. I noticed that right away," said one of the porters.

"I saw something else when he held the gun over his head and shot the ceiling of the smoking compartment, something on his right forearm. Some letters, or initials, in red and blue ink. Like a tattoo. W.L.C.," said the brakeman.

William Jeffers called Charlie at home. They talked on the telephone about what might be done if the bandit decided to rob another U.P. train. "I want you to be ready at a moment's notice to get a posse of cowboys on horseback to ride with local sheriffs on this outlaw's trail. You're the one man who knows every foot of this rangeland."

"I'm not a lawman, but I'll do what I can," said Charlie. After hanging up the receiver Charlie felt rather pleased that Mr. Jeffers had thought of him in connection with helping set a trap or locating this train robber. Charlie could, on short notice, have men, supplies, horses, or an automobile ready to go anywhere up and down the U.P. line. He thought there was something unique, even gracious, about a man who'd rob men, but not women. The bandit was a mystery man. Could just be some poor devil down on his luck, maybe needed a few dollars fast. Charlie was not too surprised about the robbery, though. Many men were finding it hard to locate jobs. More and more men were moving from one place to another because they'd been laid off from work. Without money men rode the rails or hopped a freight.

Winter moved into spring slowly that year. There were several feet of snow on the ground. Sleighs were the only vehicles that moved. Floyd and Dee Dee looked after the ranch; they kept hay spread on top of the snow for the cattle and horses that ranged in the closer pastures. Pauline and her baby were at the ranch, patiently waiting for Johnson to come home. Johnson left the Saratoga Hot Springs after a two-week stay. He went to Hardin, Montana, on the Big Horn River and hired out as a cowboy.

Charlie knew when Johnson left the Hot Springs because he no longer received a bill for his board and room. He called the doctor who'd looked after Johnson. The doctor told him he'd gone to Montana. "I believe he's headed west. Told me that when he'd made enough money cowboying, he was going to the West Coast to see about being in pictures. He's a good-looking son of a gun. I can see him as a matinee idol, a heartthrob for the ladies," said the doctor, "like Tom Mix."

"What I want to know is, how was he when he left? How was his attitude? Was he dried out? Off the booze?" yelled Charlie. "I don't want to hear an opinion that he's like Tom Mix!"

"Rational, yes, I'd say he knew what he was doing, and yes, not a drop to drink while he was here at the hotel. You can be proud of that young man, Mr. Irwin. He's just fine."

"Maybe fine for you!" shouted Charlie. "Not so fine for the family he abandoned!" He slammed the receiver, and thought to himself that if Pauline wanted, he'd go to Montana and bring Johnson back. But Pauline didn't want Charlie to go after her husband.

"Let him go. He'll come back when he wants by himself," she said with tears in her eyes.

Frank and Clara Belle had had a third little girl, Arlyne Lucille, the previous October. Frank stayed at the ranch while Clara Belle and the children stayed in Cheyenne. Charlie promised Joella's husband that when his Army duty was over, he could work with him on the ranch. "I'll get you a good piece of land, you and Joella can build on it, have some horses, and you'll do fine, right here in Wyoming." He would have given Johnson land and horses had he come back. He'd built the ranch for his children and it was time they began taking the responsibility of running it. He needed his children to keep the ranch running smoothly. He had no plans for his children to move away. To have his children leave Cheyenne and the ranch was something Charlie would not think about.

However, he did think about the train robber that had seemed to disappear without a trace. He wondered if the robber would dare strike again.

Posters were up in every U.P. depot in southern Wyoming, offering a fifteen-hundred-dollar reward for information leading to the arrest of the "Gentleman Bandit."

Charlie had heard nothing since the telephone call from Jeffers and a call in mid-February from the sheriff of Green River. The morning the sheriff called someone had found an old black wool coat in an alley. The coat had a wrinkled, white silk scarf in the pocket. "Could be the large handkerchief the bandit wore. I bet he's still here in town," said the sheriff.

"I'll come have a look around," said Charlie. He had a new Overland and was happy to have an excuse to drive it several hundred miles to show it off as soon as some of the snow melted. The automobile could go the fifty, sixty miles an hour that the trains traveled.

Two cowboys from Y6 were in town to take a couple of the horses in the Four-Mile pasture back to the ranch. Charlie said to leave the horses. He took the men with him to Green River. The sheriff had a guard in the alley where the coat had been found. The railroad yards and trains were being watched. Before any empty baggage car was sent out of town it was searched, and a search of each passenger train was made. Charlie and his men drove into town near midnight and suggested that the roads also be watched.

He went into the depot and talked with the ticket agent, who didn't believe the bandit was still in town. "We'd have found him by now. This is a small place and everybody's looking."

Just then the ticket agent looked behind Charlie and told him to step to one side because there was a man who looked like he wanted to purchase a ticket. Charlie stepped away and let the man step up next to the window.

"One way to Laramie," the man said, and turned to look directly at Charlie, who smiled. "Not much business this time of night, huh?"

Charlie nodded and said there was not much scenery between Green River and Laramie this time of night.

"I'll sleep," said the man putting a ten-dollar bill through the window. The ticket agent handed the man his ticket, took the ten dollars, and counted out change.

Charlie noticed how big the man's hands were and thought to himself, There's a fellow that's ham-handed for sure.

The man had trouble slipping the ticket into his shirt pocket. He laughed at his own clumsiness and turned to leave. Charlie smiled and put his hand on the man's shoulder. The man seemed startled for an instant.

"Friend, don't forget your change," said Charlie, taking his hand away.

The man relaxed and picked up his change. He thanked Charlie, walked out into the night, and boarded the waiting train.

No one seemed to know who owned the black coat and no other clues turned up, so after two days of wandering up and down the tracks and snow-filled ravines, Charlie and his two men left Green River and drove back to Cheyenne.

Weeks went by. Railroad officials and Sweetwater County's sheriff found nothing. Old-timers found it laughable that one man could hold up an entire train and then get away leaving no clues.

On the fourth of April more snow fell, swirling against fences, barns and houses. Charlie grumbled that winter was eating into spring. He went to bed and had barely dropped off to sleep when the telephone rang. It was Mr. W. J. McClements, chief of the Union Pacific special agents. "C.B.?"

"Yes."

"Train number one, the Overland Limited, is being robbed. She left Cheyenne twenty minutes ago. Get out there! Corlett Junction!"

"I'm on my way!" said Charlie. He thought of a dozen questions he wanted to ask. He wondered if the bandit wore a white handkerchief over his face, like a white mask. He wanted to know if he wore a brown coat, yellow corduroy trousers, and big, black buckled overshoes like the man who was so nervous he'd forgotten his change.

Charlie got in his Overland and drove along the road that paralleled the tracks on the way to the Fort Russell station. The Burlington tracks were in sight and Charlie heard the northbound, Burlington night train pull into Fort Russell. He turned off his automobile lights and got out to examine the train. He looked between the cars and underneath on the rods. He tipped his hat when the brakeman walked past. When the train let out a cloud of hissing steam into the cold night air, Charlie went back to his automobile. As the train pulled out, Charlie started up and followed along with his lights off. He followed the train out of the station, past Corlett Junction several miles. He saw nothing unusual, no one walking the tracks nor along either side of the road. He turned around, put on the lights, and headed back to Cheyenne. He did not see the figure of a lone man climb out of the culvert, walk across the road behind him, and hunch his shoulders against the wind as he headed north.

Train No. 1 was held at Laramie so that the passengers could be questioned. The conductor was congratulated by Chief McClements for slipping a message off the train at the Borie water tank, stating that there was a robbery taking place. No one blamed him that the robber was not caught.

For the next few weeks all transients were questioned and those that could not account for their whereabouts around the time of the robbery were jailed. Hobos were taken off freight trains and placed in Cheyenne's jail. A hundred men hunted around the sandhills and dunes near Cheyenne. A suspicious man was jailed, but he swore he was no bandit.

For several days Charlie rode the Overland Limited, making a study of all the passengers. He found no one that seemed suspicious. He told Chief McClements he believed the bandit had struck out on foot and was obtaining meals and lodging from the small ranchers and homesteaders. "I saw no sign of a horse or horses when I looked around the tracks west of the Fort Russell station."

"I'll send some men to look around Denver," said McClements, "and you look north of Cheyenne. Troops from Fort Russell are searching around Rawlins."

Charlie took a score of cowboys out into the brush-covered hills around Horse Creek and Iron Mountain. They searched every draw and gully, behind every sage and willow clump. He was preparing to search the small ranches near Diamond and Chugwater when the weather went into a decline and stayed near twenty degrees below zero for the best part of a week. When the temperature moderated there was a two-day blizzard. Charlie called off the hunt. The bandit had to be holed up somewhere with homesteaders or ranchers. No one could survive long in that searing cold, followed by the snowstorm.

A special train from Omaha was coming to Cheyenne with

General Superintendent Jeffers, who meant to get this man who had twice robbed a Union Pacific train. The railroad now offered a reward of fifty-five hundred dollars for the capture of the bandit, dead or alive. The state of Wyoming posted a reward of five hundred dollars.

Charlie had Frank bring horses into the Cheyenne stockyards, ready to go at any time. He left his Overland parked at the U.P. depot so that he could either drive anywhere or put the automobile in a freight car and take it anywhere along the train line.

On April twenty-first the U.P.'s train No. 21 was robbed near Hanna, near where several years before Charlie had helped U.P. men build wooden snow sheds over the tracks, so no train would be delayed in a winter snowstorm. This time Chief McClements and Cheyenne's Sheriff Roach were in charge of about three hundred men, who divided into posses all along the U.P.'s line from Cheyenne to Green River. The description of the bandit was similar to the man who'd held up the two other U.P. trains. He was tall, wore a broad-brimmed hat, a brown overcoat, well-worn yellow trousers, and a pair of large black boots, shiny new.

A young man with abnormally large hands bought a ticket and Pullman space on train No. 21, the Pacific Limited from Greeley, Colorado, to Rawlins, Wyoming. The man appeared ill and could barely speak above a whisper. He had the Pullman porter make up the berth and bring him hot lemonade at thirty-minute intervals. When the train stopped at Laramie, the man got off to mail several letters written on U.P. stationery. Then he got back on his Pullman car and pretended to read a magazine, but all the time he was checking out the passengers to see if he could pick out the Pinkerton guard that was now riding every U.P. train. He walked through the daycoach as the dining-car waiter announced first call for dinner, playing three notes on his hand-held xylophone. He looked out the window and guessed the train was near Medicine Bow. He went to the dining car, had dinner, and paid the waiter with a ten-dollar bill. While waiting for change, a man came into the car and passed so close he could see a slight bulge under his right arm. He knew right away he was the train guard.

After his meal the man approached the guard in the daycoach and struck up a conversation. He asked what the guard would do if the U.P.'s bandit were on this train.

"I hope I see him first, so that I can shoot the dirty damned coyote. Jesus, he's slippery as a mountain trout."

"Sshh, don't talk that way, there's ladies in this car. Profanity's not fit for a lady's ears," said the man. "Now, what if that bandit got the drop on you? What would you do?"

"I'd hold my hands up," said the guard with a laugh.

The man laughed and leaned toward the guard. Then in an instant he'd reached around and taken hold of the guard's revolver. He'd taken a small pistol from his pocket and held it in the other hand. "Stick 'em up!"

The guard was dumbfounded.

"Get your hat and go through the train with me. Hold the hat so the men can put their cash there," said the man. Then as he walked behind the guard, holding the muzzle of one gun at his back, he called out, "Hands up! Everybody, except you ladies! I don't want anything from you ladies, but men, dole out your cash in this hat! Nobody leave your seat or I'll shoot!"

They went into the forward car and the man told the conductor to hold his hands high. The conductor froze. The man fired his gun into the ceiling and all hands in the car went up. The man put the two guns together in his right hand. The conductor saw that the man's forefinger reached easily around to both triggers. The man reached into his left pocket and drew out a gold watch. "Here, take this to Superintendent Toucey in Cheyenne. Tell him, it'll help pay for the reward money he's got on me."

The conductor took the pocket watch and knew it was the one taken in the Overland Limited holdup.

The man took back one weapon in his left hand and turned his back on the conductor. He pushed the guard ahead, collecting money as fast as he could. Some said he got as much as four hundred dollars, others said it was closer to a thousand dollars.

The train slowed to enter the Edson tunnel east of Walcott. The man told the train guard to open the vestibule door, then the outside gate or trap door. Quickly he stuffed the money in his coat pockets and leaped off into the black night. When he landed he twisted his ankle badly, letting the two guns fly from his hands along with the wallet belonging to the train guard. He found the wallet and shoved it close to the tracks where it could easily be found. He searched for the guns, then without finding them he walked away from the railroad track. It was four hours before that the train had stopped in Laramie.

The following day the *Denver Post* received a letter written on U.P. stationery and postmarked the twenty-first from Laramie.

Denver Post:

To prove that this letter is the real thing, I am enclosing a watch-chain which I took from the last holdup out of

Cheyenne—this chain can easily be identified.

To convince the officers that they have the wrong man in jail, I will hold up a train somewhere west of Laramie, Wyoming.

The White Masked Bandit*

Charlie lost no time getting horses into a boxcar, and his automobile, along with Hughie Clark's Ford and some saddles, into another boxcar. He rounded up all the cowboys he could find and put them on his special train. Before leaving the station in Cheyenne he told S. R. Toucey, superintendent of the Wyoming division of the U.P., to telephone the Hanna station if more men and horses were needed in the Laramie and Medicine Bow area.

Toucey, who was thin, energetic, about thirty-five, motioned for Charlie to follow him inside and to his office. "C.B., wait a minute before you go. I have something, might be important—might not. Four years ago a Wilfrid Fields applied for a job as brakeman. He was hired because he said that he'd been a brakeman on the Louisville and Nashville."

"That doesn't sound like anything to do with a masked bandit," said Charlie, growing impatient and ready to leave.

"Hold it, this Wilfrid Fields was eventually fired for negligence because he was the cause for a derailment of a freight train near Borie. I was looking through the old files this morning after the paper came. I compared Fields's written application with the writing in the letter sent to the *Post* last night. See, here! I swear they are the same handwriting!"

"Let me see!" cried Charlie in a booming loud voice. He grabbed the newspaper and sat in an empty chair. "Maybe—the *T*s and rounded *r*s look alike." He studied the job application. "Say, this man's physical description, six feet tall, one hundred seventy-five pounds, is similar to the bandit's. But there's no mention of a tattoo on his right forearm, Toucey."

Toucey swiveled around in his chair to face Charlie. "Well, if I had a tattoo, I wouldn't mention it on a job application either. What do you think the letters stand for? W.L.C.? Those his real initials, or a girlfriend's?"

Charlie handed the file and newspaper back to Toucey. "You're all right. Tell me if you have any other hunches."

*Courtesy Charles M. Bennett Collection, Scottsdale, Arizona.

"You bet," said Toucey, smiling so that rays of tiny creases formed at the corners of his eyes.

Charlie didn't stay for more speculative talk; he bustled out of the office, ran down the platform, and swung himself up into the coach on his special train, which also carried McClements and Jeffers. Because of his extra weight, he gasped for breath when he was inside the car looking for a seat. Finally he found a vacant place and sat down to catch his breath. He hadn't begun to worry about the additional pounds. He'd been large all his life. He had a large frame, his mother always said. He liked good, healthful food, beefsteak, potatoes and gravy, homemade biscuits, green beans simmered all day in sweet butter. He didn't have much exercise when he was in the office working as livestock agent. However, he always trimmed down working at the ranch and when he was on the road with the show. He looked around the car and recognized Hughie Clark in a blue and gray checked shirt talking with some Union Pacific men, George Bachus, Charles Herenden, Sam Radissell, and the two Huneucker brothers, who were ranchers.

George Bachus got up. He looked like he ought to be in high school. He was short and slim. He came over and sat next to Charlie. "Some of the men think that this train robber is being protected by dirt farmers or homesteaders, or sheep men. They say that's why there's no clues. C.B., you know some of those poor homesteaders'd tell you they never saw some stranger. They'd look you straight in the eye and all the while have that stranger in their root cellar. These folks ain't real partial to the Union Pacific, troops from Fort Russell, the sheriff and his deputies, nor cowboys and big ranchers." He looked at Charlie, who was drumming his fingers on his protruding waist. "Oh, C.B., I'm sorry—oh, no, I didn't mean it that way. You know what I meant."

"Sure, I know," said Charlie with a grin. "I talked to some of those hobos and small-time farmers in Cheyenne myself. They're amused that one man had the audacity, the cleverness, to put all of us in a whirlwind."

The train stopped at Laramie. Charlie got out and went into the station. Nothing had come in on the wire. He came out, looked up and down the tracks. Suddenly he pictured the bandit mailing that letter to the *Denver Post* right here at the Laramie station. The man must have looked rather pleased with himself. In Charlie's imagination, the man looked like a dozen men Charlie knew, even dressed the same except that he had extra big hands and feet. "Jeems!" he shouted out loud. "That man in Green River! He bought a one-way ticket to Laramie! His hands —huge! His feet—I don't remember—yes—I do remember, they were like paddles! He was paddle-footed!" He waved to the engineer to go on, climbed aboard the train, squeezed past Bachus, and tried to think what the man's face looked like.

Bachus asked, "You think there'll be any messages at Hanna?"

Charlie shook his head back and forth, "Nope." He was thinking, trying to remember some facial feature, a cleft chin, a prominent nose, eye color, big ears, but nothing definite came to mind.

Bachus asked, "We stopping at Walcott? Creates a lot of excitement for the hundred and fifty townspeople. They're not used to having a train stop." He chewed a toothpick.

Charlie grinned. "We'll stop. Give those people some excitement."

Just as Charlie had predicted, there were no messages at Hanna, but in Walcott the marshal, Bill Hayes, got on the train. He had a day's growth of beard and looked like he needed sleep.

"Should have shaved before moving in with us dudes," hollered Charlie.

"I was fixing to shave when I got the idea to join you gents and go up the line to Rawlins. We'll stop there, fan out, and double back to Hanna." Hayes rubbed the stubble on his chin.

"Maybe we ought to spread out as far back as Laramie," said Charlie. Then he told the men about standing next to the bandit around midnight a couple weeks back in Green River.

"I've been looking by horseback half the night, ever since I got the word that quite a few gents on number twenty-one were robbed yesterday. I thought the man might have a horse waiting somewhere and head out for the hills or even go for Elk Mountain. I hunted up and down the ravines and started for Rattlesnake Pass, but the snow's still three foot deep there. I'd like a piece of that reward money," said Hayes. His blue eyes were serious, but his mouth turned up into a smile.

The train pulled to a siding at Rawlins. Charlie bought feed for the horses and gasoline for the two automobiles from Andy Corson. A man dressed in faded trousers and a frayed brown shirt over gray woolen long-sleeved underwear was hanging around the livery station. "You C. B. Irwin?"

"I am," said Charlie.

"Well, I'd like to offer my services. I don't have a horse

because it was taken along with my cattle a week ago. I'd like to catch that weasel."

Charlie had the man sign a voucher, which was the back of an envelope.

The man wrote, "R. L. Donnell, robbed at my ranch of a horse and of cattle. I would like to catch the cutthroat before I take my family to California."

"Come on, I'll find you a horse to ride. You'll find some action, I promise," said Charlie, giving Donnell one of the horses coming out of the baggage car. Charlie pointed to the saddles and told Donnell to put one on his horse.

"Much obliged," said Donnell. "Some of the men hanging around the depot over yonder said you treated everyone fair." His mustache moved stiffly over the corners of his mouth.

Sheriff Ruby Rivera of Carbon County showed up with a score of men on horseback. Rivera carried enough hardware to give himself kidney sores. Charlie had observed that the man who wears his holsters tied down won't do much talking with his mouth. Sheriff Rivera was an exception. Right away Rivera suggested that he take all the men on horseback south of Rawlins and that those who wished to ride in cars go with Hughie Clark or C. B. Irwin.

Charlie squinted at Rivera several seconds, then said, "The cars can carry extra grub for the men, extra feed for the horses, and equipment for staying out overnight. One car will go with you and the other will stay with me and my men on horseback. Heads up! We're on our way."

Rivera didn't move out, he reined his horse over toward the train's engine. He angled the horse in as close as it would get to the noisy steam engine and called up to the cab. "Take this train back to Cheyenne! Leave it here and it could alert that damned bandit. We'll not do anything to let him slip away this time!"

The engineer tipped his hat and looked down at Rivera. A sudden blast of steam caused Rivera's horse to whinny and rise on its hind feet and gallop off into a bunch of sage. Rivera swore and went back to his horsemen.

Charlie watched his Overland being driven out of the baggage car over a wide plank. "It's all ready the minute we get some of the grub loaded in her, sir," said one of the men.

"Thanks," said Charlie. "Load her, I'll be right back." He walked away from the milling horse and over to the track. He waved his hat at the engineer. "This train was made up on my orders."

"Yes, sir," called the engineer. "You wrote out the orders before the general manager knew you were at the Cheyenne station."

"All right. I'm still giving the orders. This train goes as far as Hanna. Hold there on a siding. First get yourself a good meal here in town. Charge it to me."

"C.B., sir. It's four-thirty in the morning. Nothing's open."

"The Merc over there's open. I bought oats, canned tomatoes, and stuff!"

"That's not my idea of a good meal."

"Jeems!" called Charlie. "See if some townsman'd be willing to take you home for biscuits and gravy, sausage and a couple of eggs, and hot coffee."

"Sure thing." The engineer shut down the engine and climbed out of the cab, followed by his fireman and brakeman.

Charlie gave him one of his U.P. livestock agent's cards. "This will get you what you need. I'll take care of whatever your meal's worth."

"Hey, C.B., my brother-in-law's place is not far from here. We'll go there. His wife, my sister, would feed you, too," said the brakeman. Then he said something that baffled Charlie. "My brother-in-law was up around the Barrett sheep camp not long ago. One of the Mexican herders told him that a young man, with green eyes and big hands, stayed at the camp overnight and laughed about holding up a train with a glass gun." He held his hands up. "Now, don't laugh. Wait until you hear this. I was on the number eighteen the night she was robbed. When we were looking out in the bushes, we found nothing but snow deep as hell. But I remember, like yesterday, kicking at broken glass on a tie. The glass was painted nickel plate and some was dark blue. Those little round, colored candies that come in glass toys was scattered in the cinders. I thought at the time it was a funny place for a kid's toy. Then I forgot about it until I heard this other story."

Charlie had to admit it was a strange story. "But what about the hole in the smoking compartment? That was made with a real pistol. I don't know about this glass-gun story. It doesn't make a lot of sense."

"Sir, the glass gun was found between Green River and Rock Springs. Maybe someone should go back and see if it's still there," said the brakeman.

"If nothing turns up today, I'll take a run toward the west and see what I can find," promised Charlie. "But right now, I'd add the story to all the other rumors that are flying around. Do you think a train robber would use a glass toy to make a holdup?"

The trainmen all shook their heads and grinned and headed across the road to Rawlins.

Charlie climbed into his car and motioned for Bachus, who was on foot, to get in beside him. He waved to Rivera, who sat mute on his horse. Charlie and his men rode out into the Rawlins hills and hunted for the sandy, dirt roads used mainly by loggers.

Several times Charlie got out of the car and traded places with a horseback rider, or walked, trying to find traces of some kind of tracks made by a large-size boot. He never dreamed that the bandit had sprained his right ankle, taken his boot off for relief, then taken the other shoe off and walked in his woolen socks.

Charlie took his automobile across the North Platte bridge, then again sought out roads close to the hills. Outside of Elmo he and the men stopped at a seepage lake, made from snowmelt coming off the foothills. They filled their canteens and Charlie passed boxes of hard tack and chipped beef among the men. He divided up the navy blue woolen U.P. Pullman blankets, one to every two men. Then he and Bachus took two of the pack horses after dividing the loads, which were tarps and the men's jackets and coats. Charlie had decided to leave the car beside the only store in Elmo, the Trading Post. He and the men would fan out toward the Medicine Bow River, and meet back in Elmo in eight hours if they found nothing.

Bachus and Charlie moseyed around by the railroad tracks for thirty minutes then they wandered out in the brush. After about twenty minutes Bachus yelled to Charlie, "C.B., lookit this here track in the dirt. And the empty tomato can." The sky was beginning to lighten. The bright stars faded.

"The can looks fresh," said Charlie. "Probably one of our own men tossed it here."

"I don't think so. This can has the label. Those you bought in Rawlins had no paper label on them. I remember Hayes saying he hoped there were no surprises in that crate of canned tomatoes," said Bachus.

"You're absolutely right," said Charlie, looking at the top of the can. "Looks like he used a pocket knife to open it. Put it in your saddle bag. Let's follow those tracks."

Bachus nodded and he watched Charlie measure the large footprint. The morning light was bright enough that they could see men on horseback a quarter of a mile on either side of them, fanning out into the Medicine Bow area. The air was cold as

Charlie and Bachus followed the tracks, which went down a steep ravine to a small creek. Bachus scrambled down, leaving Charlie at the top with the horses. Then he yelled, "C.B., the man waded across the water and he had his shoes off! The tracks are of a man in his stocking feet!"

Charlie brought the horses scrambling down the steep, rocky embankment. He examined the tracks. "Made sometime this morning. The mud isn't dry." He pinched the brim of his hat together and scooped up a long drink of water and let the horses drink for a moment before moving up the other side, which was thick with willows and sage.

"I could chew on a crust of bread and bacon rind while riding this nag," said Bachus.

"I'll give you some hard tack and chipped beef," said Charlie, rummaging around in the canvas pack on the side of his horse.

They went through more ravines and water courses filled with snowmelt. The salty meat made them stop at every water-filled depression or creek for a drink. By midmorning Charlie and Bachus caught up with Sheriff Rivera and some other men. They, too, had seen tracks, but had lost them as they wandered into rock in the foothills. They now worked together, keeping their conversation at a minimum.

Charlie looked around once and thought searchers were so thick that they were all in danger of shooting one another if anyone saw or heard something unusual.

Charlie was sure when they went into the Thatcher Bottoms that the Union Pacific would have its bandit before the day was out. He was sure the search parties had him surrounded. "What time is it?" he asked Bachus.

"Time to stop for something to eat. You start the fire and I'll get you some coffee grounds to put in a tin can."

"I wouldn't build a fire," warned Charlie. "That will only alert the robber." He looked up and saw Marshal Hayes from Walcott. "We think the man's in these bottoms somewhere."

Marshal Hayes dismounted and poked around in the brush.

Charlie looked at the sky. It was overcast, but he estimated the sun to be about overhead. "I ought to go back to Hanna and tell that engineer to wait a couple more hours. I hate to leave when it seems we are so close, but I said we'd be back in about eight hours."

"You go, I'll take care of things," said Hayes.

"Jeems, I hope you don't flush him out until I get back," said Charlie. He estimated it was at least ten to twelve miles to

Hanna. He kicked his horse and drove it up and down the gullies, across the fast-running, ice-cold creeks, through yellow sand and brush of Bat's Bottom. There he heard someone whistling and knew there were several men to his right riding through the sandy bottomland. He swung away from the posse and rode for the railroad tracks. After he'd talked to the engineer, he had the Hanna operator call Toucey in Cheyenne and tell him they'd have his man before midafternoon.

The operator asked if he could call the Dana Section House and tell those men the news. "Sure," said Charlie, "just don't send any more men into Thatcher Bottoms. Everyone's armed to the teeth in there and jumpy, ready to shoot at the first crack of a twig."

"You sure you want to go back into that kind of trap?" asked the operator.

"I wouldn't miss it for the world," said Charlie, going out to mount his horse. He hurried back into the bottom country as fast as he could. It was easy to follow his own tracks. He slowed up when he got to the creeks where there was thick brush. He rode carefully around each willow clump to make certain no one was hiding in the middle. Then he heard the soft nicker of a horse. He stopped and looked around. There was Bachus off his horse, trailing something along a stretch of rocks that had been scattered across the narrow valley by some long-gone ice floe. The path of the ice floe was invisible now, pines grew sedately among the rocks on the side of the foothills, but in the more open places were huge boulders gouged out of the hills and pushed down to a new resting place. Charlie watched Bachus several moments, then he saw that others were also scattered about. The men were checking behind each huge boulder. The ground was dry, mostly gravel. There were no prints or tracks to follow over the small rocks.

Charlie tethered his horse to a mesquite shrub, made certain the old Henry rimfire was loaded. He could hear himself breathe and feel his heart beat. He nodded to Bachus, who held his index finger crosswise to his lips, indicating silence. Then he began to feel that someone was watching him. The hairs on the back of Charlie's head prickled. Slowly he turned and looked. There was nothing except men moving slowly from rock to rock as he and Bachus were now doing. Maybe those others had been watching him, checking out the way he put his rifle around each rock before he moved it. He kept the rifle high so that the bandit would not grab it. And he held tight, so that by now his hands and arms ached. His back was tired from the tension of moving slowly and riding to Hanna. Charlie was positive the bandit was holed up here. He didn't know why he was so sure. He could smell him. But he couldn't say what he smelled like. The air was still. It was as if the wind, too, were waiting for something to happen before resuming its normal pattern of gusts.

Twenty yards ahead of Charlie, Bachus slipped and half-fell. Charlie heard him swear under his breath. Then it happened. Standing in front of Bachus was a tall man with his hands up over his head, the collar of his flannel shirt turned up close around his neck. Charlie moved faster now from rock to rock until he was at one side covering Bachus easily.

"Keep those hands high, mister," said Charlie in his booming voice.

The man looked up, straight at Charlie, seemed to recognize him, just as Marshal Hayes hit his right hand so that his revolver fell and clattered on the rocks.

"All right, you've got me," said the man.

"Don't hit him again," said Charlie, picking up the revolver and slipping it under his own belt. "Tie his hands with my lasso, and we'll take him in."

Bachus let out a long breath of air. "I knowed he was behind that rock! I saw him move there about a half-hour ago. About the same time you came back, C.B. I waited before getting to that big rock, then when I got here, I wasn't so sure I'd really seen anything." Bachus tied his hands together and wound the extra rope around the man's waist.

"He's not going to ride back on my horse," said Marshal Hayes.

"He's going to ride in front of Bachus," said Charlie. "I'd take him with me, but I don't think my horse could stand the strain."

Several of the boys who were moving in to surround the bandit laughed at Charlie's joke. The bandit looked at Charlie and smiled. His eyes softened.

Charlie asked, "What's your name, friend?"

"William L. Carlisle."

"'You're not Wilfrid Fields?" Charlie could hear some of the other men cheering and hip-hooraying, glad the bandit was found and they'd seen his capture.

"No. I never heard of him," said Carlisle.

Charlie sat in Carlisle's Cheyenne cell on the iron cot. "Mr. Carlisle, you know that I have to send in a report to the General

Superintendent of the Union Pacific. If I ask you some questions and take down some notes, my letter will be accurate. It will be better written in your favor if you tell me the truth."

"All right," agreed Carlisle. "I never shot anyone. And I never intended to take a life." Carlisle told Charlie that he was born May 4, 1890, in Pennsylvania. "I only went as far as the fifth grade."

"We have something in common. I went as far as fifth grade," said Charlie, taking off his wide-brimmed hat. "Where'd you go to school?"

"My father was a harness maker and we moved to Evans, Colorado."

"I know where that is, south of Greeley," said Charlie.

"Well, we moved west to Loveland. That's where I went to school. Then the family moved to Texas. My mother and sister still live in Texas. I sent some of the money I rustled to them." Then he stared at the floor. "I'm going to tell you some things I'm not proud of. One of my brothers served a sentence for forgery and another shot and killed a man in a quarrel over some young lady they were both interested in. My brother ran for his horse and a quick getaway, but he spurred the horse too roughly and was bucked off. He lay unconscious in the road until he was found and jailed."

Carlisle told Charlie that from 1900 to 1902 he was in the State Industrial School at Golden, Colorado, because his father said he was uncontrollable and incorrigible. His father had turned him in for stealing shoes from the small shoe store his father owned at that time. "I only took the shoes to send to my sister and mother. Pa left them in Texas with nothing and made us boys come back to Colorado with him. I always worried about my mother and sister. Pa said they were not worth worrying about, to forget them." Carlisle had tears in his eyes.

Charlie waited until Carlisle blew his nose on the heavy cotton handkerchief supplied by the prison. "Even as a young man, you realized that your father was wrong."

"Yes," said Carlisle. "That's why I changed my name when I was about fifteen and began riding the freights. I've been in thirty-eight states. My pa's name was Carlise."

"What was the first job you ever had?" asked Charlie.

"I was in Sioux City, Iowa, where an employment officer got me a job in March of 1906 with the railroad in Great Falls, Montana. But a fifteen-year-old kid is too light to work in the freight yards so the Great Northern kicked me off. That was a kick to my own confidence. I drifted around ranches in northern Montana a while." Carlisle stood up and asked the guard to bring in two glasses of water. "Mr. Irwin, I have confidence in you. I think if you write this story it will be helpful to keep the lawmen from connecting me with a lot of other robberies, which they probably think I've done."

Carlisle told Charlie that while he was in Montana he took his first step to the other side of the law. An outfit, called the Skelton Boys, mostly Indian breeds, were stealing horses in northern Montana and in Canada and making quite a bit of money. Carlisle joined them. The gang rustled horses from ranchers and then sold them on either side of the border. The outfit was trailed and shot at. They broke up. "I was arrested August seventeenth, 1914, at a ranch within twenty miles of Hardin, Montana, by the deputy sheriff. I was arrested under the name of Walter Cottrell, alias Ward Kerrigan, for stealing one horse. I was convicted and sentenced for eighteen months at the Deer Lodge Penitentiary. The warden's name was Frank Connoley. Everybody in Montana knows him. You can write him. He'll tell you the same as I have."

The water came. Carlisle drank all of his and asked for more. Charlie took a few swallows and set his glass down on the floor by his extra pencils.

"Then I headed for Wyoming. I got a job at the Smith ranch at a place called Crazy Woman in Johnson County. Then I worked at a ranch in Kaycee on the Middle Fork of the Powder River. I couldn't stay in one place for long. Before I had time to get into any trouble, I moved south to Texas, thinking I'd visit my mother and sister. The Madero revolution was taking place along the Texas border in 1910 where Francisco Madero and his guerrillas were fixing to overthrow the Mexican government. The guerrillas needed guns. I signed up and was soon running illegal guns to Juarez from El Paso. Those were the days before the border patrol. Runners like me kept an eye out for the customs men and ran the weapons across the border to guerrilla tent camps. After a close call with a smart customs official I again started jumping freights headed for the West. I didn't stay in one place more than three months. I saw a lot of the country, from the adobe, sunbaked buildings of the Southwest to the wide streets with automobiles and trolleys of Los Angeles. I liked the small towns best. The people are friendlier."

Carlisle asked Charlie if he was tired of writing all those words. Charlie looked up. "Nope, but I'm sure getting hungry."

"Say, why don't you eat with me," suggested Carlisle. He pounded on the bars of his cell. "Bring me two lunch trays. Mr. Irwin's staying for lunch."

The guard laughed loudly. "Next I suppose you'll tell me you want a table with a white cloth."

"That would be nice for my guest," said Carlisle.

Charlie did not want to stay. He'd heard about prison food. And he didn't believe it had improved much since the time of Tom Horn. Actually he didn't believe that Carlisle would be having two trays of food brought to his cell. The state of Wyoming wasn't in the business of serving guests at its prisons. He pocketed his pencils, drank the rest of his water, and stood up. He could hear the carts bringing the trays. They clanged against the floor and clanked against the walls. The guard called out, "Mr. Irwin, Sheriff Roach said if it were anyone else he'd kick him out, but you're here to do a job for the Union Pacific and he says you're all right. Enjoy your lunch." Two trays were pushed under the bars.

Carlisle brought one to Charlie and then picked up the other. The two men sat side by side and ate. Neither said a word. The food was good: creamed chicken on mashed potatoes, green beans, biscuits, canned peaches, milk and coffee. Charlie slid his empty tray under the bars to the corridor. Carlisle finished up and did the same. "Thanks, friend," said Charlie.

"Are you going to rewrite all that scratching you've been making while I talk?" said Carlisle.

"No, I'm not going to rewrite it. I'm going to have my secretary type it for me," said Charlie.

"She can read it?"

"If she can't she'll ask me. She's my oldest daughter."

"I would like to have a daughter one day," said Carlisle moodily.

"Let's finish this job first," said Charlie with a smile. "After working the Mexican-Texas border as a gun runner, what did you do?"

"I came north. One town I really like is Denver."

"I like it, too. It'll be one of the largest towns in the West one day."

"You know, if you go up Seventeenth Street from the depot, there's a string of bars and in every bar there used to be a bunch of tinhorn gamblers. You could get in a poker game easy enough," Carlisle said, "but if you got out with a cent it wasn't their fault."

Carlisle told Charlie that he went to Sheridan, Wyoming, and started work in October 1915. "I was a fireman for the Burlington Railroad. Honest. The last of November I had an accident, getting off of the engine at a water tank. I had misrepresented my references to the Burlington so did not try to go back to work for them anymore. That's when I went to Denver. I advertised for a job in the *Denver Post* and the *News*. The ad was run on December fifth, sixth, and seventh. I advertised that I was an ex-convict, but that I wanted to do better and that I wanted a steady job, as my mind would not permit me to be idle.

"I received several replies: Hugh O'Neil of the *Denver Post* will confirm all that I am telling you."

Charlie nodded, kept his eyes down, and wrote as fast as he could. Carlisle's story was moving smooth and rapid.

"I went to work for John Larson, a mine owner, in Denver. He sent me to work in his mine at Central City as a mucker. I worked there steady all winter, until June first, then they laid me off. I made two trips from Central City to Denver, which is about thirty miles. The first time I walked. The second time I borrowed the money and took the stage, that was on June fifth." Carlisle crossed his legs and asked Charlie if he had any makings.

"Sorry, I don't smoke, so I don't carry any tobacco."

"Oh, well, I'll live," said Carlisle. "I told Mr. Larson that I would have to have steady work, that my mind would not permit me to lay around. So he said that he couldn't understand why the foreman would not give me steady work. He said he'd pay me off." Then Carlisle hesitated a moment before he said, "No, my dates are wrong there, I mean that I was laid off and only worked off and on until June twenty-fifth. Then I made my first trip to Denver, telling Larson that I must have work to keep my mind occupied. He sent me back to the mine, telling me that he would give them instructions to work me steady. I went back to Denver on February fifth, 1916. I told my troubles again to Mr. Larson, mainly that the foreman would not let me work at all. That's when he paid me off. He gave me fifteen dollars, which I applied to the balance on my board bills. So then, on Saturday, February fifth, I arrived in Cheyenne and tried to get work at the livery barns around town. I could not strike anything."

"Did you go to Meanea's Saddle Shop? He keeps a list posted near the front door of ranchers and business places in the area that are looking for men, and he knows places not on the list if a man asks," said Charlie, trying to remember if he still had a call out for extra help at the ranch.

"No, I never hit that place. I ran out of money and ran on to a man in one of the saloons that I'd loaned money to in Montana. I asked him for five dollars. He gave it to me. His name was Texas. He was a ranch blacksmith and worked around at the different ranches."

"I never heard of him. I have a ranch north of Cheyenne," said Charlie. "Being Livestock Agent for the U.P. is a good job, but a man with a family could starve with only that."

"Ya, well, I just drifted around for the next few days. Then I got so hungry I thought I was going to be sick. That's when I robbed my first train, February ninth. When I saw all the posters on all the buildings and telegraph posts, I knew what a fix I was in. It was going to be life in prison or death for robbing a train. I knew they'd get me sooner or later, so I decided to have fun while I could.

"If I hadn't twisted my ankle when I landed in the soft dirt outside of Hanna the other night, I might still be out there incognito. You know I was as far as the Platte River at one time, walking barefoot or with my stockings on."

"Bachus and I found your tracks and we knew you had taken your boots off," said Charlie. "Your feet hurt?"

"No, sir, not anymore. The first two times I sneaked over the back end of the observation car and the third time I bought a ticket. You were there and saw me." His light-colored eyes twinkled once again.

"You never used a horse?" asked Charlie.

"Of course not! You can't ride a horse along beside a train and jump on, or ride beside a speeding train and grab a hold of a ladder on a freight car. A horse won't let you get that close to the side of a train. You might ride up to the rear of the train, but not the side. My friend, if you are a ranchman, you should know that."

Charlie chuckled. He shook Carlisle's hand. "I'll do the best I can for you." He'd folded up his notepaper and stuffed it in his coat pocket. "I wish you luck, friend."

"Thanks, Mr. Irwin. I won't forget you. Don't worry about me. I've always taken my medicine with a stiff upper lip."

Charlie sent an extra copy of the typewritten story Carlisle had told to Mr. Jeffers in Omaha. Charlie could not go to the ranch that weekend because if there was anything else to be written, Mr. Jeffers would get in touch with Charlie at the office or at his Cheyenne home. Charlie wished like anything he could go to the ranch. He could think better there. He wanted to think about

Carlisle. Charlie liked him. He felt that Carlisle could have made a good life for himself if way back when he was a boy, his father had not been so hard on him. Now, if he could talk with the right people, Carlisle could make something of himself. He needed some confidence and someone to praise his work.

Charlie compared Carlisle with Tom Horn and couldn't find a trait to compare. Comparisons meant similarities. The two men were different as fire and water. Carlisle was not bitter about his captors. He was learned, acted on impulse, not introspective. He was weak. He was a mover. He could not sit still in one place for long. He was not a silent stalker as was Horn. He'd never killed a man. Charlie didn't think Carlisle could muster up enough anger to want to kill anyone. He was not a ladies' man. He was a dreamer. He wished he had a little girl, a daughter. Suddenly Charlie knew something that was similar about the two outlaws. Tom Horn and William Carlisle were both loners.

On April twenty-third Charlie received two telegrams from Union Pacific officials.

Charles B. Irwin
Copy W. M. Jeffers, Cheyenne

Omaha, April 23, 1916

You are eighteen carat and a real bandit chaser. We fully appreciate your valuable assistance.

Charles Ware
General Manager U.P.R.R.
10:45 A.M.*

Chas. Irwin
Cheyenne, Wyo.

Omaha, April 23, 1916

I want to compliment you for the assistance you have given us in the capturing of the train robber. You are a human dynamo. Nothing gets away from you and we never make any mistake when we get you interested.

A. L. Mohler
10:14 A.M.*

Charlie sent letters to all the men who had been in his party during the search and capture of Carlisle. He sent the list of men in his party to Ware and suggested that they be reimbursed for

*Courtesy Charles M. Bennett Collection, Scottsdale, Arizona.

their work, at the rate of fifteen dollars a day. That would give each man thirty dollars. He also sent a voucher for the hay, oats, gasoline, and food purchased at the Trading Post in Hanna.

Charlie sent Carlisle's confession, which Joella had typed onto four sheets of paper, to Jeffers. Several days later Charlie had a telephone call from Jeffers while he was at the office in the Plains Hotel.

"C.B., I want you to go to Denver to visit Carlisle's landlady at 1758 Pennsylvania. She's Mrs. J. W. McKamy. Take a look around Carlisle's room. Let me know what you find."

"All right. You're the boss. What do you want me to look for? What's in a rented room, a bed and dresser?" said Charlie.

"Yes, and look in the closet for clothes—clothes he wore at the time of the robberies," said Jeffers.

"How about taking pictures?" asked Charlie, wondering where he'd get a photographer.

"Say, that's the ticket! Get someone from the *Denver Post* to go with you. He'll smell a story, so you won't have trouble talking him into going with you. Just tell that *Post* gent to call me before he prints any of the photos in the paper," said Jeffers.

Before taking the train to Denver, Charlie went to see Carlisle. He told him what Jeffers asked him to do. He also picked up his lasso rope from Sheriff Roach.

"C.B., there's a bankbook on top of the dresser. Take it to the bank for the fifteen dollars left there."

"All right, but you'd better write me a note for the bank." He handed Carlisle a sheet of paper from his pocket. It was U.P. stationery that he used in his office. Carlisle looked at it, but said nothing. He wrote:

> Dear Sirs—
>
> Please pay to bearer of this note, Charlie B. Irwin of Cheyenne, Wyo. $15 deposited by me. He has my bankbook.
>
> Respectfully,
> Walter L. Cottrell
> 1758 Pennsylvania Street
> Denver, Colo.*

*Courtesy Charles M. Bennett Collection, Scottsdale, Arizona.

"I'm going to write a note to my landlady. Please give me another piece of paper. Will you give it to her?" said Carlisle.

Charlie said he would.

Mrs. McKamy was a small, blond-haired woman. Charlie liked her right away. She smiled a lot and that made her blue eyes look like the sky on a clear day. "That Carlisle fellow was like a big, overgrown boy. My husband and I liked him. He called himself Walter L. Cottrell here. My, it's hard to think he was a train robber. He lived here two weeks. I guess the music, flowers, candy, and leather banners he bought for his room and the things he bought for us, lace doilies, magazines, picture postcards, was bought with money he stole from train passengers." Her hand went to her mouth. "Oh, my!"

"I need to examine his room," said Charlie, "and this man is going to take a few pictures." He motioned to the *Denver Post* photographer.

"My husband has the key to the room. We thought Mr. Cottrell—uh—Carlisle—was coming back. He's a postman, my husband, and out on his route." She smiled.

"Is there a window?" asked Charlie.

"Certainly," she said, leading the two men outside.

Charlie wrapped his handkerchief around his fist and smashed in the pane. He reached in and opened the catch and raised the lower half and crawled inside. The photographer handed Charlie his camera equipment, then crawled in himself.

"This man sure enjoyed spending other people's money," said the photographer, setting up his tripod with the big, black accordion-pleated camera on the top.

The walls of the room were covered with burnt-leather plaques of deer, elk, and bear and picture postcards and college pennants and banners. Two big boxes of chocolates were on the dresser top. There were green plants in red clay pots on the dresser and on the two bedside tables and on another little table in the room. A new guitar with new sheet music stood in one corner near the bed. Two new suits of clothes from the Cottrell Clothing Company in Denver were carefully arranged on hangers in the closet. In the top drawer of the dresser were receipts showing that the sheet music had been purchased from the Denver Music Company. The pictures were from Kendrick-Bellamy's and more than twenty dollars of things had come from the Kohlberg curio store and some jewelry had been bought from George Bell and Company.

"Look at this!" whistled the photographer. It was a blond wig and a box of theatrical makeup. "That man was going to wear a disguise the next time!"

Charlie opened the door from the inside. Mrs. McKamy came in. "I won't get in your way," she said. "That man was just a nice sort of big boy. He loved flowers and music."

"I can see that," said Charlie with a sigh, looking in the other dresser drawers.

"He was so generous to everyone. He delighted in filling the house with plants and cut flowers of all kinds. Why, on Easter Sunday, the biggest mass of roses and carnations I ever saw came here with this card." She fondled the card that was on one of the bedside tables. Then she laid it down gently.

"Cards!" yelled Charlie. "Look at them!" Charlie found a box full of cards neatly engraved with the name of Walter L. Cottrell. In the same drawer Charlie found a program to one of Innes's Sunday Auditorium Concerts and the official program issued at the field on the opening day of the baseball season in Denver.

Under the bed Charlie found a battered suitcase. He pulled it out and tossed it on top of the bed. He opened it and gasped. Inside were an old pair of shoes thick with dried mud, a pair of new, black rubber overshoes, also caked in mud so that the metal buckles were barely visible, and a pair of yellow corduroy trousers that had water marks up to the knees.

"That's what he wore when he held up the Overland Limited!" said Charlie. "Yellow—yellow corduroy pants!"

"This man was some sort of nut," said the photographer. "If you hadn't got him when you did he'd be playing more pranks, cutting up more didoes. Someone could get hurt the next time. The bird's a real mess." He pushed his blond hair out of his eyes and unbuttoned his coat. Then he spread the contents of the suitcase on the bed and took several pictures. "Sorry about that dried mud, but if you just shake the bedspread out, it'll be all right," he said to Mrs. McKamy.

Charlie reached into his suit coat. "Here, I almost forgot he sent this to you." Charlie gave the following note to Mrs. McKamy:

Dear Friends,

I was called back to Cheyenne and will be unable to return to Denver this summer. I am sending Mr. Charles B. Irwin, a personal friend, for my clothing and ornaments. Please let him have everything of mine and balance of money I left to pay bills with.

Sincerely your friend,
Walter L. Cottrell*

"He says for you to take his things to him. He doesn't say anything about holding up a train and being put in jail," said Mrs. McKamy. "But he does say you are his personal friend. So I guess you can take what he wants."

Both Charlie and the *Post* photographer read the letter.

"That bird has a rare sense of humor, I'd say," said the photographer.

Charlie called a taxi because he could not get all of Carlisle's belongings in the photographer's automobile. The taxi was filled with potted plants, a guitar, and pictures and banners. The photographer leaned over to look inside the taxi's side window. "Say, you look like a college kid come home for summer vacation. Or maybe come home because he flunked and was booted out by the dean. Thanks, Mr. Irwin, this is some story!"

"Mac, wait a minute." Charlie had forgotten the name of the photographer. "Don't put anything in the paper, no story, no pictures, until you call Mr. Jeffers at the U.P. offices in Omaha. Tell him what we found and get your go-ahead to print the story."

"I can do that," said the photographer. "This Jeffers isn't going to tell me not to print."

"I don't think so. He wants to know what we found and he wants to be told first. Oh, remember what I told you about the capture—get that straight. I've never seen a bigger mess than the things already put out by the papers on that. The U.P. caught this Carlisle. No private sleuths were in on it at all. You newspaper fellows ought to try to keep your facts true to life. All right, Mac, so long. Thanks for your help."

The two men shook hands. Charlie shook Mrs. McKamy's

*Courtesy Charles M. Bennett Collection, Scottsdale, Arizona.

hand. He reached into his pocket and took out three dollars. "To get the window fixed."

Mrs. McKamy waved from the front porch of her little two-bedroom frame house.

When Charlie returned to Cheyenne with all the things from the McKamy house, he found that Jeffers wanted to look it over and then send it to the prison authorities at the Wyoming State Penitentiary at Rawlins. Charlie unloaded the stuff in the baggage room at the depot. He paid the taxi driver and wrote out an expense report with the amount of the taxi fare from Denver to Cheyenne in it and left it on the desk for Mr. Jeffers.

When Jeffers arrived from Omaha, the first thing he asked Charlie was about all the cards they'd found in the room. "That *Denver Post* man told me that the cards had the name of Cottrell on them. He also told me you had a note from Carlisle to get some money from the bank."

"You can have the note I took to the bank." Charlie searched in his coat pockets and finally found the folded paper in his inside coat pocket. "There was no bankbook. At least I couldn't find it. The bank wouldn't give me the money without the bankbook. But the assistant cashier said Cottrell had a balance of exactly fifteen dollars. And he said Cottrell took out a lot more recently. You think Carlisle has money hidden somewhere? I guess we'll never find it unless Carlisle talks."

"I just want to get him out of my hair," said Jeffers.

On May 8, Carlisle was on trial in Cheyenne. On May 10 he was convicted of train robbery, without capital punishment, and on May 11 he was sentenced to life imprisonment in the State Penitentiary at Rawlins. Carlisle entered pleas of not guilty to five counts in the information Charlie had written based on his holdup of the Overland Limited and the other two holdups.

Before the trial Carlisle told the judge, "If I plead guilty you will remember that and sentence me to life imprisonment. If I stand trial, it will go into my record. What was said in the trial will be handy when I want a pardon. I plead not guilty because I may outlive this thing, and I want a chance if I do."

THIRTY-EIGHT

The Show Must Go On

The meadowlarks sang in the tall grass. The cowboys came in from their roundups, glad to be free of the snow and cold wind that bound them close to the home ranch for the winter months. A couple of cottontails scurried across the dirt road as Charlie's automobile kicked out dust from the rear wheels. He parked the car in front of the iron gate and hauled out a sack of flour and several boxes of groceries. Roy and Martinez came from the bunkhouse to help Charlie take the groceries into the kitchen.

"Got something for you boys after you get everything in the house and put on the shelves," said Charlie.

"Pa, I hope it's dill pickles," said Roy.

"Better," said Charlie.

"Chilies?" asked Martinez, his black eyes looking into one of the sacks.

"Nope. Tickets for the Hagenback Circus tomorrow. I got enough tickets so everybody's going."

At the supper table Dee Dee, who believed Charlie could do anything, asked if he'd fix it so she could walk the tight rope while she was at the circus. "I miss performing the high-wire act. Arrange something with the Hagenback people. Please."

Charlie put his fork on his empty plate, wiped his face, and leaned over the table. "This is not to be a performance by any of my people. I am taking everyone out for a treat—watch and enjoy. If you want to do something, look closely and get some ideas we might use to liven up our Wild West show."

"Thanks, Pa," said Floyd, taking Dee Dee's arm. "I told her it's dangerous up there, especially without a net."

"Men," said Dee Dee with a sigh. "You never think of danger when you're trick riding on a horse, sliding under its belly where you could get your head kicked or your neck broke."

"I know what I'm doing!" said Floyd. "Tell her, Pa."

"Floyd worries about you, because he loves you," said Charlie.

"I worry about him!" said Dee Dee. "What would I do without him? He's the most important thing in my life. I want Floyd to stop doing the Wild West show and just work the ranch." She looked around the table. Everyone sat like a statue.

Charlie was stunned. He wondered what he'd do without Floyd on the show. Why, his son had grown up with the Wild West show.

"Maybe Dee Dee's right," said Etta cautiously. "Floyd could run the ranch, give the two of them a chance to settle down, raise their own family. Charlie, you could find someone else to do the trick riding and roping."

"I don't want to talk about it," said Charlie. "Floyd, work with me this season and then I'll give you some time off. Now let's talk about the circus we'll see tomorrow."

Sitting in the grandstand besides Charlie's own family and some of his ranch hands were his brother Frank and his wife, Clara Belle. Clara Belle held their youngest girl, Arlyne, two months younger than Pauline's daughter. Their little girls, Maxine and Louise, waved to Charlie and Etta. Pauline held up Betts so that they could see how their cousin had grown. Sitting in the front seats of the grandstand were Charlie's older brother, Will, and his wife, Margaret, and their four children.

"I'm surprised Uncle Will's not in the bleachers," snipped Joella.

"Hush your spiteful tongue," said Etta.

"Well, Uncle Will wouldn't loan you a nickel unless you called in the Lord and his twelve disciples to sign your note."

"Hush," admonished Etta. "We're all family. Didn't he give you a nice wedding present?"

"Grandpa Joe's butter churn that's as old as the hills," said Joella.

"That's been in the Irwin family for years. It's a keepsake. Besides, Will fixed it so it works real good," said Etta.

"I'll never use it," said Joella.

"You have to admit he knows cows, front, back, and sidewise," said Floyd. "He gave Dee Dee and me a good milk cow."

"Must have thought your wife was expecting," murmured Joella.

Floyd's face turned crimson. "She's not, so be quiet!"

Charlie stood. "Everybody hush now and watch the show. We're here to have a good time."

The elephants came in first and circled around the big sawdust-filled ring once before doing their act. A girl in pink-spangled tights did a handstand on the back of the biggest elephant. Dee Dee whispered aloud, "I can do that."

Next came the trained bear act. The clowns tumbled head over heels when a man was shot out of a huge cannon. Charlie bet Roy that the man would land on his feet. He lost. The man landed on his back and did several rolling somersaults before getting to his feet. Charlie gave Roy a silver dollar.

Then came the chariot race. Each chariot was drawn by four all-white or four all-black horses. There were four chariots in the race, one was red, one blue, one yellow, and one white, all trimmed with gold paint.

The drivers wore sequined, black trousers, knee-high patent-leather boots, and a wide sequined collar around their necks. Their bare arms, backs, and chests were shiny with oil. The drivers carried bullwhips, which they cracked in the air to make the horses run faster. The white chariot was in the lead during the first lap; the red chariot came up close on the inside. The crowd was clapping. Charlie leaned far forward so that he could see the drivers better. He enjoyed any kind of horse race. The driver of the yellow chariot raised his arm and slashed the air with the long narrow tongue of his whip. The man's shoulder muscles rippled. His black, four-horse team inched forward. The yellow chariot was out in front as it came around to pass the grandstand for the fourth and final lap. The driver kept the chariot close to the inside rail, too close. Charlie held his breath as if anticipating what was going to happen. The chariot struck a tent pole.

Charlie was out of his seat in a flash. He had no time to think. Instinctively he knew what could happen. The other chariots would run head on into the yellow one, smashing it into kindling wood. He could see the driver of the yellow chariot was caught. The horses were plunging here and there, scared silly and out of control. The crowd screamed. If the other horses crashed against the same tent pole, the tent could collapse. The horses would run wild and spectators would be hurt.

Charlie pushed between Will and Margaret, who were yelling in panic, but frozen to their seats. He vaulted over the little white picket fence between the grandstand and the sawdust ring. He grabbed the bridles of the two lead horses, pulled them off the track so that the chariot and driver were off the ring. He stood protectively against the driver, who was entangled in the reins and debris of his chariot just as the three other chariots thundered past. Each driver was desperately trying to pull his team to a halt. They were halfway around the circle before the three teams were fully stopped.

Charlie unfastened the broken chariot from the nervous team. He kept up a rhythmic, "Whoa, boy, whoa, boy" that seemed to calm the horses. He pulled the driver away from the debris and the tangled reins. He was surprised to find that the driver was just a kid. The crowd was suddenly quiet. There was no screaming and no panicky rush for the exits. Charlie held up the arm of the driver to show that he was not injured. Someone came out and took the team out of the ring. The other teams and chariots were gone. The broken chariot was being picked up and hauled off.

"It's all right!" yelled Charlie. "The show goes on!"

The young chariot driver shook Charlie's hand. "Pal, you have the strength of a Goliath and quick wits of a fox. You saved my life, the collapse of the tent, the pile-up of horses, and more'n likely the life of those folks sitting in the first row or two!"

Charlie felt a weakness in his knees. He pulled the shiny-skinned, half-naked boy against himself in a quick embrace, saying in his ear, "You allow this greasy, oily stuff on your body? It may make you look good, but it smells like rotten fish oil." He let go abruptly, walked toward the stands, feeling the hushed silence of the crowd. Then it was broken like putting pinpricks in a dozen balloons. The crowd was applauding and on its feet. Charlie heard the boy behind him clapping his hands, so he turned and said, "My advice, kid, is to get a chariot that's green next time. Yellow's bad luck." His knees felt boneless. He climbed over the little fence and sat down beside Will for a few moments. He felt giddy as a schoolgirl.

Margaret said, "Thank God you were here, C.B."

Someone behind him said, "Thanks, mister. You were in the right place at the right time." Another person said, "I've never seen any one as strong as you. Are you one of the circus people?"

Charlie smiled and shook his head. "No, no. I acted without thinking."

"You saved all of us from a terrible catastrophe," said Gladys, Will's oldest daughter. "Uncle Charlie, you're a hero!"

"No, no," insisted Charlie, "I acted instinctively. I never thought about what I was doing. It all happened too fast." He got up and moved on up beside Etta. His knees felt like jelly. Etta took his hand and held it a moment without saying a word.

Someone behind him tapped his shoulder. "I closed my eyes and prayed, and when I opened my eyes the racetrack was cleared," said a woman.

"It was a miracle for sure," agreed another woman.

Charlie took a deep breath, smiled, and squeezed Etta's hand.

"You sure know how to show us a good time," said Dee Dee, laughing out loud.

The tent pole was straightened and two reinforcing boards were lashed over the break. The show went on.

Charlie's light-headedness subsided. His watery knees began to solidify. "Dee Dee, if you'd been on a high-wire when that pole was hit, you might have fallen and broken your neck. I saved your life."

Dee Dee swallowed and knew enough not to contradict her father-in-law. She'd never walk the wire with a chariot race going on underneath. She smiled. Charlie reached out and hugged her. Her face turned red. Charlie chuckled, patted her hand, and loosened his necktie. Dee Dee looked at Floyd.

Floyd said, "Pa's just blowing off steam. He cranked up a lot to move those horses and get that kid off the track. He likes you. Really. He doesn't want anything to happen. You're part of the family. He's protective with all of us."

Roy, sitting on the other side of Floyd, whispered something, excused himself, and pushed his way to the bottom of the stand. He stood in front of Will and Margaret and motioned something to them with his hands. They looked up at Etta and Charlie, then back at Roy, who cupped his hands around his mouth.

"Mister, me and my brothers"—he pointed to Will's boys, Sharkey and Gene—"didn't see what you done!" he yelled real loud. "Do it again!"

The whole arena seemed to hear and the tittering began to fan out like bees leaving a hive early in the morning, looking for clover in a meadow.

Charlie stood up, feeling fine now, a smile on his face, and waved his big ten-gallon white hat back and forth. He nodded to the German band that had come out into the ring. Then put his hat on his head, pushing the front brim up just a hair. The circus people knew what that meant. Charlie had said it before: "All's well. The show must go on."

After that incident, wherever the Hagenback Circus played, if Charlie Irwin or any of his family were in that town, they had complimentary passes to all the shows. Everybody in the Hagenback Circus knew who, big as a bass fiddle, C. B. Irwin was. For years the circus people talked about Charlie's bull strength, lightning action, and generous heart.

A few days after the circus left town, there was a knock at the door. The young boy who'd been in the chariot accident stood there, twisting his cap in his hands when Etta opened the door.

"I'd like to speak with Mr. Irwin, please, ma'am." The boy was nervous.

Etta directed him to Charlie's office in the Plains Hotel. When Charlie came home for supper, he had the boy with him.

"Etta, this is Bee Ho Gray. He's had enough of circus life, but wants to be in a Wild West show. What do you think of that?" asked Charlie, sitting the boy down at the supper table beside himself.

Etta went for another plate and silverware. She thought the youngster looked about sixteen, not much younger than Roy. "What do his folks say?"

"I never asked," said Charlie. He turned to the dark-haired, blue-eyed boy. "Have you asked your folks?"

"They're in Oklahoma on a ranch and probably think I've been stolen by Comanches." He took a gulp of milk. "I can swing a rope. I learned with a Comanche horsehair lariat."

"Eat your supper, then I'll give you a rope. If you're not spectacular, I can't use you. Irwin's Wild West show has only the best." Charlie made a wry face.

The boy's lips twitched. He took another gulp of milk and dug into the mound of mashed potatoes and gravy Etta piled on his plate.

When he was finished with supper, Etta asked, "Are you afraid of horses?"

The boy stared into space, weighted down by decision making. "No, I'm not," he decided. "It's chariots I don't like very much, and that stinkin' body grease."

"Nasty, flimsily built," agreed Charlie. "You want to juggle my rope a couple of times outside?"

Bee Ho Gray was a good rope juggler. To Charlie's surprise he could throw three ropes at one time. Charlie took the boy across the street to the horse stalls. He saddled a horse and told the boy he was going to ride toward him. "Show me what those Comanches taught you!" yelled Charlie, whipping the horse into action. The boy stood his ground, twirling the ropes as Charlie came at him full gallop. One rope went about the horse's neck, another around its four feet and the third caught Charlie.

"You're hired!" hollered Charlie. "I'll wire your folks in Oklahoma so they won't worry about you being kidnapped by Comanches."

"Phew!" said the boy with a sigh. "Thanks a heap, Mr. Irwin."

Charlie took Bee Ho Gray to the ranch so that he could work out with Floyd and Roy before going on the road with the show. In the meantime Charlie made up posters and programs and sent them to the printer for the 1916 show. He kept the most popular acts, added new ones, and dressed up some of the old ones to keep the enthusiasm high for his shows. He hired a new girl trick roper, Vera McGinnis, and a young man, Sam Garrett. He took Mabel Strickland and Reva Grey into the show for steer roping and relay racing. He hired Eloise Fox for trick riding. He continued to use the Sioux from the Pine Ridge Agency in South Dakota.

Floyd, Roy, and Gray worked on a roping act that would have audiences holding their breath and standing with their ovation each time. Roy said, "We have to give Bee Ho some kind of background, like where is he from and how did he learn roping."

"That's right. We need something to tell the newspaper reporters in the name of publicity," said Floyd. "Let's cook up some whopper about when Bee Ho lived with the Indians. The public loves that kind of adventure story."

Together the three boys made up a story about Bee Ho Gray. When he was a boy of only four years old, he was stolen from his parents' ranch in Oklahoma by raiding Comanches. He was raised in old Chief Quanah Parker's band, where he learned the Indian habits and language, and above all learned to ride the Comanche cayuse and use a braided horsehair lariat. His name, Bee Ho, according to Floyd's imagination, was Comanche and meant "Cripple's Brother." In the remainder of the publicity they turned to more factual material, stating that Gray threw three ropes at one time, an extraordinary feat.

As Charlie expected, Gray's act was a colossal success. Reporters in every town and city wanted to know how long he'd been with the Comanches before he was rescued.

"My pa was out hunting deer one fall when I was seven, and he stumbled on to me as I had my bow pulled back ready to shoot the same buck he was aimin' for with his Winchester. I recognized him, even before he'd decided I wasn't a Comanche. I went home with him then and there. But, of course, I went back several times to see my Comanche family in Parker's band. They've always been friendly. That's probably why the Comanches are so friendly with most whites to this day."

Floyd, Roy, and Gray would bend over with laughter after the reporter left. When Charlie read the paper he'd chuckle. "People love to be fooled. They want romance and adventure in their life. We give it to them. We take people out of a humdrum existence and set their imaginations to work. Imagining an exciting life gives the people happiness. Nothing wrong with making people feel good."

Etta did not go with the Wild West show for the first time that year. She stayed home to care for her grandchild Betts. "I love you," she told Charlie. "You are the best-looking, most generous man I know. I'll miss you and all the children and the cowboys. But, this is honest, I'm not as enthusiastic about the traveling show business as you are. I'm not so fond of living in a railroad car. I'll really enjoy watching after baby Betts. I love that baby."

Charlie never realized that Etta was not fond of traveling with the Wild West show. "I'll miss you, dear. I'll think of you, especially when the kids do an especially great performance."

She put her arms around him and felt the fluttering of his heart. He felt an indescribable, sad loneliness sweep over him. When he pulled away his voice was gruff. "Pauline wants us to take the show to Billings and Miles City, Montana. She thinks maybe Charley Johnson would come to town to see it if he's cowboying in the southeastern part of the state. Do you agree?"

Etta didn't hesitate. "Charley Johnson is her husband. She ought to be with him."

"But Montana? The show is scheduled to go east this year."

"Is there time to contact Johnson if he's still working on that ranch near Hardin?" asked Etta. "Charlie, write to him and ask him to be in the show this year. Send him railroad fare to Omaha. He can meet you there."

"All right, what can I lose?"

"Railroad fare to Omaha," said Etta with a laugh. "But I don't think so. Charley Johnson will ride your wildest buckers, Silver City and Rocking Chair. He'll be with Pauline this summer. But—if you want the truth—I don't think he'll come back to the Y6."

"Doesn't he want to see his little daughter?" Charlie was indignant.

"He doesn't think like you and I. He needs to be free."

"Is that because of that doggone blow on the head Frank gave him?" Charlie blurted.

"I think so," said Etta without qualms. "You and Pauline will have to let him go." There was a tenderness in her voice.

Goddamn, he said to himself. He'd never swear in front of Etta, the girls, or any other woman. Life can be rough as hell.

In the east the sky was gray and the stars were fewer and lighter. Charlie and the cowboys were loading the stock cars with the show animals. The horses stood together, softly nickering to one another in the boxcar. The other animals, steers, goats, buffalo, shifted about, snuffling to one another as they picked up bits of grass with their lips. Charlie walked from one car to the other making certain there was enough water and hay and at least two cowboys to each car. He walked past the animal droppings, like various shaped mud balls among the stubble.

"O.K. Load up. This train leaves in ten minutes!" he called.

Floyd was riding in the chair car with the Indians. He sat beside John Red Cloud, who was all smiles. "Hey, what do you know?" asked Floyd.

"I know you got a woman, brother, so I got me a woman."

"Yeah?" Floyd looked at the wooden peg leg jutting below the blue denim pants on the right side. "How's the wooden leg?"

Red Cloud kicked the peg leg out and touched Floyd's knee with it. "Fine. I don't need crutches nor a cane. I'm the only man I know that takes his leg off with his pants every night."

"Peg Leg, introduce me to your woman."

"Oh, she's with our papoose."

"You're afraid she'll find me handsome and irresistible. I let Dee Dee talk to you. She didn't find you all that handsome."

"Hey, it's not that. The papoose is sick, see."

"What's the matter?" asked Floyd, sensing that Red Cloud was worried about something.

"He don't keep his food down. He upchucks."

"Oh, that's nothing. You know my sister, Pauline? She has a baby now. A girl. That kid spits up and burps like a sick calf—smells about as sour, too."

"Yeah? Well, come on."

Floyd saw a quiet, round-faced, intelligent girl, who was re-plaiting her shiny black hair. Her eyes were on the sleeping infant on the seat next to hers. The baby was not more than five months old, thin, with patches of its soft, dark hair missing, so that he had a piebald effect. The girl's name was Clear Eyes. The baby had no formal name yet. Clear Eyes called him Papoose, or Baby.

Floyd bent over the seat and the baby curled thin, brown fingers around his index fingers. "You had a doctor look at your papoose?"

Clear Eyes spoke. "The Black Robe, the religious man at the agency, tells me to mash beans and potatoes with milk gravy and feed Papoose by spoon. My grandmother tells me he is too young for that. She tells me only nurse him. I have done both. Papoose is no better."

Floyd noticed that the baby's eyes moved jerkily and did not focus on anything for more than a few seconds. He picked up the baby, leaving the thin quilt behind. The infant was dressed in a white diaper, a flannel shirt, and bellyband. Long white, mercerized cotton stockings were pinned to the diaper. The baby was surprisingly light and limp, like a rag doll. He whimpered pathetically.

"I'm not holding him just right or he doesn't like me," said Floyd, handing the baby to Clear Eyes. "I'll talk to Pa about having a doctor look at him at one of our stops."

"A white medicine man?" asked Red Cloud.

"Sure. Why not?" said Floyd. "He'll have some medicine for kids."

"The white men asks for money, and what if I don't have enough?" asked Red Cloud.

"That's a stupid kind of question. You work for my pa, don't you? So he takes care of you." Floyd circled his hand through the air to indicate Red Cloud, his wife, and baby.

Clear Eyes held the baby on her shoulder and rocked the upper half of her body to quiet the whimpering. She whispered, "Remember the time you hid from your father? My grandmother threw a blanket over you and my grandfather sat on your back." She giggled. "All of us Sioux kids called you *Boots*. I had a crush on you."

Floyd's face brightened. "Really. I thought all the girls liked John." The toe of his boot touched Red Cloud's wooden leg.

"John Red Cloud was only a tough kid. You had talent. You rode a horse like our people did a hundred years ago, hanging low on one side or swung low underneath. You swung a rope farther than anyone I knew."

Floyd deliberately made a big frown. "You don't believe I can do all that now?"

Clear Eyes laughed. Her mouth turned up, causing dimples to appear at the corners. "You're pulling at my leg."

"Oh, no, not me, ma'am." Floyd held both his hands in the air and laughed. "But you sure have pretty eyes. Don't worry none. In a couple weeks Papoose'll be well enough to have a regular name. I'd let you call him Floyd. Floyd Red Cloud, how's that sound? Not so bad, huh?"

"Boots is better," said Clear Eyes.

Floyd and Red Cloud went down the coach talking to other performers. This was the time to compare notes and become reacquainted. Floyd was eager to tell about the new tricks he had for this year's show. He could stand free on the rump of his horse, do a handstand on the saddle horn. Dee Dee had taught him how graceful a backbend could be on a trotting horse.

Everyone liked Dee Dee right away. She sat with Clear Eyes and offered to hold the baby when he was particularly fussy.

Charley Johnson joined the show in Omaha. He paid no attention to Pauline at first. In Omaha Charlie brought a doctor out to the Indian camp at the fairgrounds to look at the Red Cloud baby. The doctor held a flashlight near the baby's mouth, ears and eyes. He thumped the baby's chest and back. He held his little brown feet in his hands and said, "Missus, your child must be allergic to something in milk. Feed him sugar water for two three days, then add a little oatmeal gruel to the water. When he takes to that, add a little condensed milk. You young mothers panic over the first big burp a baby makes."

Sugar water and oatmeal gruel were no good. The baby could keep nothing in his stomach. Dee Dee brought him condensed milk, diluted with several spoonfuls of water. The mixture came back. She added sugar. Still it came back. She tried plain warm water and it was the same. The baby fretted day and night, until he was too weak to cry, then he slept. His breathing was shallow.

The show went to Des Moines, Peoria, Indianapolis, and then to Springfield, Ohio. For two days the baby refused to nurse or eat. He no longer cried. He was so thin he seemed almost skeletal. Dee Dee was afraid to pick him up. Clear Eyes was afraid to leave him. Emma, her grandmother, was afraid to look at the baby. She told Clear Eyes that the life thread that held the baby to the earth was too fragile to last more than a few days. Emma was right. The baby died the second day the show was in Springfield.

The funeral was held the next morning. All the Wild West show people attended the ceremony at Burley's Funeral Parlor. Probably no funeral in that city had ever been attended by such a colorful gathering. There were roustabouts in polished boots, snug Levi's, and clean colorful flannel shirts. Cowboys in silk shirts, tan trousers, and wide-brimmed hats, brushed smooth and clean. Women in long skirts or dresses, with red or blue shawls over their lace collars. The Indian men were dressed like the cowboys and some of them wore a favorite bright blanket over their shoulders. The Indian women wore green or purple skirts, red and blue cotton or satin blouses, with beaded moccasins.

The Red Clouds were Catholic. Charlie found a priest in Springfield who would perform the funeral service. He kept his eye on Red Cloud and Clear Eyes to make certain they were cared for during their grief. He told them that they should take the rest of the day off. "You need not be in the afternoon or evening performance."

"But we can do nothing more for our child. It would help me and my woman if we could be in the pony race and covered-wagon attack," said Red Cloud. "No one dies of grief. One only thinks he will."

Charlie put his arms around the couple and held them when the small white coffin was lowered into the ground. "How can I leave Papoose in some strange town?" sobbed Clear Eyes.

"Hush," said Red Cloud gruffly. "The grandmothers who went before him will watch over him."

The twenty-third Psalm was repeated by everyone. "Now sing 'Away in a Manger, No Place for a Bed,'" sobbed Clear Eyes, tugging on Charlie's coat sleeve. "It is the song I sang each night to Papoose. Please sing the song to start him on his long journey to the old grandmothers."

Charlie had a lump in his throat the size of a buckeye seed. He swallowed hard to rid himself of it, but it did no good. He closed his eyes and imagined his own children, little, sitting around a Christmas tree in pajamas. He opened his mouth and began to hum. As the humming grew his hands began to perspire, and his collar seemed tight. He undid the top button of his shirt under his tie and started to sing. His voice was deep and resonant. He did not hurry the words. The song was a lullaby. Some of the Indian women joined in the second time he sang the verse. Their faces shone in the warm June sunshine as tears rolled down their cheeks.

Red Cloud wept openly with his arm around his woman.

The priest shook Red Cloud's hand and touched Clear Eyes's shoulder. He made the sign of the cross, and the earth was pushed onto the little coffin. "All mothers are broken-hearted when they lose a child," he said. "The early red mothers lost babies during severe winters, pioneer white mothers buried babies alongside the old Oregon Trail. Each mother had to leave her child and turn her face toward a new day. Help this little mother as You helped all mothers before her, Lord. Mend her heart and give her joy for the future. Give this young father peace and patience. Amen."

The Irwin Wild West show is still talked about in Springfield, Ohio. Maybe some of the old-timers still remember the colorful funeral performed at Burley's Funeral Parlor and singing a Christmas hymn at the cemetery one early June morning. All those show people dressed in their finest was almost like a parade to townfolks. However, the late-night performance was the most intriguing and mysterious of all.

The last show was over. Everyone was packing. Floyd and Red Cloud were leading the horses into their stock car on the railroad siding. Floyd stood stock still. He listened. He grabbed Red Cloud. "Do you hear something?"

On the soft, warm night air was a low chant, not the high chirping of crickets or katydids, but a kind of moaning that came in swells.

"It's the women. They accompany the baby on the first part of his journey into the grandmother land. Before they are finished, all marks on the newly dug earth will vanish."

"What do you mean, vanish?" asked Floyd, the hairs on the back of his neck standing up.

"Disappear, cease to exist, so no evil spirits will find the grave."

"How do the women do that?" asked Floyd, suddenly curious.

"Come, but don't ask questions. Don't say anything."

"All right, let's get this boxcar closed and see that Roy and Charley Johnson have the buffalo loaded."

The buffalo were acting dumb and not finding the ramp into their car. Roy was swearing. "What is that goddamned, flesh-crawling moaning out there? I know it ain't no pack of coyotes."

"It's a Sioux burial ceremony. So keep your mouth shut," said Floyd between gritted teeth.

"Say, pal, want a drink?" Charley Johnson offered Red Cloud a drink from the hip flask he carried. "Good stuff, huh? I got it from that son-of-a-bitch doctor in Omaha. His liquor's better'n his advice, huh?"

Red Cloud sputtered, spit out what was in his mouth, and went after Johnson with his fists.

Roy stepped back, his eyes wide. "Aw, Peg Leg, he didn't mean nothing."

Red Cloud paid no attention to Roy. His right fist shot into Johnson's eye. Johnson gasped and staggered back, picked up a bullwhip off the pile on the ground.

"Oh, no!" cried Floyd. "Johnson, put that whip down! Roy! Load the whips! Now!"

Roy got all the heavy whips in his arms and reached out to grab the one from Johnson. Johnson lashed out, wound the whip around Roy's upper body. Roy dropped the pile of whips from his arms, clawed at the leather whip-end around his chest. He grabbed the end and ran for the paraphernalia car. The whip unwound and bounced on the ground behind him. He threw it in the car, ran back for the other whips. He ran like his boots were on fire and threw the bullwhips in the car before Johnson grabbed another.

"See what I mean about saying anything?" said Floyd, glaring at Roy. "You talk too much and at the wrong time."

"And Red Cloud uses his fists instead of talking," snarled Roy. "This is no time to start a fight. That caterwauling has everyone on edge."

Red Cloud hiccuped and dug at his eyes with both hands. Floyd took off his neckerchief and handed it to the grieving man. Red Cloud stood with his back to Floyd. He wiped his face, drew a deep breath. He turned and grinned. "Thanks, brother. Let's vamoose."

Floyd and Red Cloud stood at the edge of the cemetery watching the Indian women moving as if in a shared trance over the little mound of fresh dirt. Their hair hung loose, their arms were held up toward the dark sky, lit only with a multitude of silver points, stars. The moaning was continuous and rhythmic, an ululation. Women moved in and women moved out of the ring that gave the illusion of contracting and expanding.

Floyd looked through the starlit darkness. Shadows moved on the other side of the women. He squeezed Red Cloud's arm and pointed.

"The men, my people, thinking thoughts suitable for a boy on a long journey," said Red Cloud, standing straight with his face toward the sky.

Floyd felt a wild, sad excitement. He did not know how long he stood beside Red Cloud, who did not move. Suddenly the keening ceased. The women were kneeling. Floyd could see that they had tramped down the mound of soft dirt until it was flat with the rest of the area. Then he saw four women standing at the corners of a square; they pulled little brooms, made of jack-pine needles, from their blouses or from under their shawls, and they swept the earth while the others crawled on hands and knees slowly backward, making the square larger and larger. The grave had no marker. Its exact location was obliterated. The bare ground looked untouched, undug, unmolested. There was no mark of any kind left behind.

Red Cloud sighed and put his hand on Floyd's shoulder. "See, no bad spirit can come near the baby. No bad spirit can find the baby. He is with the ancient grandmothers. He is free. Time for us to go."

Floyd was deeply moved. "When I die I would like to be so loved by all my friends and relatives."

"When a man or woman, someone really important to my people, dies and we want to keep his spirit from harm, the ground is brushed with sacred turkey feathers. The turkey feathers are not used often; generally the ground is brushed with those little whisk brooms. Not many people worthy of the feathers these days," said Red Cloud.

Later Floyd learned that behind the Indian men was another crowd of people. They were Charlie and his show people and some of the more curious townspeople. This third group stayed a respectful distance away, feeling the sacredness of the Sioux ceremony. The whites were so moved that the memory hung in the back of their minds forever. The legend of the burial of the Sioux baby will continue to be told!

From Springfield the Irwin Wild West show went to Pittsburgh, Pennsylvania, then to the big event of the year—the New York Stampede.

New York City was not like any other place the Irwin Wild

West show had been invited to perform. There were tall buildings, a river filled with boats and tugs, people, people everywhere, more automobiles in the streets than anyone from the West had ever seen.

This big celebration was produced by Guy Weadick, the "father of the Canadian Rodeo" and the organizer and producer of the time-honored Calgary Stampede. Weadick learned cowboying when he worked for Charlie; later he became a trick and fancy roper with the Miller Brothers 101 Real Wild West Show, and still later wrote a cowboy column for *The Billboard*. Weadick asked his old friend and mentor, Charlie Irwin, to furnish the livestock for the New York Stampede, which was to be the most grandiose Wild West show and rodeo ever produced. New York's streetcar strike and polio epidemic did not dampen the spirit of the biggest Western show in the United States.

The celebration was held at the New York Speedway, where the automobile races were held. The day before the first performances, Charlie had his crew at the speedway practicing so they would be familiar with the layout. Frances rode Joella's favorite horse, Toby Gray. The Irwin girls knew that they would be up against strong competition in the cowgirls' relay races. Frances, the youngest, needed extra practice slipping off her horse and jumping back on with no loss of movement or time.

Frances and Joella practiced moving their horses out fast and pushing them hard. The others practiced roping, steer riding, bull-dogging, trick roping, and riding. Floyd rode by with his lariat flying over his head just as Frances moved Toby Gray toward the inside fence. The horse sideswiped the fence, and Frances flew into the air, over onto the fence. Toby Gray moved on down the track riderless. Floyd jumped off his horse, gave the reins to Roy. "Catch Toby Gray!" he yelled, and ran to pick up his little sister off the fence. He carried her to the Irwin tent. Frances was doing her best not to cry.

Charlie looked at the back of her legs. They were badly scratched and cut. He was sure that some of the cuts were near the ligaments. He never expected anyone in his show to be badly hurt while practicing or performing. If there was a small problem, he firmly believed in the old motto "The show must go on." People paid good money to see the Irwin performers, and Charlie always saw to it that they got their money's worth. He took Frances to their hotel.

He examined Frances's cuts more thoroughly and decided that

none of the ligaments were cut deeply. There was nothing here that he could not care for with his years of experience in caring for cattle and horses. He did not call a doctor for Frances. He washed the cuts with warm water and alcohol and momentarily longed for Etta, when Frances cried out in pain as the alcohol hit the open wounds.

"There, there, Fran, you'll be all right, good as new by tomorrow," he said as he painted the back of her legs with tincture of iodine. Then he bandaged her knees so tightly that she could not bend her legs. "You stay right here and I'll bring your supper to you," he said. "After that you go to sleep and in the morning you'll be much better."

"But Pa! This is the night you are going to take the kids to Coney Island! I want to go!" Frances was now in tears.

Charlie wanted to hold her on his lap and comfort his youngest daughter. But she was not a little girl—she was a young lady. She was fifteen. Etta knew how to handle these things. He felt like the proverbial bull in the china shop. "You can't go with your knees all tied up, now, can you? Stay here and sleep. We'll tell you about Coney Island in the morning," said Charlie, trying to be calm and logical. "That suits the situation."

But her father's words did not suit Frances. She had planned for weeks to see Coney Island. "Put me in a cart and take me, please, Pa!"

"We can't take a cart in a taxi; that's how we'll go to Coney Island. If the streetcars were running, we'd not be able to take the cart there."

"Well, then, you're strong enough to carry me," Frances sobbed. "I'm not so heavy and look how big you are."

Now he missed Etta more than before. He told Frances how she had to be brave and take whatever came to her. "Make the best of it." He told her how she was a winner and a fighter and how she'd show up girls on other teams when she got on the back of a horse. "You'll have to grit your teeth every time you get on a horse tomorrow. Get all the rest you can tonight." He told her there were nine days of show and she'd perform all nine days and make him so proud of her. But—to do all that horseback riding she'd have to stay behind this one night.

"It isn't worth it! Pa, I just want to see Coney Island! Heck with all the horseback riding! Remember what happened to Lucille Mulhall? She got better, but she could have been a cripple. Do I have to ride until I'm a cripple?"

"Of course not. I know how disappointed you are. But I know that the contests tomorrow and the following days are more important than Coney Island tonight."

"Important to whom!" cried Frances.

"Important to me. Important to you. Important to the Irwin Wild West show. That's why I came to New York. I'm going to prove that the Irwins' show has the top entertainment and the top cowboys and cowgirls. We're the best in the country. Now is our chance to prove it."

"Pa, I can't prove anything with my legs all cut up like chopped beef."

"Yes, you can! When I was a kid I learned something that I've always remembered. You get cake when the trick works. That means you are rewarded when you do something unusual, something spectacular." His brown eyes shone. "Let your legs heal, then show what you can do on horseback."

"I feel like a stick-in-the-mud," sobbed Frances. "I want to see Coney Island. That's what I dreamed about." She buried her face in her arms.

Charlie tried to shut out his daughter's cries. He knew he wasn't heartless, but he'd sounded that way. He knew that kids had to learn to take care of whatever came to them. Parents would not be around as a guide or shield forever. Wasn't it better to learn right away that life had dark moments? Better to learn as soon as possible that you can overcome most problems. It's the quitter that gives up in the face of adversity, the average person turns away to another goal, but the best never give up, although difficulties arise at unexpected moments, until they succeed.

Charlie wanted his children to know life, to learn to be tough at the right time. Unless one is flat on his back, he must get up and get going. The sooner the better. So—Frances had to stay on her back one night so she could get up and go on the next day.

Charlie brought Frances supper, tucked her in the bed, kissed her, and hurried out the door.

Frances dried her tears, ate her supper, pushed the tray to one side, and got out of bed. Stiff-legged and in pain she shuffled to the box where the lariats were packed. She got a short rope and twirled it around her head. She had to stand well balanced, keep her back and shoulders relaxed, or the pain in her legs was excruciating. Tears streamed down her face. She did not wipe them away. She gritted her teeth and practiced until her hips were numb and her legs like red-hot pokers. She fell, exhausted, into bed and slept soundly until Joella came into the room the next morning.

"Look, I've got all these cigarettes." Joella emptied out her pockets. "Pa will kill me if he finds out. Put them in the tops of your boots. I'll bandage around them so Pa won't know."

"What about Coney Island?" asked Frances, her eyes still red and puffy from crying. Her legs ached and were stiff with or without the bandages.

"It was marvelous. We did everything. We rode the Ferris wheel. Dee Dee stood up at the top and waved to everyone below. People clapped and hollered. I almost wet my pants. We went into a house of mirrors that made us look fat, skinny, or just out of whack. We rode the merry-go-round, the loop-the-loop, ate popcorn and cotton candy. Eloise Fox, Reva Grey, and I went with the cowboys, got cigarettes, and smoked behind a hot-dog stand. Then we ate hot dogs with pepper sauce so Pa wouldn't know we'd been smoking. Come on, put your boots on."

Frances was struggling with her wool socks. Joella knelt on the floor and helped. She pushed and tugged with the boots, getting them over the bandaging that was under the socks. Once Frances was in so much pain she thought she was going to faint. "Let me lie down a minute," she said.

"Hey, sit up! We gotta get these coffin nails out of sight!" cried Joella.

"I don't think I can ride today," whispered Frances. "Maybe I can do a little fancy roping. Maybe—but that's all!"

"You can do it all, kid," said Joella. She stuffed a half-dozen cigarettes in the top of each boot, stuffed gauze bandages on top of that, and stood back to survey her handiwork. Frances stood stiff-legged, unable to move unless she twisted her hips from side to side to propel her legs forward. "Pa's getting your breakfast," said Joella. "Wait here for him."

"Where else can I go!" wailed Frances as Joella left the room.

Half an hour later Charlie came in with the breakfast tray. "Eat up. You'll need all your strength today," he said cheerfully. While she ate he sang to her. He also watched to see if she moved her legs. He was pleased to see she had her boots on and thought that was a good sign. He carried the box of ropes downstairs.

Charlie came back and carried her like a sack of flour out to the waiting taxicab. Joella, Pauline, and Dee Dee were already inside the cab. At the speedway Charlie carried Frances to the front row of the grandstand seats. There was a short racetrack made of dirt inside the long wider, cement automobile track. To protect the horses' feet and shoes, cinders were laid thick on the cement. Some of the horses were being exercised. The air was warm, the sun was bright. Frances thought her riding skirt was too heavy. Already she was hot and sweaty.

Charlie told her about all the people and the bright lights at Coney Island. "Music from the merry-go-round sounded like our old calliope."

"Pa, you're trying to make it sound like I didn't miss much," said Frances, rolling up the sleeves of her white satin blouse with the Y6 monogram on back.

"In a way," admitted Charlie. "You see, I felt awful about leaving you alone. I came back early and knocked on your door. When you didn't answer I thought you were asleep, then I heard you kind of moaning. I looked inside."

"Oh, Pa! You saw me with the short rope!" cried Frances. "Why didn't you come in? Say something at least?"

"I—I had to let you fight through the pain yourself. I was so proud of you. You're a true-blue Irwin all right." His eyes misted over. He put his arm around her.

"I don't know if I can ride today. Maybe if you stand me up out in the arena I can do some rope tricks." Then she thought of something and hesitated a moment before asking. "Could I have something for the pain? Charley Johnson takes something for his headaches."

Charlie's face flushed. He stood up and looked down at Frances. "Who told you whiskey was good for pain? It's poison to some, like Uncle Frank and Uncle Will. And it'll be the ruination of Johnson, especially if I ever catch him drinking on the job. Alcohol and cigarettes are things my children are not going to use. I know you see a lot of both, that's life to see how others live, but that doesn't make it right or pretty and certainly not ladylike! Alcohol's like swearing—makes a skunk out of a lady!"

Frances could feel the cigarettes snugged in the top of her boots. They seemed to burn her skin, like turpentine on a raw wound. She kept her head down so that Charlie could not see her face. She was sure if her father looked he'd see that she had a secret.

The grandstand and bleachers filled with men in shirtsleeves and straw hats and ladies with parasols. By a little past noon Frances was in the Irwin tent. Joella, Eloise Fox, and Sam Garrett were already there. Joella pulled out the bandaging and found the cigarettes, mashed, but not badly.

"Put them here so we can find them!" called Eloise, lifting up some of the girls' clothing that was lying in a heap where they'd changed to riding skirts and the Y6 shirts.

The other girls came in one by one. Joella helped Frances tie up her hair and put on the wide-brimmed hat. After the girls were dressed and ready to go out, Charlie came in and carried Frances to her horse called Pillow Kate. The track had been watered to keep down the dust.

"I hope I can make it through this relay race," said Frances.

"Hang on is all you have to do. The horse and handlers'll do the rest," said Charlie. He led the horse to the line-up. The other girls smiled at Frances. She nodded and brought her horse around the line where there was a vacant spot. As the horse turned to move in the spot it stumbled and Frances slipped in the saddle. She was unable to pull herself back upright, and she was afraid her horse would rear up on its hind legs if she stayed hanging at the side for too long. She dropped to the ground, both legs sticking out in front like a pair of wooden stilts. Charlie was right behind her. He set her on her feet in a hurry. "Don't let anyone see you sitting like that! Do you want to be disqualified? Get back up on that horse!"

"I can't!" said Frances. "My legs won't bend!"

Charlie took her hand and walked her stiff-legged around the horse once. Then he pushed her as he had before, so that she slid her leg, without bending, over the saddle. Charlie thought she was all right, so he stepped back, but her leg was only halfway across. She fell to the ground. "Pa!" Charlie put his leg out so that she could pull herself up using his leg for support. He did not offer his hand. "Pa! I can't ride. Take me back to the tent," said Frances quietly.

"Don't say *can't* to me, young lady," said Charlie. He knew she could get on that horse and ride better than most of the others, even with stiff legs. He flexed his hands, bent her from the waist over his knee and whacked her two, three times with his open palm.

She was shocked. She clamped her mouth and didn't let a sound come from her throat, nor a tear fall down her cheek. She'd never cry in front of all these people. By golly, she'd show her pa that she was tough and made of gritty, Irwin material.

Charlie picked her up, hoisted her on the horse, made sure the cinches were secure, put her feet in the stirrups, and gave her a wink. She did not look down at his face. She looked straight ahead at the black cinder track.

Each time she came in to change horses, the handlers let her slide off. That was the only way she could get out of the saddle. Immediately after the first round the handler realized that the child was riding with legs bandaged so tightly that they were stiff. She held her leg out, and it was easy for the handler to help her slide and then sort of push her onto the next horse's saddle. By the third time it was a game to see how smoothly she could slide and how gracefully the handler could put her back into another saddle. She learned to swing her feet into the stirrups. Frances came in third and was given a standing ovation, something the crowd had not given to Pauline, the winner. The crowd had seen that she'd not jumped smoothly and naturally from one horse to another. The crowd sensed something was wrong with the girl's legs, and they thought she was a game little cowgirl. They thought she was a cripple, riding in a relay race against women ten to fifteen years her senior.

Back in the tent after the race Joella brought out the cigarettes. "I've been waiting a coon's age to have one of these coffin nails." She lit up and coughed on the first puff. She gave Eloise one, then offered one to Frances.

"If Pa comes in here and finds the tent filled with smoke, he'll skin you girls alive. I hurt too much to add more to it," said Frances.

"If we get the cowboys to give us more, will you keep them for us?" asked Mabel Strickland, combing out her long hair.

"Oh, no! Line your own boots with the next batch of cigarettes. I'm in enough hot water. You saw how I fell off my horse just before the race got started. Pa's plenty mad about that." Frances's bottom lip quivered.

"How can you say that? You're the darling of the crowd. You heard their applause and whistles. You little twerp, your pa is so proud of you, he's out shaking hands and popping his buttons all over the grandstand right now," said Eloise.

Suddenly the girls heard Charlie's voice outside the tent. He was laughing in his booming voice as his friends talked to him. Joella and Eloise snubbed out the cigarettes. Joella stuffed all the loose cigarettes inside her own boot tops. Eloise lifted up the back wall of the tent and waved her hands to shove the smoke out as quickly as possible.

Frances sat in the corner with a scowl on her face. "Hurry,

Pa's coming in! We're going to be killed!" She spied a can of horse liniment on a trunk. She stretched and could not reach it. She scooted herself against the trunk and reached out, knocked the liniment and a box of horseshoes to the ground. The top was loose on the liniment and it oozed out over the iron horseshoes.

Charlie scratched on the outside of the tent and came in. "Jeems! It smells to high heaven in here. What's that, liniment?"

"Yes, Pa," said Frances quickly. "I was trying to unlace my boot and hang onto that trunk and my hand slipped—the can of liniment spilled."

"You little klutz!" said Eloise with a laugh. Then Joella began to laugh.

"I'll clean it up," said Frances. "Don't worry, Pa. I'll find a rag and wipe off those extra horseshoes."

"How you going to do that when you can't unlace your boots? When you can't walk? I'll clean it up. You girls get ready for the fancy roping— Eloise, Pauline, Joella. Not you, Frances, you do your trick roping tomorrow solo."

The five older girls were out of the tent in seconds, still laughing.

"Smells more like automobile exhaust in here than liniment," groused Charlie. "Girls can sure stink up a tent. This track and this tent remind me of Barney Oldfield. Wish he were here in New York."

"I bet you'd get on a horse and race him in a car," teased Frances.

"I would and I'd have the audience standing on their feet, same as you. Baby, you were wonderful! I wish your ma could have seen your performance. She'd have been proud."

"Ma would have made me stay off horseback."

Charlie wiped up the last of the phenolic-smelling liniment with an old rag he'd found.

On the second day of the Stampede celebration Charlie took Frances's advice and let her ride around the arena in a little red pony cart drawn by Gene Maddren's Appaloosa mule, Happy Jack. The mule had black and white spotted markings on the rump and loins. During the bucking bronc event Maddren rode the mule around the edge of the arena so if a person were thrown off, the mule would be a diversion for the wild horse, keeping it away from the person thrown on the ground, until that person could get to his feet and safety. When it was time for the trick rope event, Maddren helped Frances out of the little red cart, stood her firmly on her feet, and handed her the lariat.

"Throw a good zigzag for your old teacher, Chester Byers."

"Gosh, is Chester here?" asked Frances.

"Naw, just pretend he is and show him how good you are." Maddren got into the cart and started off the grounds, then stopped and turned around. He yelled to Frances. "Hey, kid, smile!"

She heard, and plastered a big grin on her face. She was all show business now. The rope worked fine. She could move easily from the waist up and her legs had no feeling as long as she didn't try to bend them. She could spread them or pull them in as needed as long as there was no strain on the healing tendons. She swung the wedding ring, the butterfly, big and small loops, flat loops, vertical loops, ocean wave. She took first in that day's ladies' fancy and trick roping. Floyd and Bee Ho Gray came out of the stands to congratulate her.

That afternoon and the next day she rode stiff-legged in the ladies' relay races. Each night her legs ached so much it was hard to sleep. Charlie rebandaged her legs each morning, always adding more iodine to the healing tendons.

"I could be one of the Indians," said Frances the morning of the last day in New York, "if only my arms and face were as brown as my legs."

On the final day it was announced that Joella had won the ladies' relay races. She whispered to Frances, "If Ma were here I'd announce something else. But I'm waiting until we're back in Cheyenne."

"What is it? You and Deeke going to move?"

"Not that I know of," said Joella, smiling.

"Then I bet you're going to buy a house in town," said Frances. "It'd be better than living in that small place you two rent now."

Joella only smiled.

The Irwin men had done well at the Stampede. They'd taken most of the steer-roping contests, the bucking-bronc contests, and the horse racing. Bee Ho Gray and Floyd had given such a spectacular exhibition of trick roping that they were each awarded special prizes.

On that final day there was a tremendous ovation when the master of ceremonies called out that there was going to be a five-hundred-dollar award for the best individual performance of any cowboy or cowgirl throughout the more than a week of shows and competition. Frances stood against the grandstand railing beside her two sisters and a couple of the other girls. They sat down to listen to the winner of the best individual performance. Frances wondered how she was going to shuffle over to the wooden bench. She looked around for Maddren or her father, but soon she didn't need either. The cowboys, who were sitting alongside the cowgirls, picked her up and held her out in front of the grandstand after the announcement: "Frances Irwin, all-around cowgirl! Best individual performer!"

Then the crowd was quiet as the youngest cowgirl in the Stampede celebration was carried to the judges' stand. "Congratulations, do you have anything you'd like to say to the crowd?" said one of the judges.

"This is much better than going to Coney Island!" cried Frances. Her eyes were misty.

"Young lady, anything is better than that," mumbled the judge as he handed her a silver plaque and five one-hundred-dollar bills.

The New York Stampede was the next to the last Irwin Wild West show of the season. Cincinnati was to be the last stop. Charlie decided that he did not want to carry a couple of extra boxcars of unbroken broncs, actually Wyoming wild horses, back across the country. These were the horses that Guy Weadick had asked Charlie to furnish for the Stampede. Charlie had been paid to bring these outlaw horses to the New York Stampede's big rodeo contests. The idea of an auction sounded better and better as he thought about it. Two days before the Stampede was over he put an ad in the New York papers that the Irwin Wild West show manager was going to auction off some of his horses to the highest bidder. Of course he did not think to mention that the horses were half-broken and half-wild. He thought that anyone who'd buy the horses would be able to see that these were true western-bred animals.

The day after the Stampede the New York pushcart peddlers flocked to the auction, pushing and pulling at one another as they looked over the animals in the roped-off area Charlie had rigged.

Aha, most thought, these horses have good clear eyes, their legs look strong, the backs are not swayed, and the coats are thick and shiny. The peddlers felt they were getting a tremendous bargain with the prices this westerner asked for his prime animals.

As each man bid and bought his selected animal, he led it away to be hitched to an apple cart, a vegetable cart, a corn fritter cart, or a cart loaded with pots and pans.

In a short time there was pandemonium and chaos. Pots and pans, fruits and vegetables, hot dogs, and upset carts were scattered along the streets of Long Island. One by one the peddlers came back shaking their hands, complaining to Charlie.

Charlie shrugged his shoulders and said, "Haven't you ever heard my old pal Will Rogers say to you folks, 'Let the buyer beware'? I sold you good Western broncs and you let them run away." He hitched his shoulders up and down and kept his face straight.

The Irwin cowboys, led by Floyd, caught each peddler as he turned away, still shaking his fist back at Charlie. Floyd and the cowboys said, "Give us five dollars for each animal we catch and bring back to you."

The peddlers nodded, that was not a bad deal. Thus some of Charlie's animals were sold twice to the cart peddlers. The rest of the runaways were picked up, and if no one claimed them for a five-dollar fee, they were loaded into the boxcars.

When all the animals were loaded and the performers were seated in the chair car, Charlie told the railroad dispatcher that his train was ready to move. "Sorry," said the dispatcher, "there's not only a streetcar strike, there's a railroad strike as well. You're not going anywhere."

Charlie had a sinking feeling. This could not happen to him. He had all these cars, one for the Indians, one for the cowboys and the Western band, one for him and his family and the cowgirls, three, four stock cars, and three, four flat cars for the circus wagons and the old calliope. He was due in Cincinnati for a show in less than a week. He went into the station and asked to talk to the general manager of the New York Central Railroad. "Listen," said Charlie, "I'm the livestock agent for the Union Pacific Railroad, and I've had my show outfit here in your town for the last nine days. We have our engagement in Cincinnati within a week. I'm leaving by rail, whether you have a strike on your hands or not!"

"Nothing is moving in any direction on our tracks," said the beefy, red-faced General Manager.

"This is a private train," argued Charlie. "Could I hire someone to run it for me?" He hesitated and saw that the man was not paying much attention to him. "There's an engine connected to my train of a dozen cars. We're taking it out this afternoon! Good day, sir!"

"You have no one to fire up the engine," said the general manager quietly.

"You are mistaken. I will do it myself," said Charlie.

"You will be a fireman?" asked the General Manager, sitting up and taking a good look at Charlie. "Then you need an engineer. Someone who can switch you out of the New York rail yards. Where did you say you were going?"

"Cincinnati."

"All right. If I can get you an engineer, and I'm not saying I can, you have to work out the payment. The New York Central won't pay a man who scabs for the damned Union Pacific during our railroad strike."

Charlie got an engineer who could switch the train out of the yards and take it on across the country to Cincinnati. He went back to his train and told all his people they were ready to leave. He went into the cowboys' car and talked a few moments. He chose one other to help him shovel coal the first day out. After that the cowboys took turns being firemen. Charlie even sat in the engineer's seat to give their hired man out of New York a rest. Charlie Irwin's train left New York City when no other trains were running. His train went to Cincinnati. Charlie and his Wild West show were able to keep their appointment for their last show of the season.

The engineer took the Baltimore and Ohio Railroad back to Pittsburgh, where he found the New York Central strike had ended.

It was like Christmas as the whole Irwin family was reunited and many people from Cheyenne came to greet the members of the Irwin Wild West show as they got off the train. There was much good-natured kidding about having seen the "big city." There was plenty of hugging and kissing.

Joella stood off to one side with her husband, Lieutenant Deeke Jones. He quickly told her about the changes in Fort D. A. Russell during the few weeks she'd been gone. Joella pulled his head down so she could whisper something in his ear. The lieutenant's face turned brick red. Next he twirled around with Joella as if dancing a jig.

The townspeople stopped and smiled at the happy couple. Charlie clapped his hands and said, "It's good for all us married people to be back with our partners." He hugged Etta close and kissed her soundly.

Joella took her husband's hand and said in a loud, clear voice, "We have an announcement! Deeke and I are going to have a baby—uh—in about four months!"

Charlie's mouth dropped. Etta looked startled. She was first to regain her composure. "You rode horseback in the show? Did trick roping? Relay racing?"

Charlie stuttered, "You—you were—were expecting! I never knew. I never suspected!"

"No one knew but me," said Joella with a smile. "I brought home some trophies. I'm fine! Oh, Pa and Ma, give me a hug!"

Charlie gave his oldest daughter a good squeeze. "You deliberately fooled me!" He did not look angry. She tossed her golden hair about her shoulders.

Etta hugged Joella and wiped a tear from her eye. "I should have kept you home with me and little Betts." Then her eyes twinkled and her voice took on the melodic sound Charlie loved to hear. "Oh, pshaw, maybe it's best I didn't know. You modern girls do all the things we old Victorian women were either afraid to try or forbidden to do. You seem to be just fine." She gave Lieutenant Jones a handshake and hugged Joella again. "We'll call your aunt Ell. She'd love to come for the delivery."

Charlie thought Joella ought to have a checkup with a doctor—make certain everything was all right. He was not thinking of her recent horseback riding; he was thinking of the old miscarriage. He opened his mouth as if to speak. Joella must have sensed his thoughts. She said, "Sshh, Pa. I'm fine. I'm going to have a real baby—a real, live baby."

Deeke put his arm around Joella's still-slim waist. He was handsome in his U.S. Cavalry uniform. "Now I have an announcement!" he shouted. "This will come as a surprise also. I'm being transferred to Portland before the year is over."

Etta gave a little cry. "Surely you're not leaving until after Christmas, with the new baby and all."

"When the U.S. Army says move—we move," said Jones. "December thirty-first."

"You'll be back—for visits," said Charlie.

"I will and with the baby," said Joella.

Before the week was out everyone was settled back in the routine of living in Cheyenne or at the ranch. Joella came to Charlie's office each day and continued as his secretary. Pauline stayed in town with her baby, living at the family house.

Charlie wondered why she did not go to the ranch with her husband, Charley Johnson. At suppertime he watched her. He wanted to talk with her, but he was uncertain what to say. He wanted her to work out her own problems. Yet he had a feeling about this situation, something he could not name, something unpleasant, uncomfortable, much worse than the nervous feeling of butterflies in his stomach. As the time for the Cheyenne Frontier Days neared, the feeling came with more urgency. Finally, trying to alleviate this feeling of some impending doom, he asked Pauline to come to his office a couple hours each afternoon to learn from Joella how to keep the books, write the reports, and type the letters.

Pauline was alert and intelligent. She paid more attention to instructions than what people wore or how they talked. Charlie was pleased. His second daughter would make an efficient secretary and tend to the business in a far more serious manner than the giddy Joella. But the feeling of anxiety intensified. Charlie could not put his finger on the cause. There were moments when he wondered if it were a premonition that the United States would be inexorably drawn into the European war. Or was it the disappointment that General John J. Pershing could not follow through on President Wilson's orders and capture Pancho Villa. Villa had executed sixteen U.S. citizens at Santa Isabel and attacked Columbus, New Mexico, killing twelve people. Pershing was given two biplanes with pilots to go into Mexico and capture Villa. But his mission failed.

Charlie decided to send a telegram to General Pershing, his old friend. At the telegraph office of the Union Pacific he wrote several drafts of his message to Pershing before he was satisfied. He took the copy to Warren Richardson. "Warren, please read my message to Pershing and tell me what you think," he said.

"Certainly," said Richardson, adjusting his glasses.

In the telegram Charlie asked Pershing to appoint him national commander in chief of all transportation of supplies for the United States Army.

"C.B., I don't think you should send this." Richardson scratched his ear. "In the first place only the President has the title Commander-in-Chief, and in the second place that could be quite a job. Suppose the U.S. goes to war with Germany? You'll have to get supplies to England and France."

"I've been selling Wyoming broncs overseas. I can procure the supplies and use the Union Pacific to ship to the East Coast. I know I can do the job, no matter what the title. It's my kind of job. It's something I can do to help in the war that's going on overseas and in Mexico."

"I don't believe you should send this wire, C.B.," said Richardson. "Instead of Livestock Agent the U.P. will change your title to General Agent. You're in charge of shipping all goods on the U.P."

Charlie sent the telegram. In a week Charlie had a reply. His offer to be in charge of all transportation of supplies for the United States Army was turned down. Pershing told him that there was no such job at present and he did not believe such a job would be made in the near future, but if it were, Charlie Irwin would be the first man to be considered.

Charlie was disappointed for a day or two. He knew he could handle the transportation of supplies in a more efficient manner than was being done at the present time by the Army. He shook off the disappointment and became the prime stock contractor once again for the bucking horses during the last week in July for the Frontier Days celebration.

When the celebration was over John Red Cloud asked Charlie if he'd help Frank Fools Crow buy an automobile. Fools Crow had won the cowboy-Indian pony race and the Indian relay races. He wanted the Model-T Ford at the Cheyenne Garage. He wore a fringed, buckskin jacket, faded Levi's, and high-topped moccasins. His long hair was chopped unevenly and topped with a high-crowned black hat, like the reservation Indians wore. The proprietor of the garage told him the Model T was worth three hundred dollars.

"Car's worth about a hundred!" cried Charlie.

The proprietor took him aside and said in a whisper. "Mr. Irwin, the thievin' redskin won three hundred dollars in the rodeo events. Money don't mean a thing to Injuns. I might as well take it off his hands."

"What if I wanted that tin lizzie? Would you give it to me for a hundred bucks?"

"Sure thing, Mr. Irwin."

"I'll pay cash, so you can take twenty dollars off the price," said Charlie.

"You're getting a real good machine here. I'll take ten percent off for cash." The proprietor slapped his hand on the hood and the car rattled like he'd dropped his tool chest. "Come inside while I make out the bill of sale."

"I'll be right there. I want to tell my friend, Fools Crow, to look around at the other used cars." Charlie asked Fools Crow for ninety silver dollars out of the scuffed, black leather satchel he carried. Charlie found a galvanized tin water bucket at the side of the garage to hold the silver. "When I come back, I'll have a piece of paper that says the Model-T is yours. Look around while you wait."

Charlie handed the startled proprietor the bucket of cartwheels.

"Only Injuns prefer silver to paper. You bought this car for that old buck Injun!"

"I did. Make sure you write on the bill of sale that Frank Fools Crow paid in full, in cash."

Charlie explained to Fools Crow that he had to keep the paper just in case a policeman asked if he was owner of the car. "This is proof," said Charlie.

Fools Crow grinned, put the paper inside the money pouch, stepped on the running board, swung his legs inside, and put his hands on the steering wheel.

"You know which road to take out of town?" asked Charlie.

"Yep. But, I don't know how to drive. Tee-hee."

Teaching Fools Crow to drive was not easy. He paid no attention to the road nor its curbing. If he admired the front yard of a house, he drove alongside it to get a better look. If he saw someone on the sidewalk he recognized, he drove up behind his friend and tooted the air horn.

Finally Charlie took him to the Four-Mile pasture where he drove the car like it was a horse, straight through any standing water and over the stubble of the hay field. He drove in reverse as fast as he did forward. Three days of driving in circles, forward and reverse, stopping and starting, left Charlie a nervous wreck. He asked Etta to pack up some bread and roast beef and a couple old wool blankets for Fools Crow.

"Take care and keep on your side of the road," said Charlie, shaking hands with his Indian friend.

"I'll see you," said Fools Crow, grinning.

"I hope he knows enough to stop for gasoline," Charlie said out loud as he watched the old Ford bounce and rattle across the alfalfa as Fools Crow headed for the highway.

The month of August was warm. Each weekend Charlie took Etta, Pauline, and the baby to the ranch, where there was a constant breeze and the nights were cool. Sometimes Pauline and Charley Johnson walked along the banks of Horse Creek and talked. Johnson's face had become sallow, his blond curly hair hung over his ears, and he had a look of despair.

"We'll work everything out as soon as your headaches are gone," said Pauline. His pathetic sight aroused a feeling of pity in her so deep that she believed it to be love. "The baby and I love you."

Her patronizing manner, gentleness, sparkling eyes, and healthy look irritated him. "Love? What do you know of love?"

"Love conquers everything," she said. "Remember the last

night in Omaha? You came to me because you wanted me. I'm pregnant. We'll be a real family with two babies."

"Love did not conquer my blasted headaches!" he shouted. "You think a soft heart, calf eyes, gentle words make me feel better? You think another bawling brat is the answer? The answer is strength. I have to be strong to endure life on this earth!"

Pauline wiped her tears away so that Johnson could not see her weakness. She rubbed his head and shoulders, trying to clear his tension. She spoke gently. "Remember how we used to be? So close we couldn't bear to be apart. Why can't we be like that again?" She pulled him down on the grass beside her, curled her arms around his neck, kissed him on his closed eyes, hard on his mouth. Her hands caressed, unbuttoned his shirt. Her lips brushed his chest, his flat, hard belly. Her hands told her that he wore no underwear. Her lips tingled. Her heart beat faster. She felt the excitement prickling in the middle of her belly. She put a leg over his thighs and unbuttoned his Levi's. "Charley Johnson, I love you," she whispered into his belly button.

Suddenly his back stiffened. His hands became fists jabbing into her face. He pummeled her shoulders and back. She rolled away. He grabbed her legs and half sat on them while he pounded on her breasts. He shouted, "The beginning is over! We can never go backward! Go away! Leave me alone!"

She grabbed at the grass, pulling herself backward. "I can't live without you!" she sobbed, heedless of the tears streaming down her cheeks.

"Go! You annoy me! You make me feel stifled!" The blows from his fists rained on her head. She twisted and rolled and got to her feet. She ran, stumbling at first, then getting her balance, she ran without looking backward.

Johnson stood up with his legs apart so the Levi's would not slip to the ground. He buttoned his shirt, tucked it into his pants, buttoned his pants, and brushed off the dust and dried grass. He wiped his face with his bandanna, straightened his hat. He walked back to the toolshed, nodded to a couple of the cowboys, filled his pockets with nails, took a hammer, and went out to mend the fence on one of the corrals.

Pauline was in the barn saddling a horse called Lady Jane. She didn't say anything to anybody. She led the horse out of the barn, threw herself up into the saddle, and galloped through the back pasture across the deep swale, up the bank, across the road, kicking up dust, sand, and stones. She rode heedlessly alongside an irrigation ditch until the horse stumbled and fell. Pauline was thrown away from the horse into a cluster of rock outcroppings. Her world turned black. She lay unconscious with a broken pelvis.

When the horse came to the barn without its rider, Roy went out to find Pauline. He found her moaning with pain in the sand pasture. Charlie took her to the hospital in Cheyenne. Dr. Henneberry told him that she was young and healthy. The pelvis bone would knit and be as strong or stronger than before. "C.B., your daughter has had a miscarriage. She was three months along at the most. Perhaps you ought not to tell her husband. I think the accident was deliberate."

"Jeems!" said Charlie. "I didn't know Pauline was in the family way. Daughters don't tell their fathers anything anymore." Charlie took a bandanna out of his back pocket and blew his nose. "Jeems—her husband—he's the young man you saw about a year ago. You know, hit on the head with a crowbar. A man doesn't know what family trouble is until his children are grown."

"C.B., this will pass. Go see your daughter. She needs your support," said Dr. Henneberry, shaking Charlie's hand.

The next day Charlie went to the ranch and talked with Johnson. He urged him to go to town to see Pauline, telling him only that her pelvis was broken.

Johnson would make no promises. He turned his head and would not look at Charlie. Charlie could smell the whiskey.

"I don't need you anymore," said Johnson. "I don't need Pauline either. I feel nothing for her. What do I care what happens to her? I have everything I need—myself."

"Yourself and a bottle of whiskey!" shouted Charlie, who was angry and hurt. "You know the rules around this place. I don't allow my cowboys to drink on the job!" He took hold of Johnson's arm. "If I smell liquor on your breath again, you're fired! You'll have to find a job elsewhere to support your wife and child! I won't help you anymore!"

"Don't be so touchy," said Johnson with a silly smile. "I'm not taking care of your daughter and a snot-nosed kid." He lurched forward and shook a forefinger under Charlie's nose. "What's more, I don't drink. Alls you can smell is Sen Sen. I don't need advice from you!" He smirked and staggered toward the bunkhouse.

* * *

Pauline was in the hospital two weeks, in bed at the Cheyenne home another two weeks. Johnson never came to town.

The third week in November Ell came from Colorado Springs to help with the birth of Joella's baby. Ell stayed with Etta in Cheyenne to give cheer to Pauline, to bring her out of her deep depression. Joella called each day from her apartment saying she was feeling fine. She was vague about coming to the house on Pioneer Street the minute she felt anything unusual. Ell said, "You get that handsome husband of yours to bring you here the minute you feel a twinge anywhere from the neck down. Or call me. I'll come get you in one of Charlie's autos. Certainly I can drive. I have a cousin at the spa that has a Rolls-Royce. He lets me drive to the market."

Pauline could talk easier with her Aunt Ell than she could with her own mother. Ell was never shocked by anything. She never criticized. She understood human foibles. Pauline confided that she'd really like to have more children.

Ell said with a deep chuckle, "You can't make cookies when you haven't got the dough."

A few days later Pauline was out of bed helping Etta in the kitchen. Ell said, "Trouble with you, Pauline, you're in a rut, making parsley tea for gas. Come on, add nutmeg to your tea. Nutmeg's good for the brain. Think. You have no husband. Johnson is gone. Don't weep. He's a bad actor. Let him go. Grandma Malinda used to say, 'A bad actor, like bad wine, leaves a worse hangover.' You're rid of the hangover. A divorce is not so bad, when you think there are worse things."

"Thanks," said Pauline. "I'm tired of crying over spilled milk." She sprinkled several nutmeg heads in the simmering tea.

The telephone rang. It was Lieutenant Jones. Etta said, "Is it Joella? Are you bringing her right over?"

"Yes, it's about Joella. No. I'm not bringing her over. She's at Memorial Hospital."

"Oh, Mercy! What's wrong?" Etta was white as a ghost.

"Nothing's wrong. We have a little girl!" Jones shouted. "She's—she's Patricia Enid!"

"When?" Etta was shaking.

"This afternoon!"

"But—but Charlie's sister's here, waiting to deliver the baby!"

"That's what I called for. I took Joella to the hospital. She wanted the best. At the last minute she insisted. I—I had to take her. She's persuasive. She's stubborn." Jones sounded regretful.

"A baby girl, born today, November twenty-four?" repeated Etta.

"That's right," said Jones.

Etta hung up the phone. She looked from Ell to Pauline. "Joella went to the hospital to have her baby. You heard, it's a girl, born this afternoon." She looked at Ell, who had her mouth open. "You came all the way up here. I'm sorry."

"Well, I'm not," said Pauline. "Joella is a self-centered bitch!" She bit her tongue. "Aunt Ell helped me see through my selfishness. She made me feel like I was somebody. She gave me self-confidence and self-respect. I'm going to divorce Charley Johnson and start over. I might get married again and I might not. I don't have to. Aunt Ell showed me that whatever I do, it is not the responsibility of someone else."

Ell looked stunned, then she grinned. "One of the best feelings is to be needed, wanted. Thanks."

"I don't know what got into Joella. She didn't realize that Aunt Ell came here to help her," said Etta. "She didn't think."

"She thought," said Pauline. "She's a taker. Ma, you know she takes advantage whenever she can. When she comes for supper, she never helps with the meal or lifts a finger with the dishes."

"All you girls are different," said Etta. "It's hard to imagine Joella with a new baby. It's hard to think of you without Johnson. I liked that boy—when he wasn't drinking."

"But Ma, he is drinking again," whispered Pauline, "and I don't want to think about him."

Ell put her arms around Pauline and Etta. "Listen, I have something to say, for what it's worth. Joella is not going to stay with this lieutenant of hers. He's not going to put up with her whims and extravagance."

Again Etta looked stunned. "Oh, laws, don't talk that way! Lieutenant Jones sounded happy today. He was running at the mouth."

"Yes, but Joella will beat him into doll rags before the year is out," said Ell. "She'll have him doing this and that for the baby until he'll lose sight of the fact that he has a wife."

"Oh, dear. I hope you overspoke yourself this time," said Etta with her hand over her mouth and a lump the size of a horse's bit roller in her throat.

"Now, I'm sorry," said Ell. "We should all be feeling good because there's a new baby in the family. This house needs babies. There's a rocking chair in most every room." She still had one arm around Pauline and one around Etta. "Don't take me too serious. Let's put pink ribbons on those flannel baby gowns."

The telephone rang again. It was Floyd. Etta said, "Joella has a baby girl. Speak up, Bud, so that I can hear what you are saying." She heard Floyd draw in his breath.

"Ma, this is important. Call Pa at his office. I'm bringing Charley Johnson to town. Now, don't panic. One of the men found Johnson in the barn with that horse, Lady Jane. He'd slit the horse's throat with his jackknife. We shot the horse and tied Johnson in a couple of bed sheets after we got him calmed a little with paregoric in his whiskey." He waited and when Etta didn't say anything, he said, "Ma, call Pa to meet me at the hospital."

"Which one?" said Etta, leaning against the wall.

"St. John's on Evans and House."

"St. John's? All right. I'll say you're bringing Johnson in right away."

Ell got up from the davenport and stood beside Etta. "Wouldn't it be better to take Johnson to Dr. Lesley Keeley on Maxwell? He specializes in drinking problems."

"Here's your aunt Ell," said Etta. "She has something to say."

Etta gave the phone to Ell and sat beside Pauline. "That's Bud. He said Johnson slit the throat of the horse you rode when you had your accident. He got kind of crazy when the men had to shoot the horse, so they're bringing him to town. Ell thinks he ought to go to that Keeley Institute. What do you think?"

Pauline was composed. She spoke slowly, choosing her words. "Yes, give him a chance to get his head straight. I'm not going to visit him." Her eyes were dry and she looked past Etta. "Bad luck comes in threes. First me, now Johnson. What's next?"

"We'll soon see," said Ell quietly.

Charlie met Floyd with Johnson at Dr. Keeley's. The doctor no longer had a large institute, but he kept a few patients in his home. Nearly twenty years before, Keeley had become famous for his use of gold chloride in the treatment of alcoholism and cocaine and tobacco addiction.

Dr. Keeley assured Charlie that Johnson would be cured in three weeks. At the end of the first week Johnson left Keeley's house, telling the cook he was heading northwest. For weeks Charlie checked with people he knew up and down the Union Pacific line, along the stage lines, cattle and sheep ranches, in

Montana, Wyoming, and found no trace of Johnson. Charlie finally advised Pauline to do what his sister, Ell, had said, file for desertion and a legal divorce.

Ell went back to Colorado Springs two days after Joella's baby was born, because the lieutenant had hired a nurse to take care of his wife and baby after they came home from the hospital. At the Cheyenne depot Pauline clung to her aunt Ell. "I'll always love that happy-go-lucky blond I first married. And this is the last time I'm going to cry over him."

Ell put her arms around Pauline and whispered, "Who marries for love without money has good nights and sorry days."

Pauline's mouth turned up at the corners, then she laughed. "Is that one of Grandma Malinda's sayings?"

"I'm not sure. The cousins give me proverbs. I hear things in the market. Listen and you'll hear people use phrases, like some kind of short philosophy. Write me about your baby, Betts, and tell me about Joella and her family. Keep me informed about everyone."

Charlie was informed that his old rival, Buffalo Bill Cody, had died of uremic poisoning in Denver on January 10, 1917. Charlie asked Pauline to take over his office in the Plains so that he could drive to Denver for the funeral.

Harry Tammen, F. G. Bonfils, Otto Floto from the *Denver Post,* the governors of Colorado and Wyoming, and other friends of Charlie's filed past the open bronze casket in the capitol building, then waited for the short funeral ceremony. The body was taken to a mortuary crypt, where it was kept until the earth thawed in June. Then the casket was to be carried to the top of the mountain overlooking Denver for its final burial.

"Ma, I've always thought Buffalo Bill shot thousands of rustlers, bank robbers, and bad men," said Pauline. "Us kids used to read the five-cent Buffalo Bill pulps by Ned Buntline. We passed them around at school."

Baby Betts, a chubby, bright-eyed toddler, went from one chair to another, intrigued with her own ability to walk. She touched everything within reach. Baby Betts, now seventeen months old, patted Pauline's knee, and said, "Ninner Mama, ninner!"

"Dinner? Betts, you can't be hungry. I fed you an hour ago. You must be sleepy." She pulled the child to her lap and let her nurse until she fell asleep.

Etta wondered why Pauline had continued to nurse the baby. She supposed it was for some kind of longing for affection. But suddenly she saw that the child's nursing was not out of affection; it was nothing more than a habit. A bad habit that couldn't give a purpose to life nor warm the heart. It drained the vital energy from Pauline.

Pauline asked for a glass of water, then said, "Go on, Ma, tell about Buffalo Bill."

Etta filled the teakettle with cold water and put it on the kitchen range. "Cody didn't have a sympathetic judge here in Cheyenne. The charges against Cody's wife, Louisa, were so farfetched that the judge couldn't give him a legal divorce. Ever since then, no one in Cheyenne thinks Buffalo Bill Cody is anything—except you kids, who read those cheap stories and the *Denver Post,* which is carrying on over his death as if he were someone to look up to. Why, he continued to call his Wild West show the Buffalo Bill Exposition of Frontier Days and the Passing of the West after your Pa got out of his jam with the Cheyenne's Frontier Committee. That committee never went after Buffalo Bill, mainly because he stayed out of Cheyenne. But people in Colorado are expected to look up to him, that's exactly why he's going to be buried on top of the mountain. The *Denver Post* wants to make a shrine out of that mountain. They're just pumping up their town for the tourist trade." Etta slapped her hands down on her knees.

Pauline began to laugh. "Ma, I read in the paper today that there was a moon eclipse on the day Buffalo Bill died."

"That's the most ridiculous thing yet. I bet you read that in the *Denver Post,*" said Etta.

Pauline was still laughing. "Ma, I see your point. The city of Denver is trying to build a hero for themselves. You saw through their scheme. What will be the upshot anyway?"

"Well, fifty years from now Buffalo Bill will be a hero. People forget and they need heroes. Which brings me to a question for you. What will be the upshot of your nursing that child until she's so big that her feet drag on the floor when you hold her?"

"Ma, you saw her. She won't go to sleep by herself unless she's nursed," said Pauline, patting the back of the sleeping child.

"She's past the weaning age. You have a job at the Plains Hotel. You ever think, it's not right to come home at night and nurse a baby as big as Betts? Let me wean her."

"Ma?" Pauline looked startled, as if someone were taking the child from her arms.

"I'll have the job done in a week," said Etta firmly. "It's best for both of you. When Charlie gets back, tell him Floyd took me and Betts to the ranch."

Etta took the baby to the ranch so she would not see her mother in the evenings. She kept the child on a strict schedule, with a nap every afternoon.

One afternoon Floyd came up the back steps with a handful of mail. "Look, here's a letter from Elsie Coble. Open it."

Etta had an occasional letter from Elsie Coble, and it usually told about some of the amusing things her children had done. She was still in California, according to the postmark. Etta turned the letter over. For some unexplainable reason she found it difficult to open this letter. Her hands shook and her throat felt dry. The letter said that five-year-old John had caught a cold which he was unable to shake off, so Elsie and the children went to California for the sunshine. The boy was treated by the best doctors, but nothing seemed to bring the color back to his cheeks. He died and would be buried next to his father in Cheyenne's Lakeview Cemetery. Elsie hoped that Etta and Charlie would come to the service.

Seeing Elsie Coble with her two little girls, Elsie, twelve, and Cathy, ten, sobbing, and the baby, Virginia, not much more than a year old, looking around, wide-eyed, frightened by all the solemn people in black, broke Etta's heart. She hung desperately to Charlie's hand and whispered, "Can't we do something for Elsie and the little girls? Give them some hope, something besides sadness to take back to California?"

The small steel casket was lowered into the six-foot hole next to old John Coble's grave. Charlie was feeling like spring ice about to crack and splinter. The rush of memories poured out of the raw earth. The days on the Coble IM ranch as foreman, the fire at the ranch house, Tom Horn, the hanging—the Miller boys and old Kels Nickell. Charlie squeezed Etta's tiny warm hand. He had not heard the preacher's words. Etta pulled at his arm.

"It's time to go," she said. "Let's take Elsie and the children to the ranch for dinner."

"Yes—yes, that's what we'll do. Get them away from here," stammered Charlie. He felt like a beefsteak himself, charred on the edges and raw in the middle. Then he remembered something. "Oh, dear! Charlie Hirsig and I are going to sell some mavericks to a French buyer. The Frenchman's coming to the ranch to look over the horses. They're to be sent overseas for the French Cavalry."

"Oh, pshaw, Charlie! Elsie knows what goes on at a ranch! I'm going to ask her to come." Etta let go Charlie's hand.

By noon the day was hot. Etta brought a wooden, folding table to the screened-in back porch, put a white cloth on it and a big bowl of potato salad, sliced ham, and a pitcher of iced tea. She brought out the highchair used by Betts. "Let Virginia sit there, and you can give her what you like from the table," she said to Elsie. "After we eat, the older girls can go with Frances and Dee Dee to watch the men sell horses to a Frenchman. We can talk. I'll tell you all about my granddaughter, Pauline's little girl. She's talking, calls Floyd 'Boy.' She can tell Floyd's footsteps the moment he comes to the back door. When I hear that high, melodic baby voice calling out, 'Boy, Boy, my Boy!' I know Floyd's come in."

Elsie took off her black shawl and veil. Etta was shocked to see that her beautiful honey-colored hair was nearly snow-white. She smiled. "Etta, my hair faded after John Senior died. It was as if all the color went from my life."

"Oh, no," said Etta gently. "You have these girls to look after. They'll bring you more color than you can imagine. Don't let grief rob you of life. Fight back."

"Etta, it's easy for you to say. You haven't lost a husband or a child," said Elsie. "I'm hollow inside, like a decorated Easter egg."

Charlie brought his brother Frank and Charlie Hirsig to the table. He told the children to eat up fast because the Frenchman and his interpreter were due any minute. "If you want to hear that Frenchman talk, you have to eat all that ham," he said to Cathy. "Ham gives you the energy you need to understand French. Watch how much ham I eat. You see, I'll understand him real good."

By the time the meal was over, Charlie had the girls laughing. He took them outside, after picking up his tally book. The horses were in the large corral on the east side of the barn.

"You have to take these broncs to the stock train?" asked Hirsig.

"Me or you," said Charlie with a shrug. "You give me the fee and I'll do it. The Frenchman turns in a copy of his bill of sale to the railroad so someone knows how many animals to expect."

Hirsig scratched his head. "Those are actually unbroken horses. How will they survive, being shipped to the East Coast and then put aboard a freighter for France?"

"It's my guess about half will survive," said Charlie, "same as if they were saddle-broke horses."

"Maybe we ought not to sell them," said Frank. "On the other hand, we're lucky to get anything for them and there's hundreds out there, eating up our grass or somebody else's."

"Of course we ought to sell them," said Hirsig, chewing on the fleshy end of a timothy stalk. "I was wondering if I could make money myself by doing the same thing. It's a good way to thin out those herds of wild horses. Look! There's a car coming up the road. Must be our Frenchman and his translator. C.B., remember I'm your bank representative. Don't sell anything unless I say it's a deal."

Frank grinned and Charlie shook his head, hoping that Hirsig knew what he was doing. Charlie felt he needed a witness to his business transaction with a foreign government. Momentarily he wondered if he'd have been better off with a lawyer instead of a bank executive, especially Hirsig. But it was too late to wonder. "Frank, get behind the barn. Brush each horse a little, if you can. Make their coats shine. Send out some real good-looking horses," said Charlie.

Then Charlie and Hirsig shook hands with the two men that got out of the car. The Frenchman was immaculately dressed in a gray wool business suit and a blue silk cravat at his throat. His name was Monsieur Rollette. The translator drank two glasses of Etta's iced tea, then said they were ready to see the horses.

In a few moments Frank came out on a big black and white horse. It was the same horse that Hirsig had ridden to the Y6 that morning. It was Hirsig's favorite saddle horse. He'd paid a high price for it. Charlie could see Frances and Dee Dee laughing and whispering to the two little girls.

"This is a riding horse of the best quality!" called Charlie. "He's worth a high price. Look how he reacts!"

Frank kind of reined the horse this way and then pulled that way, crossing the poor animal so it didn't know which way to take the first step. The horse appeared to be slow and ploddingly dumb.

Charlie scratched the horse behind the ear. "Jeems! What's happened to this great horse?"

Hirsig's face had gone from red to purple. A couple of the cowboys were watching from the corner of the barn. They tried to hide their snickers when the translator said, "Looks like that one is ready for the glue factory, no spunk. We'll give you half price."

Frank climbed down and handed the reins to the Frenchman. "Sure, I don't blame you. This one's not a good performer. Shouldn't be in our string of young horses. You might use it, but it's not worth a high price. Just hold it here. I'll get another."

Hirsig was so steamed he couldn't speak. He waved his hands and took the reins from the Frenchman. At that moment Frank came out from behind the barn, trying desperately to keep a wild roan calm enough to walk in front of the Frenchman and get his bid before going into the empty corral across the road.

"Don't sell this horse!" Hirsig managed to shout. "He's the best goddamned brute I got! He's not for sale!"

"Fifty dollars is too much for him," said the translator after talking to the Frenchman. "Monsieur Rollette sees through your little ruse. Trying to make believe the first horse was as lively as this one that just came by. Monsieur Rollette can see that it is dull. Actually he does not want it at all." The Frenchman made a rude noise in his throat and shook his finger at Hirsig. "Don't try any more clever tricks. Just bring out, one by one, the strong, active, vigorous horses. We will buy them, one hundred to one hundred and twenty dollars a head."

Charlie looked at Hirsig and his mouth curved up at the corners. "Take that old nag into the front yard and tie it to the water pump. Keep it out of the good stock. Shame on you!" Now Charlie could not keep the chuckle down inside his throat; he bent over as if to brush the dust off his boots.

Hirsig was chewing tobacco and turned away from the hot breeze to spit. When he turned back he looked up into Charlie's sparkling eyes and said, "If you had sold my horse, I would relocate your nose!"

"Take it easy! You heard the translator, it's no sale. The two gentlemen saw through our little tricks." Charlie was still laughing as he sent Frank back of the barn with the other cowboys, who eared down each wild, bucking horse as the saddle was thrown on its back. The horse was walked between two other horses around the corral a couple times. Frank rode the wild horse in front of the Frenchman. Each time Frank held his breath for fear the wild bronc would suddenly realize it was not hemmed in and go berserk, flinging its back legs into the air.

The Frenchman grinned. He was pleased; he could see that these horses had spunk, even though he thought they were saddle-broken. The minute the horse was put inside the corral and the saddle slipped off, it whinnied and sputtered and kicked. Frank scrambled for the fence. This was hard work.

When the Frenchman and his translator were gone, Charlie brought the cowboys, Hirsig, and Frank to the back porch for iced tea and to count their sales. The men were glad to get the dust washed from their throats.

Elsie Coble could not help but laugh when the little girls told her how the corral full of wild horses had been sold to a Frenchman who thought they were saddle-broken.

"They'll be tame by the time they get to France," said Charlie.

Elsie said, "This has been a wonderful day. I swan, I feel better already. I'll get some perspective to my life and work everything out." All of a sudden her face lit up. "Say, whatever happened to the drawing that cowboy from Montana, Charlie Russell, and Will Rogers, put on your barn door, C.B.? I remember John laughing about it and saying that the bull was more true to life than those two sickly looking bull Herefords that were on the wall of the old Cheyenne Club."

"I had to paint the doors years later and I can't draw, so I just covered the bull with paint. He's under there still," said Charlie with a laugh. "Just like Coble's picture stored under a covering of brown paper at the State Historical Society. I was told he hated that picture of those white-faced bulls, one standing, the other lying down under a shade tree. I guess he planned a long time to shoot one in the leg and the other in its left hoof."

Elsie said, "No, I don't think he planned it at all. It just happened. He came home from the club crowing like a rooster, not even the least bit annoyed because he'd been banned from setting foot in that place again. He'd taken some action against something he didn't care for and it made him feel good."

Charlie began to reminisce with Elsie. Etta sat in the rocker with little Virginia in her lap. Elsie said, "I feel embraced by you special people. You've given me more courage than I've had in the past few years. I have enjoyed the pleasure of your company and can now more easily bear my pain."

Charlie said, "All my life I've learned that life is sad or joyful. I've learned that we can control much of those feelings, so smile."

"Death is the fierce teacher. Life is the tranquil teacher," said Elsie.

"Oh, no," said Etta. "Death is part of life. You've had your share of death. None of us are left untouched. But Charlie's right, we should smile, at the world, at ourselves, and get on with the important business of enjoying life. Don't worry as though there were a thousand years to live."

Floyd came into the house. "Excuse me. Pa, I was wondering if I could take the Overland into town. Dee Dee and I thought we'd go in and have supper with Pauline and Betts."

Charlie stood up and took Floyd into the kitchen. "Son, your mother and I have company."

"I know that. Dee Dee has been showing the Coble girls around the ranch ever since you sold the wild horses. They're out after blackberries right now. We're going to take the berries to Pauline. Surprise her," said Floyd.

"Take the Pierce Arrow," said Charlie. "The keys are on my bedroom nightstand."

"It doesn't run. Why can't I take the Overland?" said Floyd.

"Because your mother and I have to take the Cobles back to town. Think of someone else beside yourself," said Charlie. "You and Dee Dee don't have to go into town tonight."

"Pa! We do! We are thinking of someone. I made blocks from cedar wood for Betts. I want to take them to her before you get involved with taking stock to town for the Frontier Days. Also, I'm not going to be in the celebration this year." Floyd stood still watching Charlie's face. He felt like something was coming up suddenly from his blind side. "I'm staying at the ranch."

"Floyd Leslie Irwin! This is no time for that sort of joke! Go on outside. Get out of here. Talk to me when you have some manners." Charlie's face was as red as Floyd's. Floyd's mouth quivered with the indignity of being told to leave within hearing of Elsie Coble. He let the screen door slam shut and stomped down the steps.

"Oh, C.B., why couldn't Floyd and his wife take us back to Cheyenne? Then everyone would be happy. Isn't that just what we were talking about? Oh, dear, young people's feelings are so fragile. Don't break his spirit. Call him back." Elsie was up looking for her veil and shawl. She went to the back steps, called her little girls into the house.

Charlie and Etta took Elsie Coble and her three girls back to the Plains Hotel in Cheyenne. Not much was said during the hour drive. Elsie took Charlie's and Etta's hands in her own when she said good-bye. "The two older girls will never forget the good time at your place." She laughed at their blackberry-stained faces and hands. "Today I learned to let go my fears and not be angry about this world." Then her voice lowered and was gentle and sad at the same time. "C.B., what's your most precious possession?"

Without hesitation he answered. "My wife and children, of course."

"Take care," said Elsie, her eyes steady and dry. She took the baby from Etta's arms and carried her straight into the hotel, with the two girls following like baby goslings, one behind the other.

The next day Charlie asked Floyd if he'd go out to Round Top to cut the hay out of the meadow next to the mountain. "There's a good crop of hay there and we ought to bring it in for the horses I'm going to use for Frontier Days."

"Pa, that's my favorite place. When the day is clear, I can see the ranch house from the top. Pa, don't yell at me. I'll cut the hay, but not today. Dee Dee and I are going into town. I rewired the ignition so we can take the old Pierce Arrow." He watched his father, hoping he'd understand that he wasn't running away from work, but that he was a person himself, with his own priorities.

Charlie didn't say anything at first. He felt like the world was spinning too fast. Like he was being left behind and couldn't catch up. "I thought a son obeyed his father. I asked you to cut hay. That's not such a hard job. You could be finished by noon."

"But if I'm not finished, I disappoint my wife again. We're going to town. If we're back in time, I'll go up and cut the hay in that little meadow. Tell Ma not to get lunch for us."

"I'm disappointed," said Charlie, "about you not wanting to be in the big celebration. Why, son?"

"Pa, I want to run the ranch, take care of the stock, plant some wheat and oats, get some more land, be the manager, while you go off with the Wild West shows or furnish stock for local rodeos. I've thought it over for a long time. Dee Dee and I have talked it over. I've made up my mind, but first I'm going to register for the draft. I want to go in the Army. Maybe I'll be sent to Paris with General Pershing."

"This country is not at war yet," said Charlie, knowing that troops had already been sent to France, and U.S. merchant ships sailing in European war zones were armed because German submarines had torpedoed U.S. ships with a loss of American lives. The newspapers carried front-page pictures of Uncle Sam pointing a compelling finger, saying, "You! Enlist today! Your country needs you!"

"But war is coming. I love this country and I am willing to

fight for it. I'll do my part. Then come home and run the ranch." Floyd was dead serious. "That's why I have to go into town today."

"What will your mother say? She has no idea you want to leave."

"She'll understand."

Charlie tried to remember what Elsie Coble had said and all he could remember was that children's feelings were fragile. That isn't true, he thought. Children's feelings are bold and callous. Parents' feelings are thinner than eggshells. He put his hand around his son's shoulder for a brief instant. "Listen," he said, "I'll make a bargain with you. Work the Frontier Days show for me this year, and when it's over and the stock's back on the ranch, then you can register and be in the Army."

Floyd's mouth turned up on one side. "Pa, you always have to have your own way. All right, it's a deal. I work for you until Frontier Days is over."

"Cut the hay?"

"Yup, as soon as we come back from town. I promised Dee Dee she could watch Betts play with those blocks I made." Floyd turned on his heel and strolled toward the house. Dee Dee was waiting near the back steps. She had a flour sack in one hand bulging with wooden blocks.

"Floyd!" called Charlie. But Floyd paid no attention.

Charlie went out to the meadow and cut the hay, saying to himself that Floyd could bale it and bring it to town. He felt good working in the shadow of Round Top, but he could not keep his eyes off the truncated Lookout Mountain. The windswept top was bleak and malevolent. Charlie shivered and chided himself for letting fingers of fear creep up and down his spine. A mountain cannot send ill fortune to anyone, he said to himself. I'm not a superstitious man, so this feeling is foolishness. He finished cutting hay and brought the reaper back to the ranch yard. All the while his back was turned toward Lookout Mountain he felt the wind drying his perspiration and making his back shiver with cold. When he turned toward Round Top, it seemed the wind ceased and the sun was warm and eased the ache of his muscles.

At supper that night Etta said, "Jeanette Rankin is in the House of Representatives. She'll not let this country go to war."

"What made you think of war?" asked Charlie.

"I've been thinking ever since I read in the papers that another ship, the *Housatonic,* was sunk."

"When this country is ready and the sound of the drum and

bugle is heard, our cowboys will all join up," said Charlie, feeling morose.

"Bud's going to sign up, isn't he?" said Etta. Her voice was thin, like the first trickle of a waterfall in the spring.

"Dear, your son is twenty-two and married. If he decides to join the Army, neither you nor his wife will stop him. I hope he gets in the cavalry."

A few days later Floyd went a few miles east to Pine Bluffs, Nebraska, for their annual rodeo. He won the steer- and goat-roping contests and took second money in the bucking contest. Afterward he and Dee Dee went on to the larger town of Sidney, where the Sells-Floto Circus was performing. Dee Dee wanted to meet Otto Floto's wife, Kitty, called the Lady in Red, who performed as a bareback rider. Kitty was delighted with the Irwin couple and invited Floyd to ride with her and twirl his rope in wide loops over their heads.

"The audience loved him!" Dee Dee told Charlie and Etta when they got home. "I did the high-wire act with a teeny-tiny pink parasol! Golly, it wasn't as much fun as I'd imagined. Maybe I'm ready to settle down!"

Floyd and Dee Dee planned to stay in town with Charlie and Etta during Frontier Days. Charlie brought in stock for his own show. He kept them in the barn and corrals he had at Frontier Park. Some of the Y6 cowboys stayed at the Irwin bunkhouse in town. The Pine Ridge Indians put up their tepees near Charlie's cookhouse.

Late Wednesday afternoon, before the Frontier events, Charlie asked Floyd if it wouldn't be a good idea to go to the park and make a couple practice passes at steer roping. "After all, you have as good a chance at taking the top purse during Frontier Days as anyone. And take off that sulfur-colored shirt. It's hideous."

"Geez, Pa! Can't you see I was going? I'm not a kid. I know how to rope a steer. You don't have to tell me everything. Can't I wear what I want?"

Floyd went through the kitchen, picked up his hat and rope. He told his mother what a good meal she'd fixed, kicked open the door, and said sullenly, "I don't know when I'll be home tonight!"

Floyd left home halfway sore at his father. Damnit, he thought, Pa doesn't need to tell me when to blow my nose anymore. He doesn't need me for the show either. There are plenty of men who can go on the Wild West circuit with him. He has

Roy and Bee Ho. Pa wants to mold us kids into something he's made up in his mind. Maybe Joella saw that and moved to the West Coast. Damnit, Pa! I'd like to be partners with you in running the ranch, not a snot-nosed kid being told what to wear and what to do. I'll be glad when I register for the draft. Then I'll be on my own, doing something of my own choosing.

Floyd rode his horse, Fashion, into the park and headed for a group of Y6 cowboys, who were trying to get a balking steer into the corral. He called out to them, "Let me tie that steer! I'll teach the son of a gun a lesson!"

Floyd went after the high-stepping steer. A second later he'd thrown his rope and thought it had fallen short, that is, not caught the animal. He swore and turned his horse in the opposite direction so he could swing out, turn back, and try again. All of a sudden the rope tightened and jerked his horse around hard. The rope had actually caught around one of the steer's legs.

Before Floyd could do anything, even figure out what had happened, Fashion threw its head backward, striking Floyd a terrible blow on his forehead. Floyd's skull made a loud crack, like the report of a rifle, as it was fractured. Floyd was unconscious.

"Floyd's acting as adolescent as Frank," said Charlie after Floyd slammed the kitchen door shut. "Did you know Uncle Frank's handling the show horses for the Sells-Floto Circus?" said Dee Dee, after she'd watched Floyd get on his horse, Fashion, and trot in the direction of Frontier Park.

"No! Jeems! I suppose that means Frank's not going to help with the fall roundup," said Charlie. "I can't depend on him at all. Well, the Y6 ranch'll go on without him."

"He didn't act like he had time to stand around and visit with us, but he said he'd be back in Cheyenne when Clara Belle had the baby. I thought he'd been drinking, but Floyd wouldn't talk about it."

"That's my brother," said Charlie with a sigh. "I'd bet my red suspenders he hasn't been sober since he's been with Sells-Floto. And his wife's here, half as big as a barn, trying to keep track of three little girls."

Etta said, "Charlie, the wash machine wringer won't work at Clara Belle's. When you have a chance, see if you can fix it. Leave her a little grocery money. You know Frank hasn't sent her a red cent!"

"Frank never grew up," said Charlie, picking up little Betts so that he could give her a horsie ride on his foot. Betts hung on with her chubby hands and squealed with delight. "Want to play with Grandpa's blocks?" asked Charlie.

Betts climbed down and scooted after her sack of blocks.

"No, no! I mean these!" called Charlie. He went to his bedroom, pulled an old, black satchel from under his bed, and opened it up on the living room floor. Inside were rows and rows of silver dollars. This was the Indians' payroll. The Sioux from Pine Ridge who came to work for Charlie in the Frontier Days program would not take paper money. Charlie always paid the Indians in hard cash, silver dollars.

Together he and Betts built fences, ranch houses, chicken coops, and corrals on the living room floor. Betts made small stacks of some of the coins. "Haystacks," she said.

"Let's make a henhouse with windows," he said. The telephone rang. "I'll get it." Charlie rolled over and pulled up from the floor.

"C. B. Irwin speaking," said Charlie.

The voice on the other end of the line was strange. "Mr. Irwin, this is Dr. Thomas at St. John's Hospital. Sir, you have a son, Floyd?"

"Yes. Yes, I do. He's over at Frontier Park, practicing for the coming celebration."

"Yes, he was at the park. He's here. There's been an accident."

"Oh, no! He's all right—isn't he?"

"Mr. Irwin, can you come to the hospital?"

"Yes, of course. I'll be right there." Charlie hung up the receiver. The faces in front of his eyes seemed to be in a fog. His mouth was dry. "Something's—something's happened to Floyd!"

Charlie and Dee Dee went to the hospital. Etta stayed home with Betts. Charlie said he'd call as soon as he knew anything. Etta thought about tragedy coming in threes. She prayed that Floyd was not the third tragedy. "Dear God. Take care of Bud. Keep him safe. I praise your name. I'll praise you every day from now on. Bud! My boy! Our boy!"

Charlie called to tell Etta that Floyd was still unconscious and the doctor could not tell when he'd come to.

Etta told Charlie that Pauline was back from the office. "I'm leaving Pauline home with Betts and coming to the hospital right away."

Charlie said, "First, see if you can find where Sells-Floto is.

Call Frank there and ask him to come home. Floyd might be laid up for a couple weeks, and we could use the extra hand. Tell Frank I'll pay him in advance."

Etta agreed. She stayed at the hospital all night with Dee Dee. Charlie went out to the park. He couldn't do anything at the hospital and he was restless. The town had made a municipal campground on its western edge for the thousands of automobile tourists expected to come in the next day. Not only was the Frontier Days celebration ready to open, but this was the one hundredth anniversary of Cheyenne. This double celebration would bring in a festive mood and more tourists than ever before. People had hung signs on their front windows announcing ROOM FOR RENT. The Union Pacific, Burlington, and Colorado Southern Railways had brought in full trainloads of people all weekend before the festivities.

Charlie walked past a group of revelers. Beyond the reverberation of a group singing on a street corner, he heard the whistle of the evening train and he imagined he heard the howling of a lone wolf as the near-full moon edged up over the plains. Near the park Charlie drew a deep breath, enjoying the smell of the newly mown hay, dust, and dung. Dear God, he thought, Floyd has so much to live for. He can't stay unconscious for long. He's one of the best all-around cowboys there is.

He waved to a couple of the Indians sitting in front of their tepees. "You people had supper? Come on over to the cookhouse at the park," he said. They ducked inside the tepee flaps and came out with their women and children. All called their greeting to Charlie. Several asked about Floyd. They'd heard about his accident from the cowboys who'd seen it happen.

"He's still unconscious. Foolhardy kid."

"Ah, we will pray for him," said John Red Cloud's wife, Clear Eyes.

Charlie couldn't eat. He went outside the cookhouse and looked toward the gently sloping hills that were covered with yellow-green grass. He thought of Floyd in the unlucky yellow shirt. He could see nothing but the deep-blue film of night. He could not remember how he got through the evening's events.

Next morning Charlie took Etta and Dee Dee home from the hospital. Even though Floyd had not yet regained consciousness, the doctor seemed optimistic. Charlie went out to the park. He found it hard to look at the string of Irwin horses where Fashion stood munching hay. He could not look at the catch pens holding the steers. He tried to smile at the cowboys.

Thousands of people had come to see the great Cheyenne double celebration and these people could not be let down. Frontier Days had to be a success. It was Charlie's responsibility to keep the stock moving in and out of the various events, to announce each event, and to sing or tell a joke or two between events to keep the excitement running high. He told himself he had an obligation not only to the ticket holders, but also to his son, who lay fighting for his life. Irwins were fighters. Floyd was in a battle for his life, and Charlie could do no less than fight through his worry and fears, to give the audience a thrilling afternoon. He told himself to keep his lip stiff and his back straight. He smiled, welcomed friends and strangers. He shook hands and invited people to the famous Irwin breakfast, then lunch. All the time he wanted to pull away from Frontier Park, rush to the hospital. He twisted his bandanna, while his insides twisted just as tight. He told himself that when Floyd was conscious, someone would send for him. When the final event was over that afternoon, he could wait no longer. He hurried to the hospital.

Ell came from Colorado Springs. Etta had called her after trying to locate Frank. Ell's strawberry-blond hair was in one thick braid and wound in a kind of halo around her head. Her face was sober, unlined. Her eyes looked like gray-green earth surrounded by undulating, pure-white snow. Charlie remembered when Floyd called Joella the Ice Princess. Now he thought the name better suited to his sister, Ell. She appeared cold as death. A chill went up Charlie's spine. He was afraid that Ell would make some portentous announcement that he didn't want to hear. She put her hand out toward him. "Frank will be here tomorrow, on the afternoon train. Will and Margaret send their prayers."

That night Charlie got into the Overland and drove out to the ranch by himself. He deliberately wrung the necks of all the peacocks and peahens. Then he carried them one by one out to the open pasture for the buzzards to feast on. He'd believed ever since they'd been brought to the ranch that they were harbingers of bad luck. He'd watched little Betts feed the birds cracked corn. Her eyes were big as dollars when the birds pecked at the corn her little fat fists threw out. But Charlie's stomach turned sour. He was convinced peacocks brought sorrow to anyone who owned them. He got back into his automobile, drove back into town, castigating himself for not getting rid of the sinister birds a long time ago.

Next morning he was at the cookhouse at Frontier Park. "Add a little more sausage to the griddle and put more buckwheat flour and water in the hot-cake batter if the Sioux come in again. And smile!" Charlie told the cook. Then he went outside, feeling apprehensive. He watched the cowboys pull their ropes from the roof of the cookhouse and barn. The ropes were left out all night to soak up the evening's moisture so they would be supple and soft for the day's calf roping, trick roping, or steer roping. The cowboys stretched their ropes to get the kinks out, and tied the split ends. They swung their ropes to make them limber and to limber themselves so they were loose and ready for the coming contests.

Charlie thought of the first morning of last year's celebration. Floyd had been up at 4 A.M. He had ridden his favorite horse, Fashion, out to the Indian encampment at the park. He had *kiyi*ed loudly, waking everyone. The young man, so full of life, was loved by the Indians and cowboys alike. "Hey, friends!" he had called to the sleepy Sioux, "come on to the cookhouse before the palefaces eat all the good meat!" Men, women, and children had followed this rangy, smiling cowboy, like sheep following the dominant ram, toward the spicy aroma of boiling coffee and frying bacon.

When the cowboys and Indians had come from the cookhouse, Floyd greeted each one by name. There were Sioux chiefs and subchiefs, mothers with cradleboards on their backs, mothers with shy children clinging to their skirts, cowboys, townsfolk, and that morning there were William Jeffers, now vice president of the U.P., and Damon Runyon getting a story for the *Saturday Evening Post*.

Charlie had been proud of the way Floyd organized the cowboys, cowgirls, and Indians working for the Y6 into the morning's parade. The theme of the parade was the evolution of transportation. Floyd had some of the Indians on foot, behind them came others with dogs drawing travois, each loaded with a smiling child, then Indians on painted ponies, then the cowboys and cowgirls on horseback and an ox team ahead of the prairie schooner, then had come Charlie in his old Colburn, which chugged and sputtered ahead of the long line of old motor trucks from several Cheyenne garages.

During that first day's program Charlie had felt so good in the center of the arena on a white horse called Whiteman, waving his broad-brimmed hat. He had sung with gusto "Alfalfa Hay." His joyful, booming voice had carried to the topmost bleacher seat. The audience had sung with him.

But now, Saturday morning, the last day of the 1917 Frontier celebration, Charlie was a different person. He was heavy-hearted. Floyd's unconscious, pale face floated in front of his eyes. Charlie smiled and bantered with the crowd, but his mind saw only his precious son. He sang, "She'll Be Coming Round the Mountain" in his loud, powerful voice, waved his hat, made his white horse turn in small circles as if it were dancing, and the crowd cheered. He announced the next event and shouted, "The show goes on!"

He dismounted and stood at the railing alone. His actions were mechanical. A haziness enveloped the crowd. A deafness obscured the approbation.

Roy put his hand on Charlie's arm. "Pa, come sit down with some of the boys. Uncle Frank is here from Florida. Have a cup of coffee. That nervous pacing drives me batty." Roy had no idea Charlie would give him the dickens.

"Don't ask me to sit! There's no time for self-indulgence! The show must go on! That's a law as old as Methuselah! Hitch the buffalo to the cart and ride them around the ring next! Wave to the crowd! Then take over the trained stallion act. Floyd didn't work with those horses four years to have them standing around pawing the dirt!"

When the final program was over, Charlie knew his cowboys would take care of the animals. He was first to leave. He didn't stand at the gate to greet friends and strangers, as he'd done other years. He rushed past the shiny Welty Bros. buggies, the *Denver Post* Boys' Band, the First U.S. Cavalry, old handdrawn fire-fighting apparatus, and out the huge iron gates. He was running past street dancers, hawkers, and boys chasing wood wagons, hooking rides. His head throbbed. He hurried to the hospital as fast as he could, half-sick with worry.

He clutched his hat in his hands and stared at his son lying in the stark white bed. Floyd's face was not tanned and healthy, but ghastly white. His left cheek looked like an eggplant. His head was shaved so that stitches could be sewn in the long scalp wound above his left eye. He must have been smacked so hard by the horse's head that the skin just popped open! My God! Charlie thought.

He went back to the waiting room, held Etta while she cried, put his arm around Dee Dee, and said, "I killed the peacocks and peahens."

"Why?" sobbed Dee Dee.

"My child! They're bad luck!" cried Charlie. He watched the doctor go into Floyd's room. He stood by the door so he could get the prognosis when the doctor came out.

The doctor's eyes were on the floor. He did not look up at Charlie, who drew his breath in sharply. Charlie's heart raced.

"Your son is dead. He never regained consciousness. He never suffered, never felt pain. I'm terribly sorry. There was nothing we could do." The doctor looked up. Charlie's face was drained of color. He leaned against the wall for support. He opened his mouth; no sound came out at first.

Finally his voice came from somewhere way below his chest. "You must be mistaken. I just saw my son and he was—was alive. I think he was. No, no, he's going to be all right!"

The doctor didn't reply. He took Charlie to a chair next to Etta. "Go home. It's over," he said gently. "I'll call the funeral home."

Etta said, "When? When did Bud die?" Tears rolled down her face.

"A moment ago. He stopped breathing and his heart stopped simultaneously. The blow to his head was so great, his brain could not function." The doctor's voice caught. He gave Etta the tightly rolled bundle of Floyd's clothes.

Etta sobbed silently while Charlie held her, feeling Floyd's boots, firm and hard inside the roll of clothing under her right arm.

Dee Dee, who was standing by Etta, crumpled in a heap on the floor.

Frank, who'd come to the hospital with Clara Belle, who was six months pregnant, stepped beside Dee Dee, looking at the red rose inlays next to the scalloped tops of her boots. "Geez! A pair of Luccheses! Did old Meanea order boots from Texas? No wonder Dee Dee's man's dead. It'd kill me to order a pair of boots for my wife like this." He belched.

Charlie stared at his brother, who seemed unfeeling and callous in the midst of the family's grief. Clara Belle bristled and fanned Dee Dee's face with her handkerchief.

"Get out of the way, Frank. Where's your manners since you've been in Florida," said Clara Belle, sobbing.

That night something happened that has never taken place before or since in front of the undertaker's place in Cheyenne. A semicircle of nearly one hundred Sioux Indians were squatted out in front, around a pitch-knot fire. One man in the center, with a blackened face, his hair hacked off at different lengths, dressed only in an unbuttoned, red, flannel shirt and breechclout, beat hypnotically on a drum. The drum was made from a nail keg with cowhide stretched tightly over both ends. The man beat with the legbone of some small animal. The men, some with black and white stripes or handprints on their faces, chanted deep in their throats. When they paused, the women, some with small children cradled in their arms or on their backs, wrapped in bright colored blankets, raised their voices in a high, piercing, tremulous effect. People gathered in tight little knots on the opposite side of the street to watch the Indians sway and sing to the drumbeat.

Among the onlookers were Clayton Danks, Bee Ho Gray, Jimmy Danks, Curly and Walt McGuckin, Pablo Martinez, and Charlie's brother Will. In another group were Harry Hynds, proprietor of the Plains Hotel, Bill Irvine, past president of the Wyoming Stock Growers' Association, and rancher Ora Haley, all friends of Charlie and his family.

The funeral parlor was not on a brightly lit street. The darkness and shadows, made larger than life by the flickering, yellow flames, seemed fitting for the mournful, heart-wrenching mood. A lone figure dressed in a black cape fastened together with a silver filigreed brooch and high-heeled shoes, carrying a dark suitcase, knocked on the front door of the funeral parlor. The beat of the drum continued. The woman did not look toward the crowd. She kept her face down, out of sight.

Once inside, Etta pushed back the hood of her cape. Her eyes were swollen and red. "The Indians! They're all out front! I had no idea they would take on so—"

"Come." The proprietor led Etta to a chair in a small office. "I have never seen, nor heard, anything like this in all my twenty years in business. The passing of your son marks the passing of an era for Cheyenne. Perhaps for the whole West. He was not only a fine cowboy, but a talented athlete, showman, and humanitarian. Like his father, he never looked at a man's skin nor his clothes. He was friends with all, young, old, black, red, or white, rich or poor. I heard he was about to join the Army. Your heart must be bursting with pride, Mrs. Irwin."

"My heart has burst with grief. At the moment I can feel nothing else," whispered Etta. "I brought some clothes. His tuxedo, with the black satin lapels, white vest, and white shirt and gloves, black bow tie, and I didn't know about shoes, I brought his boots and black spats."

"You keep the boots. You'll want them for the funeral procession. What's this other clothing? The dirty, brown twill pants and old yellow shirt?" The proprietor held up the last garments Floyd had worn. He wanted to hold his thin nose. The smell of urine and horse sweat was strong and acrid. His thin eyebrows raised and his mouth pursed.

"Those—those clothes the boy felt comfortable in. He bought them himself." Etta felt as though she were swimming upstream. It was hard to breathe and her eyes watered. "Give them back to him. Put them with him. You can do that?"

"Why, yes, I suppose so. I can tuck them inside somewhere under the satin coverlet." The funeral proprietor's voice was patronizing.

"Thank you." Etta sounded relieved. "The shirt's a happy, sunny color. Don't you think? It's not bad luck—yellow? Is it?" Now Etta sounded anxious.

"Yellow? Everybody likes yellow, Mrs. Irwin. My wife had the kitchen painted yellow."

Etta left the clothing on the desk. She put the boots back into the suitcase, closed it, pulled the cape around herself.

"You may go out the back door, if you wish," whispered the proprietor.

"Thank you, I'll go the way I came."

"Fool savages, they're still carrying on!"

"It's their way of handling grief. They're not expected to bottle it inside." Etta went out into the cool summer night, past the flickering, pitch-knot fire, thinking that the rise and fall of the voices and beat of the drum had not changed. People moved to let her pass, but not a word was spoken.

The next morning was something no one could forget. The concessionaires did not hawk their wares, but stood around patiently for buyers. Flags were down half-mast. Much of the colorful bunting was down completely. Cowboys wore black armbands. Indians struck, pulled down, their tepees and packed their gear. They had dark spots on their high cheekbones where they'd daubed ash mixed with grease. There were no grins. All faces were somber. Stock was sorted and put in corrals according to the owners at Frontier Park. Eyes darted here and there, each pair looking for that big man, for that kind-hearted man, with whom they wished to share their grief.

Those that knew Charlie well felt certain he'd make his presence felt in some way—probably in person. Rumors were rampant. Some predicted he'd ride in on his white horse to help with the cleanup. Some said he and Floyd's young widow, Dee Dee, would walk across the arena and check out the Irwin horses first thing.

Actually it was a few moments before anyone noticed that Charlie was among the roustabouts taking down tents, wooden bleachers, concession stands, flags. He said good-bye to all he came into contact with. "Good-bye, fellows. Good-bye, ladies. Thanks for your help. Couldn't do a thing without you. This is my last Wild West show."

"Oh, no, Mr. Irwin! Cheyenne's Frontier Days won't be the same without you," someone said, his voice cracking with emotion.

"Wild West shows are dead. Things change," said Charlie with a shrug. "It's in the cards. We play out the hand as it's dealt." He went on shaking hands, accepting condolences, and giving praises until the fairgrounds was bare and clean. Charlie's heart felt bare and raw with grief. He shook hands. He talked. His voice did not boom. His mind did not flow beyond this day.

On Tuesday the Irwin family moved from the undertaker's to the formal funeral ceremony at the Elks' Home. Reverend Leon C. Hills of Denver was invited to give the eulogy.

While the Irwin family was en route to the Elks' Home, there was another scene taking place in the front yard of their home on Pioneer. The Sioux stood in all their regalia in solemn lines between the trees and chanted. They passed their hands over the brand marks in the cement. Someone must have told them that Floyd had drawn the Y6 and his own registered brand, ^† , shortly after the family moved to the red brick house and the city put in the cement sidewalk. Several papooses cried and the women extended their cries with a shrill keening. After a few moments the Indians dispersed as quietly as they had come. They walked or rode horseback in a subdued, dignified manner to the Elks' Home. One by one they filed inside and sat in the wooden folding chairs at the back to hear the last story about their beloved young friend.

Reverend Hills referred to notes he held in his hand and spoke. "Floyd Leslie Irwin, born on April 29, 1895, in Goodland, Kansas, was only a small boy when he became a star Wild West performer. He took second place in the amateur rough-riding contest in 1911, here at Frontier Days. A year later in Vancouver, British Columbia, he made second in the trick riding and steer roping. In 1915 he was first in the bucking and trick riding at the Idaho Falls War Bonnet celebration. In 1916 he won the pony express at the Pendleton Round-Up, and that same year he defeated Otto Kline, the world's champion trick rider, in a contest at Topenish, Washington. He won the pony express race on six consecutive days at last year's New York Stampede and made the finals in the bucking contest there. Just two weeks ago he won both steer roping and goat roping and took second in the bucking contest in Pine Bluffs.

"Floyd was the only son of big C. B. Irwin and tiny Etta Irwin. He was one of the most popular figures in this town and in the Wild West celebrations. The young man was strong, generous, kindly, wholesome, and admired from one end of the western range states to the other. His untimely death was an accident. His death must not dampen the spirits of others for the sport of ropers and riders. Instead his spirit must be kept alive in the memory of all of us as we see and encourage other young men to enter the sport of rodeo."

Charlie and Etta held hands. Tears slid down their faces unchecked.

There was not a place to sit in the Elks' Home. Many people were standing against the back wall and out in the hall. There was not a dry eye; even the legendary stoic Sioux had tears in their eyes after the final prayer and hymn that paid tribute to the young showman they loved and respected so much.

Charlie and Etta were devastated. Their hearts were shattered and their spirits were smashed.

Young Floyd's funeral was one of the saddest and most touching Cheyenne ever saw. Charlie put his arms around Etta and Dee Dee. His eyes were red-rimmed, and he carried his wide-brimmed hat. Inside he felt hollow. Outside he felt numb. The cortege moved toward Lakeview Cemetery, led by Colonel Smoke of Fort D. A. Russell, then a detachment of cavalry men followed by the mounted cavalry band and the drum and bugle corps. The pallbearers carrying the bronze casket were cowboys who worked with Floyd on the Y6: Bob Lee, Ernie Green, Jelmer Johnson, John Rick, Clayton Danks, and Harry Walters. There was an honorary group of cowboy pallbearers, who were mounted and formed an honor guard.

Charlie held on to Etta's and Dee Dee's hands. He kept his head high and barely saw the people that lined the streets. The clear blue sky and trees blurred. He had to blink once or twice. He dared not speak because talking would unleash his pent-up anguish, like the rush of a blaze in dry pine needles.

Then came the Sioux on horseback, dressed in their beaded

leather tunics with wide fringe on sleeves and leggings. Their faces still carried the black ash, but beneath the high cheekbones were lines of red and yellow, signifying the continuity of life. A thin red line of vermilion was painted along the men's straight hair part. The tail of each horse was bobbed short.

In an ancient stagecoach, drawn by six black mules, were the Sioux women and children in their best beaded and quilled leather clothing. Their faces and hair parts were painted with thin red lines.

Then came fifty mounted cowboys in bright flannel shirts, tight gabardine pants, polished, high-heeled boots, and jingling spurs. Sadly alone came Floyd's horse, Fashion, carrying its master's empty boots on the right side of the empty saddle. The stirrups were reversed.

Floyd's own string of horses came next. Then came the tear-streaked cowgirls mingled with carriages and automobiles belonging to friends, townspeople and visitors who came to pay their last respects to the most popular young cowboy Cheyenne ever had.

After the short ceremony at the cemetery friends and well wishers flocked around the Irwin family. William Jeffers spoke with Charlie and Etta. "C.B., I owe you my promotion to vice-president of the railroad. It all stemmed from the good work that was done bringing in Bill Carlisle. We couldn't have done it as well, nor as quickly, without your organization, stock, and manpower." Warren Richardson gave his handkerchief to Etta, while Senator Thomas G. Powers, who came from Torrington, put his hand on Charlie's arm and said, "I understand the emptiness you feel, my friend. I lost my only son, George, last month in a swimming accident."

Charlie was deeply stirred. "I remember the incident. It happened in Rawhide Creek. Jeems, I had no idea the pain you felt. I'm so sorry." Charlie pulled Powers toward him in an embrace. Both men were too choked up to talk more.

The two men looked at each other and tears streamed down their faces.

Etta patted Richardson's hand and could not tell him how much she appreciated friends, because of the catch in her throat. She tried to smile through her tears. Then she took Charlie's arm and led him back to the graveled road. She whispered, "It's time for us to leave."

Charlie turned and looked back one more time. The raw earth of the grave was covered with flowers of all colors. There was a huge wreath shaped like a horseshoe sent by the cowboys. In the center was Floyd's brand, a rafter T: $\overset{\wedge}{\text{T}}$.

That evening, while the family was sitting around sipping tea, they heard the drumbeat.

"What's that?" asked Etta.

"It's the Sioux. They haven't started back home yet," said Roy. "Remember what they did when Red Cloud's baby died? They're out there keeping the evil spirits away from Floyd. They're giving him a proper send-off for his last journey."

"Did you take Fashion to the ranch?" asked Charlie.

"No, he's in the Four-Mile pasture," said Roy.

"Take him out there to the Sioux," said Charlie. "I can't look at him anymore. It tears my heart to little pieces."

Roy went out to the Four-Mile pasture and whistled once. Several horses neighed in response and trotted toward him. He climbed on the bare back of Fashion and rode to the cemetery. The Indian women had stopped their piercing keening and had fanned out over the grave site. All the flowers were gone. They were brushing the ground with turkey-feather fans so no trace of the newly dug grave was visible. Roy could see John Red Cloud standing with other men who'd thrown dust in their hair and were weeping openly. Roy could not hide in the treeless cemetery. The moonlight fell on him and the horse. An old brave, believed to be more than a hundred years old, called Pawnee Leggins, followed Red Cloud toward Roy.

Roy felt his throat tighten. He pointed to Fashion. "Yours," he said softly.

Roy could see Red Cloud's face paint furrowed and erased where tears had run. They shook hands. Neither young man could speak.

The old man touched their shoulders. "When the sun shines I will ride our brother's horse. When the snow falls I will follow our brother's trail. Red Cloud will ride the horse. In the land of the Happy Hunting Ground I will strike up a conversation with our brother. We will be old friends. He will know of this generosity."

THIRTY-NINE

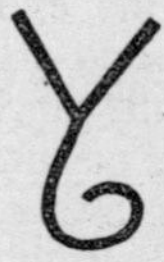

Real Western Movie

Etta found it hard to concentrate. She made one bed, swept half the kitchen, washed the breakfast silverware, leaving the cups and saucers forgotten in the sink. Neighborhood children shouted happily in the alley. Etta went to the back door to call Floyd in for a piece of fresh cake. Suddenly she'd remember Floyd was no longer here. At the ranch it was the same. She'd hear a horse gallop into the yard and the screen door slam. "Bud, if you're planning to go to town, bring me a spool of darning floss."

If it was Charlie who'd come in, he'd pull Etta against his broad chest, stroke her hair, and say, "You forgot, I'm here to run your errands."

"Oh, Charlie, I'm so sorry. The sounds, the smells, nothing's changed, only everything's changed. Sometimes I forget. For a whole day I thought Bud was out with the horses and I made his favorite sourdough rye bread. You suppose my mind's touched?" she said one day.

Charlie held her tight and said, "Dear, your reason is under a cloud. But clouds don't last." He never told her that he'd done the same thing. He'd called the cowboy that was working the blacksmith shed "Floyd." He'd daydreamed about asking Floyd if he'd signed up for a cavalry unit. He'd prepared a list of good things he'd say to Floyd about the cavalry.

Two weeks after Floyd's death Etta, teary-eyed, was knitting scarves for the men on the monitor *Cheyenne* and the battleship *Wyoming*, as were many other housewives in town. Charlie complained about "Hoover menus," so called because Herbert Hoover, who headed the War Food Administration, suggested conservation of food, "wheatless Mondays" and "meatless Tuesdays."

"No one has the right to change the diet of a good citizen. If we want to eat beef from the ranch, make bread from wheat grown on the ranch, we will," proclaimed Charlie. He stopped Etta from heeding the recommendation of cutting down on bread, meat, and sugar. "I don't see any reason to starve while my country fights a war," he said.

A small tank was transported on a railroad flatcar and exhibited from town to town promoting the sale of Victory bonds. Charlie bought bonds so that he could have a ride in the tank as it climbed over piles of brick, crossties, in and out of gullies and roadside ravines. Roy, Hippy Burmister, and the McGuckin brothers felt a great surge of patriotism. They sought out a particular U.P. employee of Russian ancestry, stripped the fellow, and painted him yellow because he refused to buy a Victory bond. Charlie posted bail to get the four men out of jail and paid their fine set by the judge and made them work the money off at the ranch.

At the suggestion of the Council of National Defense a One Hundred Percent American Club was formed in Cheyenne as well as other Wyoming towns to keep tabs on those who appeared to rebel against the government and to promote patriotism. French replaced German in the curriculum of the town's high school.

In 1918 Senator Warren was reelected, General Pershing was commander-in-chief of the American Expeditionary Forces in France, and Robert Carey, son of Joseph M. Carey, became governor of Wyoming. Wheat prices rose from seventy-two cents a bushel in 1913 to a dollar ninety-eight in 1918. Cattle prices rose from thirty-nine dollars a head in 1913 to sixty-three dollars a head at the end of 1918.

Charlie attended the Cheyenne meeting of the Wyoming Council of National Defense in February 1918. The labor shortage was the chief topic. The saloons and empty railroad boxcars harbored men who'd lost their jobs, but who now spurned lesser jobs offered them. Charlie offered these men sixty dollars a week and entrance fees if they'd ride Irwin horses in local rodeos and give Charlie half their winnings. Those that went along with Charlie made money because the Irwin horses had the speed. In fact, it was hard for an outsider to get in the winning circle at rodeos where the Irwin horses ran.

Without warning, Spanish influenza struck Wyoming, causing more deaths than all war-connected causes. Public meetings were prohibited. The schools and churches were closed. Leaf burning was stopped because it was rumored that the smoke carried the disease. Etta disliked going to town to shop because the stores that remained open were limited to five customers at a time for every twenty-five feet of store front.

Charlie sent Pauline and Frances to the ranch that summer to avoid the dreaded flu. He managed his office without a secretary. Etta went to the ranch with baby Betts, who had, according to Charlie, a bad case of summer complaint. Etta knew the baby had the deadly influenza. She wanted to keep the child at the house in town, but Charlie insisted Betts would recuperate faster at the ranch. "Everyone feels better at the ranch," said Charlie. Etta felt better in town.

Day after day Etta sat in the kitchen rocker with Betts on her lap. She sat near the door so she could look out to see who was in the backyard. She sometimes put a cool, damp cloth on the child's forehead. The child ate little and slept fitfully. After meals Etta sat in the rocker and watched Pauline and Frances put the dishes away in the cupboard that not only opened in the kitchen but also in the dining room.

"Gram's here," she whispered to the fretting child. She patted the soft brown hair. "Don't fret, honey, everything's fine. Gram's here. Sshh. Go to sleep."

Etta looked at the pie cupboard, which held two rhubarb pies and the bread that was baked on Saturday. Beyond the cupboard was the long wooden sink and the coal range. Beyond the range was the hall with the crank telephone. The call first went to the little town of Burns, and then was hooked by the operator into the Cheyenne system. Across the hall was the bathroom, with a big porcelain wash bowl and bathtub on bear-claw legs. There was a hole in the floor, covered by a heavy wooden square. The hole was always covered. In the hole was water to be used for washing dishes and bathing. Periodically this hole was emptied and left to fill up with fresh ground water, which was bitter-tasting from minerals. There was no toilet. There was an outhouse past the back steps.

Opposite the bathroom was the door to the dining room.

Beyond that was a small bedroom for the cook. Fear of influenza that year caused the cook to flee to her native state of Montana. Etta and the two girls did the cooking that summer. Farther down the hall was the front door, which was seldom used. Outside was the water pump and the fancy wrought-iron gate. Etta always had flowers growing in the front yard of the ranch house and townhouse.

Opposite the cook's bedroom was the living room on the left, in which was the stand-up Victrola. Pauline and Frances loved to wind it and listen to records by the hour. Next to the cook's bedroom was Charlie's den. On the den's floor, in front of the bookcases, was the hide of Charlie's horse, Custer, that was killed during the lightning storm in Minneapolis. The bookcase covered one wall to the ceiling. It held books about veterinary medicine, horseshoeing, range management, back copies of the *Chicago Daily Farmers and Drovers Journal* and the *Laramie Boomerang*. On the bottom shelf was a complete set of Encyclopedia Americana. Above the fireplace was the mounted head of the first buffalo that was brought in with the first stock roundup on the Y6. The other two walls were decorated with antelope and deer hides and one bear's head.

Beside the door into the den were steps leading upstairs. Etta closed her eyes and saw the small bedroom on the left. Today the walls were white and it contained an empty cot. It was Floyd's room. But Etta imagined how that tiny room would look in a soft pink with a pure white coverlet on the bed and white lace curtains at the window. The room would be for Betts when she was older and would come to the ranch house on weekends or during the summer. She patted the sleeping child's head. The largest room upstairs was at the front end. It was the ballroom. Etta remembered the good time she and Charlie had giving a dance for Frankie Warren and John Pershing several days before they were married. And the dance they'd had the night John and Elsie Coble were married. Remembering how John wanted to leave because he'd booked a room earlier at the Inter-Ocean Hotel for himself and his bride made Etta chuckle to herself. All the men had wanted to dance with the fair-haired Elsie. Coble had been able to do nothing but wait until the dancing was over. As it turned out, the Cobles had spent their first night together in Etta and Charlie's room, across the hall from the tiny bedroom. There were two other bedrooms between them and the ballroom, Pauline's room and Frances's room. Other couples had stayed over until daylight. They had slept on blankets and quilts, same as

Charlie and Etta, on the floor of the ballroom.

Those were such good days, thought Etta, before time and tragedy caught up with all of us.

The summer dragged by, hot and dusty by day, cool and buggy with mosquitoes by night.

When school began, Etta took Betts, Dee Dee, and Frances back to the red brick house in Cheyenne. Frances was in high school. Pauline and Dee Dee worked for Charlie. Betts lost so much weight Etta was almost afraid to carry the child without her being swaddled in a small comforter or carried on a pillow. At night Etta was afraid to sleep for fear the fragile child would stop breathing. She became obsessed with caring for her granddaughter.

Charlie tried to understand Etta's concern about the child. It was her way of easing the inner grief and pain over Floyd's death. But he was afraid too much concentration on the child was unhealthy. "Look, Pauline doesn't fuss about Betts as much as you. Pauline is the baby's mother. That baby knows if she lets out one whimper, you'll come running to comfort her. You are letting a two-year-old master you. That isn't right. You're bigger than she. You must master the baby."

"I lost one. I'm not losing another," Etta said, "even if it takes all my strength to heal that delicate little body."

"But, dear, in the meantime you ignore the rest of us. I realize in a way you are testing your own limitations. But you can't reach beyond those ordinary limitations unless you take a risk. Let the baby sleep one whole hour without watching her. If you come out on top of that small risk and the baby didn't cry, try two hours."

"Oh, Charlie, what if something happened to Betts when I wasn't watching? How would I feel? How would you—Pauline feel?"

"That's it. How do we feel now? You don't talk with us. You don't eat with us. You ignore us. Jeems, Etta! I want you back!"

"Charlie! Don't 'Jeems' me! Who sent our only son to Frontier Park to practice steer roping? Who encouraged that boy almost before he could walk to use a rope? I'm going to take care of the ones that are left. It's my duty to this family!"

Charlie felt his stomach muscles tighten and pull inward. He clenched and unclenched his fists. "Please don't. Don't blame me for something that was an accident. It's over. Our life now depends on how we can bridge over that terrible hole. Etta, we only live once. Isn't it better to live for all of your family and let the good Lord do some of the worrying? Etta, come back to the rest of us." He felt the tears in his eyes and his throat contract. "Have you looked at yourself in the mirror? Your hair is turning white. Oh, Etta, don't let a tiny baby pull your life away."

"I am giving life to your granddaughter."

"That's a terrible thing to tell a man. Must I choose between my wife and a granddaughter that is so tiny she's contributed nothing to this world yet?" Charlie put his hand on Etta's shoulder. She'd lost weight and probably weighed not more than a hundred pounds. He slipped his big hand across her back and the other hand under her knees. He picked up Etta, who cradled the baby in her arms, and danced around the kitchen, down the hall to the dining room, living room, and into his den. He sang, "Oh, Dem Golden Slippers." Finally he eased Etta and the smiling baby down into his big leather chair. "I choose you. And I make a promise that if you come back and choose me, we'll have this little bitty kid well before you can say the Lord is my shepherd in Hebrew."

Etta began to laugh. Betts cooed.

"Charlie, I tried to get so mad at you. Now see what you've done? You've made me laugh and Betts is saying your name over and over, 'Gramps, Gramps, Gramps.' That's it! You live life to the hilt! Living with you is—is a challenge. I was so angry with you. I blamed you for my broken heart. I wanted to lash out to blame anyone, everyone, for what happened to Bud. I still do." Tears streamed down her face and she dabbed her eyes with the corner of Betts's flannel blanket. "I'm mad! I'm mad at you! Because you made me feel happy for a moment and you made Betts laugh. I shouldn't feel happy. Should I?"

"Why not? Think what Floyd would say to you. 'Ma, let Pauline take care of her own kid. Go out to dinner with Pa. Ma, wear your blue dress and those high heels. Smile, 'cause you're the best-looking lady sipping tea in the Tivoli.'"

"Oh, oh, it's a sacrilege to talk that way. Oh, my, if I closed my eyes I could hear Bud talking as plain as if he were in this room. It takes my breath away." Etta wiped her tears with the baby's blanket again.

"You have to admit that I'm more interesting than a little bitty kid who has a limited vocabulary."

"Charlie! I don't have to admit anything, except that I love you." Etta was letting the tears stream down her face.

"I'm not boring?" asked Charlie, handing Etta his clean bandanna to blow her nose. He picked up Betts, taking off the damp flannel blanket. "Look at that! I have two girls here. One is leaking from her eyes, the other is leaking from her—"

"Stop! I'll get a diaper and you can change her. It's a miracle, this baby hasn't cried all morning." When she came back she was amazed how well Charlie could change diapers.

"Remember, we had kids of our own. It's like twirling a rope: Once you get the hang of it, you never forget. You never answered my question. Do you find me boring?" Charlie looked at Etta with his intent brown eyes. She was not sure if he was serious or teasing.

"If I pay attention to you—life is never boring. If—this is hard for me to say—if I hide within myself and leave you out, life is not half so interesting."

"Are you still mad at me?"

"Yes! No! Oh, Charlie, I can't stay mad at you."

He laid the goose-down pillow on the floor and put the baby in the middle of it. "Then come give me a kiss."

Etta leaned against Charlie and let him hold her tight. She closed her eyes and felt his wonderful, warm mouth on hers. Nothing seemed more important than this instant. A few moments before, her world was upside down and her heart was full of a festering grief. Now she felt cleansed and whole and strong enough to take care of her family. She felt secure.

Charlie felt his stomach muscles relax and the tension in the back of his neck disappear. He, too, found that the grief for his beloved son had to be changed into a feeling that he controlled his destiny. He could no longer let the pain of a hurting heart control his life. Floyd would always be missed, but the memories of his son could never be taken away. Charlie looked up in time to see Betts on hands and knees pulling books off the lower shelf. One by one the books toppled on the floor. "No matter how much you help a child, he does as he pleases when he gets away from you," Charlie said hastily. He pretended not to see Betts when the child gave him a toothless grin. He held Etta and let her kiss his eyes, mouth, and neck. This was a new beginning.

The Ringling Sells-Floto Circus came to Cheyenne from Denver.

"Late for a circus," commented Charlie. "Snow could hit the big tents any day."

Dee Dee asked to go. Etta said she thought it was improper to be seen at such entertainment so soon after the death of her husband. Dee Dee could not see that point of view. "Mr. Irwin always says a show must go on no matter what happens. The circus was part of my life."

"The people in this town look at things different. They'd think you were some kind of hussy going to see the circus right now. Wait until next year," said Etta. "Here's stockings in the basket that need darning." She shoved a wicker basket toward Dee Dee and put a wooden, black enameled darning egg in her lap.

Etta picked up Betts, who was now a healthy pink color, gaining weight and cutting teeth. Etta put a sterling silver darning thimble on her finger and rubbed it over the child's tender, swollen gums, helping the teeth to come through.

"Mrs. Irwin if Pauline and Frances went with me, would it seem so terrible?" pleaded Dee Dee.

"When I was a young girl, my mother believed that if there was a death in the family, the least that family could do to show respect was to refrain from any frivolity for a year," said Etta. "Why is that so restricting to young people nowadays?"

"Maybe because it hinders us from living the way we want," said Dee Dee. "Every time I look at the brands that Floyd traced with a horseshoe nail in the wet concrete on the front sidewalk, I feel like he marked this place. You know, like a tramp chalkmarks the curb of a house that feeds well? Like the tramps, I can always find my way back to the marks—but I don't belong here."

"You are welcome to stay as long as you like. Charlie says you are a good worker at his office," said Etta, afraid that already Dee Dee was planning to leave.

On Saturday there was a circus parade that came up Pioneer past the Irwins' house. Pauline, Frances, and Dee Dee sat on the front steps and watched the palominos strut by; the clowns with baggy pants walked in front of a group of Percherons who carried beautiful girls in spangled tights. Dee Dee waved to an old friend, Billie Burke. She told the girls how Billie Burke had worked hours each day to be able to perform acrobatics on the back of a running horse. "Same way Floyd worked hours to perfect his trick riding and his rope tricks," she said wistfully.

Then came draft horses hauling red, blue, yellow, and green parade wagons, stepping high and tossing their heads from side to side.

"I remember when you first went to the ranch," said Frances. "You got drunk as a skunk on Uncle Frank's liquor and climbed to the top of the windmill."

"Oh, I remember that," cried Pauline. "You held your arms

out over your head and walked on that railing barefoot, like some kind of ballet dancer. You never came near being knocked down by the blade, even though you glided around on that rickety rail a dozen times. My heart was in my mouth. I was afraid to breathe for fear you would fall head first to the ground. Only when I saw you climb down, quiet and graceful as a cat, could I really breathe. I wanted to pound Floyd for letting you do such a dumb thing. But the more I thought about it, the more I saw what it was you really did. You gave everyone a show and told them you had talent, you weren't afraid of high places, like most women. You showed that you were as free as a bird, no one owned your soul, not even your husband. You were like a life-sized butterfly on top of that windmill. I've never seen the likes of it before. You were better than any circus act."

Dee Dee smiled, breathing deeply. Into her nostrils came an odor of horses, sawdust and rosin, intriguing, compelling. She felt disturbed, drawn to the girls she did not recognize. The girls shivered in the cool air and the shimmering spangles on their costumes reflected the blue of their bare skin.

The next morning Dee Dee was gone. She'd left a note saying that she'd left with the Ringling Sells-Floto bunch, not to worry, she was sure she could do something more suited to her lifestyle with the circus.

Charlie sent Dee Dee money for years, whenever he knew for certain where the Ringling Sells-Floto Circus was performing. Dee Dee was once again the Iron-jawed Butterfly. As far as Charlie knew, she never remarried.

Etta felt uneasy and anxious all day after she'd found Dee Dee's note. She wondered if the anxiety was because she'd not told Charlie to go after Dee Dee. No, Dee Dee must find her own life, thought Etta. But I will miss her. Without thinking she put an extra supper dish on the table.

"Dee Dee's not coming back for supper," teased Frances. "When the circus comes back, we'll see her, huh?"

"Oh, yes," said Etta, her eyes misty.

"Someone's coming!" called Pauline. "Honest! Come look out the window. It's a taxi from the depot."

As soon as the taxi stopped, a young woman and little girl popped out the door.

Etta drew in her breath and put her hand over her mouth. She knew right away it was Joella and her little girl, Patty. She flew out the front door and down the walk. "I'm so glad to see you. Dee Dee left some time last night. How long can you stay? How is Deeke? How pretty Patty is! Like a porcelain doll." Her arms were tight around her eldest daughter, who smelled like lilies of the valley. Joella wore a brown linen suit and a brown hat with pale cream-colored flowers on the left side. She had on brown pumps and silk stockings.

"You look wonderful," said Etta. Taking Patty's hand she led them into the house. Patty, in patent-leather shoes with four button-straps over the ankle, short white stockings, and a short pink cotton dress with a shirred yoke, shivered in the cool October sunshine.

Inside the house Joella said, "Well, I'm back for good."

"For good?" said Charlie, giving his daughter a good hug and picking up Patty so he could see her better. "Is Deeke back at Fort Russell?"

"I hated the constant rain in Portland. On top of that, being Lieutenant Frank Jones's wife was nothing but servile drudgery. No one called him Deeke but me, and he told me to cut it out."

"Drudgery?" asked Charlie.

"Frank—Deeke—could eat at the officers' mess, but he came home every noon. At five he expected a hot meal with hot bread. I had to get out of bed to fix his breakfast, even if I didn't eat. I felt like a slave. When he came at noon, the house had to be spotless. He gave everything the white-glove test."

"Oh, honey!" Now Etta's eyes watered. She patted the baby Charlie held. "Come see Pauline's big girl in the high chair."

"Ma," said Joella, "don't feel bad. Deeke feels the same as me. He's the one that filed for divorce." She stood still. She'd said the word and now everyone knew she was home for good.

Charlie noticed the taxi still out front. He went out, still carrying the baby, Patty, paid the driver, and brought two huge suitcases, one by one, into the house, then went back for the several hatboxes. He looked up at the lazy clouds tinged with gold from the setting sun. The wind thrummed sadly in the electrical wires.

That winter Joella lived at the Irwin home in town with her little girl. She made hats and sold several dozen to women in Cheyenne. By spring the women from Laramie had heard about Joella's lovely hats and came to buy at Easter time.

For the past two years Martinez had been Charlie's sole jockey. He'd ridden the Irwins' seven horses in rodeos all over the northwest, like Denver, Pendleton, Walla Walla, and Calgary. The Irwin horses, Burnt Candle, Deal Carroll, Ellen Smyth, Henry Walbank, Mackinaw Belle, Panhachapi and Pickagain, won most every quarter-, half-, or three-quarter-mile race entered. By the next year Charlie bought and traded so that instead of seven horses he had fourteen. The best two he kept, Ellen Smyth and Panhachapi. Also he hired half a dozen more jockeys, who worked the horses three times a day, brushed, watered, and fed them as though they were all prizewinners. Jess Howard was hired to ride Little Spider and Paddy Button. Thompson rode Jennie Crawford and Larkin. Cassity rode Frosty Morning and Sam Connor.

Charlie began to let Will take charge of the farming and raising of the Herefords. Frank kept the jockeys in line and took care of the racehorses. Charlie continued his job as stock agent for the U.P. and thought of himself as manager of the Y6 ranch, which had grown to twenty-three thousand acres.

After Floyd's death the Wild West show wagons and calliope were stored at the Four-Mile pasture. A few times, after school, Frances took Betts and Patty out to the Four-Mile to play on the still-colorful wagons and to pretend the calliope was steamed up and ready to peal out with its lovely, rich music. The little girls decorated the wagons with handfuls of wildflowers, imagining they were in a parade along some western town's main street.

Once at the supper table Frances said, "Those kids bring offerings of Indian paintbrush, phlox, fireweed, ox-eyed daisies, and bull thistles to those old Wild West show relics. All of a sudden today it seemed like decorating the grave of some loved one. Being with those rusty wagons keeps the memories of the greatest Wild West show ever produced alive for me. Once the show was disbanded people forgot how big, how good, and how exciting the show really was. I wish there was some way to prolong and preserve the memory of the Irwin Wild West show."

Charlie said, "Fran, you're keeping it alive by taking Betts and Patty out there. They'll remember your stories and pass them along."

Charlie was concerned about the humane treatment of animals during a rodeo or Wild West show. He'd tried to instigate rules for the Cheyenne Frontier Days, but with little success. He'd become familiar with the State Veterinarian Pflaeging during the Great Endurance Race, who was an officer of the Wyoming Humane Society. Charlie applied for a commission with the society May 1918. If he were an officer in the Wyoming Humane Society, he could rule that horses had to be hackamored in corrals and led to the track in such a way that there was no danger of choking them down. This could apply to the bucking contests, and to the horse racing of all kinds.

Charlie received his commission on June 4, 1918. Several times during local rodeos and even during the Frontier Days, he warned riders about gouging the sides of their animals with spurs. Most of the riders felt his rules were most reasonable and reduced the chances for cruelty, but still did not block the excitement and daredevil actions of the contests.

During the summer of 1918 Charlie took Will's two sons, Sharkey, who was nineteen and Gene, who was eleven, on the rodeo circuit. Sharkey took first place in the bucking contest in Spokane, Washington. He won a saddle trimmed with silver. Gene spun his rope on the sidelines, hoping to attract attention. He attracted a lot of attention when he flung out his rope and caught one of the clowns by a foot.

Charlie got the rope off the clown and told Gene he'd have to sit in the stands or stay in the tack room if he swung his rope again.

"But Uncle Charlie, I want to enter the trick-roping contest!" cried the boy.

"Enter it, then. Put your name on the list today. If you don't place, you sit in the stands."

"All right!" Gene was all smiles.

Two days later Gene was in the stands, but still smiling. By the next year he would be that much better, and he knew he'd have a chance of winning the boys' trick-roping contest if his uncle Charlie continued to help him.

After the Frontier Days celebration and before school began in the fall, there was a rodeo in Cheyenne. Charlie let his men and horses enter.

Horse racing was beginning to please Charlie. Between races he'd ride in front of the grandstand on his all-white horse, Whiteman, wave his big wide-brimmed white hat. The crowd always responded with cheers and whistles.

The last rodeos of any season, like this one, were happy events, but sad when over. Everyone tried to make the fun last as long as possible. There would be no more racing nor rodeo contests until the following spring. The morning after the last rodeo Cheyenne was like a ghost town. There was a feeling all over town, and it spread out to the ranches, of a general letdown, until the fall roundups began.

Charlie wanted to buy Etta and the girls a piano for the ranch. He'd been thinking about it for a long time. The day he decided he also wanted to buy a horse named Garter from one of his cowboys was the time he decided to play poker in the bunkhouse with the cowboys. Ike Rude was called Jitney by Charlie because he worked in spurts of nervous energy exactly like the jitney engines in the U.P. switching yards. Charlie told Etta if he won enough he'd have both the piano and Rude's horse.

Etta was practical. She said, "Sell a couple of the wild broncs and buy what you what."

Charlie pulled her close. He said, "There's no challenge, no excitement, to do something so straightforward. Life needs some suspense before the joy."

"I love you, win or lose," she said. She worshipped him.

During the poker game Charlie had a winning streak. He was quick with cards. Charlie's poker games were not for nickels and dimes, but for fifty-dollar bills and one-hundred-dollar bills. On a losing streak he might give away a couple good steers and a horse. One game could wipe out a year or two savings for a young cowboy. That did not bother Charlie. His attitude was that it taught the boy a lesson. One ought to gamble big and win big. If you could not afford to lose everything, don't gamble. About midnight the men called it quits. Charlie had most of the money. "If you need money, Jitney, you can sell me your horse, Garter," Charlie said to Rude. "A thousand dollars."

"I'm not ready to sell," said Rude. He thought that in a few months there would be another game. He decided to wait until Charlie came back from racing his horses because then he'd really be worked up over the horse and he'd get twice what was offered tonight. Two thousand dollars for an old horse called Garter's not bad, he thought. And a boss who'd buy a good horse like Garter isn't so bad either, because he'd take the best care possible of the old shavetail.

In a week the ranch house had an upright piano.

"That must have been a good poker night for you," said Etta, pleased with the piano. "We'll have music wherever we are."

"You bet we will," agreed Charlie. "And I'll wait until I come back from racing my horses, then Jitney will sell his horse, Garter, to me for a song."

This was the year that Charlie found he could not control his brother Frank's drinking. Frank could not manage the jockeys nor keep the horses exercised. He slept in the barn, so Charlie was afraid he'd set the barn on fire with carelessness. "Go home to your wife and kids," said Charlie. "Clara Belle needs you and so do those four kids. She's not had money for groceries since before Frontier Days. Etta's been sending her baked goods. It's a shame to do this to someone who loves you. It's disgraceful!"

"You have no business talking to your own brother like that!" yelled Frank.

"I have if he's working for me," said Charlie.

"Well, then I quit! You find another lackey to supervise those jocks." Frank picked up his clothes and a saddle and left. Charlie did not see him at the ranch after that. Some said he went back to Florida to work around the young racetracks for room and board and twenty dollars a month. Others said he could be found around Denver and Colorado Springs training jockeys.

Charlie let Clara Belle and the children stay in Cheyenne that winter. He paid their house rent. Clara Belle wanted to go away and find a job for herself. In the spring he found a job for her in an Owl Drug Store in San Diego, California. He was in Southern California racing horses at all the small tracks. Etta kept the three girls and baby boy until Clara Belle could get enough money saved to rent an apartment and write for the children.

Shortly after the armistice with Germany was signed on November 11, 1918, ending World War I, Charlie loaded a dozen racehorses in a stock car, and took Martinez and half a dozen other jockeys and Clara Belle's four children with him to San Diego. Clara Belle met the train. She was delighted to see the children. Charlie was going to have a try at the newly built racetrack outside the United States borders, in a Mexican village, where the streets were thick with dust and yipping dogs. This was Tia Juana.

The track's owner was dark-haired, dark-eyed, smiling Sunny Jim Coffroth, who was also a friend of Will Rogers. Rogers was not surprised to see Charlie in Tia Juana. "I knew you'd wise up and see that horseracing was the most popular sport in the country."

"I'm out of the country now," said Charlie.

"Not out of your element though," said Coffroth.

"I want a place, a house for my family, near the tracks, but far enough away so I won't eat the dust of the track," said Charlie.

Charlie, Coffroth, and Rogers found a two-acre place just outside San Ysidro, a little inland, hilly town a half mile from the Mexican border. On the place was a small back road that was about a mile long and went across the border without going through San Ysidro. In the middle of the two acres was a white adobe house with a glassed-in front porch, sunken living room, fireplace, and three bedrooms. Beside the house was a three-car open garage. Built on to the garage and covered with stucco were three guest rooms, one of which was large enough to make into a room for three or four jockeys. There was plenty of room to build corrals and stalls for horses.

"Nice place," said Coffroth.

"I like it," said Rogers, "but the price is too high."

"I like it," said Charlie. "Why don't you buy it? Offer less than the asking price. See what happens." Charlie's eyes went over the rolling hills, the tan desert earth. Eucalyptus trees were in the front, almost nude with no leaves. Their bark hung in long strips as though they were molting. The land was about seven miles inland from the coast. It looked dry, with only sagebrush and cactus dotting the thin, sandy soil.

"I'll wait and make my move in the morning." Rogers winked. "Somebody may buy it before then, but I'm not going to worry."

"I'm going back to the house and see the owner," said Charlie. "I just want to talk to him. See if the title's clear—that sort of thing."

"Sure. That sort of thing," said Rogers.

"We'll wait for you," said Coffroth.

Charlie found out that the owner had bought the two acres of land from what had originally been a much larger piece—an old Spanish land grant. Charlie talked the owner down to a reasonable amount and put cash down on the table. The man signed and handed the title to Charlie.

"You got yourself a sweet place," said the man. "My wife loved it. I can't bear to look at it now that she died. I'm glad to get shut of it. I'll be out of here by tomorrow night."

Charlie shook the man's hand, then hurried back to Rogers's rented automobile. "Look at that house—she's mine."

"I'm glad I didn't worry. When'll you be ready for guests?" teased Rogers. "I suppose you want to celebrate this momentous move?"

"Well, I hadn't thought about that, but it seems like a good idea."

"There's a popular Western star of motion pictures putting on some kind of roping act in a theater in San Diego. I thought I'd go see what he looks like. How about it?" said Coffroth.

The young Western star of popular Western motion pictures was Tom Mix. Charlie was surprised. "That fellow worked for me when he didn't know one end of a horse from another. He was so clumsy he fell over his own feet. Look where he is now!"

"You're a good teacher, C.B.," quipped Rogers. "He swings a pretty good rope."

The three men talked and laughed all during the rope tricks. Finally the lady behind them poked Rogers with her knuckles and said, "Button your lip. That fellow on stage is more important than either one of you goons."

"Well, ma'am, I respect your opinion," said Rogers, "but this may change it." He got up out of his seat, ran up the aisle, and jumped on the stage with Tom Mix. "Come on, pardner, let your old buddy, Will Rogers, show the folks you aren't the only one that can twirl a rope."

The startled look on Tom Mix's face vanished when he recognized Will Rogers. Tom held up his hand so the band stopped playing. "Ladies and gentlemen, this is one of the best rope twirlers in these United States, next to me, of course. The gentleman, Will Rogers, from Claremore, Oklahoma, got his start with a circus, same as I. Give him a big hand."

The audience loved it. Rogers waved his broad-brimmed hat around, laid it on the floor, and began to twirl the rope, sideways, over his head, around his body. All the time his feet moved, as though he were a tap dancer, in time to the music. He broke into a yodel and then stopped. When the house was quiet, he pointed at the audience and said so everyone could hear, "Out there is our old friend, Mr. C. B. Irwin, alias Mr. Horse Trainer. Hi, there, C.B.!"

Charlie turned and grinned at the frowning woman behind him. He stood up and called, "If neither of you men can do the Over-the-Spoke, I'd be glad to come up and show the people exactly how it's done. Tom, be honest, tell the people you learned by sweat and hard work to ride a horse when you worked for me! Tell them honestly how green you were in those days. You thought a rope was used to hang out clothes on wash day!"

The audience roared. Before the show was over, Charlie was also up on the stage showing how to begin the loop, but keeping it small enough to go through the area between the spoke, or straight end of the rope, and the body. Charlie kept his hands about three feet apart and brought the loop down between the spoke and his necktie. The spoke slackened almost imperceptibly so that the loop rolled gently over. The loop moved slowly as it rolled, to make it easier to get it through. Charlie deliberately made the movement as slow as he could so that the audience could see the full effect of the beautiful, rolling loop.

Tom Mix sang another song. Rogers and Charlie hummed in harmony. At the end Tom Mix was between his two friends, they bowed together, and could feel the stage vibrate with the thunderous applause.

The manager met the three of them backstage and asked if either Rogers or Charlie would like to work with Tom Mix in a traveling show. Both Rogers and Charlie laughed heartily.

"I can do my own show," said Rogers.

"I raise racehorses," said Charlie. "But if I run out of work, I'll look you up."

Tom Mix shook hands with Rogers and Charlie and had to admit this show was different from any others he'd given. "I thought it was going in the waste basket at first to have you guys on the stage with me. But, by gosh, the show was a smash!" He smiled and his dark brown eyes seemed to make his tan skin look smooth as a young boy's.

Coffroth was drawn to Charlie. He admired his self-confidence.

Charlie could hardly wait to tell Etta about the new ranch he had in California. "There's room for me to build a tack room and bunkhouse for the men taking care of the horses, a feed room and five or six box stalls. I can make a couple corrals. I'll put a chicken house in the backyard and a steel fence all around the place."

"Why would you put up a steel fence? At the Y6 there's hardly any fencing, only to keep the cows or horses in their pasture." Etta was suddenly not sure she'd like this new place at all.

"Well, dear, Pancho Villa is still in Mexico, and once in a while he or his men come across the border for horses. I'd just as soon he didn't have an easy time getting at mine."

Then Etta had some surprising news for Charlie. Joella had married Captain Norman E. Waldron of the Army Remount Division. Waldron was stationed at Fort Russell. Joella did not seem to fit in with ranch life anymore. "When I meet friends in town, they ask me how Captain Waldron's wife is—Joella doesn't seem like a member of the family anymore," said Etta sadly.

"I hope to meet Captain Waldron," said Charlie.

His hope was not to be satisfied that summer. While he was on the rodeo circuit, Captain Waldron was shipped to the Philippines. He took Joella and Patty with him. The day Joella came out to the ranch to tell Etta the news was one of the busiest days on the ranch. Etta and the regular cook, Bertie, worked themselves ragged because Charlie had hired a half a dozen new cowboys just before going to the Omaha rodeo.

Joella came about nine-thirty in the morning in a chauffeur-driven army automobile. She left Patty outside feeding the chickens with Betts. Joella seated herself at the dining room table and called to Bertie, who was scrubbing the kitchen floor, "I'm ready for my breakfast!"

Bertie raised her head. Through the doorway she saw Joella in a navy-blue linen dress and high heels. "Mrs. Waldron, the cream's in the basement, if you want cereal. The rest of the stuff is in the kitchen, get it yourself. You can see I'm down on my hands and knees."

Joella's face turned bright red. She got up from her chair and went upstairs, where her mother was making beds. "Ma," she said in a high-pitched voice that was going even higher, "if I had a servant that talked like that to me, I'd fire her!"

Etta bit her tongue and sat on her bed. "Bertie works hard. If you spend one day working beside her and still feel she needs firing, then tell me."

"Ma, I'm—we're going to the Philippines. I came to say good-bye."

"How soon?"

"Tomorrow."

"I wish that your father had met Norman. Have him write. You write. Send your address, so we can write." Etta felt an emptiness in her midsection. Suddenly the room seemed too warm. "Let's go downstairs."

On the way downstairs they met Frances coming up with a load of fresh bedding. Joella stopped her sister and examined one of her hands. "It seems to me that it would be very simple for you to spend fifteen minutes a day on your nails so that they would look a little more respectable."

Frances was taken by surprise. She did not stop to make a joke of the remark, but replied immediately, "Mrs. Waldron, do a little housework yourself and see how long those long red nails last."

Etta held her breath and hoped the girls would end it right there. She thought maybe it was a good thing Joella was leaving for a while.

"I have to look presentable. I am going to Manila with Captain Waldron," Joella said with a simper.

"Oh, for gosh sakes, you won't be here when I leave for Lincoln. I'm going to the University of Nebraska this fall." Frances held up her head.

"You're going to the university? Why, that's terrific! What does Pa say about it?"

"He doesn't know. You're the first."

"He'll miss you. Pa likes to keep all the kids together now that Floyd's gone." Joella's voice had a sarcastic, cutting edge. "But we're all slipping away, one by one."

Etta sat at the dining table, her head in her hands.

"You want some tea, Mrs. Irwin?" asked Bertie.

"No, thanks, I'll get a glass of cold water in a moment," said Etta.

Bertie brought glasses of cold water in for Etta and the two girls. Joella turned up her nose. "Plain water? A slice of lemon could be floating in here, at least."

Etta smiled at her girls. "So you both have news of leaving. You said how your father feels—but do you know how I feel?"

The girls looked startled and shook their heads.

"When a person is grown, it is not right to cling to their parents. Think for yourself. Do what you want to do. Your father and I did what we thought best. We taught you to be independent. We love you, but we don't control you. If you want to come to the ranch, all right. If you don't, all right. I am going to California this winter."

"Pauline—what will she do?" asked Frances.

"She'll stay in town and take care of your father's office."

"What about Betts?" asked Joella.

"She'll come with me."

"You need some new clothes for California and a new hairstyle," said Joella. "Let's go shopping on my last day here. My car's out front. I'll make a new woman out of you."

"I don't want to be a new woman. And you're right. Your driver's waiting out in the hot sun. Remember to write."

This was the first time Etta had heard of Frances's desire to go on to school. "The University of Nebraska? Why not Wyoming?"

"I want to do something on my own. Like you said. Not be dependent on you and Pa for my thoughts."

That summer Charlie supplied stock to various rodeos and continued to enter local horse races. He had his quarter horse Sam F. that won in half-mile races in Denver and Oklahoma City and could beat any other horse at a quarter mile and most at three furlongs. He had the horse named Frank Lubbock that raced at Salt Lake in Agricultural Park. This horse won the Turf Exchange handicap in 2:10, the fastest time ever made on a half-mile track.

The jockey was a young boy Charlie had taken in for the summer, McBeth.

Now Charlie was beginning another routine. After the summer rodeos and local races, he put his best racehorses in stock cars and sent them to San Diego. He arrived about the same time and took the horses to his ranch in San Ysidro. He built a tack room and bunkhouse, and attached to that was a feed room and a half-dozen box stalls; that is, built higher than the studs and mares could see over. Then he wrote for Etta and Betts to come. Pauline stayed by herself at the house in Cheyenne. She worked in Charlie's office in the Plains Hotel. Charlie had a foreman who took care of the main ranch. Will lived at the upper ranch and took charge of the cattle.

Charlie had a new Chevrolet sedan, which he took to California in one of the stock cars.

After the new year in 1919 Charlie had many guests at his San Ysidro ranch. Will Rogers always seemed to be around so that Betts began to think his name was Uncle Will. When Charlie Russell came out to see the new place, he could not believe that Charlie liked the rolling desert with only tufty palm trees or molting eucalyptus. "The nights are hot here," complained Russell. "At least in the northwest the air cools down at night."

"Let's take Russell to a Western picture show, so he'll feel at home," said Rogers.

On Saturday after the races Charlie took everybody to see a Tom Mix thriller in San Diego. Etta held her breath as the film showed Mix on a sleek black horse chasing cattle rustlers across a long ribbon of railroad track just as the train sailed past. Mix and his horse took a flying leap onto a moving flatcar and then jumped off, upright, on the other side of the train.

"I never thought I'd see any man ride so well," said Etta.

"Any man worth his salt in the West can do that," sniffed Russell.

"It was trick photography or a dummy on the horse," said Charlie rather loudly.

Etta told Charlie to hush. "Something happens when the three of you get together," she whispered. "I'm thankful there's not a paintbrush in sight."

Rogers put his elbows into the sides of Charlie and Russell and the three men snickered, remembering the good time they had painting the bull on the barn door.

"I have to go to the rest room," said three-year-old Betts.

"I'll take her," whispered Etta, wishing Charlie could so she didn't have to miss any part of the show. They excused themselves and slipped past the people in their row. When they came back there was Mix catching up with the rustlers, chasing them pell-mell across the prairie.

"Lucky none of the horses stepped into a gopher hole," said Russell.

"Hurry, sit down," hissed Charlie. "You'll miss the good part."

"When the rustlers are strung up in a tree," said Rogers, munching popcorn.

Betts reached her hand in the popcorn as she slipped by, then stopped. "Look what I found." She held up a dollar bill.

"That piece of paper is mine. You found it! Green with white pictures. Here, I'll take it!" Rogers reached out.

"You lost it in the ladies' rest room?" asked Betts, wide-eyed.

People nearby giggled.

Rogers turned and gave those behind him a glare, then settled back with his popcorn.

"I'm going to buy a tamale," said Betts.

"I hate tamales," said Rogers.

"I like Wyoming," said Etta. "I feel unsettled here."

On the first of July 1919, Wyoming went dry; that is, the sale of any and all liquor was prohibited, on Governor Robert Carey's independent recommendation. This was six months before the state's constitutional amendment would be effective. On the thirtieth of June, Charlie told Etta he felt as useless as a .22 cartridge in a ten-gauge shotgun. "I can't keep the cowboys on the ranch. They want to go to town for a final, legal fling, to buy a drink of whiskey, a bottle of beer. I'd bet my Stetson that my brother Will is already in a saloon in Cheyenne."

"Charlie, there's all the fancy liquor you brought back from Mexico. Will you have to get rid of it?"

Charlie laughed. "No, dear, we'll leave it in the basement of the ranch house and say nothing. You and I don't use it. It's for those who come to visit and expect something—you know how it is with some."

The cowhands never made it back to the ranch until late the morning of July 1. They groaned and laughed about their headaches. The *Wyoming State Tribune* stated: "The melancholy days have come. . . . Cheyenne awoke this morning with a headache, a yearning thirst, a fuzzy taste in its mouth, and not a chance for the morning eye-opener."

Charlie came home from the office. He shook his hat before coming into the house. It was covered with the last snowflakes of the spring season, large, wet flakes. "Etta, I had a phone call this afternoon!"

From the kitchen Etta said, "Was it unusual?"

"You know that movie director that was here back in 1912 who took some shots up around Round Top and across at the sand pasture? What was the name of the show? What was the name of the director?"

"I don't remember. Why? I don't think you've been up to Round Top since—since Bud died."

"I know. It wasn't Round Top so much as the other one, Lookout. It kind of gave me the creeps. Probably my imagination. Some Hollywood producer called me today. Said he was coming out to the Y6 to make a movie. I wondered if it was the same fellow. If it is, I might tell him no to poking around those mountains again. It might not be safe."

"It might be some prank that Will Rogers is playing with you," said Etta, coming out of the kitchen. Her cheeks were red from leaning over a pot of boiling stew. Her eyes sparkled and Charlie thought she was more beautiful than when he first married her. He pulled her close and inhaled the smell of her—Shalimar perfume.

"It was no trick. This Hollywood fellow told me that he'd done some vaudeville and knew Rogers and Chester Byers. He said Byers taught him to spin a rope."

"Everyone is spinning these days."

"We're going to get into the Chevy and spin out to the ranch, because that man and a bunch of people from Hollywood are coming out there to make another movie. They'll eat and sleep at the ranch."

"Charlie! You told some stranger that he and a bunch of other strangers could stay at the ranch? You're joking."

"It's no joke. They'll be here Monday. I have to get supplies."

"I have to do some cleaning. Charlie, why didn't you ask the man his name? If I knew his name, it would be easier to make him a bed. Now I don't know whether to put him in the house, the bunkhouse, or the barn. Will he still be here when Bill Thompson and his party come on Friday in two weeks?"

Etta didn't have to wait as long as she expected to find who was coming to the Y6. Charlie didn't know the name of the producer, but the *Wyoming State Tribune* had the whole story the next day, July 11, 1919, even the news about Bill Thompson, Charlie's friend.

REAL WESTERN MOVIE FILMED NEAR CHEYENNE

Fred Stone Coming in Special Train to Make a Thriller in Heart of the Real West—No Camouflage Here

Fred Stone, world-famous comedian, and a company of motion picture stars, properties, cameramen, and all the fixin's for making a $500,000 motion picture, are coming to Cheyenne in a special train within a short time, and will go to the Y6 ranch to film a Western picture that is a Western picture, and not full of the California camouflage that is being perpetrated on the public at the present time in cowboy pictures. The company is from the Andrew Calligan Brunton Studio Company of Los Angeles.

Here for Frontier

This party will be in Cheyenne for the Frontier celebration. Mr. Stone will be the personal guest of Charles B. Irwin, owner of the Y6 ranch, both at the Frontier celebration and during his stay at the ranch near Cheyenne.

"He's going to make a real movie out there," said Charles B. Irwin today. "A picture of a real ranch, in real ranch country. There will be no orange groves for backgrounds, and no paved roads for stagecoaches to run over. We will have no California scenery in this picture."

The name of the proposed film has not been announced.

Bill Thompson Coming

Mayor William Hale Thompson of Chicago, formerly a Wyoming cowpuncher for the O Bar outfit at Elk Mountain, will arrive in Cheyenne at 8 a.m. July 25, on a special train bearing himself and a party of 125 friends.

When these men arrive in Cheyenne the whole bunch will be taken to the Y6 ranch, owned by Charlie Irwin, for a short trip. A plan is also under consideration for having Mr. Thompson and his party visit the Elk Mountain vicinity, where the Chicago mayor formerly rode night herd and was one of the best cowpunchers in this part of the country.

The party will also be here for the Frontier celebration.*

On Monday several Ford pickups came up the land to the Y6 ranch house. They were filled with cameras, trunks, and gear for the show people. Charlie pointed behind the house to the bunkhouse. "You'll stash your gear there and find there's enough bunks for everyone. We have more cots set up in the ranch house, second-floor dance hall. You'll eat at our table and call this home for the time you are here. This is Western hospitality."

Some of the cowboys were grousing about the Hollywood types who'd come in and taken over the bunkhouse. The cowboys had moved their gear to the horse barn, where they had to sleep on the hay.

Fred Stone and the cameramen stayed in the ranch house. Ranch life was a new kind of excitement for the film crew and Hollywood actors. They looked inside the barns and sheds, tramped along Horse Creek when not moving equipment or shooting scenes. The horses, cattle, and twelve buffalo used in the movie, called *The Great Southwest,* all belonged to Charlie. He charged the studio rent on the use of his livestock, the same fee he charged the Frontier Days committee.

The feeling between the cowboys and show people became tense. The cowboys resented these movie people, who took all the attention of their boss, besides their bunks. One evening at supper the cowboys decided to even things up. Roy asked, "You folks from California believe in ghosts?"

"Well, of course not," scoffed Fred Stone. He wore brown gabardine pants tucked into the tops of his leather boots. His shirtsleeves were rolled to his elbows, and he wore a red bandanna around his neck. He punched the crown of his gray felt hat so that it came to a peak at the top, like the U.S. Army service hats.

Roy's eyes glinted and he talked fast. "Well, there's a barn just up the road that is open at both ends. Some say if it's midnight and a man rides through on horseback, he sees a headless horseman ride through beside him. Ask Walt McGuckin, he's seen it more than once."

Stone ran a hand through his thinning brown hair and pointed

*Reprinted with permission of the *Wyoming State Tribune* and courtesy of the Charles M. Bennett Collection, Scottsdale, Arizona.

a finger at Roy. "No one in this day and age believes in ghosts, especially a headless horseman! Ha! Ha!"

Roy smiled and said, "Any of you Hollywood men want to go through the L5 barn at midnight? I'll bet a buck you'll come running out the other side."

"Sure, I'll take your bet," said Stone. "Some of us Hollywood movie men'll shashay through a haunted barn and come out laughing."

Stone drove out to the barn with his crew, joking and singing in an old mule-drawn wagon Charlie fixed for them. The night was cloudy, pitch black. An owl hooted and there was a rustling in the brush at the side of the road.

As soon as the movie people were out of sight the Y6 cowboys rode horseback straight across the alfalfa field to the barn. They took their places, hardly breathing. Roy wore a white sheet draped over his head. He crouched down so that it covered his boots. He was on Charlie's big white horse. Under his arm he carried the biggest watermelon he could find in Etta's garden. Other cowboys were hidden in the rafters and outside behind clumps of sagebrush. "Here they come!" someone cried.

The moving-picture people climbed out of the wagon. "I hope we don't have to be on horseback to see that ghost," someone said, and snickered. Stone walked boldly inside first. The others crowded close behind him. About halfway through nothing had happened, so they moved forward eagerly and more relaxed. Stone said, "Those cowboys just wanted to see if we'd fall for that story!"

All of a sudden white-sheeted Roy, looking as headless as Brom Bones from Sleepy Hollow, carrying the green watermelon head, galloped out along side the Hollywood folks. When his horse's hooves hit the dusty road he screamed, "Hi-yi!" The hooves of his horse made hardly a sound in the thick dust, but the heavy dust clouds drifted softly over the field in the night air.

Stone's boots slammed against the gray boards of the barn's floor. The moving-picture people ran back to the wagon. Stone frantically whipped the mules into a running pace.

When the wagon was well down the road, the cowboys bent double with laughter. They scrambled out for their horses, which waited quietly in a gulley on the far side of the road.

Next morning at breakfast Charlie asked, "You men see any ghosts last night?"

"Well—we went out to the barn—but things were pretty quiet. Roy owes me a buck," said Stone with a nervous laugh squeezed high against the back of his throat.

"I heard a racket out toward the L5 barn about midnight!" said Charlie in a booming voice. "I looked out the window and saw some bimbos hightailing it back to the bunkhouse!"

Everyone had stopped eating and the cowboys were grinning from ear to ear. Walt McGuckin couldn't keep the secret. "When you guys saw the headless horseman, you started to shake so hard you couldn't hear our horses nipping the grass at the side of the road!"

Charlie never grew tired of telling about the scene in the L5 barn at midnight. The cowboys and movie people now joked and bandied with one another in a friendly manner.

In several movie scenes Stone used Frances and Pauline and had them sing with the cowboys. In another scene he let Betts dance around the campfire while Pauline sang and someone played the guitar.

Charlie taught Stone to sing "Alfalfa Hay," and they tried to see who could outdo the other with roping tricks. Finally Charlie said, "Stone, you're all right. You're as persistent and industrious as any of my men. I noticed that if I knew a trick you never saw, you worked it over hundreds of times until you knew it. You laughed about the little joke the cowboys played on you and your people. You're a regular fellow, like Will Rogers said." Then Charlie chuckled. "When you first came I called Rogers and asked about 'the dudes from California.' He told me to give you a chance, to wait and get to know you, and I'd like you as much as he. Well, I certainly like you."

Stone sat under the tree in the front yard with Charlie. "C.B., I feel the same. We're friends!" Then he stopped smiling and looked serious again. "I bet you a spotted pony that your oldest daughter can sing as well as the two here. What's her name, Joella? What are you going to do with the talent Pauline and Frances have?"

"I'm going to let them use that talent right here on the Y6. Frances is studying accounting at the University of Nebraska so she can do the books."

"No, no! I mean the fine piano playing both girls do. And their voices are magnificent. They could be trained. Honest, I'd like to take your two girls with me to London. I'll go talk to your other girl when I'm back in California if you say the word. If she's as talented as these two, I want her also. They'd be on the stage within a year."

Charlie was so stunned he could not speak for a moment. "Really, that's not true."

"C.B., it's true as cats have kittens. When I first heard Pauline play the piano and Frances sing, I was so thrilled I tingled with excitement. I could not believe my ears. I was afraid to say a word to you at first. Then when you told me you had an older daughter who played even better than Pauline, I was speechless. I wondered why you took them around the country riding horses and swinging a rope."

"Because they're good at that. They've won all kinds of awards and prizes."

"How many people are good at more than one thing? Answer me truthfully," said Stone. "See, you can't think of anyone. You can't see the forest for the trees. Right here in your own family you have children so talented they could go from one career to another and still be tops. In a year you'll be surprised how far each will progress. No need to decide right now. Think about it. Talk it over with the little wife. In two days we leave to go back to Hollywood. There I'll join my wife and two daughters and we're off for London. See, your daughters and my daughters would be good company for one another."

"By jeems! Whatever I decide will affect the girls' whole life! Frances goes back to school this fall. Pauline is my secretary. She has Betts. Joella—I don't know—she's newly married and has a little girl. If I tell them they can go to London to study music, they'll think I'm plumb weak north of my ears. They'll believe the hot sun addled my think-box."

"C.B., don't decide now. Think about it," said Stone, smiling so that his mouth curved up in the most fascinating bow.

Charlie talked the whole proposition over with Etta that night.

"The children get their special abilities from you, Charlie," she said. "I could take care of Betts and Patty. The University of Nebraska can wait for Frances. It's an unexpected opportunity for the girls." She flushed. "I never expected, when I coaxed them to practice their piano lessons or sat at the piano and sang with each of them, that they would develop any talent. Do you believe they are really that good?"

"Dear, Stone told me in a year they'd be on stage. He has daughters himself. He sees people with musical ability every day in Hollywood. He knows they're good."

"I know they learned quickly, but I never thought it anything unusual. Imagine having daughters on the stage, or in picture shows."

"Like *The Great Southwest* and more," said Charlie.

"Did he say anything about Betts? I mean, she was so cute in that scene where she dances." Etta smiled in the dark. She reached out and put a hand on Charlie's shoulder.

"Jeems, dear! Are you going to give Stone all of our girls? Rumpelstiltskin only asked for the firstborn!" Charlie raised up on one elbow. "I was counting on Pauline and Frances to ride in the ladies' relay at the Torrington rodeo."

"Charlie, aren't you going to talk about this with the girls? Let them decide? This is something to be proud of and to brag about."

"That's what I've been thinking. If I tell them that Fred Stone, some picture-show person, said they were pretty good at the piano and they had a pretty good singing voice, they'd get a big head—a puffed-up feeling. That's nothing to brag about, is it?"

"So, deep down, do you think Mr. Stone was just blowing smoke?" asked Etta, snuggling against Charlie.

"I don't think that. He meant what he said. I want to keep the family together. We lost one. I couldn't stand to lose another."

"But Charlie, this is not the same. The girls would go to London to study. They'd be living and learning. You're the one that believes life is to be lived to the fullest. To be a success one has to forget fear, try new experiences, be different. The girls would come back. They'd be famous. They'd have their picture in the paper."

"I'm thinking about that. I'm not sure about success. But failure I know is trying to please everyone."

"Joella will never come back to stay. She's different. She's not the way I wanted her to be. She makes me angry when she's selfish and self-centered. But she's a grown person. I cannot see in her head anymore. She has to choose her own life. Wouldn't it be right and fair to tell her of this opportunity and let her choose?"

Charlie lay down and closed his eyes. He tried to picture Joella. She was golden-blond, tall and thin, like a model, well dressed in the latest fashions. She'd always been creative with her hands. She could sew, design clothes, make hats, draw, paint, play the piano, swing a fancy rope. But could she be a success? Could she pick herself up one more time than she fell down? There was only one person who could defeat Joella—and that was Joella. Charlie could never forget the screams and sobs and yes, the anger that came from Joella's mouth the night she'd miscarried. She'd blamed everyone she could lay her tongue to, except herself, for the episode. She is a taker, he thought all of a sudden, remembering what his grandmother had said about his brothers.

Pauline was dependable, but quiet. She was good at everything she tried, but she was like Etta, calm about most things. She was not pretentious. She was the best cook in the family. Pauline would not be comfortable performing on stage day in and day out.

Frances already knew what she wanted to do. She wanted to study at the university, but she wasn't studying music, piano, nor voice. She was getting an education so that she could keep records for the ranching operations. She was using her head to keep the Y6 in the family. Music and stage performances were farthest from her mind. Any performing she'd long for could be fulfilled with a ladies' relay contest or an exhibition of trick roping.

"I'll tell the girls later," said Charlie. "Life's so short. I'm keeping the girls as close to you and me for as long as possible. Etta, I'm not selfish. I'm protective. Later, if any of them wants to study music in London—all right. I'll send them myself. I can send my kids to London myself. I don't need help."

"Charlie, you're not selfish, you're protective, and also bullheaded!" said Etta. "You are wedded to the opinion that only you know what's best for your children. Why, you had no idea our girls had musical talent."

"Certainly I have opinions and principles and I hug every one of them." He gave Etta a hug. "I'm not yielding an inch! And another thing, I'll always say I knew our girls have talent. Talent runs in the Irwin family. Look at me!" He moved back so that Etta could look at him full in the face. "I put the town of Cheyenne on the map with my Wild West show. My name will go down in the history of horse racing because I intend to have the best horses for the small tracks of any man alive. That little half-pint, Pablo Martinez, will be the leading jockey in the whole United States. Last year he was on more winning horses than any other jockey. This year will be a repeat. Our girls have held all kinds of titles, Best All Around Cowgirl, World Champion Trick-Roper, Champion Relay Rider, and on and on."

"Charlie, don't get carried away with all that Irwin talent. Remember about getting blown-up and filled with hot air. Just because a handbill makes a statement doesn't make it true."

"Well, publicity makes the facts known. Haven't you noticed when something appears in the paper, people believe it was the gospel truth? How do you suppose old Bill Cody got his reputation? He hired a good publicity man. Old P. T. Barnum realized that before he was out of short pants."

Etta closed her eyes and said, "So if the girls become musicians, they'll need a publicist. Charlie, there's hardly a thing you don't know—you could—"

"One thing, dear. I don't know if women should have the right to vote in national elections."

In the morning Etta was up with the cook, Bertie, to prepare breakfast for the cowboys and Hollywood folks. She sang an old favorite, "I Would Be True."

Charlie was also up early. He went to his den with a cup of coffee in his hand. Soon he was matching his booming voice to that of Etta's so that the whole ranch house seemed to vibrate.

Fred Stone and his party left for Hollywood wide-eyed after attending a day at the Frontier Days celebration. "We need to write a story around that celebration for a picture show," said Stone. "That would keep everyone awake in the theater."

"That would cut down on the eastern crowd that comes out here every year," said Charlie. "Let Cheyenne keep this Daddy of Them All celebrations for itself. That's not any more selfish than me wanting to keep my girls around me a while longer."

"C.B., you're a real Western man, if I ever saw one," said Stone. "I'm honored to be your friend. I'm telling you."

Next morning Bill Thompson, mayor of Chicago, who used to work for the O Bar outfit, arrived at the Y6 with his party of one hundred twenty-five.

FORTY

Surprises

The telephone rang in the middle of the night at the ranch house. Charlie jumped out of bed. "Hello, C. B. Irwin here," he said, shivering.

"C.B., this is John Gale from the Union Pacific. There's a boxcar and an engine waiting for you on the siding next to the depot at Burns. How soon can you get a dozen horses, saddles, and some men here?"

"It's the middle of the night! Give me an hour. What are you so lathered up about?"

"Haven't you heard about Carlisle? Your friend Bill Carlisle has escaped."

"Oh, no!" Charlie hung up and dressed quickly in long underwear, woolen pants, a Pendelton shirt, well-greased boots, and a long sheepskin jacket. He carried his sheepskin gloves and wide-brimmed hat and went out to the bunkhouse to wake the cowboys. "You'll all come with me. Get a dozen good horses and saddles. Make it snappy!" They took all the shortcuts between the Y6 and Burns that they knew about. It was four in the morning in mid-November 1919.

Inside the boxcar Charlie smelled hay, saddle leather, and the warm bodies of horses and men. He and Al Woodruff, superintendent of the U.P.'s Wyoming Division, and Will McClement, special agent of the Secret Service for the Wyoming Division of the U.P., decided they'd begin looking for the fugitive around Medicine Bow country. They assumed that he'd not stay in the Red Desert or he'd freeze to death.

For several days they wandered out in the hills and gullies around Medicine Bow, always coming back at night tired and cold to the bone, shaking their heads. Carlisle had escaped from the Rawlins penitentiary in an empty shirt carton. On the nineteenth of November, Carlisle robbed U.P. train No. 19. A bloodstained revolver and hat was found near Medicine Bow. Nothing else.

Charlie told his boys to look around Rock River and each night call the Medicine Bow depot, as a telegrapher would be there twenty-four hours a day to advise and give or take messages. Charlie and Gale followed the telephone line to the north side of Laramie Peak and on to the Hill ranch. Hill admitted that he and his wife had given Carlisle Thanksgiving dinner, some kind of painkiller, and bandaged his hand.

Charlie and Gale stopped for food at the ranches in the area and stayed overnight when invited. They rented two trucks at the Beven place and drove in the snow to Cottonwood. They stayed at the McFarland's ranch before going on to Glendo. From what the ranchers said they were sure they were on Carlisle's trail. The snow became so deep they couldn't tell if they were driving on the road or across a hay field. They were out two days before abandoning the trucks at a ranch for a couple horses.

They tracked Carlisle to Esterbrook and from the Newells learned that Carlisle was in the Williams cabin. The trail to the cabin had been tramped recently. Wheatland's Sheriff Lon Roach was ahead of Charlie and Gale and covering the front door of the cabin. He hollered to Williams, "You got Carlisle in there?"

"Yes," Williams replied. He was a small man and blinked his eyes when he came out the door.

Roach paid no attention to Charlie and Gale coming up the trail, he bolted inside and yelled again, "Carlisle! Put your hands in the air!"

There was a shot and by the time Charlie and Gale got inside the cabin Williams was dragging Carlisle to the bed. He was bleeding all over the floor. He'd been hit in the chest.

"Stop!" cried Charlie. "Take his shirt off! Get some hot water and clean rags. We'll staunch the blood. Drag him around, you'll kill him!"

Williams scurried to the kitchen, slammed the back door shut, and hollered, "This ain't no chicken coop. I can't heat all outside with the wood I got!"

Charlie and Gale got Carlisle's shirt off and bathed and dressed the wound. Carlisle was on his side. His breathing was harsh and grating. There was a hole in his back about three inches below the shoulder blade where the shot went through.

"What's this?" asked Gale, picking up a piece of lead from the floor. "It must have fallen out of his back when Williams was pulling him."

"Or when we took his shirt off," said Charlie, looking through Carlisle's shirt. The right-hand pocket had a roll of bills, probably U.P. money, wrapped around a rabbit's foot. The shell had gone clean through the middle of the roll of bills, making three round holes in every bill. Charlie folded the shirt and held it against Carlisle's chest with firm pressure after rolling him on his back. "Roach must have used a high-powered rifle—a .20–.25. Hey, where is Sheriff Roach anyway?"

Gale got up and nearly upset the dishpan of hot water.

"Hey, you look out! You're messing up my place plenty!" cried Williams.

Roach came in from outside. "I got him, huh?"

"No argument about that," said Charlie.

They wrapped Carlisle in a blanket and boosted him on Gale's horse. Gale held him with one arm and guided the horse with the other. Charlie kept the wad of bloody bills around the rabbit's foot and the soft-lead nosed bullet Gale had found in his pocket. In Esterbrook they put Carlisle in Jesse Morris's Buick.

The shooting occurred about 11:50 A.M. on the second of December at Williams's ranch. Carlisle was at the hospital in Douglas by 1:30 P.M.

Dr. Storey talked to Charlie. "This man has lost considerable blood. The bullet went through the bottom of his right lung and left it partly filled with blood. Pneumonia may set in. And the man's nearly starved."

Charlie explained that Carlisle probably had little, if any, sleep for the past five nights. He'd been chased all over the mountains in weather that was snowy, windy, and ten or more degrees below zero.

Next morning after a good rest in a Douglas hotel, Charlie and Gale went to the hospital. Roach and a couple of his men were already there.

Carlisle had his back to them.

Dr. Storey said, "Mr. Carlisle, there are some gentlemen here to see you from the Union Pacific. They need to have your confession. Are you up to talking a few minutes?"

Carlisle moved his head and said, "Take Sheriff Roach out. He's not with the U.P. He shot an unarmed man and talks like it's the highlight of his career." He turned his head away.

Charlie went around to the other side. "Are the nurses all right?" he asked.

"So far," said Carlisle. "C.B., you got a shave since I last saw you."

"I didn't want to go home and have my wife not recognize me," Charlie said with a chuckle. "I got a beefsteak under my belt, too."

"I got a little food. Heard it was you who packed the hole in my chest and back. I owe you. If I'd lost more blood I'd of heard the owl call my name. I'd be over on the other side by now."

"You know what they say; your number wasn't on top of the heap. Will you tell me about what happened after your interesting escape? I'll take some notes so I can write a letter to Jeffers, the U.P.'s general manager."

Carlisle lay still, as if thinking. His breathing was shallow.

"I can come back tomorrow," said Charlie.

"No, stay." Carlisle's voice seemed stronger. "I only want you, C.B., to make notes from what I say. You are the only man I trust."

Charlie nodded, and Gale went out in the hall with Dr. Storey. Roach and his men had left.

That evening Charlie translated his notes and wrote his report for Bill Jeffers. When he finished he went to Gale's room. "I think Carlisle's going to make it. And I've been thinking about how Roach acted. You know, he didn't wait to see if Carlisle was armed. He didn't call in to Medicine Bow. Well, I say forget all that. Give him the publicity he wants."

Gale's mouth fell open he was so surprised.

"I believe if the Union Pacific gives the sheriff of Wheatland the five hundred dollars reward, it will do a lot of good for public relations. Too many farmers and small ranchers think the U.P. is big business, not interested in the little guy. Giving Roach the credit might help change their minds. Also, the rest of the reward money, five hundred dollars, ought to be divided among Roach's posse."

Gale gulped. He sat still for a moment. "All right. Put that in your report."

"I thought maybe you'd want to explain to Jeffers how the

reward should be divided. After all, we're in this together."

In the morning Charlie phoned Medicine Bow and told the telegrapher that he was headed home and it was time his cowboys loaded up the horses and brought them back to Cheyenne.

"Say, C.B., one of your men marked all the horses retained for emergency purposes with ear tags. It was a bright idea to keep track of all the horses the railroad kept ready for the big chase."

"Sounds good. At least everyone'll get his own horses back," said Charlie.

"Your boy, Roy, thought of the scheme. Smart boy." Then he hesitated a little. "There's something you ought to know before going on home. I hate to bring this up, but we're all friends and understand one another pretty well."

Charlie swallowed and said, "What's the trouble?"

"Your brother caused quite a ruckus in Rawlins—two nights ago."

Charlie listened carefully.

"A couple of the cavalrymen from Fort Russell were out carousing. It seems your brother got in a fight with one over some dance-hall girl, some hurdy-gurdy." He laughed at the old-fashioned term. "Both men were sent back to Cheyenne on the next train—drunk as skunks. Your brother, Frank, is not welcome in Rawlins again. In other words, if he goes there for any reason, he'll be arrested."

"I'm sorry," said Charlie.

"Oh, no need for that. It had nothing to do with you."

"He's a member of my family," said Charlie. "Thanks for telling me."

Charlie sat on a straight-backed chair inside the bunkhouse. He shuffled the deck of dog-eared playing cards on the table. He picked up a newspaper, shifted from one page to the other before noticing that it was two weeks old. He was waiting for Frank. He was undecided what he was going to say to his younger brother. He put a chunk of wood in the potbellied stove. He heard the wind howling outside and felt icy drafts come in under the door and through the cracked chinking. He blew on his cold hands and stomped his boots on the floor. He got up and went to the door. He let Frank in, then said, "It's too cold to be hauling hay out to the pastures. Wind's blown snow off most of the tablelands. Horses browse the uncovered grass."

"Yup. But snow's still deep around Lookout Mountain. Spooky the way that land's pushed up. Windy everywhere but there. Quiet on all four sides. I swear it. And if I didn't know better, I'd say the summer sun beats down on all four sides at the same time, no shade. I suppose it's the way the formation sits, but it gives me the creeps. I tried to get a bunch of horses to move over near Round Top, where there's plenty of uncovered grass. But they wouldn't budge out in the wind." Frank pulled out a wooden chair from the other side of the table. It scraped on the floor. He sat down with his back to the wall. "What's on your mind, Charlie?"

"Yeah, weird mound. I'd say the damn place was never in the sunlight. I thought I was the only one that felt uneasy about it. But old Round Top's different. Friendly."

"Like coming home. God, it feels good to be back at the ranch. See the familiar faces. But I've been colder than a Montana well-driller since I got back from the south. Blood's too thin."

"Why'd you come back, Frank?"

"I like to eat. Man, jobs are scarce. There were times my belly was as empty as a church on a Saturday night. Geez, Charlie, you didn't call me in here to throw me out, did you? I work damn hard. Ask the other cowboys. I know you didn't tell me I could come back. But I'm your kin—flesh and blood." Frank's chin quivered. He took off his gloves, shuffled the deck of dirty cards two, three times. "Jeezus, Charlie, you can't throw me out. I've got nowhere to go!"

Charlie tightened his jaw. He thought Frank was laying it on thicker than calf-splatter. "Why'd you go over to Rawlins?"

Frank opened his eyes. He looked innocent as a baby. "Oh, that! I heard Carlisle'd broken jail and you and a couple of posses were out hunting him. I remembered how you'd kept a baggage car on the siding, all ready for horses, autos, and men to trail and run down train robbers. I thought I might get me a horse or auto and lead one of them posses. I thought I might be hired by the Union Pacific."

"Those posses were volunteers. Nobody worked for pay. You should have known."

"I suppose so." Frank gazed out the smoky window toward the barn. He unbuttoned his coat.

"You made quite a fuss. Besides being embarrassed I was mad you'd come back without saying anything to me. I was told about you brawling over some lady and getting kicked out of town. If you go back to Rawlins, the sheriff'll put you in the hoosegow."

"Geez, Charlie, don't blame me! You should have seen that

gal! I knew her a couple years ago. She used to work in a saloon around Torrington. She's part Mexican or Injun—one of those dark beauties that get the blood to racing." He took off his coat and laid it on the table. "Since I wasn't around, she got acquainted with a couple cavalry wonders that're taught to ride horseback in three days at Fort Russell. Then, when I showed up, she was willin' to surrender like a willow in the wind. You know any hot-blooded jock would have done what I done. Where's it written that it's against the law to bed a good-looking woman? Huh? God, she was feisty as any wildcat. My thin blood boils in a hurry."

Charlie kept his jaw tight. He picked up the newspaper and stared at the front page, not reading a word. He was exasperated. He wondered how long he'd have to be his brother's keeper. Did kinship make it mandatory that one always look after the weaker members of the family? He searched his mind. He saw the image of his father, who took the family in a covered wagon to Kansas, to Colorado Springs, then to Cheyenne. He kept the family together. Joe never sent anyone packing. Joe never held back on the use of words. Charlie had to talk to Frank. He put the newspaper down.

"You understand your actions affect others. Think before you act. If the U.P. officials were thinking of promoting me to something with more responsibility than general agent, you nipped the idea in the bud by your fool actions in Rawlins. Frank, this is not the first time I've had to work around your drunken behavior! If you've come around here with the idea of working the rodeo circuit in the spring, forget it! I have all the jockeys I need. So, what do you expect me to do with you? I detest grit in the oil."

Frank sniffed and glared and rose to the challenge.

"I'll stay at the bunkhouse, same as any of your other hired hands." He slapped the cards on the table. "Charity begins at home."

"I will be equitable so that no one will accuse me of nepotism with you, Frank. I hire and fire at my own discretion. Shall we go to the house for dinner?" Charlie spoke in a manner that needed no reply.

Etta ignored the California ranch. She was perfectly content in the quiet, red-brick home in Cheyenne. She didn't hunger for the approbation of her family or peers as did Charlie. He was stymied when she said it was hard to pick up and leave. He didn't know what to say, because going from one racetrack to another, or one rodeo town to another, was the easiest thing in the world for him. He was invariably in the center of the big ovals that smelled like animal hide, dung, sweat, and dust. He thrived on the plaudits of his entourage and any crowd in bleacher seats or the grandstand.

Charlie assumed, without asking, that his dear Etta felt the height of satisfaction as he did when Irwin horses, kinfolk, or hired hands were winners. He took for granted that Etta was buoyed up whenever a stranger shook her hand and smiled, saying, "So, you're the wife of the famous horseman, C. B. Irwin. I've admired him for ages. You're like a pixie and he's like a bear."

Etta was so proud of Charlie. She always said he came first in her life. But deep in her heart of hearts she'd forget the ranch, the rodeos, the horse racing. She preferred to think that her husband had an office in town. He was an officer for the Union Pacific railroad. She was a homemaker with wonderful children and grandchildren. The ranch was not important to her.

"Promise me next year," called Charlie. "I like to have you with me. Then my world's complete." He grinned affectionately. He never dreamed that Etta would tangle herself up with some self-imposed limitation, such as using Betts as an excuse not to go to California.

For Christmas Fred Stone sent Betts a huge hobbyhorse, covered with regular horsehide, black with white spots, on wheels. The wheels were hidden inside the real hooves, which were polished and preserved with shellac. The tail and mane came from an actual Shetland pony. The horse had a leather bridle and saddle. Charlie brought the kitchen stool into the living room so that Betts could step up to the back of her new plaything. He neighed and pretended to kick up his heels as he pushed Betts around the house and pretended to give it oats and hay.

The winter of 1920 was one of the coldest on record. Ranchers worried about their livestock. They did everything possible to get the animals to sheltered areas, out of the strong north winds.

By the middle of January it was obvious that it was not only the coldest winter on record, but that there was more snow than normal.

There was a week of steady snow right after the first of the year. Cattle ranchers were continuously busy keeping cattle away from fences and rows of brush so they would not become foundered in deep snow, unable to move, and freeze to death.

Sheep ranchers were in deeper trouble. Their animals, bogged down in the snow, were caught in drifts with no food. They huddled against one another for warmth, but would not move out of the wind.

Charlie loaded his old Ford pickup with hay and took it to all the little valleys and meadows he could find. The pickup's high center made it easier to get in and out of places inaccessible to other vehicles. Then he loaded several empty boxcars with hay from the Four-Mile pasture. He put two men in each boxcar to toss the hay out along the track for both sheep and cattle that were stranded along the U.P. line west of Cheyenne. The boxcars were hauled at the end of freight trains. Others were sent north to Torrington and East to Gering, Nebraska.

By March there was still a lot of snow on the ground in town. On the prairie there were bare patches of dried grass exposed.

Charlie was invited to a dinner in Cheyenne given by the Wool Growers Association. He told Etta he wasn't going. "Why did those woollymonster men invite me? I'm not a sheep rancher and I never intended to be one."

"Charlie, you saved hundreds of sheep last winter. Maybe those men want to tell you thanks on Saturday night," said Etta.

"Confound it! In some ways a dumb ram reminds me of my brother Frank. He's pitiful and pulls at my heartstrings, but he makes me so angry because he doesn't think.'"

"I've seen Frank at the ranch last winter and this spring," said Etta, laughing in little fluttering notes. "He's done his share of work." She hesitated. "Only once or twice has he been to town drinking with his friends."

"I saw him once when I left the hotel after work," said Charlie derisively. "He never saw me. He looked like a man with Saint Vitus's dance." Charlie blew air out the side of his mouth. "Look here, don't get us to fighting about my brother. I know what he is. He'd go to town and let someone else do his work, then take credit for what was done while he was having a good time. I'd like to throw him out for good."

"As head of the family, it's your obligation to take care of everyone." She raised her face to him, her eyes soft.

"Will's the oldest," said Charlie, bending his head to kiss her parted lips. Her hand went around his neck. He held her until she struggled for air.

"You're the leader. Grandpa Joe recognized that!" She moved toward him again, pliant.

He kissed her hard, feeling himself swaying toward the couch.

His hand caressed her throat and he fingered the buttons beneath her collar. He loosened three, four, five buttons and slipped his hand inside her dress.

Betts came quietly into the living room dragging a flannel blanket, her hair tousled from sleep. She patted Etta's leg. "Dinner, Grammie."

Charlie and Etta sprang apart as if a shot had come through the window. Charlie felt his heart racing and saw Etta breathing rapidly so that her breast rose and fell.

Etta's hand went to her throat and she fastened her dress quickly. "Gram will take care of dinner right away, honey."

"Jeems, what time is it?" asked Charlie, loosening his tie and fanning himself with the newspaper.

"Dinnertime," she whispered. "Pauline won't be home. She's having dinner in town with a friend."

"Good for her to get out," said Charlie, throwing the blanket over Betts's head.

Betts looked out, giggling. "Peekaboo!"

During dinner Etta said, "I think Frank's turned over a new leaf. I haven't heard him complain all spring. Don't be harsh with him."

Charlie put his fork beside his plate. He wiped mashed potatoes and gravy from Betts's face. "More, please," said Betts.

He put a tablespoon of potatoes on her plate, made an indentation in the middle, and filled it with gravy. "That's a duck pond. Eat it."

"Yum," said Betts, with a mouthful.

Charlie turned to Etta. "Remember I love you, but you're naive. I used to feel like you. But I'm not soft in the head anymore. I'm a "Form" player now. Once a jackass, always a jackass. I believe what I read in the *Racing Form* about a horse. I believe in past actions. Frank finds someone to give him an excuse to come to town. He follows the first guy to the nearest saloon, like one sheep following another. When he's in trouble it's not his fault, it's the lead sheep's." Then he pointed to Betts, who had her dinner bowl upside down over her head. "Grandma, this baby needs a bath!" He laughed. Betts giggled. Etta hid her face behind her napkin, away from the mess of mashed potatoes and gravy in the little girl's hair.

"Peekaboo!" said Betts happily.

"Grandchildren! They're as disconcerting as one's own children!" grunted Charlie. "They push and pull their way into your heart, upset the status quo, change emotions and plans. Is man ever master of himself?"

Etta used a washcloth on the baby's face and hair. "I should have told you that I took your good suit to the back porch and cleaned the spots off with kerosene. It's pressed, ready to wear. One of those new white shirts with the monogram on the breast pocket would be good-looking. Go on to the dinner. Might not hurt you to know who's raising sheep. I heard the Warren ranch is testing a crossbreed called the Columbia?"

"Used to be cattlemen looked down their noses at sheep-herders. When Warren raises sheep, they become respectable," said Charlie.

Etta propped her elbows on the table to give Betts a glass of milk. "People's ideas change. Dryland farmers now irrigate sugar beets and women are going to have the privilege of voting. So why not cattlemen accepting the sheepherders?" asked Etta.

"Men talk about changes. This is what they say. The price of lambs fell from eight dollars to three dollars. Full-sized sheep are down to six dollars from ten a year ago. The wool growers are against the wall, they are looking for buyers. I'm not buying. I promise. I don't care what Senator Warren does. I'm in horse racing. I'll not be affected by a setback in the sheep market, nor in coal mining, nor oil drilling. There are rumors that the U.P. will lay off a third of its employees by year's end."

Etta put her hand to her mouth. "Charlie, can they do that to people?"

"If I were governor I'd do something about it. It all started when the banks couldn't collect on real-estate and livestock loans. If Governor Carey had done something then, we wouldn't have a crisis."

"Charlie, I honestly believe you could be governor if you really wanted to," said Etta.

Charlie found that the Wool Growers dinner was in part to thank him. He'd begun the winter "Haylift" operation and saved thousands of sheep in southern Wyoming. He was the only man there not financially involved with sheep. After dinner of lettuce salad, roast chicken, scalloped potatoes, buttered peas, biscuits, coffee, and vanilla ice cream, Charlie was called by the president of the association to the front podium. He was presented with an unexpected gift, a round golden medallion to be used as a watch fob, in commemoration of his selfless act of distributing his own hay up and down the U.P. line. The medallion was engraved with his name, the Wool Growers' motif, and the date of presentation.

He curled his toes inside his boots, shook hands with the president, a solemn-faced gentleman with a fringe of gray hair above his ears, and felt a deep contentment and an overriding thrill to be standing before fifty, sixty wool growers. His eyes twinkled with reflection from the ceiling lights whenever he moved his head. He raised his large hand and held the medallion for all to see.

"Tell the men how you feel," said the president, drawing on a rosewood tobacco pipe.

Charlie cleared his throat. "I appreciate this beautiful watch fob more than any of you know, especially since it doesn't smell one blasted bit like a sheep." His voice was deep. It carried to the four corners of the room.

The audience scraped its feet. Some people twittered, the rest of the crowd stared at Charlie to see what he'd say next.

His throat constricted a little. He took a sip of water and was again relaxed. He felt good. "I will treasure this token of our friendship. It is the beginning of a new age when the stock growers and wool growers clasp hands." Suddenly it dawned on him that many of these men had lost a lifetime of savings. It might not be mannerly to get too friendly nor sentimental. He took another sip of water and continued. "I'm wondering if you fellows could trade this little gold bauble in on a set of longjohns that will fit me? If so, I could stay out in the next snowstorm a couple of days longer, tossing hay at your dumb sheep, and not freeze my—"

"Hear, hear!" someone shouted. All the room was filled with wild applause. The men were standing one by one, spontaneously singing, "For He's a Jolly Good Fellow."

Charlie blinked. He saw the roomful of men through a cloud of blue pipe smoke. He grinned. He was elated. "If I were your governor, I'd see to it that those of you who were hurt most by the decline in the woollymonger prices received low-interest loans through the state so you could buy more stock."

The applause was thunderous.

"But if you did not pay those loans in a period of five years, you would be penalized and not be able to raise sheep again on your land. I guess you'd have to plant sugar beets, which are the state of Wyoming's next commercial crop." There was more clapping. Charlie had been an instant hit. Most of the men in the room had heard of big C. B. Irwin, but few had seen him outside of the Frontier Days activities. Some thought he truly ought to run for the governor's office next election.

Before he went home he put the gold watch fob on his gold railroad watch chain and let it hang across the front of his vest. He wore the prized medallion the rest of his life whenever he dressed in his business suit.

The following morning Warren Richardson called Charlie's office.

"Listen, C.B., this is serious. Baron de Rothschild from the Rothschild Bank of France is coming to Cheyenne on the next passenger train. The baron heard from the French cavalry that we have the best horses money can buy. He wants polo ponies to ship to France. You interested?"

Charlie exhaled. "I'll meet the baron and sell him champion polo ponies from southern Wyoming. What does he look like?"

"Your guess is as good as mine. A French banker is probably dressed to the limit. Don't be late."

Charlie went to Harrington's Men's Furnishings and bought the finest tan, beaver-fur cowboy hat he could find.

At the depot he was startled to hear French spoken by a man who looked more like a jockey than anything else. The man's suit was brown and plain. He wore a tan shirt, a tan bow tie, tan shoes, and a camel-hair overcoat.

The porter pointed his thumb toward Charlie and grinned.

Charlie nodded and held out his hand. The baron took Charlie's hand then kissed him on one cheek, then the other.

Charlie could hear the Pullman porter chuckle. Charlie said in his bellowing voice, "Only women and babies kiss in public in America; however, if you come all the way from France, it's allowed." He laughed. "Out here the sun gives a mighty glare, so I have a gift for you. We call it a ten-gallon hat. It doesn't hold ten gallons of anything, but it's sure practical and good-looking. The wide brim also keeps off rain."

The baron looked pleased. He put the hat on. "Fits like she was made for me."

"I'm glad you like it, but even more glad you speak English." Charlie led the way to his Chevy.

The baron was put up in the Irwins' guest room, Floyd's old room. Etta was up early next morning so that the men could have breakfast before going to the ranch. She made buttermilk hotcakes and fried ranch sausage. There was huckleberry jam, maple syrup, and churned butter on the table. The baron was impressed with the bold flavor of the jam. He told Etta about the blueberry wine that was a specialty in France. "Huckleberries for wine would be more *excellente*."

At the ranch Charlie did not give the baron a chance to get out of the car before he'd seen the hay pastures, grazing cattle, milk cows, and grazing horses.

The baron said, "I am surprised with the immensity of your land. *Merveilleux!* She is larger than anything I imagined."

After supper Charlie and the baron had a horse race, then raced Charlie's old Ford pickup and the Chevy. The baron won driving the Chevy across the hay field.

"This is the best time," said the baron. "You treat me like—like a real person. *Merci beaucoup*."

The next day at noon Charlie's cowboys, led by Claude Sawyer, his latest hired hand, came in with close to seventy-five of the wildest, most rambunctious horses they could find in the hills. "Mr. Irwin, I brought in some good horses for you to sell to that French dude. You want me and Roy to break them in?" Sawyer was tall, with steely blue eyes and curly salt-and-pepper hair.

"When you lead each horse out for the baron to look over, toss a saddle on its back. Take the saddle off and put it on the next one. Bring them out fast so the baron won't have time to think he wants to ride any of the hurricanes."

"Mr. Irwin, me and the boys will put bags of sand on their backs. That'll calm them so they can be taken to the stockyards and loaded into stock cars," said Sawyer.

"I sure could have used you when we were selling to the U.S. Remount," said Charlie. "We have to pay ten cents a head for brand inspection at the stockyards, so run them through the chute and use the bar iron on them. Make a talley so you are certain you're not cheated."

Sawyer was solemn. He never seemed to joke with the other cowboys.

Charlie said, "Jeems, man! Learn to laugh. You keep looking over your shoulder every once in a while as if you expect to see the devil or the sheriff on your tail. You've been on the Y6—?"

"Three months, sir."

"Well, relax. Nobody's found you. By now they're not coming."

Color ran into Sawyer's face. His eyes sparkled. "Thanks, sir."

Two days later the Baron de Rothschild left Cheyenne. He shook hands with all the cowboys around the breakfast table. He shook hands with Etta and thanked her for the good meals. He shook hands with Charlie at the U.P. depot and gave him the French salute of friendship by kissing him on both cheeks. "You come to visit my country. I show you how to play polo like the French."

"It's a deal!" called Charlie, kissing his fingers and flinging them toward the baron and laughing deep inside his chest.

* * *

Charlie read in the newspaper about a new racetrack being built in Omaha, and decided to go to the opening of the track.

He located the best hotel in Omaha for Etta and himself, then took a taxicab to the track to check on his horses.

A thoroughbred racehorse was never branded. The Irwin horses didn't have to be branded. They were easily distinguishable from most others because of their unusually strong legs. There was Riposta, Anna Lou, Art Rick, Frosty Morning, Coronado, Little Spider, and Yukon in the twenty-six horse string. Charlie's jockeys were Martinez, Mulcahy, Hurn, and McIntyre.

Charlie decided to invest in the track. The money that Charlie gave Charles B. Gardner, the secretary of the track, kept Ak-Sar-Ben racetrack out of the red the first year. A couple of years later during a newspaper interview, Gardner said, "C. B. Irwin is the best booster we could have. He brings his entire stable to our meets. Once he came up from Tia Juana with three, four carloads of horses to boost the sport here. We at Ak-Sar-Ben believe the world of racing revolves around C.B. We love him."

At the track Etta saw that most always when an Irwin horse was in a race it was a winner. Also, she saw that when a card was short, Charlie sent in horses from his stable to fill it, even when there was no chance of winning. She saw that Martinez and David Hurn were tops at the track. They rode with more confidence and consistency than any other jockey present. They rode the horses to win. Charlie came home to Cheyenne with more money than he left with, even subtracting the generous check he gave to the Omaha Race Track Association. Making money felt good to Charlie. He could dress his wife well. He could get her whatever she wanted. Etta seldom asked for anything for herself. She told Charlie to buy Ike Rude's horse, Garter. He gave Rude five hundred dollars.

"Pay off your debts, save your money. There's a chance you could buy old Garter back," said Charlie with a grin.

The 1920 Frontier Days Committee brought half a dozen Arapaho women from the Wind River Reservation in northern Wyoming to give an exhibition of tepee raising. The "squaw tepee race" was one of Etta's favorite exhibitions. She was disappointed when she found it would not be a feature the next year because the whole celebration was becoming too long.

The increased attendance to the Cheyenne celebration presented a problem. Nearly thirty thousand admission tickets were sold in a city of about thirteen thousand people. Hotels were filled during the last week in July. Many private homes rented rooms, a large number of U.P. Pullman cars were used for sleeping accommodations, and a municipal camp was opened that could hold twenty thousand automobile tourists, tents, and camping gear.

In the fall when the sheepherders drove their band to the home ranch and cut out the old ones and wethers, then took them to the Cheyenne stockyards to be sold, Charlie was rewarded with several hundred pounds of mutton. It was far more than he could use. At the ranch, the cowboys preferred beef. But he had no trouble taking the fresh meat to places where it would be used and appreciated. He knew several farmers that were having a hard time who were thankful for something to keep their children's bellies filled. He gave some of the meat to the orphanage in Torrington. While there, two scrawny, freckle-faced boys, about ten years old, followed him everywhere, even to the outside gate when he left.

"Mister," said one of the boys, "if you were looking for one of the girls to take home"—his brown eyes squinted and his mouth puckered—"well, I just thought you—a big man like you, looks smarter than that."

"Yep," said the other boy, who looked almost exactly like the first. He had the same expression, squinting, serious eyes, and tense, screwed-up mouth.

"Well, I only came to bring a truckload of white potatoes and some fresh mutton roasts for your suppers," said Charlie. "But I could use a girl in the kitchen."

"You be better off with two boys, twins, than a girl anytime," said the first boy.

Charlie began to laugh in his deepest, loudest chuckle. "You guys thought I came to look for a little girl to take home?" His brown eyes twinkled merrily. "Well, I didn't think of it until now."

"Yep," said the quiet one, pulling his hands from his trouser pockets. His mouth turned down with disappointment when he saw Charlie unfasten the gate.

"I'm Eldon and he's my brother Edwin," said the first boy, squeezing his body between his brother and the gate. "We are called Smith and we could go home with you. We wash dishes, make beds. Edwin can sew on buttons. I can iron sheets and pillowcases, sweep the kitchen."

Charlie stopped and turned around. The freckles stood out like so many spots of spattered mud on the pasty white faces. Poor tykes, they look kind of puny, thought Charlie, maybe it's from doing all that inside work. A time in the sunshine, repairing fences, could do these kids a world of good. He came back through the gate. He grinned and felt good. He'd teach these boys to rope as good as—as good as Floyd.

"Either of you been sick lately? Had the coughing sickness?"

"No, sir!" the boys said in unison.

"Well, either of you ever rustled horses lately?"

"No, sir!"

"Can you juggle a rope?"

"No, sir!"

"You like school?"

"No, sir!"

"Well, that's too bad. I know where there's a swell one-room schoolhouse with a new schoolmarm who's pretty as a little red heifer in a flowerbed." Charlie shook hands with each boy. "I'm Mr. Irwin. If you come with me, you have to go to school, work on my ranch, and learn to juggle a rope."

"Yes, sir!" Both heads of thick auburn hair bobbed up and down.

It did not take Charlie long to convince the head of the orphanage that some sweet cream, fresh vegetables, and meat would do the twin boys some good and that he'd bring them back before winter in case someone wanted to adopt them. He'd send them to the one-room schoolhouse that was near Meridan, across from the T.O. Ranch.

When Charlie and the boys were climbing into the truck, Eldon grabbed Charlie's hand. "Mister, Mister Irwin, you never told us the name of that good-looking schoolmarm."

"Molly Sawyer. And, can you believe this, Miss Molly's brother works for me?"

"Golly!" said Eldon. "Can he juggle a rope?"

The twins were given cots in the bunkhouse. Pauline went out with the clean sheets and to see if they needed clean clothes. She tried to figure out why her father brought home twin boys, such little skinny ones at that. She found Charlie sitting on the back steps, twirling his rope, when she went back to the house. She sat beside him.

"Pa, you could've brought a girl from the orphanage to help out in the kitchen. I told you Bertie and I could use more help because of all the cowboys and jockeys you've brought in. Those kids are too small to be any help. They'll get underfoot and fill up on food. It's all right to be charitable, but be sensible about it. I'm really half-angry with you."

Charlie gave Pauline a hug and laughed. "I don't blame you. I lost my head when I saw those two little boys. I thought of all the room we have at the ranch. They'll learn to do something useful. I never thought of looking for a girl until I'd already promised to take the boys home. Forgive me? Look, when I take them back I'll ask about a girl who'd like to come out here and help with the cooking and cleaning. I suppose she could sleep upstairs in the guest room, huh?"

Pauline looked at Charlie with her brown eyes wide and serious. "You won't take those boys back to the orphanage. They've twisted you around their little fingers." She laughed.

"Pauline, do I ever forget the really important things?" asked Charlie. He didn't wait for an answer but turned to watch the little boys exploring the ranch yard with Betts.

Each morning, when school began, Pauline fixed the Smith twins a sack lunch. Charlie saw that the boys had a pony to ride to school. They said they liked Miss Molly. They never complained. Whenever Charlie was at the ranch, they followed him like a pair of shadows. Etta, herself, fussed over the boys when she was at the ranch. One day she told Charlie he made them work too hard. "They're just babies. Send them to the kitchen. I baked a yellow sponge cake."

Charlie squinted his eyes and puckered up his mouth. "Yes, ma'am, Missus Irwin. I kind of wish I was only ten years old."

Etta's eyes sparkled and she giggled. "If they don't eat all the cake, you'll have some for your supper."

Before coming into the kitchen the twins washed their hands in the basin of water in the back of the house and combed their hair with their fingers, as they'd seen the cowboys do. Etta was certain they'd filled out and there was a healthy glow in their freckled cheeks. Charlie was certain the boys were smart and he was not working them too hard. He had taken them fishing in Horse Creek more than once.

The first snow came in time for Halloween. Charlie talked to Eldon and Edwin about going back to the orphanage before winter.

"We'd rather stay here, Mr. Irwin. We'll not make any trouble," said Eldon.

"Yep. Stay. We like school pretty much," said Edwin.

"But I said I'd bring you back before winter," argued Charlie, feeling his stomach pinch together and his mouth turn sour.

"No one's coming to adopt us. We'll stay here," pleaded Eldon.

"We have to stay. Who else will look after Betts when her ma goes horseback riding with Miss Molly's brother?" asked Edwin, hanging onto Charlie's arm.

The words astonished him. It was the longest sentence Edwin had ever spoken to Charlie. Pauline and Claude Sawyer? Charlie could not believe his ears. "How long you been watching over Betts?" he snapped.

"Mr. Irwin, don't yell at us," said Eldon. "We keep her out of Horse Creek and the sticker bushes. We don't let her climb to the hayloft. We let her draw pictures in the dust and let her ride her play pony in the front yard where it's level."

"You do this besides the things I tell you to do?"

"And what Miss Molly has us do, like long division," said Edwin.

"Jeems! I'm sorry. I mean, it's not fair for you to look after Betts like a sister," said Charlie. He was not thinking of the twins and Betts. He was thinking of Pauline and Sawyer. How long had they been seeing each other? Was he the last to know?

"We don't have to look after our sister. She's big," said Eldon.

Now Charlie was dumbfounded. "You have a sister? Where is she?"

"At the orphanage," said Edwin.

"Jeems! Why didn't someone tell me?" Charlie put his face in his hands. Then he looked up. "How old is she?"

"She's old. Sixteen," said Edwin.

Charlie didn't know which to do first—go after the sister of the Smith twins or talk to Pauline about seeing the cowboy, Claude Sawyer. The decision was made for him. Sawyer opened the door of the bunkhouse and came toward Charlie with long strides. He was tall and without a doubt the most handsome cowboy Charlie had at the ranch since Charley Johnson left. His hair was blond and his eyes were like blue vitriol. Today he seemed tongue-tied.

Charlie sent the twins to the bunkhouse. "You came to see me about something that's on your mind?"

"Yes, sir. It's nothing to be upset about."

"The twins tell me you've been seeing my middle daughter."

"Yes, sir."

"That what you want to talk about that won't upset me?"

"Well, I—" Sawyer wiped his face with his bandanna. "Mr. Irwin, it's about working here."

"You're surely not complaining that the work's too hard? You think thirty dollars a month and all the prunes you can eat is good pay? You get along all right with the other men? No fights?"

"No, sir, to all your questions. I'd like to stay on. To work here permanently. I could homestead some of the land that's surrounded by your sections so that it would all belong to the Y6." He held out his hand.

Charlie hesitated. "What kind of proposition are you making? Why do you want to increase the size of my land? How will that benefit you? You think if I let you homestead for the Y6 I'll let you continue to go horseback riding with my daughter? Is that your angle?"

"Yes! I mean no! Sir, I want to marry Pauline. I'm asking your permission." Sawyer jumped from one foot to the other and wiped his face again.

"What does Pauline say?" asked Charlie. His face was noncommittal.

"She said to lay it all out for you, then duck," said Sawyer, turning red as cinnabar rock.

"I mean does she—does she find you attractive?" Charlie saw Sawyer stand still and rub the back of his neck. Why don't young men just answer the questions put to them? he thought. Young people can't express themselves these days. They go by slow freight.

"I suppose she's attracted to me. She says I'm the nicest thing that's come to the ranch. That heaven can't be much better."

"Jumping beans! You don't have to tell me all that mush! You know I don't know a thing about you, except that you are good with horses. What have you been doing up to now?"

"I grew up on a ranch and rode in a couple rodeos. That's why I wouldn't mind staying here, looking after your stock, while you went to rodeos or to the racetrack."

"You applying for a job as my foreman?" Charlie stood up rigid. "I haven't had a foreman—since—since my son died."

"Yes. Pauline told me. We think—"

Charlie turned a furious eye on Sawyer. "Confound it, man! Tell me what you want! Don't tell me what you think!"

Sawyer took a deep breath. He ran his hand across his forehead. "Mr. Irwin, sir, I didn't know that asking to marry your daughter was going to be so hard. Oh, no, don't get me wrong! She's worth all the trouble."

Charlie was silent.

"Uh—after we're married we want to take care of the ranch. We want to give you time to rodeo and race horses with peace of mind. You'll know the ranch is in good hands. That's all." Sawyer held his breath.

Charlie was relieved. He thought, this man has avoided me at every turn because he didn't want me to know he wanted to court Pauline. So, that's why he's seemed so timid, skittish, like he was hiding from something. He was making a play for Pauline. The man seemed intelligent, good-looking, and plumb lady broke. It was easy to see that Pauline had him cinched up to the last hole. Charlie looked the man square in the face and wondered when he was going to draw in some air. Sawyer's face turned pink, red, then purple. Charlie bent over and guffawed. "Breathe, man, before you pass out! If you faint you won't hear what I have to say. Pauline's got you lassoed for certain. You like kids?"

"If you're talking about a little kid called Betts, I sure do!"

"She's a corker. She'll have you wound around her little finger worse'n she's done to those little Smith twins. Why, those boys will pick up those harmless, but hairy, scary, big tarantulas for her."

"I can take that, as long as she calls me Papa." Sawyer's blue eyes sparkled as deep blue as Jackson Lake.

"Then, what can I say?" said Charlie. "Except that I'm sorry I raked you over the coals with questions. It's just that—well—I guess you know, Pauline's first marriage turned rancid and that was hard on all of us. I don't want that to happen all over again." Charlie's hands rolled into fists. "There's something else you ought to keep in the back of your mind. A woman looks so darn-awful beautiful when she gets married, but a man looks scared out of his wits. They both get over it."

Sawyer said, "Mr. Irwin, I'll love Pauline as long as I live."

Pauline Irwin and Claude Sawyer were married, two weeks after beginning their courtship, in Cheyenne with Charlie's and Etta's blessing. Sawyer immediately homesteaded the land adjoining sections that belonged to the Irwin Y6.

By the end of 1920 Pauline and Sawyer were managing the ranch. Pauline kept the books and took care of the cooking after

Bertie left to care for her ailing mother. Sawyer took charge of the ranch buildings, stock, and hired hands. Little by little Charlie learned that Sawyer was born in Oklahoma Territory. He said he was born in No Man's Land that actually belonged to Quanah Parker, chief of the Comanches. When the government took over this land, Sawyer's parents moved to the Choctaw Nation to escape being identified with the grangers. He grew up on a ranch operated by his father and entered rodeos, like all the young men on Western ranches, when he was sixteen or seventeen. He also participated in rodeos and frontier exhibitions in Canada and Old Mexico. By 1914 he was a judge in many rodeo contests. The Ardmore, Oklahoma Roundup was his first experience as a judge.

Before the fall chill set in Charlie took a side of beef and a couple of gunnysacks of baking potatoes to the Torrington Orphanage. He found the twins' sister. Her name was Birdie. She had the same wavy, auburn hair as her brothers. Her eyes were pale blue. Her nose was peppered with freckles. She wore a brown print skirt which was spotlessly clean and homemade. It fit her like she'd run out of material on the sides. Her shirt was a regular store-bought man's shirt minus the collar, which could be buttoned on the neck binding. Her small feet were encased in heavy work boots that covered her ankles. Everything about her was birdlike except the brogans. Birdie counted the day Charlie Irwin came asking about her as the most lucky day of her life. She was too old for most families to adopt. She had resigned herself to feeding and bathing the orphan babies the rest of her life. When Charlie asked if she wanted to live on his ranch where her twin brothers were and help out with the household chores, she was stunned. "You can't want an old girl like me to work at your place. I'm not twelve. I'm sixteen and set in my ways."

"You know how to cook good biscuits?" asked Charlie.

"Oh, yes, and bread and cakes."

"If you want to work for me, you get board and room and thirty dollars a month, same as any hired hand."

"That's exactly what I want!" she cried, and began gathering her few belongings.

Birdie and Pauline got along well, almost like sisters. Birdie was eager to meet the other girls, Joella and Frances.

Meeting the new cook, who'd taken the place of old Bertie, was the furthest from Frances's mind while she was at the University of Nebraska. She was worried about how to tell her folks that she'd married the most intelligent man on earth, Joseph Edward Walters. She decided the best thing to do was to take Walters home for the holiday. Once the folks got to know him and like him, she'd break the big news; they were married and she was not going back to school.

First thing, when they arrived at the ranch, Charlie took Walters out to the barn and showed him the thoroughbred racehorses. "Got two new racers. Going to name one The Boy Favorite, after Pauline's husband. Maybe I ought to name the other after you?"

Walters, who was not as tall as Sawyer, was dark-haired with a little toothbrush mustache. He didn't know one horse from another. He was a business administration graduate who enjoyed keeping his nose in books. He could manipulate figures faster in his head than with a slide rule. He looked at Charlie quizzically. "Sir, how did you know? Does it show?"

"What?" asked Charlie, puzzled by this young man who knew little about ranch life, but so much about pushing numbers about on paper.

"Marriage? Does marriage show?" Walters looked about the barn nervously as though someone else might be listening. "We didn't want to say anything until later."

Charlie lowered himself on a bale of hay. "If you'll just tell me straight out in plain, everyday English right now, you won't have to save it for later."

"Well, sir, it was to be a surprise. But you've already guessed. We're married. Frances and I. We've been married a week. Gosh, sir, that's our surprise."

Charlie wondered how many more surprises his children would develop before the end of the year. What did Frances see in this Walters man, who didn't know one end of a lasso from the other? What in the world could Charlie do with a son-in-law who never rode a horse?

Walters must have read Charlie's mind because he said, "Mr. Irwin, since Frances went back to school this fall, you've been without a secretary. I'd like the job. Honest. I'd be permanent as long as you want me. I'll work with your books, type your letters, answer your phone. I'll be perfectly happy. Frances can ride horses, twirl a rope, and she'll be happy. We've talked about it."

"That's darn gallant of you. Maybe I don't like my life being run and talked about. I'm not an old man. I'm not senile. I can hire a secretary if I want one." Charlie rubbed his chin. "If you work for me, even if you push a pencil, you have to ride a horse."

"Yes, sir. That's part of being in the family?"

"You're darn tootin'! That's life! Everyone should ride a horse." Charlie took a saddle off the wall and tossed it on the back of a small black horse. "A man secretary? Now, that's something different. You think you can take care of all the stock and grain shipments that take place along the U.P. line? Keep them in a ledger, day by day, with no mix-ups?"

"I'm sure I can. Frances told me what she did last summer. Give me two weeks to prove myself."

Charlie pulled the cinch firm. "Climb up on Corncutter here. That's it. Put both feet in the stirrups. Don't hold the reins so tight. Ah-ya-ho!" He slapped his hand on the horse's hip and waved as Walters went through the barn door and looked back. His brown eyes were wide open and his lower jaw dropped so his mouth was open. "Bring Corncutter back before supper!" Charlie chuckled. He went outside to sit on the corral fence and watch Walters as long as he could. It didn't take long for him to drop down to Horse Creek and out of sight.

Thirty minutes later Charlie spotted Walters coming up the lane to the house. The horse was walking. Walters was sitting back in the saddle grinning. "Mr. Irwin! How'd I do?" he climbed off and handed the reins to Charlie. "Thank you. I may ride again after supper? May I ask Frances to ride with me—sir?"

"That's a gallant gesture. First, you tell Mrs. Irwin your surprise, then I'll name this horse the Gallant, after you." Roaring his deep belly laugh, Charlie led the horse to the barn.

Charlie barely had Walters settled in his U.P. office when he received a telegraph from Joella in San Francisco. Captain Waldron was going on some kind of training mission. Joella and Patty were coming home for the Christmas holiday. Charlie was ecstatic. The family would be together, like a family ought to be. He could hardly wait to tell Etta.

Etta went on a cleaning spree. She got the house in town and the ranch house clean as any army barracks that survived the white glove test. Canned oysters and red salmon were stacked on the pantry shelves because they were Joella's favorite.

* * *

Joella came off the Pullman car at Cheyenne wearing the latest fashion, an empire-waisted silk dress, and her long blond hair was marcelled on the ends. Little Patty wore a short, pink silk dress, short white stockings, pink silk bloomers with elasticized legs and waist, and black patent-leather shoes with half a dozen button straps up the ankle. Patty looked like a life-sized china doll, with deep blue eyes and soft golden hair.

Betts was sent to the house in town so that her cousin Patty would have a playmate. The little girls played with the silver dollars Charlie kept for the rodeo Indians' payroll in a suitcase in his study.

Christmas was celebrated at the ranch that year. Santa gave the two little girls similar dolls with clothes. The men got the usual new Stetsons. Etta received her annual bottle of Shalimar perfume and a nosegay of real violets. Charlie gave everyone, even the cowboys and jockeys, a ten-dollar gold piece.

Will and Margaret, with their two youngest, Gene and Juanita, came to Christmas dinner. Their oldest, Gladys, had married Clay Foster. The Fosters were living in Colorado. Sharkey, their older boy, was working on a ranch near Wheatland.

Pauline and Birdie said they felt like they were operating an all night restaurant, because each meal was eaten in shifts. The family had grown and now there were more cowboys and jockeys at the ranch than ever before. Etta was glad to see Frances and Joella go to the kitchen to help. But she also noticed that Joella didn't stay long. Joella spent most of her time in the dining room laughing and joking with the cowboys.

Once again Charlie and Etta were invited to the annual Governor's Ball soon after the New Year. Joella stayed on a couple weeks longer so that she could help Etta make a new ball gown from yards of blue taffeta material. This year the ball was going to be in the large reception hall of the red-brick Georgian Colonial Governor's Mansion on Twenty-first Street. The ball was a highlight for Etta and Charlie, who both liked to dance.

A week later Birdie was in the kitchen baking a birthday cake for Betts when she looked out the back door and saw Frank drive into the yard in a truck, then lead a tiny part-Shetland pony out the back end.

Frank was drunk. He had brought the pony to Charlie as a peace offering. Charlie felt torn in half. He knew he was going to tell Frank to leave. The question was, when? "Give the pony to Betts, Frank. It's her birthday."

Betts ate little for dinner, preferring to wait for the cake, iced white, with six pink candles.

"What are you going to name the pony?" asked Charlie.

"I had it named Belle," said Frank.

"Yes, Tiny Bell is the name." Betts clapped her hands. "If Tiny Bell is mine, I ought to be the one to break her."

"Amen," said Charlie. "Spoken like a real cowgirl."

Etta shot Charlie a glance that said, "Protect the child from disaster."

Everyone, except Etta and Birdie, went out to the corral to see Betts ride the white Shetland pony.

"Honey, don't let no light show between you and the horse!" hollered Sawyer.

Betts clamped her teeth together and clung to the mane. She nodded that she was ready. Charlie let go the pony and stepped back against the corral fence.

Four times she was bucked off and the last time she rolled herself underneath the fence and felt the tears sting her eyes. Her side and back hurt. Charlie leaned over her and said, "Honey, get up. You have no broken bones."

Betts didn't move.

"Well, if you're going to cry, we might as well give the pony away," said Charlie.

Betts got to her feet and looked at her grandfather. "Put me back on!"

Charlie beamed. This granddaughter had the stuff.

Betts dug her fingers into the mane and nodded. Charlie let go and the pony did not move, then it trotted a little ways around the corral and neighed. Betts clung with white knuckles and her skinny child's legs were pressed hard against its sides. Everyone was cheering. He stepped out in front and held the pony's head. "That was about perfect." He lifted Betts to the ground. "I'm real proud of your performance. Next time I'll get a halter and show you how to use the reins. You won't fall next time. This Tiny Bell knows you and likes the feel of your weight."

"Can I ride around the house?" asked Betts.

"Heavens, not in the house!" said Pauline.

"Outside, around the house," said Betts.

"Gram would have a fit if you got in her garden. She had a fit when we let you, not a sack of sand, break this pony," said Pauline.

Frank left the day after Betts broke the Shetland pony, taking all his gear from the bunkhouse, not telling anyone where he was headed.

Several days after Betts began first grade at the Gibson-Clark School, Joella had a wire from her husband, Captain Norm Waldron. He was transferred to the Philippines. Joella's green eyes glowed. "Surprise, everyone! Patty and I are going to the Philippines so Norm can be with General MacArthur!"

Etta told Charlie she was ready to see the San Ysidro ranch.

FORTY-ONE

San Ysidro, California

The Tia Juana track set the monetary pace for the great horse races of today. The track was just across the California border in Mexico. The dirt roads swirled with dust, debris, and flies. Stray dogs and half-naked children claimed the right of way. Adults took time off each afternoon for a siesta in darkened adobe huts or in the shade of a skimpy palm tree.

Charlie raced at the Tia Juana track since its opening. Sometimes he let a horse run in more than one race in a single day. That didn't bother Charlie's horses; they were winners each time. Charlie said, "Get the horses down to the track. They don't do any good in the barn. They'd rather be out there running in the fresh air."

One morning an exercise boy, Bonnie Marinelli, asked for the day off because his wife was going to have a baby. "What hospital?" asked Charlie.

"At the Mexican woman's place. She's a good baby-bringer." Marinelli pointed over the racetrack to a group of huts that looked as if they'd been put up during a hurricane.

"Bonnie, your wife belongs in a hospital. Mr. Coffroth wouldn't take his wife to such a—a hovel."

"*Sí*. Señor Coffroth owns the racetrack. He can afford a hospital."

Charlie grabbed Marinelli's arm. "You want to stop being an exercise boy and work for me as a jockey?"

"*¡Sí!*" He looked at Charlie with large brown eyes.

"When is the baby due?" asked Charlie.

"I don't know, today, tomorrow."

"Then get your stuff into the jockey's bunkhouse today. Don't worry about your wife; I'll see that she gets to a hospital," said Charlie. "Memorial in San Diego."

"*¡Sí!* Thank you!"

Charlie went to the bunkhouse before Marinelli moved in and told the men about the move. Then he passed the hat to collect money for Marinelli's wife.

Dave Hurn said, "Mr. Irwin, if you wait until the end of the week, after payday, everyone will be able to chip in more."

Charlie squinted his eyes to see Hurn better. He was little, thin, blond-haired, and looked as though he'd not yet begun shaving. "You don't know a lot about babies, do you? Dave, you can't hold a baby back until the end of the week! Babies make up their minds it's their birthday, they come. This one may come today!" He dropped a twenty-dollar bill in the bottom of his hat. Then he went to the tack room and held his hat out for the exercise boys as they came in and out. Then he went around to the trainers, and finally he went to the gates of the racetrack, where the casino, called the International Club, was always filled with gamblers, famous people, day and night. When he came away he had a hatful of money. He took Marinelli and his wife to the hospital and said, "If it's a boy, don't give him a name like *Bonnie!*"

In less than an hour the baby boy was born. Charlie said, "Kiss your wife and kid, then come on! You have a race to run." Charlie drove Marinelli back to the track and handed him a white satin shirt with the Irwin Y6 in red on back.

The first race was four and a half furlongs. Dave Hurn was on Our Leader; Martinez was on Ellen Smyth; Denny was on Audrey K.; Parke was on Commander; and Marinelli was on Riposta. If Marinelli lost, an Irwin horse would still come in first because only Irwin horses were running. Marinelli came in third and was called to ride in the seventh race. This time there were three horses from other stables in the race. Marinelli was on Phrone Ward, who had a tendency to drift. Charlie had warned him, saying, "Don't fight the drift. If you pull to keep your horse straight, it fights back and loses ground. So—let it drift and you'll see it moves only gradually toward the outside fence. The other jocks'll be watching to ride back off you. So—when you go through that last turn and come home, ride that horse like a bat coming out of you know where—let him drift! Savvy?"

Marinelli nodded. Right at the beginning he noticed how he wanted to pull the horse back as it began to drift, but he also noticed that the drift was slow and nothing to pull hard for. When he made the last turn he concentrated on speed. His horse came in first.

Charlie ran to the fence to congratulate his newest jockey. Marinelli smiled and said, "We named our boy after you, *Cholly!*"

In 1921 Pablo Martinez, still riding race horses for Charlie, was declared the all-time, all-around jockey. Martinez had won more races than any other jockey on the continent. Charlie had a big celebration in his honor at the Tia Juana Sunset Inn, where all the movie stars went for dinner on special occasions. It was not the last celebration because Martinez was declared the leading race rider in the U.S. and Mexico in 1922, 1923, 1924, and 1925.

Two weeks after Thanksgiving, on a Monday afternoon, Charlie walked inside the San Diego Owl Drug Store where Clara Belle worked. There were no horse races on Mondays. The weather was mild and sunny. Charlie felt good. He wanted to see for himself that Clara Belle was getting along all right. He took a bottle of after shave to the front counter.

"Fifty-nine cents," said Clara Belle, without looking up. She took the dollar bill. She looked wonderful. Her hair was marcelled. She wore earrings that sparkled when she moved her head. She wore an apricot-colored dress with a flowered chiffon jacket.

"How are the four kids?" Charlie asked, pushing his Stetson back on his forehead.

Clara Belle jumped. She recognized the voice instantly. "Oh, beg your pardon. Mr. Irwin! I didn't expect to see you! The kids are fine. They're in school, except for little Frank, who's staying with a friend who lives across the hall from my apartment. Did Etta come?" Her voice became soft. "I missed her more than anyone when I first came to California."

"Etta and Betts are at the San Ysidro ranch," he said. Then he had an idea. "You and the kids come to our place for Christmas. I'll send Roy around in the car." He could see her eyes light up.

On the way out Charlie couldn't help look over the youngster mopping the floor behind the soda fountain. "What's your name, son?" he asked.

"Johnnie Mulouvious. I know who you are. My pa and me follow the races. That was a nice thing you did for Marinelli and his wife."

Charlie smiled at the boy, whose brown hair needed cutting. He turned to leave but the boy said, "My pa hurt his chest when he fell off a horse. He sits home praying he'll die. Talk of dying scares me. You ever hear about a man hurting so bad that he stays home crying?"

"Sounds like he should be in a hospital," said Charlie, his brown eyes looking soft and his voice gentle.

"I don't make enough." The boy's mouth was held taut so that it would not quiver.

"Never say *don't,*" said Charlie.

The boy's face turned red. "A—a doctor told him he should be in Scripps."

"What's wrong with that? So—send him to Scripps," said Charlie, taking his hat off and looking for the drugstore manager. "Just put a twenty-dollar bill in my hat. I'll match it and everything else I get. We'll see that young Mulouvious's father gets the medical attention he needs. That boy is worried sick about his pa."

The manager's mouth hung open. "Mister, I heard that money wasn't important, but I never saw anyone who was so anxious to get rid of it as you."

Charlie felt a tingle go up his spine. "That's where you are wrong, my friend. I like money as well as the next guy, but it only gets one in trouble because someone else wants to take it away from you. So, I use my money the way I want before someone else can get his hands on it."

The manager's Adam's apple bobbed up and down. "Still you gotta admit you're not usual."

"No one should be usual," said Charlie. "No one should get tangled in some self-imposed restriction. Enjoy life!"

Charlie took his hat to every customer in the drugstore. Next day he collected more at the International Club after making a little speech about Johnnie Mulouvious's ailing pa. He collected from his friends who frequented the Tia Juana track, Fred Astaire, Jackie Coogan, and Douglas Fairbanks.

Years afterward Mulouvious still recalled the dynamic character of Charlie and said, "It was that big-hearted cowboy that let me work for him, first as an exercise boy, then as a jockey after my pa got out of Scripps. C.B. said to me, 'Don't ever be scared of anything, not even dying! Just hang on and let the wind make the crease in your cap. Let the horse run. That's what horses are made for!' "

Mulouvious became one of the well-known jockeys, years later at Santa Anita. He raced Secretariat at Hollywood Park. He always said he owed his start in the horse business to Charlie Irwin.

Etta began to love the San Ysidro ranch. However, she never did like the palm trees. She liked the large, showy purple and red bougainvillea bracts. She liked the cool, light feeling of the white adobe walls of the ranch house.

Christmas Eve, Clara Belle still looked wonderful in her apricot dress. In the morning Etta made hotcakes and fixed sausages for breakfast, then Charlie acted like Santa Claus and gave out the gifts. The boys all got new lassos, the girls dolls. Etta and Clara Belle each got a bottle of Shalimar perfume from Charlie, as well as a hundred-dollar-bill to buy clothes with. Charlie got a half-dozen monogrammed white shirts and a gold ring with a one-caret diamond from Etta. The boys in the bunkhouse gave him a silver belt buckle inlaid with turquoise, coral, and jet.

After supper Charlie told Roy it was time to take Clara Belle and the four children back to San Diego. Clara Belle had tears in her eyes as she looked at the spruce tree that touched the ceiling of the front porch. "Christmas makes me sad, too," said Charlie. "I think of the fun we had getting our own tree and putting those little white candles all around in Cheyenne."

Most every weekend Charlie brought home friends and acquaintances. Shortly after entertaining Johnnie Mulouvious and the Owl Drug Store manager and his family, Charlie brought another couple to the ranch. Will Rogers was there resting for a couple days before he completed a circuit of speaking engagements. Neither Charlie nor Rogers bothered to introduce Etta to the new guests. They probably felt the couple needed no introduction. Etta'd seen them at the Sunset Inn and the casino.

Etta was captivated with the fellow who came in a tweed sack suit. He was five-feet-eight, short compared to Rogers and Charlie. He wore a bow tie, and it seemed to accent the fullness of his mustached face. His brown eyes flashed and he vaulted over Etta's coffee table to sit on the couch beside her.

His wife was no bigger than Etta, a fraction under five feet tall, and weighed less than a hundred pounds. She was self-conscious and actually embarrassed when her husband laughed loudly and jumped over the coffee table a second time when they went to the dining room for dinner. She wore a frilly, pink organdy dress, white shoes, and a white rose in her long golden hair. Etta thought correctly that the couple had not been married for long because she still asked his advice about many things. Etta thought she was a delightful little housewife, who'd soon have a backyard full of children. Etta said, "Were you married here or in Tia Juana?"

"We were married in Glendale," said the tiny wife, bouncing her blond curls across her shoulders.

The fellow grabbed Etta's hand. "Mrs. Irwin, Etta, I'll call you Etta, you call me Doug, her mother planned the whole thing. If I'd had my way we'd been married on horseback." He spoke fast, ran his words and sentences together.

Etta laughed, charmed by the dark, swarthy man. She was glad Charlie had brought the couple home. She was sure she could become fast friends with the timid, pretty blond woman. Etta motioned for her to come out to the kitchen with her so that the men could talk. The three men were laughing, acting brash and breezy as if they'd been great friends for many years. Etta could tell that they enjoyed being together.

Suddenly Rogers got up and told the woman to sit still. He said he'd go with Etta and fix everyone a silver fizz gin cocktail. Charlie held up his hand. "No, no. Will, you know I don't drink, not even a little wine with dinner. You bring me an orange juice."

"Orange juice is what I asked for. I'm like C.B. Don't need gin to give me energy nor free my tongue," said the young fellow with a big grin.

"I'll not disappoint you, Will. Bring me something fizzy," said the young blond woman, winking at Rogers.

"Do you know the name of that couple?" Etta asked Rogers in the kitchen. "They seem so familiar, like someone I should know."

"Yes, I know,'" said Rogers, laughing. "Mrs. Irwin, you ought to have guessed by now. That's America's sweetheart and America's number one charmer. Who's America's best-loved actor? Where's your gin and fizz water?"

"Charlie Chaplin and right here in this cabinet," said Etta, getting oranges out of a paper bag and slicing them so she could put them on the juicer.

"You and Mary are alike! I can't wait to tell Doug you think

Chaplin is number one. You know Chaplin lives about a block away from the Fairbanks home in Hollywood? Ice? Where's the ice?"

"Charlie keeps that out back. In the big box. Be careful, he might have lobsters in there with the ice!" Etta called out. Then she realized who the guests were—Douglas Fairbanks and his wife, Mary Pickford. She could feel her heart beat a little faster. She made sure she took all the seeds out of the juice. Her hand shook. America's favorite movie stars at her house!

Rogers came in with a small hunk of ice. He broke it up by putting it in the center of a dishtowel and striking it on the back of one of Etta's iron frying pans. "You know who C.B. brought home?"

"Mr. and Mrs. Fairbanks! You and Charlie behave yourselves tonight at dinner. You wouldn't want them to think you two were just a couple of smart-alecky cutups."

That made Rogers laugh heartily. "Mrs. Irwin, C.B. and I are going to learn some new tricks tonight. You wait. It won't be us that cut up."

It was true. Douglas Fairbanks was the life of the party. However, Charlie and Will Rogers weren't far behind him with mischievous behavior.

Fairbanks found that Charlie did have live lobsters in the box of ice in the backyard. The lobsters were not very active in their cold environment. He took several to the bathroom and put them in the tub with a few inches of water in the bottom. Then he decided they needed salt water, so he sent Rogers in the bathroom with a salt cellar. Maria, the Irwins' Mexican cook, found the lobsters in the tub and let out a bloodcurdling scream. She thought they were overgrown cockroaches.

Etta and Mary Pickford calmed Maria so that she'd finally go to the kitchen and prepare the evening meal. While she served the dessert, Fairbanks reached around and pinched Maria on the thigh. He was so smooth that Maria thought the culprit was first Rogers then the second time Charlie. She refused to come to the dining room. Etta and Mary carried the dirty dishes to the kitchen. When the Fairbankses said it was time to leave, Charlie went to the bunkhouse to get Roy to drive them to their hotel in San Diego.

"Next time plan to stay overnight with us," begged Etta. "Mary and I get along so well."

"You'll have to come to Pickfair," said Mary. "The men can ride horseback, and you and I will play tennis, then we'll have popcorn balls and Ovaltine. You can stay in Charlie Chaplin's room. You know, he often stays with us even though he lives only a block away. I think Douglas inspires him."

"Yes," said Etta. "I can see why you were attracted to Doug. In some ways your Doug is like Charlie. They both like to see people have a good time."

"Charlie's not as impulsive as Douglas. Sometimes he really embarrasses me," said Mary, "but I can never stay angry with him."

"Embarrassing! Someday I'll tell you the story of the bull Charlie and Will painted on the barn door at the Y6 in Wyoming."

Rogers overheard and as they all walked out the back door together to the yard where Roy had the car waiting, he said to Mary, "C.B. is a man that's bigger than anything he does. And right now I'm talking about size. He's kind of like the Bible that's bigger than just the Methodist religion. You know what I mean. Why, C.B. had the best Wild West show in the world. It was head and shoulders above Buffalo Bill's, God rest his soul. C.B.'s rodeos are top drawer and his race horses are unbeatable."

Etta was touched by what Rogers said. She wiped a tear from her eye. Mary put her arm around Etta's waist and whispered, "It's all right. I understand and know you had a lot to do in making the show famous. Wives are expected to make their husbands successful. And I'm well aware of the stigma attached to any kind of show business, no matter how talented a person is."

"That's true," said Rogers. "C.B. wouldn't be what he is today if it weren't for Etta. She gives him freedom and trust and security. I come here often for rest and get much more." He took hold of Etta's hand, then took Mary's hand on the other side. "We all need good friends. If I'm at C.B.'s place in Cheyenne or San Ysidro, my manager never bothers me, unless it's an emergency."

Betts asked Rogers if he'd seen her school. "Uncle Will, you can see it from the track's grandstand."

"Wave at me when you go out for recess," said Rogers, pleased she called him Uncle Will.

The Fairbankses came and Charlie had them sit in his box seats with Etta and Will Rogers.

Rogers asked about Betts's school.

Charlie pointed and said, "It's up there, on the hill." He explained that it was built by Jim Coffroth for the children of his employees and the racing people.

Etta pointed to the large building that stood out from a low, pink adobe building. "Yes, there it is, that modern building with the shiny red roof. Nuns run the school, maybe they live in the pink adobe."

Charlie began to sputter, but before he could say anything additional, Fairbanks grabbed his arm and said, "Those lights—on the school—what do they say?"

Rogers had his hand against his forehead shading his eyes. He was grinning. "You mean the lights around that fancy red roof? Say, that must have cost a bundle. I've never seen a school with so many lights."

"I don't see any lights," said Etta, shading her eyes and squinting.

"You'd see them if it were dark," said Fairbanks, snickering and lighting a cigarette for Mary.

"You have to admit the yard is neat and clean. I love the way the sun reflects off the roof. It's not a little red schoolhouse, it's big!" Etta was pleased that Charlie had enrolled Betts in such a fine-looking school.

"Watch the race!" cried Charlie. At that moment an announcement came over the megaphone. The horse Charlie bet on, his own Woodie Montgomery, was disqualified because it had tried to shake a paper, some racing form, that had blown from the bleachers. When the horse tried to get rid of the paper that was pasted across its eyes, it had blocked other horses in the race. "Interference!" the megaphone blared.

Rogers looked crestfallen. "I bet on that horse."

Fairbanks was elated because his horse, Blind Baggage, came in first.

Charlie said, "Don't count your money until you see its color."

"Bet on Harry D. because Martinez is riding him in the next race," said Etta.

"How can you tell? You can't even see the lights around the red roof," said Rogers.

Mary was looking through opera glasses. "Etta's right!" she cried. "Doug, bet on Harry D." Then she looked up at the school as the canned music played between races. "The lights, they spell something—M-O-L-I-N-O R-O-J-O—what does that mean? Is it the name of the school?" She handed the glasses to Etta before Fairbanks could grab them.

Fairbanks's mustache twitched and his white teeth flashed into a huge grin. "Etta, I gotta tell you something. That sign says in English, 'Red Roof.'"

Charlie had his hand over his mouth, trying to hid a sheepish grin. He said, "Actually, the school is the low pink building behind—"

Rogers interrupted. "You mean the nuns run a school house next to a—"

Fairbanks let out an explosive bit of air, "If you must know, the Red Roof is a bawdy house. You know—"

Etta's face turned red. She turned to Mary, whose eyes were wide. "Did you know?" asked Etta.

"No! I never looked at the hill before. But I once heard that Coffroth built such a place to accommodate his—his employees, and that it is the most modern building in Tia Juana. Mirrors in all the bathrooms and—" Mary waved her hands.

"All those innocent kids! Right there next to a—a bawdy house!" Etta sputtered.

"Kids of all races, all nationalities in that school. They're getting the best education in the world!" said Charlie, trying to be serious.

"My granddaughter studying next to a bawdy house!" snapped Etta. "Would you permit a little granddaughter of yours to go there?" she asked Mary.

"Well—no—I—"

"I knew you wouldn't!" Etta peered through the opera glasses again. "There must be schools in San Diego!"

A week later Betts was in a boarding school in San Diego. Roy drove her to school every Sunday evening and picked her up each Friday evening so that she spent the weekends at the San Ysidro ranch.

In mid-January Betts followed Roy into the bunkhouse to give him a picture she'd drawn of a palm tree. Martinez was in bed groaning.

"Hey, Pab, I thought you were riding horses today. It's Friday."

"Sí" was all he could say.

Betts ran into the house. "Gram! Pablo's sick!"

Etta went out to the bunkhouse and found Martinez's eyes large and glassy. He was flushed. She wiped his face and arms with alcohol. He told her he'd walked all the way home from the track. He felt so weak he couldn't stay on the back of a horse.

Etta was aware of how much Charlie depended on Martinez. She was determined to have him well as soon as possible. She took him a cup of tea.

"It is strange weather. First I am hot, then cold," he said.

She put her hand on his arm and drew it back quickly. He was hot and dry. "Mr. Irwin will look at you when he comes back from today's meeting," she said.

The moment Charlie drove into the yard Etta ran out to meet him. "I think Pablo needs a doctor."

It didn't take long for Charlie to agree. "I'm taking Pab to San Diego," he told Etta. "Feed the hands. I'll get something later."

At the supper table Dave Hurn said, "Pablo didn't know enough to get sick later. The Coffroth Handicap's in a week and the stake's more'n three thousand dollars. Boy, I'd like to win that with Harry D., but the only man that can is Pablo."

Since 1917 the Coffroth Handicap was an added race in which the track management put up the money, instead of collecting it from the horsemen in the form of added entrance fees. Charlie's horses had won the Handicap for the last couple of years and he intended to do the same this year, 1922.

Charlie called Etta from the hospital in San Diego to say that Martinez had pneumonia. "He may have to stay in the hospital for a couple of weeks!"

Two days before the Handicap, Charlie said to Etta, "Pab's the only man I have that can win the Handicap. There must be some way to get him to the track."

"What about using your newest jockey, Fator, or even Dave Hurn?" asked Etta, rubbing the tension out of Charlie's shoulders.

"They're not consistent. Pab not only knows the horse he rides, but he senses what the other horses are going to do." Charlie jerked away. "Tomorrow's Saturday. I'm going to the hospital in the morning."

He was up before anyone else in the morning. He telephoned Martinez's doctor and told him it was a matter of great importance that they meet. He took a large watermelon and two smaller ones that were floating in the ice water in the backyard cooler and wrapped them in thick layers of newspaper to keep them cool. He went directly to the track and talked to several guineas and exercise boys. Smiling, he gave them an ice-cold watermelon. He found one of the stewards working early around the horse stalls and visited with him for some time, then gave him a watermelon.

At the hospital the doctor explained that Martinez was recovering nicely, but he should stay a couple more days so there'd not be a relapse. "Mr. Irwin, I don't know about your proposal. My good sense says you can't take this man out and put him on a horse this afternoon."

"Why not?" asked Charlie, his face full of innocence. "He's the only man that can ride Harry D. in the Handicap. He knows that horse inside and out. There's a big prize for this race, and lots of competition. Martinez lives for racing. He'd understand."

"I understand," said the doctor, stroking his gray beard. "Maybe, just maybe there's a way to keep Martinez quiet until he gets on the back of that horse."

"How can we keep him in bed until it's time to get on the back of Harry D.?" Charlie felt the perspiration form in the middle of his back. The men talked. Charlie waved his hands in the air and muttered how hard it was to get anything done without a lot of explanation and greasing of palms. The doctor smiled. Charlie left and was back within minutes with the biggest watermelon the doctor had ever seen. Charlie made him swear he wouldn't drop it before he reached home. They grinned and made a bargain.

The doctor arranged for Martinez to have a cup of black coffee by midmorning, Sunday. The coffee contained a little codeine, just enough to keep the jockey calm. An ambulance was called to the hospital entrance. Martinez was carried to the ambulance and put to bed. He didn't lift a finger. He looked like he was having a nap.

Charlie followed the ambulance the sixteen miles from San Diego to the small, graveled back road behind Charlie's barns and across the border, without going through San Ysidro and crossing the border on the main road. Charlie and the ambulance pulled up behind the track.

All jockeys were required to check into the jocks' room at noon, so that there couldn't be any foul play, no contact with anyone before a race. If any contacts were made, everyone knew they could be made before noon. Charlie talked with the steward he'd seen earlier and assured him that no one would make contact with the ambulance until it was time for Martinez to get dressed. Martinez would race and come immediately back to the ambulance. Two other stewards moseyed over and wanted to know what the secret was about.

Charlie crossed his fingers. Now he had to tell what was going on.

"That's the craziest thing I've ever heard," said one of the stewards. "You really got Martinez in an ambulance? I gotta see for myself," said the other.

"I'm coming," said the steward Charlie had seen early in the morning.

Charlie walked beside him. "How was the watermelon?"

"Cold and sweet. The best. But my hand still itches." He held out his hand and smiled.

Charlie groaned, but pulled a twenty-dollar bill from his pocket. The steward put the bill into his pocket. The other two stewards must have smelled money. They came alongside Charlie and smiled.

"I don't want no Mexican paper," said one. "We had a piece of that watermelon you dropped off. That was a nice thing to do." Charlie gave him a twenty-dollar bill. The steward took the money and dropped a little behind so that the other steward could walk beside Charlie and pocket twenty dollars. They looked inside the ambulance and nodded toward Martinez resting on the snow-white cot. Martinez's face cracked in the middle by a wide smile. "I came to ride my horse," he said.

"C.B. will tell you when to get dressed," said the first steward. "You look okay to me."

That night Charlie came home in a jocular mood. He danced around the supper table and sang when the meal was over.

"Charlie, none of us are getting up from the table until you tell what happened today. Don't be a big chub," said Etta.

"Big chub! I don't usually let people call me names like that." He made silly grimaces toward Etta.

"A chub's a kind of fish with a small mouth."

"Small mouth, huh? You think I'm not going to tell you about Pab riding Harry D. and winning the Coffroth Handicap? Pab and I made some money today! We have a two-foot-high silver cup! I'm going to buy a couple horses I've had my eye on. Dear, you should have seen Coffroth's face when Pab reached out and took that big silver cup. 'I though you were hospitalized!' he yelled. 'I took the day off!' Pab yelled back. When he dismounted, one of the stewards hustled him back into the ambulance. Pab's going to be in the hospital another three days."

Etta laughed until tears came to her eyes. "Charlie, that is the wildest story I've heard in a long time. No one but you could think up such a scheme and pull it off!"

* * *

When warm weather came, in the middle of April, Charlie was ready to go back to Cheyenne. This had been a good year at the track, and he'd bought a couple new horses that he hoped a season running free at the Y6 would make into strong runners. One of the horses he called Abadane, another he called Apricot for Clara Belle, another was El Roble.

That winter Charlie had spent so much money for his new horses and the bonus to his employees that he didn't have enough cash for meals for himself, Etta, and Betts. "Be thankful we have railroad passes," he told Etta, "and that the hands can all ride back in the stock cars."

Etta went to the bedroom. When she came back, she handed Charlie both her diamond and pearl earrings. "See how much that banker in San Diego will lend you for these."

"Thank you, dear. You figured out a solution. I'll put my diamond ring with your earrings and we'll have enough to get out of town." Charlie gave her a kiss and drove to the bank right away.

At several train stops Charlie bought sandwiches from the conductor and had them taken to the boxcars for his men. When the train stopped for water in Salt Lake City, he had the boxcars opened so that the men could get out and walk around, use the rest room to wash up, and get something to eat at the beanery. One hundred and twenty-four men got out of the boxcars. When they lined up to eat, the station agent announced that the beanery was closed and that none of the men were allowed to get back on the train.

Etta could not believe that the beanery did not want all that good business.

Charlie stepped forward, looked the station agent in the eye, and said, "I don't know how long you've been working for the U.P., but I've been working for this railroad for nearly fifteen years." He handed the man his card. "Now, if you will not let my men eat and get back on those boxcars I will call William Jeffers, general manager."

"It is against rules to carry more than two men in a boxcar loaded with stock," said the agent. His face was getting red.

"If the animals are in any danger, tell me," said Charlie. "They are well fed, with plenty of water, and none carries a saddle on its back. My men hang the lanterns high above the hay. They keep the cars clean. I am a member of the Wyoming Board of Human Treatment for Animals and Children. Would you like to see that card?"

"Who is superintendent of your U.P. Division?" asked the agent.

"S. R. Toucey!" snapped Charlie. "Jeems, man, let these fellows eat. They haven't had anything but sandwiches since leaving San Diego."

The agent didn't move. A vein throbbed in his neck.

"All right, where is your telephone? When I'm finished you may not have your job!" bellowed Charlie.

The station agent stepped back and motioned for the diner to open. Charlie, Etta, and Betts sat in a booth. Etta noticed that the agent had disappeared.

"That man puffed like a steam engine," giggled Betts. "Gramps told him!"

"Ssh," said Etta. "I think he's called Mr. Toucey."

"I sure hope so," said Charlie, ordering another apple pie for himself. When everyone was finished he waved the men back on the cars. Roy had found fresh hay for each car and had filled all the water buckets. Charlie looked at his pocket watch and saw that the train had waited an extra ten minutes in Salt Lake so that his men could finish eating.

Back in Cheyenne there was six inches of wet, spring snow. Betts went back to the Gibson-Clark School for the remainder of the year, which was only about six more weeks. Betts could read better, and her vocabulary was larger, than the usual second grader.

"See, I told you Tia Juana had a good school," teased Charlie. "Betts learned a lot there."

Etta made a face, but decided not to reply. She also said nothing when Charlie unpacked a dozen or more bottles of special wine from Mexico that he put in the basement saddle room at the ranch.

"It's to use for the special guests we have come out here," Charlie explained. "Don't ever worry, dear, I'm not going to become a wino."

"I've been thinking and I've decided that I want to send Betts to Sunday school," said Etta on their first Sunday back in San Ysidro.

"I can't see that that would hurt," said Charlie.

Later Betts told Etta and Charlie that she was disappointed. "The teacher told the story of Daniel, but not as good as Gramps tells it. She didn't know the names of any of the lions."

Charlie smiled.

One day before the Frontier celebration, Charlie was at the Meriden post office collecting the mail when he saw three big Brahmans in the corral by the general store. He couldn't wait to have a better look. The cow was white and the bulls were silver-gray. All three had so much loose skin at their neck and below that Charlie thought it looked like a giant turkey wattle.

Dan Donahue came out of his store and stood beside Charlie. "Ain't they somethin'! Kate's family in England sent 'em. She always said her family was well-to-do. Now I believe her."

Donahue told Charlie that the Brahmans were called Zebus in India. But he didn't tell Charlie he didn't think they were worth much. To him they were freaks, good only for showing off in some kind of circus. He knew that Charlie had a penchant for possessing anything new and different the minute he saw it. He thought that Charlie had had a couple of flush years and probably had some money in the bank. "Hold the phone!" he yelled. "I'll parade these brutes around in the field a couple of times. You watch and tell me what you think."

Charlie watched. The cow flicked her ears and lowered her head as though she had in mind to ram him against one of the gasoline pumps in front of the store. Donahue whistled and the cow looked up and followed the two bulls who followed Donahue like sheep. The creatures had a prominent hump above their shoulders, especially the bulls, the rumps drooped, and the ugly, loose pendulous skin under their throats and on their dewlaps swung back and forth.

Charlie laughed and said, "Dan, what are you going to do with such silly animals? I'll bet you people drive by here just to have a good laugh. Next thing you know they'll be laughing at you for keeping outlandish stock in your corral." Charlie drew himself up to his full six feet, four-inch height and kept his three-hundred-pound body firmly on the ground as the animals walked past him. "I'd keep those hideous animals out of sight before they're a target for somebody's rifle. They are the most ridiculous cattle I've seen in my life."

Charlie went home and told Etta about the strange-looking cattle. "I'd give my eye-teeth to own them. Wouldn't they be something to show off at Frontier? How much you think I ought to offer old Dan?"

Etta never told Charlie how much to pay for any of his stock. He knew the worth of animals much better than she. Charlie asked only to set the deal firm in his own mind.

Donahue talked with his wife, Kate. She scratched her head under her wool cap that kept the wind out of her ears. "My father went to a pack of trouble to send them. Now you want to sell?"

"C.B.'ll pay through the nose. I seen the look on his face. I could build some rental cabins by the gas pumps with the money."

"Will he dip and spray 'em against flies, grubs, and other peskies?" Kate Donahue wiped her mouth with a gingham rag she took from her apron pocket.

"You know C.B., nothing's too good for his stock. He'll pump water for 'em in drought and break ice on water holes in winter. He'll build windbreakers and plant trees for back scratching. But will these droopy-rumped critters thank him while Horse Creek's still running?" Donahue spit tobacco between his front teeth out the front door of the store.

"Let C.B. have the trouble. We'll sell." Kate pulled her cap down over her earlobes. "Build the rental cabins."

Between a couple of the Frontier events Charlie decided to show off his three Brahmans. He had a three-way megaphone through which he was singing, "When It's Springtime in the Rockies."

In the middle of the arena were a dozen cowboys sitting around waiting for the next event. Sawyer was there with Pauline and Betts, who was on hands and knees watching a couple cowboys shoot craps.

The crowd tittered, then laughed hard and clapped as Charlie led the funny-looking cattle around the arena. Then with no warning the cow began to run across the fairgrounds. Someone shouted, "Heads up!" The cow snorted and kicked up her back feet to make twin puffs of dust at quick, even intervals. Sawyer grabbed Pauline by the hand and ran for the fence. The other cowboys ran close behind. Charlie grabbed Betts and jumped over the fence. The cow was close behind. The minute it landed in the grass it stopped running and began munching.

The crowd stood and clapped, thinking it was a good piece of entertainment by C. B. Irwin.

Charlie was a showman of top quality. When he saw everyone was safe, he bellowed out over his megaphone that he'd pay five dollars to any man, woman or child who'd ride one of the new breed of cattle for a minute. The first cowboy was bucked off one of the bulls in less than ten seconds. The next rode for half a minute on the cow. Another was bucked off the cow the minute he got on. The crowd thought it was great sport. Charlie had given them a spectacular show. He thought of something new every year.

That fall at the Tia Juana track Charlie was not singing. The month of November, the rainy season, was unusually dry. Charlie rented large horse vans from the track so that he could bring his horses from the railroad boxcars, where he'd shunted them to a siding. He was afraid to leave them in the boxcars too long with little or no water. At the stables he cautioned the exercise boys to make sure his horses had plenty of water.

One weekend Betts said that the nuns had restricted the bathing to one bath a week at the boarding school because of a shortage of water.

"I hope this drought doesn't keep people away from the track," said Charlie. "If we don't have water, everything will shut down!"

"This drought is a freak," said Etta. "Ell says it won't last forever, but you'll be ankle deep in water soon."

"Ha! My sister's predictions are worth about as much as I pay for them," said Charlie.

On Friday afternoon Betts and Etta sat on the front porch watching the rolling clouds. Their whiteness seemed to be shrinking into gray overlapped with purple shadows. Betts told her grandmother she imagined the clouds were building themselves into some huge mountain filled with purple-green crags and crystal, white snow on gray boulders. Etta smiled and patted the girl's hand. Then with no warning, except the boiling clouds overhead, a sudden spray dashed against their faces like the sea spray from a crashing wave. There were little dust puffs in the yard and pockmarks left behind. There was a spattering sound as the drops struck the walk. Soon the pockmarks were filled and overflowing and washed away. There was only flat, shining brown surface. The wind came in spurts, as if undecided whether to blow now or wait to gather energy for a bigger push in the evening. Etta and Betts moved inside and smiled at the end of the drought.

"Gramps won't like the rain because of the races," said Betts.

"Oh, pshaw! That doesn't matter. This rain is a welcome sight to everyone."

By the time Charlie and the jockeys came back from the track, the rain was leaving huge pondlike puddles that were merging to form lakes. Everyone looked happy, even wading ankle deep in water.

When the rains continued at a steady pace and the winds

began to blow with hurricane force, no one was happy. Charlie could not spend Monday, his day off, at the San Ysidro ranch, he had to stay at the track to watch the horses. More than a foot of water stood on the track. Water standing on the back stretch had no place to go. The ground was saturated. The strong winds washed the track badly. The horses were moved to little hills in vans and wagons and kept in makeshift lean-tos that blew over in the wind. The stables were knee-deep in water. By Tuesday evening the rains stopped as quickly as they had come and the winds died down.

Charlie sloshed through muck and mud to make an evaluation of the damage. It was obvious the track was not going to be suitable for racing unless gravel and cinders were brought in by the truckload. All the stables and other buildings needed cleaning and repair. Charlie sought out Coffroth and said, "I believe the track can be ready for racing in three or four days. Tia Juana will carry on, even if we have to exhibit boat races instead of horse races."

Coffroth shrugged his broad shoulders. "C.B., you act like a big shot. I want my track repaired better than it was in the first place."

"All right, you let me get men and materials. I'll not only save you time, but I'll save you money and your track will be the best there is," Charlie said. "I have a stake in this place, too. My horses occupied half your stables."

Again Coffroth shrugged. He looked over Charlie's notes and said, "All right. Go ahead. I want the stables enlarged and if I don't like what I see—I throw you out and get my own labor crew."

Charlie grinned and shook Coffroth's hand and said, "All right, you're the boss."

Charlie ordered gravel, cinders, lumber, tar paper, nails, and cement. He directed each group of men. He ordered two dozen new stalls to be built in a line in front of the old ones. He made tiny walkways between the stables with dry, crushed gravel. He had wind-damaged roofs repaired. A grader filled and backfilled with gravel and clay to give a hard surface to the track. He never noticed Coffroth inspecting his work. Coffroth was not only pleased, he was surprised when he learned that the cost was about a third of what he'd expected.

When the track was finished he asked Charlie about paying the labor.

"Oh, labor's gratuitous. The men were here anyway. They worked to get the track open so they could start making real money."

Coffroth was dumbfounded. "Are things done that way in Wyoming?"

"Certainly! What other way is there?" said Charlie.

From that moment on Jim Coffroth had the highest regard for his friend Charlie Irwin. He saw that Charlie always had a box for himself and his family and guests at every race.

The evening he came home from repairing the flood damage at the track Etta said, "Charlie, if this family can sit in box seats at the races, it can have more than jelly glasses for water on the supper table."

This was the first time Charlie noticed that the water glasses were mismatched, various sizes, and colors.

"It's a disgrace to use jelly glasses when we have company. I'll get Bart to drive me to the ten-cent store in San Diego and get matching water glasses." Bart Woodward sometimes drove the car when Roy or Charlie was not available.

"That's fine," agreed Charlie. "But, dear, don't go to the dime store. I'll get some glasses for you from one of my New York catalogs."

"Charlie, I need the glasses right away."

"I'll order right away," said Charlie.

A month later a paneled truck drove into the front yard. The driver unloaded four packing barrels and left. Etta spent the rest of the afternoon unpacking glasses. There were water goblets, medium-sized glasses, down to tiny liqueur glasses. There were eight glasses of each kind in four different colors. All of them had the Y6 brand engraved on the side. Altogether there were one hundred ninety-two glasses.

"Where can I put all these glasses!" wailed Etta. "Charlie believes if I want eight, then eight times eight times eight is better!"

By the weekend Charlie had glass shelves across the two dining room windows so that Etta could put her new glasses there to catch the sunlight in rainbows on the white wall.

Charlie and Etta entertained guests at the San Ysidro ranch that Thanksgiving. Etta and Maria, the cook, prepared three big turkeys with corn-bread stuffing. Charlie could eat one whole turkey himself. The ranch hands could finish off another and the guests and rest of the family could eat the third bird.

J. Ogden Armour and his wife had come for a visit. They brought two smoked hams and several pounds of bacon to the Irwins. Mr. and Mrs. Updike from Omaha came and brought with them a young man recently out of Nebraska's law school, Howard Malcolm Baldridge.

Baldridge was in his late twenties, blond, blue-eyed, and interested in horses. "Maybe I should have been a veterinarian," he said.

"No, no," said Updike, "your training is going to suit you fine in keeping Omaha's horse-racing and livestock programs within the law."

Charlie knew that social life of Omaha centered around the Ak-Sar-Ben race track. He understood how Updike felt about keeping racing within the law. Updike wanted Baldridge to become the attorney for the city of Omaha.

Baldridge took Charlie aside and said he was not so certain he wanted to work for the city of Omaha, he would rather run for political office, such as state representative.

"Do what you want. Updike can find another young man just out of law school for his job. You'll remain friends even when you are in the House of Representatives. Never look back and regret. Go forward!"

"Thank you! That's what I needed to hear!" Baldridge shook Charlie's hand enthusiastically.*

Early in the morning on Thanksgiving Day, Charlie had a telephone call from another young man, named Tim McCoy. He explained that he was hired to be in a movie that was to have some scenes shot in Wyoming. "I heard you were from Wyoming, and I need someone to teach me Indian sign language. Can you help me?"

Charlie was like an overgrown kid. "Come on out to San Ysidro! We always have room for one more at our table. What's the name of the film?"

"The Plainsman," said McCoy. "Actually it's the first film I've been in and I wanted to impress the director that I knew the universal language all Indians understand."

"I'll teach you all I know."

*Years later Baldridge remembered Charlie's advice. After he was a Nebraska representative he became a U.S. congressman, and a colonel in the Air Corps. His son is currently Secretary of Commerce, residing in Washington, D.C.

* * *

After dinner Charlie sat in the middle of the living room floor with Tim McCoy and showed him and everyone the Indian signs he knew. McCoy learned fast and even put the signs together to make sentences. Finally he asked to see the horses Charlie had out back in the five box stalls. "I'd like you to show me how to ride. I haven't ridden a horse since I was a kid."

Charlie motioned for all the men to go outside with them. "We'll let the women get the table cleared and talk." He saddled one of the most gentle horses and put McCoy up in the saddle. He rode around the yard a few times. Updike and Armour each gave him advice.

"What if I'm chased by redskins?" McCoy hollered over his shoulder with a laugh.

"Fly low!" cried Updike.

"Run like a scalded pup!" cried Armour.

"Head for the hills!" shouted Baldridge waving his hands.

"Pray!" hollered Charlie, running after McCoy. When he caught up to the horse, he slapped it on the rump, making it trot faster and faster.

"Hey! How do you stop this thing?" called McCoy.

"Can't!" called Charlie. "It's gotta unwind by itself!"

Etta swept the bright-colored, thick wool rug Monday, the day after the company left. Charlie walked through the living room and she waved her broom at him. "If I had a sweeper that I could push back and forth, I'd get this job done better and faster."

"You're going fast enough! You're sweeping up a dust storm!" cried Charlie, backing out of her way.

"The wind blows sand through all the cracks and crannies. I'm sweeping all that grittiness back outside!" Etta called after him.

Charlie picked up the newspaper, shook off the fine particles of sand, and went to the front, glassed-in porch to read. He couldn't sit still with all the sweeping Etta was doing. He went to San Diego. In the center of San Diego's shopping district he was stopped by a policeman directing traffic. "Better slow down, Mac, before I have to give you a ticket."

Charlie put his head out the open window of his car and smiled. His face took on a boyish innocence. He drove a block farther and parked next to a shiny new Model A. It was the first time Charlie had seen such a handsome car. His Chevy looked shabby beside the new car. He ran his hand around the new paint. From the corner of his eye he saw the officer wave. Charlie smiled. The officer was walking toward him. Charlie said, "My name's not Mac. I'm C. B. Irwin. I've been to lots of state fairs and goat ropings and I never saw anything as pretty as this baby!" He patted the hood of the car. "Look at the lights and the wide running board!"

The officer began to walk around the car with Charlie, admiring things here and there. Charlie reached into his pocket, took out a handful of walnuts. He put two in his right hand, squeezed, scattered the hulls, and put the nut meats into his mouth. The officer took a pad of pink slips from his pocket. "I'm going to have to give you a ticket. You're in a No Parking zone, Mr. Irwin."

"Oh, I'm new in town," said Charlie. "I have to get a haircut and my wife a new sweeper." He reached in his pocket and handed the officer a handful of walnuts. "Watch my car for me, please. I'll be right back and move the car."

From the barber shop Charlie could see the officer leaning against his old Chevy trying to crack two walnuts together in his right hand the way Charlie did. The barber said, "What on earth did you say to that police officer?"

"I gave him something different to think about. I believe he was pleased to find someone who wasn't scared to death. I made the best of a sour situation. Not many places to park along this street," said Charlie. "Where could I go to buy a carpet sweeper?"

Charlie came out of Casey's The Store With Everything carrying a large carpet sweeper and a small one. He put the large one in the back of the car, tipped his hat to the officer, and said, "This one's good for getting corners cleaned. Here, have more walnuts. Thanks for watching my car." He got in and drove away from the curb slowly, watching the officer grinning with his mouth open.

The first thing Etta said was, "Charlie, why did you buy two sweepers?"

"My wife deserves the best there is. With two she can clean best."

"Charlie, I like both sweepers." She put her arms around his waist. The phone rang. Jim Coffroth wanted to talk with Charlie.

"C.B., you told me the other day you wished you had another car. You still want one?"

"I sure do," said Charlie. "I saw a new Model A sedan in town this morning. That baby looked tempting as sin. You want to go look at a Model A with me?"

"I can't. Some accountants are coming to look at my books.

But I want to tell you about this good deal. A trainload of cars coming to San Diego on the Southern Pacific caught fire. The cars that weren't damaged were taken off the flat cars. The railroad paid for the cars because of the fire, so it wants to recoup what it can. There's going to be an auction this afternoon. The cars will be sold for whatever they'll bring."

"What kind of cars?" asked Charlie.

"I don't know. Go and see," said Coffroth.

"I'll check it out. But I know no one is giving away something for nothing."

Charlie took Roy to the automobile auction. Charlie could find no damage to the cars, besides a little blistered paint.

Charlie looked at a Buick roadster, convertible, with a top of canvas. He thought how much he'd enjoy riding in it back and forth to the track. Then he looked over a Buick sedan, also with a canvas top, supported by metal strips and lathes. He thought Etta could drive that car to town to do her shopping. He bid on both Buicks and bought them. Roy could hardly believe Charlie'd purchased both cars. "Pa, what are you going to do with two new cars? Do you need both?"

"Son, when you see that the merchandise is good and the price is right, don't haggle. If you can use it, buy it."

"Is that the way you buy horses?" asked Roy.

"You bet," said Charlie. "And with a racehorse, if you are astute in your purchase, you'll recover your investment. That's something I learned a long time ago. You drive the roadster home." Charlie gave Roy the keys. "Then you and one of the other boys come back for the other car." He tossed the keys to the sedan to Roy. "I'm taking the Model T home."

Charlie was like a kid with new toys. He couldn't wait to show Etta both his new cars and to tell her she could use the sedan herself, whenever she wanted.

Two days before Christmas, Douglas and Mary Fairbanks came to Tia Juana to bet on the races. They sat in the Irwin box with Charlie and Etta. Charlie's sprinter, Herder, ridden by Dave Hurn, won the fourth race. His horse My Rose won the fifth race. Prince Direct was claimed out of the race for fourteen hundred dollars. It was Charlie's first claim of the season. Phrone Ward, ridden by Martinez, won by a nose over Anna Regina in the last race. Everyone felt flush with their winnings. Mary asked Etta if she and Charlie would come out to Pickfair in Hollywood for

Christmas. Etta answered yes, explaining they'd have to bring their granddaughter, Betts.

"Oh, you know I love children," said Mary. "They make Christmas the best celebration of the year."

"We'll drive the new Buick sedan," said Charlie. "What do you want for Christmas?"

"A sunshine cake!" cried Fairbanks. "It's my favorite."

The next day Charlie felt flush with his winnings. He took Etta and Betts to San Diego to buy a Christmas tree.

Then Charlie drove to Larche's Bakery and bought a dozen sunshine cakes. They were yellow sponge cakes decorated to look like Christmas wreaths.

"Gramps, can we stop at my school and leave a cake for the nuns?" asked Betts. "I want to show them you and Gram. None of my teachers believe I have a gramps who is bigger and taller than anyone and a gram who is teeny-tiny."

Charlie looked sidelong at his granddaughter. "Betts, don't tell family stuff at school."

On Christmas day Charlie drove Etta and Betts up to Hollywood. The day was mild, with soft white clouds in the sky and a gentle breeze blowing off the ocean inland. Charlie thought the palm trees along the highway were crazy-looking compared to aspen and cottonwoods and the evergreens he was used to in Wyoming. Palm trees did not look like the Christmas season to him. And sand, fine sand everywhere, was a poor substitute for snow.

Pickfair was larger than Charlie's ranch house in San Ysidro. It was brick and stucco on the outside, L-shaped, two stories, with a basement. A maid dressed in a black dress with a white apron and white cap let them inside the hallway with a blue and white tiled floor. Etta wanted to see the whole house.

"Come on," said Mary, beaming. "I'd love to show you how I've decorated." She took hold of Betts's hand and took them through the living room with its baby grand piano, the sun parlor with three lemon trees and a kumquat, all with fruit, the dining room, with a table already set for Christmas dinner, kitchen, butler's pantry, breakfast room, and back porch. Mary chattered about the furniture. She mixed oriental rugs with chintz curtains, mahogany and wicker furniture and wallpaper. She took them upstairs to a hallway that was huge and used for a sitting room. There were five bedrooms and baths and a couple porches that could be used for sleeping if cots were set up there. The furniture was modern. It was painted in white trimmed in gold, or painted in pastels, pink, yellow, or green. Mary's room was lavender, trimmed with a moss green, and Fairbanks's room was done in several shades of brown with white trim. Etta's favorite was a rose room.

"This is where Charlie Chaplin comes when he wants to meditate," explained Mary. "He often stays here overnight. You know he has his own house a block away."

Fairbanks had taken Charlie to his prized room, the place he kept all his portraits of Mary. The motion picture handbills for her films were framed and put up on one wall. He had a collection of Remington oil paintings on another wall and several Charlie Russell oil paintings in elaborate gold frames. In a glassed case were several bronze statues made by both Remington and Russell.

"Jeems!" said Charlie. "I didn't realize how realistic a painting can be. This one, by Russell, makes me feel like I'm back on the Y6."

Fairbanks took Charlie out to the back, where he had kennels for his dogs and several horses in the stables, tennis courts, a miniature golf course, several garages, a swimming pool.

After dinner they gathered around the piano. Mary and Etta took turns playing Christmas songs while everyone sang. Before going to bed they snacked on popcorn balls, chocolates, and the sunshine cake. Betts asked for Ovaltine and the maid came back with Ovaltine for everyone.

On the way back to San Ysidro the next day Charlie said, "That was a spare Christmas dinner. When we get home, bake us a ham and we'll have a dinner with sweet potatoes, cranberry sauce, green beans, mashed potatoes, and gravy. While you're doing that roast a turkey with corn bread stuffing. Ask Maria to bake some mincemeat pies. We'll have a good old-fashioned ranch dinner, and I'll think of the Russell picture I saw with snow and pine trees, and cowboys eating beans and bacon out of a frypan. Cream soup and salmon's no dinner. No wonder Mr. and Mrs. Fairbanks are so thin, they don't eat! We'll get all the boys and the rest of the sunshine cakes and have us a real feed. Etta, you think Fairbanks was pulling some kind of joke on me? Salmon for Christmas dinner? I'll get even with him. We'll have some of those giant snails next time the Fairbankses come here for supper! That'll even us on the jokes with food! I'll get that son of a gun!"

Charlie divided his horse racing into three divisions, and

called his organization Irwin Livestock and Show Company in the fall of 1923. Bob Liehe managed the first division, Harry Walters the second division, and Tom Holloway the third division. None of the managers took a veterinarian with them. They learned from Charlie how to doctor the horses. Tom Smith, who knew racehorses like the streets of his hometown, stayed with Charlie as his blacksmith. Racehorses were shod once a month or oftener if needed. As the hoof grew, it needed trimming and the shoe needed resetting.

Several years later Tom Smith decided to become a horse trainer himself. Charlie had a friend, C. S. Howard, who was looking for a trainer. Howard took Smith on Charlie's recommendation. Later Howard Smith developed the great racehorse called Sea Biscuit.

Eddie Thomas was Charlie's agent. He told him where the meetings were and where it was best to send the three division managers.

Coming from the Cheyenne ranch to the San Ysidro ranch in the fall Charlie found that the Governor's Handicap was being run in Reno the same time his train was due to arrive in that town. "I'm going to enter the filly, Lizette," Charlie told Etta.

The train was late, so when it stopped at Sparks, a town near Reno, Charlie got off and went into the depot. He asked the telegrapher to contact the race track superintendent to stall the parade to the post in Reno. "Just say that C. B. Irwin is coming a few minutes late." The superintendent knew the Irwin name was valuable to the track, so he notified the parade director and everything was stalled for a while.

Charlie and his jockey, Monty Edwards, unloaded Lizette. Edwards galloped the horse full speed to the track and directly to the barrier, which was a wide canvas and elastic band at that time. The jockey and horse arrived just as the starter sent all the horses down the track. Lizette came away from the line kicking and scratching all the way, even though she'd just run more than a mile. She won the Governor's Handicap.

Charlie got to the track by cab and missed the race. Etta stayed on the train and went on to San Diego by herself.

As far as earning money, Charlie was doing better than he'd ever done. In 1923, he had one hundred and forty-seven winners, which was a record for any horse owner in the United States. He knew it was because he was running three or four outfits at the same time. That way he could hit more races during the season.

Charlie's favorite track was Tia Juana. Ak-Sar-Ben in Omaha was a close second.

Charlie and his outfit had horses that often won over their heads. He made use of the claiming race to buy horses that no one else was interested in buying. That was how he bought Abadane. The horse was foaled in France and injured during the first World War by German shrapnel when the farm where he lived was repeatedly shelled. Both front legs were injured and he was shipped to the U.S. as a stud. Charlie let him spend a winter running free at the Cheyenne ranch. The cold and wind and constant running and foraging for food caused his legs to heal. "Leg up," Charlie called it. Abadane broke records from coast to coast. Another great race horse, Tubby A., ran five times in five days at Ak-Sar-Ben on a muddy track and won all five races.

The year 1924 seemed to be another turning point in Charlie's life. He'd bet on most anything. He was not disturbed if he lost one day, because the next he could be a winner.

It was early in the afternoon, Friday, November 28. Betts was still home on school holiday. Charlie took her to the track with him. He was going to teach his granddaughter how to bet on a good horse. He put five hundred dollars of wadded-up bills in one little fist and five hundred dollars in the other little fist. He put his hand under Betts's chin. "Now go out to that window and put this five hundred on Sea Mint to win and this five hundred on Motor Cop to place."

Betts nodded and followed the crowd down to the betting windows. In Tia Juana no one asked your age when you made a bet. They took your money and gave you a ticket.

"I want to bet five hundred on Motor Cop to win and five hundred on Sea Mint to place," she said, pushing the money through the window. She had to stand on tiptoes to pick up the tickets. When she got back to her seat she looked over the tickets, then out to the big, chalk board on the other side of the track. She couldn't breathe. She hitched over so she was sitting closer to her grandmother.

Charlie didn't seem to notice Betts's agitation. He kept his eyes on the track and hollered for Sea Mint to take longer strides. Sea Mint placed fifth—out of the running. Charlie yelled, "Pablo slept the whole time on that horse! I'm going to talk to my jockeys!"

Etta said, "Wait Charlie. Motor Cop came in first. Didn't you bet on him to place?"

"I sure did!" He sat down and grinned. "But Sea Mint was a cinch to win. Pablo is goofing off!" He stood up.

Betts knew she had to say something about the tickets clutched in her sweaty hands. "Oh, what am I going to do?" she whispered.

"What's that?" asked Charlie. "Either speak up or don't speak at all."

Betts couldn't say anything. She felt hot all over. The tickets were getting soggy. Finally she reached up and took hold of the bottom of Charlie's coat while he was standing. "Gramps?"

"Don't bother me right now, honey," he said. "I'm picking out a sure winner in this next race."

"Gramps?" she said, biting her lower lip.

"What do you want?"

"I made a mistake."

"What?"

"I got the names mixed and bet on the wrong horses."

"Let me see those tickets!"

She handed the tickets up to Charlie. He looked at them.

Betts said gritting her teeth, "I'm ready to be scolded, because I made a mistake."

Charlie was still looking at the tickets. One was no good. That was five hundred dollars down the drain. The other was on the long shot, Motor Cop, and he paid off in China! He had been a fifty to one shot. With five hundred dollars, Charlie had made twenty-five thousand dollars! He looked down at Betts and put his big hand on her shoulder. "So, that's what you were squirming around for. Jeems! The race could have gone differently and neither horse won, then if you mixed the tickets it wouldn't matter! You made a little mistake! You hear me?"

"Yes, Gramps," said Betts, with tears streaming down her face. "I'm really sorry I got it wrong. I won't do it again."

"All right. We'll see. Take this hundred dollar bill and bet on Dainty Lady to win for your grandmother."

Betts took the money and ran to the window without looking back.

While she was gone Etta told Charlie not to be so hard on the child. "She made you a wealthy man in about ten minutes."

"I'll let you buy her a new dress!" There was a wide grin on his face and a twinkle in his eyes.

Martinez rode Dainty Lady to the winner's circle at the end of the race. Betts jumped up and down with delight. "I told you I could learn to make a good bet!"

There were five races in the afternoon, and when they were over, he and Betts walked down to the bottom of the hill below the track and waited for Roy to come after them in a car. They stood close to the railroad track that separated the barns. Charlie kept his horses in a barn across the railroad tracks. Harry Walters kept some of his racehorses in a stable near the railroad tracks. Betts looked along the railroad track to see if she could find anyone she knew. Suddenly she grabbed Charlie's hand. "Gramps, there's smoke!"

Charlie hardly looked up. "That's smoke from a train, honey."

"No! The train just went by!" said Betts excitedly. She pointed to one of the barns on the slight rise called Rattlesnake Hill.

Charlie gazed over toward the barns just as someone ran out of one shabby, wooden structure and screamed, "Fire!"

He saw stable boys running to the burning barn to turn all the panicky horses loose. He thought, The barns are close. When one burns, chances are the other will also. Betts stood close to her grandfather.

She saw some of the horses plunging right back into the smoke to get inside the barn again. "Look at those stupid horses!" she cried.

Charlie wanted to run across the railroad track to the burning barn and help the stable boys. He took a deep breath and said to Betts, "Don't ever call a horse stupid for going back into the place it believes to be safe, the place where it's fed and brushed." A long silence followed as they watched the fire and smoke billowing up to the clear, blue sky like gray clouds tinged with red. "I hope someone sent for fire equipment." Charlie's face was flushed. He could hardly stand still.

Etta said, "Here comes Roy. He'll take Betts and me home. You go on over to Rattlesnake Hill and tell the stable boys their yelling is scaring the horses."

"There goes another barn!" yelled Charlie, hurrying across the tracks to send men here and there for shovels, axes, and water buckets.

The fire alarm had been sounded and Mexican soldiers were stopping all traffic at the border so that the fire engines would have plenty of room.

Charlie was on top of the highest barn directing the fire-fighting efforts in his loud, booming voice. He pointed out the buildings that needed to be watered down because there was a wind coming in off the ocean, spreading sparks to other rooftops. The wind became hot when it blew through the fire. Charlie perspired, breathed smoke, and coughed. He saw four horses go back into their burning barns. No one could get them out. Five barns blazed when the wind changed direction. He yelled at a little knot of men who were standing around talking. "Get some water over there!" Then he climbed off the roof and ran to one of the San Diego fire company trucks and asked the men to direct a stream of water on the blistering boards of the cookhouse. He sent another group of men to the southeast to beat out sparks that landed on the roofs of those stables.

One of the trainers, Pat Murphy, slipped off his stable roof and was cut about the face. Charlie examined him for broken bones. He called for Mexican soldiers to make a stretcher and carry Murphy to safety where a doctor could tape his broken ribs. Charlie wiped his face. His throat felt raw, seared from hot winds and smoke. He didn't notice that it was night time.

He formed a bucket brigade, where the fire companies could not take a truck and hose. He used an old man, Charley Beca, who was a former stable boy, to lead the chain of other stable hands to fight showers of sparks landing on two dry, wooden buildings.

Many of the horses were turned loose into the paddock behind the race track. Those that didn't head back for the barns ran off loose toward the hills beyond the far edge of town.

Mexican soldiers took drums of gasoline to an empty water pump near the grandstand where Charlie was directing more water brigades. As gasoline was poured into the water pump's engine, someone carelessly lit a cigarette. The flame ignited the vapors into an orange sheet that unfolded toward the back sky. Suddenly one of the gasoline drums exploded, knocking Charlie off his feet. He was so shaken he could do nothing but lie flat, clinging to a long board, which was a grandstand seat. He prayed the grandstand didn't catch on fire. He heard cries and shouts of men on the ground and the neighing and stomping of the horses in the paddock. Finally he felt a fine mist of water against his neck. He raised his head and saw San Diego firemen hosing the grandstand. Some of the nearby men were drenched. Some of the soldiers were trying to drive loose horses away from the paddock fence and into a ditch. The horses were wild with fear and plunged madly against the fence then into and out of the ditch.

They resisted every effort to control them. Charlie scrambled down and told the soldiers to leave the horses alone before someone was hurt. His voice was hoarse and he was bone tired. One of the soldiers told him that the fire started when some stable hands were cooking on a small oil stove and it exploded. Another said a careless match caught some papers under the grandstand. A stable boy said he'd heard a pop like a balloon, saw flames licking skyward from a rusty liniment can lying in the sun, and he was the first to cry "Fire!" Charlie was sure the fire was not intentional.

At dawn Charlie ran into Jack Akin, manager of the racetrack. Akin said he was going to make a telephone call to the Al G. Barnes Circus in San Diego. "I'm gonna ask the Barnes people to loan us some big circus tents to shelter the homeless horses."

Charlie said, "You get tents and I'll get food for everyone working here. I think part of my weak feeling is because I haven't eaten since noon yesterday!" Charlie looked at his pocket watch. "It's six in the morning!"

Charlie called Etta on the phone and told her to make as many roast beef and ham sandwiches as she could. "When you have a couple hundred, get Roy to put them in a big, cardboard box along with a change of clothes for me and bring them out to the track."

Next Charlie talked Baron Long, a thoroughbred owner with a gambler's reputation, into opening his unused, undamaged stables to some of the homeless horses. Charlie opened his own stables to homeless thoroughbreds.

The early morning sky darkened and a misty rain turned into a drenching downpour. About eight in the morning the rain slacked off to mist again. Roy brought a couple hundred sandwiches, oranges, and grapefruit to the track. Mexicans and Americans gathered around the pickup truck. Tired faces lit up as the food was passed around.

Charlie ate and talked to Roy. "Did you have trouble getting across the border?"

"No, I talked to Mr. Murkley, that short, square-shouldered customs agent. I think he recognized me as an Irwin. I gave him a sandwich and a couple of oranges. He let me across," said Roy. "He put that there sticker on the windshield." He pointed to a green square the size of a pack of cigarettes. "That makes the pickup an emergency vehicle. We can come and go across the border without being questioned."

"When you get to the ranch, call the lumber yards in San

Diego. Have them send out what lumber they can for rebuilding these barns and stables," said Charlie.

"I don't see how you can build anything unless you get the rest of that burned mess out of the way," said Roy. "The rain shoulda come last night!"

"Ya," agreed Charlie. "Tell Etta thanks for the clean clothes. I'll see her when I'm done here."

After he'd changed clothes he felt surprisingly refreshed and he went back up Rattlesnake Hill to help tear down the burned, smelly barns. The rain was still a gray mist and the wind came in unexpected gusts, causing the mist to feel like needles against the skin.

Before noon a truck carrying building material arrived. The following morning Roy brought more sandwiches and apples. Charlie kept trucks busy bringing in lumber, nails, and tar paper as men and bulldozers cleared the burned areas. The mist stopped, but the low fog, or marine layer, stayed. Electricians strung up arc lights so that rebuilding could go on through the night. Al Barnes brought in a huge tent where the horses could be kept altogether.

Monday Charlie paired John Singleton, one of his jockeys, with Harry Walters to round up as many of the horses that had gone to the hills as possible. Roy came with more food in the pickup. Some of the men clapped when they saw Roy coming alongside the track. Charlie went home with Roy.

"Oh, my arms, shoulders, and legs ache! Everything aches! I'll sleep for days!" he moaned. Charlie had not had more than ten-, fifteen-minute catnaps for three days and three nights.

By Tuesday morning the track was ready to be reopened. The only days that had been lost because of the fire were Saturday and Sunday. The track was always closed on Monday, same as any other form of live entertainment in California and Mexico. Al Barnes was back with a couple of his circus roustabouts to strike the big tent that had been loaned to the track and was no longer needed. Coffroth went out to shake Barnes's hand and tell him thanks.

In three days and three nights, not only was the fire out, but the stables were rebuilt, and hardly a thing remained to show that a disaster had taken place. Singleton and Walters replaced fifteen lost horses with twenty-four from the hills. They told Charlie that some of Pancho Villa's old soldiers were still in the hills rounding up stolen horses to sell to the Mexican Army cheap. A couple of the horses had to be shot because they'd run into the huge cactus plants that dotted the hills beyond Tia Juana and were badly injured. Extra horses were divided among owners who'd lost animals during the fire.

Coffroth, track owner, and Jack Akin, track manager, estimated that there had been seventy-five thousand dollars damage and twenty-five thousand dollars lost in horse feed and personal belongings of the stablemen. Coffroth had some insurance on the track and buildings, but not enough to cover all the damage.

Both fire fighting and construction had been a sensational effort by both Mexicans and Americans working side by side. But the most spectacular effort was shown by Charlie, who was now known as the man with a heart in his brisket as big as a saddle blanket.

Jack Akin organized a dinner at the Sunshine Inn to honor everyone who'd helped turn the disaster into a wonderful cooperative project. Al Barnes, proprietor of A. G. Barnes Circus; Talamantes, mayor of Tia Juana; Jesus Caves, Tia Juana chief of police; Lieutenant Colonel Gonzales, in charge of the Mexican Army; and Chief Almgren, San Diego Fire Department, were given special honors.

Charlie was honored with a French Petik Phillipe chiming pocket watch. The watch was also a stop watch. It was studded with diamonds and engraved with the date of the fire, Charlie's full name, and "from the Tia Juana Racing Association." Coffroth told Charlie the watch was worth more than a thousand dollars. Charlie was presented with a personal testimonial signed by one hundred and fifty horse owners, which stated, . . . "We intend this as an expression for his sterling worth as a great man and a friend."

Charlie stood up and expressed his deep gratitude and personal thanks. "I want everyone to know that there were more heroes during those three days than occur on most battlefields. There are unnamed jockeys and stable boys who worked far beyond the capacity they believed possible. This work was a team effort that the United States and Mexico should never forget. I'm so doggone proud of these international horsemen."

He was proud of Etta and her preparing food for the men fighting the fire and doing the rebuilding. Charlie decided to do something nice for her, like taking her to San Diego to see a picture show.

He loved any excuse to get dressed up and have Etta dressed in the latest fashion. He believed no expense was too great for the good clothes that he and Etta wore when they went out. He looked handsome in finely tailored suits, and shirts that were monogrammed with CBI on the left cuff. He always wore a conservative Western hat when he went out in the evening with Etta. The wide-brimmed, white Stetson was for rodeos and horse races.

This particular evening Etta wore a simple Georgette crepe in light blue. She wore diamond earrings, which Charlie bought back from the bank, a touch of Shalimar perfume, and a tiny nosegay of silk violets at her throat. She had a short ermine wrap over her shoulders and black patent-leather pumps over expensive silk stockings.

They were going to see Fairbanks's latest show, *Zorro*. Charlie loved the picture shows, especially the Westerns. He would laugh, even in the most serious episodes, at how wrong Hollywood made the cowboy and Indian pictures. He criticized the costumes, what the actors and actresses did, how they talked and rode horseback, but still he went to every new Western that came out.

This evening the temperature had dropped, causing a fog close to the warm ground. Etta fussed at Charlie's driving. "Don't go so fast!" she said several times. Then, "Charlie, we have plenty of time! Slow down!"

"Dear, when you have some place to go, it's best to get there as fast as possible. The Buick Roadster was built to have speed. If it can go forty or fifty miles an hour, why not let it. It's not speed that's unsafe. It's the driver that's not alert."

"The road is wet and slippery," she complained.

"Don't you think I'm aware of this misty fog? I adjust my driving to the conditions that prevail."

"Slow down, Charlie. You'll get us killed."

"That hurts my feelings. I would never do anything to hurt you and you know it."

Charlie didn't say anything for a while. He was concentrating on the road. Suddenly something loomed out of the darkness into the headlights. Charlie swerved to dodge it and he knew right away that had not been a good idea. He should have moved slower and not jammed his foot on the brakes. The Buick roadster skidded on the wet, slick pavement. Charlie had no control.

The car had flipped and landed on its top. Etta had been thrown out, but she was caught under the top so that one of the steel braces that held the stiff, canvas roof was bearing down on her throat. Charlie was way under the car, but not caught under one of the braces. He heard Etta moaning and making a gurgling sound. She was trying to call out to see if he was all right. Charlie felt around with his hands until he could tell exactly where Etta was. His hands shook. He couldn't see a thing.

"Dear, are you all right?"

"Eraugh!" she gasped as though being strangled.

He felt again and found the brace. It was across her throat and lower jaw. The ground was cold and damp. The dampness made it hard for him to move. He pushed himself, three, four inches at a time. It was hard work. He could feel his heart beat and smell the damp earth. He managed to move so that he was alongside Etta. Charlie's only thought now was to get the weight of the automobile off her throat. He moved so that her head and shoulders were away from the car. Then he managed to get his arms free. Etta was making strange gurgling sounds that frightened Charlie. He pushed on the brace with his free arms so that she could move out. She didn't move. He coaxed and urged. "Come on, dear, move, just a little. Move so you'll be away from that blasted brace." His arms trembled and were getting tired.

The roadside was dead quiet. He couldn't even hear Etta breathing. He couldn't see through the fog. Now he imagined he heard a car on the road, but it did not stop. His arms began to quiver violently from the tremendous weight he was holding. He moved his body under the metal brace and let it down slowly to rest on his abdomen. The pain was excruciating. For a moment Charlie thought he was going to pass out. He felt that his breathing was shallow. I am breathing, he said to himself. I can still move my arms. He could feel Etta's face with one hand. He smoothed her hair off her forehead. Her hair was wet and muddy. Her forehead was warm. That encouraged him. He talked to her, trying desperately to revive her with his voice. "Please! Say something to me! We'll get out of this. Everything will be fine."

Etta heard Charlie. Her neck hurt so much that she was afraid to swallow or push out air to talk. Saliva rolled out the side of her mouth. Tears ran down her face.

Charlie stopped talking and listened again. He felt sure he'd heard Etta breathing. "Oh, my dear, I'm so glad you are all right. Rest easy. Someone will find us. To tell the truth, I couldn't live without you." Suddenly he remembered the fog and wondered if the cars on the road could see there was an accident.

Etta tried to say something to reassure Charlie. She could not speak. Her throat felt completely closed. She braced herself, felt her toes curl in her shoes, she tried to swallow. Little by little she pushed the saliva down her throat. She'd felt the muscles move in her esophagus. Then she blacked out.

For two agonizing hours Charlie and Etta lay pinned under their Buick roadster until a rain shower cleared the fog and a driver noticed the overturned car and stopped. He walked around the car calling, "Anyone in there? Hey, anyone trapped inside?"

"We're here! Underneath!" called Charlie. "Get help. My wife can't speak!"

"Hold on!" The man said he'd send an ambulance right away.

Charlie hated to have the man leave him. But it was the only way to get help. Charlie kept his hand on Etta's face. Thank God, it's still warm, he thought. She's crying, the water on her face is warm! "Oh, dear! Can you hear me? I love you more than anything. Help is coming soon. Remember when I first saw you? You were the prettiest little thing I've ever seen in my life. I loved everything about you, the way you held your head, the way your eyes shone, the way you talked. You seemed to notice everything. You were so full of life. Jeems, where is that doggone ambulance?"

Later he could not remember if he'd fainted, but he never heard the ambulance drive up. At the hospital Charlie climbed off his stretcher. He would not let himself be carried inside. "I'm fine. Don't worry about me. Look at my wife. It's her neck." He did not want to concern himself with the ache in his stomach. He was sure it would disappear in a few days. He'd strained a muscle, sure, but it was nothing that would not heal.

Etta was X-rayed and found to have a broken left arm. Charlie insisted on being in the examining room. The doctor felt all around her neck, then had her open her mouth so he could see inside her throat. Her eyes darted from the doctor to Charlie and back to the doctor. She gagged and tears ran down her cheeks.

"Is that necessary?" asked Charlie with tears in his eyes. "Do you have to hurt her?"

"I want to make certain her neck's not broken. We'll keep your wife overnight," said the doctor. "You go home. Get some sleep."

Charlie phoned the ranch house and talked with Maria. "I'm staying in San Diego all night. I'll bring Mrs. Irwin home tomorrow. She'll be all right. The doctor is taking good care of her. Broke her arm, that's all." Charlie leaned against the wall a few moments to catch his breath. His stomach muscles felt worse than an exposed nerve and made him wince with burning pain more than once, especially when he bent over.

Next day he was at the hospital ready to take Etta home. The doctor smiled and told Charlie that Etta would have a neck that would be black and blue and sore as a boil for a few weeks. The bone fragments of her left arm had severed the outside flesh. Some of the bone had to be cut away. Etta was given the choice of having her arm heal so that she could not bend the elbow or having it heal with the elbow in a permanent bent position.

"Bent, so that I can put curlers in my hair," she said.

Charlie sent a wrecker after the roadster and had a garage look it over to make certain the car was in good working condition by the time he wanted it again. "I may run my campaign from that car, when I run for governor," roared Charlie.

After the first of the year both Charlie and Etta talked about how lucky they were.

FORTY-TWO

Family and Fortune

After the Frontier events Charlie took several of his cowboys and jockeys to the local rodeo in Rawlins, then to Las Vegas for a meeting of the Western Thoroughbred Horsemen's Association. The town was a supply post for local ranchers and had only wide, dirt roads. The men met and ate in the railroad beanery. Charlie was president of the association and set rules for safer racing conditions for both jockeys and horses. The year before he'd helped to standardize the betting rules. On the way back to Wyoming they stopped off for a couple local rodeos and for the big event in Salt Lake City. Roy won the steer-roping contest and bucking-horse contest in both Rawlins and Salt Lake. Charlie was so proud of him. In many ways Roy had taken the place of Floyd in his life.

While in Salt Lake, Charlie noticed that Roy wasn't going to town with the other men after the shows. He stayed close to the fairgrounds. Charlie assumed he was trying to save money, until he saw him with a pretty little Indian girl.

"Who's your friend?" asked Charlie.

At first Roy scowled, then he said, "She's only a friend. Smoky Morn needs someone to talk with. She's been hurt, so I kind of take care of her."

"Hope everything's going to be all right. Where's she from?"

"Oklahoma. She's Comanche."

"You're calf-eyed over a little Comanche girl?" Charlie held back his smile.

"Pa! She's a friend. Remember Harry Bowles?"

"Who could forget? He's the one raked Steamboat's sides raw!"

Roy's face turned red and he scuffed the dust with the toe of his boot. "She was Bowles's wife. At least, that's what he says. She's scared to death of him. She wants to go back to Oklahoma. I figured on buying her a bus ticket with some of my winnings. After the show today Bowles grabbed me in the tack room. He said he'd kill me if I laid a hand on Smoky Morn."

"Have you?" asked Charlie, wiping his face with a red bandanna.

"Laid a hand on her? Pa, what do you think? She's just a kid! Bowles is the one who's treated her bad."

The next day Charlie rode around the Salt Lake arena between events on his big white horse singing "Nellie Gray" and "Alfalfa Hay" through a giant bullhorn. He felt good and had the crowd singing with him. Then without warning there was a loud report, maybe two, close together. Charlie immediately thought it sounded like a revolver shot. The noise from the crowd became high-pitched like the buzzing of bees in a disturbed nest. He gave the bullhorn and reins to Sawyer and climbed from the saddle. "Announce the next event!" he called, and ducked under the grandstands and headed for the gate. There was a crowd of men milling around the stables. At the door of the tack room there was another crowd of men. Overriding the smell of hay, leather, and horse dung, Charlie could smell burnt gun powder. Someone grabbed his shoulder and shouted, "Bowles went in there about thirty minutes ago! He doesn't carry a gun!"

There was a push outward from the men closest to the door, then a third shot.

"He's killed him!" someone yelled.

"Who's he?" asked Charlie, trying to find out what was going on. He saw Ed Brown from Cheyenne waving his arms trying to get the crowd to move back. Then he stepped aside and Harry Bowles, dressed in disheveled yellow trousers and a gold shirt, slumped against Brown. Charlie drew in his breath. Bowles's face was ashen. Behind him was Roy, holding a revolver, looking scared to death.

Charlie pushed against the crowd that was moving away from the door as fast as possible. He felt the air around him hot and close. He licked his lips and felt the roughness of his tongue. He couldn't understand what anyone was saying. His heart thumped wildly. Now he could see blood dripping from the front of Bowles's shirt, down the right pants leg onto the rough wooden floor.

Charlie recognized the revolver Roy carried. It was the one kept in the tack room to be used if a horse broke a leg or had some other life-threatening accident. No one paid much attention to it hidden in a dusty cigar box on a shelf filled with liniment bottles and leather straps.

The crowd split in half to let the deputy sheriff through. He was back in a moment with Roy in handcuffs. Roy's face was white, as if bleached. His eyes met Charlie's. Charlie was dazed. He couldn't utter a word. He swayed. Someone behind him said, "You all right, C.B.?"

"I need air," Charlie moved away from the crowd. The breeze revived him. He moved. He walked. Finally he stopped. He didn't know where he was. He saw a truck load of cantaloupes come slowly up the gravel road. He stepped into the middle of the road and waved. "Say! Can you take me to the police station?"

The cantaloupe grower had a head as bald as one of his melons. "Get in, mister. I go right by there. You been robbed or somethin'?"

Charlie pulled himself inside and eased down on the seat. He didn't answer. He tried to breathe quietly, but his lungs needed great gulps of air. He felt like he'd been running. When the truck stopped, he gave the driver a five-dollar bill.

Inside the police station Charlie said he wanted to see a recent prisoner named Roy Kivett Irwin.

"Are you a relative?" asked the officer.

"I raised the boy."

"A blood relative?"

"No, sir."

"Your name?"

"Charles Burton Irwin."

"You a lawyer?"

"No, sir."

"I can't let you see the prisoner."

"What's he being held for?" Charlie licked his lips.

"Looks like first-degree murder." The officer shuffled papers.

"Bowles isn't dead! I saw him walk away from the tack room! Roy would never shoot unless it was self-defense!"

"The man died in the hospital. Looks like your man needs a good lawyer."

"I don't know any lawyers in Salt Lake!" shouted Charlie.

The officer looked up. "Call King, Schuler, and Grant Bagley. Saying around here is that they can find a cattle rustler not guilty."

Charlie had Grant Bagley at the police station in less than an hour. Bagley was dark-haired, medium build. He wore a red rubber cot over his right index finger and could page through a set of police files faster than anyone Charlie had seen.

"Looks like we've work to do, Mr. Irwin. I can't find anything on a Roy Irwin, but Harry Bowles has a record of horse thievin' in Salt Lake."

"Can I take Roy back to Cheyenne?" asked Charlie.

"No, and give me the name of the hotel where you're staying. I need witnesses. Round up some of Roy's friends—those who'd be willing to testify for him."

"I'll do anything if it helps," said Charlie.

Bagley left.

Charlie took a taxi back to the arena and helped his cowboys load the horses into boxcars. He couldn't answer all their questions. He didn't know what had happened until he read the next morning's *Salt Lake Tribune*, dated August 30, 1924. In the middle of the page was a picture of Bowles falling head first off a bucking horse at the fairgrounds minutes before he was shot in the tack room.

Kivett Faces Murder Trial—
First Degree Charges to be Filed
as Result of Killing at Rodeo.

Murder in the first degree is the charge which will be preferred in a complaint to be issued by the county attorney's office Tuesday against Roy Kivett, 24 . . . who, on Friday, shot and killed Harry Bowles, 26 . . . at the Salt Lake fair grounds. . . . Both Kivett and Bowles were riders at the rodeo.

The determination to file a first-degree murder charge followed a conference held yesterday at police headquarters . . . the nature of the information was not disclosed, it was said to be such as would justify the county attorney's office in issuing the complaint charging murder in the first degree.

At the emergency hospital, where he was taken following the shooting, Bowles denied that he had attacked Kivett with a knife. He said he had had trouble with Kivett at

> Rawlins, Wyo., about three weeks ago over his attention to Mrs. Bowles, and had threatened to 'beat him up' at that time. Since then, however, he said he had not spoken to him until they met at the fair grounds. He declared that he was unarmed, did not know Kivett was around until the man walked toward him with a gun in his hand and began shooting. Kivett claims Bowles started toward him with a knife and that he used the gun in self-defense. Kivett is also said to have claimed that he thought Bowles and his wife were divorced.*

After giving Bagley information about Roy's character, Charlie's cowboys went back to Cheyenne with the stock. Charlie remained at the Newhouse Hotel. When he was permitted to see Roy he asked him about the knife Bowles had used.

"Pa, you know I didn't shoot Bowles on purpose!" cried Roy.

"Yes, I know that. Tell me about the knife," said Charlie.

"I went to the tack room. I laid down before changing my clothes for the next event. I was thinking about winning the barrel race. Next thing I knew someone's standing beside the cot and light is flashing off a knife blade nearly blinding me." Both men sat on the edge of the narrow prison bed that had a thin mattress and one gray wool blanket. "Remember you once said, 'If you find yourself losing a tug-of-war with a tiger, throw him the rope before he gets your arm?' Well, that flashed through my mind and I reached up for that cigar box with the revolver. I threw it, box and all, at Harry. He dropped the knife. I reached for it, but he kicked it out of my reach. The revolver lay alongside the full clip. I grabbed and put them together as Harry came at me with the knife he'd picked up. He said I was too soft to pull the trigger and he lunged with the knife and I shot twice in the ceiling. He laughed. Then he came at me again. I put my foot out and he tripped. He swayed and fell. Before he could get up I threw the gun at his head, hoping to knock him cold. The gun went off when it hit the floor and the lead went into Bowles's chest. Ed Brown told me to carry the revolver out. He looked for the knife but never found it. The deputy sheriff never believed there was a knife!" Roy's shoulders shook. He put his head in his hands and sobbed.

*Reprinted with permission of *The Salt Lake Tribune* and courtesy of the Charles M. Bennett Collection, Scotsdale, Arizona.

Charlie reached out and touched Roy's arm. "I love you son. Etta and the girls love you."

"Ya, that's why I told the sheriff my name was Kivett. I didn't want to use my good Irwin name. I'd know that knife anywhere. It has a nick in the blade that looks like a tiny fish hook, otherwise it looks like yours or anybody else's pocketknife."

"Did you say that to the sheriff or the lawyer, Bagley?" asked Charlie.

"No, what's the use? They're not going to look for that knife!" cried Roy.

"Where's whatshername? Smoky Morn?"

"I gave her bus fare, maybe a little more. She left in the morning, before the shooting. Pa, she was a friend, nothing more."

Later that same day Bagley telephoned Charlie saying that Bowles's real name was Edward Vincent Bowles, Jr., and that the state had lined up a couple of men to testify as to his good character.

Charlie was livid. "That man was a bully and as crooked as a snake in a cactus bed!"

Bagley said slowly, "Mr. Irwin, tell me about this woman Roy was seeing."

"The boy is twenty-four and he doesn't ask me every time he comes and goes. I don't know that he was seeing anyone."

"Does he prefer the company of Indian women?"

"What kind of question is that? He likes people for what they are. He has good manners."

"This lady he's alleged to be seeing is alleged to have belonged to Bowles."

"No person belongs to another!" Charlie was angry.

"Roy says he thought the woman and Bowles were divorced."

"So what did Bowles say?" asked Charlie. His hands were sweaty.

"Bowles never said."

"What does the lady say?"

"We can't locate her."

"Slipped out of the loop, huh? Not unusual for an Indian, huh?"

"I couldn't have said it better," said Bagley. "I'll call you later."

Charlie sat at the small table in his hotel room and made a list of the people who'd been with Roy early the morning of August twenty-ninth; Claude and Pauline Sawyer, Ed Brown, Ed McCarty, Fred Hirsig, all from Cheyenne; Bill Wildman from Lawrenceburg, Tennessee; and Louis Kubitz from Fort Worth, Texas.

Bagley called again to say things were progressing and that he wished someone had found the knife, if there really was one. Charlie read him the list and asked what would happen when a jury heard Roy's story and there was no knife to back it up.

"No telling—each jury is different," said Bagley.

Charlie called Etta and told her not to worry. He couldn't sit still. He knew that knife was somewhere in that tack room. He called Bagley. "I want to look in the tack room for the knife, you want to come with me?" said Charlie. Bagley grunted and agreed to come.

Charlie took a taxi from the hotel. He said to the driver, "I want to check a theory I have. Let me see your pocketknife. I'll give it right back." The driver pulled a jackknife from his front pocket. The handle was black bone, the two blades were stainless steel, one long, one short. There was a corkscrew and a little spoon to clean out a pipe. "Yep," sad Charlie, handing it back. "It's like mine." He took out his handkerchief and unrolled the black, bone-handled jackknife, careful not to get his finger marks on it. He let the driver hold his knife, open it, close it. Charlie put it back in his handkerchief and slipped it in his pocket.

"Everybody carries the same kind of a pocketknife. Some have light-colored handles, only difference."

"Yep, only difference," said Charlie, looking out the window.

Bagley was waiting for him at the fairgrounds gate. The grounds were empty. The guard let them in the double gate and led them to the stables, then pointed out the tack room, which was unlocked. Charlie felt on the wall for the light switch. The day was cloudy and the window so small there was not much light coming through, except when the sun was on the side of the building in late afternoon. Charlie remembered Roy was going to enter the barrel race which was performed late in the afternoon. The sun would shine through the window and glint off a knife blade. Roy couldn't make that up. He told Bagley, who wrote something in a notebook and slipped it into his coat pocket.

Charlie moved the bed and got down on his hands and knees

to look behind. "Jeems, I wish someone would sweep these places out!" he said. He wondered how he'd drop the knife from his pocket. And if he did manage to drop it, would Bagley find it? Worse yet, would Roy realize it was not the knife with a nick in the blade? His head swirled.

Bagley moved some leather straps and mumbled that he'd already looked through that mess before. Charlie pushed around a stack of old rodeo programs and racehorse magazines, then said, "Do you know where the two men were when the gun last fired?"

"I suppose Roy was standing in front of Bowles," said Bagley, looking up at the two holes in the ceiling.

Charlie found the cigar box. It was dusty and empty. He tried to imagine the gun inside. He moved a ratty-looking saddle that was in the corner at the foot of the cot. He prayed the real knife would be found so he wouldn't have to plant his own. His head ached. He heard Bagley pushing through the old magazines and slamming them against the wall, then rummage through some worn saddle blankets.

"I agree, this place is a mess! It's a fire hazard!" cried Bagley.

Charlie pulled up a handful of forgotten hardware and opened his hand to let the junk slide out. In the center of buckles and rivets was a black, one-bladed jackknife. The long blade was exposed. The blade had a deep, curved nick in the center and looked wicked. Charlie put his hand in his pocket and felt his own pocket knife. He let out a lungful of air and cried, "Look at this baby! I could have cut my hand!"

The pretrial was scheduled for the tenth of November. Roy told Charlie to go back to Cheyenne. "I'll be all right. But write to me so I know what's going on."

"Keep your chin up. I'll be back," promised Charlie.

The next weeks were hard on Charlie and Etta. He lay in bed sleepless going over every little question and the answers he'd given to Bagley. Etta asked more questions than Bagley ever thought of. Charlie sent his managers to rodeos and horse races. Bob Liehe went to Pendleton, Oregon, with Irwin horses and Charlie took Rip Rap, Prickly Heat, General Jackson, and Sannabar to the Delmar track in St. Louis. He had with him Wee Willie Moran, one of his best jockeys. Moran astounded the St. Louis crowd by winning for Charlie three consecutive purses in one afternoon.

An eastern horse owner said, "Mr. Irwin, I hear you work your horses over much."

"I rarely work my horses," said Charlie. "My racers have the best hot mash money can buy. They appreciate good food. I know, because they never sulk in my stable. Sure, I run my horses. A horse never wins a race it doesn't enter. I let my horses find their own condition on the racetrack and when they do I keep 'em going. Never hurt a horse to race more than once a day, three, four times a week, when it's in top condition. A racehorse likes to run. When one of my horses doesn't want to run anymore I take it out to pasture or sell it to some easterner." Charlie noticed that the horse owner was well dressed and wore a diamond ring. He looked like he was making money.

The owner combed his hair and squinted up at Charlie and said, "I'd like to make you an offer you can't turn down, Mr. Irwin. I want you to be my trainer. I'll pay you a thousand dollars a week plus expenses."

Charlie was stunned. He'd never had an offer like this before. He took a deep breath, then said, "Thanks a heap. I'm honored with your offer. But I don't want to get tied up so I can't be free to hit the rodeo circuit or the small, exciting western racetracks when I feel like it. When I decide to change my routine, I'm going to run for political office." He grinned and held out his hand.

The eastern owner was disappointed, but not surprised. He shook Charlie's hand and said, "Mr. Irwin, from what I hear you could run for president of the United States and get the job."

Charlie left St. Louis thinking he was ready to face Roy's pretrial.

Charlie rode one of the horses kept in the stables in Cheyenne to the Four-Mile pasture. He couldn't stop thinking about Roy. He loved him as his own son. In many ways Roy had taken the place of Floyd in his life. Now Roy was in jail. He kept a mental image of Roy sitting alone, his hands in his lap, his face guiltless, and his spirit vulnerable.

Roy, standing there with a revolver in his hand as Harry Bowles, blood dripping from the front of his shirt, was carried from the tack room. Roy is just an innocent kid, just starting to live, thought Charlie. Roy was trying to do some good for a downtrodden human being. He'd taught his children that was the highest thing a man could do. Where did it get him? What's wrong with the world? What's wrong with our ideals, our laws? Then he remembered that this problem was only in his own mind. He was building Roy's trial into something that had not even taken place.

He leaned against a cottonwood tree and looked through its naked branches toward the sky. Looks like snow, he thought. I can't stop the snow. I can't stop what is going to take place on the eleventh. But I can be positive and give the most favorable testimony I'm able to give when called to the witness stand. I can reassure Roy. Who am I helping with this moping? Jeems! A man thinks he's strong and can handle anything. But it's not true. A man needs strength from something outside himself. My pa was a believer in God. I was raised to believe, but somehow I always thought it was something women and sick old men fell back on. I always thought I knew how to die standing up. I don't.

I'm full of knots and tighter than piano wire. I was already believing the worst. God—loosen me up and point me in the right direction. Charlie sighed. The sky had darkened and small snowflakes were falling. He held his hand out and the flakes melted. His hand was wet. He pulled his gloves from his coat pocket and put them on. He wondered how he was going to get the witnesses to Salt Lake. He thought he could drive one automobile and Pauline could drive another with them. Maybe they'd all rather go by train. He'd pay for the transportation and lodging of these people to Salt Lake and back. They were his friends, Roy's friends. Each one would have acted as Roy had done in similar circumstances. Those people believed Roy was not guilty of murder but had acted in self-defense.

Where are my thoughts getting me now?

Suddenly Charlie's thoughts took a different turn. When I'm in trouble do I call upon the Lord? When things are smooth I never think of the Lord. Do I get down on my knees and taffy up the Lord when the trouble gets so great I can't take care of it myself? I'm doing just that. Is that wrong? The Lord must know I trouble Him only when it's necessary. Other times I leave Him alone so He can take care of other poor devils in trouble. Is the Lord so egotistic that He needs praising? No, not my Lord! My Lord is strong as an ox and smart as a bunkhouse rat. If He made

Himself visible, He'd be tall with hair on His belly. He'd be gentle, slow-acting as wet gun powder, and calm as a horse trough.

With a guy like that on my side, I don't have to feel so depressed. Etta shouldn't have to call me a gloomy gus. Charlie scanned the gray-blue sky before going home. He looked at the place he always saw the ice-chip that was the morning star. There was nothing, only the gray-blue covering. The wind was sharp. He thought about the big snow that was soon to come.

The next day he met the witnesses who'd been subpoenaed from the Cheyenne area to testify on behalf of Roy. They were at the depot in time to take the morning train west to Salt Lake.

On the morning of the eleventh the courtroom was packed. In the courtroom the exhibits were displayed on a long oak table. The long underwear worn by Bowles was kind of doubled up so that only the bloody hole made by the bullet shot at close range was in plain sight. A flannel shirt was spread out, front side up to show that the hole in it matched the one in the underwear. The lead slug that had been taken from the chest of Harry Bowles. It was dark gray and looked more like a sinker used on fish line to Charlie. Next to the lead slug was a pair of blue denim pants, false teeth, an upper plate, and a map of Utah.

Exhibits on the defendant's side were a blue-black revolver tied to a cardboard, labeled Exhibit No. 1, and a black, bone-handled jackknife, with the large nicked blade extended. The knife was tied to a cardboard and marked Exhibit No. 2.

Ed Brown was called upon to answer how he heard the shots and ran into the tack room to carry out Bowles, who was struggling to get at Roy with his knife. Then John Kercher, a local cowboy, was called upon to answer questions about what he'd heard and seen. Bowles's mother and sister were called to vouch for the character of the plaintiff.

Jamison and Ensign, who were friends of Bowles and had come all the way from California, did their best to show that Bowles was always in control of his temper, but were not able to cover up the fact that he was plagued with a streak of jealousy all his life.

"Did Mr. Bowles marry, then divorce, the woman known as Smoky Morn?" asked Bagley of Jamison.

"Oh, yes, they were married in Oklahoma before Harry rodeoed at Stockton. He brought her with him and had her sit in the grandstand. Wouldn't let nobody sit with her. Poor thing."

"What does Mr. Jamison mean by 'poor thing'?" Bagley asked Ensign.

"Well, maybe he means that Harry slapped his wife around if she talked to any of us."

"Did you know that he'd divorced this woman?" Bagley asked Jamison.

"Well, yes. I know he tried to get the marriage annulled. But he wouldn't let the girl go back to her people. He told me that the Comanche will cut the nose off an adultress. So that he was keeping the woman from harm even though she no longer belonged to him."

"Mr. Bowles had altruistic motives in caring for his ex-wife. Is that right, Mr. Ensign?"

"Well, I don't know altruistic, but I do know that he beat her pretty bad, black and blue, if she even looked at another man. Harry was a drinker, and that didn't help his temper."

When the questioning of both sides was over, Judge McCrea said that the pretrial discovery was complete and the trial was scheduled for November twenty-fifth.

Charlie embraced Roy and said they'd all be back in two weeks.

"How'd I do?" asked Roy. "Pa, I was never so scared in all my life."

"You told the truth. You did the best any man could do. I can see no reason why a jury wouldn't believe your side. But don't count on luck. Etta sends her love."

The next two weeks Charlie tried to remember what the facial expression of the judge was at the end of the two days. He tried to remember if Roy was overly depressed or if he was buoyed by the pretrial. He didn't go to the ranch. He stayed in his office at the Plains Hotel from sunup to sundown. He cleaned out the files and ordered new chairs. He varnished the woodwork.

There were newspaper men and many rodeo enthusiasts who were interested in the fate of Charlie Irwin's foster son. The judge let Grant Bagley call several of his witnesses. Pauline told what a good worker Roy was on the ranch and how talented he was as a roper. "He's a brother to me," she said. "He is kind and considerate. Why, once when I was younger I cut his hair and to get even he cut mine." The court laughed softly, understanding that kind of brother-sister relationship.

The jury was given a twenty-page set of instructions, which included thirty-seven definitions, pleas, and statutes pertinent to the case of the State of Utah versus Roy Kivett. The jurors were sent out to deliberate. The judge would not let anyone leave the courtroom. He said he'd wait an hour and see what happened, then he would determine if the court should reconvene in the afternoon or the following day.

The foreman read, "We, the jurors impaneled in the above case, find the defendant not guilty."

The judge stood up, pounded his gavel once, and repeated the verdict twice. "Roy Kivett is acquitted!" he cried out.

Roy was white-faced. His bottom lip trembled.

Charlie smiled at Roy. Suddenly the lump in his throat was gone. His hands stopped perspiring and his stomach was not growling. The water in his eyes spilled over and he mopped his face. Roy smiled. Then he and Charlie were locked in a bear hug.

When Roy was safely back on the Y6, Charlie was in town with Etta. He hung around the kitchen as she did the dishes after supper. One evening he told her how good it was to be home with nothing to worry about except getting horses and men from one place to another and to find a suitable gate or starting barrier for horses at the beginning of a race. "Horses need to be kept in line so they all start at the same time."

"Some horses tend to stall before stretching out into the race," Etta laughed. "I suppose you'd like something to get those horses wound up so every one starts in a straight line."

"Stall! I'll tell you who stalls!" Charlie's voice was loud. "It's those lawyers! They stall and act like they are on to something big. I got a letter from Bagley today with a bill. It's big as an elephant! You want to know the truth. It was not one lawyer who swayed Roy's jury."

"Who then?" asked Etta putting her tiny hand over Charlie's big one.

"It was the eloquence, good sense, and plain, everyday language used by the cowboys that showed what Roy was like, even what Bowles was like. Now I have to pay a fortune to the firm of King, Schuler, and Bagley to prove that Roy was not a murderer, and we knew it all along."

"Do you resent paying them?" Etta's voice was steady, clear as a mockingbird early in the morning.

"It's not that I resent paying to have Roy acquitted, dear. It's just that I could have hunted up the evidence, called people for both sides together, talked with the jurors in less time, less words, and less typewritten sheets, and come out with the same verdict. But I had to go through the legal system! The system needs help! Its rules need changing!"

"Charlie, if you don't like the rules—change them. People can do that in this country."

"I'd change a few! Etta, don't make a funny face! When I'm governor I'll put a stop to these blamed lawyers taking months to complete litigation on a trivial case."

The telephone rang. It was Eddie Thomas on the West Coast to tell Charlie there was to be a rodeo in Chicago and could he supply men and stock. He added, "C.B., there was a flashy little number that performed in last year's Frontier, in the ladies' relay. She had that shiny stuff on her clothes."

"I know who you're talking about, Josephine Wicks," said Charlie.

"You get hold of her. Ask her to work for you." Thomas hung up.

Josephine was college-educated. Her shirts were sequined. She wore a divided skirt that not only had elastic around the waistband but also around the legs, so that when she rode the effect was a kind of balloon pants in bright colors. Charlie located her in Oklahoma. She was enthusiastic about working for the Irwin Y6 and asked Charlie if he had suggestions to improve her performance.

"Don't ever be ordinary," he said. "People are used to ordinary and don't look twice. Stay different and knock their socks off!"

When Charlie saw her again she had the most colorful boots of anyone on the rodeo circuit. The boots were tan on the foot, with blue tops inlaid with white designs. She was one of the best women relay riders Charlie ever had.

After the Chicago rodeo Charlie took his group to Des

Moines, Omaha, and Denver. Then he was back in Cheyenne for this year's Frontier. During the festivities Molly Sawyer, Claude's sister, who taught at the one-room school near Meriden, married one of the cowboys, Bill Scoon. The wedding was a big affair in the Horse Creek district.

Eddie Thomas called again to tell Charlie about a rodeo taking place in Salt Lake City. "The officials want you to be arena manager besides supplying all the men and stock for the show."

"That sounds good!" said Charlie.

That night during supper he asked Roy if he'd go to Salt Lake and enter the bronc-riding and steer-roping contests. "This is going to be a big affair. Sawyer and Pauline are coming. Even Frances is coming for the cowgirls' stake race. Sharkey's coming with Curly McGuckin, Clayton Danks—it's a big affair, same as Molly and Bill's wedding."

Roy hesitated. He felt uneasy. He had told Charlie that he'd never go back to Salt Lake as long as he lived. "I was lucky to get out of that town alive. I don't want to go back, Pa."

Charlie held his arms across his stomach and pushed inward slowly to ease the pain that seemed to be a constant reminder of that foggy night in San Diego when he had the automobile accident. "Son, you work for me. And as long as you do, you'll do as I say. Work Salt Lake one more time and I'll not ask you to go there again."

Roy's hands curled into tight balls. His mouth became thin, a straight line.

"Go on now. Get the stock ready," said Charlie.

Roy left the table and went out the back door.

Etta saw the pained look on Roy's face as he left. She said, "Let Roy stay at the ranch and work with his horses this trip. He went through a terrible ordeal in Salt Lake. His pain is still deep. The scar hasn't healed. I wish you hadn't told him he had to go." She was overcome by a sudden rush of emotion. "The spirit of Harry Bowles is still there in Salt Lake." Her throat constricted. She licked her dry lips.

Charlie wiped his mouth and pushed his chair away from the table. "Dear, you've listened to my sister, Ell, so much you sound like her. Salt Lake is a town, like any other. At their fairgrounds there are grandstands that hold ten thousand people. The old paddock is enlarged and the tack room is completely rebuilt. There's nothing left of the old place."

Etta stood up and said, "Charlie, don't make Roy go. Can't

you see how uncomfortable you've made him?"

"He has to go back to fight this thing that's in his mind. When one of the kids fell off a horse, didn't I put him back on the horse and tell him to ride again? Roy has to do the same. Like when he learned to swim. He'll be stronger for having gone back." Charlie's eyes lingered on Etta to make sure she understood. He wanted to hold her close and reassure her. He thought, Women can make themselves half sick with some soft-headed idea. "Why don't you and Betts come to Salt Lake? We'll stay at the Newhouse Hotel and see a stage play."

The grandstands were filled along with the bleacher seats the first day of Salt Lake's second annual round-up. Between acts men with drums of water on go-carts sprayed the arena's track to keep the dust down. Charlie rode his white horse and announced each event through a loud speaker. Clayton Danks was one of the arena and track judges that year.

Ike Rude, in a red and white Irwin shirt, came in third in the colt-roping contest. Pauline was first and Frances third in the cowgirls' stake race. Sawyer won the cowboys' relay race, Curly McGuckin was second. Charlie waved to Etta and Betts and sang "Singin' in the Rain." He rubbed his stomach and thought he was really feeling better. Roy came in second in the bucking-bronc contest. Charlie clapped and waved his arms. "That's Roy Kivett Irwin! That's my son!" he shouted.

During the bucking Roy's shirt was torn so he ran to the tack room to change. The next to the last event was steer roping. Sawyer had the best time until a man from Utah came in six seconds faster. Now it was up to Roy if an Irwin man was to take first in this event. Charlie boasted through the loudspeaker. "Ladies and gentlemen, the next man out of the chute is that first-class roper from Cheyenne, Roy Irwin! Give him a hearty hand!"

The crowd roared and cheered.

Charlie moved off the field so that Roy would have all the room he needed to go after his steer. Charlie felt the tingle of excitement and waved his Stetson hoping that Roy would notice and know Charlie was back of him all the way. Nothing could stop the Irwin riders this day!

Roy nodded slightly and brought his left hand down, indicating that he was seated on his horse and ready to go. The gate was opened, and in a borrowed golden silk shirt he raced his horse with great skill and confidence. He threw his lariat over the steer's horns just past the center of the arena, and just as Charlie yelled, "Son! Where'd you get that shirt? Get it off!"

Roy's horse, Beatty, backed up one or two steps after the rope was thrown so that the rope was taut. The rope was caught around the horse's leg. Roy thought the horse stumbled, but he was not certain it meant anything. He slid up and spoke softly in the horse's ear to keep it calm. Then suddenly the horse reared its head backward. Roy could not swing his weight back from the oncoming head fast enough. There was a loud crack, almost like a pistol retort.

Charlie's heart stopped beating for a moment. The crowd was on its feet, screaming. Charlie saw Roy's legs involuntarily grip the sides of the horse and hang on. The horse went down on its side and rolled to its back, pinning Roy, who was unconscious, with the front of his head split open, underneath. Instantly there were cowboys out on the field. Someone got the horse to its feet and led it away. Charlie bent over Roy, whose head was turned at an impossible angle. Charlie put his hand on Roy's forehead, then to the side of his neck. There was no pulse. He moved his thumb slowly over the warm, sweaty neck and saw the oozing red split in the head, just back of the hairline, where the horse had hit. Seven years ago and one month, Floyd was killed in the very same manner, he thought.

Etta was devastated. Roy was buried in Kansas City, where his natural mother, who had married P. H. Dunn, now lived.

Back in Cheyenne, Charlie received envelopes with a dollar or two from cowboys all over the northwest. Most of the notes asked that the money be used in some way to commemorate Roy. Charlie used the money to buy a marble headstone for his foster son's last resting place. He felt as though the breaks in his heart were almost beyond healing.

Several weeks later Etta said, "Charlie, let's go to San Ysidro tomorrow. I can get Betts ready. Can you get ready? We have to find a way to be happy again. These ups and downs do something to a body."

The first visitor at San Ysidro was Will Rogers. He said he was bushed and needed a rest.

Etta was glad to have Rogers to talk with. She told him that Frances had a baby, born on Washington's birthday, named Robert Charles. "But we've already nicknamed him Irwin. Remember Birdie Smith, sister of the twins? She went off with

Charlie's foreman, Mark Eisley. They are married and homesteading near Rockeagle."

"That reminds me that I want baking-powder biscuits and honey every morning, Mother Irwin," said Rogers.

"What are you going to do to justify such a breakfast?" Etta gave Rogers a hug.

"I'm going to keep one of your easy chairs warm and once in a while exercise one of the really tame racehorses."

That evening Charlie and Rogers talked about aeroplanes and the airmail service that was becoming an established mode of shipping between New York and San Francisco, and horse-racing gates.

Charlie thought he had a practical idea, and he put it to use at the Tia Juana track. One afternoon the horse-racing fans in Mexico were treated to the sight of one of the first wire cable barrier gates ever used on a racetrack. Coffroth gave Charlie permission to use the steel cable barrier for the first race in the 1926 Handicap. Charlie had scaffolding built on either side of the starting line. Similar to the rope or canvas barrier, the cable was to be pulled up the instant it was time for the horses to leap forward.

Baron Long told Charlie that he didn't believe horse owners had any business trying to improve horse racing. "It's been satisfactory with a line drawn in the dirt and a gun or drum to get the horses going."

"The steel cable is going to be revolutionary," said Charlie.

The steel cable almost caused a small revolution. Minutes before the Handicap, Charlie was posed on the scaffolding near the barrier. He had it pulled across the track. The horses lined up close when the clocker brought down the flag. Charlie jerked the cable up fast. It was heavy and unwieldy. The horses broke loose in some confusion. Not until the first race was over was it learned that one of Baron Long's jockeys had an ear cut off by the jerk of the cable wire.

In the four days of the Handicap, Charlie bet and lost eleven thousand dollars on his own horses. He couldn't figure out what was taking place. He became morose and depressed.

Etta decided she wasn't going to have her good dinners spoiled by Charlie with a long face. She made his favorite, a New England boiled dinner, with a big pot roast and vegetables. When Charlie and the men were seated she said, "Please don't get the potatoes mixed with the turnips. They're about the same size.

Push out the turnips if you don't care for them."

"Why put them in?" asked Rogers.

"For flavor," said Etta.

"I guess I can tell the difference between a potato and a turnip," said Rogers, making a little pile of turnips on his plate.

Charlie held his fork in the air. "For that matter I can tell the difference between good food and bad and good men and bad."

One of the men, Smith, pretended he hadn't heard and began to eat. The other men sat quietly and waited for Charlie to say what was on his mind.

"Smith! How much is Long paying you to hold back my horses?"

"I don't know what you're talking about," said Smith. His blond hair fell across his forehead and into his eyes.

"You're not even decent enough to come clean with it. My men didn't tattle on you, because the men who work for me stick together. But they knew your days were numbered. Today I saw you take a pay envelope from my place and go directly to the Long stables, stand in line, and take a pay envelope there!"

Smith's mouth fell open.

"Get your gear and get out!" shouted Charlie.

Rogers sat by the window and watched him go into the bunkhouse and come out again with a bundle of clothes under one arm and his saddle under the other. "He's gone," he said.

Everyone seemed to sigh together. Martinez broke out with a smile. "*¡Caramba!* I didn't want to be a tattletale!"

"Let's enjoy this good food!" said Rogers. "I'm glad this nonsense is over. I'm tired of spying on the bunkhouse."

Charlie ate with gusto. He put one last forkful into his mouth. The tangy, bitter taste of turnip was noticeable. He sputtered and the mouthful of turnip flew all over the rug.

Etta's face turned red. She took a deep breath and walked to Charlie's chair. She shook her forefinger at him. "I have had all I'm going to take of your feeling sorry for yourself." She bent a little closer and her forefinger touched the end of Charlie's nose each time she spoke a word. "It's time you felt good about yourself. Then the rest of us will feel good about you! The whole world will look better to all of us!"

Rogers had to keep a hand over his mouth to keep from giggling. He'd never seen Etta so angry.

She continued, "Charlie, you are going to change your disposition. You are going to be a little nicer around here!" Then, *whop!* She cracked him on the end of his nose. "And don't you ever spit anything on my good oriental carpet again!" Slowly she marched back to her chair and sat down, slid her napkin across her lap, and began to eat. There was no other sound except the rhythmic scraping of her fork against her plate.

Charlie's eyes were wide open. Etta was a Liliputian with a giant temper. She waved her left arm, permanently bent at the elbow, like a scyth cutting the air. Charlie bunched up his napkin and pushed his chair from the table and went into the living room. He prayed no one would come and see him with tears in his eyes. He was ashamed of himself. He wiped his eyes on his handkerchief and heard Etta say in a clear voice, "Everybody eat. This is good food and I don't want it to go to waste." Later he heard Etta and Rogers talking as they took the dishes into the kitchen for Maria to wash. Then Etta was standing in front of him.

"Oh, Charlie, I am so sorry. Forgive me. I didn't know any other way to snap you out of your terrible grouchy humor. You're hurting yourself and all the rest of us."

"I lost an awful lot of money and some poor kid lost an ear," he said.

"You can use that boy as one of your jockeys if Baron Long lets him go. And never mind the money. You'll make that up. And so what if you don't—we'll live off the ranch here or in Cheyenne. We'll never starve." She handed him a wet rag and a dry towel. "Go out there and clean up my carpet."

One of the men who helped with chores around the yard came in while he was on his hands and knees scrubbing the carpet. The man was called Sam Volcano, but he never showed a temper nor flared up under any circumstances. Volcano stood in the doorway and *tee-hee*ed several times. Charlie sat back on his haunches and said, "Haven't you ever seen anyone on hands and knees before?"

"Oh, yes, Mr. Irwin, ha ha, but I never expected you, the boss—ha ha!"

Charlie pushed himself to his feet, laid the towel and wet rag on the table, and went after Volcano on the back porch. Charlie shot a fist out, but missed. Volcano ducked and dodged and moved against the wall where pails, cans, and washtubs hung. He knocked off a couple pails and some cans rolled across the porch, making a terrible racket. Charlie went after Volcano again, feeling better all the time. He made a grimacing face, causing the white crescent scar on his forehead to shine. Volcano yelled as more cans and pails rattled and scattered around the porch. Charlie began to laugh. He saw men from the bunkhouse gathered out in the yard looking in. Etta and Rogers stood in the kitchen door.

A deep bellow came from the pit of Charlie's stomach. He said, "Look at the awful mess you've made here, Sam! You better pick this up. What would Mrs. Irwin say?" Then he laughed so hard his eyes watered. "Jeems! Sam, you looked so funny trying to fight off all those pails and cans and washtubs at the same time! Ha! Ha! Here, let me help you get your foot out of that pail!"

Now everybody was laughing. "Come in the house and we'll sing some songs," said Etta.

"Volcano chooses the first song!" said Rogers.

"'Yes, We Have No Bananas'!" shouted Volcano, putting his hand on Charlie's shoulder.

Later that night Etta told Charlie she'd like a little saucepan. "Something tiny to melt butter in for popcorn like we had tonight. All my pans are too big. The butter gets lost in them."

In the morning Charlie took the Buick touring car to San Diego. When he came home the back of the car was loaded with all sizes of pots and pans, two hundred dollars worth of cooking utensils.

Etta was flabbergasted. "I needed one, a little bitty saucepan. You didn't have to spend all that money. We're nearly broke."

"Fiddlesticks!" said Charlie. "You deserve the best. You mean more to me than anything. What's money? I'll make more."

Rogers came out to help put the pans in the kitchen. "If you want to be rich, give," he said.

"Who said that?" asked Etta.

"I did," said Rogers, smiling. "And I found out that the fellow called Smith put chloral hydrate in one of Charlie's watering troughs at the track. No wonder his horses couldn't run! They were drinking knockout drops!"

The next day Charlie bet five hundred dollars on Lizette in the third race to win. The horse won. One of Long's horses came in last. Charlie saw the large copper-colored stallion in the paddock and knew it should be a winner. He knew what Long was doing. A little chloral hydrate kept the horse slow until it got a reputation for being a plodder. Then it would be listed as a fifty to one shot. The day that horse is let go Long will make a lot of money, he thought. The day the horse, called Conquistador, came in a winner, Long sold it to a man from Chicago who was in Tia Juana.

Charlie's stomach cramped with gnawing spasms and he thought it was because he really wanted the big, beautiful stallion. He went to see the man from Chicago. "I hear you bought a real hay burner. I'll take it if you want to get rid of it."

"Well," said the man, who was a breeder, "the horse's hops are too broad for a good runner. He's not as good as I thought. But he's worth a fortune as a stud! That horse is the son of Man-O-War!"

"I don't have much to give for him, but I'll see if I can scrap up your asking price." The next day he was back with the twenty-five thousand dollars the man wanted. Charlie knew if he didn't buy the horse there were plenty of others who'd get the money and think they had a bargain. He was pleased to own Conquistador. He took him to the Y6 to run in the hills, feel the frost on his legs, and the rich, Wyoming grass in his belly.

During the 1927 Frontier festivities Charlie tried a new racing barrier. He'd done away with the dangerous cable and now had a flexible elastic barrier. The band was held by two men, one on each side of the track. An elaborate scaffolding was not necessary. When the signal was given the flexible barrier flew open and fell in a quivering heap that frightened the horses so they ran in panic. The audience doubled over with laughter. Before the festivities were over the barrier was called the "Irwin slingshot." However, this was the beginning of the serious racing barrier and it was used at several western tracks that summer during rodeos and horse races.

During that same summer Charlie hired several girls to work in his rodeos, including Lorena Trickey and Vera McGinnis. He'd seen Trickey win the *Denver Post*'s relay race in 1920 and 1921 in Cheyenne and knew that such a superb rider would make a smart addition to the Irwin team. The Irwin riders won the ladies' relay all four days in Pendleton, Oregon. McGinnis won the first silver loving cup Pendleton gave for the relay.

Charlie's Delco apparatus at the Y6 made the coal-oil lamps obsolete. The motor was stored in the first room of the basement. There were electric lights all over and in the bunkhouse and every shed, the chicken coup and outhouse; however, there were no electrical outlets, so the ironing was still done with flatirons. The carpet was cleaned by a push sweeper. Charlie repaired the bunkhouse that fall by putting a band of concrete outside, around the base, to keep the wind off the floor. When the concrete was still wet he wrote 'C.B.I. 10/14/26' in a corner, and it is still there.

As he worked, Etta noticed that Charlie had a hard time bending over and that he often put his hand on his stomach. One day she said, "Charlie, it's getting hard for you to get up and down, even to slide behind an automobile wheel. Why don't you have that mechanic in Cheyenne push the seat back for you, or let Bart Woodward drive all the time. You could look at the scenery."

Woodward, who was about five feet two and weighed less than one hundred fifteen pounds, said he'd be pleased to be a full-time chauffeur.

"One thing," said Charlie. "Mrs. Irwin thinks I drive too fast. You know I like to get where I'm going. So if I put my thumb in the middle of your back like this—that means hurry it up. Or if I put my arm out the window and hit the side of the car, that does not mean to put on the brake. Understand?"

"Yes, sir! You'll give me signals to step on the gas so your wife won't know you said anything to me," said Woodward.

"Exactly," said Charlie.

Charlie had a letter from the Union Pacific stating that there were changes in the organization and the job of livestock agent no longer existed, but he was to be the special representative in the Traffic Department, and his duties would be about the same as they had been. Joe Walters, who was his secretary, would no longer be employed. The railroad would assign Charlie a clerk-stenographer.

Of course, Walters was unhappy. He wondered what he would do now.

"Come on to California with us and keep the books on my racing activities," suggested Charlie. "Bring Frances and little Irwin. A winter in the sunshine will clear up the little boy's nosebleeds. Maybe the U.P. did you a favor."

When Charlie told Etta that Frances and her family were coming to California, he said, "I was thinking that Frances could ride Harry D. in Tia Juana! She's as good as any of those other jockeys."

Etta looked at him sidewise, clicked her teeth, and said, "She's going to sit on the beach, not a horse!"

Tom Holloway, against Charlie's wishes, entered Harry D. in a five-hundred-dollar claiming race as soon as they were at Tia Juana. Harry D. won the race, to the surprise of everyone. Charlie decided the horse could run, and so he bad-mouthed it, saying a single win was only a fluke. "He'll never win another race in his life," said Charlie so often that no one wanted to take his claim. Harry D. won his third, fourth, fifth, and sixth races. By then the Tia Juana fans cheered for Harry D. every time he was in a race. That horse won in rain, in mud, and on a crisp, dry track. Charlie had only one regret about that horse. The regret was that he was a gelding and could not sire other racers.

That winter Charlie became the instantaneous hero of the "guineas" at the Tia Juana track. The guineas were the stable hands, exercise boys, old jockeys that hung around the track and former owners down on their luck. The guineas conducted a "louse-ring" beside the paddock where they could see their horses run. The louse-ring was where the open books operated and the guineas could bet on their favorites. Bets from a dime up were taken.

On the first day of the Coffroth Handicap, a member of the board of directors for the track decided to abolish the louse-ring book. The stable area roared with anger and rumors ran wild. The guineas took their gripes right to Charlie. They knew he was on the side of fair play. Charlie said, "If the guineas have money and want to bet, that ought to be their privilege. That's part of racing!" Charlie and the guineas finally had their way and the louse-ring was restored. Just before the racing began a hearty cheer went up beside the paddock. Everyone on Rattlesnake Hill cheered Charlie as he walked across the track. He waved his big white hat and walked on up to his box seat with a big grin. He knew fighting for the underdog was not always popular. At times it caused Charlie to be disliked. Charlie tried to shrug off the smallness of that kind of thinking.

Near the close of the season, 1928, Charlie's friend Coffroth was forced out of business when several gamblers, headed by Baron Long, pulled out their horses and began to build a more lavish racetrack on the other side of Tia Juana. The new track was called Agua Caliente.

Coffroth had confided that he'd wanted to retire from the racetrack business for several years. Charlie said, "This is your chance. Don't look on it as disaster, but as a blessing."

The Irwin horses ran and won in the last race ever to be run on the old Tia Juana track. The afternoon, December 31, after that last race everyone moved their stock across town to the new barns at Agua Caliente. Racing was scheduled to open on New Year's Day. While the horses were being moved from the old track to the new, the Mexican laborers went on strike and walked off their jobs. All the last-minute work on the Agua Caliente track was unfinished. There was only one day before post time and Tia Juana was filled with tourists, eager to enjoy racing at the new track. Some of the large horse owners were in a frenzy. Baron Long was in a panic, and wrung his hands and complained bitterly to his men.

Charlie went to see Long and to show that he didn't hold a grudge. "I think I can get your racetrack finished by New Year's Day. Promise to pay the men I hire the same as you would pay the Mexicans and it will be done."

Long patted his slicked dark hair and laughed and said, "C.B., you act like a genius. But I know how much has to be done and it's not possible. I'd be willing to pay, but you can't do a job that's insurmountable." His teeth gleamed white in the sunlight.

"By noon tomorrow, I'll have it done for you," said Charlie tipping his hat. He talked with the guineas and anyone else he could find that was willing to donate a little back work. He sent them out in organized groups to remove all the excess building scaffolding. Other groups laid turf and put up the tote board, nailed seats tight in the grandstand, and put up the fencing. All through the night until noon on New Year's Day, Charlie was here and there, pointing out what needed to be done.

One hour before the first race was to run, Charlie called the guineas to finish up and get off the track. Agua Caliente opened on time and Charlie had several horses running in the opening race. Pegasus and Taddywawa were honored in the winner's circle. The guineas sang, "For He's a Jolly Good Fellow." Long shook Charlie's hand and said, "If you have time slips for the guineas I will pay each one."

Charlie reached into his shirt pocket and pulled out the notepad that Walters had given him. "Here's names and hours each man worked. I told the men to go around to your office tomorrow for their pay."

Charlie could tell by the astonished look on Long's face that his bluff had been called. He figured he and Long could be friends from now on.

Charlie felt so good that he took Etta to San Diego for a stage show to see their old friend Bee Ho Gray. "Watch old Bee Ho. He'll come out shiny as a June bug and do some simple rope tricks and tell a few jokes. When he's finished give him a big hand 'cause he's our friend," said Charlie.

Bee Ho came out dressed in a silk shirt, red as a turkey gobbler's neck. He wore a wide-brimmed white hat and tight blue jeans with goatskin chaps over the top. He started his rope spinning around his head. "Say, who knows how to get down off a horse?"

The audience was quiet, waiting for the punch line.

Charlie could not contain himself a minute longer. He stood up and yelled, "Tell us, Bee Ho. How do *you* get down off a horse?"

Bee Ho looked startled at first, then he smiled. "I'd recognize that voice anywhere. C. B. Irwin! You don't and I don't get down off a horse! We get down off a duck!"

The audience laughed.

"Folks," said Bee Ho, beginning to enlarge the noose of his rope, spinning from right to left, "we have in this audience a famous horse trainer and owner. C. B. Irwin ranks among the top ten owners and trainers in the U.S.A. You all should know this man!"

The spotlight went up to the loges. Charlie stood up and waved. He felt good.

Etta slid down in her seat and prayed the light would go off.

Bee Ho called out, "This big, wonderful man was for a half dozen years the champion steer roper in the entire world!"

When the applause died down Charlie hollered, "Thanks, friend. I remember when you were so green we had to tie up one leg to give you a haircut. You got any more of those old jokes?"

"I got a pocketful, C.B. First watch this trick. Bet you could come up here and show the folks a few tricks yourself."

Etta put her hands over her face and sank even farther down in her seat.

"You're looking great!" called Charlie. "Hold the rope higher. You droop. I told you that when you worked for me!"

"Old habits are hard to break. I was only a parson's boy, but I have my following. You're only a blacksmith's son, but you know how to forge ahead."

The audience loved the repartee. Some believed that C.B. was part of the show. Others had heard of him and considered it was a real treat to see C. B. Irwin in person.

Etta wished the floor would open and swallow her. She sucked in her lower lip.

Bee Ho said, "There he is folks, the living legend! Larger than life! Mr. Charles Burton Irwin!"

Etta was like a mannequin, stiff and unmoving.

Charlie smiled. He was at ease letting the light play over him. This was every bit as invigorating as the very first time Charlie was a barker in the Chillocothe medicine show. He loved to play for an audience.

"Meet me at the stage door when the show's over!" hollered Bee Ho. "Sit down now, you old wrangler, before you steal my show completely!" When he finished he bowed to all sides and said, "Thank you. I want to leave something of interest for you to do. If you've never seen a towering glacier full of frozen grasshoppers, go on over to Cooke City, Montana. Those folks will be glad to show you theirs. Right now I'm going to dinner with my friend."

Every February, Colonel Phil Chinn of the Himyar Farm in Kentucky sent a trainload of horses to be sold at auction in Tia Juana. Many racehorse owners felt they needed new blood in their stables and they looked forward to Colonel Chinn's auction. Several times Charlie had bought Colonel Chinn's horses. The auction was a huge event, held on Monday, when there was no racing.

This year Colonel Chinn was ill, so Charlie volunteered to hold the auction. Well, heck, thought Charlie, there can't be so much to getting up on a stand and rattling off a bunch of numbers while a few men and women look over the new blood. Charlie was told that he would be given a five-percent commission. "Money isn't that important," he told the Kentuckian. "I tell you what, give me a horse if you are pleased with my services."

The arrangement delighted the colonel, who made a snap conclusion that Charlie was some western hillbilly who wore suede boots with stovepipe tops and wide, blunt toes.

Charlie had Etta and Frances make cards with India ink numbers and string so that he could put each card around the neck of each horse to be auctioned. He asked Joe Walters to keep track of each horse by description and number. After each number Walters was to make a note of the bid price and who bought the horse. "Think you can keep all that in your ledger?" asked Charlie.

"Sure, no trick to bookkeeping," said Walters.

The sun was brilliant; the sky as blue as the fresh paint on the border patrol buildings between the United States and Mexico. The women wore cool, linen dresses and the men were in shirtsleeves. Charlie hammed it up so that the crowd laughed and waited for his jokes. He called through a microphone so that everyone could hear him plainly. He mispronounced names, so that Etta winced and felt embarrassed. No one else seemed to mind. Charlie read the horses' numbers with a Mexican dialect and kept everyone entertained. The bidding was kept fast and at a high pitch.

By the time the sun sank low in the west and the sky glowed with pinks and gold, Charlie had sold all the horses, except one little filly that looked almost sick. She was a two-year-old with nothing in her favor to brag about. Charlie knew this horse was his pay for the whole afternoon's work and entertainment. He was sorry that he'd not taken the offer of a commission. He led her to one of his empty stalls and read over her papers. She was from good stock. Maybe he could trade her. He began to sing, "Button Up Your Overcoat," and by the time he'd sung all the words he could remember, he'd changed his mind and decided to keep the sad, pathetic-looking little horse.

Etta said, "Charlie, why don't you name her Miss Cheyenne? After she's spent a winter at the Y6 and you find she can't race, she can pull a wagon. She'll be a reminder of the day you were an auctioneer."

So the scrawny little filly went into a boxcar with Charlie's other horses to run free in the Wyoming hills. When Miss Cheyenne went back to California the next season, she was a genuine racehorse. She won all of her races and was the darling of the Agua Caliente racetrack. She ran twelve times in fourteen days at Tanforan, Aurora, Illinois, and won twelve times. The records show that Miss Cheyenne made ninety-six starts altogether that year. Charlie told Etta that racing legged her up. "That little horse brought me luck. I'm in the money again and she's in good health."

On November 24, 1929, Frances E. Warren died at the age of eighty-five. Charlie had never thought about Warren as being old, as ever dying. Warren's death was like going to bed at night when there was sparkling white snow on the ground. In the morning the snow was gone and the ground was brown and muddy. "Death is like the Chinook wind that comes and takes the snow away. I never saw the snow melting," he told Etta.

Half the town of Cheyenne went to the funeral. Charlie thought Warren would have approved of the eulogy. "Most persons believe life's purpose is to be happy. Governor Warren believed happiness is given only to a few who discover how to use their God-given talents. The purpose of life is to make a difference."

"Amen," Charlie murmured. He took out his handkerchief and

passed it to Etta. The name of Fort D. A. Russell was changed to Fort Francis E. Warren.

To chase the dismal blues and lift their heavy hearts, Charlie's family and some of the cowboys went to the new roller-skating pavilion on Dan Donahue's place, behind his log rental cabins. Charlie didn't roller skate, but he enjoyed Donahue's tall tales.

"When me and the missus first came to Wyoming we didn't have no electric lights, you know. In the winter it was so cold the candle flame froze. I had to bury the blamed flame, so's we could sleep. Say, I feel a cold thumb and wet hair on the back of my neck!" Donahue shivered.

Charlie grinned. "It's Nipper, your dog!"

"Git!" yelled Donahue. "I don't need dog's kisses!" He threw a stick after the dog. "Say, C.B., someone told me you used to be a sprinter—half-mile. That true or some tall tale?"

"True. When I was twenty-one I ran the half-mile sprint within half a second of the world's record at that time."

"Hard to believe to look at you now." Donahue looked up and down at Charlie. "Guess you weigh about three-hundred, huh?"

"You're a good guesser. Guess who started foot races at the old rodeos and Wild West shows?"

"Cow manure! If you was to run now, you'd fly apart like a haystack in a hurricane. I remember Pettigrew. When he was a kid he was a genuine sprinter." Donahue spit tobacco juice between his front teeth.

"Want to have a race between Pettigrew and my new cowboy? His name's Charlie Bennett."

"Hold the phone! Let's put the tenderfoot to the old initiation test! He don't hold the 1930 World's Record in sprinting?"

"No! He's from the East, from Boston."

"I never heard of no cowboy from Boston." Donahue laughed. "I'm putting my money on Pettigrew."

Charlie called to a good-looking young man who leaned out of one of the openings of the six-sided, wooden pavilion. The broad-shouldered, brown-haired man carried his roller skates over his shoulder and walked toward Charlie. "You want me, Mr. Irwin?"

As soon as Donahue heard the Boston accent he was sure Pettigrew would win the race. He gave Charlie two dollars. "You hold the bets. This'll be a tortoise-and-hare affair."

Charlie took two dollars from his own pocket for his bet on Bennett.

Others gathered around and made their bets. The excitement grew. Betts kicked off her roller skates and moseyed over to see what was going on. She liked the young man from Boston. He'd wound up the Victrola on the ranch house back porch and played "Ta-ra-ra Boom-der-é" and taught her how to dance. She didn't want him to sprain an ankle running into some gopher hole. She wanted more dance lessons. She knew Pettigrew believed in keeping fit by running rain or shine, summer or winter, up and down the road around the ranch. She poured a glass of lemonade. She took it to Pettigrew, who was lean, tanned as an Indian.

"Thanks, kid," he said, gulping it down. "Gets hot on those roller skates, huh?"

"Want some more?" asked Betts.

"Don't mind if I do."

At the refreshment table she whispered to Bennett, "Don't drink that lemonade until after the race. Keep your head down. Watch for gopher holes!"

Bennett had been in foot races before. When he first came to Wyoming he worked on the Coble Two-Bar, then he went to the Jones place to dig irrigation ditches. When Charlie hired him he was working on the Hunter ranch with Bill Scoon. Bennett listened as a couple cowboys told him how good Pettigrew was. He was feeling a little nervous about this initiation.

"On your mark!" yelled Charlie. The two men stretched out and hunkered their shoulders down. "Get set!" The men touched the deep line in the dirt with their right hand fingers. "Go!" They took off like they were propelled from slingshots. The onlookers yelled, jumped up and down, and clapped their hands.

Halfway through the race it was obvious that Pettigrew had a stitch in his side. He hunched over and slowed down. Bennett ran even with him, keeping his head down. He did not look up when he passed Pettigrew.

Pettigrew looked up and saw that he was lagging behind. Panic passed over his tanned face. His heart beat faster and he sprinted forward to pass Bennett. The crowd cheered. All of a sudden Pettigrew bent double. He stopped. His head almost touched his feet. His sides moved in and out. He had the heaves.

Bennett kept running. He crossed the finish line. Charlie called out, "Winner!" and held Bennett's right hand in the air. Cowboys clapped. Donahue danced around, grabbing Charlie's arm.

"C.B., I declare you suckered me in!"

Some of the cowboys began to laugh and mimic Donahue.

"Hold the phone!" yelled Donahue. "Don't laugh at me. Horse Creek's still running. Some of you men lost money on the race, too!" He looked around to see if the womenfolks were anywhere near, then said in a whisper, "You know what I was going to do with my winnings? I was going to town to get a small kitty."

"What?" whispered a cowboy.

"You know what I mean." Donahue winked and kept his voice low. "Look there at my woman. Can you blame me? She wears that damn cap to bed." Then in an even lower voice he said, "Underneath she's bald as a hen's egg."

During the summer Charlie heard that one of his ex-jockeys, Red Puett, had actually built a starting gate that had eight separate stalls. Charlie asked the Frontier committee chairman, Bill Hass, to hire Puett to bring his starter gate for the horse-racing events.

Puett hauled his gate in the back of a truck to Cheyenne. The gate had no wheels and had to be dragged around when it was being set up. It had webbing in front that went up to release the anxious horses.

During the first race, Charlie's horse, Conquistador, was uncontrollable. It broke through the gate before starting time and ran like a streak of chain lightning, pell-mell down the dusty track.

The Frontier committee people ran Puett off the track like a flock of birds chasing a skunk out of their territory.

Charlie felt sick. He wanted to give his condolences to the dejected ex-jockey. Puett's gate was far better than rubber bands, canvas, or strands of cable stretched across the track.

A couple months later Puett figured out how to put wheels on the gate so it was easier to move. He and Charlie met again at a rodeo in Torrington. Puett said he was renting his gate for fifty dollars a day. Charlie looked the apparatus over carefully, then suggested that the gates in front of each stall ought to be powered electrically instead of mechanically. He was not surprised when Red Puett took the first closed-stall electric starting gate to Vancouver, B. C., where it was a huge success.*

* * *

*Today "Red" Clay Puett is known as having been one of the fairest stewards on the racetrack, and he is Chairman of the Board of True Center Gate Company, Inc., Phoenix, Arizona.

More and more Charlie liked to sit in his large, special-built chair in the front yard of the Cheyenne ranch house and watch the cowboys come and go at their chores. He wondered if the cramps in his legs were from carrying around so much weight.

One day he closed his eyes and let himself daydream, wondering if now wasn't the time to get into some other business. Perhaps it was time for politics. There were more than five million unemployed in the country; there was drought, bank failures, and decreased foreign trade. Charlie wondered if there was some way the state of Wyoming could organize a relief program to help the folks down on their luck. He'd been told that if he'd run for governor, most of the state would be behind him.

The end of summer 1931, Charlie was in his office in Cheyenne on Friday before the roundup. He talked to Etta, who was at the Y6, by phone about the plans for the weekend, and before he hung up, someone said, "Don't make big plans, 'cause you and me are going fishin'!" Charlie recognized the loud, jolly voice immediately.

"Will! Will Rogers! You old rope-twirling son of a gun! When did you get into town?"

"Not more than an hour ago. I flew in from San Francisco on a B-40, actually the mail plane, but you don't have to tell anybody. I came to ask if you've seen my latest picture show, *A Connecticut Yankee*."

"Etta and I saw it in San Diego. It was at the top of our list because we like shows with sound. Etta said you looked like you needed to come to the ranch and stoke up on her strawberry shortcake."

"I'm ready. I need to get away from crowds. Do a little fishing."

Charlie's smile disappeared. "I guess you are in the right place, but at the wrong time, old friend. This is the weekend before roundup. Etta and I are having company at the ranch. The meat packers, Louis Swift and his wife from Chicago, the J. O. Armours from Omaha, and the Brandeises and Updikes from Omaha, Carl Gray and his wife, you know, president of the U.P., will be there."

"No need to apologize," said Rogers. "All I need is some of Mother Irwin's cooking. I'll be just what you need at that swell party, a pair of good ears that will wring dry all those tongues."

The two friends left Charlie's office with their arms linked together, laughing and singing.

Saturday morning over breakfast at the ranch Charlie, Carl Gray, Johnathan Armour, and Louis Swift worked out a way to solicit more beef business and get the U.P. to buy more refrigerated boxcars to ship packaged beef from Omaha and Chicago to the East. The women admired Etta's flowerbeds of roses, zinnias, cosmos, poppies, and clarkias.

By midafternoon Etta had the white linen tablecloth on the dining room table. She'd brought good china and crystal goblets from the house in Cheyenne. Everything had to be nice for these important people. She'd sent Betts out with eight-year-old Irwin to pick chokecherries. Sending her grandchildren out was an excuse to get the overactive Irwin away from the final dinner preparations. She was not only going to have guests to feed, but also the cowboys and hired hands, who would eat on the back porch.

Charlie sent Frances to the cellar for some of the good Mexican wine for the guests. "Bring the wineglasses outside. Serve it before we go in to sit at the table."

When the last glass was lifted from the silver tray, Etta heard a strange chugging noise. She told Charlie to look around the side of the house and down the road. He was surprised to see clouds of dust rolling behind an old, high-centered flivver. It was the same Model-T Ford he'd helped Frank Fools Crow buy years ago!

"Now, who's that?" asked Etta. By now everyone was watching the Model T. One of its back tires was cracked, nearly broken apart. It was tied together with burlap and colored rags. The occupants were waving vigorously.

"Jeems! It looks like Fools Crow, Yellow Boy, Julia Red Bear, and friends!" Charlie waved. Rogers, standing beside him, waved, too.

Etta was horrified. "Oh, no! It can't be! Not now!" She looked at her guests. The women wore long, silk dresses. Mrs. Armour raised her lorgnette. The men in business suits looked over their wineglasses. Etta prayed that the jalopy would go right past the Y6. She watched it turn into the lane and stop in the front yard. The Sioux waved and *kiyi*ed.

Julia Red Bear leaned halfway out of the backseat and yelled, "Hallo! How are you folks? Where's my Hoonka?" This was her name for Betts, who'd been born the same day as her own daughter, whom she'd named Betty. Betty died before she was a year old of the dreaded coughing sickness. Since then, Julia always called Betts her Hoonka. The name meant a relative by choice, kind of an adopted daughter.

The finely dressed guests stood close together. Their mouths were open, but they didn't speak.

Rogers held his sides and laughed loudly as dust-streaked, barefoot children climbed out of the car and shouted, "Welcome to Mr. and Mrs. Irwin!"

Charlie said something about these people being friends. "They live in houses like most everyone else, except they don't own the land. The government owns their land. They live on a reservation." He bent and hugged each child and shook hands with the men as they piled out. The men were dressed in dusty black woolen trousers, shirts with the sleeves cut out, and leather vests. Their long hair was braided and tied with leather thongs. Fools Crow had grouse feathers stuck in the ends of his braids. Charlie Yellow Boy wore black boots. Mr. Red Bear had silver bells on his beaded moccasins that jangled every time he moved.

Before Etta could think of some explanation for her dinner guests, Julia was beside her fingering the silver tray holding the empty wineglasses. "I brought a present for my daughter, my Hoonka. Where is she?"

Etta held the silver tray tight and close to her chest. "She's, she's picking chokecherries! She's with her little cousin, Irwin!" she blurted.

"Good daughter! I have more cousins here. I show her how to pit cherries, dry them so they taste sweet." She rubbed her stomach, which jiggled up and down under her pink cotton dress.

Etta noticed that the dinner guests stayed huddled close and stared at the Sioux as if a whole tribe of wild barbarians had descended on the Y6. Etta's heart was in her throat and it pounded as if it wanted out.

"You fixing the eats?" asked Mrs. Yellow Boy, looking at the wineglasses. "We're plenty hungry and thirsty."

From the corner of her eye Etta could see Charlie introducing the men to Rogers. Rogers was motioning for the other men to come over next to the old car and meet the Sioux. Etta knew she had to shake herself into action. She had to get her mind functioning. She said, "We are so glad that you could come. You see we have other guests that are waiting to be fed. You wait here. I'll call you when it is time to eat."

"Yes, many mouths to feed. I am used to filling a big kettle with stew. I will come help you feed all these people," said Mrs. Yellow Boy. She put her brown arm around Etta's quaking shoulders. The leather band across her forehead smelled strongly of raw leather and human sweat.

"No, I would rather—no, you, too, are my guest," stuttered Etta. "Please wait. Rest in the yard where it's cool. I'll call you."

The Sioux women liked the idea of being guests and doing no work. They sat down on the front steps to wait.

Etta went over to the white women and said, "These are some of our friends from Pine Ridge. They have worked with Charlie for many years." She introduced the women and children as best she could. The Sioux women nodded, said nothing, but stared at the fine clothes. Etta prayed silently that they would not reach out and touch the white women's dresses and jewelry. The children, two boys and two girls from three to six years old, became shy and clung to their mother's skirts.

"Well," said Etta, still flustered and greatly embarrassed whenever she looked at the white women, "come inside. We'll start the meal." She watched to make certain the Sioux would stay outside.

Suddenly Rogers was at Etta's side. "Mother Irwin," he said, "the Sioux can eat on the back porch with the cowboys. They can eat in shifts." He leaned close and whispered, "Chin up. Everything will be all right." He patted Etta's arm and smiled his crooked boyish grin.

Etta bit her tongue so she wouldn't cry. "The dinner party has been ruined. I could die of humiliation."

"Humiliation never killed anyone," said Rogers. "I'll help C.B. set up extra tables on the porch. You get those nabobs seated in the dining room."

Etta nodded, then smiled as Mr. Swift helped his wife walk across the lawn in her high heels. Etta held the front door open and motioned for Frances and Pauline to come inside also. She gave the silver tray to Pauline. "Take it to the kitchen and put it in the cupboard."

Charlie and Rogers set up a couple high wooden sawhorses with boards across the top for extra tables on the back porch.

"What about chairs?" asked Rogers.

"We'll use those from the bunkhouse for the cowboys. Say, there's benches in the blacksmith shop. One is from an old sleigh. It'll have to do." Charlie hurried out to bring them in.

Rogers went to the kitchen, took a nip from the red wine bottle, put his finger to his lips and asked Frances for a covering for the boards on the sawhorses. She gave him a handful of white dishtowels. In the dining room he could hear Swift saying, "I hear people are starting to hoard gold."

Rogers spread the dishtowels, held the screen door for Charlie to bring in the seat from the sleigh. Then the two went into the dining room. Rogers sat next to Swift and said, "Out here no one hoards a thing. Everyone gives what he has to help a neighbor in need. A man's attitude here is not as self-centered as it is in the East."

Charlie entered the conversation. "We westerners don't feel the country's unemployment with any great impact. Except one thing: There's no problem hiring cowboys, there's plenty to choose from." He chuckled. Then he went on to explain that he did not raise wheat for sale on his ranch. Sure, he had a few cattle, some hogs, and Etta had some chickens, but he didn't count on them for prime income. He made money on supplying various rodeos with stock and cowboys.

"What about your racehorses, C.B.?" asked Brandeis.

"Well, yes," admitted Charlie. "I do all right raising and training racehorses for the small tracks. I'm not interested in racing the big tracks. Competition is too fierce. Agua Caliente in Mexico is the biggest I get."

For the moment everyone seemed to ignore the Sioux, who sat on the front steps and edge of the front porch. Once in a while Julia got up, cupped her hands around her face, and looked through a window inside the house.

Rogers filled his plate with mashed potatoes and gravy, roast beef and ham. When the sweet corn and glazed carrots were passed, he said he needed a second plate. Frances brought him one. He looked around the table and smiled his wide grin. "Maybe you folks don't know this. The Irwins serve the best food west of the Mississippi. It behooves you to try everything." He took two ears of corn, a serving of carrots, lettuce salad, and pickles on his second plate. He put two biscuits, butter, and honey on his bread and butter plate. He tucked his linen napkin in the front of his shirt and began to eat. "There's no better banquet than a meal with no speeches."

Everyone at the table began to relax and talk.

Gray leaned over toward Charlie and surprised everyone by suggesting that Charlie run for governor of Wyoming. "I wish someone like you, C.B., would get his hat in the ring before that Democrat, Leslie A. Miller, gets his hooks into the political machine. If Democrats have their way, you'll see your pastureland plowed into sugar-beet fields."

"What's the use of letting someone like Miller run when he's not on the right road?" said Brandeis.

"That's what I say," said Gray. "C.B., you could run for governor."

Etta drew in her breath and looked at Charlie. He never looked more handsome. He wore a navy blue suit, a white shirt, and a dark red bow tie. His brown eyes were clear. He looked at Etta a long moment before he said, "Dear, some things seem impossible until they are tried. I thought about running for mayor of Cheyenne once, then changed my mind when I became involved with horse racing. I never thought it possible that I'd ever hold a world's record of winning horses. But in 1923 I had one hundred and forty-seven wins. No one has ever done better—so far. So maybe I should think again of the impossible—running for governor sounds impossible!" He laughed to show that if he wanted to get into politics, the office of Wyoming's governor would be his first step.

Charlie got up, excused himself, went through the kitchen to the back porch. He called to the bunkhouse. "All right! Soup's on! Come and get it!" The cowboys did not have to be called a second time. They'd seen the Sioux drive up and wondered how Charlie and Etta would handle the situation. Charlie told Frances and Pauline to begin serving the cowboys. They had the same food as the dinner guests, only their plates were the everyday white graniteware and their silverware was everyday plated steel. The cowboys were not served wine. When the cowboys were concentrating more on eating than talking Charlie asked Frances, "Have we enough to serve the Sioux?"

"Yes, if we get another ham and slice it thin. We've already started more potatoes boiling." Frances pushed a lock of blond hair behind her ear. "I wish Betts would come back. Julia could make a fuss if Betts doesn't show up soon. Besides she's been gone long enough with Irwin."

Charlie put his arm around his youngest daughter. "Your mother wanted Betts to keep your little Irwin out of the way. Now you want him back. Women! There's no satisfying you!" He chuckled. "Feed the Sioux. There'll be no fuss." Charlie went out the back door, around the house, and motioned for the Sioux to follow him to the back porch.

Julia walked beside Charlie. Mr. Red Bear walked on the other side. Julia said, "What was that talk about sugar beets?" Mr. Red Bear held his nose and wrinkled his mouth to show that he did not care for the smell around sugar beet refineries.

"You shouldn't listen to others talking unless it concerns you. That's impolite," said Charlie, knowing that the Sioux did not figure it was impolite at all to overhear another's conversation.

"You can stop the plowing of pastures. You can stop the growing of beets. We make our X for you. You do better than *that* lady," said Julia. The lady she referred to was Nellie Tayloe Ross. This loyalty touched Charlie. He was sure the Indians never paid much attention to politics unless it affected their reservation lands; besides, they didn't vote.

The Sioux jostled each other to find a place to sit closest to the plate piled high with thin-sliced roast beef and ham.

Betts and Irwin burst onto the back porch, surprised to see the Sioux. "Where are the others?" asked Betts, her eyes wide. "I thought Gram was having fancy company!"

"And so!" cried Julia. "We are here! Sit beside me, Hoonka. Put your cousin with the papooses." Then Julia began to click her tongue against her teeth. "I see the little white cousin cannot yet control himself. Shame. Shame."

Betts looked around the table and saw the Indian children moving away from Irwin because his trousers were wet. "Oh, that's not what you think! He went wading in the irrigation ditch. See, my dress is still wet. I had to tuck it up in my bloomers and wade out after him. We got to laughing and splashing." She smiled at Julia. The children laughed and moved back beside Irwin.

Julia smiled and said, "So, you cared for the little boy. You are a good daughter. I brought you a beaded box for sewing things." She gave Betts a leather box with a lid beautifully decorated with colored seed beads.

"I love it!" cried Betts. "Thank you from the bottom of my heart!"

Etta came to the kitchen for more coffee for the dining room, looked at the people on the back porch, saw Betts in a mud-streaked dress, and told her to hike upstairs and change immediately. "Take Irwin with you! When you come back you can help in the kitchen!" Her serious eyes sent a chill through Betts. She gave Julia a hug and said she'd be back later. She took Irwin's hand and hurried him through the kitchen to the stairs. At the foot of the stairs she looked down and saw the little boy's nose was bleeding. "Oh, no! You could have waited until tomorrow to have a nosebleed!" she cried.

Irwin smiled. His face was white, his hair black as midnight.

His brown eyes shone like good saddle leather. He let her put clean clothes on him, then he squealed, "I have no dry shoes. Look, stocking feet!"

"That's better than bare feet," said Betts. "Don't yell. You don't want to get another nosebleed. Hold your head up. Don't look down. Maybe your pants will cover your feet so no one will notice." She changed into a yellow summer dress and went to the kitchen to ask her mother, Pauline, what to give to Julia. "She'll expect a gift."

"Give her the dress you have on! Don't wear that dress! You know how your grandfather feels about yellow. He hates the color. It's bad luck!"

Betts ran back upstairs and changed to a blue dress with a wide sash. Back in the kitchen Pauline nodded her approval and said, "When you have a chance, look at Gramps's face and at Will Rogers's face. I swear, those two are having a whale of a time. Honest!" She smoothed Irwin's hair and said, "Put him at the table with Mrs. Armour. You know the lady with the glasses and cerise dress. I heard her say she had grandchildren. She'll talk to Irwin."

Mrs. Armour helped Irwin cut his meat. She took to the little boy because he was so polite. He said, "Yes, ma'am" and "No, ma'am," when appropriate. He spoke only when spoken to. She asked him where he'd been and when she found out asked what could be done with chokecherries. "Julia Red Bear can use them in pemmican."

"What is that?" she asked.

"Dried meat pounded into a paste with lard. If it's cold it can be cut into little cakes. If it's warm it's like eating pudding made with bacon grease," explained Irwin. "The berries go in the pudding like raisins."

"Mercy! The seeds come out first!" joked Mrs. Armour.

"Yes, ma'am, and no, ma'am. Sometimes Indians forget and leave seeds in. I cracked a tooth on pemmican once." Irwin opened his mouth wide and put his face up for her to look inside.

"Close your mouth, honey," whispered Etta.

Later on after an after-dinner liqueur for those who wanted it, Mrs. Armour took Irwin around to the others, showing where he'd cracked a tooth on a chokecherry seed.

Rogers heard the story and opened his mouth. "Look back there, ma'am. You see that blank space? That's where I ate pemmican and broke a tooth clean off, myself. I just bet you a silver dollar that if you look into one of the Injun ladies' mouth, you'll find a couple of teeth missing for the same reason. Come on. I'll show you." Rogers took Mrs. Armour's arm and steered her through the kitchen to the back porch. He went to a young woman holding a little girl in a buff-colored doe-skin dress. "Mrs. Yellow Boy?" The woman nodded. Rogers explained about Robert cracking a tooth on a cherry pit. He asked if she or the little girl had done the same. Mrs. Yellow Boy understood right away and opened her mouth. She had no back molar left.

"Oh, my, you poor dear," sympathized Mrs. Armour. "There are such things as false teeth, you know, and they are very comfortable. I would think you'd like some. See if there is someone near Pine Ridge that can fit you with a set."

"I don't know these false teeth," said Mrs. Yellow Boy.

"Well, see here." Mrs. Armour took her upper plate right out.

The little girl's eyes grew large. Mrs. Yellow Boy drew in her breath. Rogers chuckled and winked at Mrs. Armour. "You're a swell sport," he said. Then he called Charlie over. "See now, Mrs. Armour is sitting with Mrs. Yellow Boy. Let's get the rest of them together. You know, I think Mrs. Armour is going to get Mrs. Yellow Boy some new teeth. Let's see what the others get or give!" He put his hand on Charlie's shoulder and said, "I agree, you ought to run for governor. Anyone that can pull off a party like this is a genius."

"But what about Etta? I think she's still a little unglued. She keeps barking orders for the girls to do this and that. She runs here and there."

"Aw, she'll be all right. You two are the best people I know. Truly! This is the most fun I've had since I went skinny-dipping in a mill pond and some girls took my clothes."

The cowboys now sat around the front of the bunkhouse. Fools Crow hollered from the back porch. "Say, when are you cowboys going to come to Pine Ridge and have a rodeo? We have boys that will beat the stuffing out of you fellows in a wild horse race!" The Sioux men ate before the women and children. Most had seconds of everything. The cowboys had eaten all of the apple pie, and Etta didn't know what to give the Sioux for dessert.

"Gram, you know what I like best?" asked Irwin, coming up in his stocking feet so that he startled her.

"What is that, honey?" she said. "Say it fast because I must think of a dessert to give the Sioux."

"Raisins and brown sugar in whipped cream," he said, licking his lips.

"Sounds like a good-enough dessert!" cried Etta. "I know there's cream in the cellar. And I have raisins and brown sugar. Thanks, honey!"

"Good cook!" called Julia, waving to Etta as she went down the cellar for the cream. Etta felt somewhat better. Over and over she'd told herself there was nothing she could do about these two different kinds of guests coming together at the same time. Each expected to be fed and made over. The cowboys didn't seem out of place with either group. Coming out of the cellar she saw they were sitting around the front of the bunkhouse braiding rope, someone played a mouth organ, and a couple were playing poker for horseshoe nails. Etta looked through the kitchen to the dining room. Those people were busy talking. Beyond, through the open front door, she saw the pink and purple sunset.

Rogers came into the kitchen and said, "Is there more of that wine left?"

"Like you had before dinner? I think so," she said.

"Serve it to your guests on the back porch. Dilute it with water if you have to. Make them feel they got everything the rest of your guests had."

"I understand," said Etta, touching Rogers arm. "You and one of the men come help."

Rogers and Louis Swift came into the kitchen. Etta opened the cupboard and showed them the water glasses and the partially empty wine bottle.

"Where are the fancy wine glasses?" asked Rogers.

"In the dishwater," said Etta.

"You wash, I'll dry," Rogers said to Swift.

The two men filled the wineglasses, half water, half red wine, and took them out to the Sioux on the silver tray. The Indians were smacking their lips over the whipped-cream dessert. Fools Crow stood up and shook Swift's hand. "I am honored," he said, raising his glass and drinking without taking a breath as he'd seen whites do with hard liquor.

"He means he's never seen men take so long washing their hands," explained Mr. Red Bear, *tee-hee*ing loudly, then grinning broadly.

Rogers explained to Swift that the Indians thought it somewhat of a joke that Charlie's male guests were washing dishes and serving food. "That's women's work." He also told Swift that the Indians thought it a great compliment to be served the red crazy water, same as the other guests.

Eldon Smith came to the back porch for the milk buckets.

"Good dinner," he said to Etta. "Say, Mrs. Irwin, do you mind if I take those Injun kids to the barn? They'd get a kick out of having milk squirted right into their mouths. I did when I first came here."

Etta nodded her approval and the Indian children followed Smith in a straight line, as if he were the mother goose and they were the goslings.

Julia found the bucket of chokecherries Betts had left in the backyard by the steps. She brought the bucket to the table inside and began squeezing out the pits between her forefinger and thumb. Each seed made two pinging sounds as it hit the porch wall and then the floor. She dropped the fruit into an empty serving bowl. Soon the other women were helping her, laughing when their seeds hit higher on the wall than the one before.

"What are they going to do with that mushy fruit?" asked Mrs. Gray with a frown. She was half appalled and half amused by the relaxed comaraderie among the Sioux women. Secretly she wished she could see how far she could shoot a cherry seed. It reminded her of shooting watermelon seeds in the yard when she was a child.

"My guess is that they'll find a rock or discarded wooden board somewhere near a campground on their way home. Spread the pulp thin to dry in the sun. When it's time to go on to Pine Ridge, someone'll scrape the dry fruit into a container. It'll go into the winter pemmican," said Charlie.

"Like raisins in mincemeat?" said Mrs. Gray.

When Charlie's Delco motor turned on a few minutes after sundown, the noise startled everyone. Rogers teasingly said, "At the Y6 you can have sunlight even after sundown!"

"And so," said Julia, coming shyly into the living room, "will Mr. Irwin give us some of this leftover sunlight so that we can see our way home in the dark?"

"A flashlight! Have you never heard of a flashlight? I guess Mr. Brandeis could send you folks some flashlights when he gets back to his store in Omaha. Come on, let's ask him." Rogers took Julia out to the front porch, where Brandeis stood with Swift.

"Certainly, I'll send a whole case of flashlights to Pine Ridge," said Brandeis.

"We will send you pemmican," said Julia.

"Please, no seeds," said Mrs. Brandeis coming out on the porch.

Soon there were promises not only of false teeth and flashlights, but electric irons and fans and canned hams to be sent to

Pine Ridge in exchange for moccasins and thick, pine-needle baskets containing pemmican. Betts finally thought of something for Julia. She took her pink flannel sheets from her bed, folded them, and took them downstairs. "They are something warm and soft to put under your buffalo robe at night," Betts said.

Julia sucked in a mouthful of air. She felt the soft flannel and her eyes watered. "An unexpected gift. It warms my heart. This cloth is like a piece of the warm pink sunset." She held the sheets up to show they matched the last baby-pink glow low on the western sky.

Betts saw Mr. Red Bear kind of squint and look away. He was disappointed there was no gift for himself. Betts thought quickly and said, "Your gift was too large to bring at the same time."

He looked up and beamed. His shoulders swaggered from side to side. Betts went after her goose-down pillow. She left the pink flannel casing on it. "Thank you," he said. "May your mouth stay wet and your feet stay dry, daughter of my woman. I have a sunset cloud I can hold." He hugged the pillow to his chest.

Before the Sioux left, Etta wrapped all the leftover biscuits in a cloth and gave them to Mrs. Yellow Boy. Rogers collected all the unsmoked cigars from the men and gave them to Charlie Yellow Boy. Charlie gave the four Sioux children each a colored bandanna.

On an impulse Mrs. Armour took out the rhinestone and tortoiseshell comb in the side of her hair and put it in the smallest girl's hair. The child tilted her head to show it off. Her eyes twinkled. The other women followed suit. They gave away their glass beads, earrings, and pins with colored glass.

The Sioux women had tears in their eyes. "We cannot repay you with such finery," said Julia, holding a hand over her mouth.

"You have paid us by coming here and sharing this day with all these friends and our cowboys," said Etta, whose tears spilled down her cheeks. Charlie put his arm around her and held her close. "We'll never forget this dinner," said Mrs. Armour. "You people are enchanting."

Julia looked puzzled. "En-chanting? You mean like singing with drums, tum-tum-tummity-tum?"

Charlie tried to translate for Julia. He said, "Mrs. Armour means tum-tum, from the heart. Enchanting means heartfelt chanting. It means you are delightful. You are sunshine to the heart. You and your people make all us whites happy. We are all friends."

"You bet your boots," said Julia with a broad smile.

Etta wrapped a dishtowel around the handle of a two-gallon tin containing the leftover gravy and mashed potatoes.

Charlie removed the burlap and colored rags, and examined the broken tire on the old Model-T. He called one of the men to find him some strips of hard leather in the blacksmith shop. He cut the leather and the men wrapped and tied and stapled with metal rivets until they had pretty well repaired the broken, solid rubber tire on the old Ford.

The Sioux scrambled up into the car. None bothered to open the doors on either side. Charlie thought perhaps the doors could not be opened. The Sioux laughed and waved and shouted, "Good-bye!"

Everyone on the lawn in front of the ranch house laughed uproariously when the single red taillight turned on as the car headed out the gate and bobbed up and down because of the bulge on the mended tire.

Later that evening, a relaxed Will Rogers smiled and said to Etta, "Life is but a gift to be enjoyed."

"Help me put cots up in the big bedroom for our guests," said Etta. "Then you and Charlie can get the sheets and blankets out and make up the cots. Let's sleep late in the morning."

"Mother Irwin, that's what I came here for," said Rogers with a crooked grin. "I'll go fishing in the afternoon."

FORTY-THREE

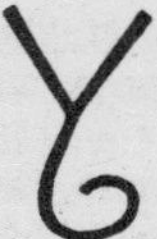

The Last Great Roundup

That winter, Will Rogers sent Charlie a telegram from Claremore, Oklahoma. "It looks like there's going to be racing in California."

The two men had talked about a racetrack in Santa Anita.

Charlie called Rogers by phone. "What's going on in Santa Anita?"

"A bunch of people with more money than you or I ever saw are going to bring that track to life. Get your ex-jockey's starting gate out there for them to see. Find out when they are going to issue bonds. I want to buy some."

"All right," said Charlie, grateful for the tip.

"When are you running for President?"

"Governor," said Charlie. "As soon as I can get my horse racing business running smooth. What are you up to?"

"C.B., I'm flying. Funny, isn't it? An old waddy like me interested in aeroplanes. Charles Lindbergh said, 'I'd rather fly than eat.' I know what he means."

"What do you know about museums?"

"Not much. Well, there's an awfully interesting gun collection in the hotel lobby here in Claremore. There's some double-barreled pistols and some old Civil War rifles. The other day I was looking at a tiny, three-inch-long, pearl-handled gun. The note beside it said that Mattie Silks carried it in her purse when she was in Abilene. Most of these guns hang on the lobby wall. They probably ought to go in a museum one day. Maybe I'll start a fund for a Museum of Western Guns."

"Doesn't that make you feel old?" Charlie frowned.

"What's that?"

"Well, finding things in museums that you have seen and used in your lifetime."

"Hey, pardner," said Rogers. "Live life to the fullest. That's our motto. Stay on fire! You with me, C.B.?"

Now Charlie smiled. "Sure. I was thinking, that's all. Jeems, life is never dull. It changes with the seasons. It's a challenge, a joy, a headache, the best creation the Lord ever made."

"Hey, you and Etta have a fight?"

"Nope. Life's too short and full of blisters for me to tangle with Etta." Charlie shifted the receiver from his right hand to his left. He scratched his nose. "Etta'd feed you, give you the shirt off her back whenever you ask. She has a great fondness for you, you old jingler."

"Then, what's eating you? You thinking of turning the Y6 into some kind of living museum about how a typical ranch ought to be run? Not a bad idea. That'll give you some place to go when the governor's mansion gets too drafty."

"I was thinking of a letter Etta had from my sister in Colorado Springs. You understand, my sister's something of a herbalist and she claims to be clairvoyant. She wrote that you and I were going to fall. You from a great height and me not so far. She had a dream about it. I don't put much faith in dreams, nor in what my sister says. But Etta's worried. She's been trying to get me to write you about it. To tell you to be careful, not to trip and fall. Jeems, it sounds silly."

"Tell Mother Irwin not to worry. When they put me in that six-foot bungalow, I'm through. That's that."

"I say the same. When I've got that wooden kimono on, that's all."

Since their automobile accident Charlie didn't want Etta out of his sight. He took her to the rodeos and horse races. Before going to San Ysidro they were going to cover the Kansas-Colorado circuit starting in Topeka. The day before it was time to leave, Charlie noticed Etta smelled of kerosene and goose grease. She had a flannel rag tied around her throat. Her face was puffy and red. She could hardly talk.

"What's the matter? Dear, take that terrible-looking rag off your neck. It smells like something I used to clean up the Delco generator."

Etta whispered, "I'm sick. I have tonsillitis."

"My gosh! Dear, we're going to Topeka tomorrow. This is no time to be sick. Can't you wait until next week to be sick?" Charlie went to the living room and sat down. He was disappointed. He was put out. In his scheme of things he had no time for sickness. He thought of all the things he depended on Etta for and finally stamped out of the house to check over the trucks he now owned and had parked along the street in front of the house in Cheyenne. There was one long-bed truck to haul the show wagons and another to haul the special stock.

The next day he put Etta on the train for Topeka. He told her to rest and get well. He didn't think she looked quite as peaked as before. Frances and Pauline were already in the driver's seats of the trucks when Charlie came back. Little Irwin was in the seat next to his mother. Next year he'd be in school. Charlie climbed in beside Frances, put Irwin on his lap, and pounded on the outside of the door, which meant the trucks were loaded and he was ready to go. He would use local men and more local stock to round out his rodeo in Topeka.

Charlie began to whistle. Everything seemed fine. Etta's two brothers, Walt and Curly, were at the ranch. Pauline's husband, Claude Sawyer, managed the ranch. Joella had gone to her husband in Fort Douglas, Utah, and Betts was in nursing school in San Diego. The Y6 ranch and the Irwin Live Stock and Show Company were making good money. "That's because I'm president and your grandmother's secretary and treasurer," he said out loud to little Irwin.

"You could be president all right, but not Ma. She's too soft, easygoing. She wants to please everyone, especially you," said Frances, looking straight ahead, following Pauline.

"If I take time off for a run in politics, nothing will change. The ranch will be run well, everybody has his job," said Charlie. He felt good.

The Topeka rodeo went well and Etta was well. Charlie bought a third big truck in Grand Junction, Colorado, so that he could carry more of his own livestock. He drove the new truck and Etta took turns riding with the three of them. On the way back to Cheyenne it began to rain. Etta, riding with Charlie, saw him nodding off and said she'd try her hand at driving a short while if he wanted to sleep.

"I'll go back to Frances and hold Irwin for a while. When you get tired, Dear, pull over. I know you don't like to drive, and this rain makes it tougher," said Charlie.

"Oh, stuff and nonsense! The road is straight and all I have to do is follow Pauline's taillights ahead. I can do that for an hour." Etta patted Charlie's arm and showed him how she'd grip the steering wheel.

"You can relax some, Dear!" he said chuckling. He looked at his pocket watch. It was two in the morning, pitch black and still raining.

Now Charlie felt wide awake. He liked the feel of his grandson, warm and sleepy in his arms. He didn't like the way the headlights seemed to melt right into the front of the road.

Frances took her hand off the wheel once to scratch her nose.

"My gosh! Don't do that!" hollered Charlie. "Scratch your nose in Pueblo, anywhere, but not here. We could drive off the road into endless blackness!"

Frances clamped both hands onto the wheel. She kept her eyes on the blackness ahead. "Dad, I want to tell you something!"

"All right, but mind your driving," said Charlie. "And don't holler, you'll wake my grandson."

"Joe and I—I, uh—you know, we haven't been together for several years. I got a divorce." Frances stopped and waited for Charlie to respond.

He didn't move. Finally he said, "Jeems, why'd you do that? I liked Joe. He was like a son. He worked at the office and at the ranch. He learned fast. We got along fine. I like the man!"

"Dad, Joe hasn't been on the ranch since 1929. Time goes fast for you," said Frances in a low voice.

"Darn tootin' it does!" he cried, and put a hand over his mouth, then took it away. "It doesn't seem long ago when you were so little you couldn't see over the dashboard of a car. Your feet wouldn't touch the pedals. Your mother called you *Noonie* and *Snooks* and *Cotton* because your hair was almost white. Beautiful, wispy hair."

"This is what I want to tell you. Last winter I ran around with Mannie Keller, you know, the track clocker at Agua Caliente. His hair is coal black. His eyes are the deepest brown and he has a cleft chin. We are opposites. He's good for me. I'm good for him. He likes little Irwin." She paused so that Charlie could think on what she'd said. Then she continued. "When I told Keller I was going back to Wyoming for the summer, he went crazy. He wanted me and Irwin to stay in San Diego. I told him I wasn't ready to stay with him. Then I thought about it. I knew I'd miss him. I wanted him to wait for me. I wanted him to be around when I got back. Dad—we got married the night before we left California."

"Where is Keller now?" demanded Charlie. His face was white.

"He lives in San Diego and works at the Caliente track," said Frances quietly. "We write."

"Jeems! What do young people think about today? I swear I can't figure it out! Young lady, if you're married to Keller, go to him. Be a wife. You can stay in the house at San Ysidro. Put Irwin in school in San Diego." Charlie breathed hard. He couldn't believe that Frances had broken off with Joe Walters. A divorce! That was so final! How could a relationship be cut apart that started so well? What happened to the promise of happiness, of caring for each other no matter what?

"I'll go to California this winter. Don't make anything complicated, Dad. It's my life. I want it simple. I want to be free to do what I feel like."

"But Joe let you do as you wanted. He was a good, honest guy. Wasn't it hard to—to let him go?" Charlie's eyes misted. He shifted the weight of the sleeping child so that his arm wasn't cramped.

"Yes, I thought about it for a long time. But look—Joella ran into problems with her first marriage. Pauline had troubles, then there's Uncle Frank—he and Clara Belle, and Uncle Will, Margaret left him."

"Margaret left because of Will's drinking. But not until the children were old enough to be on their own. They no longer had close thoughts, intimate feelings, or a sense of timelessness when they were together. Margaret and I had a talk." Charlie felt his head throb. His family was slowly unraveling. He wanted to tie the family back together. "I can't understand you. If there's a little misunderstanding, one of the partners in a marriage says, 'I want out.' You let them out? No talk? No working on a marriage? No thought of friendship, the meaning of a lifetime commitment?" He waved one hand in the air. "So—there are bound to be disagreements. But friends don't break up because of disagreements. They shake hands and start over. Kiss and make up. Why can't marriage partners realize there will be hard times. You grow together in wisdom and understanding. I should've talked with Joe. He used to come to me like I was his father." Charlie took out his handkerchief and blew his nose.

"Dad, it's too late for that. Mannie Keller and I are married," said Frances.

"What is this? A disposable society? Throw away a husband? Throw away a wife if things don't go your way? That's the most selfish thing I've heard. A marriage is for a lifetime. You have a responsibility to work at it. It is the obligation of two people. There is nothing better than a marriage that is worked at. It renews itself, gives contentment, joy. Sure there are disagreements, but nothing insurmountable. I can't understand my own children." Charlie sighed.

"Things are different nowadays than when you and Mama were young." Frances slowed the truck as it went around several curves.

"Thinking is different, but that doesn't make it right."

"I'm not responsible for Joe Walters' actions."

"If you're not, who is? That's what I mean. We don't think alike. Jeems, it's these Democrats! Roosevelt is going to ruin this country by promising to make work for everyone that can't find a job. The government's going to take responsibility for everyone's actions. That's woolly-headed thinking! That's dishonest! There used to be integrity. A man's word was his bond. A handshake as good as a signed contract."

"Dad, the government will never have to take care of me. I'm trying to tell you, people change. Remember what happened to Charley Johnson after he and Pauline were married? She had no way of knowing he'd change his personality after being hit on the head. And Joella—she seemed to grow beyond her first husband, who turned out to be paranoid, oversuspicious of anyone she made friends with. She's better off without him."

"Doesn't anyone feel old-fashioned guilt anymore? Marriage used to be a privilege. Passion's nothing to count on, but love and loyalty, they're deep and lasting." Charlie's eyes were focused into the dark distance, not on things to come, but on the things gone past.

"I don't want you upset. I'm happy with Mannie Keller. He makes me feel good." The rain came down harder.

"I'm upset. Not thinking that marriage is something special can erode society. People have to be tough. They have to believe in taking care of their own family. Today it's all right to let someone else take your wife and children? Then you can criticize the way they care for them?" Charlie was sarcastic.

"It won't be that way. Joe doesn't care what Keller does, nor what little Irwin and I do. He left us! I needed someone. Mannie needed someone."

Charlie cleared his throat. He straightened his back. "Sounds like a dog in heat! Something needed like one good jump on the first thing that comes along. That's crazy! It's primitive and undisciplined. You are a step above that kind of behavior. Sure, sex is powerful. But out of control, it's perverted. An outrage to decency!"

"Dad! Stop! It's not like that at all between Keller and myself. You're just too old to understand. Times have changed."

The blood began to surge through Charlie's veins and his face was no longer white, but it was flushed. "Young lady, nothing's changed. People are still people. They have the same feelings. I understand. It's you young people, that don't want to listen to the advice of experienced old people. You want constant gratification. You don't want to work on a strong marriage. You reject building a foundation for a lifelong commitment. You don't look ahead. Lifetime is too far. You break what is good and precious. You hurt not only yourself but those people who care most about you. You pretend you are right. But you are wrong. Dead wrong! There's none so deaf as those who won't listen!"

Frances hunched over the steering wheel. She spoke in fast, jerky sentences. "Joe left. He said he couldn't take it. He said I could do all the things on the ranch as well or better than most of the men. He couldn't compete with me. After he was fired from being your secretary at the U.P.—he—he had to ask me for money. He said he felt like he was castrated. I said he was silly. He wanted you to offer him another job. But he wouldn't ask you. He's stubborn."

"So, it was my fault. Why didn't he come and talk? Bullheadedness did him in!"

"Dad, promise to treat Keller nice?"

"Sure, baby. Don't I treat everyone right if they give me half a chance?"

The rain had eased. Frances pushed her shoulders together to relieve the tension. "Ya, Dad I know. We all depend on you for lots of things. But we have to stand on our own legs, make our own mistakes. If you were president of this country, you'd still lecture us!"

"Then show good sense. Take advantage of the good advice," said Charlie. His mouth turned up ever so slightly. "I love my kids. I loved Joe."

"Dad, let us go."

"You can't go with your head in the clouds."

"The rain's stopped. Thanks." Frances smiled.

"For what?" Charlie frowned.

"For the lecture. It gave me a lot to think about. I'm going to write to Keller and tell him the Irwins are on their way to San Ysidro in a couple of weeks."

"Let me out so that I can be on my way to take over for your mother. She's been driving more than an hour. I think that's a record for her."

As soon as the family was back from California in the spring, Charlie sent Pauline and Sawyer with some of the cowboys on the Wyoming rodeo circuit. Charlie and Etta and a few cowboys took the show wagons and some stock to a couple small towns in Oregon and Idaho for rodeos. Betts had a few weeks of vacation before her fall nursing classes started, so she helped the cook at the Y6. By late fall the family was back at the San Ysidro ranch, and Charlie made friends with Mannie Keller and devoted his time to his latest racehorses: Noah's Pride, Daphne Belle, Liolele, Mess Wagon, Voltear, Enlo, Madam Valeria, White Collar, Black Shirt, and John P. Mills.

By spring Charlie was eager to get back to Cheyenne. There were terrible floods throughout the country, with extensive damage and many lives lost. There was nothing like that in the San Diego area, but still reading about the flooding in the newspaper made Charlie nervous. Etta thought it was because he was not at the Y6 ranch when floods hit there the year before. Charlie was also upset with the passing of the Agricultural Adjustment Act, which increased farm prices along with the fact that there was an early spring drought in the country. Charlie felt that subsidy and crop-limitation efforts were unconstitutional. He was also disturbed with President Roosevelt when he devalued the dollar to fifty-nine cents. "When I get back to Cheyenne I'll have a talk with Alonzo Clark," he told Etta.

"Whyever would you want to talk to a man who was acting governor of Wyoming?" asked Etta.

Charlie grinned and stretched out his legs. "In case Clark decides not to run for governor himself in 1936. I want to ask him about putting an elevator in the governor's mansion so I won't have to go up and down stair steps."

"Charlie! Stop your teasing!" chided Etta. "You aren't seriously thinking of living in that mausoleum. Are you?" She looked at him again and suddenly saw that he really was not fooling. He was serious.

Charlie wanted to be governor of the state of Wyoming.

"I don't want you to say a word about my being interested in living in the governor's mansion until I'm dead certain that I can get a campaign committee together. Then I'll have everyone on the Y6 and in Cheyenne out stumping for C. B. Irwin. Win with Irwin!"

Etta sat up. Her eyes watered. She blinked once and her eyes looked as calm as Jackson Lake on a quiet summer day. "It's amazing, but I believe you can make it. Just think of the Governor's Balls you and I went to. Think of the many times we danced. Oh, my, it kind of takes my breath away. You're right. I'm not going to breathe a word. I'm not even going to think about it until everything is in place and ready. Well, I swan, I'm so proud to be Mrs. C. B. Irwin."

Charlie chuckled deep inside his chest and held her close against his stomach. "Let's go back to Cheyenne," he said.

They were back in Cheyenne by the first of March. Charlie had Woodward drive him to town several times so he could talk to several lawyers and to Leslie Miller, a Cheyenne businessman who was a Democratic candidate for governor. Charlie explained that he was going to apply for candidacy on the Republican ticket and he intended to run an honest and open campaign.

Charlie stood in front of the house in Cheyenne looking at the banks of snow that were still against the house. Where the snow had melted on the lawn, the grass was bright green. Something prompted him to look in the sky. He was not sure if it was the sudden gust of wind in the bare treetops or the rare sound of a motor. He put his hand up to his forehead to shade his eyes, then he called out, "Etta! Did you hear that! It was Rogers! Will just buzzed the house to tell us he's in town! I'm going across the street to the bunkhouse for Bart. We're going to the airfield!" While Charlie was shouting Etta came out and saw the plane circle one more time and tip its wings over the tree tops in front of the house.

While Charlie was gone, she took two fried chickens from the icebox and put them in the oven to warm. She made biscuit batter and set the table in the kitchen for three. She never grew tired of Rogers's visits. She thought he was more like a brother to Charlie than his own brothers.

Food was exactly what Rogers wanted. He was on a commercial air flight to Chicago. He'd talked the pilot into buzzing Charlie's house before stopping to refuel in Cheyenne.

Rogers told Etta that a fellow passenger sitting across from him ate sandwiches and apples ever since leaving Los Angeles. "He ignored my longing glances at his food. I hope you have biscuits in the oven."

"Yes, and fried chicken," said Etta.

"Put it all in a box. I have thirty minutes to get back to that aeroplane. I've thought about your wonderful cooking all the way from California. My mouth is all juiced up."

Etta looked for an empty shoe box for the food.

Charlie took Rogers's arm and led him to the back bedroom. "That hotel in Claremore still have the big gun collection?" He reached for a rifle resting on a couple of wall pegs.

"As far as I know," said Rogers. "There's a thousand or more guns there."

"You still thinking of building a museum for guns?"

"As a matter of fact, I am."

"Well, I want this old Henry rifle to go in the collection," said Charlie. "It belonged to my grandfather. Hasn't been used for years. It was quite a gun in its day. The firing pin's divided so it strikes both sides of the cartridge rim at the same time. There's no dead spot on the priming ring." Charlie caressed the rifle and took it over by the window so that Rogers could read "Henry's Patent Oct. 16, 1860," on the barrel.

"Looks like new. You sure you want to part with it?"

"It's always been something I treasured. But it's an antique. There's no use for it now—except for people to look at and admire. Rope tricks draw a bigger crowd than target shooting and that's no secret."

"I don't know what to say, pardner. For certain, I promise, there'll be a Western Gun Museum." Rogers touched Charlie's hand as he took the Henry rifle.

Charlie's eyes sparkled. "I'd better give you the gun case or that aeroplane pilot might not let you back inside." Charlie rummaged around in the top of the closet and came out with a homemade gray canvas case. "There's some forty-four cartridges in that little pocket. I always did use a rope more than a gun." Charlie had a lump in his throat. Still, it had been easier to part with the rifle than he anticipated. "My grandfather used it in the Civil War."

"Put your mind at ease. I'll take good care of it," said Rogers. He held the box Etta prepared under one arm and the rifle in the other.

At the airfield Charlie said, "Remember when those acetylene flasher lights took the place of bonfires? Many a night city folks came out to see the planes land. They parked their cars in a semicircle with headlights turned on the field."

"What will it be like in the next five years?" asked Rogers.

"There's going to be some big changes in this country. This Franklin Delano Roosevelt is for cutting back on big industry. That'll put more people out of work."

Rogers grinned, pushed his hair out of his eyes. "Even Lincoln saw the folly in that. I think he was the one that said, 'You can't lift the wage earner by pulling down the wage payer.' Charlie, my good friend, what the country needs is popular government at popular prices."

"Why, I never thought of that!" Charlie grinned to match the smile Rogers had.

"That's why I told you," said Rogers.

"Maybe there'll be restaurant service on these commercial aeroplanes in five years," said Charlie.

"Nothing as good as this!" Rogers patted the shoe box that was still warm from the fried chicken and fresh biscuits. He hitched the Henry rifle tighter into the crook of his other arm.

Charlie's eyes watered. He blinked and managed a crooked smile. "So long, old friend. Until we meet again." He waved his hat and watched the plane taxi out into the field of buffalo grass, rev its motor, then take off. He got back inside his hew red Terraplane. Bart Woodward drove him home.

At eight o'clock in the morning of the twenty-first of March, Charlie asked his son-in-law, Sawyer, to drive him into Cheyenne in the Buick coupe because Woodward had taken Etta shopping in the Terraplane. Charlie had an appointment with Perry Spencer, chairman of the Republican Central Committee and Elmer Brock, President of the Wyoming Stock Growers' Association. The Republicans were unhappy because Clark, the acting governor, had been passed over in 1933, and Miller, the Democrat, was elected governor to replace Frank Emerson, who'd died while in office.

The Republicans wanted a strong candidate for the next election, and they wanted him to begin campaigning as soon as possible. Charles Burton Irwin looked like the best man for the job.

There was a skiff of new, powdery snow on the plains. The prairie looked new and fresh. Charlie thought of purity, decency, virtue. He took the snow as a good sign.

Charlie rolled down the window of the coupe and breathed the invigorating air. He felt good, full of enthusiasm. He imagined the smell of dry grass and the faint spice aroma of flowers that cleared his head. He recalled how his brother Will would close his eyes and sneeze when the wind blew dust into the yard or blacksmith shop. Charlie did not close his eyes. There was too much to see from the car. The limbs of the buckbrush were wind-deformed. The dead twigs were misshappen and twisted.

Charlie marveled to himself how the prairie land was ever-changing with each season. He was filled with admiration for the everlasting tolerance of the plants, even though each was buffeted by wind and dried by lack of rain, to thrive in the open fields. Each plant was a survivor through its own strength and stamina.

Charlie likened the prairie plants to the enduring, tough, freedom-loving people of the Western land. Then he saw a pair of sandhill cranes ride the tail of a rising column of warm air, caused by the uneven heating of the land by the morning sun. In a few minutes the cranes dipped and dived out of sight behind a hillock. In another moment the cranes reappeared as if by magic and sailed back toward the Y6, again hunting for another thermal to ride without flapping their wings.

The car went down a long hill, pulled far to one side to pass a wagon and team of frightened horses. "Slow down! Where's the fire!" hollered the teamster.

Charlie grinned and waved back and pounded on the side of the car for Sawyer to speed up. Charlie let the wind ruffle his hair. Unexpectedly he thought of the two hills on the eastern edge of the Y6 land, Lookout and Round Top. For years the two hills were symbols to Charlie of what was good and what was disagreeable in his life. Now he compared the two hills to wild animals, one was unspoiled, the other corrupt, one was the hunter, the other the prey, producer and consumer. He equated the hills with the field plants, beneficial and poisonous, pleasing and disagreeable. He thought of insects, useful and destructive, the beautiful butterfly, the aphid-eating ladybug, the blood-sucking mosquito or deerfly. In his mind's eye he saw scorpions hiding under stones ready to attack if disturbed by a man who sought shelter by tracking a thin, red line of tiny ants to a warm, dry cave.

Charlie thought, Man has time filled with happiness, not unlike the long, bright, hot days of summer, but in time each man has his share of heartache, similar to the shivery nights of summer. Life is diversity.

When Sawyer was close to the old Warren ranch, where Charlie had first started his ranching career about thirty years before, he banged on the side of the car and yelled out in his loudest voice, "Old Governor Warren would be proud of me today!"

Sawyer, known as an especially slow driver, nodded and stepped on the gas in response to Charlie's command to go a little faster. Without warning there was a loud retort. Almost like a rifle shot. "Damn, we blew a tire!" shouted Sawyer. "It's the right front!"

"All right, just—" Charlie never finished. The car skidded on the fresh snow, left the road, flew nearly sixteen feet into the air, and crashed into a high irrigation wall. Charlie was so startled, feeling the car become airborne, that he could say nothing. From the window all he could see was blue sky and white clouds. How odd this trip has turned out to be, he thought. Then everything seemed to push inward on him and the noise was deafening, as if the whole car were shattering, falling apart. Then there was nothing, only darkness, unconsciousness.

The car crashed into a telephone pole, broke it, skidded across the road about two hundred feet, plowed into two fence posts, then stopped crossways in the drainage ditch.

A big forest-green highway-maintenance truck rolled to a stop beside the car. Five big men came over and finally pulled Charlie out of the car and laid him on the ground.

Dan Donahue was riding with Reed Koons, a state highway patrolman, when he saw his friend, C.B. Irwin, stretched out on the snow-covered ground. "Pull over!" Donahue yelled. "There's old C.B. He's been in some kind of accident!"

Donahue went over to Charlie. "Hold the phone, C.B. It's not time to cash in yet. Horse Creek's still running!"

Charlie tried to smile. His midsection was on fire. He could hardly breathe, the pain was so excruciating. Donahue took off his blanket-lined wool jacket and laid it over Charlie.

Within half an hour the ambulance arrived. Donahue got Sawyer into the backseat of his car and tried to pull his jacket down so it wasn't bunched up around his chin.

"Hey, what're you doing?" yelled Sawyer. "Leave my coat alone!"

"I was just tryin' to keep the cold air from gettin' in, that's all," said Donahue. "Besides, that's a fancy silk shirt you got on. C.B. know you're wearing a yellow shirt?"

"I didn't ask!" snapped Sawyer, holding his arms over his chest. "Make me a smoke. Makings are in my vest pocket."

"Sure," said Donahue. "C.B. has some superstition about yellow, I heard. Won't let none of his cowboys wear yellow if they're in a rodeo event or in a horse race. Won't let any of his kids wear the color around him."

"That's a lot of hooey," groaned Sawyer.

"Maybe," said Donahue, concentrating on rolling the cigarette. "Your father-in-law don't like Fridays either. I think his bank loans were due on Fridays!" Donahue chuckled.

Charlie moved in and out of consciousness. When he was put into a hospital bed, he wanted to know about Saywer. "What did you do to Claude? Please tell me!" he yelled.

Dr. Beard called Etta, who was in Cheyenne. She came to the

hospital right away. She did not wait for someone to drive her. She put her coat and hat on and walked.

The first thing Charlie said to her was, "Have you seen Claude? Who's getting things ready for the upcoming rodeo in Torrington?"

Etta had called Dr. Galen Fox to take care of Charlie. Dr. Fox had seen Charlie several times during bouts with flu. Etta thought it best to have someone who knew Charlie.

Dr. Fox came in to give Charlie a sedative to keep him quiet. He wore a long, loose white coat. He had gray hair, a big nose, and soft gray eyes. Etta left Charlie only to call Pauline at the ranch and to call Ell in Colorado Springs.

Pauline and Frances came to the hospital in the afternoon.

"How's Claude?" Charlie asked Pauline. "Is he in the hospital, too?"

"Yes. He sends you a message. He says he has educated currency that says he'll be out before you. You want to bet him?" Pauline's voice was forced cheerful.

"Tell him I'm in the home stretch," said Charlie, grinning crookedly because the sedative made him groggy.

When the girls left, Dr. Fox was back in the room. He told Charlie to sit on the edge of the bed. "I'll have someone bring you something to eat." The doctor tapped Charlie's knee and made his foot jerk forward.

"Can I get cake when that trick works?" asked Charlie with a grin. His sides were taped and still it hurt whenever he talked or took a deep breath. He knew he had several broken ribs on both sides.

"You can have anything you want," said Dr. Fox.

Charlie thought, That's surely a secret. No one ever told me I could have anything I wanted if I were a hospital patient.

The doctor listened to Charlie's heart. He suspected that Charlie was bleeding internally because he complained about feeling faint. "Lie down again, Mr. Irwin."

Charlie's color was deathly white. He laid his head down, fighting off the dizziness. He didn't want to give in to a lightheaded feeling. His abdomen hurt. He tasted the warm salty surge that was forced up into his throat. He tried to swallow. The doctor examined his legs and feet, twisted one ankle back and forth slowly, checking for any possible fractures. Charlie managed to swallow, but immediately another surge came up into his mouth. He kept his mouth shut tight. He looked at Etta and winked.

Suddenly he could not keep his mouth closed another second.

The bright-red blood gushed out, soaking the bed. Charlie fell back as everything turned black. He could not hear Etta saying, "Charlie, oh, Charlie, I love you!"

Dr. Fox called a nurse to clean the bed and Charlie, then left. The nurse put Charlie on his side, trying to make him comfortable. She slid an emesis basin under Charlie's chin. "Let it drain. Don't breathe through your mouth and suck the blood into your lungs. Don't try to talk until the drainage is stopped. It's nothing. The bleeding will stop. Then you'll start healing."

Charlie tried to indicate that he could not breathe through his nose as some of the blood had run up there. He pointed to make the nurse understand. She said to Etta that maybe running warm salt water through Charlie's nose would rinse it. "I'll check with the doctor." She took the red-stained bed linen, rolled it in a ball with Charlie's gown in the middle, then went out of the room in a brisk, efficient walk. She was back in ten minutes shaking her head.

"What did Dr. Fox say?" asked Etta.

The young nurse motioned for Etta to step out of the room. "He doesn't want to try anything just yet," she said. "We'll watch your husband closely. I—I remember when Mr. Irwin rode a white horse and sang at Frontier. I thought he had the most wonderful voice God ever created. I would have followed him anywhere, like the Pied Piper. Lots of kids felt that way." Her eyes were deep brown and sad-looking. Her lips trembled.

"Yes, I felt that way when I first met him and then I married him and have been under his magical spell for forty years."

Etta sat with Charlie all night and the next day. He was kept sedated so he wouldn't thrash around in the bed. Pauline and Frances came in to say that Sawyer was going to be all right, but his broken ribs were giving him some discomfort.

Before the dinner cart was taken from room to room, the doctor came in to look at Charlie. He took his temperature, checked his pulse and blood pressure. He compared his figures with those on the nurse's chart. He motioned for Etta to step out of the room. She could feel her heart fly to her throat. She didn't want to hear what the doctor had to say.

"He's going to be fine, isn't he? All he needs is rest so he can heal inside." She tried to sound hopeful. "Charlie's always been the strong one."

"Mrs. Irwin, I don't have much hope. I'm sorry. He's still losing blood."

"But last night—I thought he would get better." She felt herself trying to make him say Charlie would be all right.

"Yes, last night, I might have thought there was some hope the hemorrhaging would stop. That it wasn't so severe. Right now I don't know the true extent of the internal injuries. If that bleeding doesn't stop of its own accord, there's not much anyone can do."

"You can operate and patch everything together," said Etta hopefully. She felt dizzy.

"In this case, maybe not. Come sit down and let me explain." He took Etta's elbow and led her to a chair in the hallway. "You see, the whole body cavity may be filled with blood from a ruptured abdomen, spleen, intestines. He has no fascia lata or interlacing between the skin and the organs for protection like most of us. I can probe the organs easily through the skin. Everything is tender. Very painful to Mr. Irwin."

"Why? Why has Charlie no interlacing?" Etta's eyes probed the doctor.

"At some time it seems to have been torn or ripped. I don't know why. Maybe he was thrown from a horse and dragged. Maybe a horse fell on him. A great weight on his abdomen could have done this. C.B. would never discuss it with me. Was it something he wanted to forget?"

Etta grabbed the doctor's arm. "That's it. The automobile accident. Charlie was driving. The car turned over and the metal support rested on Charlie's stomach. He kept it there so that I could breathe; otherwise, it would have lain on my neck. The hospital records are in San Diego. Would they help? What can we do?" Etta was holding the doctor's arm in a viselike grip.

"Pray that the internal bleeding stops. But you should not get your hopes up. I have to be honest with you."

"Yes, I suppose so," said Etta. Tears streamed down her face. She did not try to control them. "How long?" she whispered, letting go of the doctor's arm.

He pulled away and said, "Anytime—tonight." Then he left, walking quickly up the hall.

"I'd better stay with him," Etta said out loud, and darted back inside the room.

The sad brown-eyed nurse was giving Charlie a clean basin. She ran water in the bloody one and left it on the nightstand.

Charlie seemed listless. His color was transparent gray. His beard had grown some and it looked gray, too.

"Can you breathe through your nose, Mr. Irwin?" the nurse asked. Charlie closed his mouth and a terrible gurgling was heard. He swallowed hard and waited a moment, then tried again. This time the noise was not so loud. A third time he seemed to clear the blood from his nasal passages and he tried to close his mouth. When he opened his mouth to try to talk the accumulated blood spilled out.

Sometime after midnight Etta noticed that the blood seemed to lessen and only oozed slowly from his mouth. He slept, sometimes snoring loudly. Etta had several catnaps.

The doctor was in the room at half past eight in the morning. He could not rouse Charlie.

"I'm afraid the blood is accumulating inside. It's not draining. I am surprised he's gone on this long. He has stamina." Dr. Fox's gray eyes looked from Charlie to Etta. "You need to take care of yourself. Go home and get some sleep. I'll call you if there is a change."

Etta shook her head no. She understood the doctor was trying to do his best. But she couldn't leave. She didn't want to hear the doctor tell her about Charlie's strength. She was the one who knew his strength better than anyone. She wiped her eyes and pointed to the door. "I'll call if I need you," she said.

She sat for several minutes close to Charlie so that she could put her hand on his shoulder, inside his gown. She was losing her beloved Charlie. The people of Cheyenne were losing one of the best friends they ever had. The whole country was losing one of the best horsemen that ever lived. She kissed Charlie's forehead.

Charlie seemed to sleep. He was like a man in a stupor. He moaned and groaned, but did not open his eyes.

Once Etta kissed him on the forehead. She had her chair close beside the stark, white bed. She watched Charlie's chest move up and down. She watched his grayish face so if there was any change she'd be the first to see.

About noon Charlie opened his eyes. Etta caught her breath and leaned forward. He smiled and said with a soft gurgling sound, "It's Friday."

"Yes," she said, listening. There was no sound except the rasping noise of Charlie's breathing.

"I love you, dear." Charlie's brown eyes seemed to see through Etta to something far beyond. He held one hand out as though to grasp another. Etta lay her tiny warm hand into his big, dry fist.

"I will always love you—Charlie . . . !" her voice trailed off. A big, thin bubble grew at the corner of his mouth and burst into a thousand tiny red droplets. All of a sudden she was aware that he was not breathing. His heart was still beating, but he was not breathing. The vein pulsating in his neck was slowing, slowing.

Now she could no longer see it throbbing. "Charlie!" she said close to his ear.

Dr. Fox touched Etta's shoulder. She shuddered and let the tears spill. "Do you have someone who can help you make funeral arrangements?" asked Dr. Fox.

Etta could feel his hand warm on her shoulder. "Yes. I have two grown daughters at home, and a sister-in-law and granddaughter coming."

"I will call your home. Come with me." The doctor led Etta out to the hallway and to the waiting room. "Your daughters will be here soon," he said, and left.

Ell and Joella arrived that afternoon. Ell, in a simple black dress with a pearl necklace, was sorry not to have seen her brother one last time. "But I had this feeling," she said. "This feeling of falling and nothing left but blackness. It's the same feeling I have when I think of your friend from Oklahoma, Will Rogers."

"That's weird," said Frances. "But it's a fake because nothing happened to Will Rogers, just to Dad."

Ell shrugged and smiled. Her sad, green eyes were circled with soft purple.

Joella was red-eyed from crying all the way to Cheyenne on the train. Now that she was in Cheyenne, she could not cry.

The funeral home, Hobbs, Huckfeldt, and Finkbiner, called Etta the next morning. None of the caskets they had in stock were long enough nor wide enough for Charlie's body.

Etta said, "Have a casket made that fits."

"We do not have the facilities, madam," said Mr. Hobbs, with a tremor in his voice.

"Then call someone in Denver. Have it made well and look nice." Etta felt nothing, only numbness all over.

"Yes, madam. Thank you," said Mr. Hobbs in a voice that was almost a whisper. "I will personally find someone who can make a double-size casket."

By the evening of Friday, March 23, 1934, big and little newspapers throughout the United States had the news of Charlie's death. There were thousands of stories of the lifelong accomplishments of C. B. Irwin during his fifty-nine years of a most colorful life.

Saturday morning the telegrams began pouring in for Etta and the family from all over the country from people who knew Charlie—politicians, cowboys, capitalists, railroadmen, farmers, sheepherders, movie stars, bankers, lawyers, ranchers, horsemen, rodeo and circus people, and American Indians.

Dr. Robert T. Caldwell led the simple rite assisted by Al Leslie, past exalted ruler of the B.P.O.E. Several friends of Charlie's spoke a few words. Frank Meanea said, "I never heard anybody say anything really bad about C.B." Harry Walters said, "C.B. always helped down-and-outers. I bet he's given away more money than most people earn in a lifetime." Ed McCarty said, "He never had any hate for others. He'd give you anything he had if you needed it." Harry Hynds said, "C.B. was quite a man. He loved life and knew how to get the best out of it. C.B. had electricity, an exuberance about him. I'll miss the old champ more than I can put into words."

The funeral service was held at two-thirty on Sunday, March 25. The Cheyenne Lodge No. 660, and the Cheyenne Elks arranged for the service in the junior high school auditorium. This was the only place in town that was large enough to hold all of Charlie's mourners.

Charlie's favorite hymns, "Nearer My God to Thee," "Abide With Me," and "Jesus, Lover of My Soul," were sung by a quartet of Charlie's friends, Ed Cowan, Joe Folmer, Clayton Lewis, Howard Vaughn, with Mrs. Vaughn at the piano. The same songs were sung at Floyd's funeral seventeen years before.

Thousands of mourners stood in long lines for more than three hours to pass by the wooden casket that was eight feet by three and a half feet by thirty-two inches deep. It was covered with steel-gray broadcloth and had eight handles—two more than standard. The padded inside capacity was thirty-six cubic feet, while a standard casket contains only sixteen cubic feet. Many organizations, such as the Frontier Days Committee, attended the service in a body to indicate their last good-bye to Charlie.

"If he could see this crowd, he'd give a campaign speech," said Etta. She, her daughters, and other members of the family greeted the mourners. Etta shook hands with everyone, saying, "Thank you for coming." She was oblivious to time. The whole thing seemed like a dream. When asked how she was holding up, she said, "I'll make it through this. I'll do it for Charlie."

The smell of the hundreds of floral sprays and bouquets of every hue and color permeated the whole auditorium. When the casket was closed with a sharp snap, it was covered with a blanket of red roses from Etta and the family. The casket was carried the length of the auditorium on the shoulders of nine of Charlie's cowboys: George Montgomery, Marshall McPhee, John Bell, Nels Perry, all of Cheyenne; Jelmer Johnson of Albin; Clayton

Danks of Parco; Frank Tate of Divide; John Wilkinson of Waun-eta; and King Merritt of Federal taking his place at the end. They carried the steel-gray double-size casket between lines made up of local Boy Scouts who formed a guard of honor, Cheyenne policemen, Cheyenne firemen, and Elks. The quartet sang the popular cowboy requiem, "The Last Roundup." The bronzed cheeks of the hearty westerners were wet with tears. There was not a dry eye in the hall.

Tex Sherman, a popular writer, noted, "No private citizen . . . has been accorded a more general tribute than was tendered Charlie Irwin." Charles Hirsig said, "C.B was largely responsible for the popularity of rodeo events from coast to coast, from Portland to New York, with Chicago and Omaha in between." Chief of police, T. Joe Cahill, said there were any number of old and broken-down cowpokes throughout the West who owed their very lives to Irwin. "He always kept a number of old-timers who were down on their luck working for their board and room about his place that he kept near the Tia Juana racetrack and at his Y6 ranch."

As soon as the quartet stopped singing, Betts burst into uncontrollable sobbing. Etta put her arm around her granddaughter, trying to comfort her. "Sshh, honey. Grams is here." She felt a rising lump in her throat. Tears stung her eyes. "Oh, honey! I wonder if he had a premonition," Etta sobbed.

The honorary pallbearers came two by two down the aisle behind the enormous casket. They were T. Joe Cahill, Charles Hirsig, and Warren Richardson from Cheyenne; Carl R. Gray, president of the Union Pacific Railroad; W. M. Jeffers and George Brandeis from Omaha; Henry Collins from Pendelton, Oregon; Fred Stone from New York; H. T. Palmer, William Kyse, and Ralph McArthur from San Francisco; Will Rogers from Beverly Hills; and General John J. Pershing from Washington, D.C.

A mile-long cortege followed the remains to the gravesite at Lakeview Cemetery. Charlie was buried beside his son, Floyd.

Claude Sawyer attended the funeral with red-rimmed eyes. He had to be carried on a stretcher by several Y6 cowboys. Etta went over to speak to him after the ceremony. "I'm glad the hospital made arrangements for you to come. Claude, we're all going to depend on you so much more." Her voice broke and she couldn't say anything for a few seconds. She twisted the silver-filigreed brooch at her throat.

"I'll do everything I can." Sawyer bit his bottom lip to hold the tears back.

"There's a Winchester in town. It was with the Henry rifle that Charlie gave to Will Rogers. Those guns don't mean anything to me. But they were important to Charlie. Once he told me he didn't want his brothers to have either gun. I think he was afraid Frank would ask for it. So"—she took a deep breath—"before he does, I want you to have it. You know it was Tom Horn's rifle."

Sawyer's eyes widened. He was so surprised and honored by Etta's generosity that he felt all choked up. He reached out with his hand. Etta held it. Finally she said, "Don't blame yourself. It does no good. It was a bad accident you and Charlie were in."

"I have to say this," he said in a whisper. "C.B. knew when I married Pauline that I'd served time for bank robbery. I was young and thought it was a smart, he-man kind of thing. He knew I'd learned my lesson and would never do a trick like that again. He never said a word. Not to anyone."

"I never knew." Etta wiped away the tears.

"I liked that big man. He was more than a father-in-law to me." His voice caught and he could not go on.

The cowboys took Sawyer back to Memorial Hospital.

At the graveside Etta bent to touch the flowers heaped over and around the fresh mound of earth as though she were gently caressing the only man she would ever love. There were daisies, chrysanthemums, carnations, pink, white, and red. Most were hothouse flowers. It was too early for yard flowers or wild prairie flowers. A pillow of red and white carnations formed a Y6. The pillow was from Carl Gray and his wife. A huge floral horseshoe was from the Thoroughbred Breeders Association. A wreath of red roses was from Will Rogers and Fred Stone.

Frank stood next to her. His eyes were red. "What will happen to me?" he said softly.

"You'll go on like always," said Etta.

"He sent me a hundred dollars each month. Will you continue? I think C.B. would have wanted it that way." Frank was begging. "I depend on it. Ell gave it to me. I knew it came from Charlie."

"The girls and I will go over the books and see what can be done," said Etta. "I don't want to talk about it today."

Frank took a silver flask from his back pocket. "Excuse me. I'm not well." He took several large swallows, put the top on the flask, and put it into his pocket. He wiped off his mouth and smiled. "Tonic."

"Charlie never approved of your tonic," said Etta quietly.

The three girls and their husbands talked quietly that evening to Etta about the fate of the Y6 and the Irwin Livestock and Show

Company. Etta set her mouth firmly and declared she would carry on Charlie's work of furnishing stock to rodeos and continue the racehorse business. "I'm secretary and treasurer of the company; I'll be president. Pauline will be secretary and Frances will be treasurer. Joella, you can do publicity for us. Your husbands can be managers. Everything will be up to the usual Irwin standard and everyone will be there—everyone . . . but Charlie."

Betts, Patty, and little Irwin sat huddled around the kitchen table. "You know the Indians might come to chase the evil spirits away so Gramps has a good journey into eternity," said Betts, remembering what she'd heard about her Uncle Floyd's death and burial.

"Pine Ridge is too far away," said Patty.

"Indians! Would they dance on the grave?" asked ten-year-old Irwin.

"No, I suppose not," said Betts, putting water in the teakettle and getting the jar of tea leaves from the cupboard. When the water boiled, she made tea for everyone in the living room.

Ell was saying, "I keep thinking Charlie is going to walk in the front door and laugh in his big booming voice." She put a clammy hand on Betts's arm and whispered, "Did you see him?" There were dark circles around her velvet-green eyes.

"Who?" asked Betts, watching the cup and saucer so that the tea would not spill.

"You know, my brother, Charlie, your gramps. He was sitting on the edge of the stage during the whole ceremony. He looked over all those people in the auditorium and grinned. He clapped his hands and seemed to be shouting or singing. He looked at your grandmother with that sweet look as if to say, 'Dear, see all the friends I have.' "

Betts felt a tear slide down her cheek. "I wasn't going to say anything. I thought you'd laugh. I saw him sitting on the edge of the stage with his knees crossed. I think he thoroughly enjoyed that service and the singing. Aunt Ell, I saw him get up and wave when they sang, 'The Last Roundup.' He walked toward us—then—then disappeared. I couldn't stop crying. Honestly, did we see him?"

"Yes," whispered Ell, "and the others saw him, too."

In the middle of the night Betts woke up and heard her grandmother sobbing across the hall. Then she realized the wind was blowing enough to make a sighing sound at the corners of the house. Suddenly she was on her feet and shaking Patty in the next bed.

"Wake up! You want to go to the cemetery with me?" asked Betts.

"What for?" asked Patty sleepily.

"To see if the Indians are there. Get dressed. I can drive the car." Betts was getting dressed as fast as she could. She found car keys in the kitchen. Outside it was not pitch dark; the moon was nearly full and past its zenith. The stars were bright. The few white clouds seemed like a silvery scrim. The girls drove into the spruce-lined graveled road of the cemetery, stopped the car, and got out cautiously.

"I don't see anything," said Patty. "It's cold out here." She buttoned her coat and pulled the collar up around her ears.

A rabbit scuttled from a clump of yellowed grass to some tangled leafless bushes. The high-pitched whining was heard in the spruce tops on the crest of each gust of wind.

They stood at the foot of their grandfather's grave. The smell of roses and carnations was strong as the wind gusted. Betts hunkered down and cupped a red rose in her hand. The flower was limp and cold.

"Poor Gramps. I'll never believe he's gone," said Betts. "He was the strength of the whole family. He kept us together."

Patty hunkered down as much to keep out of the wind as anything. She looked at the bare earth under her feet. There were little lines, side by side, close together, as if made with a fine-toothed rake, or even a comb. The lines went clear around the grave. "What's this?"

"Oh, my God! That's turkey feathers!" breathed Betts, crouching down to see better in the moonlight.

"Could be the way the flowers were dragged up on the grave," said Patty, clearly agitated. "No one would sweep the dirt with a feather!"

"A handful of feathers!" cried Bett's. "Lookit here!" Betts's heart was pounding fast. She had half-expected to see the lines made by the brushing of the turkey feathers. She hadn't expected to see the feathers. In the center of a jar of dried sage was a handful of turkey feathers. ,Four turkey feathers were poked through the grass into the ground. They looked like some hardy spring flower pushing through the cold soil.

"I never saw that before," said Patty. "Who put the feathers on the graves? It's like—like some ghost was here." She shivered.

"Somehow, I knew someone would be here. I knew it!" said Betts, blowing on her hands to warm them. She moved in the crouched position close to the feathers, speckled white and brown, nestled in with the brittle sage. She ran her hands along the edge of the feathers, making them look rough and unkempt. She ran her fingers up in the opposite direction and smoothed the feathers' edges. The discovery of the wild turkey feathers standing firm and proud seemed to confirm the great unbroken friendship between the Sioux and the Irwin father and son. Betts felt a great sense of reverence as if she were in a huge domed cathedral. She whispered to her cousin, "Don't step on the brush marks. They keep the evil spirits away."

The wind had died down so the air was not so cutting cold. Thin clouds scurried over the moon, diffusing the light, making it hard to make out shadows.

"Why is the spruce over there, across the yard, bowing up and down? There's no wind. Someone's there!" Patty's eyes were large and luminous. She hung on to Betts's arm. "You think someone is watching us?"

"Maybe someone's letting us look, waiting for us to leave," Betts whispered, her mouth feeling dry as cotton.

The girls stood and walked hand in hand toward the car. They quickened their steps as they passed the bowed spruce. Betts stopped, causing Patty to take one step and also stop. "Listen. Do you hear anything?"

"No."

"Stay here. I'm going to have a look," said Betts.

"Oh, no!" whispered Patty. "What if you saw someone—something—maybe an Indian."

"I have an Indian name. I'm a *hoonka*. I'm not afraid." Betts moved across the road, the gravel crunching under her shoes. Her heart was in her throat. Her palms were sweaty. There was nothing on the other side of the tree. It seemed to be bent from the weight of last winter's snow. Betts rubbed her hands against her coat and drew in a deep breath. The cold air went down into her throat before it was warmed. She breathed in more slowly. Mixed with the fresh air she smelled, in a flash of recollection, the aroma of sage and bear grease and raw leather. The smell of moccasins, or a well-worn leather tunic.

The next morning Betts told her grandmother about the feather bouquet she and Patty had seen. Etta's blue eyes seemed made of glass. They lay sunken behind wide dark circles. The lids were puffy. She reached out and gave Betts a hug. "You're spoofing me. Just like Gramps might do. You're trying to make me cheer up and smile. I was awake all night. I never heard a thing. Two giggly girls could never get past my bedroom door."

Patty said, "Gram, Betts is telling the truth. There were turkey feathers and brush marks."

"Emotions do strange things," said Etta, splashing cold water on her face with one hand, with the other she squeezed an old cork with C B I crudely carved in the top.

Weeks later Etta took fresh lilacs from the yard to Charlie's grave. She asked the caretaker if he'd seen anything on the night of March twenty-fifth.

"No, ma'am, I don't remember as I did," he said.

"My granddaughter must have dreamt the whole thing," said Etta, laughing. "Teenaged girls are so silly." She felt relieved.

Betts knew what she and Patty had seen. She had two speckled wild turkey feathers hidden in the back of her Bible.

Six days after Charlie's death, the *Wyoming State Tribune*, March 29, 1934, carried the following article by Charlie's friend, Warren Richardson:

CHARLIE IRWIN NEVER SPOKE
LIGHTLY OF WOMEN OR SWORE

Fearless Big Showman Who Had Genius for
Handling Men Did Not Drink or Use
Tobacco, Relates Friend

> . . . Charlie absolutely loved danger. His mind was quick as lightning and he always seemed to size up a bad situation and instantly do the proper and best thing to correct it. I have seen him jump in front of a crazy runaway team of horses, when it looked like sure death to do so, and stop them. No automobile could go quite fast enough to suit him, regardless of the road.
>
> His physical courage was equaled by his moral courage. I have seen him in some of the largest eastern cities, at the time he was running his Wild West Show, when he was frequently up against everything that seemed possible, but his wonderful resourcefulness never failed him. If it was necessary to talk a railroad president into carrying his trains to the next town, after a run of bad luck due to rains or other causes, he did it. 'Persistence—never give up' was Charlie's motto.
>
> He was one of the most loyal men to his friends I have ever known. A 'hale fellow well met' at all times. Regardless of what fate might have done to him he was always cheerful.
>
> I have known Charlie Irwin intimately ever since he came to Cheyenne, some thirty years ago. I have ridden many miles with him, visited him at his ranches, and I have never heard him speak lightly of a woman or utter profanity, nor have I ever seen him take a drink or use tobacco. He was a pal in his family. Charlie was proud of his charming daughters, to whom

he furnished the best horses money would buy for their performances that for years delighted thousands. His son Floyd was an early Frontier Days performer who was fatally injured at the show grounds. Charlie never recovered from the loss of his boy. Charlie's wife was his constant companion through life. He hardly ever went anywhere without her. His manner with women was always chivalrous and they all liked him.

Charlie exemplified the spirit of the old-time cowboy. If he called upon the governor he went on horseback right into his office.

. . . Illustrating Charlie's sublime confidence in himself, I remember during the early part of the World War he called me into the postal telegraph office to read me a long telegram he was about to send to General Pershing. In it he asked to be appointed commander-in-chief of all transportation of supplies for the American Army. He said, 'What do you think of that?' I said, 'Charlie, that is a pretty big job, I do not think you should send it.' His reply was, 'Why not? I can do it,' and he sent it. 'I can do it' put Charlie over lots of hurdles during his life.

All in all I have known few men who had more good qualities and less bad ones than Charlie Irwin. Big men all over the United States were his friends and always glad to see him. Charlie's big body was only equaled by his big heart, and his courage did not forsake him on the last roundup.

So long, Charlie! I will be seeing you at the races, you in the Judges stand with St. Peter, watching 'em come down the home stretch. I will surely be glad to meet you.

The *New York Herald-Tribune* in March, 1934, commented on Charlie's death. In fact, the loss of C. B. Irwin probably drew more editorial comment throughout the United States than did any citizen up to that time.

A Showman of the Track

C. B. Irwin, who died on Friday at Cheyenne, as the result of injuries in an automobile accident, was one of the most picturesque figures in the West, where he had for many years raced a stable of horses when he wasn't punching cattle or promoting rodeos. . . . There was a time when Charlie Irwin held the roping championship of the United States and was ready to back himself as a sprinter against all comers. Many a professional footrunner, masquerading as a cowpuncher, found Irwin anything but an easy mark in the impromptu matches that were decided in the dusty main street of a hamlet in Wyoming or other western states, for

Charlie's activities embraced the entire West up to the day his motor . . . somersaulted into a ditch a few miles from his ranch in Wyoming. . . .

'The boys on the hill,' as he designated the poorer class of horsemen, at Tia Juana and Agua Caliente, where Irwin raced for years, were his special charge. It was as their savior that he helped to promote the Pacific Coast Thoroughbred Horsemen's Association, of which he was once president and a director at the time of his death. . . .

The West will miss this huge man.

Will Rogers devoted one of his syndicated columns to his good friend Charlie Irwin, April 22, 1934, McNaught Syndicate, Inc.

WILL ROGERS SAYS OLD CHEYENNE WON'T SEEM THE SAME WITH CHARLEY IRWIN GONE

Believes He'll Ride Up to Heaven Like a Real Cowboy, Forking 'Steamboat' and using 'Teddy Roosevelt' for Pack Horse

Well all I know is just what I read in the papers, and what happens here and there. Have lost some fine friends lately by death. Among them a few weeks ago, Charley [sic] Irwin, the old Cowboy and Cattleman from Cheyenne, any of you that ever went to see the Big Cheyenne Frontier Show will remember Charley, he just about was the Daddy of that great Show. He had three daughters, and one son, the three daughters were wonderful relay riders. That's when you ride one horse so far, then change in front of the grand stand to another horse, then race on around, generally making three changes. They were the champs at that, for he really had fast horses, and they really rode 'em.

Exciting Times

It is absolutely the most exciting thing that has ever been invented when it is put on great, and they are all close finishing together. I have seen that old grandstand in Cheyenne just sway with cheers and excitement. It takes some real nerve, and skill to come in there at top speed and step off one of those old crazy thorobreds and keep your feet running and grab the horn on another saddle on another horse that is raring and plunging to go. Then there is the other riders and horses coming in and going out too, so you not only have to watch what you are doing, but what everybody else is doing. Then there is the mens relay. They have to change saddles, but the girls just change horses.

His son Floyd was at the time of his death just about the world's championship cowboy. He was killed roping a steer the night before the opening of the great show there. It put a great melancholy spirit over the whole celebration that year, as Floyd was a great favorite.

Raced His Horses

C. B. Irwin . . . in his later years . . . devoted his time mostly to the racetracks where he kept a big stable of horses. Always at Tia Juana, Mexico, in the winter, everybody knew him and everybody liked him, and he had the most wonderful wife in the world. Gosh what a great woman is Mrs. C. B. Irwin. And what she has had to stand for in thrills and spills with those girls and Floyd and Charley too, for he was the champion steer roper in the early days of the show. . . .

Won't Seem the Same

Ah, old Cheyenne won't seem the same. Every time I would step off an aeroplane there, (where they gas, and get meals) I would holler "Where's C.B.?" and if he was in the town he would be there. Before Cheyenne had a real aerial depot and I was going thru one night on a mail plane, he brought me a big box of fried chicken that Mrs. Irwin had cooked. Gosh it was good. I ate all the way to Omaha. He was up to see me just before he was killed in the auto accident. Buddy Sterling who had charge of my horses was one of Charley's main boys when he ran all the shows and contests. He was like Floyd, he was a top hand at anything. He gave me a race mare, a young one, that he wanted to have Buddy break for polo. Charley had a great career. He was a real cowpuncher in his day, and the greatest spirit and best company that ever lived.

That other world up there is going to hear a whoop at the gate and a yell saying, "Saint Peter, open up that main gate, for there is a real cowboy coming into the old home ranch. I am riding old 'Steamboat' bareback, and using 'Teddy Roosevelt' for a pack horse. From now on this outfit is going to be wild, for I never worked with a tame one.

The Cheyenne Chamber of Commerce glowingly praised Charlie for his work with the Frontier Days celebrations, for his foot racing, steer roping, and horse racing. The tribute concluded with these words in the April 11, 1934, *Wyoming State Tribune:*

> He was a booster in spirit and performance and sang the praises of his community and his fellow-citizens as well as extolling the virtues of that place where fate and fortune took him. That spirit was inspiring and contagious. His smile was charming, his laugh hearty and his hand-shake firm. He possessed a large melodious voice adapted to both announcing and singing to which one would listen in the arena or in the assembly room with a thrill. . . .

The *Laramie Republican* stated, "Charlie Irwin—The Great Cowpoke of Them All," on March 26, 1934:

> Charlie Irwin's death removes not only one of the most colorful figures in the West but a man who through his friendliness and open-handed generosity had endeared himself to thousands of his fellow citizens not only in Wyoming but throughout the length and breadth of the range country. Wyoming is still a cow country, and so cowmen who can preserve the old traditions will always be more or less heroes among us. Charlie Irwin was essentially a showman. He understood the game just as much as did Buffalo Bill, and like Col. Cody he was also adept and expert himself in many of the lines which entered into the sport which he followed.
>
> Whoever can forget what a figure Charlie made in the days of his prime. . . . No big man ever sat a horse better. And what horses he chose! He and one of his calico mounts supplied poetry in motion when they entered the arena of Frontier. He was a most artistic as well as effective roper, and the neatness and dispatch with which he did things, made his performances of those days a delight to watch and, when there was coupled with it the fun which he always saw in a show, he was irresistible. He will long be remembered as one of our most spectacular as well as much liked cowmen. He was in a class by himself.

Etta and the girls received thousands of telegrams and letters of condolence from the thousands of friends Charlie had made. One of the most touching letters came from one of the Sioux who had worked in the Irwin rodeos and Wild West shows, Charlie Yellow Boy of Pine Ridge, South Dakota.*

*This letter was handwritten to Pauline and is reproduced on the last page of the insert of photographs and illustrations.

During the summer of 1934 Irwin stock was sent to several local rodeos, such as Torrington and Denver, with the same good results the Irwin stock had always had. The Irwin horse stable was successful in eight days of racing at Longacres, with a horse called Instigator winning three purses. Liolele and Color Bell each won twice. Etta became the owner of the Irwin stables, Frances was manager, and her second husband, Mannie Keller, handled the jockeys. Tom Smith remained as trainer. Their prize jockey was a young man Charlie had never used, Ralph Neves. At the Tanforan track Neves rode three winners home in one day.

On the closing day, Saturday, July 28, of the 1934 Frontier Days celebration, Etta and her three daughters gave the Omaha department store owner, George Brandeis, the big, broad-brimmed, ten-gallon hat that had been especially made for Charlie by the Stetson Company more than twenty years before. Charlie had worn that big white hat to every Frontier Days festival he'd attended. There had never been another hat like that one.

Brandeis was honored to be given Charlie's hat. He told the crowd at the fairgrounds that Charlie always wore it when he came to Omaha for the Ak-Sar-Ben race meets. "Once I said to Charlie, 'That hat must have a fifteen-gallon crown. It is more like a giant sombrero. It would make any man look like a champion.' Charlie said to me, 'Well, when I die the hat is yours.'"

Charlie had not been a rich man in terms of money when he died. Etta made enough money with horse racing to pay off the debts. She knew deep in her heart that she did not have the personality nor the stamina to match Charlie's. She could not determine "good" horses to replace those that no longer ran well. She never really cared for ranch life.

Thus, a year after Charlie's death she quietly sold the twenty-three thousand acres of the Y6 ranch to Fred Petsch of Scottsbluff, Nebraska. She didn't want to sell the Y6 brand. "It was easier to buy the ranch than to negotiate for the brand," Fred Petsch admitted. Curly McGuckin, Etta's brother, worked for Petsch for a while after she sold. The Y6 is still owned and being run by Fred Petsch's two sons, Irvin Joe and Fred Lee. King Merritt bought the Four-Mile pasture.

Etta moved to Burlingame, California. She died in 1953 and was buried next to her beloved Charlie in Cheyenne.

Slightly more than a year after Charlie's tragic death, his best friend, Will Rogers, was flying with Wiley Post. The two men were killed when their plane crashed on August 15, 1935, in Alaska.

Afterword
by Dean Krakel

Lucky for me, I grew up south of Cheyenne—north of Denver, as the crow flies—in Charlie Irwin country. His tracks were all over the landscape.

During the twenties and thirties, C.B. Irwin was active in putting on Frontier Days' parades and rodeos. It was during this period that, as a young boy, I would catch glimpses of him. C.B. was a master at assembling colorful and assorted characters and historical figures. He knew most of them personally, especially the Sioux Indians. Each parade during C.B.'s years had dozens of Pine Ridge and Rosebud Sioux; in the parades they danced, chanted, and beat drums as they rode on special floats. Many were riding gaily decorated horses with blue accoutrements. Women or squaw riders often pulled travois loaded with Indian children. One special year, old Dewey High Beard, riding a fancy white horse, led the Indian delegation. High Beard was the last survivor of the Custer battle, and the war shirt he wore was decorated with cavalry scalp locks.

C.B. saw to it that the United States Cavalry was in his parades full force. Many horses pulled caissons and cannons. Fort D. A. Russell, near Cheyenne, was famous for its Black Horse Troop. One year, C.B. had General Black Jack Pershing in his parade, riding with his famous father-in-law, Senator Francis E.

Warren. C.B. Irwin had a knack for cutting through red tape to get the job done.

Another colorful figure and friend of C.B.'s was T. Joe Cahill, Cheyenne's police chief. Cahill and C.B. were involved in the life of the famous gunman Tom Horn. Cahill had been invited by Horn to be his hangman. Charlie and his brother Frank sang for Tom minutes before he was dropped through the gallows platform.

The lives of Tom Horn and C.B. Irwin were entwined through common livestock interests and through ranchers with whom they both associated—names like John Coble, Frank Bosler, Charley Hirsig, Dougald Whittaker from Horse Creek and the Jordans of Iron Mountain. Both men were outstanding steer ropers and competed in Cheyenne Frontier Days' roping contests from the turn of the century on. C.B. won the championship in 1906.

I became more involved with the Irwins as a result of my writings and research in the Tom Horn case. My book, *The Saga of Tom Horn,* was controversial. In 1950–51, I talked to practically everyone of importance in the case, including Frank Irwin, then living in Fort Collins, Colorado. The question was whether or not Horn had killed fourteen-year-old Willie Nickell. Horn was convicted of the murder. The Irwins did not believe Tom was guilty, nor did Dr. George P. Johnston, who was close to the principals, nor did John Coble. T. Joe Cahill was mechanical in his answer: "We hung Tom, didn't we?" I am not convinced that the man was guilty, but I am sure it was C. B. Irwin who tried to spring Horn from Laramie County ail. Horn bungled his jailbreak attempt because he couldn't work the firing mechanism of a German Luger.

I bumped into the Irwins during my research of the famous 1908 *Denver Post* horse race, stretching five hundred miles from Evanston, Wyoming, to Denver, Colorado. The man I was championing was W. E. Dode Wykert, a cowboy from Ault, Colorado, where I was born and raised. C.B. Irwin was backing a Cody, Wyoming, cowboy named Workman. The theme of the race was to prove which was tougher and had the greatest endurance: the range bronc or the thoroughbred. The drama set the stage for C.B. to pull off some of his greatest chicanery.

The last evidence I saw of C.B. Irwin was a huge pair of bib overalls he once wore, which were part of an exhibit held on the Wyoming State Fair Grounds in Douglas.

C.B. needs to be remembered for the many things he contributed to the West and to its heritage—all the reasons why he was elected an honoree in the Hall of Great Westerners at our National Cowboy Hall of Fame. His immortality is more heavily ensured with the publishing of Anna Lee Waldo's large book and super story based on C. B. Irwin's life and the Y6.

—Dean Krakel, Executive Vice-President of the National Cowboy Hall of Fame and Western Heritage Center, 1979 to 1985; Editor of *Persimmon Hill*, 1979 to 1985; and presently Director of the High Plains Heritage Center, Spearfish, South Dakota

Acknowledgments

I am truly grateful to Betty Steele for wanting the story of her grandfather written as a historical novel, for introducing me to the Y6 and the Pioneer Avenue homes of C. B. Irwin, for showing me the hill, Round Top, for helping me with names, dates, countless stories of ranch, rodeo, and horse-racing life and for her everlasting friendship. I thank Charlie Bennett for his generosity in letting me use his huge clipping and photograph collection. I can never thank him enough for his understanding and encouragement when they were most needed.

I wish to acknowledge my indebtedness to Odie B. Faulk for blazing the trail with his manuscript on C. B. Irwin, which I used frequently to keep my chronology correct; to Howard Leech and the Grand River Historical Society, Chillicothe, Missouri, for reprinting the *History of Caldwell and Livingston Counties, Missouri, 1886;* to Carl L. Hurd and M. C. Parker and the late Betty Walker of the Sherman County Historical Society, Goodland, Kansas, for letting me freely use the material that is in their June 1975 to January 1981 bulletins; to Mr. Bryan, Chairman of Cheyenne's 1982 Frontier Days Committee; to Robert Hanesworth for writing the story of the Frontier Days, *Daddy of 'Em All,* which was a wonderful source of reference material; to Gary Carey for his great portrayal of Douglas Fairbanks and Mary

Pickford in his book, *Doug and Mary;* to Crown Publishers for permission to use the Tom Horn letters and the song "Life's Railway to Heaven"; to Dr. J. S. Palen of Cheyenne for his stories and pictures of C. B. Irwin; and to Ferne Shulton, who published her *Pioneer Comforts and Kitchen Remedies,* and let me make use of several of her recipes.

I thank the *Wyoming State Tribune, New York Herald-Tribune,* McNaught Syndicate, Inc., *Laramie Republican, Cheyenne State Leader, Denver Post, Harper's Weekly,* and the *Salt Lake Tribune* for permission to quote the material indicated in the text by specific newspapers and dates.

Permission for photographs were obtained from the present owners and/or the Wyoming State Archives Museums and Historical Department, Cheyenne, and the Western History Research Center, Laramie. Every attempt was made to contact the original photographer or copyright holder. In many instances the early photographer could not be located nor identified. The picture of the four Irwin children may have been made at the Billie Walker Studio in Cheyenne; the picture of C. B. Irwin roping a steer was made by J. E. Stimson, Cheyenne; the picture of Clayton Danks and the horse, Steamboat, was made by Ed Tangen, Boulder, Colorado.

This book could not have been written without the help of Cathy Cooper, Associate Librarian, Keenland Library, Lexington, Kentucky; Jane Brainard, State Archives, Museums and Historical Department, Cheyenne, Wyoming; Esther Kelly and Eunice Spackman, who searched and photocopied files on C. B. Irwin, Bill Carlisle, Tom Horn, Roy Kivett, and the U. P. Railroad at the Western History Research Center, University of Wyoming, Laramie; Emmett Chisum of the American Heritage Center, University of Wyoming, who took time to show me around his research facilities and told stories of the great friendship between C. B. Irwin and his acquaintances, Francis E. Warren, General John Pershing, and Tom Horn; and Edgar R. Potter, who gave permission to use his "Cowboy Slang."

In doing research for this book, I met people such as Mrs. A. Vegelis, librarian, San Ysidro Library, San Ysidro, California; Eva Mae Emerson, postmistress, Rock River, Wyoming; Susan M. Simpson, head of public services, Albany County Public Library, Laramie, Wyoming; and John E. Witherbee, research specialist, Union Pacific Railroad Company; who were not only friendly, but more than willing to go the extra mile in helping to find information I needed.

The most unforgettable day in researching this work came when I met Irvin Joe Petsch, his wife, Donna, and his mother, Wilma. Irvin Petsch and his brother, Fred, now own the Y6 ranch. The old log bunkhouse, with C.B.'s initials in cement, still stands behind a modern ranch home. The old barn is still used every day. In the loft are several saddles once used by C.B. On an inside, red-painted wall are names and initials carved by countless cowboys who worked for C.B., including his son Floyd and son-in-law Claude Sawyer, and Will Rogers's *W. R.* Irvin Petsch gave me permission to use the Y6 brand name in this book on August 4, 1984.

Permission to use the Wyoming bucking-horse design from the Wyoming license plate was given by the Secretary of the State of Wyoming, June 20, 1984.

My husband, Bill, went south to San Ysidro, Tijuana; north to Cheyenne, Saratoga, and Encampment, Wyoming, and west to Rock Springs, Wyoming, with me and helped to gather interview notes and background information for this work. He helped to edit and proofread the manuscript and galleys and criticized my geography.

—A.L.W.

Source Material

Newspapers

In the Charles M. Bennett Collection are 472 pages of clippings photocopied from large scrapbooks kept by Etta Irwin. Most of the clippings have no identification; that is, no newspaper title nor date is indicated. However, the pages tell the story of the Cheyenne Frontier Days, Charlie Irwin and his family, Tom Horn, Bill Carlisle, Wild West Shows, Irwin Rodeos, horse racing, and the death of Charlie's son, Floyd, his foster son, Roy, and his automobile accident and death.

The following newspaper articles were selected because these clippings had full references and they established the credibility of the exploits and accomplishments of C. B. Irwin.

"Arizona Owens Takes Poison." *Sunday State Leader*, Cheyenne, August 28, 1910.

Bristol, Jack A. "Badly Injured By Shot From Sheriff Roach." *Wyoming State Tribune*, December 3, 1919.

"Carlisle Is Caught." *The Casper Daily Tribune*, December 2, 1919.

"Carlisle, Last Great Train Robber, Dies." *Rock Springs Daily Rocket*, June 20, 1964.

"Carlisle's Bold Deeds of Banditry." *The Cheyenne State Leader*, November 19, 1919.

"Carlisle's Career of Outlawry." *The Denver Post,* December 3, 1919.

"Carlisle Still Free; Is Kicked Off Train." *The Denver Times,* November 23, 1919.

"Carlisle Tells of Crime on Train 19. Statement Obtained at Bedside of Wounded Bandit Taken to Omaha by Irwin and John Gale." *Cheyenne State Leader,* December 4, 1919.

Carter, C. F. "U. P. Bandit Writes Letter to the Post as He Sits Among Intended Victims." *The Denver Post,* April 25, 1916.

"C. B. Irwin—A Big Man About the West." *Cheyenne Daily Sun,* Second Especial Edition, Summer 1979.

"C. B. Irwin—Rodeo Hill of Fame Honoree." *Cheyenne, Wyo. State Tribune-Eagle,* July 25, 1976.

"Charles B. Irwin dies of Injuries." *Casper Tribune,* March 23, 1934.

"Charles Irwin is Injured Critically in Highway Crash." *Wyoming Tribune,* March 22, 1934. Joseph F. Jacobucci Coll. 374, American Heritage Center, University of Wyoming, Laramie.

Charles M. Bennett Collection. Consists mainly of newspaper clippings and belongs to Charles M. Bennett, Scottsdale, Arizona.

"Charlie Irwin the Great Cowpoke of Them All." *Laramie Republican,* March 28, 1934.

Chrisman, George, Jr. "Losing Day at Tijuana Track Brought About Invention." *Arizona Republic,* January 30, 1979.

"Double Size Casket Made for Charlie Irwin's Body." *Denver Evening Post,* March 25, 1934.

"The Fifth Annual Frontier Celebration." *The Wyoming State Tribune,* August 31, 1901.

"Fire Destroys Four Thoroughbreds, Does Damage of $100,000." *The San Diego Union,* November 28, 1924.

Hebard, Grace Raymond Collection. B-C194-w1. Newspaper clippings from Wyoming newspapers from 1931 to 1964 about Bill Carlisle. Wyoming Clipping File, University of Wyoming, American Heritage Center, Laramie.

"Irwin Bros. Wild West Show Recalled." *Wyoming Eagle,* June 16, 18, 1970.

Irwin, Charles. "Carlisle Calmest of All Outlaws in Holdup Business." *The Denver Post,* December 3, 1919.

"Jokers Are Gumming Up Hunt For Bandit Thru False Clues." *The Denver Post,* November 24, 1919.

"Kivett Faces Murder Trial." *The Salt Lake Tribune,* August 30, 1924.

Knox, Kirk. "Coble Sisters Recall Tom Horn." *Cheyenne Republic,* August 30, 1974.

Knox, Kirk. "Saga of Tom Horn 'Hired Gun' Retold." *Wyoming State Tribune and Wyoming Eagle,* July 25, 27, 1967.

"The Last of the West." *Cheyenne Tribune Eagle,* July 24, 1977.

"Meandering Mountain Rail Line is Now Branch of U.P." *Wyoming State Tribune,* December 3, 1951.

"Mrs. Irwin Carries On With Show." *Pine Bluffs, Wyoming Post,* April 19, 1934.

"Noted Wyoming Rancher Dies of Crash Injuries." *Wyoming State Tribune,* March 24, 1934. B. F. Davis Collection, No. 484, American Heritage Center, University of Wyoming, Laramie.

"Old Timers Recall Early Days." *Wyoming Eagle,* October 29–30, 1970, Sharkey Irwin.

"Pershing Heads List of Irwin Pallbearers." *The Denver Post,* March 25, 1934.

"Real Western Movie Filmed Near Cheyenne." *Wyoming State Tribune,* July 11, 1919.

Richardson, Warren. "Charlie Irwin Never Spoke Lightly of Women or Swore." *Wyoming State Tribune,* March 29, 1934.

"Rodeo Rider is Killed in Fall." *The Salt Lake Tribune,* August 20, 1925.

Rogers, Will. "Charley Irwin, Star of the Big Cheyenne Frontier Show, Gets Final Summons." *Los Angeles Examiner,* April 29, 1934.

Rogers, Will. "Will Rogers Says Old Cheyenne Won't Seem Same With Charley Irwin Gone." *New York Herald Tribune,* March 1934. McNaught Syndicate, Inc., April 22, 1934. Hebard Collection, American Heritage Center, University of Wyoming, Laramie.

"Roosevelt Delighted With Greatest of Frontier Days." *Sunday State Leader,* August 28, 1910.

"Roy Kivett Is Killed When Horse Falls On Him At Salt Lake Rodeo." *Wyoming State Tribune,* August 20, 1925.

"Rundark Scores Initial Victory for Irwin." *The San Diego Union,* December 1, 1924.

"Scoop," "Charley Irwin Puts Over Two; Joella I. Wins." *San Diego Union,* December 7, 1922.

Shirley, Glenn. "101 Ranch, 1871–1931." *Ponca City Sunday Paper,* Aug. 22, 1971.

Shreffler, Philip A. "Jesse James Shot By 'Dirty Coward' 100 Years Ago." *The St. Louis Post-Dispatch, Sunday Magazine,* April 4, 1982.

Singular, Stephen. "The Wild Bunch." *The Denver Post Magazine,* August 5, 1984.

"Some of the Figures in Pendleton's Annual Round-Up." *East Oregonian,* September 17, 1925.

"Takes Irwins to Casper Jail." *Cheyenne Leader,* September 18, 1907.

Thompson, Martha. "Daughter Recalls Mother as World's Champion Cow Girl." *Wyoming Eagle,* December 30, 1969. Gladys Foster tells about Margaret R. Irwin.

"$1000 Prize For Body of Train Bandit." *Wyoming State Tribune,* November 28, 1919.

"Throng Pays a Last Tribute to Charlie Irwin." *Torrington Telegram,* March 29, 1934.

"Tom Horn the Noted Desperado Dies on the Gallows." *The Wyoming Tribune,* November 20, 1903.

"Trainer Irwin and His Patched-Up Winners." *The American Weekly,* January 4, 1948.

"Tribute Paid to Memory of Late Charley Irwin." *Cheyenne Tribune,* April 11, 1934.

Trimble, Sanky. "Cowboy Riding at 80, Danks Wants Name in Hall of Fame." *The Denver Post,* October 20, 1960.

"U.P. Bandit's Love of Home Comforts Revealed in Denver Rooming House." *The Denver Post,* April 25, 1916.

Urbanek, Mae. "A Poor Sheepherder Found Red Clay." *Star-Tribune,* Casper, Wyoming, March 28, 1976. About the copper mining near Encampment.

"Wyoming Man Helped Rodeo's Growth." *Casper Star-Tribune,* March 19, 1978.

Interviews on Tape

Twenty tapes made by Charles M. Bennett, Betty Steele, Odie Faulk, and A. L. Waldo, beginning 1974 through 1984, with jockeys, cowboys, and relatives about memories of life with C. B. Irwin are in the C. M. Bennett Collection, Scottsdale, Arizona.

Books and Magazines

Adams, Andy. *The Log of a Cowboy.* Lincoln: University of Nebraska Press, 1903. Bison Book printing 1964.

Adams, Ramon F., ed. *The Best of the American Cowboy.* Norman: University of Oklahoma Press, 1957.

Alexander, David. *A Sound of Horses*. New York: Bobbs-Merrill Company, 1966. Sunny Jim Coffroth. Tia Juana Race Track.

Atkinson, Ted, with Lucy Freeman. *All The Way!* Paxton/Slade Publishing Company, Inc., 1961. Introduction by James Roach, Sports Editor, *New York Times*.

Bancroft, Caroline. *Denver's Lively Past*. Boulder, Colorado: Johnson Publishing Company, 1959.

Bennett, Russell H. *The Compleat Rancher*. New York: Rinehart and Company, 1946. Summary of the Great Horse Race from Evanston to Denver.

Blakely, Reba Perry. "Frances Irwin Keller—Another Ysix Champion." *World of Rodeo and Western Heritage*, May 1980.

Blakely, Reba Perry. "Pauline Irwin Sawyer—trainer, winner." *World of Rodeo and Western Heritage*, February 1980.

Block, Eugene B. *Great Train Robberies of the West*. New York: Coward McCann, Inc., 1959. Carlisle story.

Bollinger, Edward T., and Frederick Bauer. *The Moffat Road*, Sage/Swallow Press Books, 1962. Reprint, Athens, Ohio: Ohio University Press, 1981.

Borgeson, Griffith. *The Golden Age of the American Racing Car*. New York: W. W. Norton and Company, Inc., 1966. Barney Oldfield. Tijuana, Agua Caliente, Tanforan.

Botkin, B. A., ed. *A Treasury of American Folklore*. New York: Crown Publishers, 1944.

Brown, Clark H. "Tales From Old Timers—No. 31." *The Union Pacific Magazine*, May, 1926.

Brown, William R. *Image Maker: Will Rogers and the American Dream*, Columbia: University of Missouri Press, 1970.

Byers, Chester. *Cowboy Roping and Rope Tricks*. New York: Dover Publications, Inc., 1966.

Carey, Gary. *Doug and Mary*. New York: E. P. Dutton, 1977. A biography of Douglas Fairbanks and Mary Pickford.

Carlisle, Bill. *Bill Carlisle Lone Bandit*. Pasadena, Calif.: Trails End Publishing Company, Inc., 1946. Illustrations by Charles M. Russell.

Carroll, William F. "The Days of Wicked Jenny." *Westward*, St. Louis Westerners, Vol. X, No. 2, May, 1981. Abilene and Mattie Silks.

Chapel, Charles Edward. *Guns of the Old West*. New York: Coward McCann, Inc., 1961. Henry rifle.

Chapman, Arthur. *The Story of Colorado, Out Where The West*

Begins. New York: Rand McNally and Company, 1924. Moffat Road.

Cheyenne Landmarks. Laramie, Wyoming: Laramie County Chapter, Wyoming State Historical Society, 1976.

Clark, Helen. "Clayton Danks." *The Western Horseman*, June, 1961.

Clay, John. *My Life On the Range*. Private printing by R. R. Donnelly, 1924. Reprint, New York, Antiquarian Press, Ltd., 1961.

Clymer, Floyd. *Treasury of American Automobiles, 1877–1925*, New York: McGraw Hill, 1950. Lovejoy's automobile. Barney Oldfield. Colburn. Overland. Pierce Arrow.

Coe, Charles H. *Juggling a Rope. Lariat Roping and Spinning Knots and Splices, also The Truth About Tom Horn*. Pendleton, Oregon: Hamley and Company, 1927.

Colt, Mrs. Miriam Davis. *Went To Kansas*. Watertown, Mass.: L. Ingalls and Co., 1862. Reprint, Readex Microprint Corp., 1966.

Creigh, D. W. *Nebraska*. New York: W. W. Norton, 1977. Ak-Sar-Ben.

Dary, David. *Cowboy Culture, A Saga of Five Centuries*. New York: Alfred A. Knopf, 1981. Abilene. Cheyenne Club.

Day, Beth. *America's First Cowgirl, Lucille Mulhall*. New York: Julian Messner, 1955. The Sheridan Stampede, 1915, and the Irwin sisters.

Dean, Frank E. *Trick and Fancy Riding*. Caldwell, Idaho: The Caxton Printers, Ltd., 1975.

DeYong, Joe. "Charlie and Me." *Persimmon Hill*, Vol. 11, No. 344, Summer and Fall, 1982. Note about Charlie Irwin.

Farrar, Harry. "Puett Went Into Hock To Develop Today's Automatic Stall Gate." *Horsemen's Journal*, Vol. XIV, No. IX, Sept. 1963.

Faulk, Odie B. *Bigger Than Life, The Saga of C. B. Irwin*. Unpublished manuscript, 1979, 178 pages. This manuscript was written with the aid of a grant from Charles M. Bennett. The material in Faulk's story helped in identifying and dating the clippings in the Bennett Collection, which were used as the background for both this and Faulk's work. Faulk understood that the greatness of C.B. Irwin would live on indefinitely wherever horse racing and rodeos were held. He wrote, "It is not surprising that within two years after his death many of the performers who had worked for him joined in forming the Cowboys' Turtle Association, the forerunner of the Professional Rodeo Cowboys' Association. The Turtles and their successors standardized the rules, helped set entry fees, and stipulated safety conditions to protect the entrants the way C. B. Irwin had done for his people. Without C.B. Irwin, professional rodeo would not have evolved in the way it did."

Fowler, Gene. *A Solo in Tom-Toms*. New York: The Viking Press, 1946. Story of Floyd Irwin's death.

Fowler, Gene. *Timber Line*. Garden City, N. Y.: Garden City Books, 1933. Tom Horn.

Franzwa, Gregory M. *The Oregon Trail Revisited*. St. Louis, Missouri: Patrice Press, Inc., 1972. Horse Creek Treaty.

Goldhurst, Richard. *John J. Pershing: The Classic American Soldier, Pipe Clay and Drill*. New York: Reader's Digest Press, Thomas Y. Crowell, Company, 1977.

Gray, Arthur Amos. *Men Who Built The West*. Caldwell, Idaho: The Caxton Printers, Ltd., 1945.

Gres, Kathryn. *Ninety Years Cow Country, A Factual History of the Wyoming Stock Growers Association*. Cheyenne: Wyoming Stock Growers Association, 1963.

Hall, Alice. "Buffalo Bill and the Enduring West." *National Geographic*, Vol. 160, No. 1, July 1981.

Hanes, Colonel Bailey C. *Bill Pickett, Bulldoger*. Norman: University of Oklahoma Press, 1977.

Hanesworth, Robert D. *Daddy of 'Em All, The Story of Cheyenne Frontier Days*. Cheyenne, Wyoming: Flintlock Publishing Company, 1967.

Hansen, Harry, ed. *Colorado*. New revised ed., Federal Writers' Program, American Guide Series. New York: Hastings House, 1970.

Henry, Will. *I, Tom Horn*. New York: J. B. Lippincott, 1973.

History of Caldwell and Livingston Counties, Missouri. St. Louis: National Historical Co., 1886, press of Nixon-Jones Printing Co. Becktold and Co. Book-Binders. Written and compiled from the most authentic and private sources, including a history of their townships and villages, pioneer records, biographical sketches, general and local statistics, incidents and reminiscences. Reprint, Clinton, Missouri: The Printery, 1972. Granville Brassfield. Riley Brassfield and family.

Hollenback, Frank R. *The Laramie Plains Line*. Denver: Sage Books, 1960. Laramie North Park and Western Railroad Co.

Horan, James D. *Gunfighters, The Authentic Wild West*. New York: Crown Publishers, 1976. Tom Horn.

Horn, Tom. *Life of Tom Horn, Government Scout and Interpreter, Written by Himself Together with His Letters and State-*

ments by His Friends, A Vindication. Denver: The Louthan Book Company, 1904. Reprint, Norman: University of Oklahoma Press, 1964. New York: Crown Publishers, A Jingle Bob Book, 1977.

Hyde, George. *Red Cloud's Folk*. Norman: University of Oklahoma Press, 1976.

Jones, William E., ed. *Horseshoeing*. East Lansing, Michigan: Gaballus Publishers, 1972. Horse Health and Care Series.

Kansas Writers' Program. Compiled and written by the Federal Writers' Project of the Works Projects Administration for the State of Kansas. New York: The Viking Press, 1939.

Karolevitz, Robert F. *Doctors of the Old West*. New York: Superior Publishing Company, Bonanza Book, 1967.

Kauffman, Sandra. *The Cowboy Catalog*. New York: Clarkson N. Potter, Inc. Publishers, Crown Publishers, Inc., 1980.

Kelk, Wallace. "The Puett Electric Starting Gate." *The Thoroughbred Record,* Vol. 130, No. 7, Aug. 12, 1939.

Kirkbride, Dan "Peggy." *From These Roots*. Cheyenne, Wyoming: Pioneer Printing and Stationery Co., 1972. Stories about the early ranchers north of Cheyenne.

Krakel, Dean F. "Dode Wykert and the Great Horse Race." *Colorado Magazine,* Vol. 30, No. 3, July, 1953.

Krakel, Dean F. *The Saga of Tom Horn, The Story of a Cattlemen's War*. Laramie, Wyoming: Powder River Publishers, 1954. Most complete account of the Tom Horn story including the trial and hanging.

Larson, T. A. *History of Wyoming*. Lincoln: University of Nebraska Press, 1966, 2nd ed. revised, 1978. Charlie Irwin. Much about early cattle industry, Francis E. Warren, Tom Horn, Johnson County War and Depression years.

Loomis, N. H. "Union Pacific as a Factor in United States History." *The Union Pacific Magazine,* February, 1928.

McGinnis, Vera. *Rodeo Road, My Life as a Pioneer Cowgirl*. New York: Hastings House Publishers, 1974. Story of C. B. Irwin and the three Irwin girls. Tom Smith, trainer of Seabiscuit.

McNamara, Brooks. *Step Right Up*: Garden City, N. Y.: Doubleday and Company, Inc., 1976. Medicine shows.

Mails, Thomas E. *Fools Crow*. New York: Discus, Avon Books, 1980. Cheyenne Frontier Days and Oglala from Pine Ridge.

May, Earl Chapin. *The Circus From Rome To Ringling*. Duffield and Green, 1932. Reprint, New York: Dover Publications, Inc., 1963.

Messerschmidt, Donald A., ed., adapted from Mark Junge, *The*

Grand Encampment. Encampment, Wyoming: The Grand Encampment Museum, 1972.

Michaelis, Bob. "Splinters Off the Plank Road." *Buckskin Bulletin*, Fall 1983.

Missouri. Compiled by workers of the Writers' Program of the Work Projects Administration in the State of Missouri. New York: Duell-Sloan and Pearce, 1941.

Mix, Paul E. *The Life and Legend of Tom Mix*. New York: A. S. Barnes and Company, 1972.

Monagham, Jay M. *Last Of The Bad Men*. New York: Bobbs-Merrill Company, 1946. Tom Horn story.

Moore, N. Hudson. *The Collector's Manual*. New York: Tudor Publishing Company, 1905.

Morris, Scott. "Games." *Omni*, Vol. 6, No. 7, April, 1984. Egg in a bottle.

Mothershead, Harmon Ross. *The Swan Land and Cattle Company, Ltd*. Norman: University of Oklahoma Press, 1971. Map of the lands and ranges of the Swan Land and Cattle Co. 1884–5.

Murray, William. *Horse Fever*. New York: Dodd, Mead and Company, 1976.

Nadeau, Remi. *Fort Laramie and the Sioux Indians*. Englewood Cliffs, Prentice-Hall, Inc., 1967. Horse Creek Treaty.

O'Brien, P. J. *Will Rogers, Ambassador of Good Will, Prince of Wit and Wisdom*. Copyright in Great Britain and in the British Dominions and Possessions, 1935.

O'Connor, Richard. *Black Jack Pershing*. Garden City, N. Y.: Doubleday and Company, Inc., 1961.

Olson, Ted. *Ranch on the Laramie*. New York: Little, Brown and Company, 1973.

Painter, Nell Irvin. *Exodusters, Black Migration to Kansas after Reconstruction*. New York: Alfred A. Knopf, 1977.

Peterson, Harold L. *American Knives: The First History and Collector's Guide*. New York: Charles Scribner's Sons, 1958.

Porter, Willard H. *Who's Who in Rodeo*. Oklahoma City, Okla.: Powder River Book Company, 1983.

Potter, Edgar R. *Cowboy Slang*. Seattle, Washington: Hangman Press, Superior Publishing Company, 1971.

Reed, J. O., chairman of the Centennial Historical Committee, *The Magic City of the Plains—Cheyenne, 1867–1967*. Cheyenne, Wyoming, 1967.

Rine, Josephine Z. *The World of Dogs*. Garden City, N.Y.: Doubleday and Company, Inc., 1965. Greyhound. Racing.

Riske, Milt. *Those Magnificent Cowgirls, A History of the Rodeo Cowgirls*. Cheyenne, Wyo.: Wyoming Publishing, Frontier Printing, Inc., 1983.

Rogers, Betty. *Will Rogers*. Norman: University of Oklahoma Press, 1941/1979.

Rogers, Will. "Hello Charlie, Old Hand, How Are You?" *Persimmon Hill,* Vol. 11, No. 344, Summer and Fall, 1982.

Russell, Charles M. "Charlie Tells His Own Story." *Persimmon Hill,* Vol. 11, No. 344, Summer and Fall, 1982.

Schaefer, Jack. *The Great Endurance Horse Race, 600 Miles on a Single Mount, 1908, From Evanston, Wyoming to Denver*. Santa Fe, N. M.: Stagecoach Press. C. B. Irwin and fake train robbery.

Shelton, Ferne. *Pioneer Comforts and Kitchen Remedies*. High Point, N. C.: Hutcraft, 1965.

Shelton, Ferne. *Pioneer Superstitions*. High Point, N. C.: Hutcraft, 1969.

Sherman County Historical Society. Goodland, Kansas, bulletins from Vol. 1, No. 1, June 1975, to Vol. 6, No. 3, January 1981. These bulletins were invaluable with stories of homesteaders, building a sod house, digging a well, blacksmithing, claim jumpers, the county seat battle, tooth extractor, laying railroad tracks, drought, county fairs, rainmakers, irrigation, the Farmer's Alliance, and the 1893 coursing meet.

Smith, W. H. B., and Joseph E. Smith. *The Book of Rifles*. Harrisburg, Pa.: The Stackpole Company, 1948. Henry rifle.

Spencer, D. S. "From the Diary of a 55-Year Old Timer." *The Union Pacific Magazine,* July 1929.

Sprague, Marshall. *Newport in the Rockies: The Life and Good Times of Colorado Springs*. Chicago: Sage/Swallow Press, 1961/1971/1980.

Steigleman, Walter. *Horseracing*. New York: Prentice-Hall, Inc., 1947.

Sterling, Bryan. *The Best of Will Rogers*. New York: Crown Publishers, Inc., 1979.

Stevenson, Thelma V. *Historic Hahns Peak*. Fort Collins, Colorado: Robinson Press, Inc., 1979.

Thornton, Pat. "Getting A Start In Racing." *Horsemen's Journal,* Vol. XXVIII, No. 10, October 1977. Story of Clay Puett and the starting gate. Mentions C. B. Irwin.

Vernon, Glenn R. *Man On Horseback*. New York: Harper and Row Publishers, 1964. Cheyenne roll on a saddle. Ten-gallon hats.

Watson, Aldren A. *The Village Blacksmith*. New York: Thomas Y. Crowell Company, 1968.

Williams, George. "C. B. Irwin, High Roller." *Persimmon Hill*, Vol. 7, No. 2, Spring, 1977.

Woodcock, Lyle S. "Charles Marion Russell and St. Louis." *Westward*, St. Louis Westerners, Vol. IX, No. 1, Oct., 1979.

Wyoming. Compiled by workers of the Writers' Program of the WPA in the State of Wyoming. New York: Oxford University Press, 1941.

Yost, Nellie Snynder. *Buffalo Bill, His Family, Friends, Fame, Failure and Fortunes*. Chicago: Sage Books, The Swallow Press, 1979.

Miscellaneous

Bennett, Charles M. In this collection there are dozens of miscellaneous documents, ranging from Carlisle's nine-page confession to a photocopy of the Miner family tree. The availability of these papers has been invaluable in establishing an authentic environment for the story of C. B. Irwin.

Cathey Cooper, Associate Librarian, Keenland Library, sent 13 pages of names of horses and their jockeys that were owned by C.B. Irwin from 1917 to 1933 as shown on the U.S. index of charts and the Tijuana charts.

Court case of the State of Utah vs. Roy Kivett, 95 pages, filed on Sept. 12, 1924, which include Proceedings, Warrant of Arrest, Aug. 30, 1924, Complaint, Aug. 29, 1924, Information, Subpoenas, Nov. 8, 1924, Affidavit, Oct. 29, 1924, Order, Nov. 6, 1924, Subpoenas, Instructions to the Jury, Nov. 24, 1924, Requests, Verdict, List of Exhibits, Letter on Newhouse Hotel stationery, Nov. 20, 1924 regards to payment to the witnesses, Letter to Salt Lake County Clerk, Nov. 18, 1924 in regards to payment of money.

History of the Wyoming License Plate, Saratoga Historical Museum and Cultural Center, Saratoga, Wyoming. There are some that believe the bucking horse on the license plate is the famous Steamboat. Mr. Allen T. True, who drew the horse, says he had in mind "Stub" Farlow, a rodeo figure, as the typical cowboy on his own horse, Deadman.

Program for the National Cowboy Hall of Fame banquet, Oklahoma City, Okla., December 11, 1975. C.B. Irwin was honored as that year's inductee.

Program for the Nebraska Racing Hall of Fame banquet, Ak-Sar-Ben Field, Omaha, Neb., June 25, 1979. C. B. Irwin was inducted into the Racing Hall of Fame. The citation reads as follows:

"C.B. Irwin was recognized as one of the most successful horsemen west of the Mississippi River. For more than fifteen years he ranked among the top ten owners and trainers and was the leading trainer in America in 1923 and 1930. Veteran racing observers credit Irwin for a significant contribution to Ak-Sar-Ben's early rise to national acclaim in horse racing. Among his star performers on the racetrack were Harry D., All Over, Miss Lester, Betty Luck, Lady In Black, Kippy Duncan, and the great stakes runner Abaldane. In addition to his racing and ranching, he owned his own wild west show which appeared throughout the nation."

The Steamboat Monument Project, *Wyoming Spirit,* Wyoming University, Laramie, May 1952. The project is twenty pages of pictures and documentation about the famous bucking horse, Steamboat, including a poem by Ted Olson.

Steele, Betty. This collection has three pages of onion-skin paper that is breaking apart at the fold lines, contains no date, no author, but several stories about C.B. Irwin and the following table on page 3. This table is also reproduced on page 109 of Odie Faulk's manuscript.

C. B. Irwin's Race Horse Record
From 1920 to 1927

Year	No. of racehorses that were winners	Amt. won for the year
1920	28	$ 15,336
1921	48	32,820
1922	72	52,725
1923	147	104,054
1924	51	42,825
1925	56	47,915
1926	75	69,390
1927	70	53,805

Data for the remaining of Charlie's horse racing years do not exist. Only once has the record of 147 wins in one year been topped and that was in 1937 by racehorse owner Hirst Jacobs. The years 1920, 1926, and 1927 show the second greatest number of winners on an American trainer's list.

John E. Witherbee, Research Specialist, Union Pacific Railroad Co., sent a four-page history of the Saratoga and Encampment Valley Railroad, History of the Laramie, North Park and Pacific Railroad and picture of Engine No. 101, of the Saratoga and Encampment Railway Company.